THE CRIPPLED GOD

THE CRIPPLED GOD

A Tale of the Malazan Book of the Fallen

Steven Erikson

BANTAM PRESS

LONDON · TORONTO · SYDNEY · AUCKLAND · JOHANNESBURG

TRANSWORLD PUBLISHERS
61-63 Uxbridge Road, London W5 5SA
A Random House Group Company
www.rbooks.co.uk

First published in Great Britain
in 2011 by Bantam Press
an imprint of Transworld Publishers

Copyright © Steven Erikson 2011

Steven Erikson has asserted his right under the Copyright, Designs and Patents Act 1988 to be identified as the author of this work.

This book is a work of fiction and, except in the case of historical fact, any resemblance to actual persons, living or dead, is purely coincidental.

A CIP catalogue record for this book
is available from the British Library.

ISBNs 9780593046357 (cased)
9780593046364 (tpb)

Addresses for Random House Group Ltd companies outside the UK can be found at: www.randomhouse.co.uk
The Random House Group Ltd Reg. No. 954009

The Random House Group Limited supports The Forest Stewardship Council (FSC), the leading international forest-certification organization. All our titles that are printed on Greenpeace-approved FSC-certified paper carry the FSC logo. Our paper procurement policy can be found at www.rbooks.co.uk/environment

Typeset in 10½/12pt Sabon by
Kestrel Data, Exeter, Devon.
Printed and bound in Great Britain by
Clays Ltd, Bungay, Suffolk.

2 4 6 8 10 9 7 5 3 1

Mixed Sources
Product group from well-managed
forests and other controlled sources
www.fsc.org Cert no. TT-COC-2139
© 1996 Forest Stewardship Council
FSC

Many years ago one man took a chance on an unknown writer and his first fantasy novel – a novel that had already gone the rounds of publishers a few times without any luck. Without him, without his faith and, in the years that followed, his unswerving commitment to this vast undertaking, there would be no 'Malazan Book of the Fallen'. It has been my great privilege to work with a single editor from start to finish, and so I humbly dedicate *The Crippled God* to my editor and friend, Simon Taylor.

Contents

Acknowledgements

My deepest gratitude is accorded to the following people. My advance readers for their timely commentary on this manuscript which I foisted on them at short notice and probably inopportune times: A. P. Canavan, William Hunter, Hazel Hunter, Baria Ahmed and Bowen Thomas-Lundin. And the staff of The Norway Inn in Perranarworthal, the Mango Tango and Costa Coffee in Falmouth, all of whom participated in their own way in the writing of this novel.

Also, a heartfelt thank you to all my readers, who (presumably) have stayed with me through to this, the tenth and final novel of the 'Malazan Book of the Fallen'. I have enjoyed our long conversation. What's three and a half million words between friends?

I could well ask the same question of my publishers. Thank you for your patience and support. The unruly beast is done, and I can hear your relieved sighs.

Finally, my love and gratitude to my wife, Clare Thomas, who suffered through the ordeal of not just this novel, but all those that preceded it. I think it was your mother who warned you that marrying a writer was a dicey proposition . . .

KOLANSE

WHITE SPIRES OCEAN

SES MOUNTAINS

North Citadel

Back

Danan

Hetok

ESTOBANSE PROVINCE

Gest Pass

Trelar

EAST ELAN PLAIN

Kolanse City

KOLANSE BAY

VALLEY OF BLESSED GIFT

The Spire

GLASS DESERT

PELASIAR SEA

N

DRAMATIS PERSONAE

In addition to those in *Dust of Dreams*

THE MALAZANS

Himble Thrup
Seageant Gaunt-Eye
Corporal Rib
Lap Twirl
Sad
Burnt Rope

THE HOST

Ganoes Paran, High Fist and Master of the Deck
High Mage Noto Boil
Outrider Hurlochel
Fist Rythe Bude
Captain Sweetcreek
Imperial Artist Ormulogun
Warleader Mathok
Bodyguard T'morol
Gumble

THE KHUNDRYL

Widow Jastara

THE SNAKE

Sergeant Cellows
Corporal Nithe
Sharl

THE T'LAN IMASS: THE UNBOUND

Urugal the Woven
Thenik the Shattered
Beroke Soft Voice
Kahlb the Silent Hunter
Halad the Giant

THE TISTE ANDII

Nimander Golit
Spinnock Durav
Korlat
Skintick
Desra
Dathenar Gowl
Nemanda

THE JAGHUT: THE FOURTEEN

Gathras
Sanad
Varandas
Haut
Suvalas
Aimanan
Hood

THE FORKRUL ASSAIL: THE LAWFUL INQUISITORS

Reverence
Serenity
Equity
Placid
Diligence
Abide
Aloft
Calm
Belie
Freedom
Grave

THE WATERED: THE TIERS OF LESSER ASSAIL

Amiss
Exigent
Hestand
Festian
Kessgan
Trissin
Melest
Haggraf

THE TISTE LIOSAN

Kadagar Fant
Aparal Forge
Iparth Erule
Gaelar Throe
Eldat Pressan

OTHERS

Absi
Spultatha
K'rul
Kaminsod
Munug
Silanah
Apsal'ara
Tulas Shorn
D'rek
Gallimada
Korabas

BOOK ONE

'HE WAS A SOLDIER'

I am known
in the religion of rage.
Worship me as a pool
of blood in your hands.
Drink me deep.
It's bitter fury
that boils and burns.
Your knives were small
but they were many.

I am named
in the religion of rage.
Worship me with your
offhand cuts
long after I am dead.
It's a song of dreams
crumbled to ashes.
Your wants overflowed
but now gape empty.

I am drowned
in the religion of rage.
Worship me unto
death and down
to a pile of bones.
The purest book
is the one never opened.
No needs left unfulfilled
on the cold, sacred day.

I am found
in the religion of rage.
Worship me in a
stream of curses.
This fool had faith
and in dreams he wept.
But we walk a desert
rocked by accusations,
where no man starves
with hate in his bones.

Poet's Night i.iv
The Malazan Book of the Fallen
Fisher kel Tath

CHAPTER ONE

If you never knew
the worlds in my mind
your sense of loss
would be small pity
and we'll forget this on the trail.
Take what you're given
and turn away the screwed face.
I do not deserve it,
no matter how narrow the strand
of your private shore.
If you will do your best
I'll meet your eye.
It's the clutch of arrows in hand
that I do not trust
bent to the smile hitching my way.
We aren't meeting in sorrow
or some other suture
bridging scars.
We haven't danced the same
thin ice
and my sympathy for your troubles
I give freely without thought
of reciprocity or scales on balance.
It's the decent thing, that's all.
Even if that thing
is a stranger to so many.
But there will be secrets
you never knew
and I would not choose any other way.
All my arrows are buried and
the sandy reach is broad
and all that's private

cools pinned on the altar.
Even the drips are gone,
that child of wants
with a mind full of worlds
and his reddened tears.
The days I feel mortal I so hate.
The days in my worlds,
are where I live for ever,
and should dawn ever arrive
I will to its light awaken
as one reborn.

Poet's Night iii.iv
The Malazan Book of the Fallen
Fisher kel Tath

COTILLION DREW TWO DAGGERS. HIS GAZE FELL TO THE BLADES. The blackened iron surfaces seemed to swirl, two pewter rivers oozing across pits and gouges, the edges ragged where armour and bone had slowed their thrusts. He studied the sickly sky's lurid reflections for a moment longer, and then said, 'I have no intention of explaining a damned thing.' He looked up, eyes locking. 'Do you understand me?'

The figure facing him was incapable of expression. The tatters of rotted sinew and strips of skin were motionless upon the bones of temple, cheek and jaw. The eyes held nothing, nothing at all.

Better, Cotillion decided, than jaded scepticism. Oh, how he was sick of that. 'Tell me,' he resumed, 'what do you think you're seeing here? Desperation? Panic? A failing of will, some inevitable decline crumbling to incompetence? Do you believe in failure, Edgewalker?'

The apparition remained silent for a time, and then spoke in a broken, rasping voice. 'You cannot be so . . . audacious.'

'I asked if you believed in failure. Because I don't.'

'Even should you succeed, Cotillion. Beyond all expectation, beyond, even, all *desire*. They will still speak of your failure.'

He sheathed his daggers. 'And you know what they can do to themselves.'

The head cocked, strands of hair dangling and drifting. 'Arrogance?'

'Competence,' Cotillion snapped in reply. 'Doubt me at your peril.'

'They will not believe you.'

'I do not care, Edgewalker. This is what it is.'

When he set out, he was not surprised that the deathless guardian followed. *We have done this before.* Dust and ashes puffed with each step. The wind moaned as if trapped in a crypt. 'Almost time, Edgewalker.'

'I know. You cannot win.'

Cotillion paused, half turned. He smiled a ravaged smile. 'That doesn't mean I have to lose, does it?'

Dust lifted, twisting, in her wake. From her shoulders trailed dozens of ghastly chains: bones bent and folded into irregular links, ancient bones in a thousand shades between white and deep brown. Scores of individuals made up each chain, malformed skulls matted with hair, fused spines, long bones, clacking and clattering. They drifted out behind her like a tyrant's legacy and left a tangled skein of furrows in the withered earth that stretched for leagues.

Her pace did not slow, as steady as the sun's own crawl to the horizon ahead, as inexorable as the darkness overtaking her. She was indifferent to notions of irony, and the bitter taste of irreverent mockery that could so sting the palate. In this there was only necessity, the hungriest of gods. She had known imprisonment. The memories remained fierce, but such recollections were not those of crypt walls and unlit tombs. Darkness, indeed, but also pressure. Terrible, unbearable pressure.

Madness was a demon and it lived in a world of helpless need, a thousand desires unanswered, a world without resolution. Madness, yes, she had known that demon. They had bargained with coins of pain, and those coins came from a vault that never emptied. She'd once known such wealth.

And still the darkness pursued.

Walking, a thing of hairless pate, skin the hue of bleached papyrus, elongated limbs that moved with uncanny grace. The landscape surrounding her was empty, flat on all sides but ahead, where a worn-down range of colourless hills ran a wavering claw along the horizon.

She had brought her ancestors with her and they rattled a chaotic chorus. She had not left a single one behind. Every tomb of her line now gaped empty, as hollowed out as the skulls she'd plundered from their sarcophagi. Silence ever spoke of absence. Silence was the enemy of life and she would have none of it. No, they talked in mutters and grating scrapes, her perfect ancestors, and they were the voices of her private song, keeping the demon at bay. She was done with bargains.

Long ago, she knew, the worlds – pallid islands in the Abyss – crawled with creatures. Their thoughts were blunt and simple, and beyond those thoughts there was nothing but murk, an abyss of ignorance and fear. When the first glimmers awakened in that confused gloom, they quickly flickered alight, burning like spot fires. But the mind did not awaken to itself on strains of glory. Not beauty, not even love. It did not stir with laughter or triumph. Those fires, snapping to life, all belonged to one thing and one thing only.

The first word of sentience was *justice*. A word to feed indignation. A word empowering the will to change the world and all its cruel circumstances, a word to bring righteousness to brutal infamy. Justice, bursting to life in the black soil of indifferent nature. Justice, to bind families, to build cities, to invent and to defend, to fashion laws and prohibitions, to hammer the unruly mettle of gods into religions. All the prescribed beliefs rose out twisting and branching from that single root, losing themselves in the blinding sky.

But she and her kind had stayed wrapped about the base of that vast tree, forgotten, crushed down; and in their place, beneath stones, bound in roots and dark earth, they were witness to the corruption of justice, to its loss of meaning, to its betrayal.

Gods and mortals, twisting truths, had in a host of deeds stained what once had been pure.

Well, the end was coming. *The end, dear ones, is coming.* There would be no more children, rising from the bones and rubble, to build anew all that had been lost. Was there even one among them, after all, who had not suckled at the teat of corruption? Oh, they fed their inner fires, yet they hoarded the light, the warmth, as if justice belonged to them alone.

She was appalled. She seethed with contempt. Justice was incandescent within her, and it was a fire growing day by day, as the wretched heart of the Chained One leaked out its endless streams of blood. Twelve Pures remained, feeding. Twelve. Perhaps there were others, lost in far-flung places, but she knew nothing of them. No, these twelve, they would be the faces of the final storm, and, pre-eminent among them all, she would stand at that storm's centre.

She had been given her name for this very purpose, long ago now. The Forkrul Assail were nothing if not patient. But patience itself was yet one more lost virtue.

Chains of bone trailing, Calm walked across the plain, as the day's light died behind her.

'God failed us.'

Trembling, sick to his stomach as something cold, foreign, coursed through his veins, Aparal Forge clenched his jaw to stifle a retort. *This vengeance is older than any cause you care to invent, and no matter how often you utter those words, Son of Light, the lies and madness open like flowers beneath the sun. And before me I see nothing but lurid fields of red, stretching out on all sides.*

This wasn't their battle, not their war. *Who fashioned this law that said the child must pick up the father's sword? And dear Father, did you really mean this to be? Did she not abandon her consort and take you for her own? Did you not command us to peace? Did you not say to us that we children must be as one beneath the newborn sky of your union?*

What crime awoke us to this?

I can't even remember.

'Do you feel it, Aparal? The power?'

'I feel it, Kadagar.' They'd moved away from the others, but not so far as to escape the agonized cries, the growl of the Hounds, or, drifting out over the broken rocks in ghostly streams, the blistering breath of cold upon their backs. Before them rose the infernal barrier. A wall of imprisoned souls. An eternally crashing wave of despair. He stared at the gaping faces through the mottled veil, studied the pitted horror in their eyes. *You were no different, were you? Awkward with your inheritance, the heavy blade turning this way and that in your hand.*

Why should we pay for someone else's hatred?

'What so troubles you, Aparal?'

'We cannot know the reason for our god's absence, Lord. I fear it is presumptuous of us to speak of his failure.'

Kadagar Fant was silent.

Aparal closed his eyes. He should never have spoken. *I do not learn. He walked a bloody path to rule and the pools in the mud still gleam red. The air about Kadagar remains brittle. This flower shivers to secret winds. He is dangerous, so very dangerous.*

'The Priests spoke of impostors and tricksters, Aparal.' Kadagar's tone was even, devoid of inflection. It was the voice he used when furious. 'What god would permit that? We are abandoned. The path before us now belongs to no one else – it is ours to choose.'

Ours. Yes, you speak for us all, even as we cringe at our own confessions. 'Forgive my words, Lord. I am made ill – the taste—'

'We had no choice in that, Aparal. What sickens you is the bitter flavour of its pain. It passes.' Kadagar smiled and clapped him on the back. 'I understand your momentary weakness. We shall forget your doubts, yes? And never again speak of them. We are friends, after all, and I would be most distressed to be forced to brand you a traitor. Set upon the White Wall . . . I would kneel and weep, my friend. I would.'

A spasm of alien fury hissed through Aparal and he shivered. *Abyss! Mane of Chaos, I feel you!* 'My life is yours to command, Lord.'

'Lord of Light!'

Aparal turned, as did Kadagar.

Blood streaming from his mouth, Iparth Erule staggered closer, eyes wide and fixed upon Kadagar. 'My lord, Uhandahl, who was last to drink, has just died. He – he *tore out his own throat!*'

'Then it is done,' Kadagar replied. 'How many?'

Iparth licked his lips, visibly flinched at the taste, and then said, 'You are the First of Thirteen, Lord.'

Smiling, Kadagar stepped past Iparth. 'Kessobahn still breathes?'

'Yes. It is said it can bleed for centuries—'

'But the blood is now poison,' Kadagar said, nodding. 'The wounding must be fresh, the power clean. Thirteen, you say. Excellent.'

Aparal stared at the dragon staked to the slope behind Iparth Erule. The enormous spears pinning it to the ground were black with gore and dried blood. He could feel the Eleint's pain, pouring from it in waves. Again and again it tried to lift its head, eyes blazing, jaws snapping, but the vast trap held. The four surviving Hounds of Light circled at a distance, hackles raised as they eyed the dragon. Seeing them, Aparal hugged himself. *Another mad gamble. Another bitter failure. Lord of Light, Kadagar Fant, you have not done well in the world beyond.*

Beyond this terrible vista, and facing the vertical ocean of deathless souls as if in mocking madness, rose the White Wall, which hid the decrepit remnants of the Liosan city of Saranas. The faint elongated dark streaks lining it, descending just beneath the crenellated battlements, were all he could make out of the brothers and sisters who had been condemned as traitors to the cause. Below their withered corpses ran the stains from everything their bodies had drained down the alabaster facing. *You would kneel and weep, would you, my friend?*

Iparth asked, 'My lord, do we leave the Eleint as it is?'

'No. I propose something far more fitting. Assemble the others. We shall veer.'

Aparal started but did not turn. 'Lord—'

'We are Kessobahn's children now, Aparal. A new father, to replace the one who abandoned us. Osserc is dead in our eyes and shall remain so. Even Father Light kneels broken, useless and blind.'

Aparal's eyes held on Kessobahn. *Utter such blasphemies often enough and they become banal, and all shock fades. The gods lose their power, and we rise to stand in their stead.* The ancient dragon wept blood, and in those vast, alien eyes there was nothing but rage. *Our father. Your pain, your blood, our gift to you. Alas, it is the only gift we understand.* 'And once we have veered?'

'Why, Aparal, we shall tear the Eleint apart.'

He'd known what the answer would be and he nodded. *Our father. Your pain, your blood, our gift. Celebrate our rebirth, O Father Kessobahn, with your death. And for you, there shall be no return.*

'I have nothing with which to bargain. What brings you to me? No, I see that. My broken servant cannot travel far, even in his dreams. Crippled, yes, my precious flesh and bones upon this wretched world.

Have you seen his flock? What blessing can he bestow? Why, naught but misery and suffering, and still they gather, the mobs, the clamouring, beseeching mobs. Oh, I once looked upon them with contempt. I once revelled in their pathos, their ill choices and their sorry luck. Their stupidity.

'But no one chooses their span of wits. They are each and all born with what they have, that and nothing more. Through my servant I see into their eyes – when I so dare – and they give me a look, a strange look, one that for a long time I could not understand. Hungry, of course, so brimming with need. But I am the Foreign God. The Chained One. The Fallen One, and my holy word is Pain.

'Yet those eyes implored.

'I now comprehend. What do they ask of me? Those dull fools glittering with fears, those horrid expressions to make a witness cringe. What do they want? I will answer you. They want my pity.

'They understand, you see, their own paltry scant coins in their bag of wits. They know they lack intelligence, and that this has cursed them and their lives. They have struggled and lashed out, from the very beginning. No, do not look at me that way, you of smooth and subtle thought, you give your sympathy too quickly and therein hide your belief in your own superiority. I do not deny your cleverness, but I question your compassion.

'They wanted my pity. They have it. I am the god that answers prayers – can you or any other god make that claim? See how I have changed. My pain, which I held on to so selfishly, now reaches out like a broken hand. We touch in understanding, we flinch at the touch. I am one with them all, now.

'You surprise me. I had not believed this to be a thing of value. What worth compassion? How many columns of coins balance the scales? My servant once dreamed of wealth. A buried treasure in the hills. Sitting on his withered legs, he pleaded with passers-by in the street. Now you look at me here, too broken to move, deep in the fumes, and the wind slaps these tent walls without rest. No need to bargain. My servant and I have both lost the desire to beg. You want my pity? I give it. Freely.

'Need I tell you of my pain? I look in your eyes and find the answer.

'It is my last play, but you understand that. My last. Should I fail . . .

'Very well. There is no secret to this. I will gather the poison, then. In the thunder of my pain, yes. Where else?

'Death? Since when is death failure?

'Forgive the cough. It was meant to be laughter. Go then, wring your promises with those upstarts.

'That is all faith is, you know. Pity for our souls. Ask my servant and he will tell you. God looks into your eyes, and God cringes.'

Three dragons chained for their sins. At the thought Cotillion sighed, suddenly morose. He stood twenty paces away, ankle deep in soft ash. Ascendancy, he reflected, was not quite as long a stride from the mundane as he would have liked. His throat felt tight, as if his air passages were constricted. The muscles of his shoulders ached and dull thunder pounded behind his eyes. He stared at the imprisoned Eleint lying so gaunt and deathly amidst drifts of dust, feeling . . . *mortal. Abyss take me, but I'm tired.*

Edgewalker moved up alongside him, silent and spectral.

'Bones and not much else,' Cotillion muttered.

'Do not be fooled,' Edgewalker warned. 'Flesh, skin, they are raiment. Worn or cast off as suits them. See the chains? They have been tested. Heads lifting . . . the scent of freedom.'

'How did you feel, Edgewalker, when everything you held fell to pieces in your hands? Did failure arrive like a wall of fire?' He turned to regard the apparition. 'Those tatters have the look of scorching, come to think of it. Do you remember that moment, when you lost everything? Did the world echo to your howl?'

'If you seek to torment me, Cotillion—'

'No, I would not do that. Forgive me.'

'If these are your fears, however . . .'

'No, not my fears. Not at all. They are my weapons.'

Edgewalker seemed to shiver, or perhaps some shift of the ash beneath his rotted moccasins sent a tremble through him, a brief moment of imbalance. Settling once more, the Elder fixed Cotillion with the withered dark of its eyes. 'You, Lord of Assassins, are no healer.'

No. Someone cut out my unease, please. Make clean the incision, take out what's ill and leave me free of it. We are sickened by the unknown, but knowledge can prove poisonous. And drifting lost between the two is no better. 'There is more than one path to salvation.'

'It is curious.'

'What is?'

'Your words . . . in another voice, coming from . . . someone else, would leave a listener calmed, reassured. From you, alas, they could chill a mortal soul to its very core.'

'This is what I am,' Cotillion said.

Edgewalker nodded. 'It is what you are, yes.'

Cotillion advanced another six paces, eyes on the nearest dragon, the gleaming bones of the skull visible between strips of rotted hide. 'Eloth,' he said, 'I would hear your voice.'

'Shall we bargain again, Usurper?'

The voice was male, but such details were in the habit of changing on a whim. Still, he frowned, trying to recall the last time. 'Kalse, Ampelas, you will each have your turn. Do I now speak with Eloth?'

'I am Eloth. What is it about my voice that so troubles you, Usurper? I sense your suspicion.'

'I needed to be certain,' Cotillion replied. 'And now I am. You are indeed Mockra.'

A new draconic voice rumbled laughter through Cotillion's skull, and then said, *'Be careful, Assassin, she is the mistress of deceit.'*

Cotillion's brows lifted. 'Deceit? Pray not, I beg you. I am too innocent to know much about such things. Eloth, I see you here in chains, and yet in mortal realms your voice has been heard. It seems you are not quite the prisoner you once were.'

'Sleep slips the cruellest chains, Usurper. My dreams rise on wings and I am free. Do you now tell me that such freedom was more than delusion? I am shocked unto disbelief.'

Cotillion grimaced. 'Kalse, what do you dream of?'

'Ice.'

Does that surprise me? 'Ampelas?'

'The rain that burns, Lord of Assassins, deep in shadow. And such a grisly shadow. Shall we three whisper divinations now? All my truths are chained here, it is only the lies that fly free. Yet there was one dream, one that still burns fresh in my mind. Will you hear my confession?'

'My rope is not quite as frayed as you think, Ampelas. You would do better to describe your dream to Kalse. Consider that advice my gift.' He paused, glanced back at Edgewalker for a moment, and then faced the dragons once more. 'Now then, let us bargain for real.'

'There is no value in that,' Ampelas said. *'You have nothing to give us.'*

'But I do.'

Edgewalker suddenly spoke behind him. 'Cotillion—'

'Freedom,' said Cotillion.

Silence.

He smiled. 'A fine start. Eloth, will you dream for me?'

'Kalse and Ampelas have shared your gift. They looked upon one another with faces of stone. There was pain. There was fire. An eye opened and it looked upon the Abyss. Lord of Knives, my kin in chains are . . . dismayed. Lord, I will dream for you. Speak on.'

'Listen carefully then,' Cotillion said. 'This is how it must be.'

The depths of the canyon were unlit, swallowed in eternal night far beneath the ocean's surface. Crevasses gaped in darkness, a world's death and decay streaming down in ceaseless rain, and the currents whipped in fierce torrents that stirred sediments into spinning vortices, lifting like whirlwinds. Flanked by the submerged crags of the canyon's ravaged cliffs, a flat plain stretched out, and in the centre a lurid red flame flickered to life, solitary, almost lost in the vastness.

Shifting the almost weightless burden resting on one shoulder, Mael paused to squint at that improbable fire. Then he set out, making straight for it.

Lifeless rain falling to the depths, savage currents whipping it back up into the light, where living creatures fed on the rich soup, only to eventually die and sink back down. Such an elegant exchange, the living and the dead, the light and the lightless, the world above and the world below. Almost as if someone had planned it.

He could now make out the hunched figure beside the flames, hands held out to the dubious heat. Tiny sea creatures swarmed in the reddish bloom of light like moths. The fire emerged pulsing from a rent in the floor of the canyon, gases bubbling upward.

Mael halted before the figure, shrugging off the wrapped corpse that had been balanced on his shoulder. As it rocked down to the silts tiny scavengers rushed towards it, only to spin away without alighting. Faint clouds billowed as the wrapped body settled in the mud.

The voice of K'rul, Elder God of the Warrens, drifted out from within his hood. 'If all existence is a dialogue, how is it there is still so much left unsaid?'

Mael scratched the stubble on his jaw. 'Me with mine, you with yours, him with his, and yet still we fail to convince the world of its inherent absurdity.'

K'rul shrugged. 'Him with his. Yes. Odd that of all the gods, he alone discovered this mad, and maddening, secret. The dawn to come . . . shall we leave it to him?'

'Well,' Mael grunted, 'first we need to survive the night. I have brought the one you sought.'

'I see that. Thank you, old friend. Now tell me, what of the Old Witch?'

Mael grimaced. 'The same. She tries again, but the one she has chosen . . . well, let us say that Onos T'oolan possesses depths Olar Ethil cannot hope to comprehend, and she will, I fear, come to rue her choice.'

'A man rides before him.'

Mael nodded. 'A man rides before him. It is . . . heartbreaking.'

'"Against a broken heart, even absurdity falters."'

'"Because words fall away."'

Fingers fluttered in the glow. '"A dialogue of silence."'

'"That deafens."' Mael looked off into the gloomy distance. 'Blind Gallan and his damnable poems.' Across the colourless floor armies of

12

sightless crabs were on the march, drawn to the alien light and heat. He squinted at them. 'Many died.'

'Errastas had his suspicions, and that is all the Errant needs. Terrible mischance, or deadly nudge. They were as she said they would be. Unwitnessed.' K'rul lifted his head, the empty hood now gaping in Mael's direction. 'Has he won, then?'

Mael's wiry brows rose. 'You do not know?'

'That close to Kaminsod's heart, the warrens are a mass of wounds and violence.'

Mael glanced down at the wrapped corpse. 'Brys was there. Through his tears I saw.' He was silent for a long moment, reliving someone else's memories. He suddenly hugged himself, released a ragged breath. *'In the name of the Abyss, those Bonehunters were something to behold!'*

The vague hints of a face seemed to find shape inside the hood's darkness, a gleam of teeth. 'Truly? Mael – truly?'

Emotion growled out in his words. 'This is not done. Errastas has made a terrible mistake. *Gods, they all have!'*

After a long moment, K'rul sighed, gaze returning to the fire. His pallid hands hovered above the pulsing glow of burning rock. 'I shall not remain blind. Two children. Twins. Mael, it seems we shall defy the Adjunct Tavore Paran's wish to be for ever unknown to us, unknown to everyone. What does it mean, this desire to be unwitnessed? I do not understand.'

Mael shook his head. 'There is such pain in her . . . no, I dare not get close. She stood before us, in the throne room, like a child with a terrible secret, guilt and shame beyond all measure.'

'Perhaps my guest here will have the answer.'

'Is this why you wanted him? To salve mere curiosity? Is this to be a voyeur's game, K'rul? Into a woman's broken heart?'

'Partly,' K'rul acknowledged. 'But not out of cruelty, or the lure of the forbidden. Her heart must remain her own, immune to all assault.' The god regarded the wrapped corpse. 'No, this one's flesh is dead, but his soul remains strong, trapped in its own nightmare of guilt. I would see it freed of that.'

'How?'

'Poised to act, when the moment comes. Poised to act. A life for a death, and it will have to do.'

Mael sighed unevenly. 'Then it falls on her shoulders. A lone woman. An army already mauled. With allies fevered with lust for the coming war. An enemy awaiting them all, unbowed, with inhuman confidence, so eager to spring the perfect trap.' He lifted his hands to his face. 'A mortal woman who refuses to speak.'

'Yet they follow.'

13

'They follow.'

'Mael, do they truly have a chance?'

He looked down at K'rul. 'The Malazan Empire conjured them out of nothing. Dassem's First Sword, the Bridgeburners, and now the Bonehunters. What can I tell you? It is as if they were born of another age, a golden age lost to the past, and the thing of it is: they don't even know it. Perhaps that is why she wishes them to remain unwitnessed in all that they do.'

'What do you mean?'

'She doesn't want the rest of the world to be reminded of what they once were.'

K'rul seemed to study the fire. Eventually, he said, 'In these dark waters, one cannot feel one's own tears.'

Mael's reply was bitter. 'Why do you think I live here?'

If I have not challenged myself, if I have not striven to give it all I have, then will I stand head bowed before the world's judgement. But if I am to be accused of being cleverer than I am – and how is this even possible? – or, gods forbid, too aware of every echo sent charging out into the night, to bounce and cavort, to reverberate like a sword's edge on a shield rim, if, in other words, I am to be castigated for heeding my sensitivities, well, then something rises like fire within me. I am, and I use the word most cogently, incensed.'

Udinaas snorted. The page was torn below this, as if the author's anger had sent him or her into an apoplectic frenzy. He wondered at this unknown writer's detractors, real or imagined, and he thought back to the times, long ago, when someone's fist had answered his own too-quick, too-sharp wits. Children were skilled at sensing such things, the boy too smart for his own good, and they knew what needed doing about it. *Beat him down, lads. Serves him right.* So he was sympathetic to the spirit of the long-dead writer.

'But then, you old fool, they're dust and your words live on. Who now has the last laugh?'

The rotting wood surrounding him gave back no answer. Sighing, Udinaas tossed the fragment aside, watched flakes of parchment drift down like ashes. 'Oh, what do I care? Not much longer, no, not much longer.' The oil lamp was guttering out, used up, and the chill had crept back in. He couldn't feel his hands. Old legacies, no one could shake them, these grinning stalkers.

Ulshun Pral had predicted more snow, and snow was something he had grown to despise. 'As if the sky itself was dying. You hear that, Fear Sengar? I'm almost ready to take up your tale. Who could have imagined *that* legacy?'

Groaning at the stiffness in his limbs, he clambered out of the ship's hold, emerged blinking on the slanted deck, the wind battering at his face. 'World of white, what are you telling us? That all is not well. That the fates have set a siege upon us.'

He had taken to talking to himself. That way, no one else had to cry, and he was tired of those glistening tears on weathered faces. Yes, he could thaw them all with a handful of words. But that heat inside, well, it had nowhere to go, did it? He gave it to the cold, empty air instead. Not a single frozen tear in sight.

Udinaas climbed over the ship's side, dropped down into knee-deep snow, and then took a fresh path back to the camp in the shelter of rocks, his thick, fur-lined moccasins forcing him to waddle as he ploughed through the drifts. He could smell woodsmoke.

He caught sight of the emlava halfway to the camp. The two enormous cats stood perched on high rocks, their silvered backs blending with the white sky. Watching him. 'So, you're back. That's not good, is it?' He felt their eyes tracking him as he went on. Time was slowing down. He knew that was impossible, but he could imagine an entire world buried deep in snow, a place devoid of animals, a place where seasons froze into one and that season did not end, ever. He could imagine the choking down of every choice until not a single one was left.

'A man can do it. Why not an entire world?' The snow and wind gave no answer, beyond the brutal retort that was indifference.

In between the rocks, now, the bitter wind falling off, the smoke stinging awake his nostrils. There was hunger in the camp, there was white everywhere else. And still the Imass sang their songs. 'Not enough,' Udinaas muttered, breath pluming. 'It's just not, my friends. Face it, she's *dying*. Our dear little child.'

He wondered if Silchas Ruin had known all along. This imminent failure. 'All dreams die in the end. Of all people I should know that. Dreams of sleep, dreams of the future, sooner or later comes the cold, hard dawn.' Walking past the snow-humped yurts, scowling against the droning songs drifting out around the hide flaps, he made for the trail leading to the cave.

Dirty ice crusted the rocky maw, like frozen froth. Once within its shelter the air warmed around him, damp and smelling of salts. He stamped the snow from his moccasins, and then strode into the twisting, stony corridor, hands out to the sides, fingertips brushing the wet stone. 'Oh,' he said under his breath, 'but you're a cold womb, aren't you?'

Ahead he heard voices, or, rather, one voice. *Heed your sensitivities now, Udinaas. She stands unbowed, for ever unbowed. This is what love can do, I suppose.*

The old stains on the stone floor remained, timeless reminders of blood spilled and lives lost in this wretched chamber. He could almost hear the echoes, sword and spear, the gasp of desperate breaths. *Fear Sengar, I would swear your brother stands there still. Silchas Ruin staggering back, step by step, his scowl of disbelief like a mask he'd never worn before, and was it not ill-fitting? It surely was.* Onrack T'emlava stood to the right of his wife. Ulshun Pral crouched a few paces to Kilava's left. Before them all reared a withered, sickly edifice. *Dying House, your cauldron is cracked. She was a flawed seed.*

Kilava turned upon his arrival, her dark animal eyes narrowing as would a hunting cat's as it gathered to pounce. 'Thought you might have sailed away, Udinaas.'

'The charts lead nowhere, Kilava Onass, as I'm sure the pilot observed upon arriving in the middle of a plain. Is there anything more forlorn than a foundered ship, I wonder?'

Onrack spoke. 'Friend Udinaas, I welcome your wisdom. Kilava speaks of the awakening of the Jaghut, the hunger of the Eleint, and the hand of the Forkrul Assail, which never trembles. Rud Elalle and Silchas Ruin have vanished – she cannot sense them and she fears the worst.'

'My son lives.'

Kilava stepped closer. 'You cannot know that.'

Udinaas shrugged. 'He took more from his mother than Menandore ever imagined. When she faced that Malazan wizard, when she sought to draw upon her power, well, it was one of many fatal surprises that day.' His gaze fell to those blackened stains. '*What happened to our heroic outcome, Fear? To the salvation you gave your life to win? "If I have not challenged myself, if I have not striven to give it all I have, then will I stand head bowed before the world's judgement." But the world's judgement is cruel.*'

'We contemplate a journey from this realm,' said Onrack.

Udinaas glanced at Ulshun Pral. 'Do you agree?'

The warrior freed one hand to a flurry of fluid gestures.

Udinaas grunted. *Before the spoken word, before song, there was this. But the hand speaks in broken tongue. The cipher here belongs to his posture – a nomad's squat. No one fears walking, or the unfolding of a new world. Errant take me, this innocence stabs the heart.* 'You won't like what you will find. Not the fiercest beast of this world stands a chance against my kind.' He glared at Onrack. 'What do you think that Ritual was all about? The one that stole death from your people?'

'Hurtful as his words are,' growled Kilava, 'Udinaas speaks the truth.' She faced the Azath once more. 'We can defend this gate. We can stop them.'

'And die,' snapped Udinaas.

'No,' she retorted, wheeling to face him. 'You will lead my children from here, Udinaas. Into your world. I will remain.'

'I thought you said "we", Kilava.'

'Summon your son.'

'No.'

Her eyes flared.

'Find someone else to join you in your last battle.'

'I will stand with her,' said Onrack.

'You will not,' hissed Kilava. 'You are mortal—'

'And you are not, my love?'

'I am a Bonecaster. I bore a First Hero who became a god.' Her face twisted but there was anguish in her eyes. 'Husband, I shall indeed summon allies to this battle. But you, you must go with our son, and with Udinaas.' She pointed a taloned finger at the Letherii. 'Lead them into your world. Find a place for them—'

'A place? Kilava, they are as the beasts of my world – *there are no places left!*'

'You must find one.'

Do you hear this, Fear Sengar? I am not to be you after all. No, I am to be Hull Beddict, another doomed brother. 'Follow me! Listen to all my promises! Die.' 'There is nowhere,' he said, throat tight with grief, 'In all the world . . . nowhere. We leave nothing well enough alone. Not ever. The Imass can make claim to empty lands, yes, until someone casts upon it a covetous eye. And then they will begin killing you. Collecting hides and scalps. They will poison your food. Rape your daughters. All in the name of pacification, or resettlement, or whatever other euphemistic bhederin shit they choose to spit out. And the sooner you're all dead the better, so they can forget you ever existed in the first place. Guilt is the first weed we pluck, to keep the garden pretty and smelling sweet. That is what we do, and you cannot stop us – you never could. No one can.'

Kilava's expression was flat. 'You can be stopped. You will be stopped.'

Udinaas shook his head.

'Lead them into your world, Udinaas. Fight for them. I do not mean to fall here, and if you imagine I am not capable of protecting my children, then you do not know me.'

'You condemn me, Kilava.'

'Summon your son.'

'No.'

'Then you condemn yourself, Udinaas.'

'Will you speak so coolly when my fate extends to your children as well?'

When it seemed that no answer was forthcoming, Udinaas sighed

17

and, turning about, set off for the outside, for the cold and the snow, and the whiteness and the freezing of time itself. To his anguish, Onrack followed.

'My friend.'

'I'm sorry, Onrack, I can't tell you anything helpful – nothing to ease your mind.'

'Yet,' rumbled the warrior, 'you believe you have an answer.'

'Hardly.'

'Nonetheless.'

Errant's nudge, it's hopeless. Oh, watch me walk with such resolve. Lead you all, yes. Bold Hull Beddict has returned, to repeat his host of crimes one more time.

Still hunting for heroes, Fear Sengar? Best turn away, now.

'You will lead us, Udinaas.'

'So it seems.'

Onrack sighed.

Beyond the cave mouth, the snow whipped down.

He had sought a way out. He had flung himself from the conflagration. But even the power of the Azath could not breach Akhrast Korvalain, and so he had been cast down, his mind shattered, the fragments drowning in a sea of alien blood. Would he recover? Calm did not know for certain, but she intended to take no chances. Besides, the latent power within him remained dangerous, a threat to all their plans. It could be used against them, and that was not acceptable. *No, better to turn this weapon, to take it into my own hand and wield it against the enemies I know I must soon face. Or, if that need proves unnecessary, kill him.*

Before either could ever happen, however, she would have to return here. *And do what must be done. I would do it now, if not for the risk. Should he awaken, should he force my hand . . . no, too soon. We are not ready for that.*

Calm stood over the body, studying him, the angular features, the tusks, the faint flush that hinted of fever. Then she spoke to her ancestors. 'Take him. Bind him. Weave your sorcery – he must remain unconscious. The risk of his awakening is too great. I will return before too long. Take him. Bind him.' The chains of bones slithered out like serpents, plunging into the hard ground, ensnaring the body's limbs, round the neck, across the torso, stitching him spread-eagled to this hilltop.

She saw the bones trembling. 'Yes, I understand. His power is too immense – that is why he must be kept unconscious. But there is something else I can do.' She stepped closer and crouched. Her right hand darted out, the fingers stiff as blades, and stabbed a deep hole in the man's side. She gasped and almost reeled back – was it too much? Had she awoken him?

Blood seeped down from the wound.

But Icarium did not move.

Calm released a long, unsteady breath. 'Keep the blood trickling,' she told her ancestors. 'Feed on his power.'

Straightening, she lifted her gaze, studied the horizon on all sides. The old lands of the Elan. But they had done away with them, leaving nothing but the elliptical boulders that once held down the sides of tents, and the old blinds and runs from an even older time; of the great animals that once dwelt in this plain not even a single herd remained, domestic or wild. There was, she observed, admirable perfection in this new state of things. Without criminals, there can be no crime. Without crime, no victims. The wind moaned and none stood against it to give answer.

Perfect adjudication, it tasted of paradise.

Reborn. Paradise reborn. From this empty plain, the world. From this promise, the future.

Soon.

She set out, leaving the hill behind, and with it the body of Icarium, bound to the earth in chains of bone. When she returned again to this place, she would be flush with triumph. Or in desperate need. If the latter, she would awaken him. If the former, she would grasp his head in her hands, and with a single, savage twist, break the abomination's neck.

And no matter which decision awaited her, on that day her ancestors would sing with joy.

Crooked upon the mound of rubbish, the stronghold's throne was burning in the courtyard below. Smoke, grey and black, rose in a column until it lifted past the ramparts, where the wind tore it apart, shreds drifting like banners high above the ravaged valley.

Half-naked children scampered across the battlements, their voices cutting sharp through the clatter and groan from the main gate, where the masons were repairing yesterday's damage. A watch was turning over and the High Fist listened to commands snapping like flags behind him. He blinked sweat and grit from his eyes and leaned, with some caution, on the eroded merlon, his narrowed gaze scanning the well-ordered enemy camp spread out along the valley floor.

From the rooftop platform of the square tower on his right a child of no more than nine or ten years was struggling with what had once been a signal kite, straining to hold it overhead, until with thudding wing-flaps the tattered silk dragon lifted suddenly into the air, spinning and wheeling. Ganoes Paran squinted up at it. The dragon's long tail flashed silver in the midday sunlight. The same tail, he recalled, that had been in the sky above the stronghold the day of the conquest.

What had the defenders been signalling then?

Distress. Help.

He stared up at the kite, watched it climb ever higher. Until the wind-spun smoke devoured it.

Hearing a familiar curse, he turned to see the Host's High Mage struggling past a knot of children at the top of the stairs, his face twisted in disgust as if navigating a mob of lepers. The fish spine clenched between his teeth jerking up and down in agitation, he strode up to the High Fist.

'I swear there're more of them than yesterday, and how is that possible? They don't leap out of someone's hip already half grown, do they?'

'Still creeping out from the caves,' Ganoes Paran said, fixing his attention on the enemy ranks once more.

Noto Boil grunted. 'And that's another thing. Whoever thought a cave was a decent place to live? Rank, dripping, crawling with vermin. There will be disease, mark my words, High Fist, and the Host has had quite enough of that.'

'Instruct Fist Bude to assemble a clean-up crew,' Paran said. 'Which squads got into the rum store?'

'Seventh, Tenth and Third, Second Company.'

'Captain Sweetcreek's sappers.'

Noto Boil plucked the spine from his mouth and examined the pink point. He then leaned over the wall and spat something red. 'Aye, sir. Hers.'

Paran smiled. 'Well then.'

'Aye, serves them right. So, if they stir up more vermin—'

'They are children, mage, not rats. Orphaned children.'

'Really? Those white bony ones make my skin crawl, that's all I'm saying, sir.' He reinserted the spine and it went up and down. 'Tell me again how this is better than Aren.'

'Noto Boil, as High Fist I answer only to the Empress.'

The mage snorted. 'Only she's dead.'

'Which means I answer to no one, not even you.'

'And that's the problem, nailed straight to the tree, sir. Nailed to the tree.' Seemingly satisfied with that statement, he pointed with a nod and jab of the fish spine in his mouth. 'Lots of scurrying about over there. Another attack coming?'

Paran shrugged. 'They're still . . . upset.'

'You know, if they ever decide to call our bluff—'

'Who says I'm bluffing, Boil?'

The man bit something that made him wince. 'What I mean is, sir, no one's denying you got talents and such, but those two commanders over there, well, if they get tired of throwing Watered and Shriven against us – if they just up and march themselves over here, in person, well . . . that's what I meant, sir.'

'I believe I gave you a command a short while ago.'

Noto scowled. 'Fist Bude, aye. The caves.' He turned to leave and then paused and looked back. 'They see you, you know. Standing here day after day. Taunting them.'

'I wonder,' Paran mused as he returned his attention to the enemy camp.

'Sir?'

'The Siege of Pale. Moon's Spawn just sat over the city. Months, years. Its lord never showed himself, until the day Tayschrenn decided he was ready to try him. But here's the thing, what if he had? What if, every damned day, he'd stepped out on to that ledge? So Onearm and all the rest could pause, look up, and see him standing there? Silver hair blowing, Dragnipur a black god-shitting stain spreading out behind him.'

Noto Boil worked his pick for a moment, and then said, 'What if he had, sir?'

'Fear, High Mage, takes time. Real fear, the kind that eats your courage, weakens your legs.' He shook his head and glanced at Noto Boil. 'Anyway, that was never his style, was it? I miss him, you know.' He grunted. 'Imagine that.'

'Who, Tayschrenn?'

'Noto, do you understand anything I say? Ever?'

'I try not to, sir. No offence. It's that fear thing you talked about.'

'Don't trample any children on your way down.'

'That's up to them, High Fist. Besides, the numbers could do with some thinning.'

'Noto.'

'We're an army, not a crèche, that's all I'm saying. An army under siege. Outnumbered, overcrowded, confused, bored – except when we're terrified.' He plucked out his fish spine again, whistled in a breath between his teeth. 'Caves filled with children – what were they doing with them all? Where are their parents?'

'Noto.'

'We should just hand them back, that's all I'm saying, sir.'

'Haven't you noticed, today's the first day they're finally behaving like normal children. What does that tell you?'

'Doesn't tell me nothing, sir.'

'Fist Rythe Bude. Now.'

'Aye sir, on my way.'

Ganoes Paran settled his attention on the besieging army, the precise rows of tents like bone tesserae on a buckled floor, the figures scrambling tiny as fleas over the trebuchets and Great Wagons. The foul air of battle never seemed to leave this valley. *They look ready to try us again. Worth another sortie? Mathok keeps skewering me with that hungry look. He wants at them.* He rubbed at his face. The shock of feeling his beard caught him yet again, and he grimaced. *No one likes change much, do they? But that's precisely my point.*

The silk dragon cut across his vision, diving down out of the reams of smoke. He glanced over to the boy on the tower, saw him struggling to keep his footing. A scrawny thing, one of the ones from up south. A Shriven. *When it gets too much, lad, be sure to let go.*

Seething motion now in the distant camp. The glint of pikes, the chained slaves marching out to the yokes of the Great Wagons, High Watered emerging surrounded by runners. Dust slowly lifting in the sky above the trebuchets as they were wheeled forward.

Aye, they're still upset all right.

'I knew a warrior once. Awakening from a wound to the head believing he was a dog, and what are dogs if not loyalty lacking wits? So here I stand, woman, and my eyes are filled with tears. For that warrior, who was my friend, who died thinking he was a dog. Too loyal to be sent home, too filled with faith to leave. These are the world's fallen. When I dream, I see them in their thousands, chewing at their own wounds. So, do not speak to me of freedom. He was right all along. We live in chains. Beliefs to shackle, vows to choke our throats, the cage of a mortal life, this is our fate. Who do I blame? I blame the gods. And curse them with fire in my heart.

'When she comes to me, when she says that it's time, I shall take my sword in hand. You say that I am a man of too few words, but against the sea of needs, words are weak as sand. Now, woman, tell me again of your boredom, this stretch of days and nights outside a city obsessed with mourning. I stand before you, eyes leaking with the grief of a dead friend, and all I get from you is a siege of silence.'

She said, 'You have a damned miserable way of talking your way into my bed, Karsa Orlong. Fine then, get in. Just don't break me.'

'I only break what I do not want.'

'And if the days of this relationship are numbered?'

'They are,' he replied, and then he grinned. 'But not the nights.'

Faintly, the distant city's bells tolled their grief at the fall of darkness, and in the blue-lit streets and alleys, dogs howled.

*   *   *

In the innermost chamber of the palace of the city's lord, she stood in shadows, watching as he moved away from the hearth, brushing charcoal from his hands. There was no mistaking his legacy of blood, and it seemed the weight his father had borne was settling like an old cloak on his son's surprisingly broad shoulders. She could never understand such creatures. Their willingness to martyrdom. The burdens by which they measured self-worth. This embrace of duty.

He settled into the high-backed chair, stretched out his legs, the awakening fire's flickering light licking the studs ringing his knee-high leather boots. Resting his head back, eyes closed, he spoke. 'Hood knows how you managed to get in here, and I imagine Silanah's hackles are lifting at this very moment, but if you are not here to kill me, there is wine on the table to your left. Help yourself.'

Scowling, she edged out from the shadows. All at once the chamber seemed too small, its walls threatening to snap tight around her. To so willingly abandon the sky in favour of heavy stone and blackened timbers, no, she did not understand this at all. 'Nothing but wine?' Her voice cracked slightly, reminding her that it had been some time since she'd last used it.

His elongated eyes opened and he observed her with unfeigned curiosity. 'You prefer?'

'Ale.'

'Sorry. You will need to go to the kitchens below for that.'

'Mare's milk, then.'

His brows lifted. 'Down to the palace gate, turn left, walk half a thousand leagues. And that is just a guess, mind you.'

Shrugging, she edged closer to the hearth. 'The gift struggles.'

'Gift? I do not understand.'

She gestured at the flames.

'Ah,' he said, nodding. 'Well, you stand in the breath of Mother Dark—' and then he started. 'Does she know you're here? But then,' he settled back again, 'how could she not?'

'Do you know who I am?' she asked.

'An Imass.'

'I am Apsal'ara. His night within the Sword, *his one night*, he freed me. He had the time for that. For me.' She found she was trembling.

He was still studying her. 'And so you have come here.'

She nodded.

'You didn't expect that from him, did you?'

'No. Your father – he had no reason for regret.'

He rose then, walked over to the table and poured himself a goblet of wine. He stood with the cup in hand, staring down at it. 'You know,' he muttered, 'I don't even want this. The need . . . to do something.' He snorted. '"No reason for regret", well . . .'

'They look for him – in you. Don't they?'

He grunted. 'Even in my name you will find him. Nimander. No, I'm not his only son. Not even his favoured one – I don't think he had any of those, come to think of it. Yet,' and he gestured with the goblet, 'there I sit, in his chair, before his fire. This palace feels like . . . feels like—'

'His bones?'

Nimander flinched, looked away. 'Too many empty rooms, that's all.'

'I need some clothes,' she said.

He nodded distractedly. 'I noticed.'

'Furs. Skins.'

'You intend to stay, Apsal'ara?'

'At your side, yes.'

He turned at that, eyes searching her face.

'But,' she added, 'I will not be his burden.'

A wry smile. 'Mine, then?'

'Name your closest advisers, Lord.'

He swallowed half the wine, and then set the goblet down on the table. 'The High Priestess. Chaste now, and I fear that does not serve her well. Skintick, a brother. Desra, a sister. Korlat, Spinnock, my father's most trusted servants.'

'Tiste Andii.'

'Of course.'

'And the one below?'

'The one?'

'Did he once advise you, Lord? Do you stand at the bars in the door's window, to watch him mutter and pace? Do you torment him? I wish to know the man I will serve.'

She saw clear anger in his face. 'Are you to be my jester now? I have heard of such roles in human courts. Will you cut the sinews of my legs and laugh as I stumble and fall?' He bared his teeth. 'If yours is to be my face of conscience, Apsal'ara, should you not be prettier?'

She cocked her head, made no reply.

Abruptly his fury collapsed, and his eyes fell away. 'It is the exile he has chosen. Did you test the lock on that door? It is barred from within. But then, *we* have no problem forgiving him. Advise me, then. I am a lord and it is in my power to do such things. To pardon the condemned. Yet you have seen the crypts below us. How many prisoners cringe beneath my iron hand?'

'One.'

'And I cannot free him. Surely that is worth a joke or two.'

'Is he mad?'

'Clip? Possibly.'

24

'Then no, not even you can free him. Your father took scores for the chains of Dragnipur, scores just like this Clip.'

'I dare say he did not call it freedom.'

'Nor mercy,' she replied. 'They are beyond a lord's reach, even that of a god.'

'Then we fail them all. Both lords and gods – we fail them, our broken children.'

This, she realized, would not be an easy man to serve. 'He drew others to him – your father. Others who were not Tiste Andii. I remember, in his court, in Moon's Spawn.'

Nimander's eyes narrowed.

She hesitated, unsure, and then resumed. 'Your kind are blind to many things. You need others close to you, Lord. Servants who are not Tiste Andii. I am not one of these . . . jesters you speak of. Nor, it seems, can I be your conscience, ugly as I am to your eyes—'

He held up a hand. 'Forgive me for that, I beg you. I sought to wound and so spoke an untruth, just to see it sting.'

'I believe I stung you first, my lord.'

He reached again for the wine, and then stood looking into the hearth's flames. 'Apsal'ara, Mistress of Thieves. Will you now abandon that life, to become an adviser to a Tiste Andii lord? All because my father, at the very end, showed you mercy?'

'I never blamed him for what he did. I gave him no choice. He did not free me out of mercy, Nimander.'

'Then why?'

She shook her head. 'I don't know. But I mean to find out.'

'And this pursuit – for an answer – has brought you here, to Black Coral. To . . . me.'

'Yes.'

'And how long will you stand at my side, Apsal'ara, whilst I govern a city, sign writs, debate policies? Whilst I slowly rot in the shadow of a father I barely knew and a legacy I cannot hope to fill?'

Her eyes widened. 'Lord, that is not your fate.'

He wheeled to her. 'Really? Why not? Please, *advise* me.'

She cocked her head a second time, studied the tall warrior with the bitter, helpless eyes. 'For so long you Tiste Andii prayed for Mother Dark's loving regard. For so long you yearned to be reborn to purpose, to life itself. He gave it all back to you. All of it. He did what he knew had to be done, for your sake. You, Nimander, and all the rest. And now you sit here, in his chair, in his city, among his children. And her holy breath, it embraces you all. Shall I give you what I possess of wisdom? Very well. Lord, even Mother Dark cannot hold her breath for ever.'

'She does not—'

'When a child is born it must cry.'

'You—'

'With its voice, it enters the world, and it *must* enter the world. Now,' she crossed her arms, 'will you continue hiding here in this city? I am the Mistress of Thieves, Lord. I know every path. I have walked them all. And I have seen what there is to be seen. If you and your people hide here, Lord, you will all die. And so will Mother Dark. Be her breath. Be *cast out*.'

'But we are *in this world*, Apsal'ara!'

'One world is not enough.'

'Then what must we do?'

'What your father wanted.'

'And what is that?'

She smiled. 'Shall we find out?'

'You have some nerve, Dragon Master.'

A child shrieked from somewhere down the walkway.

Without turning, Ganoes Paran sighed and said, 'You're frightening the young ones again.'

'Not nearly enough.' The iron-shod heel of a cane cracked hard on the stone. 'Isn't that always the way, hee hee!'

'I don't think I appreciate the new title you're giving me, Shadowthrone.'

A vague dark smear, the god moved up alongside Paran. The cane's gleaming head swung its silver snarl out over the valley. 'Master of the Deck of Dragons. Too much of a mouthful. It's your . . . abuses. I so dislike unpredictable people.' He giggled again. 'People. Ascendants. Gods. Thick-skulled dogs. Children.'

'Where is Cotillion, Shadowthrone?'

'You should be tired of that question by now.'

'I am tired of waiting for an answer.'

'*Then stop asking it!*' The god's manic shriek echoed through the fortress, rattled wild along corridors and through hallways before echoing back to where they stood atop the wall.

'That has certainly caught their attention,' Paran observed, nodding to a distant barrow where two tall, almost skeletal figures now stood.

Shadowthrone sniffed. 'They see nothing.' He hissed a laugh. 'Blinded by justice.'

Ganoes Paran scratched at his beard. 'What do you want?'

'Whence comes your faith?'

'Excuse me?'

The cane rapped and skittered on the stone. 'You sit with the Host in Aren, defying every imperial summons. And then you assault the Warrens with *this*.' He suddenly cackled. 'You should have seen the Emperor's face! And the names he called you, my, even the court scribers cringed!' He paused. 'Where was I? Yes, I was berating you, Dragon Master. Are you a genius? I doubt it. Leaving me no choice but to conclude that you're an idiot.'

'Is that all?'

'Is she out there?'

'You don't know?'

'Do you?'

Paran slowly nodded. 'Now I understand. It's all about faith. A notion unfamiliar to you, I take it.'

'This siege is meaningless!'

'Is it?'

Shadowthrone hissed, one ethereal hand reaching out, as if to claw at Paran's face. Instead, it hovered, twisted and then shrank into something vaguely fist-shaped. 'You don't understand anything!'

'I understand this,' Paran replied. 'Dragons are creatures of chaos. There can be no Dragon Master, making the title meaningless.'

'Exactly.' Shadowthrone reached out to gather up a tangled snarl of spider's web from beneath the wall's casing. He held it up, apparently studying the cocooned remnant of a desiccated insect.

Miserable turd. 'Here is what I know, Shadowthrone. The end begins here. Do you deny it? No, you can't, else you wouldn't be haunting me—'

'Not even you can breach the power surrounding this keep,' the god said. 'You have blinded yourself. Open your gate again, Ganoes Paran, find somewhere else to lodge your army. This is pointless.' He flung the web away and gestured with the head of his cane. 'You cannot defeat those two, we both know that.'

'But they don't, do they?'

'They will test you. Sooner or later.'

'I'm still waiting.'

'Perhaps even today.'

'Will you wager on that, Shadowthrone?'

The god snorted. 'You have nothing I want.'

'Liar.'

'Then I have nothing you want.'

'Actually, as it happens . . .'

'Do you see me holding a leash? He's not here. He's off doing other things. We're allies, do you understand? An alliance. Not a damned marriage!'

Paran grinned. 'Oddly enough, I wasn't even thinking of Cotillion.'

'A pointless wager in any case. If you lose you die. Or abandon your army to die, which I can't see you doing. Besides, you're nowhere near as devious as I am. You want this wager? Truly? Even when I lose, I win. Even when I lose . . . *I win!*'

Paran nodded. 'And that has ever been your game, Shadowthrone. You see, I know you better than you think. Yes, I would wager with you. They shall not try me this day. We shall repulse their assault . . . again. And more Shriven and Watered will die. We shall remain the itch they cannot scratch.'

'All because you have faith? Fool!'

'Those are the conditions of this wager. Agreed?'

The god's form seemed to shift about, almost vanishing entirely at one moment before reappearing, and the cane head struck chips from the merlon's worn edge. 'Agreed!'

'If you win and I survive,' resumed Paran, 'you get what you want from me, whatever that is, and assuming it's in my power to grant. If I win, I get what I want from you.'

'If it's in my power—'

'It is.'

Shadowthrone muttered something under his breath, and then hissed. 'Very well, tell me what you want.'

And so Paran told him.

The god cackled. 'And you think that's in my power? You think Cotillion has no say in the matter?'

'If he does, best you go and ask him, then. Unless,' Paran added, 'it turns out that, as I suspect, you have no idea where your ally has got to. In which case, Lord of Shadows, you will do as I ask, and answer to him later.'

'I answer to no one!' Another shriek, the echoes racing.

Paran smiled. 'Why, Shadowthrone, I know precisely how you feel. Now, what is it you seek from me?'

'I seek the source of your faith.' The cane waggled. 'That she's out there. That she seeks what you seek. That, upon the Plain of Blood and Chains, you will find her, and stand facing her – as if you two had planned this all along, when I damned well know you haven't! You don't even like each other!'

'Shadowthrone, I cannot sell you faith.'

'So lie, damn you, just do it convincingly!'

He could hear silk wings flapping, the sound a shredding of the wind itself. *A boy with a kite. Dragon Master. Ruler over all that cannot be ruled. Ride the howling chaos and call it mastery – who are you fooling? Lad, let go now. It's too much.* But he would not, he didn't know how.

The man with the greying beard watches, and can say nothing.

Distress.

He glanced to his left, but the shadow was gone.

A crash from the courtyard below drew him round. The throne, a mass of flames, had broken through the mound beneath it. And the smoke leapt skyward, like a beast unchained.

CHAPTER TWO

I look around at the living
Still and bound
Hands and knees to stone
By what we found

Was a night as wearying
As any just past?
Was a dawn any crueller
To find us this aghast?

By your hand you are staying
And this is fair
But your words of blood
Are too bitter to bear

Song of Sorrows Unwitnessed
Napan Blight

FROM HERE ONWARDS, HE COULD NOT TRUST THE SKY. THE ALTERNA-tive, he observed as he examined the desiccated, rotted state of his limbs, invited despondency. Tulas Shorn looked round, noting with faint dismay the truncated lines of sight, an affliction cursing all who must walk the land's battered surface. Scars he had looked down upon from a great height only a short time earlier now posed daunting obstacles, a host of furrowed trenches carving deep, jagged gouges across his intended path.

She is wounded but does not bleed. Not yet, at any rate. No, I see now. This flesh is dead. Yet I am drawn to this place. Why? He walked, haltingly, up to the edge of the closest crevasse. Peered down. Darkness, a breath cool and slightly sour with decay. And . . . something else.

Tulas Shorn paused for a moment, and then stepped out into space, and plunged downward.

Threadbare clothing tore loose, whipped wild as his body struck rough walls, skidded and rebounded in a knock of withered limbs, tumbling amidst hissing grit and sand, the feathery brush and then snag of grass roots, and now stones spilling to follow him down.

Bones snapped when he struck the boulder-studded floor of the fissure. More sand poured down on all sides with the sound of serpents.

He did not move for a time. The dust, billowing in the gloom, slowly settled. Eventually, he sat up. One leg had broken just above the knee. The lower part of the limb remained attached by little more than a few stretches of skin and sinew. He set the break and waited while the two ragged ends slowly fused. The four ribs that now thrust broken tips out from the right side of his chest were not particularly debilitating, so he left them, conserving his power.

A short while later he managed to stand, his shoulders scraping walls. He could make out the usual assortment of splintered bones littering the uneven floor, but these were only of mild interest, the fragments of bestial souls clinging to them writhing like ghostly worms, disturbed by the new currents in the air.

He began walking, following the odd scent he had detected from above. It was stronger down here, of course, and with each awkward step along the winding channel there arose within him a certain anticipation, bordering on excitement. Close, now.

The skull was set on a spear shaft of corroded bronze, rising to chest height and blocking the path. In a heap at the shaft's base was the rest of the skeleton, every bone systematically shattered.

Tulas Shorn halted two paces from the skull. 'Tartheno?'

The voice rumbling through his head spoke, however, in the language of the Imass. *'Bentract. Skan Ahl greets you, Revenant.'*

'Your bones are too large for a T'lan Imass.'

'Yes, but no salvation came of that.'

'Who did this to you, Skan Ahl?'

'Her body lies a few paces behind me, Revenant.'

'If you so wounded her in your battle that she died, how was it that she could destroy your body with such vigour?'

'I did not say she was dead.'

Tulas Shorn hesitated, and then snorted. 'No, nothing lives here. Either she is dead or she is gone.'

'I can hardly argue with you, Revenant. Now then, do this one thing: look behind you.'

Bemused, he did so. Sunlight fighting its way down through dust. 'I see nothing.'

'That is your privilege.'

31

'I do not understand.'

'*I saw her step past me. I heard her slide to the ground. I heard her cry out in pain, and then weep, and when the weeping was done, all that remained was her breathing, until that too slowed. But . . . I can still hear it. The lift and fall of her chest, with each rise of the moon – when its faint light reaches down – how many times? Many. I have lost count. Why does she remain? What does she want? She will not answer. She never answers.*'

Saying nothing, Tulas Shorn edged past the stake and its dusty skull. Five strides further on, he halted, stared down.

'*Does she sleep, Revenant?*'

Tulas slowly crouched. He reached down and touched the delicate rib cage lying in a shallow depression at his feet. A newborn's fossilized bones, glued to the ground by calcified limestone. *Born to the tide of the moon, were you, little one? Did you draw even a single breath? I think not.* 'T'lan Imass, was this the end of your chase?'

'*She was formidable.*'

'A Jaghut. A woman.'

'*I was the last on her trail. I failed.*'

'And is it that failure that torments you, Skan Ahl? Or that she now haunts you, here behind you, for ever hidden from your sight?'

'*Awaken her! Or better still, slay her, Revenant. Destroy her. For all we know, she is the very last Jaghut. Kill her and the war will be over, and I will know peace.*'

'There is little peace in death, T'lan Imass.' *Ah, child, the wind at night moans through you, does it? Night's very own breath, to haunt him for all eternity.*

'*Revenant, turn my skull. I would see her again.*'

Tulas Shorn straightened. 'I will not step between you in this war.'

'*But it is a war you can end!*'

'I cannot. Nor, it is clear, can you. Skan Ahl, I must leave you now.' He looked down at the tiny bones. 'Both of you.'

'*Since my failure, Revenant, I have entertained not a single visitor. You are the first to find me. Are you of such cruelty as to condemn me to an eternity in this state? She defeated me. I accept this. But I beg of you, grant me the dignity of facing my slayer.*'

'You pose a dilemma,' Tulas Shorn said after a moment's consideration. 'What you imagine to be mercy may not prove any such thing, should I acquiesce. And then there is this: I am not particularly inclined to mercy, Skan Ahl. Not with respect to you. Do you begin to comprehend my difficulty? I could indeed reach out and swing your skull round, and you may curse me for all time. Or I could elect to do nothing, to leave everything as I have found it – as if I was never here – and so earn your darkest resentment. In either case, you will see me as cruel. Now, this does not offend me overmuch. As I said, I am not stirred to kindness. The matter I face is: how cruel do I wish to be?'

'Think on that privilege I spoke of earlier, Revenant. Your simple gift of being able to turn yourself round, to see what hides behind you. We both understand that what is seen may not be welcome.'

Tulas Shorn grunted. 'T'lan Imass, I know all about looking over my shoulder.' He walked back to the skull. 'Shall I be the brush of wind, then? A single turn, a new world to unfold.'

'Will she awaken?'

'I think not,' he replied, reaching out and settling one withered fingertip against the huge skull. 'But you can try.' A slow increase in pressure, and with a grating squeal the skull swung round.

The T'lan Imass began howling in Tulas Shorn's wake as he walked back up the channel.

Gifts are never what they seem. And the punishing hand? It, too, is not what it seems. Yes, these two thoughts are worthy of long echoes, stretching into this wretched future.

As if anyone will listen.

Vengeance, held tight like an iron-shod spear in her hand, and how it burned. Ralata could feel its searing heat, and the pain was now a gift, something she could feed upon, like a hunter crouched over a fresh kill. She'd lost her horse. She'd lost her people. Everything had been taken away from her, everything except this final gift.

The broken moon was a blurred smear almost lost in the green glow of the Strangers in the Sky. The Skincut Barghast stood facing east, her back to the smouldering coals from the hearth, and looked out upon a plain that seemed to seethe in the jade and silver light.

Behind her the black-haired warrior named Draconus spoke in low tones with the Teblor giant. They talked often in some foreign tongue – Letherii, she supposed, not that she'd ever cared to learn it. Even the simpler trader's language made her head ache, but on occasion she caught some Letherii word that had made its way into the pidgin cant, so she knew they were speaking of the journey ahead.

East. It was, for the moment, convenient for her to travel in their company, despite having to constantly fend off the Teblor's clumsy advances. Draconus was able to find game where none seemed to exist. He could call water up from cracked bedrock. More than just a warrior. A shaman. And in a scabbard of midnight wood strapped to his back there was a sword of magic.

She wanted it. She meant to have it. A weapon suited to the vengeance she desired. With such a sword, she could kill the winged slayer of her sisters.

In her mind she worked through scenarios. A knife across the man's throat when he slept, and then a stab through an eye for the Teblor. Simple, quick, and she would have what she wanted. If not for the emptiness of this land. If not for the thirst and starvation that would follow – no, for the time being Draconus must live. For Ublala, however, if she could arrange a terrible accident, then she would not have him to worry about on the night she went for the sword. The dilemma of finding for the oaf a fatal demise here on this featureless plain still defeated her. But she had time.

'Come back to the fire, beloved,' the Teblor called, 'and drink some tea. It has real leaves in it and stuff that smells nice.'

Ralata massaged her temples for a moment, and then turned about. 'I am not your beloved. I belong to no one. I never will.'

At seeing the half-smile on the face of Draconus as he tossed another dung chip on to the fire, Ralata scowled. 'It is rude,' she pronounced as she walked over, squatted down and took the cup Ublala proffered, 'to talk in a language I don't understand. You could be plotting my rape and murder for all I know.'

The warrior's brows arched. 'Now, why would we want to do that, Barghast? Besides,' he added, 'Ublala is courting you.'

'He might as well give up now. I don't want him.'

Draconus shrugged. 'I have explained to him that most of what we call courting boils down to just being there. Every time you turn, you see him, until his company feels perfectly natural to you. "Courting is the art of growing like mould on the one you want."' He paused, scratched at the stubble on his jaw. 'I can't lay claim to that observation, but I don't recall who said it first.'

Ralata spat into the fire to announce her disgust. 'We're not all like Hetan, you know. She used to say she gauged the attractiveness of a man by imagining how he looked when she was staring up at his red face and bulging eyes.' She spat again. 'I am a Skincut, a slayer, a collector of scalps. When I look upon a man, I imagine what he'll look like with the skin of his face sliced away.'

'She's not very nice, is she?' Ublala asked Draconus.

'Trying hard, you mean,' Draconus replied.

'Makes me want to sex her even more than before.'

'That's how these things work.'

'It's torture. I don't like it. No, I do. No, I don't. I do. Oh, I'm going to polish my hammer.'

Ralata stared at Ublala as he surged to his feet and thumped off.

Low and in the language of the White Faces, Draconus murmured, 'He means that literally, by the way.'

She shot him a look, and snorted. 'I knew that. He has no wits for anything else.' She hesitated, and then said, 'His armour looks expensive.'

'It cost dearly, aye, Ralata. He wears it well, better than one might have hoped.' He nodded, mostly to himself, she suspected, and said, 'He will stand well, I think, when the time comes.'

She remembered this warrior killing Sekara the Vile, snapping the old woman's neck. The ease of the gesture, the way he seemed to embrace her to keep her from falling, as if her lifeless body still clung to something like dignity. He was not a man easily understood. 'What are you two seeking? You walk into the east. Why?'

'There are unfortunate things in the world, Ralata.'

She frowned. 'I don't know what that means.'

He sighed, studied the fire. 'Have you ever stepped on something unintentionally? Out through a doorway, a sudden crunching under-foot. What was it? An insect? A snail? A lizard?' He lifted his head and fixed her with his dark eyes, the embers gleaming in lurid reflection. 'Not worth a second thought, was it? Such are the vagaries of life. An ant dreaming of war, a wasp devouring a spider, a lizard stalking the wasp. All these dramas, and *crunch* – all over with. What to make of it? Nothing, I suppose. If you've a heart, you apportion out some small measure of guilt and remorse, and then continue on your way.'

She shook her head, baffled. 'You stepped on something?'

'In a manner of speaking.' He nudged the embers and watched as sparks spun upward. 'No matter. A few ants survived. No end to the little bastards, in fact. I could crush a thousand nests under heel and it'd not make a whit of difference. That's the best way of thinking about it, in fact.' He met her eyes again. 'Does that make me cold? What did I leave behind in those chains, I wonder, still shackled there, a host of forlorn virtues . . . whatever. I am having odd dreams of late.'

'I dream only of vengeance.'

'The more you dream of one particular and pleasing thing, Ralata, the quicker it palls. The edges get worn down, the lustre fades. To leave such obsessions behind, dream of them often.'

'You speak like an old man, a Barghast shaman. Riddles and bad advice, Onos Toolan was right to discount them all.' She almost looked to the west, past his shoulder, as if she might find her people and the Warleader, all marching straight for them. Instead, she finished the last of the tea in her cup.

'Onos Toolan,' Draconus muttered, 'an Imass name. A strange war-leader for the Barghast to have . . . will you tell me the tale of that, Ralata?'

She grunted. 'I have no skill for tales. Hetan took him for a hus-band. He was from the Gathering, when all the T'lan Imass answered the summons of Silverfox. She returned to him his life, ending his im-mortality, and then Hetan found him. After the end of the Pannion War. Hetan's father was Humbrall Taur, who had united the White

Face clans, but he drowned during the landing upon the shores of this continent—'

'A moment, please. Your tribes are not native to this continent?'

She shrugged. 'The Barghast gods were awakened to some peril. They filled the brains of the shamans with their panic, like sour piss. We must return here, to our original homeland, to face an ancient enemy. So we were told, but not much else. We thought the enemy was the Tiste Edur. Then the Letherii, and then the Akrynnai. But it wasn't any of them, and now we are destroyed, and if Sekara spoke truly, then Onos Toolan is dead, and so is Hetan. They're all dead. I hope the Barghast gods died with them.'

'Can you tell me more about these T'lan Imass?'

'They knelt before a mortal man. In the midst of battle, they turned their backs on the enemy. I will say no more of them.'

'Yet you chose to follow Onos Toolan—'

'He was not among those. He stood alone before Silverfox, a thing of bones, and demanded—'

But Draconus had leaned forward, almost over the fire. '"A thing of bones"? T'lan – *Tellann!* Abyss below!' He suddenly rose, startling Ralata further, and she watched as he paced, and it seemed black ink was bleeding out from the scabbard at his back, a stain that hurt her eyes. 'That bitch,' he said in a low growl. 'You selfish, spiteful hag!'

Ublala heard the outburst and he suddenly loomed into the dull glow of the fire, his huge mace leaning over one shoulder. 'What'd she do, Draconus?' He glared at Ralata. 'Should I kill her? If she's being spelfish and sightful – what's rape mean, anyway? It's got to do with sex? Can I—'

'Ublala,' Draconus cut in, 'I was not speaking of Ralata.'

The Teblor looked round. 'I don't see no one else, Draconus. She's hiding? Whoever she is, I hate her, unless she's pretty. Is she pretty? Mean is all right if they're pretty.'

The warrior was staring at Ublala. 'Best climb into your furs, Ublala, and get some sleep. I'll stand first watch.'

'All right. I wasn't tired anyway.' He swung about and set off for his bedroll.

'Be careful with those curses,' Ralata said in a hiss, rising to her feet. 'What if he strikes first and *then* asks questions?'

He glanced across at her. 'The T'lan Imass were *undead.*'

She nodded.

'She never let them go?'

'Silverfox? No. They asked, I think, but no.'

He seemed to stagger. And, turning away, he slowly sank down on to one knee, facing away from her. The pose was one of dismay, or grief – she could not be sure. Confused, Ralata took a step towards him, and

36

then stopped. He was saying something, but in a language she knew not. A phrase, over and over again, his voice hoarse, thick.

'Draconus?'

His shoulders shook, and then she heard the rumble of laughter, a deathly, humourless sound. 'And I thought my penance was long.' Head still lowered, he said, 'This Onos Toolan . . . is he now truly dead, Ralata?'

'So Sekara said.'

'Then he is at peace. At long last. At peace.'

'I doubt it,' she said.

He twisted round to regard her. 'Why do you say that?'

'They killed his wife. They killed his children. If I was Onos Toolan, even death would not keep me from my revenge.'

He drew a sharp breath, and it caught as if on a hook, and once more he turned away.

The scabbard dripped blackness as if from an open wound.

Oh, how I want that sword.

Wants and needs could starve and die, no different from love. All the grand gestures of honour and faithful loyalty meant nothing when the only witnesses were grass, wind and empty sky. It seemed to Mappo that his nobler virtues had withered on the vine, and the garden of his soul, once so verdant, now rattled skeletal branches against stone walls.

Where was his promise? What of the vows he had uttered, so sober and grim in youth, so shiny of portent, as befitted the broad-shouldered brave he had once been? Mappo could feel dread inside, hard as a fist-sized tumour in his chest. His ribs ached with the pressure of it, but it was an ache he had lived with for so long now, it had become a part of him, a scar far larger than the wound it covered. *And this is how words are made flesh. This is how our very bones become the rack of our own penance, and the muscles twitch in slick skins of sweat, the head hangs loose – I see you, Mappo – so slumped down in pathetic surrender.*

He was taken from you, like a bauble stolen from your purse. The theft stung, it stings still. You feel outraged. Violated. This is pride and indignation, isn't it? These are the sigils on your banner of war, your lust for vengeance. Look upon yourself, Mappo, you mouth the arguments of tyrants now, and all shrink from your path.

But I want him back. At my side. I swore my life to protecting him, sheltering him. How can that be taken away from me? Can you not hear the empty howl in my heart? This is a pit without light, and upon all the close walls surrounding me I can feel nothing but the gouges my claws have made.

The green sheen upon the broken land was sickly to his eyes, unnatural, an ominous imposition that made the shattering of the moon seem almost incidental. *But worlds heal, when we do not.* Mustiness clung to the night air, as of distant corpses left to rot.

There have been so many deaths in this wasteland. I don't understand it. Was this by Icarium's sword? His rage? I should have felt that, but the very ground barely breathes; like an old woman in her deathcot she can but tremble to faraway sounds. Thunder and a darkness upon the sky.

'There is war.'

Mappo grunted. They'd been silent for so long he'd almost forgotten Gruntle's presence, standing here at his side. 'What do you know of it?' he asked, pulling his gaze away from the eastern horizon.

The barb-tattooed caravan guard shrugged. 'What is there to know? Deaths beyond counting. Slaughter to make my mouth water. Hackles rise – even in this gloom I can see the dismay in your face, Trell, and I share it. War, it is what it was and always will be. What else is there to say?'

'You yearn to join the fray?'

'My dreams tell me different.'

Mappo glanced back at the camp. The humped forms of their sleeping companions, the more regular mound of the fresh burial cairn. The desiccated shape of Cartographer seated upon the stones, a tattered wolf lying at his feet. Two horses, the scatter of packs and supplies. An air of death and sorrow. 'If there is war,' he said, facing Gruntle again, 'who profits?'

The man rolled his shoulders, a habit of his, Mappo now knew, as if Trake's Mortal Sword sought to shift a burden no one else could see. 'Ever the question, as if answers meant anything, which they don't. Soldiers are herded into the iron maw and the ground turns to red mud, and someone on a nearby hill raises a fist in triumph, while another flees the field on a white horse.'

'I warrant Trake takes little pleasure in his chosen warrior's views on the matter.'

'Warrant more how little I care, Mappo. A Soletaken tiger, but such beasts keep no company, why should Trake expect anything different? We are solitary hunters; what manner of war can we hope to find? That is the irony in the whole mess: the Tiger of Summer is doomed to hunt the perfect war, but never find it. See how his tail lashes.'

No, I see that. For the true visage of war, best turn to the snarling jaws of wolves. 'Setoc,' he said in a murmur.

'She has dreams of her own, I'm sure,' Gruntle said.

'Traditional wars,' Mappo mused, 'are fomented in the winter, when the walls close in and there is too much time on one's hands. The

38

barons brood, the kings scheme, raiders plot their passages through borderlands. The wolves howl in winter. But come the season's turn, summer is born to the savagery of blades and spears – the savagery of the tiger.' He shrugged. 'I see no conflict there. You and Setoc, and the gods bound to you, you all complement one another—'

'It is more complicated than that, Trell. Cold iron belongs to the Wolves. Trake is hot iron, a fatal flaw to my mind. Oh, we do well in the bloody press, but then you must ask, how in Hood's name did we get into such a mess in the first place? Because we don't think.' Gruntle's tone was both amused and bitter.

'And so your dreams visit visions upon you, Mortal Sword? Troubling ones?'

'No one remembers the nice ones, do they? Yes, troubling. Old friends long dead stalk the jungle. They walk lost, arms groping. Their mouths work but no sound reaches me. I see a panther, my mistress of the hunt, in these dreams, by the way – she lies gored and bloody, panting fast in shock, dumb misery in her eyes.'

'Gored?'

'Boar's tusk.'

'Fener?'

'As the god of war, he was unchallenged. Vicious as any tiger, and cunning as any pack of wolves. With Fener in the ascendant, we knelt with heads bowed.'

'Your mistress lies dying?'

'Dying? Maybe. I see her, and rage fills my eyes in a flood of crimson. Gored, raped, and someone will pay for that. Someone will pay.'

Mappo was silent. *Raped?*

Gruntle then growled as befitted his patron god, and Mappo's nape-hairs stiffened at the sound. The Trell said, 'I will part this company on the morrow.'

'You seek the battlefield.'

'Which none of you need witness, I think. He was there, you see. I felt him, his power. I will find the trail. I hope. And you, Gruntle? Where will you lead this troop?'

'East, a little south of your path, but I am not content to walk at the side of the Wolves for much longer. Setoc speaks of a child in a city of ice—'

'Crystal.' Mappo briefly closed his eyes. 'A crystal city.'

'And Precious Thimble believes there is power there, something she might be able to use, to take the Shareholders home. They have a destination, but it is not mine.'

'Do you seek your mistress? There are no jungles east of here, unless they exist on the far coast.'

Gruntle started. 'Jungles? No. You think too literally, Mappo. I seek a place at her side, to fight a battle. If I am not there, she will indeed die. So my ghosts tell me in their haunting. It is not enough to arrive too late, to see the wound in her eyes, to know that all that you can hope to do is avenge what was done to her. Not enough, Trell. Never enough.'

The wound in her eyes . . . you do this all for love? Mortal Sword, do your ribs ache? Dose she haunt you, whoever she was, or is Trake simply feeding you the ripest meat? It is not enough to arrive too late. Oh, I know the truth of that.

Violated.

Raped.

Now comes the dark question. Who profits from this?

Faint huddled under her furs, feeling as if she'd been dragged behind a carriage for a league or two. There was nothing worse than cracked ribs. Well, if she'd sat up only to find her severed head resting on her lap, that would be worse. *But probably painless, all things considered. Not like this. Miserable ache, a thousand twinges vying for attention, until everything turns white and then red and then purple and finally blissful black. Where's the black? I'm waiting, been waiting all night.*

At dusk Setoc had drawn close to tell her that the Trell would be leaving on the morrow. How she knew was anyone's guess, since Mappo wasn't in any mood to talk, except to Gruntle, who was one of those men it was too easy to talk to, a man who just invited confession, as if giving off a scent or something. Hood knew, she wanted to—

A spasm. She stifled a gasp, waited out the throbs, and then sought to shift position once more, not that one was more comfortable than any other. More a matter of duration. Twenty breaths lying this way, fifteen that way, and flat on her back was impossible – she'd never imagined how the weight of her own tits could crush the breath from her, and the gentle sweep of the furs threatened to close like a vice when she thought of settling her arms. It was all impossible, and come the dawn she'd be ready to snap off heads.

'*Then Gruntle will leave us too. Not yet. But he won't stay. He can't.*'

Setoc had a way with words, the heaps of good news she stacked like the coins of a private treasure. Maybe the grasses whispered in her ears, as she lay there so gentle and damnably asleep, or the crickets and just listen to them – no, that was her spine crackling away. She fought back a moan.

So, before long, it would be the Shareholders and the barbarian, Torrent, along with the three runts and Setoc herself. She didn't count Cartographer, the wolf or the horses. Not for any particular reason, even if only the horses were actually alive. *I don't count them, that's all.* So, just them, and who among them was tough enough to fight off the next attack from that winged lizard? Torrent? He looked too young, with the eyes of a hunted hare.

And only one Bole left, and that's bad. Poor boy's miserable. Here's the deal, let's not bury any more friends, shall we?

But Precious Thimble was adamant. Raw power waited in the east. She thought she could do something with it. Open a warren, get the Hood out of here. *Can't argue with that. Wouldn't want to. Sure, she's just a cherry of a lass is our Precious. And if she's now regretting her tease, why, that will make her more careful from now on, which isn't a bad thing.*

A roll with Gruntle would be delicious. But it'd kill me. Besides, I'm all scarred up. Lopsided, hah. Who'd want a freak, except out of pity? Be rational, and don't shy from its jagged edge. Your days of crooking a finger to get a tumble are done. Find some other hobby, woman. Spinning, maybe. Butter churning – is that a hobby? Probably not.

You can't sleep through this. Face it. It'll be months before a decent night . . . sleeping. Or otherwise.

'Gruntle thinks he's going someplace to die. He doesn't want us to die with him.'

That's nice, Setoc, thanks for that.

'In the Crystal City there is a child . . . beware the opening of his eyes.'

Listen, sweetie, the little one right here needs his butt wiped and the twins are pretending not to notice but the smell's getting a tad rank, right? Take this handful of grass.

Life was so much better on the carriage, off delivering whatever.

Faint grunted and then flinched at the pain. *Gods, woman, you're completely insane.*

Let me dream of a tavern. Smoky, crowded, a perfect table. We're all sitting there, working out the shakes. Quell duck-walks to the loo. The Boles make faces at each other and then laugh. Reccanto's broken a thumb and he's putting it back in place. Glanno can't see the barman. He can't even see the table in front of him. Sweetest Sufferance is looking like a plump cat with a rat's tail hanging from her mouth.

Another pitcher arrives.

Reccanto looks up. 'Who's paying for this?' he asks.

Faint cautiously lifted one hand, moved it up to brush her cheeks. *Blissful black, you seem so far away.*

In the false dawn, Torrent opened his eyes. Some violence still rocked in his skull – a dream, but already the memory of its details faded. Blinking, he sat up. Chill air stole in beneath his rodara wool blanket, plucking at the beads of sweat on his chest. He glanced over at the horses, but the beasts stood calm, dozing. In the camp the shapes of the others were motionless in the grainy half-light.

Casting the blanket aside, he rose. The greenish glow was paling to the east. The warrior walked over to his horse, greeted it with a low murmur and settled a hand upon its warm neck. Tales of cities and empires, of gas that burned with blue flame, of secret ways through the world that his eyes could not see, all left him disturbed, agitated, though he was not sure why.

He knew Toc had come from such an empire, far away across the ocean, and his lone eye had looked upon scenes Torrent could not imagine. Yet around the Awl warrior now was a more familiar landscape, rougher than the Awl'dan, true, but just as open, sweeping, the earth levelled beneath the vast sky. What other sort of place could an honest man desire? The eyes could reach, the mind could stretch. There was space for everything. A tent or yurt for nightly shelter, a ring of stones to embrace the cookfire, the steam rising from the backs of the herds as the dawn gently broke.

He longed for such a scene, the morning's greeting one he had always known. Dogs rising from their beds of grass, the soft cry of a hungry babe from one of the yurts, the smell of smoke as hearths were awakened once more.

Sudden emotion gripped him and he fought back a sob. *All gone. Why am I still alive? Why do I cling to this misery, this empty life? When you are the last, there is no reason to keep living. All of your veins are cut, the blood drains and drains and there's no end to it.*

Redmask, you murdered us all.

Did his kin await him in the spirit world? He wished he could believe. He wished his faith had never been shattered, crushed under the heel of Letherii soldiers. If the Awl spirits had been stronger, if they had been all the shamans said they were . . . *we would not have died. Not have failed. We would never have fallen.* But, if they existed at all, they were weak, ignorant and helpless against change. Balanced on a bowstring, and when that string snapped their world was done with, for ever.

He saw Setoc awaken, watched her stand up, running fingers through the tangles in her hair. Wiping at his eyes, Torrent turned back to his horse, leaned his forehead against the slick coat of its neck. *I feel you, friend. You do not question your life. You are in its midst and know no other place, nothing outside it. How I envy you.*

She approached him, the faint crunch of stones underfoot, the slow pulse of her breathing. She came up on his left, reaching to stroke the horse in the softness between its nostrils, giving it her scent. 'Torrent,' she whispered, 'who is out there?'

He grunted. 'Your wolf ghosts are torn, aren't they? Curious, frightened . . .'

'They smell death, and yet power. So much power.'

The hide against his brow was now damp. 'She calls herself a Bone-caster. A shaman. A witch. Her name is Olar Ethil, and no life burns in her body.'

'She comes before the dawn, three mornings in a row now. But draws no closer. She hides like a hare, and when the sun's light finally arrives, she vanishes. Like dust.'

'Like dust,' he agreed.

'What does she want?'

He stepped back from his horse, ran the back of one wrist against his brow, and looked away. 'Nothing good, Setoc.'

She said nothing for a time, standing at his side, her furs wrapped tight about her shoulders. Then she seemed to shiver, and said, 'A snake writhes in each of her hands, but they're laughing.'

Telorast. Curdle. They dance in my dreams. 'They're dead, too. They're all dead, Setoc. But still they hunger . . . for something.' He shrugged. 'We are all lost out here. I feel this, like a rot in my bones.'

'I told Gruntle of my visions, the Wolves and the throne they guard. Do you know what he asked me?'

Torrent shook his head.

'He asked me if I've seen the Wolves lift a leg against that throne.'

He snorted a laugh, but the sound shook him in an unexpected way. *When did I last laugh? Spirits below.*

'It's how they mark territory,' Setoc went on, her tone wry. 'How they take possession of something. I was shocked, but not for long. They're beasts, after all. So what is it we worship when we worship them?'

'I worship no one any more, Setoc.'

'Gruntle says worship is nothing more than the surrender to things beyond our control. He says the comfort from that is false, because there is nothing comfortable in the struggle to live. He kneels to no one, not even his Tiger of Summer, who would dare compel him.' She hesitated, and then sighed and added, 'I will miss Gruntle.'

'He intends to leave us?'

'A thousand people can dream of war, but no two dreams are the same. Soon he will be gone, and Mappo, too. The boy will be upset.'

The two horses shied suddenly, stumbling in their hobbles. Stepping past them, Torrent scowled. 'This dawn,' he said in a growl, 'the hare is bold.'

Precious Thimble bit back a shriek, clawed herself awake with a gasp. Traces of fire raced along her nerves. Kicking her bedding aside, she scrambled to her feet.

Torrent and Setoc stood near the horses, facing north. Someone was

43

coming. The ground underfoot seemed to recoil in waves sweeping past her, like ripples passing just beneath the surface. Precious struggled to slow her gasping breaths. She set out to join the warrior and the girl, leaning forward as if fighting an invisible current. Hearing heavy footfalls behind her, she glanced back to see Gruntle and Mappo.

'Be careful, Precious,' Gruntle said. 'Against this one . . .' He shook his head. The barbed tattoos covering his skin were visibly deepening, and in his eyes there was nothing human. He'd yet to draw his cutlasses.

Her gaze flicked to the Trell, but his expression revealed nothing.

I didn't kill Jula. It wasn't my fault.

She spun back, pushed on.

The figure striding towards them was withered, a crone swathed in snakeskins. As she drew closer, Precious could see the ravaged state of her broad face, the emptiness of her eye sockets. Behind her Gruntle unleashed a feline hiss. 'T'lan Imass. No weapons, meaning she's a Bonecaster. Precious Thimble, do not bargain with this one. She will offer you power, to get what she wants. Refuse her.'

Through gritted teeth, she replied, 'We need to get home.'

'Not that way.'

She shook her head.

The crone halted ten paces away, and to Precious Thimble's surprise it was Torrent who spoke first.

'Leave them alone, Olar Ethil.'

The hag cocked her head, wisps of hair drifting out like strands of spider silk. 'There is only one, warrior. It is no concern of yours. I am here to claim my kin.'

'Your what? Witch, there's—'

'You cannot have him,' Gruntle rumbled, edging past Torrent.

'Stay out of this, whelp,' Olar Ethil warned. 'Look to your god, and see how he cowers before me.' She then pointed a gnarled finger at Mappo. 'And you, Trell, this is not your battle. Stand aside, and I will tell you all you need know of the one you seek.'

Mappo seemed to stagger, and then, his face twisting in anguish, he stepped back.

Precious gasped.

Setoc spoke. 'Who is this kin of yours, witch?'

'He is named Absi.'

'Absi? There is no—'

'The boy,' snapped Olar Ethil. 'The son of Onos Toolan. Bring him to me.'

Gruntle drew his swords.

'Don't be a fool!' the Bonecaster snarled. 'Your own god will stop you! Treach will not simply let you throw away your life on this. You

44

think to veer? You will fail. I will kill you, Mortal Sword, do not doubt that. The boy. Bring him to me.'

The rest were awake now, and Precious turned round to see Absi standing between the twins, his eyes wide and bright. Baaljagg was slowly coming forward, closer to where Setoc stood, its massive head lowered. Amby Bole remained close to his brother's barrow, closed in and silent, his once young face now old, and whatever love there had been in his eyes had vanished. Cartographer stood with one foot in the coals of the hearth, staring at something to the east – perhaps the rising sun – while Sweetest Sufferance was helping Faint to her feet. *I need to try some more healing on her. I can show Amby I don't always fail. I can – no, think about what is before us now! She gave Mappo what he wants, as easy as that. She bargains quick, she speaks true.* Precious faced the Bonecaster. 'Ancient One, we in the Trygalle are stranded here. I have not the power to take us home.'

'You will not interfere if I bless you with what you need?' Olar Ethil nodded. 'Agreed. Collect the child.'

'Don't even think it,' Gruntle warned, the look in his unhuman eyes halting Precious in her tracks. The barbs on his bared arms seemed to blur a moment, then grew sharp once again.

The Bonecaster said, 'The boy is mine, whelp, because his father belongs to me. The First Sword serves me once again. Would you truly desire to prevent me from reuniting the son with the father?'

Stavi and Storii rushed closer, their questions tumbling together. 'Father – he's alive? Where is he?'

Gruntle barred their way with a levelled cutlass. 'Hold a moment, you two. Something is not right here. Wait, I beg you. Guard your brother.' He turned back to Olar Ethil. 'If the boy's father now serves you, where is he?'

'Not far.'

'Then bring him to us,' Gruntle said. 'He can collect his children himself.'

'The daughters are not of his blood,' Olar Ethil replied. 'I have no use for them.'

'You? What of Onos Toolan?'

'Give them to me, then, and I will see to their disposal.'

Torrent spun round. 'Slitting their throats is what she means, Gruntle.'

'I did not say that, warrior,' the Bonecaster retorted. 'I will take the three, this I offer.'

Baaljagg was edging closer to Olar Ethil, and she beckoned to it. 'Blessed Ay, I greet you and invite you into my comp—'

The huge beast lunged, massive jaws crunching as they closed round the Bonecaster's right shoulder. The ay then spun, whipping Olar Ethil from her feet. Strips of reptile hide, fetishes of bone and shell flailed and snapped. The giant wolf did not release its grip, instead reared a second time, slamming Olar Ethil hard on to the ground. Bones splintered in its jaws, and the body struggled feebly, as would a victim stunned.

Baaljagg tore loose its grip on her crushed shoulder and closed its fangs about her skull. It then whipped her into the air.

Olar Ethil's left hand was suddenly stabbing into the ay's throat, punching through withered hide and closing on its spinal column. Even as the wolf flung her upward, she caught hold. The momentum from Baaljagg's surge added force to her grip. A sudden, terrible ripping sound erupted from the ay, and like a serpent a length of the beast's spinal column tore free of its throat, still clutched in the witch's bony hand.

The Bonecaster spun away from the ay, landing hard in a clatter of bones.

Baaljagg collapsed, head lolling like a stone in a sack.

Absi wailed.

As Olar Ethil was picking herself up, Gruntle marched towards her, his two weapons readied. Seeing him, she flung the spinal column to one side.

And began to veer.

When he reached her, she was nothing but a blur, moments from expanding into something huge. He punched where her head had been a moment earlier, and the bell hilt of the cutlass cracked hard against something. The veering abruptly vanished. Reeling back, her face crushed, Olar Ethil sprawled on her back.

'*Spit on the tiger god*,' Gruntle said, standing directly over her. 'Hood take your stupid veering, and mine!' Clashing his blades together, he brought them down in an X pattern beneath her jaw. 'Now, Bonecaster, I happen to know that if you hit even T'lan Imass bones hard enough, they shatter.'

'No mortal—'

'Piss on that. I will leave you in pieces, do you understand me? Pieces. How's it done again? Head in a niche? On a pole? The crook of a tree? No trees here, witch, but a hole in the ground, that's easy.'

'The child is mine.'

'He won't have you.'

'Why not?'

'You just killed his dog.'

Precious Thimble hurried forward, feeling half fevered, her knees wobbly beneath her. 'Bonecaster—'

'I am considering withdrawing my offers,' Olar Ethil said. 'All of them. Now, Mortal Sword, will you remove your weapons and let me rise?'

'I haven't decided.'

'What must I promise? To leave Absi in your care? Will you guard his life, Mortal Sword?'

Precious saw Gruntle hesitate.

'I came to bargain with you all,' Olar Ethil continued. 'In faith. The undead ay was a slave to ancient memories, ancient betrayals. I will not hold it against any of you. Mortal Sword, look upon your friends – who among them is capable of protecting the children? You will not. The Trell waits only to hear my words whispering through his mind, and then he will quit your company. The Awl warrior is a pup, and a disrespectful one at that. The Jhag Bolead spawn is broken inside. I mean to bring to Onos Toolan his children—'

'He's a T'lan Imass, isn't he?'

The Bonecaster was silent.

'It's the only way he would still serve you,' Gruntle said. 'He died, just as his daughters believed, and you resurrected him. Will you do the same to the boy? The gift of your deathly touch?'

'Of course not. He must live.'

'Why?'

She hesitated, and then said, 'Because he is the hope of my people, Mortal Sword. I need him – for my army and for the First Sword who commands them. The child, Absi, shall be their cause, their reason to fight.'

Gruntle, Precious saw, was suddenly pale. 'A child? Their cause?'

'Their banner, yes. You do not understand – I cannot hold on to his anger . . . the First Sword's. It is dark, a beast unchained, a leviathan – he must not be unleashed, not this way. Burn's dream, Mortal Sword, let me rise!'

Gruntle withdrew his weapons, stumbled back a step. He was muttering something under his breath. Precious Thimble caught only a few words. In the Daru tongue. *'The banner . . . child's tunic, was that it? The colour . . . began red, ended . . . black.'*

Olar Ethil struggled to her feet. Her face was barely recognizable, a crushed, splintered knot of bone and torn hide. The gouges from Baal-jagg's canines had scored deep, white grooves on her temples and the base of her mandible on both sides. The ruined shoulder slumped, its arm hanging useless.

As Gruntle backed still further, an anguished cry came from Setoc. 'Has she won you all then? Will no one protect him? Please! *Please!*'

The twins were weeping. Absi was kneeling beside Baaljagg's desiccated body, moaning in a strange cadence.

Cartographer clattered closer to the boy, one foot blackened and smouldering. 'Make him stop that. Someone. Make him stop that.'

Precious frowned, but the others ignored the undead man's pleas.

What does he mean by that? She turned to Olar Ethil. 'Bonecaster—'

'East, woman. That is where you will find all you need. I have touched your soul. I have made it into a Mahybe, a vessel that waits. East.'

Precious Thimble crossed her arms, eyes closing for a moment. She wanted to look at Faint and Sweetest, to see the satisfaction, the relief, in their eyes. She wanted to, but knew she would see nothing of the sort, not from those two. They were women, after all, and three children were being surrendered. Thrown into undead arms. *They will thank me in the end. When the memory of this moment fades, when we are all safe and home again.*

Well . . . not all of us. But what can we do?

Setoc, with Torrent at her side, was all that stood between Olar Ethil and the three children. Tears streamed down Setoc's cheeks, and in the Awl warrior's stance Precious Thimble saw a man facing his execution. He'd drawn his sabre, but the look in his eyes was bleak. Yet he did not waver. Among them all, this young warrior was the only one not to turn away. *Damn you, Setoc, will you see this brave boy die?*

'We can't stop her,' Precious said to Setoc. 'You must see that. Torrent – tell her.'

'I gave up the last of the Awl children to the Barghast,' said Torrent. 'And now they are all dead. Gone.' He shook his head.

'Can you protect *these* ones any better?' Precious demanded.

It was as if he'd been slapped. He looked away. 'Giving up children is the one thing I seem to do well.' He sheathed his weapon and grasped Setoc's upper arm. 'Come with me. We will talk where no one else can hear us.'

Setoc shot the warrior a wild look, started to struggle, and then abruptly sagged in his grip.

Precious watched him drag her away. *He broke like a frail twig. Are you proud of yourself now, Precious?*

But the path is finally clear.

Olar Ethil walked with a hitching gait she'd not shown before, joints grinding and snapping, up to where the boy knelt. She reached down with her good arm and scooped him up by the collar of his Barghast tunic. Held him out to study his face, and he in turn looked steadily back at her, dry-eyed, flat. The Bonecaster grunted. 'Your father's son all right, by the Abyss.'

She turned round and set off, northward, the boy hanging from her grip. After a moment, the twins followed, neither one looking back. *There's no end to losing everything, is there? It just goes on and on. Their mother, their father, their people. No, they won't be looking back.*

And why should they? We failed them. She came, she cut us apart, bought us like an empress scattering a handful of coins. And they were

what she bought. Them, and our turning away. And it was easy, be-
cause this is what we are.

Mahybe? What in Hood's name is that?

With horror in his heart, Mappo set out from the camp, leaving the
others, leaving behind this terrible dawn. He struggled to keep from
breaking into a run, as if that would help. Besides, if they all watched
him, they did so with consciences as stained as his own. Was there
comfort in that? Should there be? *We are nothing but our own needs.
She but showed each of us the face we hide from ourselves and everyone else. She shamed us by exposing our truths.*

He fought to remind himself of his purpose, of all that his vow
demanded, and the horrifying things it could make him do.

*Icarium lives. Remember that. Focus on it. He waits for me. I will
find him. I will make it all right once again. Our small world, closed
up and impervious to everything outside it. A world where none will
challenge us, where none will question our deeds, the hateful decisions
we once made.*

Give me this world, please, I beg you.

My most precious lies – she stole them all. They saw.

Setoc, dear gods, the betrayal in your face!

*No. I will find him. I will protect him from the world. I will protect
the world from him. And from everything else, from hurt eyes and
broken hearts, I will protect myself. And you all called it my sacrifice,
my heartbreaking loyalty – there on the Path of Hands, I took your
breaths away.*

Bonecaster, you stole my lies. See me now.

He knew his ancestors were far, far away. Their bones crumbled to
dust in chambers beneath heaped mounds of stone and earth. He knew
he had forsaken them long ago.

Then why could he hear their howls?

Mappo clapped his hands over his ears, but that did not help. The
howling went on, and on. And on this vast empty plain, he suddenly
felt small, shrinking still further with each step. *My heart. My honour
. . . shrinking, withering down . . . with each step. He's only a child.
They all are. He curled up in Gruntle's arms. The girls, they held on to
Setoc's hands and sang songs.*

*Is it not the one inescapable responsibility of an adult to protect and
defend a child?*

I am not as I once was. What have I done?

*Memories. The past. All so precious – I want it back, I want it all
back. Icarium, I will find you.*

Icarium, please, save me.

*   *   *

Torrent climbed into his saddle. He looked down and met Setoc's eyes, and then nodded.

He could see the fear and the doubt in her face, and wished he had more words worth saying, but he'd used them all up. Was it not enough that he was doing this? The question, asked so boldly and self-righteously in his own mind, almost made him laugh out loud. Still, he had to do this. He had to try. 'I will ward them, I promise.'

'You owe them nothing,' she said, hugging herself with such severity he thought her ribs might crack. 'Not your charge, but mine. Why do you do this?'

'I knew Toc.'

'Yes.'

'I think: what would he do? That is my answer, Setoc.'

Tears ran down her face. She held her lips tight, as if to speak would be to loose her grief, a wailing demon that would never again be chained, or beaten down.

'I left children to die once,' he continued. 'I let Toc down. But this time,' he shrugged, 'I hope to do better. Besides, she knows me. She will use me, she's done it before.' He glanced over at the others. The camp was packed up. Faint and Sweetest Sufferance had already begun walking, like two broken refugees. Precious Thimble trailed them by a few steps, like a child uncertain of her welcome in their company. Amby walked on his own, off to the right of the others, staring straight ahead, his stride stiff, brittle. And Gruntle, after a few words with Cartographer who once more sat on Jula's barrow, had set off, shoulders rounded as if in visceral pain. Cartographer, it seemed, was staying behind. *It comes together only to fall apart.* 'Setoc, your wolf ghosts were frightened of her.'

'Terrified.'

'You could do nothing.'

Her eyes flashed. 'Is that supposed to help? Words like that just dig big holes and invite us to jump.'

He glanced away. 'I'm sorry.'

'Go, catch up to them.'

He collected his reins, swung his mount round and tapped its flanks with his heels.

Did you gamble on this, too, Olar Ethil? How smug will you sound in your greeting?

Well now, enjoy your time, because it won't last for ever. Not if I have any say in the matter. Do not worry, Toc, I've not forgotten. For you, I will do this, or die in the effort.

He rode at a canter across the empty land, until he drew within sight of the Bonecaster and her three charges. When the twins turned and cried out in relief, it very nearly broke him.

Setoc had watched the young Awl warrior ride after Olar Ethil, saw when he reached them. An exchange of words, and then they set out once more, walking until the deceptive folds of the landscape swallowed them all. Then she turned, studied Cartographer. 'The boy was crying in grief. Over his dead dog. You told him to stop. Why? Why should that have so bothered you?'

'How is it,' the undead man said, rising from the barrow and shuffling closer, 'that the weakest among us is the only one so willing to give up his life protecting those children? I do not mean to wound you with my words, Setoc. I but struggle to understand this.' The withered face tilted to one side, pitted eye sockets seeming to study her. 'Is it, perhaps, because he has the least to lose?' He continued on in his awkward steps, to stand over the carcass of the ay.

'Of course he has,' she snapped. 'As you said, just his life.'

Cartographer looked down at the corpse of Baaljagg. 'And this one had even less.'

'Go back to your dead world, will you? It's so much simpler there, I'm sure. You can stop wondering about the things us pathetic mortals get up to.'

'I am a knower of maps, Setoc. Listen to my words. You cannot cross the Glass Desert. When you reach it, turn southward, on to the South Elan. It is not much better, but there should be enough, at least to give you a chance.'

Enough what? Food? Water? Hope? 'You are remaining here. Why?'

'In this place,' Cartographer gestured, 'the world of the dead has arrived. Here, you are the unwelcome stranger.'

Suddenly shaken, inexplicably distraught, Setoc shook her head. 'Gruntle said you were with them almost from the very beginning. Now you're just stopping. Here?'

'Must we all have a purpose?' Cartographer asked. 'I did, once, but that is done with.' His head turned, faced northward. 'Your company was . . . admirable. But I'd forgotten.' He hesitated, and she was about to ask what he'd forgotten when he said, 'Things break.'

'Yes,' she whispered, not loud enough for him to hear. She reached down and collected the bundle of her gear. Straightening, she set out. Then paused and glanced back at him. 'Cartographer, what did Gruntle say to you, at the barrow?'

'"The past is a demon that not even death can shake."'

'What did he mean by that?'

He shrugged, still studying Baaljagg's carcass. 'I told him this: I have found the living in my dreams, and they are not well.'

She turned away, began walking.

Dust devils spun and raced along, tracking her on either side. Masan Gilani knew all about this. She'd heard all the old stories of the Seven Cities campaign, how the Logros T'lan Imass had a way of just vanishing, whispering on the winds or twisting along on the currents of some river. Easy for them. Rising from the ground at the end of it all not even out of breath.

She snorted. Breath, that was a good one.

Her horse was reluctant this morning. Not enough water, not enough forage, hadn't crapped or pissed in a day and a night. Wouldn't last much longer, she suspected, unless her companions could conjure up a spring and a heap of hay or a bag or two of oats. Could they do things like that? She had no idea.

'Be serious, woman. They looked as if a sleeping dragon had rolled over them. If they could magic stuff out of nowhere, well, they'd have done something by now.' She was hungry and thirsty too, and if it came to it she'd slit her horse's neck and feast until her belly exploded. 'Put that back together, will you? Thanks.'

Not far now. By her reckoning, she'd be on the Bonehunters' trail before noon, and by dusk she'd have caught up with them – no army that size could move very quickly. They were carrying enough supplies to feed a decent-sized town for half a year. She glanced northward, something she found she was doing rather often of late. No surprise in that impulse, however. It wasn't every day that a mountain grew up out of nowhere in the course of a single day and night, and what a storm accompanied its birth! She thought to hitch to one side for a spit or two, to punctuate the sardonic wonder she'd just chewed on. But spit was worth keeping.

'Hold back one throatful,' her mother used to say, 'for Hood's own face.' Bless her, the deranged fat cow. She must have given the ragged reaper a bubbly bath the day her time came, a hair-wash, a cave mouth's spring run-off of black, stinking phlegm just gushing out, aye. Big women had a way, didn't they? Especially after their fourth or fifth decade, when all their opinions had turned to stone and chipped flinty enough to draw blood with a single glance or sneer.

She'd moved like a tree, her mother had, and just as shocking to see, too. After all, trees don't walk much, not on a sober night, just like the earth didn't move unless Burn was pitching or the man was better than he knew (and how rare was that?). Loomed, old Ma did, like midnight thunder. Death was a crowded chamber for women like her, and the crowd was the kind that parted with her first step into the room: a miracle.

Masan Gilani wiped at her face – no sweat left. Bad news, especially this early in the morning. 'I wanted to be big, Ma. I wanted to reach that ripe old age. Fifty, aye. Five bitching, rutting, terror-inspiring decades. I wanted to *loom*. Thunder in my eyes, thunder in my voice, a thing of great weights and inexorable masses. It ain't fair, me withering away out here. Dal Hon, do you miss me?

'The day I set foot on that grassy sward, the day I shoo the first mob of flies from my lips and nostrils and eyes, why, that's the day all will be right with the world once again. No, don't leave me to die here, Dal Hon. It ain't fair.'

She coughed, squinted ahead. Something of a mess up there, those two rises, the valley sprawled in between. Holes in the ground. Craters? The slopes seemed to be swarming. She blinked, wondering if she was imagining that. Deprivation played nasty games, after all. Swarming – it was swarming all right. Rats? No. 'Orthen.'

A field of battle. She caught the gleam of picked bones, took note of ashy mounds on the far ridge, from pyres, no doubt. Sound practice, burning the dead, she knew. Kept disease to a minimum. She kicked her horse into a heavy canter. 'I know, I know, not for long, sweetie.'

The dust devils whirled out past her now, spinning towards a ridge overlooking the valley.

Masan Gilani rode after them, to the top of the crest. There she reined in, scanning the wreckage filling the valley, and then the gaping entrenchments slashing across the opposite ridge, beyond which rose the humps of burned bones. Dread slowly seeped in, stealing all the day's heat from her bones.

The T'lan Imass of the Unbound solidified in a rough line on her right, also studying the scene. Their sudden appearance after so many days of dust was strangely comforting to Masan Gilani. She'd only had her horse for company for far too long now. 'Not that I'll kiss any of you,' she said.

Heads turned to regard her. None spoke.

Thank Hood for that. 'My horse is dying,' she announced. 'And whatever happened here happened to my Bonehunters and it doesn't look good. So,' she added, now glaring at the five undead warriors, 'if you have any good news to tell me, or, gods below, any explanation at all, I really *might* kiss you.'

The one named Beroke said, 'We can answer your horse's plight, human.'

'Good,' she snapped, dismounting. 'Get to it. And a little water and grub for yours truly wouldn't go amiss either. I won't be eating orthen any more, just so you know. Who ever thought crossing a lizard with a rat was a good idea?'

One of the other T'lan Imass stepped out from the line. She couldn't recall this one's name, but it was bigger than the others and looked to be composed of body parts from three, maybe four individuals. 'K'Chain Nah'ruk,' it said in a low voice. 'A battle and a harvest.'

'Harvest?'

The creature pointed at the distant mounds. 'They butchered. They fed upon their fallen enemy.'

Masan Gilani shivered. 'Cannibals?'

'The Nah'ruk are not human.'

'That makes a difference? To me it's cannibalism. Only white-skinned barbarians from the Fenn Mountains sink so low as to eat other people. Or so I hear.'

'They did not complete their feeding,' said the oversized T'lan Imass.

'What do you mean?'

'See the newborn mountain to the north?'

'No,' she drawled, 'never noticed it.'

They all studied her again.

Sighing, Masan said, 'Aye, the mountain. The storm.'

'Another battle,' said Beroke. 'An Azath was born. From this, we conclude that the Nah'ruk were defeated.'

'Oh? We hit them a second time? Good.'

'K'Chain Che'Malle,' said Beroke. 'Civil war, Masan Gilani.' The warrior gestured with a twisted arm. 'Your army . . . I do not think they all died. Your commander—'

'Tavore's alive then?'

'Her sword is.'

Her sword. Oh. That Otataral blade. 'Can I send you ahead? Can you find a trail, if there is one?'

'Thenik will scout the path before us,' Beroke said. 'It is a risk. Strangers would not welcome us.'

'I can't imagine why.'

Another protracted look. Then Beroke said, 'If our enemies should find us, Masan Gilani, before the moment of our final resurrection, then all we aspire to win will be lost.'

'Win? Win what?'

'Why, our Master's release.'

She thought about asking a few more questions, decided against it. *Gods below, you're not who I was sent to find, are you? Still, you wanted to find us, didn't you? Sinter, I wish you were here, to explain what's going on. But my gut's telling me bad things. Your Master? No, don't tell me.* 'All right. Let's ride clear of this, and then you feed us like you promised. But decent food, right? I'm civilized. Dal Honese, Malazan Empire. The Emperor himself came from Dal Hon.'

'Masan Gilani,' said Beroke, 'we know nothing of this empire of which you speak.' The T'lan Imass warrior paused, and then added, 'But the one who was once emperor . . . him we do know.'

'Really? Before or after he died?'

The five Imass regarded her once more. Then Beroke asked, 'Masan Gilani, what is the relevance of that question?'

She blinked, and then slowly shook her head. 'None, none at all, I guess.'

Another T'lan Imass spoke now. 'Masan Gilani?'

'What?'

'Your old emperor.'

'What of him?'

'Was he a liar?'

Masan Gilani scratched her head, and then she gathered up her reins, swung back on to her horse. 'That depends.'

'On what?'

'On whether you believe all the lies people say about him. Now, let's get out of this, eat and get watered, and then find Tavore's sword, and if Oponn's smiling down on us, she'll still be attached to it.'

She was startled when the five Imass bowed. Then they collapsed into dust and swirled away. 'Where's the dignity in that?' she wondered, and then looked out one more time over the battlefield and its seething orthen. *Where's the dignity in anything, woman?*

For now, keep it all inside. You don't know what has happened here. You don't know anything for certain. Not yet. Just hold on.

There's plenty of dignity in just holding on. The way Ma did.

The smell of burning grass. Wetness pressed against one cheek, cold air upon the other, the close sound of a click beetle. Sunlight, filtered through shut lids. Dusty air, seeping into his lungs and then back out again. There were parts of him lying about. In pieces. Or so it felt, but even the idea of it seemed impossible, so he discarded the notion despite what his senses were telling him.

Thoughts, nice to find he was having them. A notable triumph. Now, if he could just pull his varied bits together, the ones that weren't there. But that could wait. First, he needed to find some memories.

His grandmother. Well, an old woman, at least. Assumptions could be dangerous. One of her sayings, maybe. What about parents? What about them? Try to remember, how hard can that be? His parents. Not very bright, those two. Strange in their dullness – he'd always wondered if there wasn't more to them. There had to be, didn't there? Hidden interests, secret curiosities. Was Mother really that fascinated by what Widow Thirdly was wearing today? Was that the extent of her engagement with the world? The poor neighbour only owned two tunics and one ankle-length robe, after all, and pretty threadbare at that, as befitted a woman whose husband was a withered corpse in the sands of Seven Cities and the death coin wasn't much to live by, was it? And that old man from down the street, the one trying to court her, well, he was just out of practice, that's all. Not worth your sneers, Mother. He's just doing his best. Dreaming of a happier life, dreaming of waking something up in the widow's sad eyes.

It's an empty world without hope.

And if Father had a way of puttering about whistling some endless song and pausing every now and then to look distracted by a thought, if not thoroughly confused by its very existence, well, a man of decent years had plenty to think about, didn't he? It certainly looked like that. And if he had a way of ducking in crowds, of meeting no one's eyes, well, there was a world of men who'd forgotten how to be men. Or maybe they never learned in the first place. Were these his parents? Or someone else's?

Revelations landing with a thud. One, three, scores of them, a veritable landslide, how old had he been? Fifteen? The streets of Jakata suddenly narrowing before his eyes, the houses shrinking, the big men of the block dwindling to boastful midgets with puny eyes.

There was a whole other world out there, somewhere.

Grandma, caught a glint in your eyes. You'd beaten the dust out of the gold carpet, rolled it out into my path. For these tender feet of mine. A whole other world out there. Called 'learning'. Called 'knowledge'. Called 'magic'.

Roots and grubs and tied-off twists of someone's hair, small puppets and dolls with smeared faces of thread. Webs of gut, bundles of shedding, the plucked backs of crows. Etching on the clay floor, the drip drip of sweat from the brow. Mud was effort, the taste on the tongue that of grit from a licked stylus, and how the candles flickered and the shadows leapt!

Grandma? Your gem of a boy tore himself apart. He had fangs in his flesh and those fangs were his own, and round and round it went. Biting, tearing, hissing in agony and fury. Plummeting from the smoke-filled sky. Lifting upward again, new wings, joints creaking, a sliding nightmare.

You can't come back from that. You can't.

I touched my own dull flesh, and it was buried under bodies, all that gore draining down. I was pickled in blood. That body, I mean. What used to be mine. You don't go back, not to that.

Dead limbs shifting, slack faces turning, pretending to look at me – but I wasn't the one so rude as to drag them about. No need to accuse me with those blank eyes. Some fool's coming down, down here, and maybe my soaked skin feels warm, but that's all the lost heat from all these other corpses.

I don't come back. Not from that.

Father, if you only knew the things I have seen. Mother, if only you'd opened your own heart, enough to bless that broken widow next door.

Explain it to this fool, will you? It was a mound of bodies. They'd gathered us. Friend, you weren't supposed to interfere. Maybe they ignored you, though I can't figure why. And your touch was cold, gods it was cold!

Rats, nuzzling close, they'd snatched fragments of me out of the air. In a world where everyone is a soldier, the ones underfoot don't get noticed, but even ants fight like fiends. My rats. They worked hard, warm bodies like nests.

They couldn't get all of me. That wasn't possible. Maybe you pulled me out, but I was incomplete.

Or not. Grandma, someone tied strings to me. With everything coming down all around us, he'd knotted strings. To my Hood-damned rats. Oh, clever bastard, Quick. Clever, clever bastard. All there, all here, I'm all here. And then someone dug me out, carried me away. And the Short-Tails looked over every now and then, milled as if contemplating taking objection, but never did.

He carried me away, melting as he went.

All the butchering going on. They had a way of puttering about whistling some endless song and pausing every now and then to look distracted by a thought, if not thoroughly confused by its very existence. Like that.

So he carried me away, and where was everybody?

The pieces were back together, and Bottle opened his eyes. He was lying on the ground, the sun low to the horizon, dew in the yellow grasses close to his face, smelling of the night just past. Morning. He sighed, slowly sat up, his body feeling crazed with cracks. He looked across at the man crouched near a dung fire. *His touch was cold. And then he melted.* 'Captain Ruthan Gudd, sir.'

The man glanced over, nodded, resumed combing his beard with his fingers. 'It's a bird, I think.'

'Sir?'

He gestured at the rounded lump of scorched meat skewered above the embers. 'Just sort of fell out of the sky. Had feathers but they've burned off.' He shook his head. 'Had teeth too, however. Bird. Lizard. It's an even handful of straws in each hand, as the Strike used to say.'

'We're alone.'

'For now. We've not been gaining on them much – you start getting heavy after a while.'

'Sir, you have been carrying me?' *Melting. Drip drip.* 'How far? How many days?'

'Carrying you? What am I, a Toblakai? No, there's a travois . . . behind you. Dragging's easier than carrying. Somewhat. Wish I had a dog. When I was a child . . . well, let's just say that wishing I had a dog has been an unfamiliar experience. But yesterday I'd have cut a god's throat for one single dog.'

'I can walk now, sir.'

'But can you pull that travois?'

Frowning, Bottle twisted and looked at the conveyance. Two full length spear shafts, the pieces of two or three others. Webbing from the harnesses of leather armour, the strips stained black. 'Nothing to pull in it, sir, that I can see.'

'I was thinking me, marine.'

'Well, I can—'

Ruthan picked up the spit and waved it about. 'A joke, soldier. Ha ha. Here, this thing looks ready. Cooking is the process of making the familiar unrecognizable, and thus palatable. When intelligence was first born, the first question asked was, "Can this thing be cooked?" After all, try eating a cow's face – well, true enough, people do – oh, never mind. You must be hungry.'

Bottle made his way over. Ruthan plucked the bird from the skewer and then tore it in half, handing one section to the marine.

They ate without conversation.

At last, sucking and spitting out the last bone, licking grease from his fingers, Bottle sighed and eyed the man opposite him. 'I saw you go down, sir, under about a hundred Short-Tails.'

Ruthan raked his beard. 'Aye.'

Bottle glanced away, tried again. 'Figured you were dead.'

'Couldn't get through the armour, but I'm still a mass of bruises. Anyway, they pounded me into the ground for a while and then just, well, gave up.' He grimaced. 'Took me some time to dig free. By then, apart from the dead they were collecting, there was no sign of the Bone-hunters, or our allies. The Khundryl looked finished – never saw so many dead horses. And the trenches had been overrun. The Letherii had delivered and taken some damage, but hard to guess the extent of either.'

'I think I saw some of that,' Bottle said.

'I sniffed you out, though,' the captain said, not meeting Bottle's eyes.

'How?'

'I just did. You were barely there, but enough. So I pulled you free.'

'And they just watched.'

'Did they? Never noticed that.' He wiped his hands on his thighs and rose. 'Ready to walk then, soldier?'

'I think so. Where are we going, sir?'

58

'To find the ones still left.'

'When was the battle?'

'Four, five days ago, something like that.'

'Sir, are you a Stormrider?'

'A rogue wave?'

Bottle's frown deepened.

'Another joke,' said Ruthan Gudd. 'Let's strip what's on the travois – found you a sword, a few other things you might find useful.'

'It was all a mistake, wasn't it?'

The man shot him a look. 'Everything is, soldier, sooner or later.'

Chaos foamed in a thrashing maelstrom far below. He stood close to the ledge, looking down. Off to his right the rock tilted, marking the end of the vaguely level base of the pinnacle, and at the far end the Spar, a gnarled thing of black stabbing upward like a giant finger, seemed to cast a penumbra of white mist from its ragged tip.

Eventually, he turned away, crossed the flat stretch, twelve paces to a sheer wall of rock, and to the mouth of a tunnel where shattered boulders had spilled out to the sides. He clambered over the nearest heap until he found a dusty oilskin cape jammed inside a crevasse. Tugging it aside, he reached down and withdrew a tattered satchel. It was so rotted the base began splitting at the seams and he scrambled quickly to flat ground before the contents spilled out.

Coins pattered, baubles struck and clattered. Two larger items, both wrapped in skins and each the length of a man's forearm, struck the bedrock but made no sound. These objects were the only ones he collected, tucking one into his belt and unwrapping the other.

A sceptre of plain black wood, its ends capped in tarnished silver. He examined it for a moment, and then strode to the base of the Spar of Andii. Rummaging in the pouch at his hip, he withdrew a knotted clutch of horse hair, dropped it at his feet, and then with a broad sweeping motion used the sceptre to inscribe a circle above the black stone. Then he stepped back.

After a moment his breath caught and he half turned. When he spoke his tone was apologetic. 'Ah, Mother, it's old blood, I don't deny it. Old and thin.' He hesitated, and then said, 'Tell Father I make no apologies for my choice – why should I? No matter. The two of us did the best I could.' He grunted in humour. 'And you might say the same thing.'

He turned back.

Darkness was knotting into something solid before him. He watched it for a time, saying nothing, although her presence was palpable, vast in the gloom behind him. 'If he'd wanted blind obedience, he should have kept me chained. And you, Mother, you should have kept me a child for ever, there under your wing.' He sighed, somewhat shakily.

'We're still here, but then, we did what you both wanted. We almost got them all. The one thing none of us expected was how it would change us.' He glanced back again, momentarily. 'And it has.'

Within the circle before him, the dark form opened crimson eyes. Hoofs cracked like iron axe-blades on the stone.

He grasped the apparition's midnight mane and swung on to the beast's back. ''Ware your child, Mother.' He drew the horse round, walked it along the ledge a few strides and then back to the mouth of the tunnel. 'I've been among them for so long now, what you gave me is the barest whisper in the back of my soul. You offered scant regard for humans, and now it's all coming down. But I give you this.' He swung the horse round. 'Now it's our turn. Your son opened the way. And as for *his* son, well, if he wants the Sceptre, he'll have to come and take it.'

Ben Adaephon Delat tightened his grip on the horse's mane. 'You do your part, Mother. Let Father do his, if he's of a mind to. But it comes down to us. So stand back. Shield your eyes, because I swear to you, *we will blaze*! When our backs are against the wall, Mother, *you have no idea what we can do.*'

He drove his heels into the horse's flanks. The creature surged forward.

Now, sweet haunt, this could get a little hairy.

The horse reached the ledge. Then out, into the air. And down, plunging into the seething maelstrom.

The presence, breathing darkness, remained in the vast chamber for a time longer. The strewn scatter of coins and baubles glittered on the black stone.

Then came a tapping of a cane upon rock.

CHAPTER THREE

Time now to go out into the cold night
And that voice was chill enough
To awaken me to stillness
There were cries inviting me into the sky
But the ground held me fast –
Well that was long ago now
Yet in this bleak morning the wings
Are shadows hunched on my shoulders
And the stars feel closer than ever before
The time is soon, I fear, to set out in search
Of that voice, and I will draw to the verge
Time now to go out into the cold night
Spoken in so weary a tone
I can make nothing worthy from it
If dreams of flying are the last hope of freedom
I will pray for wings with my last breath

Cold Night
Beleager

S MOKE HUNG IN THICK WREATHS IN THE CABIN. THE PORTHOLES WERE all open, shutters locked back, but the air did not stir and the sweltering heat lapped exposed flesh like a fevered tongue. Clearing her throat against a pervasive itchiness in her upper chest, Felash, Fourteenth Daughter of Queen Abrastal, tilted her head back on the soft, if soiled and damp, pillow.

Her handmaid set about refilling the pipe bowl.

'Are you certain of the date?' Felash asked.

'Yes, Highness.'

'Well, I suppose I should be excited. I made it to my fifteenth year, let the banners wave. Not that anything waves hereabouts.' She closed her eyes for a moment, and then blinked them open again. 'Was that a swell?'

'I felt nothing, Highness.'

'It's the heat I don't appreciate. It distracts. It whispers of mortality, yielding both despondency and a strange impatience. If I'm to die soon, I say, let's just get on with it.'

'Mild congestion, Highness.'

'And the sore lower back?'

'Lack of exercise.'

'Dry throat?'

'Allergies.'

'All these aches everywhere?'

'Highness,' said the handmaid, 'are there moments when all these symptoms simply vanish?'

'Hmm. Orgasm. Or if I find myself, er, suddenly busy.'

The handmaid drew the water pipe to life and handed the princess the mouthpiece.

Felash eyed the silver spigot. 'When did I start this?'

'The rustleaf, Highness? You were six.'

'And why, again?'

'It was that or chewing your fingernails down to nothing, as I recall, Highness.'

'Ah yes, childish habits, thank the gods I'm cured. Now, do you think I dare the deck? I swear I felt a swell back then, which must yield optimism.'

'The situation is dire, Highness,' the handmaid said. 'The crew is weary from working the pumps, and still we list badly. No land in sight, not a breath of wind. There is a very serious risk of sinking.'

'We had no choice, did we?'

'The captain and first mate do not agree with that assessment, Highness. Lives were lost, we are barely afloat—'

'Mael's fault,' Felash snapped. 'Never known the bastard to be so hungry.'

'Highness, we have never before struck such a bargain with an Elder God—'

'And never again! But Mother heard, didn't she? She did. How can that not be worth the sacrifices?'

The handmaid said nothing, sitting back and assuming a meditative pose.

Felash studied the older woman with narrowed eyes. 'Fine. Opinions differ. Have cooler heads finally prevailed?'

'I cannot say, Highness. Shall I—'

'No. As you said, exercise will do me good. Select for me a worthy outfit, something both lithe and flaunting, as befits my sudden maturity. Fifteen! Gods, the slide has begun!'

Her first mate, Shurq Elalle saw, was having trouble managing the canted deck. Not enough sound body parts, she assumed, to warrant much confidence, but for all his awkwardness he moved quickly enough, despite the winces and flinches with every step he took. Pain was not a pleasant thing to live with, not day after day, night upon night, not with every damned breath.

'I do admire you, Skorgen.'

He squinted up at her as he arrived on the poop deck. 'Captain?'

'You take it with a grimace and not much else. There are many forms of courage, I believe, most of which pass unseen by the majority of us. It's not always about facing death, is it? Sometimes it's about facing life.'

'If you say so, Captain.'

'What do you have to report?' she asked.

'We're sinking.'

Well. She imagined she'd float for a while, and then eventually wander down, like a bloated sack of sodden herbs, until she found the sea bottom. Then it would be walking, but where? 'North, I think.'

'Captain?'

'The *Undying Gratitude* surely deserves a better fate. Provision the launches. How long do we have?'

'Hard to say.'

'Why?'

Skorgen's good eye squinted. 'What I meant was, I don't like saying it. Bad luck, right?'

'Skorgen, do I need to pack my trunk?'

'You're taking your trunk? Will it float? I mean, if we tie it behind the lifeboat? We only got two that'll float and both are a bit battered. Twenty-nine left in the crew, plus you and me and our guests. Ten in a launch and we'll be awash at the first whitecap. I ain't good at numbers but I think we're off some. Could be people holding on in the water. But not for long, with all those sharks hanging around. Ideal is eight to a boat. We should get down to that quick enough. But your trunk, well, that messes up my figuring.'

'Skorgen, do you recall loading my trunk?'

'No.'

'That's because I don't have one. It was a figure of speech.'

'That's a relief, then. Besides,' he added, 'you probably wouldn't have the time to pack it anyway. We could roll in the next breath, or so I'm told.'

'Errant take me, get our guests up here!'

He pointed behind her. 'There's the well-born one just coming up, Captain. She'll float high in the water, that she will, until the—'

'Lower the launches and round up the crew, Skorgen,' Shurq said, stepping past him and making her way to the princess.

'Ah, Captain, I really must—'

'No time, Highness. Get your handmaiden and whatever clothes you'll need to stay warm. The ship is going down and we need to get to the launches.'

Blinking owlishly, Felash looked round. 'That seems rather extreme.'

'Does it?'

'Yes. I would imagine that abandoning ship is one of the very last things one would wish to do, when at sea.'

Shurq Elalle nodded. 'Indeed, Highness. Especially while at sea.'

'Well, are there no alternatives? It is unlike you to panic.'

'Do I appear to be panicking?'

'Your crew is—'

'Modestly so, Highness, since we don't quite have the room needed to take everyone, meaning that some of them are about to die in the jaws of sharks. My understanding is, such a death is rather unpleasant, at least to begin with.'

'Oh dear. Well, what can be done?'

'I am open to suggestions, Highness.'

'Perhaps a ritual of salvation . . .'

'A what?'

Plump fingers fluttered. 'Let us assess the situation, shall we? The storm has split the hull, correct?'

'We hit something, Highness. I am hoping it was Mael's head. We cannot effect repairs, and our pumps have failed in stemming the tide. As you may note, to starboard, we are very nearly awash amidships. If we were not becalmed, we would have rolled by now.'

'Presumably, the hold is full of water.'

'A fair presumption, Highness.'

'It needs to be—'

A terrible groaning sound reverberated through the deck at their feet.

Felash's eyes went wide. 'Oh, what is that?'

'That is us, Highness. Sinking. Now, you mentioned a ritual. If it involves a certain Elder God of the seas, I should warn you, I cannot vouch for your well-being should my crew learn of it.'

'Really? How distressing. Well, a ritual such as the one I am suggesting may not necessarily involve that decidedly unpleasant individual. In fact—'

'Forgive me for interrupting, Highness, but it has just occurred to me that this particular contest of understatement is about to be fatally terminated. While I have thoroughly enjoyed it, I now believe you have been a truly unwitting participant. How well can you swim, since I believe we shall not have time to reach the launches . . .'

'For goodness' sake.' Felash turned about, gauging the scene on all sides. Then she gestured.

The *Undying Gratitude* shuddered. Water foamed up from the hatch. Rigging whipped as if in a gale, the stumps of the shattered masts quivering. The ship grunted as it rolled level again. To either side the water swirled. Shouts of fright came from the two launches, and Shurq Elalle heard the screams commanding axes to the lines. A moment later she saw both lifeboats pulling away, neither one fully manned, whilst the rest of her crew, along with Skorgen Kaban, bellowed and cursed from where they clung to the port gunwale. Water washed across the mid-deck.

Princess Felash was studying the lay of the ship, one finger to her plump, painted lips. 'We must drain the hold,' she said, 'before we dare lift her higher. Agreed, Captain? Lest the weight of the water break the hull apart?'

'What are you doing?' Shurq demanded.

'Why, saving us, of course. And your ship, which we still need despite its deplorable condition.'

'Deplorable? She's just fine, damn you! Or she would be, if you hadn't—'

'Now now, Captain, manners, please. I am nobility, after all.'

'Of course, Highness. Now, please save my sorry ship, and once that is done, we can discuss other matters at our leisure.'

'Excellent suggestion, Captain.'

'If you could have done this at any time, Highness—'

'Could, yes. Should, most certainly not. Once more we bargain with terrible forces. And once more, a price must be paid. So much for "never again"!'

Shurq Elalle glanced over at her first mate and crew. The deck they stood upon was no longer under water, and the sound of a hundred pumps thundered the length of the hull. *But we don't have a hundred pumps and besides, no one is down there.* 'It's Mael again, isn't it?'

Felash glanced over, lashes fluttering. 'Alas, no. The difficulty we're having at the moment, you see, stems precisely from our deliberate avoidance of that personage. After all, this is his realm, and he is not one to welcome rivals. Therefore, we must impose a physicality that resists Mael's power.'

'Highness, is this the royal "we"?'

'Ah, do you feel it, Captain?'

Thick, billowing fog now rose around the ship – the two lifeboats disappeared from sight, and their crews' cries were suddenly silenced, as if those men and women ceased to exist. In the dread hush that followed, Shurq Elalle saw Skorgen and her remaining dozen sailors huddling down on the deck, their breaths pluming, frost sparkling to life on all sides.

'Highness—'

'What a relief from that heat, don't you agree? But we must now be stern in our position. To give up too much at this moment could well prove fatal.'

'Highness,' Shurq tried again, 'who do we bargain with now?'

'The Holds are half forgotten by most, especially the long dormant ones. Imagine our surprise, then, when a frozen corpse should awaken and rise into the realm of life once more, after countless centuries. Oh, they're a hoary bunch, the Jaghut, but, you know, I still hold to a soft regard for them, despite all their extravagances. Why, in the mountains of North Bolkando there are tombs, and as for the Guardians, well—'

'Jaghut, Highness? Is that what you said? Jaghut?'

'Surely this must be panic, Captain, your constant and increasingly rude interruptions—'

'You're locking us all in ice?'

'Omtose Phellack, Captain. The Throne of Ice, do you see? It is awake once more—'

Shurq advanced on Felash. 'What is the bargain, Princess?'

'We can worry about that later—'

'No! We will worry about it right now!'

'I cannot say I appreciate such an imperious tone, Captain Elalle. Observe how steady settles the ship. Ice is frozen in the cracks in the hull and the hold is dry, if rather cold. The fog, unfortunately, we won't be able to escape, as we are chilling the water around us nigh unto freezing. Now, this current, I understand, will carry us northward, to landfall, in about three days. An unoccupied shoreline, with a sound, protected natural harbour, where we can make repairs—'

'Repairs? I've just lost half my crew!'

'We don't need them.'

Skorgen Kaban clumped over. 'Captain! Are we dead? Is this Mael's Curse? Do we travel the Seas of Death? Is this the Lifeless River? Skull Ocean? Are we betwixt the Horns of Dire and Lost? In the Throes of—'

'Gods below! Is there no end to these euphemisms for being dead?'

'Aye, and the Euphemeral Deeps, too! The crew's got questions, y'see—'

'Tell them our luck holds, Skorgen, and those hasty ones in the boats, well, that's what comes of not believing in your captain and first mate. Got that?'

'Oh, they'll like that one, Captain, since a moment ago they was cursing themselves for being too slow off the mark.'

'The very opposite to be sure, First Mate. Off you go, then.'

'Aye, Captain.'

Shurq Elalle faced the princess again. 'To my cabin if you please, Highness. The bargain.'

'The bargain? Oh, indeed. That. As you wish, but first, well, I need to change, lest I catch a chill.'

'May the Errant look away, Highness.'

'He is, dear, he is.'

Shurq watched the young woman walk to the hatch. *'Dear'? Well, maybe she's older than she looks.*

No, what she is is a condescending, pampered princess. Oh, if only Ublala was on board, he'd set her right in no time. The thought forced out a snort of amusement. 'Careful!' she admonished herself, and then frowned. *Oh, I see. I'm freezing solid. No leakage for the next little while, I guess. Best get moving. And keep moving.* She looked round, if somewhat stiffly.

Yes, the ship was on the move, riding a current already lumpy with ice. The fog embraced them, their very own private cloud. *We travel blind.*

'Captain! Crew wants t'know, is this the White Road?'

'Provisions.'

Destriant Kalyth looked across at the Shield Anvil. 'There are drones. And wagon beds where food grows. Matron Gunth Mach prepares us. We shall wander as the great herds once wandered.'

The red-bearded man rose on the Ve'Gath's stirrups of hide and bone. 'Great herds? Where?'

'Well, they all died.'

Stormy scowled. 'Died how?'

'Mostly, we killed them, Shield Anvil. The Elan were more than just keepers of myrid and rodara. We also hunted. We fought over possession of wild herds and crossings, and when we lost, why, we'd poison the beasts to spite our enemies. Or destroy the crossings, so that animals drowned on their migrations. We were one with the land.'

From her other side, Gesler snorted. 'Who's been opening your eyes, Kalyth?'

She shrugged. 'Our spirit gods starved. What did we do wrong? Nothing, we didn't change a thing. We lived as we'd always lived. And it was murderous. The wild beasts vanished. The land dried up. We fought each other, and then came the Adjudicators. Out from the east.'

'Who were they?'

Bitterness stung her words. 'Our judgement, Shield Anvil. They looked upon our deeds. They followed the course of our lives, our endless stupidities. And they decided that our reign of abuse must end.' She shot the man a look. 'I should have died with my kin. Instead, I ran away. I left them all to die. Even my own children.'

'A terrible thing,' muttered Stormy, 'but the crime was with those Adjudicators. Your people would have had to change their ways sooner or later. No, the blood is on their hands.'

'Tell us more about them,' Gesler said.

She was riding a Ve'Gath, as were her companions. The thump of the huge Che'Malle's clawed feet seemed far below her. She could barely feel their impacts on the hard ground. The sky was dull, cloudy over a grey landscape. Behind them the two children, Sinn and Grub, shared another Ve'Gath. They hardly ever spoke; in fact, Kalyth could not recall ever hearing Sinn's voice, though Grub had let on that her apparent muteness was habit rather than an affliction.

Creatures of fire. Demonspawn. Gesler and Stormy know them, but even they are not easy in their company. No, I do not like our two children.

Kalyth took a moment to gather her thoughts. 'The Adjudicators had risen to power first in Kolanse,' she said after a time. She didn't want to remember them, didn't want to think about any of that, but she forced herself to continue. 'When we first heard of them, in our camps, the stories came from caravan guards and traders. They spoke nervously, with fear in their eyes. "Not human," they said. They were priests. Their cult was founded on the Spire, which is a promontory in the bay of Kolanse, and it was there that they first settled, building a temple and then a fortress.'

'So they were foreigners?' Gesler asked.

'Yes. From somewhere called the Wretched Coast. All I have heard of this is second-hand. They arrived in ships of bone. The Spire was unoccupied – who would choose to live on cursed land? And to begin with there was but one ship, crewed by slaves, and twelve or thirteen priests and priestesses. Hardly an invasion, as far as the king of Kolanse was concerned. And when they sent an emissary to his court, he welcomed her. The native priesthoods were not as pleased and they warned their king, but he overruled them. The audience was granted. The Adjudicator was arrogant. She spoke of justice as if her people alone were its iron hand. Indeed, that emissary pointed a finger upon the king himself and pronounced his fall.'

'I bet he wasn't so pleased any more,' Stormy said with a grunt. 'He lopped the fool's head off, I hope.'

'He tried,' Kalyth replied. 'Soldiers and then sorcery – the throne room became a slaughterhouse, and when the battle was over she alone strode out from the palace. And in the harbour were a hundred more ships of bone. This is how the horror began.'

Gesler twisted in his saddle and seemed to study the two children for a moment, before facing forward again. 'Destriant, how long ago was this?'

She shrugged. 'Fifty, sixty years ago. The Adjudicators scoured out all the other priesthoods. More and more of their own followers arrived, season after season. The Watered, they were called. Those with human blood in them. Those first twelve or so, they were the Pures. From Estobanse Province – the richest land of Kolanse – they spread their power outward, enforcing their will. They were not interested in waging war upon the common people, and by voice alone they could make entire armies kneel. From Kolanse they began toppling one dynasty after another – in all the south kingdoms, those girdling the Pelasiar Sea, until all the lands were under their control.' She shuddered. 'They were cruel masters. There was drought. Starvation. They called it the Age of Justice, and left the people to die. Those who objected they executed, those who sought to rise against them, they annihilated. Before long, they reached the lands of my people. They crushed us like fleas.'

'Ges,' said Stormy after a time, 'if not human, then what?'

'Kalyth, are these Adjudicators tusked?'

'Tusked? No.'

'Describe them.'

'They are tall, gaunt. Their skin is white as alabaster, and their limbs do not move as do those of humans. From their elbows, they can bend their lower arms in all directions. It is said their bodies are hinged, as if they had two sets of hips, one stacked atop the other. And they can stand like us, or with legs like those of a horse. No weapon can reach them, and a single touch from their long fingers can shatter all the bones in a warrior's body. Sorcerous attacks drain down from them like water.'

'Is it the same for the Watered,' Gesler wanted to know, 'or just the Pures?'

'I don't know.'

'Have you seen one of these Adjudicators with your own eyes?'

She hesitated, and then shook her head.

'But your tribe—'

'We heard they were coming. We knew they would kill us all. I ran.'

'Hood's breath!' barked Stormy. 'So you don't know if they ever—'

'I snuck back, days later, Shield Anvil.' She had to force the words out, her mouth dry as dust, her thoughts cold as a corpse. 'They were thorough.' *I snuck back. But is that even true? Or did I just dream that? The broken faces of my children, so still. My husband, his spine twisted impossibly, his eyes staring. The dead dogs, the shamans' heads on poles. And the blood, everywhere – even my tears* . . . 'I ran. I am the last of my people.'

'This drought you mentioned,' Gesler said, 'had it struck before these Adjudicators arrived, or after?'

'Estobanse thrives on springs. A valley province, with vast mountains to the north and another range to the south. The sea to the east and plains to the west. The droughts were in the south kingdoms, and in the other Kolanse territories. I do not know when they started, Mortal Sword, but even in the tales from my childhood I seem to recall grief lying heavy upon the settled lands.'

'And the Elan Plains?'

She shook her head. 'Always dry, always trouble – it is why the clans fought so much. We were running out of everything. I was a child. A child gets used to things, it all feels . . . normal – for all the years I was with my people, it was like that.'

'So what brought the Adjudicators to the place,' Gesler wondered, 'if it was already suffering?'

'Weakness,' said Stormy. 'Take any starving land, and you'll find a fat king. Nobody'd weep at that slaughter in the throne room. Priests blathering on about justice. Must have sounded sweet, at least to start with.'

'Aye,' Gesler agreed. 'Still, that Spire, where they built their temple – Kalyth, you called it cursed. Why?'

'It is where a star fell from the sky,' she explained.

'Recently?'

'No, long ago, but round the promontory the seawater is red as blood – and nothing can live in that water.'

'Did any of that change once the Adjudicators installed their temple?'

'I don't know. I have never seen the place – please, I just don't know. I don't even know why we're marching in this direction. There is nothing to the east – nothing but bones.' She glared at Gesler. 'Where's your army of allies? Dead! We need to find somewhere else to go. We need—' *somewhere to hide. Ancestors forgive me.* No, her fears were all too close to the surface. A score of questions could rip through her thin skin – it hadn't taken much, had it?

'We don't know that,' Stormy said, chewing at his moustache and not meeting her eyes.

I'm sorry. I know.

'When Gu'Rull gets back,' Gesler said in a low tone, 'we'll know more. In the meantime, on we go, Destriant. No point in doing anything else.'

She nodded. *I know. Forgive me. Forgive us all.*

Their power was a dark, swirling stain, spinning out like a river at the head of the vast, snaking column. Gu'Rull studied the manifestation from above, where he was gliding just beneath the thick overcast which had spread down from the northwest. His wounds were healing, and he had travelled far, ranging out over the Wastelands.

He had observed the tattered remnants of human armies, swollen with massive trains. And south of them but drawing closer by the day another force, the ranks disciplined in their march, unblooded and, as far as such things went, formidable. Despite the commands of the Mortal Sword, neither force was of much interest to the Shi'gal Assassin. No, the knots of power he had sensed elsewhere were far more fascinating, but of them all, not one compared to that which emanated from the two human children, Sinn and Grub. Travelling there, at the very head of the Gunthan Nest.

Of course, it could be called 'Nest' no longer, could it? There was no room, no solid, protected roost for the last clan of the K'Chain Che'Malle.

Even leadership had been surrendered. To three humans. There was no doubt that without them the Che'Malle would have been destroyed by the Nah'ruk. Three humans, clad in strange titles, *and two children, wearing little more than rags.*

So many lusted after power. It was the crushing step of history, in every civilization that had ever existed. Gu'Rull had no taste for it. Better that more of his kind existed, behind every throne, to cut the throat at the first hint of mad ambition. Enough heads rolling down the ages and perhaps the lesson would finally be learned, though he doubted it.

The assassin must never die. The shadows must ever remain. We hold the world in check. We are the arbiters of reason. It is our duty, our purpose.

I have seen them. I have seen what they can do, and the joy in their eyes at the devastation they can unleash. But their throats are soft. If I must, I will rid the world of them. The power was sickly, a swathe of something vile. It leaked from their indifferent minds and fouled the sweet scents of his kin – their joy at victory, their gratitude to the Mortal Sword and the Shield Anvil, their love for Kalyth, the Destriant of the K'Chain Che'Malle. Their faith in a new future.

But these children. They need to die. Soon.

'Forkrul Assail,' whispered Grub into Sinn's ear. 'The Crystal City knew them, even the Watered ones. It holds the memory of them. Sinn, they are at the centre of the war – they're the ones the Adjunct is hunting.'

'No more,' she hissed back at him. 'Don't talk. What if they hear you?'

He sniffed. 'You think they don't know? Gesler and Stormy? Forkrul Assail, Sinn, but now she's wounded. Badly wounded. We need to stop her, or the Bonehunters will get slaughtered—'

'If there're any of them left.'

'There are. Reach with your mind—'

'That's her sword – that barrier that won't let us in. Her Otataral sword.'

'Meaning she's still alive—'

'No, just that somebody's carrying it. Could be Brys Beddict, could be Warleader Gall. We don't know, we can't get close enough to find out.'

'Gu'Rull—'

'Wants us dead.'

Grub flinched. 'What did we ever do to him? Except save his hide.'

'Him and all the other lizards. Doesn't matter. We might turn on them all, and who could stop us?'

'You could turn on 'em. I won't. So I'll be the one stopping you. Don't try it, Sinn.'

'We're in this together,' she said. 'Partners. I was just saying. It's why that assassin hates us. Nobody controls us but us. Grownups always hate that.'

'Forkrul Assail. Gesler wants to join this army to the Adjunct's – that has to be what he's planning, isn't it?'

'How should I know? Probably.'

'So we will fight Forkrul Assail.'

She flashed him a wicked smile. 'Like flies, I will pluck their legs off.'

'Who's the girl?'

Sinn rolled her eyes. 'Not again. I'm sick of talking about her.'

'She's in the Crystal City. She's waiting for us.'

'She's insane, that's what she is. You felt that, you had to. We both felt it. No, let's not talk about her any more.'

'You're afraid of her,' Grub said. 'Because maybe she's stronger than both of us.'

'Aren't you? You should be.'

'At night,' said Grub, 'I dream of red eyes. Opening. Just opening. That's all.'

'Never mind that dream,' she said, looking away.

He could feel all her muscles, tight and wiry, and he knew that this was an embrace he could not hold on to for very much longer. *She's scarier than the assassin. You in the Crystal City, are you as frightened as me?*

'Stupid dream,' said Sinn.

*　　*　　*

It was midday. Gesler called a halt. The vast column stopped en masse, and then drones stepped out to begin preparations for feeding. Wincing as he extricated himself from the scaled saddle of the Ve'Gath, noting with relief that the welts on the beast's flanks were healing, the Mortal Sword dropped down to the ground. 'Stormy, let's stretch our legs—'

'I don't need help taking a piss.'

'After that, idiot.'

Stretching out the aches in his lower back, he walked out from the column, making a point of ignoring Sinn and Grub as they clambered down. Every damned morning since the battle, he'd half expected to find them gone. He wasn't fool enough to think he had any control over them. *Torching sky-keeps like pine cones, Hood save us all.*

Stormy appeared, spitting on his hands to wash them. 'That fucking assassin doesn't want to come down. Bad news?'

'I doubt he'd quake over delivering that, Stormy. No, he's just making a point.'

'Soon as he comes down,' Stormy growled, 'my fist will make one of its own.'

Gesler laughed. 'You couldn't reach its snarly snout, not even with a ladder. What are you going to do, punch its kneecap?'

'Maybe, why not? Bet it'd hurt something awful.'

Gesler drew off his helmet. 'Forkrul Assail, Stormy. Hood's hairy bag.'

'If she's still alive, she must be having second thoughts. Who knows how many the Nah'ruk ate? For all we know, there's only a handful of Bonehunters left.'

'I doubt it,' Gesler said. 'There's standing and taking it when that's what you have to do. And then there's cutting out and setting fire to your own ass. She didn't want that fight. So they ran into her. She would've done what she needed to do to pull her soldiers out of it. It was probably messy, but it wasn't a complete annihilation.'

'If you say so.'

'Look, it's a fighting withdrawal until you can reasonably break. You narrow your front. You throw your heavies into that wall, and then you let yourself get pushed backward, step after step, until it's time to turn and run. And if the Letherii were worth anything, they'd have bled off some pressure. Best case scenario, we lost about a thousand—'

'Mostly heavies and marines – the heart of the army, Ges—'

'So you find a new one. A thousand.'

'Worst case? Not a heavy left, not a marine left, with the regulars broken and scattering like hares.'

73

Gesler glared at Stormy. 'I'm supposed to be the pessimist here, not you.'

'Get the Matron to order that assassin down here.'

'I will.'

'When?'

'When I feel like it.'

Stormy's face reddened. 'You're still a Hood-shitting sergeant, you know that? Mortal Sword? Mortal Bunghole is more like it! Gods, to think I been taking orders from you for how long?'

'Well, who's a better Shield Anvil than a man with an anvil for a head?'

Stormy grunted, and then said, 'I'm hungry.'

'Aye,' said Gesler. 'Let's go and eat.'

They set out for the feeding area.

'Do you remember, when we were young – too young? That cliff—'

'Don't go on about that damned cliff, Stormy. I still get nightmares about it.'

'It's guilt you're feeling.'

Gesler halted. 'Guilt? You damned fool. I saved your life up there!'

'After nearly killing me! If that rock coming down had hit me in the head—'

'But it didn't, did it? No, just your shoulder. A tap, a bit of dust, and then I—'

'The point is,' Stormy interrupted, 'we did stupid things back then. We should've learned, only it's turning out we never learned a damned thing.'

'That's not the problem,' Gesler retorted. 'We got busted down all those times for good reason. We can't handle responsibilities, that's our problem. We start bickering – you start thinking and that's as bad as bad can get. Stop thinking, Stormy, and that's an order.'

'You can't order me, I'm the Shield Anvil, and if I want to think, that's damn well what I'll do.'

Gesler set out again. 'Be sure to let me know when you start. In the meantime, stop moaning about everything. It's tiresome.'

'You strutting around like High King of the Universe is pretty tiresome, too.'

'Look there – more porridge. Hood's breath, Stormy, I'm already so bunged up I could pick my nose and—'

'It ain't porridge. It's mould.'

'Fungus, idiot.'

'What's the difference? All I know is, those drones are growing it in their own armpits.'

'Now you done it, Stormy. I told you to stop complaining.'

74

'Well, once I think up a reason to stop complaining, I will. But then, I'm not supposed to think, am I? Hah!'

Gesler scowled. 'Gods below, Stormy, but I'm feeling old.'

The red-bearded man paused, and then nodded. 'Aye. It's bloody miserable. I might be dead in a month, that's how I feel. Aches and twinges, all the rest. I need a woman. I need ten women. Rumjugs and Sweetlard, that's who I need – why didn't that assassin steal them, too? Then I'd be happy.'

'There's always Kalyth,' Gesler said under his breath.

'I can't roger the Destriant. It's not allowed.'

'She's comely enough. Been a mother, too—'

'What's so special about that?'

'Their tits been used, right? And their hips are all looser. That's a real woman, Stormy. She'll know what to do under the furs. And then there's that look in the eye – stop gawking, you know what I mean. A woman who's dropped a baby has got this look – they been through the worst and come out the other side. So they do that up and down thing and you know that they know they can reduce you to quivering meat if they wanted to. Mothers, Stormy. Give me a mother over any other woman every time, that's what I'm saying.'

'You're sick.'

'If it wasn't for me you'd still be clinging halfway up that cliff, a clutch of bones with birds nesting in your hair and spiders in your eye sockets.'

'If it wasn't for you I'd never have tried climbing it.'

'Yes you would.'

'Why do you say that?'

'Because, Stormy, you never think.'

He'd gathered things. Small things. Shiny stones, shards of crystal, twigs from the fruit trees, and he carried them about, and when he could he'd sit down on the floor and set them out, making mysterious patterns or perhaps no patterns, just random settings. And then he'd look at them, and that was all.

The whole ritual, now that she'd witnessed it dozens of times, deeply disturbed Badalle, but she didn't know why.

> Saddic has things in a bag
> He's a boy trying to remember
> Though I tell him not to
> Remembering's dead
> Remembering's stones and twigs
> In a bag and each time they come out
> I see dust on his hands

We choose not remembering
To keep the peace inside our heads
We were young once
But now we are ghosts in the dreams
Of the living.
Rutt holds a baby in a bag
And Held remembers everything
But will not speak, not to us.
Held dreams of twigs and stones
And knows what they are.

She thought to give Saddic these words, knowing he would hide them in the story he was telling behind his eyes, and then it occurred to her that he didn't need to hear to know, and the story he was telling was beyond the reach of anyone. *I am trapped in his story. I have flown in the sky, but the sky is the dome of Saddic's skull, and there is no way out. Look at him studying his things, see the confusion on his face. A thin face. Hollowed face. Face waiting to be filled, but it will never be filled.* 'Icarias fills our bellies,' she said, 'and starves everything else.'

Saddic looked up, met her eyes, and then looked away. Sounds from the window, voices in the square below. Families were taking root, sliding into the crystal walls and ceilings, the floors and chambers. Older boys became pretend-fathers, older girls became pretend-mothers, the young ones scampered but never for long – they'd run, as if struck with excitement, only to falter after a few steps, faces darkening with confusion and fear as they ran back to find shelter in their parents' arms.

This is the evil of remembering.

'We can't stay here,' she said. 'Someone is seeking us. We need to go and find them. Rutt knows. That's why he walks to the end of the city and stares into the west. He knows.'

Saddic began collecting his things. Into his little bag. Like a boy who'd caught something out of the corner of his eye, only to find nothing when he turned.

If you can't remember it's because you never had what it is you're trying to remember. Saddic, we've run out of gifts. Don't lie to fill up your past. 'I don't like your things, Saddic.'

He seemed to shrink inside himself and would not meet her eyes as he tied up the bag and tucked it inside his tattered shirt.

I don't like them. They hurt.

'I'm going to find Rutt. We need to get ready. Icarias is killing us.'

'I knew a woman once, in my village. Married. Her husband was a man you wanted, like a hot stone in your gut. She'd walk with him, a step behind, down the main track between the huts. She'd walk and she'd stare right at me all the way. You know why? She was staring at me to keep me from staring at him. We are really nothing but apes, hairless apes. When she's not looking, I'll piss in her grass nest – that's what I decided. And I'd do more than that. I'd seduce her man. I'd break him. His honour, his integrity, his honesty. I'd break him between my legs. So when she walked with him through the village, she'd do anything but meet my eyes. Anything.'

With that, Kisswhere reached for the jug.

The Gilk Warchief, Spax, studied her from beneath a lowered brow. And then he belched. 'How dangerous is love, hey?'

'Who said anything about love?' she retorted with a loose gesture from the hand holding the jug. 'It's all about possession. And stealing. That's what makes a woman wet, what makes her eyes shine. 'Ware the dark streak in a woman's soul.'

'Men have their own,' he muttered.

She drank, and then swung the jug back to his waiting hand. 'Different.'

'Mostly, aye. But then, maybe not.' He swallowed down a mouthful, wiped his beard. 'Possession only counts for too much in a man afraid of losing whatever he has. If he's settled he doesn't need to own, but then how many of us are settled? Few, I'd wager. We're restless enough, and the older we get, the more restless we are. The misery is, the one thing an old man wants to possess the most is the one thing he can't have.'

'What's that?'

'Add a couple of decades to that man in the village and his wife won't have to stare into any rival's eyes.'

She grunted, collected up her stick and pushed it beneath the splints binding her leg. Scratched vigorously. 'Whatever happened to decent healing?'

'They're saying magic's damn near dead in these lands. How nimble are you?'

'Nimble enough.'

'How drunk are you?'

'Drunk enough.'

'Just what a man twice her age wants to hear from a woman.'

A figure stepped into the firelight. 'Warchief, the queen summons you.'

Sighing, Spax rose. To Kisswhere he said, 'Hold that thought.'

'Doesn't work that way,' she replied. 'We flowers blossom but it's a brief blooming. If you miss your chance, well, too bad for you. This night, at least.'

'You're a damned tease, Malazan.'

'Keeps you coming back.'

He thought about that, and then snorted. 'Maybe, but don't count on it.'

'What you never find out will haunt you to the end of your days, Barghast.'

'I doubt I'll miss my chance, Kisswhere. After all, how fast can you run?'

'And how sharp is my knife?'

Spax laughed. 'I'd best not keep her highness waiting. Save me some rum, will you?'

She shrugged. 'I'm not one for promises.'

Once he'd left, Kisswhere sat alone. Her own private fire out beyond the useless pickets, her own promise of blisters and searing guilt, if that was how she wanted it. *Do I? Might be I do. So they're not all dead. That's good. So we arrived too late. That's bad, or not. And this leg, well, it's hardly a coward's ploy, is it? I tried riding with the Khundryl, didn't I? At least, I think I did. At least, that's how it looked. Good enough.*

She drank down some more of the Bolkando rum.

Spax was a man who liked women. She'd always preferred the company of such men over that of wilting, timid excuses who thought a shy batting of the eyes was – gods below – attractive. No, bold was better. Coy was a stupid game played by pathetic cowards, as far as she was concerned. *All those stumbling words, the shifting about, what's the point? If you want me, come and get me. I might even say yes.*

More likely, of course, I'll just laugh. To see the sting.

They were marching towards whatever was left of the Bonehunters. No one seemed to know how grim it was, or at any rate they weren't telling her. She'd witnessed the sorcery, tearing up the horizon, even as the hobnailed boots of the Evertine Legion thundered closer behind her. She'd seen the moonspawn – a cloud- and fire-wreathed mountain in the sky.

Was there betrayal in this? Was this what Sinter feared? Sister, are you even alive?

Of course I don't want to go back. I don't want to know. I should just say what I'm feeling. 'Go to Hood, Queen. And you too, Spax. I'm riding south.' I don't want to see their faces, those pathetic survivors. Not the shock, not the horror, not all those things you see in the faces of people who don't know why they're still alive, when so many of their comrades are dead.

Every army is a cauldron, with the flames getting higher and higher on all sides. We stew, we boil, we turn into grey lumps of meat. 'Queen Abrastal, it's you and people like you whose appetites are never sated. Your maws gape, and in we go, and it sickens me.'

When the two Khundryl riders appeared, three days past, Kisswhere had turned away. In her mind she drew a knife and murdered her curiosity, a quick slash, a sudden spray and then silence. What was the point of knowing, when knowing was nothing more than the taste of salt and iron on the tongue?

She drank more rum, pleased at the numbness of her throat. Eating fire was easy and getting easier.

A sudden memory. Their first time standing in a ragged line, the first day of their service in the marines. Some gnarled master sergeant had walked up to them, wearing the smile of a hyena approaching a crippled gazelle. Sinter had straightened beside Kisswhere, trying to affect the appropriate attention. Badan Gruk, she'd seen with a quick sidelong glance, was looking miserable – with the face of a man who'd just realized where love had taken him.

You damned fool. I can play their game. You two can't, because for you there are no games. They don't exist in your Hood-shitting world of honour and duty.

'Twelve, is it?' the master sergeant had said, his grin broadening. 'I'd wager three of you are going to make it. The rest, well, we'll bury half of 'em and the other half we'll send on to the regular infantry, where all the losers live.'

'Which half?' Kisswhere had asked.

Lizard eyes fixed on her. 'What's that, sweet roundworm?'

'Which half of the one you cut in two goes in the ground, and which half goes to the regulars? The legs half, well, that solves the marching bit. But—'

'You're one of those, are ya?'

'What? One who can count? Three make it, nine don't. Nine can't get split in half. Of course,' she added with her own broad smile, 'maybe marines don't need to know how to count, and maybe master sergeants are the thickest of the lot. Which is what I'm starting to think, anyway.'

She'd never got close to completing the thousand push-ups. *Arsehole. Men who smile like that need a sense of humour, but I'm not one to believe in miracles.*

She scratched some more with her stick. *Should've broken him, right here between my legs. Aye, save the last laugh for Kisswhere. She wins every game.* 'Every one of them, aye, isn't it obvious?'

Spax made a point of keeping his shell-armour loose, the plates clacking freely, and with all the fetishes tied everywhere he was well pleased with the concatenation of sounds when he walked. Had he been a thin runt, the effect would not have worked, but he was big enough and loud enough to be his own squad, a martial apparition that could not help but make a dramatic entrance no matter how sumptuous the destination.

In this case, the queen's command tent was as close to a palace as he was likely to find in these Wastelands, and shouldering in between the curtains of silk and the slap of his heavy gauntlets on the map table gave him no small amount of satisfaction. 'Highness, I am here.'

Queen Abrastal lounged in her ornate chair, legs stretched out, watching him from under lowered lids. Her red hair was unbound and hanging loose, freshly washed and combed out, and the Barghast's loins stirred as he observed her in turn.

'Wipe off that damned grin,' Abrastal said in a growl.

His brows lifted. 'Something wrong, Firehair?'

'Only everything I know you're thinking right now, Spax.'

'Highness, if you'd been born in an alley behind a bar, you'd still be a queen in my eyes. Deride me for my admiration all you like, it changes nothing in my heart.'

She snorted. 'You stink of rum.'

'I was pursuing a mystery, Highness.'

'Oh?'

'The onyx-skinned woman. The Malazan.'

She rolled her eyes. 'Gods below, you're worse than a crocodile in the mating season.'

'Not that mystery, Firehair, though I'll chase that one down given the chance. No, what makes me curious is her, well, her lack of zeal. This is not the soldier I would have expected.'

Abrastal waved one hand. 'There is no mystery there, Spax. The woman's a coward. Every army has them, why should the Malazan one be any different?'

'Because she's a marine,' he replied.

'So?'

'The marines damn near singlehandedly conquered Lether, Highness, and she was one of them. On Genabackis whole armies would desert if they heard they'd be facing an assault by Malazan marines. They stank with magic and Moranth munitions, and they never broke – you needed to cut them down to the last man and woman.'

'Even the hardest soldier reaches an end to their endurance, Spax.'

'Well, she's been a prisoner to the Letherii, so perhaps you are right. Now then, Highness, what did you wish of your loyal warchief?'

'I want you with me at the parley.'

'Of course.'

'Sober.'

'If you insist, but I warn you, what plagues me also plagues my

80

warriors. We yearn for a fight – we only hired on with you Bolkando because we expected an invasion or two. Instead, we're marching like damned soldiers. Could we have reached the Bonehunters in time—'

'You'd likely be regretting it,' Abrastal said, her expression darkening.

Spax tried on a scowl. 'You believe those Khundryl?'

'I do. Especially after Felash's warning – though I am coming to suspect that my Fourteenth Daughter's foresight was focused on something still awaiting us.'

'More of these two-legged giant lizards?'

She shrugged, and then shook her head. 'No, I don't think so, but unfortunately it's only a gut feeling. We'll see what we see at the parley.'

'The Malazans never conquered the Gilk Barghast,' Spax said.

'Gods below, if you show up with your hackles raised—'

'Spirits forbid the thought, Highness. Facing them, I will be like the one hare the eagle missed. I'm as likely to freeze as fill my breeches.'

Slowly, Abrastal's eyes widened. 'Warchief,' she said in wonder, 'you are frightened of them.'

He grimaced, and then nodded.

The queen of the Bolkando abruptly rose, taking a deep breath, and Spax's eyes could not help but fall to her swelling chest. 'I will meet this Adjunct,' Abrastal said with sudden vigour. Her eyes found the Barghast and pinned him in place. 'If indeed we are to face more of the giant two-legged lizards with their terrible magic . . . Spax, what will you now claim of the courage of your people?'

'Courage, Highness? You will have that. But can we hope to do what those Khundryl said the Malazans did?' He hesitated, and then shook his head. 'Firehair, I too will look hard upon those soldiers, and I fear I already know what I will see. They have known the crucible.'

'And you do not wish to see that truth, do you?'

He grunted. 'Let's just say it's both a good and a bad thing your stores of rum are nearly done.'

'Was this our betrayal?'

Tanakalian faced the question, and the eyes of the hard, iron woman who had just voiced it, for as long as he could before shying away. 'Mortal Sword, you well know we simply could not reach them in time. As such, our failure was one of circumstance, not loyalty.'

'For once,' she replied, 'you speak wisely, sir. Tomorrow we ride out to the Bonehunter camp. Prepare an escort of fifty of our brothers and sisters – I want healers and our most senior veterans.'

'I understand, Mortal Sword.'

She glanced at him, studied his face for a moment, and then returned her gaze to the jade-lit southeastern sky. 'If you do not, sir, they will.'

You hound me into a corner, Mortal Sword. You seem bent on forcing my hand. Is there only room for one on that pedestal of yours? What will you do when you stand face to face with the Adjunct? With Brys Beddict?

But, more to the point, what do you know of this betrayal? I see a sword in our future. I see blood on its blade. I see the Perish standing alone, against impossible odds.

'At the parley,' Krughava said, 'you will keep our own counsel, sir.'

He bowed. 'As you wish.'

'She has been wounded,' Krughava went on. 'We will close about her with our utmost diligence to her protection.'

'Protection, sir?'

'In the manner of hunter whales, Shield Anvil, when one of their clan is unwell.'

'Mortal Sword, this shall be a parley of comrades, more or less. Our clan, as you might call it, is unassailed. No sharks. No dhenrabi or gahrelit. Against whom do we protect her?'

'The darkness of her own doubts if nothing else. Though I cannot be certain, I fear she is one who would gnaw upon her own scars, eager to watch them bleed, thirsty for the taste of blood in her mouth.'

'Mortal Sword, how can we defend her against herself?'

Krughava was silent for a time, and then she sighed. 'Make stern your regard, banish all shadows from your mind, anneal in brightest silver your certainty. We return to the path, with all resolve. Can I make it any clearer, Shield Anvil?'

He bowed again.

'Leave me now,' she said.

Tanakalian swung round and walked down from the rise. The even rows of cookfires flickered in the basin before him, painting the canvas tents with light and shadow. Five thousand paces to the west rose another glow – the Bolkando encampment. *A parley of comrades, a clan. Or perhaps not. The Bolkando have no place in this scheme.*

They said she was concussed, but now recovers. They said something impossible happened above her unconscious form, there on the field of battle. They said – with something burning fierce in their eyes – that the Bonehunters awakened that day, and its heart was there, before the Adjunct's senseless body.

Already a legend is taking birth, and yet we saw none of its making. We played no role. The name of the Perish Grey Helms is a gaping absence in this roll call of heroes.

The injustice of that haunted him. He was Shield Anvil, but his embrace remained empty, a gaping abyss between his arms. *This will change. I will make it change. And all will see. Our time is coming.*

Blood, blood on the sword. Gods, I can almost taste it.

She pulled hard on the leaf-wrapped stick, feeling every muscle in her jaw and neck bunch taut. Smoke streaming from her mouth and nose, she faced the darkness of the north plain. Others, when they walked out to the edge of the legion's camp, would find themselves on the side that gave them a clear view of the Malazan encampment. They walked out and they stared, no different from pilgrims facing a holy shrine, an unexpected edifice on their path. She imagined that in their silence they struggled to fit into their world that dismal sprawl of dung-fires, the vague shapes moving about, the glint of banners like a small forest of storm-battered saplings. Finding a place for all that should have been easy. But it wasn't.

They would wince at their own wounds, reminded of the gaps in their own lines, and they would feel like shadows cast by something greater than anything they had known before. There was a name for this, she knew. Atri-Ceda Aranict pulled again on the stick, mindful of the bright swimming glow hovering before her face.

Some scholar once likened this to the mastery fire and all it symbolized. Huh. Some scholar was working hard to justify her habit. Stupid woman. It's yours, so just revel in it and when it comes to justifying what you do, keep your mouth shut. Philosophy, really.

Ask a soldier. A soldier knows all about smoke. And what's in and what's out, and what's the fucking difference in the end.

The Letherii had comported themselves with honour on that horrid field of battle. They had distracted the enemy. They had with blood and pain successfully effected the Malazan withdrawal – *no, let's call it what it was, a rout. Once the signals sounded, the impossible iron wall became a thing of reeds, torn loose and whipped back on the savage wind.*

Even so. Letherii soldiers walked out at dusk, or in the moments before dawn, right out to the camp's edge, and they looked across the empty expanse of scrub to the Malazans. They weren't thinking of routs, or withdrawals. They were thinking of all that had gone before that.

And there was a word for what they felt.

Humility.

'My dear.' He had come up behind her, soft-footed, as uncertain as a child.

Aranict sighed. 'I am forgetting how to sleep.'

Brys Beddict came up to stand at her side. 'Yes. I awoke and felt your absence, and it made me think.'

Once, she had been nervous before this man. Once, she had imagined illicit scenes, the way a person might conjure up wishes they knew could never be filled. Now, her vanishing from his bed wakened him to unease. *A few days, and the world changes.* 'Think of what?'

'I don't know if I should say.'

The tone was rueful. She filled her lungs with smoke, eased it back out slowly. 'I'd wager it's too late for that, Brys.'

'I have never been in love before. Not like this. I have never before felt so . . . helpless. As if, without my even noticing, I gave you all my power.'

'All the children's stories never talked about that,' Aranict said after a moment. 'The prince and the princess, each heroic and strong, equals in the grand love they win. The tale ends in mutual admiration.'

'That tastes a tad sour.'

'That taste is of self-congratulation,' she said. 'Those tales are all about narcissism. The sleight of hand lies in the hero's mirror image – a princess for a prince, a prince for a princess – but in truth it's all one. It's nobility's love for itself. Heroes win the most beautiful lovers, it's the reward for their bravery and virtue.'

'And those lovers are naught but mirrors?'

'Shiny silver ones.'

She felt him watching her.

'But,' he said after a few moments, 'it's not that even a thing, is it? You are not my mirror, Aranict. You are something *other*. I am not reflected in you, just as you are not reflected in me. So what is this that we have found here, and why do I find myself on my knees before it?'

The stick's end glowed like a newborn sun, only to ebb in its instant of life. 'How should I know, Brys? It is as if I stand facing you from an angle no one else can find, and when I'm there nothing rises between us – a trick of the light and your fortifications vanish. So you feel vulnerable.'

He grunted. 'But it is not that way with Tehol and Janath.'

'Yes, I have heard about them, and it seems to me that no matter which way each faces, he or she faces the other. He is her king and she is his queen, and everything else just follows on from there. It is the rarest of loves, I should think.'

'But it is not ours, is it, Aranict?'

She said nothing. *How can I? I feel swollen, as if I have swallowed you alive, Brys. I walk with the weight of you inside me, and I have never before felt anything like this.* She flicked the stick-end away. 'You worry too much, Brys. I am your lover. Leave it at that.'

'You are also my Atri-Ceda.'

She smiled in the darkness. 'And that, Brys, is what brought *me* out here.'

'Why?'

'Something hides. It's all around us, subtle as smoke. It has manifested only once thus far, and that was at the battle, among the Malazans – at the place where the Adjunct fell unconscious. There is a hidden hand in all of this, Brys, and I don't trust it.'

'Where the Adjunct fell? But Aranict, what happened there saved Tavore's life, and quite possibly the lives of the rest of the Bonehunters. The Nah'ruk *reeled* from that place.'

'Yet still I fear it,' she insisted, plucking out another rustleaf stick. 'Allies should show themselves.' She drew out the small silver box containing the resin sparker. The night wind defeated her efforts to scrape a flame to life, so she stepped close against Brys and tried again.

'Allies,' he said, 'have their own enemies. Showing themselves imposes a risk, I imagine.'

A flicker of flame and then the stick was alight. She took a half-step back. 'I think that's a valid observation. Well, I suppose we always suspected that the Adjunct's war wasn't a private one.'

'No matter how she might wish it so,' he said, with something like grudging respect.

'Tomorrow's parley could prove most frustrating,' Aranict observed, 'if she refuses to relent. We need to know what she knows. We need to understand what she seeks. More than all that, we need to make sense of what happened the day of the Nah'ruk.'

He reached up, surprised her by brushing her cheek, and then leaning closer and kissing her. She laughed deep in her throat. 'Danger is a most alluring drug, isn't it, Brys?'

'Yes,' he whispered, but then stepped back. 'I will walk the perimeter now, Atri-Ceda, to witness the dawn with my soldiers. Will you be rested enough for the parley?'

'More or less.'

'Good. Until later, then.'

She watched him walk away. *Errant take me, he just climbed back out.*

'When it's stretched it stays stretched,' Hanavat said in a grumble. 'What's the point?'

Shelemasa continued rubbing the oil into the woman's distended belly. 'The point is, it feels good.'

'Well, I'll grant you that, though I imagine it's as much the attention as anything else.'

'Exactly what men never understand,' the younger woman said, finally settling back and rubbing her hands together. 'We have iron in our souls. How could we not?'

Hanavat glanced away, eyes tightening. 'My last child,' she said. 'My only child.'

To that Shelemasa was silent. The charge against the Nah'ruk had taken all of Hanavat's children. *All* of them. *But if that was cruel, it is nothing compared to sparing Gall. Where the mother bows, the father breaks. They are gone. He led them all to their deaths, yet he survived. Spirits, yours is the gift of madness.*

The charge haunted Shelemasa as well. She had ridden through the lancing barrage of lightning, figures on either side erupting, bodies exploding, spraying her with sizzling gore. The screams of horses, the thunder of tumbling beasts, bones snapping – even now, that dread cauldron awakened again in her mind, a torrent of sounds pounding her ears from the inside out. She knelt in Hanavat's tent, trembling with the memories.

The older woman must have sensed something, for she reached out and settled a weathered hand on her thigh. 'It goes,' she murmured. 'I see it among all you survivors. The wave of remembrance, the horror in your eyes. But I tell you, it goes.'

'For Gall, too?'

The hand seemed to flinch. 'No. He is Warleader. It does not leave him. That charge is not in the past. He lives it again and again, every moment, day and night. I have lost him, Shelemasa. We have all lost him.'

Eight hundred and eighty warriors remained. She had stood among them, had wandered with them the wreckage of the retreat, and she had seen what she had seen. *Never again will we fight, not with the glory and joy of old. Our military effectiveness, as the Malazan scribes would say, has come to an end.* The Khundryl Burned Tears had been destroyed. Not a failure of courage. Something far worse. *We were made, in an instant, obsolete.* Nothing could break the spirit as utterly as that realization had done.

A new Warleader was needed, but she suspected no acclamation was forthcoming. The will was dead. There were no pieces left to pick up.

'I will attend the parley,' said Hanavat, 'and I want you with me, Shelemasa.'

'Your husband—'

'Is lying in his eldest son's tent. He takes no food, no water. He intends to waste away. Before long, we will burn his body on a pyre, but that will be nothing but a formality. My mourning has already begun.'

'I know . . .' Shelemasa hesitated, 'it was difficult between you. The rumours of his leanings—'

'And that is the bitterest thing of all,' Hanavat cut in. 'Gall, well, he leaned every which way. I long ago learned to accept that. What bites deepest now is we had found each other again. Before the charge. We were awakened to our love for one another. There was . . . there was happiness again. For a few moments.' She stopped then, for she was crying.

Shelemasa drew closer. 'Tell me of the child within you, Hanavat. I have never been pregnant. Tell me how it feels. Are you filled up, is that how it is? Does it stir – I am told it will stir on occasion.'

Smiling through her grief, Hanavat said, 'Ah, very well. How does it feel? Like I've just eaten a whole pig. Shall I go on?'

Shelemasa laughed, a short, unexpected laugh, and then nodded. *Tell me something good. To drown out the screams.*

'The children are asleep,' Jastara said, moving to settle down on her knees beside him. She studied his face. 'I see how much of him came from you. Your eyes, your mouth—'

'Be quiet, woman,' said Gall. 'I will not lie with my son's widow.'

She pulled away. 'Then lie with *someone*, for Hood's sake.'

He turned his head, stared at the tent wall.

'Why are you here?' she demanded. 'You come to my tent like the ghost of everything I have lost. Am I not haunted enough? What do you want with me? Look at me. I offer you my body – let us share our grief—'

'Stop.'

She hissed under her breath.

'I would you take a knife to me,' Gall said. 'Do that, woman, and I will bless you with my last breath. A knife. Give me pain, be pleased to see how you hurt me. Do that, Jastara, in the name of my son.'

'You selfish piece of dung, why should I indulge you? Get out. Find some other hole to hide in. Do you think your grandchildren are comforted seeing you this way?'

'You are not Khundryl born,' he said. 'You are Gilk. You understand nothing of our ways—'

'The Khundryl were feared warriors. They still are. You need to stand again, Gall. You need to gather your ghosts – all of them – and save your people.'

'We are not Wickans,' he whispered, reaching up to claw once more at his face.

She spat out a curse. 'Gods below, do you really think Coltaine and his damned Wickans could have done better?'

'He would have found a way.'

'Fool. No wonder your wife sneers at you. No wonder all your lovers have turned away from you—'

'Turned away? They're all dead.'

'So find some more.'

'Who would love a corpse?'

'Now finally you have a point worth making, Warleader. Who would? The answer lies before me, a stupid old man. It's been five days. You are Warleader. Shake yourself awake, damn you—'

'No. Tomorrow I will give my people into the Adjunct's care. The Khundryl Burned Tears are no more. It is done. I am done.'

The blade of a knife hovered before his eyes. 'Is this what you want?'

'Yes,' he whispered.

'What should I cut first?'

'You decide.'

The knife vanished. 'I am Gilk, as you say. What do I know of mercy? Find your own way to Hood, Gall. The Wickans would have died, just as your warriors died. No different. Battles are lost. It is the world's way. But you still breathe. Gather up your people – they look to you.'

'No longer. Never again will I lead warriors into battle.'

She snarled something incomprehensible, and moved off, leaving him alone.

He stared at the tent wall, listened to his own pointless breaths. *I know what this is. It is fear. For all my life it has waited for me, out in the cold night. I have done terrible things, and my punishment draws near. Please, hurry.*

For this night, it is very cold, and it draws ever nearer.

CHAPTER FOUR

Once we knew nothing.
Now we know everything.
Stay away from our eyes.
Our eyes are empty.
Look into our faces
and see us if you dare.
We are the skin of war.
We are the skin of war.
Once we knew nothing.
Now we know everything.

Skin
Sejaras

SWEAT ENOUGH A MAN COULD DROWN IN. HE SHIVERED BENEATH HIS furs, something he did every night since the battle. Jolting awake, drenched, heart pounding. After-images behind his eyes. Keneb, in the instant before he was torn apart, twisting round in his saddle, fixing Blistig with a cold, knowing stare. Not ten paces away, their eyes locking. But that was impossible. *I know it's impossible. I was never even close. He didn't turn, didn't look back. Didn't see me. Couldn't.*

Don't you howl at me from the dark, Keneb. Don't you stare. It was nothing to do with me. Leave me alone.

But this damned army didn't know how to break, understood nothing about routing before a superior enemy. Every soldier alone, that was what routing was all about. Instead, they *maintained order*. *'We're with you, Fist Blistig. See our boots pound. It's north we're going, is it? They ain't pursuing, sir, and that's a good thing – can't feel it no more, sir, you know: Hood's own breath, there on the back of my neck. Can't feel it. We're in good order, sir. Good order . . .'*

'Good order,' he whispered to the gloom in his tent. 'We should be scattered to the winds. Finding our own ways back. To civilization. To sanity.'

The sweat was drying, or the scraped underside of the fur skin was soaking it all up. He was still chilled, sick to his stomach with fear. *What's happened to me? They stare. Out there in the darkness. They stare. Coltaine. Duiker. The thousands beyond Aren's wall. They stare, looking down on me from their crosses. And now Keneb, there on his horse. Ruthan Gudd. Quick Ben. The dead await me. They wonder why I am not with them. I should be with them.*

They know I don't belong here.

Once, he'd been a fine soldier. A decent commander. Clever enough to preserve the lives of his garrison, the hero who saved Aren from the Whirlwind. But then the Adjunct arrived, and it all started to go wrong. She conscripted him, tore him away from Aren – they would have made him High Fist, the City's Protector. They would have given him a palace.

She stole my future. My life.

Malaz City was even worse. There, he'd been shown the empire's rotted core. Mallick Rel, the betrayer of Aren's legion, the murderer of Coltaine and Duiker and all the rest – no, there was no doubt about any of that. Yet there the Jhistal was, whispering in the Empress's ear, and his vengeance against the Wickans was not yet done. *And against us. You took us into that nest, Tavore, and more of us died. For all that you have done, I will never forgive you.*

Standing before her filled him with bile. Every time, he almost trembled in his desire to take her by the throat, to crush that throat, to tell her what she'd done to him even as the light left those dead, flat eyes.

I was a good officer once. An honourable soldier.

Now I live in terror. What will she do to us next? Y'Ghatan wasn't enough. Malaz City wasn't enough. Nor Lether either, never enough. Nah'ruk? Not enough. Damn you, Tavore. I will die for a proper cause. But this?

He'd never before known such hate. Its poison filled him, and still the dead looked on, from their places in the wastes of Hood's realm. *Shall I kill her? Is that what you all want? Tell me!*

The tent walls were lightening. This day, the parley. The Adjunct, Fists arrayed around her, the new ones, the lone surviving old one. *But who looks to me? Who walks a step behind me? Not Sort. Not Kindly. Not even Raband or Skanarow. No, the new Fists and their senior officers look right through me. I am already a ghost, already one of the forgotten. What have I done to deserve that?*

Keneb was gone. Since Letheras, Keneb had to all intents and purposes been commanding the Bonehunters. Managing the march, keeping it supplied, maintaining discipline and organization. In short, doing everything. Some people possessed such skills. *Running a garrison was easy enough. We had a fat quartermaster who had a hand in every pocket, a smiling oaf with a sharp eye, and our suppliers surrounded us and whatever needed doing, why, it was just a written request away. Sometimes not even that, more a wink, a nod.*

The patrols went out. They came back. Watches turned, gatekeepers maintained vigilance. We kept the peace and peace kept us happy.

But an army on the march was another matter. The logistics besieged him, staggered his brain. Too much to think about, too much to worry over. *Fine, we're now leaner – hah, what a sweet way of putting it. We're an army of regulars with a handful of heavies and marines. So, we're oversupplied, if such a thing even exists.*

But it won't last. She wants us to cross the Wastelands – and what waits beyond them? Desert. Emptiness. No, hunger waits for us, no matter how heaped our wagons. Hunger and thirst.

I won't take that on. I won't. Don't ask.

But they wouldn't, would they? Because he wasn't Keneb. *I really have no reason to show up. I'm worse than Banaschar in that company. At least he's got the nerve to turn up drunk, to smile in the face of the Adjunct's displeasure. That's its own kind of courage.*

Activity in the camp now, as dawn approached. Muted, few conversations, a torpid thing awakening to brutal truths, eyes blinking open, souls flinching. *We're the walking dead. What more do you want of us, Tavore?*

Plenty. He knew it like teeth sinking into his chest.

Growling under his breath, he pulled aside the furs and sat up. A Fist's tent. All that room for nothing, for the damp air to wait around for his heroic rise, his gods-given brilliance. He dragged on his clothes, collected his chill leather boots and shook them to check for nesting scorpions and spiders and then forced his feet into them. He needed to take a piss.

I was a good officer once.

Fist Blistig slipped the tethers of the tent flap, and stepped outside.

Kindly looked round. 'Captain Raband.'

'Fist?'

'Find me Pores.'

'Master Sergeant Pores, sir?'

'Or whatever rank he's decided on this morning, yes. You'll know him by his black eyes.' Kindly paused, ruminating, and then said, 'Wish I knew who broke his nose. Deserves a medal.'

'Yes sir. On my way, sir.'

He glanced over at the sound of boots drawing nearer. Fist Faradan Sort and, trailing a step behind her, Captain Skanarow. Neither woman looked happy. Kindly scowled. 'Are those the faces you want to show your soldiers?'

Skanarow looked away guiltily, but Sort's eyes hardened to flint. 'Your own soldiers are close to mutiny, Kindly – I can't believe you ordered—'

'A kit inspection? Why not? Forced them all to scrape the shit out of their breeches, a bit of tidying that was long overdue.'

Faradan Sort was studying him. 'It's not an act, is it?'

'Some advice,' Kindly said. 'The keep is on fire, the black stomach plague is killing the kitchen staff, the rats won't eat your supper and hearing the circus is in the yard your wife has oiled the hinges on the bedroom door. So I walk in and blister your ear about your scuffy boots. When I leave, what are you thinking about?'

Skanarow answered. 'I'm thinking up inventive ways to kill you, sir.'

Kindly adjusted his weapon belt. 'The sun has cracked the sky, my dears. Time for my constitutional morning walk.'

'Want a few bodyguards, sir?'

'Generous offer, Captain, but I will be fine. Oh, if Raband shows up with Pores any time soon, promote the good captain. Omnipotent Overseer of the Universe should suit. Ladies.'

Watching him walk off, Faradan Sort sighed and rubbed at her face. 'All right,' she muttered, 'the bastard has a point.'

'That's why he's a bastard, sir.'

Sort glanced over. 'Are you impugning a Fist's reputation, Captain?'

Skanarow straightened. 'Absolutely not, Fist. I was stating a fact. Fist Kindly is a bastard, sir. He was one when he was captain, lieutenant, corporal, and seven-year-old bully. Sir.'

Faradan Sort studied Skanarow for a moment. She'd taken the death of Ruthan Gudd hard, hard enough to suggest to Sort that their relationship wasn't simply one of comrades, fellow officers. And now she was saying 'sir' to someone who only days before had been a fellow captain. *Should I talk about it? Should I tell her it's as uncomfortable to me as it must be to her? Is there any point?* She was holding up, wasn't she? Behaving like a damned soldier.

And then there's Kindly. Fist Kindly, Hood help us all.

'Constitutional,' she said. 'Gods below. Now, I suppose it's time to meet my new soldiers.'

'Regular infantry are simple folk, sir. They ain't got that wayward streak like the marines got. Should be no trouble at all.'

'They broke in battle, Captain.'

'They were ordered to, sir. And that's why they're still alive, mostly.'

'I'm beginning to see another reason for Kindly's kit inspection. How many dropped their weapons, abandoned their shields?'

'Parties have been out recovering items on the backtrail, sir.'

'That's not the point,' said Sort. 'They dropped weapons. Doing that is habit-forming. You're saying they'll be no trouble, Captain? Maybe not the kind you're thinking. It's the other kind of trouble that worries me.'

'Understood, sir. Then we'd better shake them up.'

'I think I'm about to become very unpleasant.'

'A bastard?'

'Wrong gender.'

'Maybe so, sir, but it's still the right word.'

If he was still. If he struggled past the fumes and dregs of the past night's wine, and pushed away the ache in his head and sour taste on his tongue. If he held his breath, lying as one dead, in that perfect expression of surrender. Then, he could feel her. A stirring far beneath the earth's cracked, calloused skin. *The worm stirs, and you do indeed feel her, O priest. She is your gnawing guilt. She is your fevered shame, so flushing your face.*

His goddess was drawing closer. A drawn out endeavour, to be sure. She had the meat of an entire world to chew through. Bones to crunch in her jaws, secrets to devour. But mountains groaned, tilting and shifting to her deep passage. Seas churned. Forests shook. The Worm of Autumn was coming. *'Bless the falling leaves, bless the grey skies, bless this bitter wind and the beasts that sleep.' Yes, Holy Mother, I remember the prayers, the Restiturge of Pall. 'And the weary blood shall feed the soil, their fleshly bodies cast down into your belly. And the Dark Winds of Autumn shall rush in hunger, snatching up their loosed souls. Caverns shall moan with their voices. The dead have turned their backs on the solid earth, the stone and the touch of the sky. Bless their onward journey, from which none return. The souls are nothing of value. Only the flesh feeds the living. Only the flesh. Bless our eyes, D'rek, for they are open. Bless our eyes, D'rek, for they see.'*

He rolled on to his side. Poison comes to the flesh long before the soul ever leaves it. She was the cruel measurer of time. She was the face of inevitable decay. Was he not blessing her with every day of this life he'd made?

Banaschar coughed, slowly sat up. Invisible knuckles kneaded the inside of his skull. He knew they were in there, someone's fist trapped inside, someone wanting out. *Out of my head, aye. Who can blame them?*

He looked round blearily. The scene was too civilized, he concluded. Somewhat sloppy, true, sly mutters of dissolution, a certain carelessness. But not a hint of madness. Not a single whisper of horror. Normal orderliness mocked him. The tasteless air, the pallid misery of dawn soaking through the tent walls, etching the silhouettes of insects: every detail howled its mundane truth.

But so many died. Only five days ago. Six. Six, now. I can still hear them. Pain, fury, all those fierce utterances of despair. If I step outside this morning, I should see them still. Those marines. Those heavies. Swarming against the face of the enemy's advance, but these hornets were fighting a losing battle – they'd met something nastier than them, and one by one they were crushed down, smeared into the earth.

And the Khundryl. Gods below, the poor Burned Tears.

Too civilized, this scene – the heaps of clothing, the dusty jugs lying abandoned and empty on the ground, the tramped-down grasses struggling in the absence of the sun's clear streams. Would light's life ever return, or were these grasses doomed now to wither and die? Each blade knew not. For now, there was nothing to do but suffer.

'Be easy,' he muttered, 'we move on. You will recover your free ways. You will feel the wind's breath again. I promise.' *Ah, Holy Mother, are these your words of comfort? Light returns. Be patient, its sweet kiss draws ever nearer. A new day. Be still, frail one.*

Banaschar snorted, and set about seeking out a jug with something left in it.

Five Khundryl warriors stood before Dead Hedge. They looked lost, and yet determined, if such a thing was possible, and the Bridgeburner wasn't sure it was. They had difficulty meeting his eyes, yet held their ground. 'What in Hood's name am I supposed to do with you?'

He glanced back over a shoulder. His two new sergeants were coming up behind him, other soldiers gathering behind them. Both women looked like bags overstuffed with bad memories. Their faces were sickly grey, as if they'd forgotten all of life's pleasures, *as if they'd seen the other side. But lasses, it's not so bad, it's just the getting there that stinks.*

'Commander?' Sweetlard enquired, nodding to the Khundryl.

'They're volunteering to join up,' said Hedge, scowling. 'Cashiered outa the Burned Tears, or something like that.' He faced the five men again. 'I'd wager Gall will call this treason and come for your heads.'

The eldest of the warriors, his face almost black with tear tattoos, seemed to hunch lower beneath his broad, sloping shoulders. 'Gall Inshikalan's soul is dead. All his children died in the charge. He sees only the past. The Khundryl Burned Tears are no more.' He gestured at his companions. 'Yet we would fight on.'

'Why not the Bonehunters?' Hedge asked.

'Fist Kindly refused us.'

Another warrior growled and said, 'He called us savages. And cowards.'

'Cowards?' Hedge's scowl deepened. 'You were in that charge?'

'We were.'

'And you would fight on? What's cowardly about that?'

The eldest one said, 'He sought to shame us back to our people – but we are destroyed. We kneel in Coltaine's shadow, broken by failure.'

'You're saying all the others will just . . . fade away?'

The man shrugged.

Alchemist Bavedict spoke behind Hedge. 'Commander, we took us a few losses. These warriors are veterans. And survivors.'

Hedge looked round again, studied the Letherii. 'Aren't we all,' he said.

Bavedict nodded.

Sighing, Hedge faced the warriors once more. He nodded at the spokesman. 'Your name?'

'Berrach. These are my sons. Sleg, Gent, Pahvral and Rayez.'

Your sons. No wonder you didn't feel welcome in Gall's camp. 'You're now our outriders, scouts and, when needed, cavalry.'

'Bridgeburners?'

Hedge nodded. 'Bridgeburners.'

'We're not cowards,' hissed the youngest, presumably Rayez, his expression suddenly fierce.

'If you were,' said Hedge, 'I'd have sent you packing. Berrach, you're now a Captain of our Mounted – have you spare horses?'

'Not any more, Commander.'

'Never mind, then. My sergeants here will see you billeted. Dismissed.'

In response the five warriors drew their sabres and fashioned a kind of salute Hedge had never seen before, blade edges set diagonally across each man's exposed throat.

Bavedict grunted behind him.

And if I now said 'Cut' they'd do just that, wouldn't they? Gods below. 'Enough of that, soldiers,' he said. 'We don't worship Coltaine in the Bridgeburners. He was just another Malazan commander. A good one, to be sure, and right now he's standing in Dassem Ultor's shadow. And they got plenty of company. And maybe one day soon Gall will be there, too.'

Berrach was frowning. 'Do we not honour their memories, sir?'

Hedge bared his teeth in anything but a smile. 'Honour whoever you want in your spare time, Captain, only you ain't got any spare time any more, because you're now a Bridgeburner, and us Bridgeburners honour only one thing.'

'And that is, sir?'

'Killing the enemy, Captain.'

Something awoke in the faces of the warriors. As one they sheathed their weapons. Berrach seemed to be struggling to speak, and finally managed to ask, 'Commander Hedge, how do the Bridgeburners salute?'

'We don't. And as for anyone outside our company, it's this.'

Eyes widened at Hedge's obscene gesture, and then Berrach grinned.

When Hedge turned to wave his sergeants forward, he saw that they weren't quite the bloated grey bags he'd seen only moments earlier. Dread had been stripped from their faces, and now their exhaustion was plain to see – but it had softened somehow. Sweetlard and Rumjugs looked almost beautiful again.

Bridgeburners get pounded all the time. We just get back up. No bluster, just back up, aye. 'Alchemist,' he said to Bavedict, 'show me that new invention of yours.'

'Finally,' the Letherii replied. 'Funny, isn't it?'

'What is?'

'Oh, how a handful of Khundryl warriors started you all up.'

'The sergeants were in shock—'

'Commander, you looked even worse than they did.'

Oh, Hood take me, I doubt I can argue that. 'So tell me, what's the new cusser do?'

'Well now, sir, you were telling me about the Drum—'

'I what? When?'

'You were drunk. Anyway, it got me to thinking . . .'

The two newcomers walked into the squads' encampment, and faces lifted, eyes went flat. No one wanted any damned interruptions to all this private misery. Not now. Badan Gruk hesitated, and then pushed himself to his feet. 'Eighteenth, isn't it?'

The sergeant, a Genabackan, was eyeing the other soldiers. 'Which one is what's left of the Tenth?'

Badan Gruk felt himself go cold. He could feel the sudden, sharp attention of the others in the camp. He understood that regard. He wasn't a hard man and they all knew it – so, would he back down now? *If I had anything left, I would.* 'I don't know where in the trenches you were, but we met that first charge. It's a damned miracle any one of us is still alive. There's two marines left from the Tenth, and I guess that's why you're here, since you, Sergeant, and your corporal, are obviously the only survivors from your squad. You lost all your soldiers.'

At that comment Badan paused, gauging the effect of his words. He saw none. *What does that tell us? Nothing good.* He half turned and gestured. 'There, those ones, they're from Primly's squad. But Sergeant Primly is dead. So is Hunt and so are Neller and Mulvan Dreader, and Corporal Kisswhere's gone . . . missing. You're left with Skulldeath and Drawfirst.'

Trailed by his corporal, the sergeant walked over. 'On your feet, marines,' he said. 'I'm Sergeant Gaunt-Eye, and this is Corporal Rib. The Tenth is no more. You're now in the Eighteenth.'

'What?' demanded Drawfirst. 'A squad of four?'

The corporal replied. 'We're picking up two more from the Seventh, and another two from Ninth Company's Fifth.'

Ruffle limped up beside Badan Gruk. 'Sergeant, Sinter's back.'

Badan sighed and turned away. 'Fine. She can handle this, then.' He'd had his moment of spine. Nobody would have to look his way any more, expecting . . . *expecting what? Hood knows. They're just collecting up scraps now. Enough to make a rag.* He returned to the remnants of the fire, sat with his back to the others.

I've seen enough. Not even marines do this for a living. You can't die for a living. So, sew together new squads all you like. But really, just how many marines are left? Fifty? Sixty? No, better to let us soak into the regulars, sour as old blood. Hood knows, I'm sick of these faces here, sick of not seeing the ones missing, the ones I'll never see again. Shoaly. Strap Mull. Skim, Hunt, all of them.

Sinter was speaking to Gaunt-Eye, but the tones were low, level, and a few moments later she came over and squatted down at his side. 'Rider in from the Burned Tears. Kisswhere's still mending. That broken leg was a bad one.'

'They took them away?'

'Who?'

'That sergeant.'

'Aye, though it's not so much "away" as "just over there", Badan. Not enough of us to sprawl.'

Badan found a stick and stirred at the ashes. 'What is she going to do, Sinter?'

'Kisswhere?'

'The Adjunct.'

'How should I know? I've not talked to her. No one has, as far as I can tell – at least, the Fists look to be in charge at the moment.'

Badan dropped the stick and then rubbed at his face. 'We got to go back,' he said.

'That won't happen,' Sinter replied.

He shot her a glare. 'We can't just pick up and go on.'

'Keep it down, Badan. We pulled out more soldiers than we should have. We're not as mauled as we could have been. Ruthan Gudd, Quick Ben, and then what happened at the vanguard. Those things checked them. Not to mention Fid getting us dug in – without those trenches, the heavies would never have—'

'Died?'

'Held. Long enough for the Letherii to bleed off pressure. Long enough for the rest of us to disengage—'

'Disengage, aye, that's a good one.'

She leaned closer. 'Listen to me,' she hissed. 'We didn't die. Not one of us still here—'

'Can't be more obvious, what you just said.'

'No, you're not getting it. We got overrun, Badan, but we clawed through even that. Aye, maybe it was the Lady pulling in a frenzy, maybe it was all the others stepping into the paths of the blades coming down on us. Maybe it was how rattled they were by then – from what I heard Lostara Yil was almost invisible inside a cloud of blood, and none of it her own. They had to check at that. A pause. Hesitation. Whatever, the plain truth is, when we started pulling back—'

'They left us to it.'

'Point is, could have been a lot worse, Badan. Look at the Khundryl. Six thousand went in, less than a thousand rode back out. I heard some survivors have been wandering into camp. Joining up with Dead Hedge's Bridgeburners. They say Warleader Gall is broken. So, you see what happens when the commander breaks? The rest just crumble.'

'Maybe now it's our turn.'

'I doubt it. She was injured, remember, and Denul don't work on her. She needs to find her own way of healing. But you're still missing my point. Don't break to pieces, Badan. Don't crawl inside yourself. Your squad lost Skim, but nobody else.'

'Nep Furrow's sick.'

'He's always sick, Badan. At least, ever since we set foot on the Wastelands.'

'Reliko wakes up screaming.'

'He ain't alone in that. He and Vastly stood with the other heavies, right? So.'

Badan Gruk studied the dead fire, and then he sighed. 'All right, Sinter. What do you want me to do? How do I fix all this?'

'Fix this? You idiot, stop even trying. It ain't up to us. We keep our eye on our officers, we wait for their lead.'

'I ain't seen Captain Sort.'

'That's because she's just been made a Fist – where you been? Never mind. We're waiting for Fid, that's the truth of it. Same time as the parley, he's calling all of us together, the last of the marines and heavies.'

'He's still just a sergeant.'

98

'Wrong. Captain now.'

Despite himself, Badan Gruk smiled. 'Bet he's thrilled.'

'Been dancing all morning, aye.'

'So we all gather.' He looked over, met her eyes. 'And we listen to what he has to say. And then . . .'

'Then . . . well, we'll see.'

Badan squinted at her, his anxiety returning in a chill rush. *Not the answer I expected.* 'Sinter, should we go and get Kisswhere?'

'Oh, she'd like that. No, let the cow stew a while.'

'It was us being so short,' Ruffle said.

'Ey whev?'

'You heard me, Nep. Those Short-Tails were too tall. Swinging down as low as they had to was hard – their armour wouldn't give enough at the waist. And did you see us? We learned fast. We waged war on their shins. Stabbed up into their crotches. Hamstrung 'em. Skewered their damned feet. We were an army of roach dogs, Nep.'

'I een no eruch dhug, Errufel. E'en a vulf, izme. Nep Vulf!'

Reliko spoke up. 'Think you got a point there, Ruffle. We started fighting damned low, didn't we? Right at their feet, in close, doing our work.' His ebon-skinned face worked into something like a grin.

'Just what I said,' Ruffle nodded, lighting another rustleaf stick to conclude a breakfast of five others. Her hands trembled. She'd taken a slash to her right leg. The roughly sewn wound ached. And so did everything else.

Sinter settled down beside Honey. In a low voice she said, 'They had to take the arm.'

Honey's face tightened. 'Weapon arm.'

Others were leaning in to listen. Sinter frowned. 'Aye. Corporal Rim's going to be clumsy for a while.'

'So, Sergeant,' said Lookback, 'are we gonna be folded into another squad, too? Or maybe swallow up some other one with only a couple of marines left?'

Sinter shrugged. 'Still being worked out.'

Honey said, 'Didn't like what happened to the Tenth, Sergeant. One moment there, the next just gone. Like a puff of smoke. That's not right.'

'Gaunt-Eye's a bit of a bastard,' Sinter said. 'No tact.'

'Let all his soldiers die, too,' pointed out Lookback.

'Enough of that. You can't think of it that way, not this time. Heads went up, heads got blown off, and then they were on top of us. It was every soldier for herself and himself.'

'Not for Fid,' said Honey. 'Or Corporal Tarr. Or Corabb or Urb or even Hellian. They rallied marines, Sergeant. They kept their heads and so people lived.'

Sinter looked away. 'Too much talking going on around here, I think. You're all picking scabs and it's getting ugly.' She stood. 'Need another word with Fid.'

Sergeant Urb walked over to Saltlick. 'On your feet, squad.'

The man looked up, grunted his way upright.

'Collect your kit.'

'Aye, Sergeant. Where we headed to?'

Without replying, Urb set off, the heavy dropping in two steps behind him. Urb wasn't looking forward to this. He knew the faces of most of this army's marines. In such matters, his memory was good. Faces. Easy. The people hiding behind them, not easy. Names, not a chance. Now, of course, there weren't many faces left.

The marine and heavy infantry encampment was a mess. Disorganized, careless. Squads set up leaving gaps where other squads used to be. Tents hung slack from slipshod pegging. Weapon belts, battered shields and scarred armour were left lying around on the ground, amidst rodara bones and the boiled vertebrae of myrid. Shallow holes reeked where soldiers had thrown up – people complained of some stomach bug, but more likely it was just nerves, the terrible aftermath of battle. The acid of surviving that just kept on burning its way up the throat.

And around them all, the morning stretched out in its measured madness, senseless as ever. Lightening sky, the spin and whirl of insects, the muted baying of animals being driven to slaughter. One thing was missing, however. No one was saying much of anything. Soldiers sat, heads down, or glancing up every now and then, eyes empty and far away.

All under siege. By the gaps round the circle, by the heaps of tents left folded and bound with their clutter of poles and bag of stakes. The dead didn't have anything to say, either, but everyone still sat, listening for them.

Urb drew up at the foot of one such broken circle of seated soldiers. They'd set a pot on embers and the smell wafting from the brew was heady, alcoholic. Urb studied them. Two women, two men. 'Twenty-second squad?'

The elder of the two women nodded without looking up. Urb remembered seeing her. A lively face, he recalled. Sharp tongue. Malaz City, maybe, or Jakatan. Islander for sure. 'Stand up, all of you.'

He saw resentment in the faces lifting to him. The other woman, young, dark-skinned and black-haired, had eyes of startling blue, which now flashed in outrage. 'Fine, Sergeant,' she said in an accent he'd never heard before, 'you've just filled out your squad.' Seeing

Saltlick standing behind Urb, her expression changed. 'Heavy.' She nodded respectfully.

The other woman shot her companions a hard look. 'This is the Thirteenth you're looking at, boys and girls. This squad, and Hellian's, they drank lizard blood that day. So, all of you, stand the fuck up and do it now.' She led the way. 'Sergeant Urb, I'm Clasp. You come to collect us, good. We need collecting.'

The others had clambered to their feet, but the younger woman was still scowling. 'We lost us a good sergeant—'

'Who didn't listen when they said duck,' Clasp retorted.

'Always had his nose in something,' said one of the men, a Kartoolian sporting an oiled beard.

'Curiosity,' observed the other man, a short, broad Falari with long hair the colour of blood-streaked gold. The tip of his nose had been sliced off, stubbing his face.

'You all done with the elegy?' Urb asked. 'Good. This is Saltlick. Now, faces I know, so I know all of yours. Give me some names.'

The Kartoolian said, 'Burnt Rope, Sergeant. Sapper.'

'Lap Twirl,' said the Falari. 'Cutter.'

'Healing?'

'Don't count on it, not on this ground.'

'Sad,' said the younger woman. 'Squad mage. About as useless as Lap right now.'

'Still have your crossbows?' Urb asked.

No one spoke.

'First task, then, off to the armoury. Then back here, and clean up this sty. The Twenty-second is retired. Welcome to the Thirteenth. Saltlick, keep them company. Clasp, you're now corporal. Congratulations.'

When they'd all trooped off, Urb stood alone, motionless, and for a long time, unnoticed by anyone, he stared at nothing.

Someone nudged her shoulder. She moaned and rolled on to her side. A second nudge, harder this time. 'G'way. Still dark.'

'Still dark, Sergeant, because you blindfolded yourself.'

'I did? Well, why didn't you do the same, then we'd all be sleeping still. Go away.'

'It's morning, Sergeant. Captain Fiddler wants—'

'He always wants. Soon as they turn inta officers, it's do this do that alla time. Someone gimme a jug.'

'All gone, Sergeant.'

She reached up, felt at the rough cloth covering her eyes, pulled one edge down, just enough to uncover one eye. 'That can't be right. Go find some more.'

'We will,' Brethless promised. 'Soon as you get up. Someone's

101

been through the squads, doing counts. We don't like it. Makes us nervous.'

'Why?' The lone eye blinked. 'I got me eight marines—'

'Four, Sergeant.'

'Fifty per cent losses ain't too bad, for a party.'

'A party, Sergeant?'

She sat up. 'I had eight last night.'

'Four.'

'Right, four twice over.'

'There wasn't no party, Sergeant.'

Hellian tugged to expose her other eye. 'There wasn't, huh? Thas what you get for wand'ring off, then, Corporal. Missed the good times.'

'Aye, I suppose I did. We're melting a lump of chocolate in a pot – thought you might like some.'

'That stuff? I remember now. Balklo chocolate. All right, get outa my tent so I can get decent.'

'You're not in your tent, Sergeant, you're in our latrine ditch.'

She looked round. 'That explains the smell.'

'None of us used it yet, Sergeant, seeing as how you were here.'

'Oh.'

His stomach convulsed again, but there was nothing left to spit up, so he rode it out, waited, gasping, and then slowly settled back on his haunches. 'Poliel's prissy nipples! If I can't keep nothing down I'll waste away!'

'You already have, Widder,' observed Throatslitter from a few paces upwind, his voice a cracking rasp. The old scars on his neck were inflamed; he'd taken a shot to his chest, hard enough to dent his sternum with matted rows from the mail's iron links, and something from that trauma had messed up his throat.

They were away from the camp, twenty paces beyond the eastern picket. Widdershins, Throatslitter, Deadsmell and Sergeant Balm. The survivors of the 9th Squad. The regulars crouched in their holes had watched them pass with red-shot eyes, saying nothing. Was that belligerence? Pity? The squad mage didn't know and at the moment was past caring. Wiping his mouth with the back of one forearm, he looked past Throatslitter to Balm. 'You called us up here, Sergeant. What now?'

Balm drew off his helm, scratched vigorously at his scalp. 'Just thought I'd tell you, we ain't breaking the squad up and we ain't picking up any new bodies. It's just us, now.'

Widdershins grunted. 'We took a walk for that?'

'Don't be an idiot,' said Deadsmell in a growl.

Balm faced his soldiers. 'Talk, all of you. You first, Throatslitter.'

The tall man seemed to flinch. 'What's to say? We're chewed to pieces. But Kindly hogtying Fid like that, well, bloody genius. We got ourselves a captain, now—'

'There wasn't anything wrong with Sort,' Deadsmell interjected.

'Not saying there was. Definite officer, that woman. But maybe that's the point. Fid's from the ground up a marine, through and through. He was a sapper. A sergeant. Now he's captain of what's left of us. I'm settled with that.' He shrugged, facing Balm. 'Nothing more to say, Sergeant.'

'And when he says it's time to go, you gonna bleat and whine about it?'

Throatslitter's brows lifted. 'Go? Go where?'

Balm squinted and then said, 'Your turn, Deadsmell.'

'Hood's dead. Grey riders patrol the Gate. In my dreams I see faces, blurred, but still. Malazans. Bridgeburners. You can't imagine how comforting that feels, you just can't. They're all there, and I think we got Dead Hedge to thank for that.'

'How do you mean?' Widdershins asked.

'Just a feeling. As if, in coming back, he blazed a trail. Six days ago, well, I swear they were close enough to kiss.'

'Because we all almost died,' Throatslitter snapped.

'No, they were like wasps, and what was sweet wasn't us dying, wasn't the lizards neither. It was what happened at the vanguard. It was Lostara Yil.' His eyes were bright as he looked to each soldier in turn. 'I caught a glimpse, you know. I saw her dance. She did what Ruthan Gudd did, only she didn't go down under blades. The lizards recoiled – they didn't know what to do, they couldn't get close, and those that did, gods, they were cut to pieces. I saw her, and my heart near burst.'

'She saved the Adjunct's life,' said Throatslitter. 'Was that such a good thing?'

'Not for you to even ask,' said Balm. 'Fid's calling us together. He's got things to say. About that, I expect. The Adjunct. And what's to come. We're still marines. We're *the* marines, and we got heavies in our ranks, the stubbornest bulls I ever seen.'

He turned then, since two regulars from the pickets were approaching. In their arms, two loaves of bread, a wrapped brick of cheese, and a Seven Cities clay bottle.

'What's this?' Deadsmell wondered.

The two soldiers halted a few paces away, and the one on the right spoke. 'Guard's changed, Sergeant. Came out with some breakfast for us. We weren't much hungry.' They then set the items down on a bare patch of ground. Nodded, set off back for camp.

'Hood's pink belly,' Deadsmell muttered.

'Save all that,' Balm said. 'We're not yet done here. Widdershins.'

'Warrens are sick, Sergeant. Well, you seen what they're doing to us mages. And there's new ones, new warrens, I mean, but they ain't nice at all. Still, I might have to delve into them, once I get tired of being completely useless.'

'You're the best among us with a crossbow, Widder, so you ain't useless even without any magic.'

'Maybe so, Throatslitter, but it doesn't feel that way.'

'Deadsmell,' said Balm, 'you've been doing some healing.'

'I have, but Widder's right. It's not fun. The problem – for me, that is – is that I'm still somehow bound to Hood. Even though he's, uh, dead. Don't know why that should be, but the magic when it comes to me, well, it's cold as ice.'

Widdershins frowned at Deadsmell. 'Ice? That makes no sense.'

'Hood was a damned Jaghut, so yes, it does. And no, it doesn't, because he's . . . well, gone.'

Throatslitter spat and said, 'If he really died, like you say, did he walk into his realm? And didn't he have to be dead in the first place, being the God of Death and all? What you're saying makes no sense, Deadsmell.'

The necromancer looked unhappy. 'I know.'

'Next time you do some healing,' said Widdershins, 'let me do some sniffing.'

'You'll heave again.'

'So what?'

'What are you thinking, Widder?' Balm asked.

'I'm thinking Deadsmell's not using Hood's warren any more. I'm thinking it must be Omtose Phellack.'

'It's occurred to me,' Deadsmell said in a mumble.

'One way to test it for sure,' Balm said.

Widdershins swore. 'Aye. We don't know the details, but the rumour is that she's got some broken ribs, maybe even spitting up blood, and is still concussed. But with that Otataral in her, no one can do much about it.'

'But Omtose Phellack is Elder.' Deadsmell was nodding. 'We should go, then. It's worth a try.'

'We will,' said Balm, 'but first we eat.'

'And leave the Adjunct in pain?'

'We eat and drink here,' said Balm, eyes flat, 'because we're marines and we don't kick dirt in the faces of fellow soldiers.'

'Exactly,' said Widdershins. 'Besides,' he added, 'I'm starving.'

Shortnose had lost the four fingers of his shield hand. To stop the bleeding that had gone on even after the nubs had been sewn up, he had held them against a pot left squatting in a fire. Now the ends looked melted and there were blisters up to his knuckles. But the bleeding had stopped.

He had been about to profess his undying love for Flashwit, but then that sergeant from the 18th had come by and collected up both Flashwit and Mayfly, so Shortnose was alone, the last left in Gesler's old squad.

He'd sat for a time, alone, using a thorn to pop blisters and then sucking them dry. When that was done he sat some more, watching the fire burn down. At the battle the severed finger of one of the lizards had fallen down the back of his neck, between armour and shirt. When he'd finally retrieved it, he and Mayfly and Flashwit had cooked and shared its scant ribbons of meat. Then they'd separated out and distributed the bones, tying them into their hair. It was what Bonehunters did.

They'd insisted he get the longest one, on account of getting his hand chopped up, and it now hung beneath his beard, overwhelming the other finger bones, which had all come from Letherii soldiers. It was heavy and long enough to thump against his chest when he walked, which is what he decided to do once he realized that he was lonely.

Kit packed, slung over one shoulder, he set out. Thirty-two paces took him into Fiddler's old squad's camp, where he found a place to set up his tent, left his satchel in that spot, and then walked over to sit down with the other soldiers.

The pretty little woman seated on his right handed him a tin cup filled with steaming something. When he smiled his thanks she didn't smile back, which was when he recalled that her name was Smiles.

This, he decided, was better than being lonely.

'Got competition, Corabb.'

'Don't see that,' the Seven Cities warrior replied.

'Shortnose wants to be our new fist,' Cuttle explained.

'Making what, four fists in this squad? Me, Corporal Tarr, Koryk and now Shortnose.'

'I was a corporal not a fist,' said Tarr. 'Besides, I don't punch, I just take 'em.'

Cuttle snorted. 'Hardly. You went forward, no different from any fist I ever seen.'

'I went forward to stand still, sapper.'

'Well, that's a good point,' Cuttle conceded. 'I stand corrected, then.'

'I just realized something,' said Smiles. 'We got no sergeant any more. Unless it's you, Tarr. And if that's the case, then we need a new corporal, and since I'm the only one left with any brains, it's got to be me.'

Tarr scratched at his greying beard. 'Was thinking Corabb, actually.'

'He needs his own private weapons wagon!'

'I kept my Letherii sword,' Corabb retorted. 'I didn't lose anything this time.'

'Let's vote on it.'

'Let's not, Smiles,' said Tarr. 'Corabb Bhilan Thenu'alas, you're now the Fourth Squad's corporal. Congratulations.'

'He's barely stopped being a recruit!' Smiles scowled at everyone.

'Cream will rise,' said Cuttle.

Koryk bared his teeth at Smiles. 'Live with it, soldier.'

'I'm corporal now,' said Corabb. 'Did you hear that, Shortnose? I'm corporal now.'

The heavy looked up from his cup. 'Hear what?'

Losing Bottle had hurt them. Cuttle could see that in their faces. The squad's first loss, at least as far as he could recall. First from the originals, anyway. But the loss of only one soldier was pretty damned good. Most squads had fared a lot worse. Some squads had ceased to exist. *Some? More like most of 'em.*

He settled back against a spare tent's bulky folds, watched the others covertly. Listened to their complaints. Koryk was a shaken man. Whatever spine of freedom there'd once been inside him, holding him up straight, had broken. Now he wore chains inside, and they messed with his brain, and maybe that was now permanent. He drank from a well of fear, and he kept on going back to it.

That scrap back there had been horrible, but Koryk had been stumbling even before then. Cuttle wondered what was left of the warrior he'd once known. Tribals had a way of kneeling to the worst vicissitudes of civilization, and no matter how clever the cleverest ones might be, they often proved blind to what was killing them.

Maybe no different from regular people, but, to Cuttle's mind, somehow more tragic.

Even Smiles was slowly prising herself loose from Koryk.

She hadn't changed, Cuttle decided. Not one whit. As psychotic and murderous as ever, was Smiles. Her knife work had been vicious, down there beneath the swing of the lizards' weapons. She'd toppled giants that day. For all that, she'd make a terrible corporal.

Tarr had been Tarr. The same as he always was and always would be. He'd be a solid sergeant. Perhaps a tad unimaginative, but this squad was past the need for anything that might shake it up. *And we'll follow him sharp enough. The man's a bristling wall, and when that helm of his settles low over his brow, not a herd of charging bhederin could budge him. Aye, Tarr, you'll do just fine.*

Corabb. Corporal Corabb. *Perfect.*

And now Shortnose. Sitting like a tree stump, flattened blisters weeping down his hand. Drinking that rotgut Smiles had brewed up, a half-smile on his battered face. *You ain't fooling me, Shortnose. Been in the army way too long. You love the thick-skull stuff, you heavies all do. But I see the flick of those tiny eyes under those lids.*

'Hear what?' Nice one, but I saw the spark you tried to hide. Happy to be here, are you? Good. Happy to have you.

As for me, what have I learned? Nothing new. We got through it but we got plenty more to get through. Ask me then. Ask me then.

He glanced over to see Fiddler arriving. Only the neck of his fiddle left, hanging down his back, kinked strings sprung like errant hairs. Most of the red gone from his beard. His short sword's scabbard was empty – he'd left the weapon jutting from a lizard's eye socket. The look in his blue eyes was cool, almost cold.

'Sergeant Tarr, half a bell, and then lead them to the place.'

'Aye, Captain.'

'We got riders coming up from the south. Perish, a few Khundryl, and someone else. A whole lot of someone else.'

Cuttle frowned. 'Who?'

Fiddler shrugged. 'Parley. We'll find out soon enough.'

'Told you you'd live.'

Henar Vygulf smiled up at her from where he lay on the cot. But it was an uncertain smile. 'I did what you asked, Lostara. I watched.'

Her gaze faltered.

'Who are you?' he asked.

'Don't ask me that. I see that question in every face. They all look at me. They say nothing.' She hesitated, staring down at her hands. 'It was the Shadow Dance. It was *every* Shadow Dance.' She met his eyes suddenly. 'It wasn't me. I just slipped back, inside, and just like you, I watched.'

'If not you, then who?'

'The Rope. Cotillion, the Patron God of Assassins.' She grimaced. 'He took over. He's done things like that before, I think.'

Henar's eyes widened. 'A god.'

'A furious god. I – I have never felt such rage. It burned right through me. It scoured me clean.' She unhooked her belt, tugged loose her scabbarded knife. She set it down on the blankets covering his wounded chest. 'For you, my love. But be careful, it's very, very sharp.'

'The haunt is gone from your face, Lostara,' said Henar. 'You were beautiful before, but now . . .'

'An unintended gift, to be sure,' she said with some diffidence. 'Gods are not known for mercy. Or compassion. But no mortal could stand in that blaze, and not come through either burned to ashes, or reborn.'

'Reborn, yes. A good description indeed. My boldness,' he added with a rueful grimace, 'retreats before you now.'

'Don't let it,' she snapped. 'I don't take mice to my bed, Henar Vygulf.'

'I shall try, then, to find the man I was.'

'I will help, but not yet – the healers are far from finished with you.' She rose. 'I must leave you now. The Adjunct.'

'I think Brys has forgotten me. Or assumed me dead.'

'Don't think I'll be reminding him,' she said. 'You ride at my side from now on.'

'Brys—'

'Hardly. A word in private with Aranict will do the trick, I think.'

'The king's brother is collared?'

'Next time you two meet, you can compare shackles.'

'Thought you disliked mice, Lostara Yil.'

'Oh, I expect you to struggle and strain at your chains, Henar. It's the ones we can't tame that we keep under lock and key.'

'I see.'

She turned to leave the hospital tent, saw the rows of faces turned to her, even among the cutters. 'Hood's breath,' she muttered.

Pleasantly drunk, Banaschar made his way towards the command tent. He saw Fist Blistig standing outside the entrance, like a condemned man at the torturer's door. *Oh, you poor man. The wrong dead hero back there. You had your chance, I suppose. You could have been as brainless as Keneb. You could have stayed in his shadow right to the end, in fact, since you'd clearly been finding it such safe shelter for the past few months.*

But the sun finds no obstruction in painting you bright now, and how does it feel? The man looked ill. *But you don't drink, do you? That's not last night's poison in your face, more's the pity.* Sick with fear, then, and Banaschar dredged up some real sympathy for the man. A stir or two, clouding the waters, dulling the sharp edges of righteous satisfaction.

'Such a fine morning, Fist,' he said upon arriving.

'You'll be in trouble soon, High Priest.'

'How so?'

'When the wine runs out.'

Banaschar smiled. 'The temple's cellars remain well stocked, I assure you.'

Blistig's eyes lit with something avid. 'You can just go there? Any time you want?'

108

'In a manner of speaking.'

'So why do you remain? Why don't you flee this madness?'

Because Holy Mother wants me here. I am her last priest. She has something in mind for me, yes she does. 'I am dreadfully sorry to tell you this, Fist, but that door is a private one, an exclusive one.'

Blistig's face darkened. There were two guards outside the command tent, only a few paces away, well within earshot. 'I was suggesting you leave us, High Priest. You're a useless drunk, a bad influence on this army. Why the Adjunct insists on your infernal presence at these gatherings baffles me.'

'I am sure it does, Fist. But I can't imagine being such a dark temptation to your soldiers. I don't share my private stock, after all. Indeed, I suspect seeing me turns a soul away from the miseries of alcohol.'

'You mean you disgust them?'

'Precisely so, Fist.' *But we really shouldn't be having this conversation, should we? Because we could swap positions and apart from the drink, not a word need be changed. The real difference is, I lose nothing by their disgust, whereas you . . .* 'Do we await the Letherii contingent, Fist?'

'Simple courtesy, High Priest.'

You liked that idea, did you? Enough to latch on to it. Fine. 'Then I will keep you company for a time, at least until their approach.'

'Don't leave it too long,' Blistig said. 'You'd give a bad impression.'

'No doubt, and I shall not overstay the moment.'

'In fact,' resumed Blistig, 'I see the other Fists on their way. If you want your choice of seat in the tent, High Priest, best go in now.'

Well now, I can happily latch on to that. 'Tactical, Fist. I shall heed your advice.' Bowing, he turned and strode between the two guards. Catching the eye of one, he winked.

And received nothing in return.

Lostara Yil turned at the shout to see four marines approaching her. A Dal Honese sergeant, what was his name? *Balm.* Three soldiers trailed him, presumably what was left of his squad. 'You want something, Sergeant? Be quick, I'm on my way to the command tent.'

'So are we,' Balm said. 'Got a healer here who maybe could do something for her.'

'Sergeant, it doesn't work that way—'

'It might,' said the tall soldier with the scarred neck, his voice thin, the sound of stone whetting iron.

'Explain.'

Another soldier said, 'We're thinking he's using an Elder Warren, Captain.'

'A what? How in Hood's name can that be?'

The healer seemed to choke on something, and then he stepped forward. 'It's worth my trying, sir. I think Widdershins is right this time, for a change.'

Lostara considered for a moment, before nodding. 'Follow me.'

Marines weren't in the habit of wasting people's time, and asking to step into the presence of the Adjunct was, for most of them, far from a feverish ambition. *So they think they've worked something out. It'd be worth seeing if they're right. Her headaches are getting worse – you can see it.*

The command tent came into view, and she saw the Fists gathered at the entrance. They noted her approach and whatever desultory conversation had been going on a moment earlier fell away. *Fine then, even you. Go ahead.* 'Fists,' she said, 'if you would be so good as to clear a path. These marines have an appointment with the Adjunct.'

'First I've heard of it,' said Kindly.

'Well, as I recall,' said Lostara, 'the remaining heavies and marines are now under the command of Captain Fiddler, and he answers only to the Adjunct.'

'I mean to address that with the Adjunct,' said Kindly.

There's no point. 'That will have to wait until after the parley, Fist.' Gesturing, she led the marines between the company commanders. *And will you all stop staring?* Their attention tightened the muscles of her neck as she walked past, and it was a relief to duck into the tent's shadowed entranceway.

Most of the interior canvas walls had been removed, making the space seem vast. Only at the far end was some privacy maintained for the Adjunct's sleeping area, with a series of weighted curtains stretching from one side to the other. The only occupant Lostara could see was Banaschar, sitting on a long bench with his back to the outer wall, arms crossed and seemingly dozing. There was a long table and two more benches, and nothing else, not even a lantern. *No, no lantern. The light stabs her like a knife.*

As the squad drew up behind Lostara, one of the curtains was drawn back.

Adjunct Tavore stepped into view.

Even from a distance of close to ten paces Lostara could see the sheen of sweat on that pallid brow. *Gods, if the army saw this, they'd melt like snow in the fire. Vanish on the wind.*

'What are these marines doing here, Captain?' The words were weak, the tone wandering. 'We await formal guests.'

'This squad's healer thinks he can do something for you, Adjunct.'

'Then he is a fool.'

The soldier in question stepped forward. 'Adjunct. I am Corporal Deadsmell, Ninth Squad. My warren was Hood's.'

Her bleached eyes fluttered. 'If I understand the situation, Corporal, then you have my sympathy.'

He seemed taken aback. 'Well, thank you, Adjunct. The thing is . . .' He held up his hands and Lostara gasped as a flood of icy air billowed out around the healer. Frost limned the peaked ceiling. Deadsmell's breaths flowed in white streams.

The mage, Widdershins, said, 'Omtose Phellack, Adjunct. Elder.'

Tavore was perfectly still, as if frozen in place. Her eyes narrowed on the healer. 'You have found a Jaghut for a patron, Deadsmell?'

To that question the man seemed at a loss for an answer.

'The God of Death is no more,' Widdershins said, his teeth chattering as the temperature in the chamber plummeted. 'But it may be that Hood himself ain't quite as dead as we all thought he was.'

'We thought that, did we?' Tavore's lips thinned as she regarded Deadsmell. 'Healer, approach.'

One hand twisting tight to keep the man upright, Balm guided Deadsmell back outside. Throatslitter and Widdershins closed in from either side, the looks on their faces fierce, as if they were moments from drawing weapons should anyone come close.

The Fists backed away as one, and the sergeant scowled at them all. 'Make room if you please, sirs. Oh, and she'll see you now.' Without waiting a reply, Balm tugged Deadsmell forward, the healer staggering – his clothes sodden as frost and ice melted in the morning heat. Twenty paces away, behind a sagging supply tent, the sergeant finally halted. 'Sit down, Deadsmell. Gods below, tell me this'll pass.'

The healer slumped to the ground. His head sank and the others waited for the man to be sick. Instead, they heard something like a sob. Balm stared at Throatslitter, and then at Widdershins, but by their expressions they were as baffled as he was. He crouched down, one hand resting lightly on Deadsmell's back – he could feel the shudders pushing through.

The healer wept for some time.

No one spoke.

When the sobs began to subside, Balm leaned closer. 'Corporal, what in Togg's name is going on with you?'

'I – I can't explain, Sergeant.'

'The healing worked,' said Balm. 'We all saw it.'

He nodded, still not lifting his head.

'So . . . what?'

'She let down her defences, just for a moment. Let me in, Sergeant. She had to, so I could heal the damage – and gods, was there damage!

111

Stepping into view – that must have taken everything she had. Standing, talking . . .' he shook his head. 'I saw inside. I saw—'

He broke down all over again, shaking with vast, overwhelming sobs.

Balm remained crouched at his side. Widdershins and Throatslitter stood forming a kind of barrier facing outward. There was nothing to do but wait.

In the moments before the Fists trooped inside, Lostara Yil stood facing Tavore. She struggled to keep her voice steady, calm. 'Welcome back, Adjunct.'

Tavore slowly drew a deep breath. 'Your thoughts, High Priest?'

To one side, Banaschar lifted his head. 'I'm too cold to think, Adjunct.'

'Omtose Phellack. Have you felt the footfalls of the Jaghut, Banaschar?'

The ex-priest shrugged. 'So Hood had a back door. Should we really be surprised? That devious shit of a god was never one for playing straight.'

'Disingenuous, High Priest.'

His face twisted. 'Think hard on where your gifts come from, Adjunct.'

'At last,' she retorted, 'some sound advice from you, High Priest. Almost . . . sober.'

If he planned on a reply, he bit it off when Kindly, Sort and Blistig entered the chamber.

There was a stretch of silence, and then Faradan Sort snorted and said, 'And here I always believed a chilly reception was just a—'

'I am informed,' cut in the Adjunct, 'that our guests are on their way. Before they arrive, I wish each of you to report on the disposition of your soldiers. Succinctly, please.'

The Fists stared.

Lostara Yil glanced over at Banaschar, and saw something flickering in his eyes as he studied the Adjunct.

Their approach took them down the north avenue of the Malazan encampment, winding down the crooked track between abattoir tents, where the stench of butchered animals was rank in the fly-swarmed air. Atri-Ceda Aranict rode in silence beside Commander Brys, hunched against the bleating of myrid and lowing of rodara, the squeal of terrified pigs and the moaning of cattle. Creatures facing slaughter well understood their fate, and the sound of their voices crowding the air was a torment.

'Ill chosen,' muttered Brys, 'this route. My apologies, Atri-Ceda.'

Two soldiers crossed their path, wearing heavy blood-drenched aprons. Their faces were flat, expressionless. Their hands dripped gore.

'Armies bathe in blood,' said Aranict. 'That is the truth of it, isn't it, Commander?'

'I fear we all bathe in it,' he replied. 'Cities permit us to hide from that bleak truth, I think.'

'What would it be like, I wonder, if we all ate only vegetables?'

'We'd break all the land and the wild animals would have nowhere to live,' Brys replied.

'So we should see these domesticated beasts as sacrifices in the name of wildness.'

'You could,' he said, 'if it helps.'

'I'm not sure it does.'

'Nor am I.'

'I think I am too soft for all this,' she concluded. 'I have a sentimental streak. Maybe you can hide from the slaughter itself, but if you possess any imagination at all, well, there's no real hiding, is there?'

They drew closer to a broad intersection, and opposite them a sizeable troop of riders was converging on the same place, coming up from the south track. 'Well now,' said Brys, 'are those Bolkando royal standards?'

'Seems the queen has taken her escort duties well beyond her kingdom's borders.'

'Yes, most curious. Shall we await them?'

'Why not?'

They reined in at the intersection.

The queen's entourage was oversized, yet as it drew closer Brys frowned. 'Those are Evertine regulars, I think,' he said. 'Not an officer among them.'

In addition to these hardened soldiers, three Barghast warriors rode close to Abrastal, while off to the right rode two Khundryl women, one of them seven or eight months pregnant. On the left was a pair of armoured foreigners – the Perish? Aranict drew a sharp breath. 'That must be Mortal Sword Krughava. She alone could command a palace tapestry.'

Brys grunted. 'I know what you mean. I have seen a few hard women in my time, but that one . . . formidable indeed.'

'I doubt I could even lift that sword at her belt.'

With a gesture Queen Abrastal halted the entire troop. She said something to one of her soldiers, and suddenly the veterans were all dismounting, lifting satchels from their saddle horns and setting out into the Malazan camp. Aranict watched the soldiers fanning out, apparently seeking squad camps. 'What are they doing?'

Brys shook his head. 'I'm not sure.'

'They've brought . . . bottles.'

Brys Beddict grunted, and then tapped his horse's flanks. Aranict followed suit.

'Commander Brys Beddict,' said Queen Abrastal, settling back in her saddle. 'We finally meet. Tell me, does your brother know where you are?'

'Highness, does your husband?'

Her teeth flashed. 'I doubt it. But isn't this better than our meeting in anger?'

'Agreed, Highness.'

'Now, barring this Gilk oaf at my side and of course you, it seems this will be a gathering of women. Do you quake in your boots, Prince?'

'If I am, I am man enough to not admit it, Highness. Will you be so kind as to perform introductions?'

Abrastal removed her heavy gauntlets and gestured to her right. 'From the Khundryl, Hanavat, wife to Warleader Gall, and with her Shelemasa, bodyguard and One of the Charge.'

Brys tilted his head to both women. 'Hanavat. We were witness to the Charge.' His gaze momentarily flicked to Shelemasa, then back to Hanavat. 'Please, if you will, inform your husband that I was shamed by his courage and that of the Burned Tears. Seeing the Khundryl stung me to action. I would he understand that all that the Letherii were subsequently able to achieve in relieving the Bonehunters is set in humble gratitude at the Warleader's feet.'

Hanavat's broad, fleshy face remained expressionless. 'Most generous words, Prince. My husband shall be told.'

The awkwardness of that reply hung in the dusty air for a moment, and then Queen Abrastal gestured to the Perish. 'Mortal Sword Krughava and Shield Anvil Tanakalian, of the Grey Helms.'

Once again Brys tilted his head. 'Mortal Sword. Shield Anvil.'

'You stood in our place six days ago,' said Krughava, her tone almost harsh. 'This is now an open wound upon the souls of my brothers and sisters. We grieve at the sacrifice you suffered in our stead. This is not your war, after all, yet you stood firm. You fought with valour. Should the opportunity ever arise, sir, we shall in turn stand in your place. This the Perish Grey Helms avow.'

Brys Beddict seemed at a loss.

Aranict cleared her throat and said, 'You have humbled the prince, Mortal Sword. Shall we now present ourselves to the Adjunct?'

Queen Abrastal collected up her reins and swung her mount on to the track leading to the camp's centre. 'Will you ride at my side, Prince?'

'Thank you,' Brys managed.

114

Aranict dropped her mount just behind the two, and found herself riding alongside the 'Gilk oaf'.

He glanced across at her and his broad, scarified face was solemn. 'That Mortal Sword,' he muttered low, 'she comes across with all the soft sweetness of a mouthful of quartz. Well done to your commander for recovering.'

'Thank you.'

'Don't turn round, but if you did you would see tears on the face of Hanavat. I think I like your commander. I am Spax, Warchief of the Gilk Barghast.'

'Atri-Ceda Aranict.'

'That means High Mage Aranict, yes?'

'I suppose it does. Warchief, those Evertine soldiers who have gone out among the Malazans – what are they doing?'

Spax reached up and made a clawing gesture beneath his eyes. 'What are they doing, Atri-Ceda? Spirits below, they are being human.'

BOOK TWO

ALL THE TAKERS OF MY DAYS

Well enough she faces away
Walking past these dripping thrones
No one knows where the next foot
Falls
When we stumble in the shadows
Our standards bow to wizened winds
I saw that look beneath the rim
Of blistered iron
And it howled to the men kneeling
In the square and the dogs sleep on
In the cool foot of the wall, no fools there
She was ever looking elsewhere
Like a disenchanted damsel
A shift of her shoulder
Sprawls corpses into her wake
No matter
There was a child dream once
You remember well
Was she the mother or did that tit
Seep seduction?
All these thrones I built with my own
Hands
Labours of love thin over ragged nails
I wanted benediction, or the slip away
Of clothes, whichever bends my way
Behind her back
Oh we were guards then, stern sentinels,
And these grilled masks smelling of blood
Now sweat something old
We never knew what we were guarding
We never do and never will
But I swear to you all:
I will die at its feet before I take a step inside
Call me duty and be done with it
Or roll from your tongue that sweet curl
That is valour
While the dogs twitch in dream
Like children left lying
Underfoot

Adjunct
Hare Ravage

CHAPTER FIVE

She was dying but we carried her down to the shore. There was
light stretched like skin over her pain, but it was thin and fast
fraying. None of us dared note in any whisper of irony, how
she who was named Awakening Dawn was now fading in this
morning's wretched rise.

Her weak gestures had brought her down here, where the
silver waves fell like rain and the froth at the curling foot
was flecked crimson. Bodies bloated and pale fanned limbs
in the shallows, and we wondered at the fitness of her last
command.

Is it suit to face your slayer? Soon enough I will answer that
for myself. We can hear the legions mustering again behind the
flowing wall, and the others are drawing back to ready their
rough line. So few left. Perhaps this is what she came to see,
before the killing light dried her eyes.

Shake fragment, Kharkanas, Author unknown

THE BLACK LACQUERED AMPHORA EMERGED FROM THE SIDE DOOR AND
skidded, rather than rolled, diagonally across the corridor. It
struck the base of the marble banister at the top of the stairs,
and the crack echoed sharp as a split skull before the huge vessel
tilted and pitched down the steps. Shattering, it flung its shards in a
glistening spray down the stone flight all the way to the main floor.
Sparkling dust spun and twisted for a time, before settling like flecks
of frost.

Withal walked over to the edge of the steps and looked down. 'That,'
he said under his breath, 'was rather spectacular.' He turned at a sound
behind him.

Captain Brevity was leaning out from the doorway, glancing round
until she spotted Withal. 'You'd better come in,' she said.

'I was doing just that,' he replied. 'Five strides closer and she'd be a widow.'

Brevity made a face he couldn't quite read, and then edged to one side to let him pass.

The throne room was still a chamber of ghosts. Black stone and black wood, the crimson and onyx mosaic of the floor dulled with dust and dried leaves that had wandered in from some high window. It seemed to hold nothing of the now brimming power of the Teronderai, the holy sepulchre of Mother Dark, yet for all that Withal felt diminished as he stepped through the side entrance and edged out towards the centre of the room.

The throne was on his right, raised on a knee-high dais that was, he realized, the vast stump of a blackwood tree. Roots snaked down to sink into the surrounding floor. The throne itself had been carved from the bole, a simple, almost ascetic chair. Perhaps it had once been plush, padded and bold in rich fabrics, but not even the tacks remained.

His wife stood just to the other side of the throne, her arms crossed, now dragging her glare from Yan Tovis – who stood facing the throne as would a supplicant – to Withal. 'Finally,' she snapped, 'my escort. Take me out of here, husband.'

Yan Tovis, queen of the Shake, cleared her throat. 'Leaving solves nothing—'

'Wrong. It solves *everything*.'

The woman facing her sighed. 'This is the throne of the Tiste Andii, and Kharkanas is the capital of the Hold of Darkness. You are home, Highness—'

'Stop calling me that!'

'But I must, for you are of royal blood—'

'We were all of *royal* blood in this infernal city!' Sandalath Drukorlat pointed a finger at Yan Tovis. 'As were the Shake!'

'But our realm was and is the Shore, Highness, whereas Kharkanas is yours. But if it must be that there be only one queen, then I freely abdicate—'

'You will not. They are *your* people! You led them here, Yan Tovis. You are their queen.'

'Upon this throne, Highness, only one of royal Tiste Andii blood can make a true claim. And, as we both well know, there is only one Tiste Andii in this entire realm, and that is you.'

'Fine, and over whom do I rule? Heaps of dust? Mouldy bones? Blood stains on the floor? And where is my High Priestess, in whose eyes Mother Dark shines? Where is my Blind Gallan, my brilliant, tortured court fool? Where are my rivals, my hostages, my servants and soldiers? Handmaidens and— Oh, never mind. This is pointless. I don't want that throne.'

120

'Nonetheless,' said Yan Tovis.

'Very well, I accept it, and my first act is to abdicate and yield the throne and all of Wise Kharkanas to you, Queen Yan Tovis. Captain Brevity, find us a royal seal – there must be one lying around here somewhere – and parchment and ink and wax.'

The queen of the Shake was smiling, but it was a sad smile. '"Wise Kharkanas." I had forgotten that honorific. Queen Sandalath Drukorlat, I respectfully decline your offer. My duties are upon the Shore.' She nodded to Brevity. 'Until such time that other Tiste Andii return to Kharkanas, I humbly submit Captain Brevity here to act as your Chancellor, Palace Guard Commander, and whatever other duties of organization as are required to return this palace to its former glory.'

Sandalath snorted. 'Oh, clever. And I suppose a few hundred of your Shake are waiting outside with mops and buckets.'

'Letherii, actually. Islanders and other refugees. They have known great privation, Highness, and will view the privilege of palace employment with humility and gratitude.'

'And if I turn them all away? Oh yes, I see the traps you've set around me, Yan Tovis. You intend to guilt me on to that accursed throne. But what if I am a harder woman than you?'

'The burden of rule hardens us both, Highness.'

Sandalath cast Withal a beseeching look. 'Talk her out of this, husband.'

'I would if I thought I had any chance of swaying her, beloved.' He strode to the base of the dais, eyeing the throne. 'Needs a cushion or two, I should think, before you could hope to sit there for any length of time.'

'And you as my consort? Gods, don't you think I could do better?'

'Undoubtedly,' he replied. 'For the moment, however, you are stuck with me, and,' he added with a wave at the throne, 'with this. So sit down and make it official, Sand, so Yan Tovis can kneel or curtsey or whatever it is she has to do, and Brevity can get on with scrubbing the floors and beating the tapestries.'

The Tiste Andii woman cast about, as if seeking another amphora, but the nearest one stood perched on a stone cup near the side door – now an orphan, Withal saw, noting the unoccupied stone base on the entrance's other side. He waited to see if she'd make the fierce march to repeat her gesture of frustration and anger, but all at once his wife seemed to subside. *Thank Mael. That would have made her look ridiculous. Decorum, beloved, as befits the Queen of Darkness. Aye, some things you can't run from.*

'There will be two queens in this realm,' Sandalath said, coming round to slump down in the throne. 'Don't even think of curtseying,

121

Tovis.' She eyed the Shake woman with something close to a glower. 'Other Tiste Andii, you said.'

'Surely they have sensed Mother Dark's return,' Yan Tovis replied. 'Surely, they too understand that the diaspora is at last at an end.'

'Just how many Tiste Andii do you imagine are left?'

'I don't know. But I do know this: those who live shall return here. Just as the Shake have done. Just as you have done.'

'Good. First one gets here can have this throne and all that goes with it. Husband, start building us a cottage in the woods. Make it remote. No, make it impossible to reach. And tell none but me where it is.'

'A cottage.'

'Yes. With a drawbridge and a moat, and pitfalls and sprawl-traps.'

'I'll start drawing up plans.'

Yan Tovis said, 'Queen Sandalath, I beg your leave.'

'Yes. Sooner the better.'

The ex-Letherii officer tilted her head, wheeled and strode from the chamber.

Captain Brevity stepped forward to face the throne and settled on one knee. 'Highness, shall I summon the palace staff?'

'In here? Abyss take me, no. Start with all the other rooms. Go on. You are, er, dismissed. Husband! Don't even think of leaving.'

'The thought had not even occurred to me.' And he managed to hold his neutral expression against her withering scepticism.

As soon as they were alone, Sandalath sprang from the throne as if she'd just found one of those ancient tacks. 'That bitch!'

Withal flinched. 'Yan—'

'No, not her – she's right, the cow. I'm stuck with this, for the moment. Besides, why should she be the only one to suffer the burden of rule, as she so quaintly put it?'

'Well, put it that way, and I can see how she might be in need of a friend.'

'An equal of sorts, yes. The problem is, I don't fit. I'm not her equal. I didn't lead ten thousand people to this realm. I barely got *you* here.'

He shrugged. 'But here we are.'

'And she knew.'

'Who?'

'That bitch Tavore. Somehow, she knew this would happen—'

'There's no proof of that, Sand,' Withal replied. 'It was Fiddler's reading, not hers.'

She made a dismissive gesture. 'Technicalities, Withal. She trapped me is what she did. I should never have been there. No, she knew there was a card waiting for me. There's no other explanation.'

'But that's no explanation at all, Sand.'

The look she threw him was miserable. 'You think I don't know that?'

Withal hesitated. 'Listen,' he said, 'your kin are coming. Are you really certain you want me standing there at your side when they do?'

Her eyes narrowed. 'What you're really saying is: do I want to be standing at her side when they arrive? A mere human, a shortlived plaything to the Queen of Darkness. That's how you think they'll see you, isn't it?'

'Well . . .'

'You're wrong. It will be the opposite and that might be just as bad. They'll see you for what you are: a threat.'

'A *what*?'

She regarded him archly. 'Your kind are the inheritors – of everything. And here you are, along with all those Letherii and blood-thin Shake, squatting in Kharkanas. Is there anywhere you damned bastards don't end up sooner or later? That's what they'll be thinking.'

'Mael knows, they've got a point,' he said, looking away, down the length of the throne room, imagining a score or more regal Tiste Andii standing there, eyes hard, faces like stone. 'I'd better leave.'

'No you won't. Mother Dark—' Abruptly she shut her mouth.

He turned his head, studied her. 'Your goddess is whispering in your ear, Sand? About me?'

'You'll be needed,' she said, once more eyeing the lone amphora. 'All of you. The Letherii refugees. The Shake. And it's not fair. *It's not fair!*'

He took her arm as she moved to assault the crockery. Pulled her round until she was in his arms. Startled, terrified, he held her as she wept. *Mael! What awaits us here?*

But there was no answer, and his god had never felt so far away.

Yedan Derryg dragged the tip of the Hust sword, making a line in the crumbled bones of the Shore. The cascading wall of light flowed in reflection along the length of the ancient blade, like tears of milk. 'We are children here,' he muttered.

Captain Pithy hawked phlegm, stepped forward and spat into the wall, and then turned to face him. 'Something tells me we'd better grow up fast, Watch.'

Yedan clenched his teeth, chewed on a half-dozen possible responses to her grim observation, before saying, 'Yes.'

'The faces in the wash,' said Pithy, nodding at the eternally descending rain of light rearing before them, 'there's more of 'em. And seems they're getting closer, as if clawing their way through. I'm expecting t'see an arm thrust out any time now.' She hitched her thumbs in her weapon belt. 'Thing is, sir, what happens then?'

He stared into the Lightfall. Tried remembering memories that weren't his own. The grinding of molars sounded like distant thunder in his head. 'We fight.'

'And that's why you've recruited everyone with arms and legs into this army of yours.'

'Not everyone. The Letherii islanders—'

'Can smell trouble better than anyone. Convicted criminals, almost the whole lot. It's a case of the nerves all around, sir, and soon as they figure things out, they'll start stepping up.'

He eyed the woman. 'What makes you so sure, Captain?'

'Soon as they figure things out, I said.'

'What things?'

'That there's nowhere to run to, for one,' she replied. 'And that there won't be any bystanders, no – what's the word? Non-combatants. We got us a fight for our very lives ahead. Do you deny it?'

He shook his head, studied the play of light on the blade again. 'We will stand on the bones of our ancestors.' He glanced at Pithy. 'We have a queen to protect.'

'Don't you think your sister will be right here in the front line?'

'My sister? No, not her. The queen of Kharkanas.'

'It's her we're gonna die protecting? I don't get it, sir. Why her?'

He grimaced, lifted the sword and slowly sheathed it. 'We are of the Shore. The bones at our feet are *us*. Our history. Our meaning. Here we will stand. It is our purpose.' Memories not his own, yet still they stirred. 'Our purpose.'

'Yours maybe. The rest of us just want to live another day. Get on with things. Making babies, tilling the ground, getting rich, whatever.'

He shrugged, eyes now on the wall. 'Privileges, Captain, we cannot at the moment afford to entertain.'

'I ain't happy about the thought of dying for some Tiste Andii queen,' Pithy said, 'and I doubt I'm alone in that. So maybe I take back what I said earlier. There could be trouble ahead.'

'No. There won't.'

'Plan on cutting off a few heads?'

'If necessary.'

She muttered a curse. 'I hope not. Like I said before, so long as they all realize there's nowhere to go. Should be enough, shouldn't it?' When no answer was forthcoming she cleared her throat and said, 'Well, it comes down to saying the right things at the right time. Now, Watch Derryg, you might be an Errant-shitting warrior, and a decent soldier, too, but you're lacking the subtleties of command—'

'There are no subtleties in command, Captain. Neither my sister nor me is one for rousing speeches. We make our expectations plain and we expect them to be met. Without complaint. Without hesitation. It's not enough to fight to stay alive. We must fight determined to win.'

'People ain't stupid – well, forget I said that. Plenty of 'em are. But something tells me there's a difference between fighting to stay alive and fighting for a cause bigger than your own life, or even the lives of your loved ones, or your comrades. A difference, but for the life of me I couldn't say what it is.'

'You were always a soldier, Captain?'

Pithy snorted. 'Not me. I was a thief who thought she was smarter than she really was.'

Yedan considered that for a time. Before him, blurred faces pushed through the light, mouths opening, expressions twisting into masks of rage. Hands stretched to find his throat, clutched empty. He could reach out and touch the wall, if he so chose. Instead, he observed the enemy before him. 'What cause, Captain, would you fight for? In the manner you describe – beyond one's own life or those of loved ones?'

'Now that's the question, isn't it? For us Letherii, this ain't our home. Maybe we could come to want it to be, in time, a few generations soaking our blood into the land. But there won't be any time. Not enough for that.'

'If that is your answer—'

'No it ain't. I'm working on it, sir. It's called *thinking things through*. A cause, then. Can't be some Tiste Andii queen or her damned throne, or even her damned city. Can't be Yan Tovis, even though she brought 'em all through and so saved their lives. Memories die like beached fish and soon enough just the smell will do t'drive 'em away. Can't be you neither.'

'Captain,' said Yedan Derryg, 'if the enemy destroy us, they will march down the Road of Gallan. Unobstructed, they will breach the gate to your own world, and they will lay waste to every human civilization, until nothing remains but ash. And then they will slay the gods themselves. Your gods.'

'If they're that nasty, how can we hope to hold 'em here?'

Yedan nodded at the Lightfall. 'Because, Captain, there is only one way through. This stretch of beach. A thousand paces wide. Only here is the wall scarred and thin from past wounds. Only here can they hope to break the barrier. We bar this door, Captain, and we save your world.'

'And just how long are we supposed to hold 'em back?'

He ruminated for a moment, and then he said, 'As long as needed, Captain.'

She rubbed at the back of her neck, squinted at Yedan for a time, and then looked away. 'How can you do that, sir?'

'Do what?'

'Stand there, so close, just watching them – can't you see their faces? Can't you feel their hatred? What they want to do to you?'

'Of course.'

'Yet there you stand.'

'They serve to remind me, Captain.'

'Of what?'

'Of why I exist.'

She hissed between her teeth. 'You just sent a chill right through me.'

'I asked about a worthy cause.'

'Yeah, saving the world. That might work.'

He shot her a look. 'Might?'

'True, you'd think saving your world is a good enough reason for doing anything and everything, wouldn't you?'

'Isn't it?'

'People being what people are . . . we'll see.'

'You lack faith, Captain.'

'What I lack is proof to the contrary, sir. I ain't seen it yet, in all my years. What do you think makes criminals in the first place?'

'Stupidity and greed.'

'Besides those? I'll tell you. It's looking around, real carefully. It's seeing what's really there, and who wins every time, and it's deciding that despair tastes like shit. It's deciding to do whatever it takes to sneak through, to win what you can for yourself. It's also condemning your fellow humans to whatever misery finds them – even if that misery is by your own hand. To hurt another human being is to announce your hatred of humanity – but mostly your thinking is about hating back what already hates you. A thief steals telling herself she's evening out crooked scales. That's how we sleep at night, y'see.'

'A fine speech, Captain.'

'Tried making it short as I could, sir.'

'So indeed you are without faith.'

'I have faith that what's worst in humanity isn't hard to find – it's all around us, sour as a leaking bladder, day after day. It's the stink we all get used to. As for what's best . . . maybe, but I wouldn't push all my stacks of coin into the centre of the table on that bet.' She paused and then said, 'Thinking on it, there's one thing you could do to buy their souls.'

'And that is?'

'Empty out the palace treasury and bury it ten paces up the beach. And make a show of it. Maybe even announce that it's, you know, the Sword's Gold. To be divided up at day's end.'

'And would they fight to save the soldier beside them? I doubt it.'

'Hmm, good point. Then announce a fixed amount – and whatever is unclaimed on account of the soldier being dead goes back into the treasury.'

'Well, Captain, you could petition the Queen of Darkness.'

'Oh, I can do better. Sister Brevity's the treasurer now.'

'You are a cynical woman, Captain Pithy.'

'In case saving the world don't work, that's all. Make getting rich the reward and they'll eat their own children before backing a single step.'

'And which of the two causes would you more readily give your life for, Captain?'

'Neither, sir.'

His brows lifted.

She spat again. 'I was a thief once. Plenty of hatred then, both ways. But then I walked a step behind your sister and watched her bleed for us all. And then there was you, too, for that matter. That rearguard action that saved all our skins. So now,' she scowled at the Lightfall, 'well, I'll stand here, and I'll fight until the fight's left them or it's left me.'

Yedan studied her in earnest now. 'And why would you do that, Pithy Islander?'

'Because it's the right thing to do, Yedan Derryg.'

Rightness. The word was lodged in Yan Tovis's throat like shards of glass. She could taste blood in her mouth, and all that had seeped down into her stomach seemed to have solidified into something fist-sized, heavy as stone.

The Shore invited her, reached out and clawed at her with its need. A need it yearned to share with her. *You stand with me, Queen. As you once did, as you shall do again. You are the Shake and the Shake are of the Shore, and I have tasted your blood all my life.*

Queen, I thirst again. Against this enemy, there shall be Rightness upon the Shore, and you will stand, and you will yield not a step.

But there was betrayal, long ago. How could the Liosan forget? How could they set it aside? Judgement, the coarse, thorn-studded brambles of retribution, they could snag an entire people, and as the blood streamed down each body was lifted higher, lifted from the ground. The vicious snare carried them into the righteous sky.

Reason could not reach that high, and in the heavens madness spun untamed.

Rightness rages on both sides of the wall. Who can hope to halt what is coming? Not the Queen of Darkness, not the queen of the Shake. Not Yedan Derryg – oh no, my brother strains for that moment. He draws his wretched sword again and again. He smiles at the Lightfall's lurid play on the blade. He stands before the silent shrieking insanity of hatred made manifest, and he does not flinch.

But, and this was the impossible contradiction, her brother had not once in his life felt a single spasm of hatred – his soul was implacably incapable of such an emotion. He could stand in the fire and not burn. He could stand before those deformed faces, those grasping hands, and . . . and . . . *nothing*.

Oh, Yedan, what waits within you? Have you surrendered completely to the need of the Shore? Are you one with it? Do you know a single moment of doubt? Does it? She could understand the seductive lure of that invitation. Absolution through surrender, the utter abjection of the self. She understood it, yes, but she did not trust it.

When that which offers blessing predicates such on the absolute obeisance of the supplicant . . . demands, in fact, the soul's willing enslavement – no, how could such a force stand tall in moral probity?

The Shore demands our surrender to it. Demands our enslavement in the glory of its love, the sweet purity of its eternal blessing.

There is something wrong with that. Something . . . monstrous. You offer us the freedom of choice, yet avow that to turn away is to lose all hope of glory, of salvation. What sort of freedom is that?

She had held that her faith in the Shore set her above other worshippers, those quivering mortals kneeling before fickle carnate gods. The Shore was without a face. The Shore was not a god, but an idea, the eternal conversation of elemental forces. Changeable, yet for ever unchangeable, the binding of life and death itself. Not something to be bargained with, not a thing with personality, mercurial and prone to spite. The Shore, she had believed, made no demands.

But now here she was, feeling the desiccated wind rising up from the bone strand, watching her brother speaking to Pithy, seeing her brother less than a stride away from Lightfall's terrible fury, drawing his sword again and again. And the First Shore howled in her soul.

Here! Blessed Daughter, I am here and with me you belong! See this wound. You and I shall close it. My bones, your blood. The death underfoot, the life with sword in hand. You shall be my flesh. I shall be your bone. Together we will stand. Changeable and unchangeable.

Free and enslaved.

A figure edged up on her right, and then another on her left. She looked to neither.

The one on the right crooned something melodic and wordless, and then said, 'Ween decided, Queen. Skwish to stand with the Watch, an mine to stand with you.'

'An the Shore an the day,' added Skwish. 'Lissen to it sing!'

Pully moaned again. 'Y'ain knelled afore the Shore, Highness. Y'ain done it yet. An be sure y'need to, afore the breach comes.'

'Een the queen's got to srender,' said Skwish. 'T'the Shore.'

Crumbled bones into chains. Freedom into slavery. Why did we ever agree to this bargain? It was never equal. The blood was ours, not the Shore's. Errant fend, even the bones came from us!

Empty Throne, my certainty is . . . gone. My faith . . . crumbles.

'Don't my people deserve better?'

Pully snorted. 'Single droppa Shake inem, they hear the song. They yearn t'come, t'stand—'

'To fight,' finished Skwish.

'But . . .' *they deserve better.*

'Go down t'the Shore, Highness. Een you tain't above the First Shore.'

Yan Tovis grimaced. 'You think to force me, Pully? Skwish?'

'If yer brother—'

'Hadn't killed all your allies,' Yan Tovis said, nodding. 'Yes. Oddly enough, I don't think he fully comprehended the consequences. Did he? A hundred and more witches and warlocks . . . yes, they could compel me, perhaps. But you two? No.'

'Is a mistake, Highness.'

'Didn't stop you feeding on my blood, did it? Made young again, and now you roll like sluts in every man's tent.'

'Een Witchslayer says—'

'Yes, you all say. "Kneel, O Queen." "Surrender to the Shore, sister." You know, the only person here who comes close to understanding me isn't even human. And what did I do? I destroyed the friendship growing between us by forcing her on to the Throne of Dark. I fear she will never forgive me.' Yan Tovis gestured suddenly. 'Both of you, leave me now.'

'As witches we got to warn yee—'

'And so you have, Pully. Now go, before I call Yedan up here to finish what he started all those months ago.'

She listened to their footfalls in the sand, and then through the grasses.

Below, on the Shore, Captain Pithy was departing, moving off to the left, probably making her way to the Letherii encampment. Her brother remained, though now he began walking the length of the strand. *Like a caged cat.*

But remember, dear brother. The Hust sword broke.

She lifted her gaze, studied the hissing storm of light, high above the blurred shapes of Liosan warriors. She was not sure, but at times lately she'd thought she'd seen vast shapes wheeling up there.

Clouds. Thunderheads.

Rightness was a vicious word. *Is it right to demand this of us? Is it right to invite us in one breath and threaten us in the next? Am I not queen of the Shake? Are these not my subjects? You would I simply give them to you? Their blood, their lives?*

129

Errant's nudge, how I envy Sandalath Drukorlat, the Queen with no subjects.

The liquid sky of Lightfall was a thick, opaque swirl. No thunderheads today. Seeing that should have relieved her, but it didn't.

Upon the Great Spire overlooking Kolanse Bay, five Pures ascended the steep stairs carved into the crater's ravaged flank. To their right, as they climbed towards the Altar of Judgement, the slope fell away to a sheer cliff, and far below the seas thrashed, the waters raging into foaming spume the colour of mare's milk. Centuries of pounding fury had gnawed into the Spire, down to its very roots, apart from a narrow, treacherous isthmus on the inland side.

From above, foul winds bled down, pulled towards the waves in endless streams. At times Shriven had been poisoned in their pilgrimage, here on the weathered pumice steps, but the Pures could withstand such vicissitudes, and when they passed the shrivelled corpses huddled against the stairs they simply stepped over them.

The Pure who was named Reverence led the way. She was Eldest among those who remained in close proximity to the Great Spire. Tall even for a Forkrul Assail, she was exceedingly gaunt, almost skeletal. Thousands of years upon this world had turned her once white skin a sickly grey, worn through to bruised tones around her joints, including those of her double-hinged jaw and the vertical epiphysis that bisected her face from chin to forehead. One eye had been blinded centuries past in a battle with a Jaghut, a tusk slash as they struggled to tear out each other's throat, and the ferocity of that bite had dented the bones of the socket, collapsing the brow ridge on that side.

She favoured her right leg, as the effort of the ascent shot lancing pain through her left hip. A T'lan Imass sword-thrust had very nearly disembowelled her on another rise of stone steps, on a distant continent and long, long ago. Even as the flint weapon stabbed into her, she had torn the warrior's head from its shoulders. *The demands of adjudication are not for the weak*, she would say from time to time, whispered as something akin to a mantra, tempering true once more the iron of her will.

Yes, the climb had been a long one, for them all, but soon the summit would heave into view, pure and bristling, and the final death-blows would be delivered. *Judgement upon humanity. Judgement upon this broken, wounded world. We shall cleanse. It is not what we chose for ourselves. This burden in truth does not belong to us, but who will stand to defend this world? Who but the Forkrul Assail can destroy all the humans in this realm? Who but the Forkrul Assail can slay their venal gods?*

The oldest justice of all is the justice of the possible. Hunter and prey, death or escape, to feed or to starve. Each plays to what is possible and the victims strive to answer their needs, and that is all there is. All there ever need be.

I remember grasses in the wind. I remember skies filling with birds from horizon to horizon. I remember weeping at the silence in the years that followed, when these furtive killers edged out into the world and killed all they could. When they walked ancient shorelines and thrust their greed like bone knives into new lands.

We watched. We grieved. We grew into the iron of anger, and then rage. And now. Now, we are cold and certain. There will be death.

Steady breaths behind her, a source of strength, succour for her will to complete this climb, to push away the aches, the labours of a body as battered as the earth itself. She could remember the day peace was declared dead. The day the Forkrul Assail stood tall, for the first time, and saw before them the future, and the necessity they must answer.

Since then . . . so many unanticipated allies.

Above, seven steps away, the edge of the altar, the platform's white quartzite glistening in the thin light. Drawing upon her strength for this last effort, she pushed herself upward. And then, at last, she stepped on to the windswept expanse. The Altar of Judgement, white as freshly fallen snow, the carved sunburst of blood channels leading out from the centre, cut deep, shadowed into darkness.

Reverence strode forward, loosening her thick cloak as the heat bloomed up and out from the crater's mouth surrounding the Spire, rank with sulphurs. Behind her, the four other Pures spread out, finding their own paths to the centre-stone.

Her lone eye fell to that blackened, rotted abomination, the boulder that was – or, perhaps, encased – the heart of an alien god. She could see no rise and fall from its mottled form, yet to set hand upon it was to feel its stubborn life. *The sky tore him apart. Flung across half the world the flaming debris that was his body, and pieces fell and fell, upon one continent and then another. Into the shocked seas. Ah, if there had been more. If there had been enough to annihilate every human on this world, not just the ones whose hubris was so brazen, whose madness reached across the Abyss, to take this wretched thing.*

Soon, they would pierce the centre-stone, the Heart, and that alien god's blood would flow, and the power would . . . *feed us.* With that power they could fully open the gate of Akhrast Korvalain; they could unleash the cleansing storm, and it would sweep the world. *Drown on your hubris, humans. It is all you deserve.* Indeed, it would finish what the Summoners in their insanity had begun.

You chain what you can use. As the gods have done to him. But when its usefulness is at an end . . . what then? Do you simply kill? Or do you squeeze the last possible drop of blood from the carcass? Fill your belly?

Is there a use for endless pain? Let us see, shall we?

'Sister Reverence.'

She turned, studied the younger woman facing her. In the few paces between them there was a gulf so vast there was no hope of ever spanning it. 'Sister Calm.'

'If we are to hear naught but reports on the disposition of our armies, Sister, was there need for this ascent?'

'"Need." Now that is an interesting word, is it not?'

Calm's eyes remained flat, unwilling to rise. 'The siege belabours us, Sister. The Watered who command are insufficient to the task.'

'Whom do you suggest we send, Sister Calm?'

'Brother Diligence.'

Ah, next to me in seniority. My closest ally. Of course. She turned to the slope-shouldered man standing nearest the Heart. 'Brother Diligence?'

He glanced over, his pale eyes cold as the seas behind him. 'I will break the defenders, Sister Reverence. None there can hope to stand against me.'

'It remains an option,' murmured Reverence.

Again, Calm did not react.

Reverence looked to the others. 'Brother Abide?'

'It is known where blood soaks the sands,' the Mystic said, 'that other forces are arraying against us. Beyond the Glass Desert.'

'We have other armies,' said Calm. 'Enough to meet and defeat each one.'

'Sister Calm is correct,' added Sister Equity. 'Brother Diligence can destroy the humans who by treachery gained the North Keep, and indeed he can return in time for us to meet the new threats from the west.'

'But only if we do not linger too long in reaching a decision,' said Calm.

And so it divides. 'Brother Diligence?'

'The risk remains,' the warrior said, 'that we have underestimated the commander of those invaders. After all, they appeared as if from nowhere, and their successes to date have been . . . impressive.'

'From nowhere, yes,' muttered Brother Abide. 'Cause for dismay. A warren? Most certainly. But to guide an entire army through? Sister Calm and Sister Equity, we cannot discount the possibility of those in the keep simply leaving the way they came, should matters prove too precipitous. In which case, when and where will they reappear?'

'A valid point,' said Diligence. 'For as long as they are held in place, they are no threat to us.'

'Even so,' countered Calm, 'your presence and command of our besieging army will ensure that you can respond to anything unexpected. There will come a time – there *must* come a time – when it is expedient to drive them from the keep and, if possible, annihilate them.'

'Indeed there will,' agreed Reverence. 'But as Brother Abide has noted before, we are not yet certain that we have accounted for all the threats assembling against us.' She gestured. 'The Great Spire, the Altar of Judgement, this is where we remain the most vulnerable. Diligence in command of the Spire Army ensures the Spire and the Heart hold inviolate.' She paused, fixed her single eye upon Sister Calm. 'Our remaining Pures command the outlying armies inland. Do you suggest that, in the end, they shall prove unequal to the task? Sister Belie? Sister Freedom? Brothers Grave, Serenity and Aloft? Which of them falters in your regard?'

Calm glanced away. 'I hold that it is best to eliminate each threat as it arises, Sister Reverence.'

Reverence frowned. 'And should the enemy in the keep vanish as mysteriously as it arrived? Only to, perhaps, reappear here, at the very foot of the Great Spire? With Brother Diligence stranded at the far end of Estobanse Valley? What then?' she asked. *Yes, best we argue here, alone, beyond the hearing of our Watered and Shriven servants.* She resumed, this time taking in all the others. 'All of Kolanse has been cleansed – how could we have done otherwise, when, upon reaching these shores, we witnessed the terrible damage done to this land? Estobanse remains, because for the moment we require that it do so. To feed the Shriven and Watered. When the Heart is sacrificed upon this altar, brothers and sisters, even our need for human armies will be at an end. The end of the human world begins here – we must protect this place above all others, even Estobanse. Do any of you deny this?'

Silence.

Reverence met Calm's gaze. 'Sister Calm, in the name of your ancestors, patience.' At that there was finally a response. Calm's face tightened, and she rocked as if struck. Satisfied, Reverence blithely continued. 'All that is required is in motion, even as we speak. There will be rain before the storm. There must be. I ask that you set out once more, upon the dead lands, that you be our eyes so set as to forewarn us should any threat emerge from an unexpected quarter.' She gestured. 'Indeed, take Sister Equity with you.'

'Sound tactic,' said Brother Diligence, with a dry smile.

Calm bowed stiffly. 'As you wish, Sister Reverence.'

Catching something avid in the younger woman's eyes, Reverence frowned, suddenly uneasy. *Ah, have I been anticipated here? Have I stepped blind into a trap? You wish to be sent out into the Wastes, Calm. Why? What am I unleashing?*

'Our disposition, Sister Reverence?'

Curious, she nodded. 'As you desire.'

'Sister Equity shall take the south lands, then, while I journey into the west.'

Again? And what did you do there the first time out? What did you find? 'Very well,' Reverence said. 'Now, we stand upon the Altar of Judgement, once more united in our endeavours. With humility—'

'Blessed Pures!'

The shout came from the edge of the stairs, and they turned to see Watered Amiss, his face flame-flashed with exertion. They had left him at the Third Landing, against the eastern flank of the Spire.

Reverence strode towards him. 'Brother, what word do you bring us with such haste?'

He stumbled on to the altar and pointed to the east. 'Blessed Pures! In the harbour – *ships*! Many, many ships!'

Reverence noted the alarm and consternation in the faces of her kin, and felt a surge of satisfaction. *Yes, unseen threats assail you all now.* 'Brother Diligence, assemble the Defenders and awaken our warren in the Watered sub-commanders. Akhrast Korvalain shall be our bristling wall this day.' *And Sister Reverence? Ah, well, perhaps she will be the Gate.*

Calm and Equity had rushed to the eastern edge of the altar. Both stared for a moment before Equity turned round. 'Ships of war, kin. Grey as wolves upon the water.'

'Shall we descend and greet them?' Reverence asked.

Brother Diligence's smile was cruel and hard.

He knelt in the midst of Chaos. Pressures descended upon him, seeking to crack his bones. Torrid winds clawed at him, hungry to shred his soul. But he had walked here of his own accord. In his heart, such savage challenge as to face down the Abyss itself.

All is not bound to fate. It must not be.

All is not carved in stone, buried deep and for ever beyond mortal sight.

There must be more. In all the worlds, the solid laws are a prison – and I will see us freed!

He had met Chaos with fury in his being, a bristling armour of rage proof against all it flung at him. He had walked into the maelstrom seas of madness, and held tight to his own sanity. And then, at last, he had stood, unbowed, alone, and argued against the universe itself. The laws that were lies, the proofs that were false. Stone a hand could pass through. Water that could be breathed. Air as impenetrable as a wall. Fire to quench the deadliest thirst. Light that blinded, darkness that revealed. The beast within that was the heart of dignity, the sentient self that was purest savagery. In life the secret codes of death. In death the seeds of life.

He had spoken with the elemental forces of nature. Argued without relent. He had defended his right to an existence torn loose from these dread, unknowable horrors.

For his efforts, the blind uncertainty of Chaos had besieged him. How long? Centuries? Millennia? Now he knelt, battered, his armour shattered, wounds bleeding. And still it assailed him, sought to tear him apart.

The fissure that erupted from him first emerged from the centre of his head, a blast of argent fire in which he heard manic laughter. With terrible ripping sounds, the rent worked its way down his body, unfolding his throat, peeling back each side. His breastbone cracked in two, ribs bursting free. His stomach opened, spilling bitter fluids.

Then there was nothing. For how long, he never knew. When cognizance returned to him, he was standing where he had stood before, and before him two naked figures knelt, heads bowed. A man, a woman.

My children, born of anguish and need. My ever facile twins. My wretched faces of freedom. Chaos answers with its most delicious joke. Pull and prod, you godlings, you will never know what I lost in making you, this vicious bargain with uncertainty.

I will give you worlds. Yet not one shall be your home. You are cursed to wander through them, trapped in your eternal games. Lord and Lady of Chance. In the language of the Azathanai, Oponn.

My children, you shall never forgive me. Nor do I deserve forgiveness. The laws are not what they seem. Order is an illusion. It hides its lies in your very eyes, deceiving all they see. Because to see is to change that which is seen.

No, none of us will ever see true. We cannot. It is impossible. I give you a life without answers, my children. Walk the realms, spread the word in your illimitable way, Oponn. Some will welcome you. Others will not. And that, dear ones, is the joke on them. And on us.

I had a thought.

Now see what it made.

'Is this senility?'

The cavern shed its fluids, an incessant trickle and drizzle. The air stank of pain.

Sechul Lath glanced over. 'You spoke, Errastas?'

'You were far away. Memories haunting you, Setch?'

They sat on boulders, the two of them, the plumes of their breaths drifting like smoke. From somewhere in the cavern's depths came the sound of rushing water.

'Hardly. After all, as you are ever quick to point out, I am a man of modest achievements.'

'Not a man. A god. Making your pathetic deeds even more embarrassing.'

'Yes,' Sechul Lath agreed, nodding. 'I have many regrets.'

'Only fools know regret,' Errastas said, only to undermine his assertion as he unconsciously reached up towards his gaping eye socket. The brush of his fingers, the flinch of muscles in his cheek.

Hiding a smile, Sechul Lath looked away.

Kilmandaros still sat hunched, almost folded over, in the dripping blood rain of the Otataral Dragon. When exhaustion took her, the period of recovery could be long, interminably so in the eyes of the Errant. Even worse, she was not yet done with this. Lifting his gaze, Sechul Lath studied the dragon, Korabas. *She is the one law amidst the chaos of the Eleint. She is the denial of their power. She is the will set free. It's not enough to bleed her. She needs to die.*

And not even Kilmandaros can do that. Not with this one. At least, not now, while the gate is still sealed. She needs to die, but she must first be freed.

Against the madness of such contradictions, I wagered my very life. I walked into the heart of Chaos to challenge the absurdity of existence. And for that, I was torn in two.

My modest achievement.

'The Forkrul Assail,' he muttered, glancing back at Errastas. 'They cannot be permitted to actually succeed in what they seek to do. You must know that. The Assail do not kneel before gods, not even Elder Ones.'

'Their arrogance is boundless,' the Errant said, baring his teeth. 'We will exploit that, dear Knuckles. Mayhap they will slit the throats of the gods. But we are another matter.'

'We will need K'rul before this ends, I think.'

'Of us all, he best understands expedience,' Errastas agreed.

Expedience? 'And Mael. And Olar—'

'That hag has her own plans, but she will fail.'

'With a nudge?'

'It won't be hard,' the Errant replied. 'A nudge? More like a tap, the gentlest of prods.'

'Don't be premature in that. She'll serve well as a distraction, for as long as possible.'

He was touching his socket again. Seeking benediction? *Unlikely.*

'Azath,' said Sechul Lath. 'That was unexpected. How deep is your wound, Errastas?'

'More indignation than blood,' the Errant answered, grimacing. 'I was sorely used. Someone will pay for that.'

'Lifestealer?'

'Ah, Knuckles, do you think me a fool? Challenge that one? No. Besides, there were children involved. Human children.'

'Easier targets, then.'

Errastas must have caught something in Sechul's tone, for his face darkened. 'Don't you dare think them innocent!'

'I don't,' Sechul replied, thinking of his own unholy spawn. 'But it was Feather Witch who swallowed your eye, was it not? And you say that you killed her, with your own hands. How then—'

'Icarium's stupid gambit in Letheras. It's why I never found her soul. No, she carried my eye straight to him, the rotting bitch. And now he's spat out fledgling warrens, and made of my eye a Finnest for an Azath. He remains the single force of true unpredictability in this scheme.'

'Calm assures us otherwise.'

'I don't trust her.'

Finally, friend, you begin to think clearly again. 'Just so,' he said.

Errastas glanced over at Kilmandaros. 'Can we not feed her or something? Hasten this healing?'

'No. The wards Rake and the others set were profound. Tearing them down damaged her deeply, in ways no sorcerous healing can reach. Leave her in peace.'

Errastas hissed.

'Besides,' Sechul Lath continued, 'they're not all in place yet. You know that.'

'I have waited so long for this. I want us to be ready when the time comes.'

'And so we shall, Errastas.'

The Errant's single eye fixed on Sechul Lath. 'Calm is not the only one I do not trust.'

'There will be ashes and death, but survivors will emerge. They always do. They will understand the necessity of blood. We shall be unchallenged, Errastas.'

'Yet you sought to betray me. You and Kilmandaros.'

'Betray? No.' *We dismissed you.*

'That is how I see it. How can I not?'

'What you fail to understand, old friend,' said Sechul Lath, 'is that I don't care about being unchallenged. I don't care about a new world rising from the wreckage of this one. I am happy enough to wander the ruins. To mock those mortals who would try again.' He gestured. 'Leave the world to its wild ignorance – at least life was simple then. I turned my back on worshippers because I was done with them. Disgusted with them. I don't want what we *had*, Errastas.'

'But I do, Setch.'

'And you are welcome to it.'

'What of your children?'

'What of them?'

'Where do you see Oponn in the world to come?'

'I don't see them anywhere,' Sechul Lath said.

Errastas drew a sharp breath. 'You will kill them?'

'What I made I can unmake.'

'Your words please me, Knuckles. Indeed, I am relieved.'

It wasn't much of a life, my children, was it? I doubt you will object overmuch. Prod and pull, yes, but in the end – after thousands and thousands of years of that pathetic game – what is achieved? Learned? By anyone?

Chance is a miserable bitch, a hard bastard. It shows a smile, but it is a wolf's smile. What is learned? Only that every ambition must kneel to that which cannot be anticipated. And you can duck and dodge for only so long. It'll take you down in the end.

A man slips the noose. A civilization steps from the path of its own hubris. Once. Twice. Thrice even. But what of the twentieth time? The fiftieth? Triumph falters. It always does. There was never a balance.

After all, common sense will tell you, it's far easier to push than it is to pull.

'How does Kilmandaros feel,' Errastas asked, 'about killing her own children?'

Sechul Lath glanced over at his mother, and then back at his companion. 'Don't you understand anything, Errastas? She doesn't feel anything.'

After a moment, the lone eye shied away.

Now I think you understand.

What does the child want, that you did not have first? What do you own that the child does not want? Badalle had awoken this morning with these questions echoing in her head. The voice was a woman's, and then a man's. Both delivered in the same abject tones of despair.

She sat in the sun's light as it bled in from the window, banishing the chill in her bones as would a lizard or a serpent, and struggled to understand the night's visions, the dark, disturbing voices of strangers saying such terrible things.

It is what is passed on, I suppose. I think I see that.

She glanced over to where Saddic sat on the floor, his collection of useless objects arrayed around him, a lost look on his oddly wrinkled face. *Like an old man with his life's treasure. Only he's forgotten how to count.*

But what they owned, what they had, was not necessarily a good thing, a thing of virtue. Sometimes, what they had was poison, and the child's hunger knew no different. How could it? And so the crimes passed on, from one generation to the next. *Until they destroy us. Yes,*

I see that now. My dreams are wise, wiser than me. My dreams sing the songs of the Quitters, clever in argument, subtle in persuasion.

My dreams are warning me.

She turned away from the sun's light and faced the chamber. 'Is everyone ready?'

Saddic looked up guiltily, and then nodded.

Badalle twisted back and leaned out on the window ledge, craning round in order to see the western end of the plaza. Rutt was there, with Held in his arms. Others waited in the shadows of the surrounding buildings, as if figures on friezes had stepped out from their stone worlds.

It was just as well. They'd eaten all the fruit on the city's trees.

And the crystal was stealing our souls.

'Then it is time. Leave those things behind, Saddic.'

Instead, he began gathering them up.

A flash of anger hissed through Badalle, followed by fear. She didn't understand either. Sighing, she dropped down from the ledge. 'There will be Shards. Diamonds, Rubies and Opals. We will begin dying again.'

The boy looked at her with knowing eyes.

She sighed a second time. 'There are fathers among us now. We must watch them carefully, Saddic, in case they find father thoughts.'

To that he shook his head, as if to deny her words. 'No, Badalle,' he said in his broken voice. 'They just care for the young ones.'

So few words from you, Saddic. I'd thought you mute. What other things awaken in you, behind those old man's eyes, that old man's face?

She left the room. Saddic followed, his bag of useless things in his arms like a newborn babe. Down the sharp-edged steps, through the cool air of the hidden corridors, and then outside, into the blinding heat. Badalle walked without hesitation to where stood Rutt, who now watched her approach with hooded eyes. As she drew closer, the other children edged into the sunlight, clumped in their makeshift families. Hands were held, rag-ends clutched, legs embraced. She paused in her journey. She had forgotten how many still lived.

Forcing herself on, she walked until she stood before Rutt, and then she spun round and raised her arms out to the sides.

> 'The city spits us out
> We are sour and we are bitter
> To taste.
> The blind feeders-on-us turn away
> As they gorge
> As they devour all that was meant for us

All we thought to inherit
Because we wanted what they had
Because we thought it belonged to us
Just as it did to them
They looked away as they ate our future
And now the city's walls
Steal our wants
And spit out what remains
It's not much
Just something sour, something bitter
To taste.
And this is what you taste
In your mouths.
Something sour, something bitter.'

Rutt stared at her for a long moment, and then he nodded, and set out along the wide central avenue. Westward, into the Glass Desert. Behind him, the Snake uncoiled itself from its months-long slumber.

This was something the Snake understood, and Badalle could see it. In the steady, unhurried strides of the children trooping past, in their set faces, bleakness settling with familiarity in thin, wan features. *We know this. We have learned to love this.*

To walk. To slither beneath the fists of the world.

We are the Snake reborn.

In time, they reached the city's edge, and looked out on the flat glittering wastes.

Suffering's comfort. Like a dead mother's embrace.

CHAPTER SIX

'Dominant among the ancient races we can observe four: the Imass, the Jaghut, the K'Chain Che'Malle, and the Forkrul Assail. While others were present in the eldritch times, either their numbers were scant or their legacies have all but vanished from the world.

As for us humans, we were the rats in the walls and crawlspaces, those few of us that existed.

But is not domination our birthright? Are we not the likenesses of carved idols and prophets? Do these idols not serve us? Do these prophets not prophesy our dominion over all other creatures?

Perhaps you might note, with a sly wink, that the hands that carved the idols were our own; and that those blessed prophets so bold in their claims of righteous glory, each emerged from the common human press. You might note, then, that our fierce assertions cannot help but be blatantly self-serving, indeed, self-justifying.

And if you did, well, you are no friend of ours. And for you we have this dagger, this pyre, this iron tongue of torture. Retract your claims to our unexceptional selves, our gross banality of the profane.

As a species, we are displeased by notions of a mundane disconnect from destiny, and we shall hold to our deadly displeasure until we humans have crumbled to ash and dust.

For, as the Elder Races would tell you, were they around to do so, the world has its own dagger, its own iron tongue, its own pyre. And from its flames, there is nowhere to hide.'

Fragment purportedly from a translator's note to a lost edition of *Gothos' Folly*, Genabaris, 835 Burn's Sleep

THREE DAYS AND TWO NIGHTS THEY HAD STOOD AMONG THE DEAD bodies. The blood and gore dried on their tattered furs, their weapons. Their only motion came from the wind plucking at strands of hair and rawhide strips.

The carrion birds, lizards and capemoths that descended upon the field of slaughter fed undisturbed, leisurely in their feasting on rotting flesh. The figures standing motionless in their midst were too desiccated for their attentions; they might as well have been the stumps of long-dead trees, wind-torn and lifeless.

The small creatures were entirely unaware of the silent howls erupting from the souls of the slayers, the unending waves of grief that battered at these withered apparitions, the horror churning beneath layers of blackened, dried blood. They could not feel the storm raging behind skin-stretched faces, in the caverns of skulls, in the shrunken pits of eye sockets.

With the sun fleeing beneath the horizon on the third night, First Sword Onos T'oolan faced southeast and, with heavy but even strides, set out, the sword in his hand dragging a path through the knotted grasses.

The others followed, an army of destitute, bereft T'lan Imass, their souls utterly destroyed.

Slayers of the innocent. Murderers of children. The stone weapons lifted and the stone weapons fell. Faces wrote knotted tales of horror. Small skulls cracked open like ostrich eggs. Spirits fled like tiny birds.

When the others left, two remained behind. Kalt Urmanal of the Orshayn T'lan Imass ignored the command of his clan, the pressure of its will. Trembling, he held himself against the sweep of that dread tide pulling so insistently into the First Sword's shadow.

He would not bow to Onos T'oolan. And much as he yearned to fall to insensate dust, releasing for ever his tortured spirit, instead he held his place, surrounded by half-devoured corpses – eye sockets plucked clean, soft lips and cheeks stripped away by eager beaks – and grasped in both hands the crumbling madness of all that life – and death – had delivered to him.

But he knew with desolation as abject as anything he had felt before that there would be no gift of peace, not for him nor for any of the others, and that even dissolution might prove unequal to the task of cleansing his soul.

The flint sword in his hand was heavy, as if caked in mud. *If only it was.* His bones, hardened to stone, wrapped round him like a cage of vast, crushing weight.

As dawn rose on the fourth day, as the screams in his skull broke like sand before the wind, he lifted his head and looked across to the one other who had not yielded to the First Sword's ineffable summons.

A Bonecaster of the Brold clan. Of the Second Ritual, the Failed Ritual. *And if only it had failed. Knife Drip, such a sweet name, such a prophetic name.* 'This,' said Kalt Urmanal, 'is the Ritual you sought, Nom Kala. This is the escape you desired.' He gestured with his free hand. 'Your escape from these . . . children. Who would, in years to come – years they no longer have awaiting them – who would, then, have hunted down your kin. Your mate, your children. They would have killed you all without a moment's thought. In their eyes, you were beasts. You were less than they were, and so you deserved less.'

'The beast,' she said, 'that dies at the hand of a human remains innocent.'

'While that human cannot make the same claim.'

'Can they not?'

Kalt Urmanal tilted his head, studied the white-fur-clad woman. 'The hunter finds justification.'

'Need suffices.'

'And the murderer?'

'Need suffices.'

'Then we are all cursed to commit endless crimes, and this is our eternal fate. And it is our gift to justify all that we do.' *But this is no gift.* 'Tell me, Nom Kala, do you feel innocent?'

'I feel nothing.'

'I do not believe you.'

'I feel nothing because there is nothing left.'

'Very well. Now I believe you, Nom Kala.' He scanned the field of slaughter. 'It was my thought to stand here until their very bones vanished beneath the thin soil, hid inside brush and grasses. Until nothing remained of what has happened here.' He paused, and then said again, 'It was my thought.'

'You will find no penance, Kalt Urmanal.'

'Ah. Yes, that was the word I sought. I had forgotten it.'

'As you would.'

'As I would.'

Neither spoke again until the sun had once more vanished, yielding the sky to the Jade Strangers and the broken moon that was rising fitfully in the northeast. Then Kalt Urmanal hefted his weapon. 'I smell blood.'

Nom Kala stirred. 'Yes,' she said.

'Immortal blood, not yet spilled, but . . . soon.'

'Yes.'

'In moments of murder,' said Kalt Urmanal, 'the world laughs.'

'Your thoughts are harsh,' replied Nom Kala, settling her hair-matted mace in its sling draped across her back. She collected her harpoons.

'Are they? Nom Kala, have you ever known a world at peace? I know

143

the answer. I have existed far longer than you, and in that time there was no peace. Ever.'

'I have known *moments* of peace,' she said, facing him. 'It is foolish to expect more than that, Kalt Urmanal.'

'Do you seek such a moment now?'

She hesitated and then said, 'Perhaps.'

'Then I shall accompany you. We shall journey to find it. That single, most precious moment.'

'Do not cling to hope.'

'No, I shall cling to you, Nom Kala.'

She flinched. 'Do not do that,' she whispered.

'I can see you were beautiful once. And now, for the yearning in your empty heart, you are beautiful again.'

'Will you so torment me? If so, do not journey with me, I beg you.'

'I shall be silent at your side, unless you choose otherwise, Nom Kala. Look at us, we two remain. Deathless, and so well suited to this search for a moment of peace. Shall we begin?'

Saying nothing, she began walking.

As did he.

Do you remember, how those flowers danced in the wind? Three women knelt in soft clays beside the stream, taking cupped handfuls of clear water to sprinkle upon the softened pran'ag hides before binding them. The migrations were under way, velvet upon the antlers, and the insects spun in iridescent clouds, flitting like delicious thoughts.

The sun was warm that day. Do you remember?

Greasy stones were lifted from the sacks, rolled in hands around the circle of laughing youths, while the cooked meat was drawn forth and everyone gathered to feast. It was, with these gentle scenes, a day like any other.

The call from the edge of camp was not unduly alarming. Three strangers approaching from the south.

One of the other clans, familiar faces, smiles to greet kin.

The second shout froze everyone.

I went out with the others. I held my finest spear in my hand, and with my warriors all about me I felt sure and bold. Those who drew near were not kin. True strangers. If necessary, we would drive them off.

There was this moment – please, you must remember with me. We stood in a row, as they came to within six paces of us, and we looked into their faces.

We saw ourselves, yet not. Subtle the alterations. They were taller, thinner-boned. Strewn with fetishes and shells and beads of amber. Their faces did not possess the rounded comfort of Imass faces.

Features had sharpened, narrowed. The bones of their jaw beneath the mouth jutted under dark beards. We saw their weapons and they confused us. We saw the fineness of their skins and furs and leggings, and we felt diminished.

Their eyes were arrogant, the colour of earth, not sky.

With gestures, these three sought to drive us away. This was their land to hunt now. We were the intruders. Do you remember how that felt? I looked into their faces, into their eyes, and I saw the truth.

To these tall strangers, we were ranag, we were bhederin, we were pran'ag.

Killing them made no difference, and the blood on our weapons weakened us with horror. Please, I am begging you, remember this. It was the day the world began to die. Our world.

Tell me what you remember, you who stood facing these roughened savages with their blunt faces, their squat selves, their hair of red and blond. Tell me what you felt, your indignation when we did not cower, your outrage when we cut you down.

You knew you would come again, in numbers beyond imagining. And you would hunt us, chase us down, drive us into cold valleys and cliff caves above crashing seas. Until we were all gone. And then, of course, you would turn on each other.

If you dare to remember this, then you will understand. I am the slayer of children – your children – no! Show me no horror! Your hands are red with the blood of my children! You cannot kill us any more, but we can kill you, and so we shall. We are the sword of ancient memories. Memories of fire, memories of ice, memories of the pain you delivered upon us. I shall answer your crime. I shall be the hand of your utter annihilation. Every last child.

I am Onos T'oolan and once, I was an Imass. Once, I looked upon flowers dancing in the wind.

See my army? It has come to kill you. Seek out the cold valleys. Seek out the caves in the cliffs over crashing seas. It will not matter. As these shelters failed us, so they will fail you.

I see well this truth: you never expected our return.

Too bad.

Yes, he would have liked these thoughts, this blistering, righteous pronouncement that vengeance was deserved and so meted out. And that the innocence of the young was a lie, when they become the inheritors, when they grow fat on the evil deeds of their ancestors.

They were, he knew, the thoughts of Olar Ethil, whispered into the secret places of his soul. He well understood her. He always had.

The Barghast deserved their fate. They had slain his wife, his children. And he remembered the arrogance in the eyes of his family's slayers – but how had he seen that? It was impossible. He'd already been dead.

145

She creeps inside me. Olar Ethil, you are not welcome. You want me to serve you. You want – yes, I know what you want, and you dare to call it healing.

There is a dead seedling in you, Bonecaster. A shrunken, lifeless thing. In others, it lives on, sometimes frail and starving, sometimes thriving with sweet anguish. That seedling, Olar Ethil, has a name, and even the name would twist sour upon your lips. The name is compassion.

One day I will stand before you, and I will kiss you, Olar Ethil, and give you a taste of what you never possessed. And I will see you choke. Spit in bitter fury. And even then, to show you its meaning, I will weep for you.

We have fled from it for too long. Our people, our blessed, doomed people. Can you not shed a tear for them, Bonecaster? Your putative children? They lived well in their slow failing, well enough – show me the scene I never saw, the moment I never knew, when I stood before the first humans. Tell me of the blood I spilled, to echo my latest crime, to fuse the two together, as if righteousness was a mask to be worn again and again.

Do you think me a fool?

Toc, my brother, sent me away. But I think, now, he was compelled. I think now, Olar Ethil, you held him fast. I have lost a brother and I know he will never return. For his fate, I would weep.

If I only could.

Forces were gathering, to a place in the east. The ancient warren of Tellann was a thing of raging fire, like the plains lit in flames on every horizon. He could feel the heat, could taste the bitter smoke. Elsewhere – *not far* – Omtose Phellack churned awake with the thunder of riven ice. Seas cracked and valleys groaned. And closer to hand, the stench of the K'Chain Che'Malle rode the winds pungent as a serpent's belly. And now . . . yes. *Akhrast Korvalain. The pale ghosts of old once more walk the land. The Elder Warrens rise again. By all the spirits of earth and water, what has begun here?*

Olar Ethil, in what comes, the T'lan Imass shall be as motes of dust in a maelstrom. And what you seek – no, the price is too high. It is too high.

Yet he marched, as if destiny still existed for his people, as if death itself was no barrier to the glory awaiting them. *We have lost our minds. Toc Younger, what is this winter tide that so carries us forward? Ride to me, let us speak again, as we did once. Toc Younger, I forgive you. For the wounds you delivered, for all that you denied me, I cannot but forgive you.*

One last journey into the storm, then. He would lead. His lost kin would follow. He understood that much. Less than dust motes they might be, but the T'lan Imass would be there. *We shall not be forgotten. We deserve better than that.*

We were you before you were born. Do not forget us. And in your memory, I beg of you, let us stand tall and proud. Leave to us our footprints in the sand, there to mark the trail you now tread, so that you understand – wherever you go, we were there first.

In the wake of Onos T'oolan, three thousand T'lan Imass followed. Orshayn, Brold, and a score more forgotten clans – those that fell in the Wars, those that surrendered to despair.

It was likely, Rystalle Ev suspected, that Onos T'oolan was unaware that he had opened his mind to them, that the terrible emotions warring in his soul rushed out to engulf them all. The ancient barriers had been torn down, and she and all the others weathered the storm in silence, wretched, beaten into numbness.

At the field of slaughter, his howls had echoed their own, but now the First Sword was binding them in grisly chains.

They would stand with him. They had no choice. And when at last he fell, as he must, so too would they.

This was . . . acceptable. It was, in fact, just. *Slayers of children deserve no glory. The caves are emptied now, but we cannot dwell there. The air is thick with the blood we spilled. Even the flames from the hearth cannot warm us.*

She sensed that Kalt Urmanal was no longer with them. She was not surprised, and although her own anguish at his absence clawed at her, the pain felt distant, drowned beneath the torments of the First Sword. Her love had always been a lost thing, and he had ever been blind to it.

All the jealousy she had once felt lingered, a poison suffusing her being, tainting her love for him. He had been broken by the K'Chain Che'Malle long ago, when they had slain his wife and children. Her love was for a memory, and the memory was flawed.

No, it is best that he is gone. That he decided he could not go on. The truth is, I admire the strength of his will, that he could so defy the First Sword's power. Had others remained behind? She did not know, but if they had, she prayed their presence would comfort Kalt Urmanal.

What is it, to lose a love you never had?

Ulag Togtil, who had come among the Orshayn Imass as a stranger, whose blood was thickened with that of the Trellan Telakai, now reeled in the First Sword's wake, as if his limbs were under siege. There was a harshness to the Trellan that had stood him well on the day of the slaughter, but now it floundered in the depthless well that was the emotional torrent of the Imass.

To feel too deeply, oh, how the callous would mock this. Their regard, flat and gauging as a vulture's upon a dying man. Something to amuse, but even trees will tremble to cold winds; are you so bereft, friend, that you dare not do the same?

Onos T'oolan gives us his pain. He is unaware of the gift, yet gift it is. We obeyed the command of the First Sword, knowing nothing of his soul. We'd thought we had found in him a tyrant to beggar the Jaghut themselves. Instead, he was lost as we are.

But if there be unseen witnesses to this moment, if there be callous ones among them, ah, what is it that you fear to reveal? There in that tear, that low sob? You smile in superiority, but what is the nature of this triumph of yours? I wish to know. Your self-made chains draped so tight about you are nothing to be proud of. Your inability to feel is not a virtue.

And your smile has cracks.

Ulag had played this game all his life, and now he did so again, in the ashes of Tellann, in the swirling mad river of the First Sword's path. Imagining his invisible audience, a sea of blurred faces, a host of unknown thoughts behind the veil of their eyes.

And he would speak to them, from time to time.

I am the wolf that would die of loneliness if cast from the pack. And so, even when I am alone, I choose to believe otherwise.

There was no true unity in the T'lan Imass, for we had surrendered the memories of our lives. Yet even then, I refused to be alone. Ah, I am a fool. My audience belongs to future's judgement, and harsh it shall be, and when at last it speaks in that multitude of voices, I shall not be there to hear it.

Can you be at ease with that, Ulag? Can you hear the dry laughter of the Trellan? The jeering of humans?

But see how it bows you, even now. See how it batters you down.

Against the future, Ulag, you are helpless as a babe lying on a rock. And the eagle's shadow slides across the tear-filled eyes, the soft face. The babe falls silent, knowing danger is near. But, alas, it has not even learned to crawl. And Mother's hands are long gone.

For this fate, Onos T'oolan, we would all weep. If we could.

Shield Anvil Stormy picked himself up off the ground, blinking water from his eyes and probing his split cheek. 'All right,' he said, spitting blood, 'I suppose I deserved that. At least,' and he glared at Gesler, 'that's what you're going to tell me right now. It is, isn't it? Tell me it is, or so help me, Ges, I'm going to rip your head right off and throw it in the nearest cesspit I find.'

'I needed to get your attention,' the Mortal Sword replied. 'With you, subtle don't work.'

'How would you know? You ain't tried it yet. Not once, in all the years I've been cursed by your company.'

'Well,' said Gesler, squinting at the mass of Che'Malle Furies thumping past, 'turns out I got a solution for that. An end to your curse.'

'You can't run away! You can't leave me here—'

'No, it's you I'm sending away, Stormy.'

'What?'

'I'm the Mortal Sword. I can do things like that.'

'Send me where?'

'To her, to what's left of her.'

Stormy looked away, south across the empty, dismal plain. He spat again. 'You really don't like me much, do you?'

'We have to find out, Stormy. Aye, I could go myself, but you're the Shield Anvil. There will be the souls of friends, hanging around like a bad smell. Will you just leave the ghosts to wander, Stormy?'

'What am I supposed to do with them?'

'How should I know? Bless them, I suppose, or whatever it is you have to do.'

Destriant Kalyth was riding back to where they'd dismounted. She was looking at each of them in turn, back and forth, frowning at the red welt and split cheek under Stormy's left eye. She drew up her Ve'Gath mount. 'Don't you two ever just talk? Spirits below, men are all the same. What has happened?'

'Nothing,' Stormy replied. 'I have to leave.'

'Leave?'

'It's temporary,' said Gesler, swinging himself back into the bone and scale saddle that was his mount's back. 'Like a mangy pup, he'll show up again before too long.'

'Where is he going?' Kalyth demanded.

'Back to where we came from,' Gesler replied. 'Back to the Bonehunters. They got hurt bad. We need to find out how bad.'

'Why?'

Stormy glared up at Gesler, waiting for the bastard to come up with an answer to that question, but the Mortal Sword simply growled under his breath and kicked his charger into motion.

As he rode away, Kalyth fixed her attention on Stormy. 'Well?'

He shrugged. 'When there's trouble ahead, Destriant, it's good to know how your allies are faring.'

His reply clearly disturbed her, though she seemed unable to explain why. 'You will need an escort.'

'No, I won't.'

'Yes you will, Shield Anvil. Your Ve'Gath needs to eat. I will have Sag'Churok assign three K'ell Hunters to you, and two drones. When do you leave?'

He walked to his mount. 'Now.'

She hissed some Elan curse and kicked her Ve'Gath into motion.

Grinning, Stormy mounted up and set out. *Classic Malazan military structure at work here, woman. Short, violent discussion and that's it. We don't wait around. And Gesler? I'm gonna bust your jaw.*

Grub watched Stormy's departure and scowled. 'Something's up.'

Sinn snorted. 'Thanks. I was just falling asleep, and now you've woke me up again. Who cares where Stormy's going?'

'I do.'

'They're mostly dead,' she said. 'And he's going to confirm that. You want to go with him, Grub? Want to look at Keneb's corpse? Should I go with you? So I can see what the vultures have done to my brother? The truth is in your heart, Grub. You feel it just like I do. They're dead.'

At her harsh words Grub hunched down, looked away. Rows of Che'Malle, Ve'Gath soldiers, their massive elongated heads moving in smooth rhythm, their hides coated in dust that dulled the burnished gold of the scales on their necks and backs. Weapons slung down from harnesses of drone-hide, swinging and rustling. Ornate helms hiding the soldiers' eyes. *But every soldier's eyes look the same. Seen too much and more's coming and they know it.*

Uncle Keneb, it's all over for you now. Finally. And you never really wanted any of it anyway, did you? Your wife left you. All you had was the army, and you died with it. Did you ever want anything else?

But he didn't know the truth of any of that. He hadn't lived enough of his own life. He tried getting into the heads of people like Keneb – the ones with so many years behind them – and he couldn't. He could recite what he knew of them. *Whirlwind. Slaughter and flight. Loves lost, but what do I know about that?*

Keneb, you're gone. I'll never see your face again – your exasperation when you looked at me, and even then I knew you'd never abandon me. You just couldn't, and I knew it. And that is what I have lost, isn't it? I don't even have a name for it, but it's gone now, for ever gone.

He glanced over at Sinn. Her eyes were closed and she rolled in the Ve'Gath's gait, chin settling on her breast bone. *Your brother has died, Sinn. And you just sleep. The magic's carved everything out of you, hasn't it? You're just wearing that girl's face, her skin, and whatever you are, there inside, it isn't human at all any more, is it?*

And you want me to join you.

Well, if it means an end to feeling pain, then I will.

Keneb, why did you leave me?

*   *   *

Eyes closed, her mind wandered into a place of dust and sand, where the sun's fading light turned the cliffs into fire. She knew this world. She had seen it many times, had walked it. And somewhere in the hazy distances there were familiar faces. Figures seething in the hot markets of G'danisban, cooled corridors and the slap of bared feet. And then terror, servants with bloodied knives, a night of smoke and flames. And all through the city, screams pierced the madness.

Stumbling into a room, a most precious room – was that her mother? Sister? Or just some guest? The two stable boys and a handmaiden – who was always laughing, she recalled, and was laughing again, with her fist and most of her forearm pushed up inside Mother, while the boys held the battered woman down. Whatever the laughing girl was reaching for, she couldn't seem to find it.

Blurred panic, flight, one of the boys setting off after her.

Bared feet slapping on stone, the ragged beat of hard breaths. He caught her in the corridor, and in the cool shadow he used something other than his fist on her, in the same place, and by his cries he found whatever it was he'd been looking for, a moment before a strange barrier inside her head was torn through, and sorcery rushed out to lift the boy straight up, until he was pressed awkwardly against the arched ceiling of the corridor. His eyes were bulging, face darkening, the thing between his legs shrivelling and turning black as blood vessels began bursting inside him.

She'd stared up, fixing on his swollen eyes, watched them begin spraying blood in fine jets. And still she pushed. His bones cracked, fluids spurted, his wastes splashing down on to her legs to mix with the blood pooling there. As he flattened, he spread out, until it seemed he was part of the stone, a ghastly image of something vaguely human, made of skin and plaster and oozing mud.

By then, she suspected, he'd been dead for some time.

Crawling away, feeling broken inside, as if he was still there and would always be there, as if she had nothing of herself, nothing pure or untouched by someone else.

Then, much later, an assassin's face, a night of caves and demons and murder. She'd been dreaming of poison, yes, and there had been bloated bodies, but nothing cleaned her out, no matter what she tried.

Outside a city, watching the flames ever rising. Soldiers were dying. The world was a trap and they all seemed surprised by that, even though it was something she'd always known. The fire wanted her and it so wanted her, why, she let it inside. To burn her empty.

She'd wanted to believe that it had worked. That she was at last clean. But before too long she could feel that boy return, deep, deep inside her. She needed more. More fire, because fire delivered death. And in the midst of conflagration, time and again, a voice whispered to her.

'You are my child. The Virgin of Death is never what they think it is. What dies is the virgin herself, the purity of her soul. Or his. Why always assume the Virgin is a girl? So I show you what you were, but now I show you what you are. Feel my heat – it is the pleasure you have for ever lost. Feel my kiss upon your lips: this is the love you will never know. See my hunger, it is your yearning for a peace you will never find.

'You are my child. You killed him before he left you. You crushed his brain to pulp. The rest was just for show. He was still inside you, a dead boy, and this was Hood's path to your soul, and the Lord of Death's touch steals life. You killed the boy, but the boy killed you, too, Sinn. What do you feel deep in you? Give it any shape you want, any name, it doesn't matter. What matters is this: it is dead, and it waits for you, and will wait for you until your last breath leaves your body.

'When your death is already inside you, there is nowhere to run, no escape possible. When your death is already inside you, Sinn, you have nothing to lose.'

She had nothing to lose. This was true. About everything. No family, no brother, no one at all. Even Grub, her sweet Virgin, well, he would never reach her, just as she would never, ever, reach inside him, to dirty what was pure. *My precious possession, dear Grub, and him I will keep safe from harm. No one will ever touch him. No slap of bared feet, no harsh breaths. I am your fire, Grub, and I will burn to ash anything and anyone who dares gets close to you.*

That is why I rode the lizard's lightning, that brilliant fire. I rode it straight for Keneb. I didn't guide it, I didn't choose it, but I understood the necessity of it, the rightness of taking away the one person left who loved you.

Do not grieve. You have me, Grub. We have each other, and what could be more perfect than that?

Familiar faces in the distant haze. Her mind wandered the desert, as the night drew in, and somewhere down on the flats small fires lit awake, and she smiled. *We are the dead thing in the womb of the world, and we and we alone light the darkness with fire. By that you will know us. By those flames alone, the earth shall tremble.*

What is it to be raped? I am silent as the world and we will say nothing. What is it to be the rapist?

The desert at night was a cold place, except for the fires. Dark too, except for the fires.

'It plagues the young, this need to find reasons for things.'

Rud Elalle huddled, robes drawn tight around him, and edged closer to the fire. The wind up in these crags was fierce, the air thin and icy.

152

Far below, low on the slopes of the mountainsides, the edge of the tree line was visible as a black mass, thinning at the highest reaches – which seemed very far away. He shivered. 'Couldn't we at least find a cave or something?'

Silchas Ruin stood facing the high passes to the north, seemingly immune to the cold. 'Very well, come the morrow, we shall do that. Had we remained Eleint, of course—'

'I would be comfortable, yes. I know.' Rud stared at the feeble flames as they devoured the last of the wood he had carried up from below. In draconic form, the raging chaos within him would have kept him warm, inured to the elements. But his thoughts twisted wild when he was veered, when the blood of the Eleint coursed dominant in his veins. He began to lose his sense of himself as a creature of reasoning, of rational thought and clear purpose. Not that he had a clear purpose, of course. Not yet. But it wasn't healthy to be a dragon – he knew that much.

Mother, how could you have lived with this? For so long? No wonder you went mad. No wonder you all did. He glanced over at Silchas Ruin, but the figure had not moved. *How much longer?* he wanted to ask. Still . . . the Tiste Andii needed no further invitation to view him as little more than a child. A child of terrible power, true, but still a child.

And, Rud allowed, he would not be far wrong, would he? There was no sense to what they intended to do. So much was out of their hands. They hovered like swords, but whose gauntleted grasp would close on them when the time came? There didn't seem to be an answer to that question, at least not one Silchas Ruin was willing to share.

And what of this Tiste Andii, standing there as if carved from alabaster, rubies for eyes, moaning blades crossing his back? He had lost his last surviving brother. He was utterly alone, bereft. Olar Ethil had broken him for no purpose Rud could see, barring that of spite. But Silchas Ruin had finally straightened, biting on that wound in the manner of a speared wolf, and he'd been limping ever since – at least in his sembled state. It was quite possible – and indeed likely – that Silchas Ruin preferred to remain in an Eleint form, if only to cauterize the pain with the soulfire of chaos. Yet there he stood. *Because I am too weak to resist. Draconean ambitions taste bitter as poison. They want my surrender, they want to hear me howl with desire.*

'Once we find a cave,' resumed Silchas Ruin, 'I will leave you for a time. Those stone weapons of yours are insufficient for what comes. While it is true that we may have no need for swords and the like, I believe it is time for you to take to hand a proper blade.'

'You want to go and find me a sword.'

'Yes.'

'And where do you look for something like that?' Rud asked. 'A weaponsmith's in Letheras? A trader's camp near a recent battlefield?'

'None of those,' he replied. 'For you, I have something more ambitious in mind.'

Rud's gaze returned to the flames. 'How long will you be gone?'

'Not long, I should think.'

'Well then,' Rud snapped, 'what are you waiting for? I can find my own cave.'

He felt Silchas Ruin's regard upon him, and then it was gone and when he turned, so was the Tiste Andii – he had plummeted from the ledge. Moments later a buffet of wind struck him, and he saw the dragon lifting skyward, up above the ravaged peaks, blotting out stars.

'Ah, Silchas, I am sorry.'

Despondent, he held his hands out over the coals. He missed his father. Udinaas would have a wry grin for this moment, a few cutting words – not too deep, of course, but enough to awaken in Rud a measure of self-regard, something he suspected he needed. *Spirits of the stream, it's just that I'm lonely. I miss home. The sweet songs of the Imass, the fiery lure of Kilava – oh, Onrack, do you know how lucky you are?*

And where is my love? Where does she hide? He glared around, at the bare rock, the flight of sparks, the frail shelter in this crook of stone. *Not here, that's for sure.*

Well, if any man needed a woman more than he did, it was his father. *In a way, he is as alone among the Imass as I am here. He was a slave. A sailor. A Letherii. His home was civilized. Crowded with so many conveniences one could go mad trying to choose among them. And now he lives in a hut of hide and tenag bones. With winter closing in – oh, the Imass knew a harsh world.* No, none of that was fair on Udinaas, who saw himself as so unexceptional he was beneath notice. *Unexceptional? Will it take a woman to convince you otherwise? You can't find one there – you need to go home, Father.*

He could try a sending. A conjuration of will and power – was it possible to reach that far? 'Worth a try,' he muttered. 'Tomorrow morning.' For now, Rud Elalle would try to sleep. If that failed, well, there was the blood of the Eleint, and its deadly, sultry call.

He lifted his head, looked south. At the far side of the range, he knew, there was a vast green valley, slopes ribboned with terraces verdant with growth. There were towns and villages and forts and high towers guarding the bridges spanning the rivers. There were tens of thousands working those narrow fields.

They had flown so high above all of this, to a human eye they would have been virtually invisible. When they drew nearer to the rearing range north of the valley, close to its westernmost end, they had seen an encamped army, laying siege to a fastness carved into the first of the mountains. Rud had wondered at that. Civil war? But Silchas Ruin had shown no curiosity. *'Humans can do whatever they please, and they will. Count on it, Ryadd.'*

Still, he imagined it was warm inside that keep right now.

Assuming it still held against the enemy. For some reason, he was sure that it did. *Aye, humans will do whatever they please, Silchas Ruin, and they'll be damned stubborn about it, too.*

He settled down against the cold night.

His thoughts were earth, and the blood moved slowly through it, seeping like a summer's rain. He saw how the others looked at him, when they'd thought his attention elsewhere. So much larger than any of them was he, bedecked in the armour of Dalk's hide, his Ethilian mace showing a face to each of the cardinal directions, as befitted the Witch's gift from the sky.

Listening to them readying their weapons, adjusting the straps of their armour, locking the grilled cheek-guards in place on their blackened helms, he knew that, in the past weeks, he had become the mountain they huddled against, the stone at their backs, on their flanks, at the point of the spear – wherever he was needed most, there he would be.

How many of the foe had he killed? He had no idea. Scores. Hundreds. They were the Fangs of Death, their numbers were endless and that, he well knew, was no exaggeration.

His fellow invaders, who once numbered in their tens of thousands, had dwindled now. It might be that other fragments still pushed on, somewhere to the south or north, but then they did not have a Thel Akai warrior in their company. They did not have a dragon-killer. *They do not have me.*

Earth was slow in dying. The soil was a black realm of countless mouths, ceaseless hungers. In a single handful raged a million wars. Death was ever the enemy, yet death was also the source of sustenance. It took a ferocious will to murder earth.

One by one, his companions – barely a score left now – announced themselves ready, in rising to their feet, in testing their gauntleted grips on their notched, battered weapons. And such weapons! Each one worth a dozen epic songs of glory and pain, triumph and loss. If he looked up from the ground at this moment, he would see faces swallowed in the barred shadows of their cheek-guards; he would see these proud warriors standing, eyes fixed eastward, and, slowly, those grimly set mouths and the thin, tattered lips would twist with wry amusement.

A war they could not win.

An epic march from which not one great hero would ever return.

The earth within him surged with sudden fire, and he rose, the mace

155

lifting in his huge hands. *We shall have lived as none other has lived. We shall die as no other has died. Can you taste this moment? By the Witch but I can!*

He faced his companions, and gave them his own grin.

Tusked mouths opened like split flesh, and cold laughter filled the air.

Groaning, Ublala Pung opened his eyes. More dreams! More terrible visions! He rolled on to his side and blinked across the makeshift camp at the huddled form of the Barghast woman. His love. His adored one. It wasn't fair that she hated him. He reached out and drew close the strange mace with its four blue-iron heads. It looked as if it should be heavy, and perhaps to some people it was. And it had a name, its very own name. But he'd forgotten it. *A dozen and four epic songs. Songs of glore and painty, turnips and lust.*

Perhaps she was just pretending to sleep. And she'd try to kill him again. The last time Draconus had stopped her, appearing as if out of nowhere to grasp her wrist, staying the dagger's point a finger's breadth from Ublala's right eye. He'd then slapped the woman, hard enough to send her sprawling.

'Best we kill her now, Ublala.'

Rubbing the sleep from his face. 'No, please, don't do that. I love her. It's just a spat of some sort, Draconus, and as soon as I figure out what we're arguing about I'll fix it, I swear.'

'Ublala—'

'Please! We're just disagreeing about something.'

'She means to kill and then rob us.'

'She had cruel parents, and was bullied as a child, Draconus. Other girls pulled her braids and spat in her ears. It's all a misunderstanding!'

'One more chance, then. My advice is to beat her senseless, Ublala. It's likely that's how Barghast men treat murderous women, as necessity demands.'

'I can't do that, Draconus. But I'll comb her hair.'

Which was what he had been doing when she'd finally come round. Lacking a comb, he'd been using a thorny twig, which probably wasn't ideal, especially on her fine eyebrows, but they'd since taken care of the infections and she was looking almost normal again.

So maybe she really was asleep, and now that she had no weapons left, why, she was as harmless as a twill-mouse, except for the big rocks she kept close at hand every night.

At least she had stopped complaining.

Ublala twisted to see if he could find Draconus – the man never seemed to sleep at all, though he'd lie down on occasion, which is what he'd been doing when Ralata had tried knifing Ublala. Wasn't she surprised!

The man was standing facing north, something he had been doing a lot of, lately.

People like him had too many thoughts, Ublala decided. So many he couldn't even rest from himself, and that had to be a hard thing to live with. No, it was better to have hardly any thoughts at all. *Like earth. Yes, that's it all right. Dirt.*

But those tusks were scary, and that laughing was even worse!

A new scent on the cool breath drifting in from the west. Perhaps some ancient memories were stirred by it, something that left the pack agitated. She watched the lord stretching and then padding up to the rise. He possessed such power, as did all lords – he could stand on a high place, exposed to all four winds, and feel no fear.

The others remained in the high grasses of the slope, the young males pacing, the females in the shadow of the trees, where pups crawled and tumbled.

Bellies were full, but the herds wending up from the plains to the south were smaller this season, and there was a harried air to their long flight from thirst and heat, as if pursued by fire or worse. Hunting the beasts had been easy – the animal they'd brought down had already been exhausted, and the taste of old terror was in its blood.

The lord stood on the ridge. His ears sharpened and the others quickly rose – even the games of the pups ceased.

The lord staggered. Three sticks were jutting from it now, and from the slope beyond came strange excited barks. Blood threaded down from the sticks as the lord sank down, head twisting in a vain effort to reach the shafts. Then it fell on its side and stopped moving.

There was motion on all sides now, and more sticks whipped through foliage and grasses, sinking into flesh. The pack erupted in snarls of pain.

The figures that rushed in moved on their hind legs. Their skins gleamed with oil and their smell was that of crushed plants over something else. They flung more sticks. There was white around their eyes and they had small mouths from which came their wild barking.

She gasped as fire tore into her flank. Blood filled her throat, sprayed out from her nostrils and then poured from her jaws. She saw an attacker reach down and grasp a pup by its tail. He swung it and then slammed the little one against the bole of a tree.

An old scent. *They are among us again. There is nowhere to hide. Now we die.*

Vision blurred, Setoc withdrew her hand from the bleached wolf's skull they'd found in the crotch of the gnarled tree growing from the edge of the dried-up spring. The rough, tortured bark had almost devoured the bleached bone.

The first tree they'd found in weeks. She wiped at her eyes. *And this.*

It wasn't enough to grieve. She saw that now. Not enough to wallow in the anguish of blood on the hands. It wasn't enough to fight for mercy, to plead for a new way of walking the world. It wasn't enough to feel guilt.

She turned to study the camp. Faint, Precious Thimble, Sweetest Sufferance and Amby Bole, all looking for a way home. A place of comfort, all threats diminished, all dangers locked away. Where patrols kept the streets safe, where the fields ran in rows and so did trees. Or so she imagined – strange scenes that couldn't be memory, because she had no memory beyond the plains and the wild lands. But in those cities the only animals nearby were slaves or food, and those that weren't lived in cages, or their skins adorned the shoulders of fine ladies and bold nobles, or their bones waited in heaps for the grinders, to be fed into the planted fields.

That was their world, the one they wanted back.

You can have it. There is no place for me in it, is there? Very well. The sorrow within her now seemed infinite. She walked from the camp, out into the darkness. The Bonecaster had taken the children, and Torrent with them. Destinies had taken the Trell and Gruntle. Death had taken the others. *But I owe you nothing. In your company, my ghost wolves stay away. They drift like distant desires. I am forgetting what it is to run free.*

I am forgetting why I am here.

They would not miss her. They had their own haunts, after all. *I do not belong with you. I think – I think . . . I am what you left behind. Long ago.* She wondered if she too was in search of a destiny, the same as Mappo and Gruntle, but it seemed they were so much more than her, and that even the idea of a destiny for Setoc was ridiculous. *But the ghost wolves – and all the other fallen beasts – they look to me. For something. I just don't know what it is. And I need to find out.*

Is that what destiny is? Is that all it is?

It was surprisingly easy to leave them behind, the ones she'd walked with for so long now. She could have turned back right then, to face the city – all the cities and all the broken lands that fed them. She could have chosen to accept her humanness. Instead . . . *look at me. Here I walk.*

Let the Wolves cleanse this world. Let the beasts return. Above all, let the senseless killing end: we are tired of running, tired of dying. You must see that. You must feel something for that. Just how cold is your soul?

You empty the land. You break the earth and use it until it dies, and then your children starve. Do not blame me. Do not blame any of us for that.

Her breath caught and she hesitated. A sudden dark thought had flared in her mind. A knife in her hand. Throats opening to the night. Four more of the murderers dead. In a war that she knew might never end. *But what difference does that make – we've been losing for so long, I doubt we'd know the taste of victory even as it filled our mouths. Even as it drowned us in its glory.*

Could she kill them? Could she turn around, here and now, and creep back into the camp? *No pup skulls to crack open, but still. The dead-inside have to work hard at their pleasures. That burst of shock. Disbelief. The sudden laugh. So hard, to feel anything at all, isn't it?*

The thoughts were delicious, but she resumed her journey. It was not, she decided, her destiny to kill one here, another there. No, if she could, she would kill them all. *This is the war the Wolves have sought. The Hold shall be reborn. Am I to be their leader? Am I to stand alone at the head of some vast army of retribution?*

All at once, the ghost wolves were surrounding her, brushing close, and she began a loping run, effortlessly, her heart surging with strength. Freedom – she understood now – was something so long lost among humans that they had forgotten what it felt like. *Bend to your labours! Grasp those coins! Keep the doors locked and fires raging to empty the shadows behind you! Make your brothers and sisters kneel before you, to serve your pleasures. Are you free? You don't remember the truth of what once was – of what you all so willingly surrendered.*

I will show you freedom. So I vow: I will show you what it is to be free.

On all sides, the ghost wolves howled.

'She's gone.'

Faint opened her eyes, blinked at the bright morning sun. 'What? Who?'

'The girl. Setoc, with the wolf eyes. Gone.'

She stared up at Amby, frowning. And then said, 'Oh.'

'I don't think she's coming back.'

'No, Amby, I don't either.'

He moved back as she sat up. Her chest ached, her ragged scars itched. She was filthy and the taste in her mouth was thick with the rancid meat they'd eaten the night before. Amby stood like a man lost in the company of anyone but his brother – just a glance nearly broke her heart.

She looked past him. Sweetest Sufferance was still asleep, her rounded form swathed in blankets. Precious Thimble sat near the ashes of the night's fire, eyes fixed dully on Amby.

She'd heard tales of horror, amongst the shareholders who'd signed out and now sat in taverns waiting to die. They'd drink and tell of missions that had ended in disaster. A dead mage, lost in unknown lands, no way home. The few lucky ones would find a place to book passage, or perhaps another Trygalle carriage would find them, half starved and half mad, and these ones would come home broken, their eyes empty.

She stared up at the morning sky. Was the flying lizard still up there? Did it mock them with its cold eyes? She doubted it. *If we make it out of this, it will be a miracle. The longest tug of the Lady's luck this world has ever seen. And let's face it, things don't work out that way. They never do.*

'I smelled smoke,' said Amby.

'When?'

He shrugged. 'Dawn. The wind had yet to turn. Was running before the sun.'

East. She stood, studied the rumpled wastes. Was that a faint haze? No, that veil was too big. A cloud. 'Well,' she said, 'it's where we were headed, more or less.'

If the man wanted to smell things, fine. Made no difference.

'We need water,' Amby said.

Sighing, Faint turned and approached Precious Thimble. The young witch would not meet her eyes. Faint waited for a moment, and then said, 'Can you conjure water?'

'I told you—'

'Yes, the land's mostly dead. Still. Can you?'

'There's no point in trying.'

'Try anyway.'

Her eyes flashed. 'Who left you in charge?'

'You're a shareholder in the Trygalle. I have seniority here, Precious.'

'But I'm—'

'So far,' Faint cut in, 'you're nothing. Show us some magery and that might drag you up a notch or two. Open us a gate home and I'll personally crown you empress. But until then, Precious, I'm in charge.'

'It hurts.'

'What does? Listen. People die.'

But she shook her head. 'Magic. Here. The ground . . . *flinches*.'

'Precious, I don't care if it howls. Just get us some water.'

'It doesn't want us here. It doesn't want anyone here.'

'Too bad.'

Precious shivered. 'There's something . . . If it's a spirit – even the ghost of one. Maybe . . .'

'Get started on it.' Faint walked over to Sweetest Sufferance. 'Hood's breath, wake up.'

'I'm awake, cow.'

Well, turned out everyone felt as miserable as she did.

'Hungry,' said Precious Thimble.

Gods below. Faint looked to the east again. Cloud or smoke? Nearby, Amby made a groaning sound. She glanced over. Something was wrong with his face – mud streaks? Tears? No, too dark. She stepped closer. *What, is that blood?*

Nearby, the packhorse tore free of the stake tethering it and lunged away, hoofs thundering.

A rattling sound erupted from Sweetest Sufferance. Faint spun. 'Sweetie?'

The blanket-swathed form was twitching.

'Hungry,' said Precious Thimble again.

Spasms surged through Sweetest Sufferance, her limbs jumping. She kicked her way clear of the blankets, rolled on to her back. Her eyes were opened wide, filling with blood. Her face was visibly swelling. Flesh split.

'In here?' asked Precious Thimble.

Faint whirled to the witch – saw the strange tilt to her head, the drool slicking her chin. Her eyes were glazed. She rushed over. 'Get it out! Precious! Send it away!'

Sweetest Sufferance jerked upright, blood draining down from her fingertips. Bony projections had pushed through her face, closing the space for her eyes, her mouth. Her entire body shook as if something was inside, trying to escape. Tearing sounds burst from under her clothing as more bones thrust past skin, pushed at her sodden clothing.

The ground beneath the woman seemed to be cracking open.

Numb with horror, Faint backed up a step. Shock stole her will. 'Precious – please—'

Amby suddenly howled and the cry was so raw it jolted Faint awake. Twisting round once more, she rushed to Precious Thimble. Struck the woman in the face, a vicious slap, as hard as she could manage. The young witch's head rocked. Amby screamed again.

Faint glanced back at Sweetest Sufferance – but the woman was mostly gone, and in her place, rising up from the broken earth below, was a stained wrist thick as the bole of an ancient tree. The hand had pushed its fingers through the woman's body, as if fighting free of an ill-fitting glove. Gore-streaked nails clawed at the air.

The ground tilted beneath Faint, almost pitching her from her feet.

Amby staggered up to Precious Thimble – his face a mask of blood – and when his fist struck her face her entire head snapped back. She toppled. Bawling, he took her in his arms and began running.

161

The arm was reaching higher, the remnants of Sweetest Sufferance's body still clinging to the grasping hand. Blood was burning away, blackening, shedding in flakes, revealing a limb of purest jade.

Faint staggered back. A mound was rising – an entire hill – splitting the hard ground. The tree at the spring thrashed, and on its long-dead branches green suddenly sprouted, writhing like worms. Jade fruit bulged, burgeoned in clusters to pull the branches down.

Rock exploded from a ridge fifty paces to the south. High grasses waved like jade flames. A vast, gleaming boulder rocked into view – *a forehead – oh, gods below, oh, Hood. Beru – please—*

Draconus turned round, his eyes black as pools of ink. 'Wait here,' he said.

Ublala opened his mouth, but the ground was shaking, rolling like waves rushing in from somewhere to the north, and he forgot what he wanted to ask. He turned to his beloved.

Ralata was awake, crouched low on the balls of her feet. Terror filled her face as she stared past Ublala.

He turned back in time to see Draconus drawing his sword. Blackness poured from the long blade like wind-whipped shrouds, billowing out, twisting to close around the man like folding wings. Draconus disappeared inside the darkness, and the inky cloud spiralled higher, growing in size. In moments it towered over them, and then those black wings unfolded once more.

The apparition rose into the sky, enormous wings of inky smoke thundering the air.

Ublala stared after it. His mace was in his hands for some reason, and the skystone head steamed as if dipped in a forge.

He watched the huge thing fly away, northward. Not a dragon. Winged darkness. *Just that. Winged darkness.*

He licked his lips. 'Draconus?'

The brow ridges lifted clear of the shattered bedrock. Eyes blazed like emerald beacons. A second hand had thrust free, thirty paces to the west. Faint stood as if rooted to the shaking ground, as trapped as the rattling tree. Her thoughts had fled. A pressure was building inside her skull. She could hear voices, thousands, tens of thousands of voices, all speaking in a language she could not understand. They were rising in alarm, in fear, in panic. She clapped her hands to her ears, but it was no use.

They want out.

They asked. But no answers came. They begged. Pleaded. The world gave them silence. How do I know this? Their hearts – the beating – I can feel them. Feel them breaking.

Anguish tore at her soul. She could not survive this. It was too much, the pain too vast.

Icy air swept over her from behind. An enormous shadow swirled across the earth to her left. Something enshrouded in darkness, borne on vast ethereal wings, descended to where the jade head was emerging.

Faint saw the flash of something long and black, a gleaming edge, and as the darkness slammed like a tidal wave against the brow of the giant that splinter was driven forward, piercing the centre of the forehead.

Thunder cracked. Faint was thrown from her feet by the concussion. The impossible chorus of voices cried out – in pain, in shock, and something else. Beneath her the earth seemed to moan. Staggering upright once more, Faint coughed out the blood filling her mouth.

Those cries? Relief? At last. At last, an answer.

The forearm directly in front of her and the hand off to the west were suddenly motionless, the jade luminescence fading as if sheathed in dust. The tree, tilted precariously to one side, slowed its manic shivering, its branches now burdened with leaves of jade and the huge globes of fruit.

Up on the hill, the darkness coalesced, like a slowly indrawn breath, and in its place stood a tall, broad-shouldered man. His hands were clasped about the grip of a two-handed sword bleeding black streams that spun lazily in the air. She saw him struggle to pull the weapon from the jade forehead that reared like a stone wall in front of him.

He grunted when he finally succeeded. The sword slid into the scabbard slung under his left arm. He turned round, walked towards Faint. Pale skin, chiselled features, black hair, depthless eyes. As he neared her, he spoke in Daru. 'Where he came from, every god is a Shield Anvil. Woman, have you lost your mind?'

She opened her mouth for a denial, a rush of protest, but then he was walking past her. She turned, stared after him. *South? What's down there? Where are you going? No, never mind, Faint.*

Gods below, what have I just witnessed?

Her gaze returned to the sundered forehead surmounting the hill. The wound in its centre was visible even from this distance. It had nearly split the giant skull in half.

She slowly sank to her knees. *A god. That was a god. Were they both gods? Did one just murder the other?* She realized that she had wet herself. One more reek to clash with all the others. Drawing a shaky breath, she lowered her head. 'Sweetest Sufferance, I'm sorry. She warned me against it. I'm sorry, Sweetie. Please forgive me.'

She would, in a while, set out to find Amby and Precious Thimble. But not yet. *Not quite yet.*

* * *

163

Ublala watched her tying up her bedroll. 'Where are you going? We should wait. He said to wait.'

She bared her teeth but did not look at him. 'He is a demon. When he runs out of things to hunt, he'll kill and eat us.'

'No he won't. He's nice. Draconus is nice, my love—'

'Don't call me that.'

'But—'

'Be quiet. Give me back my knife.'

'I can't. You might stab me.'

'I won't. I'm leaving you both. I'm going home.'

'Home? Where is that? Can I come?'

'Only if you can swim,' she said. 'Now, at least the knife. And if you love me the way you say you do, you'll give me the rest of my weapons too.'

'I'm not supposed to.'

Venom blazed in her eyes. 'You're awake. You're holding that club. I can't hurt you. Unless you're a coward, Ublala. I can't love cowards – they disgust me.'

He hunched down. 'Just because I'm scared of you don't mean I'm a coward. I once fought five Teblor gods.'

'Of course you did. Cowards always lie.'

'And I fought against the Fangs of Death and all those tusked warriors liked me – no, that wasn't me. At least, I don't think it was.' He stared at the mace. 'But I killed Dalk. I killed a dragon. It was easy – no, it wasn't. It was hard, I think. I can't remember.'

'No end to all the lies.'

'You're right,' he said, suddenly glum. 'No end to them.'

'Give me my weapons.'

'If I do you'll die.'

'What?'

'You'll leave us, and there's no food out here unless Draconus gets it for us. You'll starve. I can't.'

'Am I your prisoner? Is that how you like it, Ublala? You want a slave?'

He looked up at her. 'Can I sex you any time if you're my slave?'

'That's not love,' she said.

'It's been so long,' he replied, 'I suppose I'll take sex instead of love. See what's happened to me?'

'Fine. I'll lie with you, if you give me my weapons afterwards.'

Ublala clutched his head. 'Oh, you're confusing me!'

She advanced on him. 'Agree to my offer, Ublala, and I'm yours—' She stopped abruptly, turned away.

He stared after her. 'What's wrong? I agree! I agree!'

'Too late,' she said. 'Your friend's back.'

Ublala twisted round to see Draconus approaching. 'He's no friend of mine,' he muttered. 'Not any more.'

'Too crowded, these Wastelands,' she said.

'Then leave us,' Torrent replied. 'We won't miss you.'

In answer, Olar Ethil picked up Absi once more, by the scruff of his neck. 'We have rested enough,' she said.

'Stop carrying him like that,' said Torrent. 'He can ride with me.'

Her neck creaked as she turned to regard him. 'Attempt to flee and I will catch you, pup.'

Torrent glanced across at the twins, who huddled together near the ring of stones where they had tried making a fire the night before. 'I won't do that,' he said.

'Sentimentality will see the death of you,' said the Bonecaster. 'Come here. Take the child.'

He strode over. When he reached for the boy, Olar Ethil's skeletal hand snapped out. Torrent was dragged close, pulled up until his eyes were less than a hand's breadth from her broken face.

'*Call upon no gods in this place,*' she hissed. 'Everything's too close to the surface. Do you understand me? Even the ghost of Toc Younger cannot withstand a summons – and he will not arrive alone.' She pushed him back. 'You have been warned – my only warning. I catch you whispering a prayer, Torrent of the Awl, and I will kill you.'

He stepped back, scowling. 'That threat's getting as old as you, hag.' He took Absi's hand and led him slowly to where his horse waited. 'And we need food – remember what that is, Olar Ethil? And water.'

He looked round but could see no sign of Telorast and Curdle – when had he last seen them? He could not recall. Sighing, he beckoned to the twins. Stavi and Storii leapt to their feet and joined him. 'Can you walk for a time?' he asked them. 'Later, you can ride, a little longer than you did yesterday. I don't mind walking.'

'Did you hear that thunder?' Stavi asked.

'Just thunder.'

'Is our father still alive?' Storii asked. 'Is he really?'

'I won't lie,' Torrent said. 'If his spirit walks the land again, he is the same as Olar Ethil. A T'lan Imass. I fear there will be little that you will recognize—'

'Except what's inside him,' said Storii. 'That won't have changed.'

Torrent glanced away. 'I hope you're right, for all our sakes.' He hesitated, and then said, 'After all, if anyone can stand up to this Bonecaster, it will be your father.'

'He'll take us back,' said Stavi. 'All three of us. You'll see.'

He nodded. 'Ready, then?'

No, he wouldn't lie to them, not about their father. But some suspicions he would keep to himself. He did not expect Olar Ethil to take them to Onos T'oolan. Absi, and perhaps even the twins, had become her currency when forcing the First Sword's hand, and she would not permit a situation where he could directly challenge her over possession of them. No, these coins of flesh she would keep well hidden.

Torrent collected up Absi, his heart clenching as the boy's arms went round his neck. The young were quick to adapt, he knew, but even then there were hurts that slipped through awareness leaving not a ripple, and they sank deep. And many years later, why, they'd shaped an entire life. *Abandon the child and all the man's tethers will be weak. Take away the child's love and the woman will be a leaf on every stream. So the older ones said. Always full of warnings, telling us all that life was a treacherous journey. That a path once begun could not easily be evaded, or twisted anew by wish or will.*

With a grinning Absi settled on the saddle, his small hands gripping the horn, Torrent collected the reins. The twins falling in beside him, he set off after Olar Ethil.

The thunder had stopped as quickly as it had begun, and the cloudless sky was unchanged. Terrible forces were in play in these Wastelands, enough to shake even the deathless witch striding so purposefully ahead of them. '*Call upon no gods in this place.*' A curious warning. Had someone prayed? He snorted. *When did praying achieve anything but silence? Anything but the pathetic absence filling the air, building like a bubble of nothingness in the soul? Since when didn't a prayer leave only empty yearning, where wishes burned and longing was a knife twisting in the chest?*

Call upon no gods in this place. Summon not Toc Anaster, my one-eyed guardian who can ride through the veil, who can speak with the voice of death itself. Why do you so fear him, Olar Ethil? What can he do to you?

But I know the answer to that, don't I?

Ahead, the Bonecaster hesitated, turning to stare at Torrent.

When he smiled, she faced forward again and resumed her walk.

Yes, Olar Ethil. These Wastelands are very crowded indeed. Step lightly, hag, as if that will do any good.

Absi made a strange grunting sound, and then sang, 'Tollallallallalla! Tollallallalla!'

Every word from a child is itself a prayer. A blessing. Dare we answer? Beware little Absi, Olar Ethil. There are hurts that slip through. You killed his dog.

You killed his dog.

*   *   *

The fabric between the warrens was shredded. Gaping holes yawned on all sides. As befitted his veered form, Gruntle moved in the shadows, a creature of stealth, muscles rolling beneath his barbed hide, eyes flaring like embers in the night. But purchase under his padded paws was uncertain. Vistas shifted wildly before his fixed gaze. Only desperation – and perhaps madness – had taken him on these paths.

One moment flowing down a bitter cold scree of moss-backed boulders, the next moving like a ghost through a cathedral forest cloaked in fetid gloom. In yet another, the air was foul with poisons, and he found himself forced to swim a river, the waters thick and crusted with brown foam. Up on to the bank and into a village of cut stone crowded with carriages, passing through a graveyard, a fox pitching an eerie cry upon catching his scent.

He stumbled upon two figures – their sudden appearance so startling him that alarm unleashed his instincts – a snarl, sudden rush, claws and then fangs. Screams tore the night air. His jaws crunched down through the bones of a human neck. A lash of one clawed paw ripped one side from a dog, flinging the dying beast into the brush. And then through, away from that world and into a sodden jungle lit by flashes of lightning – the reek of sulphur heavy in the air.

Down a bank of mud, into a charnel pit of rotting corpses, the bloated bodies of men and horses, someone singing plaintively in the distance.

A burning forest.

The corridor of a palace or temple – dozens of robed people fleeing with shrieks – and once more he tore through them. Human blood filling his mouth, the taste appallingly sweet. Dragging bodies down from behind, crunching through skulls – weak fists thumping into his flanks—

Somewhere deep inside him, he loosed a sob, tearing himself free – and once more the world shifted, a barren tundra now, someone kneeling beside a boulder, head lifting, eyes meeting his.

'Stop this. Now. Child of Treach, you lose yourself to the beast's blood.'

A woman, her long black hair thick and glossy as a panther's hide, her face broad, the cheekbones high and flaring, her amber eyes filled with knowing. A few rags of caribou skin for clothes, despite the frigid air.

'When you find me,' she continued, 'it will not be as you imagine. We shall not meet as lovers. We shall not desire the same things. It may be we shall fight, you and me.'

He crouched, sides heaving, muscles trembling, but the blind rage was fading.

She made an odd gesture with one hand. 'A cat leaps, takes the life of a bird. Another takes the life of a child playing in the garden. This *is what a cat does, do you deny this? Is there a crime in these scenes? Perhaps. For the bird, the crime of carelessness, incaution. The child? An inattentive parent? An ill-chosen place to dwell in?*

'*The chicks in their nest cry out for a mother who will not return. Her death is their deaths. The mother grieves her loss, but perhaps there will be another child, a new life to replace the one lost. Tell me, Gruntle, how does one measure these things? How does one decide which life is the more precious? Are feelings apportioned according to intelligence and self-awareness? Does a tiny creature grieve less deeply than one of greater . . . stature?*

'*But is it not natural to rage for vengeance, for retribution? Does the dead bird's mate dream of murder?*

'*Child of Treach, you have taken more than just children, on this hard path of yours. In your wake, much grief now swirls. Your arrival was inexplicable to their senses, but the proof of your presence lay in pools of blood.*

'*Be the weapon of random chance if you must. Be the unimaginable force that strikes down with no reason, no purpose. Be the taker of lives.*

'*I will await you, at the end of this path. Will we discuss vengeance? With fang and claw?*'

At the threat a low growl rumbled from his chest.

Her smile was sad. She gestured again—

Blinking, Gruntle found himself on his hands and knees, stony ground under him. He coughed and then spat to clear gobs of thick blood from his mouth, reached up and wiped his wet lips – on the back of his hand a red smear and strands of human hair. 'Gods below,' he muttered. 'That was a mistake.'

The warrens were falling apart. *Where was I going? What was I running from?* But he remembered. Betrayals. Weaknesses. The flaws of being human – he'd sought an escape. A headlong plunge into mindlessness, fleeing from all manner of remorse and recrimination. *Running away.*

'But what is the point?' he said under his breath. *To forget is to forget myself. Who I am, and that I must not surrender. If I do, I will have nothing left.*

Ah, but still . . . to be blameless. A cat above the tiny carcass of a bird. Above the corpse of a child.

Blameless.

But the bastards hunting me down don't care about that. A child has died. Mothers bow in wretched grief. Weapons are taken in hand. The world is a dangerous place; they mean to make it less so. They yearn to die ancient and withered in straw beds, at the end of a long life, with skins upon their walls proclaiming their bravery.

168

Well then, come to me if you must. To your eyes I am a monstrous tiger. But in my mind, I have a man's cunning. And yes, I know all about vengeance.

He could see now where his path was taking him. Trake's deadly gift was turning in his hands, finding a new, terrible shape. 'You would set yourselves apart, then? Not animal. Something other. Very well, then there will be war.'

Brushing at his eyes, he climbed slowly to his feet. *Admire the beast. He is brave. Even as he charges your spear. And should you then stand above my corpse, note well your own bravery, but in my lifeless eyes see this truth: what we have shared in this clash of courage, friend, was not a thing of sentience or intelligence. Skill and luck may be triumphant, but these are nature's gifts.*

Confuse this at your peril.

'Treach, hear me. I will fight this war. I see its . . . inevitability. I will charge the spear.' *Because I have no choice.* He bared his teeth. 'Just make my death worthwhile.'

Somewhere ahead, she awaited him. He still did not know what that meant.

The veil between human and beast was shredded, and he found himself looking out from both sides. Desperation and madness. *Oh, Stonny, I cannot keep my promise. I am sorry. If I could but set my eyes upon your face one more time.* He sighed. 'Yes, woman, to answer your cruel question, the bird's mate dreams of murder.'

The tears kept returning. Blurring his vision, streaming down his scarred, pitted cheeks. But Mappo forced himself onward, fighting each step he took. Two wills were locked in battle. The need to find his friend. The need to flee his shame. The war was now a thing of pain – there had been a time, so long ago now, when he had not shied from self-regard; when, for all the deceits guiding his life, he had understood the necessity, the sharp clarity of his purpose.

He stood between the world and Icarium. Why? *Because the world was worth saving. Because there was love, and moments of peace. Because compassion existed, like a blossom in a crack of stone, a fulsome truth, a breathtaking miracle.* And Icarium was a weapon of destruction, senseless, blind. Mappo had given his life to keeping that weapon in its scabbard, peace-strapped, forgotten.

In the name of compassion, and love.

Which he had just walked away from. Turning his back upon children, so as to not see the hurt in their eyes, that hardening flatness as yet another betrayal beset their brief lives. Because, he told himself, their future was uncertain, yet still alive with possibilities. *But if Icarium*

169

should awaken, and no one is there to stop him, those possibilities will come to an end. Does this not make sense? Oh yes, indeed it made sense.

And still, it was wrong. I know it. I feel it. I can't hide from it. If I harden myself to compassion, then what am I trying to save?

And so he wept. For himself. In the face of shame, grief burned away. In the face of shame, he began to lose who he was, who he had always believed himself to be. Duty, pride in his vow, his sacrifice – it all crumbled. He tried to imagine finding Icarium, his oldest friend. He tried to envision a return to the old ways, to his words of deception in the name of love, to the gentle games of feint and sleight of hand that they played to keep horrifying truths at bay. Everything as it once was, and at the core of it all Mappo's willingness to surrender his own life rather than see the Lifestealer's eyes catch flame.

He did not know if he could do that any more. A man's heart must be pure for such a thing, cleansed of all doubts, sufficient to make death itself a worthy sacrifice. But the solid beliefs of years past had now broken down.

He felt hunched down inside himself, as if folding round an old wound, leaving his bones feeling frail, a cage that could crumple at the first hint of pressure.

The wasted land passed him by on all sides, barely observed. The day's heat faltered before the conflagration in his skull.

Mappo forced himself onward. He had to find Icarium now, more than ever. *To beg forgiveness. And to end it.*

My friend. I am not enough any more. I am not the warrior you once knew. I am not the wall to lean your weary self against. I have betrayed children, Icarium. Look into my eyes and see the truth of this.

I beg a release.

'End it, Icarium. Please, end this.'

Stormy thought he could make out a pall of dust to the southeast. No telling how far – the horizons played tricks in this place. The lizard he rode devoured leagues. It never seemed to tire. Glancing back, he glowered at the drones plodding in his wake. K'ell Hunters ranged on his flanks, sometimes visible, but mostly not, lost somewhere in the deceptive folds and creases of the landscape.

I'm riding a damned Ve'Gath. The nastiest weapon of war I've ever seen. I don't need a damned escort. All right, so it needed to be fed come evening. There was that to consider. *But I'm a man. I hate the need to consider anything. It's not a problem either. Mostly.*

He preferred being just a corporal. This Shield Anvil business left a sour taste in his mouth. *Aye, there's a sentimental streak in me. I don't deny it, and maybe it's wide as an ocean like Ges says. But I didn't ask for it. I cried for a dying mouse once – dying because I tried to catch it only my hand was too clumsy and something got broken inside. Lying there in my palm, breaths coming so fast, but the tiny limbs'd stopped moving, and then the breaths slowed.*

I knelt on the stones and watched it slowly die. There in my hand. Gods, it's enough to make me bawl all over again, just remembering. How old was I? Twenty?

He leaned to one side and cleared his nose, one nostril and then the other. Then cleaned his moustache with his fingers, wiping them on his leg. Dust cloud any closer? Hard to say.

Clearing a rise, he cursed and silently ordered his mount to a halt. The basin below stretched out three hundred or more paces, and half that distance out a dozen or so figures were standing or sitting in a rough circle. As soon as he came into view the ones standing turned to face him, while the ones sitting slowly climbed upright and did the same.

They were tall, gaunt, and armoured in black chain, black scales and black leather.

The Ke'll Hunters had appeared suddenly to Stormy's right and left and were closing up at a swift lope, their massive cutlasses held out to the sides.

Stormy could taste something oily and bitter.

'Calm down, lizards,' he said under his breath, kicking the Ve'Gath into motion. 'They ain't drawing.'

Dark narrow faces beneath ornate helms tracked Stormy's approach. Withered faces. *Those bastards are tusked. Jaghut? Must be – that old bust of Gothos in Aren's Grey Temple had tusks like those. But then, these fellows ain't looking too good. T'lan? Did the Jaghut have T'lan? Oh, never mind these questions, idiot. Just ask 'em. Or not.* Ten paces between them, Stormy reined in. The Hunters halted a few paces back, settled and planted the tips of their cutlasses in the hard earth.

He studied the warriors before him. 'Ugly,' he muttered.

One spoke, though Stormy wasn't immediately certain from which one the voice came. 'Do you see this, Bolirium?'

'I see,' another answered.

'A human – well, mostly human. Hard to tell behind all that hair. But let us be generous. A human, with K'Chain as pets. And only a few moments ago, Bolirium, you had the nerve to suggest that the world was a better place than when we'd last left it.'

'I did,' Bolirium admitted, and then added, 'I was an idiot.'

Low laughter.

A third Jaghut then said, 'K'Chain and termites, Gedoran. Find one . . .'

'And you know there's a hundred thousand more in the woodwork. As you say, Varandas.'

'And with that other smell . . .'

'Just so,' Gedoran said – and Stormy found him by the nod accompanying the words. 'Dust.'

'Dreams and nightmares, Gedoran, hide in the same pit. Reach down and you're blind to what you pull out.'

They were all speaking Falari, which was ridiculous. Stormy snorted, and then said, 'Listen. You're in my way.'

Gedoran stepped forward. 'You did not come in search of us?'

'Do I really look that stupid? No. Why, should I have?'

'He is impertinent.'

'Daryft, a human riding a Ve'Gath can be as impertinent as he likes,' said Bolirium.

Hard laughter, heads rocking back.

Stormy said, 'You're in the middle of nowhere. What are you up to?'

'Ah,' said Gedoran, 'now that is a pertinent query. We have sent our commander on a quest, and now await his return.'

'You order your commander around?'

'Yes, isn't that wonderful?'

The Jaghut laughed again, a habit, Stormy decided as it went on, and on, that could prove maddening. 'Well, I'll leave you to it, then.'

The fourteen Jaghut bowed, and Gedoran said, 'Until we meet again, Shield Anvil.'

'I don't intend to ride back the way I came in.'

'Wisdom is not yet dead,' said Bolirium. 'Did I not suggest this to you all?'

'Amidst a host of idiotic assertions, perhaps you did.'

'Varandas, there must be a balance in the world. On one side a morsel of weighty wisdom, offsetting a gastric avalanche of brainless stupidity. Is that not the way of things?'

'But Bolirium, a drop of perfume cannot defeat a heap of shit.'

'That depends, Varandas, on where you put your nose.'

Gedoran said, 'Be sure to inform us, Varandas, when you finally smell something sweet.'

'Don't hold your breath, Gedoran.'

To raucous laughter, Stormy kicked the Ve'Gath into motion, steering the creature to the left to ride round the Jaghut. Once past he urged his mount into a loping trot. A short while later the K'ell Hunters drew in closer.

He could smell their unease. 'Aye,' he muttered.

He wondered who the commander was. *Must be a damned idiot. But then, anything to escape that laughing. Aye, now that makes sense.*

Why, I'd probably ride straight up Hood's arsehole to get away from that lot.

And as soon as I smell something sweet, boys and girls, why, I'll ride straight back and tell you.

That dust cloud looked closer. Maybe.

CHAPTER SEVEN

'Awaiting Restitution'
Epigraph on gravestone, Lether

'Is IT AS I SEE?' BRYS BEDDICT ASKED. 'THE FATE OF THE WORLD IN THE hands of three women?'

Atri-Ceda Aranict drew one more time on the stick and then flicked the stub into the fire. *Into flames* . . . She held the smoke in her lungs as long as she could, as if in refusing to breathe out she could hold back time itself. *I saw caverns. I saw darkness . . . and the rain, gods below, the rain* . . . Finally, she sighed. If there was any smoke left she didn't see it. 'Not three women alone,' she said. 'There is one man. You.'

They sat undisturbed before the fire. Soldiers slept. The bawling of animals awaiting slaughter had died down for the night. Cookfires dwindled as the swirling wind ate the last dung, and the air was filled with ashes. Come the dawn . . . *we leave. Broken apart, each our separate ways. Could I have imagined this? Did she know? She must have. By her sword we are shattered.*

'It was necessary,' said Brys.

'You sound as if you are trying convince yourself,' she observed, drawing a taper from her belt sheath and reaching to set one end into the flames. Watched as it caught. Brought the lurid fire closer to her face to light yet another stick.

'I understood her, I think.' He grunted. 'Well, as much as anyone could.'

She nodded. 'The look on the faces of her officers.'

'Stunned. Yes.'

She thought of Fist Blistig. 'Appalled.'

He glanced across at her. 'I worried for you, my love. Abrastal's daughter—'

'A potent child indeed, to find us from so far away.' She pulled on the stick. 'I was unprepared. The visions made no sense. They over-whelmed me.'

'Are you able to make sense of them now?'

'No.'

'Will you describe them to me, Aranict?'

She dropped her gaze.

'Forgive me for asking,' he said. 'I did not think – you should not have to relive such trauma. Ah, I am tired and tomorrow will be a long day.'

She heard the invitation in his words, but the flames of the hearth held her in place. *Something. A promise. A warning. I need to think on this.* 'I will join you, love, soon.'

'Of course. If you find me dead to the world . . .'

She flinched, recovered and said, 'I shall be careful not to wake you.'

He leaned close and she turned to meet his lips with hers. Saw the tenderness of his smile as he pulled away.

Then she was alone, and her gaze returned again to the flames. *A parley. A meeting of minds. Well.*

It had begun simply enough. Regal riders reining before the command tent, soldiers appearing to take the horses. Greetings exchanged with the Malazan officers awaiting these distinguished guests. The Adjunct was within, yes. Her wounds? She has recovered, thankfully. We're afraid there will be little formality in all this, Highness – is it not best that we each make our own introductions? Mortal Sword, Shield Anvil, it is good to see you both . . .

Fist Faradan Sort had held to her own standard of formality, Aranict supposed. Both comfortable and respectful. Whereas Fists Kindly and Blistig had said nothing, the tension between the two men palpable.

She'd stood close to Commander Brys. It was difficult to know where to look. The Khundryl women, Hanavat and Shelemasa, held back from the others, as if uncertain of their own worth. As words were exchanged between Sort and Krughava and Abrastal on the matter of who should enter first – a clash of deference, of all things – Aranict edged back a step and made her way over to the Khundryl.

They observed her approach with evident trepidation. Aranict stopped, drew out her pouch and counted out three sticks of rustleaf. She held them up with brows raised. Sudden smiles answered her.

She stood and smoked with them, a few paces back from all the others, and Aranict caught Brys's eye and was pleased by the pride she saw in her lover's regard.

It was finally determined that Queen Abrastal would be the first to enter, accompanied by the Barghast Warchief Spax, followed by the Perish. When faces turned to the Khundryl women, Hanavat gestured with one hand – clearly, now that she had something to do, she was content to wait. Shelemasa seemed even more relieved.

Brys approached. 'Atri-Ceda Aranict, if you please, would you escort the Khundryl inside once you are . . . er, done here.'

'Of course,' she replied. 'It will be my pleasure.'

Moments later the three women were alone apart from the two soldiers flanking the tent's entrance.

Hanavat was the first to speak. 'I am tempted to go back to my people. I do not belong in such company.'

'You stand in your husband's stead,' said Aranict.

She grimaced. 'It is not what I would choose.'

'No one is blind to that,' Aranict said, as gently as she could. 'But, if you like, I can invent an excuse . . .'

'No,' Hanavat said. 'Even my husband struggled in this particular duty. The Burned Tears are sworn to the field of battle, in the memory of Coltaine of the Crow clan.' She released a harsh stream of smoke. 'But it seems failure finds us no matter where we turn.' She nodded to the tent. 'I will stand before their disappointment since my husband dares not. My midwives tell me again and again that a woman's spirit is stronger than a man's. This day I mean to prove it.'

'If you like, I shall introduce you, Hanavat.'

'I expect no such formalities, Atri-Ceda. The Adjunct has more important matters to attend to in there.'

'My head is spinning,' said Shelemasa.

'It passes,' said Aranict.

A short time later they were done. Hanavat gestured for Aranict to precede them. The Atri-Ceda turned to the tent entrance, but then Hanavat said, 'Aranict.'

'Yes?'

'Thank you.'

'My commander spoke from the heart with the words he gave you earlier, Hanavat. The Khundryl have nothing to be ashamed of. Indeed, the very opposite is true.' She led them into the command tent.

In the outer chamber were the two Malazan captains, Raband and Skanarow. Muted voices came from the other side of the curtain.

Skanarow gave them all a strained smile. 'We decided we didn't want to crowd the room.'

When Shelemasa hesitated, Hanavat took the younger woman by the arm.

Aranict drew the entrance curtain to one side. The Khundryl women entered the chamber.

Conversation fell away.

As Aranict stepped in she sensed the tension. Mortal Sword Krughava's face was dark with anger – or shame. A pace behind her was the Shield Anvil, pale, clearly rattled. Brys stood to the right, his back almost brushing the curtain wall. Alarm was writ plain on his face. To the left stood the queen, taut and watchful as her sharp eyes tracked from Krughava to the Adjunct and back again. Who had just been speaking? Aranict wasn't sure.

The Fists stood to the Adjunct's left, close to the corner of the chamber. Banaschar leaned against a support pole on the other side, his arms crossed and his eyelids half lowered. Close by, as if ready to catch the ex-priest should he collapse, was Lostara Yil.

Adjunct Tavore looked hale, her expression severe, holding Krughava's glare unflinchingly.

Upon the arrival of the Khundryl, Fist Faradan Sort cleared her throat and said, 'Adjunct, it pleases me to introduce—'

'No need,' Tavore replied, setting her regard upon Shelemasa. The Adjunct stepped forward, forcing apart the Mortal Sword and the queen. 'I assume you are Shelemasa, who succeeded in rallying the survivors of the Charge, guiding the retreat and so saving many lives. It is said you were the last to leave the field. Your presence here honours us all.' She paused, and then turned to Hanavat. 'Precious mother,' she said, 'I grieve for your terrible losses. It grieves me too that, in this time, your husband dwells only upon his own losses. It is my hope that he soon awakens to the gifts remaining in his life.' Tavore looked at the others. 'Hanavat and Shelemasa are Khundryl Burned Tears, our longest-standing allies. Their sacrifice on the day of the Nah'ruk saved the lives of thousands. On this day, as upon every other, I value their counsel. Fist Kindly, find a chair for Hanavat – it is not proper that she stand with her child so near.'

Aranict saw Hanavat fighting back tears, welling up behind her astonishment, and if the two women now stood taller than they had a moment earlier . . . *Adjunct Tavore, you continue to surprise us.*

Tavore returned to her original position. 'The Bonehunters,' she said, 'have had enough time to lick their wounds. Now we must march in earnest.'

Krughava's voice was harsh with suppressed emotion. 'We are sworn to—'

'Serve me,' the Adjunct snapped. 'You have sworn to serve me, and that I need to remind you of this pains me, Mortal Sword.'

'You do not,' Krughava said in a tone like honed iron. 'Your army is damaged, Adjunct. We stand before you – all of us here – and would pledge ourselves to your cause—'

'Not quite,' cut in Queen Abrastal, 'since I don't yet understand that cause, and by the look on the face of Prince Brys I suspect he shares my unease.'

Krughava hissed a curse in her own language, and then tried again.

'Adjunct. Now is the time to coalesce our respective forces, thus bolstering our strength—'

'No.'

The word struck like a knife driven into the floor between them.

The colour left Krughava's face. 'If you doubt our loyalty or courage—'

'I do not,' Tavore replied. 'In fact, I am depending on it.'

'But this makes no sense!'

The Adjunct turned to Abrastal. 'Highness, your presence here is most unexpected, but welcome. Your kingdom, even more than that of King Tehol, has had long-term contact with those territories of Kolanse and the South Kingdoms of the Pelasiar Sea.'

'That is true, Adjunct.'

'What can you tell us of the situation there?'

The queen's brows lifted. 'I assumed you were entirely aware of where you are headed, Adjunct. If that is not the case, then I am baffled. What manner of war do you seek? What is the cause for this belligerence of yours?'

It seemed that Tavore was unwilling to answer. Silence stretched.

The one who finally spoke startled them all. 'The Worm will feed.' Banaschar slowly lifted his head. 'She will gorge on the slaughter to come.' His bleary gaze wandered among them, settled on the Bolkando queen. 'What are you worth? Any of you?' He nodded to the Adjunct. 'She thinks . . . enough. Enough worth to fight an impossible war. For you, Highness. And you, Prince Brys. And,' he faltered for a moment, as if about to be sick, 'even me.'

'I don't understand,' said Abrastal, 'but I will let the matter rest for now. To answer you, Adjunct, I must weave a tale. And,' she added, 'my throat grows parched.'

Sort walked to the curtain entrance, leaned out and ordered her captains to find some ale.

The queen snorted and then said, 'Well, I suppose ale better suits a story told than does wine. Very well, I shall begin. They came from the sea. Isn't that always the way? No matter. There was trouble in the lands long before that day, however. Decades of drought. Uprisings, civil wars, usurpations, a host of once wealthy nations now verging on utter collapse.

'In such times, prophets are known to rise. Bold revolutions, the heads of kings and queens on spear points, blood in the streets. But against a sky empty of rain no cause triumphs, no great leader from the masses can offer salvation, and before long even *their* heads adorn spikes.'

Sort arrived with a cask of ale and a dozen or so tin cups. She set about serving drinks, beginning with the queen.

Abrastal swallowed down a quick mouthful, sighed, and resumed, 'One can imagine how it must have felt. The world was ending. Civilization itself had failed, revealing its terrible fragilities – that clutter of thin sticks holding it all upright. In place of rain, despair settled upon the lands. In Kolanse, only the province of Estobanse thrived. Fed by glacial streams and rivers, sheltered from the hot winds of the south, by this one province all of Kolanse struggled on – but there were too many mouths to feed and the strain was taking its toll. If there was a solution to this strait, it was too cruel to contemplate.

'The strangers from the sea had no such qualms, and when they cast down the rulers of Kolanse they did what they deemed necessary—'

'A cull,' said the Adjunct, and that word seemed to take the life from Tavore's eyes.

Abrastal regarded Tavore a moment over the rim of her cup, drank, and then nodded. 'Just so. In the first year, they reduced the population of Kolanse by fifty per cent. The least fit, the elderly, the sickly. Another ten per cent the next year, and then, with more of their own kind coming in great ships, they sent armies into the South Kingdoms. Adjudication, they called it. They titled themselves Inquisitors, in their hands they held the justice of the land itself – and that justice proved harsh indeed.'

Abrastal hesitated, and then shrugged. 'That was pretty much the end of our trade with the east. As we are people of the land, not the sea, we sent out merchant caravans along the old south routes, but those few that returned told tales of nothing but desolation. The merchant ships we then hired ventured into the Pelasiar Sea, and found silted-in ports and abandoned cities all along the coasts. They could find no one left with whom to trade.'

'Did they travel onward to Kolanse?' Tavore asked.

'Only the first few. With reason. The Inquisitors did not welcome visitors.' She drained her cup and held it out for a refill. 'We considered war, Adjunct. Though the ships were not our own, we'd given them royal charter, and we were most displeased by the slaughter of innocents.' She glanced over at her Barghast Warchief. 'We even hired ourselves a mercenary army.'

'Yet you declared no war,' observed Brys.

'No. I sent an agent, my Eleventh Daughter. She did not survive, yet was able to send me . . . a message. These Inquisitors were not human at all.'

'Justice,' said Banaschar, pulling a small jug from his cloak, 'the sweet contradiction they took to, like . . .' he regarded the jug, 'like wine. There is no true justice, they will say, without the most basic right that is retribution. Exploit the world at your peril, dear friends. One day

179

someone will decide to speak for that world. One day, someone will come calling.' He snorted. 'But Forkrul Assail? Gods below, even the Liosan would've done better.' He tilted the jug back, drank, and then sighed. 'There were temples to D'rek once. In Kolanse.' He grinned at Tavore. 'Woe to all a priest's confessions, eh, Adjunct?'

'Not human,' repeated Abrastal. 'Their power was unassailable, and it seemed to be growing. We declared no war,' and she looked up into the Adjunct's eyes, 'but here we are.'

Adjunct Tavore faced Brys Beddict. 'Prince, I have not had the opportunity to thank you for your intervention on the day of the Nah'ruk. That the Bonehunters still exist is due to your bravery and that of your soldiers. Without you and the Khundryl, we would never have extricated ourselves from that engagement.'

'I fear, Adjunct,' said Brys, 'that we were not enough, and I am sure Warleader Gall, and indeed Hanavat here, feel the same. Your army is hurt. The stand by the heavy infantry and the marines took from you the very soldiers you need the most.' He glanced at Krughava briefly, and then continued, 'Adjunct, I share the Mortal Sword's dismay at what you now propose.'

'The Bonehunters,' said Tavore, 'will march alone.'

'Do you say then,' Brys asked, 'that you have no further need of us?'

'No, my need for you has never been greater.'

Queen Abrastal held out her cup, and as Sort refilled it she said, 'Then you have misled me, Adjunct. Clearly, you know more of the enemy – these Forkrul Assail – and their aims than do any of us. Or,' she corrected, 'you think you do. I would point out that the Inquisitors no longer appear to hold to expansionist intentions – the Errant knows, they've had enough time to prove otherwise.'

Banaschar's laugh was soft yet grating. 'The Bonehunters march alone, leaking blood with every step. Fists, captains and cooks all ask the same thing: what does she know? How does she know it? Who speaks to this hard woman with the flat eyes, this Otataral sword stolen from the Empress's scabbard? Was it Quick Ben, our mysterious High Mage who no longer walks with us? Was it Fist Keneb? Or perhaps the Empress is not the mistress of betrayal as we all believe and the Empire's High Mage Tayschrenn now creeps in step with us, a shadow no one casts.' He toasted with his jug. 'Or has she simply gone mad? But no, none of us think so, do we? She *knows*. Something. But what? And how?' He drank, weaved a moment as if about to fall, then steadied himself before Lostara Yil reached him. Noticing her, he offered the woman a loose smile.

'Or is the ex-priest whispering in her ear?' The question was asked by Fist Blistig, his tone strained and cold.

Banaschar's brows lifted. 'The last priest of D'rek has no time for whispering, my dear boneless Fist Blistig—'

The Fist grunted an oath and would have stepped forward if Kindly had not edged deftly into his path.

Smiling, Banaschar went on. 'All the chewing deafens him, anyway. Gnawing, on all sides. The dog has wounds – don't touch!' He waved with his jug in the Adjunct's direction. 'The Bonehunters march alone, oh yes, more alone than anyone could imagine. But look to Tavore now – look carefully, friends. This solitude she insists upon, why, it's not complicated at all. Are you not all commanders? Friends, this is simple. It's called . . . *tactics*.'

Aranict looked to Brys in the odd silence that followed, and she saw the glint of something awaken in his eyes, as if an unknown language had suddenly become comprehensible. 'Adjunct,' he said, 'against the Lether Empire, you struck both overland and by sea. We reeled from one direction and then another.'

'You say you need us more than ever,' said Mortal Sword Krughava then, 'because we are to invade on more than one front. Adjunct?'

'Directly east of us waits the Glass Desert,' Tavore said. 'While it offers the shortest route into the territories of the Forkrul Assail, this path is not only reputedly treacherous but by all accounts impossible for an army to traverse.' She studied the Perish. 'That is the path the Bonehunters will take. Mortal Sword, you cannot accompany us, because we cannot feed you, nor supply you with water. Beyond the Glass Desert, by Queen Abrastal's own account, the land scarcely improves.'

'A moment, please.' The Bolkando queen was staring at the Adjunct. 'The only viable overland routes are the southern caravan tracks. The Glass Desert is truly impassable. If you take your army into it you will destroy what's left of the Bonehunters – not one of you will emerge.'

'We shall cross the Glass Desert,' said the Adjunct, 'emerging to the southwest of Estobanse Province. And we mean to be seen by the enemy at the earliest opportunity. And they shall gather their forces to meet us, and a battle shall be fought. One battle.'

Something in Tavore's tone made Aranict gasp and she felt herself grow cold with horror.

'What of the Grey Helms?' Krughava demanded.

'In the Bay of Kolanse there rises a natural edifice known as the Spire. Atop this fastness there is a temple. Within this temple something is trapped. Something wounded, something that needs to be freed. The Bonehunters shall be the lodestone to the forces of the Forkrul Assail, Mortal Sword, but it is the Perish who will strike the death blow against the enemy.'

Aranict saw Krughava's iron eyes narrowing. 'We are to take the south route.'

'Yes.'

A battle. One battle. She means to sacrifice herself and her soldiers. Oh, by all the Holds, she cannot—

'You invite mutiny,' said Fist Blistig, his face flushed dark. 'Tavore – you cannot ask this of us.'

And she faced her Fists then, and said in a whisper, '*But I must.*'

'Unwitnessed,' said Faradan Sort, ghost-pale, dry-lipped. 'Adjunct, this battle you seek. If we face an enemy believing only in our own deaths—'

Banaschar spoke, and Aranict was shocked to see tears streaming down his cheeks. 'To the executioner's axe there are those who kneel, head bowed, and await their fate. Then there are those who fight, who strain, who cry out their defiance even as the blade descends.' He pointed a finger at Blistig. 'Now you will speak true, Fist: which one is Adjunct Tavore?'

'A drunken fool speaks for our commander?' Blistig's voice was vicious. He bared his teeth. 'How damned appropriate! Will you stand there with us on that day, Banaschar?'

'I shall.'

'Drunk.' The word was a sneer.

The man's answering smile was terrible. 'No. Stone sober, Blistig. As befits your one – your only – witness.'

'Hood take your damned executioner! I will have none of this!' Blistig appealed to his fellow Fists. 'Knowing what you now know, will you lead your soldiers to their deaths? If this Glass Desert doesn't kill us, the Assail will. And all for what? A feint? A fucking *feint*?' He spun to the Adjunct. 'Is that all we're worth, woman? A rusty dagger for one last thrust and if the blade snaps, what of it?'

Krughava spoke. 'Adjunct Tavore. This thing that is wounded, this thing in the temple upon the Spire – what is it that you wish freed?'

'The heart of the Crippled God,' Tavore replied.

The Mortal Sword seemed visibly rocked by that. Behind her, with eyes shining, Tanakalian asked, '*Why?*'

'The Forkrul Assail draw upon its blood, Shield Anvil. They seek to open the Gates of Justice upon this world. Akhrast Korvalain. To unleash the fullest measure of power, they intend to drive a blade through that heart when the time is right—'

'And when is that?' Abrastal demanded.

'When the Spears of Jade arrive, Highness. Less than three months from now, if Banaschar's calculations are correct.'

The ex-priest grunted. 'D'rek is coiled about time itself, friends.'

Clearing his throat, Brys asked, 'The Jade Spears, Adjunct. What are they?'

'The souls of his worshippers, Prince. His beloved believers. They are coming for their god.'

Chills tracked Aranict's spine.

'If the heart is freed,' said Krughava, 'then . . . he can return to them.'

'Yes.'

'He will leave pieces behind no matter what,' said Banaschar. 'Pulling him down tore him apart. But there should be enough. As for the rest, well, "for the rotted flesh, the Worm sings".' His laugh was bitter. He stared at Tavore. 'See her? Look well, all of you. She is the madness of ambition, friends. From beneath the hands of the Forkrul Assail, and those of the gods themselves, she means to steal the Crippled God's heart.'

Queen Abrastal gusted out a breath. 'My Fourteenth Daughter is even now approaching the South Kingdoms. She is a sorceress of considerable talent. If we are to continue this discussion of tactics, I will seek to open a path to her—'

The Adjunct cut in. 'Highness, this is not your war.'

'Forgive me, Adjunct Tavore, but I believe it is.' She turned to her Barghast Warchief. 'Spax, your warriors hunger for a scrap – what say you?'

'Where you lead, Highness, the White Face Gilk shall follow.'

'The Otataral sword I wear—'

'Forgive me again, Adjunct, but the power my daughter is drawing upon now happens to be Elder. Omtose Phellack.'

Tavore blinked. 'I see.'

Brys Beddict then spoke. 'Mortal Sword Krughava, if you will accept the alliance of Queen Abrastal, will you accept mine?'

The grey-haired woman bowed. 'Prince – and Highness – the Perish are honoured. But . . .' she hesitated, then continued, 'I must tell you all, I shall be harsh company. Knowing what the Bonehunters face . . . knowing that they will face it alone, as wounded as the very heart they would see freed . . . ah, my mood is grim indeed, and I do not expect that to change. When at last I strike for the Spire, you will be hard pressed to match my determination.'

Brys smiled. 'A worthy challenge, Mortal Sword.'

The Adjunct walked to stand once more before Hanavat. 'Mother,' she said, 'I would ask this of you: will the Khundryl march with the Bonehunters?'

Hanavat seemed to struggle finding her voice. 'Adjunct, we are few.'

'Nonetheless.'

'Then . . . yes, we shall march with you.'

Queen Abrastal asked, 'Adjunct? Shall I call upon Felash, my Fourteenth Daughter? There are matters of tactics and logistics awaiting us this day. By your leave, I—'

'I am done with this!' Blistig shouted, turning to leave.

'Stand where you are, Fist,' Tavore said in a voice like bared steel.

'I resign—'

'I forbid it.'

He stared at her, mouth open in shock.

'Fists Blistig, Kindly and Faradan Sort, our companies need to be readied for tomorrow's march. I shall call upon you all at dusk to hear reports of our status. Until then, you are dismissed.'

Kindly grasped Blistig by one arm and marched him out, Sort following with a wry smile.

'Omtose Phellack,' muttered Banaschar once they'd left. 'Adjunct, I was chilled enough the last time. Will you excuse me?'

Tavore nodded. 'Captain Yil, please escort our priest to his tent, lest he get lost.' She then shot Aranict a glance, as if to ask *Are you ready for this?* To which Aranict nodded.

Abrastal sighed. 'Very well, shall we begin?'

Aranict saw that the dung had burned down to dull ashes. She flicked away the gutted butt of her last stick, and then stood, lifting her gaze to the Spears of Jade.

We'll do what we can. Today, we promised as much. What we can. One battle. Oh, Tavore . . .

Sick and shaken as she had been, her hardest journey this day had been back through the Bonehunter camp. The soldiers, their faces, the low conversations and the occasional laugh – each and every scene, each and every sound, struck her heart like a dagger's point. *I am looking upon dead men, dead women. They don't know it yet. They don't know what's awaiting them, what she means to do with them.*

Or maybe they do.

Unwitnessed. I've heard about this, about what she told them. Unwitnessed . . . is what happens when nobody survives.

He'd intended to call them all together during the Adjunct's parley, but re-forming the squads had taken longer than he'd thought it would – a notion which, he decided, had been foolishly optimistic. Even with spaces in each campfire's circle yawning like silent howls, marines and heavies might as well have been rooted to the ground. They'd needed pulling, kicking, dragging out of their old places.

To fit into a new thing you had to leave the old thing behind, and that wasn't as easy as it sounded, since it meant accepting that the old thing was dead, for ever gone, no matter where you tried standing or how stubbornly you held fast.

Fiddler knew he'd been no different. As bad as Hedge in that regard, in fact. The heavies and the marines were a chewed-up mess. Standing over them, like some cutter above a mauled patient, trying to work out exactly what he was looking at – desperate for something even remotely recognizable – he'd watched them trickle slowly into the basin he'd chosen for this meeting. As the sun waned in the sky, as pairs of squad-mates set out to find some missing comrade, eventually returning with a scowling companion in tow – aye, this was a rough scene, resentment thickening in the dusty air.

He'd waited, weathering their impatience, until at last, with dusk fast rushing in, the final recalcitrant soldier walked into the crowd – Koryk.

Well. You can try all the browbeating you want, when the skull's turned into a solid stone wall there's no getting in.

'So,' Fiddler said, 'I'm captain to you lot now.' He stared at the faces – only half of which seemed to be paying him any attention. 'If Whiskeyjack could see me right now, he'd probably choke – I was never cut out for anything more than what I was in the beginning. A sapper—'

'So what is it,' a voice called out, 'you want us to feel sorry for you?'

'No, Gaunt-Eye. With you all feeling so sorry for yourselves I wouldn't stand a chance, would I? I look out at you now and you know what I'm thinking? I'm thinking: you ain't Bridgeburners. You ain't even close.'

Even the gloom wasn't enough to hide the hard hostility fixed on him now. 'Aye,' he said. 'You see, it was back in Blackdog that it finally clunked home that we were the walking dead. Someone wanted us in the ground, and damn if we didn't mostly end up there. In the tunnels of Pale, the tombs of the Bridgeburners. Tombs they dug for themselves. Heard a few stragglers hung on until Black Coral, and those bodies ended up in Moon's Spawn the day it was abandoned by the Tiste Andii. An end to the tale, but like I said, we saw that end coming from a long way off.'

He fell silent then, momentarily lost in his own memories, the million losses that added up to what he felt now. Then he shook himself and looked up once more. 'But you lot.' He shook his head. 'You're too stupid to know what's been beating you on the heads ever since Y'Ghatan. Wide-eyed stupid.'

Cuttle spoke up. 'We're the walking dead.'

'Thanks for the good news, Fid,' someone said, his voice muffled.

A few laughs, but they were bitter.

Fiddler continued. 'Those lizards took a nasty bite out of us. In fact, they pretty much did us in. Look around. We're what's left. The smoke over Pale's thinning, and here we are. Aye, it's my past pulling me right round till I'm facing the wrong way. You think you feel like shits – try standing in my boots, boys and girls.'

'Thought we were going to decide what to do.'

Fiddler found Gaunt-Eye in the crowd. 'Is that what you thought, Sergeant? Is that really what you thought we'd be doing here? What, we gonna vote on something? We gonna stick up our little hands after arguing ourselves blue? After digging our little holes and crouching in 'em like mummy's womb? Tell me, Sergeant, exactly what have we got to argue about?'

'Pulling out.'

'Someone rustle up a burial detail, we got us a sergeant to plant.'

'You called this damned meeting, Captain—'

'Aye, I did. But not to hold hands. The Adjunct wants something special from us. Once we get t'other side of the Glass Desert. And here I am letting you know, we're going to be our own little army. Nobody wanders off, is that understood? On the march, you all stay tight. Keep your weapons, keep sharp, and wait for my word.'

'You call this an army, Captain?'

'It'll have to do, won't it?'

'So what is it we're supposed to do?'

'You'll find out, I'm sure.'

A few more laughs.

'More lizards waiting for us, Cap'n?'

'No, Reliko, we took care of them already, remember?'

'Damn me, I miss something?'

'No lizards,' Fiddler said. 'Something even uglier and nastier, in fact.'

'All right then,' said Reliko, 's'long as it's not lizards.'

'Hold on,' said Corporal Rib. 'Captain, y'had us sitting here all afternoon? Just to tell us that?'

'Not my fault we had stragglers, Corporal. I need some lessons from Sort, or maybe Kindly. A captain orders, soldiers obey. At least it's supposed to work that way. But then, you're all different now . . . special cases, right? You'll follow an order only if you feel like it. You earned that, or something. How? By living when your buddies died. Why'd they die? Right. They were following orders – whether they liked 'em or not. Fancy that. Deciding whether or not to show up here, what was that? Must've been honouring your fallen comrades, I suppose, the ones who died in your place.'

'Maybe we're broken.'

Again, that voice he couldn't quite place. Fiddler scratched his beard and shook his head. 'You're not broken. The walking dead don't break. Still waiting for that to clunk home, are ya? We're going to be the Adjunct's little army. But *too* little – anyone can see that. Now, it's

186

not that she wants us dead. She doesn't. In fact, it might even be that she's trying to save our lives – after all, where's she taking the regulars? Chances are, wherever that is, you don't want to be there.

'So maybe she thinks we've earned a break. Or maybe not. Who knows what the Adjunct thinks, about anything. She wants what's left of the heavies and the marines in one company. Simple enough.'

'You know more than you're saying, Fiddler.'

'Do I, Koryk?'

'Aye. You've got the Deck of Dragons.'

'What I know is this. Next time I give you all an order, I don't expect to have to wait all day to see you follow it. Next soldier tries that with me gets tossed to the regulars. Outa the special club, for good.'

'We dismissed, Captain?'

'I ain't decided yet. In fact, I'm tempted to make you sit here all night. Just to make a point, right? The one about discipline, the one your friends died for.'

'We took that point the first time, Captain.'

'Maybe *you* did, Cuttle. Ready to say the same for the rest of 'em?'

'No.'

Fiddler sat down on a boulder at the edge of the basin and settled until he was comfortable. He looked into the night sky. 'Ain't that jade light pretty?'

Things were simple, really. There's only so much a soldier can do, only so much a soldier needs to think about at any one time. Pile on too much and their knees start shaking, their eyes glaze over, and they start looking around for something to kill. *Because killing simplifies. It's called an elimination of distractions.*

Her horse was content, watered and fed enough to send the occasional stream down and plant an island or two in their wake. Happy horse, happy Masan Gilani. *Simple.* Her companions were once more nowhere to be seen. Sour company besides; she hardly missed them.

And she herself wasn't feeling as saggy and slack as she'd been only a day earlier. Who knew where the T'lan Imass had found the smoked antelope meat, the tanned bladders filled to bursting with clean, cold water, the loaves of hard bread and the rancid jar of buttery cheese. Probably the same place as the forage for her horse. *And wherever that was, it was a hundred leagues away from here – oh, speak it plain, Masan. It was through some infernal warren. Aye, I seen them fall into dust, but maybe that's not what it seems. Maybe they just step into another place.*

Somewhere nice. Where at the point of a stone sword farmers hand over victuals with a beaming smile and good hale to you all.

Dusk was darkening the sky. She'd have to stop soon.

They must have heard her coming, for the two men stood waiting at the far end of the slope, staring up at her the instant she'd cleared the rise. Masan reined in, squinted for a moment, and then nudged her mount forward.

'You're not all that's left,' she said as she drew nearer. 'You can't be.'

Captain Ruthan Gudd shook his head. 'We're not far from them. A league or two, I'd wager.'

'We'd thought to just push on,' added Bottle.

'Do you know how bad it was?'

'Not yet,' said the captain, eyeing her horse. 'That beast looks too fit, Masan Gilani.'

'No such thing,' she replied, dismounting, 'as a too-fit horse, sir.'

He made a face. 'Meaning you're not going to explain yourself.'

'Didn't you desert?' Bottle asked. 'If you did, Masan, you're riding the wrong way, unless you're happy with being strung up.'

'She didn't desert,' Ruthan Gudd said, turning to resume walking. 'Special mission for the Adjunct.'

'How do you know anything about it, sir?' Masan asked, falling in step with the two men.

'I don't. I'm just guessing.' He combed at his beard. 'I have a talent for that.'

'Has plenty of talents does our captain here,' Bottle muttered.

Whatever was going on between these two, she had to admit to herself that she was happy to see them. 'So how did you two get separated from the army?' she asked. 'By the way, you both look a mess. Bottle, you bathe in blood or something? I barely recognized you.'

'You'd look the same,' he retorted, 'buried under fifty corpses for half a day.'

'Not quite that long,' the captain corrected.

Her breath caught. 'So you *were* at the battle,' she said. 'What battle? What in Hood's name happened?'

'Bits are missing,' Bottle replied, shrugging.

'Bits?'

He seemed ready to say something, changed his mind and instead said, 'I didn't quite catch it all. Especially the, er, second half. But you know, Masan, all the stories about high attrition among officers in the Malazan military?' He jerked a thumb at Ruthan Gudd. 'It ain't so with him.'

The captain said, 'If you hear a certain resentment in his tone, it's because I saved his life.'

'And as for the smugness in the captain's tone—'

'Fine,' she snapped. 'Aye, the Adjunct sent me to find some people.'

'Which you evidently failed to do,' observed Bottle.

'No she didn't,' said Ruthan Gudd.

'So all this crawling skin I'm feeling isn't fleas?'

Ruthan Gudd bared his teeth in a hard grin. 'Well no, it probably is, soldier. Frankly, I'd be surprised if you did feel something – oh, I know, you're a mage. Fid's shaved knuckle, right? Even so, these bastards know how to hide.'

'Let me guess: they're inside the horse. Isn't there some legend about—'

'The moral of which,' Rudd interjected, 'is consistently misapprehended. It's nothing to do with what you think it's to do with. The fact is, that tale's moral is "don't trust horses". Sometimes people look way too hard into such things. Other times, of course, they don't look hard enough. But most of the time by far, they don't look at all.'

'If you want,' said Masan Gilani, 'I can ask them to show themselves.'

'I've absolutely no interest in—'

'I do,' Bottle cut him off. 'Your pardon, sir, for interrupting.'

'An apology I'm not prepared to accept, soldier. As for these guests, Masan Gilani, your offer is categorically—'

Swirls of dust on all sides.

Moments later five T'lan Imass encircled them.

'Gods below,' Ruthan Gudd muttered.

As one, the undead warriors bowed to the captain. One spoke. 'We greet you, Elder.'

Gudd's second curse was in a language Masan Gilani had never heard before.

It's not what you think,' he'd said with those hoary things bowing before him. And he'd not said much else. The T'lan Imass vanished again a short time later and the three soldiers continued on as the night deepened around them.

Bottle wanted to scream. The captain's company over the past few days had been an exercise in patience and frustration. He wasn't a man for words. *Ruthan Gudd. Or whatever your name really is. It's not what I think? How do you know what I think? Besides, it's exactly what I think. Fid has his shaved knuckle, and it seems the Adjunct has one, too.*

A Hood-damned Elder God – after all, what other kind of 'Elder' would T'lan Imass bow before? And since when did they bow before anything?

Masan Gilani's barrage of questions had withered the T'lan Imass to dust with, Bottle thought, a harried haste. But things from the past had a way of refusing illumination. As bad as standing stones, they held all their secrets buried deep inside. It wasn't even a question of irritating coyness. *They just don't give a shit. Explanations? What's the point? Who cares what you think you need to know, anyway? If I'm a stone, lean against me. If I'm a ruin, rest your weary arse on the rubble. And if I'm an Elder God, well, Abyss take you, don't look to me for anything.*

But he'd ridden out against the Nah'ruk, when he could have ridden the other way. He went and made a stand. Which made him what? Another one in mysterious service to Adjunct Tavore Paran of Unta? *But why? Even the Empress didn't want her in the end. T'amber, Quick Ben, even Fiddler – they stood with her, even when it cost them their lives.*

Soldiers muttered she didn't inspire a damned thing in them. Soldiers grumbled that she was no Dujek Onearm, no Coltaine, no Crust, no Dassem Ultor. They didn't know what she was. *None of us do, come to that. But look at us, right here, right now, walking back to her. A Dal Honese horsewoman who can ride like the wind – well, a heavy wind, then. An Elder God . . . and me. Gods below, I've lost my mind.*

Not quite. I tore it apart. Only to have Quick Ben make sure most of it came back. Do I feel different? Am I changed? How would I even know?

But I miss the Bonehunters. I miss my miserable squad. I miss the damned Adjunct.

We're nothing but the sword in her hand, but we're a comfortable grip. Use us, then. Just do it in style.

'Camp glow ahead,' said Masan Gilani, who once more rode her horse. 'Looks damned big.'

'Her allies have arrived,' said Ruthan Gudd, then added, 'I expect.'

Bottle snorted. 'Does she know you're alive, Captain?'

'Why should she?'

'Well, because . . .'

'I'm a captain, soldier.'

'Who rode alone into the face of a Nah'ruk legion! Armoured in ice! With a sword of ice! A horse—'

'Oh, enough, Bottle. You have no idea how much I regret doing what I did. It's nice not being noticed. Maybe one day you humans will finally understand that, and do away with all your mad ambitions, your insipid self-delusional megalomania. You weren't shat out by some god on high. You weren't painted in the flesh of the divine – at least, not any more than anyone or anything else. What's with you all, anyway? You jam a stick up your own arse then preen at how tall and straight you're standing. Soldier, you think you put your crawling days behind the day you left your mother's tit? Take it from me – you're still crawling, lad. Probably always will.'

Bludgeoned by the tirade, Bottle was silent.

190

'You two go on,' said Masan Gilani. 'I need to piss.'

'That last time was the horse then?' Rudd asked.

'Oh, funny man – or whatever.' She reined in.

'So they bowed to you,' Bottle said as he and the captain continued on. 'Why take it out on me?'

'I didn't – ah, never mind. To answer you, no, the Adjunct knows nothing about me. But as you say, my precious anonymity is over – or it is assuming the moment we're in camp you go running off to your sergeant.'

'I'm sure I will,' Bottle replied. 'But not, if you like, to babble about you being an Elder God.'

'God? Not a god, Bottle. I told you: it's not what you think.'

'I'll keep your ugly little secret, sir, if that's how you want it. But that won't change what we all saw that day, will it?'

'Stormrider magic, yes. That.'

'That.'

'I borrowed it.'

'Borrowed?'

'Yes,' he snapped in reply. 'I don't steal, Bottle.'

'Of course not, sir. Why would you need to?'

'Exactly.'

Bottle nodded in the gloom, listening as Masan rode back up to them. 'Borrowed.'

'A misunderstood people, the Stormriders.'

'No doubt. Abject terror leaves little room for much else.'

'Interestingly,' Ruthan Gudd said in a murmur, 'needs have converged somewhat. And I'm too old to believe in coincidence. No matter. We do what we do and that's that.'

'Sounds like something Fiddler would say.'

'Fiddler's a wise man, Bottle. He's also the best of you, though I doubt many would see that, at least not as clearly as I do.'

'Fiddler, is it? Not the Adjunct, Captain?'

He heard Ruthan Gudd's sigh, and it was a sound filled with sorrow. 'I see pickets.'

'So do I,' said Masan Gilani. 'Not Malazan. Perish.'

'Our allies,' said Bottle, glaring at Ruthan Gudd, but of course it was too dark for him to see that. *Then again, what's darkness to a Hood-cursed ice-wielding Imass-kneeling Elder God?*

Who then spoke. 'It was a guess, Bottle. Truly.'

'You took my anger.'

The voice came out of the shadows. Blinking, Lostara Yil slowly sat up, the furs sliding down, the chill air sweeping around her bared breasts, back and belly. A figure was sitting on the tent's lone camp stool to her left, cloaked, hooded in grey wool. The two hands, hanging down past the bend of his knees, were pale as bone.

Lostara's heart thudded hard in her chest. 'I felt it,' she said. 'Rising like a flood.' She shivered, whispered, 'And I drowned.'

'Your love summoned me, Lostara Yil.'

She scowled. 'I have no love for you, Cotillion.'

The hooded head dipped slightly. 'The man you chose to defend.'

His tone startled her. *Weary, yes, but more than that. Lonely. This god is lonely.*

'You danced for him and none other,' Cotillion went on. 'Not even the Adjunct.'

'I expected to die.'

'I know.'

She waited. Faint voices from the camp beyond the flimsy walls, the occasional glow of a hooded lantern swinging past, the thud of boots.

The silence stretched.

'You saved us,' she finally said. 'For that, I suppose I have to thank you.'

'No, Lostara Yil, you do not. I possessed you, after all. You didn't ask for that, but then, even all those years ago, the grace of your dance was . . . breathtaking.'

Her breath caught. Something was happening here. She didn't understand it. 'If you did not wish my gratitude, Cotillion, why are you here?' Even as she spoke, she flinched at her own tone's harshness. *That came out all wrong—*

His face remained hidden. 'Those were early days, weren't they. Our flesh was real, our breaths . . . real. It was all there, in reach, and we took it without a moment's thought as to how precious it all was. Our youth, the brightness of the sun, the heat that seemed to stretch ahead for ever.'

She realized then that he was weeping. Felt helpless before it. *What is this about?* 'I took your anger, you said.' And yes, she could remember it, the way the power filled her. The skill with the swords was entirely her own, but the swiftness – the profound awareness – that had belonged to him. 'I took your anger. Cotillion, what did you take from *me*?'

He seemed to shake his head. 'I think I'm done with possessing women.'

'What did you take? You took that love, didn't you? It drowned you, just as your anger drowned me.'

He sighed. 'Always an even exchange.'

'Can a god not love?'

'A god . . . forgets.'

She was appalled. 'But then, what keeps you going? Cotillion, *why do you fight on?*'

Abruptly he stood. 'You are chilled. I have disturbed your rest—'

'Possess me again.'

'*What?*'

'The love that I feel. You need it, Cotillion. That need is what brought you here, wasn't it? You want to . . . to drown again.'

His reply was a frail whisper. 'I cannot.'

'Why not? I offer this to you. As a true measure of my gratitude. When a mortal communes with her god, is not the language love itself?'

'My worshippers love me not, Lostara Yil. Besides, I have nothing worthy to give in exchange. I appreciate your offer—'

'Listen, you shit, I'm trying to give you some of your humanity back. You're a damned god – if you lose your passion where does that leave us?'

The question clearly rocked him. 'I do not doubt the path awaiting me, Lostara Yil. I am strong enough for it, right to the bitter end—'

'I don't doubt any of that. I *felt* you, remember? Listen, whatever that end you see coming . . . what I'm offering is to take away some of its bitterness. Don't you see that?'

He was shaking his head. 'You don't understand. The blood on my hands—'

'Is now on my hands, too, or have you forgotten that?'

'No. I possessed you—'

'You think that makes a difference?'

'I should not have come here.'

'Probably not, but here you are, and that hood doesn't hide everything. Very well, refuse my offer, but do you really think it's just women who feel love? If you decide never again to feel . . . anything, then best you swear off possession entirely, Cotillion. Steal into us mortals and we'll take what we need from you, and we'll give in return whatever we own. If you're lucky, it'll be love. If you're not lucky, well, Hood knows what you'll get.'

'I am aware of this.'

'Yes, you must be. I'm sorry. But, Cotillion, you gave me more than your anger. Don't you see that? The man I love does not now grieve for me. His love is not for a ghost, a brief moment in his life that he can never recapture. You gave us both a chance to live, and to love – it doesn't matter for how much longer.'

'I also spared the Adjunct, and by extension this entire army.'

She cocked her head, momentarily disoriented. 'Do you regret that?'

He hesitated, and that silence rippled like ice-water through Lostara Yil.

'While she lives,' he said, 'the path awaiting you, and this beleaguered, half-damned army, is as bitter as my own. To the suffering to come . . . ah, there are no gifts in any of this.'

'There must be, Cotillion. They exist. They always do.'

'Will you all die in the name of love?' The question seemed torn from something inside him.

'If die we must, what better reason?'

He studied her for a dozen heartbeats, and then said, 'I have been considering . . . amends.'

'Amends? I don't understand.'

'Our youth,' he murmured, as if he had not heard her, 'the brightness of the sun. She chose to leave him. Because, I fear, of me, of what I did to her. It was wrong. All of it, so terribly *wrong*. Love . . . I'd forgotten.'

The shadows deepened, and a moment later she was alone in her tent. *She? Cotillion, listen to my prayer. For all your fears, love is not something you can forget. But you can turn your back on it. Do not do that.* A god had sought her out. A god suffering desperate need. But she couldn't give him what he desired – perhaps, she saw now, he'd been wise in rejecting what she'd offered. *The first time, it was anger for love. But I saw no anger left in him.*

Always an even exchange. If I opened my love to him . . . whatever he had left inside himself, he didn't want to give it to me. And that, she now comprehended, had been an act of mercy.

The things said and the things not said. In the space in between, a thousand worlds. A thousand worlds.

The Perish escort of two armoured, helmed and taciturn soldiers halted. The one on the left pointed and said to Bottle, 'There, marine, you will find your comrades. They have gathered at the summons of their captain.' To Masan Gilani and Ruthan Gudd, the soldier continued, 'The Adjunct's command tent lies elsewhere, but as we have come to the edge of the Bonehunter encampment, I expect you will have little difficulty in finding your own way.'

'Much as we will miss your company,' Ruthan Gudd said, 'I am sure you are correct. Thank you for guiding us this far, sirs.'

The figures – Bottle wasn't even sure if they were men or women, and the voice of the one who'd spoken gave no hint whatsoever – bowed, and then turned about to retrace their routes.

Bottle faced his companions. 'We part here, then. Masan, I expect I'll see you soon enough. Captain.' He saluted smartly.

The man scowled in reply. Gesturing to Masan, he set off for the heart of the camp.

Bottle faced the direction the guard had indicated. *What's Sort got to say to them, then? Guess I'm about to find out.*

They'd set no pickets. A small mass of soldiers were seated or standing in a basin, and at the far end, hunched down on a boulder . . . *is that Fiddler? Gods below, don't tell me this is all that's left!* Tentatively, he approached.

They made their own way through a relatively quiet camp. It was late, and Masan was not looking forward to rousing the Adjunct, but she knew Tavore would not abide any delays to any of this. *Though my report probably won't impress her. Five beat-up T'lan Imass is all I've got to show.* No, it was Ruthan Gudd who was marching into a serious mess. She hoped she'd be witness to at least some of that exchange, if only to revel in the captain's discomfort.

Elder! Well, I won't tell. But all the rest you did, Captain, now that sounded interesting. Too bad I missed it.

They passed through a few groups here and there, and Masan sensed a heightening attention from those faces turned their way, but no one accosted them. No one said a damned thing. *Strange and stranger still.*

They came to within sight of the command tent. Two guards were stationed at the flap, and the glow of lantern light painted the canvas walls.

'Does she ever sleep?' Ruthan Gudd wondered in a drawl.

'In her boots,' Masan replied, 'I doubt I would.'

The eyes of the guards were now on them, and both slowly straightened, their shadowed gazes clearly fixing on the captain. Both saluted when he halted before them.

'She probably wants to see us,' Ruthan said.

'You have leave to enter, sir,' one of them said.

As the captain moved to the entrance the same guard said, 'Sir?'

'Yes?'

'Welcome back.'

Masan followed him inside.

'Of all the luck,' muttered Ruthan Gudd upon seeing a dozing Skanarow. He held a hand to stay Masan. 'Please,' he whispered, 'don't wake her.'

'Coward,' she mouthed in reply.

Grimacing, he edged past the sleeping woman. As she neared, Masan's gaze fell to one wayward booted foot, and she gave it a kick.

Skanarow bolted upright. 'Adj— *Gods below!*'

That shout rang loud as a hammered cauldron.

At the very threshold to the inner chamber, Ruthan Gudd wheeled. Whatever he intended to say, he had no chance, as Skanarow was upon him in an instant. Such was the force of her lunge and embrace that he staggered back, splitting the curtain, into the Adjunct's presence.

Skanarow held her kiss as if glued to the captain's mouth.

Grinning, Masan Gilani edged in behind them, caught the Adjunct's astonished gaze.

Tavore was standing beside a small folding map table. She was otherwise alone, accounting for her half-dressed state – only the quilted undergarment of her armour covered her torso, and below that nothing but loose linen trousers, the knees so stained they'd have embarrassed a farmer. Her face was strangely streaked in the half-light of a single oil lamp.

'Adjunct,' Masan Gilani said, saluting. 'On my return journey, I happened upon the captain here, and a marine named Bottle, from Fiddler's squad—'

'Skanarow!' The word was sharp as a blade. 'Disengage yourself from the captain. I believe he has come here to speak to me – as for the rest, it will have to wait.'

Skanarow pulled herself from Ruthan Gudd. 'M-my apologies, Adjunct. I – with your leave, I will wait outside—'

'You will not. You will return to your tent and wait there. I trust the captain will find it without much trouble?'

Skanarow blinked, and then, fighting a smile, she saluted a second time and, with one last glance at Ruthan – a look that was either a glare or a dark promise – she was gone.

Ruthan Gudd straightened before the Adjunct and cleared his throat. 'Adjunct.'

'Your act, Captain, on the day of the Nah'ruk, broke enough military conventions to warrant a court-martial. You abandoned your soldiers and disobeyed orders.'

'Yes, Adjunct.'

'And quite possibly saved all our lives.' She seemed to become cognizant of her attire, for she turned to the tent's centre pole, where a robe hung from a hook. Shrugging into the woollen garment she faced Ruthan again. 'Entire tomes have been devoted to a discussion of these particular incidents in military campaigns. Disobedience on the one hand and extraordinary valour on the other. What is to be done with such a soldier?'

'Rank and discipline must ever take precedence, Adjunct.'

Her gaze sharpened on him. 'Is that your learned opinion on the matter, Captain? Content, are you, with distilling all those tomes in a handful of words?'

'Frankly, Adjunct? Yes.'

'I see. Then what do you suggest I do with you?'

'At the very least, Adjunct, reduce my rank. For you are accurate and proper in noting my dereliction of responsibility regarding the soldiers under my command.'

'Of course I am, you fool.' She ran a hand through her short hair, and caught Masan's gaze. The Dal Honese could not help but see the faint gleam in those unremarkable – and clearly tired – eyes. 'Very well, Ruthan Gudd. You have lost your command. Your rank, however, shall remain unchanged, but from this day forward you are attached to my staff. And if you imagine this to be some sort of promotion, well, I suggest you sit down with Lostara Yil some time soon.' She paused, eyes narrowing on Ruthan Gudd. 'Why, Captain, you seem displeased. Good. Now, as to other matters that we should discuss, perhaps they can wait. There is one woman in this camp, however, who cannot. Dismissed.'

His salute was somewhat shaky.

When he was gone, the Adjunct sighed and sat down by her map table. 'Forgive me, marine, for my improper state. It has been a long day.'

'No need to apologize, Adjunct.'

Tavore's eyes travelled up and down Masan, sending a faint tremor through her spine – *oh, I know that kind of look*. 'You look surprisingly hale, soldier.'

'Modest gifts from our new allies, Adjunct.'

Brows lifted. 'Indeed?'

'Alas, there're only five of them.'

'Five?'

'T'lan Imass, Adjunct. I don't know if they were the allies you sought. In fact, they found me, not the other way round, and it is their opinion that my bringing them here was the right thing to do.'

The Adjunct continued studying her. Masan felt trickles of sweat wending down the small of her back. *I don't know. She's a damned skinny one . . .*

'Summon them.'

The figures rose from the dirt floor. Dust to bones, dust to withered flesh, dust to chipped weapons of stone. The T'lan Imass bowed to the Adjunct.

The one named Beroke then spoke. 'Adjunct Tavore Paran, we are the Unbound. We bring you greeting, Adjunct, from the Crippled God.'

And at that something seemed to crumple inside Tavore, for she leaned forward, set her hands to her face, and said, 'Thank you. I thought . . . out of time . . . too late. Oh gods, *thank you*.'

He'd stood unnoticed for some time, just one more marine, there on the edge of the crowd. Holding back, unsure of what he was witnessing here. Fiddler wasn't saying anything. In fact, the bastard might well be sleeping, with his head sunk down like that. As for the soldiers in the basin, some muttered back and forth, a few tried to sleep but were kicked awake by their companions.

When Fiddler lifted his gaze, the marines and heavies fell silent, suddenly attentive. The sergeant was rummaging in his kit bag. He drew something out but it was impossible to see what. Peered at it for a long moment, and then returned it to his satchel. 'Cuttle!'

'Aye?'

'He's here. Go find him.'

The sapper rose and slowly turned. 'All right, then,' he growled, 'I ain't got the eyes of a rat. So show yourself, damn you.'

A slow heat prickled through Bottle. He looked round.

Fiddler said, 'Aye, Bottle. You. Don't be so thick.'

'Here,' Bottle said.

Figures close to him swung round then. A few muffled curses, and all at once a space opened around him. Cuttle was making his way over, and even in the gloom his expression was severe.

'I think Smiles sold off your kit, Bottle,' he said as he arrived to stand before him. 'At least you scrounged up some weapons, which is saying something.'

'You all knew?'

'Knew what? That you survived? Gods no. We all figured you dead and gone. You think Smiles would've sold off your stuff if we didn't?'

He could see the rest of the squad drawing up behind Cuttle. 'Well, yes.'

The sapper grunted. 'Got a point there, soldier. Anyway, we didn't know a damned thing. He just made us sit here and wait, is what he did—'

'I thought this was Faradan Sort's meeting—'

'Fid's cap'n now, Bottle.'

'Oh.'

'And since he's now a captain, official and everything, he's got decorum t'follow.'

'Right. Of course. I mean—'

'So instead of him doing this, it's me.' And with that the veteran stepped close and embraced him, hard enough to make Bottle's bones ache. Cuttle's breath was harsh in his ear. 'Kept looking at a card, y'see? Kept looking at it. Welcome back, Bottle. Gods below, welcome home.'

Stormy halted the Ve'Gath. Grainy-eyed, aching, he stared at the massed army seething in motion on the flats below as the dawn sliced open the eastern horizon. Bonehunter standards to the left, companies jostling to form up for the march – far too few companies for Stormy's liking. Already assembled and facing southeast, the Letherii legions, and with them Perish ranks, and the gilt standards of some other army. Scowling, he swung his gaze back to the Bonehunters. Positioned to march due east. 'Gods below.'

A scattering of Khundryl outriders had spotted him, two setting off back to the vanguard while a half-dozen, bows drawn and arrows nocked, rode swiftly in his direction. Seeing their growing confusion as they approached, Stormy grinned. He lifted one hand in greeting. They pulled up thirty paces away.

The ranks of the Bonehunters were all halted now, facing in his direction. He saw the Adjunct and a handful of officers emerging from the swirling dust near the column's head to ride towards him.

He considered meeting them halfway, decided not to. Twisting round, he looked back at his K'ell Hunter escort and the drones. Weapon points were buried in the hard ground. The drones had settled on their tails, tiny birds dancing on their hides and feeding on ticks and mites. From them all, a scent of calm repose. 'Good. Stay there, all of you. And don't do anything . . . unnerving.'

Horses shied on the approach, and it was quickly apparent that none of the mounts would draw within twenty long strides of the Ve'Gath. Across the gap, Stormy met the Adjunct's eyes. 'I'd dismount,' he said, 'but I think my legs died some time in the night. Adjunct, I bring greetings from Mortal Sword Gesler, Destriant Kalyth, and the Gunthan K'Chain Che'Malle.'

She slipped down from her mount and walked towards him, slowly drawing off her leather gloves. 'The Nah'ruk, Corporal, were seeking their kin, correct?'

'Aye. Estranged kin, I'd say. Saw no hugs when we all met.'

'If Sergeant Gesler is now Mortal Sword, Corporal, what does that make you?'

'Shield Anvil.'

'I see. And the god you serve?'

'Damned if I know, Adjunct.'

Tucking the gloves in her belt, she drew off her helm and ran a hand through her hair. 'Your battle with the Nah'ruk . . .'

'Malazan tactics, Adjunct, along with these beasts, gave us the upper hand. We annihilated the bastards.'

Something changed in her face, but nothing he could work out. She glanced back at her officers, or perhaps the army waiting beyond, and then once more fixed her gaze upon him. 'Shield Anvil Stormy, this creature you ride—'

'Ve'Gath Soldier, Adjunct. Only three bear these . . . saddles.'

'And your K'Chain Che'Malle army – I see Hunters behind you as well. There are more of these Ve'Gath?'

My K'Chain Che'Malle army. 'Aye, lots. We got a bit mauled, to be sure. Those sky keeps gave us trouble, but some unexpected allies arrived to take 'em down. That's what I'm here to tell you, Adjunct. Sinn and Grub found us. There was someone else, too. Never figured out who, but no matter, nobody climbed down out of the Azath when it was all done with, so I doubt they made it.'

He'd just thrown enough at her to confuse a damned ascendant. Instead, she simply studied him, and then asked, 'Shield Anvil, you now command an army of K'Chain Che'Malle?'

'Aye, and our two runts are saying they have to stay with us, unless you order 'em back to you—'

'No.'

Stormy cursed under his breath. 'You sure? They're handy, don't eat much, clean up after themselves . . . mostly – well, occasionally – but with plenty of back-of-the-hand training, why, they'd shape up—'

'Fist Keneb is dead,' she cut in. 'We have also lost Quick Ben, and most of the marines and the heavies.'

He winced. 'Them Short-Tails was bleeding when they found us. But what you're saying tells me you could do with the runts—'

'No. You will need them more than we will.'

'We will? Adjunct, where do you think we're going?'

'To war.'

'Against who?'

'"Whom", Shield Anvil. You intend to wage war against the Forkrul Assail.'

He grimaced, glanced at the Fist and captains positioned behind the Adjunct. Blistig, Lostara Yil, Ruthan Gudd. That miserable ex-priest, half slumped over his saddle. His attention returned to the Adjunct. 'Now, why would we declare war on the Forkrul Assail?'

'Ask the runts.'

Stormy sagged. 'We did that. They ain't good on explanations, those two. Grub's the only one between 'em who'll say anything to us at all. Oh, Sinn talks just fine, when it suits her. Me and Ges, we was hoping you'd be more . . . uh, forthcoming.'

A snort from Blistig.

Tavore said, 'Shield Anvil, inform Mortal Sword Gesler of the following. The Perish, Letherii and Bolkando armies are marching on the Spire. It is my fear that even such a formidable force . . . will not be enough. The sorcery of the Assail is powerful and insidious, especially on the field of battle—'

'Is it now, Adjunct?'

She blinked, and then said, 'I have spent three years amidst the archives of Unta, Stormy. Reading the oldest and obscurest histories drawn to the capital from the further reaches of the Malazan Empire. I have interviewed the finest scholars I could find, including Heboric

Light-Touch, on matters of fragmented references to the Forkrul Assail.' She hesitated, and then continued. 'I know what awaits us all, Shield Anvil. The three human armies you now see marching into the southeast are . . . *vulnerable*.'

'Where the K'Chain Che'Malle are not.'

She shrugged. 'Could we conjure before us, here and now, a Forkrul Assail, do you imagine it could command your Ve'Gath to surrender its weapons? To kneel?'

Stormy grunted. 'I'd like to see it try. But what of the runts?'

'Safer in your company than in ours.'

He narrowed his gaze on her. 'What is it you mean to do with your Bonehunters, Adjunct?'

'Split the enemy forces, Shield Anvil.'

'You have taken a savaging, Adjunct—'

'And have been avenged by you and your Che'Malle.' She took a step closer, dropping her voice. 'Stormy, when news of your victory spreads through my army, much that haunts it now will fall silent. There will be no cheers – I am not such a fool as to expect anything like that. But, at the very least, there will be satisfaction. Do you understand me?'

'Is Fiddler—'

'He lives.'

'Good.' He squinted at her. 'You've a way of gathering allies, haven't you, Adjunct?'

'It is not me, Stormy, it is the cause itself.'

'I'd agree if I could figure out what that cause is all about.'

'You mentioned a Destriant—'

'Aye, I did.'

'Then ask that one.'

'We did, but she knows even less than we do.'

Tavore cocked her head. 'Are you sure?'

'Well, she gets little sleep. Nightmares every night.' He clawed fingers through his beard, 'Aw, Hood take me . . .'

'She sees the fate awaiting us all should we fail, Shield Anvil.'

He was silent, thinking back, crossing a thousand leagues of memory and time. Days in Aren, ranks milling, recalcitrant faces, a desperate need for cohesion. *Armies are unruly beasts. You took 'us, you made 'us into something, but none of us knows what, or even what for.* And now here she stood, a thin, plain woman. Not tall. Not imposing in any way at all. *Except for the cold iron in her bones.* 'Why did you take this on, Adjunct?'

She settled the helm back on her head and fixed the clasps. 'That's my business.'

'This path of yours,' he asked, resisting her dismissal, 'where did it start? That first step, when was it? You can answer me that one, at least.'

She regarded him. 'Can I?'

'I'm about to ride back to Gesler, Adjunct. And I got to make a report. I got to tell him what I think about all this. So . . . give me something.'

She looked away, studied the formed-up ranks of her army. 'My first step? Very well.'

He waited.

She stood as if carved from flawed marble, a thing in profile weeping dust – but no, that sense was emerging from deep inside his own soul, as if he'd found a mirror's reflection of the nondescript woman standing before him, and in that reflection a thousand hidden truths.

She faced him again, her eyes swallowed by the shadow of the helm's rim. 'The day, Adjunct, the Paran family lost its only son.'

The answer was so unexpected, so jarring, that Stormy could say nothing. *Gods below, Tavore.* He struggled to find words, any words. 'I – I did not know your brother had died, Adjunct—'

'He hasn't,' she snapped, turning away.

Stormy silently cursed. He'd said the wrong thing. He'd shown his own stupidity, his own lack of understanding. *Fine! Maybe I'm not Gesler! Maybe I don't get it—* A gelid breath seemed to flow through him then. 'Adjunct!' His shout drew her round.

'What is it?'

He drew a deep breath, and then said, 'When we join up with the Perish and the others, who's in overall command?'

She studied him briefly before replying, 'There will be a Prince of Lether. A Mortal Sword of the Grey Helms, and the queen of Bolkando.'

'Hood's breath! I don't—'

'Who will be in command, Shield Anvil? You and Gesler.'

He stared at her, aghast, and then bellowed, 'Don't you think his head's swelled big enough yet? You ain't had to live with him!'

Her tone was hard and cold. 'Bear in mind what I said about vulnerability, Shield Anvil, and be sure to guard your own back.'

'Guard – what?'

'One last thing, Stormy. Extend my condolences to Grub. Inform him, if you think it will help, that Fist Keneb's death was one of . . . singular heroism.'

He thought he heard a careful choosing of words in that statement. *No matter. Might help, as much as such shit can, with that stuff. Worth a try, I suppose.* 'Adjunct?'

She had gathered the reins of her horse and had one foot in the stirrup. 'Yes?'

'Shall we meet again?'

Tavore Paran hesitated, and what might have been a faint smile curved her thin lips. She swung astride her horse. 'Fare you well, Shield Anvil.' A pause, and then, 'Stormy, should you one day meet my brother . . . no, never mind.' With that she drew her horse round and set off for the head of the column.

Blistig wheeled in behind her, as did Ruthan Gudd and then the ex-priest – although perhaps with him it was more a matter of a mount content to follow the others. Leaving only Lostara Yil.

'Stormy.'

'Lostara.'

'Quick Ben was sure you and Gesler lived.'

'Was he now?'

'But now we've lost him.'

He thought about that, and then grinned. 'Take this for what it's worth, Lostara Yil. He figured we were alive and well. He was right. Now, I've got this feeling he ain't so lost as you might think. He's a snake. Always was, always will be.'

The smile she flashed him almost made him hesitate, but before he could call out something inviting and possibly improper she was riding after the others.

Damn! Smiles like that don't land on me every day.

Scowling, he ordered his Ve'Gath round and then set off on the back trail.

The Hunters and drones fell into his wake.

One of the tiny birds tried landing in Stormy's beard. His curse sent it screeching away.

BOOK THREE

TO CHARGE THE SPEAR

And now the bold historian
Wields into play that tome
Of blistering worth
Where the stern monks
Cower under the lash
And through the high window
The ashes of heretics drift
Down in purity's rain
See the truths stitched in thread
Of gold across hapless skin
I am the arbiter of lies
Who will cleanse his hand
In copper bowls and white sand
But the spittle on his lips
Gathers the host to another tale
I was never so blind
To not feel the deep tremble
Of hidden rivers in churning torrent
Or the prickly tear of quill's jab
I will tell you the manner
Of all things in sure proof
This order'd stone row –
Oh spare me now the speckled fists
This princeps' purge and prattle
I live in mists and seething cloud
And the breaths of the unseen
Give warmth and comfort to better
The bleakest days to come
And I will carry on in my
Uncertainty, cowl'd in a peace
Such as you could not imagine

A Life in Mists
Gothos (?)

CHAPTER EIGHT

Whatever we're left with
can only be enough,
if in the measure of things
nothing is cast off,
discarded on the wayside
in the strides that take us clear
beyond the smoke and grief
into a world of shocked birth
opening eyes upon a sudden light.
And to whirl then in a breath
to see all that we have done,
where the tombs on the trail
lie sealed like jewelled memories
in the dusk of a good life's end,
and not one footprint beckons
upon the soft snow ahead,
but feel this sweet wind caress.
A season crawls from earth
beneath mantled folds.
I have caught a glimpse,
a hint of flared mystery,
shapes in the liquid glare.
They will take from us
all that we cradle in our arms
and the burden yielded
makes feathers of my hands,
and the voices drifting down
are all that we're left with
and shall for ever be enough

You Will Take My Days
Fisher kel Tath

*T*O SLITHER BENEATH THE FISTS OF THE WORLD.

Her name was Thorl. A quiet one, with watchful, sad eyes. Bursting from the cloud of Shards, her screams sounded like laughter. The devouring insects clustered where her eyes had been. They lunged into her gaping mouth, the welters of blood from shredded lips drawing hundreds more.

Saddic cried out his horror, staggered back as if about to flee, but Badalle snapped out one hand and held him fast. Panic was what the Shards loved most, what they waited for, and panic was what had taken Thorl, and now the Shards were taking her.

Blind, the girl ran, stumbling on the jagged crystals that tore her bared feet.

Children edged closer to her, and Badalle could see the flatness in their eyes and she understood.

Strike down, fists, still we slide and slither. You cannot kill us, you cannot kill the memory of us. We remain, to remind you of the future you gave us. We remain, because we are the proof of your crime.

Let the eaters crowd your eyes. Welcome your own blindness, as if it was a gift of mercy. And that could well be laughter. Dear child, you could well be laughing, a voice of memory. Of history, even. In that laugh, all the ills of the world. In that laugh, all the proofs of your guilt.

Children are dying. Still dying. For ever dying.

Thorl fell, her screams deadening to choking, hacking sounds as Shards crawled down her throat. She writhed, and then twitched, and the swarm grew sluggish, feeding, fattening.

Badalle watched the children close in, watched their hands lunge out, snatching wallowing insects, stuffing them into eager mouths. *We go round and round and this is the story of the world. Do not flee us. Do not flee this moment, this scene. Do not confuse dislike and abhorrence with angry denial of truths you do not wish to see. I accept your horror and expect no forgiveness. But if you deny, I name you coward.*

And I have had my fill of cowards.

She blew flies from her lips, and glanced at Rutt. He clutched Held, weeping without tears. Beyond him stretched out the terrible flat waste of the Glass Desert. Badalle then turned back to study the Snake, eyes narrowing. Torpor unsuited to the heat, the brightness of the sky. This was the sluggish motion of the exhausted. *Your fists beat us senseless. Your fists explode with reasons. You beat us out of fear. Out of self-loathing. You beat us because it feels good, it feels good to pretend and to forget, and every time your fist comes down, you crush a little more guilt.*

In that old place where we once lived, you decried those who beat their children. Yet see what you have done to the world.

You are all beaters of children.

'Badalle,' said Rutt.

'Yes, Rutt.' She did not face him again, not yet.

'We have few days left. The holes of water are gone. We cannot even go back – we will never make it back. Badalle, I think I give up – I – I'm ready to give up.'

Give up. 'Will you leave Held to the Shards? To the Opals?'

She heard him draw a sharp breath.

'They will not touch Held,' he whispered.

No, they won't, will they. 'Before Held became Held,' she said, 'Held had another name, and that name was Born. Born came from between the legs of a woman, a mother. Born came into this world with eyes of blue, blue as this sky, and blue they remain. We must go on, Rutt. We must live to see the day when a new colour finds Held's eyes, when Held goes back to being Born.'

'Badalle,' he whispered behind her.

'You don't have to understand,' she said. 'We don't know who that mother was. We don't know who the new mother will be.'

'I've seen, at night . . .' he faltered then. 'Badalle—'

'The older ones, yes,' she replied. 'Our own mothers and fathers, lying together, trying to make babies. We can only go back to what we knew, to whatever we remember from the old days. We make it all happen again, even though we know it didn't work the first time, it's all we know to do.'

'Do you still fly in your dreams, Badalle?'

'We have to go on, Rutt, until Held stops being Held and becomes Born.'

'I hear her crying at night.'

Her. This is her story: Born becomes Held, Held becomes Mother, Mother makes Born, Born is Held . . . And the boys who are now fathers, they try to go back, back inside, every night, they try and try.

Rutt, we all cry at night.

'We need to walk,' she said, turning to face him at last.

His visage was crumpled, a thing of slack skin and ringed eyes. Broken lips, the forehead of a priest who doubts his own faith. His hair was falling out, his hands looked huge.

'Held says, *west*, Rutt. West.'

'There is nothing there.'

There is a great family, and they are rich in all things. In food. In water. They seek us, to bless us, to show us that the future still lives. They will promise to us that future. I have seen, I have seen it all. And there is a mother who leads them, and all her children she holds in her arms, though she has never made a Born. There is a mother, Rutt, just like you. And soon, the child in her arms will open its eyes. 'I dreamed of Held last night, Rutt.'

'You did?'

'Yes. She had wings, and she was flying away. I heard her voice on the wind.'

'Her voice, Badalle? What was she saying? What was Held saying?'

'She wasn't saying anything, Rutt. She was laughing.'

Frost limned the driftwood heaped along the strand, and the chunks of ice in the shallow waters of the bay crunched and ground as the rolling waves jostled them. Felash hacked out the last of her morning cough and then, drawing her fur-lined cloak about her shoulders, she straightened and walked over to where her handmaid was building up the fire. 'Have you prepared my breakfast?'

The older woman gestured to the strange disc of sawn tree trunk they were using as a table, where waited a mug of herbal tea and a lit hookah.

'Excellent. I tell you, my head aches. Mother's sendings are clumsy and brutal. Or perhaps it's just Omtose Phellack that is so harsh – like this infernal ice and chill plaguing us.' She glanced over at the other camp, thirty paces along the beach, and frowned. 'And all this superstition! Tipped well over the edge into blatant rudeness, in my opinion.'

'The sorcery frightens them, Highness.'

'Pah! That sorcery saved their lives! You would think gratitude should trump petty terrors and imagined bugaboos. Dear me, what a pathetic gaggle of hens they all are.' She settled down on a log, careful to avoid the strange iron bolts jutting from it. Sipped some tea, and then reached for the hookah's artfully carved ivory mouthpiece. Puffing contentedly, she twisted to eye the ship frozen in the bay. 'Look at that. The only thing keeping it afloat is the iceberg it's nesting in.'

'Alas, Highness, that is probably the very source of their present discontent. They are sailors stranded on land. Even the captain and her first mate are showing their despondency.'

'Well,' Felash sniffed, 'we must make do with what we have, mustn't we? In any case, there's nothing to be done for it, is there? That ship is finished. We must now trek overland, and how my feet will survive this I dare not contemplate.'

She turned in her seat to see Shurq Elalle and Skorgen Kaban approaching, the first mate cursing as he stumbled in the sand.

'Captain! Join me in some tea. You too, Skorgen, please.' She faced her handmaid. 'Fetch us more cups, will you? Excellent.'

210

'Beru bless us,' Skorgen hissed. 'Ten paces away and the heat's melting us where we stand, but here—'

'That will fade, I am sure,' said Felash. 'The sorcery of yesterday was, shall we say, rather intense. And before you complain overmuch, I shall observe that my maid and I are no less discomforted by this wretched cold. Perhaps the Jaghut were delighted to dwell within such a climate, but as you can well see, we are not Jaghut.'

Shurq Elalle said, 'Highness, about my ship . . .'

Felash drew deeply on her mouthpiece, 'Yes,' she sighed. 'That. I believe I have apologized already, have I not? It is perhaps a consequence of insufficient education, but I truly was unaware that all ships carry in their bellies a certain amount of water, considered acceptable for voyaging. And that the freezing thereof would result in disaster, in the manner of split boards and so forth. Besides, was not your crew working the pumps?'

'As you say,' Shurq said. 'But a hundred hands below deck could not have pumped fast enough, given the speed of that freezing. But that was not my point – as you noted, we have been through all that. Bad luck, plain and simple. No, what I wished to discuss was the matter of repairs.'

Felash regarded the pale-skinned woman, and slowly tapped the mouthpiece against her teeth. 'In the midst of your histrionics two days ago, Captain, I had assumed that all was lost in the matter of the *Undying Gratitude*. Have you reconsidered?'

'Yes. No. Rather, we have walked this beach. The driftwood is useless. The few logs we found were heavy as granite – Mael knows what they used that damned stuff for, but it sure doesn't float. In fact, it appears to have neutral buoyancy—'

'Excuse me, what?'

'Push that wood to any depth you like, there it stays. Never before seen the like. We have a ex-joiner with us who says it's to do with the minerals the wood has absorbed, and the soil the tree grew in. In any case, we see no forests inland – no trees at all, anywhere.'

'Meaning you have no wood with which to effect repairs. Yes, Captain, was this not your prediction two days ago?'

'Aye, it was, and so it has proved, Highness. And as my crew can't survive on a frozen ship, on the surface of it we seem to indeed be stranded.'

Skorgen kicked sand with his good foot. 'What's worse, Highness, there's hardly any shellfish an' the like in the shallows. Picked clean long ago, I'd wager. We couldn't even walk up the coast t'get where you want us to go.'

'Most disturbing,' Felash murmured, still eyeing Shurq Elalle. 'Yet you have an idea, haven't you, Captain?'

'Maybe.'

'Please, proceed. I am not by nature averse to adventure and experimentation.'

'Aye, Highness.' Still, the woman hesitated.

Felash sent a stream of smoke whirling away. 'Come now, Captain, your first mate is turning blue.'

'Very well. Omtose Phellack, Highness – is it a true Hold?'

'I am not sure what you mean by that question.'

'A Hold. A place, a world unlike this one—'

'Where,' added Skorgen, 'we might find, er, trees. Or something. Unless it's all ice and snow, of course, or worse.'

'Ah, I see.' She tapped some more, thinking. 'The Hold of Ice, well, precisely. The sorcery – as we have all discovered – is certainly . . . cold. Forbidding, even. But if my education suffers in matters of ship building and the like, it is rather more comprehensive when it comes to the Holds.' She smiled. 'Naturally.'

'Naturally,' said Shurq Elalle, to cut off whatever Skorgen had been about to say.

'The commonest manifestation of Omtose Phellack is precisely as we have experienced. Ice. Bitter cold, desiccating, enervating. But it must be understood, said sorcery was shaped as a defensive weapon, if you will. The Jaghut were at war with an implacable enemy, and they were losing that war. They sought to surround themselves in vast sheets of ice, to make of it an impassable barrier. And as often as not they succeeded . . . for a time. Of course, as my mother used to delight in pointing out, war drives invention, and as soon as one side improves its tactical position, the other quickly adapts to negate the advantage – assuming they have the time to do so. Interestingly, one could argue it was the Jaghut's very own flaws that ensured their demise. For, had they considered ice not as a defensive measure, but as an *offensive* one – had they made it a true weapon, a force of attack and assault – why, they might well have annihilated their enemy before it could adapt. And while details regarding that enemy are murky—'

'Forgive me, Highness,' interrupted the captain. 'But, as you noted earlier, my first mate is truly suffering. If I am understanding you, the ice and cold of Omtose Phellack are mere aspects, or, I suppose, applications of a force. And, as such, they are not that force's sole characteristic.'

Felash clapped her hands. 'Precisely, Captain! Excellent!'

'Very well, Highness. I am so relieved. Now, as to those other aspects of the Hold, what can you tell me?'

Felash blinked up at the woman. 'Why, nothing.'

'Nothing?'

212

'Not a thing, Captain. The only manifestation of Omtose Phellack this world has seen has been ice-aspected.'

'Then how do you know there's more to it?'

'Captain, it only stands to reason.'

'So, this notion of there being more, it's merely . . . theoretical?'

'Dearest, that term is not pejorative, no matter the tone you have just employed.'

Teeth chattering, Skorgen Kaban said, 'So I stood here for that? You ain't got a Mael-spitting clue?'

'Hardly accurate, First Mate,' Felash said. 'It would hardly have served any of us if I'd simply said, "I don't know", would it? Instead, what I have actually said is, "I don't know, but I believe this to be a path worth pursuing."'

'So why didn't you?' he demanded.

'But I did!'

Shurq Elalle turned to Skorgen. 'That's enough, Pretty. Go back to the others.'

'An' tell 'em what?'

'We're . . . exploring possibilities.'

Felash waved one plump hand. 'A moment, please. I suggest that you both return to your fellows. The explorations that will occupy me on this day are best done alone, for I cannot guarantee the safety of any-one in close proximity. In fact, I suggest you move your camp perhaps twice its present distance from us.'

'Very well, Highness,' said Shurq Elalle. 'We shall do that.'

As they marched off, Felash turned to her handmaid. 'My dear,' she murmured, 'a journey awaits you.'

'Yes, Highness.'

'Gird yourself well,' Felash advised. 'Prepare the armour and take the throwing axes. And you will need to swim out to the ship, for a splinter of wood. But before all that, I wish a new pot of tea, and more rustleaf for this bowl.'

'At once, Highness.'

'Gods below,' Shurq Elalle muttered as they neared the crew's camp, 'but she has spectacular tits. It ever amazes me the extraordinary variation blessing us all.' She glanced at her first mate. 'Or cursing us, as the case may be.'

'I wanted to stick a damned knife in her skull, Cap'n.'

'Belay such notions, and stow them deep and dark – if one of the mates hears you, well, I don't want that kind of trouble.'

'Of course, Cap'n. Was just an impulse, anyway, like a tic under the eye. Anyway, how could you see her tits at all, under all those warm furs and such?'

'I could see just fine,' Shurq replied. 'It's called imagination, Pretty.'

'Wish I had some of that.'

'In the meantime, we need to allay some fears, and I expect moving us farther down the strand will put us in good stead right from the start.'

'Aye, it will.' He scratched at the scars puckering his neck. 'You know, Cap'n, I got me a smell that's saying that handmaiden of hers ain't as useless as she's made out to look, you know?'

'Brewing pots and lighting pipe bowls doesn't count for anything with you, Pretty? I tell you, I'm considering finding my own handmaiden once we get home. Of course,' she added, 'there's no rule says it has to be a woman, is there?'

A flush crept up the man's misshapen face.

Shurq clapped him on the back. 'You're right about her, Pretty. I'm thinking she's as mean a sorceress as the Princess herself, and probably a lot more besides. That woman hides herself well, but one glimpse of her wrists . . . well, unless she's throwing bales of hay around when no one's looking – and given the scars on her hands those bales got knives in them – well, aye, she's more than she seems.'

'What's her name anyway?'

'No idea.' Shurq grunted. The sailors at the camp were watching them now. 'All right, Pretty, let me do the talking.'

'Aye, Cap'n, better you'n me.'

'And if I mess up, you can beat on some heads.'

'T'bring 'em round, like.'

'Exactly.'

Cool beneath the umbrella, Felash watched her handmaid crawl up from the water. 'You need more fat on you, dear,' she observed. 'I'm sure the sun will warm you up soon enough, as it has done me. In any case,' she gestured with the mouthpiece, 'the passage awaits you.'

Gasping, the older woman slowly worked her way well clear of the water line. In her right hand was a splinter of wood, black against her bluish knuckles. Behind her, in the shallows, the ice was fast melting as the last remnants of Omtose Phellack faded. At the bay's outer edge, where the shelf fell away to deeper water, the *Undying Gratitude* was settling lower into her glittering, weeping nest.

Once the handmaid had recovered enough to begin moving, she dressed herself in quilted undergarments and then the heavy scaled armour retrieved from bundles of waxed canvas. Taking up the paired throwing axes, a leather-sheathed short sword, an underarm holster of four throwing knives, and her helm, she completed her attire by tucking the wood splinter into her belt. 'Highness, I am ready.'

'Well said. My patience was wearing ominously thin.' Sighing, Felash set the mouthpiece down and rose. 'Where did you put the last of the sweets?'

'Beside the brick of rustleaf, Highness.'

'Ah, I see. Wonderful. See how thin I'm getting? It's an outrage. Do you recall your own childhood, dear, when your chest was flat and all your bones jutted every which way?'

'No, Highness, I was never boy-thin, thank the Errant's nudge.'

'Nor me. I have always been suspicious of grown men who seem to like that in their women. What's wrong with little boys if they're into pallid bony wraiths?'

'Perhaps it appeals to their protective natures, Highness.'

'Protecting is one thing, diddling is entirely another. Now, where was I? Oh yes, throwing you into the Hold of Ice. Best unsheathe at least a few of your weapons, dear. Who knows what you'll land in.'

The handmaid drew her axes. 'I am ready.'

'. . . that condescending, patronizing cow doesn't deserve tits like that, or that soft blemish-free skin and lustrous hair. And the way those hips swing, why, I'm amazed she doesn't throw out her back with every step, and those damned luscious lips look ready made to wrap themselves round— Gods, what was that?'

The thunderclap shivered the water in the bay, set the sand to blurry trembling. Shurq Elalle turned to see an enormous white cloud billowing out and up from Felash's camp. The sailors – well out of earshot behind her – were now on their feet, shouting in alarm.

'Stay here, Skorgen. And calm those fools down!' She set off at a run.

The camp was a mess, gear flung about as if a whirlwind had erupted in its midst. Princess Felash was slowly picking herself up from the blasted sand. Her hair was awry, her clothes dishevelled. Her face was red, as if she'd been repeatedly slapped.

'Highness, are you all right?'

The girl coughed. 'I believe the theory has proved itself, Captain. It seems there is far more to Omtose Phellack than a few chunks of ice. The passage I found, well, it's hard to say where precisely it led—'

'Where is your handmaiden, Highness?'

'Well, let us hope she is exploring in wonder and delight.'

'You sent her through?'

A flash from her stunning eyes. 'Of course I sent her through! Did you not insist on the necessity, given our terrible plight? Can you begin to imagine my sacrifice, the appalling extremity of the service we are providing here?'

Shurq Elalle studied the plump girl. 'What if she doesn't come back?'

'I shall be most displeased. At the same time, we shall have before us evidence to support certain other theories about Omtose Phellack.'

'Excuse me, what other theories?'

'Why, the ones about shrieking demons, clouds of madness, flesh-eating plants, treacherous voles and a hundred other nightmares in a similar vein. Now, please be so kind as to rebuild my fire here, will you?'

She reached for her last throwing knife, found the sheath empty. Cursing, she ducked beneath the scything slash and threw herself to the left, shoulder-rolling until she came up against the bulk of the first fiend she'd slain. Her hands scrabbled up its muricated hide, found the wedge of one of her axes. Grunting as she tugged it free, she rolled over the body – it quivered as six swords punched into it in the spot where she'd been a moment earlier – and regained her feet in time to send the axe flying.

It crunched into the demon's brow, rocking its head back.

She lunged for it, tugging away one of the heavy swords gripped by the closest hand, which was twitching as the huge beast sagged on to its knees. Blade clashing as she beat away the swords flailing about at the ends of the five other arms, she chopped into its thick neck, once, twice, three times, until the head rolled free.

Spinning, she looked for more of the damned things. Five corpses and nothing more. Apart from her heavy breaths, the glade was silent.

From one fire straight into another – she'd landed in the middle of a camp – and it was her luck that she'd been ready when they clearly were not. The fire burned on here and there, where the hottest embers had scattered. If she was not careful, she'd end up burning down the forest – and all the wood the captain and her crew sorely needed.

The handmaid retrieved her weapons, and then stamped out the smouldering flames.

She cursed as something bit into the back of her neck. Scrabbling with one hand, she closed her fist about something small and furry, brought it round for a closer look. A vole, with a mouthful of her flesh. Snorting, she flung the thing away.

'Well, Highness,' she muttered, 'seems I've found some trees.'

Some beast shrieked close by, and the cry was echoed by a half-dozen more, surrounding the glade, drawing closer.

'Errant's bunghole, those things sound vicious.'

Pointless hanging around here, she decided. Choosing a direction at random, she ducked into the forest.

Absurdly dark, and the air was damp and cold. Plunging forward, she held her axes at the ready. A shriek sounded directly behind her and she whirled round. Something skittered on the forest floor. Another damned vole. She watched it pause, tilt its head back, and loose another curdling shriek.

A short time later she'd left the voracious things behind. The huge boles of the trees thinned out, with more undergrowth now impeding her way. She caught glimpses of the sky, a sweep of stars, no moon. A dozen paces ahead the ground fell away. She came to the edge, looked down into a ravine crowded with treefall, the trunks grey as bones.

Clumps of low fog wandered the length of the channel, glowing like swamp gas.

The channel was the product of flash flooding, and those trees had been savagely uprooted, flung down and carried along in the tumult. Studying the wreckage, she caught a shape in the ravine's gloom, twenty or so paces downstream. At first she'd assumed it was a barrier of knotted branches and trees, but that detritus had fetched up against something else . . . a hull.

She drew out the splinter of wood in her belt. It seemed to be sweating in her hand.

Boots skidding, she half slid, half stumbled down the steep bank of the ravine. Avoiding the fog as best she could, she clambered and climbed her way closer to the ship. How it had made it this far down this treacherous, winding channel without being torn to pieces was something of a mystery, but she knew enough to trust this sorcerous link. Whatever shape it was in, there would be enough of it to be of some use.

At last she reached the hull, set her hand against it. Not rotten. She thumped it, was rewarded with a faint hollow sound. Five arm-spans above her was an ornately carved gunnel, the heavy rail formed in the shape of entwining serpents running the length of the ship – which she judged to be somewhere between fifteen and twenty paces.

She glanced down then, to see the fog rising up to swallow her knees. And in that fog, small clawed hands reached out to grasp her thighs, the talons stabbing deep, the limbs writhing like worms. Gasping at the pain, she pulled out her sword and began hacking.

Her thighs were shredded and streaming blood by the time she cut herself loose and worked her way up the side of the hull, using the clutter of trees and branches for foot- and handholds. Gasping, she lifted herself over the gunnel and thumped down on the slanted deck.

And found herself in the midst of a squall of black-haired, scaled apes. Howling, the dog-sized creatures bared dagger-long fangs, eyes flashing lurid yellow, and raised their knotted clubs. Then they rushed her.

From somewhere up the length of ravine, there came a deep, rumbling roar. But she had no time to think about that.

*   *   *

'My ootooloo thinks this is sex – how strange.'

Felash glanced sidelong at the captain, her lids slowly settling in a lazy blink. 'Back in the palace, there are exquisite mouthpieces carved in the semblance of a penis.' She gestured with one hand. 'All part of a princess's education—'

Shurq set the mouthpiece down. 'Enough of that, I think, Highness. I leave you to your . . . devices.'

'Adventure arrives in all manner of guises, Captain. Had your ootooloo a brain, I am sure it would most avidly concur.'

'But that's the whole point about, er, desire. It's mostly brainless. Most of the world's tragedy is found in this one misunderstanding. We tie too much to it, you see. Things like loyalty and precious intimacy, love and possession, and sooner or later it all goes wrong. Why, I knew men – and I do mean "knew" – who'd come to me twice a week hungry for the brainless stuff, and afterwards they'd babble on about their wives.'

'What would they tell you? Please, I must know.'

'Starved for gossip, are you?'

'The palace seems terribly far away at the moment.'

'Just so, Highness. Well. Some would tell me about all the sorcery of love being gone between them, the embers of desire cold as stone now. Others would complain about how complicated it had all become, or how rote, or how fraught. And still more would talk of their wives as if they were possessions, to be used when it suited the men and otherwise left alone, but the very notion of those wives perhaps doing what the husband happened to be doing – there with me – well, that could light a murderous rage in their eyes.'

'So, while being with you, most of them still missed the point?'

'Very astute, Highness. Yes, they missed the point entirely.'

'Because what you offered was sex without complications.'

'Exactly.'

'Brainless.'

'Yes. And that freed them, and freedom made them happy – or anyway forgetful – at least for a short time. But once the flush was past, well, that old world and all its chains just came rattling back down. They'd leave as if they were condemned to swim the canal.'

'You have led a varied and extraordinary life, Captain.'

'Life? Wrong word, Highness.'

'Oh, one doesn't have to be breathing to be alive – and before you comment on how ridiculously obvious that statement seems, I do implore you to give it a second consideration, as I was not referring to your condition.'

'Then I am indeed curious as to what you might mean, Highness.'

'In my years of education, I have—'

A roar drowned out her next words, and they swung round to see a torrent of muddy, foaming water pounding into the bay just beyond the shallows. Rushing from a gaping wound almost swallowed in gouts of steam, the flood thundered aside the slabs of floating ice, clearing a broad swathe. A moment later what seemed half a forest exploded out from the wound, snapped branches and sundered trees, and then the prow of a ship lunged into view, outward like a thrust fist, and then plunging down to the bay's churning waters.

The raucous flow drove the ship straight for the reef.

'Errant's bitch!' swore Shurq Elalle.

Abruptly, in wallows of spume and steam, the ship heeled, came about, and they saw a figure at the stern rudder, pushing hard against the current.

The wound thundered shut, cutting off the wild flow. Branches and logs skirled in the spinning water.

Felash watched the captain run into the shallows.

The strange ship had crunched briefly against the coral shelf before pulling clear. It was fortunate, the princess decided, that the seas were calm, but it was obvious that one woman alone could not manage the craft, and that disaster still loomed. Glancing to the right, she saw the crew pelting along the strand, clearly intent on joining the captain.

Felash looked back to the ship. 'Dearie, couldn't you have found a prettier one?'

Spitting out silty water, Shurq Elalle pulled herself on to the deck. Something slimy beneath her boots sent her down on to her backside with a thump. She held up one palm. Blood. Lots and lots of blood. Swearing, she regained her feet and made for the bow. 'Is there an anchor?' she shouted. 'Where's the damned anchor?'

From the stern, the handmaid yelled back, 'How should I know?'

Shurq saw her crew now plunging into the shallows. *Good.*

'We're drifting back to that reef,' the handmaiden cried. 'How do I stop it doing that?'

'*With a damned anchor, you stupid cow!*'

Failing to find anything, and feeling somewhat bad about her outburst, Shurq turned about and began making her way back to the stern. One clear look at the handmaiden stopped her in her tracks. 'Gods, woman, what happened to you?'

'It's the damned voles,' she snarled. 'This – that thing – is that what you call a sea-anchor?'

Shurq forced her eyes away from the woman to where she was pointing. 'Mael's kiss, aye, it is!' Five quick steps along she halted yet again. 'Is that water I'm hearing below? Are we taking on water?'

The handmaiden leaned on the rudder's handle and looked over with red-shot, exhausted eyes. 'You're asking me, Captain?'

Shurq whirled, reached the landward gunnel. Glared down at her thrashing crew. 'Get aboard, you lazy pigs! Man the pumps! Fast!'

Back on shore, Felash settled down on the log, careful once more to avoid the iron spikes. Drawing on her hookah, she watched the antics with some contentment. As she exhaled a stream of smoke, she heard and felt a rattle in her throat.

Almost time for her afternoon cough.

He kicked his way through the clutter, the crumpled helms, the crushed iron scales, the bones that crumbled into dust and lifted grey clouds to swirl about his legs. Ahead, across an expanse of level land buried in corpses, was a mound of the same twisted bodies, and from the top of that mound rose the trunks of two trees, bound at the centre to form an upright X. The remnants of a body hung from it, flesh in shreds, black hair hanging down over the desiccated face.

Silchas Ruin could see, even from this distance, the long-shafted arrow buried in the figure's forehead.

Here, in this place, realms folded one upon another. Chaos and madness in such profusion as to stain time itself, holding horror in an implacable grip. Here, the skin of a hundred worlds bore the same seared brand. He did not know what had happened at this battle – this slaughter – to leave such a legacy, nor even the particular world in which the actual event had taken place.

He slowly crossed the killing field, towards the mound and its grisly shrine.

Other figures moved about, walking as if lost, as if seeking friends amidst the faceless thousands. At first he'd thought them ghosts, but they were not ghosts. They were gods.

His passage caught the attention of one, and then another, and then still more. Some simply looked away again, resuming whatever it was they were doing. A few set out to intercept him. As they drew closer, he heard their voices, their thoughts.

'A stranger. Interloper. This is not his world, this is not his curse, this is nothing to him.'

'He comes to mock us, the fragments of us snared here.'

'He does not even hear the cries that so deafen us, all these chains of desire . . .'

'And despair, Shedenul, so much despair . . .'

Silchas Ruin reached the base of the mound, studied the twisted bodies before him, a steep slope of solid bone, leathery flesh, armour and shattered weapons.

A half-dozen gods gathered around him.

'Tiste Liosan?'

'No, Beru. Tiste Andii. His white skin mocks the darkness within him.'

'Does he belong in the war? He is dangerous. We don't want him anywhere near us when we slay the Fallen One. When we feed and so free ourselves—'

'Free?' growled one in a thick, heavy voice. 'Mowri, from the legacy of our followers we shall never be free. This is the bargain we made—'

'I made no such bargain, Dessembrae!'

'Nevertheless, Beru. Mortal desire gave us shape. Mortal desire dragged us into all their realms. It was not enough that we ascended, not enough that we should seek out our own destinies. I tell you, though most of me still walks a distant world – and his howls of betrayal deafen me – in curse and prayer I am knotted here like a fist. Do I desire worship? I do not. Do I seek ever greater power? I have been shown its futility, and now all my purpose settles like ash upon my soul. Here, we are trapped, and so we shall remain—'

'Because that fool Master sanctified Kaminsod's theft! The Fallen One was wounded. Made useless with pain. And with that Master's cursed blessing he raised the House of Chains, and with those chains he bound us all!'

Dessembrae snorted. 'Long before the first rattle of those chains, we were in shackles – though we amused ourselves by pretending that they did not exist. The Master of the Deck and the Fallen One dispelled the illusion – no, they dispelled our delusions – and with them all their sweet, precious convenience.'

'I do not need an upstart like you telling me all I already know!'

'You do, when you would feed your reason with false indignation. We shall soon gather in another place little different from this one, and there we shall commit murder. Cold, brutal murder. We shall slay a fellow god. Before his heart is sundered, before the Unknowable Woman can ever reach the Fallen One, or attempt whatever it is she intends, we shall kill him.'

'Do not so easily discard that woman, Dessembrae,' said a new voice, a woman's, thin and crackling. 'She is sibling to the Master of the Deck – a Master who hides himself from us all. How can this be? How has he managed to blind us to his whereabouts? I tell you, he hovers over all of this, as unknowable as his sister. This wretched family from that wretched empire—'

A cane cracked against bones, splintering them, and Silchas turned to see that a new god had arrived. Indistinct, a smear of shadow. 'Dessembrae,' this one hissed, 'and dearest Jhess. Beru, Shedenul, Mowri. Beckra, Thilanda, see how you crowd this Tiste Andii? This

221

brother of Anomander Rake? Do you imagine he cannot hear you?'
The cane jabbed at Dessembrae. 'Look at us, so fey in reflection of
our once-mortal selves. The Empire, yes! Our empire, Dessembrae,
or have you forgotten? That wretched family? Our very own
children!'

'Oh, look around, Shadowthrone,' snarled Jhess, her face of skeined
wool, cotton, hemp and silk twisting and knotting as she bared web-
shrouded teeth. 'D'rek has come and gone from this place. She knows
and makes for us a true path. Your damned children cannot hope to
defeat us. Leave them to the Forkrul Assail! May they devour each
other!'

Shadowthrone giggled. 'Tell me, Jhess, do you see your cousin anywhere near? Where is the Queen of Dreams in this place of death?'

'She hides—'

'She is not here, Jhess,' said Shadowthrone, 'because she is awake.
Awake! Do you understand me? Not sleeping, not dreaming herself
here, not plucking all your mad tails, Jhess, to confuse mortal minds.
You are all blind fools!'

'You mean to betray us!' shrieked Shedenul.

'I care nothing for any of you,' Shadowthrone replied, with a laconic
gesture of one ethereal hand. 'Betray? Too much effort over too little
of worth.'

'You come here only to mock us?'

'I am here, Beru, because I am curious. Not about any of you. You're
nothing but gods, and if the Assail succeed you will all vanish like farts
in the wind. No, my curiosity is with our unexpected guest, our Tiste
Andii.' The cane waved at Silchas Ruin. 'O brother of heroes, why do
you bless Coltaine's Eternal Fall with your presence?'

'I seek a weapon.'

'The two you carry are not enough?'

'For a companion. This battle you all seem so eager to join, I could
warn you against it, but I admit that I see little use in that. You are all
determined to join the fray, leaving me to wonder.'

'Wonder what?' demanded Beru.

'When the dust settles, how many of your corpses will I see upon
that field?' Silchas Ruin shrugged. 'Do as you will.'

'Your brother slew our strongest ally.'

'He did? And of what significance is that to me, Beru?'

'You are as infuriating as he was! May you share his fate!'

'We shall all share his fate,' Silchas Ruin replied.

Shadowthrone giggled. 'I have found you a weapon, but only if the
one who wields it is worthy.'

Silchas Ruin looked round. 'From this place?'

'No, not from here. There is nothing to the weapons here but *memories of failure.*' A sword appeared from the shadows swirling round the god and clattered at the Tiste Andii's feet.

Looking down, he drew a sharp breath. 'Where did you come by this?'

'Recognize it?'

'A Hust . . . but no.' He hesitated. 'I feel that I should, knowing well that sacred forge. The draconic theme is . . . distinctive. But the ferrules remind me of Hust's earliest period of manufacture, and I thought I knew all of those so made. Where did you come by this?'

'Of little relevance, Prince. You note the draconic theme, do you? What is the term? Pattern weld? So you might think, to see those scales glittering so prettily along the length of the blade.' He giggled. *'So you might think.'*

'This weapon is too good for the one I intended to arm.'

'Indeed? How . . . unfortunate. Perhaps you could convince your friend to take the ones you now wield? And for yourself, this singular weapon. Consider it a gift to you, from Shadowthrone.'

'And why should you so gift me?' Silchas Ruin asked.

'Perhaps the others here bemoan the loss of Hood. I do not. He was hoary and humourless, and ugly besides. Thus. If I cannot convey my best wishes to Hood's noble slayer, then his brother shall have to do.'

Silchas Ruin looked back down at the Hust sword. 'When we were children,' he muttered, 'he used to steal my things all the time, because he liked to see me lose my temper.' He paused, remembering, and then sighed. 'Even then, he was fearless.'

Shadowthrone was silent. The other gods simply watched.

'And then,' Silchas Ruin whispered, 'he stole my grief. And now, what is there, I wonder . . . what is there left to feel?'

'If I suggested "gratitude", would that be insensitive?'

Silchas Ruin shot the god a sharp look, and then said, 'I accept the gift, Shadowthrone, and in return I offer you this.' He waved at the other gods. 'This mob ill suits you. Leave them to their devices, Shadowthrone.'

The god cackled. *'If I was blood kin to this family, I'd be the uncle slumped drunk and senseless in the corner. Luckily – dare I risk that word? – I am not kin to any of them. Rest assured I will humbly heed your advice, Prince.'*

Silchas Ruin picked up the weapon. He looked at the gods, his crimson eyes slowly moving from one ghastly face to the next. And then he vanished.

Dessembrae wheeled on Shadowthrone. 'What was all that? What scheme are you playing at?'

Shadowthrone's cane snapped out, caught the Lord of Tragedy flush across the bridge of his nose. He stumbled back, fell on to his backside.

Shadowthrone hissed, and then said, 'The best part of you wanders the mortal world, old friend. Long ago, he surrendered that emptiness called pride. At last, I see where it fetched up. Well, it seems one more lesson in humility shall find you.' He glared at the others. 'All of you, in fact.'

Beru growled. 'You snivelling little upstart . . .'

But then his voice fell away, for the Lord of Shadows was gone.

'Busy busy busy.'

Cotillion paused on the road. 'It's done?'

'Of course it's done!' Shadowthrone snapped, and then grunted. 'Here? What are we doing here?'

'Recognize the place, then.'

'Pah! Not more regrets from you. I'm sick of them!'

'I am marking this site one more time—'

'What, like a Hound pissing against a fence post?'

Cotillion nodded. 'Crude, but apt.'

'What of you?' Shadowthrone demanded. 'Did you return to Shadowkeep? Did you send her off? Did she need a few slaps? A punch in the nose, a quick roger behind the keep?'

'She needed only my invitation, Ammanas.'

'Truly?'

'Of all the wolves on one's own trail,' Cotillion said, 'there is always one, the pack's leader. Cruel and relentless. Show me a god or a mortal with no wolves on their heels—'

'Enough talk of wolves. This is me, after all. Fanged, eyes of fire, foul fur and endless hunger, a hundred beasts, each one named Regret.'

'Just so.' Cotillion nodded.

'So you put her on a horse and gave her a blade, and sent her back down her own trail.'

'To kill the biggest, meanest one, aye.'

Shadowthrone grunted again. 'Bet she was smiling.'

'Find me a fool who'll take that bet,' Cotillion replied, smiling himself.

The Lord of Shadows looked round. 'See none hereabouts. Too bad.'

The air filled with the cries of gulls.

Tiste Liosan. The Children of Father Light. A star is born in the dark, and the heavens are revealed to all. Withal ran his hand along the pitted plaster, fragments of damp moss falling away where his fingers scraped it loose. The painted scene was in a primitive, awkward style, yet he suspected it was more recent than those glorious works in the city's palace. Light like blood, corpses on the strand, faces shining beneath helms. A sky igniting . . .

A few survived the chaos, the civil wars. They cowered here in this forest. In coloured plaster and paint, they sought to make eternal their memories. He wondered why people did such things. He wondered at their need to leave behind a record of the great events witnessed, and lived through.

Sure enough, a discovery like this – here in the forest above the Shore, at the base of a vast sinkhole his errant step had inadvertently discovered – well, it led to questions, and mystery, and, like the missing patches and the thick clumps of moss, he found a need to fill in the gaps.

For we are all bound in stories, and as the years pile up they turn to stone, layer upon layer, building our lives. You can stand on them and stare out at future's horizon, or you can be crushed beneath their weight. You can take a pick in hand and break them all apart, until you're left with nothing but rubble. You can crush that down into dust and watch the wind blow it away. Or you can worship those wretched stories, carving idols and fascinating lies to lift your gaze ever higher, and all those falsehoods make hollow and thin the ground you stand on.

Stories. They are the clutter in our lives, the conveniences we lean upon and hide behind. But what of it? Change them at will – it's only a game in the skull, shaking the bones in the cup to see if something new shows up. Aye, I imagine such games are liberating, and the sense of leaving oneself behind is akin to moving house. A fresh start beckons. A new life, a new host of stories, a new mountain to build stone by stone.

'What makes you happy, Withal?'

Long stretches of time, Sand, free of alarm.

'Nothing else?'

Oh, beauty, I suppose. Pleasure to caress the senses.

'You play at being a solid and simple man, Withal, but I think it is all an act. In fact, I think you think too much, about too many things. You're worse than me. And before long, all that chaos gets so thick it starts looking solid, and simple.'

Woman, you make my head ache. I'm going for a walk.

Rubbing at his bruised hip, he brushed twigs and mud from his clothes, and then carefully made his way up the sinkhole's side, grasping roots, finding footholds from the blocks of cut stone hiding in the gloom. Pulling himself clear, he resumed his journey down to the Shore.

Twenty or more paces up from the strand, the forest edge had been

225

transformed. Trees cut down, trenches dug in banked ripples facing the imminent breach in Lightfall. Figures swarming everywhere. Weapons in heaps – swords, spears and pikes – with Shake and Letherii crews busy scrubbing the rust from the ancient iron, rolling new grips from strips of soaked leather. The wood of the hafted weapons seemed to have been unaffected by the passage of time, the black shafts as strong as ever. Hundreds of helms formed vaguely disturbing mounds here and there, awaiting oil and refitting.

Working his way past all this, Withal reached the strand. He paused, searching among the crowds. But he could not find the one he sought. Seeing a familiar face ahead, he called out, 'Captain Pithy!'

The woman looked up.

'Where is he?' Withal asked.

She straightened from the leather map she'd laid out on the sand, wiped sweat from her face, and then pointed.

Withal looked in that direction. Saw a lone figure seated atop an old midden, facing Lightfall. With a wave to Pithy, he set off in that direction.

Yedan Derryg was taking bites from a lump of cheese, his jaws working steadily as he studied the cascading light. He glanced over as Withal approached, but only briefly. Boots crunching on the ghastly white bone fragments of the beach, and then the slope of the midden, where amidst larger pieces of bone there were husks of some forest nut, more recent gourds and pieces of pottery, Withal reached the prince's side, whereupon he sat down. 'I didn't know we had any cheese left.'

Yedan plopped the last bit into his mouth, chewed a moment, swallowed and then said, 'We don't.'

Withal rubbed at his face. 'I expect to feel the salt, the freshened sea breezes. Instead, the air feels as close as the hold of a ship.' He nodded to Lightfall. 'There is no breath from this, none at all.'

Yedan grunted. 'There will be soon enough.'

'The queen was wondering about that.'

'Wondering?'

'All right. Fretting. Well, more like a cornered cat, come to think of it, so not fretting at all. Snarling, all claws out, fear blazing in her eyes.'

Yedan's jaws bunched, as if he was still chewing cheese, and then he said, 'Is that what you wake up to every morning, Withal?'

He sighed, squinted at Lightfall. 'Never been married, have you? I can tell.'

'Not much interested.'

'In any of that?'

'In women.'

'Ah. Well, among the Meckros, men marry each other all the time.

226

I figure they see how men and women do it, and want that for themselves.'

'Want what, exactly?'

'Someone to be the cat, someone to be the dog, I suppose. But all official like.'

'And here I thought you'd go on about love and commitment, Withal.'

'No, it's all down to who lifts a leg and who squats. And if you're lucky, that goes back and forth. If you're unlucky, you end up trapped in one or the other and life's miserable.'

'Your winning description of marriage, Withal, has fallen somewhat short for me.'

'Sorry to hear that, Yedan.'

'Something to do, I suspect, with the lack of sincerity.'

Withal grinned. 'Anyway, the queen is eager for reassurance. Do you feel ready? And how . . . how soon?'

'There is no true measure of readiness until we are engaged, Withal, until I can see what my army can do, or is willing to do. Of the two, I will take the latter and hope for the former. As for how soon . . .' He paused, and then pointed at Lightfall. 'There, do you see that?'

A strange dull spot formed in the descending streams of light. It bled outward like a stain, reaching down to the very base, before the brighter edges began soaking back in. 'What was that?'

'Dragons, Withal.'

'*What?*'

'Soletaken, or allies. The sorcery of the Eleint that some call their *breath*. They assail the barrier with that chaotic power, and with each breath the ancient wound thins, the skin weakens.'

'Mael save us, Yedan – you mean to stand against *dragons*? How?'

'When the wound opens, it will be at the base – to open the way for their foot soldiers. A beachhead will need to be established – we need to be driven back from the wound. For a dragon to physically come through the breach will take all of its power, and when it does it will be on the ground, not in the air. And when a dragon is on the ground, it is vulnerable.'

'But if the beachhead has driven you back—'

'We must in turn overrun them.'

'To reach that first dragon.'

'Yes.'

'And kill it.'

'Ideally, halfway through the wound. And not killed, but dying. At that moment, my sister and the witches need to . . . pounce. To take that draconic life force—'

'And seal the breach.'

227

Yedan Derryg nodded.

Withal stared at the man, his angled profile, his dark, calm eyes fixed so steadily upon Lightfall. *Beru's sweet piss, does nothing rattle him? Prince Yedan Derryg, your soldiers will look to you, and now at last I begin to see what they will see. You are their own wall, their own Lightfall.*

But are you wounded, too?

'Yedan, can it be done? What you describe?'

The man shrugged. 'My sister refuses to kneel before the First Shore. It is the act that sanctifies the queen of the Shake, and she will not do it.'

'Why ever not?'

His teeth bared in a brief grin, Yedan said, 'We are a contrary lot, us royals. A queen who defies sanctification, a prince who will never produce an heir, and what of Awakening Dawn? What of our Sister of Night? Gone, for ever gone. Yan Tovis and me, we are all that's left. Have you ever been in a Letherii city, Withal?'

'Well, yes.'

'Have you ever seen a Shake walk through a Letherii crowd?'

'No, I don't think so.'

'They keep their eyes on the cobbles. They shift and slide from anyone in their path. They do not walk as would you, tall, filling the space you need.'

'I believe that has changed, Yedan – what you and your sister have done here—'

'And sticking a sword in their hand and telling them to stand here, to fight and to die without a single backward step, will turn mice into snarling leopards? We shall find out the answer to that soon enough.'

Withal thought for a time on all that the prince had said, and then he shook his head. 'Is it just your royal blood, then, that makes you and your sister the exceptions to the image you paint of the Shake? You are not mice.'

'We trained as officers in the Letherii military – we considered that a duty, not to the king of Lether, but to the Shake. To lead we must be seen to lead, but more than that we needed to learn *how* to lead. This was the Letherii military's gift to us, but it was a dangerous one, for it very nearly swallowed up Yan Tovis – perhaps it has, given the reluctance she now displays.'

'If she does not kneel to the Shore,' asked Withal, 'can the witches alone seal the wound?'

'No.'

'And if there were more of them?'

Yedan glanced over. 'If I hadn't murdered them, you mean?' He seemed to find something left over in his mouth, worked it loose with his tongue, chewed and swallowed. 'Hard to say. Possibly. Possibly not. Venal rivalries plagued them. It's more likely they would have usurped my sister, or even killed her. And then they'd set about killing each other.'

'But couldn't you have stopped them?'

'I did.'

Withal was silent for a moment, and then he said, 'Surely she understands the danger?'

'I imagine so.'

'You've not tried to persuade her?'

'In her own way, my sister is as stubborn as I am.'

'Another wall,' Withal muttered.

'What?'

He shook his head. 'Nothing of import.'

'There. Another pass comes – look—'

A dark shape was descending behind Lightfall, a thing huge and blurred. Lunging to sweep past the heart of the wound. Something struck the barrier like a massive fist. Light sprayed like blood. Red cracks spread out from the dark stain.

Yedan stood. 'Go back to the queen of Kharkanas, Withal,' he said, drawing his sword. 'One more pass, if that, and then this begins.'

'Begins?' Withal asked, as if struck dumb.

He saw Pithy and Brevity running up the strand. A sudden chill flooded through him. Terrible memories. Of his younger days, of battles upon the decks of the Meckros. Fear weakened his legs.

'Tell her,' continued Yedan, his tone as steady as ever, 'we will hold as long as we can. Tell her, Withal, that once more the Shake stand upon the Shore.'

Spear points thrust out from the wound, a shivering, bristling horror – he could see figures, pushing, crowding, could almost hear their howls. Light spurted like ropes of gore. Light flooded out on to the strand, illuminating the crushed bones. Light lit faces beneath helms.

Tiste Liosan. The Children of Father Light. A star is born in the dark, and the heavens are revealed to all.

'Go, Withal. We are breached.'

We can hold against nothing. We can only crumble, like sand before the devouring wave. Yedan calls to his officers, his officers rush and shout, ranks form up, these would-be soldiers struggle and steady themselves. The Shake – my Shake – stand pale, eyes wide, straining to see what's happening at the breach, where the Letherii, dreaming of riches, meet the thrusting spears.

Screams now rise from the wound. There are Tiste Liosan, their faces broken masks of fury, and all the madness of war is down there, at the breach. Life's blood even now spilling down.

We cannot hold. Look at my people, how their eyes track my brother now, but he's only one man, and even he cannot defeat this enemy. Long ago, there were enough of us, enough to hold, enough to last and to die to save this realm. But no longer.

Pully and Skwish loomed in front of her. They were shouting, screaming, but she was deaf to them. The clash of weapons grew desperate, like a thousand knives upon a single whetstone. *But you are flesh, my brother. Not a whetstone. Flesh.*

'You must kneel!'

Yan Tovis frowned at the young woman before her. 'Is it blood you want?'

Eyes widened.

She held out her wrists. 'This?'

'You need to kneel before the Shore!'

'No,' she growled. 'Not yet. Go away, I'm done with you. The islanders are fighting – go down to them, kneel yourselves. In the sand beside the wounded and the dying – both of you. Look in their faces, and tell them it was all worth it.' Yan Tovis lunged forward, pushing them so that they staggered. 'Go! Tell them!'

You want me to kneel? To sanctify all of this? Shall I be yet one more ruler to urge my subjects to their deaths? Shall I stand tall and bold, shouting fierce promises of glory? How many lies can this scene withstand? Just how empty can words be?

'Kneel,' she whispered. 'Yes. Everyone. *Kneel.*'

CHAPTER NINE

I am fallen prey
There was a time
When fangs sank deep
My body dragged
And flesh howled
Fear's face was cold
With instinct's need
There was a time
When strangers took me
And the unfamiliar
Whispered terror
And the shock of desires
We could not expect
Lit eyes so like our own
There was a time
When a friend twisted
Before my eyes
And all my solid faiths
Washed free underfoot
Unknowing the world
With new and cruel design
There was a time
When kin drew the knife
To sever sacred law
With red envy
And red malice
The horror visits
The heart of home
Do you see this journey?
What began in shadows
And dark distance
Has drawn ever closer

Now I am fallen prey
To the demon in my soul
And the face twisting
Is my own
Railing at failures
Of flesh and bone
The spirit withers
And I fall prey
We have listed
A world of enemies
And now we fall prey
We fall prey

Faces of Fear
Fisher kel Tath

BROKEN AT LAST, THE BODY SLUMPS AND THE SPIRIT PULLS FREE, THE spirit wings away in flight and the sound of its wings is a sigh. But this, he knew, was not always the case. There were times when the spirit staggered loose with a howl, as broken as the body left behind. Too long inside tortured flesh, too long a sordid lover of punishing pain.

The sound of his horse's hoofs was hollow, the creak of its tendons like the settling of an old, familiar chair, and he thought of a warm room, a place heady with memories threaded through with love and grief, with joy and suffering. But there was no pocket within him to hold tears, nothing he could squeeze in one fist just to feel the wet trickling down between his fingers. No gestures left to remind himself of who he had once been.

He found her rotted corpse, huddled in the lee of a boulder. There were red glints in her hair, beneath wind-blown dust. Her face was tucked down, sunken cheeks pressed against the knees. As if in her last moments she sat, curled up, staring down at the stumps of her feet.

It was all too far gone, he told himself. Even this felt mechanical, but disjointed, on the edge of failure; a measure of stumbling steps, like a man blind and lost, trying to find his way home. Dismounting, boots rocking as the bones inside them shifted and scraped, he walked to her, slowly sat down on the boulder, amidst the creaks of tendon, bone and armour.

Broken-winged, the spirit had staggered from this place. Lost even to itself. How could he hope to track it? Leaning forward, he settled his face into his hands, and – though it made no difference – he closed his one eye.

Who I am no longer matters. A chair, creaking. A small room, acrid with woodsmoke. Crows in the rafters – what mad woman would invite them into this place? The hunters have thundered past and the wolf no longer howls. She has no breath for such things, not now, not running as she must. Running – gods, running!

She knows it's no use. She knows they will corner her, spit her with spears. She knows all about hunting, and the kill, for these were the forces of law in her nature. So too, it seems, for the ones pursuing her.

And the woman in the chair, her eyes are smarting, her vision blurs. The chimney needs cleaning, and besides, the wild is dead, for ever dead. And when next the hunters thunder past, their quarry will be on two legs, not four.

Just so.

Do you dream of me, old woman? Do you dream of a single eye, flaring in the night, one last look of the wild upon your face, your world? Gods below, I am tearing apart. I can feel it.

The horns sound their triumph. Slain, the beast's heart stills its mad race.

In her creaking chair, the old woman reaches up one hand, and gouges out one of her eyes. It rests bloody in her palm while she gasps with pain. And then she lifts her head and fixes her one remaining eye upon him. 'Even the blind know how to weep.'

He shakes his head, not in denial, but because he does not understand.

The old woman throws the eye into the fire. 'To the wild, to the wild, all gone. Gone. Loose the wolf within you, Ghost. Loose the beast upon the trail, and one day you shall find her.'

'Who are you?'

'Smell that? Wax in the fire. Wax in the fire.'

'What place is this?'

'This?' The chair creaks. She reaches up to her other eye. 'Love lives here, Ghost. The Hold you have forgotten, the Hold you all yearn to find again. But you forget more than that.' She pushed her nails into her other eye. 'Where there is love, there is pain.'

'No,' he whispered, 'there must be more to it than that.' He lifted his head, and opened his eye. Wretched wasteland, a boulder, a huddled form. 'But she threw it into the flames.' *Wax. Wax in the fire.*

Looking down, he studied the corpse beside him, and then he rocked to his feet, walked over to his lifeless horse, and pulled from the saddle a roll of sacking. Laying it out, he went back to her, lifted her gently from her snarled nest of greening grasses. On to the cloth, drawing up the edges and binding them tight, and then gathering the sack and slinging it across the horse's rump just behind the saddle, before climbing astride the motionless mount.

Collecting up the reins, Toc closed his remaining eye.

Then opened the missing one.

The day's light vanished abruptly, the mass of bruised clouds climbing, billowing outward. A savage gust of wind bowed back the trees lining the north ridge and a moment later rushed down the slope and up on to the road. Her horse shied and then quivered to the impact, and she hunched down over the saddle as the gale threatened to lift her from the animal's back. Driving her heels into its flanks, she urged her mount onward.

She was still half a day from the city – the warrens had a way of wandering, and gates could never be counted on, and this particular gate had opened a long, long way from where it had begun. Exhausted, filled with doubts and trepidation, she pushed on, her horse's hoofs cracking sparks on the cobbles.

Some things could haunt a soul; some things needed undoing. The toe of a boot searching ashes – but no, she'd gone beyond that. She was here, regrets like hounds at her heels.

Thunder pounded; lightning flashed and sent jagged fissures of argent light splitting the black clouds. Somewhere behind her a strike detonated on the road and her horse stumbled. She steadied it with a firm rein. The gusts of wind felt like fists pummelling the left side of her face, and all down that side of her body. She swore, but could barely hear her own voice.

The darkness had swallowed the world now and she rode half blind, trusting her mount to stay on the road. And still the rain held back – she could taste it on the air, bitter with the salt whipped up from the seas beyond the ridge.

Her cloak pulled loose from the thigh strings and snapped out wild as a torn sail behind her. She shouted a curse as she was nearly yanked from the saddle. Teeth grinding, she forced her upper body forward once again, one hand holding tight on the hinged saddle horn.

She'd ridden into the face of sandstorms – gods, she'd damned near spat into the face of the Whirlwind itself – but nothing like this. The air crackled, groaned. The road shook to the thunderous reverberations, like the hoofs of a god descending.

Howling now, giving voice to her fury, she drove her horse into a churning gallop, and the beast's breaths snorted like drums in the rain – but the air was charnel hot, tomb-dry – another blinding flash, another deafening detonation – her horse wavered and then, muscles bunching, bones straining, it regained its purchase on the road –

– and someone was now riding beside her, on a huge, gaunt horse black as the sky overhead.

She twisted round to glare at him. 'This is you?'

A flash of a grin, and then, 'Sorry!'

'When will it end?'

'How should I know? When the damned gate closes!'

He then added something more, but thunder smashed to splinters whatever he'd said, and she shook her head at him.

He leaned closer, shouted, 'It's good to see you again!'

'You idiot! Does he even know you're here?'

And to that question, his only answer was another grin.

Where had he been? The man had ever infuriated her. And now here he was, at her side, reminding her of all the reasons she'd had the first time round for doing . . . for doing what she did. Growling another curse, she shot him a glare. 'Will this get any worse?'

'Only when we leave!'

Gods below, the things I'll do for love.

'North,' the withered hag had said, her bent and broken visage reminding Torrent of an uncle who'd taken a hoof to the side of his face, crushing jaws and cheekbone. For the rest of his days, he'd shown to the world the imprint of that hoof, and with a twisted, toothless grin, he'd laugh and say, *'My best friend did this. What's the world come to when you can't even trust your best friends?'*

And if the horse had outlived him, if his wife had not wept at his byre as a widow should, instead standing dry-eyed and expressionless, if he'd not begun chasing little girls . . . Torrent shook his head. Any rider who called his horse his best friend already had a few stones knocked loose in his skull.

For all that, Torrent found himself tending to his mount with a care bordering on obsession. And he grieved to see it suffer. Poor forage, not enough water, the absence of its own kind. Solitude weakened a horse's spirit, for they were herd animals as much as humans were, and loneliness dulled the eye.

'The desert glitters with death,' continued Olar Ethil. 'We must go round it. North.'

Torrent glanced over at the children. Absi had ventured a few strides on to the plain, returning with a shard of crystal that painted prisms up his bared arm. He held up his trophy, waved it back and forth as if it was a sword, and then he laughed. The twins looked on, their wan faces empty of expression.

He had no skills when it came to children. Redmask had set him to care for the Awl children, that day long ago, knowing well his awkwardness, his discomfort. Redmask had been punishing him for something – Torrent could no longer remember what, not that it mattered any more. From where he had been, he'd seen the fall of the great leader. From where he had been, he'd witnessed the death of Toc Anaster.

It was a measure of human madness, he realized, that children should be made to see such things. The pain of the dying, the violence of the slayer, the cruelty of the victor. He wondered what the twins had seen, since that night of betrayal. Even Absi must bear scars, though he seemed oddly immune to long bouts of sorrow.

No, none of this was right. But then, maybe it had never been right. Did there not come to every child that moment when the mother, the father, loses that god-like status, that supreme competence in all things, when they are revealed to be as weak, as flawed and as lost as the child looking on? How that moment crushes! All at once the world becomes a threatening place, and in the unknown waits all manner of danger, and the child wonders if there is any place left in which to hide, to find refuge.

'North,' said Olar Ethil again, and she set off, limping, pieces hanging from her battered form. The two skeletal lizards scampered into her wake – he'd wondered where they'd been, since it had been days since he'd last seen them, but now the damned things were back.

Torrent turned from his horse and walked over to the children. 'Absi and Stavi this time,' he said. Stavi rose and took her brother's hand – the one not gripping the shard – and led him over to the horse. She clambered into the saddle, and then reached down to Absi.

Watching her lift the boy from the ground and set him down on the saddle in front of her reminded Torrent of how these children had changed. Wiry, all fat burned away, their skins darkened by the sun. A newly honed edge of competence.

Redmask left me to guard the children. But they are gone, now. All of them. Gone. So I promised Setoc to ward these ones. So bold, that vow. And I don't even like children. If I fail again, these three will die.

Storii's calloused hand slipped into his own. He looked down to meet her eyes, and what he saw in them made his stomach twist. *No, I am not your unflawed protector, not your guardian god. No, do not look at me like that.* 'Let's go,' he said gruffly.

She could feel her power growing, her senses reaching out through stony ground, along the sodden sands of buried streams. Again and again, she touched the signs of her chosen children, the Imass, and even those from the Eres'al – who dwelt in the times before the Imass. And she could hear the echoes of their voices, songs lost to ancient winds

236

now, there on the banks of extinct rivers, in the lees of hills long since worn down and eaten away.

The tools were crude, it was true, the stone of poor quality, but no matter. They had lived in this place; they had wandered these lands. *And they shall do so once again. Onos T'oolan, you refuse to understand what I seek for you, for you and all your kin. Silverfox has led so many away, far beyond my reach, but First Sword, those who follow you shall find salvation.*

Heed not the summons of the First Throne – she may be a child of the Emperor, she may even stand in the shadow of secrets – but her power over you is an illusion. What urges you to obey is the stain of Logros, the madness of his desperation. Yes, you knelt before the First Throne, there with all the others, but the Emperor is dead. The Emperor is dead!

Listen to me, Onos T'oolan! Turn your people back – the path you are on shall see you all destroyed. Find me – let us end this war of wills. First Sword, see through my eyes – I have your son.

I have your son.

But still he pushed her away, still his own power seethed and roiled around him, raw with the force of Tellann. She sought to force her way through, but his strength defied her. *You damned fool! I have your son!*

She snarled, paused to glare back at the humans trailing her. *And what of your daughters, Onos? Shall I open their throats? Will that compel you? How dare you defy me! Answer me!*

Nothing but the moaning wind.

Must I abandon them? Must I find you myself? Tell me, is your power sufficient to rebuff a dragon? I will come to you, First Sword, in the raging fire of Telas—

'If you harm them, Olar Ethil, a thousand worlds of Telas fire shall not keep you safe from me.'

She laughed. 'Ah, now you speak.'

'Do I?'

The Bonecaster hissed in fury. 'You? Begone, you one-eyed corpse! Go back to your pathetic army of worthless soldiers!'

'Reach so with your powers, Olar Ethil, and there is no telling whom you might find. In fact, consider this a warning. You are far from alone in this land. There are wings in the darkness, and the morning frost holds in every droplet a thousand eyes. On the wind, scents and flavours, and the breath of ice—'

'Oh, be quiet! I see what you're doing! Do you imagine me unable to hide?'

'You failed in hiding from me, a one-eyed corpse.'

'The longer you linger,' she said, 'the more you lose of yourself. That

237

is *my* warning to *you*. You fall away, Toc Anaster. Do you understand me? *You fall away.*'

'*I shall hold on long enough.*'

'*To do what?*'

'*What's needed.*'

It proved easy for her will to evade him, slipping to rush past, thundering like a flash flood. Pouring, like water, like fire. She would assail the First Sword's Tellann. She would shatter the barrier. She would take him by the throat—

Ahead, a line of horse soldiers across her path, silent and dark upon the plain. Dirty, limp banners, torn standards, helms above gaunt, withered faces.

Her power hammered into them, crashed and broke apart like waves against a cliff. Olar Ethil felt her mind reeling back. She was stunned by the will of these revenants, these usurpers of the Throne of Death. As she staggered back, one guided his horse out from the line.

The grey of his beard was spun iron, the cast of his eyes was stone. He reined in before her, leaned forward on his saddle. 'You are treading foreign land, Bonecaster.'

'You dare challenge me?'

'Anywhere, any time.'

'He is mine!'

'Olar Ethil,' he said, drawing his sword, 'when you argue with death, you always lose.'

Shrieking her fury, she fled.

Torrent walked to stand beside the kneeling creature. 'You nearly deafened us,' he said. 'Is something wrong?'

She slowly straightened, then lashed out an arm across the front of his chest. Thrown back, he was flung through the air. He struck the ground hard, the breath driven from his lungs.

Olar Ethil walked to him, reached down and closed a hand round his throat. She pulled him upright, thrust her mangled face forward, and in the sockets of her eyes he could see fires raging. 'If I kill them all,' she hissed, 'here and now . . . what use are you? Tell me, pup, what use are you?'

He gasped, trying to regain his breath. Snarling, she thrust him away. 'Do not mock me again, Awl.'

Torrent staggered, dropped to one knee.

Close by, the two skeletal reptiles laughed.

Storii ran to his side. 'Don't,' she pleaded, her face tear-streaked. 'Don't, please. *Don't leave us!*'

He shook his head, his throat too bruised for words.

His horse moved up behind them, nudged Torrent's shoulder.
Spirits below.

It had been a long time since he'd last unleashed the full power of
Tellann, dragging his hold on the Warren with him with each heavy,
scraping step. Within its deadened heart, nothing could reach Onos
T'oolan; even the furious assault of Olar Ethil felt muted, a muffled
rage made indistinct by layer upon layer of the First Sword's will.

He recalled a desert, a salt flat's verge of sharp stones. There were
rents in the line. There were clans with but a few warriors left to stand,
there on that cold, still morning. He stood before Logros, bereft of his
kin, and all that held him there was the binding of duty, the knotted
webs of loyalty. He was the First Sword, after all.

The last Jaghut in the Odhan had been hunted down, butchered.
The time had come to return to the Malazan Empire, to the Emperor
who had seated himself on the First Throne. And Onos T'oolan knew
he would soon return to the side of Dassem Ultor, his mortal shadow
who had taken for himself – and for his closest followers – the title of
First Sword. Prophetic inspiration, for they would soon all be dead – as
dead as Onos T'oolan, as dead as the T'lan Imass. Or if not dead, then
. . . *destroyed.*

Instead, Logros had lifted one hand, a splay of gnarled fingers all
pointing at Onos. 'You were once our First Sword,' he said. 'When we
return to the mortal empire, we shall avow service to Dassem Ultor,
for he is your heir to the title. You shall surrender the name of First
Sword.'

Onos T'oolan considered that for a time. Surrender the title? Cut
through the bindings? Sever the knots? *Know freedom once more?* 'He
is mortal, Logros. He does not know what he has done in taking for
himself the title of First Sword.'

'In service,' Logros replied, 'the T'lan Imass sanctify him—'

'You would make of him a god?'

'We are warriors. Our blessing shall—'

'*Damn him for eternity!*'

'Onos T'oolan, you are of no use to us.'

'Do you imagine' – and he recalled the timbre of his voice, the seething outrage, and the horror of what Logros sought to do . . . *to a mortal
man, to a man destined to face his own death, and that is something
we have never done, no, we ever ran from that moment of reckoning –
Logros, the Lord of Death shall strike at the T'lan Imass, through him.
Hood shall make him pay. For our crime, for our defiance –* 'Do you
imagine,' he'd said, 'that your blessing could be anything but a curse?
You would make him a god of sorrow, and failure, a god with a face
doomed to weep, to twist in anguish—'

'Onos T'oolan, we cast you out.'

'I shall speak to Dassem Ultor—'

'You do not understand. It is too late.'

Too late.

The Adjunct Lorn had believed that it was the murder of the Emperor that had broken the human empire's alliance with Logros T'lan Imass. She had been wrong. *The spilled blood you should have heeded was Dassem Ultor's, not Kellanved's. And for all that neither man truly died, but only one bore the deadly kiss of Hood in all the days that followed. Only one stood before Hood himself, and learned of the terrible thing Logros had done to him.*

They said Hood was his patron god. They said he had avowed service to the Lord of Death. They said that Hood then betrayed him. They understood nothing. Dassem and his daughter, they were Hood's knives, striking at us. What is it, to be the weapon of a god?

Where are you now, Logros? Do you feel me, so fiercely reborn? My heir – your chosen child – has rejected the role. His footfalls now mark the passing of tragedy. You have made him the God of Tears, and now that Hood is gone he must hunt down the next one who made him what he was. Do you tremble, Logros? Dassem is coming for you. He is coming for you.

No, the world could not reach through to Onos T'oolan. Not a tremor of pain, not a tremble of grief. He knew nothing of rage. He was immune to every betrayal delivered upon him, and upon those whom he had loved with all his once-mortal heart. He had no desire for vengeance; he had no hope of salvation.

I am the First Sword. I am the weapon of the godless, and upon the day I am unsheathed, dust shall take your every dream. Logros, you fool, did you think you and all the T'lan Imass were proof against your new god's deadly kiss? Ask Kron. Ask Silverfox. Look upon me now, see how Olar Ethil seeks to wrest me away from Dassem's curse – but she cannot. You gave him mastery over us, and these chains no Bonecaster can shatter.

We march to our annihilation. The First Sword is torn in two, one half mortal and cruel in denial, the other half immortal and crueller still. Be glad Dassem has not found me. Be glad he seeks his own path, and that he will be far from the place where I shall stand.

And here is my secret. Heed this well. The weapon of the godless needs no hand to wield it. The weapon of the godless wields itself. It is without fear. It is empty of guilt and disdainful of retribution. It is all that and more, but one thing it is not: a liar. No slaying in the name of a higher power, no promises of redemption. It will not cloak brutality in the zeal that justifies, that absolves.

And this is why it is the most horrifying weapon of all.

No one could reach him, and he could feel his power seething, emanating from him in radiating waves – and beyond it the world trembled. He was no longer interested in hiding. No longer concerned with stratagems of deceit.

Let his enemies find him. Let them dare his wrath.

Was this not better? Was this not more comforting than if he'd ignited his rage? Tellann did not demand ferocious fires, engulfing the lands, devouring the sky. Tellann could hide in a single spark, or the faint gleam in an ember's soul. It could hide in the patience of a warrior immune to doubt, armoured in pure righteousness.

And if that righteousness then blazed, if it scorched all who dared assail it, well, was that not just?

Ulag Togtil bowed under the assault of the First Sword's thoughts, this searing flood of bright horror. He could feel the waves of anguish erupting from his fellow warriors, swirling like newborn eels in the maelstrom of their leader's rage.

Was this destroying them all? Would Onos T'oolan at last find his place to embrace annihilation, only to turn round and discover nothing but ashes in his wake? His followers incinerated by all that roiled out from him? *Or will this anneal us? Will this forge us all into his weapons of the godless?*

We felt you, Olar Ethil, and we too reject you and all that you promise. Our time is over. The First Sword understands this. You do not.

Go away. The blood you demand from this world is too terrible, and to spill it in our name is to give final proof to this theme of tragedy, the dread curse born of the mortal named Dassem Ultor.

Logros, could I find you now, I would tear your limbs off. I would twist your skull until your neck snapped. And I would bury that skull in the deepest, darkest pit, so that you witness naught but an eternity of decay.

Yes, we understand the First Sword now.

We understand, and we cannot bear it.

Rystalle Ev struggled to reach Ulag's side. She needed his strength. The First Sword was devouring himself, his thoughts both gaping, snapping maw and mangled, bloody tail. He was a serpent of fire, wheeling inexorably forward. The current swept his warriors after him; they staggered, blind in the deluge of terrible power.

Ulag, please – are we not done with weapons? Is peace nothing but a lie?

First Sword – you vow to shatter us all, but what will it win us? Is this the only legacy we can offer to all who follow? We die, tokens of useless defiance. The kings will still stride the earth, the slaves will still bow in chains, the hunters will hunt and the hunted will die. Mothers will weep for lost children – First Sword, can you offer us nothing but this?

But there was no room in the thoughts of Onos T'oolan to heed the fears of his followers. He was not even listening, chewing on the pathetic game of implacability – this mad diffidence and the absurdity of the unaffected. No, none of them could reach him.

But we follow. We can do nothing else.

She stumbled against Ulag. He reached out, steadied her.

'Ulag?'

'Hold on, Rystalle Ev. Find something. A memory you can hold on to. A time of joy, of love even. When the moment comes . . .' he paused, as if struggling with his words, 'when the time comes, and you are driven to your knees, when the world turns its face from you on all sides, when you fall inside yourself, and fall, *and fall*, find your moment, your dream of peace.'

'There is none,' she whispered. 'I remember only grief.'

'Find it,' he hissed. 'You must!'

'He will see us all destroyed – that is the only peace I now dream of, Ulag.'

She saw him turn away then, and sorrow filled her. *See us? We are the T'lan Imass. We are the glory of immortality. When oblivion comes, I shall kiss it. And in my mind, I shall ride into the void on a river of tears. On a river of tears.*

Gruntle followed a trail old beyond imagination, skirting sheer cliffs, the tumbled wreckage of sharp rocks and shattered boulders. In this place of dreams the air was hot, smelling of salt marshes and vast tidal flats. It was a trail of the dead and the dying, a trail of clenched jaws and neck muscles taut as bands of iron. Limbs scraped, knocked against stone, and that deep, warm miasma that so bound the minds of the hunted, the victims, filled the air like the breath of ghosts trapped for ever in this travail.

He reached the cave, paused just outside it, head lifted, testing the air.

But all this was long past, generation folded upon generation, a procession that promised to repeat again and again, for all time.

An illusion, he well knew. The last giant cat that had dragged its prey into this cave was bones and dust, so scattered by the centuries that he could not identify its scent. A leopard, a tiger, a cave lion – what did it matter, the damned thing was dead. The cycle of hunting, breeding and rearing had long ago snapped clean.

He edged into the cave, knowing what he would find.

Bones. Gnawed skulls. Eres'al skulls, and those of other apes, and here and there a human child, a woman. This was proof of a time when the world's future tyrants were nothing but victims, cowering, eyes wide at the flash of feline eyes in the darkness. They fell to savage fangs, to talons. They hung slack by the neck from the jaws of the great tawny beasts haunting their world.

Tyranny was but a gleam in the eye back then, and each day the sun lifted to light a world of ignorance. How sweet must that have been.

Gruntle snorted. Where was the mind that dreamed of unimagined possibilities – like hands groping in the dark? Groping – was that a flare of distant light? Was that a promise of something, something . . . wonderful? In the moment before the low growl – hackles snapping – and the sudden lunge. *Better to die reaching for dreams than reaching for . . . for what? That tick under the armpit of the smelly creature huddled against you?*

I have heard that rock apes gather on the cliff edges to watch the sun set and rise. What are they thinking? What are they dreaming? Is that a moment of prayer? A time to give thanks for the glory of life?

A prayer? Aye: 'May all these two-legged hunters chew straight up their own arses. Give us spears of fire and lightning to turn this battle – just once, we beg you. Just once!'

He reached out a massive barbed paw and slapped at a small skull, watched it skid and then slowly spin in place. *Got you, I see. Fangs went crunch, dreams went away. Done.* With a low growl, he slipped past the heaps of bones until he found the place where the ancient cats had slept, bellies full, running through the wild grasses of their dream worlds – which were no different from this one. *Imagine dreaming of a paradise no different from the one in which you happen to live. What moral might hide in that?*

All these worlds, all these fraught warrens, mocked him with their perfect banality. Patterns without revelation, repetitions without meaning. It was not enough to imagine worlds without humans or other sentient fools; the simple act of imagining placed his all-too-human sensibility upon the scene, his very own eyes to witness the idyllic perfection of his absolute absence. For all that, it was easy to harbour such contradictions – *when I hold on to this humanity within me. When I refuse the sweet bliss of the tiger's world.*

No wonder you forgot everything, Trake. No wonder you weren't ready for godhood. In the jungles of ancient days, the tigers were gods. Until the new gods arrived. And they were far thirstier for blood than the tigers ever were, and now the jungle is silent.

This night, he knew, here in this cave, he would dream of the hunt, the perfect stalking of the perfect prey, and dragging his victim up the trail and into this cave, away from the hyenas and jackals.

As dreams went, it wasn't that bad. As dreams went.
Black fur, the taste of blood in my mouth . . .

He had found him outside the walls of a dead city. Kneeling on a dusty road, collecting the shattered remnants of an old pot, but it was not just one pot that had broken apart, it was hundreds. A panicked flight, smoke and flames rising to blacken the limestone cliffs against which the city had cowered, the blurred passing of wretched faces, like broken husks and flotsam in a river. Things fell, things fell apart.

He was trying to put the pieces back together, and as Mappo drew nearer he looked up, but only briefly, before returning to his task. 'Good sir,' he said, with one finger pushing shards back and forth, endlessly rearranging, seeking patterns, 'Good sir, have you by chance some glue?'

The rage was gone, and with it all memory. Icarium knelt with his back to a city he had destroyed.

Sighing, Mappo set his heavy satchel down, and then crouched. 'Too many broke here,' he said, 'for you to repair. It would take weeks, maybe even months.'

'But I have time.'

Mappo flinched, looked away – but not at the city, where capemoths crowded window sills in the slope-walled buildings leaning against the cliff walls, where the scorch marks streaked the stone like slashes into night. Not at the city, with its narrow streets filled with rubble and corpses, and the rhizan lizards swarming the cold, rotting flesh, and the bhok'arala clambering down to lick sticky stains for the salt and snatching up bundles of clothing with which to make nests. And not at the gate, the doors blasted apart, the heaps of dead soldiers swelling inside their armour as the day's heat burgeoned.

He stared instead southward, to the old caravan camps marked only by low stone foundations and pens for sheep and goats. Never again would the desert traders travel to this place; never again would merchants from distant cities come seeking the famous Redworm Silks of Shikimesh.

'I thought, friend,' Mappo said, and then he shook his head. 'Only yesterday you spoke of journeying. Northeast, you said, to the coast.'

Icarium looked up, frowned. 'I did?'

'Seeking the Tanno, the Spiritwalkers. They are said to have collected ancient records from as far back as the First Empire.'

'Yes.' Icarium nodded. 'I have heard that said, too. Think of all that secret knowledge! Tell me, do you think the priests will permit me entry to their libraries? There is so much I need to learn – why would they stop me? Do you think they will be kind, friend? Kind to me?'

Mappo studied the shards on the road. 'The Tanno are said to be very wise, Icarium. I do not imagine they would bar their doors to you.'

'Good. That's good.'

The Trell scratched at the bristle on his jaw. 'So, it shall be Icarium and Mappo, walking across the wastes, all the way to the coast, there to take ship to the island, to the home of the Spiritwalkers.'

'Icarium and Mappo,' the Jhag repeated, and then he smiled. 'Mappo, my friend, this seems a most promising day, does it not?'

'I shall draw water from the caravan wells, and then we can be on our way.'

'Water,' said Icarium. 'Yes, so I can wash this mud off – I seem to have bathed in it.'

'You slid down a bank yesterday evening.'

'Just so, Mappo. Clumsy of me.' He slowly straightened, cupped in his hands a score of fragments. 'See the beautiful blue glaze? Like the sky itself – they must have been beautiful, these vessels. It is such a loss, when precious things break, isn't it?'

'Yes, Icarium, a terrible loss.'

'Mappo?' He lifted eyes sharp with anguish. 'In the city, I think, something happened. Thousands have died – thousands lie dead in that city – it's true, isn't it?'

'Yes, Icarium, a most tragic end.'

'What awful curse was visited upon it, do you think?'

Mappo shook his head.

Icarium studied the shards in his hands. 'If I could put it all back together, I would. You know that, don't you? You understand that – please, say that you understand.'

'I do, friend.'

'To take what's broken. To mend it.'

'Yes,' Mappo whispered.

'Must everything break in the end?'

'No, Icarium, not everything.'

'Not everything? What will not break in the end? Tell me, Mappo.'

'Why,' and the Trell forced a smile, 'you need not look far. Are we not friends, Icarium? Have we not always been friends?'

A sudden light in the Jhag's grey eyes. 'Shall I help you with the water?'

'I would like that.'

Icarium stared at the shards in his hands and hesitated.

Mappo dragged his satchel over. 'In here, if you like. We can try to put them together later.'

'But there's more on the road, all about – I would need—'

'Leave the water to me, then, Icarium. Fill the satchel, if you like, as many as you can gather.'

'But the weight – no, I think it would prove too heavy a burden, friend, this obsession of mine.'

'Don't worry on that account, friend. Go on. I will be back shortly.'

'You are certain?'

'Go on.'

With a smile, Icarium knelt once again. His gaze caught on his sword, lying on the verge a few paces to his right, and Mappo saw him frown.

'I cleaned the mud from it last night,' Mappo said.

'Ah. That was kind of you, friend.'

Shikimesh and the Redworm Silks. An age ago, a thousand lies ago, and the biggest lie of all. A friendship that could never break. He sat in the gloom, encircled by a ring of stones he had rolled together – an old Trell ritual – with the gap opening to the east, to where the sun would rise. In his hands a dozen or so dusty, pale blue potsherds.

We never got round to putting them back together. He'd forgotten by the afternoon, and I made no effort to remind him – and was that not my task? To feed him only those memories I judged useful, to starve all the others until they vanished.

Kneeling that day, he had been like a child, with all his games in waiting before him – waiting for someone like me to come along. Before that, he was content with the company of his own toys and nothing more. Is that not a precious gift? Is that not the wonder of a child? The way they have of building their own worlds, of living in them, and finding joy in the living itself?

Who would break that? Who would crush and destroy such a wondrous thing?

Will I find you kneeling in the dust, Icarium? Will I find you puzzling over the wreckage surrounding you? Will we speak of holy libraries and secret histories?

Shall we sit and build us a pot?

With gentle care, Mappo returned the shards to his satchel. He lay down, set his back to the gap in the ring of stones, and tried to sleep.

Faint scanned the area. 'They split here,' she announced. 'One army went due east, but it's the narrower trail.' She pointed southeast. 'Two, maybe three forces – big ones – went that way. So, we have us a choice to make.' She faced her companions, gaze settling on Precious Thimble.

The young woman seemed to have aged decades since Jula's death. She stood in obvious pain, the soles of her feet probably blistered, cracked and weeping. *Just like mine.* 'Well? You said there was power . . . out here, somewhere. Tell us, which army do we follow?'

Precious Thimble hugged herself. 'If they're armies, there must be a war.'

Faint said, 'Well, there was a battle, yes. We found what was left. But maybe that battle was the only one. Maybe the war's over and everyone's going home.'

'I meant, why do we have to follow any of them?'

'Because we're starving and dying of thirst—'

The young woman's eyes flashed. 'I'm doing the best I can!'

Faint said, 'I know, but it's not enough, Precious. If we don't catch up with somebody, we're all going to die.'

'East, then – no, wait.' She hesitated.

'Out with it,' growled Faint.

'There's something terrible that way. I – I don't want to get close. I reach out, and then I flee – I don't know why. I don't know anything!'

Amby was staring at her as if studying a strange piece of wood, or a broken idol. He seemed moments from spitting at its feet.

Faint ran her hands through her greasy hair – it was getting long but she welcomed that. Anything to fend off the infernal heat. Her chest ached and the pain was a constant companion now. She dreamed of getting drunk. Falling insensate in some alley, or some squalid room in an inn. Disappearing from herself, for one night, just one night. *And let me wake up to a new body, a new world. With Sweetest Sufferance alive and sitting beside me. With no warring gods and swords through foreheads.* 'What about to the southeast, Sorceress? Any bad feelings in that direction?'

Precious Thimble shook her head, and then shrugged.

'What does that mean?' Faint hissed in exasperation. 'Is it as nasty as what's east of us, or isn't it?'

'No – but . . .'

'But what?'

'It tastes of blood! There! How's that, then? It all tastes of blood!'

'Are they spilling it or drinking it?'

Precious Thimble stared at Faint as if she'd gone mad. *Gods, maybe I have, asking a question like that.* 'Which way will kill us quickest?'

A deep, shuddering breath. 'East. That army – they're all going to die.'

'Of what?' Faint demanded.

'I don't know – thirst, maybe. Yes, thirst.' Her eyes widened. 'There's no water, no water at all – I see ground, glittering ground, blinding, sharp as daggers. And bones – endless fields of bones. I see men and women driven mad by the heat. I see children – *oh gods* – they come walking up like nightmares, like proof of all the crimes we have ever committed.' Abruptly, horrifyingly, she howled, her hands to her face, and then staggered back and would have fallen if not for Amby, who stepped close to take her weight. She twisted round and buried herself in his embrace. Over her head, he stared at Faint, and gave her a jarring smile.

Madness? Too late, Precious Thimble – and thank the gods you can't see what we're seeing. Shivering, Faint turned to the southeast. 'That way, then.' *Children. Don't remind me. Some crimes cut close to the bone, too close. No, don't remind me.*

In her mind she saw Sweetest Sufferance, a face splitting into a smile. *'Finally,'* she muttered, *'a decision. Get on with it, Faint.'*

Faint nodded for Amby to follow with the sorceress, and then she set out with her hobbling, wincing gait. *If they've gone too far, we won't make it. If we get much worse . . . blood. We'll either spill it or drink it.*

She wondered at the armies ahead. Who in Hood's name were they, and why go this deep into the Wastelands just to fight a stupid battle? And why then split up? *And you poor fools marching east. Just a glimpse of where you're headed tears at her sanity. I pray you turn back before you leave too many lying lifeless on the ground.*

Wherever you're going, it can't be worth it. Nothing in this world is worth it, and you'd be hard pressed to convince me otherwise.

She heard a grunt and glanced back.

Amby was carrying Precious Thimble in his arms, the smile on his face stretched into a rictus travesty of satisfaction, as if in finding his heart's desire he was forcing himself to take its fullest pleasure. Precious Thimble's head lolled against his upper arm, her eyes closed, her mouth half open.

'What's wrong with her?'

Amby said, 'Fainted . . . Faint.'

'Oh, sod off, you lump of lard.'

Ten thousand furred backs, black, silver and grey, the bodies lean and long. Like iron swords, ten thousand iron swords. They seethed before Setoc's eyes, they blurred like the honed edges of waves on an angry sea. She was carried along, driven to rearing cliffs, to up-thrust fangs of rotted rock.

The wind roared in her ears, roared in and through her, trembling like thunder through every bone of her being. She felt the beasts crashing ashore, felt their fury assailing insensate stone and all the brutal laws that held it in place. They bared teeth at the sky, they bit and chewed shafts of sunlight as if speared through. They howled against the coming of night and in the hunt they stalked their own senseless savagery.

We are what we are, and facing this enemy what we are is helpless.

Who will fight for us? Who will peel lips back to reveal swords of sharp iron?

The cliffs ahead reverberated to the onslaught – she drew ever closer. *Wolves of Winter, do you see me? Blessed Lord, Proud Lady, is this your summons? Does there await a cave in that ravaged wall? And inside, a Hold of Thrones?*

There is a smell to the wild, a smell that makes the hairs stand on end, that rushes like ice through human veins. There are trails crossing the path, secret passages beneath the canopy. Mice dance on the beaten floor in the instant before we arrive, and we are blind to it all.

And all the spaces carved out by our fires and our weapons and our axes and our ploughs, we must then fill with that sweating, bitter flood that is pride. In the wastelands of our making we will ourselves to stand as would one exalted and triumphant.

Thrones of the Wild, thrones of bones and hides and lifeless eyes. Tall as mountains, these Beast Thrones.

Who assails us? Who hunts us? Who slays us?

Everyone.

She raced for the jagged rocks. Annihilation, if it came, would arrive as a blessing. The heat of the beasts carrying her was sweet as a loving kiss, a safe embrace, a promise of salvation. *I am the Destriant of the Wolves. I hold in my chest the souls of the all the slain beasts, of this and every other world.*

But I cannot hold them for ever.

I need a sword. I need absolution.

Absolution, yes, and a sword. Ten thousand iron swords. In the name of the Wolves of Winter, in the name of the Wild.

Sister Equity walked across lifeless sand, far to the south of the Spire, far away from the eyes of everyone. She had once dreamed of peace. She had lived in a world where questions were rare, and there had been comfort in that. If there was a cause worthy enough to which she could devote her life, it was to journey from birth to death without confrontation. Nothing to stir her unease, nothing to deliver pain or to receive it. Although the Forkrul Assail had long ago lost their god, had long ago suffered the terrible grief of that god's violent end – the murder for which no penance was possible – she had come to harbour in her own soul a childish hope that a new god could be made. Assembled like the setting of bones, the moulded clay of muscles, the smooth caress of a face given form, given life by her own loving hands. And this god she would call Harmony.

In the world of this god life would not demand a death. There would be no need to kill in order to eat. There would be no cruel fate or random tragedy to take one before her time, and the forests and plains would seethe with animals, the skies with birds, the seas, lakes and rivers with fish.

The wishes of a child were fragile things, and she now knew that none ever survived the hard, jostling indifference that came with the bitter imperatives of adulthood: the stone-eyed rush to find elusive proofs of worth, or to reach at last the swollen satiation that was satisfaction. Virtues changed; the clays found new forms and hardened to stone, and adults took weapons in hand and killed each other over them. And in that new world she had found herself growing into there was no place – no place at all – for peace.

She recalled walking from the ship into the city, into the midst of these clamouring humans with the frightened eyes. On all sides, she could see how they dwelt in war, each one an exhausted soldier battling demons real and imagined. They fought for status, they fought for dignity, and they fought to wrest both away from their neighbours, their mates, their kin. In fact, the very necessity that held families together, and neighbourhoods, provinces and kingdoms, was fraught with desperation and fear, barricaded against the unknown, the strange and the threatening.

The Forkrul Assail had been right in shattering it all. There would be peace, but in the making of peace there must be judgement, and retribution. The people of Kolanse and the kingdoms to the south must all be returned to their childlike state, and then built anew. They could not, would not, do it for themselves – too many things got in the way, after all. They always did.

It was unfortunate that to achieve a sustainable balance many thousands had to die, but when the alternative was the death of *everyone*, who could argue against the choice made? Populations had been dismantled, selectively culled. Entire regions laid waste, not a single human left, to free the land to heal. Those who were permitted to live were forced into a new way of living, under the implacable guidance of the Forkrul Assail.

If this had been the extent of the redress, Equity would have been content. Things could be made viable, a balance could be achieved, and perhaps even a new god would arise, born of sober faith in reality and its very real limitations, born of honest humility and the desire for peace. A faith to spread across the world, adjudicated by the Pures and then the Watered.

If not for the Heart, if not for that fist of torment dredged up from the depths of the bay. All that power, so raw, so alien, so perfect in its denial. Our god was slain, but we had already found a path to vengeance – the Nah'ruk, who had broken their chains and now thirsted for the blood of their masters. So much was already within our reach.

250

*But for the Heart, so firing Reverence, Serenity and the other elders,
so poisoning their souls. No balance could be perfect – we all knew
that – but now a new solution burned bright, so bright it blinded them
to all else. The Gate, wrested away from the K'Chain Che'Malle,
cleansed of that foul, ancient curse. Akhrast Korvalain, returned once
more to the Forkrul Assail, and from that gate – from the power of the
Heart – we could resurrect our god.*

We could be made children once again.

*Sacrifices? Oh yes, but everything of worth demanded that. Bal-
ance? Why, we shall do away with the one force eternally intent on
destroying that balance – humanity.*

*Our answer is annihilation. Our cull shall be absolute. Our cull
shall be the excision of an entire species.*

*'Raise up the Heart! Hold it high so that its dread beat is heard by
all! Against the depredations of humanity, think you not that we shall
find allies?'*

Allies. Yes, Reverence, we have found allies.

*And I tell myself that I see peace in the future – the peace of my
childhood, the peace of harmony, the peace of a silent world. All we
need to reach it, is a little blood. A little blood.*

*But, Sister Reverence, then I look into your ancient eyes, and I see
how the hunger of our allies has infected you. The Tiste Liosan, the
Eleint, the Lord and Lady of the Beast Hold – but all they desire is
chaos, anarchy, destruction, the end of the Age of Gods and the Age
of Humans. Like you, they thirst for blood, but not a little blood. No.
Oceans, oceans of blood.*

*Sister Reverence, we shall defy you when the time comes. Calm has
found a weapon, a weapon to end your insane ambitions.*

Her footfalls were a whisper in the sand, but in her mind the ground
trembled beneath her tread. The sun's heat was fierce on her white
face, but the fire of her thoughts was hotter still. And the voices from
the beach, not far ahead now, should fall in futility before her hard
intransigence, yet in them she found . . . hope.

'Balance,' she said under her breath. 'Sister Reverence, you force this
upon us. In your extremity, we must counter you. Calm has found the
weapon we need. Reach for your fiercest madness, we shall match it –
and more.'

In truth, she cared nothing for the fate of humanity. If they all
perished, so be it. No, what was important, here and now and in the
future to come, was *principle. Balance has an eternal enemy, and its
name is ambition. You have forgotten this, Sister Reverence, and it
falls to us to remind you. And so we shall.*

She climbed the high bank above the beach. Below, fifteen paces
away, a dozen humans had gathered, and it seemed an argument was

under way. In the bay beyond sat a ship, its arcane lines sending a sudden chill through Equity. *Jaghut. The fools!*

She marched down on to the beach.

The first two sailors who saw her both shrieked. Weapons flashed, and all at once the humans were rushing towards her.

'I would speak—'

A cutlass lashed out for her face. She edged aside, caught the wrist and clenched until bones split. The man howled, and she closed, driving her fingers into his throat. Blood sprayed from his gaping mouth, his eyes bulging as he fell back. A knife-thrust sought her stomach. Her mid-section bent to one side, evading the attack. She sent one hand snapping out to grasp the woman's forehead and crushed it like the shell of an egg.

A cutlass struck her left shoulder, rebounded as if from dense wood. Hissing, Equity twisted round. Two swift blows broke the man's neck. Scowling now, she waded forward. Bodies spun to her lashing hands. The screams were deafening—

And then the survivors were fleeing along the beach, their weapons flung away, and down by the water, thirty paces distant, stood four figures: a man, three women. Equity marched towards them.

Sorcery erupted from the shortest of the women. A wave of blistering cold crashed into the Forkrul Assail, driving her back a step.

One of the other women had drawn two short-hafted throwing axes and was fast closing.

Sweet kiss of the Abyss, are they all suicidal? 'Cease your attack!'

One axe flew straight for her. She slipped from its path, only to grunt as the second axe struck her in the chest, its iron blade lodged in her breast bone. Agony ripped through her. The second wave of Omtose Phellack lifted her from the sand, flung her five paces back. She landed hard on her back, rolled, and then regained her feet. The bones of her chest plate convulsed, rejecting the axe blade, and she straightened in time to meet the attack of the axe-throwing woman.

Long-bladed knives, a blur of hissing blades.

Equity blocked the attacks, one after another, but was driven back, one step, two.

She awakened her voice. '*STOP!*'

The woman staggered, and then, with a growl, she pushed forward. '*STOP THIS!*'

Blood spattered from her attacker's nose. Blood blossomed in her eyes. She stumbled, then lifted her weapons once more.

Snarling, Equity stepped close and slapped the woman, hard enough to snap her head round. She collapsed in a heap. The Forkrul Assail stood over her, contemplating driving a heel into the human's throat.

An arrow glanced across her left temple, scoring a red slash. '*CEASE ALL ATTACKS!*'

The woman at her feet moaned, tried to rise. Exasperated, Equity reached down, picked her up and threw her into the sea ten paces to her right. She stabbed a long finger at the sorceress. 'I will speak to you!'

The other woman with her shouted, 'Then stop killing my crew!'

Equity ran a finger along the gash in her temple – the wound was already mending. She sighed. Her chest ached, but the bones had begun healing and the pain was fading to an itch. 'They attacked me,' she said. 'I simply defended myself. Indeed,' she added, cautiously approaching, 'if I desired to kill them all, I would have done so.'

'I see five bodies over there—'

'As I said, I would have killed them all.'

The woman thrashing in the shallows was climbing unsteadily to her feet. Equity regarded her for a moment. 'If she comes at me again, I will kill her.' She faced the sorceress. 'Make that plain to her – she belongs to you, does she not?'

The short, plump mage made a strange wiggle with the fingers of one hand. 'I am hard pressed to keep her from carving your head from your rather bony shoulders. You certainly have a way with words, Inquisitor, but that will not work a second time.'

Equity narrowed her attention on the other woman in the group. She snorted. 'It is said the Realm of Death is sundered. Do your kind now plague the world?'

'I carry no plague,' the woman replied.

The Forkrul Assail frowned. Was she a simpleton? Often, she well knew, the brain decayed irreparably in such creatures.

The man standing beside the undead woman was now staring at her with his one working eye. 'Did she say y'got the plague, Cap'n?'

'No, Pretty, she said you're an idiot. Now be quiet – better yet, gather up the crew, now that they've scattered every which way, and detail a burial party, and all that other stuff. Go on.'

'Aye, Cap'n.' Then he hesitated, and said in a hoarse whisper that all could hear, 'It's just, this one, she looks like she's got a plague, don't she? All white and all those veins on her arms, and—'

'Go, Kaban. Now.'

Nodding, the man limped off.

Equity watched the woman who'd attacked her set about retrieving her weapons.

'Inquisitor,' said the sorceress, 'we have no interest in suffering your . . . adjudication. Indeed, we proclaim you our enemy.'

'Is blind hatred your only recourse?' Equity demanded. 'You name me "Inquisitor", telling me that you know certain details of local significance. Yet that title is a presumption. You assume that all

Forkrul Assail are Inquisitors, and this is ignorant. Indeed, most of the Inquisitors we set upon the peoples of this land were Watered – as much human blood in their veins as Assail. We discovered a rather sweet irony in observing their zeal, by the way.'

'Nevertheless,' the sorceress retorted, even as she made imperative gestures towards her servant, 'we must view you as our enemy.'

'You still do not understand, do you? Your enemies are the Elders among the Pures, who seek the utter destruction of you and your kind, not just on this continent, but across the entire world.'

'I am sure you understood why we might object to such desires,' the sorceress said, and now her servant arrived, delivering into the young woman's plump hand a clay pipe. She puffed for a moment, and then continued, 'And while you appear to be suggesting that you do not share the zeal of your Elder Pures, I cannot help but wonder what has brought you here, to me.'

'You have bargained with the Jaghut,' said Equity.

'They share our aversion to your notions of justice.'

Frowning, Equity said, 'I cannot understand what value the Jaghut see in you, a silly little girl playing at deadly magics, and beside you a lifeless abomination harbouring a parasite.' She fixed her gaze upon the servant. 'Is there a glamour about this one? If so, it is too subtle for me. Tell me, Sorceress, is she Jaghut?'

'My handmaid? Goodness, no!'

Equity's eyes settled upon the ship in the bay. 'Is he there?'

'Who?'

'Your ally – I would speak to him. Or her.'

Smoke billowed and streamed. 'I'm sorry, what ally?'

'Where hides the Jaghut?' Equity demanded.

'Ah, I see. You misapprehend. I struck no bargain with any particular Jaghut. I merely sacrificed some blood for the privilege of Omtose Phellack—'

The undead captain turned on the sorceress. 'You did what? Errant's nudge – that storm! You can't—'

'Necessity, Captain Elalle. Now please, cogitate in silence for the moment, will you?'

'I am astonished,' admitted Equity. 'I did not imagine you to be so ... thick.'

'Thorns and rocks—'

'You cannot bargain with Omtose Phellack – you are not Jaghut. No, you need a blessing, or personal intervention, and this is as true of a mortal as it is of an Elder God. That ship is Jaghut – its kind has not sailed the seas of this world for millennia. Where has it come from?'

'From the realm of Omtose Phellack itself,' said the sorceress.

'No, that is not possible. Unless a Jaghut has journeyed into the warren – but no, there is naught but ice – yonder ship was built in this world. Do you see now why this makes no sense?'

'Not just ice, apparently.'

'You have seen Omtose Phellack?'

'My handmaid,' said the sorceress. 'It was she who journeyed through the gate. It was she who entered Omtose Phellack and returned with the ship.'

Equity studied the woman with the bruised eyes. 'Describe the place where you were, please.'

'Enlighten her,' ordered the sorceress when the handmaid hesitated.

A shrug, and then, 'Forest. Demons. Ravines. Vicious apes.'

'You did not journey to Omtose Phellack,' Equity pronounced. 'The gate opened upon another realm, a different warren.'

'That cannot be,' objected the sorceress. 'My ritual fed on the power of Omtose Phellack.'

'Enough of all this,' drawled the captain, crossing her arms. 'This Forkrul Assail has come here to negotiate. She seeks to betray her Elders. Obviously, she's come looking for allies, though why she would seek us out remains something of a mystery, since she clearly knew nothing about your making use of Omtose Phellack, Princess. So, unless your skills in sorcery are such that even the gods tremble, I admit to having some trouble understanding what she wants from us.'

Equity sighed. 'We felt the touch of an Elder Warren, but could not determine which one.'

'Then it was the Elder Pures who dispatched you?'

'No, those who remain close to the Spire are mostly blind to distant powers. When I spoke of "we" I meant myself and my comrades; we have journeyed many times well beyond the influence of the power emanating from the Spire, else we would not have detected these . . . intrusions.'

'And now you want to forge some kind of alliance,' said the captain.

'You seek the Spire, and that which lies upon its altar—'

'Not precisely,' interjected the sorceress, pausing to pull hard on her pipe before adding, 'we seek to prevent whatever it is you're all planning.'

'And how do you expect to do that?'

'I believe the term you have already used will suffice: allies.'

'If you – and your allies – would have any hope of succeeding, you will need our help.'

'And if we do not trust you?' the captain asked.

'This is proving a waste of time,' said Equity. 'I will speak to the Jaghut now.'

'There isn't one,' said the sorceress, behind a veil of smoke.

'Then he or she is hiding even from you. Open the gate, Princess – the one you used for your servant. The presence is very close – I can feel it. I felt it when you unleashed Omtose Phellack against me. Open the gate, and let us all see who has come among us.'

Hissing, the sorceress held out her pipe. The handmaid took it. 'Very well. It will be a feeble gate; indeed, I might well fail—'

'It won't.'

The sorceress walked a short distance away, her rounded hips swaying. She lifted her hands, fingers moving as if plucking invisible strings.

Bitter cold flooded out, the sand crackling as if lit by lightning, and the gate that erupted was massive, yawning, towering. Through the billowing icy air flowed out a sweeter, rank smell. The smell of death.

A figure stood on the threshold of the gate. Tall, hunched, a withered, lifeless face of greenish grey, yellowed tusks thrusting up from the lower jaw. Pitted eyes regarded them from beneath a tattered woollen cowl.

The power cascading from this apparition sent Equity stumbling back. *Abyss! A Jaghut, yes, but not just any Jaghut! Calm – can you hear me? Through this howl? Can you hear me? An ally stands before me – an ally of ancient – so ancient – power! This one could have been an Elder God. This one could have been . . . anything!* Gasping, fighting to keep from falling to one knee, from bowing before this terrible creature, Equity forced herself to lift her gaze, to meet the empty hollows of his eyes.

'I know you,' she said. 'You are Hood.'

The Jaghut stepped forward, the gate swirling closed behind him. Hood paused, regarding each witness in turn, and then walked towards Equity.

'*They made you their king,*' she whispered. 'They who followed no one chose to follow *you*. They who refused every war fought *your* war. And what you did then – what you did—'

As he reached her, his desiccated hands caught her. He lifted her from her feet, and then, mouth stretching, he bit into the side of her face. The tusks drove up beneath her cheek bone, burst the eye on that side. In a welter of blood, he tore away half of her face, and then bit a second time, up under the orbitals, the tusks driving into her brain.

Equity hung in his grip, feeling her life drain away. Her head felt strangely unbalanced. She seemed to be weeping from only one eye, and from her throat no words were possible. *I once dreamed of peace. As a child, I dreamed of—*

Shurq Elalle stared in horror as the Jaghut flung the corpse away. From his gore-drenched mouth fell fragments of scalp and skull.

Then Hood faced them, and in a dry, toneless voice he said, 'I have never much liked Forkrul Assail.'

No one spoke. Felash stood trembling, her face pale as death itself. Beside her, the handmaid had set her hands upon the axes at her belt, but seemed unable to move beyond that futile, diffident gesture.

Shurq Elalle gathered herself, and said, 'You have a singular way of ending a discussion, Jaghut.'

The empty pits seemed to find her, somehow, and Hood said, 'We have no need of allies. Besides, I recently learned a lesson in brevity, Shurq Elalle, which I have taken to heart.'

'A lesson? Really? *Who taught you that?*'

The Jaghut looked away, across the water. 'Ah, my Death Ship. I admit, it was a quaint affectation. Nonetheless, one cannot help but admire its lines.'

Princess Felash, Fourteenth Daughter of Bolkando, fell to her knees and was sick in the sand.

CHAPTER TEN

What is it about this world
That so causes you trouble?
Why avow in your tone
This victim role?
And the plaintive hurt
Painting your eyes
Bemoans a life's struggle
Ever paying a grievous toll

We gathered in one place
Under the selfsame sun
And the bronze woman
Holding the basin,
Her breasts settled in the bowl,
Looked down with pity
Or was it contempt?
She is a queen of dreams
And her gift is yours to take
Pity if you choose it
Or contempt behind the veil
I would have polished those eyes
For a better look
I would have caressed those roses
For a sweeter taste
When we drink from the same cup
And you make bitter recoil
I wonder at the tongue in waiting
And your deadening flavours
So eager to now despoil

What is it about this world
That so causes you trouble?
What could I say to change
Your wounded regard?
If my cold kiss must fail
And my milk run sour
Beneath the temple bell
That so blights your reward?

Ten thousand hang from trees
Their limbs bared roots
Starved of hope in the sun
And the wood-cutters are long gone
Up to where the road gives way
To trails in the dust
That spiral and curl
Like the smoke of fires
They are blazing beacons
In the desert night.
It was said by the lepers
Huddled against the hill
That a man with no hands
Who could stare only
As could the blind
Upon the horrors of argument
Did with one hand gone
Reach into the dark sky
And with the other too gone
He led me home

Wood-Cutters
Tablets II & III
Hethra of Aren

THE EDGE OF THE GLASS DESERT WAS A BROKEN LINE OF CRYSTALS AND boulders, for all the world like an ancient shoreline. Aranict could not pull her gaze from it. She sat slumped in the saddle of her wearily plodding horse, a hood drawn over against the blistering sun, off to one side of the main column. Prince Brys rode somewhere ahead, near the vanguard, leaving her alone.

The desert's vast, flat stretch was blinding, the glare painful and strangely discordant, as if she was witnessing an ongoing crime, the raw lacerations of a curse upon the land itself. Stones melted to glass, shards of crystal jutting like spears, others that grew like bushes, every branch and twig glittering as if made of ice.

Rolled up against the verge there were bones, heaped like driftwood. Most were shattered, reduced to splinters, as if whatever had befallen the land had taken in a massive fist each creature and crushed the life from it – it felt like a deliberate act, an exercise in unbelievable malice. She thought she could still taste the evil, could still feel its rotted breath on the wind.

Waves of nausea spread out from her stomach again and again, slow as a creeping tide, and when it washed its way back, when it retreated, it left a residue in her own bones. *This place, it wants to kill me. I can feel it.* Her skin was clammy and cool beneath her cloak. *It wants inside. Eager as an infection. Who could have done this? Why? What terrible conflict led to this?*

She imagined that if she listened carefully enough, if all the sounds of thousands of soldiers marching and hundreds of wagons rolling were to suddenly fall away, if even the wind moaned into silence, she might hear still the droning words of the ritual that had ignited the fires, creating the desecrating cruelty that would become the Glass Desert.

This is what despair leads to, the kind of despair that steals light from the world, that mocks life's own struggle to exist, to persist. Denying our desire to heal, to mend all that we break. Refusing hope itself.

If despair has a ritual, it was spoken here.

Riding this close to the glistening edge, to the banks of bones and cracked boulders, she felt as if she was taking it inside herself, as if deadly crystals had begun growing within her, whispering awake in the echoes of ancient words. *When all you are is made wrong. This is how it feels.*

Brys Beddict's army was many days behind the other two, for the prince had made certain he was the last to leave the Bonehunters. They had marched with them to the desert's very edge. Eight days through an increasingly parched and forbidding land. She wondered if he'd been hoping to change the Adjunct's mind, to convince her of the madness of her determination to cross the Glass Desert. Or perhaps he had been considering accompanying that doomed force. For the first time since they had become lovers, Brys had closed himself to her. *And not just me. To everyone.*

And on the day we parted from them, he stood near Tavore, but he said nothing. Nor as we all watched the Bonehunters form up and set out, crossing that ghastly midden of crystals and bones, into the harsh glare beyond; we all watched, and not one of us – not one in the entire mass of soldiers – had a thing to say.

When the last burdened wagon rocked over the berm, and the last of the dust swirled away in the Malazans' wake; when the column wavered and smeared in the fierce glare and rising heat, Brys had turned to face her.

The look in his face shocked her, cut through her every defence. Whatever he had thought to do to dissuade the Adjunct, the moment had passed. No, a thousand moments. Eight days' worth, and not one grasped, not one taken in hand like a weapon. The brittle wall of silence had defeated him, defeated them all. That look . . .

Helpless. Filled with . . . Abyss below, filled with despair.

She was a singular woman, was Tavore Paran. They could all see that. They had all witnessed the terrible majesty of her will.

And her soldiers followed – that had been for Aranict the hardest thing to witness. The squads fell in, the companies formed up, and as they marched past Prince Brys they offered him a sharp, perfect salute. *As if on a parade ground. Eyes hidden in the shadow of their helms, that closed fist on the chest, expressions chiselled from stone – gods, I will never forget that, any of it. Those faces. Horrifying in their emptiness. Those soldiers: veterans of something far beyond battles, far beyond shields locked and swords bared, beyond even the screams of dying comrades and the desolation of loss.*

Veterans of a lifetime of impossible decisions, of all that is unbearable and all that is without reconciliation.

Brys Beddict rode to the head of the column then, to lead his soldiers south, along the very edge of the Glass Desert. It was clear that as soon as they reached its southernmost end, he would swing the army eastward, and the pace would become savage. They were a week or more behind the Perish and the Evertine Legion.

Aranict lit another stick of rustleaf. Her neck ached, as she found it impossible to face forward, to look ahead. The Glass Desert held her.

They're out there. Do they reel beneath its onslaught? Has its madness infected them? Are they even now killing each other, frenzied with fever? It has been three days. They might already be dead, every one of them. More bones to crush, to push towards the shoreline – the only retreat left to them. She looked again at the bleached splinters. *Did you all try to cross the desert?*

The very notion chilled her. Shivering beneath her cloak, she forced her gaze away from the horror on her left, only to see its mangled verge stretching ahead, southward alongside the column, until the two seemed to merge in the hazy distance.

Brys, my love, from all of us what will you now forge? We Letherii have known too many defeats of late. And we tasted our own blood yet again, against the Nah'ruk. Not so bitter that time, for we saved the Bonehunters. Still, we pale beside our allies. In their shadow we are diminished.

And yet . . . they saluted us.

She could not get that moment out of her mind. The faces haunted her and she feared they would do so for the rest of her life.

Whose army are they? These Bonehunters. What is their cause? And the strength within them, where does it come from? Is it held in the soul of the Adjunct? No – at least, I don't think so. Oh, she is the focus for them all, but they have no love for her. They see her, if at all, as no different from a mountain, a column of storm clouds, a bitter grey sea – they see her as part of the natural world, a thing to be borne, to be weathered.

I saw in their faces the erosion of her will, and they bore it. They bore it as they did all else. These Malazans, they shame the gods themselves.

'Coming up on us fast, Highness, out of the northwest.'

Brys nodded. 'Draw in the flying wing, Preda. I will take out our standard-bearer and my Atri-Ceda – when you see us ride out from the column, fall the wing in behind us.'

'Yes, Highness.'

Brys listened to the Preda dispatching riders, one out to the flanking wing of light cavalry, another to retrieve Aranict from down the column. The standard-bearer rode up beside the prince, his face pale and drawn. 'No need for alarm, soldier,' Brys said to the young man. 'This shall be a meeting of allies.'

'But . . . lizards, sir!'

'K'Chain Che'Malle. Not Short-Tails – I am sure you have heard, the army now approaching us subsequently defeated the Nah'ruk.'

The young man nodded, nervously licking his lips.

Brys studied him. 'Soldier, our clash with the Nah'ruk – was that your first taste of battle?'

'Yes, sir.'

'You bore this standard?'

'No, sir. Well, I was the third to take it up that day, and by then we were in full retreat—'

'Withdrawal,' Brys corrected. 'Trust me, a full retreat is a far messier thing than what we managed.'

'Yes, sir.'

Brys glanced up at the standard and fought down a groan, reminded once again of his brother's perverse humour. *Not a legion's standard. No, the Imperial Standard, no less.* Depending from a cross-bridge of iron, the cloth was a tattered rectangle of colourless wool – it was, in fact, a fair copy of Tehol's blanket, almost to scale. And where one might expect some elegant or proud heraldic crest at centre, there was instead the new royal sigil of King Tehol the Only of Lether: a three-

262

quarter-on rendition of his brother's roof-top bed, and if one looked carefully one would see cowering beneath that bed a row of six plucked – but living – hens. Eyeing it, Brys recalled his meeting with Tehol upon the unveiling.

'*You would have our armies fight under that?*'

'*Well, I did. The bed, I mean. And so did the chickens – can you imagine the extent of their holy dread, knowing that God wanted to cook them? All right, not* their *god, not precisely. Though we cannot actually be sure of that, can we? Bugg, are you worshipped by hens and cocks?*'

'*Not both at the same time, sire.*'

'*Thank you. Most enlightening.*'

'*My very reason to exist, sire. You are welcome.*'

'*Tehol—*'

'*Yes, Brys?*'

'*I understand your notion that dignity cannot be found in the . . . er, material – not a throne, not a crown, not even a fine estate or whatnot – but when it comes to the military—*'

'*Oh, that's all I ever hear from you, brother! "It's not that way in the military, Tehol", "The enlisted won't go for that, Tehol", "They don't like pink, Tehol". The pathetic conservatism of that hoary institution is, frankly, embarrassing.*'

'*I don't recall any mention of pink, sire.*'

'*There wasn't, Bugg. I was being illustrative.*'

'*What kind of illustration did you have in mind? Shall I summon the court artist again?*'

'*Abyss no! After that debacle with my wife and that pretty guard—*'

'*Ex-guard, sire.*'

'*Really? By whose order? I demand to know!*'

'*Your wife, the queen, sire.*'

'*That interfering cow . . . oh, don't look at me like that, beloved – I was but referring to you in your official capacity. Thus, while I rail at the queen, my love for my beautiful wife remains in its usual beaming manner for ever untarnished—*'

'*Too bad the same cannot be said for that poor young woman, husband.*'

'*I never tarnished her – not once!*'

'*Tehol, have you seen that damned painting?*'

'*Only once, dearest, since you went and burned the only copy. And – that's right, you look well at this wagging finger – that artist has been depressed ever since—*'

'*More like running scared,*' suggested Bugg.

'*Tehol, about this Imperial Standard—*'

'Not *again*, Brys. I *thought we were past all that. It's lovely and most apt—'*

'But who will rally under it?'

'Brys, *if an army must rally, one must presume it is in dire straits, yes? Well then, where better to hide than under the king's bed?'*

'With all the other chickens,' added Bugg. 'Well now, sire, that's clever.'

'Hold on,' said the queen, 'What did you mean by "the only copy"?'

'Brys! Rally the troops!'

Sweating under the bright sun, the king's brother snorted – but how he missed those days now. The chaotic palace of King Tehol seemed very far away. He squinted up at the standard, and smiled.

Aranict arrived, reining in. 'Prince, it pleases me to see you smiling. What so amuses you?'

'Nothing, Atri-Ceda. That is, nothing of import. We have been found by the K'Chain Che'Malle – such a motley collection of allies we make, don't you think? No matter. Ride with me. I would become acquainted with our new commanders.'

The woman frowned. 'Are they not two common marines, sire? Anyone can acquire a title – it hardly makes them fit to demand the obedience of a prince, not to mention the queen of the Bolkando.'

'Gesler and Stormy are far more than just Malazan marines, Aranict. And I am not referring to their new titles.'

'I don't recall meeting them.'

'I will be pleased to introduce you, if you like.'

With the standard-bearer twenty paces ahead, they set out side by side, horse hoofs thumping as if on hollow ground. 'Brys, do you hear that?'

'We ride across an ancient lake bed,' he said. 'Often the lake remains, but only beneath the surface, and I think that must have been the case here, once. But now . . .'

'The water's gone.'

'Yes. Gone.'

'Might we all fall through?'

He shrugged.

'So now even the ground under us is uncertain.'

'I am sorry, Aranict. I have been neglecting you.'

'Yes, you have.'

The flying wing was swinging in behind them, thirty Bluerose lancers in perfect formation. Brys thought about the soldier he'd lost – *to love, no less.* Henar Vygulf now marched with the Bonehunters. *And if I have sent him to his death . . . I do not think he will curse my name.* 'I am not very good with grief, Aranict. When our parents died, well, without Tehol and Hull I don't think I would have made it through. Kuru Qan once told me that grieving had nothing to do with the ones gone, and everything to do with the ones left behind. We feel the absences in our life like open wounds, and they never really close, no matter how many years pass.'

'Do you grieve then for the Adjunct and the Bonehunters?'

'It makes no sense, does it? She . . . well . . . she is a difficult woman to like. She views a human gesture as if it was some kind of surrender, a weakness. Her responsibilities consume her, because she will allow herself nothing else.'

'It was said she had a lover,' said Aranict. 'She died saving Tavore's life.'

'Imagine the wound that made.'

'No one wants to be un-liked, Brys. But if it must be so, one can strive for other things. Like respect. Or even fear. Choices fall away, without you even noticing, until there are very few left, and you realize that you are nothing but what you are.'

Brys thought about that, and then sighed. 'I should have liked her. I should have found something – beyond her competence, beyond even her stubbornness. Something . . .'

'Brys, what is it that you grieve over? Is it your own failure to find in Tavore the reasons you need for following her?'

He grunted. 'I should have talked to you days ago.'

'You were too busy saying nothing.'

'I stayed close, as long as I could. Like a man dying of thirst – was she my salvation? Or just a mirage?' He shook his head.

'We won't turn back, will we?'

'No, we won't.'

'We'll see this through.'

'Yes, and so I must hide my uncertainty – from my officers, from my soldiers—'

'But not from me, Brys.'

He turned to study her face, was shocked to see tears streaking her dusty cheeks. 'Aranict?'

'Never mind this,' she said, as if angry with herself. 'Do you want to be like her, Brys? Do you want your responsibilities to consume you?'

'Of course not.'

'And since we began marching with the Bonehunters, what has the Adjunct given you?'

'Not much—'

'Nothing,' she snapped. 'Nothing but silence. Every time you needed something else, she gave you silence. Brys, you've said little to anyone for days. Don't take on someone else's wounds. Don't.'

Chastened, he looked ahead. The dark stain of legions in the hazy distance, and a nearer group, humans and lizards both, drawing closer.

When the Guardian of the Names came for me, the sea ran from him like tears. But I was dead by then. I saw none of that. Only upon my rebirth did these visions find me. I see poor Rhulad Sengar lying cut and broken on the blood-spattered floor, crying out to his brothers. I see them turn away. I see my body slumping down against the dais. I see my king sitting lifeless on his throne.

Could we but have left him there, so useless to resist the puppet-masters who ever gather to symbols of power – are they all so blind as to not see the absurdity of their ambitions? The pathetic venality of all their petty scheming? Grasp those dead limbs, then, and make him do your will.

I have dreamed the names of a thousand lost gods. Will I ever speak them? Will I break upon this world one last time those names of the fallen? Is that enough, to give remembrance to the dead? A name upon my breath, spoken out loud, a whisper, a bold shout – will a distant soul stir? Find itself once more?

In speaking a god's name, do we conjure it into being?

'Brys.'

'Aranict?'

'Did you hear me?'

'I did, and I will heed your warning, my love. But you should bear in mind that, sometimes, solitude is the only refuge left. Solitude . . . and silence.'

He saw how his words left her shaken, and was sorry. *Shall I by name resurrect a god? Force its eyes to open once more? To see what lies all about us, to see the devastation we have wrought?*

Am I that cruel? That selfish?

Silence. Tavore, I think I begin to understand you. Must the fallen be made to see what they died for, to see their sacrifice so squandered? Is this what you mean – what you have always meant – by 'unwitnessed'?

'Now it is you who weep – Errant's shove, Brys, what a wretched pair we make. Gather yourself, please – we are almost upon them.'

He drew a shaky breath and straightened in his saddle. 'I could not have stopped her, Aranict.'

'Did you really expect to?'

'I don't know. But I think I have figured something out. She gives us silence because she dares not give us anything else. What we see as cold and indifferent is in fact the deepest compassion imaginable.'

'Do you think that is true?'

'I choose to believe it, Aranict.'

'Well enough, then.'

Brys raised his voice. 'Bearer!'

The young man reined in and swung his mount out to the right. Brys and Aranict drew up alongside him.

The two marines had dismounted, joining a woman, a boy and a girl. The woman was middle-aged, possibly an Awl by birth. The children were Malazans, though clearly unrelated. Had he seen these two before? In the palace? Possibly. Behind them all stood a half-dozen K'Chain Che'Malle, including three of the saddled creatures. Two of the remaining lizards were not as robust, yet bore huge blades instead of hands, while the third one was broader of snout, heavier of girth, and unarmed. Two ragged-looking dogs wandered out from between the legs of the lizards. The humans approached.

'Aranict,' said Brys under his breath, 'tell me what you see.'

'Not now,' she said, her voice hoarse.

He glanced across to see her setting alight a stick of rustleaf, her hands shaking. 'Tell me this at least. Shall a prince of Lether relinquish command to these ones?'

Smoke hissed out, and then, 'The marines . . . yes, for one simple reason.'

'Which is?'

'Better them than those two children.'

I see.

At five paces away they halted, and the clean-shaven marine was the first to speak. His eyes on the standard, he said, 'So it's true.'

Brys cleared his throat. 'My brother the king—'

'Has no respect at all for the institutions of the military,' said the marine, nodding. 'Hood take me, for that reason alone I'd follow him anywhere. What think you, Stormy?'

The man scowled, scratched his red beard, and then grunted. 'Do I have to?'

'Do what? You oaf, I was saying—'

'And I wasn't listening, so how do I know what you was saying, Gesler? And do I even care? If I did, I'd probably have listened, wouldn't I?'

Gesler muttered something, and then said to Brys, 'Prince, I'd beg you to excuse my companion's boorish manners, but then he ain't five years old and I ain't his dada, so feel welcome to regard him with disgust. We do, all of us here, ain't that right, Stormy?'

'I ain't listening.'

'Prince Brys, about the chain of command the Adjunct wants—'

'I am content, Mortal Sword Gesler, to accede to her wishes.'

'Well, we ain't.'

'Y'got that right,' Stormy growled. 'It's all right Ges handling the Che'Malle – it's all down to smells, y'see? All he needs to do is fart or whatever and all the swords come out, which come to think of it, is just like old times. In the barracks, why—'

'It's down to trust,' said the boy. The bigger of the two dogs had drawn up next to him. Belligerent eyes glared out from a mangled face.

No one spoke. The silence stretched.

'You'd better explain that, Grub,' said Gesler, his expression dark.

Brys started to speak but Aranict stayed him with a hand on his arm.

'It's down to the people she knows best,' Grub continued. 'That's all.'

'We saved their lives!' blurted the standard-bearer, his face flushed.

'That's enough, soldier,' said Brys. 'What the boy says makes sense, Gesler. After all, what can she make of our motives? This is her war, it always has been. Why are we here? Why does Queen Abrastal seem intent on making this her cause as well? The Bonehunters brought the Letherii to their knees – might we not harbour resentment over that? Might we not contemplate betrayal? As for Bolkando, well, from all accounts the Khundryl laid waste to vast regions in that kingdom, and spilled the blood of the queen's subjects. Together with the Perish, they effectively subjected Bolkando to outright extortion.'

'So why should she have any better reason to trust *us*?' Gesler demanded. 'We got snatched, and now we're commanding our own damned army of lizards. The fact is, we deserted the—'

'I ain't deserted nothing!' Stormy shouted. The smaller of the two dogs barked.

Brys noted the growing alarm on the face of the Awl woman. He caught her eye and said, 'You are the Destriant?'

'I am Kalyth,' she said. 'I do not understand what is going on. The way you use the trader's tongue – there are words I don't know. I am sorry.' She faced Gesler. 'He is Mortal Sword of the K'Chain Che'Malle. He is defender of Matron Gunth Mach. We must fight to stay alive. There are old wounds . . . old . . . crimes. We cannot escape. Gunth Mach cannot escape. We fight, will fight.'

'And somehow,' Brys mused, 'the Adjunct understands the truth of that. How?'

Kalyth shook her head. 'I do not know her. But' – and she pointed at the girl standing near Grub – 'where this one goes, there will be fire.'

Gesler rubbed at his face with both hands. 'Our . . . Ceda. Sinn. Without her sorcery, and Grub's, the Nah'ruk would have defeated us. Not on the ground, but from the sky keeps. So,' he sighed, 'Sinn and Grub saved us all. The Adjunct said we'd need them—'

'No,' corrected Stormy, 'she said they'd be safer with us than with her.'

Gesler said to Brys, 'We've been thinking of going after them – into that desert.'

'She will not be swayed,' said Brys. 'And she wants none of us to follow her. It is her conviction that we will be needed elsewhere.'

'I can't assume command,' said Gesler. 'I'm a Hood-damned marine, a fucking sergeant.'

'You was a damned *Fist*, Gesler!' Stormy said.

'For three days—'

'Till they busted you down, aye! And why was you busted down? No, you don't want to say, do you?'

'Leave it—'

'I won't!' Stormy jabbed a finger at his companion. 'You went and thought you could be another Dassem! You went and got us all to swear our souls to a damned god! This ain't your first time as a Mortal Sword, is it?'

Gesler wheeled on Stormy. 'How should I know? It's not like Fener reached down and patted me on the head, is it? And what about you, *Adjutant*? You lied to the damned Empress!'

'I did what Cartheron and Urko asked me to do!'

'You betrayed the Empire!'

Ceda Sinn was laughing, but it was a cold, cruel laugh.

Kalyth had gone white and had backed up a step, her eyes wide as she looked from Gesler to Stormy and back again.

Sinn said to Gesler. 'That's why you'll be needed. But you won't like it. Hah! You won't like any of it!'

Gesler made to advance on the girl but Stormy stepped into his path and shoved him back.

'*Will all of you stop it!*'

Aranict's shout halted everyone.

Swearing under his breath, Gesler turned away from Stormy's challenging glare. 'Prince, this ain't what I was looking for. I wanted you to take overall command – you or Krughava. Gods, even that queen you talked about. I don't want any of this.'

'The matter,' said Brys, 'has proved far more complicated than even I had thought. But I mean to hold to my agreement with the Adjunct. Nor do I expect Queen Abrastal to change her mind, either. Our royal titles are nothing but a product of circumstance. They confer no special talent or ability, and we are both aware of that. Mortal Sword Gesler, it is undeniable that you are in command of the most formidable army in this alliance, and as such, the full weight of command must fall on you.'

The man looked miserable.

Snarling, Stormy swung round and stamped back to the waiting K'Chain Che'Malle. The small hairy dog followed.

Gesler shrugged. 'We liked it the way we'd made it – gods, so long ago now. Hiding in some foul garrison in a smelly fishing village. We'd ducked down so far it looked like the world had forgotten us, and that was just how we wanted it. And now look at us. Gods below.'

Brys cocked his head. 'You have been with the Adjunct ever since that time?'

'Not quite. We got pulled in with the Whirlwind – a mutiny. We blame the Imperial Historian, that's who we blame. Never mind, none of it's worth knowing – it's just a sordid tale of us staggering and stumbling this way and that across half the damned world. We did nothing of note, except maybe staying alive, and see where it's got us.'

'If you and your friend are feeling so trapped,' said Brys, 'why not just leave? Did you not already call yourself and Stormy deserters?'

'Wish I could. I really do. But we can't, and we know it.'

'But . . . why?'

Gesler looked down abjectly at Grub. 'Because,' he whispered like a man condemned, '*she trusts us.*'

'Now didn't that go well,' said Aranict as they rode back towards the column at a slow trot.

Brys regarded her. 'There was considerable alarm in your voice, Aranict, when you so startled us all.'

'Where do gods come from, Brys? Do you know?'

He shook his head, unwilling to stir awake his memories of the seabed, the forgotten menhirs so bearded in slime. He had lost a lifetime wandering the muddy, wasted depths. *I slept, and so wanted to sleep – for ever. And if this is not the death others find, it was the death that found me. Such weariness, I'd lost the will to drag myself free.*

'Gesler and Stormy,' said Aranict, 'they are almost within reach.'

'I'm sorry, what?'

'Of godhood.'

'You speak of things Kuru Qan used to talk about. The ancient First Empire notion of ascendancy.'

'The Destriant spoke of fire.'

He struggled to stay on the path she seemed to be taking. 'The girl, Sinn . . .'

Aranict snorted. 'Yes, her. Fire at its most destructive, at its most senseless – she could have burned us all to ash and given it not a moment's thought. When you hold such power inside you, it burns away all that is human. You *feel* nothing. But Brys, you don't understand – the Adjunct wants Sinn with them.'

'As far away from her as possible? I don't think Tavore would—'

'No no, that wasn't her reason, Brys. It's Gesler and Stormy.'

'You are right in saying that I don't understand.'

'Those two men have walked in the Hold of Fire, in what the sages of the First Empire called *Telas*. Tavore wants Sinn with them because no one else can stand against that child, no one else could hope to survive her power, for when Sinn awakens that power, as Kalyth said, *there will be fire.*'

'The Adjunct warned of betrayal—'

'Brys, Gesler and Stormy are on the edge of ascendancy, and they can feel it. They're both holding on for dear life—'

'Holding on to what?'

'To their humanity,' she replied. 'Their fingers are numb, the muscles of their arms are screaming. Their nails are cracked and bleeding. Did you see how the boy watched them? The one named Grub? He stands beside Sinn like her conscience made manifest – it is truly outside her now. She could push it away, she could crush the life from it – I don't know why she hasn't already. For all the fire in her hands, her heart is cold as ice.'

'Are you saying the boy has no power of his own?'

She shot him a look. 'Did the Adjunct speak of him? The boy?'

Warily, he nodded.

'What did she say?'

'She said he was the hope of us all, and that in the end his power would – could – prove our salvation.'

She searched his face. 'Then, Brys, we are in trouble.'

Betrayal. When the face before us proves a lie, when the eyes deceive and hide the truths behind them. Will there be no end to such things?

He thought back to the seabed, as he knew he would. *I have these names, deep inside me. The names of the fallen. I can hear each one, there with its own, unique voice. Yet so many sound the same, a cry of pain. Of . . . betrayal. So many, and so many times.* 'She trusts those two marines,' he said. 'She trusts them not to betray her. It's all she has. It's all she can hope for.'

'Yes,' said Aranict. 'And, worse than that, that Awl woman – Kalyth – who said she didn't understand anything, well, she understands all too well. Like it or not, she holds the fate of the K'Chain Che'Malle in her hands. She is the Destriant to the Matron – do you imagine she trusts Sinn? With all their lives? With the Matron's and all the other K'Chain Che'Malle? Hardly. She is in the same position as we are – it's all down to Gesler and Stormy, and she is watching those two men fight for everything.'

'It must be breaking her heart.'

'She's terrified, Brys. And so alone, so alone. With all that.'

He rubbed at his face. Their horses had slowed to a slow amble, directionless. Unaware, the standard-bearer had ridden on and was now closing on the column. At this distance, the standard looked like a white flag. 'Aranict, what can we do?'

'No matter what happens,' she said, 'we must stand with them. With Gesler and Stormy, and Kalyth and the K'Chain Che'Malle. But if it comes down to who can we save, if we're left with that awful choice, then . . . it must be the boy.'

'Those two men are at each other's throat – there must be—'

'Oh, *that*. Brys, they are like brothers, those two. They'll snap at each other, even come to blows. They'll shout each other down, but things would be a lot worse if none of that was happening. What we saw was their humanity – the very thing they're desperate to keep. That was all like . . . like a ritual. Of caring. Love, even.'

'As if married . . .'

'Brothers, I'd say. Bound by blood, bound by history. When we witness them argue, we only hear what's said out loud – we don't hear all the rest, the important stuff. Kalyth is only beginning to understand that – when she does, some of her terror and anxiety will go away.'

'I hope you are right.' Brys reined in, and then dismounted. He turned to observe the Bluerose lancers, waved them back to their flanking patrol. To Aranict he said, 'Let us walk. The vanguard will survive without me a while longer, I'm sure.'

He could see her curiosity, but she shrugged and slipped down from her horse. Leading their mounts, they began walking, parallel to the column.

'My love,' said Brys, 'I have known a silence deeper – and more crushing – than anyone could imagine.'

'You need not speak of it—'

'No, you are wrong. But what I must tell you is more than finding a new intimacy between us, though that will be part of it. What I will describe is important – it bears on what you have just said, and – with your help – I hope it will guide us to a course of action. Tell me, what do you know of my death?'

She paused to light a new stick from the stub of the old one. 'Poison. An accident.'

'And my corpse?'

'A revenant stole it.'

'Stole? Perhaps it seemed that way. In truth, I was *retrieved*. I was carried back to a place I had been to before. My very name was carved upon a standing stone. Joined to countless others.'

She frowned, seemed to study the wiry grasses on the ground before them. 'Is this what happens, then? To all of us? Our names set in stone? From death to life and then back again? As some sages have claimed?'

'I do not know what happens, in truth. Whether what I experienced was fundamentally different from what others go through. But I sense there was something to it that was . . . unique. If I was inclined to blame anyone, it would have to be Kuru Qan. He invoked a ritual, sending me to a distant place, a realm, perhaps – a world upon the floor of the ocean – and it was there that I first met the . . . revenant. The Guardian of the Names – or so I now call it.'

'And this was the one who came for you? In the throne room?'

He nodded.

'Because he possessed your name?'

'Perhaps – but perhaps not. We met in the clash of blades. I bested him in combat . . .'

'He failed in his guardianship.'

'Yes.'

'When he came for you,' said Aranict, 'it was to set you in his stead.'

'You have the truth of it, I think.' *Or so it seemed.*

'The "names" you speak of, Brys – does no one guard them now?'

'Ah, thus leading us to my resurrection. What do you know of the details surrounding it?'

Aranict shook her head. 'Nothing. But then, almost no one does.'

'As you might imagine, I think about this often. In my dreams there are memories of things I have never done, or seen. Most troubling, at least at first. Like you, I have no real knowledge of my return to the realm of the living. Was there an invitation? A sundering of chains? I just don't know.'

'The power to achieve such a thing must have been immense.'

'Something tells me,' he said with a wry smile, 'even an Elder God's power would not have been enough. The desires of the living – for the return of the ones they have lost – cannot unravel the laws of death. This is not a journey one is meant to ever take, and all that we were when alive we are not now. I am not the same man, for that man died in the throne room, at the very feet of his king.'

She was studying him now, with fear in her eyes.

'For a long time,' Brys said, 'I did not think I was capable of finding anything – not even an echo of who I had once been. But then . . . you.' He shook his head. 'Now, what can I tell you? What value does any of this have, beyond the truths we have now shared? It is, I think, this: I was released . . . to do something. Here, in this world. I think I now know what that thing is. I don't know, however, what will be achieved. I don't know why it is so . . . important. The Guardian has sent me back, for I am his hope.' He shot her a look. 'When you spoke of Tavore's belief in the boy, I caught a glimmer . . . like the flickering of a distant candle, as if through murky water . . . of someone in the gloom. And I realized that I have seen this scene before, in a dream.'

'Someone,' murmured Aranict. 'Your Guardian?'

'No. But I have felt that stranger's thoughts – I have dreamed his memories. An ancient house, where once I stood, but now it was empty. Flooded, dark. Like so much upon the bed of the oceans, its time was past, its purpose . . . lost. He walked inside it, wanting to find it as he once found it, wanting, above all, the comfort of company. But they're gone.'

'"They"? People dwelt in that house?'

'No longer. He left it and now walks, bearing a lantern – I see him like a figure of myth, the last soul in the deep. The lone, dull glow of all he has left to offer anyone. A moment of' – he reached up to his face, wiped at the tears – 'of . . . light. Relief. From the terrible pressures, the burdens, the *darkness*.'

They had halted. She stood facing him, her eyes filled with sorrow. She whispered, 'Does he beckon you? Does he beg your company, Brys?'

He blinked, shook his head. 'I – I don't know. He . . . waits for me. I see the lantern's light, I see his shadow. All a thing of myth, a conjuration. Does he wait for the souls of the drowned? It seems he must. When we flounder, when we lose the sense of what is up and what is down – is that not what often happens when one drowns? And we see a lightness in the murk, and we believe it to be the surface. Instead . . . his lantern calls us. Down, and down . . .'

'Brys, what must you do?'

'There is a voice within me,' he said, his throat suddenly hoarse, thick with emotion. 'All that the seas have taken – the gods and mortals – all the . . . the *Unwitnessed*.' He lifted his gaze to meet her wide eyes. 'I am as bound as the Adjunct, as driven on to . . . something . . . as she. Was I resurrected to be brother to a king? A commander of armies? Am I here in answer to a brother's grief, to a *wish* for how things once were? Am I here to feel once more what it is to be human, to be alive? No. There is more, my love. There is more.'

She reached up one hand, brushed his cheek. 'Must I lose you, Brys?'

I don't know.

Aranict must have seen his answer though he spoke it not, for she leaned against him, like one falling, and he closed an arm round her.

Dear voice. Dear thing that waits inside me – words cannot change a world. They never could. Would you stir a thousand souls? A million? The mud kicked up and taken on the senseless currents? Only to settle again, somewhere else.

Your shadow, friend, feels like my own.

Your light, so fitful, so faint – we all stir in the dark, from the moment of birth to the moment of death. But you dream of finding us,

274

because, like each of us, you are alone. There is more. There must be more.

By all the love in my veins, please, there must be more.

'Do not lecture me, sir, on the covenants of our faith.'

So much had been given to the silence, as if it was a precious repository, a vault that could transform all it held, and make of the fears a host of bold virtues. *But these fears are unchanged.* Shield Anvil Tanakalian stood before Krughava. The sounds of five thousand brothers and sisters preparing camp surrounded them.

Sweat trickled under his garments. He could smell his own body, rank and acrid with his wool gambeson's lanolin. The day's march felt heavy on his shoulders. His eyes stung; his mouth was dry.

Was he ready for this moment? He could not be sure – he had his own fears with which he had to contend, after all. *But then, how long must I wait? And what moment, among all the moments, can I judge safest? The breath before the war cry? Hardly.*

I will do this now, and may all who witness understand – it has been a long time in coming, and the silence surrounding me was not my own – it was where she had driven me. Where she would force us all, against the cliff wall, into cracks in the stone.

Iron, what are your virtues? The honed edge kisses and sparks rain down. Blood rides the ferule and splashes on the white snow. This is how you mark every trail. Tanakalian looked away. Seething motion, tents rising, tendrils of smoke curling up on the wind. 'Without a Destriant,' he said, 'we cannot know their fate.' He glanced back at her, eyes narrowing.

Mortal Sword Krughava stood watching seven brothers and sisters assembling her command tent. The skin of her thick forearms, where they were crossed over her breasts, had deepened to bronze, a hue that seemed as dusty as the patches of bared earth all around them. The sun had bleached the strands of hair that escaped her helm, and they drifted out like webs on the hot wind. If she bore wounds from the parley with the Adjunct, she would not show them. 'Sir,' she said, 'Commander Erekala is not one for indecision. This is precisely why I chose him to command the fleet. You invite uncertainty and think that this is the time for such things – when so much has been challenged.'

But, you damned fool, Run'Thurvian saw what was coming. We shall betray our vow. And I see no way out. 'Mortal Sword,' he began, struggling to keep the anger from his voice, 'we are sworn to the Wolves of Winter. In our iron we bare the fangs of war.'

She grunted. 'And there shall indeed be war, Shield Anvil.'

When you stood before the Adjunct, when you avowed service to her and her alone, it was the glory of that moment that so seduced you, wasn't it? Madness! 'We could not have anticipated what the Adjunct intended,' he said. 'We could not have known she would so deceive us—'

She turned then. 'Sir, must I censure you?'

Tanakalian's eyes widened. He straightened before her. 'Mortal Sword, I am the Shield Anvil of the Perish Grey Helms—'

'You are a fool, Tanakalian. You are, indeed, my greatest regret.'

This time, he vowed, he would not retreat before her disdain. He would not walk away, feeling diminished, battered. 'And you, Mortal Sword, stand before me as the greatest threat the Grey Helms have ever known.'

The brothers and sisters at the tent had halted all activity. Others were joining them in witnessing this clash. *Look at you all! You knew it was coming!* Tanakalian's heart was thundering in his chest.

Krughava had gone white. 'Explain that, Shield Anvil.' Her voice was harsh, grating. 'On your life, *explain that.*'

Oh, how he had longed for this moment, how he had conjured this scene, where stood the Shield Anvil, face to face with Krughava. Witnessed and so remembered. *This precise scene.* And in his mind he had spoken all he would now say, his voice hard and bold, solid and unwavering before this wretched tyrant's ire. Tanakalian drew a slow breath, watched the Mortal Sword tremble with rage, and was not cowed. 'Adjunct Tavore is one woman. A mortal woman – that and nothing more. It was not your place to avow service to her. We are Children of the Wolves, not that damned woman! And now see what has happened! She sets our course and it stabs at the very heart of our faith!'

'The Fallen God—'

'Hood *take* the Fallen God! "When the bhederin is wounded and weak, the wolves shall close in!" So it is written! In the name of our gods, Mortal Sword, he should *die* by our hand! But none of that matters – do you truly imagine Tavore gives a damn about our faith? Does she kneel before the Wolves? She does not.'

'We march to the final war, sir, and such a war demands us. The Perish. The Grey Helms – without us, there can be no final war! And I will not abide—'

'A final war? Don't be ridiculous. There's no such thing as a *final* war! When the last human falls, when the last god breathes his last breath, the vermin shall lock jaws over the carcasses. There is no end – not to anything, you mad, vain fool! This was all about you standing on a heap of corpses, your sword red as the sunset. This was all about Krughava and her insane visions of glory!' He gestured furiously at the soldiers gathered round them. 'And if we must all die for your precious, shining moment, why, is it not the Shield Anvil who stands ready to embrace the souls?'

'*That is your role!*'

'To bless your wilful murder of our brothers and sisters? You want me to sanctify their sacrifice?'

Her left hand was on the grip of her sword, the blade was half drawn. She had gone from white to bright red. *The berserk rage is almost upon her. She is moments from killing me. By the Wolves, see what she is!* 'The Shield Anvil, sir, shall not question—'

'I will bless us, Mortal Sword, in the name of a *just* cause. Make your cause just. I plead with you, before all these witnesses – before our brothers and sisters – *make this cause just!*'

The sword scraped. The iron sank down, vanished into the scabbard. The fires in her eyes suddenly ebbed. 'So we are divided,' she said. 'We are driven apart. The crisis I have feared is finally upon us. The Adjunct spoke of betrayal.' Her cold eyes scanned the crowd. 'My children, what has befallen us?'

Captain Ikarl, one of the last veterans among them, spoke. 'Mortal Sword. Two sides of an argument can make the complicated seem simple, when it is anything but simple. A third voice can offer reason, and indeed wisdom. We must acclaim a Destriant. To bridge this divide, to mend this wound.'

She cocked her head. 'Sir, do you voice the doubt of many? Do my brothers and sisters question my leadership?'

He shook his head, but there was no telling what that negation referred to. 'Mortal Sword, we are sworn to the Wolves of Winter – but without a Destriant we cannot reach them. We are severed from our gods and so we suffer. Krughava, daughter of Nakalat, do you not see how we suffer?'

Shaken, her eyes bleak, she regarded Tanakalian once more. 'Shield Anvil, do you counsel betrayal of the Adjunct Tavore?'

And so it is laid bare. At last, it is laid bare. He raised his voice, forcing himself to remain firm, calm, revealing no hint of triumph. 'The Wolves howl in the name of war. Our worship was born in the snows of our homeland, in the winter's cruel, icy breath. We came to honour and respect the beasts of the wild, the wolves who shared the mountain fastnesses, the dark forests, with our kind. Even as, in our early days, we hunted those very beasts. We understood them, or so we liked to believe—'

'These words are unnecessary—'

'No, Mortal Sword. They are necessary. They are, in fact, *vital.*' He eyed the others – all had gathered now, a silent mass. *Five thousand. Brothers, sisters all. You hear me. You will hear me. You must hear me.* 'We find ourselves divided, but this crisis has waited for us, and we must face it. A crisis created by the Mortal Sword's vow to the Adjunct. We shall face it. Here. Now. Brothers, sisters, we have looked into the eyes of the beast – our chosen wildness – and in bold presumption, we proclaimed them our brothers, our sisters, our kin.'

Voices cried out – angry, harsh with denial. Tanakalian raised his hands, held them high until silence returned. 'A presumption,' he repeated. 'We cannot know the mind of a wolf, no more than we can know the mind of a dog, or a dhenrabi of the north seas. Yet we took upon ourselves the most ancient of gods – the Lord and Lady of the frozen winter, of all the beasts, of the world's wildness. We vowed ourselves to a House – a Hold – *where we do not belong—*'

The protests were louder this time, reluctant to die away. Tanakalian waited. 'But *war*, ah, we knew that well. We understood it, in a manner no wolf of the forest could. Was this to be our cause, then? Were we to be the sword of the wilds, the defender of wolves and all the beasts of forest, sea, plain and mountain?' He faced Krughava. 'Mortal Sword?'

'The earliest sentiments whispered of such things,' she replied, 'as we all know. And we have not gone astray, sir. *We have not.*'

'We have, Mortal Sword, if we continue to follow the Adjunct, if we stand beside her in this war she seeks. At last, it is time for me to speak of Destriant Run'Thurvian's final warning, uttered to me moments before his death, hard words, accusing words, even as he denied my embrace.'

The shock was palpable, like thunder so distant it was not heard, but felt. A tremble in the very bones. *And all that comes, all that now rushes towards us . . .*

Krughava's eyes were wide and he could see her confusion. 'Tanakalian – he refused you?'

'He did. He never approved of me – but you could hardly have been unaware of that. He must have worked on you, I think, day and night, undermining your decision to make me the Shield Anvil. And when he died, his fears and doubts took root in you.'

The look she was giving him was one he'd never seen before.

Ikarl asked, 'Shield Anvil, tell us of the Destriant's warning.'

'Betrayal. He said she would force us to betray our gods – I could not be certain of whom he spoke. The Adjunct?' He faced Krughava. 'Or our very own Mortal Sword? It was difficult, you see, for his dislike of me proved an obstacle. That, and the fact that he was dying before my very eyes.'

'You speak truth,' Krughava said, as if astonished.

'Mortal Sword, do not think I do not love my brothers and sisters. Do not think I would stand here and lie. I am the Shield Anvil, and for all Run'Thurvian's doubts – for all *your* doubts, Krughava – I hold to my duty. We are divided, yes. But what divides us is so fundamental that to put it into words could strike one as absurd. Upon the side of the Adjunct, we are offered a place among mortals, among humans – flawed, weak, uncertain in their cause. Upon the other side, our covenant of faith. The Wolves of Winter, the Wolves of War. The Lord and the Lady of the Beast Hold. And in this faith we choose to stand alongside the beasts. We avow our swords in the name of their freedom, their right to live, to share this and every other world. The question – so absurd – is this: are we to be human, or are we to be humanity's slayers? And if the latter, then what will come of us should we win? Should we somehow lead a rebellion of the wilds, and so destroy every last human on this world? Must we then fall upon our own swords?'

He paused then, suddenly drained, and met Krughava's eyes. 'Run'Thurvian was right. There will be betrayal. In fact, in choosing one side, we cannot but betray the other. Mortal Sword, you set your sword down before the Adjunct. But long before that moment you pledged that selfsame weapon in the name of our gods. No matter how strong the sword's forging,' he said, 'no weapon can long withstand contrary pressures. It weakens. It shatters. No weapon has ever bridged a divide, and once drawn, a sword can only cut. For all the virtues of iron, Mortal Sword, we are flesh and blood. What awaits us, Krughava? Which path shall you lead us upon? Shall it be to your personal glory, there at the Adjunct's side? Or shall it be in the name of the gods we are sworn to serve?'

She reeled at his words, seemed unable to speak.

The virtue of iron, woman, is that when it strikes, it strikes true! He faced the crowd. 'Sisters! Brothers of the Grey Helms! There are many gods of war – we have crossed half this world and we cannot deny the thousand faces – the thousand masks worn by that grim bringer of strife. We have seen mortals kneel before idols and statues – before the likeness of a boar, a striped tiger, or two wolves. We have heard the cries upon the battlefield.' He paused and half smiled, as if remembering. 'The field of battle, yes. By those beseeching cries alone, we might imagine that the greatest god of war is named *Mother*.' He held up his hands again to stay his listeners. 'I meant no disrespect, dear kin. I speak only to find what sets us apart – from all those other blood-soaked cults. What do they seek, there in violent battle, those savage faiths? Why, they seek death – the death of their enemies – and if death must come to themselves, then they pray it is a brave one, a glorious one.'

He strode past Krughava, was pleased to see her step aside, and faced Ikarl and the others: scores of faces, eyes fixed upon him now, eyes that slipped over the Mortal Sword as if she had ceased to exist. He could not believe the suddenness, the sheer *immensity* of this usurpation.

She was fatally weakened. There in the Adjunct's command tent. She sought to show none of it, and hid it well indeed. Yet all I needed to do was prod, just once. And see what has happened.

Tavore, your denial broke Krughava, and Krughava was a woman for whom trust was everything. How could I have not heard the splintering of her spine? Right then and there? How could I not have understood the moment when she grasped the notion of strategy, of tactics, and made bold her renewed zeal? It was . . . desperate. No matter. 'But we are not the same as the others. We are not simply one cult of war among many. It is not glory we seek – not in our name, at least. It is not even the death of our enemies that so gladdens us, filling our drunken nights with bravado. We are too sombre for such things. It is not in us to swagger and bluster. *War,* my brothers, my sisters, is the only weapon we have left.

'To defend the wilds. I tell you, I would defy Run'Thurvian's last words! Betray the Wolves? No! Never! And the day of our battle, when we stand free upon the corpses of our fellow humans, when we have delivered once more the wildness upon all the world, well, then I shall bow to the Wolves. And I shall with humility step aside. For it is not *our* glory that we seek.' He swung to stare at Krughava. 'It never was.' Facing the others again. 'Must we then fall upon our own swords? No, for as I said earlier, *there is no such thing as a final war.* One day we shall be called upon again – that is the only certainty we need to recognize.

'Brothers, sisters! Are you sworn to the Wolves of Winter?'

The roar that answered his question rocked him back a step. Recovering, he spun round, marched up to Krughava. 'Mortal Sword, I sought you out to ask you about Commander Erekala and the fleet. You chose him, but I must know, is he a loyal servant to the Wolves? Or does he worship *you?*'

He might as well have slapped her. *Yes, I do this before witnesses. All the public slights you visited upon me – at last I can deliver the same to you. How does it feel?*

Krughava straightened. 'Erekala is most devout, sir.'

'The fleet should have arrived,' he said. 'Blockading the harbour and so isolating the Spire. Yes?'

She nodded.

'And there they await us.'

'Yes, Shield Anvil.'

'Mortal Sword, will you return to the fold? Will you lead us in the war to come? Our need for you—'

She lifted her eyes, silenced him with their icy regard. A sneer curled her lips. 'Is clearly past, Shield Anvil.' She turned to the crowd. 'I relinquish the title of Mortal Sword to the Wolves. In my vow to the Adjunct, I seem to have betrayed you all. So be it, sirs. Let it be written that the betrayal – so forewarned by Destriant Run'Thurvian – belonged not to the Perish Grey Helms, but to Mortal Sword Krughava. The crime is mine and mine alone.'

Gods, the supreme egoism of this creature! Even in defeat, she will stand upon the mound, alone. I divest her of everything – I drive the knife into her very heart – and now she is suddenly transformed into a figure of breathtaking tragedy! How does she manage it? Every time!

'How it shall be written,' he said in a loud voice, 'remains to be decided. Should you rediscover your faith, Krughava—'

She bared her teeth. 'Should you discover your *humanity*, Tanakalian, should you find the courage – Hood knows where – to see the crisis in your own soul, then do come to me. Until then, I shall ride alone.'

He snorted. 'And will you raise your own tent, too? Cook your own breakfast?'

'I have ever given thanks to my brothers and sisters, Shield Anvil, for such kindnesses as they volunteer.' She cocked her head. 'I wonder . . . how long before doing the same slips from your mind, Tanakalian?'

As she walked away, he turned to the tent. 'Here, my children, shall I help you with that?'

'*Usurpation?*'

Krughava swept past Spax, flung her helm into a corner of the tent, and followed it with her gauntlets. 'I would drink, Highness.'

Abrastal gestured savagely and Spax shook himself, went over to collect a jug. 'Woman, you have the right of it. Get drunk, and then come to my bed. I vow to make you forget all your ills.'

The stern woman regarded the Barghast with a measuring stare, as if contemplating his offer. Spax felt sudden sweat upon the small of his back. He quickly poured out a goblet and handed it to her.

Queen Abrastal sank back into the heap of cushions. 'Well, that didn't take long.'

Krughava's eyes flashed. 'If I am too shameful in your eyes, Highness—'

'Oh be quiet and drink that down. Spax, be ready to pour her another. I was but musing out loud, Mortal Sword, on my sense of the Adjunct's—'

'Her? And if it pleases, I am no longer Mortal Sword. No, none of this can be cast at Tavore's feet—'

'By all the river gods, woman, sit down and drink – in other words, be quiet! Leave me to do all the talking.'

'What of me, Firehair?'

'Should the miraculous moment ever arrive when you can say something of value, Spax of the Gilk, be sure to leap right in. Meanwhile,

I return to my point. The Adjunct. I can't even guess at the manner of it, but clearly she somehow managed to bind you all to her – until the day of the parley, when she went and tore it all apart. Thus, not long – do you see? What she made she then un-made, and I do wonder at her appalling sense of timing.'

Krughava's eyes were level above the rim of the goblet. 'Highness, what did you make of her?'

'Spax, hand me that damned jug if all you can do is stare – no, give it to me. Throw yourself down by the curtain – we might need to wipe our feet by the time the night's done. Now, the Adjunct. Krughava – I swear, I will have you weeping, or whatever else I can wring from you. To hold it all inside as I see you doing will kill you.'

'Tavore Paran, Highness.'

Abrastal sighed, watching Spax settle down near the curtain. 'I miss the Khundryl,' she muttered. She blinked and then looked away, seemed to study one of the thick tapestries hanging from the tent frame. Spax squinted at it. Some faded coronation scene, figures stiff as statues, the kind of formality that spoke of artistic incompetence or the absurdity of genius. He could never make up his mind over such things. *It's just a stupid circlet of gold and silver and whatnot. It's just a stupid proclamation of superiority – look at all the bowed heads! Where's the real message here? Why, it's with those guards lining the walls, and the swords under their hands.*

'It is difficult,' Abrastal said, frowning still at the tapestry. 'Where does loyalty come from? What causes it to be born? What lifts one person above all the others, so that one chooses to follow her, or him? Is it nothing but our own desperation? Is it, as the Khundryl say, that vast crow's wing stretching over us? Do we yearn for the shelter of competence – real or imagined, true or delusional?'

Spax cleared his throat. 'In times of crisis, Firehair, even the smallest group of people will turn their heads, finding one among them. When we have no answers, we look to one who might – and that hope is born of qualities observed: of clearest thought, of wisdom or bold courage – all that each of us wishes to reflect.'

Krughava shifted to regard Spax, but said nothing.

'Reflect, is it?' Abrastal grunted, drank down a mouthful of wine. 'Is this queen a mirror? Is that all I am? Is that all you are, Warchief Spax? A mirror for your people?'

'In many ways, yes. But in looking into that mirror they ever choose, I think, to see only what they want to see.'

'Sir,' rumbled Krughava to Spax, 'you invite an untenable position, for all who would command, who would take the lead, from the smallest band of warriors to the vastest empire.' She scowled at her goblet and held it out to Abrastal, who leaned forward to refill it. 'Among the

Perish, upon nights overcast and moonless, twenty hunters each would take to rath'avars and row out beyond the fiords. They would light bright lanterns, suspending them on poles out over the black, icy waters, and by that light they would call from the deeps the three-jawed nitals – a terrible fish that in vast numbers hunt the dhenrabi, and are able to strip those leviathan creatures down to the bones in a single sounding. The nitals, you see, hunt by the moon's glow. And when they rose to the light, the hunters would spear them.' She fell silent, lids lowering for a time.

Spax scratched at the bristle on his jaw, trying to work out the significance of that tale. He glanced at Abrastal, but the queen seemed fixated on the old tapestry.

'Those fish would rise to the surface,' Krughava said in a voice like gravel under a boot heel, 'and the light would blind them, freeze them. There was no bravery in slaying them – it was nothing but slaughter, and would only end when the arms and shoulders of the hunters burned like fire, when they could no longer lift their harpoons.'

Spax snorted, nodding. 'Yes, it does feel like that, at times.'

'When I think of the wilds,' she continued as if not hearing him, 'I think of the nitals. We humans stand as the brightest light, and before us every living beast of this world freezes in place. My Shield Anvil has reawakened all the rage in my people, a rage confounded with guilt. We are to be the slaughterers defending the slaughtered.'

'The Wolves of War—'

'It is a damned cult!' snapped Krughava, and then she shook her head. 'The savagery of the wolf inspired us – is that so surprising?'

'But there must be tenets of your faith,' Spax persisted, 'that do indeed cry out for retribution.'

'Delusions, sir. Highness, speak of the Adjunct. Please.'

'A most driven woman, Krughava. Desperation. And terrible need. But is she a mirror? And if so, what are we all meant to see?'

Krughava looked up, studied Abrastal. 'The thought alone makes me want to weep, but I know not why.'

'To reflect,' said Spax, 'a mirror is made hard, polished, unflawed.'

'Find us more wine, Spax,' Abrastal growled, 'this one is done. Krughava – you swore allegiance to the Adjunct. Why?'

'We were troubled. Questions had begun to plague us, especially the Destriant and his highest seneschals – those who had given their lives to the philosophy of our religion. We trained to be the weapons of war, you see, but we had begun to wonder if the only gesture of humanity was the one that delivered violence. Destruction. We wondered at the seemingly insurmountable might of vengeance, retribution and righteous punishment.' Her eyes were bleak. 'Is that all we possess? Is there nothing else that might challenge such weapons?'

'Then,' ventured Abrastal, 'you must have seen something. In her. In Tavore Paran—'

But Krughava shook her head. 'All that I knew of her, in that moment when I pledged my service and that of the Grey Helms – all that I knew, well, it came from the visions of the seneschals. The Fallen God was damaged. In terrible pain. Like a beast – like any of us – he lashed out at his tormentors. In that, he was more the wolf than we were. Or could ever hope to be. Highness, a knife to his throat would be a mercy, for so many – you must understand this – so many had now gathered to feed on his pain, to drink the sweet venom of his fevered blood. More than that, in witnessing his imprisonment, and his agony, they felt themselves elevated – it made them feel powerful, and in that power the only currency was cruelty. After all, is that not always our way?'

'The dreams of the seneschals, Krughava? What did they offer?'

The iron-haired woman nodded. 'An alternative. A way out. In those dreams stood a woman, a mortal woman, immune to all magics, immune to the seduction of the Fallen God's eternal suffering. And she held something in her hand – it was small, indeed, so small that our dreamers could not discern its nature, but it haunted them – oh, how it haunted them!'

'What was she holding?' Abrastal demanded, leaning forward. 'You must have an idea.'

'An idea? Oh, hundreds of those, Highness. What she held had the power to free the Fallen God. It had the power to defy the gods of war – and every other god. It was a power to crush the life from vengeance, from retribution, from righteous punishment. The power to burn away the *seduction of suffering* itself.' Her eyes glittered in the lantern light. 'Can you imagine such a thing?'

Spax leaned back. 'I have seen her enough times. I see nothing in her hand.'

Krughava had set the cup down. She now sat, her left hand held out, palm up, resting on her knee. She gazed down at it, as if seeking to conjure all that she needed. 'That,' she whispered, 'is not a mirror. But . . . oh, how I wish it to be one.'

'Krughava,' Abrastal said in a low, almost tentative voice. 'In the moment you stood before her, was there not doubt? Was there not even a single instant of . . . uncertainty?'

'I thought – in her eyes, so flat . . . something. And now I wonder – I cannot help but wonder now if all that I thought I saw was nothing more than what I wanted to see.' The hand slowly curled, closed like a dying flower. '*The mirror lies.*'

Those last words shook Spax to his very core. He climbed to his feet, feeling blood rushing into his face. 'Then why didn't you accept your Shield Anvil's argument? Krughava! Why are you even here?'

With desolate eyes, she looked up at him. 'I wanted a just war. I wanted it to be the last war of all wars. I wanted an end. One day the wolves will run only in our memories, our dreams. I do not want to live to see that day.'

'There was something there,' Abrastal insisted. 'In her hand – your seers saw it, Krughava. They saw it. You must find out what it was – for all of us to do this, to do as she bids – for *us*, Krughava, you must find it!'

'But I know what it is, Highness. In this moment, I have found my answer. And I see now how I have watched it weaken. How I have watched its light fade from the world. You see the Adjunct's desperation – oh yes, she is desperate. We are too few. We are failing. That precious thing she found, she paid a price for it, and that price is now proving too high. For her, for the Bonehunters, for us.'

Spax bared his teeth. 'Then the mirror did not lie.'

'The lie is in the faith, sir. The faith that it can win, that it can even survive at all. You see, she is indeed but one woman, a mortal, and her strength is no greater than anyone else's. She has been at war – I now think – all of her life. Is it any wonder she now stumbles?'

Spax thought back to that parley, and then shook his head. 'From somewhere, Krughava, she is finding strength. I saw it – we all did, damn you—'

'She turned me away.'

Abrastal snorted. 'You feel slighted? Is that where all this has come from?'

'Highness.' Krughava's tone hardened. 'From the very beginning, I saw myself as the reflection of her faith. I would be her one unshakeable ally – sworn to her and her alone, no matter where she would lead us. And I knew that we understood each other. And that as much as I needed her – and what she held inside – she in turn needed *me*. Do you grasp any of this? I was the source of her strength. When her faith faltered, she needed only to look at me.' Krughava held her palms against her face, covering her eyes, and slowly leaned forward. Muffled, she said, 'She turned me away.'

Spax looked over at Abrastal and met the queen's steady gaze. The Gilk Warchief slowly nodded.

'You leave me in a difficult position,' Abrastal said. 'Krughava. If I understand you correctly, it is now your thought that in denying you, the Adjunct has in effect lost her faith. Yet was this not a matter of disposition? Two objectives, not one, and so we are to be divided in strength. And given the nature of the Glass Desert—'

But Krughava was shaking her head behind her hands. 'Do you truly imagine that she believes she can cross it? With her army?'

Spax loosed a stream of Barghast curses, and then said, 'What would be the point of that? If she intends suicide – no, her ego cannot be so diabolically monstrous that she'd take all her soldiers with her!'

'You are yet, I think,' and Krughava's hands fell away as she looked up at him, 'to acquaint yourself with the third voice in this eternal argument.'

'What do you speak of?'

'I speak of despair, sir. Yes, she would will herself and her army across the Glass Desert, but she does so without faith. It is gone, driven away—'

Abrastal said, 'Sincerely as you may have seen yourself as the true and unshakeable reflection of Tavore's faith, I believe your conviction that Tavore saw you the same way – in those precise terms – is itself an article of faith. This place of despair where you now find yourself is entirely of your own making.'

Krughava shook her head. 'I have watched it weaken. I have watched its light fade from the world. And I have seen her desperation. We are too few. We are failing. That shining thing, there in her hand, is dying.'

'Tell me its name,' Abrastal whispered. 'This argument of yours. You name one side *faith* and another *despair*. Speak to me of what she holds. This failing, dying thing.'

Spax turned to Abrastal in surprise. 'Why, Firehair, you do not yet know? That which fades from the world? Its name is *compassion*. This is what she holds for the Fallen God. What she holds for us all.'

'And it is not enough,' Krughava whispered. '*Gods below, it is not enough.*'

BOOK FOUR

THE FISTS OF THE WORLD

If there was a better place
Would you seek it out?
If peace was at hand
Would you reach for it?
And on this road stand thousands
Weeping for all that is past
The journey's at an end
We are done with our old ways
But they are not done with us
There is no air left
In this closed fist
The last breath has been taken
And now awaits release
Where the children sit waiting
For the legacy of waste
Buried in the gifts we made
I have seen a better place
I have known peace like sleep
It lies at road's end
Where the silts have gathered
And voices moan like music
In this moment of reaching
The stone took my flesh
And held me fast
With eyes unseeing
Breath bound within
A fist closed on darkness
A hand outstretched
And now you march past
Tossing coins at my feet
In my story I sought a better place
And yearned so for peace
But it is a tale untold
And a life unfinished

Wood-Cutters
Tablet IV
Hethra of Aren

CHAPTER ELEVEN

On that day I watched them lift high
In the tallness of being they shouldered years
And stood as who they would become
There was sweat on their arms and mad jackals
Went slinking from their bright eyes
I see a knowledge sliding beneath this door
Where I lean barred and gasping in horror
And for all that I have flung my back against it
They are the milling proofs of revelation
Crowding the street beyond like roosting prophets
And as the children wandered off in the way of gods
The small shape was unmoving at suffering's end
On this day I watched them lift high
Tomorrow's wretched pantheon around stains
On the stone where a lame dog had been trapped
In a forest of thin legs and the sticks and bricks
Went up and down like builders of monuments
Where the bowls are bronze and overflowing
And marble statues brood like pigeons
Have you seen all these faces of God?
Lifted so high to show us the perfection
Of our own holy faces but their hands are empty
Of bricks and sticks now that they're grown
Is there no faith to scour away the cruelty of children?
Will no god shield the crying dog on the stone
From his lesser versions caging the helpless
And the lame? If we are made as we would be
Then the makers are us. And if there stands
A god moulding all he is in what we are
Then we are that god and the children
Beating to death a small dog outside my door

Are the small measures of his will considered
And in tasting either spat out or consumed
In the ecstasy of the omnipotent

Children Like Gods
Fisher kel Tath

*T*HE RAMPS HAD BEEN LAID OUT, THE CREWS SINGING AS THEY HEAVED *on the ropes. Columns of black marble, rising in a ring around the glittering mound. The dust in Spindle's mouth tasted like hope, the ache in his shoulders and lower back felt like the promise of salvation.*

He had seen her this day and she had been . . . better. Still a child, really, a sorely used one, and only a bastard would say it had all been for the good. That the finding of faith could only come from terrible suffering. That wisdom was borne on scars. Just a child, dammit, scoured clean of foul addictions, but that look remained, there in her ancient eyes. Knowledge of deadly flavours, a recognition of the self, lying trapped in chains of weakness and desire.

She was the Redeemer's High Priestess. He had taken her in his embrace, and she was the last ever to have known that gift.

The digging around the mound had scurried up offerings by the bucketload. T'lan Imass, mostly. Bits of polished bone, shells and amber beads had a way of wandering down the sides of the barrow. The great plaster friezes they were working on in Coral now held those quaint, curious gifts, there in the elaborate borders surrounding the Nine Sacred Scenes.

Spindle leaned against the water wagon, awaiting his turn with a battered tin cup in one cracked, calloused hand.

He'd been a marine once. A Bridgeburner. He'd trained in military engineering, as much as any Malazan marine had. And now, three months since his return from Darujhistan (and what a mess that had been!) he'd been made a pit captain, but as in his soldiering days he wasn't one to sit back and let everyone else do all the hard work. No, all of this felt . . . good. Honest.

He'd not had a murderous thought in weeks. Well, days then.

The sun was bright, blistering down on the flood plain. On the west road huge wagons were wending up and down from the quarries. And as for the city to the south . . . he turned, squinted. Glorious light. Kurald Galain was gone. Black Coral was black no longer.

Gone. The Tiste Andii had vanished, that red dragon with them, leaving everything else behind. Books, treasures, everything. Not a word to anyone, not a single hint. Damned mysterious, but then what was odd about that? They weren't human. They didn't think like humans. In fact—

'Gods below!'

From the high palace, from the towers, a sudden conflagration, swirling darkness that spread out in roiling clouds, and then broke into pieces.

Shouts from the crews. Fear, alarm. Dread.

Distant cries . . . raining down.

Spindle was on his knees, the tin cup rolling away from trembling hands. The last time . . . gods! The last time he'd seen—

Great Ravens filled the sky. Thousands, spinning, climbing, a raucous roar. The sun momentarily vanished behind their vast cloud.

Shivering, his peace shattered, he could feel old tears rising from some deep well inside. He'd thought it sealed. Forgotten. But no. 'My friends,' *he whispered.* 'The tunnels . . . oh, my heart, my heart . . .'

Great Ravens, pouring out from the high places of the city, winging ever higher, massing, drifting out over the bay.

'Leaving. They're leaving.'

And as they swarmed above the city, as they boiled out over the sea to the east, a hundred horrid, crushing memories wheeled into Spindle, and there took roost.

Only a bastard would say it had all been for the good. That the finding of faith could only come from terrible suffering. That wisdom was borne on scars. Only a bastard.

He knelt.

And as only a soldier could, he wept.

Something had drawn Banaschar to the small crowd of soldiers. It might have been curiosity; at least, that was how it must have looked, but the truth was that his every motion now, from one place to next, was his way of fleeing. *Fleeing the itch. The itch of temple cellars, of all that had been within my reach. If I could have known. Could have guessed.*

The Glass Desert defied him. That perfect luxury that was a drunk's paradise, all that endless wine that cost him not a single coin, was gone. *I am damned now. As I swore to Blistig, as I said to them all, sobriety has come to pass for poor old Banaschar. Not a drop in his veins, not a hint upon his fevered breath. Nothing of the man he was.*

Except for the itch.

The soldiers – regulars, he thought – were gathered about an overturned boulder. They'd been rolling it to pin down a corner of the kitchen tent. There'd been something hiding under it.

Banaschar edged in for a look.

A worm, coiled in sleep, though it had begun to stir, lifting a blind head. Long as an eel from Malaz Harbour, but there the similarity ended. This one had mouths all over it.

'Can't say I like the look of that thing,' one of the soldiers was saying.

'Looks slow,' observed another.

'You just woke it up. It crawls by day, is my guess. All those hungry mouths . . . Hood's breath, we better turn all the rocks in camp. The thought of lying down to sleep with them out hunting whatever . . .'

Someone glanced up and noticed Banaschar. 'Look, that useless priest of D'rek's here. What, come for a look at your baby?'

'Myriad are the forms of the Autumn Worm—'

'What's that? A myrid worm, y'say?'

'I've seen the like,' Banaschar said, silencing them all. *In my dreams. When the itch turns to something that bites. That chews and gnaws and I can't see it, can't find it. When I scream in the night.* 'That was good advice,' he added. 'Scour the camp – spread the word. Find them. Kill them all.'

A boot heel slammed down.

The worm writhed, and then uncoiled and lifted its head as would a spitting serpent.

Soldiers backed away, swearing.

Banaschar was jostled to one side. Iron flashed, a sword blade descending, slicing the worm in two. He looked up to see Faradan Sort. She glowered at the ring of soldiers. 'Stop wasting time,' she snapped. 'The day grows hotter, soldiers. Get this done and then find some shade.'

The two sections of the worm had squirmed until contacting one another, at which point they constricted in mortal battle.

Someone threw a coin down, puffing dust. 'The shorter myrid.'

'I'll see you on that.' A second coin landed near the first one.

Faradan Sort's sword lashed down, again and again, until bits of worm lay scattered glistening in the white dust. 'Now,' she said, 'the next bet I hear placed – on anything – will see the fool hauling water from here to the Eastern Ocean. Am I understood? Good. Now get to work, all of you.'

As they hurried off, the Fist turned to Banaschar, studied him critically. 'You look worse than usual, Priest. Find some shade—'

'Oh, the sun is my friend, Fist.'

'Only a man with no friends would say that,' she replied, eyes narrowed. 'You're scorched. There will be pain – I suggest you seek out a healer.'

'I appreciate your advice, Fist. Do I anticipate pain today? I do. In fact, I think I welcome it.'

He saw a flash of disgust. 'Gods below, you're better than that.'

'Am I? Nice of you to say so.'

Faradan Sort hesitated, as if about to say something more, but then she turned away.

He watched her making her way deeper into the camp of the regulars, where soldiers now hurried about, dislodging rocks with knives and short swords in hand. Blades flashed and curses sounded.

The exhaustion of this place left him appalled. Shards of crystal born in screams of pressure, somewhere far below, perhaps, and then driven upward, slicing through the skin of the earth. Looking round, he imagined the pain of all that, the unyielding will behind such forces. He lifted his gaze, stared into the east where the sun edged open like a lizard's eye. 'Something,' he whispered, 'died here. Someone . . .' The shock had torn through this land. And the power unleashed, in that wild death, had delivered such a wound upon the Sleeping Goddess that she must have cried out in her sleep. *They killed her flesh. We walk upon her dead flesh. Crystals like cancer growing on all sides.*

He resumed his wandering, the itch biting at his heels.

Fist Blistig pushed his way past the crowd and entered the tent. *Gods below.* 'Everyone out. Except for the quartermaster.' The mob besieging Pores, where he sat behind a folding table, quickly departed, with more than one venomous look cast at the clean-shaven man now leaning back on his stool. Brows lifting, he regarded Blistig.

The Fist turned and dropped the tent flap. He faced Pores. 'Lieutenant. Master-Sergeant. Quartermaster. Just how many ranks and titles do you need?'

'Why, Fist Blistig, I go where necessity finds me. Now, what can I do for you, sir?'

'How much water did we go through last night?'

'Too much, sir. The oxen and horses alone—'

'By your reckoning, how many days can we go without resupply?'

'Well now, Fist, that depends.'

Blistig scowled. 'All the soldiers who were in here, Pores – what were they doing?'

'Petitioning, sir. Needless to say, I have had to refuse them all. It is quickly becoming apparent that water is acquiring a value that beggars gold and diamonds. It has, in short, become the currency of survival. And on that matter, I am glad you're here, Fist Blistig. I foresee a time – not far off – when begging turns to anger, and anger to violence. I would like to request more guards on the water wagons—'

'Are you rationing?'

'Of course, sir. But it's difficult, since we don't seem to have any reliable information on how many days it will take to cross this desert. Or, rather, nights.' Pores hesitated, and then he leaned forward. 'Sir, if you were to approach the Adjunct. The rumour is, she has a map. She knows how wide this damned desert is, and she's not telling. Why is she not telling? Because—'

'Because it's too far,' Blistig growled.

Lifting his hands in a just-so gesture, Pores leaned back. 'My carefree days are over, sir. This is now in deadly earnest.'

'You have the right of that.'

'Did the Adjunct send you, Fist? Have you been requested to make a report on our provisions? If so, I have a tally here—'

'How many days before we're out of water?' Blistig demanded.

'At fullest rationing, and allowing for the beasts of burden, about five.'

'And without the animals?'

'Without the oxen at least, we'd end up having to pull the wagons ourselves – hard work, thirsty work. I cannot be certain, but I suspect any gains would be offset by the increased consumption among the pull-crews—'

'But that would diminish over time, would it not? As the barrels emptied.'

'True. Fist, is this the Adjunct's command? Do we slaughter the oxen? The horses?'

'When that order comes, soldier, it will not be going through you. I am prepared to strengthen the guard around the wagons, Pores.'

'Excellent—'

'Reliable guards,' Blistig cut in, fixing Pores with his eyes.

'Of course, sir. How soon—'

'You are to set aside a company's supply of water, Quartermaster. Initial the barrels with my sigil. They are to be breached only upon my personal command, and the portions will be allotted to the names on the list you will be given. No deviation.'

Pores's gaze had narrowed. 'A company's allotment, Fist?'

'Yes.'

'And should I assume, sir, that your extra guards will be taking extra care in guarding those barrels?'

'Are my instructions clear, Quartermaster?'

'Aye, Fist. Perfectly clear. Now, as to disposition. How many extra guards will you be assigning?'

'Ten should do, I think.'

'Ten? In a single shift of rounds they'd be hard pressed to keep an eye on five wagons, sir, much less the scores and scores—'

'Redistribute your other guards accordingly, then.'

'Yes sir. Very good, sir.'

'I am trusting to your competence, Pores, and your discretion. Are we understood?'

'We are, Fist Blistig.'

Satisfied, he left the tent, paused outside the flap to glower at the dozen or so soldiers still lingering. 'First soldier caught trying to buy water gets tried for treason, and then executed. Now, you still got a reason to see the quartermaster? No, didn't think so.'

Blistig set out for his tent. The heat was building. *She's not going to kill me. I ain't here to die for her, or any other fucking glory. The real 'unwitnessed' are the ones who survive, who come walking out of the dust when all the heroes are dead. They did what they needed to live.*

Pores understands. He's cut from the same cloth as me. Hood himself knows that crook's got his own private store squirrelled away somewhere. Well, he's not the only smart bastard in this army.

You ain't getting me, Tavore. You ain't.

Frowning, Pores rose and began pacing, circling the folding table and the three-legged stool. Thrice round and then he grunted, paused and called out, 'Himble Thrup, you out there?'

A short, round-faced but scrawny soldier slipped in. 'Been waiting for your call, sir.'

'What a fine clerk you've become, Himble. Is the list ready?'

'Aye, sir. What did Lord Knock-knees want, anyway?'

'We'll get to that. Let's see your genius, Himble – oh, here, let me unfold it. You know, it's amazing you can write at all.'

Grinning, Himble held up his hands. The fingers had been chopped clean off at the knuckles, on both hands. 'It's easy, sir. Why, I never been a better scriber than I am now.'

'You still have your thumbs.'

'And that's it, sir, that's it indeed.'

Pores scanned the parchment, glanced at his clerk. 'You certain of this?'

'I am, sir. It's bad. Eight days at the stretch. Ten days in pain. Which way do we go?'

'That's for the Adjunct to decide.' He folded up the parchment and handed it back to Himble. 'No, don't deliver it just yet. The Fist is sending us ten handpicked thugs to stand guard over his private claim – a company's supply – and before you ask, no, I don't think he means to share it with anyone, not even his lackeys.'

'Just like y'said, sir. That it weren't gonna be just regulars snivelling for a sip. Is he the first?'

'And only, I should think, at least of that rank. We'll get a few lieutenants in here, I expect. Maybe even a captain or two, looking out for the soldiers under them. How are the piss-bottles going?'

'Being d'sturbeted right now, sir. You'd think they'd make faces, but they don't.'

'Because they're not fools, Himble. The fools are dead. Just the wise ones left.'

'Wise, sir, like you 'n' me.'

'Precisely. Now, sit yourself down here and get ready to scribe. Tell me when you're set.' Pores resumed pacing.

Himble drew out his field box of stylus, wax tablets and wick lamp. From a sparker he lit the lamp and warmed the tip of the stylus. When this was done he said, 'Ready, sir.'

'Write the following: "Private missive, from Lieutenant Master-Sergeant Field Quartermaster Pores, to Fist Kindly. Warmest salutations and congratulations on your promotion, sir. As one might observe from your advancement and, indeed, mine, cream doth rise, etc. In as much as I am ever delighted in corresponding with you, discussing all manner of subjects in all possible idioms, alas, this subject is rather more official in nature. In short, we are faced with a crisis of the highest order. Accordingly, I humbly seek your advice and would suggest we arrange a most private meeting at the earliest convenience. Yours affectionately, Pores." Got that, Himble?'

'Yes sir.'

'Please read it back to me.'

Himble cleared his throat, squinted at the tablet. '"Pores to Kindly meet in secret when?"'

'Excellent. Dispatch that at once, Himble.'

'Before or after the one to the Adjunct?'

'Hmm, before, I think. Did I not say "a crisis of the highest order"?'

Himble squinted again at the tablet and nodded. 'So you did, sir.'

'Right, then. Be off with you, Corporal.'

Himble packed up his kit, humming under his breath.

Pores observed him. 'Happy to be drummed out of the heavies, Himble?'

The man paused, cocked his head and considered. 'Happy, sir? No, not happy, but then, get your fingers chopped off an' what can y'do?'

'I have heard of one of your companions getting a special leather harness made—'

'Only one hand was done with 'im, sir. I lost the shield side in the first stand, and then the sword one in the fourth push.'

'And now you're a clerk.'

'Aye, sir.'

Pores studied him for a moment, and then said, 'On your way, Himble.'

Once he'd left, Pores continued pacing. 'Note to self,' he muttered, 'talk to the armourer and weaponsmith. See if we can rig up something. Something tells me Himble's old talents will become necessary before too long. With respect to the well-being and continued existence of one

Pores, humble, most obedient officer of the Bonehunters.' He frowned. *Eight at the stretch. Ten in pain. May the gods above help us all.*

Fist Kindly ran a hand over his head as if smoothing down hair. For a brief instant Lostara Yil found the gesture endearing. The moment passed when she reminded herself of his reputation. In any case, the man's worried expression was troubling, and she could see quiet dismay in his eyes.

Faradan Sort set down her gauntlets. 'Adjunct, that was a difficult march. This broken ground is pounding the wagons, and then there're the oxen and horses. Seven draught animals have come up lame and need slaughtering. Two horses among the Khundryl and another from the command herd.'

'It's only going to get worse,' muttered Kindly. 'This Glass Desert is well named. Adjunct,' and he glanced at Faradan Sort and then Ruthan Gudd, 'we would speak to you of our misgivings. This course of action could well shatter us. Even should we manage to cross this wretched land, our effectiveness as a fighting force will be severely compromised.'

Faradan Sort added, 'The mages are united in their opinion that no water is available, unless we were to halt for a few days and try sinking some deep wells. Very deep wells, Adjunct. And even then, well, the problem is that the mages have nothing to draw on. They're powerless. Not a single warren is available to them, meaning they don't know if there's water far down under us, or not.' She paused, and then sighed. 'I wish I had some good news – we could do with it.'

The Adjunct stood over her map table. She seemed to be studying the lands of Kolanse, as marked on oiled hide by some Bolkando merchant fifty years ago, the notes etched in a language none here could read. 'We shall have to cross a range of hills, or buttes, here' – she pointed – 'before we can enter the valley province of Estobanse. It's my suspicion, however, that the enemy will reach us before then. Either from the passes or from the east. Or both. Obviously, I'd rather we did not have to fight on two fronts. The passes will be key to all this. The threat from Estobanse is the greater of the two. Fist Kindly, kill all the command horses but one. Request the Khundryl to cull their herd down to one mount per warrior with ten to spare. Fist Sort, begin selecting crew to pull the supply wagons – those oxen won't last many more nights.'

Kindly ran a hand over his scalp again. 'Adjunct, it seems that time is against us. In this crossing, I mean. I wonder, could we push the duration of each night's march? Up past two bells after dawn, and a bell or more before the sun sets. It'll wear on us, to be certain, but then we are facing that anyway.'

'Those wagons that empty of provisions,' Faradan Sort added, 'could take the soldiers' armour and melee weapons, relieving some of their burden. We could also begin divesting the train of extraneous materiel. Reduce the armourers and weaponsmiths. All of that is more or less in decent repair – the soldiers didn't waste much time getting stuff mended or replaced. If we dropped seventy per cent of the raw iron, most of the forges, and the coal, we could redistribute the food and water on to more wagons, at least to start, which will relieve the oxen and the crews, not to mention reducing the damage to the wagons, since they'll ride lighter.'

'We could triple soldiers up in the squad tents,' Kindly said.

'We keep all the tents and cloth,' the Adjunct said without looking up. 'As for your suggestions, Faradan, see to them. And, Fist Kindly, the longer marches begin, starting this evening.'

'Adjunct,' said Kindly, 'this is going to be . . . brutal. Morale being what it is, we could face trouble, soon.'

'The news of the Nah'ruk defeat helped,' Sort said, 'but the half-day and full night we've just walked have sapped the zeal. Adjunct, the soldiers need something more to hold on to. Something. Anything.'

At last, Tavore raised her head. She gazed levelly at Faradan Sort with red-rimmed eyes. 'And what, Fist,' she asked in a dull voice, 'would you have me give them?'

'I don't know, Adjunct. The rumours are chewing us to pieces—'

'Which rumours would those be?'

Faradan Sort hesitated, looked away.

'Kindly,' said Tavore, 'your fellow Fist seems to have lost her voice.'

'Adjunct.' Kindly nodded. 'The rumours, well. Some are wild. Others strike rather close to the bone.'

Ruthan Gudd spoke up. 'We're in league with the Elder Gods, and you mean to spill the blood of your soldiers in a grand, final sacrifice – all of them – to achieve your own ascendancy. There's another one, that you've made a secret pact with the High Houses and the younger gods. You will bargain with them using the Crippled God – that's why we intend to snatch him, to steal what's left of him away from the Forkrul Assail. There are plenty more, Adjunct.'

'You possess hidden knowledge,' said Kindly, 'acquired from who knows where. And because no one knows where, they all invent their own explanations.'

'But in each,' said Ruthan Gudd, now eyeing Tavore, 'you are kneeling before a god. And, well, what Malazan soldier doesn't get a bitter taste from that? What Malazan soldier doesn't know the story of Dassem Ultor? Homage to a god by a commander is ever served by the blood of those under his or her command. Look around, Adjunct. We're not serving the Malazan Empire any more. We're serving *you*.'

In a voice little more than whisper, the Adjunct said, 'You are all serving me, are you? You are all about to risk your lives for *me*? Please, any of you here, tell me, what have I done to deserve *that*?'

The tone of her question left a shocked silence.

Tavore Paran looked from one to the next, and in her eyes there was no anger, no outrage, no indignation. Rather, in her eyes Lostara Yil saw something helpless. Confused.

After a long, brittle moment, Kindly said, 'Adjunct, we march to save the Crippled God. The problem is, as far as gods go, he's not much liked. You won't find a single worshipper of him in the Bonehunters.'

'Indeed?' Suddenly her voice was harsh. 'And not one soldier in this army – in this *tent* – has not suffered? Not one here has not broken, not even once? Not wept? Not grieved?'

'But we will not worship that!' Kindly retorted. 'We will not kneel to such things!'

'I am relieved to hear you say so,' she replied, as if the fires inside had died down as quickly as they had flared. Eyes on the map, trying to find a way through. 'So look across, then, across that vast divide. Look into that god's eyes, Fist Kindly, and make your thoughts hard. Make them cold. Unfeeling. Make them all the things you need to in order to feel not a single pang, not a lone tremor. *Look into his eyes, Kindly, before you choose to turn away.* Will you do that?'

'I cannot, Adjunct,' Kindly replied, in a shaken voice. 'For he does not stand before me.'

And Tavore met his eyes once more. 'Doesn't he?'

One heartbeat, and then two, before Kindly rocked back. Only to turn away.

Lostara Yil gasped. *As you said he would.*

But Tavore would not let him go. 'Do you need a temple, Kindly? A graven image? Do you need priests? Sacred texts? Do you need to close your eyes to see a god? So noble on his throne, so lofty in his regard, and oh, let's not forget, that hand of mercy, ever reaching down. Do you need all of that, Kindly? You others? Do you all need it in order to be blessed with the truth?'

The tent flap was roughly pulled aside and Banaschar entered. 'Was I summoned?' And the grin he gave them was a thing of horror, a slash opening to them all the turmoil inside the man, the torment of his life. 'I caught some of that, just outside. Too much, in fact.' He looked to the Adjunct. '"Blessed with the truth." My dear Adjunct, you must know by now. Truth blesses no one. Truth can only *curse*.'

The Adjunct seemed to sag inside. Gaze dropping back down to the map on the table, she said, 'Then please, Septarch, do curse us with a few words of truth.'

'I rather doubt there's need,' he replied. 'We have walked it this night, and will again, beneath the glow of the Jade Strangers.' He paused and frowned at those gathered. 'Adjunct, were you under siege? And have I, by some unwitting miracle, broken it?'

Kindly reached for his helm. 'I must assemble my officers,' he said. He waited, standing at attention, until Tavore lifted a hand in dismissal, her eyes still on the map.

Faradan Sort followed him out.

Lostara Yil caught Ruthan Gudd's eye, and gestured him to accompany her. 'Adjunct, we shall be outside the tent.'

'Rest, both of you,' said Tavore.

'Aye, Adjunct, if you will.'

From the plain woman, a faint smile. 'Soon. Go.'

Lostara saw Banaschar settling on to the leather saddle of a stool. *Gods, with company like his, is it any wonder she is as she is?*

The High Priest pointed a finger at Ruthan Gudd as he stepped past, and made a strange gesture, as if inscribing in the air.

Ruthan Gudd hesitated for a moment, and then, with a wry expression, he combed one hand through his beard, and went out of the tent. Lostara fell in behind him.

'Are you all right?' Faradan Sort asked.

Kindly's expression darkened. 'Of course I'm not all right.'

'Listen,' she said. 'We tried—'

'You can't ask soldiers to open their hearts. If they did they'd never take another life.' He faced her. 'How can she not understand that? We need to harden ourselves – to all that we have to do. We need to make ourselves harder than our enemy. Instead, she wants us to go soft. To *feel*.' He shook his head, and she saw that he was trembling – with fury or frustration.

She turned as Ruthan Gudd and Lostara Yil emerged from the command tent.

Kindly looked at Ruthan. 'Whoever you really are, Captain, you'd better talk some sense into her – because it's turning out that no one else can.'

Ruthan Gudd frowned. 'What sense would that be, Fist?'

'We kill people for a living,' Kindly growled.

'I don't think she wants that to change,' the captain replied.

'She wants us to bleed for the Crippled God!'

'Keep it down, Kindly,' warned Faradan Sort. 'Better yet, let's walk a little way beyond camp.'

They set out. Ruthan hesitated, but was nudged along by Lostara Yil. No one spoke until they'd left the haphazard picket stations well behind. Out under the sun, the heat swarmed against them, the glare blinding their eyes.

'It won't work,' announced Kindly, crossing his arms. 'There will be mutiny, and then fighting – over the water – and before it's all done most of us will be dead. Not even the damned marines and heavies at full strength could keep this army together—'

'You clearly don't think highly of my regulars,' said Faradan Sort.

'Just how many volunteered, Sort?'

'I don't know.'

'Malazan policy is to take the eager ones and make 'em marines or heavies. The convicts and the destitute and the press-ganged, they all end up as regulars. Faradan, are you really certain of your soldiers? Be honest – no one here is likely to indulge in gossip.'

She looked away, squinted. 'The only odd thing about them that I have noticed, Kindly, is that they don't say much. About anything. You'd have to twist an arm to force out an opinion.' She shrugged. 'They know they're faceless. They always have been, most of them, long before they ended up in the military. This – this is just more of the same.'

'Maybe they say nothing within range of your hearing, Sort,' Kindly muttered, 'but I'd wager they have plenty to say to each other, when no one else is around.'

'I'm not sure about that.'

'Have you forgotten your own days as a lowly soldier?'

She flinched, and then said, 'No, Kindly, I have not forgotten. But I can stand fifty paces from a campfire, close enough to see mouths moving, to see the gestures that accompany argument – and there's none of it. I admit, it's uncanny, but my soldiers seem to have *nothing to say*, not even to each other.'

No one spoke for a time.

Ruthan Gudd stood combing his beard with his fingers, his expression thoughtful yet somehow abstracted, as if he'd not been listening, as if he was wrestling with something a thousand leagues away. *Or maybe a thousand years.*

Faradan Sort sighed. 'Mutiny. That's an ugly word, Kindly. You seem ready to throw it at the feet of my regulars.'

'It's what I fear, Faradan. I am not questioning your command – you do know that, don't you?'

She thought about that, and then grunted. 'Well, actually, that's precisely what you're questioning. I'm not Fist Blistig, and I dare say my reputation is decent enough among my soldiers. Aye, I might be hated, but it's not a murderous hate.' She regarded Kindly. 'Didn't you once speak about making a point of being hated by your soldiers? We are to be their lodestones, and when they see us bear it, when they see how none of it can buckle us, they are in turn strengthened. Or did I misunderstand you?'

'You didn't. But we're not being looked at like that any more, Sort. Now, they're seeing us as potential allies. Against *her*.'

Ruthan Gudd's voice was dry, 'Ready to lead a revolt, Kindly?'

'Ask that again and I'll do my level best to kill you, Captain.'

Ruthan Gudd's grin was cold. 'Sorry, I'm not here to give you an easy way out, Fist.'

'No, you're not giving any of us anything.'

'What would you have me say? She doesn't want her soldiers weeping or bleeding out all over the ground because they've gone soft. She wants them to be the opposite. Not just hard.' He eyed the three of them. 'Savage. Unyielding. Stubborn as cliffs against the sea.'

'In the command tent—'

'You missed the point,' Ruthan cut in. 'I now think you all did. She said to look across, into the eyes of the Crippled God. To look, and to *feel*. But you couldn't do it, Kindly, could you? Could *you*, Fist Sort? Lostara? Any of you?'

'And what of you?' Kindly snapped.

'Not a chance.'

'So she knocked us all down – *what was the point of that?*'

'Why shouldn't she?' Ruthan Gudd retorted. 'You asked for more from her. And then I nailed her to a damned tree with that madness about *serving* her. She struck back, and that, friends, was the most human moment from the Adjunct I've yet seen.' He faced them. 'Until then, I was undecided. Would I stay on? Would I ride out, away from all this? And if I left, well, it's not as though anyone could stop me, is it?'

'But,' said Faradan Sort, 'here you are.'

'Yes. I'm with her now for as long as she needs me.'

Fist Kindly raised one hand, as if to strike out at Ruthan Gudd. 'But why?'

'You still don't get it. None of you. Listen. We don't dare look across into the eyes of a suffering god. But, Kindly, she dares. You asked for more from her – gods below, what more can she give? She'll feel all the compassion none of you can afford to feel. Behind that cold iron, she will *feel* what we can't.' His eyes went flat on Kindly. 'And you asked for more.'

The stones ticked in the heat. A few insects spun on glittering wings.

Ruthan Gudd turned to Faradan Sort. 'Your regulars are not saying anything? Be relieved, Fist. Maybe they're finally realizing, on some instinctive level, what she's taken from them. What she's holding inside, for safekeeping. The best they have.'

Faradan Sort shook her head. 'Now who is the one with too much faith, Ruthan Gudd?'

He shrugged. 'It's hot out here.'

They watched as he headed off, a lone figure trudging back to the pickets, and to the camp beyond. There was no dust in the air – this desert didn't make dust.

Eventually, Kindly turned to Lostara Yil. 'Did you suspect he was about to bolt?'

'What? No. The man's a damned cipher, Fist.'

'How,' asked Faradan, 'is this going to work? When I need to stiffen the spines of my soldiers, what in Hood's name can I say to them?'

After a moment, Lostara Yil cleared her throat and said, 'I don't think you have to tell them anything, Fist.'

'What do you mean? And don't go spewing out Ruthan's words – he places far too much in the hearts and minds of the common soldier. Just because your life is devoted to killing, it doesn't accord you any special wisdom.'

'I don't agree with that,' Lostara said. 'Look, just by standing with her, with the Adjunct, you're saying all that needs saying. The real threat to this army is Fist Blistig, who's hardly kept secret his opposition to the Adjunct, and by extension to all of you. If he starts gathering followers . . . well, that's when the trouble will start.'

Kindly reached up and wiped the sweat from his brow. 'There *is* wisdom, Faradan. The wisdom that comes with knowing – right to the very core of your soul – just how fragile life really is. You earn that wisdom when you take someone else's life.'

'And what about the ones who don't think twice about it? Wisdom? Hardly. More like . . . a growing taste for it. That dark rush of pleasure that's so . . . addictive.' She looked away. *I know. I stood the Wall.*

Lostara pointed. 'There's a runner coming . . . for one of us.'

They waited until the thin, round-faced soldier arrived. A soldier with mutilated hands. He saluted with the right one and proffered Kindly a wax tablet with the other. 'Compl'ments of Lieutenant Master-Sergeant Quartermaster Pores, sir.'

Kindly took the tablet and studied it. 'Soldier,' he said.

'Sir?'

'The sun's heat has melted the wax. I do hope you committed the message to memory.'

'Sir, I have.'

'Let's hear it.'

'Sir, the missive was private.'

'From Pores? I really don't have time for this. We're past all the duelling. Spit it out, soldier.'

'Sir. To quote: "Private missive, from Lieutenant Master-Sergeant Field Quartermaster Pores, to Fist Kindly. Warmest salutations and congratulations on your promotion, sir. As one might observe from

303

your advancement and, indeed, mine, cream doth rise, etc. In as much as I am ever delighted in corresponding with you, discussing all manner of subjects in all possible idioms, alas, this subject is rather more official in nature. In short, we are faced with a crisis of the highest order. Accordingly, I humbly seek your advice and would suggest we arrange a most private meeting at the earliest convenience. Yours affectionately, Pores."' The soldier then saluted again and said, 'I'm t'wait yer answer, sir.'

In the bemused silence that followed, Faradan Sort narrowed her eyes on the soldier. 'You were heavy infantry, weren't you?'

'Corporal Himble Thrup, Fist.'

'How stands the rank and file, soldier?'

'Standin' true, Fist.'

'Do the enlisted say much about the Adjunct, soldier? Off the record here.'

The watery eyes flicked momentarily to her, then away again. 'Occasionally, sir.'

'And what do they say?'

'Not much, sir. Mostly, it's all them rumours.'

'You discuss them.'

'No sir. We chew 'em up till there's nothing left. And then invent new ones, sir.'

'To sow dissension?'

Brows lifted beneath the rim of the helm. 'No, Fist. It's . . . er . . . entertainment. Beats boredom, sir. Boredom leads to laziness, sir, and laziness can get a soldier up and killt. Or the one beside 'im, which is e'en worse. We hate being bored, sir, that's all.'

Kindly said, 'Tell Pores to find me at my command tent, whenever he likes.'

'Sir.'

'Dismissed, soldier.'

The man saluted a third time, wheeled and set off.

Kindly grunted.

'That's a heavy for you,' Faradan Sort muttered, and then snorted. 'Inventing nasty rumours for fun.'

'They're only nasty, I suppose, once someone decides one's for real.'

'If you say so, Kindly. As for my regulars, well, now I know where the barrage is coming from.'

'Even if it is coming down on them,' observed Lostara Yil, 'from what you said it's not stirring up much dust.'

Faradan met Kindly's eyes. 'Are we panicking over nothing, Kindly?'

'To be honest,' he admitted, 'I don't really know any more.'

* * *

Ruthan Gudd drew off his gambeson and paused to luxuriate in the sudden escape from unbearable heat as his sweat-slicked skin cooled.

'Well,' said Skanarow from her cot, 'that woke me up.'

'My godlike physique?'

'The smell, Ruthan.'

'Ah, thank you, woman, you've left me positively glowing.' He unclipped his sword belt and let it fall to the ground, then slumped down on the edge of his cot and settled his head in his hands.

Skanarow sat up. 'Another one?'

Through his fingers he said, 'Not sure how many more of those she can weather.'

'We're barely two days into the desert, Ruthan – I hope she's tougher than you think.'

He let his hands fall and glanced at her. 'So do I.' He studied her for a moment and then said, 'I should probably tell you, I was considering . . . leaving.'

'Oh.'

'Not you. This army.'

'Ruthan, I'm *in* this army.'

'I planned on kidnapping you.'

'I see.'

He sighed. 'Today, she changed my mind. So, my love, we're in this till the bitter end.'

'If that's a marriage proposal . . . I kind of like it.'

He studied her. *Gods, I'd forgotten . . .*

Loud clattering came from behind the cook tents, where the scullions were scrubbing pots with handfuls of rocks and pebbles. Cuttle cinched tight a strap on his kit bag. Straightening, he arched his back and winced. 'Gods, it's a young un's game, ain't it just. Koryk, you giving up on those?'

The Seti half-blood had thrown his military issue hobnailed boots to one side, and was using a rounded stone to work out the creases in a pair of worn, tribal moccasins. 'Too hot,' he said.

'Won't those get cut to shreds?' Smiles asked from where she sat on her pack. 'You start limping, Koryk, don't look to me for help.'

'Toss the boots on to the wagon,' Cuttle said. 'Just in case, Koryk.'

The man shrugged.

Sergeant Tarr returned from the company command tent. 'Finish loading up,' he said. 'We're getting a quick start here.' He paused. 'Anybody managed to sleep?'

Silence answered him.

Tarr grunted. 'Right. I doubt it'll be the same come tomorrow. It's a long haul ahead of us. Weapons fit to use? Everybody? Shortnose?'

The heavy looked up, small eyes glittering in the gloom. 'Yah.'

'Corabb?'

'Aye, Sergeant. Can still hear her moaning from the whetstone—'

'It ain't a woman,' said Smiles. 'It's a sword.'

'Then why's she moaning?'

'You never heard a woman moan in your life, so how would you know?'

'Sounds like a woman.'

'I don't hear any moaning anyway,' she replied, drawing out a brace of fighting knives. 'Weapons good, Sergeant. Just give me some sweet flesh to stick 'em in.'

'Hold the thought,' Tarr advised.

'For, like, five months, Smiles.' Koryk looked up, studied her from under his unbound hair. 'Can you do that?'

She sneered. 'If it's going to take five months to cross this desert, idiot, we're deader than dead.' She rapped one blade against the clay jug slung by braided webbing on her pack. 'And I ain't drinking my own piss neither.'

'Want mine?' Bottle asked from where he was lying, eyes closed, hands behind his head.

'Is that an offer to swap? Gods, Bottle, you're sick, you know that?'

'Listen, if I have to drink it, better it be a woman's, because then, if I work real hard, I might be able to pretend I like it. Or something.' When no one said anything, Bottle opened his eyes, sat up. 'What?'

Cuttle made to spit, checked himself, and turned to Tarr. 'Fid have anything new to say, Sergeant?'

'No. Why, should he have?'

'Well, I mean, he figures we're going to make it across, right?'

Tarr shrugged. 'I suppose so.'

'Can't do that mission if we don't.'

'That's a fair point, sapper.'

'He say anything about all this drinking our own piss?'

Tarr frowned.

Koryk spoke up, 'Sure he did, Cuttle. It's all in that Deck of Dragons of his. New card. Piss Drinker, High House.'

'High House what?' Smiles asked.

Koryk simply grinned, and then looked up at Cuttle and the smile became cold. 'Card's got your face on it, Cuttle, big as life.'

Cuttle studied the half-blood, the ritual scarring and tattoos, all in the glyph language of the Seti that Koryk probably only half understood. The ridiculous moccasins. His view was suddenly blocked, and his gaze flicked up to meet Tarr's dark, deceptively calm eyes.

'Just leave it,' the sergeant said in a low mutter.

'Thought I was gonna do something?'

'Cuttle . . .'

'Thought I was going to rip a few new arseholes in him? Shove my last sharper up inside and then throw him into yonder wagon? Something like that, Sergeant?'

From behind Tarr, Koryk snorted.

'Load your pack on the wagon, Cuttle.'

'Aye, Sergeant.'

'Rest of you, get your gear up and get ready – the night beckons and all that.'

'I might sell my piss,' said Smiles.

'Yeah,' said Koryk, 'all that silver and gold, only it won't go on the wagon, Smiles. We need to keep the bed clear for all the booty we're going to scoop up. No, soldier, you got to carry it.' He pulled on the first moccasin, tugged the laces. Both strings of leather snapped in his hands. He swore.

Cuttle heaved his pack on to the wagon's bed, and then stepped back as Corabb followed suit with his own gear, the others lining up, Koryk coming last wearing two untied moccasins. The sapper stepped past the corporal, Bottle, and then Smiles.

His fist caught Koryk flush on the side of the man's head. The crack was loud enough to make the oxen start. The half-blood thumped hard on the ground, and did not move.

'Well now,' Tarr said, glowering at Cuttle, 'come the fight and this soldier beside you, sapper, you going to step sure then?'

'Makes no difference what I done just now,' Cuttle replied. 'Beside him, in the next battle, I ain't gonna step sure at all. He mouthed off in the trench – to Fiddler himself. And he's been mopin' around ever since. Y'can have all the courage you want on the outside, but it ain't worth shit, Sergeant, when what's inside can't even see straight.' The speech had dried out his mouth. He lifted his right hand. 'Gotta see a cutter now, Sergeant. I broke the fucker.'

'You *stupid* . . . go on, get out of my sight. Corabb, Bottle, get Koryk on to the wagon. Wait. Is he even alive? All right, into the wagon. He probably won't wake up till the night's march is done.'

'Just his luck,' muttered Smiles.

Horns sounded. The Bonehunters stirred, shook out, fell back into column, and the march was under way. Bottle slipped in behind Corabb, with Smiles on his left. Three strides in their wake walked Shortnose. Bottle's pack was light – most of his kit had gone into general resupply, and as was true of armies the world over, there was no such thing as oversupply, at least not when it came to useful gear. *Useless stuff, well, that's different. If we were back in Malaz, or Seven Cities, we'd have plenty of that. Quills and no ink, clasps but not a sewing kit to be found, wicks and no wax – still, wouldn't it be nice to be back in Malaz? Stop that, Bottle. Things are bad enough without adding pointless nostalgia to the unruly mess.* In any case, he'd lost most of his useful gear. Only to discover that he really didn't need it after all.

The clay jug rolled in its webbing alongside his hip, swinging with each stride. *Well, it made sense to me anyway. I could always ask . . . I don't know. Flashwit. Or . . . gods below, Masan Gilani! I'm sure she'd—*

'Get up here beside me, Bottle.'

'Sergeant?'

'Fid wanted me to ask you some questions.'

'We already went over what I remembered—'

'Not that. Ancient history, Bottle. What battle was that again? Never mind. Drop back there, Corabb. No, you're still corporal. Relax. Just need some words with Bottle here – our squad mage, right?'

'I'll be right behind you then, Sergeant.'

'Thanks, Corporal, and I can't tell you how reassuring it is to feel your breath on the back of my neck, too.'

'I ain't drunk no piss yet, Sergeant.'

Once past the corporal, Bottle scowled back at him over a shoulder. 'Corabb, why are you talking like Cuttle's dumber brother these days?'

'I'm a marine, soldier, and that's what I am and this is how us marines talk. Like the sergeant says, what battle was that again? Ancient history. We fight somebody? When? Like that, you see?'

'The best marines of all, Corporal,' Tarr drawled, 'are the ones who don't say a damned thing.'

. . .

'Corporal Corabb?'

'Sorry, what, Sergeant? Like that?'

'Perfect.'

Bottle could see Balm and his squad a dozen paces ahead. Throat-slitter. Deadsmell. Widdershins. *That's it? That's all that's left of them?*

'No warrens around here, right?'

'Sergeant? Oh, aye. None at all. These Fid's questions?'

'So it's dead as dead can be.'

'Aye. Like a sucked bone.'

'Meaning,' Tarr resumed, 'no one can find us out here. Right?'

Bottle blinked, and then scratched at the stubble on his jaw. His nails came away flecked with burnt skin and something that looked like salt crystals. He frowned. 'Well, I suppose so. Unless, of course, they've got eyes. Or wings,' and he nodded upward.

Breath gusted from Tarr's nostrils, making a faint whistling sound.

'For that, they'd have to be out here, doing what we're doing. But this desert's supposed to be impassable. No one in their right minds would ever try and cross it. That's the view, isn't it?'

The view? It ain't opinion, Tarr. It's a fact. No one in their right minds would try and cross it. 'Is there someone in particular, Sergeant, who might be trying to find us?'

Tarr shook his head. 'Captain's the one with the Deck, not me.'

'But they'll be cold here, those cards. Lifeless. So, what we're talking about is a reading he did before we crossed over. Was someone closing in, Sergeant?'

'No point in asking me that, Bottle.'

'Listen, this is ridiculous. If Fiddler wants to ask me stuff, he can just hump down here and do it. That way, I can ask stuff back.'

'Are they blind, Bottle, is what Fid wanted to know. Not us. Them.'

Them. 'Aye. Wide-Eyed Blind.'

Tarr grunted. 'Good.'

'Sergeant . . . can you remember who came up with our name? Bone-hunters?'

'Might have been the Adjunct herself. The first time I heard it was from her. I think.'

But this is impossible. Aren. She couldn't have known. Not then.

'Why, Bottle?'

'No reason, just wondering. Is that it? Can me and the corporal switch round again?'

'One more question. Is Quick Ben alive?'

'I already told Fid—'

'This question ain't his, Bottle. It's mine.'

'Listen, I don't know – and I told Fid the same thing. I got no sense with those people—'

'Which people?'

'Bridgeburners. Those people. Dead Hedge, Quick Ben – even Fiddler himself. They aren't the same as us. As you and me, Sergeant, or Corabb back there. Don't ask me to explain what I mean. The point is, I can't read them, can't scry for them. Sometimes, it's like they're . . . I don't know . . . ghosts. You poke and you go right through. Other times, they're like a solid mountain, so big the sun itself can't climb over them. So I don't know, is my answer.'

Tarr was squinting across at him. 'You say all that to the captain?'

'I don't know if Quick Ben's dead or alive, Sergeant, but if I was to wager on it, well, I can think of a few hundred Bonehunters happy to go against me, more than a few hundred, in fact. But if I was to take that bet to Hedge, or Fiddler . . .' Bottle shook his head, slapped at something biting his neck.

'You're wagering that he's dead?'

'No, I'm betting he's alive. And I'm betting more than that. I'm betting he's still in this game.'

The sergeant suddenly grinned. 'Great to have you back, Mage.'

'Not so fast, Tarr – Sergeant, I mean. Don't forget, I didn't see him at the end there. And from what I've heard, it was ugly.'

'The ugliest.'

'So . . . that's why I'm not making any wagers.'

'Hood knows what Fid ever saw in you, soldier. Go on, get out of my sight.'

When he'd exchanged places in the line with Corabb, Cuttle fell in on his left. 'Listen—'

'Who in Hood's name am I these days, Fisher himself?'

'What? No. It's something Koryk said—'

'Which thing? The thing about the Piss Drinker? Fid doesn't make his own cards, Cuttle. He's not that kind of Deck monger. So—'

'About booty, soldier. That thing about booty.'

'I think that was sarcasm.'

On his right, Smiles grunted, but offered nothing more.

'That's just it,' Cuttle said. 'Now, it was Dassem Ultor who really came down on the whole pillaging stuff—'

'We were conquering, not raiding. When you occupy a city, it's bad practice to loot and rape the citizens. Riles them, and before you know it your occupying garrison soldiers start getting murdered on night patrol.'

'So, we weren't in the habit of it anyway, but even then we still had a chance to get rich. Every company got itself a scribe and everything was portioned out. Collected weapons and armour. Horses, all that. Winning a battle meant bonuses.'

'All very well, Cuttle,' nodded Bottle. 'But we here got us a temple treasury. The pay rolls are still being maintained. The fact is, sapper, we're all stinking rich.'

'Assuming we live to get it.'

'That's always how it is. I don't see your point.'

The sapper's small eyes glittered. 'Tell me,' he said in a rough voice, 'do you give a Nacht's ass about it? Do you, Bottle?'

He considered. Four, five, seven strides. 'No,' he admitted, 'but then, I never did care much. Not in it for wealth.'

'You're young, aye. It's the adventure that tugs you along. But you see, get to a certain age, seen enough of all that's out there, and you start thinking about your life when it's all done with. Y'start thinking about some cosy cottage, or maybe a decent room above a decent tavern. Aye, you know it'll probably never be, but you dream about it anyway. And that's where all the coin comes in.'

'And?'

His voice dropped lower. 'Bottle, I ain't thinking past next week. I ain't thought about my pay in months. You hearing me? No cottage, no tavern. No nice little fisher boat or, gods forbid, a garden. None of it.'

'That's because we're the walking dead, right?'

'I thought so, what with what Fid said the other night, but now I don't.'

Curious, Bottle eyed the sapper. 'Go on, then.'

Cuttle shrugged, as if suddenly uncomfortable. 'Something's happened to us, that's all. The Bonehunters. Maybe it was invading Lether. Maybe it was Malaz City, or even Y'Ghatan, I don't know. Look at us. We're an army not thinking about loot. Why do you think Koryk went and mocked Smiles here about charging for her piss?'

'Because he's broke,' Smiles answered. 'And jealous.'

'It's because no one cares about silver and gold, or buying stinking estates, or breeding horses or taking up sea trades. We're probably the only army in the world that doesn't.'

Smiles snorted. 'Hold on, sapper. You don't think that when we've chopped up whoever and we're standing there on that battlefield – don't you think we're gonna start cutting off fingers and all the rest? Loading up on torcs and rings and decent swords and whatever?'

'No. I don't, Smiles.'

'I think I agree with Cuttle on this one,' said Bottle. 'Then again, maybe *you* will—'

'Why should I?' she retorted. 'I wasn't talking about me at all—'

'Another first,' Bottle muttered.

'Oh, I'm gonna walk around checking bodies, aye,' she said, nodding. 'Find one still breathing, and slit goes the throat. Rings and shit? Forget it.'

'Just what I been saying,' Cuttle said, and he fixed wide eyes upon Bottle. 'It's exactly it, Bottle. This army has gone insane.'

'Fid's captain now,' Balm growled. 'What more do you need to know? He'll do us right. He was a Bridgeburner, wasn't he? Look at his old squad, lads – didn't lose a damned one of them. If that ain't the kind eye of a god looking down, what is?'

Widdershins crowded up behind Throatslitter, Deadsmell and the sergeant. 'Did any of you hear Bottle back there? That stuff about our name?'

Throatslitter scowled. 'What?'

'He was asking about how we got our name.'

'So?'

'So, I just think . . . well . . . I think it's important. I think Bottle knows something, but he's keeping it quiet—'

'Bottled up?' Deadsmell asked.

Throatslitter's high-pitched laugh triggered curses up and down the line. The assassin hissed under his breath. 'Sorry, that just came out.'

'So give him a shake, Wid,' pressed Deadsmell, 'until it all gushes out. He's got a cork somewhere, go and find it.'

Throatslitter snorted, and then choked as he held down another squeal.

'Stop that, Deadsmell,' Balm ordered. 'I mean it.'

'But I've just scratched the surface of possibilities, Sergeant—'

'You saw what Cuttle went and did to Koryk? I'll lay you out, Deadsmell—'

'You can't do that – you're our sergeant!'

'Meaning I *can* do it, idiot.'

Widdershins said, 'Bottle's a mage, just like me. We got us a common bond. Think I might talk to him after all. There's something he's not saying. I know it.'

'Well,' mused Deadsmell, 'the man did somehow survive the Nah'ruk kitchen tent, so that's kind of impressive.'

'And he came in with Captain Ruthan Gudd. There's an inner circle, you see. I suspected it from way back.'

'Widdershins, you may have hit on something there,' said Deadsmell. 'People in the know. Knowing . . . something.'

'More than us, right.'

'Probably got it all mapped out, too. Even how we're going to get across this desert, and then take down another empire just like we took down Lether.'

'Just like we crushed the Whirlwind, too. And got ourselves out of Malaz City. So now you ain't making fun of me no more, Deadsmell, are ya?'

As one, the four marines twisted round to glare at the squad trudging behind them. Sergeant Tarr's brows lifted.

'You hearing this, Tarr?' Balm called back.

'Not a word of it, Balm.'

'Good.'

Facing forward again, Widdershins tried to press even closer. 'Listen,' he whispered, 'we can work out who's in the know. Fid, and Ruthan Gudd—'

'And Bottle,' said Deadsmell, 'because he's Fid's shaved knuckle.'

'Masan Gilani—'

'What? Really?'

'Another one attached to the Adjunct's retinue – they didn't kill her horse, did you know that? They kept her two of 'em, in fact.' Widdershins rubbed at his face. 'Gets cold with the sun down, don't it? Then there's Lostara Yil, who did that Shadow Dance – that one for sure. Who else?'

312

'Keneb but he's dead,' said Balm. 'Quick Ben, too.'

Widdershins barked a low laugh. 'I'm with Bottle on that one. He's out there, somewhere. Maybe with Gesler and Stormy—'

'Of course!' Balm cut in. 'Ges and Stormy! And don't they have the runts with them?'

'Sinn and Grub, aye.'

Widdershins nodded. 'Could be the whole conspiracy right there, then. The inner circle I was talking about—'

'The conniving cabal,' said Deadsmell.

'Aye—'

'The secret sneaks.'

'Just so.'

'The shifty-eyed sentinels of truth—'

Throatslitter's laugh pierced the night.

Sinter winced at the cry behind them. 'Gods, I wish he'd stop doing that.'

'Nothing very funny about this,' Badan Gruk agreed. 'But then it's Throatslitter, isn't it? That man would laugh over his dying sister.' He shook his head. 'I don't get people like him. Taking pleasure in misery, in torture, all that. What's to laugh about? Talk about a messed-up mind.'

She glanced at him curiously. His face was lit in the green glow of the Jade Spears. Ghoulish. Ethereal. 'What's eating you, Badan?'

'That conspiracy of Wid's.' He shot her a suspicious look. 'It's got to include you, Sinter, don't it?'

'Like Hood it does.'

'You had a chat with Masan Gilani – and' – he nodded towards the wagon rocking and creaking just ahead of them – 'your sister.'

'We was just trying to work out stuff to help the Adjunct—'

'Because you knew something. Those feelings you get. You knew we were in trouble, long before the lizards showed up.'

'Little good it did us. Don't you see? I knew but I didn't know. Do you have any idea how helpless that made me feel?'

'So what's coming, Sinter?'

'No idea – and that's just how I want it.' She tapped her helm. 'All quiet, not a whisper. You think I'm in some inner circle? You're wrong.'

'Fine,' he said. 'Forget it.'

The silence stretched between them, and to Sinter it felt like a cocoon, or a web they were snared in. Struggling just made it worse. In the hills high above the savanna of her homeland there were ancient tombs carved into cliff faces. Barely past her first blooding, she'd journeyed with her sister and two others to explore those mysterious caves.

Nothing but dust. The stone sarcophagi were stacked a dozen to each chamber, and Sinter remembered standing in the relative chill, one hand holding a makeshift torch, and in the flickering, wavering orange light staring at the lowest coffin in a stack rising before her. Other peoples buried their dead, instead of gifting the corpse to the vulture goddess and her get. Or sealed them beneath heavy lids of stone. And she remembered thinking, with a chill rippling through her: *but what if they got it wrong? What if you weren't dead?*

In the years since, she'd heard horrifying tales of hapless people buried alive, trapped within coffins of stone or wood. Life in the barracks was rife with stories intended to make one shiver. Worse than the haranguing threats from priests behind a pulpit – and everyone knew those ones were doing it for the coin. And all that delicious sharing out of fear.

And now . . . now, I feel as if I'm about to wake up. From a long sleep. From my mouth, a sighing breath – but all I see is darkness, all I hear is a strange dull echo all around me. And I reach up, and find cold, damp stone. It was the drops that awakened me. The condensation of my own breathing.

I am about to wake up, to find that I have been buried alive.

The terror would not let her go. *This desert belongs to the dead. Its song is the song of dying.*

In the wagon lumbering a few strides ahead sat her sister. Head lolling as if asleep. Was it that easy for her? That leg was slow in mending, and now that they were in this lifeless place no healer could help her. She must be in pain. Yet she slept.

While we march.

The deserter never deserted after all. Who could have guessed she'd find something inside, something that reached out beyond, outside her damned self? We can never know, can we? Can never know someone else, even one of our own blood.

Kisswhere. You should have run. Limped. Done whatever you needed to do. I could manage all of this, I could. If I knew you were safe – far away.

She thought back to when her sister had appeared, in the company of the Khundryl – that ragged, wretched huddle of survivors. Young mothers, old mothers, crippled warriors, unblooded children. Elders tottering like the harbingers of shattered faith. And there she was, struggling with a makeshift crutch – the kind one saw among broken veterans on foreign streets as they begged for alms. *Gods below, at least the Malazan Empire knew how to honour their veterans. You don't just up and forget them. Ignore them. Step over them in the gutters. You honour them. Even the kin of the lost get coin and a holyday in their honour . . .*

There were, she knew, all kinds of coffins. All kinds of ways of finding out you've been buried alive. How many people dreaded opening their eyes? Opening them for real? How many were terrified of what they would find? That stone box. That solid darkness. The immovable walls and lid and the impossible weight.

Her sister would not meet her eye. Would not even speak to her. Not since Kisswhere's return to the ranks. *But return she did. And soldiers saw that. Saw, and realized that she'd gone to get the Khundryl, to find help for that awful day.*

They understood, too, how Kisswhere must feel, there in that ruined haggle of survivors. Aye, she'd sent the rest of them to their deaths. Enough to destroy the strongest among them, aye. But look at her. Seems able to bear it. The broken leg? She was riding Hood-bent for leather, friends – would've been in that fatal charge, too, if not for her horse going down.

No, they now looked on Kisswhere with a seriousness to their regard that spoke tomes about finally belonging, that spoke of seeing on her the fresh scars from the only rite of passage worth respecting – *surviving, with the coin paid in full for the privilege.*

Well. That is my sister, isn't it? No matter what, she will shine. She will shine.

Kisswhere could feel her teeth grinding, on the edge of cracking, as the wagon clunked over yet another rock, and with breath held she waited for the rush of stunning pain. Up from the bones of her leg, spreading like bright flowers through her hips, rising through her torso like a tree with a thousand stabbing branches and ten thousand needled twigs. Higher still, the mad serrated leaves unfurling in her skull, lacerating her brain.

She rode the manic surge, the insane growth of agony, and then, as it pulsed back down, as it ebbed, she slowly released her sour breath. She stank of suffering; she could taste it on her swollen tongue. She leaked it out on the grimy boards beneath her.

They should have left her behind. A lone tent in the rubbish of the abandoned camp. That would have been an act of mercy. But since when did armies think about that? Their whole business was the denial of mercy, and like a water mill the huge stone wheel of destruction rolled on, and on. No one allowed to get off, on . . . on what? She found herself grinning. *On pain of death, that's what.*

Staring at her own knees, at the thick bundling of myrid skins surrounding her splinted leg. Hair hanging down, hiding from her eyes Badan Gruk, Sinter and all the rest, so useless in their clumping along, so bitter in all the ghosts they now carried, the weight bowing them down.

315

Was it Pores or Kindly? Yes, Pores. 'Grow that hair, woman!' Or was it 'Cut it'? I can't remember – how can I not remember? Was it that long ago?

Pores, pretending to be Kindly. Where does that kind of courage come from? That . . . audacity? That knowing look will be in his eye right up until he's shoved through Hood's Gate. It will, won't it?

How I admire people like that. How I wanted to be like them.

Badan Gruk, take a lesson from Pores, I beg you. No more of the sad eyes, the hurt look. I see it and I want to stab deeper. Lash out. I want to make true all your miserable worries, all those wounds upon your heart. Let's see them bleed!

The wagon jarred beneath her. She gasped. Flowers and trees, leaves of fire igniting behind her eyes. No time to think. Every thought tried running, only to explode in the forest. *Bursting awake all the leaves, high in the canopy, and every thought wings away.* Like birds into the sky.

The leg was infected. There was fever, and nothing anyone could do about it. Herbs fought the good war, or they would if there were any. If she asked for them. If she told someone. Pastes and poultices, elixirs and unguents, all the ranks of grim-faced soldiers, banners waving, marching into disease's grinning face.

No one's allowed to get off. On pain of death, aye.

Stay right here, this rocking wagon, the rank sweat of the oxen so sweet in our nostrils. We got us a war, comrades. Can't stop and chat. We got us a war, and no one's allowed to get off. No one's allowed to get off. No one's allowed to—

Badan grunted and looked up.

'Shit,' said Sinter, starting forward.

Kisswhere had been leaning forward over her thighs, one leg dangling off the wooden tail, the other splinted straight, thrust out at an angle. She'd just fallen back, head cracking as it bounced on the slats.

Sinter clambered on to the wagon. 'Gods below, she's on fire. Badan – get us a cutter, fast.' Straightening, she faced forward and leaned over the bundles of gear. 'Ruffle! Pull this thing over to one side – hurry! Out of the line!'

'Aye, Sergeant!'

'They're pulling outa line, Sergeant. Should we go back and see what's up?'

Hellian scowled. 'Just march, Corporal.'

It was dark but not so dark as it maybe should be. People glowed green, but then, could be that was how it always was, when she didn't

316

drink. *No wonder I drink.* 'Listen, all of you,' she said, 'keep an eye out.'

'For what?' Breathy asked.

'For a tavern, of course. Idiot.'

They'd gotten two transfers. From the Seventh Squad. A pair of swords, one of them with a bad knee and the other one with the face of a gut-sick horse. *Limp's the name of one of them. But which one? That other one . . . Crump. A sapper? Is Crump the sapper? But sappers ain't worth much now, are they? Big enough to be a sword, though, unless Crump is the one with the bad knee. Imagine, a sapper with a bad knee. Set the charge and run! Well, hobble. Fast as you can. Guess you looking like a horse was some kind of joke, huh?*

Sappers. Nothing but a bad idea that stayed bad. Bust up one leg on all of 'em, that'd make the breed extinct quick enough.

Aye, Limp's the sapper. Crump's the other one. Crump goes the knee. Limp goes the sapper. But wait, which one's got the bad knee again? I could turn round. I suppose. Turn round and, say, take a look. Which one's limping? Get the limper sorted and I got Crump, meaning the sapper's the other one, with the bad knee. Limp, then. He's named Limp on account of the bad knee of his buddy's, since he has to help the fool along all the time. But then, if he got that name at the start, why, he'd not make it as a soldier at all. He'd of been drummed out, or planted behind a desk. So, the sapper didn't run fast enough from some fuse, that's how he earned his name. Got the name Crump, on account of a crumpling knee. Now I get it. Whew.

But what's the point of a horse with a bad knee?

''S getting cold, Sergeant.'

Hellian's scowl deepened. 'What do you want me to do about it, fart in your face?'

'No. Was just saying. Oh, and Limp's lagging – we should've stuck 'im on the wagon.'

'Who are you again?'

'I'm Maybe, Sergeant. Been with you since the beginning.'

'Which door?'

'What?'

'The street we lived on in Kartool City. Which door was you in?'

'I ain't from Kartool, Sergeant. I meant, the beginning of the squad. That's what I meant. Aren. Seven Cities. The first time we marched across a Hood-rotting desert.'

'Back to Y'Ghatan? No wonder I'm so thirsty. Got water in that jug there, soldier?'

'Just my piss, Sergeant.'

'Lucky you ain't a woman. Try pissing into a bottle when you're a woman. Y'Ghatan. Gods below, how many times do we got to take that place?'

'We ain't marching to Y'Ghatan, Sergeant. We're – oh, never mind. It's a desert for sure, though. Cold.'

'Corporal Touchless!'

'Sergeant?'

'What you got in that jug there?'

'Piss.'

'Who's selling that stuff anyway? Bloody genius.'

Maybe said, 'Heard the quartermaster was tying bladders on the Khundryl stallions.'

Hellian frowned. 'They'd explode. Why would he do that? And more to the point, how? Stick your hand up its—'

'Not the horse's bladder, Sergeant. Waterskins, right? Cow bladders. Tied to the stallion's cock.'

'Duck, you mean.'

'What?'

'Horses hate cocks, but they don't mind ducks. But that bladder would slow 'em down something awful. Quite the farm where you grew up, Maybe.'

'I ain't fooled, you know,' said Maybe, leaning close. 'But I see the point, right? You're keeping us entertained. It's like a game, pieces jumping every which way.'

She eyed him. 'Oh, I'm just fooling with ya, am I?'

He met her gaze, and then his eyes shied away. 'Sorry, Sergeant. Feeling it, huh?'

Hellian said nothing. *Glowing green, aye. And all those rocks and shards out there, where the spiders are. Tiny eyes all heaped up, all watching me pass. I'm sober. Can't pretend they're not there, not any more.*

And not a tavern in sight.

This is going to be bad. Very bad. 'Hear that?' she asked. 'That was a damned hyena.'

'That was Throatslitter, Sergeant.'

'He killed a hyena? Good for him. Where's Balgrid anyway?'

'Dead.'

'Damned slacker. I'm going to sleep. Corporal, you're in charge—'

'Can't sleep now,' Brethless objected. 'We're walking, Sergeant—'

'Best time for it, then. Wake me when the sun comes up.'

'Now that ain't fair how she does that.'

Brethless grunted. 'You hear about them all the time, though. Those veterans who can sleep on the march.' He mused, and then grunted a second time. 'Didn't know she was one of them.'

'Sober now,' Maybe muttered. 'That's what's new with her.'

'Did you see her and Urb and Tarr heading back into the trench? I'd just about given up, and then I saw her, and she pulled me along as if I was wearing chains round my neck. I had nothing left – me and Touchy – remember, Touchy?'

'Aye. What of it?'

'We were finished. When I saw Quick Ben go down, it was like someone carved out my gut. I went all hollow inside. Suddenly, I knew it was time to die.'

'You were wrong,' said Maybe in a growl.

'We got us a good sergeant, is what I'm saying.'

Maybe nodded, and glanced back at Crump. 'You listening, soldier? Don't mess it up.'

The tall, long-faced man with the strangely wide-spaced eyes blinked confusedly. 'They stepped on my cussers,' he said. 'Now I ain't got any more.'

'Can you use that sword on your belt, sapper?'

'What? This? No, why would I want to do that? We're just marching.'

Lagging behind, breath coming in harsh gasps, Limp said, 'Crump had a bag of munitions. Stuck his brain in there, too. For, uh, safe-keeping. It all went up, throwing Nah'ruk everywhere. He's just an empty skull now, Maybe.'

'So he can't fight? What about using a crossbow?'

'Never seen him try one of those. But fight? Crump fights, don't worry about that.'

'Well, with what, then? That stupid bush knife?'

'He uses his hands, Maybe.'

'Well, that's just great then.'

'We're just marching,' said Crump again, and then he laughed.

Urb glanced back at the squad trudging five paces behind his own. She had nothing to drink now. She was waking up. To who she really was. And maybe she didn't like what she saw. Wasn't that what drinking was all about to begin with? He rubbed the back of his neck, faced forward again.

Sober now. Eyes clear. Clear enough to see . . . well, it wasn't like she'd really shown any interest. And besides, did he really want to get tangled with someone like that? Standing up only to probably fall down again. It was a narrow path for people like her, and they needed to want to walk it. If they didn't, off they went again, sooner or later. Every time.

Of course, if what Fid had said was true, what did any of it even matter? They were the walking dead, looking for a place to finish up with all the walking. So in the meantime, if there was a chance at anything, why not take it? She'd not be serious about it, though, would she? She'd just mock the whole idea of love, of what he would end up cutting out and slapping down wet and red on the table between them – she'd just laugh.

He wasn't brave enough for that. In fact, he wasn't brave at all, about anything. Not fighting Nah'ruk, or Letherii, or Whirlwind fanatics. Every time he had to draw his sword, he went cold as ice inside. Loose, quaking, dread shivering out from his stomach to steal the heat from his limbs. He drew his sword expecting to die, and die poorly.

But he'd do what he could to keep her alive. Always had. Always would. Usually she was too drunk to even see it, or maybe she was so used to him being there when it counted that he was no different from a stone wall for her to throw her back against. But wasn't even that enough for him?

It would have to be, because he didn't have the courage for anything more. Being the walking dead didn't have a thing to do with bravery. It was just a way of looking at the time left, of ducking down and pushing on and not complaining. He could do that. He'd been doing that all his life, in fact.

I've been the walking dead all along, and I didn't even know it. The thought left him weakened, as if some hidden knife had just pushed deep inside, piercing his soul. *I've been telling myself this was being alive. This here. This . . . hiding. Wishing. Dreaming. Wanting. And all the while, what does anyone else see when they look at me?*

Quiet Urb. Not much going on in there, is there? But a fair soldier. Adequate. Made sergeant, sure, but don't ever think he'll go higher. Hasn't got it inside, you see. It's quiet as a cave in there, but you got to, well, admire him. He's a man without troubles. He's a man who lives it easy, if you know what I mean.

That's Sergeant Urb. He'll do until a better sergeant comes along.

Hiding ain't living. Hiding's just walking dead.

He looked up into the jade-lit night sky, studied those grim slashes cleaving the darkness. Huge now, seeming ready to slice into the face of this very world. Urb shivered. *But if I'm the walking dead, why am I still so afraid?*

Corporal Clasp dropped back from her position alongside Urb, until Saltlick, who'd been taking up the rear, reached her, and she fell in beside him. 'Can I have a quiet word with you?' she asked.

He glanced over, blinked. 'I can be quiet.'

'I'd noticed, Saltlick. Is that how it is in this squad?'

'What do you mean?'

She nodded ahead. 'Sergeant Urb. You and him are the same. You don't say anything, don't give yourselves away. You know, we all knew there was a . . . well, a kind of elite group. Squads and a few heavies. Somehow all closer to Fiddler, back when he was a sergeant. Closer than the rest of us. We knew it. We could see it. Fiddler, and round him Gesler and Stormy, Balm and Hellian, Cord and Shard. And Urb. With Quick Ben dropping in, and then Hedge. And finally, some of you heavies. Shortnose, Mayfly, Flashwit. You. I know, it was all about Fiddler, and the ones he drew in around him. The ones he picked.'

Saltlick was staring at her now.

Clasp grimaced. 'Look at my soldiers,' she said under her breath. 'Look at Sad. You know what she is? A damned Semk witch. *Semk*. You know what she does when she gets ready for a fight? Never mind. You'll see for yourself, assuming we survive this desert. Then there's Burnt Rope. Sapper. But he surprised me at the trench. So did our cutter – you know, he once went and sought out Gesler and Stormy – fellow Falaris, right? We sent him. We sent Lap Twirl to Ges and Stormy, to test them out. To see if we could get in.'

'Get in?'

'To those elites. To the insiders, right? Well, he didn't get anywhere. They were friendly enough, and the three of them got drunk – it was in Letheras. Got beastly drunk, and hired up a whole whorehouse of women. But Lap kept a bit of himself cold sober, and when he judged it right he just went and asked. Asked in. You know what Gesler said?'

Saltlick shook his head.

'The bastard denied it to Lap's face. Said it didn't exist. Lied to Lap's face. That's how we know there's no getting in.'

Saltlick continued studying her. 'So,' he said after a few strides, 'why are you telling me?'

'Urb's one of the finest sergeants we marines got left to us. We know that. In fact, it's got us pissing in our boots. The pressure's getting unbearable, Saltlick. We can't get a word outa him. And you can see in his eyes – he's damned disappointed to be saddled with us.'

'All right,' said Saltlick.

She frowned up at him. 'All right what?'

'You're in, Corporal. You and your soldiers. You're all in.'

'Really? You sure?'

'You're in.'

Smiling, she moved ahead again, paused to glance back and nod. He nodded back, saw the lightness in her step. Watched as she leaned in close to Lap Twirl, and the two soldiers spoke in whispers and gestures, and a moment later Sad and Burnt Rope closed up to listen in. Faces turned, looked back at him.

He waved.

I can't wait till Flashwit hears this one.

Saltlick shifted uncomfortably. He'd sweated a lot in his tent, and now his sack was chafing. He could almost feel the skin peeling off. *Fuck, that stings. Better air out my balls tomorrow.*

The sergeant was glaring at her, gesturing. Flashwit frowned.

Mayfly nudged her. 'Wants to talk to you.'

'Why?'

'He has seven questions. How would I know? Go on, Princess. The idiot lost his whole squad. He probably wants to try and explain. So he doesn't get a knife in his back.'

'I wouldn't stick a knife in his back,' Flashwit said, shaking her head. 'No matter what he did.'

'Really?'

'If he killed them all and told me about it, I'd just break his neck. A knife in the back, that's cowardly.'

'No it ain't,' Mayfly objected. 'It's making a point. Victim's not worth a look in the eye when y'kill him. Victim's not s'posed to know what ended it, just that it ended, and there's Hood's Gate calling 'im .'

'But sometimes you miss.'

'Better go, he's gettin' cross.'

Grunting, Flashwit made her way up to Sergeant Gaunt-Eye. Wasn't a friendly face, that one. But a face a person would remember anyway. For all the wrong things in it. 'Sergeant?'

'You don't know the hand-talk, soldier?'

'What talk? Oh, that. Yah, I know it. Mostly. Advance. Stop. Hit the ground. Fight. Go fuck yourself. Like that.'

'A marine should know how to put together whole sentences, Flashwit.'

'Yah? I'm a heavy, Sergeant.'

'Tell me about the girly one.'

'Using my hands? Can't, Sergeant. I mean, I'd have to try and ask, "What girly one?" and I don't know how to do that.'

'Skulldeath. Talk to me, soldier. With words – but keep your voice down.'

'I ain't never raised my voice, not once, Sergeant, in my whole life.'

'Skulldeath.'

'What about him?'

'Why's he so girly, for one?'

'He's a prince, Sergeant. From some tribe in Seven Cities. He's the heir, in fact—'

'Then what in Hood's name is he doing here?'

She shrugged. 'They sent him to grow up somewhere else. With us. T'see the world and all that.'

Gaunt-Eye bared crooked teeth. 'Bet he's regretting that.'

'No reason why,' Flashwit said. 'Not yet, anyway.'

'So, he grew up all pampered and perfumed, then.'

'I suppose.'

'So how did he get that stupid name?'

Flashwit squinted at the sergeant. 'Beggin' yer pardon, Sergeant, but where was you and your squad? Back at the Trench, I mean.'

He shot her a vicious look. 'What difference does that make?'

'Well, you couldn't have not seen him then. Skulldeath. He jumps high, y'see. He was the only one of us cutting Nah'ruk *throats*, right? Jumps high, like I said. See those eight notches on his left wrist?'

'Those burns?'

'Aye. One for each Nah'ruk he personally throat-cut.'

Gaunt-Eye snorted. 'A liar, too, then. About what I figured.'

'But he never counted, Sergeant. Never does. Eight is what we saw him do, those who saw him at all, I mean. We talked about it, comparing and all that. Eight. So we told him and he burned those marks on his wrist. When we asked him how many he gutted, he said he didn't know. When we asked him how many he hamstrung, he didn't know that either. The rest of us couldn't come up with numbers on those. Lot more than eight, though. But since we seen him burn himself, we decided not to tell him how many. He'd be one big burn now, right? And since he's so pretty, well, that'd be a shame.'

She fell silent then, to catch her breath. She'd broken three or so ribs in the fight, so talking hurt. More than breathing, which hurt bad enough. Talking was worse. That had been the most words she'd used all at once since the battle.

'Drawfirst and Mayfly,' said Gaunt-Eye, 'and you. All heavies.'

'Aye, Sergeant.'

'Get back in line, Flashwit.'

She gave him a bright smile that seemed to startle him, and then fell back, past one-armed Corporal Rib – who eyed her with something like suspicion – and then Drawfirst and Skulldeath, before positioning herself beside Mayfly.

'Well?' Mayfly asked.

'You was wrong,' Flashwit said with deep satisfaction.

'About what?'

'Hah. He only asked *six* questions!'

Gaunt-Eye was throwing more looks back at his squad.

'Who's he want now?' Mayfly wondered.

And then the sergeant pointed at Skulldeath. 'You blow me one more kiss, soldier, and I'll wrap your guts round your Hood-damned neck!'

'Well now,' Flashwit muttered.

Mayfly nodded. 'The prince ain't missed yet, has he?'

*   *   *

323

Hedge could hear howling laughter behind him, and the breath gusted from him. 'Listen to that, Bavedict! Fid slapped 'em up and down all right – I knew it!'

The Letherii alchemist tugged again on the ox lead. 'Alas, Commander, I don't know what you mean by that.'

'Bet he gave 'em the old "Walking Dead" speech. It's like cutting shackles, that one. There was a night, you see, when Dujek Onearm himself came into the Bridgeburners' camp. We was working Pale then, the tunnels – I never shifted so many boulders in my life. He came in, right, and told us what we already knew.' Hedge drew off his scorched leather cap and scratched at his fresh-shaven scalp. 'We was the walking dead. Then he left. Left us to figure out what we were going to do about it.'

'What did you do?'

Hedge tugged on the cap again. 'Well, most of us, er, died. Before we even had a chance. But Whiskeyjack, he wasn't going to turn his back on any of it. And Quick Ben and Kalam, gods, they just wanted to start the killing. Y'ain't got nothing to lose once you're the walking dead.'

'I do admit, Commander, that I don't much like being described in that manner.'

'Got cold feet now?'

'I always appreciate your wit, sir,' said Bavedict. 'But cold feet are precisely what I don't want, if you understand me.'

'So buck up, then. Besides, what Fid had to say to his Bonehunters, well, that's up to him. Got nothing to do with us Bridgeburners—'

'Presumably because the Bridgeburners have been walking dead since, er, Pale.'

Hedge slapped him on the back. 'Exactly. It's not like it's an exclusive club, right?'

'Sir,' ventured Bavedict, 'was it just this afternoon that you were complaining how your old friend had turned his back on you? That you were feeling like a leper—'

'Things are easier when you're dead. I mean, for him. He could put me away, on some shelf in his skull, and leave me there.' Hedge gestured carelessly with one hand. 'I get it. I always did. I just don't like it. I feel *insulted*. I mean, I'm back. Anyone can see that. Fid should be happy. And Quick Ben – well, you saw what he did at the battle, before he skipped out. Went and did a Tayschrenn on us. Next time we meet, him and me are going to have some words, we are.'

'My point, sir, was that Fiddler has actually drawn himself closer to you, if indeed he spoke of his soldiers being among the walking dead.'

'You might think that,' Hedge said, nodding. 'But you'd be wrong. When you're dead, Bavedict, you ain't got no brothers. Nothing holds ya together. At least, not that I ever seen. Aye, the dead Bridgeburners are all together, but that's just old memories, chaining 'em all to each other. It's just ghostly echoes, from back when they were alive. I'm telling you, Alchemist, keep doing all you can to stay alive, for as long as you can. Because the dead got no friends.'

Bavedict sighed. 'I do hope you're wrong, Commander. Did you not say the Realm of Death has changed – that the Reaper himself surrendered the Unliving Throne? And that this Whiskeyjack—'

'You never knew him. Whiskeyjack, I mean. So you'll just have to take me at my word, he's a stubborn bastard. Probably the stubbornest bastard ever to walk this world. So, maybe you got a point. Maybe he can make it all different. If anyone can, it's him.' Another slap on Bavedict's shoulder. 'You gave me something to think about there. Fid never did that, you know. In fact, I can't remember what he ever did for me. I'm thinking now, I never really liked him at all.'

'How unfortunate. Did you like Whiskeyjack?'

'Aye, we was the best of friends. Plenty there to like, basically. In both of us. Fid was the odd one out, come to think on it.'

'And now Whiskeyjack rides among the dead.'

'Tragic, Bavedict. A damned shame.'

'And you loved him deeply.'

'So I did. So I did.'

'But Fiddler is still alive.'

'Aye—'

'And you never really liked him.'

'Just so—'

'In fact, you love *all* the dead Bridgeburners.'

'Of course I do!'

'Just not the last one left alive.'

Hedge glared, and then slapped the man on the side of the head. 'Why am I talking to you? You don't understand nothing!'

Off he marched, up to where his company trudged.

Bavedict drew out a small jar. Porcelain and studded jewels. He unscrewed the top, dipped one fingertip in, drew it back and examined it, and then rubbed it across his gums. 'Die?' he whispered. 'But I have no intention of dying. Not ever.'

Jastara finally found them, up near the head of the Khundryl column. It was impressive, how Hanavat managed to keep up this pace, the way she waddled with all that extra weight. It was never easy being pregnant. Sick to start, and then hungry all the time, and finally big as a bloated bhederin, until it all ends in excruciating pain. She recalled her first time, going through all that so bright-eyed and flushed, only to lose the damned thing as soon as it came out.

'The child did what she had to do, Jastara. Showed you the journey

325

you will know again, and again. She did what she had to do, and is now returned to the black waters.'

But other mothers didn't have to go through that, did they? It was hardly as if Jastara was blessed with a life of greatness, was it? *'Married Gall's favourite son, though, didn't she? That woman has ambitions, if not for herself, then for her get.'* Ambitions. That word now dangled like a bedraggled crow from a spear point, a rotted, withered clutch of shredded feathers and old blood. *'Watch out for widows. See how she took Gall in? What are they doing at night, when the children are asleep? Hanavat had better beware, especially as vulnerable as she is now, with a child about to drop, and her husband fled from her side. No, look hard at that Gilk, Widow Jastara.'*

There were measures of disgust, and they came close and one recoiled, and then they came back a second time, and one didn't recoil quite so far. And when they crept back a third time, and a fourth, when the hand reached out from the darkness to caress her bared thigh, to probe under the furs . . . well, sometimes disgust was like a mourner's shroud, suddenly too heavy to wear any more. *'Look hard at her now. You can see it in her eyes.'*

Comfort a broken man and you take the breaking inside. What woman didn't know that? The cracks spread outward, whispering into everything within reach. It was the curse of drunks and d'bayang addicts, and womanizers and sluts. The curse of men who spoiled young boys and girls – their own get, sometimes. Spoiled them for ever.

Accusations and proof and then all that shame, kneeling in the dirt with hands over his eyes. Or *her* eyes. And suddenly all the disgust comes back, only now it tastes familiar. No, more than familiar. It tastes *intimate*.

Do I feel soiled? Do I dare look into Hanavat's eyes? The question held her back, not ten paces behind Gall's wife. *My mother-in-law. Oh yes, look at Jastara now. But you forget, she lost the man she loved. She too was wounded. Maybe even broken. Of course, she couldn't show it, couldn't indulge in it, because while wife she may no longer be, mother she remains.*

What of me? My pain? His arms are the wrong arms, but the embrace is still warm, and strong. His shoulder has taken my tears. What am I to do?

So she held back, and the others looked at her, and whispered things to each other.

'Her courage has failed her,' murmured Shelemasa.

Hanavat sighed. 'Perhaps tomorrow, then.'

'I don't know what she thinks she can say,' the younger woman said. 'To make this right. Cast him out is what she should do.'

Hanavat glanced across at Shelemasa. 'So that is what everyone is saying, is it? That hard tone, those hard words. The most plentiful coin, spent so freely, is also the most worthless one.'

Shelemasa frowned. 'What do you mean?'

'When you are judgemental, all the paint in the world cannot hide the ugliness of your face. The viciousness inside pushes through and twists every feature.'

'I – I am sorry, Hanavat. I was thinking of you—'

'And you would take what you imagine to be my feelings and speak them back to me. You proclaim yourself the warrior at my side, the line standing firm, to give comfort to me – I understand all that, Shelemasa. Yet what I hear from you – what I see in the eyes of the others – has nothing to do with me. Have I asked for pity? Have I asked for allies in this hidden war? Is there even any war at all? You presume much.'

'She will not speak to you—'

'And how brave would you be in her stead? Her father-in-law has seduced her, taken her to his bed. Or she him, either way makes no difference. Do you think I do not know my own husband? He is difficult to resist in the best of times, and now in his pain and his need . . . well, not a woman or man here could defeat his will. But you see, you are all safe. From him. Freeing you to cast judgement upon the one woman now in his snare. Not upon my husband, however – for what might that say about me? Do not speak to me of sides in this. There are none. There are but people. People of all sorts, each doing what they can to get by.'

'And if what they do hurts others? Hanavat, will you martyr yourself? Will you weep for Jastara, too, who hides every day in his arms?'

'Ah, see how I have stung you? You in your cruel judgement. My husband in his need. Jastara in her weakness. They are one and all acts of selfishness. Acts of *pushing away*.'

'How can you say that? I despise what they've done to you!'

'And it tastes sweet, yes? Listen to me. I too am a widow, now. And a mother who has lost her children. Have I need for an embrace? A stolen moment of love? Should I feel hatred for Gall and Jastara, for finding what I cannot?'

Shelemasa's expression was appalled. Tears streaked down through the white paint on her face. 'Is it not your husband you should look to for that?'

'While he still faces away from me, I cannot.'

'Then *he's* the coward!'

'To look into my eyes,' Hanavat said, 'is to see all that we once shared, and have now lost. It is too much to bear, and not just for my husband. Yes,' she added, 'I carry his last child, and if that child is not his, well, that is for me to know, in my heart, but never to be spoken.

327

For now, I have that much – I have what I need to hold on, Shelemasa. And now, so does Gall.'

The younger woman shook her head. 'Then you stand alone, Mother. He has taken his son's widow. That is unforgivable.'

'Better, Shelemasa. Much better. You see, Jastara does not deserve your hate. Not those looks, those whispers behind her back. No, instead, to be true sisters to her, you must go to her. Comfort her. And when you have done that – when all of you have done that – then I shall go to her, and take her into my arms.'

Henar Vygulf remembered the day he acquired his first horse. His father, whose shattered hip five years earlier had ended his riding days, had limped at his side, using his cane, as they made their way out to the pasture. A new herd had been culled from the wild herds of the high mountain plateaus, and twenty-three of the magnificent beasts now moved restlessly about in the enclosure.

The sun was high, shrinking shadows underfoot, and the wind swept steady down the slopes, combing the high grasses, warm and sweet with the flavours of early autumn. Henar was nine years old.

'Will one see me?' he'd asked his father. 'Will one choose me?'

The tall Bluerose horse-breeder looked down, dark brows rising. 'It's that new maid, isn't it? The one with the watermelon tits and wide eyes. From the coast, yes? Filling your head with all sorts of rubbish.'

'But—'

'There's not a horse in the wide world, Henar, happy to choose a rider. Not one beast eager to serve. Not one is delighted at being broken, its will beaten down. Are they any different from you, or me?'

'But dogs—'

'By the Black-Winged Lord, Henar, dogs are *bred* to be four-legged slaves. Ever seen a wolf smile? Trust me, you don't want to. Ever. They smile right before they lunge for your throat. Never mind dogs.' He pointed with his cane. 'Those animals are wild. They have lived in utter freedom. So, see one you like?'

'That piebald one, off to the left on its own.'

His father grunted. 'A young stallion. Not yet strong enough to contest the ranks. Not bad, Henar. But I'm . . . well, surprised. Even from here, one animal stands out. Really stands out. You're old enough, have been around me enough, too. I would've thought you'd see straight off—'

'I did, Father.'

'What is it, then? Do you feel you do not deserve the best out there?'

'Not if it means breaking them.'

328

His father's head had rocked back then, and he'd laughed. Loud enough to startle the herd.

Recalling that moment of his youth, the huge warrior smiled. *Remember that day, Father? I bet you do. And if you could see me now. See the woman walking at my side. Why, I can almost hear that beautiful roar of your laughter.*

One day, Father, I will bring her to you. This wild, free woman. We'll step on to that long white road, walk between the trees – they must be big by now – and up through the estate gate.

I'll see you standing by the front entrance, like a statue commanding the stone itself. New lines on your face, but that hooked grin still there, in a beard now gone grey. You're leaning on your cane, and I can smell horses – like a flower's heady scent on the air, and that scent will tell me that I've come home.

I'll see you studying her, noting her height, her lithe confidence, the boldness in her eyes. And you'll wonder if she's broken me – not the other way round – you can see that. Not the other way round. But then you'll look into my eyes, and your smile will broaden.

And you'll tilt back that majestic head. And laugh to the heavens.

It will be the sweetest sound in the world. It will be the voice of our triumph. All of us. You, me, her.

Father, I do miss you.

Lostara's calloused hand found his own, and he took some of her weight as she leaned one shoulder against him. 'Bless Brys Beddict,' she said under her breath.

Henar nodded. 'I suspect a streak of the sentimental in my commander.'

'Be glad of it. I am.'

'It was . . . unexpected.'

'Why? I fought for you, Henar. Not the Adjunct. You. He understood—'

'No, not all that, beloved. All . . . this. Where we have found ourselves. And how we have found each other, for that matter.'

She looked up at the Strangers in the night sky. 'So, he gives us what time there's left to us. Less sentimental, then, more . . . pity. You've a dour streak, Henar – I think I prefer Brys's sentimental one. Maybe I'll get rid of you and ride back to him.'

'You'd have to fight Aranict for him, I should think.'

'Oh, you're right, and I couldn't do that. Wouldn't. I like her far too much. Well then, seems I'm saddled with you.'

He smiled. *Saddled. Hah.*

'Henar.'

'Yes?'

'I fear we won't be coming back from this journey.'

329

He nodded, not because he agreed with her, but because he knew what she feared.

'We're going to die,' she said. 'In fact, we may not even make it across this desert.'

'There is that risk.'

'It's hardly fair.'

'I had a maid, once, at the country estate. Watermelon tits and big eyes—'

'*What?*'

'My father is terrible with names. So he came up with, er, memorable descriptions. Anyway, she used to tell me stories at night. Long, rambling tales of heroes. Loves lost, loves won. She'd make every ending sweet. To make the night's dreams the same, you see?'

'Just what a child needs.'

'I suppose. But those stories weren't for me. They were for her. She was from the coast, and she'd left behind a man she loved – this was Lether, don't forget, and her whole community was trapped in the Indebted way of life. It's why she came to work for our family. As for the young man, well, he was sent to sea.' He was silent for a moment, remembering, and then he said, 'Every night, she told me how she wanted her life to turn out – though of course I didn't realize that at the time. But the truth of it was, she wanted that happy ending. She needed to believe in it. For her, and for everyone else.'

Lostara sighed. 'What happened to her?'

'As far as I know, she's still there, at the country estate.'

'Are you trying to break my heart, Henar?'

He shook his head. 'My father worked the system as best he could, and he was not unkind with his Indebted. About a year before I left to train with the Lancers, watermelon tits with big eyes married the son of one of our horse-trainers. My last vision of her, her belly was out to here and those tits were even bigger.'

'She'd given up on her man from the sea, then. Well, probably wise, I suppose. Part of growing up.'

Henar eyed her, and then away, out over the rocky landscape. 'I think about her, every now and then.' He grinned. 'I even used to fantasize about her, yes, in the way young men will do.' The grin faded. 'But mostly I see her sitting on the edge of the bed, her hands flying and her eyes getting wider, and in that bed is her own child. A boy. Who will dream sweet dreams. And when the lantern is turned down, when she's standing by the door to his room, that's when the tears will run down her cheeks. And she'll remember a young man on the edge of the sea.' Lostara's breathing had changed, somehow, and her face was hidden from his view. 'My love?'

Her reply was muffled. 'It's all right. Henar, you keep surprising me. That's all.'

'We'll survive this, Lostara Yil,' he said. 'And one day I will lead you by the hand up to my father's house. And we'll see him, standing there, waiting for us. And he will laugh.'

She looked up, wiping at her cheeks. 'Laugh?'

'There are pleasures in the world, Lostara Yil, that go beyond words.' *I heard one of those pleasures once. And I will hear it again. I will.*

'Before I reached the lofty position of inexhaustible masturbation that is Demidrek Septarch of the Great Temple,' Banaschar was saying, 'I had to follow the same rituals as everyone else. And one of those rituals was to counsel commoners – who knows why they'd ever seek out a priest of the Autumn Worm, but then, the truth of it is, the real and true function of priests of all colours is simply that of listening to a litany of moans, fears and confessions, all for the betterment of someone's soul – never could figure out whose, but no matter.' He paused. 'Are you actually listening, Adjunct?'

'It appears that I have little choice,' she replied.

The Glass Desert stretched ahead of them. A small flanking troop, scouts, he assumed, were slightly ahead and to the left – north – of the vanguard, moving on foot as was everyone else. But directly before Banaschar and the Adjunct there stretched nothing but a broken plain studded with crystals, beneath a ghoulish sky.

The ex-priest shrugged. 'Now isn't this an interesting turn. Blessed woman, will you hear my tales of mortal woe? Will you give counsel?'

The look she cast at him was unreadable and it occurred to him, an instant later, that it was just as well.

He cleared his throat. 'Occasionally, one of them would complain. About me. Or, rather, about us sanctimonious shits in these ridiculous robes and whatnot. You know what they'd be so irritated about? I'll tell you. *Love.* That's what.'

A second glance, even briefer than the first one.

He nodded. 'Precisely. They asked: "You, priest – you, with that hand beneath the vestments – what in Hood's name do you know about love? More to the point, what do you know about *romance*?" You see, most people end up moaning about relationships. More than being poor, or lame or sick, more than any other topic you could imagine. Lovers, husbands, wives, strangers, sisters – endless confessions and desires and betrayals and all the rest. That's why the question would eventually come round – being priests we'd excused ourselves from the whole mess. Hardly a strong position from which to dispense inane truisms passing as advice. Do you follow me so far, Adjunct?'

'Have you nothing to drink, Banaschar?'

He kicked at a cluster of crystals, expecting them to break. They didn't. Cursing in pain under his breath, he hobbled for a few strides. 'What did I know about romance? Nothing. But, after enough years of listening to every possible iteration on the subject, ah, eventually things start getting clearer.'

'Do they now?'

'They do, Adjunct. Shall I expound on love and romance?'

'I'd rather you—'

'It's actually a mathematical exercise,' he said. 'Romance is the negotiation of possibilities, towards that elusive prize called love. There, you see? I wager you expected me to go on and on, didn't you? But I'm done. Done discussing love and romance.'

'Your description lacks something, Banaschar.'

'It lacks *everything*, Adjunct. All that confuses and clouds, that makes murky what is in fact both simple and stupidly elegant. Or elegantly stupid, depending on your attitude to the subject.'

They continued on, neither speaking, for some time. The clatter and groan of the column behind them was incessant, but apart from a lone burst of laughter a while back there was none of the ribald songs and chants, the running jests or arguments. While it was true that the Adjunct had set a stiff pace, Banaschar knew that these soldiers were hardened enough to think little of it. The quiet was unnerving.

Got a desert to cross. It's cold and it's not nearly as dark as it should be. And that alien glow whispers down on us. If I listen carefully enough, I can hear words. Drifting down. In all the languages of the world – but not this world, of course. Some other one, where faces lift hopefully to the heavens. 'Are you there?' they ask. And the sky answers not.

While here I walk. Here I look up and I ask: 'Are you there?' and down come the voices. 'Yes. We are here. Just . . . reach.'

'I was a sober priest back then,' he said. 'A serious one. I listened. I counselled.'

Eventually, she looked over, but said nothing.

Fiddler glanced to the right. Southward, forty paces distant, the head of the column. The Adjunct. Beside her the priest. Behind the two of them, a pair of Fists.

Eight Khundryl youths walked with Fiddler, ushered out from under their mother's skirts. They'd spotted him walking alone and had drawn closer. Curious, maybe. Or wanting to be doing something that might be important. Scouting, guarding the flank.

He didn't send them away. Too many had that lost, hopeful look in their eyes. Dead fathers, brothers, mothers, sisters. Massive absences through which winds howled. Now they hovered, flanking him as if he was the column itself.

Fiddler was silent – and they'd taken up that silence as if it would make them older – so the only sounds were the stones shifting underfoot, the scuff of moccasins, the thump of his boots. And the grind of the column.

He'd seen the map. He knew what lay ahead. *Only the impossible. Without water, we will never leave this desert. Without water, all of her plans die here. And the gods will close like jackals, and then the Elder Gods will show their hand, and blood will spill.*

The Crippled God will suffer terribly – all the pain and anguish he has known up to now will be nothing but prelude. They will feed on his agony and they will feed for a long, long time.

On your agony, Fallen One. You are in the Deck of Dragons. Your House is sanctified. If we fail, that decision will prove your gravest error. It will trap you here. It will make suffering your holy writ – oh, many will flock to you. No one likes to suffer in isolation, and no one likes to suffer for no reason. You will answer both, and make of them an illness. Of body, of spirit. Even as the torturing of your soul goes on, and on.

I never said I'd like you, Fallen One. But then, you never said I had to. Not me, not the Adjunct, not any of us. You just asked us to do what's right. We said yes. And it's done. But bear in mind, we're mortal, and in this war to come, we're fragile – among all the players, we're the most vulnerable.

Maybe that fits. Maybe it's only right that we should be the ones to raise your standard, Fallen One. And ignorant historians will write of us, in the guise of knowledge. They will argue over our purpose – the things we sought to do. They will overturn every boulder, every barrow stone, seeking our motives. Looking for hints of ambition.

They will compose a Book of the Fallen.

And then argue over its significance. In the guise of knowledge – but truly, what will they know? Of each of us? From that distance, from that cold, cold distance – you'd have to squint. You'd have to look hard.

Because we're thin on the ground.

So very . . . thin.

Children always made him feel awkward. Choices he'd put aside, futures he'd long ago surrendered. And looking at them left him feeling guilty. *They were crimes of necessity, each time I turned away. Each time we all did. Whiskeyjack, remember once when we stood on the ramparts at Mock's Hold? Laseen had just stepped out from . . . the shadows. There was a child, some son of some merchant. He was bold. You told him something, Whiskeyjack. Some advice. What was it? I can't recall. I don't even know why I'm remembering any of it.*

Mothers were looking on from that column – their eyes were on their children, these young legacies, and would grip tight as talons if they could. *But spaces now gape, and the children edge ever closer to them, to fill what has been lost. And the mothers tell themselves it will be enough, it must be enough.*

Just as I tell you now, Fallen One, whatever we manage to do, it will have to be enough. We will bring this book to an end, one way or another.

And one more thing. Something I only realized today, when I chanced to glance across and see her, standing there, moments from signalling the beginning of this march. From the very first, we have lived the tale of the Adjunct. First it was Lorn, back in Darujhistan. And now it is Tavore Paran.

The Adjunct never stands in the centre. She stands to one side. Always. The truth of that is right there, in her title – which she will not relinquish. So, what does it mean? Ah, Fallen One, it means this: she will do what she has to do, but your life is not in her hands.

I see that now.

Fallen One, your life is in the hands of a murderer of Malazan marines and heavies.

Your life is in my hands.

And soon she will send us on our way.

In that Malazan Book of the Fallen, the historians will write of our suffering, and they will speak of it as the suffering of those who served the Crippled God. As something . . . fitting. And for our seeming fanaticism they will dismiss all that we were, and think only of what we achieved. Or failed to achieve.

And in so doing, they will miss the whole fucking point.

Fallen One, we are all your children.

CHAPTER TWELVE

Word came, and in the ashes I finally straightened and looked
upon those few of my children left standing. The Throne of
Shadows was no more and out from the twilight flew dragons,
filling the air with cries of rage and frustration.

I knew then that he had done it. He had cheated them all,
but at what cost? I looked at the heaps of corpses, a monstrous
high water mark upon this cursed strand. Blood ran in streams
down the slope to where crimson-streaked light cascaded,
where all the wounds still gaped. Another wave was coming.
We could not hold.

Down from the forest, at that moment of deepest despair,
came a trio of figures. I faced them, and from my ravaged soul
there was born hope's glimmer . . .

Excerpt
Book Eleven
Throne, Sceptre and Crown
Rise Harat
(Coral Trove)

PITHY STAGGERED CLEAR, SHEATHED IN BLOOD. THE BLISTERING WHITE
of the strand shocked her, tilting and rocking before her eyes. She
fell to her knees, and then on to her side. She let go of her sword
but the grip clung to her hand a moment longer, before sobbing loose.
With her other hand she tugged off her helm. The blade cut was a slit
scoring right through the dented iron. Strands of bloody hair and the
tufted padding of her under-helm filled the gap.

She let her head drop back, the terrible sounds of battle fading. Overhead the sky spun. Torn fragments of light drifted in the gloom. *Ah,
Brev. He warned us. In that way of his, he warned us. Back and forth*

*he walked, drawing and sheathing and drawing that damned sword.
Over and over again.*

*You can think about what's to come. You can try and picture it in
your mind. What warriors did. What soldiers walked into. But none
of it readies you. None of it.*

The screaming seemed far away now. The surge and terrible clatter,
the maw of the breach a mass of blades, spear and sword, knife and
axe, and all that mouth did was chew people to bloody bits, those iron
fangs clashing and grinding – there was no end to its appetite.

So long as there're more people to shove into it.

Her body felt hot, the sweaty gambeson chafing under her arms. She
could smell her own reek.

*So we called ourselves captains, did we, Brev? Good at giving orders.
Good at standing around looking important. There with the prince.
With his knot of elite soldiers he now calls his Watch. Me and you,
Brevity, we were officers.*

In an army of fools.

Blood ran warm to pool in her ears, first the one on the left, then the
one on the right. Other sounds were drowned in the deluge. *Is that the
ocean I'm hearing? An ocean of blood? Is this, I wonder, the last thing
we ever hear? Dear ocean, then, call my soul. I would swim the waters
again. Let me swim the waters again.*

Something trembled the sands beneath her. *No, they won't quit.
They want through. Just like he said.*

She was no captain. She knew nothing about what being a real
captain meant. From that first moment, when the breach opened, when
light flared out like a tongue of fire, and all those voices from beyond
the barrier ripped through . . .

She saw Yedan Derryg marching down to the breach. His Watch
had been arrayed, positioned as squad leaders in the forward line of
Letherii volunteers. And there was Withal, moving quickly back up the
ravaged slope, into the forest. *Word to the queen of Kharkanas: the
battle begins.*

Pithy's attention returned to the breach. *Stick the mercenaries to the
front, in a place where there's no retreat except through your more
loyal soldiers. They're there for the loot to come. But loot never held
any man or woman, not for long, not when it all rips open. These
Letherii islanders – they're my people. Mine.*

She took up her sword as she ran down to that first high berm.
The weapon in her hand never felt right. It frightened her, in fact.
She dreaded spitting herself as much as she did some snarling enemy's
spear thrust. Where was Brevity? Somewhere in the rush – *we're like a
kicked-over nest of termites.*

336

Someone was wailing – a mother whose child has just pulled loose from her embrace, has just vanished into the press with a sword and shield, a spear or a pike. *It's a scene of the world. Every world. On the other side of the barrier, some mother screams her fear, loses sight of her cherished one.* She stumbled, dropped to one knee, vomited into the crushed bones of the beach. Coughing, spitting, feeling a strange hollowness inside, blossoming outward, until it felt as if her brain was attached to nothing, floating free of her body.

She could hear a roar. The sound of battle – no, she'd never heard it before, not like this. The flight from the coast back in Lether had been nothing like this. Back then, the voices and the will had come from pain and fear, from broken needs. It had possessed a plaintive timbre. Against the discipline of Yedan Derryg and his elites, those wretched foes had not stood a chance.

This was different. The sound that erupted from the breach was by itself enough to drive the defenders back a step. Triumph and rage – they were through! At last, through! And the hated enemy would not stop them, would not even slow them. With the mass of their comrades driving them from behind, with the slashing spear points dropping horizontal before them, the Tiste Liosan poured from the wound.

Pithy forced herself back on to her feet, forced herself forward. She was still floating free, but her vision seemed impossibly sharp. She saw the front line of Letherii lifting bizarrely into the air, saw their heads tilting back, their mouths wide open. Lifted on the spears of the enemy.

The sword slipped from her hand. Numbed, confused, she spun to retrieve it. Someone collided with her, knocked her down. She coughed on a lungful of dusty sand. Where was her sword? There. She crawled over to it. The grip was gritty, biting into her palm. Pithy wiped at her hand. Looked over at the breach.

Somehow, the Letherii line was still there. They were fighting back. They were holding the Liosan on the berm's slope. The press from their own side was vicious, pushing to hold and then pushing to advance. Gaps opened here and there and torn bodies were carried back out, limbs dragging.

The two witches were now among the wounded. Each held a dagger in one hand. Pithy watched Skwish kneel beside an injured woman, leaning close to examine a wound. With a shake of her head she slid the knife into the Letherii's chest, straight into her heart, then moved on to the next casualty.

You fucking murderers.

Pully was stuffing bandages into a hole in a man's side, shouting for stretcher-bearers. A second station for the wounded was forming higher up the strand, where cutters worked to staunch bleeding, stitch

337

gashes and saw off ruined limbs. Nearby was a pit dug into the sand, for those severed limbs and for those wounded no one could save.

It's . . . organized. They planned for this. Yes, I remember now. We all planned for this. For what's happening right now.

Pithy scrambled forward again. 'They're holding,' she gasped. 'They're holding!'

'Captain!'

A boy ran up to her. She'd never seen him before. He was frighteningly thin, with sores crusting his mouth. A Letherii. 'Who sent you?' she demanded.

'Corporal Nithe of the Watch, right anchor, has been wounded and pulled from the line, sir. The prince needs you to immediately take up command of those flank squads, sir.'

Errant's push. She licked her lips. Her bladder was stinging as if everything it held had turned into acid. She looked down at her sword.

'Sir?'

The damned boy was staring at her. Those weeping sores around his mouth, the smears on his face. She could see that he was terrified. An orphan whose new family was being killed before his very eyes. He had carried the prince's words. He had found her, done what Yedan had asked of him. He was doing what he was supposed to be doing. *Following orders. Holding on to duty, as desperate as the rest of us. Stop looking at me like that.* 'Lead me through,' she said.

And like a boy eager for the beach, he took her hand and led her forward.

The smell of the heaving press made her choke. The sweat and spewed vomit, the fear and the shit and the piss. How could anyone fight in this? Pithy almost pulled herself loose from the boy's cold grip. But now hands were pushing at her from behind. Faces lunged close, shouting things. Eyes met her own, filled with pleading. Panic roiled in like a grey, grainy cloud.

Her knees found a figure down on all fours. As she struggled to step over him, she looked down. Unwounded by any weapon but terror itself. The realization triggered a surge of fury. She halted and twisted round. '*Get up, you worthless pile of shit! They're dying up there! For you! On your feet!*' And this time she managed to prise her hand loose from the boy's. Reaching down, she took the man by the hair. 'Stand up! You're with me – let's go!'

Those close by were watching. Staring. She saw things harden in their eyes and wondered what that was about. 'Lead on, lad! Front line, quick! You, soldier, don't even think of pullin' back!'

Listen to me! Like I know what I'm doing. Like I done this before.

She heard voices around her now.

'*Look, Captain's here—*'

'*Cap'n Pithy – see her? There—*'

'*She choked a coward—*'

'*Killed him!*'

'*Pithy killed a coward – right in front of my eyes!*'

'Gods below,' she muttered. The boy glanced back at her as he struggled to push between two Letherii men. His eyes were suddenly bright.

And then, all at once, she could see spear points, flashing as they rocked up from impacts with shields, lashing out, clashing with swords and Andiian pikes. For the first time, she caught a glimpse of a Liosan face. Long, narrow, stretched – but – *Errant! They look like the Andii! They look just like them!*

White-skinned instead of black-skinned. *Is that it? Is that the only fucking difference?*

Those eyes locked on her own, pale blue and frighteningly young, above the struggling press between them. And she saw his fear. His terrible, horrifying fear. 'No,' she murmured. *Don't do this. Go back. Please—*

An axe blade slammed into the side of the Liosan's head. Bones folded in around sundered flesh. Blood sprayed from eye, nose and mouth. The lone visible eye still staring at her suddenly went blank, sightless, and he fell down, out of her sight.

Pithy moaned. Tears rose inside her. Her sinuses closed up, forcing her breaths to her mouth – she couldn't get enough air. She could barely see through the blur. And the light was pouring down, mottled by shadows. Pouring down and down—

A Letherii woman reached back and closed a bloody grip on her wrist. Pulling her forward. 'Corporal Nithe said he'd be back soon, sir.'

Was this going to be a conversation? She could see the fighting – right there, almost within reach. Where had the boy gone? Nowhere in sight. Her coward? There, suddenly in the front line and screaming as he brought a shield round to block a savage thrust. 'What happened to him?'

'Captain?'

'Nithe! What happened to him?'

'Got a hand cut off, sir. Went to get it scabbed – said he'd be back soon.' The woman faced front again, raised her voice. 'Captain Pithy's in command!'

No one seemed to heed that announcement.

And then Pithy felt the air change, as if her ears had popped. Something seethed, up around her, and then outward. From nowhere and everywhere there came a roar, and the flank lurched, heaved into the face of the Liosan front.

As if caught in a current, Pithy was pulled forward.

She stepped on something that rolled underfoot. Looked down.

The boy stared up at her. But no, he was staring up at nothing. Around his gaping mouth, the sores were black with dirt.

No, clean those up—

And then the bodies underfoot were Liosan, twisted, curled round welters of blood and gaping wounds. Broken spear shafts, soiled clothing. Empty faces.

She could hear other roars, and she knew – *she knew* – that the entire Letherii line was driving forward, one section after another. *Go back to your hole, you poor miserable dogs!* 'Go back!' she shouted. 'Back! This is ours! This is ours!'

And all at once, that cry was taken up.

She saw the Liosan reel before it, saw the enemy ranks buckling as the Letherii surged into them, again and again.

A sudden gap before her. A Liosan, settling on one knee, one shoulder sliced open, down through the joint, the arm hanging. Seeing her, he struggled to rise. He was old, his face lined, and the look in his eyes was bleak.

Pithy's sword swing was awkward, but all of her strength was behind it. She clipped the edge of his jaw before the blade cut deep into his neck. Blood spurted, gushed all over her. Shocked by the hot deluge, she stepped back—

And that one step saved her life. A spear thrust caught her head, bit into her helm. She felt the blade edge cut into her scalp, grind along the bone of her skull – and then she was pulled away.

A burly man dragged her close. 'Never mind that – y'still got your head, don't you? Seen my sword?' he asked. 'I dropped the fucker – you'll know it 'cause it's still in my hand – never mind—' He bent down and came up with a wood-cutter's axe. 'Errant's horse-humped earhole, what the fuck is this? Never mind – to the back line with you, Captain Pithy. I started this and I mean to finish it up.'

Nithe? Never Mind Nithe? Is that what they call you?

'This is ours!' The chant went on and on.

Hands took hold of her. She was being pulled out. Her first engagement against the Liosan. Her first taste – of everything. The slaughter. The hurt. The anger. The falling light. *All of it. All of it. Oh, gods, all of it!*

Suddenly she stumbled clear.

Winced at the blinding glare of the strand, as tendrils of agonizing light writhed overhead. Down, on to her knees. Down, on to her side. Sword and helmet away. Sounds, dimming, fading . . .

Someone drove a pair of knees against her left hip. Blinking, she looked up at Skwish, saw the knife in the witch's gore-drenched left hand. 'Don't even think it,' Pithy said in a growl.

The witch grinned.

Then was gone.

The last end of the rout, a scattering of Liosan, converging as they dragged wounded comrades back through the breach, vanishing into blinding light. Yedan Derryg's sword was unaccountably heavy in his hand, so he let the tip crunch down into the soaked strand.

'Prince!'

'Address that front line, Sergeant – get our wounded and dead out of there.' He glared at the breach. The blackened, weeping mar in Lightfall. Too damaged to do anything as miraculous as heal before his eyes, but the first probe of the enemy had been denied.

The Liosan had taken as many of their dead and dying with them as they could, but there were still scores and scores, bodies heaped up at the base of the first berm. 'Get a crew to start piling them up, against the breach. Make a wall, but tell them to be careful – make sure the fallen are actually dead or near enough as to make no difference.'

'Yes, sir.'

He lifted his gaze as a shadow crossed the Lightfall, just above the wound. Bared his teeth.

A new voice spoke beside him. 'That was closer than I liked, Prince.'

He turned. 'Bedac. Was it you behind that last push?'

'Far right flank,' the woman said.

'Nithe? Could've sworn that was a woman's shout.'

'Nithe got his hand chopped off. Didn't bleed out, thankfully. Captain Pithy took that flank command, sire. Nithe made it back in time to drive a wood-axe into the skull of one of the last Liosan on that side. Hard enough to break the handle.'

Yedan frowned. 'What's a wood-axe doing in our ranks? My orders on weapon choices were clear enough. That reminds me – Sergeant! Collect up the better Liosan weapons, will you?'

'Got plans with your trophy, Prince?'

'What trophy?'

She nodded down at his sword.

He glanced at it. A Liosan head was impaled on the blade, from the top of the skull down and out through the neck, which had already been half severed. He grunted. 'No wonder it felt heavy.'

Yan Tovis stood at the forest verge. Watching them dragging bodies clear, watching others tossing limbs and rolling corpses into the pit.

None of it seemed real. The triumphant and suddenly exhausted Letherii ranks along the berm were settling to catch their breaths, to check on weapons and armour, to take the skins of water from the youths now threading through the ranks. *They think they've won.*

Without Yedan and his Watch, that front line would have quickly crumpled. Instead, the survivors now felt bold, filled to bursting. In this one clash, something had been tempered. She knew what she was seeing. A fighting force cannot be simply assembled. It needed that brutal forge and it needed all its fires quenched in the blood of battle. Her brother was making something here.

But it would not be enough.

She could see how her own Shake were looking on, no different from Yan Tovis herself. Yedan was not about to expend the Letherii ranks as if they were useless skirmishers, not with what he'd now made of them. He would pull them back, holding them in reserve during the next battle.

They probed to test our mettle. Next time, we will see their true fury. And if that beachhead is established, then the first dragon will come through.

Her Shake watched, yes, and thought about their own time to come, their own stand against the Liosan. Few of the Letherii were trained as soldiers, and that was no different from the Shake. But Yedan's Watch would be there, solid as standing stones. *Until they start falling. They can only do so much. They're Yedan's most precious resource, but he must risk them each time. And, as they begin to fall, why, he'll have a new crop of veterans to draw upon. These very Letherii here, and then from among our own Shake.*

It's so very . . . logical. But, dear brother, it's what you do best, isn't it?

How can I kneel to this? By doing so, do I not make it all . . . inevitable? No. That I will not do. But I will take my place among my people, on that berm. I know how to fight. I might not be Yedan's equal in that, but I'm damned close.

It's carved into the souls of the royal line. To stand here, upon the First Shore. To stand here, and to die.

They were stacking Liosan corpses, making a wall across the breach. The contempt of that gesture was as calculated as everything else Yedan did. *Rage is the enemy. Beware that, Liosan. He will make your rage your downfall, if he can.*

You cannot make my brother angry. He's not like you. He's not like any of us. And his army will follow his lead. They will look to him and take inside what he gives. It's cold. Lifeless. They'll take it in and it will change them all.

Your army, brother. My people. I can't win this, but neither can you.

She collected her sword belt from the stump of a felled tree, strapped it on. Settled the helm on her head and fastened the clasp. Tugged on her gauntlets.

Her people took note. They faced her now, and watched as their queen prepared to fight.

But what are they thinking?

Why do they even look to us? My brother? Me? See where our love for them has taken them. See all those limp, lifeless bodies tumbling into the pit.

They watched this calm, silent woman readying for battle.

They didn't know, of course, about all the howling going on in her head, the anguished screams and the poisoned helplessness eating at every hidden edge. No, they knew nothing about any of that.

She saw her brother. Gesturing, giving orders.

He turned then, and across the distance he faced her.

Should she lift a hand? Acknowledge his achievement? This first triumph? Should she draw her sword, perhaps, and lift it high? Would he respond in kind?

Not a chance. But then, look at me. We see each other, yes, and neither of us does a thing to reach across. How can we? We are co-conspirators in the slaughter of all these people. Yan Tovis turned, found one of her messengers. 'Aras, deliver the news to Queen Drukorlat. The breach was repelled. Acceptable losses. We await their next attack.'

The young girl bowed and then hurried off, into the forest.

When Twilight looked back down to the strand, her brother was nowhere in sight.

It was now a road, of sorts. The white dust soaked in blood, churned into reddish-brown mud, straight as a spear shaft between Saranas' Wedding Gate and the Breach. Shivering, Aparal Forge watched the wagons burdened with the wounded drawing closer. To either side of the narrow track the massed legions prepared for the real assault. Heads turned to watch the broken remnants of the Forlorn Hope file past.

Well, that was proof enough, was it not? Kharkanas was occupied once more. The infernal Shake had returned, or someone much like them, and were determined to contest the breach. Madness, all of it. Glancing up, he saw four of the Thirteen still veered, their vast wings flashing gold in the ceaseless light. The Draconean blood had finally taken them, he knew. They had surrendered for ever to the chaos. Among them was Iparth Erule, who had once been a friend. 'Son of Light,' he whispered, 'beware your chosen, now that the blood of the Eleint rises, to drown all that we once were.'

The door behind him swung open, cracking against the stone wall. Aparal flinched, but did not turn round.

'If you had followed, brother—'

'But I did, Son of Light.'

Kadagar Fant swore, was suddenly beside Aparal, hands settling on the alabaster merlon. 'That last pass – we were almost through! See my children still on the wing? Where are the others?'

'Lord, the Mane of Chaos frightens them. If they surrender to it for too long . . . Son of Light, you could lose control of them—'

'When I am veered they well comprehend my power – my domination. What more is needed to bend them to my will? Do you truly believe that I do not understand the nature of the Eleint?'

'The risk, Lord—'

'It frightens you, does it, brother?'

'I fear we might lose control of our own people, Lord, and not through any flaw in our purpose, or leadership. Iparth Erule and his sisters no longer semble. The blood of the Eleint has taken them, it has stolen their minds. When they cease to be Tiste Liosan, how soon before our cause becomes meaningless? How soon before they find their own ambitions?'

Kadagar Fant said nothing for some time. Then he leaned forward over the wall and looked straight down. 'It has been some time,' he said in a musing tone, 'since we last set a traitor upon the White Wall. Brother, do you think my people begin to forget? Must I remind them again?'

Aparal Forge thought about it. 'If you feel it necessary, Lord.' He held his gaze on the column crawling towards the Wedding Gate.

'This is new,' the Son of Light said.

'Lord?'

'I see no answering fear in you, brother.'

The Mane of Chaos, you fool. It devours fear like bloody meat. 'I am as ever your servant, Lord.'

'So much so, I now see, that you would risk your own life to speak your mind.'

'Perhaps.' *As I once did, long ago, when we were different people, not yet who we are now.* 'If so, then I will add this. The day you cease to hear me will be the day that we will have lost.'

Kadagar's voice was so quiet that Aparal barely made out what he was saying. 'Are you that important, brother?'

'I am now, Lord.'

'Why?'

'Because I am the last among your people to whom you still listen, Lord. You look down upon this cursed wall and what do you see? Brave warriors who disagreed with you. The rotting remnants of our priesthood—'

344

Kadagar whispered, 'They opposed the path of the Eleint.'

'They did, Lord, and now they are dead. And four of the Thirteen will not return.'

'I can command them.'

'As it pleases them to appear loyal, so that shall remain, Lord.'

Veiled eyes lifted to meet his gaze. 'You draw close, brother Aparal Forge, so very close.'

'If my counsel is treason, then condemn me, Lord. But you will not see fear, not in me. Not any more and never again.'

Kadagar Fant snarled and then said, 'There is not time for this. The legions are ready, and I need you down there, commanding the assault. The enemy beyond the breach was surprisingly weak—'

'Weak, Lord?'

'I will accept bold words from you, brother, but not outright rudeness.'

'Sorry, Lord.'

'Weak. Indeed, it seems they are not even true Shake. Devoid of Tiste blood entirely. It is my thought that they are mercenaries, hired because the Andii now in Kharkanas are too few to personally oppose us. In fact, I now believe that the Shake are no more. Gone, like a nightmare before the dawn.'

'They fought surprisingly well for mercenaries, Lord.'

'Humans are like that, brother. Decide on something and there's no moving them. You have to cut down every last one of them. Until not one is left breathing.'

'The surest way to win an argument,' Aparal commented.

Kadagar reached over and gripped his upper arm. 'Better! Return to the living, old friend! Today, we shall gain the Shore. Tonight, we shall dine in the High Palace of Kharkanas!'

'Lord, may I descend to take command of the legions?'

'Go, brother! You shall see me soon enough, flying above you.'

Aparal hesitated. 'Lord, might I speak one last word of advice?'

Kadagar's face clouded, but he nodded.

'Do not be the first of our Thirteen through the breach. Leave that to Iparth Erule, or one of his sisters.'

'But why?'

'Because the enemy knows that we are here. Soletaken or true Eleint. They will have plans to deal with our eventual arrival, Lord. Use Erule to discover it. We cannot risk losing you, Son of Light.'

Kadagar's pale eyes searched his, and then he smiled. 'Friend, it shall be as you say. Go now.'

Father Light, is this what you want? What was in your mind when you walked out from the city, through the gate that would be named for

345

the day of your wedding, for your procession's path into the realm of Dark? Did you ever imagine that you would bring about the end of the world?

Take the Sceptre in hand. Walk to the Throne. There is an old saying: every crown leaves a circle of blood. I always wondered what it meant. Where was that circle? Surrounding the one now ruling, or closer still, like razors against the brow?

Aparal Forge walked along one verge of the blood path. He could have veered into his dragon form. He could have wheeled out from the high wall and in moments settled before the breach, those old scattered stones of the toppled edifice, with all the joyous carvings. But what would that be saying to his warriors? *You are indeed led by dragons, by the blood-tainted, by the devourers of Kessobahn.* But was he not Tiste Liosan? *I am. For now, for as long as I can hold on. And I'd rather show them that. I'd rather they see me, here, walking.*

The soldiers were ready. He could see as much. He sought to draw strength from them, reassurance, all the confidence he would need to in turn command them. As they in turn did when seeing him.

I must speak to them. Fashion words. What shall I say? Mercenaries await us. Humans. They can be broken, for their will has been bought, and if it is to be something to bargain with, like a comforting robe, then that will cannot be worth much, when all comfort vanishes. No, make it simpler. Tell them that coin cannot purchase righteousness. Against our will the humans shall falter.

We must simply push hard enough for long enough.

Speak with confidence, yes.

And then I will think of loves lost, to empty out all the places inside me. Ready to be filled with fury and desire.

The Liosan knew enough about humans. Through the piercing of the veil such as a priest or mage occasionally achieved, they had ventured into human worlds. 'Testing the notions of justice', as one old scout had once said. Small parties, of aimless purpose or singular intent. Journeying often enough for these explorers to return with knowledge of the strange, weak but profligate human creatures. Short-lived and truncated of thought. Incapable of planning ahead beyond a few years at most, and more commonly barely capable of thinking past a mere stretch of days.

There were always exceptions, of course. Great leaders, visionaries. Tyrants. But even among them, the legacy they sought was more often than not a selfish one, the private glory of immortal notoriety or fame.

Pathetic.

As he approached the breach, Aparal wondered whether there was a great leader among these humans, these mercenaries. It was of course possible, but he doubted it.

The once glorious gate had been shattered long ago. It had commemorated a marriage that had spilled more blood than could be imagined. *Shattered three civilizations. Destroyed an entire realm. Father Light, could you but have known, would you have turned away? Would you have sacrificed your happiness for the sake of your people? And hers?*

I like to think you would have. Yes. You would have sacrificed yourself, because you were better than all of us.

And now your children yearn to avenge your failure. But nothing we can do, nothing we can ever do, will make it better. No matter. We're not interested in healing old wounds – look at that gate for proof of that!

A space had been left clear before the breach. Of the wound itself, there was naught to be seen but stacked corpses, dim and ethereal through Lightfall's incessant bleeding. Seeing those bodies, Aparal scowled, and from deep inside him surged a rush of rage. Liosan. Draconean.

He stepped into the space, turned towards his kin. 'Brothers! Sisters! See what these humans have done to our fallen! They choose not to honour us as worthy foes. They imagine this dread wall will wound us!

'The Son of Light looks down upon us from the White Wall's rampart. The Son of Light has said that on this day we shall conquer the Realm of Dark! We shall conquer Kharkanas! We know they are waiting. Shall we seek them out? Brothers! Sisters! Shall we seek them out?'

The roar that answered him felt like a physical blow, but he welcomed it. *Their anger is without measure. Their justness is unassailable. Kadagar is right. We shall win through.*

He faced the ruined gate, glared at the breach. Drawing his sword, he held it high. 'Seventh Legion, Arrow Formation! Who leads?'

A harsh voice called out behind him. 'I lead, Aparal Forge! Gaelar Throe shall lead!'

Gaelar. I should have known. 'Gaelar. There is a commander among the humans. Find him. Kill him.'

'I so vow, Aparal Forge! I so vow!'

The power massing behind him made Aparal tremble. This assault would sweep aside the humans. Up and into the forest beyond. To the city itself. The palace splashed in blood. The Son of Light triumphant upon the Throne, Sceptre in hand.

And if Mother Dark dwelt in the temple, they would kill her.

We will not be stopped. Not this time.

Shadows from above. He looked up. Three dragons, and then a

347

fourth. *So eager. Iparth Erule. I think you want that throne. I think you mean to take it.*

'Liosan! Seventh Legion, level spears!' He turned, moved to the right. Gaelar was ready. They were all ready, bristling, straining for the signal, desperate to lunge forward. Burst through the wall of corpses, burst out on to the Shore.

And begin the slaughter.

Silent, Aparal Forge swung down the sword.

Sandalath Drukorlat, Queen of High House Dark, ruler of Kharkanas, walked alone in the palace, wondering where all the ghosts had gone. They should be crowding these ancient halls, whispering along the corridors and passages, lurking in recesses and doorways. Struggling to recall what needed doing, calling out for loved ones in faint, echoing voices. She ran her hand along a wall as she walked, feeling the hard, polished stone. She was far beyond the rounds of the paltry staff now resident in the palace.

Hunting ghosts. Stone like skin, but the skin is cold.

She could remember when it was different. Alive. Guards and guests, petitioners and servants, priestesses and midwives, retainers and scholars. Hostages. Swirling in their own precious currents, each and every one of them, like blood in a beating heart.

Her worn boots echoed as she made her way down a narrow corridor. Smaller now, this passage, and the steps she reached were shallow and worn, wending up in a tight spiral. She halted, gasping as a faint draught came down from above. *I remember this. The downdraught. I remember it. Against my face, my neck. Down round my bared ankles – I used to run – when was that? I must have been a child. Yes, a child. When was that?* Her right shoulder brushed against the wall again and again as she climbed. The sloped stone over her head felt oppressively close.

Why did I run?

Perhaps some inkling of the future. But for that child, there was no refuge. How could there be? Here she was, and the centuries upon centuries in between were now carved solid as this stone. *Stop running, child. It's done. Stop running, even the memory hurts.*

Sandalath reached the top floor, a small flagstone landing, a black-wood door set into an archway. The iron handle was shaped from three lengths of linked chains entwined, stiff enough to form a ring. She stared at it, remembering how at first she'd had to reach up to grasp it, and tug hard to swing back the door. *Hostage Room. Born into it, imprisoned within it, until the day you are sent away. The day some-one comes and takes you. Hostage Room, child. You didn't even know what that meant. No, it was your home.*

Reaching out, she grasped the ring. A single tug and something broke on the other side, fell with a clunk. *Oh . . . no, no, no—*

She opened the door.

The bed had partially collapsed. Insects had chewed the covers until they fell to dust. Thousands of generations of those insects had dwelt in the mattress, until it too crumbled to nothing. The creatures had eaten the wax candles in the silver sticks still standing on the solid blackwood dresser. Above the dresser, the polished mirror was mottled with midnight stains. The broad windows had been shuttered tight; now little of that remained but heaps of fittings on the floor.

Sandalath stepped inside. She could not see it yet, but she knew it was there.

Locked from the inside.

In the passageway leading to the Tutor Chamber she found the small, frail bones of this room's last hostage. The mice had eaten most of the child, until little more than grey stains marked its position – a body sprawled between the two chambers. Teeth lay scattered like the beads of a broken necklace.

I know how it was for you. I know. Slaughter in the citadel, screams rising from below, the smell of smoke. The world was ending. *Mother Dark turned away. Anomander's dreams of unification fell like dust through his fingers. The people were fleeing – fleeing Kurald Galain itself. The end of the world.*

She crouched down in the narrow corridor, stared down at the remnants. *Child? Are you me? No. I was long gone from here by then. Sent off to serve my purpose, but that purpose failed. I was among a mass of refugees on Gallan's Road. Blind Gallan shall lead us to freedom. We need only follow the sightless seer. We need only trust in his vision. Oh yes, child, the madness of that was, well, plain to see. But Darkness was never so cold as on that day.*

And on that day, we were all blind.

The child hostage would not have left this room. She had learned obedience before all else. Told to stay, she had set the flimsy lock that she had believed would bar the outer door – *we all believed it, each in our turn. It was our comfort. Our symbol of independence. It was a lock a grown Andii could break in one hand.*

But no one came to challenge your delusion of safety.

The lock was proof against everything going on outside this room. It was, in fact, the strongest barrier of all.

She sank down further, leaned one shoulder against the passage wall.

I am queen and I am hostage both. No one can take me. Until they decide to. No one can break my lock. Until they need to. In the meantime, see me sitting so regal on my throne. Frozen like an image in a frieze. But she would not weep, not for herself. All that running had taken her precisely to this place, this moment in time. *All that running.*

After some time, she climbed to her feet, went back into the outer room. Stared at what remained of herself in the mottled mirror. Fragments, pieces, an incomplete map. *Look at me. Are you looking at me, now, at last? I sense the stirring in your mind. Impatience, the wanting to be away, off somewhere else – anywhere but in this skull, anywhere but behind these eyes. What in your life has so chilled your heart, that you so quickly refuse another's pain, another's loss?*

Run, then. Go on. Run away, skip down the passage, find all the places that stab deep enough to make you feel.

Sandalath turned away. Back to the door, down the spiralling descent. One didn't need ghosts, she decided. Not a single ethereal glimpse was necessary. Empty corridors and echoing chambers were in themselves ghosts, emerging in the instant of her arrival, only to fade away once she was past. *Like the rooms of memory. Step inside, conjure what you see, wonder at what you feel, and then leave. But you take something with you. You always take something with you. Swirling, raising up dust.* She wanted to howl.

'Mother Dark, I understand now. Once again, I am a hostage.' She had died – drowned? – in the rolling surf of a distant shore. The end of a long, harrowing journey, such an ignoble, pathetic end. Thrashing in darkness, shocking cold filling her lungs – was that how it was? It must have been.

Silchas Ruin came to us upon that road. Wounded, stricken, he said he had forged an alliance. With an Edur prince – or was he king? If so, not for long. Emurlahn was destroyed, torn apart. He too was on the run.

An alliance of the defeated, of the fleeing. They would open a gate leading into another realm. They would find a place of peace, of healing. No throne to fight over, no sceptre to wield, no crown to cut the brow. *They would take us there.*

Salvation.

She was in the habit, she realized, of rolling ashore, only to be dragged back into deeper waters. A place to drown, a place of peace, an end to the running. Was it coming again? *Then, Mother Dark, I pray to you, make this time final. Grant me blessed oblivion, a place without war.*

Messengers found her in the hallway. Urged her to return to the throne room. There was news of the breach. Withal awaited her. She walked as one dulled by d'bayang, panelled scenes marching past on either side, as mottled as the mirror she had stared into so long ago now. Centuries ago. *Draconean blood proved a dark tomb, didn't it?*

350

See how my thoughts wander? See how these memories haunt? Do you truly dream of resurrection? Alas, I cannot recommend it.

Her husband's eyes studied her. 'Sand—'

'I was exploring,' she said, walking directly to seat herself on the throne. 'How bad, then?'

'The first assault was denied,' he replied. 'Yedan's Letherii line held, and then pushed the Liosan back through the wound. The Watch—'

'The Watch, yes.' *I remember now. It was already in me. Growing. Wanting my love. But how could I love?* 'The Shake have held, Lord. The Watch commanded. They have driven the Liosan back through the wound. The priestesses believe they have devised a means of sealing the rent, Lord—'

'Then they had better set about achieving that, Kellaras, for the Liosan shall launch another assault soon. And then another, and another. They will keep coming until they are through, or until they are all dead.'

'Lord, is such the fury of Osseric against you that—'

'Commander Kellaras, this is not Osseric's doing. It is not even Father Light's. No, these are children who will have their way. Unless the wound is healed, there will be no end to their efforts.' And then Anomander's eyes found her. 'Hostage,' he murmured, gesturing all the others to leave. He rose from the throne. 'I did not see you there. He released you then – I did not think—'

'No, Lord,' she said, 'he did not release me. He . . . abandoned me.'

'Hostage Drukorlat—'

'I am a hostage no longer, Lord. I am nothing.'

'What did he do to you?'

But she would not answer that. Could not. He had enough troubles, did he not? Wars upon all sides, armies advancing on Kharkanas. It was dying, all of it. Dying, and in his eyes she could see that he knew it.

'Sandalath Drukorlat.' *And with her name he reached out, settled a cool hand upon her brow. And took from her the knowledge he sought.* 'No,' *he whispered,* 'this cannot be.'

She pulled away then, unable to meet his eyes, unwilling to acknowledge the fury now emanating from him.

'I will avenge you.'

Those words could well have driven a spear through her, for the impact they made. She reeled, with pain a raging fire within her. Shaking her head, she staggered away. Avenge? I will have my own vengeance. I swear it.

He called out to her, but she fled the throne room. And ran.

Shallow steps climbing . . . a wooden door. A lock.

'Sandalath?'

351

'The priestesses can heal the wound.'

'What priestesses?'

'The Liosan won't stop. Nothing can make them stop. The Watch knows – all the Shake do. They have accepted it. They are going to die for us. Every last one of them. We cannot permit that. Where is Gallan? Where is Silchas? Where is my brother—'

Then Withal's arms were about her, lifting her from the throne, holding her tight. She felt weak as a child, but he was strong – stronger than she'd ever imagined was possible for a human. She felt something crumble within her and let out a soft gasp.

'I went looking for ghosts,' she said. 'I – I found them, I think. Mother help me. Save me – it's too much—'

'*Sand.*' The word was a sob.

'We need to run,' she said. 'That's all we need to do, my love. Run. Tell Twilight – raise a flag of truce – I will yield Kharkanas to the Liosan. They can have it, and I hope they *burn it to the fucking ground*!'

'Sand – this is Yedan's battle now, and he will not parley with the Liosan. He is a Shake prince. He wields a Hust blade – it was the witches who explained to me what that meant—'

'Hust? A Hust sword?' *Did I know that? I must have. Did I?*

'Forged to slay Eleint – without them the Andii could never have killed all those dragons at the Sundering. They could never have fought back. Yedan's sword knows what's coming—'

'*Stop it!*'

'It's too late—'

'Yedan—'

'He knows, Sand. Of course he knows. The witches are desperate – Yan Tovis accepts none of this—'

'Because she's not a fool!' Sandalath pushed Withal back. '*We need to run!*'

He shook his head.

She glared round. Guards looked away. Servants ducked their heads. She bared her teeth. 'You must think me mad. Do you? But I'm not. I see now, as clearly as Yan Tovis does. Is this all the Shake are to be to us? Wretched fodder doomed to fail? How dare we ask them to fight?' She spun, glared at the domed ceiling. 'Mother Dark! *How dare you?*'

The shout echoed, her only reply.

'The Shake will fight,' said Withal into the silence that followed. 'Not for you, Sand. Not for the Queen of High House Dark. Not even for Kharkanas. They will fight for their right to live. This once, after generations of retreating, of kneeling to masters. Sand – *this is their fight.*'

'Their deaths, you mean. Don't you? Their deaths!'

'And they will choose where it is to be, Sand. Not me. Not you.'

What makes us do this? What makes us set aside the comforts of peace?

'Sand,' Withal said in a quiet voice, 'this is their freedom. This one thing. Their freedom.'

'Go back to them, then,' she croaked, turning away. 'Be their witness, Withal. They've earned that much at least. Remember all that you see, for as long as there's life left to you.'

'My love—'

'No.' She shook her head, walking from the throne room.

Hostages. We are all hostages.

Yedan Derryg leaned the blade of his sword against his shoulder, his jaws bunching rhythmically, his eyes narrowing as he studied the breach. 'Signal the front lines. They're coming.'

The blurred shapes of the dragons skittered like wind-torn clouds behind the veil of Lightfall. He counted five in all, but suspected there were more. 'It will be in strength this time,' he said. 'They will seek to advance ten paces to start, and then form a crescent as the ranks behind them spill out, spread out. Our flanks need to deny that. Push in along the Lightfall itself, sever the vanguard.'

'That's asking a lot,' muttered Brevity beside him.

Yedan nodded.

'Maybe too much,' she continued. 'We're none of us trained as soldiers. We don't know what we're doing.'

'Captain, the Liosan are no different. Helmed and armed doesn't make an army. They are conscripts – I could see as much the first time.' He chewed on the thought and then added, 'Soft.'

'You saying they don't want any of this?'

'Like us,' he replied, 'they have no choice. We're in a war that began long ago, and it has never ended, Captain.'

'Pithy says they look no different from the Tiste Andii, barring their snowy skin.'

He shrugged. 'Why should that matter? It's all down to disagreeing about how things should be.'

'We can't win, can we?'

He glanced at her. 'Among mortals, every victory is temporary. In the end, we all lose.'

She spat on to the white sand. 'You ain't cheering me at all, sir. If we ain't got no hope of winning against 'em, what's the point?'

'Ever won a scrap, Captain? Ever stood over the corpses of your enemy? No? When you do, come find me. Come tell me how sweet victory tastes.' He lifted the sword and pointed down to the breach. 'You can win even when you lose. Because, even in losing, you might still succeed in making your point. In saying that you refuse the way they want it.'

'Well now, that makes me feel better.'

'I can't do the rousing speeches, Captain.'

'I noticed.'

'Those words sound hollow, all of them. In fact, I do not believe that I have ever heard a commander or ruler say anything to straighten me up. Or make me want to do for them what they wanted done. So,' he said amiably, 'if I won't die for someone else, how can I ask anyone else to do so?'

'Then what're we gonna die for here?'

'For yourselves, Captain. Each and every one of you. What could be more honest than that?'

After a time, she grunted. 'I thought it was all about fighting for the soldier beside you. And all that. Not wanting to let them down, I mean.'

'What you seek not to let down, Captain, is your sense of yourself. How you see yourself, even when you see yourself through the eyes of the people around you.' He shook his head. 'I won't argue against that. So much comes down to pride, after all.'

'So, we're to hold against the Liosan – we're to hold the First Shore – out of some kind of feeling of pride?'

'I would like to hear a truly rousing speech, one day,' Yedan mused. 'Just once.' Then he sighed. 'No matter. One can't have everything, can one?'

'I see 'em – coming through!'

Yedan started walking down the slope. 'Hold back the Letherii until I need them, Captain.'

'Yes sir!'

The Liosan vanguard burst through the breach with a roar.

Seeing the shadows wheeling above the Liosan, Brevity flinched. *Dragons. That ain't fair. Just ain't.* She turned and made her way down to the Letherii legion.

They were like Pithy now. They had that thing in their eyes – Brevity could not find words to describe it. They'd fought for their lives, but not in that daily struggle to put food on the table, not in those quiet moments when the body surrendered to some illness. This was a sudden thing, a savage thing. That look she saw now, she didn't know what it was.

But she wanted some of it.

Errant's nudge, I must be mad.

*   *   *

354

Sharl had always been the older sister, the capable one. When her mother had wandered off in the way drunks did, leaving them on their own, Sharl had reached out to take in her two younger brothers.

The Shake understood the two sides of the Shore. The drawing close, the falling apart. Those sides lived in their blood, and in all the ghettos where dwelt the remnants of her people the fates washed back and forth, and sometimes it was all one could do to simply hang on.

She had led them out of childhood. But more than that, she had tried to lead them away from something else, something far crueller. The sense of failure that hung thick in the neighbourhood, the kind of failure that slunk through alleys with drawn knives, that stepped over bodies lying in the rubbish. The kind of failure that unleashed hatred upon those who would seek a better life, those who would dare rise above their wretched station.

She had seen a clever boy beaten to death outside her shelter. By his cousins.

Letherii missions sent people into the communities. Building roads out, roads to take the Shake away from their misery. It was pointless. Sharl had seen as much, again and again. Outsiders never understood how a people could eat themselves from the inside out.

She was thinking about that as she set her boots in the sand and adjusted the heavy pike in her hands. Flanked by her brothers, with all of the Shake formed up to face this enemy of strangers. They stood on the First Shore, bathed in the eerie rain of Lightfall, and she wondered if this was to be the last moment for her and the boys. How quickly would her family vanish from the world of the living? Which of them would be the first to fall? Which the last?

I'm scared. By the deeps, I am scared.

Capable Sharl, oh, see how that lie shines on this day. I will try to keep them alive. I will do all I can.

Mother, they said they found your body in a ditch outside the town. Where were you going? What road were you building?

'Casel, Oruth, I love you both.'

She felt their eyes as they looked upon her, but she held her gaze fixed on the breach.

Someone shouted, 'Here they come!' But the cry was unnecessary, as the wound split to the first spear points, and the Liosan surged out with terrifying howls. A tall warrior was in the lead. His face twisted, his eyes lit like fire, his mouth stretched open as he brought up his spear.

He was staring at Sharl, who stood opposite as he lunged forward.

She would have run if a path were open to her. She would have fallen to her knees if mercy were possible. She would have shouted, pleaded for an end to this terrible need to fight, to kill. She would have done anything to end this.

Her brothers screamed, and those cries were so raw with terror that Sharl felt buffeted, battered by this instant of utter, horrifying vulnerability—

Mother, weaving, stumbling down the road. Her clothes reeking, her breaths a wet rattle.

The Shake cannot run from themselves.

'Sharl!'

She lifted the pike at the last moment. The warrior had not even noticed the weapon, or its deadly length. Even as he lifted his spear, the broad iron head took him just beneath his sternum.

The impact rocked her back, thundered through her bones.

The surprise in his face made her want to weep, so childlike, so helpless.

His sagging weight pulled the pike down. She tore it free, her breaths coming so fast the world was spinning. *He didn't see it. How could he not have seen it?*

All at once there was fighting along the line, spreading out from the centre. The Liosan were trying to push them back. Their fury deafened her. They fought like rabid dogs. She stabbed out again and again with the pike. The point scored off shields, was batted aside by bronze-sheathed shafts. Liosan ducked past it, only to be met by the hacking swords of her brothers.

Piss drenched the inside of her left thigh – *shame, oh, shame!*

They yielded a step – the entire line – as if by command. But she heard nothing beyond the roar engulfing her, the clash of weapons, the grunts and gasps. This was a tide, driving them back, and like the sand beneath them the Shake were crumbling.

The pike's long shaft was slick with blood. The point was wrapped in gore.

The muscles of her forearms and shoulders burning, she raised the weapon once more, saw a face, and stabbed into it. Edge grating past teeth, biting into the back of a mouth, the flaring flanges slicing through cheeks. Blood poured from the Liosan's nose, misted up into his eyes. He snapped his head back, choking, dropping his weapons as he fell to his knees. His hands went to his shattered mouth, seeking to hold in place the dangling lower jaw, the flaps of tongue.

Casel lunged low and pushed his sword's point into the Liosan's neck.

And then her brother was falling. An animal cry came from his throat and he twisted as a Liosan advanced to stand over him, grinding her spear point down through Casel, who writhed like a pinned eel.

Sharl swung the pike, and she screamed as the point slashed the Liosan just under her chin, opening her windpipe.

Hands took Casel's ankles and dragged him back. A stranger came up to take her brother's place.

No – not a stranger—

A marled sword blade swung past her, caught a Liosan closing on her. Sliced through him from shoulder to hip. The backswing sent the top half of a head and helm spinning away. A third swing severed two hands gripping a spear. Three fallen Liosan, opening a gap.

'Follow me,' Yedan Derryg said, stepping forward.

And around Sharl and Oruth, the Watch drew up, huge soldiers in heavy armour, blackened shields like an expanding wall, long-bladed swords lashing out.

As they advanced, they carried Sharl and her brother with them.

Into the face of the Liosan.

Pithy reached Brevity. Her face was flushed, slick with sweat, and there was blood on her sword. Gasping, she said, 'Two companies of Letherii, sister – to relieve the centre of the Shake line. They've been savaged.'

'He's pushing straight for the wound,' Brevity said. 'Is that right? That's Yedan down there, isn't it? Him and half his Watch – gods, it's as if the Liosan are melting away.'

'Two companies, Brev! We're going to split the enemy on this side, but that means we need to push right up to the fuckin' hole, right? And then hold it for as long as we need to cut 'em all down on the flanks.'

Licking dry lips, Brevity nodded. 'I'll lead them.'

'Yes, I'm relieving ya here, love – I'm ready to drop. So, what're you waitin' for? Go!'

Pithy watched Brev lead a hundred Letherii down to the berm. Her heart was finally slowing its mad jackrabbit dance. Jamming the point of her sword in the sand, she turned to regard the remaining Letherii.

Nods answered her. They were ready. They'd tasted it and they wanted to taste it again. *Yes, I know. It terrifies us. It makes us sick inside. But it's like painting the world in gold and diamonds.*

From the breach the roar was unceasing, savage as a storm against cliffs.

Dear ocean, then, call my soul. I would swim the waters again. Let me swim the waters again.

CHAPTER THIRTEEN

There was a love once
I shaped it with my hands
Until in its forms
I saw sunlight and streams
And earthy verges sweet with grass

It fit easily into my pack
And made peaceful
The years of wandering
Through forests in retreat
And down the river's tragic flow

On the day we broke
Upon the shore of a distant land
I fled cold and bereft
Fighting curtains of ash
Up through the snows of the pass

In the heaps of spoil
Among an enemy victorious
My love floundered
In the cracked company of kin
Broken down blow upon blow

And now as my days lower
Into the sleep of regret
I dream of fresh clay
Finding these old hands
Where the wind sings of love

Forests in Retreat
Fisher kel Tath

THE PASSAGE OF THOUSANDS OF HOBNAILED BOOTS HAD WORN through the thin grasses, lifting into the air vast clouds of dust. The breeze had fallen off and, coming down from the north, tracked the columns at virtually the same turgid pace, blinding them to the world.

The horses were growing gaunt, their heads hanging, their eyes dull. When Aranict turned her mount to follow Brys, the beast felt sluggish beneath her, slow to canter. They rode out to the west side of the marching troops and made their way back down the line's ragged length. Dusty faces lifted here and there to watch them pass, but mostly the soldiers kept their gazes on the ground before them, too weary to answer any stir of curiosity.

She knew how they felt. She had done her share of plodding on foot, although without the added burden of a pack heavy with armour and weapons. They had marched hard to draw up close to the Bolkando Evertine Legion, who in turn had already fallen a third of a day behind the Perish. Shield Anvil Tanakalian was if anything proving harsher than Krughava in driving the Grey Helms. Their pace was punishing, sparing no thought for their putative allies.

Brys was worried, and so was Queen Abrastal. Was this nothing more than the lust for glory, the fierce zeal of fanatics? Or was something more unpleasant at work here? Aranict had her suspicions, but she was not yet willing to voice them, not even to Brys. Tanakalian had not been pleased with the Adjunct's insistence that Gesler take overall command. Perhaps he intended to make the position irrelevant, at least in so far as regards the Perish. *But if so, why would he do that?*

They pulled free of the last block of wagons and through the drifting dust they saw the rearguard, a dozen Bluerose lancers, drawn up around three figures on foot. Aranict rose in her saddle and looked westward – the K'Chain Che'Malle were out there, she knew. Out of sight yet still moving in parallel with the Letherii. She wondered when next Gesler, Stormy and Kalyth would visit them. *More arguments, more confusion thicker than these clouds of dust.*

She shook her head. *Never mind all that.* Since the morning strangers had been tracking them. *And they've just bitten our tail.* Aranict returned her attention to the three dishevelled newcomers. Two women and one man. They'd arrived with little evident gear or supplies, and as Aranict drew closer she could see their sorry state.

But they were not wearing uniforms. *Not Malazan deserters, then. Or worse: survivors.*

Brys slowed his horse, glanced back at her, and, seeing his relief, she nodded. He'd feared the same. But in some ways, she realized, this was even more disturbing, as if the Bonehunters had truly vanished, their fate unknown and possibly unknowable. Like ghosts.

She had to struggle against thinking of them as being already dead. In her mind rose visions of hollowed eye sockets, withered skin splitting over bones – the image was horrifying, yet it haunted her. She could see the edge of the Glass Desert off to the east, heat shimmering in a wall, rising like a barrier beyond which the soil lost all life.

They reined in. Brys studied the three strangers for a moment, and then said, 'Welcome.'

The woman in the front turned her head and spoke to her comrades. *'Gesros Latherii stigan thal. Ur leszt.'*

The other woman, short and plump but with the blotchy, sagging cheeks that denoted dehydration, frowned and said, *'Hegoran stig Daru?'*

'Ur hedon ap,' replied the first woman. She was taller than the other one, with shoulder-length dark brown hair. She had the eyes of someone used to pain. Facing Brys again, she said, 'Latherii Ehrlii? Are you Ehrlii speak? Are you speak Latherii?'

'Letherii,' Brys corrected. 'The language of the First Empire.'

'First Empire,' the woman repeated, matching perfectly Brys's intonation. 'Slums – er, lowborn stig— dialect. Ehrlitan.'

The plump woman snapped, *'Turul berys? Turul berys?'*

The first woman sighed. 'Please. Water?'

Brys gestured to the preda commanding the lancers. 'Give them something to drink. They're in a bad way.'

'Commander, our own supplies—'

'Do it, Preda. Three more in our army won't make much difference either way. And find a cutter – the sun has roasted them.' He nodded to the first woman. 'I am Commander Brys Beddict. We march to war, I'm afraid. You are welcome to travel with us for as long as you desire, but once we enter enemy territory, unless you remain with us, I cannot guarantee your safety.'

Of course he didn't call himself a prince. Just a commander. Noble titles still sat uneasily with him.

The woman was slowly nodding. 'You march south.'

'For now,' he replied.

'And then?'

'East.'

She turned to the other woman. *'Gesra ilit.'*

'Ilit? Korl mestr al'ahamd.'

The woman faced Brys. 'I named Faint. We go with you, *tu*— please. *Ilit*. East.'

Aranict cleared her throat. The inside of her mouth was stinging, had been for days. She was itchy beneath her soiled garments. She spent a moment lighting a stick of rustleaf, knowing that Brys had twisted in his saddle and was now observing her. Through a brief veil of smoke

360

she met his eyes and said, 'The younger one's a mage. The man – there's something odd about him, as if he's only in the guise of a human, but it's a guise that is partly torn away. Behind it . . .' She shrugged, drew on her stick. 'Like a wolf pretending to sleep. He has iron in his hands.'

Brys glanced over, frowned.

'In the bones,' she amended. 'He could probably punch his way through a keep wall.'

'*Iron*, Atri-Ceda? Are you sure? How can that be?'

'I don't know. I might even be wrong. But you can see, he carries no weapons, and those knuckles are badly scarred. There's a taint of the demonic about him—' She cut herself off, as Faint was now speaking quickly to the young mage.

'*Hed henap vil nen? Ul stig "Atri-Ceda". Ceda ges kerallu. Ust kellan varad harada unan y? Thekel edu.*'

Eyes fixed on Aranict and everyone was silent for a moment.

With narrowed gaze the young sorceress addressed Faint. '*Kellan varad. V'ap gerule y mest.*'

Whatever she'd said did not seem to warrant a reply from Faint, who now spoke to Aranict. 'We are lost. Seek Holds. Way home. Darujhistan. Do you *kerall*— er, are you, ah, caster magic? Kellan Varad? High Mage?'

Aranict glanced at Brys, who now answered her earlier shrug with one of his own. She was silent for a moment, thinking, and then she said, 'Yes, Faint. Atri-Ceda. High Mage. I am named Aranict.' She cocked her head and asked, 'The Letherii you speak, it is high diction, is it not? Where did you learn it?'

Faint shook her head. 'City. Seven Cities. Ehrlitan. Lowborn tongue, in slums. You speak like whore.'

Aranict pulled hard on her rustleaf, and then smiled. 'This should be fun.'

The ghost of Sweetest Sufferance held up her clay pipe, squinted at the curls of smoke rising from it. '*See that, Faint? That's the perfect breath of every life-giving god there ever was. Holier than incense. Why, if priests filled their braziers with rustleaf, the temples would be packed, worshippers like salted fish in a barrel—*'

'Worshippers?' Faint snorted. 'Addicts, you mean.'

'*Variations on a theme, darling. You've stopped wincing with every breath, I see.*'

Faint leaned back on the heap of blankets. 'You heard Precious. That Aranict is tapping Elder magic—'

'*And something else, too, she said. Newborn, she called it – what in Hood's name is that supposed to mean?*'

'I don't care. All I know is I've stopped aching everywhere.'

'Me too.'

Sweetest puffed contentedly for a time, and then said, '*They were nervous round Amby though, weren't they?*' She glanced over at the silent man where he sat close to the tent's entrance. '*Like they never seen a Bole before, right, Amby?*'

The man gave no sign of having heard her, which Faint found something of a relief. *He must think I've gone mad, having a one-way conversation like this. Then again, he might be right. Something snapped in me, I suppose.*

Sweetest Sufferance rolled her eyes at Faint.

'Did you see the tack on that commander's horse,' Faint asked in a low voice. 'A different rig from what the lancers had. The set-up was different, I mean. That over-tug inside the horn. The stirrup angle—'

'*What're you going on about, Faint?*'

'The prince's horse, idiot. He had his tack worked in the Malazan style.'

Sweetest Sufferance frowned at Faint. '*Coincidence?*' She waved a hand. '*Sorry, pretend I didn't say that. So, that is strange, isn't it? Can't think the Malazans ever got this far. But maybe they did. Oh, well, they must have, since you saw what you saw—*'

'Your head's spinning, isn't it?'

'*I might crawl out and throw up soon,*' she replied. '*Amby, don't be blocking that flap, right? Now, Malazan tack. What do you think that means?*'

'If Precious and Aranict can work out a way of talking to each other, we might find out.'

'*We ever use the Holds, Faint?*'

'Not on purpose. No. Master Quell had some stories, though. The early days, when things were a lot wilder than what we go through – when they didn't know how to control or even pick their gates. Every now and then, one of the carriages would plunge into some world nobody even knew existed. Got into lots of trouble, too. Quell once told me about one realm where there was virtually no magic at all. The shareholders who ended up there had a Hood's hole of a time getting back.'

'*Yeah, we had it easy, didn't we?*'

'Until our master got eviscerated, yes, Sweetie.'

'*You know, I doubt Precious is going to get much that's useful from that High Mage.*'

'Why do you say that?'

Sweetest shrugged. '*It's not like we got anything to offer them, is it? Not like we can bargain or make a deal.*'

'Sure we can. Get us back home and the Trygalle will offer 'em a free delivery. Anything, anywhere.'

'You think so? Why? I can't think we're that important, Faint.'

'You ain't read all the articles, have you? If we're in trouble, we can bargain with the full backing of the Guild, and they will honour those bargains to the letter.'

'*Really? Well now, they know how to take care of their share-holders. I'm impressed.*'

'You have to hand it to them,' Faint agreed. 'I mean, excepting when we're torn off the carriage on a run and left behind to get ripped apart and eaten. Or cut down in a deal that goes sour. Or we run up a whopping tab in the local pit. Or some alien disease takes us down. Or we lose a limb or three, get head-bash addled, or—'

'*Giant lizards drop outa the sky and kill us, yes. Be quiet, Faint. You're not helping things at all.*'

'What I'm doing,' Faint said, closing her eyes, 'is trying not to think about those runts, and the hag that took them.'

'*It's not like they were shareholders, dearie.*'

Ah, now that's my Sweetest. 'True enough. Still. We got stretched out plain to see that day, Sweetest, and the rack's tightening still, at least in my mind. I just don't feel good about it.'

'*Think I'll head out and throw up now,*' Sweetest said.

Slipping past Amby was easy, Faint saw, for a ghost.

Precious Thimble rubbed at her face, which had gone slightly numb. 'How are you doing this?' she asked. 'You're pushing words into my head.'

'The Empty Hold is awake once more,' Aranict replied. 'It is the Hold of the Unseen, the realms of the mind. Perception, knowledge, illusion, delusion. Faith, despair, curiosity, fear. Its weapon is the false belief in chance, in random fate.'

Precious was shaking her head. 'Listen. Chance is real. You can't say it isn't. And mischance, too. You said your army got caught in a fight nobody was looking for – what was that?'

'I dread to think,' Aranict replied. 'But I assure you it was not blind chance. In any case, your vocabulary has improved dramatically. Your comprehension is sound—'

'So you can stop shoving stuff in, right?'

Aranict nodded. 'Drink. Rest now.'

'I have too many questions for that, Atri-Ceda. Why is the Hold empty?'

'Because it is home to all which cannot be possessed, cannot be owned. And so too is the *throne* within the Hold empty, left eternally vacant. Because the very nature of rule is itself an illusion, a conceit and the product of a grand conspiracy. To have a ruler one must choose to be ruled over, and that forces notions of inequity to the fore, until they

363

become, well, formalized. Made central to education, made essential as a binding force in society, until everything exists to prop up those in power. The Empty Throne reminds us of all that. Well, some of us, anyway.'

Precious Thimble frowned. 'What did you mean when you said the Hold was *awake* once more?'

'The Wastelands are so called because they are damaged—'

'I know that – I can't do a damned thing here.'

'Nor could I, until recently.' The Atri-Ceda plucked out a stick of rolled rustleaf and quickly lit it. Smoke thickened the air in the tent. 'Imagine a house burning down,' she said, 'leaving nothing but heaps of ash. That's what happened to magic in the Wastelands. Will it ever come back? Ever heal? Maybe that's what we're seeing here, but the power doesn't just show up. It grows, and I think now it has to start in a certain way. Beginning with . . . wandering. And then come the Holds, like plants taking root.' Aranict gestured. 'Much wandering in these Wastelands of late, yes? Powerful forces, so much violence, so much *will*.'

'And from Holds to warrens,' muttered Precious, nodding to herself.

'Ah, the Malazans speak of this, too. These *warrens*. If they are destined to appear here, they have yet to do so, Precious Thimble. And is there not concern that they are ill?'

'Malazans,' Precious hissed. 'You'd think they *invented* warrens, the way they go on. Things got sickly for a time, sure, but then that went away.'

'The Holds have always been the source of magical power on this continent,' Aranict said, shrugging. 'In many ways, we Letherii are very conservative, but I am beginning to think there are other reasons for why there has been no change here. The K'Chain Che'Malle remain. And the Forkrul Assail dominate the lands to the east. Even the creatures known as the T'lan Imass are among us now, and without question the Hold of Ice is in the ascendant, meaning the Jaghut have returned.' She shook her head. 'The Malazans speak of war among the gods. I fear that what is coming will prove more terrible than any of us can imagine.'

Precious licked her lips, glanced away. The tent seemed to have closed round her, like a death-shroud being drawn tight. She shivered. 'We just want to go home.'

'I do not know how I can help you,' Aranict said. 'The Holds are not realms one willingly travels through. Even drawing upon their power invites chaos and madness. They are places of treachery, of deadly traps and pits leading down into unknown realms. Worse, the more powerful rituals demand blood.'

Precious gathered herself, met the Atri-Ceda's gaze. 'In the east,' she said. 'Something's there – I can feel it. A thing of vast power.'

'Yes,' Aranict said, nodding.

'It is where you are going, isn't it? This army and the war to come. You are going to fight for that power, to take it for yourself.'

'Not quite, Precious Thimble. That power – we mean to set it free.'

'And if you do? What happens then?'

'We don't know.'

'You keep speaking of the Malazans. Are they here? Are they one of the armies marching to this war?'

Aranict seemed about to say one thing, then changed her mind and said, 'Yes.'

Precious sat back on her haunches. 'I am from One-Eye Cat, a city of Genabackis. We were conquered by the Malazans. Winning is all that matters to them, Atri-Ceda. They will lie. They will backstab. Whatever you see on the surface, don't believe it. Don't. With them, nothing is as it seems, not ever.'

'They are a complicated people—'

Precious snorted. 'Their first emperor was where it all started. The sleight of hand, the deadly misdirection – everything the Malazan Empire became infamous for started with *him*. And though he's now dead and gone, nothing has changed. Tell your commander, Aranict. Tell him. The Malazans – they'll betray you. *They'll betray you.*'

Brys glanced up as she entered the tent. 'You were able to speak to her?'

'I was, after some curious work – it's as I said, the power of the Holds ever grows. I was never before able to manipulate the Empty Hold the way I did this night. In fact –' she settled down on the bed mat, started pulling off her boots – 'I don't feel very good about what I had to do. By the time I was done not even her innermost thoughts were hidden from me. I feel . . . sullied.'

He moved closer, slipped an arm round her. 'Was there no other way?'

'I don't know. Maybe. But this was the quickest. She had some interesting opinions on the Malazans.'

'Oh?'

'Doesn't trust them. Her people didn't fare well during the Malazan conquest of Genabackis. Yet for all that resentment, a part of her recognizes that some good came of it in the end. The enforcement of laws and justice, and so on. Hasn't dulled her hatred, though.'

'Trust,' Brys mused. 'Always a difficult issue.'

'Well,' Aranict said, 'Tavore *is* hiding something.'

'I believe what she is hiding is her awareness of just how wretched her chances are, Aranict.'

'But that's just it,' Aranict said. 'From what I gleaned from Precious Thimble, the Malazans *never* do something at which they're likely to fail. So if Tavore's chances look as bad as we all seem to think, what are we missing?'

'Now that is an interesting question,' Brys admitted.

'Anyway,' Aranict said, 'they'll be coming with us to Kolanse.'

'Very well. Can we trust them?'

Aranict settled back on the mat with a heavy sigh. 'No.'

'Ah. Will that prove a problem?'

'I doubt it. If Precious Thimble attempts to draw upon a Hold, she'll get her head ripped off by all that raw power. Too young, and doesn't know what she's doing.'

'Hmm. Could such a personal disaster put anyone else at risk?'

'It could, Brys. Good thing you brought me along, isn't it?'

He lay down beside her. 'Whatever happened to the shy, nervous woman I made my Atri-Ceda?'

'You seduced her, you fool.'

'Errant's push!' She sank down on to her knees, head hanging, her breath coming in gasps.

Spax drew up his leggings, stepped away from where she knelt close to the tent's back wall. 'Best dessert there is,' he said. 'Better run off now. I have to see your mother, and if she catches a glimpse of you anywhere near here, she'll know.'

'What if she does?' Spultatha snapped. 'It's not as if she's opened *her* legs to you, is it?'

He snorted. 'Like a royal vault, she is.'

'You're not good-looking enough. And you smell.'

'I smell like a Gilk White Face Barghast, woman, and you've hardly complained.'

She rose, straightening her tunic. 'I am now.'

'Your mother is growing ever more protective of her daughters,' he said, scratching with both hands at his beard. 'Spirits below, this dust gets everywhere.'

Spultatha slipped past him without another word. He watched her head off into the night, and then made his way round the royal train's equipment tent. Opposite waited the queen's tent, two guards stationed out front.

'Is she ready for me?' Spax asked as he approached.

'Too late for that,' one replied, and the other grunted a laugh. They stepped clear to allow him passage. He went inside, and then through to the inner chamber.

'Can she walk?'

'Highness?'

Abrastal drank down the last of her wine, lifted up the goblet. 'My third in a row. I'm not looking forward to this, and having to listen to one of my own daughters squeal like a myrid with a herder's hand up its arse has hardly improved my mood.'

'She's untutored in the ways of real men,' Spax responded. 'Where do you want me for this?'

Abrastal gestured to one side of the tent. 'There. Weapons drawn.'

The Warchief raised his brows, but said nothing as he walked over to where she had indicated.

'This will be a kind of gate,' Abrastal said, folding her legs as she settled back in her chair. 'Things could come through, and to make matters worse it'll be hard to make out what we're seeing – there will be a veil between us. If the situation sours, it can be torn, either by whatever is on the other side, or by you going through.'

'Going through? Highness—'

'Be quiet. You are in my employ and you will do what you're told.'

Swamp shit, we really did put her in a foul mood. Oh well. He drew his long knives and crouched down. 'If I'd known I would have brought my axes.'

'What do your shamans tell you, Spax, about your Barghast gods?'

He blinked. 'Why, nothing, Firehair. Why should they? I'm the Warchief. I deal in matters of war. All that other rubbish is for them to worry over.'

'And are they?'

'Are they what?'

'Worried.'

'They're warlocks, they're always worried.'

'Spax.'

He grimaced. 'The Barghast gods are idiots. Like sixteen children locked in a small room. For days. They'll start eating each other next.'

'So there are sixteen of them?'

'What? No. That was a just a number I threw out – spirits below, Firehair, you keep taking me literally – I'm Spax, remember? I make things up, to entertain myself. You want me to talk about my gods? Well, they're worse than me. They probably made *themselves* up.'

'What do your shamans say?'

Spax scowled. 'I don't care what they say!'

'Is it that bad?'

He shrugged. 'Could be our gods suddenly get smart. Could be they realize that their best chance of surviving what's to come is to keep their heads down. Could be they can cure the world's ills with one sweet kiss, too.' He held up his knives. 'But I ain't holding my breath.'

'Don't pray to them, Spax. Not tonight, not now. Do you understand me?'

'I can't even remember the last time I prayed to them, Highness.'

Abrastal poured herself another goblet of wine. 'Grab those furs over there. You'll need them.'

Furs? 'Firehair, I—'

A stain darkened the space in the centre of chamber, and an instant later bitter cold air spilled out, frosting everything in sight. The Warchief's lungs burned with every breath. Pottery stacked against one wall cracked, then shattered, and what it contained fell out in frozen lumps.

Through pained eyes, Spax saw shapes take form within the gelid stain. In the forefront, facing Abrastal, was a short, curvaceous woman – young, he thought, though it was difficult to be sure. *Felash. Is that her? Yes, must be her, who else would it be?* Upon her left stood a taller woman, though the only detail he could make out was what appeared to be a glittering diamond set in her brow, from which extraordinary colours now flowed.

Then a shape coalesced to the Fourteenth Daughter's right. Unnaturally tall, dressed in black, the hint of chain armour beneath the slashed cloak. A hood was drawn back, revealing a gaunt, demonic face. Stained tusks rose from the lower jaw, thrusting outward like curved knives. The pits of its eyes were dark. *A damned Jaghut. Leaving me to wonder just how many more of my childhood terrors are real?*

The Jaghut seemed to study Abrastal for a time, and then the head turned and Spax found himself staring into those lifeless pits. Withered lips peeled back, and the apparition spoke. *'Barghast.'* Voiced as if it was an insult.

Spax growled a low curse. Said, 'I am Gilk. We have many enemies, all of whom fear us. You are welcome to be one of them, Jaghut.'

'Mother,' said the daughter. 'I see you are well.'

Abrastal tipped her goblet. A solid lump of wine fell out. 'Is this really necessary? I think I am frozen to my chair.'

'Omtose Phellack, Mother – the Hold's ancient king has returned. He stands beside me.'

'He's dead.'

The Jaghut faced the queen again. 'I have heard better insults from my pets, mortal.' He then pointed at Spax. 'Speaking of pets, what do you intend to do with yours?'

'A precaution,' Abrastal said, shrugging.

The other woman, the one Spax did not know, then spoke. 'Highness, only a few days ago this Jaghut here bit off the face of a Forkrul Assail.' She edged a step back to take in the Barghast. 'Do not clash those blades, warrior – they will shatter.'

Felash said, 'Mother, we have found a new ally in our . . . endeavours. The king of the Hold of Ice now stands with us.'

'Why?'

The other woman said, 'I don't think they like the Forkrul Assail, Highness.'

'You must be Captain Shurq Elalle,' the queen said. 'I have heard interesting things about you, but that will have to wait until another time. Fourteenth Daughter, are you once again upon the seas?'

'We are. On a Ship of the Dead. You think *you're* cold?' One hand fluttered. 'We're less than two weeks from the Teeth.'

'What of the Perish fleet?'

Felash shook her head. 'No sign. We must assume they have arrived – whether a blockade now exists . . .' she shrugged. 'Mother, be careful. The Forkrul Assail know we are coming – all of us. *They know.*'

'Can we maintain this line of communication?'

'Not much longer,' Felash replied. 'Once we draw closer to the Assail's demesne, their Hold will dominate.'

Spax snorted. 'Even against the king of the Hold of Ice? Now, how pathetic is that?'

The Jaghut faced him once more. 'When Draconus stepped on to this world, he missed a few of your kind underfoot. He has grown careless in his old age. When next you and I meet, Barghast, we shall have words on the matter.'

'Have you a name, Jaghut?' Spax asked. 'I want to know who to curse. I want the name of this miserable rotting carcass I'm looking at right now.'

The mouth stretched once more. 'Can you not guess, Barghast? As you squat shivering in my breath?'

Felash said, 'Mother, are you sure you want to go on with this? Against the forces now gathering, we're *nothing.*'

'I think,' said Abrastal, 'the time has come to be more forthright regarding our allies here in the Wastelands. We seem to have acquired a force of, well, lizards. Large, powerful, well armed. They call themselves the K'Chain Che'Malle, and they are commanded by two Malazans—'

She stopped them, since the Jaghut had begun laughing.

The sound reached into Spax's bones until he felt them rattling like frozen sticks. His glare, fixed upon the Jaghut, suddenly widened. *His breath? But how – no, yes, see that cloak, see that cowl.* He straightened, chest swelling. 'I have never feared you,' he said.

Hood ceased laughing, regarded the Barghast. 'Of course not, Warchief Spax of the Gilk. But then, once I am known to you, fear is irrelevant, isn't it?'

'Especially when you're already dead!'

One long, bony finger lifted into view, wagged at the Warchief. 'Ah, but how would you know? Imagine dying, and then finding yourself asking, "What now?" The day you stand on the wrong side of death, Spax, come and find me, and in the bitter truth of equals you and I shall discuss *real* fear.' Hood laughed a second time.

Moments later all three apparitions were gone. The biting chill remained, mists roiling in the chamber. Queen Abrastal fixed Spax with a hard stare. 'What was all that about, Warchief?'

He scowled. 'I don't for an instant doubt that captain's claim. Bit off an Assail's face, did he? I'm surprised it wasn't its whole damned head.' Spax fought off another shiver. 'Too many swords in the fire, Highness. Things are going to break. Badly.'

'Second thoughts?'

'More than I dare to count.' Breath gusted from his nostrils. 'It's time to offer counsel, whether you like it or not. I know you are committed to this venture, and nothing I can say will dissuade you – we're about to wage war against the Forkrul Assail.' He studied her with narrowed eyes. 'You've wanted that for some time. I see the truth of that. But listen, there are times when a course decided upon gathers a power of its own. A momentum that sweeps us all along. Firehair, this river we're on seems calm enough for now. But the current grows and grows, and soon even if we seek the safety of shore, it will be too late.'

'A fine speech, Spax. The Gilk Warchief advises caution. So noted.' Abruptly she rose. 'My Fourteenth Daughter is not one you could tumble behind the equipment tent. That said, I do not think she invited that undead Jaghut into our alliance – rather, I suspect she had little say in the matter.'

'And the current grows bold.'

She eyed him. 'Journey to the Letherii camp. Inform Prince Brys of this turn of events.'

'Now?'

'Now.'

'What of the Perish?'

The queen frowned, and then shook her head. 'I will not see one of our few fit horses run to death just to bring word to the Grey Helms. I don't know what they're trying to prove with that torrid pace—'

'I do.'

'Indeed? Very well, Spax, let's hear it.'

'They seek to make us irrelevant, Firehair. You, Brys, and especially the K'Chain Che'Malle.'

'They want the glory for themselves?'

'Shield Anvil Tanakalian,' he said, adding a disgusted grunt. 'He's young, with too much to prove. But that is not what is bothering me,

Highness. I no longer trust his motives – I cannot say if the goal he seeks is at all related to the Adjunct's. These Grey Helms, they are the avatars of war, but it is not the war between peoples that they serve, it is the war of nature against humans.'

'Then he is a greater fool than we can even imagine,' Abrastal said. 'He cannot win that war. Nature cannot win – it never could.'

Spax was silent for a moment, and then in a low voice he said, 'I believe that it is the other way round, Highness. This is a war *we* cannot win. All of our victories are temporary – no, illusory. In the end we lose, because, even in winning, we still *lose*.'

Abrastal walked from the chamber. Brows lifting, Spax followed her.

Outside, under the green-lit night sky, past the two guards.

She continued down the centre aisle between the officers' tents, out past the kitchen camps, the offal pits, the latrine rows. *Like peeling back the orderly façade, down now among the foul rubbish of our leavings. Ah, Firehair, I am not so blind as to miss the meaning of this journey.*

When at last she halted, they were beyond the northeast pickets. For Spax to make his way to the distant Letherii encampment, he need only strike out northward, angling slightly to the west. He could see the fitful glow from the prince's position. *Like us, they're running out of things to burn.*

Abrastal faced east, to where just beyond a ribbon of white bones the Glass Desert was a sea of sharp, glittering stars lying as if scattered in death, bathed in emerald light. 'The Wastelands,' she murmured.

'Highness?'

'Who won here, Spax?'

'As we can see. No one won.'

'And in the Glass Desert?'

He squinted. 'It hurts the eye, Firehair. Blood was spilled there, I think. Immortal blood.'

'Would you throw the crime at the feet of humans?'

He grunted. 'Now you split reeds, Highness. It is the wilful mind that is Nature's enemy, for out of that wilfulness comes arrogance—'

'And contempt. Warchief, it seems we will all face a terrible choice, then. Are we worth saving? You? Me? My children? My people?'

'Do you now waver in your resolve?'

She faced him. 'Do you?'

Spax scratched his beard with both hands. 'All that Krughava said when she was ousted. I have considered it, again and again.' He grimaced. 'Now it seems that even Spax of the Gilk can revise his views. A time of miracles to be sure. I will, I think, choose to see it this way: if nature must win in the end, then let the death of our kind be sweet and slow. So sweet, so slow, that we do not even notice. Let us fade and dwindle in our tyranny, from world to continent, from continent to country, from country to city, city to neighbourhood, to home, to the ground under our feet, and finally down to the pointless triumphs inside each of our skulls.'

'These are not the words of a warrior.'

He heard the harsh emotion in her tone and nodded in the darkness. 'If it is true and the Grey Helms seek to be the swords of nature's vengeance, then the Shield Anvil has missed the point. Since when is nature interested in revenge? Look around.' He waved a hand. 'The grass grows back where it can. The birds nest where they can. The soil breathes when it can. It just goes on, Highness, the only way it knows how to – with what's left.'

'The same as us,' she said.

'Maybe this is what Krughava could see so clearly, and Tanakalian can't. When we war against nature, we war against ourselves. There is no distinction, no dividing line, no enemy. We devour everything in a lust for *self*-destruction. As if that is intelligence's only gift.'

'Only curse, you mean.'

He shrugged. 'I suppose there is a gift is in being able to see what we're doing, even as we do it. And in seeing, we come to understand.'

'Knowledge we choose not to use, Spax.'

'I have no answer to that, Firehair. Before our inaction, I am as helpless as the next man. But it may be that we *all* feel that way. Smart as we are individually, together we become stupid, appallingly stupid.' He shrugged again. 'Even the gods cannot find a way through this. And even if they had, we'd not listen, would we?'

'I see her face, Spax.'

Her face. Yes. 'It's not much of a face, is it? So plain, so . . . lifeless.'

Abrastal flinched. 'Find another word, please.'

'Bleak, then. But she makes no effort, does she? Nothing regal in her clothes. Not a single item of jewellery. No paint on her face, or her lips, and her hair – so short, so . . . ah, Highness, why does any of that even bother me? But it does, and I don't know why.'

'Nothing . . . regal,' Abrastal mused. 'If what you say is true – and yes, so it seems to me as well – then why, when I look upon her, do I see . . . well, something . . .'

That I did not see before. Or that I did not understand. She ever grows in my mind, this Adjunct Tavore. 'Noble,' he said.

She gasped. 'Yes!'

'She doesn't fight against nature, does she?'

'Is it just that? Is that all it is?'

Spax shook his head. 'Highness, you say you keep seeing her face. It is the same for me. I am haunted and I do not know why. It floats behind my eyes and I fix upon it again and again, as if I'm waiting. Waiting to see the expression it will assume, that one expression of truth. It's coming. I know it is, and so I look upon her and I cannot stop looking upon her.'

'She has made us all lost,' Abrastal said. 'I did not anticipate I would feel so troubled, Spax. It's not in my nature. Like some prophet of old, she has indeed led us out into the wilderness.'

'Until she leads us home.'

Abrastal turned and stepped closer, her eyes glittering. 'And will she?'

'In that nobility, Firehair,' he replied in a whisper, 'I find faith.' *Against the despair. As did Krughava. And in the Adjunct's small hand, like a wispy seed, there is compassion.*

He watched her eyes widen, and then her hand was behind his head, pulling him close. One hard kiss, and then she pushed him away. 'It's getting cold,' she said, setting off for camp. Over a shoulder she added, 'You should be able to reach the Letherii before dawn.'

Spax stared after her. *Very well, it seems we will do this, after all. Hood, the Lord of Death, stood before me and spoke of fear. The fear of the dead. But if the dead know fear, what hope do we have?*

Tavore, does a god stand in your shadow? Ready to offer us a gift, for the sacrifices we will make? Is this your secret, the thing that takes away all your fear? Please, lean close, and whisper it to me.

But that face, there behind his eyes, might have been as far away as the moon. And if the gods came at last to crowd round her, would they too look down, in perilous wonder, at that frail magic in the palm of her hand? Would it frighten them?

When it so frightens the rest of us?

He looked out over the Glass Desert's offering of dead stars. *Tavore, do you now shine bright among them, just one more of the fallen?* And would there come a time when her bones came crawling to this shore to join all the others? Spax, Warchief of the Gilk Barghast, shivered like a child left naked in the night, and the question pursued him as he set out for the Letherii camp.

She had always considered the notion of penance to be pathetic self-indulgence, and those that set out upon such a course, choosing isolation and abnegation in some remote cave or weathered hut, were to her mind little more than cowards. The ethics of the world belonged to society, to that fraught maelstrom of relationships, where argument and fierce emotions waged eternal war.

Yet here she sat, alone beneath a green-limned sky, with a slumbering horse her only company, and all her private arguments were slowly drifting away, as if she walked through one room after another, leaving ever further behind some regal chamber echoing with raucous debate. The irritation that was futility was finally gone, and in the silence ahead she sensed the gift of peace.

Krughava snorted. Perhaps all those hermits and aesthetes were wiser than she had ever suspected. Tanakalian now stood in her place, there at the head of the Grey Helms, and he would lead them where he willed. She had been caught out by the logic of his argument, and, like a wolf brought to bay by hounds, she had found herself assailed as he closed in.

Contradiction. In the rational realm, the word was a blistering condemnation. Proof of flawed logic. To expose it in an adversary's position was akin to delivering a deathblow, and she well recalled the triumphant gleam in his eyes in the instant he struck. But, she wondered now, where was the crime in that most human of capacities: to carry in one's heart a contradiction, to leave it unchallenged, immune to reconciliation; indeed, to be two people at once, each true to herself, and neither denying the presence of the other? What vast laws of cosmology were broken by this human talent? Did the universe split asunder? Did reality lose its way?

No. In fact, it seemed that the only realm wherein contradiction had any power at all was the realm of rational argument. And, Krughava admitted, she had begun to doubt that realm's self-proclaimed virtue. Of course, Tanakalian would argue that her terrible crime had led the Perish Grey Helms into crisis. Upon whose side would they stand? How could they serve more than one master? *'Will we not fight for the Wolves? Will we not fight for the Wild? Or shall we commit sacrilege by kneeling before a mere mortal woman? This crisis, Krughava, is of your own making.'* Or words to that effect.

Perhaps it was at that – of her own making. *And yet . . .* Within her there had been no conflict, no brewing storm awaiting them. She had chosen to walk at Tavore Paran's side. Together they had crossed half a world. And, Krughava had been certain, at the very end they would have remained side by side, two women against a raging conflagration. In that moment, success or failure would lose all relevance. The triumph was in the stance. *In the defiance. Because this is the essence of life itself. Human and wild, in that moment we are all the same. Contradiction, Tanakalian? No. I would show you this final gift. Human and wild, we are the same. I would have shown the wolf gods the truth of this. Whether they liked it or not.*

And this contradiction of yours, Shield Anvil, would have vanished like a puff of smoke.

What did I seek in our faith? I sought to mend the impossible crisis that is our worship of the Wild, our worship of all that we have left behind and to which we can never return. I sought reconciliation. An

374

acceptance of the brutal contradiction of our human lives.

But then the Adjunct had rejected her. There was an old saying among the Perish that a room full of women was a knife-seller's vision of paradise. *'There will be betrayal.'* Oh yes indeed. Betrayal. So unexpected, so hurtful that Tavore might as well have slit open Krughava's throat, watched her bleed out on the floor of the command tent.

And now the Mortal Sword was lost.

Contradiction. You would choose only the worthy to embrace, Shield Anvil? Then what you do is not an embrace, sir. It is a reward. And if you are to taste the flavour of naught but virtuous souls, how will you ever find the strength to best the flaws within your own soul? Shield Anvil Tanakalian, you are headed into difficult times.

She sat alone, head lowered, her fur cloak drawn tight about her. Weapons laid out to one side, hobbled horse behind her. *Run'Thurvian, are you there, old friend? You refused his embrace. Your soul is left to wander where it will. Have you walked with me? Can you not hear my prayer?*

I was betrayed, and then betrayed a second time. If I am cruel, then your untimely death could mark the first of three. And all about me I see . . . contradiction. You were the Destriant. From you comes the voice of our gods. But now the gods can tell us nothing, for you are silent. The Grey Helms are led by a Shield Anvil who has elected himself the sole arbiter of righteousness. I avowed service to the Adjunct Tavore Paran, only to have her send me away.

Nothing is as it seems –

Her breath caught. *Ice upon the surface of the lake seems solid, and we might slide quickly from place to place. But the ice is thin and that is the danger, the price of carelessness. Did I not question the contradiction's criminality?*

She rose and faced the Glass Desert. 'Adjunct Tavore,' she whispered. 'Have I skidded too sure upon the ice? If I am untroubled by my own contradictions, why do I choose to see yours as a crime? As betrayal?'

That Gilk Warchief – was it he who spoke of Tavore's surrender to despair? Her expectation of failure? Her desire to spare us the witnessing of that failure?

Or was it all nothing more than what she said it was: a tactical necessity?

'Destriant – old friend. Shall it be my own people who become the betrayers? Are we to be the knife that fatally strikes Tavore Paran and her Malazans? Run'Thurvian, what must I do?'

You could ride back to the camp, woman, and slide an arm's length of cold iron through the bastard.

She shook her head. The Grey Helms were bound to strict laws and would not permit themselves to be led by a murderer. No, they would execute her. *But at least there would be no Tanakalian. Who would take command? Heveth, Lambat? But then, would they not feel bound to their last commander's intentions?*

Listen to yourself, Krughava! Actually considering outright murder of a fellow Grey Helm!

No, that was the wrong direction, the wrong path. She would have to leave the Perish to whatever fate Tanakalian found for them. But the betrayal – well, that would not be set at her feet.

Krughava faced the Glass Desert. *I will ride to her. I will warn her. And I will stand at her side until the very end.*

All doubt vanished from her mind. She collected up her weapons. *See how clear the ice has become, Run'Thurvian? I can see its thickness. Upon this, an entire army could march without fear.*

Krughava drew a deep breath of cold night air, and then turned to her horse. 'Ah, friend, I have one thing left to ask of you . . .'

The Ve'Gath stood with their heads tilted downward, as if contemplating the lifeless earth at their feet, but Gesler knew it was simply the way they slept – or, rather, rested, since as far as he could tell the huge reptilian warriors never closed their eyes. It was unnerving, leading an army like this. *Like commanding ten thousand hounds. But they're smarter than hounds, which makes it even worse.* The wings of K'ell Hunters remained well beyond the encampment, seemingly immune to the vicissitudes of food, water and rest – their endurance made him feel soft. *But not as soft as Stormy. Listen to that bastard snore – they can probably hear him over in the Letherii camp.*

He knew he should be sleeping, but there had been dreams. Unpleasant ones. Disturbing enough to drag him out from his furs, with dawn still two bells away. Now he stood looking upon the massed Ve'Gath legions. They were halted in formation, like vast assemblies of brooding statues, grey as dulled iron beneath the uncanny night sky.

He had been kneeling, as if broken, and the dreamscape surrounding him was a charnel house of torn bodies. The blood had soaked up through his leggings and now thickened against the skin of his knees and shins. Somewhere fire was pouring from the very bedrock and roiling gouts of deadly gases coiled skyward – and in that sky, as he'd looked up, he'd seen . . . *something.* Clouds? He could not be sure, but there was something monstrous about them, something that ripped like talons into his chest. He'd seen motion, as if the sky itself was heaving. *A gate? Could be. But no gate could be as big as that. It took the whole sky. And why did it feel as if I was to blame for it?*

Gesler might have cried out then. Enough to rattle him awake. He'd lain beneath the furs, sweat-soaked and shivering. From the nearby ranks of Ve'Gath came a stirring motion, as the flavours of his distress agitated the sleeping K'Chain Che'Malle. Muttering under his breath, he'd risen to his feet.

An army encamped without cookfires, without tents, or roped pens or the ragged sprawl of followers. It didn't seem proper. In fact, it didn't seem *real*.

The Wickan cattledog, Bent, had found him then. Misshapen snout, one clouded eye, the gleam of canines and splintered teeth – he'd never seen so many scars on a single animal. But as the beast drew up, Gesler remembered back to a late afternoon on the Aren Way.

Hunting survivors. And how pathetic was that – two damned dogs. Among so many corpses the memory haunts me to this day. Two damned dogs.

And then that Trell, there on the wagon.

All of us on the bed, me, Stormy, Truth and that Trell. Willing two dying animals back to life. Truth – he was weeping, but we knew what it was all about. We knew it because we felt it. So many had been taken from us that day. Coltaine. Bult. Lull.

Duiker – gods, finding him crucified like that, at the road's end, staked to the last of those ghastly trees – no, we couldn't tell Truth about that. It's what made the name we'd given him sting us so afterwards. We kept it from him, me and Stormy – but that Trell saw through us. And was good enough to say nothing.

We saved the lives of two dumb dogs, and it was like a new dawn.

He looked down at Bent. 'Remember that day, you ugly horror?'

The wide head lifted, the motion stretching the torn lips back from the crooked teeth, the misaligned jaw that should have made the dog look comical, but didn't. No. Instead, it broke the heart. *All you did in our name. Too loyal for your own good. Too brave to know any different. And still you failed to protect them. Would you have been happier if we'd let you die? Freed your spirits to run with the ones you loved?*

Did we hurt you that day? Me and Stormy and Truth and that Trell? 'I hear you,' he whispered, studying the dog. 'The way you wince when you get up after another night on cold ground. I see you limping at day's end, Bent.' *You and me, we're both breaking down. This journey will be the last of us, won't it? You and me, Bent. The last of us.* 'I'll take your side when the time comes,' he said. 'In fact, I will die for you, dog. It's the least I can do.' The promise sounded foolish, and he looked round to make certain no one else was near. Their only company was the other dog, Roach, digging frantically at some mouse hole. Gesler sighed. *But who says my life's worth any more than this dog's? Or that its life is worth less than mine? Who stands around measuring these things? The gods? Hah! Good one. No. We do, and that's the sorriest joke of all.*

Feeling chilled, he shook himself.

Bent sat down on his left, yawned with a grinding, grating sound.

Gesler grunted. 'We seen a lot, ain't we? All that grey in our muzzles, hey?'

Aren Way. The sun was hot, but we could barely feel it. Truth brushing the flies from the wounds. We don't like death. It's as simple as that. We don't like it.

He heard soft footpads and turned to see Destriant Kalyth approaching. When she settled down on Bent's other side and rested a hand on the beast's head, Gesler flinched. But the dog did not move.

He grunted. 'Never seen Bent accept that from anybody, Destriant.'

'South of the Glass Desert,' she said. 'We are soon to enter the homeland of my people. Not my tribes, but our kin. The Elan lived on the plains that enclose the Glass Desert on three sides. My own clan was to the north.'

'Then you can't be certain they're all dead – these ones in the south.'

She shook her head. 'I am. The voice-slayers from Kolanse hunted down the last of us. Those that didn't die from the drought, I mean.'

'Kalyth, if you got away, others did too.'

'I hope not,' she whispered, and she set to massaging the cattledog, along the shoulders, down the length of the beast's back to the hips, and under her breath she chanted something in her own language. Bent's eyes slowly closed.

Gesler watched her, wondering at the meaning of her reply. Whispered like a prayer. 'It seems,' he muttered after a moment, 'that us survivors all share the same torment.'

She glanced up at him. 'That is why you and the Shield Anvil always argue. It's like watching your children die, isn't it?'

A clutch of pain inside made him look away. 'I don't know why the Adjunct wants it this way, but I do know why she's keeping it all inside. She has no choice. Maybe none of us do – we are what we are, and no amount of talking or explaining is going to make a difference to anything.'

Bent was lying down now, breathing slow in sleep. Kalyth slowly withdrew her hands.

'You just took away his pain, didn't you?'

She shrugged. 'My people kept such animals. As children, we all learned the songs of peace.'

'"Songs of peace,"' Gesler mused. 'It'd be nice to hear a few more of those in the world, wouldn't it?'

'Not any time soon, I fear.'

'They just found you, didn't they? In their search for people to lead them.'

She nodded, straightening. 'It wasn't fair. But I'm glad of it, Mortal Sword.' She faced him. 'I am. And I am glad of you. And Stormy – and these dogs. Even Grub.'

But not Sinn. No one is glad of Sinn. Poor girl – she probably knows it, too. 'Sinn lost her brother,' he said. 'But she might have been unhinged long before that. She was caught in a rebellion.' He glanced down at Bent. 'No one came through it unscarred.'

'As you said, the curse of surviving.'

'Making us no different from the K'Chain Che'Malle,' he observed. 'I'm surprised it took them so long to realize it.'

'Gunth Mach's mother realized it, and for that she was deemed insane. If we do not fight together, we end up fighting each other. She died before she could witness the fruits of her vision. She died believing she had failed.'

'Kalyth, the winged assassin, Gu'Rull, does it remain guarding us?'

She looked skyward, eyes narrowing at the Jade Strangers. 'I sent the Shi'gal to scout our approach.'

'Into Kolanse? Isn't that risky?'

She shrugged. 'In truth, Gu'Rull serves Gunth Mach – it is by her command that she releases him to us. This time, however, the Matron and I agreed. Mortal Sword, from the visions Gu'Rull has given me, I do not think the Grey Helms accept your command.'

Gesler snorted. 'Pious bores – I'm glad of that, truth be told. Oh, Krughava looked to be capable and all that, but I tell you, all that Wolf-worshipping made me uneasy.' Noting her raised brow he shrugged and said, 'Aye, I went and picked my own god of war, so it's a bit much to be going on about the Perish. The thing is, Kalyth, it makes sense for a soldier to choose a god of war. It doesn't make sense when a god of war makes soldiers of an entire people. It's the wrong way round, right? Well, there's something skewed about it – though I can't really tell you why I feel that way.'

'So they are free to do as they please?'

'I suppose so. I don't know much about this Tanakalian, except that he'd have done well in the Malazan court, if there's any truth to the story of how he usurped Krughava. People like that, Kalyth, I don't trust. It's what got me in so much trouble all those years ago. Anyway, if Tanakalian wants to take his Perish right up the arsehole of the Forkrul Assail, well, he's welcome to light his own torch and go to it.'

'What are your thoughts on the Letherii prince, Mortal Sword?'

'Him I like. Aranict, too. Solid people, those two. From what I heard back in Letherii, before his brother took the throne, Brys was some kind of special bodyguard to the Letherii emperor. Unmatched with the sword. That tells me more about him than you think.'

'In what way?'

'Anyone who has mastered a weapon – truly mastered it – is a humble man or woman. More than that, I know how he thinks, and something of what he sees. The way his brain works. And it seems that making him a prince hasn't changed him any. So, Kalyth, worry not about the Letherii. Come the day, they'll be there.'

'Leaving only the Bolkando—'

'She defers to Brys, I think. She doesn't want to, but that's just how it is. Besides,' Gesler added, 'she has red hair.'

Kalyth frowned. 'I don't understand.'

'Me and Stormy, we're Falari. Plenty of red-haired people in Falar. So, I'll tell you what Abrastal is like. Deadly temper, glowing-hot iron, but being a mother she's learned the wisdom of knowing what's in her control and what isn't. She doesn't like it but she lives with it. Likes her sex, too, but prone to jealousy – and all of that bluster, why, it's all for show. Inside, she's just looking for a man like me.'

She gasped. 'But she's married! And to a king!'

Gesler grinned. 'Was just seeing if you were still listening, Destriant. Saw your attention drifting there.'

'A Hunter found me – you're closed off and Stormy is sleeping. A rider was seen, out from close to the Perish camp, riding into the Glass Desert.'

'Any more detail than that?'

'You can see what the Hunter saw, Mortal Sword.'

'Right, I can, can't I?' He concentrated for a moment, and then swore under his breath. 'Krughava.'

'Where—'

'To the Adjunct, I'd wager. But she'll never make it.'

'What should we do?'

Gesler scratched his jaw, and then wheeled round. 'Stormy! Wake up, you fat bearded ox!'

BOOK FIVE

A HAND UPON THE FATES

'I have had visions of the future, and each and every one of them ends up in the same place. Don't ask me what it means. I already know. That's the problem with visions of the future.'

Emperor Kellanved

CHAPTER FOURTEEN

Where is the meaning in this stride foot following foot?
Why must the land crawl so beneath us in our journey?
All to take us to the place where we began so long ago
Only to find it strange and unknown and unredeemed
Who has blazed this trail and how weary must I become
Before the rain grows gentle and soft as tears on the brow?
Until the valley unfolds into a river the sweet colour of sand
And trees ribbon the sky overhead with dusty leaves?
How weary must you become as you rattle the chains
And drown in the banners of meaning and rueful portent?
If I make you share my torment foot following foot
Know that this is my curse of the swallowed key
And cruel desire
And when our blood mixes and drains in the grey earth
When the faces blur before our eyes in these last of last days
We shall turn about to see the path of years we have made
And wail at the absence of answers and the things left unseen
For this is life's legion of truth so strange so unknown
So unredeemed and we cannot know what we will live
Until the journey is done
My beautiful legion, leave me to rest on the wayside
As onward you march to the circling sun
Where spin shadows tracing the eternal day
Raise stones to signal my passing
Unmarked and mysterious
Saying nothing of me
Saying nothing at all
The legion is faceless and must ever remain so
As faceless as the sky

Skull's Lament
Anomandaris
Fisher kel Tath

383

WHITE AS BONE, THE BUTTERFLIES FORMED A VAST CLOUD OVER-head. Again and again their swirling mass dimmed the sun with a blessed gift of shadow that moments later broke apart, proving that curses hid in every gift, and that blessings could pass in the blink of an eye.

An eye swarming with flies. Badalle could feel and indeed see them clustering at the corners; she could feel them drinking her tears. She did not resent their need, and their frenzied crawl and buzz felt cool against her scorched cheeks. Those that crowded her mouth she ate when she could, the taste bitter when she crushed them, the wings like patches of dry skin almost impossible to swallow.

Since the Shards had left, only the butterflies and the flies remained, and there was something pure in these last two forces. One white, the other black. Only the extremes remained: from the unyielding ground below to the hollow sky above; from the push of life to the pull of death; from the breath hiding within to the last to leave a fallen child.

The flies fed upon the living, but the butterflies waited for the dead. There was nothing in between. Nothing but this walking, the torn feet and the stains they left behind, the figures toppling and then stepped over.

In her head, Badalle was singing. She sensed the presence of others – not those ahead of her or those behind her, but ghostly things. Invisible eyes and veiled thoughts. An impatience, a harsh desire for judgement. As if the Snake's very existence was an affront. To be ignored. Denied. Fled from.

But she would not permit any to escape. They did not have to like what they saw. They did not have to like her at all. Or Rutt or Held or Saddic or any of the bare thousand still alive. They could rail at her thoughts, at the poetry she found in the heart of suffering, as if it had no meaning to them, no value. No truth. They could do all of that; still she would not let them go.

I am as true as anything you have ever seen. A dying child, aban-doned by the world. And I say this: there is nothing truer. Nothing.

Flee from me if you can. I promise I will haunt you. This is my only purpose now, the only one left to me. I am history made alive, holding on but failing. I am everything you would not think of, belly filled and thirst slaked, there in all your comforts surrounded by faces you know and love.

But hear me. Heed my warning. History has claws.

Saddic still carried his hoard. He dragged it behind him. In a sack made of clothes no longer needed by anyone. His treasure trove. His *... things.* What did he want with them? What meaning hid inside that sack? All those stupid bits, the shiny stones, the pieces of wood. And the way, with every dusk, when they could walk no further, he would take them all out to look at them – why did that frighten her?

Sometimes he would weep, for no reason. And make fists as if to crush all his baubles into dust, and it was then that she realized that Saddic didn't know what they meant either. But he wouldn't leave them behind. That sack would be the death of him.

She imagined the moment when he fell. This boy she would have liked for a brother. On to his knees, hands all entwined in the cloth sleeves, falling forward so that his face struck the ground. He'd try to get back up, but he'd fail. And the flies would swarm him until he was no longer even visible, just a seething, glittering blackness. Where Saddic had been.

They'd eat his last breath. Drink the last tears from his eyes which now just stared. Invade his open mouth to make it dry as a cave, a spider hole. And then the swarm would explode, rush away seeking more of life's sweet water. And down would descend the butterflies. To strip away his skin, and the thing left – with its sack – would no longer be Saddic.

Saddic will be gone. Happy Saddic. Peaceful Saddic, a ghost hovering, looking down at that sack. I would have words for him, for his passing. I would stand over him, looking down at all those fluttering wings so like leaves, and I would try, one more time, to make sense of the sack, the sack that killed him.

And I would fail. Making my words few. Weak. A song of unknowing. All I have for my brother Saddic.

When that time comes, I will know it is time for me to die, too. When that time comes, I will give up.

And so she sang. A song of knowing. The most powerful song of all.

They had a day left, maybe two.

Is this what I wanted? Every journey must end. Out here there is nothing but ends. No beginnings left. Out here, I have nothing but claws.

'Badalle.' The word was soft, like crumpled cloth, and she felt it brush her senses.

'Rutt.'

'I can't do this any more.'

'But you are Rutt. The head of the Snake. And Held, who is the tongue.'

'No. I can't. I have gone blind.'

She moved up alongside him, studied his old man's face. 'They're swollen,' she said. 'Closed up, Rutt. It's to keep them safe. Your eyes.'

'But I can't see.'

'There's nothing to see, Rutt.'

'I can't lead.'

'For this, there is no one better.'

'Badalle—'

'Even the stones are gone. Just walk, Rutt. The way is clear; for as far as I can see, it's clear.'

He loosed a sob. The flies poured in and he bent over, coughing, retching. He stumbled and she caught him before he fell. Rutt righted himself, clutching Held tight. Badalle heard a soft whimper rising from them both.

No water. This is what is killing us now. Squinting, she glanced back. Saddic was nowhere in sight – had he already fallen? If he had, it would be just as well that she'd not seen it. Other faces, vaguely familiar, stared at her and Rutt, waiting for the Snake to begin moving once again. They stood hunched over, tottering. They stood with backs arched and bellies distended as if about to drop a baby. Their eyes were depthless pools where the flies gathered to drink. Sores crusted their noses, their mouths and ears. Skin on cheeks and chins had cracked open and glistened beneath ribbons of flies. Many were bald, missing teeth, their gums bleeding. And Rutt was not alone in being blind.

Our children. See what we have done to them. Our mothers and fathers left us to this, and now we leave them, too, in our turn. There is no end to the generations of the foolish. One after another after another and at some point we all started nodding thinking this is how it has to be, and so we don't even try to change things. All we pass down to our children is the same stupid grin.

But I have claws. And I will tear away that grin. I swear it.

'Badalle.'

She had begun singing out loud. Wordless, the tone low and then building, thickening. Until she could feel more than one voice within her, and each in turn joined her song. Filling the air. Their sound was one of horror, a terrible thing – she felt its power growing. *Growing.*

'Badalle?'

I have claws. I have claws. I have claws. Show me that grin one more time. Show it, I'm begging you! Let me tear it from your face. Let me rip deep, until my talons score your teeth! Let me feel the blood and let me hear the meat splitting and let me see the look in your eyes as you meet mine let me see I have claws I have claws I have claws—

'Badalle!'

Someone struck her, knocked her down. Stunned, she stared up into Saddic's face, his round, wizened face. And from his eyes red tears tracked down through the dust on his leathery cheeks.

'Don't cry,' she whispered. 'It's all right, Saddic. Don't cry.'

Rutt knelt beside her, groped with one hand until his fingers brushed her forehead. 'What have you done?'

386

His tone startled her. *The cloth is torn.* 'They're all too weak,' she said. 'Too weak to feel anger. So I felt it for them – for all of you—' She stopped. Rutt's fingertips leaked blood. She could feel crystal shards digging into her back. *What?*

'You moved us,' Saddic said. 'It . . . hurt.'

She could hear wailing now. The Snake was writhing in pain. 'I went . . . I went looking.'

'For what?' Rutt demanded. *'For what?'*

'For claws.'

Saddic shook his head. 'Badalle. We're children. We don't have claws.'

The sun dimmed then and she squinted past Saddic. But the butterflies were gone. *Flies, look at all the flies.*

'We don't have claws, Badalle.'

'No, Saddic, you're right. We don't. *But someone does.*'

The power of the song still clung to her, fierce as a promise. *Someone does.* 'I'm taking us there,' she said, meeting Saddic's wide eyes.

He drew back, leaving her to stare up at the sky. Flies, roiling in a massive cloud, black as the Abyss. She clambered to her feet. 'Take my hand, Rutt. It's time to walk.'

She crouched, staring up at the gate. Beneath it the crumbling ruin of Kettle House was like a thing crushed under a heel. Something like blood oozed out from its roots to carve runnels down the slope. She believed it was dead, but of course there was no way to know for sure.

There was no glory in failure. Kilava had learned that long, long ago. The passing of an age was always one of dissolution, a final sigh of exhaustion and surrender. She had seen her kin vanish from the world – the venal mockery that were the T'lan Imass hardly weighed as much as dust upon the scales of survival – and she well understood the secret desires of Olar Ethil.

Maybe the hag would succeed. The spirits knew, she was ripe for redemption.

Kilava had lied. To Onrack, to Udinaas, to Ulshun Pral and his clan. There had been no choice. To remain here would have seen them all slain, and she would not have that on her conscience.

When the wound was breached, the Eleint would enter this world. There was no hope of stopping them. T'iam could not be denied, not with what was coming.

The only unknown, to her mind, was the Crippled God. The Forkrul Assail were simple enough, as bound to the insanity of final arguments as were the Tiste Liosan. Kin in spirit, those two. And she believed she knew what her brother intended to do, and she would leave him to it,

387

and if her blessing meant anything, well then he had it, with all her heart. No, the Crippled God was the only force that troubled her.

She remembered the earth's pain when he was brought down from the sky. She remembered his fury and his agony when first he was chained. But the gods were hardly done with him. They returned again and again, crushing him down, destroying his every attempt to find a place for himself. If he cried out for justice, no one was interested in listening. If he howled in wretched suffering, they but turned away.

But the Crippled God was not alone in that neglect. The mortal realm was crowded with those who were just as wounded, just as broken, just as forgotten. In this way, all that he had become – his very place in the pantheon – had been forged by the gods themselves.

And now they feared him. Now, they meant to kill him.

'Because the gods will not answer mortal suffering. It is too much . . . work.'

He must know what they intended – she was certain of it. He must be desperate in seeking a way out, an escape. No matter what, she knew he would not die without a fight. Was this not the meaning of suffering?

Her feline eyes narrowed on the gate. Starvald Demelain was a fiery red welt in the sky, growing, deepening.

'Soon,' *she whispered.*

She would flee before them. To remain here was too dangerous. The destruction they would bring to this world would beggar the dreams of even the Forkrul Assail. And once upon the mortal realm, so crowded with pathetic humans, there would be slaughter on a colossal scale. Who could oppose them? She smiled at the thought.

'There are a few, aren't there? But too few. No, friends, let them loose. T'iam must be reborn, to face her most ancient enemy. Chaos against order, as simple – as banal – as that. Do not stand in their path – not one of you could hope to survive it.'

What then of her children?

'Dear brother, let us see, shall we? The hag's heart is broken, and she will do whatever she can to see it healed. Despise her, Onos – the spirits know, she deserves nothing else – but do not dismiss her. Do not.'

It seemed very complicated.

Kilava Onass looked up at the wound.

'But it isn't. It isn't anything like that at all.'

Rock cracked in Kettle House, startling her. Reddish mists roiled out from the sundered walls.

'She was flawed, was Kettle. Too weak, too young.' *What legacy could be found in a child left alone, abandoned to the fates? How many truths hid in the scatter of small bones? Too many to bear thinking about.*

Another stone shattered, the sound like snapping chains.
Kilava returned her attention to the gate.

Gruntle slumped against a massive boulder, in the full sun, and leaned his head back against the warm stone, closing his eyes. *Instinct's a bitch.* The god who had damned him was a burning presence deep inside, filling him with an urgency he could not understand. His nerves were frayed; he was exhausted.

He had journeyed through countless realms, desperate to find the quickest path to take him . . . where? *A gate. A disaster about to be unleashed. What is it you so fear, Trake? Why can you not just tell me, you miserable rat-chewing bastard? Show me an enemy. Show me someone I can kill for you, since that seems to be the only thing that pleases you.*

The air stank. He listened to the flies crawling on the corpses surrounding him. He didn't know where he was. Broad-leafed trees encircled the glade; he had heard geese flying overhead. But this was not his world. It felt . . . different. Like a place twisted by sickness – and not the sickness that had taken the twenty or so wretched humans lying here in the high grasses, marring their skin with weeping pustules, swelling their throats and forcing their tongues past blistered lips. No, all of that was just a symptom of some deeper disease.

There was intention. Here. Someone summoned Poliel and set her upon these people. I am being shown true evil – is that what you wanted, Trake? Reminding me of just how horrifying we can be? People curse you and the pestilence of your touch ruins countless lives, but you are not a stranger to any world.

These people – someone used you to kill them.

He thought he'd seen the worst of humanity's flaws back in Capustan, in the Pannion War. An entire people deliberately driven insane. But if he understood the truths behind that war, there had been a wounded thing at the very core of the Domin, a thing that could only lash out, claws bared, so vast, so consuming was its pain.

And though he was not yet ready for it, a part of him understood that forgiveness was possible, from the streets of Capustan to the throne in Coral, and probably beyond – there had been mention of a being trapped in a gate, sealing a wound with its own life force. He could track an argument through all that, and the knowledge gave him something close to peace. Enough to live with.

But not here. What crime did they commit – these poor people – to earn such punishment?

He could feel his tears drying on his cheeks. *This is . . . unforgivable. Is it my anger you want, Trake? Is this why I am here, to be reawakened? Enough of the shame, the grief, the self-recrimination, is that what you're telling me?*

Well then, it hasn't worked. All I see here is what we're capable of doing.

He missed Ganoes Paran. And Itkovian. Friends to whom he could speak. They seemed to belong to a different life, a life long lost to him. *Harllo. Ah, you should see your namesake, my friend. Oh, how you would have loved him – she'd have to fight you off, brick up the doors to keep you from being his father. You'd have shown her what it meant to love a child unconditionally.*

Stonny, do you miss Harllo as much as I do?

But you've got the boy. You've got your son. And I promised I would come back. I promised.

'What would you do here, Master of the Deck?' His question was swallowed by the glade. 'What choice would you make, Paran? We weren't happy with our lots, were we? But we took hold of them anyway. By the throat. I expect you've yet to relinquish your grip. Me? Ah, gods, how I've messed it up.'

In his dreams he had seen a blackened thing, with claws of red and fangs dripping gore. Lying panting, dying, on churned-up earth. The air was brittle cold. The wind whipped about as if warring with itself. What place was that?

That place? Gods, it's where I'm going, isn't it? I have a fight ahead. A terrible fight. Is she my ally? My lover? Is she even real?

It was time. An end to these morbid thoughts, this brush with self-indulgence. He knew well that to give voice to certain feelings, to expose them in all their honesty, made him vulnerable to derision. *'Don't touch us with what you feel. We don't believe you.'* His eyes blinking open, he looked around.

Crows on the branches, but even they were not yet ready to feed.

Gruntle climbed to his feet, walked to the nearest corpse. A young man, skin of burnished bronze, braided hair black as pitch. Dressed like some Rhivi outlander. Stone tools, a wooden club at his waist – beautifully carved, shaped like a cutlass, the edge oiled and gleaming. 'You loved that sword, didn't you? But it didn't help you. Not against this.'

He turned, took in the glade, and spread his arms. 'You died miserable. I now offer you something more, a second way.'

The hair on the back of his neck lifted. Their spirits had drawn close. 'You were warriors. Come with me and be warriors once again. And if we are to die, then it shall be a better death. I can offer this but nothing more.'

The last time he had done this, his followers had been alive. Until this moment, he had not even known that this was possible, this breaching of death's barrier. *It's all changing. I don't think I like it.*

The spirits drifted back to their bodies. The flies scattered.

Moments later, limbs twitched, mouths opened to dry rasps. *Now, Trake, we can't have them like this, can we? Heal their flesh, you piece of immortal dung.*

Power filled the glade, an emanation that pushed back the vile curse of this realm, all the exultant expressions of evil that seemed to thrive unopposed in this place. Swept away. Refuted.

He remembered sitting at a campfire, listening to Harllo going on about something, and a fragment of words returned to him now. The face across the fire, long and flickering. '*War, Gruntle. Like it or not, it's the spur of civilization.*' And then that lopsided grin.

'Hear that, Trake? I just figured out why you've granted me this gift. It's all nothing but expedience with you. One hand blesses but the other waits for the coin. And you'll be paid, no matter what. No matter what.'

Twenty-one silent warriors now faced him, their sores gone, their eyes bright. He could be cruel now and just take them. 'He'll have made sure you can understand me. He'll have done that, I think.'

Cautious nods.

'Good. You can stay here. You can return to your people – if any are still alive. You can try to seek vengeance against the ones who killed you. But you know you'll lose. Against the evil now in your land, you are doomed.

'You're warriors. When you run with me, know that a fight awaits us. That is our path.' He hesitated, and then spat to one side. 'Is there glory in war? Come with me and let's find out.'

When he set off, twenty-one warriors followed.

And when he awakened his power they rushed closer. *This, my friends, is called veering. And this, my friends, is the body of a tiger.*

A rather big one.

The three strangely garbed strangers they found walking on the trail ahead barely had time to lift their long clubs before Gruntle was among them. Once he passed, there wasn't much left of those three pale men, and he felt the pleasure of his companions. And shared it. *There's only one thing to do with evil. Take it in your jaws and crush it.*

Then they were gone from the world.

What place washes bones up like driftwood? Mappo's gaze narrowed on the flat, blinding stretch awaiting him. Shards of quartz and gypsum studded the colourless, dead ground, like knots of cacti. The horizon was level behind shimmering waves of heat, as if this desert reached to the very edge of the world.

I have to cross it.

He crouched, reached down and picked up a long bone, studied it. *Bhederin? Maybe. Not yet fully grown.* He collected another. *Wolf or dog jaw. So, this desert was once prairie. What happened?* The bones fell with a clatter. Straightening, Mappo drew a deep breath. *I think . . . I think I am getting tired of living. Tired of the whole thing. Nothing is working like it used to. Flaws are appearing, signs of things breaking down. Inside. The very core of my spirit.*

But I have one thing left to do. Just one thing left, and then I can be done with all this. He found himself drifting off, not for the first time, finding that place in his head where every thought rattled like chains, and he could only drag himself in crooked circles, the weight stealing his strength, his willingness to go on.

One thing left. It's down to managing resources. Harbouring the will. Navigating between all the sour truths. You can live that long, Mappo. You have no choice but to live that long, or all this will be for nothing.

I see the world's edge. Waiting for me.

He tightened the straps of his sack, and then set out. At a steady jog. *It's just a desert. I've run across a few in my day. I won't go hungry. I won't go thirsty, and whatever exhaustion comes to me, well, it'll end when it's all over.*

With each footfall his nerves seemed to recoil from the contact. This was a damaged place, one vast scar upon the earth. And for all the death lining the desert's bizarre shore behind him, there was life here. Inimical, unpleasant life. And it possessed *intent.*

You feel me, don't you? I offend you. But it is not my desire to offend. Leave me to pass, friend, and we will be done with each other.

Flies buzzed round him now. He had settled into a dogtrot, his breathing steady and deep. The insects kept pace, gathering in ever greater numbers. *Death is not punishment. It is release. I have seen that all my life. Though I did not wish to, though I told myself stories to pretend otherwise. Every struggle must end. Is the rest that follows eternal? I doubt it. I doubt we'd ever get off that easily.*

Hood, I feel your absence. I wonder what it means. Who now waits beyond the gate? So much anguish comes in knowing that each of us must pass through it alone. To then discover that once through we remain alone – no, that is too much to bear.

I could have married. Stayed in the village. I could have fathered children, and seen in each child something of my wife, something of me. Is that enough meaning to a life? A cloth of unending folds?

I could have murdered Icarium – but then, he has instincts for such things. His madness awakens so fast, so utterly fast, that I might have failed – and after killing me his rage would have sought a new target, and many others would have died.

There really was no choice. There never was. Is it any wonder I am so tired?

The flies swarmed him in a thick, glittering cloud. They sought out his eyes, but those had closed to slits. They spun round his mouth, but the gusts of breath from his nostrils drove them off. His people had been herders. They understood flies. He ignored their seething embrace. It meant nothing, and on he ran.

But then my death would have made my loved ones grieve, and there is nothing pleasant in grieving. It is hot and dry to the touch. It is weakness taken inside. It can rise up and drown a life. No, I am glad I never found a wife, never fathered children. I could not bear to be the cause of their sorrow.

How can one give so freely of love to another, when the final outcome is one of betrayal? When one must leave the other – to be the betrayer who dies, to be the betrayed left alive. How can this be an even exchange, with death waiting at the end?

He ran, and time passed. The sun tracked across half the sky. The warm ache in his legs had shaken off the torment of his thoughts again and again, leading him into a world emptied of everything. *How perfect is running? This grand delusion of flight? Away from our demons, ever away, until even the self sobs loose, spins lost in our wake.*

Perfect, oh yes. And a thing to despise. No distance can win an escape; no speed can outrun this self and all its host of troubles. It's only the sweet exhaustion that follows that we so cherish. An exhaustion so pure it is as close to dying as we can get without actually doing so.

Poets could speak knowingly of metaphors; if life is walking, then running is a life's entire span speeded up, and to act out birth to death in a single day, over and over again, has the flavour of perfect habit, for it mimicks undeniable truths. *Small deaths paying homage to the real one. We choose them in myriad forms and delight in the ritual. I could run until I wear out. Every joint, every bone and every muscle. I could run until my heart groans older than its years, and finally bursts.*

I could damn the poets and make the metaphor real. We are all self-destructive. It is integral to our nature. And we will run even when there's nowhere to run to, and nothing terrible to run from. Why? Because to walk is just as meaningless. It just takes longer.

Through the screen of whizzing flies he saw something in the sky ahead. A darker cloud, a towering, swirling thing. Dust storm? There was no dust. A whirlwind? Maybe. But the air was still. It was in his path, although still some distance away. He watched it, to track its path.

The cloud remained directly ahead. *Just bigger.*

It's coming straight at me.

More flies?

The insects surrounding him were suddenly frenzied – and he caught something in their manic buzzing. *You're part of this, aren't you? The finders of life. And once found, you . . . summon.*

He could hear that cloud now, a deeper, more frightening drone quickly overwhelming the swarming flies.

Locusts.

But that makes no sense. There is nothing for them to eat. There is nothing here at all.

All of this felt wrong. Mappo slowed his run, halted. The flies spun round him a moment longer, and then fled. He stood, breathing deep, eyes on the vast spinning pillar of locusts.

And then, all at once, he understood. 'D'ivers.'

Something that looked like white foam was spreading from the base of the locust cloud, surging in tumultuous waves. *Gods below. Butterflies.* 'You're all d'ivers. You're all one thing, one creature – the flies, the locusts, the butterflies – and this desert is where you live.' He recalled the bones upon the edge. 'This desert . . . is what you made.'

The butterflies reached him, whipped round him – so many he could no longer see the ground at his feet. The frantic breaths of their wings stole the sweat from his skin, until he began shivering. 'D'ivers! I would speak to you! Semble! Show yourself to me!'

The locusts blighted half the sky, devouring the sun. Spinning overhead, and then, in a wave of rage, descending.

Mappo dropped to his knees, buried his face beneath his arms, hunched down.

They struck his back like a deluge of darts.

As more poured down, he grunted at their weight. Bones creaked. He struggled for breath, clenched his jaws against the pain.

The locusts stabbed again and again with their jaws, driven mad by the feel and scent of living flesh.

But he was Trell, and his kind had skin like leather.

The locusts could not draw blood. But the weight grew vast, seeking to crush him. In the gap his arms made for his face he stared at inky darkness, and his gasps snatched up dust from the ground. Deafened by the futile clack of bladed jaws, buried in riotous darkness, he held on.

He could feel the mind of the d'ivers now. Its fury was not for him alone. *Who stung you so? Who in this desert drove you away? Why are you fleeing?*

The being was ancient. It had not sembled in a long time – thousands of years, perhaps more. Lost now to the primitive instincts of the insects. *Shards opals diamonds gems leaves drinkers* – the words slithered into him as if from nowhere, a girl's sing-song voice that now echoed in his mind. *Shards opals diamonds gems leaves drinkers – go away!*

With a deafening roar the vast weight on Mappo's back burst apart, exploded outward.

He sat up, tilted back his head. 'Shards opals diamonds gems leaves drinkers – go away. Go away. Go!'

A song of banishing.

The cloud heaved upward, twisted, and then churned past him. Another seething wave of butterflies, and then they too were gone.

Stunned, Mappo looked round. He was alone. *Child, where are you? Such power in your song – are you Forkrul Assail? No matter. Mappo thanks you.*

He was covered in bruises. Every bone ached. *But still alive.*

'Child, be careful. This d'ivers was once a god. Someone tore it apart, into so many pieces it can never heal. It can't even find itself. All it knows now is hunger – not for you or me. For something else. Life itself, perhaps. Child, your song has power. Be careful. What you banish you can also summon.'

He heard her voice again, fainter now, drifting away. *'Like the flies. Like the song of the flies.'*

Grunting, he climbed to his feet. Drew his sack round and loosened the drawstrings, reached in and lifted out a waterskin. He drank deep, sighed, drank a second time and then stuffed the skin back into the sack. Tightening the shoulder straps again, he faced east, and resumed running.

For the edge of the world.

'Nice sword.'

'Alas, this one I must use. I will give my two Letherii swords to you.'

Ryadd Eleis leaned back against the knobby stone of the cave wall. 'How did they get the dragons on that blade?'

Silchas Ruin continued studying the weapon he had unsheathed. The flames of the hearth danced up and down its length. 'There is something wrong with this,' he said. 'The House of Hust burned to the ground with everything else – not Kharkanas itself, of course, that city didn't burn. Not precisely. But Hust, well, those forges were a prize, you see. And what could not be held had to be destroyed.'

Ryadd glanced away, at the pearl sky beyond the cave mouth. Another dawn had arrived. He'd been alone for some time. Awakened to find that the Tiste Andii had returned sometime in the night, blown in like a drift of snow. 'I don't understand what you're saying.'

The white face took on an almost human hue, bathed as it was in the firelight. But those red eyes were as unnerving as ever. 'I thought I knew all the weapons forged by the Hust. Even the obscure ones.'

'That one does not look obscure, Silchas,' said Ryadd. 'It looks like a hero's weapon. A famous weapon. One with a name.'

'As you say,' Silchas agreed. 'And I am not so old as to forget the ancient warning about trusting shadows. No, the one who gave me this sword is playing a game.'

'Someone gave it to you? In return for what?'

'I wish I knew.'

Ryadd smiled. 'Never bargain knowing only the value of one side of the deal. Onrack said that to me once. Or maybe it was Ulshun Pral.'

Silchas shot him a look.

Ryadd shrugged, lifting himself to his feet. 'Do we now resume our journey?'

Sheathing the sword, Silchas straightened as well. 'We have gone far enough, I think.'

'What do you mean?'

'I needed to take you away from Starvald Demelain, and now I have done so.' He faced Ryadd. 'This is what you must learn. The Eleint blood within you is a poison. I share it, of course. My brother and I chose it for ourselves – we perceived a necessity, but that is the fatal lure of power, isn't it? With the blood of T'iam within our veins, we could bring peace to Kurald Galain. Of course, that meant crushing every House opposing us. Regrettable, but that sentiment was as far as the poison would permit us to go in our thoughts. The thousands who died could not make us hesitate, could not stop us from continuing. Killing thousands more.'

'I am not you, Silchas Ruin.'

'Nor will you ever be, if I can help it.'

Ryadd walked to the cave's edge, looked out on bleak, jagged rock and blinding sweeps of snow where the sun's light marched down into the valley below. Elsewhere, in shadow, the snow was as blue as the sky. 'What have you done, Silchas?'

Behind him, the Tiste Andii replied, 'What I deemed . . . necessary. I have no doubt that Kilava succeeded in forcing your people out of that realm – they won't die, not there, not then. Udinaas is a clever man. In his life, he has come to understand the pragmatism of survival. He will have led the Imass away from there. And he will find them a home, somewhere to hide from humans—'

'How?' Ryadd demanded. 'It's not even possible.'

'He will seek help.'

'Who?'

'Seren Pedac,' Silchas replied. 'Her old profession makes her a good choice.'

'Her child must have been born by now.'

'Yes. A child she knows she must protect. When Udinaas comes to her, she will see how her need and his can be resolved together. She will guide the Imass to a hidden place, and in that place she too will hide, with her child. Protected by Onrack, protected by the Imass.'

'Why can't we be just left alone?' Ryadd heard the anguish in his own voice and closed his eyes against the outside glare.

'Ryadd Eleis, there is a kind of fish, living in rivers, that when in small numbers – two or perhaps three – is peaceful enough. But when the school grows, when a certain threshold is reached, these fish go mad. They tear things apart. They can devour the life in a river for a league's length, and only when their bellies start bursting do they finally scatter.'

'What has that to do with anything?' Ryadd turned to glare at Silchas Ruin.

The Tiste Andii sighed. 'When the gate of Starvald Demelain opens, the Eleint will come through in vast numbers. Most will be young, by themselves little threat, but among them there will be the last of the Ancients. Leviathans of appalling power – but they are incomplete. They will arrive hunting their kin. Ryadd, if you and I had remained, seeking to oppose the opening of that gate, we would lose our minds. We would in mindless desire join the Storm of the Eleint. We would follow the Ancients – have you never wondered why, in all the realms but Starvald Demelain itself, one will never find more than five or six dragons in one place? Even that many demands the mastery of at least one Ancient. Indeed, to be safe, Eleint tend to travel in threes.' Silchas Ruin walked up to stand beside Ryadd, and stared out at the vista. 'We are the blood of chaos, Ryadd Eleis, and when too many of us gather in one place, *the blood boils.*'

'Then,' Ryadd whispered, 'the Eleint are coming, and there's no stopping them.'

'What you say is true. But here you are safe.'

'Me? What of you?'

Silchas Ruin's hand found the grip of his scabbarded sword. 'I must leave you now, I think. I did not plan it, and I am not pleased at the thought of abandoning you—'

'And all that we spoke of before was a lie,' cut in Ryadd. 'Our perilous mission – all of it, a lie.'

'Your father understood. I promised him that I would save you, and I have done so.'

'Why did you bother?'

'Because you are dangerous enough alone, Ryadd. In a Storm . . . no, I could not risk that.'

'Then you intend to fight them after all!'

'I will defend my freedom, Ryadd—'

'What makes you think you can? With what you said of the Ancients—'

'Because I *am* one, Ryadd. An Ancient.'

Ryadd stared at the tall, white-skinned warrior. 'Could you compel me, Silchas Ruin?'

'I have no desire to even so much as attempt it, Ryadd. Chaos seduces – you have felt it. And soon you may witness the fullest expression of that curse. But I have learned to resist the seduction.' He smiled suddenly, and in an ironic tone added, 'We Tiste Andii are skilled at denying ourselves. We have had a long time to get it right, after all.'

Ryadd drew his furs close about himself. His breath plumed in the bitter cold. He concentrated a moment, was answered by a billowing of the hearth's flames behind him. Heat roiled past.

Silchas glanced back at the sudden inferno. 'You are indeed your mother's son, Ryadd.'

He shrugged. 'I was tired of being chilled.' He then looked across at Silchas. 'Was she an Ancient Eleint?'

'The first few generations of Soletaken count among the Ancients, yes. T'iam's blood was at its purest then, but that purity is short-lived.'

'Are there others like you, Silchas? In this world?'

'Ancients?' He hesitated, and then nodded. 'A few.'

'When the Storm arrives, what will they do?'

'I don't know. But we who were not trapped within Starvald Demelain all share our desire for independence, for our freedom.'

'So they will fight, like you.'

'Perhaps.'

'Then why can I not fight beside you?'

'If I must defend you while defending myself – well, it is likely that I would fail on both counts.'

'But I am Menandore's son—'

'And formidable, yes, but you lack control. An Ancient will see you – will see all that you are – and it will take you, tearing out your mind and enslaving what remains.'

'If you did the same – to me – imagine how powerful you would then be, Silchas.'

'Now you know why dragons so often betray one another in the heat of battle. It is our fear that makes us strike at our allies – before they can strike at us. Even in the Storm, the Ancients will trust not one of their equals, and each will possess scores of lesser slaves, as protection against betrayal.'

'It seems a terrible way to live.'

'You don't understand. It is not simply that we are the blood of chaos, it is that we are *eager* to boil. The Eleint revel in anarchy, in toppling regimes among the Towers, in unmitigated slaughter of the vanquished and the innocent. To see flames on the horizon, to see the enkar'l vultures descending upon a corpse-strewn plain – this charges our heart as does nothing else.'

'The Storm will unleash all that? On this world?'

Silchas Ruin nodded.

'But who can stop them?'

'My other swords are beside your pallet, Ryadd Eleis. They are honourable weapons, if somewhat irritating on occasion.'

'*Who can stop them?*'

'We'll see.'

'How long must I wait here?'

Silchas Ruin met his eyes with a steady, reptilian stare. 'Until the moment you realize that it's time to leave. Be well, Ryadd. Perhaps we will meet again. When next you see your father, do tell him I did what I promised.' He hesitated, and then added, 'Tell him, too, that with Kettle, I believe now that I acted . . . hastily. And for that I am sorry.'

'Is it Olar Ethil?'

Silchas Ruin frowned. 'What?'

'Is she the one you're going to kill, Silchas Ruin?'

'Why would I do that?'

'For what she said.'

'She spoke the truth, Ryadd.'

'She hurt you. On purpose.'

He shrugged. 'What of it? Only words, Ryadd. Only words.'

The Tiste Andii leaned forward then, over the cliff's edge, and slipped out of sight. A moment later he lifted back into view, a bone-white dragon, white as the snow below, where his winged shadow slipped in pursuit.

Ryadd stood a moment longer, and then turned away from the cave mouth. The fire blazed until the swords started singing in the heat.

'Look at you, squatting in your own filth like that. What happened to Fenn's great pride – wasn't that his name? Fenn? That Teblor warking? So he died, friend – doesn't mean you have to fall so low. It's disgusting is what it is. Head back into the mountains – oh, hold on a moment there. Let's see that mace – take the sheath off, will you?'

He licked chapped, stinging lips. His whole mouth felt swollen on the inside. He needed a drink, but the post's gate had been locked. He'd slept against it through the night, listening to the singing in the tavern.

'Show it to me, Teblor – could be we can make us a deal here.'

He straightened up as best he could. 'I cannot yield this,' he said. 'It is an Eleint'aral K'eth. With a secret name – I walked the Roads of the

Dead to win this weapon. With my own hands I broke the neck of a Forkrul Assail—'

But the guard was laughing. 'Meaning it's worth four crowns, not two, right? Harrower's breath, you people can spin 'em, can't you? Been through Death's Gate, have ya? And back out again? Quite a feat for a drunk Teblor stinking of pigshit.'

'I was not always this way—'

'Of course not, friend, but here you are now. Desperate for drink, with just me standing between you and the tavern. This could be Death's Gate all over again, come to think of it, hey? 'Cause if I let you through, why, the next time you leave it'll probably be by the heels. You want through, Teblor? Gotta pay the Harrower's coin. That mace – hand it over then.'

'I cannot. You don't understand. When I came back . . . you cannot imagine. I had seen where we all ended up, you see? When I came back, the drink called me. Helps me forget. Helps me hide. What I saw broke me, that's all. Please, you can see that – how it broke me. I'm begging—'

'Factor don't take to beggars, not here. Y'got nothing to pay your way in, be off – back into the woods, dry as a hag's cubbyhole, true enough. Now, for that mace, well, I'll give ya three crowns. Even you couldn't drink three crowns' worth in a single night. Three. See, got 'em right here. What do you say?'

'Father.'

'Get lost, lad, me and your da's working out a business transaction here.'

'No deal, Guard, not for that weapon—'

'It's your da's to do with as he pleases—'

'You can't even lift it.'

'Wasn't planning on lifting it. But up on the wall of my brother's tavern, well, that'd make quite a sight, don't you think? Pride of place for you Teblor, right over the hearth.'

'Sorry, sir. I'm taking him back to the village now.'

'Until tomorrow night – or next week – listen, lad, you can't save them that won't be saved.'

'I know. But the dragon-killer, that I can save.'

'Dragon-killer? Bold name. Too bad dragons don't exist.'

'Son, I wasn't going to sell it. I swear that—'

'I heard, Father.'

'I wasn't.'

'The Elders have agreed, Father. The Resting Stone waits.'

'It does?'

'Hey now, you two! Boy, did you say Resting Stone?'

'Best you pretend you never heard that, sir.'

400

'That vicious shit's outlawed – king's command! You – Da – your son says the Elders are going to murder you. Under a big fucking boulder. You can claim sanctuary—'

'Sir, if you take him inside the fort, we will have no choice.'

'No choice? No choice but to do what?'

'It's better if none of this ever happened, sir.'

'I'm calling the captain—'

'If you do that, this will all come out. Sir, do you want to start the Teblor on the path to war? Do you want us to burn your fledgling colony to the ground? Do you want us to hunt down and kill every one of you? Children, mothers, the old and wise? What will the First Empire think of a colony gone silent? Will they cross the ocean to investigate? And the next time your people come to our shore, will we meet you not as friends, but as enemies?'

'Son – bury the weapon with me. And the armour – please . . .'

The youth nodded. 'Yes, Father.'

'This time when I die, I shall not return.'

'That is true.'

'Live long, son, as long as you can.'

'I shall try. Guard?'

'Get out of my sight, both of you.'

On to the forest trail. Away from the trading post, the place where Teblor came down to surrender everything, beginning with dignity. He held his son's hand and did not look back. 'There is nowhere to drink in the realm of the dead.'

'I am sorry, Father . . .'

'I'm not, my son. I'm not.'

Ublala sat up, wiping at his eyes. 'They killed me! Again!'

Ralata stirred beside him, twisting to lift her head and study him with bleary eyes. A moment later her head disappeared again beneath the furs.

Ublala looked round, found Draconus standing nearby, but the warrior's attention remained fixed on the eastern horizon, where the sun's newborn light slowly revealed a rocky, glittering desert. Rubbing at his face, the giant stood. 'I'm hungry, Draconus. I'm chilled, my feet hurt, I got dirt under my nails and there's things living in my hair. But the sexing was great.'

Draconus glanced over. 'I had begun to doubt she would relent, Toblakai.'

'She was bored, you see. Boredom's a good reason, don't you think? I think so. I'll do more of that from now on, with women I want to sex.'

One brow arched. 'You will bore them into submission, Ublala?'

'I will. Soon as we find more women. I'll bore them right to the ground. Was that a dragon you turned into? It was hard to see, you were all blurry and black like smoke. Can you do that whenever you like? You gods got it good, I think, being able to do things like that. Hey, where did that fire come from?'

'Best begin cooking your breakfasts, Ublala, we have far to walk today. And it will be through a warren, for I like not the look of that desert ahead.'

Ublala scratched his itchy scalp. 'If you can fly, why don't you just go where you're going? Me and my wife, we can find someplace else to go. And I can bury the mace and the armour. Right here. I don't like them. I don't like the dreams they give me—'

'I will indeed leave you, Ublala, but not quite yet. As for the weapons, I fear you will need them soon. You will have to trust me in this, friend.'

'All right. I'll make breakfast now – is that half a pig? Where's the other half? I always wonder that, you know, when I'm in the market and I see half a pig. Where's the other half? Did it run away? Haha – Ralata? Did you hear me make a joke? Haha. As if half-pigs can run! No, they'd have to kind of hop, wouldn't they? Hop hop hop.'

From under the furs, Ralata groaned.

'Ublala.'

'Yes, Draconus?'

'Do you believe in justice?'

'What? Did I do something wrong? What did I do? I won't make jokes no more, I promise.'

'You've done nothing wrong. Do you know when something is unfair?'

Ublala looked round desperately.

'Not at this moment, friend. I mean, in general. When you see something that is unjust, that is unfair, do you do something about it? Or do you just turn away? I think I know the answer, but I need to make certain.'

'I don't like bad things, Draconus,' Ublala muttered. 'I tried telling that to the Toblakai gods, when they were coming up out of the ground, but they didn't listen, so me and Iron Bars, we had to kill them.'

Draconus studied him for some time, and then he said, 'I believe I have just done something similar. Don't bury your weapons, Ublala.'

He had left his tent well before dusk, to walk the length of the column, among the restless soldiers. They slept badly or not at all, and more than one set of red-shot, bleary eyes tracked Ruthan Gudd as he made his way to the rear. Thirst was a spreading plague, and it grew in the mind like a fever. It pushed away normal thoughts, stretching out

402

time until it snapped. Of all the tortures devised to break people, not one came close to thirst.

Among the wagons now, where heaps of dried, smoked meats remained wrapped in hides, stacked in the beds. The long knotted ropes with rigged harnesses were coiled up in front of each wagon. The oxen were gone. Muscle came from humans now. Carrying food no one wanted to eat. Food that knotted solid in the gut, food that gripped hard with vicious cramps and drove strong men to their knees.

Next on the trail were the ambulance wagons, burdened with the broken, the ones driven half-mad by sun and dehydration. He saw the knots of fully armed guards standing over the water barrels used by the healers, and the sight distressed him. Discipline was fraying and he well understood what he was seeing. Simple need had the power to crush entire civilizations, to bring down all order in human affairs. *To reduce us to mindless beasts. And now it stalks this camp, these soldiers.*

This army was close to shattering. The thirst gnawed ceaselessly.

The sun cut a slice on the western horizon, red as a bloodless wound. Soon the infernal flies would stir awake, at first drowsy in the unwelcome chill, and then rushing in to dance on every exposed area of skin – as if the night itself had awakened with a hundred thousand legs. And then would come the billowing clouds of butterflies, keeping pace overhead like silver clouds tinted jade green – they had first arrived to feed on the carcasses of the last slaughtered oxen, and now they returned each evening, eager for more.

He walked between the wagons with their moaning cargo, exchanging occasional nods with the cutters who moved among their charges with moistened cloths to press against blistered mouths.

No pickets waited beyond the refuse trench – there seemed to be little point in such things – only a row of grave mounds, with a crew of a dozen diggers working on a few more with picks and shovels. Beneath the ground's sun-baked surface there was nothing but stone-hard white silts, deep as a man was tall. At times, when the pick broke a chunk loose, the pressed bones of fish were revealed, of types no one had ever seen before. Ruthan Gudd had chanced to see one example, some massively jawed monstrosity was etched in rust-red bones on a slab of powdery silt. Enormous eye sockets above rows upon rows of long fangs.

He'd listened to the listless conjecture for a short time, and then wandered on without adding any comment of his own. *From the deepest ocean beds,* he could have told them, but that would have slung too many questions his way, ones he had no desire to answer. *'How the fuck do you know that?'*

403

Good question.

No. Bad question.

He'd kept silent.

Out past the diggers now, ignoring them as they straightened to lean on shovels and stare at him. He walked on to the trail the column had made, a road of sorts where the sharp stones had been kicked clear by the passage of thousands of boots. Twenty paces. Thirty, well away from the camp now. He halted.

All right, then. Show yourselves.

He waited, fingers combing through his beard, expecting to see the dust swirl up from the path, lift into the air, find shape. The simple act of setting eyes upon a T'lan Imass depressed Ruthan Gudd. There was shame in making the wrong choice – only a fool would deny that. And just as one had to live with the choice, so too was one forced to live with the shame. Well, perhaps *live* wasn't the right word, not with the T'lan Imass.

Poor fools. Make yourselves the servants of war. Surrender every- thing else. Bury your memories. Pretend that the choice was a noble one, and that this wretched existence is good enough. Since when did vengeance answer anything? Anything of worth?

I know all about punishment. Retribution. Wish I didn't but I do. It all comes down to eliminating that which offends. As if one could empty the world of bastards, or scour it clean of evil acts. Well, that would be nice. Too bad it never works. And all that satisfaction, well, it proves short-lived. Tasting like . . . dust.

No poet could find a more powerful symbol of futility than the T'lan Imass. Futility and obstinate stupidity. *In war you need something to fight for. But you took that away, didn't you? All that you fought to preserve had ceased to exist. You condemned your entire world to oblivion, extinction. Leaving what? What shining purpose to drive you on and on?*

Oh yes, I remember now. Vengeance.

No swirls of dust. Just two figures emerging from the lurid, dust- wreathed west, shambling on the trail of the Bonehunters.

The male was huge, battered, hulking. His stone sword, carried loosely in one hand, was black with sun-baked blood. The female was more gracile than most T'lan Imass, dressed in rotted sealskins, and on her shoulder a small forest of wood, bone and ivory harpoons. The two figures halted five paces from Ruthan Gudd.

The male bowed his head. 'Elder, we greet you.'

Ruthan scowled. 'How many more of you are out there?'

'I am Kalt Urmanal, and the Bonecaster at my side is Nom Kala of the Brold. The two of us are all that are here. We are deserters.'

'Are you now? Well, among the Bonehunters, desertion is punishable

404

by death. Tell me, since that obviously won't work, how do the T'lan Imass punish deserters, Kalt?'

'They don't, Elder. Deserting is punishment enough.'

Sighing, Ruthan Gudd looked away. 'Who leads the T'lan Imass army, Kalt? The army you fled?'

The female, Nom Kala, answered. 'First Sword Onos T'oolan. Elder, there is the smell of ice about you. Are you Jaghut?'

'Jaghut? No. Do I look like a Jaghut?'

'I do not know. I have never seen one.'

Never – what? 'I haven't washed in some time, Nom Kala.' He combed his beard. 'Why did you follow us? What do you want with the Bonehunters? No, wait, let us return to that later. You say that Onos T'oolan, the First Sword, leads an army of T'lan Imass – which clans? How many Bonecasters? Do they walk this same desert? How far away?'

Kalt Urmanal said, 'Far to the south, Elder. Of Bonecasters there are few, but of warriors there are many. Forgotten clans, remnants of armies broken on this continent in ancient conflicts. Onos T'oolan summoned them—'

'No,' said Nom Kala, 'the summons came from Olar Ethil, in the making of Onos—'

'*Shit*,' Ruthan swore.

Both T'lan Imass fell silent.

'This is turning into a real mess.' Ruthan clawed again at his beard, glared at the undead warriors. 'What is she planning? Do you know?'

'She intends to wield the First Sword, Elder,' Nom Kala replied. 'She seeks . . . redemption.'

'She has said this to you, Bonecaster?'

'No, Elder, she has not. She remains distant from Onos T'oolan. For now. But I was born on this soil. She cannot walk it with impunity, nor hide the power of her desires. She journeys eastward, parallel with Onos T'oolan.' Nom Kala hesitated, and then added, 'The First Sword is also aware of her, but he remains defiant.'

'He is a Childslayer, Elder,' said Kalt Urmanal. 'A black river has drowned his mind, and those who chose to follow him can no longer escape its terrible current. We do not know the First Sword's intent. We do not know the enemy he will choose. But he seeks annihilation. Theirs or his own – he cares not how the bones will fall.'

'What has driven him to such a state?' Ruthan Gudd asked, chilled by the warrior's words.

'She has,' Nom Kala replied.

'Does he know that?'

'He does, Elder.'

'Then could Olar Ethil be the enemy he chooses?'

405

Both T'lan Imass were silent for a moment, and then Kalt Urmanal said, 'We had not considered that possibility.'

'It seems she betrayed him,' Ruthan observed. 'Why shouldn't he return the favour?'

'He was noble, once,' said Kalt. 'Honourable. But now his spirit is wounded and he walks alone no matter how many follow behind him. Elder, we are creatures inclined to . . . excess. In our feelings.'

'I had no idea,' Ruthan said in a dry tone. 'So while you have fled one nightmare, alas, you have found another.'

'Your wake is filled with suffering,' Nom Kala said. 'It was an easy path to follow. You cannot cross this desert. No mortal can. A god has died here—'

'I know.'

'But he is not gone.'

'I know that, too. Shattered into a million fragments, but each fragment lives on. D'ivers. And there is no hope of ever sembling back into a single form – it's too late and has been for a long time.' He waved at the flies. 'Mindless, filled with pathetic need, understanding nothing.' He cocked his head. 'Not so different from you, then.'

'We do not deny how far we have fallen,' said Kalt Urmanal.

Ruthan Gudd's shoulders sagged. He looked down. 'So have we all, T'lan Imass. The suffering here is contagious, I think. It seeps into us, makes bitter our thoughts. I am sorry for my words—'

'There is no need to apologize, Elder. You spoke the truth. We have come to you, because we are lost. Yet something still holds us here, even as oblivion beckons us with the promise of eternal peace. Perhaps, like you, we need answers. Perhaps, like you, we yearn to hope.'

He twisted inside at that, was forced to turn away. *Pathetic! Yield them no pity!* Struggling against tears, he said, 'You are not the first. Permit me to summon your kin.'

Five warriors rose from the dust behind him.

Urugal the Woven stepped forward and said, 'Now we are seven again. Now, at last, the House of Chains is complete.'

Hear that? All here now, Fallen One. I didn't think you could get this far. I really didn't. How long have you been building this tale, this relentless book of yours? Is everyone in place? Are you ready for your final, doomed attempt to win for yourself . . . whatever it is you wish to win?

See the gods assembling against you.

See the gates your poison has frayed, ready to break asunder and unleash devastation.

See the ones who stepped up to clear this path ahead. So many have died. Some died well. Others died badly. You took them all. Accepted their flaws – the weak ones, the fatal ones. Accepted them and blessed them.

And you weren't nice about it either, were you? But then, how could you be?

He knew then, with abject despair, that he would never comprehend the full extent of the Crippled God's preparations. How long ago had it all begun? On what distant land? By whose unwitting mortal hand? *I'll never know. No one will. Win or fail, no one will. In this, he is as unwitnessed as we are. Adjunct, I am beginning to understand you, but that changes nothing, does it?*

The book shall be a cipher. For all time. A cipher.

Looking up, he found that he was alone.

Behind him, the army was struggling to its feet.

'Behold, night is born. And we must walk with it.' You had the right *of that, Gallan.* He watched the burial crew rolling wrapped corpses into the grave pits. *Who were those poor victims? What were their names? Their lives? Does anyone know? Anyone at all?*

'He's not broached a single cask?'

Pores shook his head. 'Not yet. He's as bad off as the rest of us, sir.'

Kindly grunted, glanced over at Faradan Sort. 'Tougher than I'd have expected.'

'There are levels of desperation,' she said. 'So he hasn't reached the next one yet. It'll come. The question is, what then, Kindly? Expose him? Watch our soldiers tear him limb from limb? Does the Adjunct know about any of this?'

'I'm going to need more guards,' said Pores.

'I will speak to Captain Fiddler,' Kindly said. 'We'll put the marines and the heavies on those posts. No one will mess with them.'

Pores scratched something on his wax ledger, read over what he'd written and then nodded. 'The real mutiny is brewing with the haul teams. That food is killing us. Sure, chewing on dried meat works up some juices, but it's like swallowing a bhederin cow's afterbirth after it's been ten days in the sun.'

Faradan Sort made a choking sound. 'Wall's foot, Pores, couldn't you paint a nicer picture?'

Pores raised his eyebrows. 'But Fist, I worked on that one all day.'

Kindly rose. 'This night is going to be a bad one,' he said. 'How many more are we going to lose? We're already staggering like T'lan Imass.'

'Worse than a necromancer's garden party,' Pores threw in, earning another scowl from Faradan Sort. His smile was weak and he returned to the wax tablet.

'Keep an eye on Blistig's cache, Pores.'

407

'I will, sir.'

Kindly left the tent, one wall of which suddenly sagged.

'They're folding me up,' Pores observed, rising from the stool and wincing as he massaged his lower back. 'I feel thirty years older.'

'We all do,' Sort muttered, collecting her gear. 'Live with it.'

'Until I die, sir.'

She paused at the tent entrance. Another wall sagged. 'You're thinking all wrong, Pores. There is a way through this. There has to be.'

He grimaced. 'Faith in the Adjunct untarnished, then? I envy you, Fist.'

'I didn't expect you to fold so quickly,' she said, eyeing him.

He stored his ledger in a small box and then looked up at her. 'Fist, some time tonight the haul crew will drop the ropes. They'll refuse to drag those wagons one more stride, and we'll be looking at marching on without food, and when that happens, do you understand what it will mean? It will mean we've given up – it'll mean we can't see a way through this. Fist, the Bonehunters are about to announce their death sentence. That is what I will have to deal with tonight. Me first, before any of you show up.'

'So stop it from happening!'

He looked at her with bleak eyes. 'How?'

She found she was trembling. 'Guarding the water – can you do it with just the marines?'

His gaze narrowed on her, and then he nodded.

She left him there, in his collapsing tent, and set out through the breaking camp. *Talk to the heavies, Fiddler. Promise me we can do this. I'm not ready to give up. I didn't survive the Wall to die of thirst in a fucking desert.*

Blistig glared at Shelemasa for a moment longer, and then fixed his hate-filled eyes on the Khundryl horses. He could feel the rage flaring inside him. *You bitch – look what you're doing to us, all for some war we don't even want.* 'Just kill them,' he commanded.

The young woman shook her head.

Heat flushed his face. 'We can't waste the water on horses!'

'We aren't, Fist.'

'What do you mean?'

'The horses get our allotted water,' Shelemasa said. 'And we drink from the horses.'

He stared, incredulous. 'You drink their piss?'

'No, Fist, we drink their blood.'

'Gods below.' *Is it any wonder you all look half dead?* He rubbed at his face, turned away. *Speak the truth, Blistig. It's all you have left.* 'You've had your cavalry charge, Khundryl,' he said, watching a troop

408

of heavies marching past – going the wrong way. 'There won't be another, so what's the point?'

When he turned back he saw that she had gone white. *The truth. Nobody has to like it.* 'The time has come for hard words,' he said. 'You're done – you've lost your warleader and got an old woman instead, a pregnant one at that. You haven't got enough warriors left to scare a family of berry-pickers. She just invited you along out of pity – don't you see that?'

'That's enough,' snapped another voice.

He turned to see Hanavat standing behind him. Blistig bared his teeth. 'I'm glad you heard all that. It needed saying. Kill the damned horses. They're useless.'

She studied him with flat eyes. 'Fist Blistig, while you hid behind Aren's precious walls, the Wickans of the Seventh Army fought a battle in a valley, and in that battle they mounted a charge upslope, into a wall of the enemy. They won that battle when it seemed they could not. But how? I will tell you. Their shamans had selected a single horse, and with tears in their eyes they fed on its spirit, and when they were done that horse was dead. But the impossible had been achieved, because Coltaine expected no less.'

'I hid behind a fucking wall, did I? I was the garrison commander! Where else would I be?'

'The Adjunct has asked us to preserve our horses, and this we shall do, Fist, because she expects no less from us. If you must object, deliver your complaint to the Adjunct. As for you, as you are not the Fist in command of the Khundryl, I tell you now that you are no longer welcome here.'

'Fine. Go ahead and choke on that blood, then. I spoke out of concern, and in return you do nothing but insult me.'

'I know the reasons behind your words, Fist Blistig,' Hanavat said levelly.

He met her eyes unflinching, and then, shrugging, he said, 'The slut speaks.' He turned and left them.

As the Fist walked away, Shelemasa drew a shaky breath and stepped close to Hanavat. 'Mother?'

She shook her head. 'I am fine, Shelemasa. The fever thirst is on Fist Blistig. That and nothing more.'

'He said we were *done*. I will *not* be pitied! Not by anyone! The Khundryl—'

'The Adjunct believes we are still of worth, and so do I. Now, let us tend to our beasts. Do we have enough fodder?'

Shelemasa shook herself, and then nodded. 'More than we need, in fact.'

'Good. And our water?'

She winced.

Hanavat sighed, and then arched her back with a groan. 'I'm too old to think of her as my mother,' she said, 'and yet I do. We still breathe, Shelemasa. And we can still walk. For now, that must be enough.'

Shelemasa stepped closer, as close as she dared to get. 'You have borne children. You have loved a man—'

'Many men, truth be told.'

'I thought that, one day, I could say the same for myself. I thought I could look back and be satisfied.'

'You don't deserve to die, Shelemasa. I could not agree with you more, and so you shall not. We will do whatever must be done. We will live through this—' She cut herself off then and Shelemasa looked up to see her staring back at the Khundryl camp. She followed the older woman's gaze.

Gall had appeared, and at his side stood Jastara, his eldest son's widow. Shelemasa moved to block Hanavat from their view, and then walked over. 'Warleader,' she hissed, 'how many times will you wound her?'

The warrior seemed to have aged a dozen years since she had last seen him, but it did nothing to cool her fury. And in his unwillingness to meet her eyes she saw only cowardice.

'We go to our sons this night,' he said. 'Tell her that. I do not mean to wound. Tonight, or the next. Soon.'

'Soon,' said Jastara, her tone harsh. 'And I will see my husband again. I will walk at his side—'

Shelemasa felt disgust twisting her face. 'After sleeping with his father? Will you, Jastara? Is his spirit here? Does he see you? Does he know all that you have done? Yet you tell yourself you will be at his side again – you are mad!' A hand settled on her shoulder and she turned. 'Hanavat – no—'

'You are so quick to defend me, Shelemasa, and for that I am ever grateful. But I will speak to my husband.'

Jastara had backed away at Shelemasa's words, and a moment later she fled, pushing through the crowd that had gathered. A few of the older women spun to strike at her when she rushed past. A dozen youths gathered nearby laughed and one reached down for a stone—

'Belay that, scout!'

At the bark, the girl froze.

Captain Fiddler was walking into the Khundryl camp, to collect his scouts. He glanced over at Gall, Hanavat and Shelemasa and for an instant it seemed he was simply going to continue on to his charges, but then he altered his path and approached.

'No disrespect intended, Mother Hanavat, but we don't have time for all this shit. Your histories are just that – a heap of stories you keep dragging everywhere you go. Warleader Gall, all that doom you're bleating on about is a waste of breath. We're not blind. None of us. The only question you have to deal with now is how are you going to face that end? Like a warrior, or on your Hood-damned knees?' Then, ignoring the crowd, Fiddler made his way towards his troop. 'We're on point this night, scouts. Take up those spears and let's get moving. The column's about to march.'

Shelemasa watched the Malazan lead the youths away.

From Hanavat, a low laugh, and then, 'No disrespect, he said. And then he went and slapped us all down.'

'Mother—'

'No, he was right, Shelemasa. We stand here, naked but for our pride. Yet see how heavy it weighs. Well, this night, I think, I will try to step lighter – after all, what have I left to lose?'

Your child.

As if Hanavat had read her mind, she reached up and brushed Shelemasa's cheek. 'I will die first,' she whispered, 'and the one within me shall quickly follow. If this is how it must be, then I must accept it. As must we all.' She faced her husband then. 'But not on our knees. We are Khundryl. We are the Burned Tears.'

Gall said, 'If I had not led us down to Aren, our children would still be alive. I have killed our children, Hanavat. I – I need you to hate me.'

'I know, husband.'

Shelemasa could see that beseeching need in Gall's reddened eyes, but his wife gave him nothing more.

He tried again. 'Wife, the Burned Tears died at the Charge.'

Hanavat simply shook her head, then took Shelemasa's hand and led her into the camp. It was time to leave. They had to see to the horses. Shelemasa spared one glance back and saw Gall standing alone, hands covering his face.

'In grief,' murmured Hanavat, 'people will do anything to escape what cannot be escaped. Shelemasa, you must go to Jastara. You must take back your words.'

'I will not.'

'It is not for you to judge – yet how often is it that those in no position to judge are the first to do so, and with such fire and venom? Speak to her, Shelemasa. Help her find some peace.'

'But how can I, when just to think of her fills me with disgust?'

'I did not suggest it would be easy, daughter.'

'I will give it some thought.'

'Very well. Just don't wait too long.'

*   *   *

The army lifted into motion like a beast mired in mud, one last exhausted heave forward, weight dragging it down. The wagons lurched behind the teams of haulers as they strapped on their harnesses and took up the ropes. Scores of tents were left standing, along with a scattering of cookpots and soiled clothing lying like trampled flags.

Flies roiled in clouds to swarm the hunched-over, silent soldiers, and overhead the glow of the Jade Strangers was brighter than any moonlight, bright enough for Lostara Yil to see every detail on the painted shields of the regulars, which they now carried to keep the flies from their backs. The lurid green painted drawn, lined faces with a ghastly corpulent hue, and made unearthly the surrounding desert. Clouds of butterflies wheeled above like ever-building storms.

Lostara stood with Henar Vygulf at her side, watching the Adjunct draw on her cloak, watching her lifting the hood. She had taken to leading the vanguard herself, five or six paces ahead of everyone else, excepting Captain Fiddler's thirty or so Khundryl youths who ranged ahead a hundred paces, scouts with nothing to scout. Lostara's eyes stayed on the Adjunct.

'In Bluerose,' said Henar, 'there is a festival of the Black-Winged Lord once every ten years on winter's longest night. The High Priestess shrouds herself and leads a procession through the city.'

'This Black-Winged Lord is your god?'

'Unofficially, under the suspicious regard of the Letherii. Highly proscribed, in fact, but this procession was one of the few that they did not outlaw.'

'You were celebrating the year's longest night?'

'Not really. Not in the fashion that farmers might each winter, to celebrate the coming of the planting season – very few farms around Bluerose; we were mostly seafaring. Well, maritime, anyway. It was meant to summon our god, I suppose. I was not much for making sense of such things. And as I said, it was once every ten years.'

Lostara waited. Henar wasn't a talkative man – *thank Hood* – but when he spoke he always had something useful to say. Eventually.

'Hooded, she'd walk silent streets, followed by thousands equally mute, down to the water's edge. She would stand just beyond the reach of the surf. An acolyte would come up to her carrying a lantern, which she would take in one hand. And at the moment of dawn's first awakening, she would fling that lantern into the water, quenching its light.'

Lostara grunted. 'Curious ritual. Instead of the lantern, then, the sun. Sounds like you were worshipping the coming of day more than anything else.'

'Then she would draw a ceremonial dagger and cut her own throat.'

412

Shaken, Lostara Yil faced him, but found she had nothing to say. No response seemed possible. Then a thought struck her. 'And that was a festival the Letherii permitted?'

'They would come down and watch, picnicking on the strand.' He shrugged. 'For them it was one less irritating High Priestess, I suppose.'

Her gaze returned to the Adjunct. She had just set out. A shrouded figure, hidden from all behind her by that plain hood. The soldiers fell in after her and the only sound that came from them was the dull clatter of their armour, the thump of their boots. Lostara Yil shivered and leaned close to Henar.

'The hood,' Henar muttered. 'It reminded me, that's all.'

She nodded. But she dreaded the thought of that story coming back to haunt them.

'I can't believe I died for this,' Hedge said, wanting to spit but there wasn't enough in his mouth to do it, and of course he'd have to be mad to waste the water. He turned and glared at the three oxen pulling Bavedict's carriage. 'Got any more of that drink you gave 'em? They're looking damned hale, Alchemist – we could all do with a sip or three.'

'Hardly, Commander,' Bavedict said, one hand on the hawser. 'They've been dead for three days now.'

Hedge squinted at the nearest beast. 'Well now, I'm impressed. I admit it. Impressed, and that can't be said often of old Hedge.'

'In Letheras,' Bavedict said, 'there are dozens of people wandering around who are in fact dead and have been for some time. Necromantic alchemy is one of the most advanced of the Uneasy Arts among the Letherii. In fact, of all the curse elixirs I sold, the one achieving everlasting undeath was probably the most popular – as much as anything costing a chestful of gold can be popular.'

'Could you do this for a whole army?'

Bavedict blanched. 'C-commander, such things are, er, prohibitively difficult to achieve. Preparing a single curse-vial, for example, involves months of back-breaking effort. Denatured ootooloo spawn – the primary ingredient – well, you'd be lucky to get three drops a night, and harvesting is terribly risky, not to mention exhausting, even for a man reputedly as skilled as myself.'

'Ulatoo spawn, huh? Never heard of it. Never mind, then. It was just a notion. But, you got any more of that stuff?'

'No sir. I judged as greatest the need of the Bridgeburners for the munitions in this carriage—'

'Shh! Don't use that word, you fool!'

'Sorry, sir. Perhaps, then, we should invent some other term – something innocuous, that we could use freely.'

Hedge rubbed at his whiskered jaw. 'Good idea. How about . . . kittens?'

'Kittens, sir? Why not? Now then, our carriage full of kittens is not something that can be abandoned, is it, sir? And I should tell you, the entire company of Bridgeburners has not the strength to haul it.'

'Really? Well, er, just how many kittens you got stuffed in there?'

'It's the raw ingredients, sir. Bottles and casks and vials and . . . er, tubing. Condensers, distillation apparatuses. Um, without two cats of opposite gender, sir, making kittens is not an easy venture.'

Hedge stared for a moment, and then nodded. 'Oh, ah, of course, Alchemist. Just so.' He glanced to his right, where a squad of marines had just come up alongside them, but their attention was on the wagon loaded with food and water that they were guarding, or so Hedge assumed since they were resting hands on hilts and looking belligerent. 'Well, keep at it then, Bavedict. Never can have too many kittens, can we?'

'Precisely, sir.'

Six paces behind the two men, Rumjugs leaned close to Sweetlard. 'I had me some kittens once, you know.'

Sweetlard shot her an unsurprised look. 'Errant knows, you'll take coin from anybody, love.'

He had a swagger, I remember that much. And how I'd get sick, my stomach burning like I'd swallowed coals, every time he came into the house. Ma, she was a bird, really, the kind that flits about as if no branch gives comfort, no leaf makes perfect shade. And her eyes would leap to him and then away again. But in that one look she'd know if something bad was on the way.

If it was, she'd edge closer to me. The jay is in the tree, the chick is in danger. But there was nothing she could do. He weighed twice as much as she did. He once threw her through the shack's flimsy wall. That time was something of a mistake for old Da, since it took outside what went on inside, so people saw the truth of it all. My little family.

There must've been a neighbour, someone on the street, who'd seen and decided he didn't much like it. A day later Da was dragged back to the house beaten close to death, and there we were, Ma and her two boys – that was before my brother ran away – there we were, nursing him back.

How stupid was that? We should've finished what that right-thinking neighbour had started.

But we didn't.

That swagger, and Ma darting about.

I remember the last day of all that. I was seven, almost eight. Quiet Ginanse, who lived up the street and worked as a knife-sharpener, had

414

been found strangled in the alley behind his shop. People were upset. Ginanse had been solid, an old veteran of the Falar Wars, and though he had a weakness for drink he wasn't a violent drunk. Not at all. Too much ale and he wanted to seduce every woman he saw. A sweet soul, then. That's what Ma used to say, hands fluttering like wings.

So people were upset. He'd been drunk the night before. In no shape to defend himself. The rope that had killed him was horsehair – I remember how people talked about that, as if it was important, though I didn't know why at the time. But they'd found horsehairs in Gin's neck.

The old women who shared a house on the corner, three of them, seemed to be looking at us again and again – we were outside, listening to everybody talking, all those emotions running high. Ma was white as plucked down. Da was on the bench beside the shack's door. He'd gotten a rash on his hands and was slowly melting a lump of lard between them. There'd been a strange look in his eye, but for once he wasn't offering any opinion on the matter.

Horsehair. A tradition among the outliers, the wood-cutting camps east of the city. 'How adulterers are hung, aye?' And the old women nodded. 'But old Ginanse, he ain't never—' 'No, couldn't, y'see? Got burned down there – was on a ship that caught fire when they took Falar Harbour. He couldn't do nothing.'

The drunk seducer with nowhere to take it. How shit-fouled miserable is that? Breaks the heart.

And he'd always a kind word for Ma, when she went to him to get the one knife we owned sharpened. Hardly charged a thing either. 'That blade a mouse couldn't shave with, hah! Hey, boy, your ma ever let you shave a mouse? Good practice for when one shows up under yer nose! Few years yet, though.'

'So,' said someone in the crowd, 'a jealous man – no, make it a jealous, stupid man. With wood for brains.' And a few people laughed, but they weren't pleasant laughs. People were working up to something. People knew something. People were figuring it out.

Like a bird in a thorn bush, Ma slipped inside without a sound. I followed her, thinking about poor old Ginanse and wondering who was gonna sharpen Ma's knife now. But Da got up right then and went in a step before me. His hands were dripping melted fat.

I don't remember exactly what I saw. Just a flash, really. Up close to Da's face, just under his huge, bearded jaw. And he made a gurgling sound and his knees bent as if he was about to sit down – right on me. I jumped back, tripped in the doorway and landed in the dust beside the bench.

Da was making spitting sounds, but not from his mouth. From his neck. And when he landed on his knees, twisting round in the

415

doorway as if wanting to come back outside, the front of his chest was all wet and bright red. I looked into my father's eyes. And for the first and only time in my life with him, I actually saw something alive in there. A flicker, a gleam, that went out for good as he slumped on the threshold.

Behind him, Ma stood holding that little knife in her right hand.

'Here y'go, boy, hold it careful now. It's sharp enough to shave a mouse – Bridgeburner magic, what I can do with decent iron. Give us another smile, sweet Elade, it's all the payment I ask, darling.'

'Well now, recruit, y'ever stand still? Seen you goin' round and round and round. Tell me, was your old man a court clown or something?'

No, Master-Sergeant, my da was a wood-cutter.

'Really? Outlier blood? But you're a scrawny thing for a wood-cutter's son. Not one for the trade then?'

He died when I was seven, Master-Sergeant. I was of no mind to follow his ways. I ended up learning most from my ma's side of the family – had an aunt and uncle who worked with animals.

'Found you a name, lad.'

Master-Sergeant?

'See, I wrote it right here, making it official. Your name is Widdershins, and you're now a marine. Now get out of my sight – and get someone to beat those dogs. That barking's driving me mad.'

'How's the stomach, Wid?'

'Burns like coals, Sergeant.'

A half-dozen regulars were coming up alongside them. The one in the lead eyed Balm and said, 'Fist Blistig assigned us t'this one, Sergeant. We got it in hand—'

'Best under a blanket, Corporal,' said Balm.

Throatslitter piped an eerie laugh, and the squad of regulars jumped at the sound.

'Your help's always welcome,' Balm added. 'But from now on, these wagons got details of marines to help guard 'em.'

The corporal looked nervous enough for Widdershins to give him a closer look. Now that's an awfully plump face for someone on three tiny cups a day.

The corporal was stubborn or stupid enough to try again. 'Fist Blistig—'

'Ain't commanding marines, Corporal. But tell you what, go to him and tell him all about this conversation, why don't you? If he's got a problem he can come to me. I'm Sergeant Balm, Ninth Squad. Or, if I rank too low for him on all this, why, he can hunt down Captain

416

Fiddler, who's up ahead, on point.' Balm cocked his head and scratched his jaw. 'Seem to recall, from my basic training days, that a Fist outranks a captain – hey, Deadsmell, is that right?'

'Mostly, Sergeant. But sometimes, well, it depends on the Fist.'

'And the captain,' added Throatslitter, nudging Widdershins with a sharp elbow.

'Now there's a point,' Balm mused. 'Kinda sticky, like a hand under a blanket.'

Throatslitter's second laugh sent them scurrying.

'Those soldiers looked flush,' Widdershins muttered once they'd retreated into the gloom. 'At first, well, the poor fools were just following orders, so I thought you was being unkind, Sergeant – but now I got some suspicions.'

'That's an executable offence,' said Deadsmell. 'What you're suggesting there, Wid.'

'It's going to happen soon if it hasn't already,' Widdershins said, grimacing. 'We all know it. Why d'you think Fid nailed us to these wagons?'

Throatslitter added, 'Heard we was getting our heavies for this, but then we weren't.'

'Nervous, Throaty?' Widdershins asked. 'Only the four of us, after all. The scariest thing about us is your awful laugh.'

'Worked though, didn't it?'

'They went to moan at their captain or whoever,' Balm said. 'They'll be back with reinforcements, is my guess.'

Widdershins jabbed Throatslitter with his elbow, avenging that earlier prod. 'Scared, Throaty?'

'Only of your breath, Wid – get away from me.'

'Got another squad on the other side of these wagons,' Balm pointed out. 'Anyone see which one?'

They all looked over, but the three lines of wretched haulers mostly blocked their view. Throatslitter grunted. 'Could be Whiskeyjack himself. If we get in trouble they won't be able to get through—'

'What's your problem?' Balm demanded.

Throatslitter bared his teeth. 'This is *thirst* we're dealing with here, Sergeant – no, all of you! Where I came from, droughts hit often, and the worst was when the city was besieged – and with Li Heng, well, during the scraps with the Seti that was pretty much every summer. So I know about thirst, all right? Once the fever strikes, there's no stopping it.'

'Well isn't that cheery? You can stop talking now, Throatslitter, and that's an order.'

'I think it's Badan Gruk's squad,' said Deadsmell.

Balm snorted.

Widdershins frowned. 'That's a problem, Sergeant? They're Dal Honese just like you, aren't they?'

'Don't be an idiot. They're from the southern jungles.'

'So are you, aren't you?'

'Even if I was, and I'm not saying I wasn't, or was, that'd make no difference, you understand me, Wid?'

'No. Tayschrenn himself couldn't have worked out what you just said, Sergeant.'

'It's complicated, that's all. But . . . Badan Gruk. Well, could be worse, I suppose. Though like Throaty said, we'd both have trouble supporting the other. I wish Fid ain't pulled the heavies from us. What d'you think he's done with 'em?'

Deadsmell said, 'It was Faradan Sort who come up after Kindly, to talk to the captain. And I wasn't deliberately eavesdropping or nothing. I just happened to be standing close. So I didn't catch it all, but I think there might be some trouble with the food haulers on the back end. I'm thinking that's where the heavies went.'

'What, to lighten the loads?'

Throatslitter yelped.

Lap Twirl scratched at the end of his nose where the tip had once been. 'Kind've insulting,' he muttered, 'them calling themselves Bridge-burners.'

Burnt Rope glanced over at the company marching on his left. Squinted at the three oxen plodding the way oxen plodded the world over. *It's how it looks when y'get someone doing something nobody wants t'do. Draught animals. Of course, it's all down to stupidity, isn't it? Do the work, get food, do more work to get more food. Over and over again. Not like us at all.* 'I don't care what they call themselves, Lap. They're marching just like us. In the same mess, and when we're all bleached bones, well, who could tell the difference between any of us?'

'I could,' Lap Twirl said. 'Easy. Just by looking at the skulls. I can tell if it's a woman or a man, young or old. I can tell if it's a city-born fool or a country one. Where I apprenticed, back in Falar, my master had shelves and shelves of skulls. Was doing a study – he could tell a Napan from a Quon, a Genabackan from a Kartoolian—'

Corporal Clasp, walking a step ahead, snorted loudly and then half turned, 'And you believed him, Lap? Let me guess, that's how he made his living, isn't it? Wasn't it you Falari who had that thing about burying relatives in the walls of your houses? So when rival claims to some building came up, why, everyone ran to the skull-scriers.'

'My master was famous for settling disputes.'

418

'I just bet he was. Listen, working out a man or woman, old or young – sure, I'll buy that. But the rest? Forget it, Lap.'

'Why are we talking about skulls again?' Burnt Rope asked. When no one seemed able to come up with an answer, he went on, 'Anyway, I'm thinking it's all right that we got them Bridgeburners so close, instead of 'em regulars – if we get mobbed at this wagon here, we could call on 'em to help.'

'Why would they do that?' Lap Twirl demanded.

'Can't say. But Dead Hedge, he's a real Bridgeburner—'

'Yeah,' drawled Clasp, 'I heard that, too. Pure rubbish, you know. They're all dead. Everyone knows that.'

'Not Fiddler . . .'

'Except Fiddler . . .'

'And Fiddler and Hedge were in the same squad. Along with Quick Ben. So Hedge is for real.'

'All right, fine, so it isn't pure rubbish. But him helping us is. We get in trouble here, we got no one else to look to for help. Tarr's squad is on the other side of the haulers – no way t'reach us. So, just stay sharp, especially when the midnight bell sounds.'

From ahead of them all, Sergeant Urb glanced back. 'Everyone relax,' he said. 'There won't be any trouble.'

'What makes you so sure, Sergeant?'

'Because, Corporal Clasp, we got Bridgeburners marching beside us. And they got kittens.'

Burnt Rope joined the others in solemn nodding. Urb knew his stuff. They were lucky to have him. Even with Saltlick sent off back-column, they would be fine. Burnt Rope glanced enviously at that huge Letherii carriage. 'Wish I had me some of them kittens.'

If anything, letting go was the easiest among all the choices left. The other choices crowded together, jostling and unpleasant, and stared with belligerent expressions. Waiting, expectant. And he so wanted to turn away from them all. He so wanted to let go.

Instead, the captain just walked, his scouts whispering around him like a score of childhood memories. He didn't want them around, but he couldn't send them away either. It was what he was stuck with. It's what we're all stuck with.

And so there was no letting go, not from any of this. He knew what the Adjunct wanted, and what she wanted of him. *And my marines, and my heavies. And none of it's fair and we both know it and that's not fair either.* Those other choices, willing him to meet their eye, stood before him like an unruly legion. *'Take us, Fiddler, we're all that you meant to say, a thousand times in your life – when you looked on and remained silent, when you let it all slide past instead of taking a step*

419

right into the path of all that shit, all that cruel misery. When you . . . let it go. And felt bits of you die inside, small ones, barely a sting, and then gone.

'But they add up, soldier. Don't they? So she says don't let go this time, don't sidestep. She says – well, you know what she says.'

Fiddler wasn't surprised that the chiding voice within him, the voice of those hardened choices ahead, was Whiskeyjack's. He could almost see his sergeant's eyes, blue and grey, the colour of honed weapons, the colour of winter skies, fixing upon him that knowing look, the one that said, 'You'll do right, soldier, because you don't know how to do anything else. Doing right, soldier, is the only thing you're good at.' And if it hurts? 'Too bad. Stop your bitching, Fid. Besides, you ain't as alone as you think you are.'

He grunted. Now where had that thought come from? No matter. It was starting to look like the whole thing was useless. It was starting to look like this desert was going to kill them all. But until then, he'd just go on, and on, walking.

Walking.

A small, grubby hand tugged at his jerkin. He looked down.

The boy pointed ahead.

Walking.

Fiddler squinted. Shapes in the distance. Figures appearing out of the darkness.

Walking.

'Gods below,' he whispered.

Walking.

CHAPTER FIFTEEN

And all the ages past
Have nothing to say
They rest easy underfoot
Uttering not a whisper
They are dead as the eyes
That looked upon them
Riding the dust that gathers
In lost and forgotten corners
You won't find them
Scratched in scrolls
Or between the bindings
Of leather-bound tomes
Not once carved
On stelae and stone walls
They do not hide
Waiting to be found
Like treasures of truth
Or holy revelation
Not one of the ages past
Will descend from the heavens
Cupped in the hand
Of a god or clutched tight
By a stumbling prophet
All these ages past
Remain for ever untouched
With lessons unlearned
By the fool who can do nothing
But stare ahead
To where stands the future
Grinning with empty eyes

Helpless Days
Fisher kel Tath

TIME HAD BECOME MEANINGLESS. THEIR WORLD NOW ROLLED LIKE waves, back and forth, awash with blood. Yan Tovis fought with her people. She could match her brother's savagery, if not his skill. She could cut down Liosan until the muscles of her arm finally failed, and she'd back away, dragging her sword behind her. Until the rainy, flat blackness unfurled from the corners of her vision and she staggered, chest screaming for breath, moments from slipping into unconsciousness, but somehow each time managing to pull herself back, pushing clear of the press and stumbling among the wounded and dying. And then down on to her knees, because another step was suddenly impossible, and all around her swirled the incessant tidal flow and ebb, the blur of figures moving from body to body, and the air was filled with terrible sound. Shrieks of pain, the shouts of the cutters and stretcher-bearers, the roar of endless, eternal battle.

She understood so much more now. About the world. About the struggle to survive in that world. In any world. But she could find words for none of it. These revelations were ineffable, too vast for the intellect to conquer. She wanted to weep, but her tears were long gone, and all that remained precious could be found in the next breath she took, and the one after that. Each one stunning her with its gift.

Reaching up one trembling forearm, she wiped blood and grime from her face. A shadow passed over her and she lifted her head to see the close pass of another dragon – but it did not descend to the breach, not this time, instead lifting high, seeming to hover a moment behind the curtain of Lightfall before backing away and vanishing into the glare.

Relief came in a nauseating rush that had her leaning forward. Someone came to her side, resting a light arm across her back.

'Highness. Here, water. Drink.'

Yan Tovis looked up. The face was familiar only in that she'd seen this woman again and again in the press, fighting with an Andiian pike. Grateful, yet sick with guilt, she nodded and took the waterskin.

'They've lost the will for it, Highness. Again. It's the shock.'

The shock, yes. That.

Half of my people are dead or too wounded to fight on. As many Letherii. And my brother stands tall still, as if it's all going to plan. As if he's satisfied by our stubborn insanity, this thing he's made of us all.

The smith will bend the iron to his will. The smith does not weep when the iron struggles and resists, when it seeks to find its own shape, its own truth. He hammers the sword, until he beats out a new truth. Edged and deadly.

'Highness, the last of the blood has shattered. I – I saw souls, trapped within – breaking apart. Highness – I saw them screaming, but I heard nothing.'

Yan Tovis straightened, and now it was time to be the one giving comfort. Yet she'd forgotten how. 'Those lost within, soldier, will for ever stand upon the Shore. There are . . . worse places to be.' If she could, she would flinch at her own tone. So lifeless, so cold.

Despite that, she felt something like will steal back into the young woman. It seemed impossible. *Yedan, what have you made of my people?*

How long ago was it? In a place where days could not be measured, where the only tempo was the wash and flood of howling figures, this tide seething into the heart of midnight, she had no answer to this simplest of questions. Lifting the waterskin, she drank deep, and then, half in dread, half in disbelief, she faced Lightfall.

And the wound, where the last of the Liosan still alive on this side were falling to Shake swords and Andiian pikes. Her brother was down there. He had been down there for what seemed for ever, impervious to exhaustion, as units disengaged and others stumbled forward to relieve them, as the warriors of his Watch fell one by one, as veterans of the first battle stepped to the fore in their place, as they too began to fall, and Shake veterans arrived – like this woman at her side.

Brother. You can kill for ever. But we cannot keep up with you. No one can.

I see an end to this, when you stand alone, and the dead shall be your ground.

She turned to the soldier. 'You need to rest. Deliver this news to Queen Drukorlat. The blood wall has shattered. The Liosan have retreated. Half of us remain.'

The woman stared. And then looked around, as if only now realizing the full extent of the horror surrounding them, the heaps of corpses, the entire strand a mass of supine bodies under blood-soaked blankets. She saw her mouth the word *half*.

'When in the palace, rest. Eat.'

But the soldier was shaking her head. 'Highness. I have one brother left to me. I cannot stay in the palace – I cannot leave his side for too long. I am sorry. I shall deliver your message and then return at once.'

Yan Tovis wanted to rail at her, but she bit down on her fury, for it was meant not for this woman, but for Yedan Derryg, who had done this to her people. 'Tell me then, where is your brother?'

The woman pointed to a boy sleeping in a press of Shake fighters resting nearby.

The vision seemed to stab deep into Yan Tovis and she struggled to stifle a sob. 'Be with him, then – I will find another for the message.'

'Highness! I can—'

She pushed the waterskin into the woman's arms. 'When he awakens, he will be thirsty.'

Seeing the soldier's wounded expression as she backed away, Yan Tovis could only turn from her, fixing her eyes once more upon the breach. *It's not you who has failed me*, she wanted to say to that soldier, *it is I who have failed you*. But then she was alone once more and it was too late.

Brother, are you down there? I cannot see you. Do you stand triumphant once more? I cannot see you.

All I can see is what you did. Yesterday. A thousand years ago. In the breath just past. When there are none but ghosts left upon the Shore, they will sing your praises. They will make of you a legend that none living will ever hear – gods, the span of time itself must be crowded with such legends, for ever lost yet whispered eternally on the winds.

What if that is the only true measure of time? All that only the dead have witnessed, all that only they can speak of, though no mortal life will ever hear them. All those stories for ever lost.

Is it any wonder we cannot grasp hold of the ages past? That all we can manage is what clings to our own lives, and what waits within reach? To all the rest, we are cursed to deafness.

And so, because she knew naught else to do, in her mind Yan Tovis reached out – to that moment a day past, or a breath ago, or indeed at the very dawn of time, when she saw her brother lead a sortie into the face of the Liosan centre, and his Hust sword howled with slaughter, and, with that voice, summoned a dragon.

She tightened the straps of her helm and readied her sword. Down at the breach the Liosan were pouring like foam from the wound, and Yan Tovis could see her Shake buckling. Everywhere but at the centre, where her brother hacked his way forward, and all the enemy reeling before him seemed to be moving at half his speed. He could have been cutting reeds for all the resistance they offered him. Even from this distance, blood washed like a bow wave before Yedan's advance, and behind him Shake fighters followed, and she could see how his deadliness infected them, raised them into a state of frenzied fury.

From one flank two Letherii companies pushed in to bolster her people, and she watched the line stiffen, watched it plant its feet and hold fast.

Yan Tovis set off for the other flank, increasing her pace until she was jogging. Anything faster would have instilled panic in those who saw her. But the longer she took, the closer that flank edged towards routing, and the more of her people died beneath the Liosan attackers. Her heart thundered, and trembling took possession of her entire body.

Into the press, shouting now, forcing her way through. Her fighters found her with wild, frightened eyes, fixed upon her with sudden hope.

But they needed more than hope.

She lifted her sword, and became a queen going to war. Unleashed, the battle lust of her royal line, the generation upon generation of this one necessity, this nectar of power, rising within her, taking away the words in her voice, leaving only a savage scream that made those close to her flinch and stare.

Huddling in a corner of her mind was a bleak awareness, observing with an ironic half-smile. *Do you hear me, brother? Here on your left? Do you nod in satisfaction? Do you feel my blood reaching to meet yours? Rulers of the Shake, once more fighting upon the Shore.*

Oh, we have never been as pathetic as we are at this moment, Yedan. Pathetic in our fate, trapped in our roles, our place in things. We were born to this scene. Every freedom was a lie. A terrible, heart-crushing lie.

The enemy was suddenly before her. She greeted them with a smile, and then the flash of her sword.

To either side, her people rallied. Fighting with their queen – they could not let her stand alone, they could not leave her, not now, and what took hold of their lives then was something unruly and huge, a leviathan bristling awake. They struck back, halting the Liosan advance, and then pushed forward.

Light exploded like blood from the wound.

Yedan and his wedge of Shake fighters vanished in the gushing wave.

She saw her brother's followers flung back, tumbling like rag dolls in a hurricane. Weapons flew from hands, helms were torn loose, limbs flailed. They were thrown up against the shins of their kin holding the centre line, even as it reeled back to a howling wind that erupted from the wound.

In the fiery gale, Yedan stood suddenly alone.

Yan Tovis felt ice in her veins. *Dragon breath—*

A massive shape looming in the breach, filling it, and then out from the fulminating light snapped a reptilian head, jaws open in a hissing snarl. Lunging down at her brother.

She screamed.

Heard the jaws impact the ground like the fist of a god – and knew that Yedan was no longer there. Her own voice now keening, she slashed forward, barely seeing those she cut down.

Manic laughter filled the air – *Hust! Awake!*

She broke through, staggered, and saw—

The dragon's head was lifting in a spray of blood-soaked sand, the neck arching, the jaws stretching wide once more, and then, as if from

425

nowhere, Yedan Derryg was directly beneath that enormous serpent head, and he was swinging his laughing sword – and that glee rose to a shriek of delight as the blade's edge chopped deep into the dragon's neck.

He was a man slashing into the bole of a centuries-old tree. The impact should have shattered the bones of his arms. The sword should have rebounded, or exploded in his hands, spraying deadly shards.

Yet she saw the weapon tear through that enormous, armoured neck. She saw the blood and gore erupt in its wake, and then a fountain of blood spraying into the air.

The dragon, its shoulders jammed in the breach, shook with the blow. The long neck whipped upward, seeking to pull away, and in the welling gape of the wound in its throat Yan Tovis saw the gleam of bone. Yedan had cut through to the dragon's spine.

Another gloating shriek announced his backswing.

The dragon's head and an arm's length of neck jumped away then, off to one side, and the yawning jaws pitched nose down and hammered the strand as if mocking that first lunge. The head tilted and then fell with a trembling thump, the eyes staring sightlessly.

The headless neck thrashed upward like a giant blind worm, spitting blood in lashing gouts, and on all sides of the quivering, decapitated beast black crystals pushed up from the drenched sand, drawing together, rising to form faceted walls – and from every corpse that had been splashed or buried in the deluge ghostly forms now rose, struggling within that crystal. Mouths opened in silent screams.

Dodging the falling head, Yedan had simply advanced upon the trembling body filling the breach. Using both hands, he drove the Hust sword, point first, deep into the beast's chest.

The dragon exploded out from the wound, scales and shattered bone, yet even as Yedan staggered beneath the flood of gore the blood washed from him as would rain upon oil.

Hust. Killer of dragons. You will shield your wielder, to keep your joy alive. Hust, your terrible laughter reveals the madness of your maker.

Yedan's desire to trap the corpse of a dragon in the breach was not to be – not this time – for she could see the ruined body being dragged back in heaving lunges – *more dragons behind this one, crowding the gate.*

Will another come through? To meet the fate of its kin?

I think not.

Not yet.

Not for some time.

The Liosan on this side of the wound were dead, bodies heaped on all sides. Her Shake stood atop them, two, three deep under their

426

unsteady feet, and she saw the shock in their faces as they stared upon Yedan Derryg, who stood before the wound – close enough to take a step through, if he so desired, and take the battle into the enemy's realm. And for a moment she thought he might – nothing was impossible with her brother – but instead he turned round, and met his sister's eyes.

'If you had knelt—'

'No time,' she replied, shaking the blood from her sword. 'You saw that. They know what you would seek to do, brother. They will not permit it.'

'Then we must make it so that they have no say in the matter.'

'They were impatient,' she said.

He nodded, and then faced the fighters. 'They will clear the gate and re-form. Captains! Draw your units back and reassemble to the rear. Sound the call to the Letherii. Shake – you have now stood the Shore, and you stood it well.' He sheathed his weapon, silencing its chilling chuckle. 'This is how we shall measure our last days. Here, on this border drawn with the bones of our ancestors. And none shall move us.

'Shake! Tell me when you have come home – tell me when that truth finally comes to you. You are *home*.'

The words horrified her, but more horrifying still was the answering roar from her people.

Yedan seemed surprised, and he turned to her then, and she saw the truth in his eyes.

Brother, you do not feel it. You do not feel that you have come home. You do not feel as they do!

A flash of something in his gaze, something private between them that shook her as had nothing else. Longing, fear, and despair.

Oh, Yedan. I did not know. I did not know.

Kadagar Fant, Lord of Light, stood trembling before the corpse of Iparth Erule. This was his third visit to the marshalling area before the gate, his third time down from the high wall to stand before the headless dragon lying on its side at the end of a curling swathe of broken black shards. The golden scales had dulled, the belly was bloating with gases, and capemoths clustered in the gaping mouth of the severed neck, a mass of fluttering white wings – as if flowers had burst from the corpse in some manic celebration.

Aparal Forge looked away from his lord, not ready for him yet. He had sent legion after legion through the breach, and with growing despair watched each one retreat, torn and bloody. Hundreds of his soldiers were lying on dripping cots beneath canopies – he could hear their cries amidst the clatter of weapons being readied for the next assault – and thrice their number rested for ever silent in neat rows beyond the cutter trenches. He had no idea how many were lost beyond the breach – a thousand? More? The enemy had no interest in treating Liosan wounded, and why would they? *We would kill their wounded just as quickly, and call it mercy. These are the mechanics of war. It's where logic takes us, every time.*

Overhead sailed three dragons. Like birds startled into the sky, they refused to come down, and had been up there since Iparth's death. Aparal could feel their rage, and something like hunger – as if some part of them, something reptilian and soulless, wanted to descend and feed on that rank carcass. The remaining seven, sembled since the morning, had established discrete encampments on the barrows to either side of the Great Avenue, with their bespoke legions settled around them. The elites, the true Liosan warriors, yet to draw weapons, yet to advance upon the gate, awaiting only Kadagar's command.

When would it come? When would their lord decide that he'd seen enough of his citizens die? Common dwellers of the city, commanded by nobles trapped below the select ranks of the Soletaken, soldiers only in name, and oh how they died!

Fury seethed in him at the thought. *But I will not look to my lord. I will not beseech him yet again. Will he only relent when they're all dead? For whom, then, this victory?* But he knew the answer to that question.

If Kadagar Fant stood alone at the end of all this; if he sat in the gloom of an empty throne room in an empty palace, in an empty city, he would still count it a triumph. Winning Kharkanas was meaningless; what mattered to the Lord of Light was the absolute annihilation of those who opposed him. *On both sides of the breach.*

Do you remember, Kadagar, the day the stranger came to Saranas? We were still children then, still friends, still open to possibilities. But even we shared our shock at his nerve. A human, almost as tall as a Liosan, wearing beneath a tattered woollen cloak a coat of mail that reached down to his ankles, a bastard sword slung under his left arm. Long grey hair, snarled with indifference, a beard stained the hue of rust beneath the thin lips. He had been smiling – they all agreed on that, from the scouts beyond the walls to the guards at the South Gate, to those in the streets who halted to watch him stride towards the citadel at the heart of Saranas.

And he was still smiling when he stepped into the throne room, and your father leaned forward on the High Throne, making the bonewood creak.

It was Haradegar – your uncle – who growled and reached for his sword. Too much arrogance in this stranger. Too much contempt in that smile.

But your father lifted a hand, staying his Weaponmaster, and he spoke to the stranger in a tone we'd not heard before.

'Kallor, High King, welcome to Saranas, last city of Tiste Liosan. I am Krin Ne Fant, Champion of High House Light—'

'Serap's son?'

Their lord flinched, and Kadagar, I saw the shame in your eyes.

'My . . . grandmother, High King. I did not know—'

'She'd have no reason to tell you, would she?' Kallor looked round. 'She was virtually a prisoner here – they even sent her handmaids away. Arrived as a stranger, and as a stranger you were determined to keep her. Is it any wonder she fled this shit-bucket?'

Haradegar's sword hissed free.

Kallor looked over at the Weaponsmith, and grinned, and whatever Haradegar saw in the High King's eyes stole his courage – oh, shame upon shame, Kadagar! Were these your first wounds? I think now that they were.

The High King faced Krin once more. 'I promised her, and so I am here. Krin Ne Fant, your grandmother Serap, of the Issgin line, is dead.'

Krin slowly settled back on the throne, but he now looked shrunken, withering in that bonewood cage. 'What – what happened?'

Kallor grunted. 'What happened? I just told you. She died. Is that not enough?'

'No.'

Shrugging, the High King said, 'Poison. By her own hand. I found her at dawn on the first day of the Season of Flies, cold and still on the throne I made for her with my own hands. Krin Ne Fant, I am her murderer.'

I remember the silence that followed. I remember how dry my mouth was, and how I could not look anywhere but at this terrible, grey man who stood as one without fear, yet spoke words inviting violence.

But Fant was shaking his head. 'If . . . you said "by her own hand"—'

The smile turned into a snarl. 'Do you truly believe suicide belongs solely to the one taking his or her own life? All that rot about selfishness and self-hatred? The lies we tell ourselves to absolve us of all blame, of all the roles that we played in that wretched death?' He raised one chain-clad hand, pointed a finger first at Krin and then with a sweeping gesture at all who stood in the throne room. 'You all had your parts to play in her death. The doors you kept locked. The loyal servants and friends you took from her. Your ill-disguised whispers behind her back or when she stepped into a room. But I have not come to avow vengeance on her behalf. How can I? The freshest blood of guilt is the pool I now stand in. I could not love her enough. I can never love enough.

'I killed her. One drop of poison each day, for a thousand years.

'By her wishes, I return to Saranas. By her wishes, I bring you this.' And then he drew from beneath his grey cloak a bedraggled rag doll. Flung it so that it slid to the foot of the dais.

And in that time word had travelled out, and now standing inside the doors, twenty paces behind Kallor, stood your father's mother. Serap's daughter.

Did Kallor know she was there? Listening to his words? Would it have changed anything?

'She was making this for her daughter,' Kallor said, 'and took it with her when she fled. Unfinished. In fact, little more than knotted cloth and wool. And so it remained, for all the centuries I knew and loved her. I surmise,' he added, 'she found it again by accident. And decided it needed . . . finishing. On the dawn when I found her, it was settled into her lap like a newborn child.'

Behind him, Krin's mother made a wounded sound and sank to her knees. Her servants rushed close.

Smiling once more, Kallor unstrapped his weapon harness and let it fall to the tiled floor. The clash rang hollow in the chamber. 'My words are done. I am the killer of Serap, and I await your kiss of righteous vengeance.' And then he crossed his arms and waited.

Why do I remember this now, Kadagar? Of course, for all the miserable tragedy of that moment, was it not what came next that truly filled my chest with ashes?

Krin, his hand lifted, fingers pressed against temple, not even looking up as he gestured with his other hand. And whispered. 'Go, Kallor. Just . . . go.'

And how then I finally understood the High King's smile. Not a thing of pleasure. No, this was the smile of a man who wanted to die.

What did we do? We denied him.

I remember how he reached down to collect his sword, how he turned away, his back to the throne and the man seated upon it, and walked out. I saw him walk past the huddle of retainers and the woman kneeling in their midst, and he paused, looked down at her.

If he said anything then, we did not hear it. If he uttered soft words, none within range ever spoke of them. And then he was walking onward, out and beyond their sight.

Four years later you swore that you would never sire a child. That all the Liosan would be your children, come the day you ascended to the throne. And I might have laughed, too blind to the future awaiting us all these centuries later. I might have wounded you, as children often do.

'Beloved brother.'

Aparal turned. 'Lord.'

'Your thoughts were far away. What were you thinking, that could so drag you from this place?'

Was there longing in Kadagar's eyes? He didn't think so. 'Lord, no more than weariness. A moment's rest.' He looked to the assembled legions. 'They are ready. Good.'

As he moved to join his retinue Kadagar stayed him with one hand and leaned close to whisper, '*What were you thinking about, brother?*'

A rag doll. 'Old friend, it was a moment empty of dreams. A place of grey dust. That and nothing more.'

Kadagar let go, stepped back. 'Aparal – is it true?'

'Lord?'

'The laughter—'

'Yes, Lord. A Hust waits for us, in the hands of a Shake warrior.' He pointed at the carcass of the dragon. 'Two passes of the blade, to slice through Iparth Erule's neck.'

'He must be killed! This Shake warrior!'

'Yes, Lord.'

Kadagar lifted one hand to his brow, reminding Aparal of the father, of poor, lost Krin Ne Fant. 'But . . . how?'

Aparal cocked his head. 'Lord? Why, when all the others have fallen, when he alone remains. When twelve dragons break through. Sire, this is not a legion of Hust. It is one sword.'

And Kadagar was nodding now, eyes flooding with relief. 'Just so, brother.' He glanced back at the carcass. 'Poor Iparth Erule.'

'Poor Iparth Erule.'

Kadagar Fant, Lord of Light, then licked his lips. 'Such a terrible waste.'

In every echo that reached Sandalath Drukorlat, she heard ghosts laughing. Withal sat close, down on the stone of the dais, almost at her feet, but it seemed he was dozing, exhaustion making a mockery of his vigil. She did not mind. Mortal failure was ever tinged with irony, was it not?

She closed her eyes, listening, waiting for the visions to return. Were these sendings from Mother Dark? Or just the cluttered rag-ends of all those lives surrendered to these walls and floors of stone? *Mother, I doubt there is anything of you in these scenes. The gloom is of their own making, and those hard voices rocking so back and forth in my skull, well, I know them all.*

One side crimson with blood, Anomander Rake straightening to face the Hust Legion. 'The invasion has just begun,' he told the waiting warriors. 'We risk being overwhelmed.' He drew a slow, deep breath, jaws briefly clenching in pain. 'I shall wait for them beyond the Rent, to deny them the Throne of Shadow. This leaves the gate itself. Hust Legion! You shall march to the gate. You shall march through it. You shall take the battle to them, and hold them there. And,' he scanned the rows of helmed faces, 'when the last five of you remain, you must give your lives to sealing that wound. You shall, Hust-armed and Hust-armoured, for ever close Starvald Demelain.'

Wailing shrieks from blades and scaled breastplates, from helms, from greaves and gauntlets, a deafening chorus that shattered into wild laughter. But within that insane glee, the faces of the Andiian warriors were expressionless. And with solemn salutes they acknowledged their lord's command.

Hust Legion, we never saw you again.

But the Eleint stopped coming.

Hust Legion, how many did you kill on that other side? How many bones lie in heaps upon that alien plain? There at the gate? I can almost . . . almost see them, a felled forest of bones.

But now shadows slide over them, shadows from the sky.

Anomander Rake, 'for ever' was a lie. But you knew that. You were just buying time. Thinking we would ready ourselves for the next invasion. Did we? Did anyone?

But then, a suspicion whispers in my skull. You made her face us once again. Well, not us. Me.

Killed yourself a dragon, did you, Yedan Derryg?

Feel up to a thousand more?

Withal knew he was dreaming. The Meckros city where he had been born was nothing like this, a place of smoky dark quartzite and walls sheathed in mica and anthracite, and even as the groaning rise and fall beneath his feet told him the city was indeed floating on unseen seas, beyond the canted avenue lining the high sea wall on his left he could see nothing. No stars above, no cresting foam below.

Cordage creaked, the only sounds surrounding him. The city was abandoned, and he was alone.

'*Mortal. She will not listen. She is lost in ages past.*'

He looked round, and then grunted, irritated with himself. She was the Goddess of Dark. What else would he see of her, if not this empty abyss on all sides? 'And me, an island city, untethered and unanchored and caught on unknown currents. Mael knows, Withal, even your dreams lack the subtle touch.'

'*Despair is a curse, Withal of the Meckros. You must warn her—*'

'Forgive me for interrupting, Mother Dark, but she is past listening to me. And to be honest, I don't blame her. I have nothing worth saying. You have made her the ruler of an empty city – how do you expect her to feel?'

Too bold, perhaps, for there came no reply from the surrounding darkness.

He stumbled forward, unsure of his destination, but feeling the need to reach it. 'I have lost my belief in the seriousness of the world. Any world. Every world. You give me an empty city, and I feel like laughing. It's not as if I don't believe in ghosts. I do. How could I not? As far as I'm concerned, we're *all* ghosts.' He paused, set a hand upon the cold, damp stone of the sea wall. 'Only this is real. Only this lasts from moment to moment, stretching on for years. Centuries. We – we just pass through. Filled with ephemeral thoughts—'

'*You surrender too much of yourself, Withal.*'

'It's easy,' he replied, 'when nothing I own is worth a damned thing.'

'*This island city is the ghost. Its truth lies broken on the seabed. It drifts only in your memory, Withal.*'

He grunted. 'The ghost dreams of ghosts in a ghostly world. This is what I've come to understand, Mother Dark. From the Tiste Andii – and these Liosan. The way you can take a hundred thousand years and crush it all in one hand. There is no truth to time. It's all a lie.'

'*She agrees with you, Withal. She was born a hostage to secret fates, born a hostage to a future she could not imagine, much less defy. In this, it was understood by all, she symbolized every child.*'

'But you took it too far,' he said, shaking his head. 'You never let her grow up.'

'*Yes, we would keep them children for ever.*'

The Meckros city ended with a ragged edge, as if it had been torn in half. Withal continued walking until his steps sent him pitching down through darkness.

He started, head snapping up, and looked round. The throne room of Kharkanas, Sandalath on the throne, hands to her face, sobbing uncontrollably. Swearing under his breath, he rose, unfolding stiff, aching limbs, and went up to take her into his arms.

'They're all dying! Withal! On the Shore – *they're all dying!*'

He held her tight.

Her words muffled by his shoulder, she said, 'Five thousand warriors. From the mines, from the prisons. From the gutters. Five thousand. The Hust Legion – I saw them marching out from the burning city.' She lifted her head, stared at him with tortured eyes. '*Their swords howled. Their armour sang with joy. No one stood by and wept. No. Instead, they ran from the laughter, they fled the streets – those not already dead. The sound – so terrible – the Hust Legion marched to their deaths, and no one watched them go!*'

He slapped her, hard enough to knock her to the floor at the foot of the throne. 'Enough of this, Sand. This palace is driving you mad.'

She twisted round on to her knees, a knife in her hand, eyes blazing with rage.

'Better,' he grunted, and then backed away from the slashing blade. 'Too many wretched ghosts in your skull, woman. They all think they got something useful to tell you, but they don't. They're damned fools, and you know how I know they're damned fools? Because they're still here.'

Warily, he watched her straighten, watched her lick the blood from her lips. Then sheathe the knife. Her sigh was ragged. 'Husband, it's this waiting. Waiting for them all to die, for the Liosan legions to enter the city – the palace. And then they will kill you, and I cannot bear it.'

'Not just me,' he said. 'You, as well.'

'I have no regret for that. None.'

'There are other Tiste Andii. There must be. They are coming—'

'To what end?' She slumped at the foot of the throne. 'To avenge me? And so it goes on and on, back and forth. As if it all meant something.' She looked up. 'Do these walls care? This floor? No, but I will make it different this time, Withal.' She met his eyes with a fierce challenge. 'I will burn this palace down to the ground before they ever get here. I swear it.'

'Sandalath, there is nothing here to burn.'

'There are other ways,' she whispered, 'to summon fire.'

The killing ground was once more clear of corpses, broken weapons and pieces of torn flesh, but the once-white sand was brown as mud. Captain Pithy studied it for a moment longer, and then resumed examining the grip of her sword. The leather cord was loose – twice in the last fight the weapon had shifted in her grip. Looking up, she saw one of the Letherii youths Yedan was using to scavenge decent weapons. 'You! Over here!'

The girl struggled up with her sled and stepped to one side as Pithy began rummaging through the blood-spattered array of weapons. 'Hear any chuckling from any of these, girl?' She looked up and winked. 'Didn't think so, but one can always hope.'

'You're Captain Pithy.'

'So far, aye.' She found a Liosan sword and lifted it clear, testing its weight and balance. Then peering at the honed edge, before snorting. 'Looks a hundred years old, and neglected for half that.' She returned it to the sled. 'Why aren't there any Letherii weapons here?'

'The Liosan steal them, sir.'

'Well, that's one way to beat us – a mass exchange of weapons, until all we're left with is that useless crap they brought from the other side. Better send word to the prince – we need to deny them these particular spoils, and make a point of it.' Pithy retrieved her old sword. 'Here, you got small fingers – see if you can thread that strip through on the end here, where it's pulled loose. Just thread it and I'll do the rest.'

Instead of her fingers, the girl used her teeth, and in moments had managed to tug the leather strip through.

'Smart lass.' Pithy tugged hard on the strip and was pleased to see the coil draw tighter to the wooden handles encasing the tang. 'There, should do for the next fight or two. Thanks for helping fix my sword. Now, off you go – I see 'em massing again on the other side.'

The girl took up the ropes and hurried off with her sled, the ivory runners sliding easily across the strand.

Captain Pithy walked to her place in the line. 'Now,' she said in a loud voice, 'it's Nithe's day off, the lazy shit. He probably thinks he's earned those five whores and the jug of wine sharing his bed, but that was just me feeling sorry for him.'

'Cap'n's a pimp!' someone shouted from a few rows back.

Pithy waited for the laughter to die down. 'Can't make piss on the coin they pay officers in this army, so don't begrudge me something on the side.'

'Never you, Captain!'

Horns sounded and Pithy faced the breach. 'Coming through, soldiers! Harden up now like a virgin's dream! Weapons ready!'

A vague mass of shapes, pushing and then slashing through bruised light thin as skin. Then the blades drew back.

What's this? Something different – what are—

From the wound, three enormous Hounds bursting through. Blood-thick sand sprayed as the creatures skidded. One twisted to one side, shot off towards the Shake line on Pithy's right, a white blur, huge as a bull. Another charged for the other flank, and the one directly before Pithy met her eyes in the instant before it lowered its broad head, and she felt the strength leave her body in a single, soft breath. Then the Hound lunged straight at her.

As the jaws stretched wide, revealing canines long as daggers, Yan Tovis ducked low and swung her sword. The blade bit into the left of the beast's neck, and then rebounded in a splash of blood. Beside her, a Shake warrior shrieked, but the cry was short-lived, vanishing when the beast bit down, its jaws engulfing his head. Bones crunching, the man was lifted from his feet as the Hound reared back, fangs sawing through his neck. Gore sprayed as the headless corpse fell to the sand and rolled on to its back.

Yan Tovis thrust her sword, but the point skidded across the beast's chest.

Snarling, it swung its head. The impact sent Yan Tovis spinning.

Landing hard, she rolled on to her side, seeing Liosan ranks plunging through the breach not fifteen paces from her. She'd lost her sword, and her groping hand found nothing but clumps of blood-glued sand. She could feel her strength faltering, draining away, pain spreading across half her body.

Behind her, the Hound began killing her people.

It ends. As simple as that?

'Pikes!' someone screamed – *was it me?* As the massive Hound leapt for her, Pithy dropped to the sand, twisted as the beast passed directly over her, and thrust her sword into its belly.

The point was punched back out as if fired from a crossbow, driving her elbow into the ground. One of the Hound's back legs lifted her from the sand, carried her flailing forward. She heard the clash of pike shafts close in on all sides. Half stunned, she curled up beneath the beast. Its snarls filled her world, along with the crunch of bones and the shrieks of dying Letherii. She was kicked again, this time spilling her out to one side.

Teeth grinding, she forced herself into a crouch. She still held her sword, glued to her hand now by streams of blood – she was cut somewhere – and she made herself close on the thrashing demon. Lunged.

The blunted, battered tip of the sword caught the Hound in the corner of its left eye. With an almost human scream, the beast lurched away, sending figures sprawling. It was scored with slashes from countless pike-thrusts, white hide streaming crimson, and more soldiers pressed in, pursuing. The Hound stumbled over a corpse, twisted round to face its attackers.

Its left eye was filled with blood.

Got you, you heap of dung!

Someone leapt close, swinging a wood-cutter's axe. The impact on the beast's skull drove it to its knees. The axe handle shattered, and Pithy saw the wedge blade fall away. The Hound's skull gleamed, exposed across half its head, a torn flap of skin dangling down past its jaw.

One-handed Nithe flung the broken handle away, reached for a knife.

The Hound snapped out, jaws hammering into the man. Canines punched through chain, tore deep into his chest. As they ripped free, Nithe's ribs seemed to explode outward in their wake. He spun, landed on his knees.

Pithy shrieked.

The Hound's second bite tore Nithe's face off – forehead, cheekbones, his upper jaw. His mandible dropped down, hanging like a bloody collar. Both his eyes were gone. He pitched forward.

Weaving drunkenly now, the Hound stumbled back. Behind it, Liosan warriors advanced in a bristling line, faces lit with desire.

'*Drive them back!*' Pithy screamed.

Pikes levelled, her Letherii pushed forward.

'*The queen! The queen!*'

Shake warriors suddenly surrounded Yan Tovis. She heard the Hound somewhere behind her, snarls, weapons striking, shafts shattering, terrible cries of pain – a knot of madness tearing ever deeper through the ranks. But protecting her now, a score of her people, forming up to face the Liosan soldiers.

To defend their queen. No, please – don't do this—

There weren't enough of them. They would die for nothing.

The Liosan arrived like the crest of a wave, and in moments rushed round to isolate Yan Tovis and her warriors.

Someone crouched to hand her a sword.

Her throat thick with nausea, she forced herself to her feet.

Seeing the Hound charging for his line on the left flank, Yedan Derryg ran to meet it. The Hust sword loosed a manic, ululating cry, and it seemed that the chilling sound checked the beast – for the briefest of instants – before it launched itself at the prince.

When its jaws reached for him, the head was driving down, anticipating that he would come in low. Instead, Yedan leapt high, twisted parallel with the ground, legs thrown out, and rolled in the air, over the Hound's shoulders, and as he spun, down swung the sword.

The Hust blade shrieked as it bit, athwart the beast's spine, driving down through vertebrae and then spinal cord.

He glanced off its hip coming down, and that hip fell one way and Yedan the other. Striking the ground, he rolled and came to his feet, eyes still on the Hound.

Watched as it toppled, body thumping on the sand, head following. Its eyes stared sightlessly. And beyond the dead beast, rows of faces. Letherii. Shake. Gape-mouthed like fools.

He pointed at Brevity. 'Captain! Advance the flank – shallow wedge! Push into the Liosan and push hard!'

With that he turned and ran across the strand. He'd seen two more Hounds.

Ahead, a wedge formation of Liosan soldiers had closed with Pithy's Letherii and neither side was yielding. Yedan could not see the Hound – had they killed it? No – there, trying to retreat to Lightfall's wound. Should he let it go?

No.

But to reach it, he would have to carve through a score of Liosan.

They saw him, and recoiled.

The Hust sword's laugh was shrill.

Yedan cut the first two down and wounded another before he was temporarily slowed by the rest of them. Swords hacked at him, slashed for his face. Others thrust for his belly and thighs. He blocked, countered. Twisted, pushed forward.

Severed arms and hands spun, releasing the weapons they'd held. Blood sprayed and spat, bodies reeled. Flashes of wild expressions, mouths opening in pain and shock. And then he was past them all, in his wake carnage and horror.

The Hound was three strides from the breach, struggling to stay upright.

He saw its head turn, looked into its eyes, both of which wept blood. Torn lips formed ragged black lines as it snarled at him, heaving to meet him—

But not in time. A thrust. A slash. The Hound's guts billowed out and spilled to the ground in a brown splash of fluids.

It sank down, howling.

Yedan leapt on to its back –

– in time to see a fourth Hound lunge through the gate.

The prince launched himself forward, through the air, sword's point extended.

Into the Hound's broad chest, the blade sliding in with gurgling mirth.

The beast's countering bite hammered him to the ground, but he refused to let go of the sword, dragging it with him. The Hound coughed blood in thick, hot sprays, pitched forward, head lolling.

Yedan kicked it in the throat to free his sword, turned then, and found a mass of Liosan wheeling to face him. No quick way through – both flanks had closed up. *Slow work ahead—*

And then, from the wound behind him, a sudden presence that lifted the hairs on the back of his neck. Looming, foul with chaotic sorcery.

Dragon.

Swearing under his breath, Yedan Derryg swung round, and plunged into Lightfall's wound.

Half her warriors had gone down, and Yan Tovis could feel herself weakening. She could barely lift her sword. *Gods, what is wrong with me? How badly was I injured? I ache – but . . . what else?* She staggered, sagged down on to one knee. The fighting closed in around her. *What—*

Concussions from beyond the Shake line. The Hound screaming in fury and pain.

Head spinning, she looked up.

A grey, miasmic wave of sorcery erupted from the edge of the flank closest to Lightfall, the spitting, crackling wave rushing close to strike the press of Liosan. Bodies erupted in red mist.

Shouting – someone had hold of Yan Tovis under each arm, was dragging her back to the re-formed Shake line – and there was Skwish, rushing to join them.

'*Blood of the queen! Blood of the queen!*' The witch looked ten years old, a child of shining gold. 'Get her clear! The rest a you! Advance!'

And then, from the wound, a reverberation that sent them all to their knees.

Deafened by a sudden, thunderous *crack!* from the breach, Aparal Forge saw his Soletaken kin rearing back. Eldat Pressen, the youngest and boldest of them all, so eager to follow in the wake of the Hounds of Light, was pulling her head back from the wound, and in that recoiling motion blood fountained.

He stared, aghast, as brains and gore sprayed down from her shattered skull.

Her body shook in waves of savage trembling, her tail thrashing, claws digging into and then tearing up the ground. A blind sweep of her tail sent broken bodies flying.

Her huge torso collapsing with massive shudders, Eldat's neck and head writhed, and Aparal could now see the terrible sword blow that had struck her head, splitting the skull open, destroying her and all that she had once been – a bright-eyed, laughing woman. He loosed a sob, but could not turn away. *Eldat. Playing in the garden, in another age. We were thinking only of peace then. But now I wonder, did it ever exist? That age? Or were we just holding our breath? Through all those years, those decades – she grew into a beautiful woman, we all saw that. We witnessed and it gave us pleasure.*

And oh how we all longed to bed her. But she'd set her heart upon the only one of us who would take no woman – or man – into his arms. Kadagar had no time for such things, and if he broke her heart again and again, well, that was the price of serving his people. As father to them all, he could be lover to none.

Kadagar, you stand on the battlements once more.

You look down upon her death, and there is no swift mercy here, no sudden stillness. Her mind is destroyed, but her body refuses to yield. Kadagar Fant, what meaning do you dare take from this?

He struggled to regain self-control. 'Clear the area,' he said to his officers, his voice breaking. He drew a deep breath, cleared his throat. 'She will not die quickly. Not now.'

Ashen-faced, the soldiers set off to relay the commands.

Aparal looked back at the gate. *Hust. You came to meet her, before*

439

she was across the threshold. Where, then, are my soldiers on the other side? Where – gods below – are the Hounds?

In cascading streams of light, Yedan Derryg groped blindly. His sword's laughter was slowly dying away. This was the real danger. Getting lost within Lightfall. But he'd seen little choice, and now he needed to return. One Hound remained. How many of his soldiers were dying even now? Whilst he stumbled blindly in this infernal light?

He could feel the wound's terrible pain, a vicious, biting thing, desperate to heal.

Yedan halted. A wrong step now could take him on to the Liosan plain, facing tens of thousands of the enemy. And more dragons.

Heavy, buffeting currents from behind him. He whirled.

Something, coming through—

The Hound exploded from the light.

He dropped low into a crouch, blade slashing. Cutting through both front legs. The beast stumbled – he twisted and chopped down on its neck. The Hust blade sliced through, leapt out from under its throat with a delighted yelp. The head slammed into the ground at Yedan's feet.

He stood for a moment, staring down at it. Then he sheathed his sword, reached down. His back creaked as he strained to lift the head into his arms. He faced the direction the Hound had been heading and then, with a running start that spun him round, he heaved the head out into the light.

Facing the opposite direction, he set off for the wound.

Aparal's eyes had been on the gate, and he was not alone in seeing the Hound's severed head sailing out to thump and roll on the ground. Shouts of dismay and horror sounded on all sides.

He stared in horror.

It cannot be just one man. It cannot!

A Hust legion waits for us. Hundreds of the cursed slayers, each one driven mad by their weapons. Nothing will stop them, nothing can defeat them.

We cannot win this.

Unblinking, he stared at the huge head, the empty eyes, and then he turned to the dying dragon. It had lurched up against the corpse of Iparth Erule. Had bitten into his rotting flank. But now the motions were slowing, losing that frenzied strength. *Eldat, please die. Please.*

'Not long now,' he whispered. *Not long now.*

Waves of sorcery had pursued the Hound back to the wound, Pully and Skwish advancing behind them, clambering over corpses and torn-up soldiers still in the process of dying. Pithy staggered in their wake. She'd taken a slash to her right shoulder and the bleeding wasn't slowing. Her arm was sheathed in red, with thick threads draining from her fist. Colours were fast fading from the world.

She saw Brevity leading a solid wedge of Letherii, coming up from the left flank. Where was the prince?

And what was that thunder in the breach?

Nearby was the carcass of a Hound, and nearer the breach another one of the horrid, giant beasts, still alive, still kicking where it lay on its side. Soldiers were closing on it, readying their pikes. Killing it was going to take some time.

I'm so tired. All at once the strength left her legs and she sat down. *Bad cut. A fang? A claw? I can't remember – can't twist round enough to see it. But at least the pain's gone.*

'Captain!'

Pithy looked down at the sword in her hand. Smiled. *You did all right. You didn't fail me. Where's that girl? Need to tell her.*

'Someone get one of the witches! Quickly!'

That voice was loud, almost right next to her ear, but it seemed muffled all the same. She saw Brevity running towards her now, but it was hard work, getting over all those bodies, and Pithy wondered if she'd arrive in time.

In time for what? Oh. This.

She settled, tried lying down, found herself cradled in someone's arms.

'Her back's bitten half off! *Where are the witches?*'

'Spent.'

'We need—'

A roaring sound filling her head, Pithy looked down at her hand, the one holding the sword. She willed it to let go, but it refused. She frowned. But a moment later the frown faded. *I understand. I am a soldier. Not a thief. Not a criminal. A soldier. And a soldier never lets go of the sword. Ever. You see it in their eyes.*

Can you see it in my eyes? I bet you can.

It's true. At last, it's true. I was a soldier.

Brevity was still ten paces away when she saw her friend die. She cried out, sagged down amidst the corpses. Crossing this killing field had been a nightmare, a passage of unrelenting horror. Letherii, Shake, Liosan – bodies were bodies, and death was death, and names didn't mean shit. She was soaked in what had been spilled, what had been lost. The abattoir reek was thick enough to drown in. She held her head in her hands.

Pithy.

441

Remember the scams? How we took 'em for all they had? It was us against the world and gods, it felt good those times we won. It never hurt us, not once, beating 'em at their own game. Sure, they had law on their side, making legal all they stole. But then, they'd made up those laws. That was the only difference between us.

We used to hate their greed. But then we got greedy ourselves. Served us right, getting caught.

Island life, now that was boring. Until those Malazans showed up. It all started right then, didn't it? Leading up to here. To now.

They sent us tumbling, didn't they? Fetching us up on the Shore. We could've gone off on our own, back into everything we knew and despised. But we didn't. We stayed with Twilight and the Watch, and they made us captains.

And now we fought us a war. You did, Pithy. I'm still fighting it. Still not knowing what any of it means.

Ten paces, and I can't look over at you. I can't. It's this distance between us. And while I live, I can't cross it. Pithy, how could you leave me so alone?

Yedan Derryg emerged from the wound in Lightfall. The laughter of his sword chewed the air. She stared across at him, thinking how lost he looked. *But no. That's just me. It's just me. He knows what he needs to know. He's worked it all out. It comes with the blood.*

Sergeant Cellows stumped up to Yedan. 'Prince – she's alive, but unconscious. The witches used her—'

'I know,' he replied, studying the killing field.

The sergeant, burly and hulking – a touch of Teblor blood in him – followed his gaze and grunted. 'They hurt us this time, sire. The Hounds mauled the centre and the right flank. One of the beasts reached the wounded before Pully drove it back. But our losses, sire. They hurt us. Nithe, Aysgan, Trapple, Pithy—'

Yedan shot him a hard look. 'Pithy?'

Cellows pointed with a finger that had been cut off just below the knuckle. 'There.' A figure slumped in a weeping soldier's arms. Brevity kneeling nearby, head lowered.

'See to what needs to be done, Sergeant. Wounded. Weapons.'

'Yes, sire – er, Prince?'

'What is it?'

'Seems I'm the last.'

'The last?'

'From your original company, sir. Coast Patrol.'

Yedan felt something crunch at the back of his mouth. He winced, leaned over and spat. 'Shit, broke a tooth.' He lifted his eyes, stared across at Cellows. 'I want you in reserve.'

442

'Sire?'

'For when I need you the most, Sergeant. For when I need you at my side. Until then, you are to remain out of the fight.'

'Sire—'

'But when I call, you'd better be ready.'

The man saluted, and then strode away.

'My last,' Yedan whispered.

He squinted at Brevity. *If all these eyes were not upon me, I would walk to you, Brevity. I would take you in my arms. I would share your grief. You deserve that much. We both do. But I can show nothing like . . . that.*

He hesitated, suddenly unsure. Probed his broken tooth with his tongue. Tasted blood. 'Shit.'

Brevity looked up as the shadow fell over her. 'Prince.' She struggled to stand but Yedan reached out, and the weight of his hand pushed her back down.

She waited for him to speak. But he said nothing, though his eyes were now on Pithy and the soldiers gathering around the fallen woman. She forced herself to follow his gaze.

They were lifting her so gently she thought her heart would rupture.

'It's no easy thing,' murmured Yedan, 'to earn that.'

Aparal Forge saw the enclaves encamped on the surrounding mounds slowly stirring awake, saw the soldiers assembling. *This will be the one, then. When we throw our elites through the gate. Legions of Light. Lord Kadagar Fant, why did you wait this long?*

If they had gone through from the first, the Shake would have fallen by now. Make the first bite the deepest. Every commander knows this. But you wouldn't listen. You wanted to bleed your people first, to make your cause theirs.

But it hasn't worked. They fight because you give them no choice. The pot-throwers dry their hands and the wheel slows and then stops. The weavers lock up their looms. The wood-carvers put away their tools. The road-menders, the lamp-makers, the hawkers of songbirds and the dog-skinners, the mothers and the whores and the consorts and the drug-peddlers – they all set down the things they would do, to fight this war of yours.

It all stops, and for so many now will never start again.

You've ripped out the side of your people, left a gaping wound – a wound like the one before us. And we flow through it like blood. We spill out and scab up on the other side.

The Soletaken were all sembled now. They knew what needed to be done. And as the ranks drew up, Aparal saw his Eleint-fouled kin take position, each at the head of his or her own elite soldiers.

But a Hust Legion awaits us. Slayers of Hounds and Dragons, in all the mad laughter of war.

This next battle. It will be our last.

He looked up to the battlements, but Kadagar was not there. And from his soldiers resting on all sides, his commoners so bloodied, so utterly ruined, Aparal heard the same words. *'He comes. Our lord shall lead us.'*

Our lord. Our very own rag doll.

'Water, Highness. Drink.'

She barely had strength to guide the mouthpiece to her lips. Like rain in a desert, the water flowed through the ravaged insides of her mouth. Lacerated tissues stung awake, her throat opened in relief. She pulled it away, gasping.

'What's happening? Where am I?'

'The witches and your brother, Queen, they killed the Hounds.'

Hounds.

What day is this? In a world without days, what day is this?

'They're little girls now,' her companion said.

Yan Tovis blinked up at her. A familiar face. 'Your brother?'

The woman looked away.

'I'm sorry.'

She shook her head. 'I will see them soon, my queen. That's what I look forward to now.'

'Don't think that way—'

'Forgive me, Highness. I took care of them all my life, but against this, I wasn't enough. I failed. It's too much. From the very start, it was too much.'

Yan Tovis stared up at the woman's face, the dry eyes, the absence of expression. *She's already gone.* '"They await you on the Shore."'

A brittle half-smile. 'So we say over our dead, yes. I remember.'

Over our dead.

'Tell the witches – if they do that to me again – if they use me like that – *ever again* – I will kill them both.'

The woman flinched. 'They look ten years old, Highness.'

'But they aren't. They're two old women, sour and bitter and hateful of the world. Go, give them my warning, soldier.'

With a silent nod, the young woman rose.

Yan Tovis settled her head, felt the sand grinding against the back of her skull. *Empty sky. Dreams of darkness. If I had knelt to the Shore, they couldn't touch me. Instead, they punished me.*

'But if they hadn't,' she whispered, 'those Hounds would have killed hundreds more. Which of us, then, is sour and bitter? Hateful of the world?'

I will go to her. To Kharkanas. I will beg her forgiveness. Neither of us can withstand the weight of this crown. We should cast it off. We can find the strength for that. We must.

Oh, I am a fool. Yedan will not yield. The lives lost must mean something, even when they don't. So, it seems we must all die. It seems we have no choice. Not the Shake, not the Letherii, not Sandalath Drukorlat, Queen of High House Dark.

She reached down and came up with a handful of white sand – crumbled bones. 'It's all here,' she whispered. 'Our entire history, right here. From then . . . to now. To what's coming. All . . . here.' And she watched, as she closed that hand into a fist, as if to crush it all.

CHAPTER SIXTEEN

Stone whispers
Patience
But we take chisel in hand
Child begs
Not yet
But the sands have run out
Sky cries
Fly
But we hold our ground
Wind sings
Free
But roots bind us down
Lover sighs
Stay
But we must be gone
Life pleads
Live
But death is the dream
We beg
Not yet
But the sands have run out
Stone whispers
Patience...

Incantation
Gallan of Kharkanas

'THERE WILL COME A TIME,' VENTURED SECHUL LATH, 'WHEN WE shall be all but forgotten.'

'Speak for yourself,' growled Errastas.

'*And they shall drink blood.* Remember that? Book of Elders. And that is the last memory of us that will remain. As drinkers of blood. A tyranny of thirst. If it is not for us to save our worshippers, then who will – who will save all these wretched mortals?'

Behind them, feet thumping the ground like a drum of war, Kilmandaros said, 'They cannot be saved. They never could.'

'Then what use are we? To any of them?'

Errastas spat on the ground, and replied with contempt, 'Someone to blame, Setch. For all the ruin they themselves commit. On each other. On themselves. Anyway, enough. We've chewed on this too many times.'

Sechul Lath glanced back. 'Are we far enough, do you think?'

Kilmandaros's eyes were hooded with exhaustion, and she did not bother following his gaze. 'No.'

'A warren—' Errastas began.

She cut him off with a snort. 'The wounding to come shall strike through every warren. Young and Elder. Our only hope is to get as much distance between us and her as we can.'

Errastas shrugged. 'I never much liked K'rul anyway.'

'To begin,' Kilmandaros said, 'this but wounds. If she is not slain in time, then K'rul will indeed die, and the world shall be unmade. The death of sorcery, and more.'

Sechul Lath smiled across at Errastas. 'And so the coin is cast, and it spins, and spins still.'

'She is no longer our problem,' he replied, one finger probing the empty socket of his stolen eye. 'Her sister will have to deal with her. Or someone else.'

'And on this our fate rests – that someone else cleans up the mess we make. I dare say our children will not appreciate the burden.'

'They'll not live long enough to appreciate much of anything,' Errastas said.

I truly see our problem, friends. We don't want the future, we want the past. With a new name. But it's still the past, that invented realm of nostalgia, all the jagged edges smoothed away. Paradise . . . for the drinkers of blood.

'Draconus seeks to do me harm,' said Kilmandaros. 'He waits for me.'

'Don't be a fool,' snapped Errastas. 'He will join with T'iam in slaying the Otataral Dragon. He may have vowed eternal war against chaos, but even he would not welcome its end. Besides, a battle with you risks too much – you might kill him. He's been imprisoned in a sword for how long? You think he'd risk his freedom so soon? Perhaps indeed he has old scores to settle with you, Kilmandaros, but he is about to discover far more immediate threats.'

'Unless he gleans our purpose.'

Sechul Lath glanced back at her. 'Mother, I assure you, he has done that. But I think Errastas judges rightly. Draconus will see the threat posed by the release of the Otataral Dragon, and her presence will be his lodestone. Hopefully a fatal one.'

'Many have tried to kill her,' Errastas agreed, 'and all have failed. Even the imprisonment demanded an elaborate trap – one that took centuries for Rake to devise.'

'He wasn't alone,' rumbled Kilmandaros.

'And what was made you have now unmade,' Errastas said, nodding. 'And Anomander Rake is dead, and there remains no one to match his insane obsessions—'

Kilmandaros had drawn close during the conversation, and her hand was a sudden blur in the corner of Sechul's vision, but the blow she struck Errastas was impossible to miss, as ribs snapped and he was thrown from his feet. He struck the ground, rolled once, and then curled up around the damage to his chest.

She moved to stand over him. 'You will cease speaking ill of him,' she said in a low voice. 'We did not always agree. Often we quarrelled. But the Son of Darkness was a man of integrity and honour. No longer will I permit you to spit on his name. He is dead, and your voice lives on like the cry of a cowardly crow, Errastas. You were never his match, and even in death he stands taller than you in all your guises. Do you think I do not hear your resentment? Your envy? It disgusts me.'

Sechul Lath felt a trickle of power from Errastas, as the Elder God healed himself. Slowly, he regained his feet, and, not looking at either of them, resumed walking.

After a moment, Sechul fell in behind the Errant, followed by Kilmandaros.

She said, loud enough for both to hear, 'Rake once said to me that Draconus was a man of great honour. Before the betrayal. Before his day of rage. I believe him.'

Sechul turned and studied his mother. 'You believe he will leave the Otataral Dragon to T'iam. That he will seek you out, not to settle old scores, but to punish you for what you have done here. To punish you for releasing her.'

'Punish me?' She bared her tusks. 'He will seek to kill me, my son. And I am frightened.'

The admission was like ice in Sechul's veins. *Mother?* 'We should never have done this,' he whispered.

'A common prayer,' she muttered in reply.

'Farther still?' Errastas demanded.

Kilmandaros glanced behind them. 'Farther still.'

*   *   *

448

The dragon circled him twice before descending to the broken tundra two hundred paces ahead. As Tulas Shorn walked closer, he watched it eyeing him warily. Scales like plates of ice, milky and translucent in places, blinding white where the sun's light struck them full. Eyes red as blood. With less than fifty strides between them, the dragon sembled.

Tulas maintained his steady approach until ten paces away, and then he halted in alarm. 'Is that a Hust blade you carry, Silchas Ruin? Such was not your style.'

The weapon was moaning, sensing the nearness of one possessing the blood of Eleint. *One other than its wielder, that is.*

Silchas Ruin's expression was flat. 'It seems that you evaded their bargain – for there was a bargain, was there not? Between my brother and the Lord of the Slain. There had to have been.'

'I imagine you are correct.'

'Was your prison Hood's realm, Prince, or Dragnipur?'

Tulas straightened, tilted his head. 'You refuse me my proper title.'

'I see no throne, Tulas Shorn. Was "prince" not honorific enough? Would you prefer *pretender*?'

'If I was not bound still – and eternally so, I fear – to this state of undeath, Silchas Ruin, I might take offence at your words.'

'If you wish, we could still cross blades, you sperm-clouded abomination of darkness.'

Tulas considered the proposition. 'You are returned to this world, Silchas, leading me to the inescapable conclusion that the Azath do indeed know how to shit.'

'Tulas,' said Silchas Ruin as he strode closer, 'do you remember the night of the whores?'

'I do.'

'You are such a rotted mess now, I doubt a kingdom's wealth could buy you their favour.'

'As I recall, they blindfolded themselves before lying with you – what did they squeal? Oh yes. *"He has the eyes of a white rat!"* Or words to that effect.'

They faced one another.

'Tulas, would a smile crack what's left of your face?'

'Probably, old friend, but know that I *am* smiling – in my heart.'

Their embrace was savage with memories thought for ever lost, a friendship they'd thought long dead.

'Against this,' Silchas whispered, 'not even Hood can stand. *My friend.*'

After a time, they drew apart.

'Do not weep for me,' said Tulas Shorn.

Silchas made a careless gesture. 'Unexpected joy. But . . . too bad about the war.'

'The war in which we did our level best to kill each other? Yes, those were bad times. We were each caught in whirlpools, friend, too vast and powerful for us to escape.'

'The day Emurlahn shattered, so too did my heart. For you, Tulas. For . . . everything we then lost.'

'Do you know, I do not even remember my own death? For all I know, it could well have been by your hand.'

Silchas Ruin shook his head. 'It was not. You were lost in the shattering – so even I do not know what happened to you. I . . . I searched, for a time.'

'As I would have done for you.'

'But then Scara—'

'Curse of the Eleint.'

Silchas nodded. 'Too easily embraced.'

'But not you. Not me.'

'It pleases me to hear you say that. Starvald Demelain—'

'I know. The Storm will be a siren call.'

'Together, we can resist it.'

'This smile upon my soul, it grows. At last, my heart's dream – we shall fight side by side, Silchas Ruin.'

'And the first to fall . . .'

'The other shall guard.'

'Tulas.'

'Yes?'

'He saw my grief. He joined with me in my search.'

Tulas Shorn looked away, said nothing.

'Tulas, Anomander—'

'No, friend. Not yet – I – I am not yet ready to think of him. I am sorry.'

Silchas Ruin's breath was ragged. He lifted a hand to his face, looked away, and then nodded. 'As you wish.' He laughed harshly. 'It matters not, anyway. Not any more. He is dead.'

'I know that,' Tulas said, reaching out to grasp Silchas's right shoulder. 'And more than ever, *it matters*. If we do not speak of your loss – for a time – it does not mean I feel nothing of your grief. Understand me, please.'

'Very well.'

Tulas eyed the Tiste Andii. 'Curse of the Eleint,' he said.

But his friend flinched. Neither spoke for a time. The Hust sword at Silchas's belt was muttering in its scabbard. Then Silchas looked up. 'Oh, there is one other thing – a spawn of Menandore—'

'An enemy?'

'He was born this side of Starvald Demelain.'

'Ah, then a potential ally. Three . . . a good number. Does this child command the power inside him, does he rule the rage within?'

'If he did, he would be here with us now.'

'I see. Then what shall be his fate?'

'I have not yet decided.'

They began walking north. The tundra stretched out on all sides. Small birds flitted among the low growth, and spinning clouds of midges lifted from the path they took. In the vast distance stretched a gleaming white line, marking the edge of the ice fields.

'I sense the hand of Elder Gods in all this,' Tulas Shorn said after a time.

'Yes.'

'What do they want?'

'What they always want. A return to power.'

'In the time of my deathlessness, Silchas, I came to understand the truth of that old saying: you cannot go back.'

'They know it, but it won't stop them from trying. And in trying, they may well destroy this world and countless others. They may well kill K'rul himself.'

'A bold gamble, then.'

Silchas nodded. 'The boldest.'

'Sechul Lath, then?'

'And Errastas, yes.'

'So, Sechul Lath casts the die, and Errastas nudges the last tip – the game is rigged, friend.'

'Just the way they like it, yes.'

'Will you still play?'

Silchas looked thoughtful, and then he sighed. 'They consider themselves masters at cheating. But then, I think this will be the first time that they sit at a table with mortal humans facing them. Cheating? When it comes to that, the Elder Gods are as children compared to humans. Since the time of my return, this much at least I have learned.'

'The game is in danger of being turned?'

Silchas glanced across at him, and grinned. 'I think . . . yes: just watch, Tulas. Just watch.'

In the scabbard, the sword gurgled. Laughter or, Tulas mused, choking.

'My friend, how did you come by that weapon?'

'A gift.'

'From whom? Are they mad?'

'Shadow.'

Tulas found he had nothing to say. *Struck speechless*, as the fire tellers used to say. Grimacing, he struggled, desperate to voice a warning – anything.

Silchas glanced over. 'Not Edgewalker, Tulas.'

Edge— *No, it cannot be – he could not have – oh, wonders of the Abyss!* His voice cracked when at last he managed to speak. 'I forgive him.'

Silchas frowned across at him. 'Who?'

'Your brother,' Tulas replied in a broken rasp. 'I forgive him – for all of it – for my anger, now proved so . . . so *misplaced*. Gods below, Silchas! He spoke true! But – how? *How did he manage it?*'

Silchas was still frowning. 'I don't understand, Tulas. How did he manage what?'

Tulas stared at Silchas Ruin. A moment's disbelief, but then he shook his head. *He said nothing, then, not even to his beloved brother. He was true to his word. He held the secret close and not once yielded a single word, not a single hint – else it would be known by now. It would be known!*

'Tulas?'

'I forgive him, Silchas.'

'I – I am so pleased. I am . . . humbled, friend. You see, that day, I remain convinced that it was not as it seemed—'

'Oh, indeed, it was not.'

'Can you explain, then?'

'No.'

'Tulas?'

They had halted. The sun was low on the horizon, painting the northern ice lurid shades of crimson. The midges whined in agitated clouds.

Tulas sighed. 'To tell you, my friend, would be to betray his last secret. I forgive him, yes, but I already fear that he would not forgive me, if he could. For my words. My rage. My stupidity. If I now yield his last secret, all hope for me is lost. I beg you to understand.'

Silchas Ruin's smile was tight. 'My brother had a secret he kept even from me?'

'From everyone.'

'Everyone but you.'

'It was to me that he vowed to say nothing, ever.'

The Tiste Andii's eyes narrowed. 'A secret as dangerous as that?'

'Yes.'

Silchas grunted, but it was a despairing sound. 'Oh, my friend. Does it not occur to you that, with a secret as deadly as you seem to suggest, my brother would do all he needed to to prevent its revelation?'

'Yes, that has occurred to me.'

'Including killing you.'

452

Tulas nodded. 'Yes. You may have explained my demise. Your brother murdered me.' *And to complete the deception, he helped his brother look for me.*

'But—'

'Still, Silchas, I forgive him. Between your brother and me, after all, I had clearly announced myself the unreliable one. I know it is difficult for you to accept that he would keep this from you—'

Silchas barked a laugh. 'Dawn's fire, Tulas, you are out of practice. I was being ironic. My brother kept things from me? Hardly a revelation to crush me underfoot. Anomander had many lessons to give me about pride, and, finally, a few of them have stuck.'

'The world is vast yet—'

'—truths are rare. Just so.'

'And,' Tulas added, 'as the whores whispered about you, a man of giant aspirations but tiny capacities.'

'Tell me, Prince Puke of the Eleint, shall I introduce you to this Hust blade?'

'Best save that line for the next whore you meet, Silchas.'

'Ha! I will!'

'Prince Silchas of the Laughing Cock. Could be a while before we find a—'

'Wrong, friend. We go to meet the biggest whore of them all.'

Tulas felt dried skin rip open as he laid bare his teeth. 'T'iam. Oh, she won't like that title, not one bit.'

'Mother's sake, Tulas. Irony!'

'Ah,' he nodded after a moment. 'Yes. After all, if she's a whore, then that makes all of us Soletaken—'

'Makes us all whorespawn!'

'And this amuses you?'

'It does. Besides, I can think of no better line with which to greet her.'

'Silchas, a lone Hust blade? Now you are too bold. An entire legion went out to do battle with her, and did not return.'

'Yes they died, Tulas, but they did not fail.'

'You said, a gift from Shadow?'

'Yes. But not Edgewalker.'

'Then who?'

'He is pompous in his title. A new god. Shadowthrone.'

Shadowthrone. Ahh, not as pompous as you might think. 'Do not underestimate him, friend.'

'You warn me against someone you have never met?'

'I do.'

'What gives you cause to do so?'

Tulas pointed down at the scabbarded sword. 'That.'

453

'I will admit to some unease, friend.'

'Good.'

'Shall I show you the dragon-patterned welding?'

Oh dear.

Father?

The scene was murky, stained like an old painting, yet the figure looked up from the chair he was slumped in. Tired eyes squinted in the gloom. *'If this is a dream, Rud . . . you look well, and that is good enough for me.'*

Where are you?

Udinaas grimaced. *'She's a stubborn one, as bad as me. Well, not quite.'*

The home of Seren Pedac. Then . . . Silchas judged rightly. You went to her. For help.

'Desperation, Rud. Seems to be driving my life these days. And you, are you well?'

My power grows, Father. Blood of the Eleint. It scares me. But I can reach you now. You are not dreaming. I am unharmed.

Udinaas rubbed at his face, and he looked old to Ryadd's eyes, a realization that triggered a pang deep inside. His father then nodded. *'The Imass are in hiding, north of the city. A forest abandoned by the Teblor. It is perilous, but there's no choice. I comfort myself with the thought of these ancient people, ancestors of us all, perhaps, crouching unseen in the midst of humanity. If this is possible, then so are many other unlikely possibilities, and perhaps the world is not as empty as we think we have made it.'*

Father, Kilava sent you away because she will not resist the sundering of the gate.

Udinaas looked away. *'I suspected something like that.'*

She's already given up—

'Rud, I think it was her desire all along. In fact, I do not think Kettle's mortal wounding came from the other side of Starvald Demelain. The Azath was young, yes, but strong. And with the Finnest of Scabandari, well – do you remember our confidence? But then, suddenly, something changed . . .'

Ryadd thought about that, and felt a surge of anger building within him. *That was wrong,* he said.

'She pushed the Imass back into the world of the living—'

That was *a living world!*

'It was a dream, doomed to go round and round and never change. In the eyes of nature, it was an abomination. But listen, Rud' – and he leaned forward – *'Onrack loves her still. Do nothing rash. Leave her be.'*

And if you all die? If the Imass are discovered and then hunted down?

'Trust in Seren Pedac. She will find a place for us. Rud – stay away from the dragons. When they come – stay as far away from them as you can.'

Silchas so warned me, Father.

'Is he with you?'

No.

Udinaas nodded. 'I'm not very free with my trust, but he did as he promised. I will give him that. Still, I'm glad he's gone.'

Father, Seren Pedac must protect her child – he's in great danger. Offer her the protection of the Imass.

Udinaas lifted his brows. 'That just might work. Good thinking, there.'

Not me, Father. Silchas Ruin.

'You begin to fade from my eyes, Rud—'

I grow weary.

'Be safe. I lo—'

And then he was gone. Ryadd blinked his eyes clear, stared round at the grim cave walls. 'A place to hide,' he whispered. *It's all we ask. It's what we all would ask, had we the voice. Just leave us alone.*

'She means to kill us,' Stavi said, with eyes that did not belong to a young girl. 'Me and Storii. She only wants Absi.'

The dusk was drawing its shroud. Torrent had found some bhederin dung, years old, and they huddled around the flickering flames. He watched the strange flashes of colour coming from the crystal shard Absi was playing with.

'She won't,' he assured the twins. 'She means to use you to bend your father to her will.'

'She only needs Absi for that,' said Storii. 'She'll kill one of us first, to get his attention. And then the other, to leave him with only his son. And then our father will kneel before her. He will surrender.'

'You're thinking too much – both of you. We're still a long way from anything happening.'

'You're wrong,' Stavi said. 'It's much closer than you think, Torrent.'

To that he had nothing to say. *Even my lies fail me.* He threw another chip on to the fire. 'Wrap up now, in each other's arms – Absi, go to your sisters. This night will be a cold one.'

'She took us north.'

'Yes, Stavi.'

'Why?'

'I don't know – we couldn't cross that desert.' He looked around.

'This might be a Hold, for all I know. I do not recognize the stars – and those jade spears are gone.'

'A warren,' said Storii, with some impatience. 'We already knew that. But still she took us north.'

'Go to sleep, all of you.'

When the three children settled down, Torrent threw the one fur skin they possessed over them, and then rose to stretch his legs and back. Glancing over at the witch, huddled fifteen paces away, he was reminded of a corpse he'd once found – one of the old women of the village, who'd walked out in the winter cold to find a place to die in solitude. A few of the old ones still did such things, though for most the custom had faded. A withered creature, rising from the spring thaw's deep snows, kneeling in the fold of a hillside.

Maybe it wasn't a bad way to die. Alone, freezing until all feeling went away, and then sleep, offering one last, warm sigh. The winds had torn her up, he recalled, and ice shards had broken through her skin from the inside, and the crows had found her eyes, lips and ears. And what was left . . .

Olar Ethil lifted her head, regarded him across the distance.

Torrent turned away.

'Do not wander too far,' she warned behind him. 'In this warren, it is easy to get lost – and I will not go looking for you.'

Because we're almost there, aren't we?

'If you choose to run away, pup, do not think I will take you back.'

He set out, with no intention of going too far. *Don't leave us, they begged. I won't. Promise.* Ten paces on, he glanced back. 'Spirits below!' The camp had vanished – now, nothing but flat tundra, stretching away into the darkness.

Then he caught a glimmer – *the fire. I was just looking in the wrong direction.* Torrent ran towards it. Halfway there he slowed, and then halted. *Too far away – I never walked this far. I barely walked at all!*

But he could see a figure seated before the feeble flames. Shivering, Torrent slowly approached. *Olar Ethil? Is that you? No.*

Not unless you've been hiding that red waistcoat.

The man was reaching into one voluminous sleeve, drawing forth silver wine cups, a large decanter, and then a host of candied fruit and baked desserts.

I am dreaming. All of this. I am sleeping close to the children right now, and my moans are heard by none but the hag.

The man looked up. His face was round, softened by years of indolence. A city dweller's face. He gestured with a plump hand. 'Quickly, Kruppe gestures – see? There is little time. Come. Sit. Before Kruppe awakens to a miserable and fraught dawn in his beleaguered city. You are the keeper of my daughters?'

456

'What? I—'

'Kruppe would be there, if he could. Pah! It is ever our excuse, and paltry and pathetic it is. But then, Kruppe is famous for his energetic seed – why, it has been known to swim a league upriver to impregnate a baron's pretty daughter not three months before her scandalous marriage. Well, the marriage proved scandalous six months later, anyway, and how that husband was castigated and, indeed, disowned! Now, if he'd been as adventurous as she would have liked, why, Kruppe's seed would have come to the door only to find it barred, yes? So, the husband got all that he deserved, or so Judge Kruppe pronounces.'

'*Your* daughters . . . spirits take me, I see the resemblance – the eyes, the gestures with the hands – but Hetan—'

'Delicious Hetan, memories return in a stew of desire and alarm – no matter. Grievous the fate of their mother. Perilous the fate of her children – and we must do something about that. Why are you not eating? Drinking? Baruk's finest fare.'

Torrent pointed. 'They . . . vanished.'

'Oh my. The dread curse of unmindfulness. Perhaps next time, my barbarian friend. But time, it grows short, but Kruppe is shorter still.' He fluttered a hand. 'Tell me, what do you now see there?'

Torrent squinted. 'A bow. Quiver. Arrows.'

'Rhivi. To this day they yearly ply me with useless gifts, for reasons that, while obscure, are no doubt well deserved. In any case, I give them all away as a measure of my extraordinary generosity. Are these not finer weapons than the ones you now possess?'

'My bow split. I had nothing with which to repair it. The arrow shafts have dried and warped – I'd intended to harden them one last time but forgot. The fletching—'

'Before you go on, good sir, by your list Kruppe can conclude that yes, indeed, this Rhivi offering is superior to that which you now possess.'

'I just said that.'

'Did you? Excellent. Take them and be off with you. Quickly. Let it never be said that Kruppe is a neglectful father, no matter what that baron's daughter later claimed in court. And if Kruppe had not dramatically revealed that she was now sleeping with her advocate, why, Kruppe would be a much thinner man than the one you now see fading before you, red waistcoat and all . . .'

'Wait! I'm lost! She said—'

'Behind you, O wily scout.'

New weapons in hand, Torrent slowly turned, to see, twenty paces away, the dying fire, the children knotted up beneath the fur, and Olar Ethil slumped on the far side. He swung back to thank the man, but he was gone, and with him his modest hearth. He lifted the weapons for a closer look. *These are from no dream. These are real, and finely made.* He set the string and tested the draw. *Spirits! These Rhivi must be giants!*

Olar Ethil barely stirred when he returned to the fire. 'Changed your mind, did you?'

Torrent set the bow and quiver down beside him. 'Yes,' he said.

'Just as well, pup. Warrens are dangerous places for fools such as you. If you would honour the vow you made, you would do well to stay close to me.'

Torrent tossed the last chip of dung into the fire, watched sparks lift into the night. 'I shall, Bonecaster.'

Her head settled once more. He stared across at her. *When sleep offers its final sigh, old hag, I'll be there to wake you.*

Absi rolled over in his sleep and in a soft, sing-song voice, said, 'Kralalalala. Yip.'

But Torrent could see that his eyes were closed, and on his face there was a contented smile. The child licked his lips.

Saved them for him, did you, Kruppe? Well done.

Onos T'oolan halted, slowly turned. Limned in jade light, a thousand T'lan Imass stood facing him. *So many? And, swirling there, the dust of hundreds more. Strangers. Summoned by the unveiling of Tellann. Is this what I want? Is this what I need?* All at once he felt the weight of their attention, fixed so remorselessly upon him, and almost buckled. *Needs, wants, they are irrelevant. This is what I will. And by that power alone, a world can be destroyed. Or shaped anew.* He slowly straightened, restored by the thought, and the strength that came with it.

When I am done, dust shall be dust. Nothing more. Not a thing alive with secrets. Or thick with grief and horror. Simply dust. 'Do you understand me?'

'We do, First Sword.'

'I will free you.'

'Not yet, First Sword.'

'I would walk alone.'

'Then you shall.'

His army fell in cascading clouds, save two figures that had been standing well back in the T'lan legion.

Onos considered them for a time, and then beckoned.

They approached, and the female spoke. 'First Sword, I once walked these lands – yet I did not.'

'You are named Rystalle Ev.'

'Yes.'

'Your words make no sense.'

458

She shrugged, pointed northward. 'There. Something . . . troubling.'

'Olar Ethil—'

'No, First Sword. This is closer.'

'You are curious, Rystalle Ev?'

The warrior beside her, Ulag Togtil, spoke. 'There are lost memories within her, First Sword. Perhaps they were taken from other Imass – from those who once lived here. Perhaps they are her own. That which will be found to the north, it is like the awakening of an old wound, but one she cannot see. Only feel.'

'What you seek,' Rystalle Ev said to Onos, 'is threatened. Or so I fear. But I cannot be certain.'

Onos T'oolan studied the two of them. 'You resist me well – and I see the strength you find in each other. It is . . . strange.'

'First Sword,' said Ulag, 'it is *love*.'

Onos was silent, struggling to comprehend the warrior's statement.

'We did not discover it from within ourselves,' Rystalle Ev said. 'We found it—'

'Like a stone in a stream,' Ulag said. 'Bright, wondrous—'

'In the stream, First Sword, of your thoughts.'

'When the mountains thunder, and the ice in the high passes at last shatters to spring's warmth.' Ulag lifted a withered hand, let it fall again. 'The stream becomes a torrent, sweeping all down with it. Cruel flood. And yet . . . a stone, glimmering.'

'This is not possible,' said Onos T'oolan. 'There is no such thing within me. The fires of Tellann have burned hollow my soul. You delude yourselves. Each other.'

Rystalle Ev shrugged. 'Delusions of comfort – are these not the gifts of love, First Sword?'

Onos regarded the female. 'Go, then, the two of you. Find this threat. Determine its nature, and then return.'

Ulag spoke, 'You ask nothing more of us, First Sword?'

'Rystalle Ev, does it hunt us?'

'No, First Sword. I think not. It simply . . . is.'

'Find this memory of yours, Rystalle Ev. If it is indeed a threat to me, then I shall destroy it.'

Onos T'oolan watched the two T'lan Imass trudge northward. The First Sword had drawn the power of Tellann close, protective – wearying of Olar Ethil's assaults, he had made it an impenetrable wall. But there was risk to this. The wall left him blind to all that lay beyond it.

Threats to what I seek, to the fate I desire for us. Olar Ethil stands alone against me. I can think of no one else. After all, I do not flee destruction, but strive to meet it. To find it, in the place of my choosing. Who would deny me that?

Rystalle Ev, memories are powerless – did the Ritual not teach us this? Find what troubles you, then come back.

Ulag Togtil, in your language of flowers . . . I would know more of this glimmering stone, this wondrous impossibility.

He resumed his walk. Now alone on the ravaged plain, sword tip striking sparks from stones lying embedded in the ground. In his wake, a building wall of dust. Alive with secrets. Thick with grief and horror. Rising higher.

Rystalle Ev glanced back, watched the First Sword making his solitary way eastward, the dust seething behind him.

'He does not know, does he?'

'He is closed too much within himself,' Ulag Togtil said.

'See the cloud. We began as only a few hundred. We left a thousand to march behind him, as he demanded. But he has awakened Tellann. He has summoned.'

'How many now, Rystalle Ev?'

'Five thousand? Ten?'

'That wall, Rystalle Ev, it is vast.'

'Yes,' she whispered.

Another moment passed, and then they turned and set off northward.

The mists cleared and Gruntle found himself padding through fresh snow. A thousand paces to his left two splintered masts jutted from a white mound, the windblown snow heaped in a high dune around the wreckage of a ship. Directly ahead, rocky outcroppings marked the foot of a range of cliffs split by narrow gorges.

At the flat foot of the outcroppings a scattering of skeletal hut frames crouched in the lee of the cliffs. The breath of raw magic was heavy in the air.

There was an answering thunder in his chest, and he could feel the warrior souls within him gathering close, awakening their power. He drew closer.

Hearing a coughing grunt, he halted, and tensed upon seeing two thick-shouldered cats emerge from a cave. Their hide was banded grey and black, like shadows on stone. Their upper canines reached down past their lower jaws. The beasts eyed him, small ears flattening back against their broad skulls, but made no other move.

Gruntle stretched his jaws in a yawn. Just beyond the huts, a rockfall had made a crevasse into a cave, and from that dark mouth drifted unsettling emanations. Fixing his eyes upon that passage, he padded forward.

The two sabre-toothed cats loped towards him.

Not Soletaken. Not d'ivers. These are true beasts. Hunters. But they look . . . hungry. At the cave mouth, Gruntle hesitated, glancing back as the big cats approached. *Are you that fearless? What do you want with me?*

Having drawn closer until flanked by the hooped frames of two huts, the cats halted, the one on the left sitting down on its haunches, and then flopping on to the thin snow and rolling on to its back.

Tension eased from Gruntle. *Hungry for company.* He faced the cave once more, and then slipped into the darkness. Instead of bitter cold, he felt heat, gusting damp and fetid from further within.

She is here. She is waiting for me.

Oh, how I have waited for this moment. Trake, I never asked for this. I never asked for you. And when you chose me, I told you, again and again, it was a mistake. Stonny, if you could see me now, you'd understand. You'd know the why . . . of all of this.

I can almost see it – that one, quick nod – to tell me it's all right. I won't be coming back, but it's all right. We both know there are some places you can't come back from. Not ever.

He considered sembling and then decided against it. She would meet him as she chose, but he was Trake's Mortal Sword – at least on this day. A voice whispered inside him, distant, hollow, commanding him to turn round, to flee this place, but he ignored it.

The crevasse narrowed, twisting, before opening out into a vast, domed cavern.

She stood facing him, a squat, muscular woman cloaked in the fur of a panther, but otherwise naked. Her hooded eyes held glints of gold, her round face was framed in thick, long black hair. Her broad, full-lipped mouth was set, unwelcoming.

Behind her, on a cracked hump of stone, was the ruin of a house. Walls had caved in and it seemed that an ancient tree had grown up from beneath the structure, shattering the foundations, but the tree was now dead. Sorrow drifted down from the broken edifice, bitter to Gruntle's senses.

Above it, just under the dome, steam roiled, the clouds lit from behind – as if the cavern's roof was glowing, hot enough to melt the stone. Staring up at this manifestation, Gruntle felt on the verge of falling upward – pulled into a realm unimaginably vast. *Vast, yes, but not empty.*

She spoke in his mind, that now familiar deep, liquid voice. 'Starvald Demelain, Mortal Sword, now commanding this place, transforming the very stone itself. No other gate remains. As for you . . . is this your god's panic? You should not be here. Tell him, Mortal Sword – tell my child – I will not permit your interference.'

Your child? You claim to be Trake's mother, do you?

He sensed a flash of irritation. *'First Swords, First Empire, First Heroes – we were a people proud of such things, for all the good it did us. I have birthed many children. Most of them are now dead.'*

So is Trake.

'First Heroes were chosen, Mortal Sword, to become gods, and so escape death. All that he surrendered that day on the Plains of Lamatath was his mortal flesh. But like any god, he cannot risk becoming manifest, and so he created you. His Mortal Sword, the weapon of his will.'

Remind me to thank him for that.

'You must stand aside here,' she said. *'The Eleint are coming. If you seek to oppose them, you will die, Mortal Sword.'*

No, what you fear is that I shall succeed.

'I will not permit that.'

Then it is you and I who shall fight in this cavern, as I have seen in my dreams—

'Dreams? You fool. I was trying to warn you.'

Black fur . . . blood, a dying breath – woman, these were not your sendings.

'There is little time left! Gruntle, do not challenge this!' She lifted her arms out to the sides. *'Look at me! I am Kilava Onass, a Bonecaster of the Imass. I defied the Ritual of Tellann, and my power beggars that of your human gods. What will occur here not even I can prevent – do you understand me? It is . . . necessary . . .'*

He had expected such words, but still his hackles rose. *It's what we always hear, isn't it? From generals and warlords and miserable tyrants. Justifying yet another nightmare epoch of slaughter. Of suffering, misery and despair. And what do we all do? We duck down and weather it. We tell ourselves that this is how it must be – I stood on the roof of a building, and all around me people were dying. And by my hand – gods! That building wept blood!*

For what? They all died – the whole fucking city – all those people – they just died anyway!

I told Trake he chose wrongly. I was never a soldier – I despise war. I detest all the sordid lies about glory and honour – you, Kilava, if you have lived as long as you say you have, if Trake is your get, then you have seen a child of yours kneel to war – as if war itself was a damned god!

But still, you want him to live – you want your child-god, your First fucking Hero, to go on, and on. Wars without end. And the sword shall swing down and they shall fall – for ever more!

'Gruntle, why are you here?'

He advanced, feeling the blood within him rise to a boil. *Haven't you guessed? I'm going to fight. I'm going to bring your son down – here and now. I'm going to kill the bastard. An end to the god of slaughter, of horror, of rape—*

Kilava howled in sudden rage, vanished inside a blur of darkness. Veered into a panther as huge as Gruntle himself, she coiled to spring.

In his mind, he saw a single, quick nod. *Yes.* Baring his fangs, Gruntle lunged to meet her.

Far to the northeast, something glittered. Mappo stood studying it for a long time, as the sun swelled the horizon behind him, and then slunk, red and sullen, down past the edge of the world. That distant, flashing fire held on for a while longer, like burning hills.

He drew the waterskin from his sack, drank deep, and then crouched down to probe his lacerated feet. The soles of the boots had been torn away by the fierce assault of crystal shards. Since noon he had been trailing blood, each smear vanishing beneath a frenzied clump of cape-moths, as if flowers sprang from his every footprint. *Such is the gift of life in this tortured place.* He drew a deep breath. The muscles of his legs were like clenched fists beneath him. He could not push on for much longer, not without a full night of rest.

But time is running out.

Mappo drank once more and then stored the waterskin. Shouldering the pack, he set off. Northeast.

The Jade Spears slashed a path into the night sky, and green light bled down, transforming the desert floor into a luminescent sea. As he jogged, Mappo imagined himself crossing the basin of an ocean. The bitter cold air filled his lungs, biting like ice with each indrawn breath. From this place, he knew, he would never surface. The thought disturbed him and with a growl he cast it from his mind.

As he ran, shooting stars raced and flared overhead, growing into an emerald storm, criss-crossing the heavens. He thought that, if he listened carefully enough, he might hear them, hissing like steam as they skipped, and then igniting with a crack of thunder once they began their final descent. But the rasping was only his own breath, the thunder nothing but the drum of his own heart. The sky stayed silent, and the burning arrows remained far, far away.

The sorrow in his soul had begun to taste sour. Aged and dissolute, moments from crumbling. He did not know what would come in its wake. Resignation, as might find a fatally ill man in his last days? Or just an exultant eagerness to see it all end? At the moment, even despair seemed too much effort.

He drew closer, eyes fixing on what seemed a range of tall crystals, green as glacial ice, rising to command the scene ahead. His exhausted mind struggled to make sense of it. *Something . . . order, a pattern . . .*

Oh, gods, I've seen its like before. In stone.

Icarium—

Immortal architect, builder of monuments, you set out to challenge the gods, to defy the weavers of time. Maker of what cannot die, but with each edifice you raise the things that you need the most – the memories the rest of us guard so zealously – and they arrive stillborn in your hands. Each one as dead as the one before.

And look at us, we who would pray to forget so much – our regrets, our foolish choices, the hurts we delivered over a lifetime – we think nothing of this gift, this freedom we see as a cage, and in our rattling fury we wish that we were just like you.

Raiser of empty buildings. Visionary of silent cities.

But how many times could he remind Icarium of friendship? The precious comfort of familiar company? How many times could he fill once more all those empty rooms? *My friend, my bottomless well. But should I tell you the truth, then you would take your own life.*

Is that so bad a thing? With all that you have done? Is it?

And now you are threatened. And helpless. I feel this. I know it as truth. I fear that you will be awakened, in all your rage, and that this time there will be more than just humans within reach of your sword. This time there will be gods.

Someone wants you, Icarium, to be their weapon.

But . . . if I reach you first, I could awaken you to who you are. I could speak the truth of your history, friend. And when you set the point of the dagger to your chest, I could stand back. Do nothing. I could honour you with the one thing I still had – myself. I could be the witness to your one act of justice.

I could talk you into killing yourself.

Is it possible? That this is where friendship can take us?

What would I do then?

I would bury you. And weep over the stones. For my loss, as friends will do.

The city was his genius – Mappo could see that truth in every line – but as he drew closer, squinting at the strangely flowing light and shadows in the facets of crystal, he saw evidence of occupation. His steps slowed.

Broken husks of fruit, fragments of clothing, the musty smell of dried faeces.

The sun was beginning to rise – had it been that far? He approached the nearest, broadest avenue. As he passed between two angular buildings, he froze at a flicker of movement – there, reflected from a facet projecting from the wall to his right. And as he stared, he saw it again.

Children. Walking past.

Yet no one was here – *no one but me.*

They were wending their way out of the city – hundreds upon hundreds of children. Stick-thin limbs and bellies swollen with starvation. As he watched the procession, he saw not a single adult among them.

Mappo walked on, catching glimpses in the crystals of their brief occupation, their squatting presence amidst palatial – if cold – splendour. *Icarium, I begin to understand. And yet, cruellest joke of all, this was the one place you could never find again.*

Every time you said you felt close . . . this city was the place you sought. These crystal machines of memory. And the trail you hunted – it did not matter if we were on another continent, it did not matter if we were half a world away – that trail was one of remembering. Remembering this city.

He went on, piecing together the more recent history, the army of children, and many times he caught sight of one girl, her mouth crusted with sores, her hair bleached of all colour. And huge eyes that seemed to somehow find his own – but that was impossible. She was long gone, with all the other children. She could not be—

Ah! This is the one! Voicing songs of incantation – the banisher of the d'ivers. Opals gems shards – this is the child.

He had come to a central square. She was there, looking out at him from a tilted spire of quartz. He walked until he stood in front of her, and her eyes tracked him all the way.

'You are just a memory,' Mappo said. 'It is a function of the machine, to trap the life passing through it. You cannot be looking at me – no, someone has walked my path, someone has come to stand before you here.' He swung round.

Fifteen paces away, before the sealed door of a narrow structure, Mappo saw a boy, tall, clutching a bundled shape. Their eyes met.

I am between them. That is all. They do not see me. They see each other.

But the boy's eyes pinned him like knife points. And he spoke. 'Do not turn away.'

Mappo staggered as if struck.

Behind him, the girl said, 'Icarias cannot hold us. The city is troubled.'

He faced her again. A boy had come up beside her, in his scrawny arms a heap of rubbish. He studied the girl's profile with open adoration. She blew flies from her lips.

'Badalle.' The tall boy's voice drifted past him. 'What did you dream?'

The girl smiled. 'No one wants us, Rutt. Not one – in their lives they won't change a thing to help us. In their lives they make ever more of

465

us, but when they say they care about our future, they're lying. The words are empty. Powerless. But I have seen words of *real* power, Rutt, and each one is a weapon. *A weapon.* That is why adults spend a lifetime blunting them.' She shrugged. 'No one likes getting cut.'

When the boy spoke again, it was as if he stood in Mappo's place. 'What did you dream, Badalle?'

'In the end we take our language with us. In the end, we leave them all behind.' She turned to the boy beside her and frowned. 'Throw them away. I don't like them.'

The boy shook his head.

'What did you dream, Badalle?'

The girl's gaze returned, centring on Mappo's face. 'I saw a tiger. I saw an ogre. I saw men and women. Then a witch came and took their children away. And not one of them tried to stop her.'

'It wasn't like that,' Mappo whispered. But it was.

'Then one rode after them – he wasn't much older than you, Rutt. I think. He was hard to see. A ghost got in the way. He was young enough to still listen to his conscience.'

'*It wasn't like that!*'

'Is that all?' asked the boy named Rutt.

'No,' she replied, 'but he's heard enough.'

Mappo cried out, staggered back, away. He shot a look back and saw her eyes tracking him. And in his skull, she said, '*Ogre, I can't save you, and you can't save him. Not from himself. He is your Held, but every child wakes up. In this world, every child wakes up – and it is what all of you fear the most. Look at Rutt. He has Held in his arms. And you, you go to find your Held, to fill your arms once more. Look at Rutt. He is terrified of Held waking up. He's just like you. Now hear my poem. It is for you.*

> '*She made you choose*
> *which child to save.*
> *And you chose.*
> *One to save,*
> *the others to surrender.*
> *It is not an easy choice*
> *But you make it every day*
> *That is not an easy truth*
> *But the truth is every day*
> *One of us among those*
> *You walk away from*
> *Dies*
> *And there are more truths*
> *In this world*

466

Than I can count
But each time you walk away
The memory remains
And no matter how far or fast
You run
The memory remains.'

Mappo spun, fled the square.

Echoes pursued him. Carrying her voice. *'In Icarias, memory remains. In Icarias waits the tomb of all that is forgotten. Where memory remains. Where he would have found his truth. Do you choose to save him now, Ogre? Do you choose to bring him to his city? When he opens his own tomb, what will he find?*

What do any of us find?

Will you dare map your life, Ogre, by each dead child left in your wake? You see, I dreamed a dream I cannot tell Rutt, because I love him. I dreamed of a tomb, Ogre, filled with every dead child.

It seems, then, that we are all builders of monuments.

Shrieking, Mappo ran. And ran, leaving a trail of bloody footprints, and on all sides, his reflection. Forever trapped.

Because the memory remains.

'Will you ever tire, Setch, of gloom and doom?'

Sechul Lath glanced across at Errastas. 'I will, the moment you tire of all that blood on your hands.'

Errastas snarled. 'And is it your task to ever remind me of it?'

'To be honest, I don't know. I suppose I could carve out my own eyes, and then bless my newfound blindness—'

'Do you now mock my wound?'

'No, forgive me. I was thinking of the poet who one day decided he'd seen too much.'

Behind them, Kilmandaros asked, 'And did his self-mutilation change the world?'

'Irrevocably, Mother.'

'How so?' she asked.

'Eyes can be hard as armour. They can be hardened to see yet feel nothing, if the will is strong enough. You've seen such eyes, Mother – you as well, Errastas. They lie flat in the sockets, like stone walls. They are capable of witnessing any and every atrocity. Nothing gets in, nothing gets out. Now, that poet, he removed those stones. Tore away the veil, permanently. So what was inside, well, it all poured out.'

'But, being blinded, nothing that was outside could find a way in.'

'Indeed, Mother, but by then it was too late. It had to be, if you think about it.'

467

'So it poured out,' grumbled Errastas. 'Then what?'

'I'd hazard it changed the world.'

'Not for the better,' Kilmandaros muttered.

'I have no burning need, Errastas,' said Sechul Lath, 'to cure the ills of the world. This one or any other.'

'Yet you observe critically—'

'If all honest observation ends up sounding critical, is it the honesty you then reject, or the act of observation?'

'Why not both?'

'Indeed, why not both? Abyss knows, it's easier that way.'

'Why do you bother, then?'

'Errastas, I am left with two choices. I could weep for a reason, or weep for no reason. In the latter we find madness.'

'And is the former any different?' Kilmandaros asked.

'Yes. A part of me chooses to believe that if I weep long enough, I'll weep myself out. And then, in the ashes – in the aftermath – will be born something else.'

'Like what?' Errastas demanded.

Sechul Lath shrugged. 'Hope.'

'See this hole in my face, Knuckles? I too weep, but my tears are blood.'

'My friend, at last you have become the true god of all the living worlds. When you finally stand at the very pinnacle of all creation, we shall raise statues marking your holy wounding, symbol of life's ceaseless suffering.'

'This I will accept, so long as the blood leaking down my face isn't my own.'

Kilmandaros grunted. 'No doubt your worshippers will be happy to bleed for you, Errastas, until the Abyss swallows us all.'

'And I shall possess a thirst to match their generosity.'

'When we—'

But Kilmandaros's hand suddenly gripped Sechul's shoulder and spun him round. 'Friends,' she said in a rumble, 'it is time.'

They faced the way they had come.

From the ridge where they stood, the basin to the west stretched out flat, studded with rocks and tufts of wiry grass, for as far as they could see. But now, under the mid-morning light, the vista had begun to change. Spreading in a vast, curved shadow, the ground was bleaching, all colour draining away. From grey to white, until it seemed that the entire basin was a thing of bone and ash, and in the distance – at the very centre of this blight – the earth had begun to rise.

'She awakens,' said Kilmandaros.

'And now,' whispered Errastas, his lone eyes glittering bright, 'we shall speak of dragons.'

468

A hill where no hill had been before, lifting to command the horizon, bulging, swelling – a mountain—

They saw it explode, a billowing eruption of earth and stone.

Huge cracks ripped across the basin floor. The entire ridge rippled under them and all three Elder Gods staggered.

As the column of dust and ashes rose skyward, as the cloud opened like a mushroom to fill half the sky, the sound finally reached them, solid as a rushing wall, igniting stunning agony inside their skulls. Sechul and Errastas were battered to the ground, sent tumbling. Even Kilmandaros was thrown from her feet – Sechul stared across at her, saw her mouth opened wide in a terrible scream that he could not hear amidst the howling wind, the crushing thunder of that eruption.

Twisting round, he stared at the vast, roiling cloud. *Korabas. You are returned to the world.*

Within the maelstrom spinning vortices of dirt, dust and smoke had begun to form. He watched them coil, pushed out to the sides as if buffeted by some unseen column of rising air at the very centre. Sechul frowned.

Her wings? Are those made by her wings? Elder blood!

As the roar died away, Sechul Lath heard Errastas. Laughing.

'Mother?'

Kilmandaros was climbing to her feet. She glanced across at her son. 'Korabas Otataral iras'Eleint. Otataral, Sechul, is not a thing – it is a title.' She turned to Errastas. 'Errant! Do you know its meaning?'

The one-eyed Elder God's laughter slowly died. He looked away. 'What do I care for ancient titles?' he muttered.

'Mother?'

She faced the terrible blight of earth and sky to the west. 'Otas'taral. In every storm there is an eye, a place of . . . stillness. Otas'taral means the Eye of Abnegation. And now, upon the world, we have birthed a *storm.*'

Sechul Lath sank back down, covered his face with dust-stained hands. *Will I ever tire? Yes. I have. See what we have unleashed. See what we have begun.*

Errastas staggered close, falling to his knees beside Sechul, who looked up into that ravaged face and saw both manic glee and brittle terror. The Errant smiled a ghastly smile. 'Do you see, Setch? They have to stop her! They have no choice!'

Yes, please. Stop her.

'She has begun to move,' Kilmandaros announced.

Sechul pushed Errastas to one side and sat up. But the sky revealed nothing: too much dust, too much smoke and ash – the pall had devoured two-thirds of the heavens, and the last third looked sickly, as if in retreat. The unnatural gloom was settling fast. 'Where?' he demanded.

His mother pointed. 'Track her by the ground. For now, it is all we can do.'

Sechul Lath stood.

'There,' she said.

A broad swathe of bleached death, stretching in a line. 'Northeast,' he whispered, watching the slow, devastating blight cutting its slash across the landscape. 'All that lies beneath her . . .'

'Where she passes,' said Kilmandaros, 'no life shall ever return. The stillness of matter becomes absolute. She is the Eye of Abnegation, the storm's centre, where all must die.'

'Mother, we have gone too far. This time—'

'It's too late!' shrieked Errastas. 'She is the heart of sorcery! Without the Eye of Abnegation, there can be no magic!'

'What?'

But Kilmandaros was shaking her head. 'It is not as simple as that.'

'What isn't?' Sechul demanded.

'Now that she is freed,' she said, 'the Eleint must kill her. They have no choice. Their power is magical, and Korabas will kill all that magic depends upon. And since she is immune to their sorcery, it must be by fang and claw, and that will demand every Eleint – every *storm*, until T'iam herself is awakened. And as for K'rul, well, he can no longer refuse the Errant's summons – he was the one who harnessed the chaos of the dragons in the first place.'

'*They have to kill her!*' cried Errastas. The blood leaking from his eye was now black with dust.

Kilmandaros grunted non-committally. 'If they truly kill her, Errastas, then the storm dies.' She faced him. 'But you knew this – or at least guessed the truth. What you seek is the death of all sorcery bound to laws of control. You seek to create a realm where no mortal can hurt you, ever again. A realm where the blood is sacrificed in our name, but in truth we have no power to intervene, even if we wanted to. You desire worship, Errastas, but one where you need give nothing in return. Have I guessed right?'

Sechul Lath shook his head. 'They cannot kill her—'

Errastas wheeled on him. 'But they must! I told you! I will see them all destroyed! The meddling gods – *I want our children dead!* K'rul will understand – he will see that there's no other way, no way to end this venal, pathetic tragedy.' He stabbed a finger at Sechul. 'You thought this was a game? Cheating with the knuckles, and then a wink to the moll? I *summoned* the Elder Gods! K'rul thinks to ignore me? No! I have forced his hand!' He suddenly cackled, his fingers twitching. 'She is a blood clot let loose in his veins! And she will find his brain, and he will die! I am the Master of the Holds, *and I will not be ignored!*'

Sechul Lath staggered back from Errastas. 'They chained her the first time,' he said, 'because killing her was not an option – not if they wanted to keep the warrens alive.' He whirled on Kilmandaros. 'Mother – did you – did . . .'

She turned away. 'I grew tired of this,' she said.

Tired? 'But – but the heart of the Crippled God—'

Errastas spat. 'What do we care about that dried-up slab of meat? He'll be as dead as the rest of them by the time this is done! So will the Forkrul Assail – and all the rest who'd think to challenge me! You didn't believe me, Setch – you chose to not take me seriously – *again*.'

Sechul Lath shook his head. 'I understand you now. Your real enemy is the Master of the Deck of Dragons. Dragons who *are* warrens – all that new, raw power. But you knew that you could not hope to match that Master – not so long as the gods and warrens remained dominant. So you devised a plan to kill it all. The Deck, the sorcery of the Dragons, the Master – the gods. But what makes you think that the Holds will somehow prove immune to the Eye of Abnegation?'

'Because the Holds are *Elder*, you fool. It was K'rul's bartering with the Eleint that made this whole mess – that brought the warrens into the realms, that forced order upon the chaos of the Old Magic. K'rul's conniving that saw one dragon selected among the Grand Clan, chosen to become the Negator, the Otataral, while all the others would chain themselves to aspects of magic. They brought *law* to sorcery, and now I will shatter that law. For ever more!'

'K'rul sought peace—'

'He sought to trump us! And so he did – but that ends today! Today! Sechul Lath, did you not agree to end it all? By your words, you agreed!'

I wasn't serious. I'm never serious. That's my curse. 'So, Errastas, if you will not seek the heart of the Crippled God, where will you go now?'

'That is my business,' he snapped, turning to study the bleached scar crossing the land. 'Far away.' He faced Sechul again. 'Mael finally comprehends what we have done here – but tell me, do you see him? Does he charge towards us now in all his fury? He does not. And Ardata? Know that she too now schemes anew. As does Olar Ethil – the Elders once more approach ascension, a return to rule. There is much to be done.'

The Errant set off, then. Southward.

He flees.

Sechul turned to Kilmandaros. 'I see my path now, Mother, from this moment onward. Shall I describe it for you? I see myself wandering, lost and alone. With only a growing madness for company. It is a vision – I see it clear as day. Well,' and his laugh was dry, 'every pantheon needs a fool, drooling and wild-eyed.'

'My son,' she said, 'it is only a plan.'

'Excuse me? What?'

'The Errant. What we have unleashed here cannot be controlled. Now, more than ever, the future is unknown, no matter what he chooses to believe.'

'Can she be chained again, Mother?'

She shrugged. 'Anomander Rake is dead. The other Eleint who partook of the chaining, they too are now dead.'

'K'rul—'

'She is loose *within* him. He can do nothing. The Eleint who come will fight her. They will seek to take her down – but Korabas has long ago surrendered her sanity, and she will fight them to the bitter end. I expect most will die.'

'Mother, *please*.'

Kilmandaros sighed. 'You will not stay with me, my son?'

'To witness your meeting with Draconus? I think not.'

She nodded.

'Draconus will kill you!'

She faced him with burning eyes. 'It was only a plan, my beloved son.'

BOOK SIX

TO ONE IN CHAINS

If you knew where this path led
Would you have walked it?
If you knew the pain at love's solemn end
Would you have awakened it?

In darkness the wheel turns
In darkness the dust dims
In red fire the wheel burns
In darkness the sun spins

If you knew the thought in your head
Would you have spoken it?
If by this one word you betrayed a friend
Would you have uttered it?

In darkness the wheel turns
In darkness the dust dims
In red fire the wheel burns
In darkness the sun spins

If you knew the face of the dead
Would you have touched it?
If by this coin a soul's journey to send
Would you have stolen it?

In darkness the wheel turns
In darkness the dust dims
In red fire the wheel burns
In darkness the sun spins

Sparak Chant
Psalm VII 'The Vulture's Laugh'
The Sparak Nethem

CHAPTER SEVENTEEN

The faces all in rows will wait
As I take each in my hands
Remembering what it is
To be who I am not.
Will all these struggles
Fade into white?
Or melt like snow on stone
In the heat of dawn?
Do you feel my hands?
These weathered wings
Of dreams of flight
– stripped –
Are gifts worn down.
Still I hold fast and climb sure
Through your eyes –
Who waits for me
Away from the ravaged nests
The scenes of violence
Any searching will easily find
The broken twigs
The tufts of feather and hair
The spilled now drying –
Did you spring alight
Swift away unharmed?
So many lies we leave be
The sweet feeding to make us strong
But the rows are unmoving
And we journey without a step
What I dare you to lose
I surrendered long ago
But what I beg you to find
Must I then lose?

In these rows there are tales
For every line, every broken smile
Draw close then
And dry these tears
For I have a story to tell

The Unwitnessed
Fisher kel Tath

*T*HESE SOLDIERS. THE TWO WORDS HUNG IN HER MIND LIKE MEAT
from butcher hooks. They twisted slowly, aimlessly. They
dripped, but the drips had begun to slow. Lying on her side
atop the packs of wrapped food, Badalle could let her head sink down
on one side and see the rough trail stretching away behind them. Not
much was being left behind now – barring the bodies – and beneath the
light of the Jade Strangers those pale shapes looked like toppled statues
of marble lining a long-abandoned road. Things with their stories gone,
their histories for ever lost. When she tired of that view, she could set
her gaze the opposite way, looking ahead, and from her vantage point
the column was like a swollen worm, with thousands of heads upon its
elongated back, each one of them slave to the same crawling body.

Every now and then the worm cast off a part of it that had died, and
these pieces were pushed out to the sides. Hands would reach down
from those walking past, collecting up fragments of clothing which
would be used during the day, stitched together to make flies – gifts
of shade from the dead – and by the time those discarded pieces came
close to her, why, they'd be mostly naked, and they'd have become
marble statues. *Because, when things fail, you topple the statues.*

Directly before her, the bared backs of the haulers glistened with
precious sweat as they strained in their yokes. And the thick ropes
twisted as they went taut and gusted out breaths of glittering dust
all down their length. *They call these soldiers heavies. Some of them
anyway. The ones who don't stop, who don't fall down, who don't die.
The ones who scare the others and make them keep going. Until they
fall over dead. Heavies. These soldiers.*

She thought back. The sun had been spilling out along the horizon.
The day was going away, and it had been a day when no one had
spoken, when the Snake had been silent. She had been walking three
paces behind Rutt, and Rutt walked hunched over around Held, who
was huddled in his arms, and Held's eyes were closed against the glare
– but then, they were always closed, because so much in the world was
too hard to look at.

This would be their last night. They knew it – the whole Snake knew

476

it. Badalle had said nothing to change their minds. Perhaps she too had given up – it was hard to know for certain. Defiance could hold its shape, even when it was made of nothing but cinders and ash. Anger could look hot to the touch, when in truth it was lifeless and cold. In this way, the world could deceive. It could lie, and in lying it invited delusion. It invited the idea that what it *was* was true. In this way, the world could make belief a fatal illness.

She stared down at the backs of the heavies, and remembered more.

Rutt's steps wavered. Halted. His voice cracked as it made a wordless sound, and then it cracked a second time, and he said, 'Badalle. The flies are walking now.'

She looked down at her legs, to see if they could take her up alongside him, and, slowly, agonizingly, they did. And far ahead, to the place where he was looking with his blinded, closed-up eyes, she saw swarming shapes, black as they came out of the sunset's red glare. Black and seething. Flies, walking on two legs, one clump, then another and another, emerging from the blood-light.

'The flies,' said Rutt, 'are walking.'

But she had sent them away. Her last command of power, the one that used her up. And now, this day, she had been blowing nothing but air from her lips.

Badalle squinted.

'I want to be blind again, Badalle.'

She studied the puffed masses filling his sockets. 'You still are, Rutt.'

'Then . . . they are in my head. The flies . . . *in my head.*'

'No. I see them too. But that seething – it is just the sun's light behind them. Rutt, they are people.'

He almost fell then, but widened his stance and, with terrible grace, he straightened. 'Fathers.'

'No. Yes. No.'

'Did we turn round, Badalle? Did we somehow turn round?'

'No. See, the west – we have walked into the sun, every day, every dusk.' She was silent then. The Snake was coiling up behind the two of them, its scrawny body of bones drawing together, as if that could keep it safe. The figures from the sunset were coming closer. 'Rutt, there are . . . children.'

'What is that, upon their skin – their faces?'

She saw the one father among them, his beard grey and rust, his eyes suffering the way the eyes of some fathers did – as they sent their young ones away for the last time. But the faces of the children drew her attention. *Tattoos.* 'They have marked themselves, Rutt.' *Droplets, black tears. No, I see the truth of it now. Not tears. The tears have dried up, and will never return. These marks, upon face and hands, arms and neck, shoulders and chest. These marks.* 'Rutt.'

'Badalle?'

'They have claws.'

A ragged breath fell out from him, left him visibly trembling.

'Try now, Rutt. Your eyes. Try to open them.'

'I – I can't—'

'Try. You must.'

The father, along with his mob of clawed children, drew closer. They were wary – she could see that. *They did not expect us. They did not come looking for us. They are not here to save us.* She could see their suffering now, the thirst that gripped their faces like taloned, skeletal hands. *Claws will make you suffer.*

Yet the father, now standing before Rutt, reached down to the water-skin strapped to his sword belt. There was little water in it – that was obvious by its thinness, the ease with which he lifted it. Tugging the stopper free, he held it out to Rutt.

Who in turn thrust out Held. 'Her first,' he said. 'Please, the little one first.'

The gesture was unambiguous and without hesitation the father stepped up, and as Rutt pulled the cloth from in front of Held's small, wizened face the bearded man leaned close.

She saw him recoil, saw him look up and stare hard into Rutt's slitted eyes.

Badalle held her breath. Waited.

Then he shifted the waterskin, dipped the mouthpiece over Held's mouth, and the water trickled down.

She sighed. 'This father, Rutt, is a good father.'

One of the clawed children, a year or two older than Rutt, came up then and gently took Held from Rutt's arms – he might have resisted, but did not have the strength, and when the babe was in the cradle of the strange boy's arms Rutt's own arms remained crooked, as if he still held her, and Badalle saw how the tendons at his elbows had shrunk, drawn tight. And she thought back, trying to recall when she had last seen Rutt not holding Held, and she couldn't.

The baby was a ghost in his arms now.

The father was weeping – she could see the tracks down his dark-ened, pitted cheeks – and he guided the mouthpiece into Rutt's mouth, forced it past the boy's lips. A few drops, and then out again.

Rutt swallowed.

The other children with claws slipped past them, into the coiled Snake, each pulling out their own waterskins. But there were not enough of them. Still they went.

And now Badalle saw a new Snake, coming out of the sunset, and this one was of iron and chains, and she knew that she had seen it before, in her dreams. She had looked down upon this glittering serpent. *Fathers and mothers, but children all. And there – I see her – that is their one mother – I see her. She comes.*

People spilled out around the woman, with more waterskins.

She halted close to the bearded father, her eyes on Badalle, and when she spoke it was in the language of Badalle's dreams. 'Fiddler, they are walking the wrong way.'

'Aye, Adjunct.'

'I see only children.'

'Aye.'

Standing behind this woman was another soldier. 'But . . . Adjunct, who do they belong to?'

She turned. 'It doesn't matter, Fist, because they now belong to us.'

Rutt turned to Badalle. 'What are they saying?'

'They're saying we have to go back.'

The boy mouthed the last word. *Back?*

Badalle said, 'Rutt, you did not fail. You guided the Snake, and your blind tongue flicked out and found these strangers who are strangers no longer. Rutt, you led us from death and into life. Rutt,' she stepped close, 'you can rest now.'

The bearded man – whose name was Fiddler – managed to break Rutt's fall, but both went down to their knees.

The Adjunct took a half-step. 'Captain? Does he live?'

He looked up after a moment. 'If his heart still beats, Adjunct, I can neither feel nor hear it.'

Badalle spoke in their language. 'He lives, Father. He has just gone away. For a time.'

The man Mother had called Fist, who had been standing back, now edged forward and said, 'Child, how is it you speak Malazan? Who are you?'

Who am I? I don't know. I've never known. She met Mother's eyes. 'Rutt led us to you. Because you are the only ones left.'

'Only ones?'

'The only ones who will not turn away from us. You are our mother.'

At that the Adjunct seemed to step back, her eyes flaring as if struck to pain. And then she looked away from Badalle, who then pointed at Fiddler. 'And he is our father, and soon he will go away and we will never see him again. It is the way of fathers.' That thought made her sad, but she shook her head against the feeling. 'It is just the way.'

The Adjunct seemed to be trembling and unable to look upon Badalle. Instead, she turned to the man beside her. 'Fist, broach the reserve casks.'

'Adjunct! Look at them! Half will die before dawn!'

'Fist Blistig, I have given you an order.'

'We cannot spare any water! Not for these – these . . .'

'Obey my command,' said the Adjunct in a weary tone, 'or I will have you executed. Here. Immediately.'

'And face open rebellion! I swear it—'

Fiddler had straightened and now he walked to stand in front of Fist Blistig, so close that the Fist took a step back. He said nothing, only smiled, his teeth white amidst that tangle of rusty beard.

Snarling an oath, Blistig swung round. 'On your heads, then.'

The Adjunct spoke. 'Captains Yil and Gudd, accompany Fist Blistig.'

A man and a woman who had been hanging back swung round to flank Blistig as he marched back into the column.

Fiddler returned to where Rutt was lying. He knelt beside the boy, settled one hand to one side of the thin face. Then he looked up at Badalle. 'He led you?'

She nodded.

'How far? How long?'

She shrugged. 'Kolanse.'

The man blinked, looked over at the Adjunct for an instant, and then back to Badalle. 'How many days, then, to water?'

She shook her head. 'To Icarias, where there are wells . . . I – I can't remember. Seven days? Ten?'

'Impossible,' said someone from the crowd gathered behind the Adjunct. 'We have a day's supply left. Without water, three days at the most – Adjunct, we cannot make it.'

Badalle cocked her head. 'Where there is no water, there is blood. Flies. Shards. Where there is no food, there are children who have died.'

Someone said, 'Fist Blistig is right this time, Adjunct. We can't do this.'

'Captain Fiddler.'

'Aye?'

'Have your scouts guide the ones who can walk back to the food wagons. Ask the Khundryl to attend to those who cannot. See to it that everyone gets water, and food if they can manage any.'

'Aye, Adjunct.'

Badalle watched him ease his arms under Rutt, watched him lift the boy. *Rutt is now Held. He carried Held until he could carry her no longer, and now he is carried, and this is how it goes on.*

'Adjunct,' she said as Fiddler carried Rutt away, 'I am named Badalle, and for you I have a poem.'

'Child, if you stand there unattended to for much longer, you are going to die. I will hear your poem, but not now.'

Badalle smiled. 'Yes, Mother.'

And for you I have a poem. She stared at the straining backs, the shedding ropes, the toppled statues by the wayside. Two nights now since that meeting, since the last time Badalle had seen the Adjunct. Or the man named Fiddler. And the water was now gone, and still Rutt would not wake, and Saddic sat atop the bales putting his things in patterns only to pack them away again, until the next time.

And she listened to the arguments. She heard the fighting, saw the sudden roiling eddies where fists lashed out, soldiers grappled, knives were drawn. She watched as these men and women stumbled towards death, because Icarias was too far away. They had nothing left to drink, and now those who drank their own piss were starting to go mad, because piss was poison – but they would not bleed out the dead ones. They just left them to lie on the ground.

This night, she had counted fifty-four. The night before there had been thirty-nine, and on the day in between they'd carried seventy-two bodies from the camp, not bothering to dig a trench this time, simply leaving them lying in rows.

The children of the Snake were on the food wagons. Their walking was done, and they too were dying.

Icarias. I see your wells. They were almost dry when we left you. Something is taking the water away, even now. I don't know why. But it doesn't matter. We will not reach them. Is it true, then, that all mothers must fail? And all fathers must walk away never to be seen again?

Mother, for you I have a poem. Will you come to me? Will you hear my words?

The wagon rocked, the heavies strained. Soldiers died.

They were on a path now. Fiddler's scouts had little trouble following it. Small, bleached bones, all the ones who had fallen behind the boy named Rutt, the girl named Badalle. Each modest collection he stumbled over was an accusation, a mute rebuke. These children. They had done the impossible. *And now we fail them.*

He could hear the blood in his own veins, frantic, rushing through hollow places, and the sound it made was an incessant howl. Did the Adjunct still believe? Now that they were dying by the score, did she still hold to her faith? When determination, when stubborn will, proved not enough, what then? He had no answers to such questions. If he sought her out – *no, she's had enough of that. They're on her constantly. Fists, captains, the cutters.* Besides, talking was torture – lips split open, the

481

swollen tongue struggled, the back of the throat – tight and cracked – was pained by every uttered word.

He walked with his scouts, not wanting to drop back, to see what was happening in the column. Not wanting to witness its disintegration. Were his heavies still pulling the wagons? If they were, they were fools. Were any of those starved children left? That boy, Rutt – who'd carried that thing for so long his arms looked permanently crippled – was he still in a coma, or had he slipped away, believing he'd saved them all?

That would be the best. To ride the delusion into oblivion. There are no ghosts here, not in this desert. His soul just drifted away. Simple. Peaceful. Rising, carrying that baby – because he will always carry that baby. Go well, lad. Go well, the both of you.

They'd come looking for a mother and a father. A thousand children, a thousand orphans – but he was beginning to see, here on this trail, just how many more there had once been – in this train Badalle had called the Snake, and the comprehension of that twisted like a knife in his chest. *Kolanse, what have you done? To your people? To your children? Kolanse, had you no better answer than this? Gods, if we could have found you – if we could have faced you across a killing field. We would give answer to your crimes.*

Adjunct, you were right to seek this war.

But you were wrong thinking we could win it. You cannot wage war against indifference. Ah, listen to me. But am I dead? Not yet.

The previous day, when the entire camp was silent, soldiers lying motionless beneath the flies, he had reached into his pack, settled his hand upon the Deck of Dragons. *And . . . nothing. Lifeless.* This desert was bereft and no power could reach them. *We have made the gods blind to us. The gods, and the enemy ahead. Adjunct, I see your reason for this. I did then and I do now. But look at us – we're human. Mortal. No stronger than anyone else. And for all that you wanted to make us something more, something greater, it seems that we cannot be what you want.*

We cannot be what we want, either. And this, more than anything else, is what now crushes us. But still, I am not yet dead.

He thought back to the moment when they'd found the children; the way his scouts – not much older themselves – moved so solemnly among the refugees, giving all the water they carried – their entire allotment for the night's march given away, from one mouth to the next, until the last drops had been squeezed from the skins. And then the Khundryl youths could only stand, helpless, each surrounded by children who reached out – not to grasp or demand, but to touch, and in that touch give thanks. *Not for the water – that was gone – but for the gesture.*

How far must one fall, to give thanks for nothing but desire? Empty intent?

The ones who drove you away . . .

But we have allies, and there is no barrier before them, nothing to slow their march on Kolanse. Gesler, show Stormy the truth of this, and then cut his leash. Leave him to voice a howl to make the Hounds themselves cower! Let him loose, Ges, I beg you.

Because I don't think we can make it.

The bones of his neck grinding, Fiddler looked up, glared at the Jade Strangers. They filled the night sky now, blazing slashes across heaven's face. *Omens make me puke. I'm sick of the miserable things. But . . . what if you're nothing like that, you up there? What if your journey belongs to you and you alone, no destination, no reason or purpose? What if, tomorrow or the next day, you finally descend – to wipe out all of us, to make pointless our every struggle, our every great, noble cause? What is it then, O glorious universe, that you are telling us?*

Destiny is a lie.

But, then, do I even care? Look at these bones we step over. We go as far as we can go, and then we stop. And that is how it is. That is all it is. So . . . now what?

'Snakes,' said Banaschar, blinking against the hard clarity of sober vision. *It was better when everything was blurred. Much better.* 'That might have been my first fear, the one that had me stumbling right into the pit of vipers we so blithely call the Temple of D'rek. Face what you fear, isn't that the sage advice? Maybe that's sobriety's real curse, the recognition that being frightened is not character-building after all, and that the advice was shit and the world is full of liars.'

The Adjunct was silent as she walked beside him. Not that he was expecting a reply, since he was no longer certain that his words were actually getting past his throat. It was possible, indeed, highly likely, that everything he'd been saying for the past two days had been entirely in his own mind. But then, it was easier that way.

'Rebellion. Even the word itself makes me . . . envious. I've never felt it – here, in my soul. Never experienced a single moment of defiant fury, of the self demanding its right to be just the way it wants to be. Even when it doesn't know what that being looks like. It just wants it.

'Of course, drinking is the sweet surrender. The sanctum of cowards – and we're all cowards, us drunks, and don't let anyone try to convince you otherwise. It's the only thing we're good at, mostly, because it's both our reason and the means by which we run away. From everything. Which is why a drunk needs to stay drunk.'

He glanced across at her. Was she listening? Was there anything to listen to?

483

'Let's move on – that subject makes me . . . cringe. Another grand notion awaits us, as soon as I can think of one. *Snakes, you ask?* Well, of course it was a grand notion – the girl giving us names like that. Theirs. Ours. Snakes in the desert. It's bold, if you think about it. Snakes are damned hard to kill. They slide past underfoot. They hide in plain sight.

'So . . . hmm, how about knowledge? When knowing becomes a fall from grace. When truth is seen to condemn rather than liberate. When enlightenment shows nothing but the dark pathos of our endless list of failures. All that. But these attitudes, well, they come from those who want to encourage ignorance – a vital tactic in their maintenance of power. Besides, real knowledge forces one to act –

'Or does it?'

He paused then, trying to think it through. Only to feel a spasm of fear. 'You're right, let's move on yet again. If there's one thing I know it's that about some things I don't want to know anything. So . . . ah, in keeping with unexpected guests, shall we speak of heroism?'

Smiles staggered to one side and dropped to one knee. Bottle took up position behind her, guarding her back. The short sword in his hand seemed to be trembling all on its own.

He watched Tarr bull his way back through the milling press. His visage was darker than Bottle had ever seen before. 'Koryk!' he snapped.

'Here, Sergeant.'

'You'll live?'

'Caught a look in an eye,' the man replied, edging into view. One side of his face was sheathed in blood, but it wasn't his own. 'Seen hyenas looking saner.' He pointed with a bloodied long knife. 'That corporal there gave 'im a nudge . . .'

The man Koryk indicated was on his knees. A regular. Burly, broad-shouldered, with a knife handle jutting from the right side of his chest. Blood was streaming from his mouth and nostrils, filled with bubbles.

Tarr glared round, his eyes catching Bottle. He walked over. 'Smiles – look at me, soldier.'

She lifted her head. 'Like Koryk said, Sergeant – we ain't blind and we ain't stupid. Caught the same nudge, so I gave him my knife.'

Tarr met Bottle's eyes.

Bottle nodded. 'Twelve paces between 'em, in the dark, in a crowd.'

The dying corporal had dropped his bearded chin to his chest and seemed to be staring at his knees. Corabb edged closer and gave the man a push. He fell over. The thudding impact, as he landed on the ground, spurted one last mass of foam from his mouth and nose.

'Two down?' Tarr asked.

Bottle could feel the hatred in the eyes of the regulars crowding the scene, and he flinched when Corabb said, 'Three, Sergeant. The first two were the distraction – two more came in low from behind, making for the wagon. I got the first one, then Cuttle chased the last one away – still after him, I guess.'

'He's out there?' Tarr demanded. 'Hood's breath!'

Smiles straightened and, moving drunkenly, made her way to the dead corporal, where she retrieved her knife. 'It ain't right,' she muttered. She faced the crowd. 'We're guarding empty casks, you damned fools!'

Someone called out, 'Wasn't us, marine. That was the Fist's gang.'

Bottle scowled. *Blistig. Gods below.*

'Just leave us alone,' Smiles said, turning away.

Cuttle returned, caught Tarr's eye and with one hand casually brushed the crossbow slung down behind his left arm.

The sergeant faced the haulers. 'Pull up the ropes, soldiers – let's get this moving again.'

Smiles came up to Bottle. 'Killing our own – it ain't right.'

'I know.'

'You had my back – thanks.'

He nodded.

The crowd of regulars was melting away. The wagon started rolling, the squad falling in alongside it, and the bodies were left behind.

'It's the madness,' said Corabb a short time later. 'In Seven Cities—'

'You don't need to tell us,' Cuttle interrupted. 'We was there, remember?'

'Aye. Just saying, that's all. The madness of thirst—'

'That was planned out.'

'The corporal, aye,' Corabb said, 'but not that fool going for Koryk.'

'And the ones coming in from behind? Planned, Corabb. Someone's orders. That ain't madness. That ain't anything of the sort.'

'Mostly, I was talking about the rest of them regulars – the ones closing in on the smell of blood.'

No one had any response to that. Bottle found that he was still holding his short sword. Sighing, he sheathed it.

Shortnose took the blood-stained shirt and pushed it beneath the collar of the leather yoke, stuffing it across the width of his collar bones where his skin had been worn away and things were looking raw. Someone had brought him the shirt, sopping wet and warm, but all that blood didn't bother him much – he was already adding to it.

The wagon was heavy. Heavier now with children riding atop all the bundles of food. But for all their numbers, not as heavy as it should have been. That was because they were mostly starved down to bones. He didn't like thinking about that. Back when he'd been a child he remembered hungry times, but every one of those times his da would come in with something for the runts, Shortnose the runtiest of them all. A scrap. Something to chew. And his ma, she'd go out with other mas and they'd be busy for a few days and nights and then she'd come back in, sometimes bruised, sometimes weeping, but she'd have money for the table, and that money turned into food. His da used to swear a lot those times she did that.

But it was all down to feeding the runts. *'My beautiful runts,'* his da liked saying. And then, years later, when the garrison had up and left town, suddenly Ma couldn't get the money the way she used to, but she and Da were happier for all of that anyway. Shortnose's older brothers had all gone off by then, two of 'em to war and the other one to marry Widow Karas, who was ten years older than him and who Shortnose secretly loved with all his might, so it was probably a good thing he ran away when he did, since his brother wouldn't have taken kindly to that trouble behind the barn with Karas drunk, or maybe not, and anyway it was all in good fun –

He noticed a boy walking beside him. Carrying a sack. His hands were bloody and he was licking them clean.

Brought me that shirt, did you? 'Ain't good, runt,' he said. 'Drinking blood.'

The boy frowned up at him, and went on with his licking until his hands were clean.

– and he'd heard later how one of his brothers got killed outside Nathilog and the other one came back with only one leg, and then the pensions came through and Ma and Da stopped having to struggle so, especially when Shortnose joined up himself and sent two-thirds of his pay back home; half of that went home to Da and Ma; the other third went to his brother and his wife, because he felt guilty about the baby and all.

Still, it wasn't good being hungry so young, and starving was worst of all. His da used to say, *'If ya can't feed 'em, don't have 'em. Hood's proud pole, it don't take a genius to see that!'* It sure don't, and that was why Shortnose kept paying for his runt, and he'd still be paying for it if it wasn't for them being fired and made outlaws and deserters and all the other names the military came up with for not doing what they told you to do. By now, though, that runt would be old enough to work all on its own, so maybe his brother would have called off the bounty on his head. Maybe everything was all right by now, the dust settled and all.

It was nice to think so. But now he'd gone and fallen in love with Flashwit and Mayfly and wasn't that silly, since there were two of them and only one of him. Not that he saw that as a problem. But women could get funny about things like that. And lots of other things too, which was why they were so much trouble.

The hauler on his right stumbled. Shortnose reached down one-handed and lifted the woman back on to her feet. She gasped her thanks.

Now women. He could think about women all—

'You're Shortnose, aren't ya?'

He glanced down at her. She was short, with big, strong-looking legs – now that was bad luck for her, wasn't it? The one thing that made proper men drool turned out getting her yoked like a – like a – 'Yah, that's me.'

'Been tryin to look, y'see?'

'No.'

'I heard you got the same ear bitten off twice.'

'So?'

'Well, er, how's that possible?'

'Don't ask me. It was all Bredd's fault.'

'Bredd? Nefarias Bredd? You were fighting him?'

'Might have been. Save your breath, soldier. See this runt here? He ain't saying a thing, cause he's smart.'

'It's because he doesn't understand Malazan.'

'As good an excuse as any, I always say. Anyway, just keep pulling, and think about things you like to think about. To distract ya from all the bad stuff.'

'What are you thinking about?'

'Me? Women.'

'Right,' she said in a strangely cold tone. 'So I guess I'll think about handsome, clever men.'

He smiled down at her. 'You don't have to do that, lass – you got one walking right beside you.'

The boy went away and came back a short time later with some more cloth, which he gave to Shortnose so that he could stop his bleeding nose.

Like his da used to say, *There ain't no figurin' the ways of women.* Too bad too. She was kinda pretty and, even better, she could swear the hide off a bhederin. Could there be a sexier combination? He didn't think so.

'You'd think I was some kind of leper. It ain't my fault I been dead once, and maybe being dead once means things like getting thirsty don't hurt as much – I don't know.'

'I have been condensing everything in sight,' Bavedict said. 'That's what's been keeping me going.'

Hedge eyed the alchemist quizzically, and then he shrugged. 'Beats talking all day, I suppose.'

Bavedict opened his mouth and then shut it again.

'How are the kittens?'

'The kittens are just fine, Commander.'

'We got enough of 'em?'

'For more than one engagement? Hard to say, sir. I'm comfortable with one battle, using what we need and not holding back.' He glanced back at the carriage, and then said, 'I have given some thought to strategies, sir, with respect to alchemical . . . er . . . kittens. I don't think being misers with them works. You want to go the opposite way, in fact. Flood the field of battle, hit them so hard the shock overwhelms them—'

'I thought you wasn't going to talk all night? Listen, we worked that out years ago. Walls and waves, we called it. Walls when you was holding a line or position. Waves when you was on the advance. And there ain't no point in holding back – except the one with your own name on it, of course. Because every sapper will tell you, if you're gonna kill 'em they're gonna kill you at the same time, guaranteed. We call it disincentive.'

Bavedict glanced back a second time, frowned at the troop stumping along beside the carriage. The captains weren't doing well. Thinning out, but not in a good way. They'd not said much in days. Behind them walked the Khundryl, still leading their horses – *so I wasn't quite telling Hedge the truth. I didn't just dose the oxen but you'd think they'd see—*

'Still nervous?' Hedge asked him. 'I'd be, if I was you. Khundryl like their horses. A lot. Between a warrior's horse and his mother, it's even odds which one he'd save, if it came down to choosing. Then you just went and killed 'em.'

'They were dying anyway, sir. In a single day, a horse needs more water than four soldiers, and those Khundryl were running out. Try bleeding a dehydrated animal, sir – it isn't easy.'

'Right, so now they got undead horses and still no water, meaning if you'd done that a week ago, why, all that sacrifice wouldn't have been necessary. They want to kill you, alchemist – it took me half a day to talk 'em out of it.'

Bavedict glared at Hedge. 'You just said, between horses and their mothers—'

'They'd save their mothers, of course. What are you, an idiot?'

The alchemist sighed.

'Anyway,' Hedge continued after a moment, 'we're all Bridgeburners now. Now it's true, we killed a few officers every now and then, if they was bad enough. Who wouldn't? Get a fool in charge and they're likely to get you all killed, so better top 'em first, right? But you ain't done nothing to earn that. Besides, I need you and so do they. So it's simple and all – nobody's gonna cut your throat.'

'I am most relieved, Commander.'

Hedge moved closer, dropping his voice. 'But listen. It's all about to fall apart – can you see that? The Bonehunters – those regulars – they're losing it.'

'Sir, we're not much better off.'

'So we don't want to get caught up in the slaughter, right? I already told my captains. We're gonna pull out hard as soon as it starts up – I want a hundred paces between us before they start looking for somebody new to kill.'

'Sir, do you think it will get that bad?'

Hedge shrugged. 'Hard to say. So far, the marines are holding 'em all in check. But there's gonna come a scrap, any time now, when a marine gets taken down. And the smell of blood will do it, mark my words.'

'How would the Bridgeburners have handled this, sir? Back in the day?'

'Simple. Sniff out the yappers and kill 'em. It's the ones who can't stop bitching, talking it up, egging on the stupider ones to do something stupid. Hoping it all busts out. Me' – he nodded to the column walking beside them – 'I'd jump Blistig and drag him off into the desert – and for a whole damned day nobody'd be sleeping, 'cause of all the screaming.'

'No wonder you all got outlawed,' Bavedict muttered.

The sky to the east was lightening, the sun rising to wage war with the Jade Strangers before they plunged beneath the north horizon. The column broke down in sections, clumps of soldiers spilling away on to the sides of the trail. Sinking down, heads lowered, weapons and armour clashing as packs dropped to the ground. The haulers stopped, struggled out of the heavy yokes. Wailing from the Khundryl as yet another horse stumbled and fell on to its side – and out flashed the knives, and this day there would be plenty of blood to drink, but no one rejoiced among the Burned Tears.

Where the wagons halted, the marines settled, red-eyed and slack-faced with exhaustion. On all sides, the soldiers moved like old men and women, fighting to raise tarps and flies, roll out bedding, pausing to rest between tasks. Weapons were slowly drawn, the day's damage repaired with oiled whetstones, but the act was almost mindless: gestures of instinct observed by dull, sullen eyes.

And then out from the wagons came the children, in ones and twos, into the midst of the soldiers. They came not to beg or plead, but simply to sit, watching over the soldiers as they slept. Or suffered with staring eyes. Or, in the case of some, quietly died.

Sergeant Sinter observed this as she sat leaning against the wheel of the wagon they'd been guarding. The tremulous arrival of a child into every knot of soldiers seemed to have a strange effect upon them. Arguments fell away, glaring eyes faded, resentments sank down. The sleepless rolled on to their sides and surrendered to weariness. Pain was swallowed back and those who sat weeping without tears eventually settled into silence.

What gift was this? She did not understand. And when a soldier awoke in the closing of dusk, and found curled at his or her side a small, still form, cool and pale in the dying light, she'd seen how the squad then gathered to set shards of crystal over the lifeless child, raising a glittering mound. And the soldiers would then cut fetishes free from their belts and harnesses – the bones they'd carried since Aren – and set them upon the pathetic heaps of rock.

'They're killing us.'

She looked over at her sister, who sat against the back wheel, her splinted leg stretched out. 'Who is it this time, Kisswhere?'

'They come and share the last moments. Ours. Theirs. It's not fair, what they bring.'

Sinter's eyes narrowed on Kisswhere. *You've gone away, sister. Will you ever come back?* 'I don't know what they bring,' she said.

'You wouldn't.'

A dull awakening of anger, which then drained away. 'Why do you say that?'

Kisswhere bared her teeth, the back of her head resting between two spokes, her eyes closed. 'What you always had, Sinter. What I never had. That's why you can't see it. Can't recognize it. It'd be like seeing into your own soul, and that's something nobody can do. Oh, they say they can. Talk about revelation, or truth. All that shit. But inside us, something stays hidden. For ever.'

'There's nothing hiding inside me, Kisswhere.'

'But those children – sitting, watching, lying close – it hurts you to see them, doesn't it?'

Sinter looked away.

'You fool,' Kisswhere sighed. 'They bring *dignity*. Same as you. Same as the Adjunct herself – why do you think so many of us hate her? Hate the sight of her? She shows us everything we don't want to be reminded of, because there's nothing harder for most of us to find than dignity. Nothing. So, they show us how you can die with dignity – they show us by dying themselves, and by letting us die while being watched over.'

'The Adjunct said *unwitnessed*. These children don't agree.'

But it's all pointless anyway.

490

Kisswhere went on, 'Did you think this would be easy? Did you think our feet wouldn't start to drag? We've walked across half a world to get here. We stopped being an army long ago – and no, I don't know what we are now. I don't think there's a person in this world who'd be able to give us a name.'

'We're not going to make it,' Sinter said.

'So what?'

Sinter looked across at her sister. Their eyes briefly locked. Just past Kisswhere, Corporal Rim sat hunched over, rubbing oil into the stump of his right arm. He made no sign of listening, but she knew he was. Same for Honey, lying shrouded under stained linen to keep the sun from her eyes. 'So you don't care, Kisswhere. You never did.'

'Surviving this ain't the point, Sinter. It stopped being the point some time ago.'

'Right,' she snapped. 'So enlighten me.'

'You already know. You said it yourself – we're not going to make it. And those children, they come among us, like homunculi. Made up of everything we surrendered in our lives – all that dignity, and integrity, and truth – all of it, and look at them – starved down to bones and not much else. We ain't been too good with the best in us, sister, have we?'

If tears had been possible, Sinter would have wept them. Instead, she sank down on to the hard ground. 'You should've run,' she said.

'I bet the Adjunct says that to herself a thousand times a day.'

The Adjunct? Sinter shook her head. 'She's not the running type.'

'No, and neither are you. And now, it turns out, neither am I.'

This is not my sister.

'I think,' Kisswhere resumed, 'tomorrow will be our last march. And you know, it's all right. It was worth the try. Someone should tell her that. It was worth the try.'

'No spiders,' said Hellian, settling her head back on the bedroll. 'This is the best there is. This desert, it's paradise. Let the flies and capemoths take my corpse. Even those damned meat-eating locusts. You won't find a spider making a nest in my skull's eye sockets – what could be better than that?'

'What got you so scared of 'em, Sergeant?'

She thought about that. But then her mind wandered away, and she saw heaps of skulls, all of them smiling. And why not? Oh, yes, no spiders. 'My father tells a story, especially when he's drunk. He thinks it's damned funny, that story. Oh, wait, is that my father? Could be my uncle. Or even my stepfather. Might even be my brother's father, who lives down the lane. Anyway, it was a story and how he laughed. You got to know Kartool, Maybe. Spiders big enough to eat gulls, right?'

'Been there once, aye, Sergeant. Creepy place.'

'The redbacks are the worst. Not big, not much poisonous by themselves. One at a time, I mean. Thing is, when they hatch, there's thousands, and they stick together for days, so they can kill big prey and all of them feed on it, right? And the egg-sacs, why, they can be hidden anywhere.

'So, I was maybe two. Spent all day in a crib, every day, since my mother had another baby on the way only she kept getting fevers and eventually she went and lost it, which was stupid, since we had a good healer down the street, but Father drank up all the coin he made. Anyway. I had this doll—'

'Oh gods, Sergeant—'

'Aye, they came out of its head. Ate right through the stuffing, and then out through the eyes and the mouth and everywhere else. And there I was: food. It was my half-brother who came in and found me. My head was swollen to twice its size – couldn't even see my eyes – and I was choking. Counted two hundred bites, maybe more, since they were mostly in my hair. Now, as far as prey goes, I was too big even for a thousand redback babies. But they tried damned hard.'

'And that story made him laugh? What kind of fucked-up—'

'Watch it, that's my father you're talking about there. Or uncle, or stepfather, or the guy down the lane.'

'Now I see it, Sergeant,' said Touchy. 'It's all right. I see it. That'd scar anyone for life.'

'The story ain't finished, Corporal. I ain't got to the whole point of it. Y'see, I was eating them damned spiders. Eating 'em like candy. They said my belly was more swollen than my head, and that's why I was choking so bad – they were biting me all the way down.

'So they brought in the healer, and she conjured up big chunks of ice. Into my mouth. Back of the throat. And all around my neck, too. Story goes that I had a stroke, from all that ice. Killed the part of my brain that knows when it's time to stop.' She stared up at the brightening sky. 'They say I stole my first jug from my father's stash when I was six. Got so drunk they needed to bring the healer back a second time. And that's when she scried me inside and said I was in for a life of trouble.'

A hand brushed her upper arm. 'That's a heartbreaking tale, Sergeant.'

'Is it?' *I suppose it is. Of course, I just made it up. Tug those heartstrings, see all that sweet sympathy in their sweet little faces. They'll forgive me anything now.*

Why do I hate spiders? Gods, who doesn't? What a stupid question.

*   *   *

'Faces in the Rock,' said Urugal the Woven, crouching to scrape patterns in the hard ground. 'Seven of the Dying Fires. The Unbound. These are our titles – we T'lan Imass cast out from our clans. We who failed in the wars. We who were cursed to witness.'

Nom Kala shifted to look back upon the human camp – a dissolute column forming a jagged line across the hardpan. All motion was dying away there, the growing heat stealing all that was left. The humps of prostrate bodies stretched long shadows.

'We chose a Knight of Chains,' Urugal went on, 'and by his will we were freed from our prison, and by his will the chains shall one day shatter. Then we awaited the sanctification of the House of Chains.'

'This knight,' rumbled Kalt Urmanal, 'is he among us now?'

'No, but he awaits us,' replied Urugal. 'Long has been his journey, and soon the fate of us all will fall at his feet. But, alas, the Fallen One does not command him, and the King in Chains has turned his back on our cause – for the King of the House is cursed, and his chains will never break. It is our belief that he will not sit long upon that throne. Thus, we discard him.'

Beroke Soft Voice said, 'The Knight is a despiser of chains, but understanding eludes him still. Many are the chains that cut cruel, that enslave with malice. Yet other chains also exist, and these are the ones we each choose to wear – not out of fear, or ignorance. These are the noblest of chains. Honour. Virtue. Loyalty. Many will approach the House of Chains, only to falter upon its threshold, for it demands within us strengths rarely used. When suffering awaits, it takes great courage to stride forward, to enter this unrelenting, unforgiving realm.'

Urugal had scraped seven symbols on the ground. He now pointed to each in turn and said, 'The Consort. She who is known to us. The Reaver – there are two faces. One man. One woman. Knight, we have spoken of. The Seven of the Dead Fires, the Unbound – we T'lan Imass, for now, but that will change. Cripple, he whose mind must crawl to serve the sacred life within him. Leper, that which is both living and dead. Fool, the threat from within. All, then, but the Knight walk among the mortals in our keeping. Here. Now.'

Nom Kala studied the symbols. 'But Urugal, they are all dying.'

'And there is no wind to carry us,' Beroke said. 'We cannot travel to what lies ahead.'

'Thus, we cannot give them hope.'

Kalt Urmanal grunted at Urugal's conclusion. 'We are T'lan Imass, what know we of hope?'

'Are we then lost?' Nom Kala asked.

The others were silent.

'I have a thought,' she said. 'It is as Kalt says – we are not creatures of hope. We cannot give them what we surrendered so long ago. These mortal humans will die, if we cannot save them. Do any of you dispute that?'

'We do not,' said Urugal.

'And so' – Nom Kala stepped forward and with one skeletal foot broke the patterns in the dirt – 'the House of Chains will die.'

'In another age, it will awaken once more.'

'If it must be us – and we do wish it to be us, do we not? If it must be us, Unbound, then we have no choice. We must go to the Adjunct.'

'And say what?' Urugal demanded.

'Why, we must lie to her.'

None spoke for a time.

Nom Kala studied the camp, the stretched shadows. 'Let us seek to steal one more day.'

'To what end is one more day?'

'I cannot say, Urugal the Woven. Sometimes, hope is born from a lie. So be it. To her, we shall lie.'

Ruthan Gudd's eyes tracked Lostara Yil as she approached the Adjunct. The two women stood studying the east as if to defy the savage dawn. He wondered what kept Tavore on her feet. Each night she set out, marching without rest, and by her will alone she dragged an entire army in her wake. If she would not stumble, then neither would the soldiers behind her. It had become a battle, a silent war. *And she's winning it. Every body left behind is testament to that.*

But how much longer can she keep this up? Look at that rising run, Adjunct, and the emptiness beneath it. Sometimes, when people speak of forbidding, deadly places, it's not just a story. Sometimes, it's all true, and the warnings are honest warnings. There are places that will kill you. And we have found one.

'What are they saying, do you think?' Skanarow asked.

He looked down at her, eyes tightening. 'Sleep, my love.' He watched her settle her head back on the hard ground, her eyes closing.

Not much longer. And now it's too late – I can't save you. I can't just steal you away, because you won't make it. He wondered if he would walk out of this desert alone. One survivor left, leaving behind six thousand corpses. A damned Otataral sword in one hand, for the day when he'd need it. *Aye, Ruthan Gudd, he's been a one man army before, after all. Here he goes again.* Lifting his gaze, he studied the two women standing twenty paces away, and frowned. *Lostara – she's been possessed by a god. Does that make her tougher than she used to be? Who knows? But she's looking in better shape than Skanarow. Better than the Adjunct, too.*

'Please, lie beside me.'

Ruthan flinched. He combed through his beard. 'I will. In a moment.'

'Beloved?'

'A moment.' He walked over to Tavore and Lostara.

If they were in a conversation, it wasn't one using words. The Adjunct heard him approaching and turned to regard him. 'Captain. The ice armour you conjured—'

'Not here, Adjunct. Nothing works here.'

Her eyes flattened. 'But you will . . . persevere.'

Lostara Yil coughed, and then said, 'Ruthan, the T'lan Imass bow to you. They title you *Elder.*'

'I am not a god, Elder or otherwise, Lostara. I'm sorry. Wouldn't it be nice to be one, though? For each and every one of us. Just to be . . . outside all this. The T'lan Imass will manage, when—'

'So will you,' the Adjunct cut in. 'Yet you are not a god.'

'We do not choose to whom we are born.'

'Indeed not. Who, then, are your parents?'

He scratched his beard vigorously. 'Adjunct, does it matter? It may be that this desert doesn't kill me. It's equally likely that it will.'

'You will reach the city with the wells.'

'Will I?' Ruthan shook his head. 'Let me be honest with you – I cannot fathom how those children got as far as they did. What did Badalle say? Ten days away? But Icarias is two, even three weeks' march from here.'

'How do you know this?'

He grimaced. 'I was once a guest of the Jaghut who dwelt in Icarias along with a refugee enclave of K'Chain Che'Malle. The simple fact remains, the only way those children could have come as far as they have, Adjunct, is by *warren.*'

Tavore turned to Lostara. 'Get the girl. Bring her to me.'

'Aye, Adjunct.'

When she'd departed, Tavore fixed Ruthan with a hard stare. 'A warren.'

'Which is impossible. I know.' He saw a glitter of hope in her eyes and shook his head. 'Do not, Adjunct. The desert is sucked dry, and if you're not careful things are likely to get much worse.'

'Worse? Explain to me how this could get worse, Captain.'

He looked away, back to where Skanarow slept, and sighed. 'Draw your sword, Adjunct.'

'What?'

'Unsheathe your Otataral blade.'

She had the sword half out of the scabbard before Ruthan reached out and grasped her wrist. And then, retching, he fell to his knees, turning his head away.

Tavore slammed the weapon back down and staggered back a step. '*Gods!*' she gasped.

Ruthan spat, and then used the back of his wrist to wipe at his beard. 'It's what none of you ever understood,' he said, staring down at his trembling hands, studying the smears of blood in what he'd coughed up. 'It's not just some damned metal that just happens to devour magic. Otataral is *aspected*.' He pushed himself back on to his feet. 'The next time you draw that weapon, Adjunct, the act will *summon*. She is loose upon the world now, the dragon that is the source of all Otataral – the living heart of that which takes life. She has been freed.'

Tavore took another step back, shaking her head. 'What has been done?' she demanded, her voice breaking.

He saw panic rising within her – vast cracks in her armour – and held out a hand. 'Wait – listen to me. Tavore Paran, listen! It will be answered – everything is answered. Everything!'

And now, all at once, it was as if a child was standing before him. Lost, frightened. The sight tore at his heart. 'They're not interested in the Crippled God. Do you understand me? The ones who did this – they don't care what happens to him. They're reaching for something bigger – and they think they will sweep all this aside. You, the Fallen One, the Forkrul Assail – all of it, swept away!

'But they're fools. Do you understand me? Anomander Rake is gone, but Draconus now walks the world. Do you see? *Everything is answered.*' *And that is the true madness of this – the Otataral Dragon cannot remain unchained. Draconus will have to kill it – him or the Eleint – and by killing it they will end all magic. They will cast us all out into a world devoid of sorcery.*

She had turned away from him, was now staring into the east. 'This is what he meant,' she murmured.

'Adjunct?'

'He said my sword would not be enough – we argued that, again and again. He said . . . he said—' She faced him, eyes suddenly shining, and Ruthan was struck by a sudden beauty in her face, a thing that seemed to rise as if from nowhere. 'He said . . . "*it will be answered.*" His words, the same as yours.'

'Who are you talking about?' he demanded. *Who's been scheming this nightmare all along? What raving, lunatic idiot—*

'Ben Adaephon Delat.'

He stared, disbelieving, thunderstruck at his own stupidity. 'That name . . .'

'High Mage Quick Ben, Captain. He vowed he would save Burn, and that was one vow he would not surrender. He said the cancer needed cutting out – Ruthan? What is wrong?'

But he had turned away, struggling to hold it all in. Struggling –

496

and then failing. Laughter burst from him. Disbelieving, wondrous laughter. 'Delat? Adaephon Delat? *Quick* Ben – oh, by the Abyss! The bloody nerve of him! Was it a glamour, that made me so thick? No wonder he stayed away from me!'

'Captain?'

He stared at her, and he could feel his mouth stretched wide in a manic, helpless grin. 'And down he went, in the battle with the Short-Tails? Like Hood he did!'

Her lips thinned into a straight line. 'Captain Ruthan Gudd, even you could not be so dense. Of course he isn't dead.' She pointed to a nearby figure perched atop an outcrop of rock. 'Ask our resident Septarch of D'rek. He will tell you, since he at last has figured it out.'

As if commanded, Banaschar rose then, tottering as he walked to them. He wagged a finger at Ruthan Gudd, and through cracked, bleeding lips, he said, 'This is Quick Ben's game, O Elder. The bones are in his sweaty hands and they have been for some time. Now, if at his table you'll find the Worm of Autumn, and the once Lord of Death, and Shadowthrone and Cotillion, not to mention the past players Anomander Rake and Dessembrae, and who knows who else, well – did you really believe a few thousand damned Nah'ruk could take him down? The thing about Adaephon Delat's game is this: *he cheats.*'

He turned to the Adjunct and managed a faint bow. 'Lady Tavore, it is fair to say that I will remember the light in your eyes – as I am privileged to see it now – for the rest of my days. Did I not speak of heroism? I believe I did, though in your despond perhaps you were not listening.'

'By your words, High Priest, I found the strength for the next step. Forgive me if I could give you nothing in return.'

He cocked his head and regarded her, and then said softly, 'My lady, have you not given enough?'

Ruthan Gudd clawed at his beard. The delight was fast fading, and he feared stirring the ashes and finding that hope had been nothing but a lone spark, already gone. 'We still face a dilemma, and oh how I wish Delat was here, though I think even he would have no answers for our plight. This desert will have us.'

Tavore said, 'Captain, if I fall – take up my sword.'

'If I do, Adjunct – and if indeed a time comes when I must draw that weapon – it will kill me.'

'Then as you have said, you must not be an Elder God.'

'As I said,' he agreed wryly. 'But the matter is simpler than that. I have lived a long time, and that is by magic alone. Without sorcery, I would be less than dust.' He glanced at Banaschar. 'Delat is not the only one to have gamed at the table of the gods.'

'I would know your story some day, Ruthan Gudd,' said Banaschar, with a sad smile.

Ruthan Gudd shrugged. 'To be honest, too sordid to tell.'

They were silent, as if so thoroughly wrung out by all that had been said – and felt – that nothing remained.

Lostara then returned, and at her side was the girl named Badalle, and a boy carrying a sack.

Nom Kala walked through a silent camp, bodies lying motionless on all sides, half-closed eyes tracking her as she strode past. She saw suffering on a scale that made long-dead emotions tremble inside her, and she remembered the fate of her own kind, when walls of ice closed in, when the animals died out or went away, when there was nothing left to eat, when the humans hunted them down.

Their answer had been the Ritual, an escape that proved a prison. But such a thing was not available to these mortals. *Another day. A lie to give them that, if one is even possible. See how weak they are. See how they fail. Another day – but would that be a gift? The marching, the dragging steps, the ones falling to the side to surrender. Will they thank me for those extra moments?*

Perhaps her desire to help was in fact one of cruelty—

'So, how does it feel?'

At the faint voice she halted, looked round, saw a soldier sitting near-by, studying her. 'How does what feel?' she asked.

'Being . . . dust.'

She did not know how to answer him and so was silent.

'We'll be joining you soon enough, I suppose.'

'No, you won't. No memory will remain, nothing to draw you back.'

'But I have strings, T'lan Imass. That's my private curse. I *will* be pulled back together – or they'll try, anyway. Over and over again.'

Nom Kala studied the man, and then shook her head. 'I see no strings, mortal. If they once existed, now they are gone. Nothing holds you. Not the will of gods, not the lies of destiny or fate. You are severed from everything but that which lives within you.'

'Truly? No wonder I feel so lonely.'

'Yes,' she said. 'That is the reason.'

'But . . . you are not alone, are you, T'lan Imass?'

'No, but that is no salvation. Together, we but share our loneliness.'

He snorted. 'Not sure that makes sense, but I think I understand you anyway. Listen, do us a favour. Once the last of us has fallen, don't fall to dust, don't give up just yet. Walk out of this desert. *Walk out of it.* Please, will you do that?'

'Because it is said that this desert cannot be crossed. Yes, I understand you, mortal.'

'Will you do it?'

'We shall.'

He settled back on his bedroll with an uneven sigh. 'Good. Prove them wrong. It's good enough, I think.'

Nom Kala hesitated, and then said, 'Do not give up, soldier. One more march.'

Eyes closed, he asked, 'What would be the point of that?'

'Push your comrades on – through this next night. Do this, please. As I have agreed to do as you wish, I ask that you reciprocate.'

He opened his eyes, squinted at her. 'Is it that important?'

'Suffering is a chasm. But there is the other side, and upon that side waits the Fallen God. I am one of the Seven now. I am one among the Unbound. The Fallen One understands suffering, mortal. In that you are not alone. In that, neither are the T'lan Imass alone.'

'Aye, I'll grant you that he knows a thing or two about suffering. That you do, as well. I just don't see the comfort in that kind of sharing.'

'If not comfort, then find *strength*.'

'To keep bearing that suffering? What for?'

Yes, Nom Kala, what for? Do you have an answer? Does anyone? 'When you at last reach across that chasm, mortal, and grasp tight the hand of the Fallen One, ask him your question.'

He managed a sour smile. 'Convenient.' And he closed his eyes once more.

She continued on, troubled, heavy with anguish. *The T'lan Imass have seen civilizations rise and fall. We have seen lands die, only to be reborn. We have seen the seas rise and we have walked ancient seabeds. We have witnessed life's myriad struggles. From the lone creature suffering its last moments to thousands dying in a bleak season.*

And what have we learned?

Only that life is its own purpose. And that, where there is life, there shall be suffering. Has it any meaning? Is existence reason enough?

I am an Unbound. I am free to see, and what is it that I see?

I see . . . nothing.

Ahead, at the vanguard of the column, there were figures. Standing. *Now, I must find a worthy lie. And if my name is to be cursed in the last breaths of these humans, so be it. My crime was hope. My punishment is to see it fail.*

But the T'lan Imass have weathered that punishment for a long time, and the failure of hope has a name: it is called suffering.

'Words,' said Badalle, meeting the Adjunct's eyes. 'I found power in words. But that power is gone. I have nothing left.'

Mother turned to her companions, but said nothing. There was almost no life left in her plain face, her plain eyes, and seeing that hurt Badalle somewhere inside. *I had a poem for you. But it is gone. Dried up.*

A man combed his beard with filthy fingers and said, 'Child . . . if your strength returns – another day . . .'

'It is not that kind of strength,' Badalle replied. 'It is gone, perhaps for ever. I do not know how to get it back. I think it has died.' *I am not your hope. I cannot be. It was meant to be the other way round, don't you see that? We are children. That and nothing more.* 'The god that died here, it was the same.'

Mother frowned. 'Can you explain that, Badalle?'

She shook her head.

The other man – the one with the haunted eyes – then spoke. 'What can you tell us of that god, Badalle?'

'He broke apart.'

'Did he just break apart or did someone break him apart?'

'He was murdered by his followers.'

The man reacted as if he'd been struck in the face.

'It is in the Song of the Shards,' she continued. 'The god sought to give his people one last gift. But they refused it. They would not live by it, and so they killed him.' She shrugged. 'It was long ago, in the age when believers murdered their gods if they didn't like what the god had to say. But it's all different now, isn't it?'

'Aye,' the bearded man muttered. 'Now we just ignore them to death.'

'It's not the gods that we ignore,' said the woman standing beside Mother, 'just their gifts of wisdom.'

The other man spoke. 'Do that long enough and the gods just wither and die. So it takes longer, but in the end, it's still murder. And we're just as vicious with mortals who have the nerve to say things we don't want to hear.' He cursed, and then said, 'Is it any wonder we've outstayed our welcome?'

Mother met Badalle's eyes and asked, 'This city – Icarias – who dwells there?'

'Only ghosts, Mother.'

Beside her, Saddic had seated himself on the ground, taking out his useless things, but at the mention of Icarias he looked up and then pointed at the bearded man. 'Badalle,' he said. 'I saw this man. In the crystal caves beneath the city.'

She considered this, and then shrugged. 'Not ghosts, then. Memories.'

'For ever frozen,' the bearded man said, eyeing the boy. He faced Mother. 'Adjunct, they cannot help you. Look at them – they're dying just as we are.'

'Would that we could have done better by them,' said the other man.

Mother hesitated, and then nodded, as if in defeat.

This is not how it should be. What am I not seeing? Why do I feel so helpless?

The bearded man was still watching Saddic, and then he said, 'Send them back to their beds, Adjunct. This is all too . . . cruel. The sun and heat, I mean.'

'Lostara—'

'No, I will escort them, Adjunct.'

'Very well, Captain. Badalle, this man, Ruthan Gudd, will take you back now.'

'Yes, Mother.'

The captain settled into a crouch, facing Saddic. 'Here,' he said gruffly, 'let me help with these toys.'

Badalle stared, suddenly breathless, watching as Ruthan Gudd and Saddic filled the tattered bag. Something made Saddic look up then, his eyes meeting hers.

'Badalle? What is it? What did he say?'

She struggled to breathe, struggled to speak. Something fierce and wild rushed through her. She fell to her knees, snatched the bag from Saddic's small hands. She spilled the objects back out and stared down at them in wonder.

'Badalle?'

The captain had leaned back, startled by the vehemence in her gesture, yet he said nothing.

'Badalle?'

'Saddic – these things – *they're toys.*'

He looked up at her, the colour leaving his face. Showing her, bared and raw, wretched astonishment. Then that shattered, and she could see that he was about to cry.

I'm sorry. I'd . . . forgotten.

She watched as Saddic's attention returned to the collection of objects spilled out on the ground before him. He reached out as if to touch one – a bundle of twine and feathers – and then snatched back his hand. 'Toys,' he whispered. 'They're toys.'

The captain climbed to his feet and backed away. His dark eyes met her gaze, and she saw the horror in them, and she understood. *Yes, this is what we lost.* 'Thank you, Captain,' she said quietly. 'We will go back. Just . . . not yet. Please?'

He nodded, and then led the other adults away, and though it was obvious that they were confused, that they had questions, not one of them said a word.

Badalle moved to kneel across from Saddic. She stared down at

501

the array, weakened by a sudden feeling of helplessness. *I – I don't remember.* Yet, when she reached down to pick up the pommel from a knife or sword, when she hesitated and looked over at Saddic, he simply nodded his invitation.

Thirty paces away, hot but dry-skinned in the burgeoning heat, Ruthan Gudd stood watching, his only company the Adjunct. In a few terse, difficult words, he had explained his sense of what had just happened.

Neither spoke for some time.

It wasn't fair. Of all the crimes he had seen in a life almost too long to comprehend . . . *this one surpasses them all. The look on her face. On the boy's when she told him. That pathetic collection, carried like a treasure, and is it not a treasure?* Finally, he wiped a hand before his eyes and said, 'We spoke of murdering gods, with a strange diffidence, almost a bluster – and what did they show us? Adjunct, what are we, when we murder *innocence*?'

Tavore's sigh was ragged. 'It will be answered.'

He saw her take on the burden, in the settling of her shoulders, recognized the breathtaking courage in the way she lifted her head, the way she refused to look away from the scene – *of two children, trying to remember what it is to play. Adjunct – do not do this. You cannot carry anything more—*

Hearing someone behind them, they both turned.

A T'lan Imass. Ruthan Gudd grunted. 'One of our deserters.'

'Nom Kala,' the apparition replied. 'Now in the service of the Fallen One, Elder.'

'What do you wish to tell me?' Tavore asked.

'Adjunct. You must march for another night – you cannot stop here. You cannot give up. One more night.'

'I intend to march for as many nights as we can, Nom Kala.'

She was silent, as if nonplussed.

Ruthan Gudd cleared his throat. 'You don't want us to give up – we understand that, Nom Kala. We are the Fallen One's last hope.'

'Your soldiers fail.'

'They're not interested in worshipping the Crippled God,' he said. 'They don't want to give their lives to a cause they don't understand. This confusion and reluctance weakens their spirit.'

'Yes, Elder. Thus, there must be one more night of marching.'

'And then?' the Adjunct demanded. 'What salvation will find us by tomorrow's dawn?'

'The Seven of the Dying Fires shall endeavour to awaken Tellann,' Nom Kala replied. 'We have begun our preparations for a Ritual of Opening. Once we have created a gate we shall travel through, to a place where there is fresh water. We shall fill the casks once more and return to you. But we need another day.'

'There are but seven of you,' Ruthan said. 'In this desert, that is not enough.'

'We shall succeed in this, Elder.'

Ruthan cocked his head. 'If you say so.'

'I do. Now, please inform your soldiers. One more march.'

'To reach salvation,' said the Adjunct.

'Yes.'

'Very well, Nom Kala.'

The T'lan Imass bowed to them both, turned and then strode back into the camp.

When she was gone, the Adjunct sighed. 'In your obviously long life, Captain, did you ever throw dice with a T'lan Imass?'

'No, and I used to think that wisdom on my part.'

'And now?'

Ruthan Gudd shook his head. 'They are terrible liars.'

'Still,' she said under her breath, 'I appreciate the effort.'

'We don't need it, Adjunct. To keep us all going – we don't need it.'

'We don't?'

'No.' And he pointed to Badalle and Saddic. 'I will go among the troops this day, Adjunct, for I have a story to tell. Two children, a sack of toys.'

She eyed him. 'These children?'

He nodded. 'These children.'

CHAPTER EIGHTEEN

Down on the strand where the sea meets the land
Where fishermen kneel over wounds that won't heal
And the water weeps at the end of the day
      In the mirror you walk away

Among the red trees and the long dead leaves
The axeman wanders but cannot remember
And the earth runs like tears and will not stay
      In the mirror you walk away

In the silent season high on the hill's bastion
In the burning rain and the soul's dark stain
Where the children lie where they lay
      In the mirror you walk away

Along the furrows of his heels a long shadow steals
Down from the altar pulled all the destinies fulfilled
Tell the tale another god has had his day
      And in the mirror you walk away

When on the grey fields the troubles fall still
Another soldier's cause dies for what never was
Drifting past the dreams now gone astray
      In the mirror you walk away

Soiled the sacrament and broken the monument
Sullied the sculpture and soured the rapture
Beauty lives but brief its stay
      And in the mirror you walk away

Gods will give and then take away
If faith tastes of blood
drink deep when you pray
Beauty lives but brief its stay
And when it all goes away
and there's nothing left to save
In the mirror you walk away
In the mirror you walk away

Song of the Last Prayer
(in the age of adjudication)
Sevul of Kolanse

H*E FELT THE NUDGE AND IMAGINED HIMSELF IN THE HOLD OF A SHIP,*
rolling in heavy swells. When the nudge came a second time,
he thought of drunken nights, sprawled beneath a table with
someone's booted foot thudding against him. With the third nudge –
harder this time, delivered with irritation or impatience – he muttered
a curse. But something had gummed together his lips, so the word
came out as a moan.

He decided it was time to open his eyes.

That too proved a struggle, lids pulling apart as if glued, stinging
viciously once he blinked his way clear. Gloom, blurred shapes, some-
thing like a face hovering over him. The air smelled of decay. The taste
in his mouth was of old, old blood. And something else. Bitter. It was,
he decided, the taste of failure.

'Get up.'

Another figure, now kneeling beside him. A soft hand pressing
against the side of his face – but his beard was stiff and it crackled
under the palm, and the hand slipped away. Only to come back, hard
enough to rock his head.

And a woman said, 'We don't have time for this. The door's open.
Some people round here got a feel for things like that.'

The first speaker said, 'Poison's gone inert. Long ago. But he ain't
moved in a while.'

'The guardian should've—'

'Off wandering the warrens, is my guess. Lucky us.'

'Just help him to his feet, will you?'

Hands under his arms, a grunt, and he felt himself leave the stone
floor except for his heels. Sudden pain in his lower back and his legs
as they tried to take his weight. He couldn't remember being this heavy
– was he ever this heavy?

'Stand up, damn you – I can't hold you up long.'

505

'How do you think I felt?' the woman asked beside him. 'He made all my bones creak.'

He swore at the sharp stabs lancing out from his legs, tottered—

'There, back a step – lean against the wall. Good, like that. Now look at me, idiot. Look at me like you know me.'

It was dark, but he could make out the man's face now. Studied the eyes fixing on his own, and frowned.

'What's my name?' the man demanded.

He worked until he had some spit in his mouth, pushed with his tongue to force open his lips. 'I know you,' he managed to say. 'Your name . . . Blob.'

'Blob?' The man's head turned towards the woman. 'He says my name is Blob.'

'Should I slap him again?'

'Blur,' he now said, blinking at the woman. 'Blob and Blur. I remember now. You got me drunk. Took advantage of me. I should probably kill you both. Where are my trousers?'

Still leaning against the wall, still using it to prop himself up, he glared at the man and the woman, watched them both back off a step. They were all in a corridor, and to his right was a thick wooden door, pushed open, revealing a snarled lumpy mess of a yard just beyond, and a cool draught was slinking in, smelling of brackish water and rubbish.

The man spoke slowly, as if to a child. 'You're wearing your trousers.'

'Of course I am. Think I can't dress myself? Where are my knives?'

The woman swore under her breath and then said, 'The fool's lost his mind. Not hard, since it wasn't great to begin with, but it's gone now. He's useless to us – Cotillion lied. Just wanted me out from underfoot, so he sent me riding wild as a she-witch – all for nothing!'

'I'd agree with you on that assessment,' said the other man, now crossing his arms, 'except for one thing.'

'What?'

'Blob and Blur? The bastard's having us on, Minala. And he thinks it's funny, too. See that glare? Like every ocean storm's come home to roost on his forehead. Thing is, Kalam never glares. Almost never scowls. Kalam's got the face of an assassin.'

Kalam sneered. 'I'm having you on, am I? Tell you what, Wizard, am I having you on the way you had me on when I cracked that acorn and you never showed? With about a hundred Claws closing in on me?'

'Not my fault. Besides, look at you. You came out the other end still walking—'

'Crawling, actually,' corrected Minala. 'According to Shadowthrone,

I mean. In fact, the wispy runt had to drag Kalam up to the door here. It's a wonder he even managed it.'

Quick Ben snorted. 'So you ain't nearly as good as you think you are. What a shock. Look at your clothes and armour – you're chopped to pieces, O mighty assassin. A handful of Laseen's weasels made a mess of you, and you've got the nerve to blame me.'

'So where is she?' Kalam demanded.

'Who?'

'Laseen. I got to settle with her – she cut Tavore loose. She said the Wickans have to be sacrificed – and Korbolo Dom. I want that bastard's knobby head bouncing down every step from Mock's Hold to the mouth of the sewer – where the fuck are my knives?'

Minala drew out a belted brace and flung the gear at his feet. 'So I come riding through a thousand warrens, nearly get blasted by lightning, and you ain't got a single word for your Hood-damned wife?'

'You threw me out, remember?'

'Remember? I'm remembering why, is what I'm remembering. This is all Cotillion's fault.'

Quick Ben said, 'She won't say it, but she misses you—'

She rounded on him. 'You stay out of this!'

'I'd love to, but we haven't got time. Look, Kalam, she's sincere – she even found you a horse—'

'What do I need a horse for? We're in Malaz City! If Laseen's run away, I don't need a horse – I need a ship.'

'Kalam, listen to me. Shadowthrone delivered you to the Deadhouse. You were dying. Poisoned. And then you were just, er, left here. Lying there on the floor. For some time – well, a fair bit of time, in fact.'

'Did you kill Laseen, then? Did you avenge me? And you have the nerve to call yourself my friend – you didn't kill her, did you? Did you?'

'No I didn't – just close that trap of yours and try listening for a change. Never mind the Malazan Empire. Never mind the Regent or Protector or whatever title Mallick Rel's come up with. And maybe Laseen got killed like they say she did, or maybe she didn't – it doesn't matter. We're not hanging around, Kalam. We're needed elsewhere. Do you understand what I'm saying?'

'Not a word. But it sounds to me like we're wasting time.' He looked at Minala. 'So you got me a horse, did you? Is it big enough? Better not be a stallion – you know how they get jealous when I'm around you.'

'I wasn't picky,' she said. 'But if I'd thought about it, I'd have gotten you a fat one-eared three-legged ass, and you could take turns riding each other. Not that anybody'd tell the difference.'

'Gods below, you two!' hissed Quick Ben, with a sharp look out into the yard. 'Trying to wake up the whole waterfront? We've got to go. Now.'

Kalam collected the weapon belt, checked to confirm that the sheaths held his long knives. But his memory still wasn't the way it should have been, so he couldn't be sure. But they looked to be decent weapons anyway. 'Fine. Shut up the both of you and let's get going.'

Outside, beneath a strangely green cloudy night sky, Quick Ben led the way down the winding path between overgrown mounds and dead trees. They reached the gate and the wizard gestured off to their left.

The horses were tethered to a hitching post in front of a sunken tavern thirty paces away. Rising waters had flooded the taproom, leaving the place abandoned and dark. As they set off for them, Kalam narrowed his gaze on one of the beasts. His steps slowed. 'Hold on,' he whispered, 'that ain't a horse.'

'Best I could do,' Quick Ben muttered. 'Don't worry, it's mine.'

Four paces from the rail and a hulking, armoured figure stepped out from the tavern's nearest alley. Two heavy blades clashed together, and then lifted threateningly.

Quick Ben swore. 'Look, Temper, I knocked. Nobody home.'

The visored face swung to study the Deadhouse, and then a deep voice rumbled out. 'I might have to kill you three anyway.'

'Why?' yelped Quick Ben.

Temper pointed with one of his huge swords. 'You didn't close the fucking door.'

'I'll be right back.'

They watched the wizard hurry back to the Deadhouse.

Temper turned to Kalam. 'He never fooled me, you know. I don't know what Whiskeyjack was thinking.'

'You smell of Coop's Ale,' said Kalam. 'I'm thirsty. Listen, Minala – when Quick gets back, tell him—'

'Don't even try,' she said in a growl. 'Besides, here he comes.'

'Done,' said Quick Ben when he returned. His teeth flashed white as he smiled.

Temper slid his weapons back into their sheaths. 'I suppose I don't really need to say this to any of you. But . . . don't come back. We like it sleepy here. I see any of you again . . .'

Quick Ben's smile vanished and he sighed and shook his head. 'Temper, you should've bolted to the Bridgeburners when you had the chance.'

'I hear they're all dead.'

The wizard swung atop his ethereal horse and grinned down. 'Exactly.'

Examining the natty gelding Minala had found for him, Kalam

glanced over. 'Do you like being retired, Temper? No, it's an honest question. Do you like it?'

'Night like this . . . seeing you all eager to ride out . . . into serious trouble, no doubt . . . aye, Assassin, I like it. And if you want to do the same, I'll stand you a tankard of Coop's in yonder inn, before throwing you into the harbour.'

'I'll get back to you on that,' Kalam replied, mounting up. He looked across to Minala, and then Quick Ben. 'All right, unless these horses can run on water, someone needs to crack open a warren.'

'Well,' said Quick Ben, 'mine can.'

'Smug as ever, I see.'

'In any case, warrens are my business—'

'And how's business?' Kalam asked.

'Awful. But that's all about to change.'

'Really? How?'

'Gods below, Kalam. Because I'm back, that's why. Now stop talking and leave me to it, will you?'

When the three riders were gone, and the tattered wisps of foul-smelling smoke had drifted away, Temper swung round, stepped back into the gloom of the alley, and studied the wraith-like figure standing amidst the rubbish. 'Old loyalties,' he said. 'The only reason I let them go. The Deadhouse isn't a damned toll booth, Emperor.'

A cane cracked its silver heel hard on the grimy stones. 'Emperor? I left that behind long ago. And as for the days when I gave kindly advice, well, they never existed. But for this once, and for you alone, Temper, a word of caution. Watch how you talk to gods, mortal, lest they . . .' he suddenly giggled, 'take umbrage.'

Temper grunted, said nothing for a dozen heartbeats, and then: 'Umbrage . . . huh.' He turned to leave, and Shadowthrone struck the cobbles again. The huge warrior paused, looked over.

Shadowthrone hissed. 'Well? Is that it?'

'Is what it?'

'That's all you have to say? This is a momentous scene, you fat fool! This is where everything really, truly, finally begins! So squeeze the ale from your brain, mortal, and say something worthy of your kind. You stand before a god! Speak your eloquence for all posterity. Be profound!'

'Profound . . . huh.' Temper was silent for a long moment, studying the cobbles of the alley mouth. And then he lifted his helmed head, faced Shadowthrone, and said, 'Fuck off.'

Sister Belie watched the man pick his way carefully through the mass of rubble that had once been the citadel gate. He wasn't especially tall.

He had nothing of the brawn common to a veteran soldier, though a white scar was visible climbing one side of his jaw, up to a clipped ear – that didn't look like a sword cut, she decided. *Something bit him. Would Sister Reverence appreciate that? A Jaghut's tusk, perchance? Not likely.* No, there wasn't much to this man, nothing to explain the source of his defiance, his infuriating resistance to the will and voice of the Watered.

This was about to change, of course. The enemy commander had just made a fatal error in agreeing to this parley. For Sister Belie's blood was not watered, and this man was about to discover the power in the voice of a pure-born Forkrul Assail.

The smoke-stained, cracked walls of the citadel were proof of the effort the Watered commanders had made in seeking to conclude this siege; and the thousand or so rotting corpses lying on the killing ground beneath those walls marked the savage determination of the Shriven. But every assault thus far had ended in defeat.

Yes, the enemy has done well. But our patience is at an end. It is time to finish this.

The fool was unguarded. He came out alone – not that it would have mattered, for she would have used his own bodyguards to cut him down. Instead, she would make him take his own life, here, before the horrified eyes of his soldiers lining those battlements.

The enemy commander picked his way past the corpses and then drew to within ten paces of where she stood. Halting, he eyed her curiously for a moment, and then spoke in passable Kolansii. 'A Pure, then. Is that the correct term? Not mixed blood – the ones you call *Watered*, as in "watered down", presumably. No, you are a true Forkrul Assail. Have you come to . . . adjudicate?' And he smiled.

'Human arrogance ever takes my breath away,' Sister Belie observed. 'Perhaps, under certain circumstances, it is justified. For example, when dealing with your own kind, whom you have made helpless and at your mercy. Or in the matter of dealing with lesser beasts, when they presume to defy your tyranny. In the palace of the now dead king of Kolanse, there is a vast chamber crowded with stuffed trophies – animals slain by those of the royal line. Wolves, bears, cats. Eagles. Stags, elk, bhederin. They are given postures of ferocity, to mark that final moment of defiance – their presumption to the right to their own lives, one supposes. You are human – as human as was the king of Kolanse. Can you explain to me this sordid need to slay animals? Are we to believe that each and every beast in that chamber sought to kill its slayer?'

'Well now,' the man replied, 'I admit to having a personal opinion on such matters, but you have to understand, I never could comprehend the pleasure of slaughter. Those whom I have met who have enjoyed such activities, well, the reasons they tend to give don't make much sense to me. You could have simply asked the king of Kolanse.'

'I did,' Sister Belie said, nodding.

His brows lifted. 'And?'

'He said it made him feel one with the animal he killed.'

'Ah. I've heard similar.'

'Accordingly,' she resumed, 'I killed all his children and had them stuffed and displayed in the same chamber. It was my wish that he feel one with his offspring, too.'

'I imagine that wasn't very successful.'

She shrugged. 'Let us hear your opinion, then.'

'Some needs are so pathetic they cannot be satisfied except by killing. I don't mean those among us who hunt out of necessity. That's just food. But let's face it, as soon as you start planting fields and keeping livestock, you don't need to hunt for food any more.'

'The king also said it was his means of worshipping nature.'

'By destroying it?'

'Just my thought, human. But then, is that not your principal means of worship?'

'Now that is a perceptive, if slightly painful, observation. But consider this – in killing and stuffing those children, were you not expressing the same detestable arrogance that so offended you in the first place?'

'It was an experiment to see if I too could feel one with those I had slain. Alas, I did not. I felt . . . sad. That I should have such power in my hands, and should choose to use it for destructive ends. And yet I discovered something else – a truth about myself, in fact. There is pleasure in destroying, and it is a most sordid kind of pleasure. I suspect this is what is confused with the notion of "oneness" by such chronic slayers.'

'You're probably right.'

'Because they are, in fact, not particularly intelligent.'

'I assumed you would arrive at that opinion sooner or later.'

'Why?'

'Well, it sounds as if you feel a need to justify killing us, and while you have pity for the lesser beasts of this world, your definition of "lesser beasts" does not include humans. Yet, ironically, your justification is predicated on the very same notion of arrogant superiority that you found so reprehensible in the Kolanse royal family. The beast that knows no better can be slain with impunity. Of course, there is no logic to that notion at all, is there?'

Sister Belie sighed. 'That was most enjoyable. Now I need you to take your own life, so that we may end this pointless battle. I would like to be able to tell you that your army will be well treated, and so on. But the truth is, I will command them – just as I command the Shriven.

And with the power of my voice I will set them against my enemies, whoever they may be, and they will fight without fear. They will fight with a ferocity the like of which has never been seen among your kind, because I intend to *use* them, the way you use horses, or war dogs. In other words, like well-trained beasts.'

'What a depressing notion, Forkrul Assail. Those pathetic needs I talked about? They all come down to power. The king killed those animals because he had the power to do so, and expressing that power made him feel good. But it never lasts long, so out he goes to kill some more. I find it pathetic. And all that you have just said to me here, well, it's really the same old shit. By your voice and the sorcery of Akhrast Korvalain you will seek to fill that void in your soul, the void that is the hunger for control, when the bitter truth is, you really control nothing, and the universe is destined to swallow you up just as it does everything else.'

'You do not believe in the power to do good? To do what is right?'

'The Hold of the Beasts wants vengeance. It wants to redress the balance of slaughter. Messy as that would be, at least I see the logic of it. But I fear it's too late. Their age is past, for now.'

'We will prove the lie of your words, human.'

'No, you won't. Because, Forkrul Assail, you are going to fail, and in failing you fail your allies as well, and for them the misery simply goes on and on. The only end to the tragedy of the beasts will come at the hands of humans – and to the Wolves I would advise patience. They need do nothing more, because we humans *will* destroy ourselves. It may take a while, because there's lots of us, but we'll do it in the end, because we are nothing if not thorough. As for you and your kind – you're not even relevant.'

'Draw your knife, human. Kneel.'

'I am sorry, but I can barely hear you.'

She blinked. 'Draw your knife!'

'Barely a whisper, I'm afraid.' He drew out a small wooden card. 'I am Ganoes Paran. I was a soldier in the Malazan army, a marine, to be precise. But then I became the Master of the Deck of Dragons. I didn't ask for the title, and had no real understanding of the role for quite some time. But I'm getting the hang of it now.' He held up the card. 'This is where your voice is going. It's another realm, where the only things hearing you – or, rather, succumbing to your power – are insects and worms in the mud. They're confused. They don't know what a *knife* is. They don't even know how to kneel.'

Sister Belie stepped forward. 'Then I shall break you with my hands—'

He seemed to lean back, and suddenly he was gone. The card fell, clattered on the stones. She reached down, picked up it. The image

512

was little more than a scratching of lines, a rough landscape, a hint of ground, low plants – and there, vague in the gloom, stood the man. He beckoned and in her mind she heard his voice.

'*Come after me, Forkrul Assail. I invite you to do battle with me here. No? Well, it was foolish of me to think you were that stupid. After all, I need only step out of this wretched place, leaving you trapped – and it'd be a long, long time before you found your way home. Well. We have now met. We are enemies known to one another, as it should be.*

'*You cannot enslave my army. If you want to defeat us, you'll have to do it the hard way. Oh, by the way, I enjoyed our little talk. I think I now understand you better than you do me, which is an advantage I intend to exploit. Oh, if you could see your expression now—*'

With a snarl she snapped the card in half, flung the pieces to the ground. Whirling, she marched back to where her officers waited. 'Summon Brother Grave – assemble the legions. We shall end this!'

One of the Watered stepped forward tremulously and bowed. 'Pure, we need reinforcements—'

'And you shall have them. We shall sustain this assault – give them no rest. Brother Grave waits with three legions. I will have that human's hide nailed to the wall of this citadel.'

The Watered grinned. 'A worthy trophy, Pure.'

She faced the edifice once more. '*I will*,' she whispered, '*because I can.*'

'You fool,' snapped Noto Boil. 'She almost had you, didn't she?'

Paran wiped at the mud caked on his boots. 'Find Fist Bude. Get the reserves ready. This one's going to be messy. And tell Mathok to mount up for a sortie – before the bastards get a chance to set up.'

'Did she seek to command you?'

'I told you, I had an answer to that. But you're right, those Forkrul Assail move damned fast. It was close. Closer than I would have liked, but then,' he smiled at the healer, 'we've stirred them up. Got *two* pure-bloods over there now – and more legions to boot.'

'Let me guess – all according to your plan.'

'Where's Ormulogun? I need him to work on that etching – in case we need to get the Hood out of here.'

Noto Boil sighed, and set off to look for the Imperial Artist. He chewed on his fish spine until he tasted blood.

'*You always could pick them, couldn't you, woman?*' She'd been walking in her sleep again, this time out and down the steps into the cellar, where waited a dead friend. He was sitting on one of the kegs Antsy called the Sours – one of those that held bodies of damned Seguleh.

Not that they were there any more, but that pickling concoction was still one of the foulest brews she'd ever smelled.

Was it Bluepearl who'd given it a taste? She couldn't remember, but . . . probably.

He was sitting working a knife tip under filthy fingernails.

'Am I sleeping again?' Picker asked.

'Yeah,' Bluepearl replied. 'But I'm telling ya, Pick, getting dragged into your dreams like this ain't much fun.'

'You know what's happened to this city?'

He grimaced, frowned at his nails. 'I voted against settling here – do you remember that? But the count didn't go my way – story of my life. And then Darujhistan went and killed me.'

'But you didn't know why, did you? I can tell you why now, Bluepearl. I know why now.'

He sheathed his knife and the sound the weapon made as it locked in the scabbard was sharp enough to make her breath catch. Looked across at her and said, 'We resanctified this place, did you know that? Spilling all that blood – it was stirring when we moved in, but then we went and drenched the stones in that red stuff.'

'Meaning?'

He shrugged, drew out his knife again and began cleaning his nails, each gesture the same as the time before. 'In here, Pick, we're safe.'

She snorted. 'Maybe for you.'

'You got to go soon, Sergeant. Out of the city. Will there be trouble, you doing that?'

'You called me Sergeant.'

'Aye, I did. Because I'm passing on orders here. That's all.'

'Whose orders?'

He examined his nails. 'There's no such thing, Picker, as retiring from the Bridgeburners.'

'Go back to Hood!'

He grunted in amusement, clicked his knife home, the sound louder and more disturbing than the first time. 'Where Hood's at I ain't going, Pick. We got us the right commander again, the one we should've had right from the start. By whose order, Sergeant?' He drew out his knife and set to his nails again. 'Whiskeyjack.'

'What's he got to do with any of this? I know who I'm supposed to find. I even know where he's holed up – and staying outa Darujhistan tells me he's smarter than he looks.' Lifting an arm, she caught a flash of silver. Stared in horror at the torcs now encircling her upper arms. 'Gods below! How did these come back! Get 'em off me!'

'Treach needs you now. Tiger of Summer and all that.' He grinned at her. 'It's all brewing up, my love.'

'Shit! I just put 'em on because they looked nice!'

514

He was studying her, head cocked. 'Getting fat on us, Sergeant?'

She scowled. 'Taken to wearing chain under everything.'

'Even when you're asleep? And you say you ain't a Bridgeburner no more?'

'What kind of dream is this?'

He sheathed his dagger. This time the click was sharp enough to make her flinch. 'The important kind, Sergeant. Look at it this way. Hood's gone. Death's Gate was just . . . gaping. But someone sanctified us. We've seen more death than a sane person could stand. But we ain't sane, are we? We're soldiers. Veterans. We're past sane. We're in that other place, where all the insanity's been storming around us for so long it can't touch us no more either. Meaning we're outside both. What makes us perfect for Death's Gate? Simple, Picker. It don't matter what we look at, we don't blink.'

'I can get out of the city,' she said. 'But it won't be easy.'

He began cleaning his fingernails, the knife blade flashing dull in the misty gloom. 'Glad to hear all that confidence has come roaring back. Thing is, we ain't in the mood to challenge what's going on here. Besides, we're kinda busy at the moment.'

'So I'm on my own, is that it?'

'Not quite. We arranged for a reliable . . . guide.' He rose. The dagger slammed back into its scabbard—

The sound startled her awake. Lying tangled in sweaty blankets, Blend snoring at her side. Something was at the door, trying to get in. Cursing under her breath, Picker collected up the sword propped beside the bed.

She saw the latch flick once – the same sound Bluepearl's dagger had been making.

Whoever was trying to open that door wasn't having much luck. 'What a fine guide you sent there, Whiskeyjack. Can't even open a stupid door.'

'Mmm?'

'Go back to sleep, love.' She rose and walked to the door, turned the latch with her sword point and stepped back to let the door swing open.

A mangy cat sat in the corridor.

Mangy? 'The ugly thing's dead. A Hood-damned undead cat – gods below.'

The creature had a collar made of thick hide or leather, twisted into a coil. A tarnished silver coin or medallion hung from it. Picker crouched, reached out and dragged the cat closer, frowning when it made no effort to walk, just sliding in its sitting position. 'Gods, you stink.'

Rotted eye sockets offered her about as much expression as any living cat might manage. She bent closer, took hold of the medallion. Feeble scratching marred both sides, a name in archaic Gadrobi or Rhivi. She frowned at it. 'Tufty?'

So Blend and Antsy weren't just making stuff up. They were telling the truth. They'd found that Jaghut a damned dead cat.

Then her eyes narrowed on the collar. Skin, mottled here and there by red-ochre tattoos. 'Oh,' she muttered, 'let me guess. T'lan Imass?'

From the room behind her, Blend called out. 'Pick?'

'It's fine,' Picker said, straightening. 'Just the cat.'

'Did you feed it? I didn't feed it – oh, gods, I can't remember when I last fed the cat!'

Picker walked into the room. Sure enough, Blend was still sleeping. Having one of those *dreams. She went over and settled down on the mattress. Leaned closer and whispered. 'It's true, Blend. You forgot. For months!'*

The woman moaned, distress twisting her features, but her eyes remained shut.

'You've made a real mess, Blend. That poor cat. I just found it, and Hood knows it ain't a pretty sight.'

'You could've fed it, Picker – why didn't you feed it?'

Something sharp pricked under Picker's chin and she froze.

'Better answer me,' Blend said in a casual tone. 'You see, I loved that cat. Got it for my sixth birthday. It was my favourite cat.'

'Bluepearl?' Picker called out. 'Can you fix this, please? Bluepearl?'

No answer. Picker knew that if she tried to pull away, Blend's deadly instincts would answer with a fatal thrust – up through her brain. She thought furiously. 'I was only joking, love. Tufty's fine.'

Blend's brow wrinkled. 'Tufty? Who's Tufty?'

'Uh, the cat I forgot to feed.'

The knife vanished beneath the blankets, and Blend rolled over. 'You never was good with animals,' *she mumbled, and then added,* 'Bet it hates you now. No more cuddles for you, Pick.' *A moment later she was snoring.*

Picker's sigh was ragged. Wiping sweat from her eyes, she glared across at the ugly thing in the doorway. 'Lords above, I hope so.'

And then she discovered the silver torcs.

The waters calmed, as they were wont to do whenever he came up from below deck. Shurq Elalle watched the Jaghut approach. The rest of her crew – the few that still lived – sat or sprawled amidships tracking the tall, ghastly warrior with a fascination she almost envied. Here was the once-god of death and the exquisite irony of her meeting Hood

516

was simply delicious. Back in Letheras, she'd have wagered her entire fortune that this was one encounter she would never have.

Instead, she was captaining Hood's Ship of the Dead, or whatever it was he called it. Vessel of Souls? Death Ship? Something ominous, anyway. Not that she had much to do by way of giving orders and the like. Whatever propelled the craft wasn't slave to winds, canvas and cordage. And not an oar in sight.

Suddenly, the seas had become uninteresting. As if all her skills – and possibly it was the same with her crew – all their skills had become irrelevant. And for all the ease and comfort that came with this kind of sailing, her sense was one of tragic loss. At this moment, her respect for the sea wavered, as if fatally weakened, and she wondered if, before long, there would come to humans a true conquest of the waves, spelling the end of humility. *And let's face it, humanity without humility is a dangerous force. Don't know why I'm thinking as if I'm seeing the future, but that's how it feels. Some future time when sorcery does too much, when it solves all our problems – only to invent new ones. If this is to be the real future, I don't want it.*

'There is a darkness upon your thoughts, Captain Elalle.'

She glanced over at him. Burnished tusks, mottled with unimaginable age. Worn, leathery skin stretched gaunt over sharp bones. Deep-set eyes, haunted in shadow, the vertical pupils barely visible – but they'd not been there when he'd first appeared, so it seemed that life was returning to the Jaghut. 'You can sense such things, Hood?'

'You are the captain.'

'I don't see the relevance of that – the title has lost all meaning.'

'To the contrary,' Hood replied. 'It is by the currents of your thoughts that we find our course.' He pointed ahead.

She squinted. A smudge building on the horizon. 'I've conjured up a storm?'

'Out of witless boredom I created ships like this one, and I set captains upon them, choosing those among the dead for whom death has become an obsession.'

'I imagine you'd have plenty to choose from. How can the dead not obsess over their being dead?'

'I am not responsible for small minds, Captain Elalle. Indeed, I always possessed a kind of admiration for those who refused their fate, who struggled to escape my dreadful realm.'

'Enough to let them go?'

'Go? I can tell you that all those who *have* escaped my realm now exist in misery. For their path ahead is no longer a mystery, and for them hope does not exist. They know that no paradise awaits them, and that no amount of diligent worship, sacrifice, or piety can change that.'

'That is . . . awful.'

'What it is, Captain, is inexcusable.'

She considered his words, and then considered them some more. 'The gods take, but give nothing in return.'

'Ah, see how the storm dissipates? Excellent, Captain . . . oh dear, it now returns, much more virulent than before. Captain, I would advise—'

'Advise me nothing! Couldn't you have forced their hand? Done something?'

The strange, terrible eyes fixed on her. 'But I have.'

'Then . . . was it necessary for you to leave the realm of death? Is that why you're here? It must be. You have set something in motion.'

'I have not acted alone, Captain.'

'I would hear more, Hood. If there is a reason for all this, I – I need to know it.'

Hood said nothing for a time, studying the roiling clouds marring the way ahead. Then he spoke. 'I so dislike moments of revelation, Captain. One is invited to infer all manner of deliberation leading us to this place, this time. When the truth of it is chance and mischance rule our every step.' He sighed. 'Very well, I am not indifferent to your . . . needs. This possibility only gained life when two usurpers reawakened the remnants of Kurald Emurlahn – the Realm of Shadow – and then set out to travel the warrens, and indeed the Holds. Seeking knowledge. Seeking the truth of things. What they eventually discovered did not please them. And in the boldness of their . . . youth, they decided that something must be done.'

'Two new gods,' Shurq Elalle murmured. 'They came to you?'

'Not at first. Instead, they sought out loyal allies among the mortals they had once commanded. Well, perhaps "mortals" is not quite accurate in some instances. No matter. Let us call it a wondrous conflagration of circumstance and character, a kind of audacity which made anything possible. Before long, they found the need to gather additional allies. Shall I list them for you?'

'Why not?'

'The Son of Darkness, who understood the true burden of a surrendered future, the fatality of empty faith. The Warlord of the Sleeping Goddess, who would defy the eternal patience of the earth itself, and Stonewielder, the One who stood facing Caladan Brood, ensuring the world's balance. These two are destined to walk disparate paths, but what they seek is much the same. The Queen of Dreams, whose pool had grown still as death itself. The Lord of Tragedy – and, well, a host of others, all drawn into the fold.'

'Those you have named – are they gods?'

Hood shrugged. 'Ascendants. The complexity of this beggars belief, to be honest. The sheer scale of contingencies . . . well, for all his peculiarities, let no one accuse Shadowthrone of failings in the matter of intelligence. The same can be said for Cotillion, for the patron of assassins well comprehended that just as certain individuals deserve a knife through the heart, so too do certain . . . ideas.'

'Yet mortals are part of this plan, too.'

'Indeed.'

'The Adjunct Tavore Paran?'

Hood was silent for a moment. 'This congress, Captain, is not above cruel use of mortals.'

'That is . . . unfair.'

'But consider what may be won here, Shurq Elalle.'

'I have – I am, Hood. But . . . no. *That is unfair.*'

'The storm, Captain—'

'Why does that surprise you?' she retorted. 'Try telling me something that doesn't break my heart, then. Try telling me something that doesn't make me furious – at your arrogance. Your contempt.'

'We do not hold the Adjunct Tavore Paran in contempt.'

'Really?' she asked, the word dripping with derision.

'Captain, she takes our arrogance and humbles us.'

'And what's her reward?' Shurq demanded.

Hood looked away, and then shook his head. 'For her, there is none.'

'Tell me,' Shurq said in a rasp, 'tell me she did not agree to this.'

'To that, Captain, I shall say nothing.' He stepped past her then and raised his hands. 'We cannot survive the violence your thoughts have conjured, Captain. Thus, I have no recourse but to intervene. Fortunately,' he turned to eye her briefly, 'Mael concurs.'

'Push it away, then,' Shurq Elalle snapped. 'But I will bring it back, I swear it. To so use an innocent woman . . .'

'You begin to try me, Captain Elalle. If you intend to fight me for the rest of this voyage, I must find us another captain.'

'Please do, Hood. I barely knew the Adjunct, but—'

He twisted round. 'Indeed, you barely know her. I will tell you this, then. I looked out through her sister's eyes, through a helm's visor – in the moment that she died – and I stared up at my slayer, the Adjunct Tavore Paran. And the blood dripping from her sword was mine. You will speak to me of innocence? There is no such thing.'

Shurq Elalle stared at Hood. 'So, in using her now . . . is this punishment?'

'Consider it so, if it eases your conscience.'

'She murdered her sister?'

'Yes.'

'Is it guilt that drives her now, Hood? Does she seek redemption?'

'I imagine she does.'

'Will she find it?'

Hood shrugged.

What is it you're not telling me? I can sense . . . something. The sister . . . a helm's visor. 'Hood, that murder – was it an accident?'

The Jaghut did not reply.

Shurq stepped closer. 'Does Tavore even know she killed her own sister?'

'Irrelevant, Captain Elalle. It is the ignorant who yearn most for redemption.'

After a moment, she stepped back, went to the side rail, stared out over the rolling grey swells, what Skorgen called swollen waters. 'If we had met in your realm, Hood,' she said, 'I would not have refused my state. I would not have sought to escape. Instead, I would have tried to kill you.'

'Many have, Captain.'

'Good for them.' *Swollen waters.* 'Hood, if she never discovers the truth – if she is made to carry that ignorance for the rest of her days . . . do you even care?'

'Do you imagine that knowledge would be a gift?'

'I . . . don't know.'

'The truth may hide at your feet. The truth may lie coiled in high grasses. But it still has claws, it still has fangs. Be careful, Captain, where you step.'

'Food reserves are dwindling,' Felash said, and then sighed and looked up at her handmaiden. 'Straits are dire for dear Mother.' She sat straighter, arched her back and groaned. 'Do you advise rest? These journeys through troubled realms, by Jaghut's cold breath or not, do take their toll upon my delicate self. But I must refuse your concerns, my dear. Necessity demands – is that wine you're pouring? Excellent. I'd thought that long gone.'

'I made a request, Highness.'

'Indeed? Of whom?'

'It seems,' the woman said, passing over a cup, 'libations in the name of death continue unabated, and if the once-god of that dread underworld is not above trespassing in his old . . . er, haunts, well, far be it from us to complain.'

'Just so. Nonetheless, sweetie, I dislike the notion of you consorting with that hoary creature. Best keep a respectful distance, matching my own wise caution in this matter.'

'As you wish.'

'But I must say, superb wine, given its provenance – I trust you have acquired a decent supply.'

'Luckily, yes, Highness.'

'The other news is almost as dire, I'm afraid. We have cause now to mistrust the motivations of the Perish Grey Helms. Most disturbing.'

The handmaid's eyes narrowed as she set to filling a bowl of rustleaf. 'Are we not at this moment sailing to a rendezvous with the Perish fleet, Highness?'

'Assuming no calamity had struck, yes. But what is their disposition? The answer to that question is now paramount.'

'Perhaps I could scry—'

'No, we cannot risk that. The warren of the Forkrul Assail waxes full – hmm, was I being poetic there, or succumbing to cliché?'

'I wouldn't know,' murmured the handmaiden, concentrating on lighting the pipe.

'We have been careless in your education. Never mind. Too late now, for it is well known that a person's brain ossifies at a certain age, becoming incapable of new acquisition, barring simple matters such as languages, martial skills and so on. There is a moment when true genius is within the reach of any and every child, and the gauge of that moment's duration is in fact the only means of defining intelligence. Thus, while you are naturally bright, and therefore it is probable that the time of your receptivity could have been measured in months, if not years, we have done all we thought to do at that juncture, and the time for regrets is past – my dear, what was in this wine? My mouth seems to be running all by itself. For most people, of course, that moment of receptivity was sadly brief. A day? Half a day? And alas, once gone, it can never return.'

'Excuse me, Highness, your pipe is lit.'

'Good. Give it over. About this wine—'

There was a knock upon the cabin door, and a moment later the latch lifted and First Mate Skorgen Kaban the Pretty loomed in the doorway, knuckling his brow. 'Princess, Highest of Highs, beg yer pardon. Got urgent happenings up top, if you please. Cap'n requests yer presence.'

Felash sighed. 'Very well, assuming I am able to, uh, stand. Umph, some assistance—'

The handmaid reached out to steady her.

'Lead on, Skorgen,' Felash said with a careless wave of one hand. 'And if you must ogle my tits, try being subtle about it, will you?'

'Sorry, Highness. Only got the one good eye, y'know.'

They paused and waited while the handmaid got over a sudden fit of coughing.

Shurq Elalle turned as her first mate clumped up to her.

'Captain! The Squall Witch – she's drunk!'

'Pretty, was that meant to be a whisper? Greetings, Highness.'

'Drunkenness lies in the purview of the lowborn. Captain, allow me to assure you that I am neither drunk nor lowborn. But, I must ask, where is our Jaghut guest?'

Shurq grunted. 'Thought you'd have passed him on the way up. There is the matter of keeping at least one knife well hidden, you see.'

'No, Captain. I am afraid I do not.'

'Ah, of course.' Shurq pointed ahead. 'We have been sighted by that ship and it now bears down on us. Not a Throne of War. Kolansian, one presumes.'

Somewhat unsteadily, the princess made her way to the captain's side. 'Oh dear,' she said, 'that is an Assail ship. At the very least, a Lesser Watered will be commanding. Most distressing, of course, are the implications.'

'As in,' ventured Shurq Elalle, 'where is the Perish fleet?'

'Precisely. And if that is not sufficiently alarming, I am afraid that I have been engaged in exhausting rituals this day. If we must fight, I will be of little use. We have already experienced the danger posed by Forkrul Assail, by both their physical prowess and the sorcery of their voice.'

'I need no reminders, Highness. And while I proved immune to such magics, the same cannot be said for my crew. And now you tell me that you are unable to defend us. So much for hiding one knife, Highness.'

'We shall see. We have, after all, my handmaid.'

Shurq glanced over at the woman, recalling her attacks upon Sister Equity. 'She did not fare so well against a Pure, Highness.'

'Well, a Higher Watered's Assail blood is, er, watered down, and is not quite as powerful. In any case, it remains to be seen how this will play out. After all, this could be one of the betrayers among the Assail. In the meantime, Captain, may I suggest your first mate gather your crew and make for the hold.'

'Skorgen, take 'em down and keep 'em quiet.'

'Aye, Captain.'

There was something skeletal about the Assail ship. Two types of wood were visible, one bone white and the other dull black. The hull was narrow of beam and high-castled, and with the two masts offering minimal canvas, Shurq suspected that it had been built to ply sheltered waters. An open sea gale could well swamp such a ship. At twice the mass of her old raider, the *Undying Gratitude*, Shurq judged it to have a complement of seventy or so sailors on board, along with twenty or more marines, and as the craft came around and fell off before the wind on the port side of the Death Ship she stepped to the rail and looked across. A tall, spectral figure was staring down on her, flanked by two helmed guards cloaked in chain surcoats.

A few paces behind the captain, Princess Felash said, 'Dearie, those marines.'

'Yes, Highness,' the handmaid replied.

'Captain?'

'Highness?'

'Why not ask them what they want?'

Shurq turned to eye the princess. Before she could say anything, however, there were shouts from the Assail ship, and she swung back to see the handmaid scrambling up the side. *Shit, wish I'd seen that leap.* The craft was wallowing at least six paces away. 'Princess, what is that woman doing?'

The handmaid drew herself up and over the rail. The deck was an eye-hurting maze of black and white wood, like a shattered mosaic. Six more helmed, chain-clad marines stood near the main mast, now drawing heavy cutlasses.

The Assail half-blood commander wore a heavy, jewelled cloak, the thick oiled wool dyed a deep blue. Torcs of gold collared her long neck, and her head was shaved, emphasizing the angled planes of her skull. She was unarmed, and she now faced the handmaid with a look of amused surprise, lifting a hand to stay her soldiers.

Looking round, the handmaid saw recent storm damage – much of the rigging had been torn away, and mounds of cordage and shattered stays littered the deck. There seemed to be less than a score of hands working on repairs.

'Inform your captain,' said the Assail half-blood, 'that having entered territorial waters, she must abide by the laws of High Kolanse. I am Lesser Watered Intransigent, Inquisitor of the Southern Fleet.'

'Not much of a fleet,' the handmaid observed.

The Inquisitor blinked. 'A sudden storm has temporarily scattered us. To resume my message to your captain, she and her crew – including all passengers – must accept adjudication.'

'By "adjudication" do you mean killing?'

The pale-skinned woman smiled, the expression seeming to fold the two sides of her face slightly inward. 'The Proclamation of Restitution has been sanctioned. We continue the task.'

'And did this fate befall the Perish?'

'Yours is not a Perish ship.' She frowned. 'I sense enmity from your vessel – and that fat little girl with the pipe, she is a mage, is she not? We shall adjudicate her first.'

The handmaid walked back to the rail and leaned over. 'Highness,' she called down, 'they're being a little cagey regarding the Perish. Might be you were right.'

'Anything else that might be important?' Felash asked.

'No, Highness. Only that they want to kill us.'

'Very well. Carry on.'

The handmaid turned round.

The Lesser Watered spoke, 'Reach not for your weapons. Kneel. For each and every one of you, the healing of the world begins with your death. Among all the reasons to die, is there one more worthy than this? Be thankful that we give meaning to your end. Kneel.'

The handmaid shook her head. 'A Pure already tried all that. Caught me off guard . . . for a moment or two. My will is not yours to command.'

She moved then, rather faster than they'd expected, her hands thrusting outward, striking the bodyguards in the chest. Both warriors were lifted from their feet. Over the rail, plummeting to the waters below. She ducked at that instant, evading the Lesser's lashing attack, and kicked at the second joint on the woman's left leg, folding it halfway between the knee and the ankle. Her attacker stumbled, and the handmaid slipped past her, spinning round and out to one side to meet the six marines.

Behind them others were coming up from below, she saw.

She drew her fighting knives. She needed bigger weapons. The marine closest to her wielded a nice pair of cutlasses. She would take those.

Shurq Elalle loosed a startled oath and then leaned forward to watch the two armoured guards plunge into the choppy waters between the ships. Both men vanished in a froth of bubbles. Turning to Felash, she asked, 'Does she need help over there?'

Plucked brows lifted. 'I certainly hope not!'

The sounds of fighting – blades clashing, shouts and then screams – came from the deck of the other ship. 'Princess, this handmaid of yours, where did she come from?'

'Ah, now that is a mystery.'

'Enlighten me.'

'Do we have the time? Well, I suppose we do.' She puffed on her pipe, her face disappearing briefly behind a plume of smoke, and then said, 'My mother's account, this. There were seven of them. Six remain – the seventh, well, there was some kind of private challenge that, um, failed. No matter. Now, I will grant you, they appear young, but do not let that deceive you. My mother concluded that alchemies constituted a worthwhile investment in maintaining the vigour of her six eldest daughters' handmaids. And we daughters are of course sworn to secrecy in all such matters, perpetuating the illusion that we have simply grown up with our loyal companions, and so on . . .'

She paused then when another chain-clad marine spun head first over the rail, trailing blood over the side. A loud splash followed.

'They were most recalcitrant about divesting themselves of their horrid masks, but in the end my mother's will prevailed.'

Shurq Elalle frowned. *Masks?*

The sailors made a mess of things as the Lesser Watered, in her pain and panic, used the sorcery of her voice to command them, and it was some time before the handmaid worked her way through the howling mob. Frenzied rage had shock value, and the crew's utter lack of the instinct for self-preservation made things rather frantic for a few moments, but there was nothing tactical in their efforts to bring her down. When at last the handmaid stepped over a sprawl of bleeding bodies and approached the Inquisitor, she was breathing hard and sweat stung her eyes.

The woman facing her cradled a broken arm, stood hunched over a dislocated shoulder, and glared across at the handmaid. 'What manner of demon are you?' she demanded in a ragged hiss.

'For an answer to that,' the handmaid replied with a half-smile, 'best look elsewhere.'

The Inquisitor scythed out one leg. The handmaid leapt high, swung down, and severed the limb just above the knee. As she came down, her other cutlass cut into the vertical hinge of the woman's face, splitting it in two. A back-swing with the pommel of the first cutlass slammed into the side of the Inquisitor's skull, punching through.

Pouring out blood, the corpse crumpled at her feet. The handmaid looked round. No movement among any of the other bodies. *Just as Mother taught.* She glanced down at the cutlasses in her hands, and then let them fall with a clatter. *Pieces of shit.* She went looking for her knives.

Hood returned to the deck once they were under way. The once-god of death looked back, frowned at the burning ship in their wake.

'Would've stopped her firing it,' Shurq Elalle muttered, following the Jaghut's gaze, 'if I'd had the chance.'

'Oh? Why is that, Captain?'

'Well, that column of smoke can be seen from a long way off.'

'Indeed.' And Hood turned to her then, and smiled.

'I must leave you now.'

Ublala grunted. 'I knew you weren't my friend.'

'I assure you,' Draconus said, 'that I am, Ublala Pung. But events have occurred that now force my hand. As for you, a different destiny awaits.'

'I hate destiny.'

'Do you understand the meaning of the word?'

Ublala looked across at Ralata and scowled. 'Of course I do. It's the place where you end up. Everyone knows that.'

'In a manner of speaking, perhaps. I fear you have mistaken it for "destination". Ublala, destiny is the fate you find for yourself. Many hold to the belief that it is preordained, as if the future was already decided and there is nothing you can do to escape it. I do not. Each of us is free to decide.'

'Then I'm going with you. My wife can go somewhere else. She keeps talking about babies but I don't want babies – they get in the way of having fun, and people who end up having them spend all day talking about how great it is, but they look miserable even when they're smiling. Or worse, there're those ones who think their baby is the God of Genius reborn and even its poo smells like flowers, and all they do is talk about them for ever and ever and it's so boring I want to run away, or break their necks, or drown them all in the slop bucket.'

'A rather uncharitable view, Ublala.'

'I don't give nothing for free, that's for sure. Whole people disappear when a baby arrives. Poof! Where'd they go? Oh, I know, they're crawling around making baby noises. It makes me sick.' He ducked the rock Ralata threw at him and continued, 'So I'm going with you and if you were a real friend you'd take me because if I make a baby my life is over. Over!'

'Can you fly, Ublala?'

'That's not fair!'

'Nevertheless, and no, I will not carry you. Now, listen to me. We have gone as far west as needed – now you must strike northward.'

'Why?'

Draconus glanced away, eyes narrowing, and then he sighed and said, 'Your innocence is a gift, Ublala Pung. A rare gift. It must endure. It must be protected, but that I can no longer do. Walk northward, that is all I ask.'

'Where am I going?'

'I cannot say for certain,' Draconus admitted. 'Nothing is certain, especially now.'

'Will you come back?'

Draconus hesitated, and then he shook his head. 'I do not think we will meet again, no. And for that I truly grieve.'

'Are you going somewhere to die?'

'Do not weep, friend. I do not know what awaits me.' He stepped close to Ublala. 'I have left you sufficient food and water for a week's travel. Beyond that, well.' He shrugged, and then held out a hand. 'Now, let us clasp arms.'

Instead, Ublala wrapped the god in a fierce hug.

After a moment, Draconus pulled himself free. 'You give reason, friend, for what I must attempt. If sorcery must die, the magic in the mortal soul will persevere – or so I choose to believe.'

Ralata hissed, 'Kill him, Ublala! Kill him now – you can do it! Snap his neck! Take that sword!'

Ublala winced and then shrugged. 'She's always going on like this. She don't mean anything by it, Draconus. Honest.' He wiped at his eyes. 'Goodbye. I'll never see you again.' And this time he burst into tears, wailing with his hands over his eyes.

When Ralata rushed to him, scrabbling to draw his knife, Ublala batted her away between sobs. She was thrown back, sailing through the air and then landing hard, limbs flailing, before falling still.

Frowning, Draconus walked over. Crouched down. 'Unconscious. Well, that is something, I suppose.'

Sniffling, Ublala said, 'Women always get jealous about man friends. Sometimes they say bad things about them. Sometimes they try to knife them. Sometimes they sex them. Sometimes they run away with them. Sometimes they get so mad they just up and die. But it's all just stupid.'

Draconus straightened, walked a short distance away, and then turned to face Ublala one more time. 'Be well, Ublala Pung.'

'Don't die, Draconus.'

The god smiled. 'I shall try not to.'

Ublala watched his friend disappear inside a bloom of black, ethereal darkness, watched as the darkness found shape – spreading wings, a long serpent neck, a massive head with rows of scimitar-length fangs, eyes of lurid yellow.

The dragon lifted into the sky, the vast wings hissing with the sound of cold water on hot stones as the creature wheeled and set off.

With an uneven sigh, the Teblor collected the pack containing the food, and then the heavy waterskins. Along with his weapons and armour, the burden was enough to make him grunt when he straightened.

Grasping Ralata by one ankle, he began walking.

The way she was right now, why, a wife was as bad as a baby.

Brother Diligence arrived well ahead of the retinue, his boots echoing as he strode the length of the throne room. All the blood stains remained – splashed and smeared across the marble tiles, along the pillars to either side and the walls behind them, and upon the throne itself, where sat Sister Reverence.

Restitution had begun here, in this very chamber, and it was proper to remind all who would enter. Halting before Reverence – the only other person present – he said, 'We must assume that they are lost to us, Sister.'

'I smell smoke, Brother.'

'Indeed.'

'Excellent.' She paused and then said, '"Lost." Now that is a curious word. Are they dead, or are they now treasonous to our great cause?'

'If the former, Sister, we must then reconsider the enemies arrayed against us.'

'And if the latter, then we must re-evaluate the loyalty *among* us.'

'The issue lies with Sister Calm,' said Brother Diligence. 'Equity but follows.'

'Not precisely true, Brother. Equity is the heart of the ideals which they would hold, but it is Calm who adheres to the practical. Her long imprisonment, horrific as it must have been, has greatly damaged her spirit, I am afraid. We must, indeed, hope that she is dead, more so than poor, misguided Equity.'

'I have received a missive from the siege, Sister. The assault failed.'

Reverence sat straighter. 'But how can this be?'

'Sister Belie informs me that Akhrast Korvalain is ineffectual against the commander of the besieged.'

'Impossible – unless, is he a god? An ascendant?'

'Neither, I am told. This man – a mortal – titles himself the Master of the Deck of Dragons. He commands the warrens, in ways Sister Belie cannot quite understand. But what she describes at last explains the sudden appearance of that army. They arrived via a portal, travelling by warren. Incidentally, this is why they could not get closer to us here at the Spire, where our sorcerous influence is strongest.'

'I see. Then this master's power cannot challenge us.'

'He and his army represent a military threat nonetheless. I now advise we dispatch another three legions, commanded by another Pure.'

'Ready the legions, Brother, but do not send them to Estobanse. Not yet. The challenge posed by the Master of the Deck of Dragons . . . intrigues me. I will think some more on how to deal with him.'

'As you wish, Sister.'

The doors swung open then and Diligence turned to observe the approach of the retinue. Flanked by two Pures, the heavily armoured warriors marched towards the throne, a full dozen of the highest-ranking officers.

Brother Diligence murmured, 'Most formidable, are they not, Sister Reverence?'

'Indeed, Brother.'

Ten paces from the dais the contingent halted.

Brother Diligence studied them briefly, and then said to one of the escorting Pures, 'Brother Serenity. They have anchored their ships in the harbour?'

'They have, Brother. They are now servants of the Restitution.'

Sister Reverence then spoke. 'Welcome, Grey Helms of the Perish. Your gesture has left no doubt in our minds as to the veracity of your claims.'

One of the commanders tipped his head and said, 'We have discussed your arguments at length, Sister Reverence, and we are agreed. Our Mortal Sword committed blasphemy in swearing fealty to the Malazans. Furthermore, we are certain that our Shield Anvil has concluded much the same, and that he is now at odds with the Mortal Sword.'

'And who will win this wrestling for control of your land-based army?'

'There is no ambiguity, Sister Reverence. The Mortal Sword shall be made to accept her crime, and do penance. If she refuses, she will be divested of her title and the privileges it affords. The time has come. The vengeance of the Wolves of Winter must now begin.'

'All very delightful,' Sister Reverence purred, and then she leaned forward. 'Unfortunately, the Forkrul Assail demand something more than an alliance of forces that just happen to share – for the moment at least – a common cause.' She raised her voice. 'Now, you shall kneel. You shall avow your service to the will of the Forkrul Assail.'

Even Brother Diligence felt buffeted by the power of Sister Reverence's sorcery. Against this, no mere human, no matter how pious or disciplined, could stand.

The chamber echoed with the creak and clatter of armour as the Perish warriors knelt on the bloodstained tiles of the throne room.

Diligence turned to Reverence. 'Sister, I look forward to using these subjects. And it pleases me to know that yet more are on their way.'

She nodded, leaning back. 'What are wolves but dogs not yet beaten into submission?'

Diligence frowned. 'Their cause is just, Sister Reverence.'

'It is indeed, Brother. But wildness is without discipline. Even savagery must be controlled, given direction and focus. We shall be the guiding hand.'

'As you say, Sister.' He regarded the still-kneeling Perish.

'You look thoughtful, Brother.'

'I was contemplating setting these warriors against the Master of the Deck of Dragons.'

Reverence arched her brows, and then said, 'Brother Serenity, what think you of that notion?'

'I only ask that I be granted the privilege of commanding them, Sister. It is my understanding that the offending army is composed of Malazans, and I have a history with Malazans.'

'Send them, Brother Diligence. Break their defences, Serenity, and if you can, drive them out into the open. I dare say even mastery of the warrens would not save them then. At that moment, we shall discover what other resources the man possesses, if any.'

'Do you want him delivered in chains before you, Sister?'

She considered, and then said, 'No. His head will suffice.'

The swarm of Shards twisted as it lifted high into the air, blotting out a third of the sky. The shadow it cast spread across the ravaged, lifeless desert, flowing like black water. The scent of suffering was in the air, and the hunger of the locusts was, as ever, desperate.

The shadow found the prey, but even the sudden cooling of air was not enough to awaken it to the threat fast closing, and the locusts rushed towards it. As the vast cloud hovered a moment it seemed to tremble, and then out from its heart burst a winged creature. It plummeted down upon the unconscious form lying sprawled on the parched ground, and in its wake descended the Shards, their wings voicing a roar.

Taloned hands reached down, grasped hold of the body, lifted it effortlessly. Wings thundering, the creature rose back into the sky. Behind it, the locusts spun in confusion.

From the body he held, Gu'Rull could taste the flavour of life, but that flavour was weakening. He wondered if he'd end up delivering a corpse to Gesler and Stormy. It made little difference to the Shi'gal Assassin. This one, this Mortal Sword of the Grey Helms, had lost her command, and such failures revealed flaws of character – better that such flaws be exposed now rather than later, when the lives of thousands might be at stake.

A waste of time, this. I was drawing closer to the enemy. The Destriant should not have called me back.

The Shi'gal was looking forward to the imminent war. The bitter flavour of ancient memories remained strong in the K'Chain Che'Malle. There could be no convenient rewriting of histories, such as seemed common among humans. No invented myths of past glory and honour that never was. The crimes committed back then were as sordid as those committed now, or those to come. And in the moment of slaughter, none of that really mattered. Who struck the first blow all those thousands of years ago was without relevance. The only thing that counted was who would strike the *last* blow.

This contingent of Forkrul Assail – these Pures so twisted away from their own history as to imagine themselves an entire world's arbiters – was perhaps the most powerful remnant of that species left. And could not the same be said for Gunth'an Wandering? *Are we not the last K'Chain Che'Malle? Is it not fitting that we meet for one more battle, a final clash between Elder powers?* That this war would make use of humans on both sides was incidental. That entire civilizations might fall – or, indeed, *every* civilization – well, Gu'Rull would not shed a single drop of oil in grief. Among humans, every faith was nothing but smoke, at times thick enough to blind and at other times cynically thin. And every belief was a fire that devoured its own fuel, until nothing but ashes remained. As far as Gu'Rull could determine, the only virtue humans possessed was a talent for starting over, with stern resolve restored in the sudden glow of renewed optimism, in complete disregard of whatever lessons past failures might offer. And he had no choice but to acknowledge the power of that virtue. *It is contingent upon collective amnesia, but as everyone knows, stupidity needs no excuse to repeat itself.*

The body he carried voiced a faint moan, and the assassin looked down at her with his lower eyes. She had not fared well in her idiotic attempt to find the Bonehunters. Gu'Rull had found the skeleton of her horse less than a third of a day's march from the trail the army had made, and making use of the carnivorous locusts he'd tracked her to the trail itself.

He felt a faint disquiet at the thought of the Bonehunters. High in the sky above the desert, he had seen their churned-up, broken path stretching eastwards. Hundreds of corpses and carcasses left behind, but he could see no end to that trail. *Surely they must all have died by now.*

He crossed the edge of the desert, banked southward.

'Reduce the rations again,' Queen Abrastal commanded, and then watched her officers bow obeisance and make their way back to their companies.

Beside her Spax turned to glare for a moment at the setting sun, and then he grunted. 'They're suffering, Firehair. The Barghast are used to such deprivations – for generations we've been pushed to the poorest regions. We learned what it is to starve.'

'Tomorrow,' she said, 'we shall reach the southern provinces of Kolanse. But I fear we shall find no salvation there.'

He silently agreed with that observation. They had come upon the remains of refugee trains. Camps cluttered with withered rubbish and desiccated corpses. Firepits filled with human bones, many of them belonging to children. Only yesterday a pack of emaciated dogs had attacked a Gilk scouting party, and every animal had to be cut down – desperation had gnawed away all fear, all sense of self-preservation.

'We shall begin killing the draught animals,' Abrastal said. 'Warchief, I think I now understand the Adjunct's recognition of all that we would face, and the manner in which such truths wounded her. We must divest ourselves of all hope of ever returning from this war.'

He scratched at his beard, considered her words, and then said, 'The

531

White Faces set out seeking a final battle, a moment of perfect glory. Our young gods stood before us, blackened faces smeared with filth, their hair the colour of blood. From the deepest beds of peat they rose to confront us. And from the ancient burial ships they brought forth the finest weapons of our ancestors. "Our enemies await us," they said.'

She studied him with narrowed eyes. 'And yet you Gilk broke away. Abandoned the destiny that brought you to this continent.'

'Ah, I shall tell you the truth of that, Highness. When Humbrall Taur died, we saw the end of the White Face alliance. There was no flaw in Onos Toolan, who was raised in Taur's place. Indeed, if certain rumours are to be believed, that warrior is older than our gods, and of his prowess with that flint sword I have no doubt at all. No, he accepted the title out of love – for Humbrall's only daughter. He possessed nothing of the zeal the younger warriors so desired in their warleader. His eyes did not shine with glory, and his voice – no matter how wise the words – held nothing of fire.'

'In short, he was no politician.'

Spax grimaced. 'You'd think tribes beaten down by centuries of defeat, clans rotted with feuds and mutual hatreds, you'd think, wouldn't you, that we'd listen to measured wisdom – that we'd heed his warnings against self-destruction.'

'And if Humbrall Taur had not drowned—'

'Even Taur was barely holding the clans together. I cannot even say for certain that his drowning was an accident – I was not witness to it. In any case, we Gilk saw nothing evil in Onos Toolan, only in what was likely to be done to him. Among the Barghast, Firehair, a leader is not simply ousted, cast adrift. He is killed. And so too his family – his entire bloodline is slaughtered. We Gilk would not be party to that.'

'And did you warn Onos Toolan before you left?'

'No, for it is possible that he would have sought our support in the power struggle to come. And, had he asked, well, how could I have looked him in the eye and refused? It's my thought now that he would not have asked. But even then, it's likely I would have offered nonetheless.'

She was frowning at him thoughtfully. 'You chose the coward's path.'

'Perhaps you see it that way. Perhaps many did, and still do. But what I did, I did to save my people. And this only Onos Toolan understood – for he did not pursue me, even when he had his chance.'

'And now, perhaps alone among all the White Face Barghast, you have found that final war to fight, in the name of your bog gods.'

He sighed. 'And nightly I pray that when the battle begins, Onos Toolan will be there. To lead the Barghast.'

'But it is not to be, Spax.'

'I know, Highness. I know. And the Gilk shall stand alone, the last clan, the last of the White Faces.'

'Will you call upon your gods, Spax, upon the charge?'

'I doubt it.'

'Then, what shall you do? To inspire your warriors?'

He shrugged loose the tension in his shoulders, felt weariness draining in behind it. 'I believe, Highness, *I shall shame them.*'

As Faint swung herself astride the gaunt horse, she glanced back to see the ghost of Sweetest Sufferance standing at the edge of the camp. A shiver whispered through her, and she looked across to Precious Thimble. 'Tell me you don't see her.'

'I don't see her, Faint. Let's go, else we lose them in the dark.'

They set off at a canter. Overhead, heavy clouds obscured the Jade Strangers, enough to mute the green glow that had haunted every night for what seemed to be months, if not years. 'Typical, isn't it? The one night we could do with that ghoulish light.'

'Are they rain clouds? That's what I want to know. Are they, Faint?'

'What am I, a weather scrier? I don't know. But I don't smell rain. I smell . . . dust.'

'Thanks,' snapped Precious Thimble.

Faint could just make out the two riders ahead. Brys and Aranict. A K'ell Hunter had arrived with dusk, delivering a message scratched on a wax tablet, and now they were riding to the Che'Malle encampment. Aranict's invitation had come as a surprise, but Faint was eager to see these huge lizard warriors who'd be fighting at their side. *Fighting – well, not us shareholders – we're just along for the ride, yee hah. But a good look at the Letherii allies just might put me at ease. At least there's one army that isn't starving and half dying of thirst. Or so I've heard.*

But for all their complaining, and Hood knows there's been plenty of it, seems no one can get too heated up about it. Not with that Malazan army trying to cross a real desert. No matter how bad we've got it . . .

'I still hate horses,' Precious Thimble said beside her.

'You've got to roll with the animal under you, girl. Just think about making love.'

'What's that supposed to mean?'

Faint looked across at her. 'Gods below, don't tell me you're a damned virgin.'

'Then I won't – and no more talking about that. They're letting us catch up to them.'

533

Ahead, Brys and Aranict had slowed their horses to a fast trot. 'The mounts are winded, Precious. We're all in bad shape.'

Before long, they drew up alongside the prince and the Atri-Ceda. 'Where's this army, then?' Faint demanded. 'I thought they were camped close.'

'They are, Faint,' Aranict replied. 'They simply have no need of cookfires, or lanterns.'

And now Faint made out a darker stain covering the low hills before them, and the dull gleam here and there of iron, or maybe reptilian eyes. Another shiver rippled through her. 'How confident are you in these allies?' She could see massive, elongated heads lifting now, eyes fixing upon them. She could see serrated rows of fangs.

'They are commanded by three humans, Faint, and two of them were once soldiers in the Bonehunters.'

Precious Thimble muttered something under her breath, probably a curse.

Aranict glanced at the young sorceress, and then over at Faint. 'Do you share your colleague's mistrust of Malazans, Faint?'

'Well, they tried conquering Darujhistan once. But then they turned round and crushed the Pannion Domin – and the Pannions were headed towards Darujhistan, with bad intentions.' She shrugged. 'I don't see them as any better or worse than anyone else.' Turning to Precious, she said, 'Besides, I visited One-Eye Cat before it got conquered, and that place was a hole.'

'But at least it was *my* hole!' Precious snapped.

'Did you just say—'

'Oh, be quiet, will you? You know what I meant!'

The prince and the Atri-Ceda said nothing and managed to hold their expressions – at least as far as Faint could discern in the heavy gloom. *Darkness our saviour!*

Thirty paces ahead, at the mouth of an avenue between ranks of silent, motionless K'Chain Che'Malle stood two men and a woman. The woman knelt and lifted the shutters on an oversized lantern, bathing the area in light.

As the riders drew closer, Faint studied these . . . commanders. The men were the soldiers, clad in the uniforms of Malazan marines, and though at first Faint took them to be Falari – with that red and yellow hair – there seemed to be a strange hue to their skin, somewhere between bronze and gold, almost lit from within. The woman was a tribal of some sort. Like the Rhivi, only bigger-boned, her face broad, slightly flat, her eyes dark and glittering like obsidian.

Prince Brys dismounted, followed by Aranict and then Faint. Precious remained seated on her horse, glowering at the Malazans.

'Sergeant Gesler,' Brys began, and then stopped. 'Are you certain you prefer that modest rank? As Mortal Sword to the—'

'Forgive me for interrupting, Commander,' Gesler said, 'but Stormy insists. He won't even talk to me otherwise. Leave all the fancy titles to other people—'

'He got busted down for good reasons,' Stormy cut in. 'And he ain't fixed none of those that I can see. In fact, he's gotten worse. If he showed up in a recruiting line right now I'd send him to the cook staff, and if they was feeling generous they might let him scrub a few pots. As it is, though, he's a sergeant, and I'm a corporal.'

'Commanding seven thousand K'Chain Che'Malle,' Aranict observed, lighting a stick of rustleaf from a small ember-box.

Stormy shrugged.

Sighing, Brys resumed, 'Sergeant Gesler. Your message – I take it she is awake.'

'Aye, and she's not particularly happy. Commander, she's got something to say, something she needs to tell you.'

'I see. Well then, lead on, Sergeant.'

As they made their way through the camp, with Gesler out front and Stormy carrying the lantern a few paces behind, Faint found herself walking alongside the tribal woman.

'You are the Destriant.'

'Kalyth, once of the Elan. And you are one of the strangers who found the Letherii army.'

'Faint, of the Trygalle Trade Guild. That miserable girl riding behind us is Precious Thimble. She doesn't like Malazans.'

'From her,' Kalyth said, 'the flavour is one of fear.'

'With good reason,' Precious retorted.

'It's this war we can't make any sense of,' Faint said. 'The Malazans fight when and where it suits them. They're a damned empire, after all. It's all about conquest. Expansion. They don't fight for noble causes, generally. Even taking down the Pannions was politically expedient. So we're finding it hard to work out what they're up to. From all that we've heard, Kolanse is not worth the effort. Especially with a bunch of Forkrul Assail laying claim to it now.'

Those dark eyes fixed on Faint's. 'What do you know of the Forkrul Assail?'

'Not much,' she admitted. 'An ancient race – back in Darujhistan, where I come from, most people think of them as, well, mythical. Ruling in an age when justice prevailed over all the world. We've long since fallen from that age, of course, and much as people might bemoan our state no one wants it back, if you know what I mean.'

'Why not?'

'Because then we'd actually be taken to task for all the terrible stuff we do. Besides, being fallen excuses our worst traits. We're not what we once were, too bad, but that's just how it is. Thank Hood and all the rest.'

Kalyth was slowly nodding. 'Then is it your belief that we can be no better than who and what we are now?'

'Something like that.'

'What if I were to tell you that the Malazans seek to change that? That they seek to rise higher, taller? That, once fallen, they now wish to stand? One more time. Perhaps the last time. And not just for themselves, but for all of us.'

A snort from Precious.

Faint frowned, and then shook her head. 'Then why fight the Forkrul Assail?'

'Because the Forkrul Assail have judged us – they came among my people, so this I know all too well. And in that judgement, they have decided that we must all die. Not just in Kolanse, not just on the Plains of Elan. But everywhere.'

'Given our history, that's not too surprising.'

'But, Faint of the Trygalle Trade Guild, the Forkrul Assail are in no position to judge. I have tasted the ancient flavours of the K'Chain Che'Malle, and it is as if that history was now my own. The Age of Justice – and the time of the Forkrul Assail – ended not at the hand of enemies, or foreign races, but at the hands of the Forkrul Assail themselves.'

'How?'

'They judged their own god, and found him wanting. And for his imperfections, they finally killed him.'

Ahead was a large tent, and the prince, Aranict, and the Malazans entered, taking the lantern's light with them. Faint held back in the darkness, Kalyth at her side. Behind them, Precious Thimble reined in, but still did not dismount.

Kalyth continued, 'There was war. Between the K'Chain Che'Malle and the Assail. The causes were mundane – the hunger for land, mostly. The Forkrul Assail had begun wars of extermination against many other races, but none had the strength and will to oppose them as did the K'Chain Che'Malle. When the war began to turn against the Assail, they turned on their own god, and in the need for yet more power they wounded him. But wounding proved not enough. They took more and more from him.

'The K'Chain Che'Malle nests began to fall one by one, until the last surviving Matron, in her desperation, opened a portal to the heart of chaos and set her back against it, hiding its presence from the advancing Assail. And when at last she stood facing them, when the tortured god's power rushed to annihilate her and all her kind, she surrendered her life, and the gate, which she had sealed with her own body, her own life force, opened. To devour the Assail god's soul.

'He was too wounded to resist. What remained of him, in this realm, was shattered, mindless and lost.' Her eyes glittered. 'You have seen the Glass Desert. That is where all that remains of that god now lives. If one could call it a life.'

'What happened to the Assail, Kalyth?'

The woman shrugged. 'Their power spent, they were broken. Though they blamed the Matron for the loss of their god, it was by their judgement that he was wielded as would one wield a weapon, a thing to be used, a thing not worthy of anything else. In any case, they had not the strength to exterminate the K'Chain Che'Malle. But the truth was the war had destroyed both races, and when other races appeared through the cracks of chaos – which could now reach this and every realm – neither could stop the invasions. More wars, defeats, betrayals, until the age itself crumbled and was no more.'

'This has the sound of legend, Kalyth,' Faint said.

'The memory of every Matron is passed down in the blood, the oils – the secretions. Nothing is lost. Gunth Mach has offered me some of their flavours. Much of it I cannot be certain of – there was a time, between the stars . . . I don't know. And it may be that I did not fully understand the tale I have just told. It may be that many truths were lost to me – our senses are so limited, compared to those of the K'Chain Che'Malle.'

'You have given reason for why the K'Chain Che'Malle seek to fight the Forkrul Assail. Because their war never ended.'

'We are each the last of our kind.'

'Is there not room enough for both of you?'

'The K'Chain might wish it so, but the Assail do not. Their memory is just as long, you see. And they do see their cause as being just.'

Behind them, Precious spoke in a dark, gleeful tone. 'You're using them! The Malazans and all their pathetic arrogance! You K'Chain Che'Malle – *you're using them!*'

The Destriant turned. 'Does it seem that way, sorceress? I taste in you the pleasure of that thought.'

'Why not? It's all they deserve.'

'If it is all that *they* deserve, then it is all that *we* deserve.'

'Just use them, Destriant. Use them up!'

For some reason, Faint was no longer interested in entering the tent. She nodded towards it. 'What's going on in there, Destriant?'

'Krughava, once Mortal Sword of the Perish Grey Helms, speaks to Prince Brys Beddict. She warns him of betrayal. The Perish vowed to serve the Adjunct Tavore. Instead, they will draw swords against us. They will fight under the banner of the Forkrul Assail.'

'Gods below – why would they do that?'

But Precious was laughing.

Kalyth sighed. 'The truth is this: the standard of justice can be raised by many, and each may lay rightful claim to it. How are these claims weighed? Gesler would answer quickly enough. They are weighed on the field of battle. But . . . I am not so sure. The Perish claim to worship ancient war gods, and these—'

'Which war gods?' Faint demanded.

'They are called Fanderay and Togg, the Wolves of Winter.'

Faint turned, stared up at Precious, and then back at Kalyth. 'And Krughava was the Mortal Sword. Who now commands?'

'The Shield Anvil, Tanakalian.'

'And the Destriant? There should be a Destriant among them, right?'

'He died on the voyage, I am told. The position is still vacant.'

'No it isn't.'

'Leave it, Faint,' said Precious. 'You don't know. You can't be certain—'

'Don't be an idiot. You saw her eyes – those were a wolf's eyes. And all her talk about the ghosts, and the old crimes, and all the rest.'

Kalyth spoke. 'I do not understand. Of whom do you speak?'

Shit. Faint turned back to the tent. 'Seems I need to go in there after all.'

'The forgiving embrace must be earned,' Shield Anvil Tanakalian said. 'Am I of such little worth that the cowards and fools among you can *demand* my blessing?' He scanned the faces before him, saw their exhaustion, and was disgusted. 'You come to me again and again. You ask, is this not the time to elect a new Mortal Sword? A new Destriant? Perhaps it is. Perhaps I am but waiting . . . for one of you to rise above the others, to show us all your worthiness. Alas, I am still waiting.'

The eyes regarding him from beneath the rims of the helms were bleak, beaten down. The camp behind these officers had lost its orderliness. Discipline had given way to bestial indifference, the torrid pace of the march their only excuse. They had crossed the border into Central Kolanse two days past, trudged down a road already overgrown, through towns little more than burned stains. This was a land returning to the wild, yet it stank of death.

'It must be,' said Tanakalian, 'that for now one man shall suffer the burden of all three titles. I did not ask for this. I do not welcome it. Ambition is a poison – we all saw what it did to Krughava. Must we now invite a return to that madness? I am not—'

He stopped then, as a sudden breath of ice flowed past him. He saw the officers facing him recoil, saw a stirring ripple through the ranks

538

assembled behind them. Mists lifted from the ground, curled and roiled on all sides.

What is this? Who has come among us? He started – something caught in the corner of his eye. A flash of movement. Then another. Low, the whisper of fur, a lurid glint from burning eyes. Sudden shouts from the Perish, the ranks losing formation, weapons hissing from scabbards.

Tanakalian could feel the buffeting tide sweeping past him. Invisible forms slid past his legs, pushed him off balance. He spun round, glared into the darkness. 'Show yourselves!'

A figure, coming up from beyond the road's berm. A girl, wearing rags. But he could see the flowing shapes now, the ethereal forms surrounding her. *Wolves. She comes in a sea of wolves.* But they were not real. Not living. Not breathing. These beasts were long dead. They bore wounds. Stains in the fur, gashes in the hide. The glow from their eyes was otherworldly, like holes burned through a wall – and what lay beyond was rage. *Incandescent rage.*

She drew nearer, and her eyes were the same. Torn through by fury. One blazed yellow, the other was quicksilver.

Horror filled Tanakalian at the moment of recognition. *The Wolves of Winter – they are within her. They are there, inside her – those eyes! They stare out at me from the Beast Throne. Fanderay. Togg. Our gods are among us.*

All strength left his limbs when those terrible eyes fixed on him and sank into his skull like fangs, forcing him to his knees.

All at once she stood before him. Those fangs dug deeper, tearing into his brain, ripping loose every secret, every hidden hunger. Raping him with cold remorselessness. As if he was carrion. Something washed back, thick as blood, and it was filled with contempt. An instant later and he was dismissed, made irrelevant. Her gaze lifted past him, to the Grey Helms – and he knew that they too knelt, abject, helpless, their courage drained away, their souls made cold with fear.

When she spoke in their minds, the voice was a multitude of howls, a sound more terrible than anything they had ever heard.

'I am the voice of the Wolves of Winter. Listen well to these words. We will not be judged.' She looked down at Tanakalian. *'You would wield my swords, mortal? Are you the one to lay waste to a thousand realms in my name? I think not. Pettiness consumes your thoughts. Vanity commands your every vision.*

'Look well upon this child. She is Setoc. Destriant. She is our voice. She is our will.'

The girl raised her eyes once more, addressed the entire army. *'Your kin kneel before the Forkrul Assail in the palace of Kolanse. The Assail would force the Perish Grey Helms to serve them, and they eagerly await your arrival, and the moment when you, too, must kneel in obeisance.*

'This . . . *offends us.*

'*When Sister Reverence summons Destriant Setoc, when she seeks to wrest this army from us, she shall know the wrath of the Wolves.*'

One of the officers suddenly found the courage to call out, 'Blessed Wolves – do you wish us to destroy the Forkrul Assail? Did the Mortal Sword speak true?'

'*Around us, mortal, there are only enemies. But we are among you now, and in the moment of battle the ghosts shall rise, in numbers beyond counting, and before us every army shall fall. Before us, every city shall burn. Before us, there shall be slaughter to redress the balance.*

'*Think on your faith, my children. Think well on the imbalance of which I speak. The millennia of slaughter at your human hand. We shall give answer. In every realm, we shall give answer!*'

Before the power of his gods, Tanakalian bowed his head. To hide his eyes. He was seething, his time of glory ripped away from him, his dreams of power stolen, his ascension left in ruins by this . . . this *girl*.

She had walked past him now, into the midst of his soldiers. But no, they were no longer his, were they? 'It will not end this way,' he whispered. '*It will not end this way!*'

She staggered away, blood pouring from her wounds.

Gruntle sought to rise, to lift his huge form one more time, but will was not enough. The pain was fading, a dullness seeping in, and in his bloodied nostrils all he could smell was burned fur, scorched flesh. The time surrounding him now, slowly closing in, seemed a force vast beyond countenance. It felt thick, unyielding, and yet he could see its expanse, the way it stretched behind him – but not ahead. No, there, almost within reach, it vanished into dark mists.

If he could, he would have laughed. The irony of life's end was found in all the truths suddenly discovered, when it was too late to do a damned thing about them. It was said that in the moments before death, there arrived an acceptance, a willingness to see it come to an end, and an indifference to the anguish and grief of the living. *If I have let go, why can't you? It's these truths, you see, and my helplessness in answering them. I would laugh, but in laughter there is pain. I would bless, but in blessing there is loss. This is not how anyone wants it. But then, it never is.*

Don't you see that, Stonny? In all your fraught moments – and isn't every moment fraught? – in all of them, you miss the chance of peace. The calm of all these truths, the ones us dying discover, and even then we can say nothing. Offer nothing.

540

This time. It's all past. No. It's my past. And with it, I can do nothing.

They had fought with terrible savagery. For how long he could not guess. Two indomitable beasts spilling out their hot, steaming blood, lashing out in rage, staggering in pain. Claws tearing, slashing deep. Fangs punching through hide and thick muscle. The stone floor of the chamber had grown slick, the air hot and fetid.

And overhead, looming above the ruined carcass of the Azath house, the huge wound fulminated, the edges burning, sizzling as if weeping acid.

Gruntle did not even see the moment the first of the dragons came through. He and Kilava were locked together, claws raking each other's flanks down to the bone, when something like a hurricane wind slammed them down on to the unyielding ground. Pulverized rock billowed out, filling the chamber even as enormous cracks opened on the rough walls.

Stunned by the thunderous concussion, Gruntle pulled away from Kilava. Yet the rage would not leave him, and he felt his god howling somewhere deep inside his chest – a creature held back for too long by Kilava's denial – and now it clawed its way free. She could no longer resist him, could no longer find the strength to defy what was coming.

I warned you.

The dragon filled the chamber, impossibly huge, wings hammering at the walls. Gruntle understood, then, that the creature was trapped – by the ancient, heavy stone of the cavern walls. It needed to unleash its sorcery – to shatter these confines, to open the way for the hundreds of other dragons crowding the gate.

He must strike now.

The roar that tore out from his throat was Trake's own, a god's call to war. The power within him becoming a thing of agony, Gruntle's limbs coiled, lowering him into a crouch, and then he leapt.

The dragon's neck arched, the head snapped down, jaws opening wide.

He slammed into the creature's neck. Claws sinking deep, his fangs burying themselves in the dragon's throat. Scales broke as Gruntle's jaws tightened, closing on the windpipe.

The dragon reared in shock, and with the convulsive motion blood poured into Gruntle's mouth. As he clung to the creature's writhing neck, his weight began to pull the dragon down. Wings cracked on the stone floor. Talons gouged wounds in the rock and then scraped frantically. The impact when the dragon struck the ground almost tore Gruntle loose, but he managed to hold on, the muscles of his shoulders, neck and jaws bunching until they creaked. He could hear the desperate wheezing of breath, and tightened his death grip.

The dragon reared a second time, lifting Gruntle into the air.

And then Kilava struck him with all the force of a battering ram. The dragon's throat was ripped wide open in a torrent of gore, but Gruntle was falling, Kilava's own fangs scoring deep across his shoulder blades.

They pounded against the stone floor, burst apart, Gruntle scrabbling to find his footing, twisting to find Kilava – to kill her once and for all—

The dying dragon was not yet done. Its jaws slammed down on Gruntle. Fangs long as scimitars impaled him. He was lifted from the ground, and then flung through the air.

Bones exploded inside his mangled flesh when he struck the wall. Leaving a glittering crimson streak, he slid down the stone to slump gasping, too broken to move.

The dragon staggered, head swinging round, eyes blazing as they fixed on him. Jaws opened, and sorcery roiled out in a torrent.

Gruntle heard Trake's death cry, and that howl itself seemed to catch fire in the conflagration of draconic magic. It raged around him, tore deep into his ruined body. And all at once his god left him, stumbling away, away from this realm. A trail, another cave, a place of darkness, a place to lie down and die.

Again. You damned fool. You never learn. And now . . . now it's too late.

The dragon careened against the far wall, sank down, spilling out the last of itself.

But above it, in that tearing wound, another was clawing its way through.

The cavern simply disintegrated as Eleint sorcery annihilated the last barriers surrounding Starvald Demelain. Beyond, the deep snows erupted in clouds of scalding steam. The ground itself was torn away, leaving nothing but swirling chaos.

In clouds of spinning dust and pelting rubble, in the wild fires of chaotic magic, the dragons returned to the world.

In my dreams, a blackened cat, a thing lying bleeding, gasping, dying. Blackened. In my dreams, I saw not her, but myself.

Dear Kilava, you did warn me. And I did not listen.

And when I warned Trake, Tiger of Summer and god of war, he did not listen. You fool. You needed wisdom in the one you chose, Trake. Not just another damned version of you. With all the same, useless, deadly flaws.

All that time, stretching away behind me now. Solid as stone, every shape, every rise and every dip, worn away in these winds of dying. Stonny, see what I have done? Or failed to do. You were right to refuse me. I always thought bigger than I could deliver. I always wanted what I could not hold.

And I saw it in your eyes – the day I stood before you, when I promised that I would come back. I saw in your eyes you knew I wouldn't. You knew you would never see me again. Ah, my love, so many truths, come too late.

And this love, it is the last thing I have left, the last thing to hold on to. All I ever wanted – feel it slip away, slip away.

Woman, you should never have let me go. I should have given you that power over me. If I had, you would've understood. You would have believed my love for you. And if you had believed, in that moment . . . I would have believed, too. How could I not?

This is my fault. I saw that then and I see it now. My fault.

Stonny, my love, I am sorry.

Time, that stretched behind him for ever, that closed in and became solid, that beckoned ahead with a darkness almost within reach, then ended.

By the time she staggered to his side, she saw that he was dead. Sembled into her Imass form, she sat down weakly beside his carcass, lifted her gaze to the empty, dust-wreathed sky.

The last of them, gone now. Out into the world. She had known that there would be hundreds of them, but still, the sight of that exodus had stunned her.

Blood pooled beneath her, mixing with that of Gruntle, this noble fool lying so still beside her. There was nothing more heartbreaking than to look upon a dead beast, a thing stripped of its terrible strength, its perfect majesty. And there was something still crueller when that beast was a hunter, a predator. *A rival.* Not killed for food. No. Killed for existing, killed for the presumption of competition. *The predator fights to the last. It refuses to surrender. Hunt it down. Corner it. See those bared fangs. Listen to its fury and its fear and its noble defiance.*

You understood all of this, Gruntle. You understood the inescapable, profound tragedy that is the beast that hunts, that dares to challenge our domination.

I did not mean to take your life.

She knew she was badly hurt. She knew she might not survive this. Even without the power of his god – whom she had kept away until the dragon's arrival – he had been . . . extraordinary. Had he not turned upon the Eleint . . . *yes, he would have killed me.*

Gruntle, I will remember you. This I swear. Here, in the cracks in my heart. I will curse Trake until the end of my days, but you, brother of the hunt, I will remember.

Hearing a scrabble of stones, she lifted her head.

The pair of emlava had returned, and now edged towards her. She sensed their distress. Their grief. 'He lives,' she whispered. 'My husband lives. For now. As for what comes . . .' *I wish I had an answer.*

The realm was dying on all sides. Disintegrating into dust, as all dreams must do, when the last dreamer is gone.

When she leaned back, closed her eyes, she felt the world shifting beneath her. So . . . gentle now, sweet as the rocking of a ship. *Husband. Was I wrong to do this?* She looked over to see the two sabre-toothed cats lying down beside Gruntle's carcass. As if to give him warmth.

As if to make him their own.

CHAPTER NINETEEN

'Not even the dead know the end to war.'

Iskar Jarak

'WHAT ARE YOU DOING?' Withal cinched tight the last straps, and reached for the black-scaled gauntlets. 'I can't just sit here any more,' he said. 'Since it seems we're all going to die anyway.' He glanced up at her, and shrugged.

Her lips were dry, chapped. Her eyes were ringed in red, hollowed with exhaustion. 'What of me?' she asked in a whisper. 'You will leave me . . . alone?'

'Sand, there are no chains on that throne—'

'*But there are!*'

'No. And there's no law says you got to sit there until the end. Why give them the glory of dragging you down from it, their delight at seeing fresh Andiian blood splashing the dais steps? Piss on them! Come with me. Die with the ones giving their lives to defend you.'

She looked away. 'I do not know how to fight.'

'Doesn't matter,' he said, rising from where he'd been sitting on the stone steps at the base of the throne. He took up the heavy mace he'd found – along with this arcane armour – in a dust-thick crypt far below the palace. 'Look at me. Too old for this by half.' He picked up the shield, slipping his arm through the straps.

She did look at him then. 'That's not Andiian armour.'

'Didn't think it was,' he replied, 'else it would never have fitted me. Better yet, it's not the kind that needs two people to put on. And the leather bindings – they don't seem to have aged at all.'

'How could I bear it, Withal? Seeing them die.'

'You sit here fighting your own war, Sand. If their dying in your imagination is easier for you to bear, it's because you don't see the blood. You don't hear the cries. The price they're paying you won't even deign to witness.'

'Did I make any bold claims to courage?'

'You make plenty of claims,' he said wearily, 'but none of them come close to courage.'

'Go then,' she hissed. 'I am done with you.'

He studied her, and then nodded.

Walked from the throne room.

Sandalath Drukorlat leaned back on the throne, closed her eyes. 'Now,' she muttered, 'I have my very own ghost.' The life that was, the one she had just killed. 'There's courage in doing that. And if it felt easy, well, we know that's a lie. But a gentle one. Gentle as a kiss never taken, a moment . . . slipping past, not touched, not even once.'

The soldier who walked in then, why, she knew him well. She could see through his armour right through to his beating heart, and such a large, strong heart. She could see, too, all his bones, scarred with healed breaks, and beyond that the floor of the chamber. Because this soldier's arrival had been a long, long time ago, and the one seated on this throne, before whom he now knelt, was not Sandalath Drukorlat.

The soldier was looking down, and then he was laughing. The sound was warm with love, softened by some unknown regret.

'Gods below,' said a voice from the throne, seeming to come from the dark wood behind her head. 'How is it I cannot even remember your name?'

The soldier was grinning when he looked up. 'Lord, when was the last time a Warden of the Outer Reach visited the throne room of Kharkanas? Even I cannot answer that.'

But Anomander was not yet prepared to excuse himself this failing. 'Have I not seen you before? Did not your commander at the Reach speak to me of you?'

'Perhaps, Lord, the praise was faint, if it existed at all. Shall I ease your dismay, Lord?'

Sandalath saw a hand rise from where one of her own rested on the arm of the chair. *His hand. Pointing – no, just a gesture, just that.* 'No need. Warden Spinnock Durav.'

The soldier smiled and nodded. 'Upon word of your summons, Lord, I have come, as at that time I was the ranking officer in the Reach.'

'Where then is Calat Hustain?'

'An event at the gate, Lord.'

'Starvald Demelain? I have heard nothing of this.'

'It has been only a week, Lord, since he set out for it.'

'What manner of event was this – do you know?'

'The word that came to us from the Watchers did not suggest urgency, or dire threat, Lord. An awakening of foreign energies. Modest, but worth closer examination.'

'Very well. Then, Spinnock Durav, it shall be you.'

'I am ever at your call, Lord. What is it that you wish me to do?'

Anomander's answer stole all humour from the soldier's face. And, she recalled, it was never to return.

The peace of the forest belied the horror waiting ahead. Water dripped from moss, ran like tears down channels in the lichen covering the boles of the trees. Somewhere, above the canopy, heavy clouds had settled, leaking rain. Withal would have welcomed the cool drops, the sweet kisses from heaven. He needed to be reminded of things beyond all this – the throne room and the woman he had left behind, and before him the First Shore with its heaps of corpses and pools of thickening blood. But this forest was too narrow to hold all that he wanted, and to pass from one misery to the next took little effort, and it was not long before he could hear the battle ahead, and between the towering trunks of the ancient trees he now caught flashes of shimmering light – *where the world ends.*

For all of us.

He was done with her haunting his dreams, done with all the demands that he make his love for Sandalath into some kind of weapon, a thing with which to threaten and cajole. And Sand had been right in rejecting him. No, she was Mother Dark's problem now.

The chewed-up trail dipped before climbing to the ridge overlooking the First Shore, and as he scrabbled his way up the slope the sounds of fighting built into a roar. Two more steps, a thick root for a handhold, and then he was on the ridge, and before him was a scene that stole the strength from his legs, that closed a cold hand about his heart.

Who then has seen such a thing? Before him, seven thousand bodies. Letherii. Shake. And there, along the base of Lightfall – to either side of that breach – how many dead and dying Liosan? Ten thousand? Fifteen? The numbers seemed incomprehensible. The numbers gave him nothing. In his mind he could repeat them, as if voicing a mantra, as his gaze moved from one horror to the next, and then down to where the knot of defenders fought at the very mouth of the wound – fought to deny the Liosan a single foothold upon the Shore – and still, none of it made sense. Even when it did.

It is the last stand. That is what this is. They keep coming. We keep falling. An entire people, face to face with annihilation.

All at once he wanted to turn round, march back to Kharkanas, to the palace, into the throne room, and . . . and *what? It's not her fault. There's nothing here she ever wanted. Gods below, Sand, I begin to understand your madness. No one here will accept surrender, no matter what you say. You could open your own throat there on that throne, and it wouldn't matter. These people will die defending a corpse. A corpse on a throne, in a corpse of a city. The cause stopped meaning anything some time ago.*

I should have seen that.

Two girls were among the dead and dying, stumbling from body to body. They were painted head to toe in crimson. One of them was shrieking, as if seeking to tear her own voice to pieces, to destroy it for all time. The other careered among the corpses, hands over her ears.

There were no reserves. All who remained standing were at the breach, where Yedan Derryg still stood, still fought. But what of Yan Tovis? What of the queen of the Shake? If she was in that dreadful press, Withal could not see her. If she had died, she was buried beneath her fallen subjects.

He found that he was breathing hard, his heart pounding. The grip of the mace was slick in his hand. He set it down, reached for the ornate, full-visored helm slung from his knife belt. Fumbled to loosen the clasp – as if his fingers had forgotten how to work. Finally tugging it free, he worked the helm on to his head, felt its weight settle. He closed the clasp under his chin, the iron hoop tearing at the beard on his throat.

The sounds of the battle dulled then, faint as distant breakers on some unseen strand. A louder squeal when he set the visor and locked it in place, and the scene before him was suddenly split, broken up by the chaotically angled bars. His breaths now filled the confined space.

Withal collected the mace, straightened. Brought the shield round to guard his left side, and lurched into motion.

Someone else had wrested control of his body – his legs, now carrying him down on to the strand; his eyes, searching for a path through the pale, motionless bodies; the hand holding his weapon and the forearm bearing the weight of the shield – they no longer belonged to him, no longer answered to his will. *You do not willingly walk into a battle like this. How can you? No, some other force takes you there, moves you like a pawn, a puppet. And you watch yourself going ever forward, and you are baffled, disbelieving. And all that fear, it's hollowed out – just an empty place now. And the roar outside is lost to the roar inside – your own blood, your breaths – and now your mouth is parched and you would kill your own mother for a drink of water. But of course you won't, because that would be wrong – and that thought makes you want to laugh. But if you do, you know that you will lose it, you know that if that laughter starts it won't stop.*

Was this how it was in my first battle? Was this why I could remember so little – only frozen moments, those moments that reach up and take you by the throat? That make you see all that you don't want to see, remember all that you pray to forget?

Is this how it was?

He was clambering over the heaped bodies now, the flesh beneath him cold, taking the imprints of his feet and knees like damp clay – he looked back at the dents and wondered at their wrongness. And then he was moving on, and before him was a ragged wall, Letherii and Shake on their knees, or bent over, or trying to drag themselves out from a forest of legs, shielding wounds – he thought he would see weeping faces, bawling despair, but the pain-twisted faces were dry, and every cry that clawed past his own roaring self was one of raw pain. *Just that. Nothing more. A sound without complications, can you hear it?*

If there could be one god, with one voice, this is the sound it would make – to stop us in our endless madness.

But look on, Withal. See the truth. We do not listen.

He made his way past these exhausted and wounded comrades, pushed his way into the heaving mass. The stench rocked him. Abattoir, sewer, cutter's floor. Thick enough to choke him. He struggled against vomiting – here inside this helm – no, he would not do that. Could not.

Faces now, on all sides. None speaking, and the look in their eyes was flat, flatter than anything he'd ever seen. And they were all straining towards the front line, moving up to take their places, to fill the gaps, the unending gaps, as if to say *If you will kill us all, kill me next. But do not think it will be easy.*

Suddenly, he felt ready for this. *Walk until something bars your path. Then stand, until you fall. Whoever said life was complicated?*

The channels and currents had carried him to the left flank, well away from that immovable knot at the centre, where a sword's laughter had taken for itself all the Shore's madness, every last scrap of it.

He saw Brevity, though at first he did not recognize her – that solid, handsome face, the wry look in her eyes, all gone. In their place a mask of wet blood over dried blood, over blood that had turned into black tar. A slash had opened one cheek, revealing two rows of red molars. There was nothing sardonic left, but she commanded that front line, her will clenched like a fist.

Off her shield side, two Shake fell and three Liosan pushed in to widen the gap.

Eyes widening at the perfect, breathtaking simplicity of what was needed of him, Withal surged to meet them.

This was something new. Yan Tovis could feel it. Yedan Derryg had advanced the line to the very edge of the breach, and there they had held against the Liosan. This time there was to be no foothold. He would refuse them a single step upon the strand.

He had explained nothing, and as she fought, crowded hard against that wound – from which Liosan poured like blood – she began to realize that, this time, there would be no respite, not until one side or the other fell, to the very last soldier. What had begun would not end until the last sword swung down, or sank deep in writhing flesh.

How had he known? What had he done on the other side of the gate? What had he seen?

She caught glimpses of her brother, there, where the terrifying pealing laughter went on and on, where blood fountained, where Liosan bodies piled ever higher and they stood on them, fighting for balance, face to face, weapons flashing. Glimpses. A face she barely knew, so twisted was it, the Hust sword dragging him past exhaustion, past all reason of what the human body could withstand. Of his face, she could see the white bones beneath translucent flesh, could see all the veins and arteries and the root-mat of vessels, could see the bloody tears that streamed down from his eyes.

Night had come to the Shake. The sand had measured the time, in a kind of stillness, a kind of silence that was beneath all this, and the grains slipped down, and now had come the eternity just before dawn, the time of the Watch. He stood. He fought, his stance wide to find purchase on a hill of bodies.

See him. In the eternity before dawn. When among mortals courage is at its weakest, when fear sinks talons on the threshold and will not let go. When one awakens to such loneliness as to twist a moan from the chest. But then . . . you feel it, breath catching. You feel it. You are not alone.

The Watch stands guard.

They would not break, would not yield – all those who stood now with him. Instead, at his sides they died, and died.

She was a thing of ash and blood, moulded into something vaguely human-shaped, tempered by the crushed bone of her ancestors, and she fought on, because her brother would not yield, because the very border that was Lightfall, and the wound, had now become the place where it would be decided.

And still the Liosan came, lunging wild-eyed from the swirling chaos – most did not even have time to react, to make sense of the nightmare world into which they had just stumbled, before a pike plunged into them, or a sword lashed down. And so they died, there on that threshold, fouling those who came after them.

She had no idea how many of her people were left, and a vision that had come upon her a century ago, maybe longer, of Yedan Derryg standing alone before the breach, the very last to fall, now returned to her, not as some dreadful imagining, but as prophetic truth.

And all because I would not kneel to the Shore.

There was no dragon challenging the breach. If one came, she now would not hesitate. She would fling herself down, trusting in Yedan to kill the damned thing, trusting in the power of her own blood to claim that dying creature, hold it fast, grasp hold of its blood and lift it, higher, yet higher, to make a wall, to seal this gate.

Why did I wait? Why did I resist?

Why did I believe my freedom was worth anything? Why did I imagine that I had the right to choose my destiny? Or choose to deny it?

Only the defeated kneel. Only slaves, the ones who surrender their lives – into the hands of others.

But now . . . I would do it. To save my people, this pitiful remnant. Come to me now, my child-witches. See me kneel. Bleed me out. I am ready.

A Liosan fell to her sword, on to his knees before her, as if mocking her sudden desire, and over his head she saw her brother – saw him turn, saw him find her. Their gazes locked.

Yan Tovis loosed a sob, and then nodded.

Yedan Deryyg threw out his arms to the sides. Roared, 'Back! Ten paces!'

And hail welcome to the dragon.

She watched Spinnock Durav enter the throne room yet again, and wondered at the absence of his smile. That face did not welcome solemn regard, wore it like an ill-fitting mask. Made it lined where it should be smooth, made the eyes flinch when he looked up to meet the gaze of the one seated on this throne.

He smelled of burnt wood, as if he had dragged the death of a forest behind him, and now the smoke swirled round his legs, his kneeling form, like serpents only she could see.

'Highness,' he said.

'Speak to me,' said a strained, half-broken voice, 'on the disposition of my legions.'

'Certain leaders among us,' Spinnock replied, eyes lowering to fix on the dais, or perhaps a pair of booted feet, 'are in their souls unleashed. 'Tis the scent upon this wind—'

'If the fire draws closer, the city will burn.'

'Against that conflagration, Highness, only you can stand, for it is by your will – we see that now. We see your grief, though we do not yet understand its meaning. What pact have you made with Silanah? Why does she lay waste to all the land? Why does she drive ever closer to proud Kharkanas?'

'Proud?' The word was a sneer. 'I am now one ghost among many, and it is only ghosts who belong here. If we are to be forgotten, the city must fall. If we are to be forgiven, the city must swallow our crimes. If we are to be dust, the city must be ash. That is how to end this.'

'We have journeyed long, Highness. From the Outer Marches, on a hundred hidden paths only a thief would remember. And then the violence took our leaders. *The blood of Eleint.*'

'Cursed blood!'

'Highness?'

'No! It poisoned me once – you know that, Spinnock Durav! You were there!'

He bowed his head still further. 'I saw what was done, yes. I saw what you sought to hide away.'

'I did not ask them to come back. I didn't!'

He lifted his gaze, tilted his head. 'I sense . . . this is important. Highness. *Who did you not ask to come back?*'

Hard, cold hands closed on her face. She felt them like her own, felt the long fingers like prison bars, smelled the wax of melted candles. 'Can't you hear it?'

'Hear what, Highness?'

'Their screams. The dying! *Can't you hear it?*'

'Highness, there is a distant roar. Lightfall—'

'*Lightfall!*' Her eyes widened but she could not speak, could not think.

'What is happening?' he demanded.

What is happening? Everything is happening! 'Are they in disarray? Your troops?'

He shook his head. 'No, Highness. They wait on Blind Gallan's Road.'

Blind Gallan's Road? There was no such road. Not then. Not when Spinnock Durav came to kneel before his lord. I have lost my mind. A sudden whimper, and she shrank back in the throne. 'Take off that mask, Spinnock Durav. You were never so old.'

'Who did you ask not to come back?'

She licked her lips. 'She should have taken the throne. She was a true queen, you see. Of the Shake. And the Letherii, the ones she saved. I don't belong here – I told them—'

But Spinnock Durav was on his feet, a growing horror on his face. 'Highness! Sandalath Drukorlat! What is that roar?'

She stared at him. Moved her mouth to make words. Failed. Tried a second time. 'The breach. They've come again – tell Anomander – tell him! No one can stop them but him! The Shake – *dying.* Oh, Mother bless us. DYING!'

Her shriek echoed in the vast room. But he was already leaving. Out

552

in the corridor now, shouting orders – but that voice, too desperate, too frantic. Not like Spinnock Durav at all.

Lord Nimander Golit Anomandaris, firstborn of the fraught union of Son of Darkness and the First Daughter of Draconus, fell to his knees. His body trembled as he struggled against the blood of the Eleint and its terrible need, its inescapable *necessity*. Where was Skintick? Desra? Nenanda?

The stones of the river bed crunched beside him, and he felt hands clutch his shoulders. *'Resist this, Lord. We're the last two left. Resist the call of the Eleint!'*

He lifted his head, baffled, and stared into Korlat's ancient eyes. 'What – who?'

'She has commanded Silanah. She has summoned the Warren of Fire, and set upon the dragon the madness of her desire – do you understand? *She would burn this realm to the ground!*'

Gasping, he shook his head. 'Who sits upon the throne? Who would do this in Mother Dark's name?'

'Can you not smell the blood? Nimander? There is war – here – I don't know who. But souls are falling, in appalling numbers. And on the Throne of Darkness sits a queen – *a queen in despair.*'

He blinked. *A queen?* 'Where is Apsal'ara?'

Korlat looked across the river. 'Into the city, Lord.'

'And Spinnock?'

'He has followed – to beseech the queen. To make sense of this – Nimander, listen to me. Your Soletaken kin, they have succumbed to Silanah's power – she now commands a Storm. If we now veer, you, myself, Dathenar and Prazek – we shall be forced to fight them. In the skies above Kharkanas, we shall annihilate each other. *This must not be.*'

Nimander forced himself to his feet. 'No. Silanah. She must be stopped.'

'Only the Queen can command her to stop, Nimander.'

'Then . . . take me to her.'

When Korlat hesitated, he studied her, eyes narrowing. 'What is it, Korlat? Who is this Queen of Darkness?'

'I fear . . . no matter. Go, then, Nimander. Convince her to release Silanah.'

'But – where will you go?'

'The war. I will go with Dathenar and Prazek. Lord, I believe I know where the battle will be found. I hope that I am wrong. But . . . go. *Walk where your father walked.*'

*   *   *

553

How long ago was it? She could not remember. She was young. The night before she had taken a boy to her bed, to remind herself that not everything was pain. And if she later broke his heart, she'd not meant to. But this was a new day, and already the night just past seemed centuries away.

She'd been with her brother's hunting party. On the spoor of tenag. The day was warm, the sun bright and pleased with itself.

They heard his laughter first, a deep thing, hinting of thunder, and they followed it down into a depression thick with chokecherry and dogwood. A figure, lying against a slope. He was Imass, like them, but they did not recognize him, and this in itself was startling. Disturbing.

She could see at once, when she and her kin gathered close, that his wounds were fatal. It was a wonder he still lived, and an even greater wonder that he could laugh as he did, and through all the agony in his eyes, that mirth still shone when he looked up at them.

Her brother was first to speak, because that was his way. 'What manner of stone do you wear?'

'Stone?' the dying man replied, showing a red smile. 'Metal, my friends. Armour. A Tel Akai gift.'

'Where have you come from?'

'Clanless. I wandered. I came upon an army, my friends.'

'There is no army.'

'Jaghut. Tel Akai. Others.'

They were silenced by this. The Jaghut were despised. Feared. But an army of Jaghut? Impossible.

Were they now at war? Her clan? Her people? If so, then they would all die. An army of Jaghut – the words alone opened like Omtose Phellack in her soul.

'I joined them,' said the man, and then, lifting a mangled hand, he added, 'Set no crime at my feet for that. Because, you see, I am the last left. They died. All of them. The Jaghut. The Tel Akai. The Jheck. All . . . dead.'

'What enemy has come among us?' her brother asked, his eyes wide with fear.

'None but that has always been with us, friends. Think well on my words. When you slay a beast, when you hunt as you do now, and blood is spilled. When you close upon the beast in its dying, do you not see its defiance? Its struggle to the very last moment? The legs that kick, the head that tries to lift, the blood frothing from the nostrils?'

They nodded. They had seen. And each time they had felt something fill their hearts, choke in their throats. One needed to bite back on that. Things were as they were.

'Bless the Jaghut,' the stranger said, his head falling back. He laughed,

but it was short, frail. 'Why defy death, when you cannot help but fail? They would tell you why. No. They would show you why – if only you had the courage to see, to stand with them, to understand the true enemy of all life.' His eyes found her, her alone, and once more he managed a smile. 'Now I will die. I will . . . fail. But I beg of you,' and his eyes glistened, and she saw that they were beautiful eyes, especially now, 'a kiss. Many a woman cursed me in my youth. Even as they loved me. It was . . . glorious.'

She saw the life draining from those eyes, and so she leaned forward, to catch its leaving. With a soft kiss. His breath was of blood. His lips were cracked, but they were warm.

She held that kiss, as that warmth left. Held it, to give him as much of her as she could.

Her brother pulled her away, held her in his arms the way he used to, when she was much younger, when she was not so guarded with her own body.

They took the armour, before leaving his body to the wild. And she claimed that armour for her own. For that kiss.

And now, she wanted it back. Hissing in frustration, Apsal'ara scanned the empty chamber. She was far beneath the ground floor of the palace. She was where they'd put her armour and her mace, the first time she'd been captured in their midst. They'd been amused by her – it was always that way, as if Kharkanas held nothing worth stealing, as if the very idea of theft was too absurd to countenance.

But someone had stolen her armour!

Seething with outrage and indignation, she set out in search of it.

All reason had left the face of their lord. Froth foamed the corners of his mouth as he screamed his rage, driving the ranks into the maw of the gate, and it was indeed a maw – Aparal Forge could see the truth of that. The fangs descended again and again. They chewed his people to bloody shreds and splintered bones. And this was an appetite without end.

They could not push past, not a single damned step – denying the legions a foothold, a place into which their Soletaken masters could come, could veer and, in veering, at last shatter the opposition.

The commander on the other side had anticipated them. Somehow, he had known the precise moment at which to modify his tactics.

Aparal watched the mangled bodies being pulled from the swirling maelstrom of the gate, watched the way those bodies floundered like wreckage, bobbing on human hands and shoulders, out to the deep trenches already heaped high with the dead. Apart from the elite companies, hardly any soldiers remained. *This iron mouth has devoured the population of an entire city. Look well, my*

Soletaken kin, and ask yourself: whom will you lord it over now? Who will serve you in your estates? Who will raise the food, who will serve it, who will make your fine clothes, who will clean your shit-buckets?

None of this was real. Not any more. And all the ordered precision of existence was now in shambles, a bloodied mess. There was nothing to discuss, no arguments to fling back and forth, no pauses in time to step back and study old tapestries on the walls and pray for the guidance of heroic ancestors.

Saranas was destroyed, and when this was done it would be as empty, as filled with ghosts, as Kharkanas. *Light finds the face of Darkness, and lo, it is its own. Is this not what you wanted, Kadagar? But, when you finally possess what you wanted, who, O Lord of Ghosts, who will sweep the floors?*

And now, at last, the elite ranks were pushing up against the gate – all the fodder had been used up. Now, then, arrived the final battle.

Aparal made his way down to where the wounded were being left, abandoned, alongside the trenches. The chorus of their cries was horrible beyond measure – to enter this place was an invitation to madness, and he almost welcomed that possibility. He pushed past the staggering, dead-eyed cutters and healers, searching until he found one man, sitting cradling the stump of his left arm, the severed end of which trailed wisps of smoke. A man not screaming, not weeping, not yet reduced to a piteous wretch.

'Soldier. Look at me.'

The head lifted. A shudder seemed to run through the man.

'You have been through the gate?'

A shaky nod.

'How many left – among the enemy? How many left?'

'I – could not be sure, Lord. But . . . I think . . . few.'

'This is what we keep hearing, but what does that mean? Fifty? Five thousand?'

The soldier shook his head. 'Few, Lord. And, Lord, *there is laughter!*'

'Hust weapons, soldier. Possessed blades. Tell me what is *few*?'

The man suddenly bared his teeth, and then, with deliberation, he spat at Aparal's feet.

All who return from the other side are subjects no longer. Mark this, Kadagar. Aparal pointed at the legions now crowding the gate. 'More than them? Look, damn you!'

Dull eyes shifted, squinted.

'*That*, soldier, is seven thousand, maybe eight. On the other side, as many? More? Less?' When the man simply returned his stare, Aparal drew his sword. 'You have been through the gate. You have seen – *assess the enemy's strength!*'

The man grinned, eyes now on the weapon in Aparal's hand. 'Go ahead.'

'No, not you, soldier.' He waved with the blade of the sword, the gesture encompassing a score of other wounded. 'I will kill them, one after another, until you answer me.'

'Do you not see, Lord, why we refuse you? You have already killed us. All of us. Surviving these wounds will not change that. Look at me. I am already dead. To you. To all the world. Now fuck off. No, better yet – take yourself through to the other side. See for—'

Aparal did not know where the rage came from, but the savage strength of his blow lifted the soldier's head from his neck, sent it spinning, and then bouncing, until it fetched up against another wounded soldier – who turned her head, regarded it for a moment, then looked away again.

Trembling, horrified by what he had done, Aparal Forge backed away.

From one side he heard a weary chuckle, and then, 'Barely a thousand left, Lord. They're done.'

He twisted round, sought out the one who spoke. Before him was the trench, piled with corpses. 'Is it the dead who now speak?'

'As good as,' came the reply. 'You don't understand, do you? We don't tell you because we honour our enemy – they're not Tiste Andii. They're humans – who fight like demons.'

He saw the man now. Only the upper half of his body was visible, the rest buried under bodies. Someone had judged him dead. Someone had made a mistake. But then Aparal saw that half his skull was gone, exposing the brain. 'The Hust Legion—'

'Oh, you'd like that, wouldn't you? But there's no Hust Legion. There's one man. One Hust sword. Slayer of dragons and slayer of hounds, slayer of a thousand Liosan . . . *one man*. And when you finally break through, Lord, may he cut you down – you Soletaken, you betrayers. Every one of you.'

If you stood here, Kadagar Fant . . . if you stood here, you would finally see what we have done.

Aparal retreated, made his way towards the gate. Yes, he would push through. He would step out on to that foreign shore. And, if he could, he would destroy this lone warrior. *And then it will be over. Because that is all I want, now, for this to be over.*

He spied a messenger corps, a dozen or so runners standing just beyond the nearest legion. 'Words to my kin!' he barked. 'Less than a thousand remain on the other side. And there is but one man with a Hust sword. Inform our lord – *the time is now.*'

557

An end. Bless me, an end.

Sheathing his bloody sword, he fixed his gaze on the gate. 'There,' he whispered. '*Now.*'

Halfway across the bridge, Nimander paused, stared at the keep's massive gates. The air was filling with smoke, and he could now hear the detonations. The sorcery of dragons, the Eleint doing what they did best. *Destroying everything in their path.*

The return of the Tiste Andii should not have been like this. In flames, in annihilation. He had felt his kin being torn away from him. They had veered over the Outer Marches: they had been flying in the company of Silanah. To honour her, of all things. She was of the royal household now, or so Nimander had wanted – *another foolish conceit. In Draconic form, she was my father's lover – but that was long ago.* But Anomander Rake's hunger for awakening the blood of the Eleint within him had waned. Even when faced with the ruination of Moon's Spawn, he had not surrendered to it.

Nimander could not even imagine the will that had denied such a . . . gift. Above Pale, he could have killed Tayschrenn – Korlat had said as much. He could have flown down from Moon's Spawn, Silanah at his side, and brought fire and devastation to the Malazans. The sudden descent of terror from the skies, scattering the enemy, shattering the opposition arrayed against him.

Instead, he waited, and when at last he veered into his Draconic form, it was to save a different city.

'*He would have done so for Pale, if not for the betrayal.*'

'*But, Korlat, it was only the mages who broke their vow. Not the people of the city.*'

She had nodded then, and looked across to her two companions. Prazek Goul, who had once been Orfantal's swordmaster. And Dathenar Fandoris, abandoned spawn from a High Priestess and then, much later, Korlat's own Mistress of Assassination. The three of them, all that remained of his father's cadre of Soletaken dragons.

Prazek had said, '*No matter what, there would have been terrible destruction visited upon Pale. Had Anomander Rake veered into a dragon, Tayschrenn would have had no choice but to turn his fullest powers upon him. By the time the two were done, all of Pale would have been ashes. Instead, our lord descended into the city, and hunted down those wizards, taking them one by one. So, in truth, he did indeed save Pale.*'

'*Although,*' added Dathenar, '*he could not have anticipated the revenge of the Moranth upon Pale's citizens.*'

'*The Malazans could have stopped that,*' countered Prazek.

And the three had nodded.

Blinking, Nimander drew a deep breath, pushing away that gnawing hunger within him – to veer, to rise up, to join the Storm. Then he made his way across the bridge, and into the palace.

From the shadows of the entrance, Apsal'ara stepped out to block his path. 'Lord Nimander, there is a Tiste Andii woman upon the throne.'

'So Korlat told me. She has bound Silanah – I must convince her—'

'She is Korlat's mother, Lord. Once a Hostage, now the Queen of High House Dark. But madness has taken her. It may be, Lord, that you will have to kill her.'

'*What?* Where is Spinnock?'

'Returned to your legions. There is war upon the First Shore. The Tiste Liosan seek to invade, and those who oppose them are few.'

'There are other Tiste Andii?'

She shook her head. 'No. They are Shake.'

Shake? The island prison – gods, no. He stood, his desire suddenly torn in two directions.

'Make the Queen yield, Lord,' said Apsal'ara. 'Spinnock will lead your people in battle.' She stepped closer, reached up and brushed Nimander's cheek. 'My love, do this.'

'I will not usurp the Queen of High House Dark! Do we return, only to spill Andiian blood all over again?' He shook his head in horrified denial. 'No, I cannot!'

'Then convince her to release Silanah – the Storm will be needed. To save Kharkanas – to save the Shake.'

'Come with me.'

'No, Nimander. I will go to the First Shore. I will fight. Find me there.' Her hand slipped behind his head now and drew his face down to her own. She kissed him hard, and then pushed him away, and was past him, out on to the bridge.

The thunder of Silanah's rage was drawing closer.

Nimander rushed inside.

The elders and the young remained camped near the bank of the river, though Spinnock knew that before long they would have to retreat into the city. If Silanah could not be stopped. Glancing back, up the road, it seemed that half the sky was aflame. Forests were burning, the ground itself erupting into fountains of molten rock. He caught a dark shape sailing amidst the smoke.

Drawing on his gauntlets, he faced his warriors, and saw that all eyes were upon him. At Spinnock's back was the forest, and beyond it waited the First Shore. They understood what was to come. He need tell them nothing.

And yet . . .

Anomander, old friend. Do you now sit at your mother's side? Do you now look down upon us? Are you helpless, unable to reach across, to still Silanah's savage fury? Or have you ceased to care?

And yet.

'*Anomander, old friend. Do you now sit at your mother's side? Do you now look down upon us? Are you helpless, unable to reach across, to still Silanah's savage fury? Or have you ceased to care?*'

Spinnock straightened, scanned the helmed faces before him. And then he drew his sword. Caught the eye of Captain Irind, gestured the burly man forward. 'Face to me your shield, Captain, and hold well your stance.'

The man's eyes narrowed slightly, and then he took position, raising the shield between them and settling his shoulder beneath its rim, head turned away.

Spinnock half turned, as if dismissing Irind, and then he whirled. The sword cracked hard against the shield, staggering the captain. The reverberation echoed, out into the forest, and then fell back like rain among the troops.

'When he led you and your ancestors from this place,' Spinnock said, pitching his voice loud enough to carry – though in truth a sudden silence had taken the scene, and it seemed not even the Storm could reach through, 'from smoke, from fire, from ruin, Mother Dark had turned away. Before you, before your lord Anomander Rake, there was . . . *nothing.*'

Again his sword struck. Again Irind staggered but held his ground.

'Prepare to advance. We will not form up once clear of the forest.' He bared his teeth. 'There is no time for that. Captain Irind, stay at my side.'

Spinnock led the way into the ancient wood. Behind him the ranks spilled out, order almost immediately broken by the boles of trees, by sinkholes and tree-falls. The air was heavy with mists. Water streamed down every trunk, every branch, every dark-veined leaf.

He raised his voice as he advanced, knowing that they would hear him, knowing that Mother Dark had given him this. *For her people. For this day, this most fraught day.* 'Lord Nimander has gone to the palace. He seeks to turn Silanah from her path. What value winning the battle if we lose the war? If not for that, he would be here. He would be speaking to you. But he is not. And . . . this time, *this one time,* it is well – for like many of you, I was *born* in this realm.'

Irind was beside him, ready for the blow. The sword hammered the shield, the sound a shout of iron.

'Lord Anomander Rake led you to another world. He fought to give you purpose – a reason to live. And for many, in that he failed. But those of you here – for you, *he did not fail.*'

He swung the sword again, the impact shivering up his arm.

'He asked you to fight wars that were not yours to fight. He asked you to bow to causes not your own. A hundred banners, a hundred cities – allies who welcomed you and allies who did not. Allies who blessed you and allies who feared you. And your kin died, oh, how they died – they gave up their lives in causes *not their own*.'

The sword cracked again, and this time Irind almost buckled beneath the blow. Spinnock could hear his harsh breaths.

'They were all different, and they were all the same. But the cause – the true cause he offered you – *did not change*.'

The blow sent Irind to his knees.

Another soldier moved up, readying his own shield. Bodily dragged Irind back, and then took his place. The sounds from the advancing warriors behind Spinnock was a susurration – breaths, armour, boots scrabbling for purchase.

'Your lord was thinking – each and every time – he was thinking . . . *of this moment*.'

Again flashed the sword.

'Each time, every time. *The cause was just*.'

Crack!

'He needed to keep reminding you. For this day!'

Crack!

'Today, this is not foreign soil! Today, this cause is your own!'

Crack!

'*Today, the Tiste Andii fight for themselves!*'

And this time other weapons found the rims of shields.

CRACK!

'*Your home!*'

CRACK!

'*Your kin!*'

CRACK!

The sword shivered in his hand. The soldier stumbling beside him fell away, his shield split.

Gasping, Spinnock Durav pushed on. *Anomander Rake – do you witness this? Do you look into these faces – all these faces behind me?*

'*This time! Strangers fight in your name! Strangers die for you! Your cause – not theirs!*'

CRACK!

The reverberation shoved him forward, shivered through him like something holy. '*Children of Dark, humans are dying in your name!*'

CRACK!

The very air trembled with that concussion. A torrent of water – clinging to high branches, to needles and leaves – shook loose and rained down in an answering hiss.

Ahead, Spinnock could hear fighting.

Do you see, Anomander? Old friend, do you see?

This is our war.

CRACK!

Through the boles a glimmer of falling light. A vast shape lifting high. The sudden roar of a dragon.

Gods, no, what have they done?

CRACK!

Anomander Rake entered the throne room. Sandalath Drukorlat stared at him, watching as he strode towards her.

His voice held a hint of thunder outside. 'Release Silanah.'

'Where is your sword?'

The Son of Darkness drew up momentarily, brow clouding. One hand brushed the grip of the weapon slung at his belt.

'Not that one,' she said. 'The slayer of Draconus. Show me. *Show me his sword!*'

'Highness—'

'Stop that! This throne is not mine. It is yours. Do not mock me, Lord. They said you killed him. They said you cut him down.'

'I have done no such thing, Highness.'

A sudden thought struck her. 'Where is Orfantal? You took him to stand at your side. Where is my son? My beloved son? Tell me!'

He drew closer. He looked so young, so vulnerable. And that was all . . . wrong. *Ah, this is much earlier. He has not yet killed the Consort. But then . . . who am I?*

'Release Silanah, Sandalath Drukorlat. The Storm must be freed – the destruction of Kharkanas will make all the deaths meaningless.'

'Meaningless! Yes! It is what I have been saying all along! *It's all meaningless! And I am proving it!*'

He was standing before her now, his eyes level with her own. 'Korlat—'

A shriek shattered his next words. Sandalath recoiled, and only then realized that the cry had been torn from her own throat. *'Not yet! Where is Orfantal? Where is my beloved son?'*

She saw something in his face then, an anguish he could not hide. She had never known him to be so . . . weak. So pathetically unguarded. She sneered. 'Kneel, Anomander, Son of Darkness. *Kneel before this Hostage.*'

When he lowered himself to one knee, a sudden laugh burst from her. Disbelief. Shock. Delight. 'I proclaim my beloved son Knight of Darkness – you, I cast out! You're kneeling! Now,' and she leaned forward, *'grovel.'*

'Release Silanah, Highness, or there can be no Knight of Darkness.'

'Why not?'

'Because you're destroying Kharkanas!'

She stabbed a finger at him. 'As you did! When you made Mother Dark turn away! But don't you see? I can save you from all that! I can do it first!' She bared her teeth at him. '*Now* who is the hostage?'

He rose then, and she shrank back in the throne. She had gone too far – she could see it in his eyes. His trembling hands. He seemed to be struggling to speak.

'Just tell me,' Sandalath whispered. 'The truth. Where is my son?'

It was as if the question delivered a mortal wound. Anomander Rake staggered to one side, like a broken man. Shaking his head, he sank down, one hand groping for the edge of the dais.

And she knew then. She had won.

Back ten paces.

In the space left by their retreat from the breach, bodies made a floor of trampled, bloody flesh, shattered spears, broken swords. Here and there, limbs moved, hands reaching, feet kicking, legs twitching. Mouths in smeared faces opened like holes into the Abyss, eyes staring out from places of horror, pain, or fading resignation.

Sharl, who had failed in keeping her brothers alive, and who had, thus far, failed in joining them, stood beside Captain Brevity. She held a sword, the point dug into a corpse under her feet, and knew she would not be able to lift it, not again. There was nothing left, nothing but raging agony in her joints, her muscles, her spine. Thirst clawed at her throat, and every desperate breath she drew deep into her lungs was foul with the stench of the dead and the dying.

'Stiffen up, lads and lasses,' growled Brevity. 'They're suspicious, is my guess. Not sure. But count on this: they're coming.'

Someone moved past them then, burly, heavy in armour. Sergeant Cellows, the last of the prince's own soldiers.

He made his way to position himself on Yedan Derryg's left, drawing round and setting his shield, readying the heavy-bladed sword in his other hand. For some reason, his arrival, so solemn, so solitary, chilled Sharl to the core. She looked to her left and saw Yan Tovis. Standing, watching, a queen covered in blood – and how much of it belonged to her own subjects? But no, the question no longer mattered. Nor the fact that she had led them to this end.

'We all end somewhere,' she whispered.

Brevity heard and glanced over, spat blood, and then said, 'That's the truth of it, all right. The only truth there is.'

Sharl nodded, and somehow raised once more the sword in her hand. 'I am ready, Captain.'

'We all are, soldier.'

Behind them Sharl heard a low murmuring, the words *we all end somewhere* rippling out, taking hold, and soldiers slowly straightened, drawing up their weapons.

When the words followed the curve of waiting soldiers and at last reached Yan Tovis, Sharl saw her flinch as if struck, and she turned to look upon her people, saw them straightening, readying, saw the look on their battle-aged faces.

Their queen stepped back, then, into the gap. One stride, and then another, and all at once all eyes were upon her. Lightfall streamed down behind her. It could have been a thing of beauty and wonder. It could have been something other than a manifestation of terror and grief. But it was as if it ceased to exist for Yan Tovis as she scanned the faces, as she fixed her eyes upon the last thousand subjects of her realm.

And then, with even her brother looking on, the queen knelt. Not to the First Shore – not to this horror – but to her people.

In the swirling wound eight paces behind her, a row of spear points lashed out, scything empty air. And then, pushing through the miasma, fully armoured soldiers.

'Shit,' muttered Brevity. 'That's heavy infantry.'

Yan Tovis rose, swung to face her ancient foe. For a moment she seemed deaf to her soldiers, shouting for her to rejoin the line. For a moment, Sharl thought she might instead advance to meet them, and she saw the flank behind bristling up, as if to rush to join her – one last, suicidal rush. To die beside their queen. And oh, how Sharl longed to join them.

Then Yan Tovis turned her back on the enemy, re-joined her soldiers.

The first row of Liosan stepped clear of the wound, another following. They were shouting something, those Liosan, shouting in triumph a single word – but Sharl could not make it out.

Yedan Derryg's voice rang out above their cries. 'All lines! Advance five!'

And there, four rows back of the Liosan front rank, a knot of officers, a single figure among them waving his sword – as if to cut down his own people – and they pressed back on all sides. And there, off to the right, another widening swirl of humanity, making space – and there, upon the left, the same. Sharl stared, unable to understand what they were—

The three isolated warriors then dissolved into blinding white light – and the light burgeoned, and inside that light, massive, scaled shapes, taking form. The flash of blazing eyes. Wings snapping out like galley sails.

And the dragon at the centre then rose into the air.

We all end somewhere.
We all end here.

As the centre ranks rose up to collide with the Liosan front line, Yedan Derryg, with Sergeant Cellows at his side, pushed forward. Five lines between him and that veering dragon. His only obstacle. But these were the elites, heavily armoured, perfectly disciplined.

He saw the other two Soletaken, one on each side, but there was nothing he could do about them. Not yet.

The Hust sword howled as he slammed into the front line. The blade was gorged on draconic blood. It had drunk deep the red wine of Hounds' blood. It had bathed in the life-ends of a thousand Liosan soldiers. Now it shook off the chains of constraint.

So swiftly did it slash that Yedan almost lost his grip. He grunted to see the soldier before him cut through, shield, sword, chain, flesh and bone, diagonally down his torso, gore exploding out to the sides. A back swing split open the chests of the man to either side. Like a cestus, Yedan and the soldiers closest to him drove into the Liosan ranks.

The Hust sword spun, lashed out in blurs, blood sprayed. Yedan was tugged after it, stumbling, at times almost lifted from his feet as the weapon shrieked its glee, slaughtering all that dared stand before it.

All at once, there was no one between him and the Soletaken. The wreaths of white fire were pouring off the shining scales, the solid bulk of the dragon rising to fill Yedan Derryg's vision.

Shit. Miscalculated. It's going to get clear. Sister – I'm sorry. I'm too late.

The head lunged.

He leapt.

The sword sank deep into the dragon's chest. The creature roared in shock and pain, and then the wings hammered at its sides, scattering Liosan and Shake alike, and the Soletaken lifted into the air.

Hanging from his sword, Yedan scrambled, fought his way on to the dragon's shoulders. He tore his weapon free. Cut two-handed into its neck.

Twenty reaches above the melee, the creature pitched, canted hard and slammed into Lightfall.

The concussion thundered.

Yedan Derryg slid down over the dragon's right shoulder, down between it and Lightfall.

The dragon's neck bowed and the jaws plunged down to engulf him.

As they closed, the Hust sword burst from the top of the dragon's snout. Wings smashing the wall of light, the giant reptile reared its head back, Yedan tumbling free, still gripping the sword.

He was caught by the talons of the Soletaken's left foot, the massive claws convulsively clenching. Blood sprayed from the body it held.

Again the dragon careered into Lightfall, and this time a wing collapsed under the impact. Twisting, pitching head first, the creature slid downward. Slammed into the ground.

Yedan Derryg was thrown clear, his body a shattered mess, and where he fell, he did not move. At his side, the Hust sword howled its rage.

The journey through the forest by Rake's last three Soletaken – Korlat, Prazek Goul and Dathenar Fandoris – had been as savage as fighting a riptide. Silanah was among the most ancient of all living Eleint. Her will tore at them, drove them to their knees again and again. Silanah called upon them, called them by name, sought her own summoning. Still, they managed to resist, but Korlat knew that to shift into draconic form would simply make it worse, the blood of the Eleint awakening in each of them, chaos unfurling in their souls like the deadliest flower. At the same time, she knew that there were Soletaken at the First Shore. She could feel them. And what could the Shake do against such creatures?

Only die.

The Liosan Soletaken would be able to resist Silanah – at least for a time – or perhaps indeed they could even defy her, if their own Storm, when it broke upon this world, was strong enough. And she feared it would be. *This is not the taste of one or two Soletaken. No – gods, how many are there?*

'Korlat!' gasped Dathenar.

'I know. But we have no choice, do we?'

Prazek spat behind her and said. 'Better to die in Kharkanas than anywhere else.'

Korlat agreed.

As they reached the rise, they saw a frenzied battle at the wound in Lightfall, and the Liosan soldiers now pouring from that breach vastly outnumbered the defenders. They saw a man do battle with a dragon rising skyward. Saw two Liosan warriors veering to join their winged kin.

They did not hesitate. Darkness bloomed, erupted like black smoke under water, and three black dragons rose above the strand.

As they closed, eight more Liosan veered, and the air filled with the roars of dragons.

Yan Tovis dragged herself over corpses, trying to reach her brother's horrifyingly motionless form. The two witches were taking the last from her – she felt each sorcerous wave they lashed into the flanking dragons, heard the Soletaken screaming in pain and outrage, and knew that all of it was *not enough*.

But they were stealing from her this one last act – this journey of love and grief – and the unfairness of that howled in her heart.

Soldiers fought around her, sought to protect their fallen queen. Bodies fell to either side. It seemed that the Liosan were now everywhere – the Shake and Letherii lines had buckled, companies driven apart, hacked at from all sides.

And still he seemed a thousand leagues away.

Draconic sorcery detonated. The bed of bodies beneath her lifted as one, and then fell back with a sound like a drum. And Yan Tovis felt a sudden absence. *Skwish. She's dead.*

A trickle of strength returned to her, and she resumed pulling herself along.

Her bones were rattling to some distant sound – or was it inside her? *Yes, inside, yet still . . . distant. As far away as hope. And that is a shore I will never reach.* It shook through her. Shook even the corpses beneath her, and those to the sides.

Two stood to either side of her, two of her own, the last two, fighting.

She did not have to look to know who they were. The love filling all the empty spaces inside her now could take them in, like flavours. Brevity, who imagined that her friend Pithy was still with her, still fighting for the dignity they had always wanted, the dignity they'd once thought they could cheat and steal their way to find. Sharl – sweet, young, ancient Sharl, who knew nothing of fighting, who knew only that she had failed to save her brothers, and would not fail again.

There were all kinds of love, and, with wonder, she realized that she now knew them all.

Before her, five simple paces away – could she walk – lay the body of her brother.

Another concussion.

Pully. I am sorry.

There is no glory in dying young, unless you were old first.

No witches now to steal her strength. She lifted herself up, on to her hands and knees, and made for Yedan. As she drew up alongside, she saw the hand nearer her move.

Pulled herself up, knelt at his side, looked down into his face, the only part of him that had not been chewed and crushed beyond recognition. She saw his lips moving, leaned close.

'Beloved brother,' she whispered, 'it is Yan.'

'I see it,' he whispered.

'What do you see?'

'I see it. Yan. It's there, right before me.' His broken lips smiled.
'Yedan?'
'At last,' he sighed, 'I am . . . home.'

Their queen and the body of their prince, they were now an island upon the sea, and the last of them gathered round, to hold its ever shrinking shoreline. And, above it all, three black dragons warred with ten white dragons, and then there were only two against ten.

Surrounding the island and its shore, the Liosan pushed in on waves of steel and fury. Theirs was the hunger of the ocean, and that was a hunger without end.

But the ground trembled. It shivered. And the source of that steady, drumming thunder was coming ever closer.

Leaning like a drunk on the dais, Nimander struggled for a way through this. It would seem that he had to veer, and soon, and then he would have to somehow resist Silanah's will. He would have to fight her, try to kill her. But he knew he would fail. She would send his own kin against him, and the horror of the blood that would then spill was too much to bear.

Sandalath Drukorlat still sat on the throne, muttering under her breath. *I could kill her. After all, do I not already have Tiste Andii blood on my hands? And then, should we by some miracle prevail here, why, a usurper could take this throne. That, too, has been done before.*

And the new kingdom of Kharkanas shall be born in the ashes of murder. Yes, I could do that. But look upon her, Nimander – she does not even remember you. In her madness, I am my father. Sandalath, do you truly not remember? Withal and I – we lied to you. A terrible accident, the suicide that never was.

Shall I lie to you again?

No, I cannot.

There were ghosts in this palace – in this very room. He had never before felt such palpable presence, as if countless ages had awakened to this moment. As if all of the fallen had returned, to witness the end of every dream.

'Apsal'ara,' he whispered. 'I need you.'

Came an answering whisper, *'It's not her you need.'*

Smiling down on the broken form of Anomander Rake, Sandalath slowly drew her dagger. *But he doesn't have the sword. He hasn't done what he vowed to do. How can I kill him now?*

Look at him, though! This . . . thing. Against mighty Draconus? Impossible. I suspected it, back on the island. That broken window, the

*body lying on the cobbles. How few his followers then, how pathetic
his lack of control.*

A new voice spoke. 'Orfantal will die if you do not release Silanah.'

Sandalath looked up. Her eyes widened. A ghost stood before her,
where Anomander – in that bold, deceitful moment of bluster – had
been a moment earlier. A woman, young, and she knew her – *no, I do
not. I will not. I refuse. How can my thoughts summon?*

Silanah? Who was speaking of her? Was it me?

To the ghost standing before her, she growled, 'I do not know you.'

Smiling, the ghost said, 'But you do. You knew me all too well, as I
recall. I am Phaed. My brother,' and she gestured down to Anomander,
'is of such honour that he would rather give you your end, here and
now, than hurt you further. Nor will he threaten you with what he
cannot do in any case – no matter what the cost – to his people, to those
doomed humans upon the First Shore.'

'I only want my son,' Sandalath whispered. 'He took him, and I want
him back!'

'This is not Anomander Rake,' Phaed said. 'This is his son. How can
you not remember, Sandalath Drukorlat? Upon the islands, across the
vast seas – you took us in, as if we were your children. Now Nimander
is here, begging you to release Silanah – to end the destruction of
Kharkanas.'

Sandalath sneered. 'I can taste lies – they fill this room. Ten thousand
lies built this keep, stone by stone. Remember what Gallan said? "At
the roots of every great empire you will find ten thousand lies." But he
was not blind then, was he? I never trusted you, Phaed.'

'But you trusted Nimander.'

She blinked. *Nimander?* 'You are right – he does not lie. What a
damned fool, just like his father, and see where it has got us.'

'Your son Orfantal will die, Sandalath Drukorlat, unless you release
Silanah.'

'Orfantal! Bring him to me.'

'I will, once you relinquish the throne and all the power it grants you.
Once you free Silanah from your will.'

She licked her lips, studied the ghost's strangely flat eyes. *I remember
those eyes, the knowing in them. Knowing that I knew the truth of her.
Phaed. Venal, conscienceless.* 'You are the liar among us!'

Phaed cocked her head, smiled. 'I never liked you, it's true. But I
never lied to you. Now, do you want to see your son or not? This is
what I offer.'

She stared at the ghost, and then looked down at Anoman— no,
Nimander. 'You have never lied to me, Nimander. Does your sister
speak true?'

'Do not ask *him*!' Phaed snapped. 'This negotiation is between you

569

and me. Sandalath, you of all people should understand what is going on here. You know the way of Hostages.'

'Orfantal is not a Hostage!'

'Events have changed things – there are new powers here.'

'That is not fair!'

Phaed's laugh stabbed like a knife. 'The Hostage whimpers at the unfairness of it all.'

'Don't.'

'Oh, shall I show some mercy, then?'

'Stop it!'

'Very well,' said Phaed, 'I will give you this . . . gift. Retire to the chamber in the tower, Sandalath. You know the one. Lock the door from within, so that no one else may enter. Remain there. Await your son. And when he comes, why, then you can unlock your door. To take him into your arms.'

My room. My sweet, perfect room. If I wait there. If I hide there, everything will be all right. Tears streamed down Sandalath's face. 'Yes,' she whispered. 'My son.'

'Will you yield the throne?' Phaed asked. 'It must be now. Once you have done that, then you can go to your room, Sandalath. Where you will be safe, and where you can wait for him.'

There was no end, it seemed, to what could spill down from her eyes. She rose, the dagger falling to clatter on the stones. *My room, yes. It's safe there. I have the lock, there at the door. The lock, to keep me safe.*

Silanah – hear me. I will see my son! They will bring him to me! But first, I must release you. Eleint, you are free.

And soon, we will all be free. All of us hostages. We will finally be free.

After Sandalath Drukorlat, making sounds like an excited child, had rushed from the throne room, Nimander looked across at the ghost of Phaed.

Who stared back, expressionless. 'I vowed to haunt you. My brother. My killer. To torment you for the rest of your days. Instead, you deliver me . . . home.'

His eyes narrowed on her, suspicious – as he knew he would always be, with this one.

'Join your kin, Nimander. There is little time.'

'What of you?' he demanded.

Phaed seemed to soften before his eyes. 'A mother will sit in a tower, awaiting her son. She will keep the door locked. She will wait for the sound of boots upon the stairs. I go to keep her company.'

'Phaed.'

The ghost smiled. 'Shall we call this penance, brother?'

Blows rang, skittered off his armour, and beneath the banded ribbons of iron, the scales and the chain, his flesh was bruised, split and crushed. Withal swung his mace, even as a spear point gouged a score above the rim of his helm, twisting his head round. He felt a shield shatter beneath his attacking blow, and someone cried out in pain. Half blinded – blood was now streaming down the inside of his helm, clouding the vision of his left eye – he pushed forward to finish the Liosan.

Instead, he was shield-bashed from the side. Stumbling, tripping in a tangle of dead limbs, Withal fell. *Now I'm in trouble.*

A Liosan loomed over him, thrust down with his sword.

A strange black flash, blocking the blow – a blur, and the Liosan howled in agony, toppling back.

Crouching now over Withal, a half-naked woman, her muscles sheathed in sweat, an obsidian knife in one hand, dripping blood. She leaned close, her face pressing against the visor's bars.

'Thief!'

'What? I – what?'

'My armour! Your stole it!'

'I didn't know—'

'But you stood long – and there's more standing ahead, so get off your arse!'

She grasped him by the collar of his hauberk, and with one hand pulled him to his feet. Withal staggered for balance. Brought his shield round and readied the mace.

They were surrounded. Fighting to the last.

Overhead, two black dragons – *where in Hood's name did they come from?* – were at the centre of a storm of white- and gold-hued dragons. They were torn, shredded, hissing like gutted cats, lashing out in fury even as they were being driven down, and down.

The half-naked woman fought beside him with serpentine grace, her ridiculous obsidian knives whispering out like black tongues, returning wet with blood.

Confusion roared through Withal. This woman was a stranger – but that was impossible. Through the grille of his visor, he shouted, 'Who in Hood's name are you?'

Sharl sank back, knees folding, and suddenly she was lying on the ground. Figures crowded above her, twisted faces, thrusting spear shafts, feet fighting for purchase. She'd lost her sword, and blood was welling from somewhere below her rib cage. Her fumbling fingers probed, found a puncture that went in, and in.

'Ah, I am slain.'

'Can you breathe? Take a breath, woman! A deep breath, and that's an order!'

'C-captain?'

'You heard me!'

Sharl couldn't see her – somewhere behind her head – and her voice was barely recognizable, but who else would it be? Who else could it be? The ground trembled beneath her. Where was that trembling coming from? Like a thousand iron hearts. Beating. *Beating*. She drew fetid air into her lungs. Deeper, and deeper still. 'Captain! I can breathe!'

'Then you'll live! Get up! I want you with me – till the end, y'understand?'

Sharl tried to sit up, sank back in gasping pain. 'Been stabbed, Captain—'

'That's how y'get into this damned club! Stand up, damn you!'

She rolled on to her side – easier this way to draw up her legs, to make her way to her hands and knees.

Brevity was gasping out words. 'Girl without a friend . . . Nothing worse! Know what happens when a girl's got no friend?'

'No, Captain.'

'They get married!'

Sharl saw a sword nearby – a corpse was gripping it. She reached out and prised the weapon free. 'All right, Captain,' she said, 'I'll be your friend.'

'Till the end?'

'Till the end.'

'Swear it!'

'I swear! I swear!'

A hand reached under an armpit, lifted her up. 'Steady now, love. Let's go kill us some men.'

Zevgan Drouls had killed his debt-holder, and then the bastard's whole family. Then he had burned down the estate and with it all the records of the hundreds of families swindled into indebtedness by a man who thought he had the right to do whatever he damn well pleased with as many lives as he could chain and shackle. Zevgan had gone on to burn down the bank, and then the Hall of Records – well, only half of it, to be sure, but the right half.

Not that anyone could prove a single thing, because he was no fool. Still, enough suspicions ended up crowding his feet, enough to get him sent to the prison islands. Where he'd spent the last twenty-one years of his life – until the exodus. Until the march. Until this damned shore.

Too old to fight in the ranks, he now knelt on the berm overlooking the First Shore, alongside a dozen or so others in the Children's Guard. The lame, the ancient, the half blind and the half deaf. Behind them, huddled in the gloom of the forest edge, all the young 'uns and the pregnant women, and those too old or, of late, too badly wounded to do any more fighting – and there were lots of those.

Zevgan and his crew – and the ten or so other squads – waited to give their lives defending the children of the Shake and the Letherii islanders, the children and those others, but it was the children Zevgan kept thinking about.

Well, it wouldn't be much of a defence, he knew – they all knew it, in fact – but that didn't matter. *Why should it? Those are children behind us, looking up to us with those scared eyes. What else counts?*

Mixter Frill pushed up closer beside him, wiping at his nose. 'So you're confessing, are ya?'

'Y'heard me,' Zevgan replied. 'I did it. All of it. And I'd do it again, too. In fact, if they hadn't a stuck me on that island, I would never have stopped. I woulda burned down all the banks, all the Halls of Records, all the fat estates with their fat lenders and their fat wives and husbands and fat whatevers.'

'You murdered innocents, Zev, is what you did. They shoulda hung you.'

'Hung. Tortured, turned me inside out, roasted my balls and diced up my cock, aye, Mix. Errant knows, messing with how things are made up for the people in power – why, there's no more heinous crime than that, and they'd be the first to tell you, too.'

'Look at 'em dying out there, Zev.'

'I'm looking, Mix.'

'And we're next.'

'We're next, aye. And that's why I'm confessing. Y'see, it's my last laugh. At 'em all, right? Ain't strangled, ain't inside out, ain't ball-roasted, ain't dick-diced.'

Mix said something but with all the noise Zev couldn't make it out. He twisted to ask but then he saw, on all sides, figures rushing past. And there were swords, and that raging forest behind them, with all that deafening noise that had been getting closer and closer, and now was here.

Mix was shouting, but Zev just stared.

Skin black as ink. Tall buggers, all manner of weapons out, hammering the rims of shields, and the look in their faces – as they threaded through the camp where all the children huddled and stared, where the pregnant women flinched and shied – the look on their faces – *I know that look. I saw it in the mirror, I saw it in the mirror.*

The night I took 'em all down.

The two black dragons would not last much longer – it was a wonder they still lived, still fought on. Leaving them to his kin,

Kadagar Fant descended to fly low over the Shore. He could see the last of the hated enemy going down to the swords and spears of the elites – they were surrounded, those wretched murderers, stupidly protecting their leaders – the dead one and the woman kneeling at his side.

Soon he would land. He would semble. Kadagar wanted to be there when that woman was the only one left. He wanted to cut her head off with his own hands. Was she the queen? Of all Kharkanas? He believed she was. He had to acknowledge her bravery – to come down to the First Shore, to fight alongside her people.

But not all bravery was worthy of reward, or even acknowledgement, and the only reward he intended for this woman was a quick death. *But a squalid one. Maybe I'll just choke the life from her.*

This realm was thick with smoke, distant forests alight, and Kadagar wondered if the enemy sought to deny him the throne by perniciously burning the city to the ground. He could easily imagine such perfidy from this sort. *But I will rebuild. And I will loose the light upon this realm. Scour away the darkness, the infernal shadows. Something new will be born of this. An age of peace. Blessed peace!*

He saw one of the black dragons spin past, pursued by two of his kin. That one, he knew, was moments from death.

Aparal, you should never have gone through first. You knew he would be waiting for you. But his brother, his most loyal servant and friend, was now sembled, a lone, motionless body lying at the foot of Lightfall. From this height, pathetically small, insignificant. And this was improper – he would raise a monument to Aparal's sacrifice, to the glory of his slaying the wielder of the Hust sword. There, at the base of Lightfall itself, he would—

Black as midnight, a tide was flooding out from the forest edge below. Kadagar stared in horror as it rushed across the strand and slammed into his Liosan legions.

Tiste Andii!

He wheeled, crooked his wings, awakening the sorcery within him, and sped down towards his hated foes. *I will kill them. I will kill them all!*

Something spun past him in a welter of blood and gore – one of his kin – torn to shreds. Kadagar screamed, twisted his neck and glared upward.

To see a red dragon – a true Eleint, twice the size of his kin – close upon a brother Soletaken. Fire poured from it in a savage wave, struck the white dragon. The body exploded in a fireball, torn chunks of meat spinning away trailing smoke. And now, more black dragons sailed down from the sky.

He saw two descend on the kin that had been pursuing the lone dragon, saw them crash down on them in a deluge of fangs and claws.

The lone hunter below them banked then, and, wings thundering the air, rose towards Kadagar.

Against him, she would not last. Too wounded, too weakened – he would destroy her quickly, and then return to aid his kin. *This cannot end this way! It must not!*

Like a fist of stone, something hammered down on him. He shrieked in agony and rage as enormous talons tore ragged furrows deep across his back. Jaws snapped down, crushed one of his wings. Helpless, Kadagar plunged earthward.

He struck the strand in a shower of crushed white bone, skidding and then rolling, slamming up against the unyielding wall of Lightfall. The sand pelted down, filling his ragged wounds. Far overhead, the death cries of his kin. A thousand paces away, the battle at the breach. He was alone, hurt, broken.

Kadagar sembled. Dragged himself into a sitting position, setting his back to Lightfall, and watched the black dragon that had been rising to meet him now landing thirty paces away, shedding blood like rain.

High overhead, the red Eleint killed another of his Soletaken kin – taking hold of it like a small bird, ripping its limbs off, crushing its skull in its massive jaws.

Before him, she had sembled, and now she walked towards him.

Kadagar closed his eyes. *My people. My people.* The sound of her boots. He looked up. She had a knife in one hand.

'My people,' he said.

She showed him a red smile. 'Your people.'

He stared up at her.

'Give me your name, Liosan.'

'I am Kadagar Fant, Lord of Light.'

'Lord of Light.'

'I call upon the ancient custom of Hostage.'

'We have no need of hostages. Your army is destroyed, Lord.'

'I will speak for the Liosan. There shall be peace.'

The woman nodded. 'Yes, there shall be peace. Lord Kadagar Fant, on behalf of the Tiste Andii, *welcome to Darkness.*' The knife flashed up towards his eye.

A sudden sting of pain and then . . .

Korlat stared down at the dead man, at her knife, pushed to the hilt in his right eye socket, and then she stepped back, turned away.

At the breach, her Tiste Andii kin were slaughtering the last of the Liosan. They had driven them back to the wound itself, and when the enemy retreated into the miasma she saw ranks of Andii follow. There would be an end to this. *An end.*

Overhead, Nimander and his kin were descending, along with Prazek. Dathenar had fallen earlier. Korlat had felt her death cry and its howl still echoed in her soul. Silanah remained high overhead, wheeling like a huntress. Not one of the Liosan Soletaken remained.

She looked down the strand, eyes narrowing at the motley remnants of the Shake – three, four hundred at the most – now hunched over, slumping, some falling, in a ragged circle surrounding a kneeling figure. Her gaze drifted momentarily from this company of survivors, travelled over the solid carpet of bodies spreading out on all sides. And, slowly, the magnitude of the slaughter, here upon the First Shore, found resolution.

Gods below.

She set out for those survivors. A woman dripping blood from too many wounds to count, and beneath her feet, in a steady drizzle, crimson rain.

Impossibly, the sound was gone, and the silence now surrounding them had thickened. Withal knelt, bent over, struggling to find his breath, but some blow had broken ribs, and he was afraid to move, afraid to inhale too deeply.

The half-naked woman settled down beside him, tortured him by leaning against him. 'Now that was a fight, thief. And for you, maybe not over.'

He was having trouble with his eyes – the blood was drying, seeking to close them up. 'Not over?'

'If you don't give that armour back, I will have to kill you.'

He reached up, dragged his helm free and let it tumble from his hands. 'It's yours. I never want to see it again.'

'Ill words,' she chided. 'It saved your life a dozen times this day.'

She was right in that. Still. 'I don't care.'

'Look up, man. It's the least you can do.'

But that was too hard. 'No. You did not see them here from the beginning. You did not see them die. How long have they been fighting? Weeks? Months? For ever?'

'I can see the truth of that.'

'They weren't soldiers—'

'I beg to differ.'

'*They weren't soldiers!*'

'Look up, old man. In the name of the Fallen, look up.'

And so he did.

He and the Shake, the Letherii, the Queen Yan Tovis, Twilight –

these few hundred – were surrounded once more. But this time those facing them were Tiste Andii, in their thousands.

And not one was standing.

Instead, they knelt, heads bowed.

Withal twisted round, made to rise. 'I'm not the one needs to see this—'

But the woman beside him caught his arm, forcibly pulled him back down. 'No,' she said, like him looking across to Yan Tovis – who still knelt over the body of her brother, and who still held shut her eyes, as if she could hold back all the truths before her. 'Not yet.'

He saw Sergeant Cellows sitting near the queen, the Hust sword balanced across his thighs. He too seemed unable to look up, to see anything beyond his inner grief.

And all the others, blind to all that surrounded them. *Oh, will not one of you look up? Look up and see those who have witnessed all that you have done? See how they honour you . . . but no, they are past such things now. Past them.*

A group of Tiste Andii approached from up the strand. Something familiar there – Withal's eyes narrowed, and then he hissed a curse and climbed to his feet. Nimander. Skintick. Desra. Nenanda. But these were not the frail creatures he had once known – *if they ever were what I thought they were. If it was all hidden away back then, it is hidden no more. But . . . Aranatha? Kedeviss?*

'Withal,' said Nimander, his voice hoarse, almost broken.

'You found your people,' Withal said.

The head cocked. 'And you yours.'

But that notion hurt him deep inside, and he would not consider it. Shaking his head, he said, 'The Shake and the Letherii islanders, Nimander – see what they have done.'

'They held the First Shore.'

And Withal now understood that hoarseness, all the broken edges of Nimander's voice. Tears were streaming down his cheeks. For all that he had seen – that he must have seen, for surely he numbered among the black dragons – of this strand, this battle.

Nimander turned as another Tiste Andii staggered close. A woman, half her clothes torn away, her flesh flensed and gashed. 'Korlat. She did what was needed. She . . . saw reason. Will you go to your mother now?'

'I will not.'

Withal saw Nimander's sudden frown. 'She sits upon the throne of Kharkanas, Korlat. She must be made to know that her daughter has returned to her.'

Korlat's eyes shifted slowly, fixed upon the kneeling form of Yan Tovis. 'Her son was the only child that ever mattered to my mother,

Nimander. And I failed to protect him. She set that one charge upon me. To protect her son.'

'But you are her daughter!'

Korlat raised her voice, 'Twlight, queen of the Shake! Look upon me.'

Slowly, Yan Tovis lifted her gaze.

Korlat spoke. 'I have no place in the palace of my mother, the queen of Kharkanas. In ancient times, Highness, there stood at your side a Sister of Night. Will you take me – will you take Korlat, daughter of Sandalath Drukorlat?'

Yan Tovis frowned. Her gaze wandered from the Tiste Andii woman standing before her, wandered out to the kneeling Tiste Andii, and then, at last, to the huddle of her own people, her so few survivors. And then, as if borne by an impossible strength, she climbed to her feet. Brushed feebly at the sand clinging to her bloody clothes. Straightened. 'Korlat, daughter of Sandalath Drukorlat, the Sister of Night in the House of the Shake is not for one of the pure blood—'

'Forgive me, Queen, but my blood is not pure.'

Yan Tovis paused, and then continued, 'The blood of the Eleint—'

'Queen, *my blood is not pure.*'

Withal suddenly comprehended Korlat's meaning. Cold dread curled in his chest. *No, Korlat will have no place in the palace of Queen Sandalath Drukorlat.* And how was it, after all that had happened, here on the First Shore, that his heart could still break?

One more time.

Oh . . . Sand.

Yan Tovis spoke. 'Korlat, Daughter of Sandalath Drukorlat, I welcome you into the House of the Shake. Sister of Night, come to me.'

One more time.

'What are you doing?' Sharl asked. She was lying down on the ground again, with no memory of how she'd got there.

'Pluggin' the hole in your gut,' Brevity said.

'Am I going to die?'

'Not a chance. You're my new best friend, remember? Speaking of which, what's your name?'

Sharl tried to lift herself up, but there was no strength left in her. She had never felt so weak. All she wanted to do was close her eyes. And sleep.

Someone was shaking her. 'Don't! *Don't you leave me alone!*'

Her body felt chained down, and she wanted free of it. *I never knew how to fight.*

'No! I can't bear this, don't you understand? I can't bear to see you die!'

I'm sorry. I wasn't brave enough for any of this. My brothers, they died years ago, you see. It was only my stubbornness, my guilt – I couldn't let them go. I brought them with me. And those two boys I found, they didn't mind the new names I gave them. Oruth. Casel.

I couldn't stop them dying. It was hunger, that's all. When you have no land, no way through, when they just step over you in the street. I did my best. We were not good enough – they said so, that look in their eyes, stepping over us – we just weren't good enough. Not clever enough, not brave enough.

Casel was four when he died. We left him in the alley behind Skadan's. I found a bit of sacking. I put it over his eyes. Oruth asked why and I said it was what they did at funerals. They did things to the body. But why? he asked. I said I didn't know. When Oruth died a month later, I found another piece of cloth. I put it over his eyes. Another alley, another funeral.

They were so little.

Someone was crying. A sound of terrible, soul-crushing anguish. But she herself was done with that. *Let the chains fall away. And for my eyes, a cloth.*

It's what they do.

With the Sister of Cold Nights standing close, Yan Tovis sat once more beside the body of her brother. She looked down on his face, wondering what seemed so different about it now, wondering what details had now arrived, here in death, that made it seem so peaceful.

And then she saw. The muscles of his jaw were no longer taut, bunched by that incessant clench. And suddenly he seemed young, younger than she'd ever seen him before.

Yedan Derryg, you are beautiful.

From all sides, she now heard, there rose a keening sound. Her Shake and her Letherii were now mourning for their fallen prince. She let the sound close round her like a shroud.

Welcome home then, brother.

CHAPTER TWENTY

'We stood watching the bodies tumbling and rolling down the broad steps. Half the city was on fire and out in the farmholdings terrified slaves were dragging the diseased carcasses into enormous heaps while lamplighters wearing scarves poured oil and set alight the mountains of putrid flesh, until the black columns marched like demons across the land.

'In the canals the corpses were so thick we saw a filthy boy eschew the bridge for a wild scramble, but he only made it halfway before falling in, and the last we saw of him was a small hand waving desperately at the sky, before it went down.

'Most of the malformed and wizened babies had already been put to death, as much an act of mercy as any kind of misplaced shame, though there was plenty about which we rightly should be ashamed, and who would dare argue that? The animals were gone, the skies were empty of life, the waters were poisoned, and where paradise had once beckoned now desolation ruled, and it was all by our own righteous will.

'The last pair of politicians fell with hands around each other's throat, trailed by frantic toadies and professional apologists looking for a way out, though none existed, and soon they too choked on their own shit.

'As for us, well, we leaned our bloodied pikes against the plinth of the toppled monument facing those broad steps, sat down in the wreckage, and discussed the weather.'

Sadakar's Account
The Fall of Inderas

THE SUN HAD SET. THE BOY, AWAKE AT LAST, TOTTERED INTO THE Khundryl camp. He held his arms as if cradling something. He heard the woman's cries – it was impossible not to – and all

580

the Khundryl had gathered outside a tent, even as the rest of the army pushed itself upright like a beast more dead than alive, to begin another night of marching. He stood, listening. There was the smell of blood in the air.

Warleader Gall could hear his wife's labour pains. The sound filled him with horror. Could there be anything crueller than this? *To deliver a child into this world. By the Fall of Coltaine, have we not shed enough tears? Do we not bear their scars as proof?*

He sought to roll over in his furs, wanting none of this, but he could not move. As if his body had died this day. And he but crouched inside it. *Born to a dying mother. Who gathers round her now? Shelemasa. The last of the surviving shoulder-women. But there are no daughters. No sons with their wives. And there is not me, and with this child, this last child, for the first time I will not witness my wife giving birth.*

A knife pressed against his cheek. Jastara's voice hissed in his ear. 'If you do not go to her now, Gall, I will kill you myself.'

I cannot.

'For the coward you are, I will kill you. Do you hear me, Gall? I will make your screams drown out the world – even your wife's cries – or do you forget? *I am Semk.* This whole night – I will make it your eternal torment. You will beg for release, and I shall deny it!'

'Then do it, woman.'

'Does not the father kneel before the mother? In the time of birth? Does he not bow to the strength he himself does not possess? Does he not look into the eyes of the woman he loves, only to see a power strange and terrible – how it does not even see him, how it looks past – or no, how it looks *within? Does not a man need to be humbled?* Tell me, Gall, that you refuse to see that again – one final time in your life! Witness it!'

He blinked up at her. The knife point had dug deep, now grazing the bone of his cheek. He felt the blood running down to drip from the line of his jaw, the rim of his ear. 'The child is not mine,' he whispered.

'But it is. You fool, can't you see that? It will be the last Khundryl child! The last of the Burned Tears! You are Warleader Gall. It shall be born, and it shall look up into your face! *How dare you deny it that?*'

His breath was coming in gasps. *Do I have this left in me? Can I find the strength she demands of me? I . . . I have lost so much. So much.*

'This is our final night, Gall. Be our Warleader one last time. Be a husband. Be a father.'

A feeble, trembling hand fumbled with the furs covering him – he caught its movement, wondered at it. *My own? Yes.* Groaning, he struggled to sit up. The knife slipped away from his bloody cheek. He stared across at Jastara.

581

'My son . . . did well by you.'

Her eyes went wide. The colour left her face. She shrank back.

Gall pushed the furs away, reached for his weapon belt.

Summoned by a mother's cries, Badalle walked with her children. Saddic stumbled at her side. They were all closing in, like an indrawn breath.

The army was on the move. She had not believed these soldiers capable of rising yet again, to face the wastes ahead. She did not understand the source of strength they had found, the hard will in their eyes. Nor did she understand the way they looked at her and Saddic, and at the other children of the Snake. *As if we have been made holy. As if we have blessed them. When the truth is, it is they who have blessed us, because now we children will not have to die alone. We can die in the arms of men and women, men and women who for that moment become our fathers, our mothers.*

But, here in the Khundryl camp, a new child was about to come into the world.

When she arrived, the clawed warriors surrounded the birth-tent. She saw the corpse of a horse nearby and walked over to stand upon it.

Her children saw and they faced her, for they knew what was coming. Looking down, she met Saddic's shining eyes, and nodded.

Badalle awakened her voice. 'There is a mother this night.'

Warriors turned to her – they had no choice. She would make them listen, if only to give them the one thing that she had left. *Where it all began, so it ends. This is what I have, the only thing I ever had. Words.*

> 'There is a mother this night
> In the desert of dreams
> Beneath stars burned blind
> And soldiers must march where
> She leads them on the dead trail
> By this truth we are all bound
> Past the bodies left in the ditch
> She looks up where we fail
> And the sky is without end
> Follow her for the time of our birth
> Is a birth still to come
> There is a mother this night
> Who leads an army of children
> What will you ask of her
> When dawn awakens?

What will you demand of her
That she would give
If only she could?
There is a mother in the night
For a child lost in the dark'

Faces stared up at her, but she could make no sense of what she saw in them. And she could barely remember the words she had just spoken, but when she looked down at Saddic he nodded, to tell her that he had them, gathered like the toys in the sack dangling from one hand. *And when he is a man, he will write this down, all of this, and one night a stranger will find him, a poet, a singer of tales and a whisperer of songs.*

He will come in search of the fallen.

Like a newborn child, he will come in search of the fallen.

Saddic, you will not die here. Not for many, many years. How do I know this? And the woman who sleeps in the other room – who has loved you all her life – who is she? I would see that, if I could.

The mother's cries were softer now.

A man appeared. Walked through the silent crowd that parted from his path. Strode into the tent. Moments later, the mother inside was weeping, a sound that filled the world, that made Badalle's heart pound. And then, a small, pitiful wail.

Badalle sensed someone standing near her. She turned to see the Adjunct.

'Mother,' Badalle said, 'you should be leading your children.'

'Did you truly think I would miss this?'

Sighing, Badalle stepped down from the carcass of the horse. Reached out and took the Adjunct's hand.

She flinched as if stung, stared down at Badalle as if in shock. 'Don't do that,' she said.

'Mother, when will you let yourself feel?'

The Adjunct backed away, and moments later she was gone, lost in the crowd. If it made a path for her, Badalle couldn't see it.

'There is a mother this night,' she whispered, 'but to her the stars are blind.'

Koryk reached up and with one finger probed the line of his gums. When he withdrew the finger and looked down, he saw that it was smeared with blood. And that was a good joke. He was dying of thirst, just like all the others, but he'd been drinking his own blood for two days now. Wiping his finger clean on his thigh, he glanced over at the others.

Smiles was going to outlast them all. Women were stronger in ways no man dared admit. But then they had to be.

There was more blood running down the back of his nose. He could never quite manage to get his throat clear of it, no matter how many times he swallowed. *They had to be. A house of whores. I saw all I ever needed to see. Better than any tutor's endless droning on about history. Better than all the sages and prophets and agitators and rebels. Aye, those ones made fists and shook them, punching walls at the injustice of it all – but those walls, they were just the boxes they'd built for themselves, the boxes they lived in. They could never see past. And for most of them, that box was their whole world. They had no idea there was anything outside it.*

But the whores knew. Laughter for the moment, but take the stretch of years and it's all heartbreak. A woman gives up her body when she has nothing else left to give. She gives it up like a man his last copper. In a whore's eyes, you'll find everything that we do to each other. Everything.

He'd killed a fellow Bonehunter last night. A man trying to steal an empty cask. But he wasn't thinking about that. That damned face so twisted with need, or the sigh that left the man on that last breath. No, he was thinking about whores.

They could have schooled me in shame. But they didn't. And now, gods help me, I wish they had. Because then, he would understand what it was that forced his comrades back to their feet, that gave them the strength to pick up their gear one more time, knees bending under that weight. 'The Malazan soldier carries on his back all that's needed for war.' Dassem's credo for campaigns. *But what if there's no war? What if the enemy is inside you? And what if this burden doesn't belong to just you? What if it belongs to a whole damned world? What then?*

He'd listened to that captain, Ruthan Gudd. Lying dry-skinned in the unbearable heat, shivering beneath the last blanket he still owned, he heard about the boy and the girl and the toys spilled out on the ground between them. They'd forgotten the word. *Toys.* But even finding it again hadn't helped much, because they'd also forgotten how to *play*.

There's a secret few would guess. In a house of whores, the love for children is as close to sacred as a mortal can get. Too precious to mock, because every whore remembers the child she once was. Maybe they were sad memories, maybe they were bittersweet, but it was all before the last thing was given away. So they know. It's innocence that is sacred.

Nothing else.

On holy days, priests used to incite mobs to stone whores. No one would go out – he remembered all the women hiding in their rooms, speaking only in whispers lest some sound escape past the shutters, or out under the door. And he used to cower with them, terrified, and on those days he came to learn a hatred for priests, for temples, for all those hunters of the unworthy.

So, Crippled God. Fallen One. If I could kill you with my bare hands, I would. If I could kill every priest, and every god, and all those others stalking the streets with stones in their hands, I would. For the whores and all you took from them. And for the children.

He rose, shouldering his pack, his useless weapons, his useless armour, and faced the others, seeing that they too were ready, and when Tarr gestured they fell in one by one.

One more night. In the name of innocence.

Bottle's joints were on fire. Swollen and red, they made every step agony. Since when was a story enough to keep someone alive? No matter how heartbreaking, no matter how tragic. No matter how incensed the listener might become. The world lacked such simplicity. He'd never believed in speeches, was ever suspicious of that power to incite. Dreams could be voiced, desires could be uttered and then whispered back with fervour, but in the end most people eventually turned away and the crowd dispersed, and it was back home and getting on with living.

For all the boldness of believers on the front line, when the fires ebbed and no one was looking, it was time again to hide away. *But maybe we need that. Our little hole to climb down into. For some respite, where all the clamouring voices in your head can just die away. For blessed silence.*

And the ones who never get to that, who are so consumed they can find nowhere to hide, no place to rest, see what happens to them – see the fever in their eyes. They have made their lives torture, they have made the voice of their spirit one long, unbroken howl.

Fevered, aye. He was that, and more. 'We're the walking dead.' Fiddler's words, or someone's, anyway. Maybe Cuttle. No matter. The walking dead didn't feel pain like this. The walking dead didn't carry on their backs a thousand questions – questions with no answers.

His grandmother was now hobbling beside him. She didn't belong on this trail, in this desert, but there she was. And maybe she wasn't his grandmother at all, just some other wax witch twisting reeds in her arthritic hands, making dolls for the children in the village ahead. Gifts.

Charms. I remember you giving them away. Toys, you said, head bobbing. Free toys! And they all ran up to you, laughing.

But you wove protections into those dolls. Blessings, wards against illness. Nothing powerful, nothing to stop, say, a flash flood or an avalanche. But the father that lashed out with his fists. The uncle who slipped under the blankets in the dead of night. Those ones paid for what they did.

And the cuts that healed. The fevers that went away.

So, Grandmother, I'll walk this last walk. In your memory. Make me a doll, for this pain.

And take this child by the hand. And tell him again, how they will pay for what they did.

For years, before her nails were worn down to bloody shreds by all that she clawed at, Smiles had carried a dream, carried it around like a pearl inside a battered shell. Of a day in the future when she was a mother, and she'd given birth to twins. Two girls, squalling and hissing the way girls do. Playing on the beach under her watchful eye.

And then, in a dark, desolate season – with the skies grey and the seas swollen – the older ones would come to her. *'The fish are gone,'* they'd say. *'The spirits must be appeased. Choose one, Mother, and make of her the gift of our people, our gift to the thirsty waters.'* And she would walk away, calling her daughters back to the hut.

They were lowborn. The whole family. Her husband and the father of the twins was gone, maybe dead. It was all down to her. One child to be blessed, the other cursed. Yet arguments could be made as to who was which. She knew all about that.

A night of bitter winds, of fires doused by spray. And Smiles would set out, knives in hand. And she would kill every one of those elders – in all their hunger, in all their needs now that they were too old to fish, now that the only authority they still possessed came with their threats and warnings about angry, vengeful spirits. Aye, she would show them a vengeful, angry spirit, and the gifts it would make to the hungry sea would appease a thousand spirits of the deep.

Those kinds of dreams were honey on the tongue, heady with the juices of pleasure and satisfaction. She suspected such dreams hid in the hearts of everyone. Desires for justice, for redress, for a settling of the scales. And of course, that sour undercurrent of knowledge, that none of it was possible, that so much would rise in opposition, in self-preservation even, to crush that dream, its frail bones, its pattering heart – even that could not take away the sweet delight, the precious hope.

Wells for the coin, league-stones for the wreaths, barrows for the widdershins dance – the world was filled with magical places awaiting wishes. And empires raised lotteries, opened games, sought to lift high heroes among the common folk – *and everyone rushes up with their dreams. But stop. Look back. Gods, look around! If all we seek is an escape, what does that say about the world we live in? That village, that city, that life?*

586

We are desperate with our dreams. What – oh, what – does that say?

So those two children had forgotten about toys. She wasn't surprised. She remembered the day she sat with the last dolls she owned, but across from her sat no one. Where was her sister? They'd taken her. *But how can I play?*

'*Child, she was taken long ago. You cannot remember what you never had. Go out now and play with Skella.*'

'*Skella is highborn – she just orders me around.*'

'*That's the way it is, child. Best you get used to it.*'

In her dream, she saved murdering Skella for last.

Cuttle's brothers had been on the wall when it came down. He remembered his shock. Their city was falling. His brothers had just died defending it. Hengese soldiers were in the gap, clambering over the wreckage, coming out of the dust howling like demons.

Lessons, then. No wall was impenetrable. And the resolute in spirit could die as easily as could the coward. He would have liked to believe it wasn't like that, none of it – this whole mess. And that children could be left to play and not worry about the life ahead. To play the way he and his brothers had played, unmindful of the irony as they charged each other with wooden swords and fought to defend a midden behind the fishworks, dying one by one like heroes in some imagined last stand, giving their lives to save the swarming flies, the screeching gulls and the heaps of shells. Where knelt a helpless maiden, or some such thing.

Maiden, stolen crown, the jewelled eye of a goddess. They wove fine stories around their deeds, didn't they? In those long winters when it seemed that all the grey, sickly sky wanted to do was collapse down on the whole city, crush it for ever, they lived and died their shining epics.

A backside kick sent him out from childhood. He'd not forgotten those games, however. They lived with him and would until this – his last damned day. But not for the obvious reasons. Nostalgia was like a disease, one that crept in and stole the colour from the world and the time you lived in. Made for bitter people. Dangerous people, when they wanted back what never was. *And it wasn't even our innocence back then – we never felt innocent.* They spent day after day living older than their years, after all. And no, not even the ties of family blood, those so-familiar faces he grew up alongside, and all the safety and protection and comfort they offered. No, those games stayed with him because of something else, something he now understood to have been with him, undying, since those days.

Maiden, stolen crown, the jewelled eye of a god. Die for a reason.

That's all. Cuttle, you're the last brother left who can do this. The others didn't make it, not to this epic's end. So you carry them now, here on your back, those boys with their flushed faces, you carry them. You're carrying them right past their useless deaths on that wall in a war that meant nothing. Take them now to where they need to go.

We're going to die for a reason. That's not too much to ask, is it?

You should've seen our last stands. They were something.

Corabb was thinking about Leoman of the Flails. Not that he wanted to, but that evil, lying, murdering bastard was like a friend you didn't want any more who just kept showing up with a stupid grin on his ugly face. He was covered in dust, too, and he had no idea why and no, he didn't care either.

That's what came of believing in people. All sorts of people, with their foreheads all hot and burning and not a drink of water in sight. The man burned a city to the ground. Tried killing fifty million people, too, or however many were in Y'Ghatan when the army broke through and the temple caught fire and the priest's head was rolling around on the floor like a kick-ball with a face on it.

Corabb had wanted to be good. He'd grown up wanting that and nothing else. The world was bad and he wanted it to be good. Was that stupid? What was that his tutor used to say, after the man had cried himself dry and in his fists were tangled clumps of his own hair – what was his name again? Baldy? He'd look over at young Corabb and say, 'Good? You don't know the meaning of the word. In fact, you're about the worst student I have ever had the horror of entertaining.'

That was fine. He didn't entertain very good either, Corabb recalled, old Baldy. In fact, he was the most boring man in the whole village, which was why they voted him to teach the young ones, because the young ones were causing so much trouble getting underfoot and all the grown-ups decided they needed to be talked at until they turned into motionless lumps and their eyes fell out and rolled like marbles.

But those fists, holding clumps of hair. That was exciting. Birds could use that for nests. So maybe Baldy really *was* entertaining, when he did his red-face thing and bounced around on his stool.

Leoman was no better. It was just Corabb's luck, all these bad teachers.

He remembered the day he made his mother cry. The Gafan brothers had been teasing him, for what he couldn't recall, so he'd chased them down, softened them up a bit, and then used a rope he stole from a rag man to tie them all together, wrist to ankle, the four of them, their faces like burst gourds, and dragged them into the house. 'Ma! Cook these!'

Grunter Gafan had shown up to get his children back. Had the gall to threaten Corabb's mother, and since Canarab his father was still off in the wars it fell to Corabb to stand up to the pig-faced bully. But she'd been cooking a stew in that pot, and besides, once Grunter's head was inside it there was no more room for the boys. They said he smelled like onions for weeks.

It was the spilled supper that made his ma cry. At least, that's what Corabb worked out, eventually. Couldn't have been anything else, and if they had to move to get away from the Gafan clan, the new neighbourhood was nicer anyway. And the day Grunter got killed, well, he should've known better than trying to slide all the way under that wagon, and Corabb's kicking him in the head a few times had nothing to do with his tragic end. Nobody liked Grunter anyway, though Corabb probably shouldn't have used that for his defence at the trial.

So it was the priest pits for young Corabb. Cutting limestone wasn't that bad a job, except when people got crushed, or coughed their lungs out spraying blood everywhere. And this was where he started listening to stories people told. Passing the time. It had been a mistake. Of course, if not for the uprising he'd probably still be there, getting crushed and coughing his lungs out. And the uprising – well, if he looked back on it, that had been the beginning of his own rebellion, which later led him to join the bigger one. All because people told stories about freedom and the days before the Malazans. Stories that probably weren't even true.

Leoman. Leoman of the Flails. And Sha'ik, and Toblakai. And all the fanatics. And all the bodies. Nothing good in any of that. *When you believe people telling all those lies.*

Was the Adjunct any different? He wasn't sure any more. He didn't understand all this business about being unwitnessed. That was what he'd been fighting against all his life.

But now I got a kick-ball head and it's burning up in the sun. And by dawn we'll all be done with, finished. Dead and no one left to see. Is that what she meant? But . . . what's the point of that?

He had been born stubborn. Or so everyone said. Maybe it had made for problems in his life, but Tarr wasn't one to dwell on them. Here, this night, stubbornness was all he had left. Sergeant to a squad of marines – he'd never thought he'd make it this far. Not with Fiddler there, taking care of everything that needed taking care of. But now Fid wasn't running this squad any more. *Now it's mine. I'm the one gets to walk it into the ground. I'm the one gets to watch them die like flies on the sill.*

He planned on being the last to go down – he had his stubbornness, after all. His way of pushing, and pushing, until he pushed through.

He remembered the day they formed up, officially, in Aren. The chaos, the guarded looks, all the bitching that went on. Unruly, unhappy, close to falling apart. Then a few veterans stepped up. Fiddler. Cuttle. Gesler, Stormy. And did what was needed. *And that's when I knew that I was going to stick with this. Be a soldier. I had them to follow, and that was good enough.*

It still is. It has to be.

Fiddler's up ahead somewhere. Cuttle's right behind me. Only ever had the Adjunct as commander, and she's kept me alive this long. She wants another march, she'll get it. No questions, no complaining.

He twisted round, glared at his squad. 'First one falls, I will personally curse to the Thirteen Gates of the Abyss. Am I understood?'

'That calls for a drink,' said Cuttle.

The others laughed. It wasn't much of a laugh, but for Tarr it was good enough. *They'll make it through this night. Past that, I won't ask them for a damned thing.*

Unless I need to.

Himble Thrup had picked up a new name. Shorthand. He liked it. The old family line of Thrups, well, his brothers were welcome to it. That long, ropy thing tying him to where he'd come from, and who he'd been, well, he'd just cut it. Gone. All the shit going one way, all the shit going back the other way, the rotted birth cord no Thrup dared touch. *Snick. Gone. Good riddance.*

Shorthand it is, on account of my short hands, y'see? A damned giant lizard took 'em. No, boys, it's all true. A giant lizard. Chain Kemalles they was called, but we called 'em Stumpies, on account of their tails. This was back when I was a heavy. Aye, I don't look like a heavy. I know that. But it ain't just size makes a heavy. In fact, I know a Dal Honese heavy no bigger than a toad, and no prettier either. It's all attitude.

Just look at the ones hauling those ropes – the ones just up ahead. What in Hood's name are they doing, dragging these wagons? It don't matter. They're heavies and someone told 'em, 'Haul these wagons,' and so that's what they're doing. Y'see? Attitude.

Aye, we stopped 'em cold, those Stumpies. They swung high, we ducked low. They gave us the blade, we gave 'em the shield. That's how it's done. True, I won't lie, not many of us left. We was outnumbered, badly outnumbered.

These days? I'm working for Master-Sergeant Lieutenant Quartermaster Pores. He's just gone back to check on a cracked axle three wagons back. Be with us shortly. Me? I'm waiting for our squad of marines, t'stand guard, aye. But they had a scrap last night, got cut up a bit, but it never went further, since nobody's got the strength to take

it further, if you see what I mean. Still, needed some sewing and the
like. I'm expectin' them any time.
The name's Shorthand—
Something hard as stone smashed into the side of his head.

Rackle lowered the mace, watched as Stull and Bester dragged the body
off to one side. A score or so regulars had looked up at the scuffle, and
now watched with dull eyes as they went, their legs dragging them
along as if those legs were the last parts of them still working.

Rackle wasn't ready to be like that. Hood take 'em all, he wasn't. 'So
much for the bodyguard,' he said.

'Quiet!' hissed Bester, nodding ahead to the lines of haulers. 'Get up
on the wagon, Rack, but go slow and careful – they're going to feel the
extra weight no matter what.'

Rackle grunted. 'Oafs are past feeling anything, Best.' But he edged
up close to the wagon, reached up one hand and set a foot on the
helper, and as the wagon rolled ahead he let it lift him from the ground,
nice and slow the way Best wanted it.

Rackle watched as Stull re-joined Bester, and the two melted away
into the gloom.

So far so good. Somewhere in this wagon, probably packed dead
centre, were Blistig's special casks. Time had come for a drink. He
drew himself higher up, leaning against the bales as he did so, reaching
for more handholds. That water – he could smell it. Close.

Pores crawled out from under the wagon. 'Cracked right through,' he
said, climbing to his feet. 'What's in this one?' he asked the man beside
him.

The once-company cook scratched at his beard. 'Some lantern oil.
Horseshoes. Wax, grease—'

'*Grease?* And it didn't occur to you to maybe *use* some of it on this
damned axle?'

'We was saving it for when it got real bad, sir. Aye, maybe that was
a mistake.'

'All right,' Pores sighed. 'Cut the haulers loose and send them on. I'll
take a closer look at what else is up there.'

'Aye, sir, but I don't think anybody's going to come back for whatever you think we still need.'

Pores looked round. They'd been left behind by the train. *Shit.* 'Even
so – there might be a child hiding under the blankets, the way they
come crawling out of the unlikeliest of places. Or too sick to move.'

'I'll be on with it then, sir.'

'Spread the haulers out with the rest.'

'Aye sir.'

Pores watched him go, and then heaved himself up on to the bed of the wagon. Trying to ignore the fire someone had lit in the back of his throat, and his growing sense of helplessness, he set to exploring.

The kegs of grease were pretty much empty – with only a few handfuls of the rancid gunk left – so it probably wouldn't have been enough to save the axle anyway. He tried pushing clear a cask filled with horseshoes, but he no longer had the strength left to do that. Clambering over it, he thumped the nearest bale. 'Anyone down there? Wake up or get left behind!'

Silence.

Pores drew his dagger and slit open the bale. *Spare uniforms? Gods below! If the haulers find out they'll skin me alive.* He cut open a few more. Tick for mattresses. Lead shot packed in wool for slingers – *we don't have any slingers. Who's quartermaster of this mess? Oh, me. Right.* 'That's it, then,' he muttered, 'Master-Sergeant Pores, fire Quartermaster Pores. Can I do that, Lieutenant? You can, because I'm telling you so, or do I need to take this to Fist Kindly? Please, sir, no, don't do that. He hates me! Odd, he doesn't hate *me*, Master-Sergeant. Really, sir? I'm certain of it, Master-Sergeant. Reasonably. I hope. All right, no more excuses for the old man – he hates us all. This is what happens to a bald man who starts collecting combs—'

'Quartermaster Pores.'

He looked up. Saw Fist Blistig standing at the back of the wagon. 'Fist?'

'I need to speak to you.'

'Aye, sir. What can I do for you?'

'You can give me my casks.'

'Casks? Oh, those casks.'

'Get over here, Pores, I ain't in the mood to be looking up at you.'

He clambered his way to the back of the wagon, dropped down on to the ground – at the impact his knees folded under him and he swore as he sank lower.

And the knife meant for his heart went into his upper chest instead.

Pores fell back, sliding from the blade. Blood sprayed, pattering the dusty ground like raindrops. He found himself staring up at the Jade Strangers.

'Bleeder,' Blistig said, moving into his line of sight and looking down at him. 'That'll do.'

He listened to the Fist walking away, and he wanted to laugh. *Saves me a night's march.*

Things were quiet for a time, as he felt himself fading away. And then he heard the crunch of a foot stepping close to the side of his head. He blinked open his eyes. *Look. It's the Grey Man, the Harrower, come for me. I knew I rated special attention.* The rotted skeleton crouched down to stare at him with black, empty sockets.

Pores smiled. 'Just leave it by the door.'

Balm looked round, scowling. 'So where is he?'

Throatslitter hacked out a dry cough that left him doubled over. On one knee, he gasped for a time and then said in a voice like sifting sand, 'Probably running an errand for Pores, Sergeant.'

Deadsmell snorted. 'Errand? You lost your mind, Throat? Nobody's running errands any more. He should be here. No, I don't like this.'

Balm drew off his helm and scratched at his scalp. 'Throat, climb up and give it a look over, will you?'

'There ain't nothing worth stealing up there, Sergeant.'

'I know that and you know that, but that don't mean anybody else knows it. Go on.'

Groaning, Throatslitter slowly straightened. Made his way over to the side of the wagon.

'Widdershins,' said Balm, 'go up and talk to the haulers, see what they know.'

'What they know is the sight of their own feet, Sergeant.'

'I don't care.'

The mage made his way to the front of the wagon.

'Down to a crawl,' Balm observed, eyeing the wagon's wobbly wheels rocking past. 'We'll be lucky making two leagues tonight.'

Throatslitter pulled himself on to the sideboard.

The crossbow quarrel coming out of the darkness caught him in the right buttock. He howled.

Balm spun round, bringing up his shield. A quarrel slammed into it, skittered up past his face, slicing cheek and ear. 'Ambush!'

The wagon trundled to a halt.

Throatslitter had dropped back down, only to fall on to his side, a stream of curses hissing from him. Deadsmell threw himself down beside him. 'Lie still, damn you – got to cut it out or you're useless t'us!'

But Throatslitter had managed to get one hand around the quarrel's shaft. He tore it loose, flung it to one side.

Deadsmell stared at the man – he hadn't made a sound.

With bloodied hands, Throatslitter signalled: *Someone in wagon.*

The healer nodded, looked round – Balm had squatted down behind his shield, short sword readied. Widdershins was nowhere to be seen. The last of the regulars on this flank had simply melted away, and though the glow from the Strangers was now painting the desert pan a luminous green their attackers were nowhere to be seen.

Deadsmell collected a pebble and flung it at Balm. It struck his hip and the sergeant's head snapped around.

More hand signals.

Balm backed until he was pressed against the wagon's front wheel. With his tongue he was trying to lap up the blood trickling down his cheek. He flung a series of gestures off to his right, and then glanced back at Deadsmell and, tongue snaking out yet again, he nodded.

Thank Hood. Deadsmell met Throatslitter's eyes, jerked his head upward. *Make a show.*

Drawing his knives, Throatslitter gathered into a crouch.

Rackle held himself perfectly still. Not quite the way they'd planned this. One wounded to show so far. The Fist wouldn't be happy, but maybe he could salvage this mess.

He heard the wounded one hiss, 'Get up on top, Deadsmell, and take a look around.'

'You lost your mind, Throat?'

'Just do it,' growled the sergeant.

The weight of the wagon shifted. *Here he comes. Hey, Deadsmell, I got me a nice surprise waiting for you.* He tightened his grip on the mace in his right hand.

A sound from the back of the wagon. He twisted round to see the wounded one sliding up into view. *Shit!*

Another shudder of the wagon, as Deadsmell began pulling himself up the side.

Rackle looked across at Throatslitter, saw the man grin.

Time to leave. He rose, spun round—

Widdershins gave the bastard a smile as he drove his short sword into the man's gut, and then up under his heart.

'Stay low, Wid!' Throatslitter hissed.

He let the body's weight pull him down behind some bales. 'Where's the other one?' he asked.

'More than one,' Deadsmell replied, sliding in from the side. 'Two, I'd guess. Snipers with crossbows, probably lying in shallow pits somewhere out there.'

The wagon rocked violently from the opposite side and a moment later Sergeant Hellian was staring down at them. 'You lads in trouble?'

'Head low, Sergeant!' Throatslitter hissed, 'Snipers!'

'Oh yeah? Where?'

'Out in the desert.'

She squinted in the direction he pointed, and then twisted round. 'Spread out, squad – we're going to advance on some dug-in positions. Gopher hunting time. Oh, and shields up – they got crossbows.'

Deadsmell stared across at Throatslitter, who simply shook his head.

'Listen, Sergeant—'

'You got a wounded man here, healer,' Hellian pointed out, and then she clambered across, followed by two soldiers from her squad. Others had gone round the wagon, advancing slowly on the flank. Hellian dropped down. 'Sergeant Balm, hold fast will ya? We got this.'

'You won't find 'em,' Balm replied. 'Saw a couple of shadows running off.'

'Really? Which way?'

'Into the regulars. We lost 'em, Hellian.'

The woman sagged. 'What were they after?'

'Hood knows.'

Having observed all this from atop the wagon, Deadsmell turned back. 'Nice work, Wid, though it would've been good to have taken him alive.'

'Wasn't interested in talking,' Widdershins replied. 'They probably killed Shorthand.'

Deadsmell was silent. He should've thought of that. 'We need to look for him.'

'And leave the wagon?' Throatslitter demanded.

'There ain't nothing on this wagon!'

'Right, sorry. Got caught up, somehow. Anyway, I doubt I can walk, so I can stay behind and, er, guard.'

'Where'd you get it, Throat?' Widdershins asked.

'Where it means I can't walk, Wid.'

'In the butt,' Deadsmell explained. 'It ain't bleeding – did that quarrel hit bone?'

'Don't think so.'

'Miracle, with your skinny—'

'Just go find Shorthand, will you?'

Deadsmell nodded over at Widdershins, and the two of them climbed down from the wagon.

As all of this had been going on, the rest of the column had simply gone round them. On this flank, Sergeant Urb's squad had arrived, and after a few words with Balm and Hellian Urb led his marines onward. Balm faced his two soldiers.

'We was targeted specifically,' he said.

'The marked casks,' said Widdershins. 'Don't matter that we used it all up on the children. They still think we're holding back.'

'Blistig,' said Deadsmell.

Balm's face twisted in distaste and he reached up to wipe more blood from his cheek. Then he licked his fingers. 'Killing officers is one thing . . . but a Fist? I don't know.'

'Who'd complain?' Deadsmell demanded.

'It's mutiny.'

'We ain't going against the Adjunct's command in this—'

'Wrong. In a way that's exactly what we're doing. She made him Fist.'

'But now he's trying to kill his own soldiers!'

'Aye, Deadsmell.'

Widdershins hissed to get their attention. 'T'lan Imass coming, Sergeant.'

'Now what?'

The figure halted before Deadsmell. 'Healer, there is need for you.'

'You're way past helping—'

'The one named Pores is dying from a knife wound. Will you come?'

Deadsmell turned to Balm.

'All right,' the sergeant said. 'I'll go find Kindly.'

Shortnose had been cut loose. The rest agreed it should be him, and he went and found Flashwit and Mayfly, and a little while later Saltlick joined them. None of them said much, but it was clear that Shortnose was in charge. He didn't know why but he wasn't in the mood to argue anyway so it was him whether he wanted it to be or not.

He led them into the press of the regulars, where soldiers melted from their path and with eyes all hollow and haunted tracked them as they went past.

Maybe they'd been harnessed like oxen, but that didn't mean they weren't paying attention to whatever was going on around them. Most of it wasn't worth chewing on, but sometimes some unguarded comment hung around and then, when something else arrived, it came back, and things started making sense.

They weren't oxen. They were heavies. And word had reached them that Shorthand had a broken skull and probably wasn't going to last the night, and that a squad of marines had been ambushed, with one of them down but luckily not dead. Looked like the one who busted Shorthand's head got himself gutted by a marine, but at least two more attackers had gotten away.

There weren't just two of them, Shortnose knew. Two with crossbows, aye, stolen from a wagon. At least seven others with them, though. Fist Blistig's gang of thugs.

Every army had them. They were only trouble when some fool put 'em all together in one place, and Blistig had done just that.

Head-breaking a heavy? And from behind, too? That needed answering. Shorthand had been a knot in the saw of the Stumpies. He'd blunted a lot of teeth on that saw. Bad luck about the fingers, but cutting wood's a dangerous business, almost – Shortnose frowned – almost as dangerous as being a heavy.

Too bad that Blistig wasn't with his crew when they found it. They wouldn't have killed him, though. Just let him watch as they waded into his gang, disarming them and breaking arms and legs, with at least one stamp-down from Mayfly crushing a fool's pelvis, making him squirt in both directions. Aye, it would have been great for the Fist to see when Saltlick found one of the stolen crossbows and tried to jam it butt-end first down a thug's mouth. Things tore and snapped and broke but he got it as far down as the middle of the throat, which was something. They left it there.

Shortnose and Flashwit just used their fists and pounded faces into bloody pulps, and that took a lot of punches, but the only people looking on were regulars and eventually those regulars just started walking again, since there was nothing else to be done.

Somebody blindsided a heavy. That wasn't done. Ever.

But even Shortnose was surprised when a regular, a sergeant leading his squad past, looked down on the bodies of the thugs, and spat at the nearest one – no real spit, just the sound, the stab of his head, clear enough to take its meaning. And Shortnose looked across to Flashwit and then Saltlick and they nodded back.

Just as the heavies weren't all oxen, the regulars weren't all packmules. They'd seen, they'd listened. They'd made up their minds. And that was good.

Better that than killing them all, wasn't it? *That'd take all night. Or even longer.*

'Found him, Fist,' said Captain Raband.

Kindly turned to Balm. 'Pull everybody back now – this is between me and Blistig, understood?'

The sergeant nodded, and then hesitated. 'Fist? You're going to kill him, ain't ya?'

'Sergeant?'

'Well, sir, it's just . . . if you ain't gonna, cause of some rules or something, a word to Throatslitter, or Smiles who's in Tarr's squad, or—'

'Marine, listen well to what I'm about to say. Unless you want to see one of your marines executed, you will not touch Fist Blistig. Am I understood?'

'Begging your pardon, Fist, but come the sun's rise, we're all gonna be crawling, if that. So that kinda threat don't mean much, if you see what I mean. We got us a list under Blistig's name, Fist, and we're expecting you to carve a nice red line right through it, starting with him.'

'You are talking mutiny, Sergeant.'

'Ugly word, that one, sir. What did the Bridgeburners call it? *Culling.*

Old Malazan habit, right? Picked it up from the Emperor himself, in fact, and then the Empress, who did the same.'

'As she sought to do with the Wickans, Sergeant, or have you forgotten?'

'Aye, easy to get carried away, sir. But tonight we're talking one man.'

Kindly glanced across at Raband, who stood waiting. 'Is the Fist alone, captain?'

'No sir. Fist Sort and Captain Skanarow are with him, along with Captain Ruthan Gudd. There's been an accusation voiced, sir – I was planning on telling you on the way, but,' and he shot Balm a look, 'Ruthan Gudd says there's blood on Blistig's knife. Pores's blood.'

Balm swore. 'Togg's bloody jowls! *By his own hand?*'

Raband shrugged.

'Lead on, Captain,' Kindly said, so quiet the words barely carried.

Balm watched them go.

Deadsmell followed a pace behind his guide. Ahead, the other T'lan Imass had raised a tarp. Lanterns were lit, shutters slipped back, wicks turned up and blazing. It had been a long way back along the trail, forty or more paces. Nearby squatted a wagon. In the harsh light beneath the tarp, he saw Pores's body.

Blood everywhere. He won't survive this. He edged past the T'lan Imass and made his way under the tarp, falling to his knees beside Pores. Studied the wound. *This is a bleeder. Above the heart. He should be already dead.* But he could see the faint pulse, pushing out thinning trickles of blood. The man's breathing was shallow, rasping. *Not a lung, too. Please, not a lung.* 'I've got no magic here,' he said, looking up and seeing nothing but withered, lifeless faces staring back down at him. *Shit, no help there.*

He stared back down at Pores. 'Seen the insides of plenty of people,' he muttered. 'Living and dead. Well. Had a teacher, once, a priest. Dresser of the dead. He had some radical notions. Gods, why not? He's going to die either way.'

Deadsmell drew out his sewing kit. 'Said it should be possible to go right inside a body, clamp the bleeder, and then sew it back together, right there inside. Not that it'll help much if he's got a punctured lung too. But no blood froth at the mouth. Not yet. So . . . I guess I'll give it a try.' He looked up. 'Two of you, I need your hands – I need the wound held open, wide as you can make it – gods, those are foul-looking fingers you Imass got.'

'There is nothing living on our hands,' said one of them.

'What's that got to do with anything?' Deadsmell asked.

'We will carry no infection into his flesh, healer.'

'No, but the knife blade that did this probably has.'

'His bleeding has cleaned the wound, healer. The greatest risk of infection will be from your hands, and your tools.'

Threading a needle with gut, Deadsmell scowled. 'That old priest shared your opinion. But there's nothing I can do about that, is there?'

'No.'

Deadsmell's vision spun momentarily, and then steadied once more. *Unbelievable. I'm dying, even as I'm trying to save another man from doing the same. And really, is there any point to this?*

Two Imass had knelt, reaching to prise open the wound.

'Dig your fingers in – I need to see as much as I can. No, wait, now all I can see are your fingers.'

One spoke. 'Healer. One of us shall hold open the wound. The other shall reach inside and find the two severed ends of the vessel.'

'Yes! That's it! And once you've got them, pinch hard – stop the blood flow – and then bring them together so I can see them.'

'We are ready, healer.'

'He's lost a lot of blood. He's in shock. This probably won't work. Surprised he's not already dead. I might just kill him. Or he'll die later. Blood loss. Infection.' He trailed off, looked across at blank, staring, lifeless faces. 'Right, needed to get all that out of the way. Here goes.'

They were waiting well off to one side of the trail. The column's ragged end had already passed. Blistig stood facing the others, arms crossed.

Kindly and Raband made their way over.

Overhead, the Jade Strangers blazed with a green light bright enough to cast sharp shadows, and it seemed the desert air itself was confused, not nearly as chill as it should have been. There was no wind, and stillness surrounded the group.

Blistig met Kindly's eyes unflinchingly. 'I executed a traitor tonight, Kindly. That and nothing more. I was holding on to reserves of water – knowing a time of great need would come.'

'Indeed,' Kindly replied. 'How many casks was it again? Four? Five?'

'For the officer corps, Kindly. With some, if we so judged, to the marines and heavies. It wouldn't have been much, granted, but something . . . maybe enough. Didn't the Adjunct make it plain? The marines and the heavies before everyone else. In fact, the rest of them don't matter.'

'Lieutenant Pores was not under your command, Blistig.'

'Acts of treason fall under the purview of any commanding officer who happens to be present, Kindly. I acted within military law in this matter.'

'That water,' said Ruthan Gudd, 'was doled out to the children of the Snake. By the Adjunct's direct command.'

'The Adjunct knew nothing about it, Captain Gudd, so what you're saying makes no sense.'

Faradan Sort snorted. 'We all knew about your stash, Blistig. We've just been waiting for you to make your move. But you can't reclaim what was never yours in the first place, never mind that it's now all gone. If there was any treason here, Blistig, it was yours.'

He sneered. 'That's where you've lost the track – all of you! All this "we're in this together" rubbish – so that a lowly latrine digger gets the same portion as a Fist, or a captain, or the damned Adjunct herself – that's not how the world is, and with good reason! It's us highborn who've earned the greater portion. On account of our greater responsibilities, our greater skills and talents. *That's* the order of the world, friends.'

'Never knew you were highborn, Blistig,' commented Faradan Sort.

The man scowled. 'There's other paths to privilege, Sort. Look at you, after all, a deserter of the Wall, now here you are, a damned Fist. And Kindly here, straight up from the regular ranks, and that climb wasn't exactly meteoric, was it? Decades of mediocrity, right, Kindly? You ended up just outlasting everyone else.'

'Everything you're saying, Blistig,' said Ruthan Gudd, 'is undermining your original argument. Seems there's not one highborn among us here. In fact, only the Adjunct can make that claim.'

'A woman who betrayed her own class,' Blistig said, with a cold grin. 'Treason starts at the top when it comes to the Bonehunters.'

'You plan on killing everyone, then, Blistig?'

'Kindly, turns out I don't have to, do I? We're finished. All those warnings have proved true. This desert can't be crossed. We've failed. In every way, we've failed.' He shook his head. 'I did Pores a damned favour. I made it quick.'

'Expecting one of us to make it as quick for you?' Ruthan Gudd asked him.

Blistig shrugged. 'Why not? I don't care any more. I really don't. She's already killed us all. Will it be your blade, Captain Gudd? Do me a favour – make it the icy one.'

'No one will be killing you this night,' Kindly said. He unclipped his sword belt and threw it to one side. 'We bear these titles. Fists. Let's find their original meaning, you and me, Blistig.'

'You're joking, old man.'

Faradan Sort turned to Kindly in alarm. 'What are you doing? Let's just drag him up before the Adjunct. Kindly!'

But the man bulled forward. And Blistig moved to meet him.

Two men too weak to do any real damage to the other. The fight was pathetic. Punches that couldn't break skin, blows that could barely bruise. Three or four exchanges and both men were kneeling three paces apart, gasping, heads held down.

When Kindly looked up, Blistig threw sand into his eyes, lurched forward, grasped Kindly's head and drove it down on to one knee.

Sort moved to intervene but Ruthan Gudd reached out and held her back.

The impact should have shattered Kindly's nose, but it didn't. He punched Blistig's crotch.

The man let out a strangled grunt, sagged down on to his side.

Kindly tried to get up, fell back down, and then rolled on to his back, eyes squeezed shut, his chest heaving for breath.

'That's it,' Ruthan Gudd said. 'They're done.'

'Stupid!' Faradan Sort snapped, pulling her arm out of Gudd's grip. She went to stand over the two men. 'What was the point? If the soldiers up there had seen this – you useless fools! Blistig, if we weren't all of us about to die, I *would* kill you. But you don't deserve that mercy – no, you're going to suffer through this night just like everyone else.' She turned. 'Captain Raband, help your Fist.'

Blistig managed to work himself back on to his knees, and he slowly sat up. 'She's killed us all. For nothing.' He moved his glare from one face to the next. 'Aye, I see it in your eyes, every one of you, you ain't got a thing to say to make it different. She's killed us. You know it the same as me. So, you want to kill me? You want to do her work for her?' He climbed, with difficulty, to his feet. 'Give me the dignity of dying on my own.'

'You should have understood the value of that,' said Ruthan, 'before you stuck a knife in Pores, Fist Blistig.'

'Maybe I should have. But he lied to me, and I don't like being lied to.' He pointed a finger at Kindly. 'We're not done, you and me. I'll be waiting for you at Hood's Gate, old man.'

'Pathetic,' hissed Faradan Sort.

They left Blistig where he was, and the way he held himself, it would be a while before he'd be ready to start walking again. Skanarow moved alongside Ruthan Gudd.

'I was hoping we'd just kill him,' she said, low under her breath. 'The man's a murderer, after all. Pores wasn't even wearing a weapon belt, and his knife was jammed hilt deep in a bale on the wagon.'

'If anyone will be looking for Blistig at Hood's Gate, it will be Lieutenant Pores, don't you think?'

But Skanarow shook her head. 'I never believed in retribution beyond Death's Gates. Nobody is squatting on the other side weighing and balancing a life's scales.' She stumbled slightly and Ruthan moved to catch her. Felt her momentarily sag against him. 'Shit, I may not last the night.'

'You will, Skanarow. I'm not letting you die, do you understand me?'

'There's no way out, and you know it, my love. You know it – you can't hide what I see in your eyes.'

He said nothing, because there was nothing to say.

'You'll forget me, won't you? Eventually. Like . . . all the rest.'

'Don't say that, Skanarow – it's the wrong thing to think. For people . . . like me . . . it's not forgetting that is our curse. It's remembering.'

Her smile was faint, and she disengaged herself from his half-embrace. 'Then I beg you, love, do all that you can to forget me. Leave no memory behind to haunt you – let it all fade. It shouldn't be hard – what we had didn't last long, did it?'

He'd heard such words before. *And this is why remembering is a curse.*

Blistig faced back the way they'd come. Off in the distance he could make out the glow of lanterns, the lights swinging low to the ground. Frowning, he watched as they came closer.

She killed us. Come the dawn, when we're all finished, unable to take another step, I'm going to go to her. I'm going to stick a knife in her. Not a fatal wound, not right away, no. In the stomach, where the acids will all leak out and start eating her up from the inside out. And I'll kneel over her, staring down into her pain, and that will be the sweetest sight I will ever see. A sight to carry me right into death.

But even that won't be enough, not for what she's done to us. Kindly, at Hood's Gate, you're going to have to wait, because I won't be finished with Tavore Paran of House Paran.

T'lan Imass, carrying a makeshift stretcher on which lay a swaddled body. Beside this, a marine with blood covering his hands and forearms.

Blistig squinted as they drew closer.

The T'lan Imass walked past him and the Fist looked down at the pale face of the man on the stretcher. He grunted.

The marine halted before him, saluted. 'Fist,' he said.

'Pores ain't dead yet? What was the point of that, healer?'

Blistig's answer was a fist smashing into his face, hard enough to crush his nose, send him reeling back. Stumbling, falling to the ground. Blood gushing down, he lay stunned.

The healer moved to stand over him. 'Thing is, Fist,' he said, massaging his hand, 'what with all the shit Pores has gone through because of you, we decided to make him an honorary marine. Now, you go sticking a knife in a fellow marine and, well, we're out for you now. Understand me, sir? The marines are out for you.'

Blistig listened to the man walk off in the wake of the T'lan Imass.

He made it on to his side to spit out slime and blood, and then grunted a laugh. *Aye, and a man is measured by his enemies.*

Do your worst, marines. So long as I get to her first.

It was some time before he managed to regain his feet, but when he set off after the column, his strides were stiff, jerking, filled with a strength past anything he had known before. In his head three words made a mantra. *To see her. To see her. To see her.*

The Khundryl camp was being packed up, but the people doing the task moved with aching slowness. The claws upon their skin seemed to be dragging them down, and Badalle watched in the midst of twenty or so of Rutt's children, as everything that was coming along for this final night was put in its proper place – everything but for the mother's tent, and she was yet to emerge.

The midwives and other women had come out earlier, expressions guarded, and, though she could not be certain, in Badalle's mind she saw but three figures remaining inside. The father, the mother, and the baby. Would this be their final home, then?

A Khundryl child came up to Saddic, pressing into his hands yet another toy – a bone top or whistle, she couldn't quite see it before Saddic slipped it into his sack and smiled his thanks. A new sack, too big to carry now. The Khundryl children had been bringing him toys all day.

The times she'd watched that procession, she'd wanted to cry. She'd wanted Saddic to cry. But she didn't understand why she wanted that – they were being kind, after all. And she didn't know why she saw those Khundryl children as if they were but servants to something greater, something almost too big for words. Not at the instigation of adults, not even mothers and fathers. Not at the behest of pity, either. Didn't they want their toys? She had seen such precious things settle into Saddic's hand, had seen bright shining eyes lift shyly to Saddic in the moment of giving, and then fall away again – children running off, too light-footed, flinging themselves into their friends' arms, and this went on and on and Badalle didn't understand, but how her heart ached. How she wanted Saddic to weep, how she wanted to feel her own tears.

She spoke a poem under her breath.

> 'Snakes do not know how to cry.
> They know too much
> and yearn for darkness.
> They know too much
> and fear the light.
> No one gives gifts to snakes,
> and no one makes of them a gift.

They are neither given
nor received.
Yet in all the world,
snakes do not know how to cry.'

Saddic studied her and she knew that he had heard. Of course it was for him, this poem, though she suspected that he did not know that. *But the man who will find him will. Maybe he'll cry, when we cannot. Maybe he will tell this tale in such a way as to make his listeners cry, because we cannot.*

A Khundryl elder came up then and helped Saddic load his bag of toys on to a wagon. When the boy glanced over at Badalle, she nodded. He climbed up to settle himself beside his treasure. And there, he believed, he would die.

But it is not to be. How will he survive? I wish I knew the answer to that, because a secret hides inside it.

The birth-tent's flap was swept aside then, and the father emerged. His eyes were raw with weeping, yet there was a fire in them. *He is proud. He is defiant in his pride, and would challenge us all. I like this look. It is how a father should look.* Then behind him, out she came, unsteady on her feet, sagging with exhaustion, and in her arms a small bundled form.

Badalle gasped upon seeing Rutt walking towards them – where had he come from? Where had he been hiding?

With his crooked arms, with a terrible need in his ancient face, he walked to stand before the mother.

Anguish gripped Badalle's heart and she staggered in sudden weakness. *Where is Held? Held is gone. Held was gone long ago. And what Rutt carried in his arms was us, all that way. He carried us.*

The mother looked across at this boy, and Badalle saw now that she was old – and so too was the father, old enough to be grandparents – she looked at Rutt, his empty arms, the ravaged face.

She does not understand. How can she? He cannot hurt anyone, not Rutt. He carried our hope, but our hope died. But it wasn't his fault, it wasn't his fault. Mother, if you had been there – if you had seen—

And she stepped forward then, that old woman, that mother with her last ever child, this stranger, and gently laid her baby into Rutt's waiting arms.

A gift beyond measure, and when she settled an arm about his shoulders, drawing him forward, so that he could walk with them – her and her husband – and they set out, slowly as it was all she could manage, in the wake of the nearest wagon, and all the Khundryl began to move . . . Badalle stood unmoving.

Saddic, I will tell you to remember this. These are the Khundryl, the givers of gifts. Remember them, won't you?

And Rutt walked like a king.

From where he sat, Saddic watched as they made space on a Khundryl wagon for the mother, and for Rutt and her child that he held, and then set out to catch up with the rest of the army. The man who was the father took the lead yoke at the wagon's head, and strained as if he alone could shoulder this burden.

Because it was no burden.

As Saddic well knew, gifts never are.

Ahead, the desert stretched on. Fiddler could see no end to it, and now believed he never would. He remembered that ancient shoreline of bones, the one they had left behind what seemed a century ago. No clearer warning could have been granted them, yet she had not hesitated.

He had to hand it to her. The world was her enemy, and she would face it unblinking. She had led them on to this road of suffering in the name of the Crippled God, and, to that god, what other path could there have been? She was making of them her greatest sacrifice – was it as brutal and as simple as that? He did not think her capable of such a thing. He wanted to refuse the very thought.

But here he walked, fifty or more paces ahead of them all. Even the Khundryl children were gone, leaving him alone. And behind him, a broken mass of humanity, somehow dragging itself forward, like a beast with a crushed spine. It had surrendered all formation, each soldier moving as his or her strength dictated. They carried their weapons because they had forgotten a time when they didn't. And bodies fell, one by one.

Beneath the ghoulish light of the Jade Strangers, Fiddler set his eyes upon the distant flat line of the horizon, his legs scissoring under him, the muscles too dead to feel pain. He listened to his own breaths, wheezing as the air struggled up and down a swollen, parched windpipe. In so vast a landscape he felt his world contracting, step by step, and soon, he knew, all he would hear would be his own heart, the beats climbing down, losing all rhythm, and finally falling still.

That moment waited somewhere ahead. He was on his way to find it.

Whispering motion around him now, drifting out from a fevered mind. He saw a horseman at his side, close enough to reach out, if he so wanted, and set a hand upon the beast's patched, salt-streaked shoulder. The man riding the beast he knew all too well.

Broke his leg. A toppling pillar, of all things. Mallet – I see you – you wanted to work on that leg. Got damned insubordinate about it, in fact. But he didn't listen. That's his problem, he only listens when he feels like it.

Trotts, you're still the damned ugliest Barghast I ever saw. They bred 'em that way in your tribe, didn't they? To better scare the enemy. Did they breed your women to be half blind, too? Keep the stones balanced, that's the only way to make it through.

So where's Quick Ben? Kalam? I want to see you all here, friends.

Hedge, well, he's stepped out of this path. Can't look him in the eye these days. It's the one bad twist in this whole thing, isn't it. Maybe you can talk to him, Sergeant. Talk him back to how it should be.

'Hedge is where we want him, Fid.'

What?

'We sent him to you . . . to this, I mean. He's walked a lonely path back, sapper.'

Mallet then spoke. 'Bet he thought he'd made it all the way, too, when he stood before you, Fiddler. Only to have you back away.'

I . . . oh, gods. Hedge. I better find him, chew it all out, come the dawn – we'll make it that far, won't we, Sergeant?

'Until it rises, aye, sapper. Until it rises.'

And then?

'You're so eager to join us?'

Whiskeyjack – please – where else would I go?

'If we were just waiting for the dawn, soldier, you'd have to ask, what in Hood's name for? You think we'd see you put through all of this for nothing? And then there's Hedge. He's here to die beside you and that's it? We sent him to you so you could just kiss and make up? Gods below, Fiddler, you're not that important in this wretched scheme.'

'Well,' said Mallet, 'he might be, Sergeant. Made Captain now, didn't he? Got himself his own company of marines and heavies. Bloody insufferable now, is old Fid.'

'Sky's paling,' Whiskeyjack said.

Because you're on damned horses. I can't see it.

'False dawn,' growled Trotts. 'And Fid's fading, Sergeant. We can't hold on here much longer. Once he stops thinking past his feet . . .'

I was a mason's apprentice. Had dreams of being a musician, getting fat and drunk in some royal court.

'Not this again,' someone said among the crowd. 'Someone find him a fiddle, and me a hanky.'

Glad you're all here with me. Well, most of you, anyway. The Bridgeburners deserved a better way to die—

The rider made a derisive sound. 'Don't be such an idiot, sapper. In your heads you've all built us up into something we never were. How quickly you've forgotten – we were mutinous at the best of times. The rest of the time – and that would be almost *all* the time – we were at

606

each other's throats. Officers getting posted to us would desert first. It was that bad, Fiddler.'

Look, I ain't done nothing to make this fucking legend, Sergeant. I ain't said a damned thing.

'You don't have to, and that's just my point. People can talk up anything, can make a snivelling dollop of shit the god's own mountain, given enough time and enough lies and enough *silences*.'

I'm a Bonehunter now. Got nothing to do with any of you any more – which is what I was trying to tell Hedge.

'Fine. Now go hunt down some bones.'

Sure, why not? Whose bones do you want us to hunt for?

Whiskeyjack rode slightly ahead and swung his mount round, blocking Fiddler's path. But his old sergeant wasn't looking good – he was a damned half-mummified corpse, and his mount wasn't much better off. 'Whose do you think, Fid?' And yet that voice was his – no question. *Whiskeyjack.*

'Where'd you come by that name, Fid?' And that was Mallet, but he was badly chopped up, the wounds crusted with dried blood.

The name? Bonehunters? It was finger bones, I think.

'Whose hand?'

What? Nobody's – lots of people. Nameless ones, long dead ones – just nameless bones!

They were all fading from his vision now. But he wanted them to stay. They were supposed to be here with him, to take up his soul when he died.

Whiskeyjack was backing his horse even as he grew translucent. 'Bones of the fallen, Fiddler. Now, *who fell the furthest?*'

Before him now nothing but that distant, flat line. Nothing but the horizon. Fiddler rubbed at his face. *Fucking hallucinations. Least they could've done was give me a drink of water.*

He resumed walking. No reason to. No reason not to.

'Who fell the furthest. Funny man, Whiskeyjack.' *But maybe it was so. Maybe she made us and named us to hunt down the bones of a damned god. Maybe she was telling us what she wanted all along, and we were too thick to know it.*

But look at that line. That perfect flat line. Just waiting for our bones to make us a shore, and once we've made it, why, we go no farther.

Almost time.

Hedge, I'll find you if I can. A few words. A clasp of hands, or a clout upside the head, whichever best suits the moment.

Bonehunters. Oh. Nice one.

Lostara Yil wanted her god back. She wanted to feel that flow of strength, that appalling will. To take her out of here. To feel a sudden, immortal power filling her body, and she would reach out to draw Henar Vygulf under her shadowy wing. Others too, if she could. This whole army of sufferers – they didn't deserve this.

Henar walked close by her side, ready to steady her when she stumbled. He had seemed indomitable, but now he was bent like an old man. Thirst was crushing them all, like a vast hand pressing down. The Adjunct was ten paces ahead, Banaschar off to her right, and far ahead walked Fiddler, alone, and she imagined she could hear music from him, a siren call pulling them ever forward. But his fiddle was broken. There was no music, no matter what she thought she heard, just the sluggish dirge of her own blood, the rasps of their breaths and the crunch of their worn boots on the hard ground.

The Jade Strangers hung now over the northern sky, casting confused shadows – those terrible slashes would circle round over the course of the day, now visible even through the sun's bright glare, making the light eerie, unearthly.

The Adjunct's march was unsteady, drifting to the right for a time, and then back to the left. It seemed only Fiddler was capable of managing a straight line. She remembered back to the reading. Its wild violence – had it all been for nothing? A rush of possibilities, not one realized, not one borne out in the days to follow. It seemed the Adjunct – who alone warranted no card – had taken them all from their destinies, taken them into a place with no end but death, and a death bereft of glory or honour. If that was so, then Fiddler's reading had been the cruellest of jokes.

Was he walking out there, ahead of the rest of them, out of some desperate desire? To drag them all into the truth of his visions? But the desert still stretched empty – not even the bones of the children of the Snake could be seen – they had lost them, but no one knew precisely when, and the path that might have led them to the mythical city of Icarias was now nowhere to be seen.

Her gaze found the Adjunct again, this woman she had chosen to follow. And she didn't know what to think.

Beyond Tavore, the horizon, pale as the water of a tropical sea, now showed a rim of fire. Announcing the end of the night, the end of this march. Shadows spun round.

Fiddler halted. He turned round to face them all.

The Adjunct continued until she was ten paces from him and then slowed, and with her last step, she tottered and almost fell. Banaschar moved close but stopped when Tavore straightened once more.

Henar took hold of Lostara's left arm, and they were still, and she looked down at the ground, as if to make it familiar to her eyes, knowing that from this place she would not move, ever again. Not her, not Henar. *This, this is my grave.*

The Fists and their officers were arriving. Faradan Sort with Skanarow and, beside her, Ruthan Gudd. Kindly, his face puffy and red, as if he'd stumbled and driven it into something. Raband standing close, one hand on his sword as he eyed Fist Blistig. That man, Lostara saw, had taken a punch – the evidence was plain in his swollen, misaligned nose, his split lips and the smears of dried blood. Bruises had spread out under his reddened eyes, and it seemed as if those eyes were nailed to the Adjunct. Fevered, burning with malice.

Behind them all, the army slowly ground down into something motionless, and she could see the faces of the nearest soldiers – this legion of old men and old women – all staring. Equipment bags slumped to the ground. A few, here and there, followed their kit to the ground.

It's done, then.

All eyes were on the Adjunct.

Tavore Paran suddenly looked small. A person none would notice on a street, or in a crowd. The world was filled with such people. They bore no proof of gifts, no lines of beauty or grace, no bearing of confidence or challenge. *The world is filled with them. Filled. For ever unnoticed. For ever . . . unwitnessed.*

Her plain face was ravaged by the sun, blistered and cracked. The weight she had lost made her gaunt, shrunken. Yet she stood, weathering this multitude of stares, the rising heat of hatred – as every need was refused, as every hope was answered with nothing but silence.

Now the T'lan Imass arrived. They held their weapons of stone in their lifeless hands, drawing closer to the Adjunct.

Blistig snarled. 'Bodyguards, bitch? Can they kill us all? We'll get to you. I swear it.'

The Adjunct studied the man, but said nothing.

Please, Tavore. Give us some words. Give us something. To make this dying . . . palatable. We tried, didn't we? We followed where you led. That was duty. That was loyalty. And all you kept asking of us, the battles, the marches . . . we did them. See how many have died for you, Tavore. See us who remain. Now we too will die. Because we believed.

Gods below, say something!

The Adjunct twisted round, to where Fiddler was standing, and then she faced Ruthan Gudd. 'Captain,' her voice was a dull croak, 'where lies Icarias?'

'South and east of us, Adjunct. Nine, ten days.'

'And directly east? Where is the edge of this desert?'

He clawed at his beard, and then shook his head. 'Another ten, eleven days, if we continue angling northeast – if we continue following this shallow basin as we have been doing since yesterday.'

'Is there water beyond the desert, Captain? On the Elan Plain?'

'Not much, I would warrant, or so the children have told us.'

Tavore looked to the T'lan Imass. 'Upon the Elan Plain, Beroke, can you find us water?'

One of the undead creatures faced her. 'Adjunct, we are then within the influence of Akhrast Korvalain. It is possible, but difficult, and the efforts we make will be felt. We would not be able to hide.'

'I understand. Thank you, Beroke.'

She still thinks we can make it. Ten more days! Has she lost her mind?

Blistig laughed, a sound like the tearing open of his own throat. 'We have followed a mad woman. Where else would she lead us?'

Lostara could not understand where Blistig found the energy for his rage, but he now raised his arms, shouted, 'Malazans! She gave us nothing! We pleaded – we begged! In the name of our soldiers, in the name of all of you – *we begged her!*' He faced the army. 'You saw us! Marching to her tent again and again – all our questions she spat back into our faces! Our fears, our concerns – they *told* us this desert was impassable – but she ignored them all!'

Before him stood the ranks, and from them, not a sound.

Blistig spun, advanced on the Adjunct. 'What power is this? Within you, woman? That they now die without a complaint?'

Kindly, Raband, Sort and Skanarow had all drawn closer, and all at once Lostara knew that if Blistig sought to attack Tavore now he would never reach her, never mind the T'lan Imass. Yet, for all that, those officers kept looking to the Adjunct, and Lostara saw the yearning in their eyes.

No one could withstand this much longer – even a god would fall to his knees. But still the Adjunct stood. 'Banaschar,' she said.

The ex-priest limped over to Lostara. 'Captain,' he said, 'your kit bag, please.'

She frowned at him. 'What?'

'Can I have your kit bag, Captain?'

Henar helped her lift it off her shoulders. They set it down.

Kneeling before it, Banaschar fumbled at the straps. 'She judged you the strongest,' he murmured. 'Gift of a god? Possibly. Or,' and he glanced up at her, 'maybe you're just the most stubborn one of us all.' He pulled back the sun-cracked flap, rummaged inside, and then drew out a small wooden box.

Lostara gasped. 'That's not—'

'You stayed close,' Banaschar said. 'We knew you would.'

He struggled to straighten, nodding his thanks when Lostara helped him, and then he walked slowly over to the Adjunct.

In Lostara's mind, a memory . . . a throne room. That Ceda. The king . . . *complaining, such a plain gift, that dagger. And what did the Ceda tell her? Dire necessity . . .*

Banaschar opened the box. The Adjunct reached in, withdrew the dagger. She held it before her.

'"When blood is required. When blood is *needed*."'

Tavore glanced over at her, and Lostara realized that she had spoken those words aloud.

Banaschar said, 'Adjunct, the king's Ceda—'

'Is an Elder God, yes.' Tavore continued studying the knife, and then, slowly, she looked up, her gaze moving from one face to the next. And something flickered in her expression, that parched mask of plainness. A crack through to . . . *to such hurt.* And then it was gone again, and Lostara wondered if she'd ever seen it, wondered if she'd imagined the whole thing. *She is only what you see. And what you see isn't much.*

Banaschar said, 'Your blood, Adjunct.'

She saw Fiddler then, well behind the Adjunct, saw him turn away as if in shame.

The Adjunct was studying them all. Lostara found herself at Tavore's side, with no memory of moving, and she saw the faces before her, all fixed upon the Adjunct. She saw their broken lips, the glint of unbearable need in their eyes.

And beside her, in a voice that could crush stones, Tavore Paran said, '*Haven't you drunk enough?*'

Fiddler could hear music, filled with such sorrow that he felt everything breaking inside. He would not turn round, would not watch. But he knew when she took that knife and cut deep into her hand. He felt it as if that hand was his own. The blood was bright on that simple iron blade, covering the faint swirling etching. He could see it in his mind's eye – there was no need to lift his head, no need to look over at them all, the way they stood, the thirst and the wound she had delivered so raw in their eyes.

And then, in the weight of a silence too vast to comprehend, blood flowing, the Adjunct fell to her knees.

When she drove that knife into the hard ground, Fiddler flinched, and the music deepened its timbre, grew suddenly faint, and then, in a whisper, returned to him.

His knees were cold.

Lostara Yil lifted her head. Were they killing the last of the horses? She'd not even known that any were left, but now she could hear them, somewhere in the mass of soldiers. Stepping forward, her boot skidded.

Beside her, Henar cursed under his breath – but not in anger. In wonder.

Now voices cried out, and the sound rippled through the army.

There was a whispering sound, from below, and she looked down. The ground was dark, stained.

Wet.

Banaschar was at the Adjunct's side, lifting her to her feet. 'Fists!' he snapped. 'Have them ready the casks! Move it!'

Water welled up beneath them, spread over the ground. As the sun's light brightened, Lostara could see, on all sides, a glistening tide flowing ever outward. Through the holes and tears in her boots she could now feel it, cold, almost numbing. Rising to her ankles.

What did Ruthan Gudd say? We're in a basin? How deep is this going to get?

She fell to her knees, drew her head down, and like an animal in the wilds, she drank.

And still the water rose.

Chaos in the army. Laughter. Howls, voices lifted to gods. She knew there would be those – fools – who drank too much too quickly, and it would kill them. But there were officers, and sergeants, and hands would be stayed. Besides, most of the fools were already dead.

With casks full, with all the waterskins heavy and sweating . . . could they march another eleven days? They would eat, now, and soak in as much water as they could. They would feel strength return to their limbs. Their thoughts would awaken from the sluggish torpor they had known for days now.

Still the water rose.

Horns sounded. And suddenly, the Bonehunters were on the move. Seeking high ground. For all they knew, that knife had delivered an entire sea.

Thick as blood, the smell of water filled the air.

BOOK SEVEN

YOUR PRIVATE SHORE

Lie still!
The jagged urgent heat
The horn-twisted acts
So unconscionable
I have run far from the mob
Torn the veil and bled in holes
Under your very feet
Take my word not for a day
Not a year not a century
What I will say charges the echo
Of a thousand years unchained
And all the pillagers of derision
Pacing the mouths of caves
March legions of dust
Back and forth
Like conquerors
And the juddering ways
The skittered agitations
The bridled and the umbraged
My tears appease not your thirst
My blood was never for you
I am running still
Alone as I have ever been
And this kissing air on my face
From here to for ever
Is clean and pure
As wonder

Legions of Dust
Atalict

CHAPTER TWENTY-ONE

'He was not a modest man. Contemplating suicide,
he summoned a dragon.'

Gothos' Folly
Gothos

'*E*VEN SHOULD YOU SUCCEED, COTILLION. BEYOND ALL EXPECTATION,
beyond, even, all desire. They will still speak of your failure.'
He stood in the place where the Whorl had manifested – a
wounding in the fabric of Shadow, a place now slowly healing. There
was nothing else here, nothing to give evidence to the struggles that
had occurred, the blood that had been spilled. Still, Chaos felt closer
than it ever had, as if moments from erupting once again. *The madness
of sorcerers, the ambitions of the starved . . . we're surrounded by
fools wanting more than what they have. And, alas, it's all too familiar
company, and the ugly truth is that we may not be out of place in that
crowd.* Edgewalker's words haunted him. The breathtaking ambition,
the sheer verve of all that they had set in motion. *But now we have
finally arrived – it's all cut loose, and so much – so much – is out of
our hands.*

He saw footprints in the grey dust, reminding him that there were
other arenas, distant places where battles raged on. Nothing was
simple, and in the spilling of blood no one could guess the myriad
channels it would carve.

*Shadowthrone, old friend, we have done what we could – but the
game is much bigger than we ever imagined. This gamble . . . gods, this
gamble.* One hand drifted to one of the knives at his belt. And then he
shook himself, straightening.

Take a deep breath, lad. Here goes . . .

*　　*　　*

615

'What you ask of me, it is too much. Yes, of course I see the necessity – I may have sickened, even threatened, but magic is not my enemy. It never was. Indeed, I envy its gifts to this world. Upon my own . . . ah, no matter. Belief can be rotten. All it takes is one betrayal to steal away an entire future.

'You would not have recognized me in my anger. It shone blinding bright. There remain those, among the multitudes I left behind, who imagine themselves gods, for all their mortal trappings. They would maintain a tyranny such as no true god could ever imagine. They would enslave generation upon generation – all those sharing the same soil, the same water, the same air. They conspire to keep them on their knees. Bowed in servitude. And each slave, measuring his or her life, can see – if they dare – only the truth, and so most of my world, most of my children, live a life of despair and suffering, and ever growing rage.

'Is this all there must be? The tyrants would have it so. I sometimes dream . . . yes, I know you have little time . . . I dream of returning, swords blazing with holy vengeance. I dream, Shadowthrone, of murdering every one of those fuckers. Is this what it means to be a god? To be an implacable weapon of justice?

'Wouldn't that be nice. I agree.

'No, I'm not that much of a fool. It will be no different. And should you achieve the impossible with your handful of mortals, should you free me . . . and find the path, the moment I take my first step upon the soil of my home they will emasculate me. Bleed me. Gut me, and then stretch my hide overhead. They'll need shade from the torrid heat of all the fires they themselves lit. That is the problem with tyrants, they outlive us all.

'I will do what you ask. Rather, I shall try. Pieces of me remain missing and I despair of ever seeing them again. It is my understand- ing that the one named Skinner, usurper and tyrant king of my House of Chains, has many enemies. He can now count me among them. Do you imagine he loses sleep?

'No, I don't either. Betrayers never do.

'Shadowthrone. You will not betray me, will you?'

'Karsa Orlong, where are all the gods of peace?'

He stepped outside, straightening. 'I know not.'

Picker turned to face the city. Many troubles there. Perhaps at last they had begun to settle. But . . . all that boiled beneath the surface, well, that never went away. 'Do you know how to get there?'

He eyed her. 'I know how to get there.'

She drew a deep breath – she could hear movement inside the hut behind the giant. Picker lifted her gaze until it locked with the

Toblakai's. *'I call upon the vow you made long ago, Karsa Orlong of the Teblor. When you walk to where you must go, a crippled priest will find you. In the street, a broken man, a beggar, and he will speak to you. And by his words, you shall understand.'*

'I already understand, Malazan.'

'Karsa—'

'There are too many gods of war.' And then he took up his sword, and inside the hut a woman began weeping. *'And not one of them understands the truth.'*

'Karsa—'

His teeth were bared as he said, *'When it comes to war, woman, who needs gods?'*

She watched as he set off. And under her breath she whispered, *'Darujhistan, I beg you, do not get in this man's way.'*

Dust roiled over the distant encampment. Squinting, Paran took another bite of the alien fruit his foragers had found, and wiped at the juices dribbling down into his beard.

'That is not helping, High Fist.'

He glanced over. Ormulogun was scratching desperately on a bleached board with his willow charcoal stick. At his feet squatted a fat toad, watching his efforts with gimlet eyes.

'Nothing will help that,' the toad sighed.

'Posterity!' snapped the Imperial Artist.

'Posterity my ass,' Gumble replied. 'Oh, was that not droll of me? Critics are never appreciated for what they truly are.'

'What? Leeches sucking on the talent of others, you mean?'

'It is my objectivity that you so envy, Ormulogun.'

'And you,' the artist muttered, 'can stick that objectivity up your posterity, toad.'

Paran took a last bite of the fruit, examined the furry pit, and then flung it over the wall. He wiped his hands on his thighs and turned. 'Fist Rythe Bude.'

The woman was leaning out over a parapet. She straightened. 'Sir?'

'Assemble the companies at their stations. It's time.'

'Aye, sir.'

Lounging nearby, Noto Boil drew the fish spine from between his front teeth and stepped forward. 'Is it truly?'

'Weapons,' said Paran. 'Kept hidden away. But there comes a time, Noto, when they must be unsheathed. A time, in fact, to put proof to the pretensions.' He eyed the cutter. 'The gods have been kicking us around for a long time. When do we say *enough*?'

'And in their absence, High Fist, will we manage things any better?'

617

'No,' Paran said, walking past him, 'but at least then we won't have the option of blaming someone else.'

Sister Belie scanned the distant walls. Suddenly, not a soldier in sight. 'They've quit,' she said. 'Now, the question is, do they leave the way they came, or do they march out from the gate – or what's left of it – and try to break the siege?'

Standing beside her, Watered Exigent glanced back at the camp. 'If the latter, Sister, then we are, perhaps, in trouble.'

Sister Belie pretended not to hear him. If his seed of doubt thirsted for water, he would have to find it elsewhere. *Another week. That is all we need. And then Brother Serenity will be here, with five thousand heavily armoured foreigners.* The besieging forces were damaged – that last assault had been brutal. She was down to half strength. Her hold on them was fragile, and this was not a familiar feeling.

'I see no movement at the gate, Sister Belie.'

There was a barrier to dismantle, and that would take time. *But . . . I feel it. They're coming for us.* 'Assemble the companies, Exigent. That gate is the bottleneck. If we can lock them there, we hold them until they're exhausted, too mauled to force the issue.'

'And if they break us instead?'

She turned, studied him. 'Do you doubt the power of my will? Do you imagine that this Master of the Deck can manage anything more than fending me off? I will not yield, Exigent. Understand that. And if it means that every single one of our Shriven – and every single one of their Watered commanders – ends up a corpse on the field, then so be it.'

Watered Exigent paled, and then he saluted. 'I will inform the commanders that we shall advance.'

'Have them ready, Exigent. The command to advance shall be mine and mine alone.'

'Of course, Sister Belie.'

After he had left, she returned her attention to the keep. Still no activity at the barricade. *Perhaps my feeling about this is wrong. Perhaps indeed he flees through a warren, and just like that, the siege is done. But he will return. Somewhere – this thorn is yet to leave our side, I am certain of it.*

Her eyes narrowed, and she blinked rapidly to clear a sudden blurring of her vision – but the problem was not with her eyes. To either side of the barricaded gate, the massive walls had grown strangely smudged, all along the breadth, as if stone had become water.

And from these places, troops appeared in formation, and then skirmishers and archers, fanning out from main ranks. The five-deep lines then unfolded and began linking up with those to either side.

Cavalry thundered into view on the far left flank, riding hard for a rise to the west.

She heard the shouts of confusion from her commanders, felt the recoiling fear of the Shriven. *He opened gates through the walls. He knew we would be studying the barricade, waiting for them to begin dismantling it. He knew we wouldn't advance until they did so. And now we are not ready.*

Sister Belie swung round. 'Form a line! Form a line!' *My voice will take their souls, and I will drive the Shriven forward, like wolves unleashed. They will ignore their wounds. Their fear. They will think only of slaughter. By the time my last soldier falls, the enemy will have ceased to be a military threat. This I swear!*

She saw her Watered commanders taking control of their companies, their voices powerful as iron-toothed whips. She could feel it now – the cold, implacable sorcery of Akhrast Korvalain, gathering, and she was pleased at its burgeoning strength.

And then someone shrieked, and Sister Belie staggered. *What? I have lost one of my commanders! How?*

She saw a swirl of soldiers, closing in to where one of the Watered had been standing a moment earlier. Terror and confusion rippled outward.

Forty paces distant from that scene, another commander suddenly died, his chest blossoming wounds.

They have infiltrated assassins! She awakened her voice. 'FIND THEM! ASSASSINS! FIND THEM!'

The companies were in chaos. 'FACING RANKS, PREPARE FOR THE ENEMY!'

She saw Exigent, heard his shouts as he struggled to reassert order on his milling Shriven. As she moved to join him, there was a blossom of darkness behind the man. Sister Belie shrieked a warning, but – too late. Knives sank home. Exigent arched in shock, and then was falling.

Akhrast Korvalain, I call upon your power! She set off down the slope. The darkness had vanished, but then, as magic heightened her vision, she could see its swirling path – there would be no hiding from her, not now. *A mage. How dare he!* 'NO POWER BUT MINE!'

And she saw that whirling black cloud stagger, saw it pinned in place, writhing in sudden panic.

Hands twitching in anticipation, she advanced on it. Off to her right, she could hear the enemy's horns announce the attack – she would deal with that later. *I can still save this. I must!*

The darkness convulsed in the grip of her power.

Now only six paces between her and the hidden mage. 'NO POWER BUT MINE!'

The sorcery erupted, vanished with a thunderous detonation, and she saw before her a man staggering, sinking down to his knees. Dark-skinned, bald, gaunt – *not the Master of the Deck*. No matter. She would rend him limb from limb.

Four paces, her boots crunching on gravel, and he looked up at her. And smiled. 'Got you.'

She did not even hear her killer as he came up behind her, but the long knives that burst from her chest lifted her from her feet. She twisted, balanced on two hilts, as her slayer raised her yet higher. Then, with a low grunt, he flung her to one side. She was thrown through the air, landing hard, rolling across sharp stones.

The bastard had severed the veins beneath both her hearts. And now, lying in her last moments, her head lolled and she saw him. Burly, ebon-skinned, the long-bladed knives dripping in his hands.

Her Watered were all dead. She heard the enemy ranks smashing into her disordered forces. She heard the slaughter begin.

Faintly, she caught the mage speaking to the assassin. 'Sheathe that Otataral blade, Kalam, and be quick about it.'

And he rumbled a reply, 'Done. Now . . . make me invisible again.'

Their voices grew more distant. 'Do you think it's easy? She damned near broke my back with that command.' They were walking away.

'Just feeling a tad exposed here, Quick – behind enemy lines and all.'

'What lines?'

Sister Belie closed her eyes. *Otataral? You unsheathed Otataral? Oh, you fool.* And these, her last thoughts, bubbled with a kind of dark pleasure.

The enemy broken, routed, Warleader Mathok rode up to Paran's position near the westernmost rise, and reined in. 'High Fist! The last have fled east, down into the valley. Shall we pursue?'

'No,' Paran replied, watching as Quick Ben and Kalam approached from across the killing field. 'Mathok, begin gathering up forage for your horses. Send parties deeper into the valley if needed – but for resupply only, no chasing down. I fear we shall have to ride hard now.'

'Where?'

'South, Mathok. South.'

The Warleader wheeled his mount round, yelling commands at his second, T'morol, who waited a short distance back with a wing of cavalry, and then rode off in the direction of his main force. Mathok's raiders had been eager, and they had acquitted themselves well. Watching the Warleader ride away, Paran rubbed at the back of his neck. 'No wonder you winced at every move, Dujek,' he said under

620

his breath. 'I'm a mass of knotted ropes.' *Still, the enemy broke at first contact, and what could have been a nasty scrap turned into a slaughter. A mere handful of casualties, and most of those from idiots falling on weapons in their haste to pursue.* Ensorcelled voices were all very well, but if that was where all the discipline and courage came from . . . *now, we can see the flaw in that, can't we?*

'High Fist,' said Quick Ben, walking up like a man who'd taken a beating. His face was drawn, his eyes skittish with something that might be pain.

Paran nodded. 'High Mage. Was it as bad as it looks?'

'Not really. Just out of practice. Lost touch with being subtle, I think.'

A curious thing to say, Paran reflected, and then he faced Kalam. The assassin's weapons were sheathed, and he looked rather pleased with himself. For no reason he cared to discover, Paran found he wanted to take that smugness down a notch or two. *You've been killing people, after all.* He regarded him for a moment longer before saying, 'Your wife wishes your attention.'

The man scowled. 'Now?'

That was easy. 'Since you're covered in blood, Corporal, you might want to wash first.'

Quick Ben snorted. 'I'd forgotten, Kalam. You're a lowly *corporal* – meaning I can order you around.'

'Just try it, you Hood-bitten snake.'

After the assassin had left them, the High Mage turned to Paran. Hesitated, and then said, 'Felt something, far to the southwest . . .'

'As did I, Quick Ben.'

That skittish look returned. 'Do you know what it was?'

'Do you?'

The High Mage sighed. 'Back to that, then, is it?'

Paran cocked his head. 'When I asked Shadowthrone for Kalam, I admit that I didn't expect you to be the delivery man. My last sense of you was in the company of my sister's army, keeping your head down.'

Quick Ben nodded, looking thoughtful. 'You were able to sniff out things like that? I'm impressed, Ganoes Paran. You have come a long way from the nervous, gut-sick captain I remember from Black Coral.'

'I'm still gut-sick, High Mage,' he said. 'And as for sensing distant powers, alas, that's been growing ever more uncertain. And obviously, since coming within the influence of the Assail warren I have been effectively blind. But with my sister, it was never easy in the best of circumstances—'

'Her sword.'

'Her sword, yes. And . . . other things.'

621

Quick Ben's nod was sympathetic. 'Sisters, aye.' Then his gaze sharpened. 'That . . . manifestation we felt. Do you think . . . was it her?'

Paran frowned. Just the mention of his stomach had delivered a nip of pain, and then vague nausea, reluctant to fade. *And look at us, still stepping round each other. Forget all that, Paran. Be honest, see what happens.* 'I don't know, High Mage. But I mean to find out.'

Quick Ben studied the mass of soldiers moving through the enemy supplies, and then he rubbed at his eyes. 'Ganoes Paran, what are we? Here, what are we?'

Paran felt his face twisting as anxiety gnawed again at his stomach. 'Quick Ben, we're soldiers of the Emperor. It's all we ever have been.'

Quick Ben shot him a look. 'You were just a child when he ruled.'

Paran shrugged. 'Nonetheless.'

'Aye,' the High Mage muttered like a man trying to swallow bad news, '*nonetheless*. But . . . that empire is gone, Paran. If it ever existed at all.'

Now that's a sharp observation. 'Nothing lasts, Quick Ben. Speaking of which, how do you warrant Kalam and Minala's chances?'

Quick Ben grunted and the sound might have been wry laughter, or sympathy. 'I don't. And while I think they'd be good together, they keep trying to wear each other's skin, if you know what I mean.'

'Sort of.'

'It's not love that's the problem.'

'It's all the rest.'

Quick Ben nodded, and then he shrugged. 'So tell me, O Master of the Deck of Dragons, what awaits us now?'

'That depends.'

'On what?'

'Gods below, where do I begin?'

'Start with the worst it could get.'

The worst? 'How much do you already know?'

Quick Ben rubbed vigorously at his face, as if trying to rearrange his own features. *And, maybe, become someone else.* 'Not as much as you might believe,' he said. 'Shadowthrone's not yet gotten over some past slight I offered him – though for the life of me I can't recall what it might have been. In any case, we're not exactly whispering in each other's ear.'

'Still,' Paran said, not quite convinced.

'Well. You have to understand – I usually work alone. And if I need help, I make sure the bargain I make is mutually beneficial . . . to keep down the chances of taking a knife in the back. I admit it, High Fist, I really trust no one.'

'No one at all?'

'The trust I have . . . for some people . . . comes down to how well I know them, and then it's a matter of my trusting them to do what I think they're going to do.'

'That's a rather cynical take on trust,' Paran observed.

'It's the safest. It doesn't take much insight to realize that most people are only looking out for themselves. And once you figure out what they want, you can—'

'Manipulate them?'

The wizard shrugged. 'Am I that much of a mystery? I have twelve souls in me. Think about that. All those lives, all those desires, regrets, hurts. Whatever you feel about your life, I have that a dozen times over. And some of those souls in me . . . *are old*.'

'Yet, of necessity, you all have to work together, for a common purpose.'

'If you say so.'

Paran studied the man. *Mystery? What mystery?* 'Right. Very well. The worst? Here goes, then. Kurald Galain falls to vengeful Tiste Liosan, and they walk that path right into the heart of Shadow, ousting Shadowthrone, and from there they march onward, to this world, joining with the Forkrul Assail in a tide of slaughter, until not one city is left standing, not one field planted, not one human child born into the world. Do you want the rest?'

'There's more?'

'The Elder Gods, having at last freed the Otataral Dragon, succeed in the annihilation of magic, barring that paid for in blood – unless of course Korabas is killed, but if that happens it will mean that the Eleint, who are now or will soon be loose in this realm, will have killed it – and they will in turn seek domination, not just of this realm, but of all realms, delivering chaos wherever they go. And so, even with us wiped from the earth, terrible powers will contest the claim to our legacy. The gods will be dead, magic a thirst only fools would dare invite, and . . . well, should I go on?'

Quick Ben licked dry lips. 'Parts of Burn are dying – on our way here, whenever we touched the soil of this world, I could feel her skin searing, drying and shrivelling into something . . . lifeless.'

'The Otataral Dragon, yes.'

'I probably already knew that,' Quick Ben muttered. 'Just trying not to think about it and hoping it would all go away. Hood's breath! Ganoes Paran – tell me what we can do to prevent all this?'

The High Fist's brows rose. 'How unfortunate. That is the question I was going to ask you, Quick Ben.'

'That's not funny.'

'Wasn't meant to be.'

'Your sister—'

'Aye, my sister. You were with her, wizard. She must have explained her plan.'

Quick Ben looked away. 'She would free the Crippled God.'

'And that's it?'

'How should I know? Was your whole family like her? Nobody saying a damned thing to each other? Dead silence at the dinner table? Is that how you managed to get along, assuming you got along in the first place?'

Paran grimaced. 'Can't say we did, much. Got along, I mean.'

'What might she be holding inside?'

'I wish I knew.'

Quick Ben's growing agitation was evident in his waving hands, his sudden pacing, the sharp, wide-eyed looks he threw at Paran. 'I thought you two had this *planned*!'

'Had *what* planned?'

'You're the Master of the Deck of Dragons!'

'So I am. Why, you want to play?'

For a moment it seemed Quick Ben's eyes would burst from their sockets. And then, with sudden hope: 'A reading! Yes – that's it! I'd take a damned reading right now – why not?'

But Paran was shaking his head. 'You don't want that, High Mage. Trust me, you don't. There are too many rogue players in this game. Icarium. Draconus. The First Sword of the T'lan Imass. Olar Ethil, Silchas Ruin, Tulas Shorn, Kilava – even Gruntle, the Mortal Sword of Treach. And now the Eleint, and how many dragons have come or are coming through the gate? A hundred? A thousand? Oh, and the Elder Gods: Errastas, the past Master of the Tiles, and Kilmandaros and her son . . .'

Quick Ben was staring as if Paran had lost his mind.

Paran scowled. 'What now?'

'They – they're *all here*?'

'I have the Deck of Dragons in my damned skull, remember. I caught the first winds of convergence some time ago. Trust me when I say this will be the biggest the world has ever seen, bigger even than the chaining of the Crippled God. Nobody said it'd be easy, High Mage. The question is, what do you have to offer me?'

Quick Ben snarled. 'Why, more good news, what did you think?'

'What do you mean?'

The High Mage threw up his hands. 'Let's just add the K'Chain Che'Malle and the Jaghut, and oh, we should probably mention Hood himself – no longer dragging the Throne of Death by one ankle. And who knows how many slavering fanatics of the Wolves of Winter! And what about the Crippled God himself – will he go quietly? Why should he? If I was him, even if you showed me the inviting door at the far end, I'd be slicing throats all the way down the corridor. I'd have damn well earned the right to as much vengeance as I could muster!'

Paran grunted. 'All right, it's rather more complicated than I had imagined, then.'

Quick Ben seemed to choke on his reply. After a bout of coughing, and then spitting, he shook his head and, eyes watering, he rubbed at his face again. Then he took a deep, settling breath, and said, 'We need a secret weapon, Paran.'

'I have a gut feeling about that—'

'The one burning a hole in your stomach?'

I hope not. 'I think we might have *two* secret weapons, High Mage.'

'Please, I am begging you, go on.'

'Quick Ben, tell me, who was the toughest Bridgeburner you ever knew? Think back, and think carefully. Get your ego out of the way. Ignore your favourites and the ones who spent all their time looking mean. Not the callous shits, not the back-stabbers, none of the posers. The *toughest*, Quick Ben. Day in, day out, good times, bad. Tell me. Who?'

The High Mage squinted, glanced down at the ground at his feet, and then he sighed and nodded, looking up as he said, 'I didn't need that list, Ganoes. I knew my answer right from the start. We all knew.'

'Who?'

'Fiddler. There's no tougher man alive.'

Paran looked away. 'My family . . . aye, we were something of a mess. But I will tell you this, this one thing I know without any doubt, and it starts with a memory – my sister had an area of ground cleared for her at the country estate, and it was where, beginning when she was barely five years old, she used toys to fight battles from every history book and scroll she could find. And the times when my father entertained High Fists in his horse-selling ventures, he'd make it a kind of challenge to those veteran commanders – take to the field against little sallow-faced Tavore, with all those toy soldiers. Count your attrition honestly, and see what happens. My sister, Quick Ben, from about seven onward, never lost to a single commander. And when their corpses were dragged away, she went deeper into the histories, she started taking the loser's sides, and then won those, too.'

'Tavore, then.'

'Think of all the great military leaders – Dassem, Coltaine, K'azz, Dujek, Greymane – for what it is worth, I would pit my sister against any of them. Gods below, against *all* of them.' He continued staring into the southwest. 'There you have it, High Mage. Fiddler and my sister. Our two weapons.' When he looked back he saw Quick Ben studying him.

The High Mage said, 'The ascended Bridgeburners hold the gates of death.'

'I know.'

'Except for Hedge. Whiskeyjack sent Hedge back – to Fiddler.'

'Did he now?'

'Remember Pale, Ganoes Paran?'

'As much of it as I could, which wasn't much.'

'Right – you weren't there yet, not when we got together on a hill outside the city, to shake things down one more time. Or, if you *were* around, Sorry was sticking a dagger in your back about then.'

'What about it, Quick?'

'It's just . . . we were all there. Trying to make sense of things. And now I've got this feeling . . . we're all going to meet again. To bring it all to an end.'

'One way or another.'

'Aye.'

'How do you gauge our chances, High Mage?'

'Miserable.'

'And our weapons?'

'With me vouching for Fiddler, and you for your sister,' he said, with a wry grin, 'the best we could hope for, I suppose.'

'And here I have two more – the infamous Kalam and Quick Ben. You know, if I wasn't such a realist, I'd be feeling confident right now.'

A scowl replaced the grin. 'Did you really have to put it quite that way, High Fist?'

He felt her eyes on him as he swung on to the horse. Settling in the saddle, gathering the reins, he squinted at the broad, terraced valley stretching away to his right. Rich lands, he mused. Then he glanced across at her. 'What?'

Minala shook her head. 'He's going to get you killed for real one of these days. You know that, don't you?'

Kalam snorted. 'Whatever you think you've seen, Minala, you'll just have to take my word: you really have no idea what we've survived, me and Quick.'

'Fine. Impress me.'

'Probably not possible, but I'll try anyway. Jaghut and Crimson Guard Avowed in Mott Wood. Tiste Andii assassin-mages and highborn demons in Darujhistan. More Claw than you could count.' Looking across at her, seeing her flat expression, he sighed. 'And we ain't so bad on our own, neither. Icarium, the Pannion Domin, K'Chain Nah'ruk and Soletaken dragons – Quick's faced down them all. As for me . . . if I could raise up every person and every demon and every whatever I've personally killed, I'd have an army

626

big enough to drown the Forkrul Assail in piss, never mind a knock-down fight.'

She continued staring at him, and then she said, inflectionless, 'You are both insufferable.'

'Some nerve,' he rumbled, 'after all that attention I just gave you.'

On all sides, Paran's Host was forming up, preparing to march – they had a third of a day's light left and it seemed the High Fist wasn't much interested in resting his troops. *In a hurry. That's always bad. Decent-looking soldiers, though. Lots of North Genabackan and Malazan mainlanders. And then there's those Seven Cities horsewarriors – tribals. Tribals always scared me.*

Minala took a drink from her waterskin and then spoke again. 'Were all you Bridgeburners the same? Arrogant, self-important, narcissistic?'

'Aye, and we earned every strut.'

'Rubbish.'

'In fact,' Kalam went on, ignoring her comment, 'it's probably why they decided to wipe us out. Every officer they threw at us couldn't hold up. We were a company run by the sergeants, Whiskeyjack first and foremost, but even then the sergeants voted on stuff, the orders they'd give to the captains and lieutenants, the orders to go down to the rest of us. As you might imagine, the high command didn't much like that. Oh, we might listen to a few, the ones we knew would do right by us – Dassem, Dujek, the ones we knew were worth their salt. But the rest? Not a chance.'

'Meaning you were ungovernable.'

'Meaning we were actually thinking of taking down the Empress. Aye, looking on it that way, Laseen had to wipe us out. She had no choice, and if it didn't sit well with her – having to kill off her toughest soldiers – well, I suppose we gave her few options.'

'Well now,' Minala said, 'finally, a little honesty.'

'So now I'm with the Host, wife. Which brings me to the question, what are you doing here? It ain't safe, wherever we're going.'

'Shadowthrone's children,' she said. 'Those that survived, I mean. I couldn't look them in the eye, not after what happened. I couldn't bear it any longer. And I could see – Cotillion and Shadowthrone, they were up to something. But mostly,' she seemed to shudder, 'the children, and what happened outside the throne room. I'll grant you, Quick Ben didn't hesitate, even when it looked like he was going to die. He didn't hesitate.'

'Icarium,' Kalam muttered. 'Maybe one day I'll face off against him, and we'll see.'

Minala snorted. 'That'd put a quick end to your arrogance, Kalam Mekhar.'

A signaller waved a banner, and it was time to ride down to join the vanguard. Kalam thought about Minala's last words, and sighed.

They kicked their horses into motion.

And Kalam asked, 'Love, tell me again, about that Tiste Edur with the spear . . .'

Commander Erekala of the Grey Helms entered the tent to find Brother Serenity standing in a corner at the back, draped in shadows and facing the canvas wall. There was no one else present and Erekala was brought up short.

'Pure?'

Serenity slowly turned. 'Have you ever been buried alive, Erekala? No, I would imagine not. Perhaps, in the occasional nightmare . . . no matter. Earlier this day I felt the murder of Sister Belie. And every one of her officers – all dead. The siege has been shattered, and our enemy is now loose within our demesne.'

Erekala blinked, but said nothing.

'Take off your helm,' Serenity said. 'Do you see, over there? A carafe. Foreign wine. I admit to having acquired a taste for it. It serves well in easing my . . . misgivings.' And he went over to pour himself a goblet. He poured a second goblet and gestured to it.

Helm now unstrapped and under one arm, Erekala shook his head and said, 'Misgivings, Pure? Is not the cause just?'

'Oh indeed, Erekala, there will be justice in our tide of retribution. But there will also be crime. We do not spare the children. We do not ask them to remake their world, to fashion a new place of humility, respect and compassion. We give them no chance to do better.'

'Pure,' said Erekala, 'as the teachings of the Wolves make plain, each and every generation is given a new chance. And each time, they but perpetuate the crimes of their fathers and mothers. "From the blow that strikes the innocent child to the one that lays waste to a forest, while the magnitude of the gesture may vary, the desire behind the hand does not." So the Wild would say, if it but had the words to speak.'

Serenity's eyes glittered in the shadows. 'And you see no presumption?'

Erekala cocked his head. 'Pure, the presumptions of the Perish Grey Helms are unending. Yet if we refuse or are unable to comprehend the suffering of the innocent – be it babe or beast – what do our words replace, if not all that we would not hear, would not countenance, lest it force us to change our ways, which we will never do. If we would speak for the Wild, we must begin with the voice of human conscience. And when conscience is not heeded, or is discarded, then what choice remains to us?'

'How clearly you enjoy such debate, Erekala. You remind me of better days . . . peaceful days. Very well, I will consider what the world would be like, for all within it, if conscience was more than just a whispering voice. If, indeed, it could raise a hand in anger. And, when even a sound beating is not enough, it might then close that hand about a throat and take the life from the transgressor.'

'It is our greatest presumption, Pure,' said Erekala, 'that we be the hand of conscience.'

'Holding a sword.'

'And finally driven to use it, yes.'

Serenity drained his goblet and replaced it with the other one. 'Yet your fellow humans – your *victims* – could not but see you as evil, as terrible murderers of the innocent – in fact, the very notion of guilt or innocence would be without relevance, in their eyes.'

'If we are to be evil, then we but balance the evil that opposes us.'

'Seeking . . . negation.' And Serenity smiled.

'Sister Reverence made us kneel, Pure. But we are not so naïve as to have come to you expecting anything but the opportunity to give our lives in the name of that which we believe to be right. You will use us, until none of us are left. She did not need to compel the Perish.'

'I believe you, Erekala. And I find in you and your people much to admire. I will regret sending you all to your deaths. But, as you might well understand, the Wild poses a threat even to us Forkrul Assail, should it truly be unleashed upon the world.'

'Pure, with my own Thrones of War I have carried your most dangerous enemy to this land. I know well what is coming. It is my judgement – and I am confident that the Mortal Sword and the Shield Anvil will concur – it is my judgement, Pure, that in the war now begun we will *all* lose. And in our losing, the Wild shall win.'

Serenity was silent for a time, studying the Perish commander, the unearthly eyes unwavering. Then, a small catch of breath. 'Do I err in understanding you, Erekala? You crossed the field of battle . . . to *help even the scales?*'

'By all means, Pure, send us to our deaths. Upon the other side, we shall await you.'

Serenity advanced a step. 'I know well these Malazans. And I *will* welcome them!'

'The Mortal Sword Krughava stood before the Adjunct Tavore and placed her sword in the Adjunct's hands. Before *her*, Pure, we did not kneel.'

'Sister Reverence forced you to kneel, you pompous fool!'

Erekala cocked his head. 'Did she?'

'You resisted!'

'Pure, why would we resist? You forget, we came to you, not the other way round.'

Serenity turned, faced the back wall again. His head tilted as he emptied the goblet of wine. 'Tomorrow we double our pace, Commander. We will hunt down the foreign army – the murderers of Sister Belie. And your Perish will fling themselves into the battle, and fight and not yield. If it takes the life of every single one of you, the enemy shall be destroyed.'

'Precisely,' Erekala replied.

'Dismissed.'

Donning his helm once more, Erekala left the tent.

Hips aching, Sister Reverence made her way along the ridge overlooking the now-withered farmland. She could see where Brother Diligence had established revetments, arbalest sangers, berms and trenches. She could see how he intended to funnel the enemy to the place of killing. Only the forward echelons and the engineer corps of the Shriven Army were present, the rest remaining closer to the city where supplies could readily accommodate them.

Such an army. Fifty thousand for this one battle, says Brother Diligence. And soon, more Perish Grey Helms. Five thousand heavy infantry, fanatical, and entirely subject to my desire – and Brother Diligence's. And surrounding the Spire, twenty thousand more, entrenched, immovable. What foe would dare this?

She saw her commander ahead, surrounded by officers and messengers. Old as he was, Brother Diligence seemed to have shed years now that a battle was imminent. As she drew closer, she heard him addressing his officers. '. . . shall be starving – we well know how unproductive the southlands are. And in this weakened state, they will gamble everything on a single cast of the die, a solitary, determined, desperate advance. We need but hold them until their energy is spent, for once that strength is gone they will have nothing in reserve. And then, and only then, shall we advance. Ah, Sister Reverence. Welcome.'

'Brother Diligence. All that I see here pleases me.'

He tilted in head in acknowledgement. 'Sister, has there been any word from Sisters Calm and Equity?'

'No, but I am not unduly concerned. In truth, we can manage quite well without them.'

He frowned, but nodded.

They walked a short distance from the officers.

'Brother Diligence,' she said, studying the preparations, 'I am aware of the Spire defences, and of this, your main army. Where are the reserve armies?'

'Sister Freedom and Brother Grave command twenty thousand Kolanse infantry positioned ten leagues to the west. To support them, Brother Aloft oversees fifteen thousand Shriven auxiliaries. These combined forces are so positioned as either to respond to a break-out from the enemy holding the keep, or to drive south to engage the enemy marching here – should we perceive the need for them, which I do not.' He fell silent then, and Reverence saw that his attention had been drawn downslope, to where a rider was fast approaching.

'News comes,' Reverence said. 'In haste.'

'From my southern outlying pickets, Sister.'

The Shriven's horse was lathered, straining with exhaustion as it lumbered up the slope. When the rider reined the beast in, it stumbled and barely recovered. The man, soaked in sweat, dismounted and stood before Diligence. 'Inquisitor,' he said, struggling to catch his breath.

'A moment,' Diligence said. 'I see you have ridden hard, Shriven, and such efforts tax your imperfect bodies. Gather yourself, and when you are ready, begin.'

The man gulped air for a dozen or so heartbeats, and then nodded. 'Inquisitor, a report by relay. Six days to the south, an army approaches.'

'And the size of this army?'

'Perhaps seven thousand, Inquisitor.'

Diligence gestured one of his officers over. 'Watered Hestand, prepare a single mounted battalion and a full support train – water and food for at least three legions. You are to make haste to intercept the army now marching up from the south. These foreigners are our allies, the land-based element of the Perish Grey Helms. Treat them with respect, Hestand, on your life.'

'Yes sir. Shall I deliver a message from you?'

'A simple welcome will do, until such time as we meet in person. However, it is certain that they will have news of our enemy's disposition, and that I wish to hear immediately. Be sure to have with you a full cadre of messengers and mounts.'

The Watered saluted and left.

Sister Reverence sighed. 'Soon, then.' She was silent for a moment, and then she faced Diligence. 'It must be understood, Brother, that the Heart shall be secured above all else. We well know that the gods are gathering, and that they will through force or deceit seek to wrest that organ from us. Failing that, they will attempt to destroy it.'

'None can hope to come close, Sister. The power of Akhrast Korvalain denies them and shall continue to do so. Their only possible path to the Heart is through their mortal servants.'

She feared she was missing something, however. Something . . . *vital*. 'I shall attend the Heart,' she said. 'I shall not leave its side.'

'Understood, Sister Reverence. You will then be accorded a fine view of the battle here, and may well realize our victory before do we on the field.'

'If instead I see failure, Brother, I shall by my own hand destroy the Heart.'

'Prudent,' he said.

Is this enough? What else can I do? And why – why this sudden unease? She stared southward, eyes narrowing. 'Why, Brother, do we now face such opposition? Another year, perhaps two, and Akhrast Korvalain would be of such power as to dominate this world. And then we could unleash righteous adjudication upon every land, in cleansing wrath.'

'The Fallen God has forced their hand, Sister Reverence. We cannot determine precisely how, chained and weakened as he is, but I remain convinced that he is behind this gambit.'

'Perhaps that is as it should be,' she mused. 'After all, is not his creed the very antithesis of our own? The flawed, the helpless and the hopeless . . . daring to stand before holy perfection. The weak of spirit against the indomitable of spirit, the broken against the complete. What astonishes me, Brother Diligence, is their audacity in thinking they could defeat us! Before they even arrive, why, by their very doubts and mutual mistrust, they are already lost.'

Diligence's gaunt face pinched into a faint smile. '"In a war between fanatics and sceptics, the fanatics win every time."' At her frown he shrugged. 'In the vaults of the palace, Sister, our archivists came upon some ancient Jaghut scrolls. *Gothos' Folly.* I have been acquainting myself with its peculiar perspective.'

She grimaced. 'Fanaticism, Brother Diligence, is the harbour of delusions. While to others we may appear no different from fanatics, we are. Fundamentally different, for our cause is a justice beyond our own selves, beyond even our kind. And for all that we Forkrul Assail can but aspire to true perfection, justice stands outside and its state of perfection cannot be questioned.'

'"When wisdom drips blood fools stand triumphant."'

Reverence shot him a look. 'Have those scrolls burned, Brother Diligence. That is a command, not a request.'

He bowed. 'It shall be done at once, Sister Reverence.'

'And I would hear no more of this Gothos' folly, am I understood?'

'You are, Sister Reverence. Forgive me.'

Her hips throbbed with old pain. *We have walked so far. But at last, we make our stand. And we become the fulcrum of the world. And where but upon the fulcrum shall justice be found?* Clouds of dust from the work crews lifted to roll over their position. Discomforted by the sting in her eyes and the bitter taste in her mouth, she turned away. 'Carry on, Brother Diligence.'

*   *   *

Lying prone in the withered grasses with his gaze fixed on the vast camp sprawled in the plain below, Stormy swore under his breath, reached under his belly and dragged free a sharp stone. Beside him, Gesler scratched at his nose and said, 'That looks ominous, doesn't it?'

A troop of Perish were marching a half-dozen of their comrades – these ones stripped down weaponless and wearing only their undergarments – out to a trench from which diggers were only now climbing. When they were formed into a line facing that trench, they were made to kneel. Sword blades flashed. Heads rolled and bodies fell.

Gesler grunted. 'Explains Bent and Roach going mad over those long mounds yesterday.'

Sighing, Stormy said, 'If we practised that, instead of arguing all the time, Ges, we'd have killed each other a thousand times by now.'

'Some people hate it when the party ends.'

'Exactly.'

'Listen,' said Stormy, 'we caught us up with the shits – we should do like Gu'Rull says and cut 'em all down, starting with Tanakalian.'

'In her worst moments, Krughava might agree. If we didn't have her under guard, sooner or later she'd be down there trying to do it personally,' muttered Gesler, 'but it'd still be wrong. Not . . . tactical.'

'Oh, here we go again. High First Fist Sword Prancing Gesler the Great talking tactics again. Lay a wager the rest of them Perish aren't already waiting in the Assail capital – so instead of taking down five thousand Grey Helms here and now we'll have to take down twice that number a week from now. How does that make tactical sense?'

'Krughava thinks she can turn them back, Stormy. But now's not the time.'

'She also thinks the sun sets up her ass every night and comes out of her mouth every morning. She's unhinged, Ges. You can see that, can't you? Mad as a five-eyed one-whiskered cat—'

'Hold on . . . who's that?'

'Who? Where?'

'That girl.'

Stormy fell silent, watching. He could see Tanakalian approaching her, was stunned when the Shield Anvil knelt before her. They were too distant to hear, but by the girl's gestures – pointing at the trench where the bodies and heads had been dumped – she wasn't happy about something. And she was giving that backstabbing shit an earful.

'That must be her,' Gesler said. 'The one Faint told us about.'

'Destriant,' Stormy grunted. 'But the question is, how in Hood's name did she get here?'

'Warren. She was spat out by the Wolves.'

'If Krughava's going to have to face anybody down, it'll be her.'

'You're probably right, Stormy.' Gesler edged back down the slope of the ridge, and then sat up. After a moment Stormy slid down to join him. 'It's this,' Gesler said, wiping dirt from his hands. 'The Wolves of War, right? So how come that army's acting like they don't even know we're half a day behind them?'

Stormy scratched in his beard. 'Wolves do the hunting. They don't get hunted.'

'Except by us humans.'

'Still, might be just never occurred to them to take a look back.'

'So maybe the Adjunct had it right,' Gesler said. 'This army of K'Chain Che'Malle is ready to come down like a knife in the middle of the table.'

'More like we're like snakes in the grass, and our fangs are fuckin' dripping.' Stormy smiled without humour. 'Excited yet, Mortal Sword?'

Gesler's eyes were bright. 'You?'

'Nah, you're bound to mess it all up.'

'That didn't last. Thanks.'

'Just keep your head level, Ges, that's all I'm asking.'

Gesler's expression was incredulous. 'Now that's rich, Stormy, coming from you.'

'I'm more battle-hardened these days, Ges. All my wisdom I earned the hard way.'

'How are you managing to keep a straight face?'

'That's what us battle-hardened veterans do best. Now, let's get back to camp. My mouth is watering at the thought of more armpit fungi and a big tankard brimming with gland juice.'

There is treachery in his heart. Setoc stared down at the beheaded brothers and sisters, feeling the fury of the Wolves, struggling to contain its wild wrath. The presence of the beast gods within her surged mindless as a storm, and again and again she felt as if she was moments from drowning in the deluge. *I am Setoc. Leave me to be your voice! Blind rage is pointless – for all that your cause is just, it must be a human mind that guides us all into the war to come.*

And this was what Tanakalian did not understand. Or, perhaps, what he feared the most. *We must be free to speak – all of us. We must be free to object, to argue – even the Wolves do not understand this. Look at these bodies – they spoke out against the cruel pace . . . among other things. Above all, they spoke out of fear for the readiness of their fellow soldiers – this army is exhausted.*

She turned, faced south, her eyes narrowing on a grassy ridge opposite. *If they came for us now, these lizard warriors, we would fall like myrid to the neck-hooks. If they came for us now, I would have to awaken the Wolves. But . . . the footfall of gods upon the land shall summon like drums of war. Power draws power – too soon, too far away.*

Still . . . I wonder. Why do they not attack?

She turned to see Tanakalian approaching. *Another audience. Shall I drive him to his knees again, humiliate him? No. That can wait.* She set off to take the two of them a fair distance from the camp, well beyond earshot. *Still . . . treachery in his heart.*

Even before he caught up to her he began speaking. 'Destriant, you must understand. The Perish are bound by strict rules of behaviour. It is this discipline which gives us our strength.'

'You are destroying this army, Shield Anvil.'

'The K'Chain Che'Malle—'

'Have already caught up to us.'

His eyes widened, but for once he did not question her. 'The Wolves must be sent against them, Destriant! We cannot hope to—'

'Now that our soldiers can barely stand, no, you're right: we cannot.'

He drew himself up. 'This threat was ever present in my mind, Destriant. It was my hope that the K'Chain Che'Malle would be content with escorting the Letherii and Bolkando. But I knew that I could not gamble the lives of my brothers and sisters on that assumption. This is why I drove my soldiers as hard as I did – we must reach the safety of the Forkrul Assail as soon as possible.'

'But you have failed to do so, Shield Anvil. And what manner of welcome, do you imagine, will the Assail accord us when we arrive with an army already half-dead?'

He was pale and she could see the venom in his eyes. 'I had no choice.'

'You were impatient, Shield Anvil. You exulted in your betrayal and in so doing you revealed your true nature too soon – your once-allies know the truth of you now. And they have had time to adjust their tactics.'

'This is Krughava's fault! All of it!'

'There shall be no more executions, Shield Anvil. Worse, your denial of their embrace has made a mockery of your title. I look upon you and I can see, at last, the path that led to the Forkrul Assail.'

Shock twisted his face. 'What does that mean? I am sworn to the Wolves of Winter!'

'You are drunk on justice, Shield Anvil, and for all that you imagine you walk a straight line, in truth you stumble and weave. Now you stand before me, deluded in your righteousness, and upon the path where you walked' – she gestured back towards the bodies in the trench – 'the corpses of the innocent.'

'The delusions,' he said in a low rasp, 'are not mine, child.'

Setoc smiled. 'Go on. I am intrigued.'

'Do you truly believe you can withstand the will of the Forkrul Assail? We shall be brought to heel – but that is not how it was supposed to be. Their aims are petty compared to ours. For all their claims, Destriant, the truth is, I intended to *use* them. They demand that we kneel? So be it. It matters not. The Wolves are blind to all of this – we think in ways they cannot comprehend, and this game will not be won with slavering jaws and berserk rage. Against us, that has *never worked*. No, the Wolves of Winter are better off hiding in the forest, in the dark shadows. Leave us to do what must be done, and when all the players are weakened, then shall come the time for our gods to attack – after all, is that not the way of the wolves in the wild?'

'Tanakalian,' said Setoc, 'I agree with you. But alas, I cannot choose the times when the gods speak through me. I will have no control over their power the day it steals my will. Their anger will overwhelm, and through their eyes they will see nothing but blood.'

'That is not how to fight a war.'

'I know.'

He stepped forward, a sudden hope in his eyes. 'Then you must work with me, Destriant! We can win this – win it in truth! Warn the Wolves – if they manifest, within reach of the Forkrul Assail, they will be *murdered*. Or worse, enslaved.'

'Then stand before me now as a true Shield Anvil. It is not for you to judge, not for you to deny your brothers and sisters. And above all, it is not for you to take their lives.'

Tanakalian pointed back to the bodies in the trench. 'They would have deserted, Destriant. They would have fled back to Krughava, carrying with them vital information. Their crime was treason.'

'They sought to raise a new Mortal Sword,' she said. 'For the field of battle, they sought a veteran to command them. You killed them because of a personal slight, Tanakalian.'

'Matters were far more complicated than you realize.'

She shook her head. 'You face a crisis, Shield Anvil. Your soldiers have lost confidence in you. It is crucial that you understand – if not for me, this army would return to Krughava.'

'Unleash the Wolves upon the K'Chain Che'Malle – buy us the time we need.'

'It will not be.'

'Why not?'

'Because they refuse, Shield Anvil.'

'But . . . why?'

Setoc shrugged. 'The K'Chain Che'Malle were never the enemy of the beasts. They were never so insecure as to feel the need to slaughter everything in sight. They were never so frightened, so ignorant, so . . . pathetic. I believe the Wolves do not see them as deserving of slaughter.'

'And will they change their minds when those lizards attack us?'

She fixed on him a sharp, searching stare. 'What will the Wolves witness? K'Chain Che'Malle cutting down . . . *humans*.'

'But we Perish are to be their swords of vengeance!'

'Then we can only hope that we do not face the K'Chain Che'Malle on a field of battle.'

'Do you finally comprehend the necessity, the burden upon us, Destriant? We must stand in the shadow of the Forkrul Assail. We must be free to *choose* where and when to fight, and indeed whom we shall face. Let the Assail believe they have us well shackled and compliant, eager even.'

'You balance everything on the thinnest knife edge, Shield Anvil.'

'We are the Grey Helms, Destriant, and we *shall* serve the Wolves.'

'Indeed.'

'And that is why we must continue marching at this pace – leave the lizards no time to think about what to do about us. And if they chase our tails right into the Assail army, well, the moment those two ancient foes set sight upon each other . . .'

'We need only step aside.'

He nodded.

Dismissing him for the moment, Setoc turned away. *Perhaps. Is this the treachery I sense in Tanakalian? And if I cannot agree with his methods, must I then reject his intentions? But the game he would play . . . poised between two such deadly enemies . . . is it possible?*

No, ask yourself this instead, Setoc: what alternative do we have? When she turned he was standing as he had been, facing her, and in his face, blind need. 'Are you clever enough for this, Shield Anvil?'

'I see no other way, Destriant.' He hesitated, and then he said, 'Each night, I pray to the Wolves of Winter—'

She turned away again, and this time with finality. 'You waste your breath, Shield Anvil.'

'*What?*'

'They don't understand worshippers,' she said, closing her eyes. '*They never did.*'

Once more, staggering lost – the darkness and the unbearable pressure, the raging currents that sought to rend the flesh from his bones, and on all sides the half-buried wreckage of the lost. He stumbled over rotted planks from broken hulls, kicked up bleached bones that flashed and spun in milky clouds. Silt-painted amphorae, ingots of tin and lead, a scattering of hundreds of round shields, hammered bronze over crumbling wood. Banded chests collapsed and spilling out their gems and coins – and everywhere the remains of sea creatures, their insensate bodies dragged down into the depths, and the rain from above was unending.

Brys Beddict knew this world. Was this yet another dream? A haunting from his memories? Or had his soul at last returned, to this place he would learn to call *home*?

Above all, the greatest pressure he felt, the one force which neither the strength of his legs nor the stolid stubbornness of his will could withstand, was that of immense, devastating loneliness. *Into death we step alone. Our last journey is made in solitude. Our eyes straining, our hands groping – where are we? We do not know. We cannot see.*

It was all he needed. It was all anyone needed. *A hand to take ours. A hand reaching out from the gloom. To welcome us, to assure us that our loneliness – that which we knew all our lives and so fought against with each breath we took – that loneliness has at last come to an end.*

Making death the most precious gift of all.

A thousand sages and philosophers had closed desperate fingers about the throat of this . . . this one thing. Even as they recoiled in horror, or, with a defiant cry, leapt forward. *Tell us, please – show us your proofs. Tell us oblivion has a face, and upon it the curve of a smile, the blessing of recognition. Is that too much to ask?*

But this, he knew, was the secret terror behind all faiths. The choice to believe, when to *not* believe invited the horror of the meaningless, all these lives empty of purpose, all these hopes relinquished, dropped from the hand, left to sink in the thick mud – *with silts raining down until everything is buried.*

I knew a man who studied fossils. He had made this pursuit his entire life. He spoke with great animation about his need to solve the mysteries of the distant past. And this guided his life for decades, until, in a confession written the night he took his own life, he finally spoke of the truth he had at last discovered. 'I have found the secret, the one secret that is the past. The secret is this. There are more life forms in the history of this world than we could ever imagine, much less comprehend. They lived and they died and what little remains tells us only that they once existed. And therein hides the secret, the terrible secret. It's all for nothing. Nothing but fragments of bone. All of it . . . for nothing.'

Easy enough to understand how this could have unleashed the black dogs, when comprehension yielded only a vast abyss.

But then Brys found a familiar face rising before him, there in his beleaguered memories, or dream-world – whichever this was. Tehol, and that look in his eyes that one might see the moment before he spat in the face of every god that ever existed, only to then move on to the dour mendics and philosophers and wild-haired poets. *Damn them all, Brys. No one really needs an excuse to give up on life, and all the ones you hear you might as well pluck out of a hat. Surrender is easy. Fighting is hard. Brother, I remember once reading about deadly swords that, in the moment of war, would howl with laughter. What better symbol of human defiance than that?*

Sure, Brys, I remember that bone collector. He got it all wrong. With that secret he discovered, he had a choice. Despair or wonder. Between the two, which would you choose? Me, I look at the idiocy and futility of existence and how can I not wonder?

Every creature dies, brother – you should know. I'd wager that each and every one of those creatures set out into the darkness, soul crouched and timid, not knowing what waited ahead. Why should us smart animals be unique? Death levels us with the cockroaches and the rats and the earthworms. Faith is more than turning our backs on the abyss and pretending it's not there, Brys. It's how we climb up above the cockroaches, top of the ladder, lads! And those seven rungs make all the difference! Eight? Eight rungs, then. Up here, the gods can finally see us, right?

Remember that other sage who said the soul is carried from the body by maggots? Crush a maggot kill a soul. And damn but they'd have to crawl far, so the gods gave them wings, to carry them up into the heavens. Makes for a strangely logical theory, don't you think? Where was I, brother?

More to the point, where are you?

The face of Tehol drifted away, leaving Brys alone once more. *Where am I, Tehol? I am . . . nowhere.*

He stumbled, he groped blindly, he staggered beneath unimaginable weights – too ephemeral to shrug off, yet heavy as mountains nonetheless. And on all sides, unrelieved darkness—

But no . . . is that light? Is that . . .

In the distance, a lantern's yellow flame, murky, flaring and ebbing in the currents.

Who? Do . . . do you see me?

A hand reaching out, the curve of a smile on a welcoming face.

Who are you? Why do you come for me, if not to bless me with revelation?

The stranger held the lantern low, as if no longer caring what it might reveal, and Brys saw that he was a Tiste Edur, a grey-skinned warrior wearing tattered leathers that streamed behind him like tentacles.

Step by step, he drew closer. Brys stood in the man's path, waiting.

When the Edur arrived, he looked up, dark eyes staring with an inner fire. His mouth worked, as if he'd forgotten how to speak.

Brys held up a hand in greeting.

The Edur grasped it and Brys grunted as the man leaned forward, giving him all his weight. The face, pitted and rotted, lifted to his own.

And the Edur spoke. 'Friend, do you know me? Will you bless me?'

When his eyes snapped open, Aranict was ready for him, ready for the raw horror of his expression, the soul exposed and shaken to its very core, and she took him tight in her arms. And knew, in the pit of her heart, that she was losing him.

Back. He's on his way back, and I cannot hold on to him. I cannot. She felt him shudder, and his flesh felt cold, almost damp. *He smells of . . . salt.*

It was some time before his breathing calmed, and then once more he was asleep. She slowly disengaged herself, rose, throwing on a cloak, and stepped out from the tent. It was near dawn, the encampment still and quiet as a graveyard. Overhead, the Jade Strangers cut a vast swathe across the night sky, poised like talons about to descend.

She drew out her tinder box and a stick of rustleaf. To ease the gnawing hunger.

This land was ruined, in many ways far worse than the Wastelands. All around them were signs of past prosperity. Entire villages now empty, abandoned to weeds, dust and the scattered remnants left by those who had once lived there. The fields surrounding the farms were blown down to rocks and clay, and not a single tree remained – only stumps or, here and there, pits where even the stumps had been dug out. There was no animal life, no birds, and every well they examined, every stream bed her minor mages worked over, seeking to draw water from the depths, yielded little more than soupy sludge. Their few remaining horses were suffering and might not even make it into Kolanse proper. *And the rest of us aren't doing much better. Low on food, exhausting ourselves sinking wells, and knowing that somewhere ahead a well-rested, well-fed army waits for us.*

She drew hard on the stick, looked eastward to the distant camp of the Bolkando. No fires. Even the standards tilted like the masts of some foundered ship. *I fear we won't be enough, not to do what the Adjunct needed, what she wanted. It may prove that this entire journey will end in failure, and death.*

Brys came out of the tent to stand beside her. He took the stick from her fingers and drew on it. He'd begun doing that a few weeks past, seeking, perhaps, to calm his nerves in the wake of his nightmares. But she didn't mind. She liked the company.

'I can almost taste the thoughts of my soldiers,' he said. 'We will have to kill and eat the last horses. Won't be enough – even sparing the water to make a stew . . . ah, if we could have scavenged, this might have succeeded.'

'We're not done yet, my love.' *Please, I beg you, do not answer that with yet another sad smile. With each one, I feel you slip further away.*

'It is our growing weakness that worries them the most,' he said. 'They fear we won't be fit to fight.'

'The Perish, if anything, will be even worse off.'

'But they will have some days in which to recover. Besides which, Aranict, one must fear more the Assail army.'

She lit a second stick, and then gestured with one hand. 'If all of Kolanse is like this, they won't *have* an army.'

'Queen Abrastal assures me that Kolanse continues to thrive, with what the sea offers, and the fertile valley province of Estobanse continues to produce, sheltered from the drought.'

And each night the nightmares take you. And each night I lie awake, watching you. Wondering about all the other paths we could have taken. 'How have we failed her?' Aranict asked. 'What more could we have done?'

Brys grimaced. 'This is the risk when you march an army into the unknown. In truth, no commander in his or her right mind would even contemplate such a precipitous act. Even in the invasion of new territories, all is preceded by extensive scouting, contact with local elements, and as much background intelligence as one can muster: history, trade routes, past wars.'

'Then, without the Bolkando, we would truly be marching blind. If Abrastal had not concluded that it was in her kingdom's interest to pursue this – Brys, have we misjudged the Adjunct from the very beginning? Did we fall into the trap of assuming she knew more than she did, that all that she had set out to do was actually achievable?'

'That depends.'

'On what?'

He reached over and took the new stick of rustleaf. 'On whether she has succeeded in crossing the Glass Desert, I suppose.'

'A crossing that cannot be made.'

He nodded. 'Yes.'

'Brys, not even the Adjunct can *will* her Malazans to achieve the impossible. The world sets physical limits and we must live by them, or those limits will kill us. Look around – we are almost out of food and water. And this land has nothing to give us, and just as the farmers and villagers all fled or perished, so too are we faced with the same, hard reality. The country is destroyed.'

He seemed to be studying the sky. 'My father was not an imaginative man. He could never understand me and Tehol – especially Tehol.

Our brother Hull, well now, he started out as the perfect eldest son, only to be pronounced dead in the eyes of Father.' He was silent for a few moments, smoking, and then he resumed. 'Beyond all the tutors foisted upon us, it was our father who insisted on delivering his one lesson. Even if it killed us, he would teach us the value of pragmatism. Which is, as I am sure you well understand, nothing more than a cogent recognition of reality: its limits, its demands and its necessities.'

Aranict cocked her head, wondering at the direction of his thoughts. 'Beloved, of all men, the name of Tehol does not come to mind when I think *pragmatic*.'

He glanced across at her. 'And what of me?'

'In you, yes. You are a weaponmaster, after all. I never knew Hull, so of him I cannot say.'

'So, you conclude that of the three Beddict brothers, I alone absorbed our father's harsh lessons in pragmatism.'

She nodded.

Brys looked away again, this time to the southeast. 'How far away, do you think, lies the coast?'

'Proper marching, three days – if the queen's maps are at all accurate.'

'Oh,' he murmured, 'I am sure they are.'

'It's almost dawn,' Aranict said.

'We will not march today, my love.'

She shot him a look. 'A day's rest – at this point – could prove counterproductive.'

He flicked away the stick, eyes tracking the glowing end. 'Before he . . . changed his mind about things, Tehol became the wealthiest man in Lether, Aranict. Ask yourself, how could he have done that, if in pragmatism he was an utter failure?' He faced the camp. 'Today, we eat the last of our food, and drink the last of our water.'

'Brys?'

'I think,' he said, 'I will walk over to the Bolkando camp. Will you join me, love?'

'Mud of the gods, woman, what are you doing?'

Abrastal looked up. 'What does it look as if I'm doing, Spax?'

Her fiery tresses lay heaped on the tent floor. She was wrapped in her blanket and as far as he could tell, naked underneath. He watched as she resumed slashing long lengths away with her knife. 'I witness,' he said, 'the death of my lust.'

'Good. It's about time. I was never going to bed you, Barghast.'

'Not the point. It was the *desire* I took so much pleasure in.'

'That's pathetic.'

Spax shrugged. 'I am an ugly man. This is how ugly men get through each damned day.'

'You've been bedding my daughter.'

'She only does it to infuriate you, Highness.'

Abrastal paused with her knife, looked up at him. 'And has it succeeded?'

Grinning, Spax said, 'So I tell her every night. All about your rants, your foaming mouth, your outrage and fury.'

'Ugly and clever, a deadly combination in any man.'

'Or woman, I would wager.'

'What do you want?'

'My scouts have returned from the coast, Highness. With news.'

Finally, she sensed something in him, in his tone, or the look in his eyes, for she slowly straightened. 'Are we flanked, Warchief?'

'No enemy in sight, Highness.'

'Then what? As you can see, I'm armed, and my patience is getting as short as my hair.'

'Ships were sighted. A rag-tag fleet.'

'*Ships?* Under what flag?'

'Letherii, Highness.'

Suddenly she was on her feet. Her hair only half shorn, she flung the knife away. The blanket slipped down and Spax found himself staring at her magnificent body.

'Highness, I could live with that short hair.'

'Get out of here – and send a messenger to Brys.'

'No need, Highness – about the messenger, I mean. He and Aranict are even now approaching camp.'

She was casting about for her clothes. Now she paused. 'This was planned!'

Spax shrugged. 'Possibly. But then, why not tell us? I'm more inclined to think this gesture was made by the king, entirely on his own.'

She grunted. 'You might be right. What else did the scouts see?'

'Landings, Highness. Battalion strength, Letherii infantry and auxiliaries. And more supplies than any single battalion would ever need.'

'Was the Imperial Standard flying? Does King Tehol command?'

'No, only the battalion colours were present, as far as my scouts could determine. In any case, just this last night, my scouts realized that riders were on their trail. They too will be upon us shortly.'

She was still standing before him, in all her glory. 'What are you still doing here?'

'Answering your questions, Highness.'

'I am finished with my questions. Get out.'

'One more detail you might be interested in learning,' Spax said. 'Among the auxiliaries, Highness, there are Teblor.'

Abrastal and Warchief Spax were waiting outside the queen's tent, and Aranict studied them as she and Brys approached. Both were arrayed in their full regalia, the queen looking imperial though the hair on one side of her head was shorn away, and the Gilk Warchief festooned in weapons and wearing an ankle-length cloak made of turtle shells. *What is this? What has happened?*

Abrastal was the first to speak. 'Prince Brys, it seems we shall be entertaining guests shortly.'

'Before you ask,' Brys replied, 'this was not arranged beforehand. However, the last messengers I sent back to my brother detailed what we then knew of our route. At the time, we were ten days into the Wastelands.'

'Still,' she said, 'the timing of this is . . . extraordinary.'

'My brother's Ceda is able to sense, even at a great distance, sorcerous efforts seeking groundwater.' He turned slightly to nod at Aranict. 'As you know, our legion mages have been engaged in such rituals ever since we left the Wastelands.'

Abrastal's voice was flat. 'Your Ceda was able to track us based on the drawing of water from the ground . . . while he sits ensconced in the palace in Letheras? You expect me to give credit to that explanation, Prince? Not even a god could reach that far.'

'Yes, well.'

They could hear horses now, coming in from the southeast, and the Bolkando camp was suddenly stirring, as exhausted, suffering soldiers left their bivouacs to line the main avenue between tent rows. Voices were lifting – and now Aranict could see the vanguard. She squinted at the pennants. 'Sire,' she said to Brys, 'Letherii, yes, but I do not recognize the heraldry – what battalion is that?'

'A new one, I would hazard,' Brys replied.

The battalion commander halted his troop with a gesture and then rode forward until he was ten paces from Brys and the others. He dismounted in a clatter of armour, removed his helm and then walked to kneel before the prince.

'Idist Tennedict, sire, commanding the Chancel Battalion.'

'Please stand, Commander,' said Brys. 'Your arrival is most welcome. Idist Tennedict – I believe I know that family name though at the moment I cannot place it.'

'Yes, sire. My father was one of your brother's principal stake-holders, and numbered among the first to go under on the Day of Losses.'

'I see. It seems, however, that the Tennedict family has recovered from its . . . misfortune.'

'Yes, and the king has seen fit to reward us, sire –'

'Excellent.'

'– in the form of community service, under his new programme of Indebtedness to the Community, sire. As the middle son and facing few prospects, I elected to take the military route for my community service, while the rest of the Tennedict family set to reforming the impoverished conditions of the indigents out on the Isles.'

Abrastal made a sound somewhere between disbelief and disgust. 'Forgive my interruption, Commander. Am I to understand that the king of Lether, having ruined your family's wealth, has since seen fit to demand from you a period of public service?'

'That is correct, Highness.'

'How is *that* even remotely fair?'

Idist managed a faint smile as he regarded her. 'On the matter of fairness, Queen, King Tehol had much to say to my father, and all those others who profit from the debts of others.'

Abrastal scowled. 'Speaking from a position of great privilege, I find that offensive.'

'Highness,' said Idist, 'I believe that was the point.'

Brys spoke. 'Commander, you bring not only yourselves, but also resupply, is that correct?'

'It is, sire. In addition, I carry a written missive from the king, addressed to you.'

'Do you have it with you?'

'I do, sire.'

'Then, please, read it to us.'

The young commander's brows lifted. 'Sire? Perhaps, some privacy . . .'

'Not at all, Commander. You seem to have the voice of a drill sergeant as it is. Lend it to my brother's words, if you please.'

All at once the man was sweating, and Aranict felt a sudden sympathy. She leaned close to Brys. 'You might want to reconsider, love. This is your brother, after all.'

'Yes, and?'

'His own words, Brys.'

The prince frowned. 'Ah, right.'

But Idist had begun. '"Greetings to Prince Brys from King Tehol the Only of Lether. Dearest brother, have you slept with her yet?"' Wisely, he paused then and looked up at the prince. On all sides, from the soldiers within earshot to Abrastal and Spax, there was deathly silence. Sighing, Aranict lit a stick of rustleaf.

Brys stood, one hand over his eyes, and then, with a helpless gesture, bade Idist continue.

'"Never mind, we can talk about that later, but let it be known that as king I can command from you every detail down to the very last, er, detail, all the while promising that my wife will never hear a single word of any of it. Since, as I am sure you have now discovered, pillow talk can be deadly.

'"Best I turn now to the dull, official content next, so that we can later return to the juicy details. I feel justified in such expectations since I have discovered that women actually engage in the most horrendously explicit discussions of their menfolk when in the company of their bosomed friends, inviting tit for tat, and what tit could be more inviting than tat?"'

Spax burst out a harsh laugh, and then ducked. 'Sorry, that was just me, being appalled.'

Idist resumed. '"Official now. Bugg formed up his own battalion, found an able commander for it, and then hired a fleet to transport said reinforcements along with all the resupply he could wedge into the holds. And then, following my proclamation of the sovereignty of the indigents out on the Isles, Bugg oversaw all the Teblor who, strangely, rushed to join the Letherii military with the aim of accompanying the Chancel fleet. Between you and me, the Teblor have to be the most contrary people I have ever known. Anyway, with all of Bugg doing this and Bugg doing that, I am understandably exhausted and I graciously accept your sympathy. To continue, the battalion now has three hundred Teblor in its auxiliaries. I believe some ancient prophecy has them in an advanced state of excitement.

'"Just as my very own prophecy of your impending love-life having now come true (I trust), why, *I* am left in an advanced state of excitement – but not improperly so, I assure you. That would be sick. Never mind tales of war and mayhem, brother, spin me a romance! Trapped in a palace and chained to a wife, well, you can imagine my desperation here.

'"Sincerely as I am to put into practice a new period of austerity here in the palace, I have just discovered the error of dictating this missive to my wife. So I will take this moment, before fleeing the room, to send to you all my love, and to extend my warmest greetings to everyone else whom you have forced into the awkward position of hearing this.

'"With deepest affection, your loving brother, King Tehol."'

'Prince Brys,' murmured Abrastal, 'you have my sympathies.'

Brys sighed, and then, in a remarkably calm and steady voice, he addressed Idist. 'Commander, when will the battalion arrive?'

'They have already begun their march, sire. Two days behind us. I left orders to push on into the night and rise before dawn, so with luck they will arrive by dusk tomorrow.'

'Thank you, Commander.'

As they walked back to the Letherii encampment, Idist and his troop maintaining a respectful distance behind them, Aranict took Brys's hand. 'All that cheering and laughter – that was in gratitude. You do realize that, don't you?'

He frowned.

'Brys.'

'He does it on purpose, you know. Sees me as far too serious – but then, it just so happens I am about to lead my soldiers into war. We have marched a long way and have suffered deprivations, and our enemy awaits us, fit, rested and probably thoroughly entrenched. That enemy will be choosing the ground, and to make matters worse they will probably outnumber us by a wide margin.'

'Nothing he said made light of that,' she responded. 'And by his gesture alone, you must know that he worries for you. This resupply gives us a fighting chance.'

'I know. And of course I'm grateful – how could I not be?'

'Idist did warn you.'

Brys shook his head. 'It's not the letter, Aranict.'

'It isn't?'

'What just happened back there played out in Tehol's mind even as he dictated the lines to his wife. He knew I would want his words read out loud – my brother is diabolical and thoroughly shameless. I have spent my whole life walking wide-eyed into his snares, and none of it bothers me. In fact, I cannot help but admire his genius. Every time.'

Aranict was baffled. 'Brys, what is it then?'

'I cannot recall, Aranict – and I have been trying – I cannot recall Tehol ever saying that he loved me. And that alone is the measure of his concern, and it's shaken me to the core.'

'Brys—'

'Tehol fears we will not see each other again. For all its mundane silliness, he came as close to saying goodbye as anyone could without using the word itself. And so, as you perhaps can now imagine, I miss him. I miss him dearly.'

She held tight on to his hand. As if that could help, when she knew that it could not. But she had nothing to say to him – her mind was blank, echoing in the wake of what had just rushed through it. *He expects to die. My love expects to die.*

The relief wagons rolled into the camp, and for the first time, Shield Anvil Tanakalian set eyes upon a Forkrul Assail – or so he thought, only to subsequently discover that the man was but a half-blood, a Watered. No matter, there was something of a nightmare about him – the skin white as papyrus, the way he moved, his arms crooking like snakes, the sinuous flow of his strides, and the ghastly coldness in his pallid eyes.

These are the deadliest of allies. I am not blind to the contempt you have for us, when you look upon our beleaguered, battered condition. But we shall recover, and swiftly, and when the time comes to do what is necessary, we shall be ready.

He saw Setoc standing apart, ignoring the Watered and his officers, ignoring everyone and everything. Was she caught in the grip of the Wolves? Did they stare out now from her mismatched eyes? *She is a liability. But it's not her fault – the Wolves have taken her, they use her – she is nothing more than a portal, and when the gods choose to manifest in this world they will tear right through her. I doubt she will even survive.*

If necessary, I will seal that portal. I will stop the Wolves from coming. I will do this to save their lives.

So his prayers went unanswered. By her words she had made plain that the priests of the Grey Helms were all fools, self-deluded in believing they could touch the mind of the Wild. And generations of Perish who gave their lives to the Wolves . . . *a waste. All that blood spilled. And the struggles for power, those precious titles of Mortal Sword, Shield Anvil, Destriant, they all meant nothing.*

And therein lurks the cruellest truth of all. In the end, we are no different from every other cult, every other religion. Convincing ourselves of the righteousness of our path. Convincing ourselves that we alone hold to an immutable truth. Secure in the belief that everyone else is damned.

But it was all a game, the sacred a playground for secular power struggles, venal ambition.

What's left to believe in?

His thoughts swirled, spun in a vortex, taking him down and down . . . to Krughava. *Did you see through it all? Did you decide that personal glory was all there was, the only thing worthy of aspiration? Are you, Krughava, the reduction of the argument?*

Make your last stand. Die neck-deep in integrity and honour and duty – those words are borne on a flag, in three shades of red, and you will rally to that standard and once there you will happily die. Very well, Krughava, I can make sense of you now. It does not help, because still I will not follow you. But at least I understand.

They didn't need Setoc. The Grey Helms would be the wrath of the Wolves, the fury of the Wild, but without risk to the Wolves. *Yes, this is war, but do not come here. Not to this one. If you do, they will take you. If you do, gods will die on that day.*

I will not have it.

He realized that he stood between the two – between Krughava and Setoc, between the profane and the sacred, and yet to neither would he give his embrace. *Poised on the knife edge indeed. I am the Shield*

Anvil, and the virtue of blessing is my one and my only virtue, yet here I stand, trapped, unwilling to reach out to either one.

It seems that the glorious death shall be mine, after all.

'Shield Anvil.'

He turned, found himself facing the Watered commander. 'Yes?'

'I suggest you rest and feed for this night. Come the dawn we can begin our march to Blessed Gift—'

'Excuse me, where?'

'Blessed Gift is the old name for the plain where awaits the Kolanse army. It was a land once rich with wheat.'

Tanakalian smiled, looked away. 'Very well.'

'Shield Anvil.'

He glanced back. 'What is it?'

The Watered tilted his head. 'I was about to comment on the impressive courtesy in the manners of your soldiers.'

'Forgive me,' said Tanakalian, voice tight, 'I am . . . distracted.'

'Of course. Brother Diligence wishes to know, are those pursuing you the only threat we should expect?'

Those pursuing . . . but I say nothing of the K'Chain Che'Malle. Not to you, not to any of you. 'I believe so. However . . .'

'Shield Anvil?'

'There was an army of foreigners – but they attempted to cross the Glass Desert. It is probably safe to assume that they have failed.'

'I agree. We have sensed nothing impinging upon us from that direction.'

Tanakalian nodded. 'Well, I doubt you would have anyway, but it pleases me to hear your certainty in your assessment that the Glass Desert cannot be crossed.'

'A moment, Shield Anvil – you say to me that you do not think we would sense their appearance. Why is that?'

Tanakalian's eyes wandered past, settled once more on Setoc. He shrugged. 'Their commander wields an Otataral sword. Not that it could save—' He stopped then, for the Watered was marching back to his entourage, shouting commands in the Kolansii language. In moments, three riders wheeled their mounts and set out at a gallop northward.

When he glanced back at Setoc, he found her staring at him.

The Shield Anvil realized that he was sweating, his heart beating fast in his chest. 'It's just an Otataral sword,' he muttered, baffled at the Watered's obvious alarm, unnerved by Setoc's sudden attention.

Calm yourself. Hold to the knife's edge. Breathe deeply . . . breathe . . .

CHAPTER TWENTY-TWO

'Even a man who has lived a life of sorrows will ask for one more day.'

Prayers of the Condemned
Kolanse Imperial Archives
Anonymous

CALM STOOD MOTIONLESS, FACING SOUTHWEST. THE SKY WAS EMPTY, cloudless, the blue washed out and tinged green by the Strangers. Empty, and yet . . . *Death comes. I see a road built from bones and dust, a road slashing the flesh of the earth. It comes with the speed of the wind. It comes in the shadow of . . . gods below!* Confusion erupted within her. Then terror and dread. *Korabas! Unchained! But why? Who would do such a thing? Who has summoned this power? It is madness!* For an instant, she felt once more the unyielding weight of the stone that had once imprisoned her – suffocating, the horror of limbs she could not move, the darkness and the terrible, terrible solitude. And she knew what this was; she knew this sensation, this animal terror. Panic. *No! No one will take me again!*

Trembling, she struggled to regain control.

Korabas. You are freed – I feel your bitter exultation. Perhaps I alone can truly understand it.

But they will come for you. Can you not feel them? The Eleint are upon this world. They will kill you.

Do not seek us. Do not pierce the skin of Akhrast Korvalain. We must not be wounded – not now, Korabas, I beg you.

But she knew that there would be no reasoning with such a creature. From the moment of its creation, the Otataral Dragon had been doomed to an eternity of anguish and rage. Unmatched in power, yet that power was abnegation. Its only food was sorcery, but life itself was a manifestation of magic, and so all it touched it killed. Only the Eleint possessed the will to withstand that.

Such . . . loneliness. The ordeal of existence . . . so unrelenting in its refutation. Yes, Korabas, I could look into your eyes. Without flinching. For I know the truth of your turmoil.

She knew she could not alter the dragon's deadly path. Her brothers and sisters had no idea what was now winging towards them, and against the Otataral Dragon . . . *they might all die. Reverence, Diligence, Serenity . . . all my pure kin. And all that we sought to achieve will be destroyed.* No, she could not stop Korabas.

But I can avenge the deaths of my brothers and sisters.

She was camped three days from the bound body of Lifestealer. Three days from the one weapon capable of matching the Otataral Dragon. *Icarium. I will awaken you. If the Eleint fail – if they do not come in time – I leave Korabas to you.*

The two would seek each other out – they could do naught else. *The dragon is negation. But Icarium is an open wound into Chaos itself. When his self shatters, when his so-called rage is unleashed, he is but a conduit, a portalway. This is why he cannot be stopped – he is not even there. Shall you do battle against chaos itself? Impossible.*

They will clash, and that battle shall destroy the world.

Good.

Even Sister Reverence does not understand: there is more than one path to justice.

She set out.

Beneath her feet, the earth's screaming now reached her senses – she could feel the tremors of the assault being inflicted upon it. The sudden blighting, the eruptions of dust, the vast fissures opening below Korabas. *Where she passes, there shall be no life. Where she passes, all that is living shall die.*

Eleint, find Korabas. Kill the Otataral Dragon. That is all I ask. And then we can bargain, for I shall have Icarium – I shall have a force of chaos to match your own. We can strike a perfect balance, in a world scoured empty of meddling gods . . . imagine what can be achieved!

We can give the inheritors true freedom, and by their each and every deed we can watch them hang themselves. No gods to blame, no excuses to build up, no lies to hide behind. Such a glorious world it will be! Such a righteous place – a place where justice never blinks.

We can share such a world, Eleint.

Climbing a slope to a ridgeline, she found two figures standing in her path.

T'lan Imass.

Ancient rage flared incandescent in Calm, and once more panic rattled through her, just as quickly crushed down. 'You would dare this?'

In answer they readied their stone weapons.

'*He is mine!*'

'He is no one's, Forkrul Assail,' said the female. 'Turn back.'

Calm barked a laugh as she quested with her power. 'I sense no others in this soil, nor on the winds – there are just the two of you. You must be fools to think you can stop me. I held the Stone Stairs against hundreds of your kind. I *ended* their war.'

The two T'lan Imass stepped out to the sides, the huge male hefting a flint-studded bone mace, the female shifting her grip on a stone spear.

Calm moved with stunning speed, lunging at the female, her torso writhing to evade the thrusting weapon. Her hands snapped out, one plunging into the undead warrior's chest amidst shattering ribs, the other lashing at her face – catching the lower jaw and tearing it off.

She twisted past, evading the downward swing of the male's weapon, and with one hand now gripping the spine, she spun the female round, lifting her off her feet and flinging her into the male's path. Even as he stumbled, he swung the mace in a diagonal slash. The Forkrul Assail stepped inside the attack, blocking the bone shaft with her wrists, turned to face him and thrust upward with the heels of her hands, catching each side of the warrior's lower jaw. The strength of the blow exploded the vertebrae of his neck, launching the skull into the air.

As the huge, headless warrior toppled, Calm closed once more on the female, who was feebly trying to regain her feet. Grasping her right arm, the Forkrul Assail tore it from the shoulder socket. Using the arm as a weapon, she swung it hard into the side of the female's head. The ball of the humerus punched a hole in the warrior's temple.

The T'lan Imass staggered to one side.

Calm struck again. Plates of the skull splintered, broke away. A third blow crushed the woman's face. She fell. The Forkrul Assail stepped forward and with one booted foot rolled the T'lan Imass on to her back. Then she swung the arm down repeatedly on what was left of the face and skull. The ninth blow split the arm bone. Calm flung it away in disgust and used the heel of her boot.

Long after the wretched spirit of the female warrior had left the remains on the ground, Calm continued battering at that hated face.

Some time later, she resumed her journey.

Such a glorious world it will be.

Kilmandaros fled. She could not even remember when she had begun running, or when she had breached her way into the first of innumerable warrens. The landscape she now crossed was bleak, colourless, the ground underfoot hard uneven clay that had been chopped up by thousands of hoofs. Two small moons tracked the night sky.

Half a league ahead, she saw hills of red sand, rippling as they climbed to the horizon. No places in which to hide – no caves, no forests – she would have to leave this realm soon. And yet – Kilmandaros glanced back over one shoulder.

A storm of darkness, boiling to consume half the sky.

Close! Close! Her breath tore at her throat. Her hearts pounded like the thunder of clashing stormclouds. She stumbled on torn, bloodied feet, her muscles burning like acid.

Where? Where to hide?

'I've done a terrible thing. And now I will pay – it was all Errastas! All his fault, not mine! I did not want her freed – I swear it!'

The slope of the nearest hill loomed before her, a sweep of red sand – how she hated this place!

'A terrible thing. *A terrible thing!*'

Darkness foamed up on either side. Crying out, Kilmandaros staggered to a halt, wheeled round, lifting her hands—

He struck from the sky.

Wings like flames of night. The blaze of argent reptilian eyes. Talons lunging down, impaling her shoulders, snatching her from the ground.

Kilmandaros shrieked, fists closing to smash upward into the dragon's ridged chest. The sound the impacts made was thunder.

And then, trailing ropes of blood, she was falling.

His shadow passed over her, a wheeling, plummeting presence, looming huge – jaws snapping out from a head above a lashing neck. Fangs sank into one thigh and she was thrown upward once more. Spinning, she saw gleaming bone where the muscles of her left thigh had been – saw blood spraying out from her leg. Howling, she fell earthward once more.

This time, he left her to strike the ground. She landed on her feet with the sound of exploding trees. Bones snapped, splinters driving up into her pelvis and torso. The impact threw her forward. On to her chest, and then over. Lying stunned, helpless, Kilmandaros stared upward to see Draconus descending.

Not fair.

A soft hand settled against her cheek. Blinking, she found herself looking up into her son's face. 'No! Leave here! Beloved son – *flee!*'

Instead, he straightened, drawing a sword.

Kilmandaros heard Draconus speak from only a few paces distant. 'Where is Errastas, Sechul?'

'Gone,' her son replied.

'Where?'

'I don't know. Into hiding, of course. You won't find him, not any time soon. Shall I caution you against uttering any vows, Draconus, or would the sting of that prove too much?'

'You always were chained to his ankle, Sechul Lath, but if you are determined to oppose me here, I will kill you.'

'I will defend my mother.'

'Then you will die with her.'

She saw his sad smile, his lopsided shrug. 'Draconus, I have nothing left. No one but her. If you will kill her this day, then . . . there is no reason for me to go on. Do you understand?'

'Pathetic,' growled Draconus. 'You would spend an eternity under your mother's wing? Step away, find some light – some light of your own, Sechul.'

'Ah, I see, so this is my opportunity, is it? This is what you are offering me, Draconus? You never did understand acts of generosity, did you?'

There was a long pause, and Kilmandaros knew that their gazes had locked, and then Draconus said, 'Ready your weapon.'

She would have cried out then, would have begged for the life of her son – but when she opened her mouth her throat filled with blood, and she was suddenly drowning.

She heard the *whish* of a blade, a scuffling of boots on the hard scrabble, and then a terrible, grinding sound. A sword fell to the ground, and someone made a small, childish sound.

Footsteps, drawing closer.

She couldn't breathe, felt herself dying. Her eyes, glaring upward – seeing those damned moons so puny in that vast night sky – and then that vision was blocked out and Draconus stared down on her. *He left you no choice, yes . . . but you do not say it. What need is there to say it?*

His eyes shone like silvered pools at midnight, and there was, she realized with a start, such beauty in them – *with the darkness flowing round, falling like tears, but you can see how they could turn. You can see it. Such a terrible thing . . .*

Errastas, you have killed us.

Was it mercy when he set the sharp tip of his sword into the hollow of her neck? She looked again into his eyes, but saw nothing. *Yes. Let us call it that. Mercy.*

When he thrust the blade through her throat, it was cold as ice and hot as fire, and all that she saw suddenly faded, from the inside out.

I – I'm leaving.

My son. Even at the last, you disappoint me.

Draconus pulled free the sword, and then turned. A knot of shadows, vaguely human in form, stood opposite him. To either side was a

654

Hound, and he caught a motion off to his right and then on his left – more of the beasts, encircling him.

Eyes narrowing on the apparition, Draconus leaned on his sword. 'Usurper, does Tulas know you stole his dogs?'

The silver head of a walking cane flashed briefly before the shadows hid it again, like a fisherman's lure in dark water. The apparition spoke in a thin, wavering voice, 'There is little civility in you, Old One.' A sudden giggle. 'Your . . . inheritor . . . once stood before me, just as you are doing now. He too held an infernal sword – oh, was it yours? How careless of you.'

'If you force me,' Draconus said, 'I will kill these Hounds.'

'How goes the poem? "The child and his dog . . ."'

Draconus stepped forward, blade lifting. 'Who in the name of the Azathanai are you?'

A frail, wispy hand gestured vaguely. 'Your pardon, did I offend?'

'What do you want?'

'Only a question for you, Old One.' The cane reappeared, bobbing in the direction of Kilmandaros's corpse. 'Where next? Or,' and he giggled again, '*who next?*'

'Why should it matter to you?'

'Only this . . . leave Korabas. Leave the Forkrul Assail – in fact, leave that whole mess. Even the Eleint. If you show up, it'll only complicate matters.'

'You are the one, then,' Draconus said, lowering the sword and stepping back.

'I am? Why, yes, I am.'

'The spider at the centre of this web. Hood. Rake—'

'And they were true to their words – now *that* was a rarity. Perhaps of greater relevance is this. Anomander Rake spoke well of you, Draconus. Can you imagine such a thing? But it goes even beyond that, for he also said that you would be true to your word. Will you, Draconus? Be true to your word?'

'I do not recall giving it to you on any matter here,' Draconus replied.

The cane's heel thumped on the ground. 'Excellent! Now, as to that . . .'

A short time later, with Draconus gone, the Hounds drew closer to the corpses of Kilmandaros and Sechul Lath, sniffing with their hackles raised like spines. Shadowthrone watched their agitated circling, and then glanced across to find Cotillion standing nearby.

The patron god of assassins looked . . . shaken.

Shadowthrone sighed, not without sympathy. 'The Elders are so *implacable*. Look upon these two tragic victims. How many ages have they survived? To come to an end' – he waved the cane – 'here. Wherever *here* is. Even the Hounds were hard pressed to track them.'

'You convinced him?'

Shadowthrone hissed, lifting the cane to examine the silver head. 'He thought me . . . audacious.'

'Just you?'

'Us.'

'We've lost her,' Cotillion said. 'Or so I fear. It was too much, friend, too much – they have not walked our path. They are mortals. That and nothing more. They have not *seen*. The necessity has not . . . not gnawed at their souls, the way it has with us.'

'Paths? Gnawing? Souls? None of this means anything to me. We concluded that things had to change, that is all.'

'They had to because our position was too perilous,' Cotillion replied. 'Everything that's followed – this whole insane scheme – it all began with our need to secure our place in the pantheon.'

'Precisely.'

'But then it all *changed*.'

'Maybe for you,' Shadowthrone muttered.

'Liar.'

'Shadows never lie.'

They were both silent for a moment, and then Shadowthrone tilted his head back and let loose a wild laugh. Fighting a smile, Cotillion looked away.

'Are you done with your moment of doubt?' Shadowthrone asked. 'Good. It ill-suited you. Listen, she's a woman, and that alone makes her the most terrifying force in all the realms.'

'Yes,' Cotillion said, 'I am well aware of your long-standing fear of the swaying sex.'

'I blame my mother.'

'Convenient.'

'I don't know which of us dreads more our visits.'

'She's still alive? Don't be ridiculous, Ammanas.'

'Listen, I wasn't always this old, you know. In any case, every time we end up in the same room I can see the disappointment in her eyes, and hear it in her voice. "Emperor? Oh, *that* empire. So now you're a god? Oh dear, not *Shadow*? Isn't it broken? Why did you have to pick a *broken* realm to rule? When your father was your age . . ." Aagh, and on and on it goes! I've been on the run since I was nine years old, and is it any wonder?'

Cotillion was studying him bemusedly.

'They will walk out from that desert, friend,' Shadowthrone said. 'I feel it in my bones.'

'Didn't know you had any.'

'Sticks, then. I feel it in my sticks. Hmm, doesn't sound sufficiently assuring, does it?'

'Assuring? No. Creepy? Yes.'

Shadowthrone thumped the cane down, looked round. 'We're still here? Why are we still here?'

'A few last thoughts for the departed, perhaps?'

'Is it the thing to do? I suppose it is.'

Studying the corpses now, Cotillion grunted. 'Not interested in just a slap on the wrist, was he?'

'Children who can't be touched end up getting away with murder.'

'That's your last word to them? It doesn't make any sense, Shadow-throne.'

'But it does. The Elder Gods were like spoiled children, with no one to watch over them. The only nonsensical thing about them was that they weren't all killed off long ago. Just how much can any of us tolerate? That's the question, the only question, in fact.' He gestured with the cane. 'There's one man's answer.'

'I suppose,' Cotillion mused, 'we should be thankful that Draconus was chained up inside Dragnipur for all that time. If Rake hadn't killed him . . .'

'Every wayward child should spend a few hundred lifetimes dragging a wagon filled with bodies.' Shadowthrone grunted. 'Sounds like something my mother might say. "Only a hundred lifetimes, Kellan? Too weak to handle a thousand, are you? Why, your father . . ." Aagh! Not again!'

Sechul Lath found himself lying on the ground. His eyes were closed, and he felt no desire to open them. Not yet, anyway.

He heard footsteps, coming closer. Two sets, halting to stand on either side of him.

'Oh my,' said a woman's voice on his left. 'I suppose it had to happen, eventually. Still . . . tell me, brother, are you feeling anything?'

'No,' replied the man on his right. 'Why, should I?'

'Well, we *are* what was the best of him, and we *shall* live on.'

'Do you think he can hear us, sister?'

'I imagine so. Do you remember once, we sent a coin spinning?'

'Long ago now.'

'If I listen hard . . .'

'Probably just your imagination, my love. Some games die with barely a whisper. And as for this new one – I want no part of it.'

She made a sound, something like a laugh. 'Is that wisdom I'm hear-ing?'

'Look at our father,' he said. 'When he opens his eyes, when he climbs to his feet, there will be no going back.'

'No, no going back. Ever again.'

Sechul's son sighed. 'I think we should hunt down the Errant, beloved. In our father's name, we should teach him about the lord's push.'

'Draconus will find him. You can be certain of that.'

'But I want to be there when he does.'

'Better we should be like this, brother. Come to welcome him before the gates of death. We could help him to his feet, reminding him that our father waits on the other side.'

'We could guide him to the gate.'

'Just so.'

'And then give the Errant—'

'A nudge.'

His children laughed, and Sechul Lath found himself smiling. *Son, daughter, what a fine gift you give me, before I am sent on my way.*

'Sister . . . I see a coin with two heads, both the Errant's. Shall we send it spinning?'

'Why not, brother? Prod and pull, 'tis the way of the gods.'

When at last he opened his eyes, they were gone.

And all was well.

Where her draconic shadow slipped over the land below, the ground erupted in spumes of dust and stones. Fissures spread outward jagged and depthless. Hills slumped, collapsed, their cloak of plants withering, blackening. Where she passed, the earth died. Freedom was a gift, but freedom filled her with desperate rage, and such pain that the rush of air over her scales was agony.

She had no doubt that she possessed a soul. She could see it deep inside, down a tunnel through cracked bedrock, down and ever down, to a crushed knot lying on the floor. *There. That.* And the screams that howled from it made the roots of the mountains shiver, made seas tremble. Made still the winds and lifeless the air itself.

Before her birth, there had been the peace of unknowing, the oblivion of that which did not exist. She neither felt nor cared, because she simply wasn't. Before the gods meddled, before they tore light from dark, life from death, before they raised their walls and uttered their foul words. *This is, but this is not. There shall be magic in the worlds we have made, and by its power shall life rise and in looking upon its myriad faces, we shall see our own – we shall come to know who and what we are. Here, there is magic, but here, there is not.*

She could never give her face to the gods – they would not look, they would only turn away. She could awaken all the power of her voice to cry, *I am here! See me! Acknowledge me – your one forgotten child!* But it would achieve nothing. *Because even the vision of the gods must have a blind spot. And what will you find there? Only me. A crushed knot lying on the floor.*

Her living kin were hunting her now. She did not know how many, but it did not matter. They sought her annihilation. *But . . . not yet. Leave me this freedom . . . to do something. To do a thing . . . a thing that does not destroy, but creates. Please, can I not be more than I am? Please. Do not find me.*

Below her, her flight made a bleeding scar in the earth, and where her eyes reached out, where they touched all the beauty and wonder ahead, her arrival delivered naught but devastation. It was unconscionable. It was unbearable.

See what comes, when every gift is a curse.

A sudden pressure, far behind her, and she twisted her neck round, glared into her own wake of devastation.

Eleint.

So many!

Rage gave voice to her cry, and that voice shattered the land for leagues on all sides. As its echoes rebounded, Korabas flinched at the damage she had unleashed. *No! Where is my beauty? Why is it only for you? No!*

I will have this freedom! I will have it!

To do – to do – to do something.

Her wings strained with the fury of her flight, but she could fly no faster than she was already flying, and it was not enough. The Eleint drew ever closer, and Korabas could see that crushed knot flaring with an inner fire, blazing now with all the anger she had ever felt, had ever taken inside – bound for so long. Anger at the gods. At the makers – *her* makers – for what they did to her.

Eleint! You would kill me and call it freedom? Then come to me and try!

Her rage was waiting for them, waiting for them all.

Mathok reined in, dust and stones scattering from his horse's hoofs. As the cloud lifted around him he cursed, spat and then said, 'They're in the pass, High Fist. The bastards! How did they anticipate us?'

'Calm down,' Paran said, turning to glance back at the column. 'We are in the manifestation of Akhrast Korvalain. The Assail can track our every move.' He faced the Warleader again. 'Mathok – are they well placed?'

'Dug in, sir. And these ones, High Fist, are heavily armoured. Not local – the Assail have hired mercenaries.'

Fist Rythe Bude, standing beside Paran – somewhat too close, as he could smell the spices in her hair – asked, 'Could you see their standards, Warleader?'

Mathok made a face. 'Wolf furs, Fist. Wolf skulls too. I didn't get close enough, but if they had the carcasses of wolf puppies hanging from their ear lobes it wouldn't have surprised me.'

Paran sighed. 'Togg and Fanderay. Now that complicates things.'

'Why should it complicate things?' Noto Boil demanded, withdrawing the fish spine from his mouth and studying its red tip. 'There's nothing complicated about any of this, right, High Fist? I mean, we're marching double-quick for who knows where but wherever it is it won't be pretty, and once we get there we're aiming to link forces with someone who might not even be there, to fight a war against an Elder race and their human slaves for no particular reason except that they're damned ugly. Complicated? Nonsense. Now Seven Cities . . . *that* was complicated.'

'Are you done, Boil?'

'*Noto* Boil, sir, if you please. And yes, I am. For now.'

'What makes this complicated,' Paran resumed, 'is that I have no real interest in fighting worshippers sworn to the Wolves of Winter. In fact, I sympathize with their cause, and while I might disagree with the means by which they intend to express their particular faith—' He turned to Rythe Bude. 'Gods, listen to me. I'm starting to sound like Boil!'

'*Noto* Boil.'

'The point is, we need to get through that pass. Mathok – any other routes through the south mountains?'

'How the Hood should I know? I've never been here before!'

'All right, never mind. Silly question.'

'Let's just pound right through 'em, High Fist. I figure just under five thousand—'

Fist Rythe Bude choked, coughed and then said, '*Five thousand?* Entrenched? Gods, this will be a bloodbath!'

Noto Boil cleared his throat. 'High Fist, a modest suggestion.'

'Go on.'

'You're Master of the Deck of Dragons, sir. Talk to the Wolves of Winter.'

Paran lifted a brow. 'Talk to them? Tell you what – the next pit full of wolves you get thrown into, try a little negotiating, Noto.'

'Noto *Boil*.'

'You could swap bones.' This from Gumble, where he was lying sprawled atop a flat rock. 'Sniff their butts – they like that, I'm told. Lie on your back, maybe.'

'Somebody find us a big snake,' Mathok growled, glaring at the toad.

Gumble sighed loudly, his bloated body deflating to half its normal size. 'I sense my comments are not viewed as constructive, leading me to conclude that I am in the company of fools. What's new about that, I wonder?'

Paran withdrew his helm and wiped grimy sweat from his forehead. 'So we do this the hard way. No, Fist Bude, not straight-into-the-teeth kind of hard way. Signal the corps – we're marching straight through the night. I want us formed up opposite the enemy come the dawn.'

'Sounds like straight into the teeth, sir.'

'And that's what it will *look* like, too. There might end up being some fighting, but with luck, not much.'

'And how's that going to work out, sir?'

'I intend to make them surrender, Fist. Gumble, get your fat lump off that rock and find your erstwhile artist and tell him it's time. He'll know what that means.'

'He's hardly mine, High Fist, and as for erstwhile—'

'Go, before Mathok decides to skewer you with that lance.'

'To raucous cheers from friend and foe alike,' Noto Boil muttered, the fish spine working up and down with every word.

'Look at him go,' Rythe Bude commented. 'Didn't know he could scramble that fast.'

Paran walked back to his horse, took the reins from one of the foundling children now accompanying the army. Swinging into the saddle, he looked down at the dirty-faced boy. 'Still want your reward?'

A swift nod.

Paran reached down, lifted the boy up behind him. 'Hold tight, we're going to canter. Maybe even gallop. You ready for this?'

Another nod, but the thin arms closing about Paran were tight.

'Let's go see this pass, then.' Kicking his horse forward, Paran glanced across at Mathok as the Warleader pulled up alongside him. 'Well?'

'Well what?' the warrior growled.

'That's hardly a happy expression you're wearing.'

'You got a sharp eye there, High Fist.'

'So what's the problem?'

'There's only a problem, sir, if you pull this off.'

'Are you always this hungry for a fight, Mathok?'

'Sharp eye, dumb mouth.'

Paran grinned. 'Can't have everything, you know.'

'So I'm learning, High Fist.'

'Would've made us a decent captain,' Kalam observed, as he walked with Quick Ben. They were watching Paran, flanked by a mob of Seven Cities horse-raiders, ride off towards the foot of the raw, worn range of mountains ahead. The assassin drew his cloak tighter over his broad shoulders. 'Too bad he came to us too late.'

'Did he?' the wizard wondered. 'If he'd arrived before Pale, he would've been down in the tunnels when they collapsed.'

'Maybe.'

'Why are you walking with me, Kalam? Where's Minala?'

The assassin's only answer was a low growl.

'Well,' Quick Ben said, 'it's just as well that you're here. We need to work out our next moves.'

'Our next what? We're here to kill Forkrul Assail. There's no other moves to talk about, and those ones don't need talking about.'

'Listen, that last Pure damn near killed me.'

'Rubbish.'

'Well, all right. It hurt, then.'

'Get over it, wizard. We're back fighting a real war. Old style. Ugly magic, toe to toe, the works. Don't tell me you've forgotten how to do this.'

'I haven't. But . . . where's Fiddler? Hedge? Mallet, Trotts, Whiskeyjack? Where are all the ones we need to cover our backs? Paran's sending us out into the enemy camp, Kalam. If we get in serious trouble, we're finished.'

'So fix it so that we can get back out if we have to.'

'Easy for you to say.'

Sighing, Kalam scratched at the stubble on his jaw, and then said, 'Something happened, Quick, back in Malaz City. In Mock's Hold. In that damned chamber with Laseen and the Adjunct. Well, just afterwards. Tavore and me . . . she asked me to make a choice. Laseen had already offered me whatever I wanted, pretty much. Just to turn away.'

Quick Ben was studying him with narrowed eyes. 'Everything?'

'Everything.'

'Knocking Topper off his perch?'

'Aye. She was giving me the Claw, even though I had a feeling it was rotten through and through, even then – and I found out the truth of that later that night.'

'So something had the Empress desperate.'

'Aye.'

'Fine. So . . . what did Tavore offer you instead?'

Kalam shook his head. 'Damned if I know – and I've been thinking about it. A lot. There was a look in her eyes – I don't know. A need, maybe. She knew that Laseen was going to try to kill her on the way back to the ships. We all knew it.'

'She wanted your help – is that so surprising? Who wants to die?'

'As simple as that? Quick Ben, she was asking me to die in her place. That's what she was asking.'

'Just as desperate as Laseen, then. The two of them, they asked you

662

to choose between two mirror reflections. Which one was real? Which one was worth serving? You still haven't explained how Tavore did it.'

'She did it the way she seems to get all of us to do what she needs us to do.'

'Well now, that's been the one mystery no one's been able to answer, hasn't it? But, just like you, we follow. Kalam, I wish I could have seen you on that night in Malaz City. You must have been the holiest of terrors. So, just like the rest of us, you gave her everything you had. How does she do it?'

'She simply asks,' Kalam said.

Quick Ben snorted. 'That's it?'

'I think so. No offers – no riches, no titles, nothing any of us can see as payment or reward. No, she just looks you straight in the eye, and she asks.'

'You just sent a shiver up my spine, Kalam, and I don't even know why.'

'You don't? More rubbish.'

The wizard waved his hands, 'Well, Hood knows it ain't chivalry, is it? She won't even nudge open *that* door. No fluttering eyelashes, no demure look or coy glance . . .'

Kalam grunted a laugh at the image, but then he shook himself. 'She asks, and something in your head tells you that what she's doing is right – and that it's the only reason she has to live. She asked me to die defending her – knowing I didn't even like her much. Quick, for the rest of my life, I will never forget that moment.'

'And you still can't quite work out what happened.'

The assassin nodded. 'All at once, it's as if she's somehow laid bare your soul and there it is, exposed, trembling, vulnerable beyond all belief – and she could take it, grasp it tight until the blood starts dripping. She could even stab it right through. But she didn't – she didn't do any of that, Quick. She reached down, her finger hovered, and then . . . gone, as if that was all she needed.'

'You can stop now,' the wizard muttered. 'What you're talking about – between two people – it almost never happens. Maybe it's what we all want, but Kalam, it almost *never* happens.'

'There was no respect in what Laseen offered,' the assassin said. 'It was a raw bribe, reaching for the worst in me. But from Tavore . . .'

'Nothing *but* respect. Now I see it, Kal. I see it.'

'Quick?'

'What?'

'Is she alive? Do you think . . . is Tavore still alive?'

Quick Ben kicked a stone from his path. 'Even her brother can't answer that. I just don't know.'

'But do you – are you . . .'

'Do I have faith? Is that what you're asking?' He waved about. 'Look around! This whole damned army is marching on faith! We just have to get on with it, right?'

'Fine then,' Kalam growled. 'Let me ask you this: can Paran pull it off on his own? If he has to?'

Quick Ben rubbed at his face. Scowling, he spoke under his breath. 'Listen. Have you been paying attention?'

'To what?'

'Just . . . when he walks through camp. Or rides. Do you hear the soldiers – calling up to him as he passes? Jests flying back and forth, laughter and nods, all of it. They're here because following him is what they need, what they want. The Host lost Dujek Onearm – that should've finished them, but it hasn't, has it? Our old captain here is now leading the whole army. You say Tavore *asks* because for her that's what's needed. But her brother, he just *expects*.'

Kalam slowly nodded. 'Five coins to that, Quick. Still' – and he shot the wizard a sharp look – 'Shadowthrone sent you here, didn't he?'

Quick Ben made a face. 'The Emperor's drawing in all the old webs – frankly, I'm appalled how he can still do that, you know? What kind of knots did he tie on to us anyway? Gods below.'

'Do you trust him?'

'Shadowthrone? Are you mad?'

The assassin paused, shook himself, and said, 'That's it, then. Kalam is done with his questions – you, wizard, you cover my back and I'll do the same for yours. Let's go and kill Forkrul Assail. Lots of them.'

'It's about time you regressed to your usual brainless bear-like self. So, there will be a camp up there, where the officers are all gathered. Well behind the entrenchments. Watered and Pures and whatever. We need to find the Pures first this time – take them out of the way and the rest won't be as bad.'

'Right. So what's all this about me not sheathing my Otataral knife? Why should that be a problem?'

Quick Ben shrugged. 'How does one make Otataral?'

'No idea.'

'Of course you haven't!' the wizard snapped. 'You make it by pouring as much magic into one place at one time as you possibly can, and if you're lucky a threshold is crossed – a firestorm that burns everything out, making—'

'Otataral.'

'Will you stop interrupting me? My point is, what happens when ten thousand dragons and a few hundred Elder Gods decide to get together and do the same thing?'

'Otataral Island? Off Seven Cities? No wonder there's so much—'

'Be quiet! No. Not Otataral Island – that was just some localized

664

scrap a million or so years ago. No. What you get, Kalam, is an Otataral Dragon.'

'Hood take me – wait, don't tell me they went and did that?'

'Fine, I won't. But that's still not the point, Kalam.'

'So what is the point, Quick Ben?'

'Only that the dragon's free and it's headed this way and, most important, it can *smell* Otataral. So, every time you use it— *Aack!*'

Kalam had his hands round the wizard's throat. He dragged his friend close. 'Hedge was right about you,' he whispered, as Quick Ben's eyes bulged and his face darkened. 'You're insane, and worse, you think it's funny!' Feeble hands clawed at Kalam's wrists. Snarling, the assassin flung Quick Ben away.

Staggering, the wizard fell to his knees, coughing, gasping to draw breath.

Three soldiers came running up, but Kalam held out a hand to halt them. 'Return to your ranks. He'll live, and if I kick him while he's down, it'll only be once or twice.' Seeing the look in their eyes, the assassin snorted. 'Aye, he's the High Mage. My point exactly. Now,' his expression hardened, '*get lost.*'

The soldiers retreated.

Kalam turned to glare at Quick Ben. 'Hedge always kept a sharper back, you know. Had your face painted on it. He used to tell us, if you went and killed him with one of your schemes, with his last act he was going to wing it at the back of your head. You know, I used to think that was a bit extreme.'

Leaving the gagging man on his hands and knees, Kalam resumed his walk.

My brother could not have planned for this. To see so much of his work . . . unravelled. He understood the necessity of balance, but he also understood the wonder that is life itself. No, he could not have meant this to happen. Silchas Ruin glanced over to where Tulas Shorn stood on the bluff's edge. *Escape from death is never the escape you think it is.* 'Would we have done it?' he called over.

The undead warrior's head turned, tilted slightly. 'We were young. Anything was possible.'

'Then . . . one of us would have knelt before the body of the other, weeping.'

'That is likely.'

'But now . . . Tulas, it seems we shall fight side by side, and there will be none to kneel by our bodies, none to weep for us.'

'My Hounds are wandering – I can feel them. Hunting interlopers, dreaming of the chase. They wander the broken fragments of Kurald Emurlahn.'

Silchas Ruin was silent, wondering where his friend's thoughts were taking him.

Tulas Shorn sighed, the breath a long, dry rattle. 'Do you know what I envy most about my Hounds? Their freedom. Nothing complicated in their lives. No . . . difficult choices.'

Nodding, Silchas looked away. 'We face one now, don't we?'

'The Eleint will be driven to frenzy. Their entire being will be consumed with the need to kill Korabas – can you not feel it in your own blood, Silchas?'

Yes.

Tulas continued, 'We are left to a matter of faith. I doubt even Anomander could have anticipated that the Elder Gods would be so desperate, so vengeful.'

'And this is what is troubling me,' Silchas Ruin admitted. 'We cannot assume that *all* the Elder Gods acceded to the unchaining of the Otataral Dragon.'

'Does it matter?'

'I'm not sure.'

Tulas Shorn walked back from the edge. 'Will any of them regret the annihilation of the gods? I doubt it. Once their children are gone, their resurrection is assured.'

'To inherit what, Tulas?'

'Ah, yes, but they do expect the Eleint to kill Korabas. They *require* it, in fact.'

'Must we satisfy them?' Silchas asked.

Tulas Shorn was silent for a while, and his face taken into death could give no expression, and the eyes were closed doors. 'My friend, what choice have we? If Korabas survives, this realm will die, and it will be the first of many.'

'Leaving in its wake a land without magic. But even in such places life will return.'

'We cannot be certain of that. For all that we have explored the secrets of sorcery, we still know so little. We have flown over lifeless flesh – we have seen what happens when everything is truly stripped away.'

Silchas Ruin studied his friend for a moment, then lowered himself into a squat and stared out over the valley to the south. 'Am I fooling myself?'

'About what?'

Silchas started, unaware that he had spoken out loud. 'My brother knew well the Elder Gods. He'd clashed with them often enough.'

'It may be that his answer to the threat posed by the Elder Gods was to free Draconus.'

Draconus. 'Then what will Draconus do?'

'I do not know, but even thinking about it fills me with fear. We know well what comes when Draconus is awakened to true anger – his solution may prove worse than the problem. Abyss knows, friend, we have seen that for ourselves. Still, since you have asked, I will give the matter some thought. Draconus . . . freed. Who can oppose him, now that your brother is dead? I don't know – this world has moved on. What would he do first? He would hunt down and kill the ones who freed Korabas. He always took retribution seriously.'

Silchas Ruin was nodding. 'And then?'

The undead warrior shrugged. 'Kill Korabas?'

'Leaving a realm filled with Eleint?'

'Then . . . perhaps he would stand back and watch the two elemental forces collide and maul each other, until one emerged victorious – but so weakened, so destroyed, that he need only act expeditiously, without rage. It may be that this is what your brother demanded of Draconus, in exchange for his freedom.'

Silchas Ruin held his hands up to his face. After a moment he shook his head. 'Knowing my brother, there was no demand. There was only giving.'

'Friend,' said Tulas Shorn, 'what is it that is in your mind?'

'That there is more to the unchaining of Korabas than we know. That, in some manner we have yet to fathom, the Otataral Dragon's freedom serves a higher purpose. Korabas is here because she needs to be.'

'Silchas – your living senses are sharper than my dead ones. How many Eleint have come into this world?'

The white-skinned Tiste Andii lowered his hands from his face and looked over at Tulas Shorn. 'All of them.'

Tulas Shorn staggered back a step, and then turned away – almost as if his every instinct was demanding that he flee, that he get away. *Where? Anywhere.* And then he faced Silchas again. 'Korabas does not stand a chance.'

'No, she does not.'

'The Eleint will conquer this world – who is there to stop them? My friend – we have been made irrelevant. All purpose . . . gone. I will *not* surrender to T'iam!'

The sudden anger in Tulas made Silchas straighten. 'Nor will I.'

'What can we do?'

'We can hope.'

'What do you mean?'

'You say you sense the Hounds of Shadow—'

'Not close—'

'And you tell me that they possess a new master, the usurper of Kurald Emurlahn—'

'Who commands nothing.'

'No. Not yet. There is a game being played here – beyond all that we think we understand of this situation. You say the Hounds are wandering. The question that needs to be asked is: *why?* What has Shadow to do with any of this?'

Tulas Shorn shook his head.

Silchas Ruin drew out his Hust sword. 'That usurper gave this weapon to me, as I told you. See the blade? Watermarked and etched with dragons. But there is more – there is my brother's sacrifice. There is the return of Mother Dark.'

'And now Draconus. Silchas – your brother, he cannot have meant to—'

'But I think he did, Tulas. We children were as responsible for what happened between Mother Dark and her consort as anyone was – even Osserc. My friend – *they set something into play.* Anomander, this Shadowthrone, even Hood, and perhaps many other gods hidden from our view, for ever veiled.'

'Draconus will never return to Mother Dark – do you truly believe those wounds could *ever* heal?'

'Tulas, the Eleint must be faced down – they must be driven back. They are the Children of Chaos, and who has always stood against Chaos? What was Dragnipur, Tulas, if not a broken man's attempt to save the woman he had lost? It failed – Abyss knows how it failed – but now, at last, Draconus has been freed – his own chains for ever cut away from him. Don't you see? My brother ended Mother Dark's vow of isolation – once again she faces her children. But why should it stop there? Tulas! My brother also freed Draconus.'

'Anomander would force the wounds to heal? The arrogance of the man!'

'He forces nothing, Tulas. He but opens the door. He makes possible . . . *anything*.'

'Does Draconus understand?'

Now that is the question, isn't it? 'When he is done killing the Elder Gods he feels should be killed, he will pause. He will ask himself the question, *what now?* And then, perhaps, it will come to him. The fullest recognition of Anomander's gift.'

'My friend, if I truly had breath, you would have taken it from me. But . . . how can you be certain? Of any of this?'

Silchas Ruin studied the sword in his hand. 'I think I know who crouches at the centre of this mad web. Tulas, when I veer, what happens to this Hust sword?'

'It becomes one with the fibre of your flesh and bone – as you well know, Silchas.'

'Yes . . . but this is a *Hust* – a slayer of dragons.'

668

'Was the usurper trying to tell you something, do you think?'

'I begin to suspect the gift wasn't the sword. The gift was what the sword meant – what it *means*.' He sheathed the weapon. 'The time has come, friend, for our last stand. War we shall now wage.'

Another rattle from Tulas Shorn's dry throat, but this time it was laughter. 'I delight in this irony, beloved blade-brother. Very well, let us go and kill some dragons.' Then he paused and cocked his head at Silchas. 'Korabas . . . will she thank us?'

'Do you expect her to?'

'No, I suppose not. Why should she? We will fail.'

'Now,' Silchas mused, 'you give me reason to wonder. After all, will this not be the first time that she does not fall alone?'

Tulas was silent for a moment, and then he said, 'My friend, our deaths shall be our gift to her.'

'Tulas, can two Ancients make a Storm?'

'We shall have to try.'

Anomander, I believe I shall see you soon. And Andarist, too.

'Since we are about to die, Silchas, will you tell me what happened to the Throne of Shadow?'

Silchas Ruin smiled and shook his head. 'Perhaps, if the throne so desires, it will one day tell you itself.'

'Thrones cannot speak.'

'That is true, and it's just as well, don't you think?'

'It is a good thing we are going to die side by side,' Tulas Shorn growled, 'else I would be forced to fight you after all.'

They had moved well apart, and now they veered.

And two Ancient dragons, one living, the other undead, lifted into the empty sky.

Olar Ethil crouched in the grasses like a hare about to be flushed by a hawk. Torrent studied her for a moment longer, struggling to disguise his dark satisfaction, and then turned to check once more on the three children. They slept on – the hag had done something to them. It was just past midday and they'd not travelled far since the dawn. Behind him, the Bonecaster was muttering to herself.

'Too many came through – nowhere to hide. I know now what is being attempted. It cannot work. I want it for myself – I will have it for myself! There are Ancients in the sky, but I am the most ancient one of all. I will see them driven back . . . but first, Korabas needs to die. They need to fail!'

Torrent walked over to his horse. Examined the primitive-looking arrows in the quiver strapped beside the bow. Then he glanced back at Olar Ethil. 'What are we waiting for?'

Her battered face lifted. 'I will not be part of this fight.'

He looked round, seeing nothing but empty plains. 'What fight?'

'You are as good as dead already, pup. Soon I won't need you any more. I have gifts to give. And he will forgive me – you'll see, he'll forgive me.'

'How can I see anything if I'm to be dead soon?'

She straightened, kicked at the grasses. Two skeletal lizards dodged out, evading her gnarled foot. He heard their clacking jaws as they scampered past him, down the slope and away.

'That's it then,' Olar Ethil rasped, watching them flee. 'They're gone. Good. I never trusted them – GO!' She hobbled to the edge of the ridge, shouted after them, 'Find the great Storm of T'iam! As if that will help you, hah!' Then she wheeled and stabbed a crooked finger at Torrent. 'I am watching you, pup!'

Torrent sighed. 'It's all going wrong, isn't it?'

'Errastas was a fool! And all the Elders who listened to him – his madness will kill them all! Good! So long as he leaves me alone.'

'You've lost your mind, hag.'

'Wake them up!' Olar Ethil snapped. 'We need to go south – and we must hurry!'

'I smell the sea on this wind,' Torrent said, facing east.

'Of course you do, you fool. Now get the runts up – we must go!'

You are losing your grip, witch, and you know it, don't you? You think that whatever you set out to do will be enough, that it will solve everything – but now you're discovering that it won't. I hope I do live for a while longer – long enough to be standing over your corpse.

'Your mind leaks, pup.'

It only leaks what I let through.

She shot him a look. Torrent turned away, went to awaken the children.

Telorast lunged and leapt alongside Curdle. 'We'll be safe there, Curdle, won't we? The chains of our curse – broken in the Storm! Right?'

'What I planned from the very start, Telorast – and if you weren't so thick you'd have guessed that long ago.'

'It was that priest of the Worm, that clever drunk one – better than Not-Apsalar, better by far! He told us everything we needed to know, so I don't have to guess, Curdle, because between us I'm the smarter one.'

'The only smart thing you ever did was swindling me into being your friend.'

'Friend lover sister or better half, it's all the same with us, and isn't that the best, Curdle? This is what it means to live a life of mystery and adventure! Oh – is my leg coming off? Curdle! My leg!'

'It's fine. Just wobbly. Soon it won't matter. Soon we will have the bodies to match our egos and won't that be a scary thing? Why, I can smell us a throne, Telorast. Can you?'

But Telorast had skidded to a halt. 'Wait! Curdle, wait! That Storm – it'll devour us!'

'So we get eaten – at least we'll be free. And sooner or later, the Storm will break up. It has to.'

'More like tear itself apart,' Telorast hissed. 'We've got to be careful then, Curdle, so we don't get eaten for real.'

'Well of course we'll be careful. We're brilliant.'

'And sneaky.'

'That's why creatures like us never lose, Telorast. We overflow with talents – they're spilling out everywhere!'

'So long as my leg doesn't fall off.'

'If it does I'll carry you.'

'Really?'

'Well, drag you.'

'You're so sweet, Curdle.'

'It's because we're in love, Telorast. Love is the reason I'd drag you anywhere. We love ourselves and so we deserve two thrones – at least two! We deserve them so we'll have them, even if we have to kill ten thousand babies to get to them.'

'Babies? Killing babies?'

'Why not?'

They resumed their swishing rush through the grasses. 'I can almost see them, Telorast! An army of babies between us and those thrones. They can swing their bone rattles all they like – we'll chew through them like cheese!'

'And kittens and puppies and small mice, too!'

'Stop it, Curdle – you're making me hungry! And save your breath – we'll need it to kill Korabas.'

'Can't kill Korabas with our breaths, Telorast – she's Otataral, remember? We've got to do it the hard way – piece by bloody piece, until she's raining down from the sky!'

'It will be great. Won't it? Curdle, won't it?'

'The best, Telorast. Almost as good as eating babies!'

'How long is this going to take? Are we there yet, Curdle? My legs are about to fall off, I swear it.'

'Hmm, maybe we should veer. For a bit, I mean. Just a bit, and then back down, and then we run for a while, and then veer again – what do you think?'

'I think you're almost as clever as me.'

'And you're almost as clever as *me*. We're almost as clever as each other! Isn't that great?'

*　　　*　　　*

671

Paran reined in to let the boy off. Ordering the rest of the troop to remain where they were, he waved Mathok to accompany him as he rode closer to the foot of the pass. The old mountains formed a saddle neck ahead, and the slope gave them a clear view of the trenches, berms and redoubts crowding there.

Figures swarmed the defences.

'We've been seen,' Mathok said.

Five hundred strides from the base of the rough slope, Paran halted. Studied the vista. A cobbled road worked its way up the pass. At the first line of defences a half-ring of staked earthworks curled to face inward on that road – to attempt an assault there would invite a deadly enfilade. But the rest of the ground to either side of that road was rough and broken, almost a scree.

'Had a wife once,' Mathok muttered, 'just like this.'

'Excuse me?'

'The closer I got the uglier she looked. One of the many pitfalls in getting drunk at the full moon. Waking up to the horrors you've committed, and then having to live with them.'

There were two distinct tiers to the defences, and the closer one bore the standards of Kolanse. 'Shriven auxiliaries,' Paran said. 'We'll have to go through them to get to the Wolf army. Now that's an unexpected complication.'

'But you know, I loved that woman with all my might – she was my best wife, it turned out.'

'What happened to her?'

'She inherited and left me for a prettier man. You see, she woke up that morning feeling the same horror as me, and the closer I got . . .'

'Mathok, looks like we're going to have a fight on our hands after all.'

'Your words make me happy.'

'We need to overwhelm and rout the Shriven. Then we can deal with the mercenaries. As it turns out,' he added, collecting his reins, 'that might be just what we need to convince them to surrender.'

'There'll be a Pure up there, High Fist. More fun for Kalam and your High Mage.'

'We'll draw up tonight. Mathok, your warriors won't be much use if they stay mounted.'

The man shrugged. 'Why do raiders ride horses, High Fist? Because it's the quickest means of getting away.'

'You're not just raiders any more, Mathok.'

'We'll skirmish if that's what you need, but we won't like it. Now, that road, that's a wide road, a military road. Clear the flanks and we can ride straight up it.'

'Into the waiting teeth of those mercenaries? And uphill at that? I'll not see you wasted. Sorry, no matter how thirsty you are for blood, you may have to wait a while longer.'

The warrior grimaced and then shrugged. 'We're thirsty for blood, yes, but not if most of it is our own.'

'Good,' Paran grunted. 'Keep your mob in check, that's all I ask.'

Mathok was studying him in a peculiar fashion. 'High Fist, I've heard a lifetime of tales about the Malazan army. And I've run from a few close calls in my day, ended up getting chased for weeks.' He jutted his chin at the pass. 'But this – even those Shriven look to be enough to not only stop us dead, but hurt us bad in the doing.'

'Your point?'

'I fear for the Host, that's all.'

Paran nodded. 'Come the morning, Mathok, find a high vantage point for you and your warriors. And I will show you everything you need to know about the Malazan army.'

Two turns of the sand after the sun had set, the Host drew up a short distance from the base of the pass. Beneath the luminous green glow of the Jade Strangers, the companies broke out into their bivouacs. Forward pickets were established, although no probes were expected from the enemy. Soldiers ate a quick meal, and then rested. Most slept, although a few attended to their weapons and armour, their leather harnesses, their shields and footwear. Trailed by Fist Rythe Bude, Paran walked among the camps, exchanging words here and there with those soldiers too charged up or nervous to sleep.

He had never expected to be commanding an army. He had never expected to take the place of Dujek Onearm. He thought often of that man, and took from Dujek all he could. The Host had known bad times. It deserved better, but Paran suspected that this sentiment was felt by every commander.

When he and Rythe Bude finally retired to the command tent, they found Kalam and Quick Ben awaiting them. It was two turns before dawn.

The assassin was wrapped in black muslin, pulling on his stained and worn leather gloves, and though he was wearing chain beneath the cloth, there was almost no sound while he paced. Quick Ben sat on the ground leaning back against a squat four-legged chest, his legs stretched out, his eyes half shut.

Paran stared down at the wizard. 'Well?'

'Well what?'

'Are you ready? Usually I can smell when there's been magic going on, and I can't smell a thing, High Mage.'

Quick Ben opened one eye to regard him. 'If you can tell, High Fist, then so can the Pures up there. Trust me. We're ready.'

Paran glanced across at Rythe, who simply shrugged in reply. He squinted at her. 'Get some sleep, Fist.'

'Yes sir.'

After she'd left, Paran stepped into Kalam's path. Muttering an oath, the assassin halted. Bared his teeth and said, 'You're getting on my nerves, High Fist.'

Quick Ben spoke. 'Do you have that card ready, High Fist?'

Paran nodded, edging to one side so that Kalam could resume pacing.

'Good,' said the wizard. He sat up, reached for a leather satchel lying beside him. Rummaged inside it for a moment and then drew out a crooked stick on which was tied an arm's length of twine. One end of the stick had been hacked into something resembling a point. Quick Ben stabbed that end into the floor. Then he removed from his satchel two small balls of weighted, knotted cloth, one black, the other gold. He bound these to the string, moving them away from the stick until the twine stretched straight. 'Kalam,' he said, 'it's time.'

The assassin halted, shook himself like a bear.

Climbing to his feet, Quick Ben faced Paran. 'Don't you even blink, sir. Understand?'

'I will be vigilant, High Mage,' Paran assured him. 'But you have me a little concerned here. What do you think awaits you?'

'Beyond one or two Pure Forkrul Assail?' Quick Ben snorted, and then scowled. 'Not sure. Something.'

'Let's get on with this,' Kalam growled.

Paran drew off his helm, set it down on the map table. In battle, he would attach the full face grille. It was an arcane piece, Untan, a gift from Rythe Bude, but he still wasn't used to its full weight. Turning to face the two men he began, 'I think we should—' and then fell silent. He was alone in the tent. 'Gods below, he's good.'

Heart suddenly pounding, nips of pain flaring in his stomach, he drew out the wooden card Ormulogun had prepared. Studied it in the lantern light. *The first truly Malazan card for the Deck of Dragons. Artist, you did me proud.* A single misshapen, vaguely polished object in the centre of a dark field.

'Behold,' Paran said under his breath, 'the Shaved Knuckle in the Hole.'

Invisible to all eyes, even those of the Pures, Kalam made his way silently up the cobbled road. *Well, hopefully invisible to the Pures. Either way, we'll soon find out.* To his right and left now, deep foxholes where sentries stood, chests against the pit side, looking down on the foreign invaders. At their feet, the dull glow of signal lanterns. Past them, the first berms fronting the lead trench: mounded rocks and earth, high enough to provide cover from arrows and quarrels, treacherous enough underfoot for the attackers to lose their balance and slow their charge.

The trenches themselves were solid with Kolanse soldiers, well armoured and armed with pikes. Seven paces behind them, higher up the slope, ran a long slit trench, stepped for the archers. They would loose their arrows at nearly point-blank range, over the heads of the first line of defenders and taking the Malazans at the top of the berm.

Kalam hoped that Paran's damned card was working. He hoped that the High Fist was now seeing what he was seeing. *This could be brutal. There's a decent commander up here, somewhere. Quick Ben – I don't think this is the work of a Forkrul Assail. This has the feel of a professional campaigner. Probably the Wolves commander. I hope you're thinking what I'm thinking.*

Hold on . . . mercenaries wearing wolf furs? No, couldn't be them. Just some other bastards. Got to be.

Two more tiers to match the lead line, with levelled ramps allowing for retreat, should the first trench be overrun. And plenty of reserves, positioned in three fortified camps just above the last tier. Kalam judged there to be at least six thousand Shriven here. *Glad I'm not you, Paran.*

Higher still, where at last Kalam thought he could see the summit's edge, beyond which the pass levelled out. A massive stone gate straddled the road, with a low skirting wall above a moat stretching out to either side, effectively blocking the entire pass. And this area was well lit, revealing companies of heavy infantry. They were awake, divided into squads of ten, each squad forming a circle facing inward – the soldiers were praying.

Fanatics. That's bad. We've seen this before, too many times. Surrender? Not a chance. Hold on . . . They were still too far away for him to be certain. He looked for standards, but none were raised. *There, a fully armoured soldier near the gate. Gods below! Fucking Perish!* Kalam paused, his mind racing, sweat suddenly trickling beneath his garments. *They turned on us? Krughava? I can't believe this – soldiers of the Wolves. Gods, who else could they have been? Kalam, you idiot. Hood take me, Hood take us all.*

But . . . if Krughava's here, it's no wonder the defences are bristling.

All right, woman. He began moving forward once more. *Betray us and you get what you deserve.*

The gateway was barred, with projecting spikes, all blackened iron. The lowest row of spikes, ankle-high, jutted a hand's length beyond the higher ones, except for a matching row at eye level. There was a lone Perish sentry standing behind the gate, visor lowered, heavy spear leaning against one shoulder.

Ten paces away, Kalam slipped down from the road, made his way along the drainage ditch, and down into the moat. At the bottom, short wooden spikes were jammed between sharp-edged rocks. The bank furthest from the wall was soaked in pitch. *Firewall. Nothing nice here, nothing at all. Hope you're close, Quick Ben. Hope you know what I'm going to have to do here.*

He carefully picked his way across the moat. Waited a moment, and then whispered the chain-word the wizard had given him. Sudden weightlessness. Reaching up, he made his way up and over the wall. At he touched ground on the other side, the weightlessness faded. *Well, no alarm yet. So far, Quick's promise of being able to hide magic seems to be holding.* Ahead, more guards, but widely spaced enough for the assassin to slip easily between them. He set out, made his way into the camp.

Past the squad circles, the soldiers still praying, to an empty marshalling area in the centre, and opposite it, two command tents, the one on the right surmounted by a wolf skull atop the centre pole. *Grey Helms all right. But . . . this can't be all of them. Unless Tavore made them pay dearly for the treachery. But if she did, then she's probably dead. She never got her chance.*

Well then. If vengeance is all we have left, let's get started . . .

The other tent was larger, of the same style as those in the besieging camp outside the keep. It was lit from within and two guards flanked the front flap, both Kolansii.

Drawing two throwing knives, Kalam advanced on them, moving fast. At five paces away, he raised both weapons and threw them simultaneously in a single fluid motion. Each found the base of a throat. Bodies buckled, blood splashing down, but before they could fall Kalam had reached them, grasping the knife grips to hold both men up before carefully settling them to the ground.

How much noise? Oh, who cares?

Leaving the daggers where they were, the assassin drew his two long knives, slashed the flap's draw strings, and then bulled through.

He clearly caught the Pure by surprise – nothing stealthy or subtle in this approach after all – and collided hard with the Forkrul Assail. One long knife plunged deep directly beneath the heart. The other, moving up to slash across the throat, was blocked by a forearm hard as iron. Even as the Assail stumbled back, his hands lashed out.

The first blow caught Kalam high on his right shoulder, spinning him off his feet. The second one slammed into his chest on the left side, crushing chain, breaking at least two ribs and fracturing others. The impact flung the assassin backwards. He rebounded from the tent wall to the left of the entrance.

Half stunned with pain, Kalam watched the Assail pull the long knife from his chest and fling it away.

'Oh,' he gasped, 'did I make you mad?'

Snarling, the Assail advanced on him.

The ground disappeared beneath his feet. With a howl, the Pure plunged from sight. There followed a thud.

Quick Ben materialized just on the other side of the hole. Drew out a small round ball of black clay. Leaned over to peer down. 'Compliments of the marines,' he said, and dropped the ball.

The wizard had to lunge backward as a gout of fire shot from the hole, and all at once the tent ceiling was aflame, and Quick Ben was nowhere to be seen.

Swearing, Kalam retrieved his long knife – he'd somehow held on to the other one – and leapt for the entrance.

Rolling clear, groaning at the blinding agony exploding in his chest, he staggered to his feet. On all sides, Perish soldiers were rushing to the burning tent. He saw them drawing their swords.

'Quick Ben! I'm invisible, right? Quick Ben!'

He heard a hiss: '*Sheathe that damned knife!*'

Hood's breath! Kalam spun and ran from the nearest attacker. Slammed the knife back into its scabbard. 'Try again!' he bellowed.

He stumbled, fell with a grunt. There was blood in his mouth. *Not good.*

A hand settled on his back. 'Don't move,' came Quick Ben's whisper.

The Perish were retreating now from the raging flames, and the fire was almost close enough to reach out and touch, but Kalam felt no heat. 'Can we talk?' he asked.

'Now we can, aye.'

'You said a sharper!'

'I changed my mind. Needed to make certain. Besides, the sharper's pretty loud.'

'A Hood-damned *burner*, though? Now *that's* keeping things nice and quiet! Any more Pures?'

'No. Shh – something's close. Tracking us.'

'How?'

'Don't know.'

'I wanted to go after the Perish commander – Krughava or whoever it is.'

'You're bubbling blood with every breath, Kalam. You're in no shape for anything.'

'Stabbed the bastard in the heart and it didn't do a damned thing.'

'I'm sure it did. But they've got two hearts.'

'Thanks for telling me.' Kalam grimaced, fought down a cough. 'These *are* the Perish, aren't they?'

'Aye. Now, be quiet, and let me drag you away. That fire's starting to burn through what I threw up around us.'

But the mage dragged Kalam for only two tugs before the assassin felt Quick Ben's hands suddenly grip tight. 'Shit, it's here.'

Blinking, Kalam twisted, looked round. 'I don't see—'

'Smells like an enkar'l, feels like a Toblakai.'

Not a chance – oh, gods below, what's it doing here? He could feel it now. A massive, looming presence. 'What's it doing?' he hissed.

'Er, sniffing you.'

Kalam felt his skin crawl. 'Why can't I see it?'

'Because it doesn't want you to.'

The assassin almost shouted when a sharp talon tracked gently across one cheek, ending up directly beneath an eye. He forced himself to lie perfectly still.

'A servant of the Wolves, I think.'

Aye. Don't tell me what I already know.

Then the hand pressed down on Kalam's chest, directly over his shattered ribs. But there was no pain, just a sudden heat. A moment later the hand was gone. And then—

'Hood take me,' Quick Ben muttered a few heartbeats later. 'Gone. Never seen the like. It fucking healed you, Kalam. Why did it do that?'

Feeling shaken, fragile, as if he'd inhaled a fist and had only just now coughed it back out, the assassin slowly regained his feet. There was chaos on all sides of the burning tent, and he saw a Perish officer, one of Krughava's ship commanders. He was standing staring at the tent with an odd, almost satisfied expression on his lean face.

'Ready to try for him?' Quick Ben asked.

Kalam shook his head. 'No. We don't touch the Perish.'

'What do you mean?'

'Unless you want that thing to come back, a whole lot madder.'

'Good point.'

'You're sure there aren't any more Pures?'

'No.'

'Time to go, then.'

They set out, winding unseen through the crowd of soldiers. At the skirting wall, the assassin paused and glanced back. And nodded. 'Always an even trade . . .' *Not that I can remember what I did to make him so happy.*

*　*　*

In his tent, Paran slowly sat back, carefully setting down the wooden card. He could have pulled them out, right at the moment the demon closed on them. But something had held him back. *That was a chosen servant of the Wolves of Winter. I felt its anger, and then I felt its . . . what* was *it? Solicitude? I didn't know they could even feel things like that.*

He straightened, walked over to the stick, took it in his hand, and pulled it from the ground. The balls on the string snapped after it.

A thunderous concussion in the confines of the tent, clouds of dust, and Quick Ben and Kalam staggered into view. The wizard's expression twisted with outrage. He glared across at Paran. 'That was a little late, High Fist! We were already halfway back.'

Paran waved at the dust. He could hear footsteps from beyond the flap and called out, 'Everything's fine!'

From outside, a soldier's voice hissed, 'Hear that, Gebbla? When a High Fist farts the whole world shakes!'

'Shh, y'damned idiot!'

The footsteps retreated.

Paran sighed. 'I got impatient waiting for you. Sorry. I didn't know retrieving you was going to be so messy.'

'It was for *emergencies*, sir. I feel like I've been pulled inside out.'

'Aye to that,' Kalam growled, moving over to sit down heavily on the chest. The stout legs snapped and the chest thumped down hard. The assassin winced. 'Just what my old bent spine needed, gods below.' He started pulling off his gloves.

'My sister's allies, then – am I correct, Kalam?'

'Good guess.'

'Allies no longer,' said Quick Ben, and now he was the one pacing in the confines of the tent. 'But that was Erekala, not the Mortal Sword. Didn't see the Shield Anvil either. This force is the one that came from the sea. The soldiers left to travel with the fleet.'

'So it could be that Krughava has no idea they've turned,' Kalam said.

'That alliance always had me nervous,' Quick Ben said. 'Fanatical worshippers of a world without humans – how does that make any sense? Even if Krughava hasn't turned, it's only a matter of time – all they have to do is follow their faith to its logical conclusion. I warned Tavore—'

'Now you're lying,' Kalam said in a growl.

The wizard turned on him. 'How would you know?'

'Just guessing. Because I know you, remember? You're just mad at yourself because you never anticipated this happening.'

'Fine. Have it your way then. The point is, Tavore is in trouble. She could get backstabbed at any time, and there's no way we can warn her.'

'Maybe there is,' Paran said. 'Once we get through this pass, I want you and Kalam riding ahead, fast as your horses can take you. Find my sister.'

'Did you see those defences, sir?' Kalam demanded. 'How do you hope to get the Perish to surrender? They can stop the Host right here, right now.'

But Paran was frowning. 'Why didn't that demon tear you to pieces, Kalam?'

The assassin looked away, shrugged. 'Met it before. Did it a favour. Maybe. I think. Can't remember exactly. But it was back in Seven Cities, the middle of the Whirlwind. Things happened.'

'You weave a fine tale, Kalam,' Quick Ben observed.

'I leave the endlessly flapping mouth to you, wizard.'

'Clearly a wise decision. But next time, just summarize.'

Six High Watered officers stood uneasily before Erekala, twenty paces behind them the blackened stain and charred wreckage of the Pure's tent, from which embers still blinked open and closed like glowing eyes amidst the ashes, and smoke lifted its black pall.

The times the Perish commander had had occasion to engage with these mixed-bloods, they had looked upon him with disdain. Now such superiority had been swept away, in a conflagration of fire. Brother Serenity was dead. But uttering that statement was akin to stating the impossible. One rank below Reverence and Diligence, Serenity's power had been immense, matched only by that of Calm – or so Erekala had been led to believe.

And Serenity has this night fallen to two Malazans. And come the dawn, we shall face in battle eight thousand more. But did the Pure Brother heed my caution? He did not. 'We have found blood trails leading out from the Pure's tent,' he now said. 'It is fair to assume that Brother Serenity fought hard against his assailants; indeed, that he might have seriously wounded them, perhaps even killed one.'

But he could see no effect from these words. Sighing, Erekala continued, 'Will you elect one among you to assume command of the Shriven? Alternatively, you can place yourselves under my command. Dawn is fast approaching, sirs, and we shall soon be locked in battle.'

One of the officers stepped forward. 'Sir, in all matters tactical, Brother Serenity instructed us to obey your commands.'

Erekala nodded. 'As you have done.'

'Sir,' the officer began, and then hesitated.

'Speak your mind.'

'The Pures have felt Brother Serenity's death. They are wounded,

680

confused, and from them we receive no guidance. Indeed, Akhrast Korvalain itself has been damaged here.'

'Damaged?' This was unexpected. 'How so?'

'Another Hold manifested here, last night.'

'Indeed?' He scanned the faces before him. 'Perhaps you too readily discounted the efficacy of seven thousand Perish praying to their gods.'

'We do not speak of the Beast Hold, sir.'

Erekala was silent, for now he was the one left shaken. In a quiet voice he asked, 'And have you identified the intruder, sir?'

'Not us, Commander. Sister Reverence, however – from the storm of her thoughts, we sense her . . . *recognition*.'

'Go on.'

The man shook his head. 'This is all we have, sir.'

'Is it now your thought that another ancient Hold has set itself against Akhrast Korvalain?'

'We would know more of these Malazans, sir.'

Erekala frowned. 'Have you become uncertain regarding my preparations here?'

'No, Commander. Today, the enemy shall be savaged, possibly shattered. But we seek to understand – are these Malazans nothing more than humans?'

'No different from us Perish, you mean?'

'Then . . . do they too serve an Elder God?'

'The Malazan Empire long ago outlawed cults of war in its military . . . but that is not to say that there are no secret believers among the ranks.' He studied the faces arrayed before him. 'Has it not occurred to the Forkrul Assail that, in so forcefully asserting the power of Akhrast Korvalain, they would invite the attention of the other Elder Holds?'

'It was our understanding that across most of this realm the Holds were abandoned, giving way to a younger ascendancy.'

Erekala cocked his head. 'And was this the case for the Perish?'

At last, a faint sneer from the officer. 'You were judged an aberration.'

The commander smiled. 'We can resume this discussion at a later time. You will descend among the Shriven and take command of your companies.'

The officers saluted.

Watching them march off, Erekala gestured to one of his aides. 'Sister Staylock, make the soldiers aware that we may face more than one enemy this day.'

The young woman frowned. 'Sir?'

'And then assure them that the Wolves shall guard us against all threats.'

'Yes sir.'

Alone once more, Erekala made his way to the viewing platform he'd had raised fifty paces to the left of the gate. From there, he would have an unobstructed view of the enemy assault upon his defences. *Malazans. To utter the name alone is sufficient to pale the most hardened soldier – especially among those who have faced them. What is it about these foreigners, these blades of empire, that so sets them apart?*

As he reached the ladder, he paused, recalling all that he had seen of that terrible withdrawal from Malaz City. *Adjunct Tavore, did you know you would come to this land to find other Malazans awaiting you? Are they your allies, or some other gambit orchestrated by Empress Laseen? Are they hunting you? Or is this simply another invasion?* A sudden chill tracked through him. *If allies . . . then all of this must have been planned.* The thought frightened him.

He quickly climbed upward. Reaching the platform – the smell of fresh pine sharp in the air – he crossed the raw wooden boards to the rail facing north. The sky was lightening around him, although the approach to the pass remained in shadow. He could see enemy ranks now arrayed in five distinct wedges at the base. *Can they not see what awaits them? Perhaps they will succeed in taking the first trench – but the second? It is impossible. The Grey Helms will not even draw weapons this day.* His unease deepened. *Call the Malazans every vile name there is, but do not call them fools.*

He stood, alone on the platform, and waited to see what would come.

Grainy-eyed from lack of sleep, Ganoes Paran walked until he was opposite the disordered mob. This was always the problem, he reflected, when trying to manage four hundred sloppy, unruly marines. The hard eyes, the weathered faces, the sense that they were all half wild and straining at the leash. To make matters worse, this lot slouched before him on this chill morning were, one and all, sappers.

Paran glanced back to the mass of wooden crates laid out behind him. There were no guards stationed around them. This entire gathering was taking place two hundred paces north of the camp's edge. *With good reason.* He felt a trickle of sweat work its way down his spine.

Facing the sappers once more, and with a glance at Noto Boil, and then Captain Sweetcreek who stood well off to one side, Paran cleared his throat, and began. 'I am well aware of your frustration – I held you back from the keep defences, set you to doing repairs and nothing else. I dare say your swords are rusted in their scabbards by now . . .' Paran paused, but saw no reaction from them, not a smile, not a nod. He cleared his throat again. 'I decided that it would be to our tactical advantage to withhold you sappers, along with your particular . . . talents, for as long as possible.'

There was not a sound from the assembled troops, and all eyes were fixed on Paran. He glanced again at Noto Boil. The man was standing a few paces behind and off to one side, fish-spine moving up and down in his mouth. Staring back at the sappers.

Sighing, the High Fist resumed. 'In retrospect, perhaps I should have delayed my raid on that Moranth warehouse, and not just for reasons of safety, though as I am sure you all know, the Moranth are very efficient and careful when storing munitions. Nonetheless, transporting them in bulk and overland entails undeniable risks. Fortunately, here we are.' And he gestured behind him. 'And there *they* are.'

He had been waiting for a heightening of tension, a stirring of anticipation. The first of broadening smiles, soldiers finally straightening to attention, even. Instead . . . Paran's gaze narrowed. *Nothing.*

I might as well be describing the weather. What's wrong with them?

Thought they respected me. Thought that maybe I'd finally earned the rank I was saddled with. But now . . . feels like it was all a sham.

'You may be pleased to know that your waiting is at an end. This morning, you will avail yourselves of these munitions, and return to your squads. The marines will lead the assault. You are to break the defences and, if possible, advance to the second trench. This assault must be rapid and sustained . . .' His words trailed away as he caught something at the corner of his eye.

Standing in the front row off to his right, where the sun's light slanted across unobstructed, a grizzled corporal, his broad, flat face seamed with scars visible even from where the High Fist stood. Paran squinted at the man. Then he gestured to Noto Boil. The cutter walked over, pulling the spine from his mouth.

'Noto Boil,' Paran said in a low tone.

'Sir?'

'Walk over to that corporal – that one there – and take a closer look, and then report back to me.'

'Is this a test?'

'Just do it.'

The cutter reinserted the spine and then headed over to halt directly in front of the corporal. After a moment, he swung round and made his way back.

'Well?' Paran demanded.

Noto Boil removed the spine. 'The man is crying, High Fist.'

'He's crying.'

'So it seems, sir.'

'But . . . *why* is he crying?'

Noto Boil turned back to regard the corporal once more. 'Was just the one tear. Could be anything.'

Swearing under his breath, Paran marched over to stand before the corporal. The marine's stare was fixed straight ahead. The track of that lone tear, etching its way down from his right eye, was already dulled with grit and dust. 'Something in your eye, Corporal?'

'No sir.'

'Are you ill?'

'No sir.'

'You're trembling.'

The eyes flicked briefly in their thinned slits, locked for an instant with Paran's own. 'Is that so? Didn't know that, sir. Beggin' your pardon.'

'Soldier, am I blocking your view?'

'Yes sir, that you are, sir.'

Slowly, Paran edged to one side. He studied the sapper's face for a half-dozen heartbeats, and then a few more, until . . . *oh, gods below!* 'I thought you said you weren't sick, Corporal.'

'I'm not, sir.'

'I beg to differ.'

'If you like, sir.'

'Corporal.'

Another flicker of the eyes. 'Sir?'

'Control yourselves. Be orderly. Don't blow any of us up. Am I understood?'

A quick nod. 'Aye, sir. Bless you, sir.'

Startled, Paran's voice sharpened, '*Bless* me?'

And from the mob of sappers came a muttered chorus, echoing the corporal's blessing. Paran stepped back, struggled for a moment to regain his composure, and then raised his voice. 'No need to rush – there's plenty for everyone.' He paused upon hearing a faint whimper, then continued, 'In one turn of the sand I want you back with your squads. Your sergeants have been apprised of this resupply so you can be sure that the word has gone out. By the time you get back to them they will all have done with their prayers, sacrifices, and all the rest. In other words, they'll be ready for you. The advance begins two turns of the sand from now. That is all.'

He set off, not looking back.

Noto Boil came up alongside him. 'High Fist.'

'What?'

'Is this wise? That's more munitions than any of them has ever seen.'

'In those crates are just the sharpers, burners and smokers. I haven't even let them *see* the cussers and redbolts—'

'Excuse me, sir, the *what* bolts?'

'It turns out, Noto, that there exists a whole class of munitions exclusive to the Moranth. Not for export, if you understand me. Through a card I was witness to the demonstration of some of them. These ones, which I have called redbolts, are similar to onager bolts. Only they do not require the onager.'

'Curious, High Fist. But if you haven't shown them to any sapper yet, how will anyone know how to use them?'

'If we need to fight the Perish, well, it's possible that a crash course will be necessary. For the moment, however, why distract them?'

They were approaching the camp edge, where two companies of regulars and heavies were assembled, one to either side of the cobbled road. Between them and awaiting their arrival was Fist Rythe Bude.

Noto Boil said, 'One more question, sir.'

Paran sighed. 'What?'

'Those cussers and redbolts, where did you hide them?'

'Relax. I made my own warren for them – well, to be more precise, I walled off a small area in a different warren, accessible only to me, via a card.'

'Ormulogun?'

'Excuse me? Did he paint the card? Of course.'

'Did he use a funny red slash, sir? Like lightning, only the colour of blood?'

Paran frowned. 'Redbolt symbol, yes. How did you know that?'

Noto Boil shrugged. 'Not sure, sir. Seen it somewhere, I suppose. No matter.'

Corporal Stern wiped at his eyes. Crates were being cracked open, the sappers working quickly. He scanned the remaining boxes, swore under his breath, and then turned. 'Manx, get over here.'

The Dal Honese shaman waddled over. 'Just what we figured! Only the small stuff. That bastard don't trust us.'

Stern grunted. 'You idiot. *I* don't trust us. But listen, if we—'

Manx held up a hand in front of Stern's face. 'Got it covered. See?'

The corporal tilted his head back, studied the tattoo blazoned across the hand's palm. A blood-red jagged slash. 'That's it? That's all you need?'

'Should do. We made sure the toad described it in detail.'

'Right. Has he recovered?'

'Well, we roasted him a bit crispy here and there, but he'll survive. It all kind of went wrong for a bit – I mean, we had 'em both trussed up, and we figured just threatening the toad would be enough to make the artist break down and talk. We was wrong. In fact, it was Ormulogun

685

who suggested the roasting bit – never seen the old lunatic happier. We thought they was friends—'

'Be quiet, will you? You're babbling. I don't care what happened, so long as you didn't kill either of them.'

'They're alive, I told you. Trussed up and gagged for now. We'll let 'em go later.'

Stern looked round, raised his voice, 'Sappers! Leave room for a cusser or two!'

'Ain't no cussers, Stern.'

'Never mind that. It's taken care of. Now let's get this done – and carefully. We make a mistake here and we don't take none of the bad guys with us on the way out, and that'll send our souls to the fiends of the Sapper's Torment for ever – and nobody wants that, do they?'

A sudden hush, a renewed attention to caution, and here and there, a few subtle gestures warding against the curse of the Sapper's Torment.

Satisfied, Stern nodded. 'Manx, stay close to me from now on.'

'We ain't never used one of those redbolts, Stern.'

The man grunted. 'Show me a munition I can't figure out and I'll show you the inside of the Cobra God's nose.'

Manx shot him a look. 'Figured you had north Dal Hon blood in you.'

'What's in my blood don't matter. I just know that when a sapper steps on to the field of battle, they'd be wise to call on every god they ever heard of.'

'Amen and a spit in the eye t'that.'

Stern hesitated, and then nodded. 'Amen and a spit in the eye back. Now, you ready? Good. Let's go find our squad. The sarge is gonna love this.'

'No he ain't!'

'Sarge loves what I tell him to love, Manx. Credo of the Sapper's Knuckle.'

'"Who's holding the sharper?" Aye, Sapper's Knuckle. Hey, Stern.'

'What?'

The shaman was grinning. 'See what this means? Us sappers. We're back to what we never were but could've been, and don't that taste sweet?'

'It's only sweet if we don't mess this up. Now pay attention where you're stepping. I seen gopher holes.'

'Ain't gophers, Stern. These are prairie dogs.'

'Whatever. Stick a foot in one of those and we all go up.'

Commander Erekala could feel the wind freshening, down from the north, funnelling up the narrow approach to the pass. Carried on that breeze was the smell of iron, leather, sweat and horses. Sister Staylock stood at his side, with a half-dozen messengers stationed behind them should commands need to be sent down to the flag stations positioned along the wall.

The enemy forces were shaking out, seething motion all along the front lines. The medium and heavy infantry that had been positioned there in solid ranks since dawn were now splitting up to permit new troops to move forward in ragged formation. These newcomers bore no standards, and most of them had their shields still strapped to their backs. From what Erekala could make out, they were armed with crossbows and short swords.

'Skirmishers?' asked Staylock. 'They don't look light on their feet, Commander – some of them are wearing chain. Nor are they forming a line. Who are these soldiers?'

'Marines.'

'They appear . . . undisciplined, sir.'

'It is my understanding, Sister Staylock, that against the Malazan marines the armies of the Seven Holy Cities had no counter. They are, in fact, unlike any other soldier on the field of battle.'

She turned to eye him quizzically. 'Sir, may I ask, what else have you heard about these marines?'

Erekala leaned on the rail. 'Heard? Yes, that would be the word.'

They were advancing now, broken up into squads of eight or ten, clambering steadily over the rough ground towards the first trench, where waited masses of Shriven – Kolansii regulars. Solid enough soldiers, Erekala knew. Proficient if not spectacular, yet subject to the sorcery of the Forkrul Assail. Without the Pure, however, there would be no power sufficient to unleash in them any battle frenzy. Still, they would not buckle so long as the mixed-blood commanders held their nerve.

'I don't understand you, sir.'

He glanced across at her. 'The night of the Adjunct's disengagement from the docks of Malaz City, Sister – where were you stationed?'

'The outer screen of ships, sir.'

'Ah. Do you recall, did you by chance happen to hear thunder that night – from the island?'

Frowning, she shook her head. 'Sir, for half that night I was in my sling, fast asleep.'

'Very well. Your answer, Sister, is not long in coming, I fear.'

Thirty rough and broken paces below the first berm now, the squads thinning out, those wielding crossbows raising their weapons.

On the Shriven side, the pikes angled down, readying for the enemy to breach the top of the berm. The iron points formed a bristling wall. From the second trench the archers had moved up, nocking arrows but

687

not yet drawing. Once the Malazans reached the ridge line, coming into direct line of sight, the arrows would hiss their song, and as the first line of bodies tumbled, the archers would begin firing in longer arcs – to angle the arrows down the slope. And the advance would grind to a halt, with soldiers huddling under their shields, seeking cover from the rain of death.

Twenty paces now, where there was a pause in the advance – only an instant – and then Erekala saw arms swinging, tiny objects sailing out from the hands.

Too soon.

Striking the bank two-thirds of the way up. Sudden billowing of thick black smoke, boiling out, devouring the lines of sight. Like a bank of fog, the impenetrable wall rolled up and over the berm's topside.

'Magery?' gasped Staylock.

Erekala shook his head.

And from that rising tide of midnight, more objects sailed out, landing amidst the pike-wielding press of Shriven.

Detonations and flashes of fire erupted along the entire length of the trench. The mass of Kolansii shook, and everywhere was the bright crimson of blood and torn flesh.

A second wave of munitions landed.

The report of their explosions echoed up the slope, followed by screams and shrieks of pain. The smoke was rolling into the trench, torn here and there by further detonations, but this just added dust and misted blood to the roiling mix.

Along the second trench, the archers were wavering.

'Begin firing blind,' Erekala murmured. 'Do it *now.*'

And he was pleased to see Watered officers bellowing their commands, and the bows drawn back.

A sleet of quarrels shot out from the smoke and dust, tore into the archers. And the heads of many of these quarrels were explosive. The entire line disintegrated, bodies tumbling back to the crouching loaders.

More grenados arced after the quarrels, down into the trench. Closer now, Erekala could see limbs, ripped clean from bodies, spinning in the air.

Higher up the slope, the reserve companies boiled into motion, rushing down towards the third trench, while those troops who had been stationed in that position were now foaming up over their own berm, to begin a downhill charge. The line of archers dug in above the third trench were swept up in the wholesale advance.

'What are they doing?' demanded Staylock.

'The trenches are proving indefensible against these munitions,' Erekala replied. 'The half-blood officers have correctly determined the proper response to this – they must close with the marines. Their elevation and their numbers alone should win the day.'

The marines, he now saw beneath the fast thinning smoke, had overrun the archers' trench, and looked to be digging in all along the line – but Erekala had ensured that the earthworks were designed in such a manner as to expose them to attack from higher up the slope. Those trenches offered them nothing. The marines began scurrying in full retreat.

'They're panicking,' hissed Staylock. 'They've run out of toys, and now . . .'

The descending, elongated mass of Kolansii was like an avalanche racing after the straggly marines.

'Hold up at the lowest trench,' Erekala pleaded. 'Don't follow the fools all the way down!'

The sound of that charge, past the archers' trench and into the dip of the first trench, was like thunder.

There were officers in the lead ranks. Erekala saw them checking their soldiers—

The whole scene vanished in multiple eruptions, as if the entire slope had exploded beneath the Kolansii forces. The concussion rolled upwards to shake the summit, fracturing the wall and shaking the stone gates, taking hold of the wooden platform Erekala and the others stood on and rattling it so fiercely that they all lost their footing. Rails snapped and men and women tumbled over the sides, screaming.

Erekala grasped one side post, managed to hang on as successive shock waves slammed up the slope. *Wolves protect us!*

Twisting now on the strangely tilted platform, he saw the clouds lifting to blot out the view to the north – dust and dirt, armour and weapons and sodden strips of clothing – all of it now swept down towards them, a grisly rain of devastation.

Unmindful of the deadly deluge, Erekala pulled himself upright. One of the legs of the platform had snapped and he was alone – even Staylock had plummeted to the broken ground below.

A sword tip stabbed deep into the pine boards just off to his left, the blade quivering with the impact. More rubble rained down.

He stared downslope, struggling to make sense of what he was seeing. All but the highest, nearest trench – along with the levelled ground behind it – was torn chaos, the ground wounded with overlapping craters steaming amidst chewed-up corpses. Most of the Kolansii army was simply . . . *gone.*

And then he saw movement once again, from the downward end – the same marines, swarming back up the slope, into the huge bites in the earth, up and over. Squads advancing, others drawing into tight clumps and beginning work on something.

Streams of Kolansii survivors, stunned, painted crimson, were retreating up towards the stone wall, clumping on the cobbled road. Most of the soldiers had flung away their weapons.

Just like that, the Kolansii are finished.

Strange crackling bursts of fire from the marines, and Erekala's eyes widened to see streaks of flame race out from squad positions, sizzling as they lunged up and into the air, arcing upslope.

Of the dozen terrifying projectiles launched, only two directly struck the crowded road.

The platform under Erekala pitched back, flinging him round. He lost his grip, slid past the embedded sword, and then he was falling. There was no sound. He realized that he had been deafened, and so in sweet, perfect silence, he watched the ground race up to meet him. And overhead, shadow stole the morning light.

Staylock had only just picked herself up – bruised and aching – when a closer detonation threw her back to the ground. The wall before her rippled, punching away the soldiers huddled against its protective barrier. And then, with a roar of fire, something descended on the gate to her right. The stones disintegrated in a flash of light. The sound of the impact threatened to crush her. Stunned, she staggered away from the blazing gate – saw Commander Erekala lying not ten paces away, in the wreckage of the toppled platform. Vague motions from his body drew her to him.

'Brother Erekala!' she cried.

His eyes were open, but the whites were crazed with blood. His mouth opened and closed like that of a beached fish, but she could hear no breaths going in or out.

Just as she reached his side she heard a desperate gasp from the man, and all at once he was on his side, coughing.

'Commander!'

But he did not hear her – she could see that. She looked up – entire companies of Perish had been thrown to the ground by multiple impacts.

This is not war.

This is slaughter.

And in her skull, she thought she could hear the howling of her gods. A sound of impotent rage and blind defiance. A sound that understood nothing.

A gloved hand grasped Stern by the shoulder and spun him round. Snarling, he reached for his sword, and then stared. 'Fist!'

'Cease the bombardment immediately!'

The corporal looked up and down the rough line of redbolt stations. The crates positioned behind them had each been cracked, and bundles of fleece-packed padding lay torn and scattered between the crates and the launch sites. He did a quick count of the nearest ones. 'Still got four or five salvos left, sir – right down the line!'

'I said stop! The High Fist does not want the Perish engaged!'

Stern blinked. 'But we ain't engaging the Perish!'

'Have you any idea how far those bolts are going?'

The corporal turned to spit grit from his mouth – there was another taste there, bitter, new to his tongue. 'We're softening up that wall, that's all. Not one's gone beyond it, Fist. On my word!'

'Pass it down, *cease your fire!*'

'Aye, Fist! – oh, Fist – did you see that Fiddling Hedge Drum? Gods below – in all my days left I'll never forget—'

He stopped when he saw the black rage in her face. 'We wanted them *broken*, sapper – not all dead!'

Stern scowled. 'Sorry, Fist, but nobody told us that.'

For a moment he thought she might attack him. Instead, off she stormed. Stern watched her head laterally across the slope to where regulars and heavies were drawing up, struggling to stay on what was left of the cobbled road. *Shit, we're going to have to rebuild that, aren't we? But isn't that the secret truth of everything in the military? Order us to blow it up, and then order us to rebuild the fucker. Ah, the sapper's lot . . .*

Manx crunched down at his side, his face flash-burned and smeared with greasy smoke. 'Why're we holding up? Got plenty left!'

'Fist's orders, Manx. Listen, pass word along – repack the crates, use all that extra padding.' He straightened, arched out the ache in his lower back, and then looked round. Enormous holes in the earth, huge craters steaming, heaps of shattered bodies, dust and dirt and blood still raining down through the choking smoke. He sighed. 'Looks like our work here is done.'

Staylock helped Erekala to his feet. There was a storm in his head, a droning rush as if the heavens had opened to a deluge, and beneath that pounded the labouring drum of his own heart. Looking up, squinting through the pall of smoke and dust, he saw his soldiers swarming like wasps – officers were shouting, straining to assert some order in the chaos. 'What – what is happening?' He heard his own question as the faintest of whispers.

Staylock replied from what seemed a thousand paces away. 'There are Malazans on the other side of the pass, Commander – at least four companies.'

'But that's impossible.'

'They simply appeared, sir. Now we are trapped between two armies!'

Erekala shook his head, struggling to clear his thoughts. *This cannot be. We were told there was no other way through the mountains.* 'Form up into hollow squares, the wounded in the centre.' Staggering, he set out towards the southern stretch of the pass. Behind him, Staylock was shouting orders.

Pushing through his soldiers – appalled at their shattered discipline – Erekala moved through the camp, still half dazed, until he was beyond the last of the Perish tents. The smoke and dust flowed past him, carrying with it the stench of burnt meat and scorched cloth and leather. He thought back to what he had seen down among the trenches and shivered. *What has come to us? What have we become, to do such things?*

Within sight of the Malazans, he halted. There was no mistaking this – the companies he now looked upon were the same as those he had seen earlier, down on the north side of the pass. *Warren. But . . . no one has such power – I doubt even the gods could open such gates. Yet, how can I deny what I see with my own eyes?* The enemy was drawn up, presenting a curious mix of heavy infantry, marines with crossbows, regulars and skirmishers. Beyond them a single small tent had been raised, around which soldiers clustered.

A messenger ran up to Erekala from behind. 'Sir! The enemy has reached the highest trench and continues to advance.'

'Thank you,' Erekala replied. He saw two figures emerging from the ranks, walking side by side, one tall, the other almost as tall but much broader across the shoulders. The ebon sheen of their skin cut a stark contrast to the bleached landscape. *Dal Honese or southeast Seven Cities – ah, I know these two men. The thin one – I remember him standing at the prow, facing down the Tiste Edur fleet. The High Mage, Quick Ben. Meaning the other one is the assassin. They do not belong here. But, among all the flaws afflicting me, blindness is not one of them.* Ignoring the soldier behind him, the commander set out to meet the two men.

'Look at us now,' Quick Ben muttered.

'Never mind us,' Kalam growled in reply. 'I see the commander – that's Erekala, right? See the ranks behind him? They're a mess.'

'You know,' the wizard said, 'I didn't think it was possible. Opening two gates at the same time like that, and the size of them! Gods below, he really *is* the Master of the Deck.'

Kalam glanced across at him. 'You were sceptical?'

'I'm always sceptical.'

'Well, impressive as it was, Paran came out half dead – so even he has his limits.'

'Minala's all over him – jealous, Kalam?'

The assassin shrugged. 'That's one bone I never had in my body, Quick.'

'Her and Rythe Bude – what is it with Ganoes Paran anyway? All these women slobbering all over him.'

'He's younger,' Kalam said. 'That's all it takes, you know. Us old farts ain't got a chance.'

'Speak for yourself.'

'Wipe that grin off, Quick, or I'll do it for you.'

They were closing on Erekala now, and would meet approximately halfway between the two armies. The way it should be. 'Look at us,' Quick Ben said again, low, under his breath. 'What do we know about negotiating?'

'So leave it to me,' Kalam replied. 'I mean to keep it simple.'

'Oh, this should be fun.'

They halted six paces from the Perish commander, who also stopped, and the assassin wasted no time. 'Commander Erekala, High Fist Paran extends his greetings. He wants you to surrender, so we don't have to kill all of you.'

The man looked like he'd been caught in the blast-wave of a cusser or sharper. His face was speckled with tiny cuts and gashes. Dust covered his uniform and he'd lost one chain-backed gauntlet. Erekala opened his mouth, shut it, and then tried again. 'Surrender?'

Kalam scowled. 'Those sappers have only just started. You understanding me?'

'What have you done?'

Kalam grimaced, glanced away, hands now on his hips, and then looked back at the commander. 'You're seeing how it's going to be – the old way of fighting is on its way out. The future, Erekala, just stood up and bit off half your face.'

Erekala was clearly confused. 'The future . . .'

'This is how it'll be. From now on. Fuck all the animals – they'll all be gone. But we'll still be here. We'll still be killing each other, but this time in unimaginable numbers.'

The commander shook his head. 'When all the beasts are gone—'

'Long live the cruellest beast of all,' Kalam said, suddenly baring his teeth. 'And it won't end. It'll never end.'

Erekala's eyes slowly widened, and then his gaze shifted past Quick Ben and Kalam, to the waiting ranks of Malazan soldiers. 'When all the beasts are gone,' he whispered, and then raised his voice, once more addressing Kalam. 'Your words . . . satisfy me. Inform your High Fist. The Perish Grey Helms surrender.'

'Good. Disarm – we'll collect your weapons on our way through. Sorry we can't help with your wounded, though – we're in something of a hurry.'

'And what do you intend to do with my brothers and sisters?'

Kalam frowned. 'Nothing. Just don't follow us – your role in this whole Hood-damned mess is now done. Look,' the assassin added, 'we had to get through the pass. You got in our way. We got no qualms killing the Assail and their Shriven – that's what we're here to do. But you Perish – well, the High Fist made it clear enough – you ain't our enemy. You never was.'

As they made their way back Quick Ben shot Kalam a look. 'How did you know?'

'Know what?'

'The thought of us humans slaughtering each other for ever and ever – how did you know that he'd settle with that?'

The assassin shrugged. 'I just told him how it was going to be. Soon as he heard it, he knew the truth of it. They may be fanatics but that don't make them fools.'

Quick Ben snorted. 'Beg to differ on that one, Kalam.'

Grunting, Kalam nodded and said, 'Soon as I said it . . . all right, try this. Even a fanatic can smell the shit they're buried in. Will that do?'

'Not really. They're fools because they then convince themselves it smells sweet. Listen, you basically told him that his sacred beasts were finished.'

'Aye. Then I made it taste sweet.'

Quick Ben thought about that for a time, as they approached the ranks, and finally he sighed. 'You know, Erekala ain't the only fool around here.'

'What's that smell? And I thought you were smart, wizard. Now, get us some horses while I report to Paran.'

'Tavore?'

'If she's alive, we'll find her.'

With an enraged scream, Korabas snapped her head down, jaws closing on the Eleint's shoulder. Bones exploded in her mouth. With the talons of one of her feet, she scythed the beast's underbelly, and then struck again, claws plunging deep. Blood and fluids gushed down as she tore loose the dragon's guts. With its carcass still in her jaws, she whipped it to one side, into the path of another Eleint.

Claws scored across her back. The Otataral Dragon twisted round, lashing with her talons. Puncturing scaly hide, she snatched the dragon close, bit through its neck, and then flung it away. Jaws crunched on one ankle. When her own jaws lunged down, they closed sideways around the back of the Eleint's head. A single convulsive crunch collapsed the skull. Another dragon hammered down on her from above. Talons razored bloody tracks just beneath her left eye. Fangs chewed at the ridge of her neck. Korabas folded her wings, tearing loose and plummeting away from the attacker. A dragon directly below her took the full impact of her immense weight. It spun away, one wing shattered, spine snapped, and fell earthward.

Thundering the air, she lifted herself higher once more. Eleint swarmed around her, like crows surrounding a condor, darting close and then away again. The air was filled with their reptilian shrieks, the Ancients among them roaring their fury.

She had killed scores already, had left a trail of dragon corpses strewn on the dead ground in her wake. But it was not enough. Blood streamed from her flanks, her chest creaked with her labouring breath, and the attacks were growing ever more frenzied.

The change was coming. She could taste it – in the gore sliming her mouth, shredded between her fangs – in the frantic furnaces of her nostrils – in the air on all sides. *Too many Eleint. Too many Ancients – the Storms are still in collision, but soon they will merge.*

Soon, T'iam will awaken.

Another Storm struck. Howling, Korabas lashed out. Crushing chests, tearing legs from hips, wings from shoulders. Ripping heads from necks. She bit through ribcages, sent entrails spilling. Bodies fell away, trailing tails of ruin. The air was thick with blood, and much of it her own. *Too much of it my own.*

T'iam! T'iam! Mother! Will you devour me? Will you devour your child so wrong, so hated, so abandoned?

Mother – see the coming darkness? Will you hear my cries? My cries in the dark?

There was terrible pain. The blind rage surrounding her was its own storm, all of it whirling in and down to ceaselessly batter her. She had not asked to be feared. She had not wanted such venom – the only gift from all of her kin. She had not asked to be born.

I hurt so.

Will you kill me now?

Mother, when you come, will you kill your wrong child?

Around her, an endless maelstrom of dragons. Weakening, she fought on, blind now to her path, blind to everything but the waves of pain and hate assailing her.

This life. It is all that it is, all that I am. This life – why do I deserve this? What have I done to deserve this?

The Storms ripped into her. The Storms tore her hide, rent vast tears in her wings, until her will alone was all that kept her aloft, flying across these wracked skies, as the sun bled out over the horizon far, far behind her.

See the darkness. Hear my cries.

CHAPTER TWENTY-THREE

On this grey day, in a valley deep in stone
Where like shades from the dead yard
Sorrows come forth in milling shrouds
And but a few leaves grey as moths
cling to branches on the shouldered hillsides,
Fluttering to the winds borne on night's passing
I knelt alone and made voice awaken
to call upon my god

Waiting in the echoes as the day struggled
Until in fading the silence found form
For my fingers to brush light as dust
And the crows flapped down into the trees
To study a man on his knees with glittering regard
Reminding me of the stars that moments before
Held forth watchful as sentinels
On the sky's wall now withdrawn
behind my eyes

And all the words I have given in earnest
All the felt anguish and torrid will so sternly
Set out like soldiers in furrowed rows
Hovered in a season's sundering of birds
With no song to beckon them into flight
Where my hands now spreading like wings
Bloodied in the passion of prayer
Lay dying in the bowl
of my lap

My god has no words for me on this grey day
Pallor and pallid dust serve a less imagined reply
Mute as the leaves in the absence of bestir
And even the sky has forgotten the sun
Give me the weal of silence to worry answers
From this tease of indifference – no matter
I am done with prayers on the lip of dawn
And the sorrows will fade
with light

My Fill of Answers
Fisher kel Tath

H E'D BROUGHT THE BUNDLED FORM AS CLOSE AS HE DARED, AND now it was lying on the ground beside him. The cloth was stained, threadbare, the colour of dead soil. Astride his lifeless horse, he leaned over the saddle horn and with his one eye studied the distant Spire. The vast bay on his left, beyond the cliffs, crashed in tumult, as if ripped by tides – but this violence did not belong to the tides. Sorceries were gathering and the air was heavy and sick with power.

It had all been unleashed and there was no telling how things would fall. But he had done all that he could. Hearing horse hoofs behind him he twisted round.

Toc saluted. 'Sir.'

Whiskeyjack's face was cruel in its mockery of what it had once been, in the times of living. His beard was the hue of iron below a gaunt, withered face, like the exposed roots of a long-dead tree. The eyes were unseen beneath the ridge of his brows, sunken into blackness.

We are passing away. Sinking back from this beloved edge.

'You cannot remain here, soldier.'

'I know.' Toc gestured with one desiccated hand, down to the shrouded form lying on the ground. Behind Whiskeyjack the Bridgeburners waited on their mounts, silent, motionless. Toc's eye flitted over them. 'I had no idea, sir,' he said, 'there were so many.'

'War is the great devourer, soldier. So many left us along the way.'

The tone was emptied of all emotion and this alone threatened to break what remained of Toc's heart. *This is not how you should be. We are fading. So little remains. So little . . .*

When Whiskeyjack wheeled his mount and set off, his Bridgeburners following, Toc rode with them for a short distance, flanking the solid mass of riders, until something struck him deep inside, like the twist of a knife, and he reined in once more, watching as they continued on.

Longing tore at his soul. *I once dreamed of being a Bridgeburner. If I had won that, I would now be riding with them, and it would all be so much simpler. But, as with so many dreams, I failed, and nothing was how I wanted it.* He drew his mount round and stared back at that now distant shape on the ground.

Fallen One, I understand now. You maimed me outside the city of Pale. You hollowed out one eye, made a cave in my skull. Spirits wandered in for shelter time and again. They made use of that cave. They made use of me.

But now they are gone, and only you remain. Whispering promises in the hollow of my wound.

'But can't you see the truth of this?' he muttered. 'I hold on. I hold on, but I feel my grip . . . slipping. It's slipping, Fallen One.' Still, he would cling to this last promise, for as long as he could. He would make use of this one remaining eye, to see this through.

If I can.

He kicked his horse into motion, swinging inland, into the wake of the Guardians of the Gate. The hamlets and villages of the headland were grey, abandoned, every surface coated in the ash from the Spire. Furrowed fields made ripples of dull white, as if buried in snow. Here and there, the jutting cage of ribs and hip bones made broken humps. He rode past them all, through the hanging dust cloud left behind by the Bridgeburners. And in the distance ahead, rising above banks of fog, the Spire.

Huddle close in this cave. It's almost time.

Once, long ago, the treeless plains of this land had been crowded with vast herds of furred beasts, moving in mass migrations to the siren call of the seasons. Brother Diligence was reminded of those huge creatures as he watched the bulky provision wagons wheel upslope on the raised tracks, away from the trenches and redoubts. Feeding almost fifty thousand soldiers had begun to strain the logistics of supply. Another week of this waiting would empty the granaries of the city.

But there would be no need for another week. The enemy was even now marshalling to the south, with outriders riding along the far ridge on the other side of the valley's broad, gentle saddle.

The dawn air was brittle with surging energies. Akhrast Korvalain swirled so thick it was almost visible to his eyes. Yet he sensed deep agitation, alien currents gnawing at the edges of the Elder Warren's manifestation, and this troubled him.

He stood on a slightly raised, elongated platform overlooking the defences, and as the day's light lifted he scanned yet again the complicated investment of embankments, slit-trenches, machicolations, fortlets and redoubts spread out below him. In his mind, he envisioned the enemy advance, watched as the subtle adjustments he'd had made to the approaches funnelled and crowded the attackers, punishing them at the forefront by onager defilade, and then taking them on the flanks by enfilading arrow fire from the mounded redoubts. He saw the swarming waves of enemy soldiers thrust and driven this way and that, chewing fiercely at the strongpoints only to reel back bloodied.

His eyes tracked down to the centre high-backed earthworks where he had positioned the Perish Grey Helms – they were locked in place, thrust down on to the flatland, with few avenues for retreat. Too eager to kneel, that Shield Anvil. And the young girl – there had been a feral look in her eyes Diligence did not trust. But, they would fight and die in one place, and he was confident that they would hold the centre for as long as needed.

By all estimations his defenders outnumbered the attackers, making the enemy's chances for success virtually non-existent. This invasion had already failed.

The planks underfoot creaked and bowed slightly and Brother Diligence turned to see that Shield Anvil Tanakalian had arrived on the platform. The man was pale, his face glistening with sweat. He approached the Forkrul Assail as if struggling to stay upright – and Diligence smiled upon imagining the man flinging himself prostrate at his feet. 'Shield Anvil, how fare your brothers and sisters?'

Tanakalian wiped sweat from his upper lip. 'The Bolkando forces possess a mailed fist in the Evertine Legion, Brother Diligence. Commanded by Queen Abrastal herself. And then there are the Gilk Barghast—'

'Barghast? This is your first mention of them.' Diligence sighed. 'So they have at last come to the home of their ancient kin, have they? How fitting.'

'They see themselves as shock troops, sir. You will know them by their white-painted faces.'

Diligence started. 'White-painted faces?'

Tanakalian's eyes narrowed. 'They call themselves the White Face Barghast, yes.'

'Long ago,' Diligence said, half in wonder, 'we created a Barghast army to serve us. They sought to emulate the Forkrul Assail in appearance, electing to bleach the skin of their faces.'

Frowning, the Shield Anvil shook his head. 'There was, I believe, some kind of prophecy, guiding them across the seas to land north of Lether. A holy war to be fought, or some such thing. We believe that only the Gilk clan remains.'

'They betrayed us,' Diligence said, studying Tanakalian. 'Many Pures died at their hand. Tell me, these Gilk – are they in the habit of wearing armour?'

'Turtle shell, yes – most strange.'

'Gillankai! Their hands are drenched in the blood of Pures!'

Tanakalian backed a step in the face of this sudden fury. Seeing this, Diligence narrowed his gaze on the Shield Anvil. 'How many warriors among these Gilk?'

'Three thousand, perhaps? Four?'

Snarling, Diligence turned to face the valley again. 'The weapons of the Forkrul Assail are our hands and feet – the Gillankai devised an armour to blunt our blows. Shield Anvil, when they come, concentrate against these Barghast. Break them!'

'Sir, I cannot command the presentation of enemy forces. I came here to tell you it is my suspicion that the Evertine Legion will engage the Grey Helms – a clash of heavy infantry. We shall lock jaws with them and we shall prevail. As such, sir, we leave the Gilk, the Saphii and other assorted auxiliaries to your Kolansii. In addition to the Letherii, of course.'

'Any other threats you've yet to mention, *Brother?*'

'Sir, you vastly outnumber the attackers. I expect we shall make short work of them.'

'And does this disappoint you, Shield Anvil?'

Tanakalian wiped again at the sweat beading his upper lip. 'Provided you do not seek to use your voice, sir, to demand surrender, we shall welcome all the blood spilled on this day.'

'Of course. It is the slaughter you so desire. Perhaps I shall indulge you in this. Perhaps not.'

The Shield Anvil's eyes flicked away momentarily, and then he bowed. 'As you will, sir.'

'Best return to your soldiers,' Diligence said. 'And keep a watchful eye on that Destriant. She is not what she would like us to believe she is.'

Tanakalian stiffened, and then bowed again.

Diligence watched the fool hurry away.

Watered Hestand thumped up on to the platform and saluted. 'Blessed Pure, our scouts report the advance of the enemy – they will soon crest the ridge and come into view.'

'Very well.'

'Sir – there are not enough of them.'

'Indeed.'

As Hestand hesitated, Diligence turned to eye the officer. 'Your thoughts?'

'Sir, surely their own scouts have assessed our numbers, and the completeness of our defences. Unless they hold some hidden knife or weapon, they cannot hope to best us. Sir . . .'

'Go on.'

'The High Watered among us have sensed the sudden absence of Brother Serenity, far to the northwest. Clearly, the forces that emerged from the keep are now advancing, and – somehow – they are proving their worth against even the most powerful Pures.'

'Hestand.'

'Sir.'

'This is not the day to fret over distant events, no matter how disquieting they may be.'

'Sir, it is my thought – perhaps the enemy now arraying before us possess similar efficacy, when it comes to the Forkrul Assail.'

After a long moment, Diligence nodded. 'Well said. I appreciate your persistence on this matter. By your courage you chastise me. Hestand, you are wise to awaken caution. As you have observed, the enemy before us cannot hope to prevail, nor can they be so blind that they cannot see the hard truth awaiting them. Raising the question, what secret do they possess?'

'Sir, what can we do?'

'Only wait and see, Hestand.' Diligence turned back to the valley, tracked with his eyes down the paths leading to the centre redoubt – and the wolf standards of the Perish. 'Perhaps I should compel the Shield Anvil. He is holding something back – I see that now. What I took for nerves before battle – I may have misread him.'

'Shall I retrieve the Perish commander, sir? Or perhaps send a squad down to arrest him?'

Diligence shook his head. 'And invite a mutiny among the troops holding our centre? No. I believe I must undertake this task in person.'

'Sir – is there time?' And Hestand now pointed to the south ridge.

The enemy were presenting in a solid line along the crest. Diligence studied the distant scene for a moment, and then he nodded. 'There is time. Await me here, Hestand. I shall not be gone long.'

She had ascended the Spire and now stood, her back to the altar and the Heart it held, facing out on to the bay. The fleet of anchored Perish ships rocked like wood chips in a cauldron of boiling water, and as she watched she saw a trio of masts snap in a writhing fury of shredded stays. The white spume of the waves sprayed high into the air.

Sister Reverence found that she was trembling. *There is something down there, in the depth of the bay. Something building to rage.*

Strangers have come among us.

Spinning, she faced inland, eyes darting as she studied the vast array of defences crowding the approach to the narrow isthmus. Twenty thousand elite Kolansii heavy infantry, their pikes forming thick bands of forest in solid ribbons all down the tiered descent. Fifteen hundred onagers clustered in raised fortlets interspersed among the trench lines, each one capable of releasing twelve heavy quarrels in a single salvo, with reloading time less than forty heartbeats. The defilade down the choke-point ensured devastation should any attacker strive to close on the lowest fortifications.

There was a taste of bitter metal in her mouth. Her bones ached despite the gusts of hot, rancid air belching out from fissures in the stone on all sides. *I am afraid. Should I reach out to Brother Diligence? Should I avail myself of all these unknown terrors? But what enemy can I show him? An unruly bay – that vague bank of fog or dust to the south? These things are nothing. He prepares for a battle. He has his mind on real matters – not an old woman's gibbering imagination!*

She should never have sent Brother Serenity away. And now he was dead. She had shared his last visions – raging fire, the flames blackening his once-white skin, scouring the flesh of his face, boiling the water of his eyes until the balls burst – *and his cries! Abyss below, his cries! The fire filling his mouth, the flames sweeping in, sucked past charred lips, igniting his lungs! Such a terrible death!*

These humans were an abomination. Their brutal ways shook her to the core. There was no end to their capacity for cruel destruction, no end to their will to deliver horror and death. The world would find a clean breath once they were all gone, finally, a clean and blessedly innocent breath.

Akhrast Korvalain, attend me! This is the day we are challenged! We must prevail!

Reverence walked to stand before the altar. She glared down at the knotted object set in the surface of the stone. Awakening her sorcerous vision, she studied the now visible chains binding the Heart down – all her ancestors, their bones given new shapes, but their strength had not changed. There was no weakness in what she saw. The sight relieved her. *No one shall take this from us. If I must, I will destroy it by my own hand.*

The warren surrounding the Heart had kept it hidden for all this time. What had changed? How had it been found? *Not even the gods could sense it, not hidden here at the heart of our warren. And yet we are about to be attacked. We are about to be besieged. I feel the truth of this! Who could have found it?*

A sudden thought struck her, clenching like a fist in the centre of her chest. *The Fallen One! But no – he is too weak! Bound by his own chains!*

What gambit is he playing? To think that he could challenge us! No, this is madness! But then, was the Crippled God not mad? Tortured in agony, broken, ripped apart – fragments of him scattered across half

702

the world. *But I am the one holding his heart. I have . . . stolen it. Ha, and see how deep and how vast my love! Watch as I squeeze it dry of all life!*

A marriage of justice with pain. Is this not the torture of the world? Of all worlds? 'No,' she whispered, 'I will never relinquish my . . . my *love*. Never!' *This is the only worship worthy of the name. I hold in my hand a god's heart, and together, we sing a thousand songs of suffering.*

Distant eruptions drew her round. The Perish ships! Torn from their anchors, the huge vessels now lifting wild on the heaving swells – white foam spouting skyward, splinters as ships collided, broke apart, the wolfheads drowning on all sides – she saw the Kolansii ships in the harbour directly below, moored to the moles and the inside of the breakwater, all stirring, like beasts milling in blind confusion. Waves hammered the stone breakwater, lifting enormous sheets into the air. And yet. And yet . . . *there is no wind.*

There is no wind!

Grub was almost lost in the moulded scale saddle behind the shoulders of the Ve'Gath, and yet, as the beast loped forward, he was not tossed about as he would have been if on a horse. The scales were still changing, growing to shield his legs, including his thighs, as if the saddle sought to become armour as well – he was amazed at seeing such a thing. Flanged scales now rose to encircle his hips. He had a moment of fear – would this armour, extruded out from the beast he was riding, eventually encase him in entirety? Would it ever release him?

He turned his head to the rider travelling beside him, to see if the Ve'Gath's thick hide was growing up in the same way, but no – there it remained an ornate saddle, that and nothing more. And Mortal Sword Krughava rode it with all the ease and familiarity of a veteran. He envied such people, for whom everything came so easily.

My father was not like that. He was never a natural fighter. He had nothing of the talent of, say, Kalam Mekhar. Or Stormy or Gesler. He was just an average man, forced to be more than he was.

I am glad I did not see him die. I am glad my memories see him as only alive, for ever alive.

I think I can live with that.

I have no choice.

They had left the K'Chain Che'Malle army halfway through last night, and now they were swiftly closing on the Letherii and Bolkando armies. If he stretched up – as far as the sheathing armour round his thighs would permit – he could see directly ahead the dark, seething stain of the troops ascending to the ridge. Grub glanced again across at Krughava. She was wearing her helm, the visor dropped down and the hinges locked. The wolfskin cape was too heavy to skirl out behind her, despite the swift pace the Ve'Gath were setting, but still it flowed down with impressive grace along the horizontal back of the K'Chain Che'Malle, sweeping down to cover its hips and the projecting mass of its upper leg muscles, so that the fur rippled and glistened as the muscles bunched and stretched.

She would have made a frightening mother, he decided, this Krughava. Frightening, and yet, if she gave a child her love, he suspected it would be unassailable. *Fierce as a she-wolf, yes.*

But I have no mother. Maybe I never had one – I don't remember. Not a single face, swimming blurry in my dreams – nothing. And now I have no father. I have no one and when I look ahead, into my future, I see myself riding, for ever alone. The notion, which he trucked out again and again, as if to taste it on his tongue, stirred nothing in him. He wondered if there was something wrong with him; he wondered if, years from now, on that long journey, he might find it – that wrongness, like a corpse lying on the ground on the path ahead. He wondered what he would feel then.

Thinking back on their parting from the K'Chain army, Grub tried to recall the reasons behind his decision to leave Sinn's side. Something had pulled him to Brys Beddict and all the Letherii and Bolkando, a vague belief that he would be more useful there, though he had no idea what he might do, or if he had anything to give. It was easier thinking of this like that, instead of the suspicion that he was fleeing Sinn – fleeing what she might do.

'No one can stop me, Grub. No one but you.' So she'd told him, more than once, but not in a reassuring way, not in a way that told him that he mattered to her. No, it was more like a challenge, as if to ask: *What have you got hidden inside you, Grub? Let's see, shall we?* But he didn't want to know what he had inside him. That day they'd come to do battle with the Moons, that day when there had been fire and stone and earth and something cold at the centre of it all, he had felt himself falling away, and the boy who had walked at Sinn's side was somebody else, wearing his skin, wearing his face. It had been . . . terrifying.

All that power, how it poured through us. I didn't like it. I don't like it.

I'm not running away. Sinn can do what she likes. I can't really stop her, and I don't want her to prove it, to spite her own words. I don't want to hear her laughing. I don't want to look into her eyes and see the fires of Telas.

They had been seen, and now the warrior-beasts under them were shifting their approach, angling towards a small party that had ridden out to one side. Prince Beddict. Aranict. Queen Abrastal and Spax, and three people he'd not seen before – two women and a tall, ungainly-looking man with a long face. Just behind this group, standing alone and impossibly tall, was a woman shrouded in a cloak of rabbit-skins, down to her ankles, her hair a wild, tangled mane of brown, her face looking like it had been carved from sandstone.

The thumping gait of the Ve'Gath fell off as they drew nearer. Glancing down, Grub saw that the armour formed a high collar up past his hips, flaring out just beneath his ribs. And behind his back, an upthrust of overlapping scales formed a kind of back-rest, protecting his spine.

The K'Chain Che'Malle halted, and Grub saw Brys Beddict studying Krughava.

'You are a most welcome sight, Mortal Sword.'

'Where are my Perish positioned?' Krughava demanded in a voice like grating gravel.

Queen Abrastal replied. 'Centre, nearest line of defences and a little way past that. Mortal Sword, their position is untenable – they are provided no avenues of retreat. With a little pushing, we can attack them on three sides.'

Krughava grunted. 'We are meant to maul ourselves on this studded fist, sirs. And should they all die, my Perish, it is of little interest to the Forkrul Assail.'

'We more or less worked that one out,' Spax said. The Gilk Warchief was in full turtleshell armour, his face painted white, the eyes rimmed in deep red ochre.

The Mortal Sword was momentarily silent, her gaze moving from one figure to the next, then slipping past to narrow on the huge woman standing fifteen paces back. 'You have found new allies, Prince. Toblakai?'

Brys glanced back, made a face. 'Gods below, I've never known a woman as shy as her. She is Teblor and she commands three hundred of her kind. She is named Gillimada.'

'Where will you place them?' Krughava's tone was, if anything, yet harsher than it had been a moment earlier.

Grub saw them all hesitating, and this confused him. *What is wrong?*

Aranict lit a new stick from her old one and flung the latter away, speaking all the while, 'Mortal Sword, there are over forty thousand Kolansii on the other side of the valley.'

'*Forty thousand?*'

'We are faced with a challenge,' Brys Beddict said. 'We must endeavour to engage the entirety of this force, for as long as possible.'

Queen Abrastal spoke. 'Once the Pure commanding here learns of the real assault – the one upon the Spire – he will seek to withdraw as many of his troops as he can safely manage. We judge three bells to fast-march to the isthmus – in other words, they can reach that battle in time, Mortal Sword, and strike at Gesler's flank. As yet, we can determine no way in which to prevent this happening.'

'I will turn the Perish,' pronounced Krughava. 'I will pull them from their position and wheel them round, placing them to block the way east. We need only slow the enemy, sirs, not stop them.'

'If you so succeed in regaining your command of the Grey Helms,' said Brys, 'will you welcome the company of the Teblor?'

Krughava's thinned eyes switched to the Teblor commander. 'Sirs,' she said, loud enough for all to hear, 'to fight alongside the Teblor would be an honour unsurpassed on this day.'

Grub sought to see the effect of these words, but from Gillimada there was no reaction at all.

'Mortal Sword,' said Queen Abrastal, 'are you confident that you can resume command of the Grey Helms? And before you answer, this is not the time for unrealistic bravado.'

Krughava stiffened at that. 'Do you imagine that I do not understand the severity of this moment, Highness? I will speak plainly. I do not know if I will succeed. But I will give my life in the effort – would you ask more of me?'

Abrastal shook her head.

'We must, however,' said Brys, 'present ourselves to the enemy in such a manner as to deal with either eventuality.'

A loud voice suddenly boomed, 'They talk bad!'

Gillimada was suddenly among them, her eyes level with the mounted men and women.

'Excuse me?'

She fixed the prince with her gaze, her brow fiercely knotted. 'The fish-faces. They use words that hurt. If this fight goes bad, the fish-face will speak, and make us kneel. Make us kill our own anger. You – you must be stubborn! You must say no and shake your heads no! You must see the fish-face in your head, and then you must push him or her to the ground, and then you must squat, and then you must shit on that fish-face! I have spoken!'

A short time of awkward silence, and then Grub saw that Aranict was staring straight at him.

He felt a strange shiver track up his spine. 'I don't know,' he said in a small voice.

All eyes fixed on him and he felt himself shrinking inside his peculiar half-armour.

Aranict spoke. 'Grub, we have heard what you achieved when you joined the battle between the K'Chain factions. The Teblor commander speaks of the power of Akhrast Korvalain – this sorcery of the voice –

706

and we are uncertain if we will face that power today. Nor do we know how to oppose it if it should come.'

'Shit!' bellowed Gillimada. 'I have spoken!'

Grub shook his head. 'At the battle of the Moons . . . that was Sinn. Most of it. She just used me. As if I was a knife in her left hand. I don't know what I can do.'

'We shall deal with that threat when it comes,' announced Brys Beddict. 'For now, I would welcome suggestions on the engagement. Queen Abrastal, what are your thoughts?'

The Bolkando woman scowled. She unstrapped and drew off her helm, revealing a shaved head. 'I think we should ignore the Perish – long may they sit in their holes, or' – and she shot a glance at Krughava – 'spin their standards round, should the Mortal Sword reassert her authority. Either way, we leave the centre alone.'

Brys was nodding. 'I was thinking much the same. I have no taste for spilling Perish blood, and in truth the Assail commander has done us a favour by so isolating them. This said, we must weight our right flank – the moment we see the enemy splitting to form up and fast-march towards the Spire, we need to contest that move, with as much ferocity as we can manage. Accordingly, I would the Teblor form the centre of that intercept.'

'The rest will need only a handful to hold us off the trenches,' Spax muttered.

'So we engage with but a handful,' Brys retorted, 'and peel off rank on rank as fast as we are able to.'

'That will have to do,' said Abrastal. 'No offence, Prince, but I will place the Evertine Legion on the right of centre.'

'None taken, Highness. You are correct in assessing your legion as our elites. Once we start that wheeling of reserves, the enemy might well advance pressure on your side, to break through and cut off our motion eastward.'

'I would do the same,' Abrastal replied. 'We shall be ready for that.'

'Very well.' Brys looked round. 'That's it, then? So be it. All of you, in the tasks awaiting you, fare well.'

Krughava said, 'Prince, I will ride with you to the ridge.'

Brys nodded.

As the group dispersed, Grub allowed his Ve'Gath to fall in behind Krughava's. He looked up at the sky. The Jade Strangers blazed directly overhead, the point of each talon as bright as the sun itself. The sky was too crowded, and, in a flash, he suddenly knew that it would get much more crowded before this day was done.

*   *   *

707

'What the fuck is this?'

'Careful,' muttered Stormy. 'Your language is offending our Destriant.'

Growling under his breath, Gesler pulled his feet from the scale stirrups and clambered to stand balanced on the Ve'Gath's back. 'A Hood-damned army all right, but I see no camp, and they're looking . . . rough.'

'Gods below, Ges, sit back down before you fall and break your scrawny neck.' Stormy turned to Kalyth. 'Halt 'em all, lass, except for Sag'Churok – we'll take the K'ell Hunter with us and check this out.'

The woman nodded.

As the vast K'Chain Che'Malle army ceased its advance, Gesler gestured and led Stormy and Sag'Churok forward at what passed for a canter.

The mysterious army stood motionless on a treed hill at the edge of an abandoned village. Squinting, Gesler looked for the usual flash of armour and weapons, but there was none of that. 'Maybe not an army at all,' he muttered as Stormy rode up alongside him. 'Maybe refugees.'

'Your eyes are getting bad, Ges.'

'What do you mean?'

'Old man, you've gone blind as Hood's own arsehole. Those are T'lan Imass!'

Aw, shit. 'Who invited those hoary bastards?' He shot Stormy a glare. 'Was it you, O Carrier of Flint Fucking Swords?'

'I know nothing about 'em, Gesler, I swear it!'

'Right. Playing friendly on ships and now look! You never could just stay out of other people's business, Stormy. A soul stuck in the sky – oh! Let me fix that!'

'This ain't them, Gesler. Can't be. Besides, that debt was paid up. Back in Malaz City – you was there! I gave that sword back!'

Off to one side, Sag'Churok suddenly clashed his massive swords, and both men looked over.

Gesler snorted. 'Think he just told us to shut up, Stormy.'

They were fast closing on the hill with its grey, silent mass of undead warriors. *That hill – that's a cemetery. Well, where else would they be?* Gesler saw one warrior setting off down the lumpy hillside, dragging its stone sword as a child would an oversized branch. 'That one,' he said. 'Wants to talk to us.'

'Better than rising up under our feet and cutting us to pieces.'

'Aye, much better. What do you think, Stormy? We got ourselves unexpected allies?'

'Pity the Assail if we have.'

Gesler spat. 'This ain't the day for pity. Sag'Churok! Don't do anything stupid like attacking it, all right?'

They slowed to a walk thirty paces from the lone T'lan Imass. At fifteen the K'ell Hunter halted and planted the tips of his swords in the ground. Gesler and Stormy continued on, halting five paces from the undead warrior.

Gesler called out, 'What clan?'

For a moment it seemed the T'lan Imass would ignore the question, but then, in a heavy, rasping voice, the warrior said, 'Logros, Malazan. I am Onos T'oolan.'

'Onos—' Gesler began, then snapped his mouth shut.

Stormy muttered a curse. 'Can't be. The First Sword? How many cronies of that long-dead rat-faced Emperor are involved in this?'

More T'lan Imass were coming down from the hill, ragged and slow, like the grinding of stones, and Gesler sensed something wretched in this scene, something . . . appalling. *What are they doing here?*

Onos T'oolan spoke. 'Logros's banishment of me was without meaning, Malazan. I knelt before a mortal human on the Throne of Bones, and there is none other whom I shall serve. This is what Olar Ethil did not comprehend. Bound once more to the Ritual of Tellann, I am returned to the shadow of the Emperor.'

Gesler felt sick inside. He knew he was getting only a taste of what all this meant, but it was already breaking his heart. 'He sent you, First Sword?'

'I am invited to my own death, Malazan. The manner of it remains to be decided. If the One upon the Throne could see into my soul, he would know that I am broken.'

'Broken, you say?' Stormy interrupted. 'Now that's an interesting fact, Onos T'oolan.'

The ancient warrior tilted his head. 'I do not understand your meaning.'

Stormy pointed north. 'See that spire of rock, First Sword? Right up top of that, there's something else – something just as broken as you are. The Forkrul Assail are guarding it – but we mean to take it from them. You say Kellanved ordered you here – so we got to know, First Sword, are you here to fight? And if you are, will it be against us or at our side?'

'You are Malazans.'

'The army behind us ain't.'

Onos T'oolan was silent for a time, and then he said, 'The K'Chain Che'Malle hunted Imass, from time to time.'

'Just like you hunted bhederin, or elk, or whatever. What of it?'

'When we were mortal, we had cause to fear them.'

'And elk will run when it sees you. But then, you're not mortal any more, are you?'

'I am here, Malazans, seeking a war. And yet only now do I realize that I have walked in shadow, all this time, since I first rose from the dust outside the city of Pale. I thought I was abandoned. And each time I sought a new path, that shadow followed me. That shadow *found* me, as it must. I am the First Sword of the T'lan Imass, and from this there is no escape.'

Gesler cleared his throat, blinked to work the water from his eyes. 'First Sword, am I understanding you? Are you placing yourselves under our command – just because we happen to have come from the Malazan Empire? Before you answer, you've got to understand – Kellanved is long dead, and that empire has since outlawed us. We're not here because of any damned throne, and we're not at the beckoning of anyone who's sitting in it either.'

'Tell me, then, human, why *are* you here?'

Gesler looked up, studied the hundreds of T'lan Imass crowding the hillside, spilling out into the streets and avenues of the village. Lifeless faces were turned to him, and their regard was a crushing weight. *Gods below.* 'It sounds . . . stupid, you know,' he said, now eyeing Stormy, 'when you just out and say it.'

'Go on,' growled Stormy, his face reddening as emotions rose within the huge man – Gesler could see it, and he was experiencing the same thing. The air itself seemed to swirl with feelings of appalling force. 'Go on, Gesler, and if it makes us fools . . . well, we can live with that, can't we?'

Sighing, he faced Onos T'oolan. 'Why are we here? The truth is, we're not even sure. But . . . we think we're here to right an old wrong. Because it's the thing to do, that's all.'

Silence, stretching.

Gesler turned back to Stormy. 'I knew it'd sound stupid.'

Onos T'oolan spoke. 'What do you seek on that spire, Gesler of the Malazans?'

'The heart of the Crippled God.'

'Why?'

'Because,' Stormy replied, 'we want to free him.'

'He is chained.'

'We know.'

Onos T'oolan said nothing for a moment, and then: 'You would defy the will of the gods?'

'Fast as spit,' Stormy said.

'Why do you wish to free the Fallen One?'

When Stormy hesitated, Gesler shifted in the scaled saddle and said, 'Hood take us. We want to send him home.'

710

Home. The word very nearly drove Onos T'oolan to his knees. Something was roaring in his skull. He had believed it to be the sound of his own rage – but now he could sense a multitude of voices in that cacophony. More than the unfettered thoughts of the T'lan Imass following him; more than the still distant conflagration that was the Otataral Dragon and the Eleint; no, what deafened him here was the unceasing echoes of terrible pain – this land, all the life that had once thrived here, only to falter and suffer and finally vanish. And there, upon that tower of rock, that cracked spire that was the core of a restless volcano – where the earth's blood coursed so close to the surface, in serpentine tracks round its fissured, hollowed base – another broken piece of a broken, shattered god, a being that had been writhing in torment for thousands of years. *No different from the T'lan Imass. No different from us.*

The shadow of a throne – is that not a cold, frightening place? And yet, Kellanved . . . do you truly offer succour? Dare you cast a shadow to shield us? To protect us? To humble us in the name of humanity?

I once called you our children. Our inheritors. Forgive my irony. For all the venal among your kind . . . I had thought – I had thought . . . no matter.

In his mind, he reached among his followers, found the one he sought. She was close – almost behind him. '*Bonecaster Bitterspring, of the Second Ritual, do you hear me?*'

'*I do, First Sword.*'

'*You are named a seer. Can you see what awaits us?*'

'*I have no true gift of prophecy, First Sword. My talent was in reading people. That and nothing more. I have been an impostor for so long I know no other way of being.*'

'*Bitterspring, we are all impostors. What awaits us?*'

'*What has always awaited us,*' she replied. '*Blood and tears.*'

In truth, he'd had no reason to expect anything else. Onos T'oolan drew his flint sword round, dragging a jagged furrow through dirt and stones. He lifted his gaze to the Malazans. 'Even the power of Tellann cannot penetrate the wards raised by the Forkrul Assail. We cannot, therefore, rise in the midst of the enemy in their trenches. This will have to be a direct assault.'

'We know that,' the one named Gesler said.

'We shall fight for you,' Onos T'oolan said, and then he was silent, confused at seeing the effect of his words on these two men. 'Have I distressed you?'

Gesler shook his head. 'No, you greatly relieve us, First Sword. It is not that. It's just . . .' and he shook his head. 'Now it's my turn to ask. Why?'

'If by our sacrifice – yours and mine,' said Onos T'oolan, 'the pain of one life can be ended; if, by our deaths, this one can be guided home . . . we will judge this a worthy cause.'

'This Crippled God – he is a stranger to us all.'

'It is enough that in the place he calls home, he is no stranger.'

Why should these words force tears from these two hardened soldiers? I do not understand. Onos T'oolan opened his mind to his followers. *'You have heard. You have shared. This is the path your First Sword chooses – but I will not compel you, and so I ask, will you fight at my side this day?'*

Bitterspring replied. *'First Sword, I am chosen to speak for all. We have seen the sun rise. It may be that we shall not see it set. Thus, we have us this one day, to find the measure of our worth. It is, perhaps, less time than many might possess; but so too is it more than many others are privileged to know. One day, to see who and what we are. One day, to find meaning in our existence.*

'First Sword, we welcome the opportunity you have given us. Today, we shall be your kin. Today, we shall be your sisters and brothers.'

To this, Onos T'oolan could find no words. He floundered for what seemed a long, long time. And then, from the depths of his being, there arose a strange feeling, a sense of . . . *of recognition.* 'Then you shall be my kin on this day. And among my kin, am I not, at last, home?' He had spoken these words out loud, and turning, he saw surprise on the faces of the two Malazans. Onos T'oolan stepped forward. 'Malazans, make it known to your K'Chain Che'Malle. Each in our time, we two peoples have warred against the Forkrul Assail. On this day, for the very first time, we shall do so as allies.'

Fifteen paces back the K'ell Hunter straightened then, and lifted high both swords, and Onos T'oolan felt its reptilian eyes fixed solely upon him. And he raised his own weapon.

One more gift, then, on this final day. I see you, K'Chain Che'Malle, and I call you brother.

Gesler wiped at his eyes – he could not fathom the rawness of his emotions. 'First Sword,' he called out in a roughened voice, 'how many of your warriors are here?'

Onos T'oolan hesitated, and then said, 'I do not know.'

Another T'lan Imass, who had been standing behind Onos T'oolan, then spoke, 'Mortals, we are eight thousand six hundred and eighty-four.'

'Hood's black breath!' Stormy swore. 'Gesler – T'lan Imass in the centre? With Ve'Gath to either side, and K'ell screening our flanks?'

'Aye,' Gesler nodded. 'First Sword, do you know the Jagged Teeth—'

'Gesler,' Onos T'oolan cut in, 'like you, I am a veteran of the Seven Cities campaigns.'

'Guess you are, aren't you?' Gesler grinned. 'Stormy, suck some oil and get our lizards back up and moving. I don't see any point in wasting any time on this.'

'Fine – but what about you?'

'Me and Sag'Churok – we're riding ahead. I want to see the lay of the land, especially at the base of the Spire. You catch us up, right?'

Stormy nodded. 'Good enough. How come that winged snake's not around again?'

'How should I know? Get going – I'll see you on whatever high ground I find. Make sure we draw up in formation – I don't plan on posing for the bastards.'

Kalyth stood close to Matron Gunth Mach. The Destriant had crossed her arms and knew the gesture to be protective, though it did little good – not in the face of what was coming. Wars were not part of the Elan heritage – skirmishes, yes, and feuds, and raids. But not wars. But already she had been in the midst of one, and now here she was, about to join another.

The frail woman stumbling from the camp so long ago now would have quailed at the thought, would have wept, helpless with fear.

It was the flavours of the K'Chain Che'Malle that now made her resilient, resolute—

'You are wrong in that, Destriant.'

She turned in surprise, studied the huge reptilian head hovering at her side, close enough to caress. 'It is *your* courage,' Kalyth insisted. 'It has to be. I have none of my own.'

'You are mistaken. It is your courage that gives us strength, Destriant. It is your humanness that guides us into the waiting darkness of battle.'

Kalyth shook her head. 'But I don't know why we're here – I don't know why we're going to fight this battle. We should have led you away – somewhere far from everyone else. Somewhere you don't have to fight, and die. A place to live. In peace.'

'There is no such place, Destriant. Even in isolation we were assailed – by our own doubts, by all the flavours of grief and despair. You and the Mortal Sword and the Shield Anvil, you have led us back into the living world – we have come from a place of death, but now we shall take our place among the peoples of this world. It is right that we do so.'

'But so many of you will die today!'

'We must fight to earn our right to all we would claim for ourselves. This is the struggle of all life. There are those who would deny us

713

this right – they feel it belongs to them alone. Today, we shall assert otherwise. Be free this day, Destriant. You have done what was needed – you have guided us here. The Mortal Sword and the Shield Anvil shall lead us into battle – and by the wind's scent, we shall be joined by T'lan Imass, in whom the hope for redemption is no stranger.'

Thinking about Stormy and Gesler, Kalyth shivered. 'Protect them, I beg you.'

'They shall lead. It is their purpose. This too is freedom.'

Motion in the corner of her eye drew Kalyth's attention – Sinn, slipping down from the back of her Ve'Gath, racing forward a few steps in the manner of any carefree child. And then she whirled, like a dancer, and faced Kalyth.

'The worm is burning – can't you taste it? Burning!'

Kalyth shook her head. 'I don't know what you mean, Sinn.'

But the girl was smiling. 'You can't leave fire behind. Once you've found it, you carry it with you – it's in the swords in your hands. It's in the armour you wear, and the food you eat, and the warmth of the night and the way to see through the dark. And it never sits still – it's always moving. It moved away from the Imass when they turned from it. But now they'll see that the fire they once knew didn't *leave* them – it just *spread out*. But maybe they won't understand anyway – they're not even alive, after all. You forget so much when you stop living.' She waved her arms in her excitement. 'That's what was wrong with the lizard camps! No fires!' She jabbed a finger at the Matron, hissed, *'You need reminding about fire.'*

The words were bitter as ice, and Kalyth found her arms wrapping yet tighter about her chest. And from beside her the flavour of Gunth Mach's oil suddenly soured – and the Destriant knew it for what it was.

She is afraid. The Matron is afraid.

Sister Reverence stared to the south. *At last, the enemy shows its face.* Still too far to make out anything more than the solid, dark mass of advancing legions. *Those numbers are paltry. They need fifty or sixty thousand to even hope to break the defences. And from the looks of it, these are cavalry – imagine the forage they must have carried with them!*

She glanced to the left, but the storm in the bay was unchanged, the cauldron ferocious yet striking her as strangely . . . impotent. *The one hiding there can come no closer. Akhrast Korvalain is too powerful, drinking deep of the Fallen One's heart. It is too late for all of them – we have grown too strong. We have achieved what we sought.*

A Watered was on the stairs below, using both feet and hands to make his way up, his gasps sounding torn and raw. Sister Reverence awaited him with impatience. *Even with our blessed blood – their humanness makes them so weak!*

'Beloved Sister!'

'I am here,' she replied.

'Our scouts have returned! The army to the south!'

'I see it, yes.'

'They are giant lizards! Thousands of giant lizards!'

Sister Reverence staggered back a step. Then, in a surge of suddenly febrile power, she quested out towards that army – her mind reaching, reaching, *there! A presence . . . a little further, reaching . . . touch—* She cried out. 'A Matron! *But there are no matrons left! The Nah'ruk promised! The K'Chain Che'Malle are destroyed!*' She realized that she was shouting out loud, and looked down into the wide eyes of the man kneeling at the edge of the stairs. 'Return to the defences – have the onagers loaded. The Che'Malle will waste no time – they never do. Go!'

Alone once more, Reverence closed her eyes, sought to slow the savage twin beats of her hearts that now seemed to clash in discordant panic. *Brother Diligence, hear my cry. We are deceived! The foe you face is but a feint – ignore them. I summon you and as much of the army as you can relinquish – we face K'Chain Che'Malle!* Releasing her power, she waited, breath held, for her brother's reply.

And received . . . nothing.

With hooded eyes, Setoc crouched atop a berm, facing upslope, and watched the descent of Brother Diligence. 'This is not your place,' she whispered. 'Can you feel that yet? The Wolves have claimed this den – this den you so kindly made for us. And here we will wait, until the chosen time.'

She pivoted and scanned the brothers and sisters. She could smell their distress, rising up rank and sour from the maze of trenches, from these dusty holes carved down through stone and dead soil. Many were looking out, across the width of the valley, to where the Bolkando and Letherii armies were even now beginning the descent. She saw how the soldiers reacted in dismay upon seeing no enemy element positioning itself at the centre. Well, not all dismay – she saw quickly hidden expressions of relief, and the scent of that was a looser, thinner emanation.

When the wolf becomes you, you hear and taste and smell so much more, making vision seem like a lesser power, a weakling subject to blindness in the face of truths. No, it is better with the ghosts gathered within me now. So much better.

Down came Brother Diligence, and there was Tanakalian, climbing into view, turning first to study the approaching Forkrul Assail, and then facing Setoc. He made his way closer – but not so close that should she leap, her fangs would find his throat. She noted that, and was not surprised.

'Destriant Setoc. We are about to be challenged.'

She bared her teeth.

His face knotted in a scowl. 'Listen to me! It is of no use if you can do little more than lift hackles and growl! He will use Akhrast Korvalain – do you understand me?'

'And what is it about that to cause fear, Shield Anvil?'

'The Assail know nothing of the K'Chain Che'Malle – do you see? I have kept that from them.'

'Why?'

'It does us no good if the Assail win on this day, does it?'

She cocked her head. 'It doesn't?'

'We remain balanced on the knife's edge – or have you forgotten? By what we do, by what we say or do not say, it all falls to us. Here. Now.'

'Shield Anvil' – she paused to yawn – 'Shield Anvil, why did you banish the Mortal Sword?'

'She broke our holy vow, Destriant. I have already told you this.'

'By swearing fealty to this Adjunct woman.'

'Yes.'

'And these Letherii and Bolkando – they are her allies? This Adjunct's allies?' She could see the growing frustration in the man, and was unmoved.

'I told you this!'

'Do you fear Brother Diligence? I see that you do. Should he . . . compel us. But, Shield Anvil, I want to know, which do you fear the most? The Adjunct or the Brother? Think of it as a contest if that helps. Which one is it?'

Tanakalian looked back up the slope, to where Diligence was coming ever nearer to their earthen fort, and then back again. 'The Adjunct is dead.'

'You do not know that, and besides, that doesn't matter – it's not relevant to the question I asked.'

A sneer curled his lips. 'If it is a question of immediacy, then it must be Brother Diligence.' His tone dripped venom, and she understood that as well – all the reasons, all the emotions raging back and forth in this man.

Setoc nodded, and then straightened from her crouch. She arched her back, stretched out her limbs. 'Immediacy, it's such a lie. One is close, the other is far away. So . . . fear more the one who is close. But, you see, there are two sides to immediacy. The one you're seeing is the one now, but there is another one, the one you only find at the end of things.'

Tanakalian's eyes narrowed on her, and she could see that he was startled, that he was thinking, and thinking hard now.

'So,' Setoc continued, 'let's forget the now for the moment, and go to the end of things. At the *end* of things, Shield Anvil, whom will you fear the most? Yon Brother Diligence, or the Adjunct?' Hearing voices from the trenches – filled with surprise and something like excitement – she smiled and added, 'Or our Mortal Sword, who even now rides for us?'

Suddenly white, Tanakalian climbed the nearest berm, faced the valley called Blessed Gift. For a dozen heartbeats, he made no move. And then he looked back down at Setoc. 'Where will you stand in this, Destriant?'

'I stand with the Wolves.'

Triumph flashed in his eyes.

'But,' she continued, 'that is only half the question, isn't it?'

He frowned.

'You must then ask me, where stand the Wolves?'

He half snarled – *and all the beasts beneath now awaken!* – and said, 'I know well their position, Destriant.'

'Well,' Setoc corrected, 'you thought you did.' She leapt down then, crossed the back edge of the fort to come opposite the narrow stepped track down which the Forkrul Assail was descending. Lifting her gaze, she held out her arms and shouted, 'Brother! Come no closer! You are not welcome here!'

Diligence was still fifty or more steps away, but he halted in obvious surprise.

She felt him awakening the sorcery in his voice.

And in the moment that he released it, Setoc opened her own throat to the howl of ten thousand ghost wolves.

The sound was a detonation, rising up to slam Diligence down on to his back on the earthen steps. In the numbed silence that followed, Setoc shouted again, 'You are not welcome! Go back to your slaves, Brother!'

There was no sign that the Forkrul Assail had heard. He was lying sprawled on the track, unmoving. Shriven were rushing towards him from both sides and from above. In moments they had closed, and then were lifting him up, carrying him back up the steps.

Satisfied, Setoc turned round.

The entire Perish army was facing her, every soldier. Among those closest to her, she saw blood at their ears, and trickling down from nostrils. She saw faces that looked bruised, and eyes shot with red. When Setoc spread out her arms again, they visibly flinched back. 'No foreign magic can compel us,' she said, and then she pointed. 'The Mortal Sword approaches. We shall welcome her. And in the making of this day, we shall know our fates.'

'Destriant!' someone shouted from one of the trenches. 'Who do we choose? Who do we follow?'

Tanakalian wheeled round at that, but there was no way to find the speaker amidst the press.

'I am Destriant of the Wolves,' Setoc replied. 'I am not a Grey Helm, not a sister to any of you. I am not one of your pack, and in this matter, who is to rule the pack is not for me to say.'

'Who do we fight? Destriant! Who do we fight?'

Setoc dropped her gaze to Tanakalian, just briefly, and then she answered, 'Sometimes even wolves know the value of *not fighting at all.*'

And there, she had given him what he thought he would need, for the challenge to come. Because Setoc could smell that Mortal Sword, and that woman – *that woman was a thing of war.*

Inside, the ghost wolves huddled close, giving her their immeasurable warmth. The echoes of their howl whispered back and forth – even they had been surprised at its power. *But I wasn't. This is my den and we shall defend it.*

Ears ringing at that holy cry, Krughava slowed her mount to a slow canter. Before her, lining the top of the front berm, stood her brothers and sisters – those she had known and loved for years. It was still too far for her to make out their expressions, to see if her arrival was welcome or cause for fury. But even the latter would not dissuade her. She was coming to fight for her people, and for all of Tanakalian's gleeful mocking of her belief in heroism – and indeed, in heroism lay her one and only true *faith* – she knew that the next few moments would test her as no battle had ever done.

If I am to be a hero, if I have such capacity within me, let it come now.

They said nothing when she reined in at the foot of the mound. Dismounting, Krughava looped the reins about the saddle's horn, pulled the horse round until it faced the valley once more, and with a hard slap on his rump sent it on its way. Was the gesture lost on the witnesses? *No, it most assuredly was not.*

Drawing off her helm, Mortal Sword Krughava swung round and looked up at her estranged brothers and sisters. She raised her voice. 'I would speak to Shield Anvil Tanakalian.'

An old veteran replied in a toneless voice, 'He awaits you within. Come forward in peace, Krughava.'

They have not chosen a new Mortal Sword . . . but neither will they give me my old title. So then, it all remains to be decided. So be it.

A knotted rope slithered down the steep ramp side. She took hold of it, and began climbing.

Precious Thimble drew closer to Faint's side. They remained on the valley's ridge, watching the ranks of Letherii marching down into the basin. Far to their right the Evertine Legion and its auxiliaries were doing the same. *All that marching, for this. This and only this. I'll never understand soldiers.*

'Faint?'

'What is it, Precious? You're going to tell me that you can use all this power, to carve us out a gate back home?' She glanced over, studied the pale, round face. 'No, I thought not.'

'What can you feel?'

Faint shrugged. 'My skin is crawling, and I'm no mage.'

'Exactly! You have no idea how this is feeling! Even Amby Bole is a mass of nerves, though he won't talk to me any more. I think he's become unhinged—'

'He never was hinged in the first place,' Faint cut in. 'So, what do you want from me?'

'That boy.'

'What boy?'

'The one half swallowed up by that giant lizard – who did you think I was talking about?'

Faint twisted kinks from her back, wincing. 'Fine. What about him? I'll grant you he's cute enough, but—'

'You think all this sorcery that's making us sick is coming from the Assail? You're *wrong*.'

'What?' Faint stared at Precious. 'Him?'

'It's only making us sick because he doesn't know what to do with it.'

'He's Malazan, isn't he?'

'I don't think he's anything.'

'What's that supposed to mean?'

But the witch's eyes were wide, staring at seemingly nothing. 'Can an idea find flesh? Bone? Does it have a face – is that even possible? Can people *build* a saviour, with handfuls of clay and withered sticks? If their need for a voice is so terrible, so . . . demanding – can a people build their own god, Faint? Tell me – have you ever heard such a thing? Has anyone ever even *thought* it?'

Faint reached out, pulled Precious Thimble round to face her. 'What in Hood's name are you talking about? What do you see in that boy?'

Precious Thimble's face twisted. '*I don't know!*' she cried, pulling herself away.

Faint turned, scanned the mass of troops – where was he, then?

That strange boy? But the dust was rising in walls, slipping across like curtains in the hesitant wind tracking the length of the valley. She looked to the prince's command position – off to her left – but saw only mounted messengers, signallers and the prince's staff. Her eyes narrowed on Atri-Ceda Aranict. 'Precious – come with me.'

She set out.

The ghost of Sweetest Sufferance was suddenly walking at her side. *'You should listen to the witch, love.'*

Faint glared at the ethereal form, and then shot a look back over one shoulder – to see Precious trailing half a dozen paces behind, walking like a drunk. 'Sweetest,' Faint whispered, 'how can I listen to her? She's talking nonsense!'

'I'm just saying, her ideas are intriguing. Maybe she's on the right track – I doubt that boy's even got a belly button. Have you looked? He's probably old enough for a roll in the grasses, a little schooling from Mistress Faint – what do you think? Can I watch? Just to see if he's got one, of course.'

Breath hissed from between Faint's teeth. 'Gods below. I can't even see the runt. Besides, in case you hadn't noticed, this whole valley is about to erupt in a bloodbath – and you want me to tickle his damned sack?'

'Never mind the whole belly thing, then. It was just a thought. I'm sure he's got one. Everyone does. Precious is panicking, that's all. When the Forkrul Assail unleash Akhrast Korvalain, when they awaken that deadly voice, well, who's here to fight against that? Yon Atri-Ceda and Precious herself, and that's it. Is it any wonder she's gibbering?'

'Stop talking, Sweetest.' Faint was almost upon the Atri-Ceda – the woman was standing on the very edge of the descent into the valley, dragging on a rustleaf stick as if it held the blood of immortality and eternal youth. And for all Faint knew, maybe it did.

'Atri-Ceda.'

Aranict turned, and almost immediately her eyes shifted past Faint, fixing on Precious Thimble. 'Greetings, witch. Be so good as to awaken a circle round us – and I would ask that you add your talents to my efforts in the defence to come.' She pulled hard on the stick. 'Failing that, we fall that much sooner.'

Precious Thimble made a whimpering sound.

Aranict's expression darkened. 'Courage, child. Where is your boy-friend? We will need him here – he possesses a natural disinclination to sorcerous attacks.'

Licking dust-dry lips, Faint cleared her throat. 'Atri-Ceda, your words do not elicit confidence over the outcome of this battle.'

Lighting another stick, Aranict waved one hand, as if distracted. Sending a blast of smoke into the air she said, 'I would advise that you run, but then there is nowhere to run to.' She pointed with a hand visibly trembling. 'See the prince – down there, on the horse behind the last ranks? That is the man I love, and he is about to die. Precious – listen to me. Defend this position with all that is within you, because all my power will be down there, with him. Once the Pure finds me, he will make every effort to shred me alive.'

Faint took a step back, appalled by the heart-rending rawness of the woman standing before her, so much exposed, so much ripped open for all to see. *And yet . . . and yet . . . if I could find a love like that. If I could find such a love.* 'Aranict,' she now said in a soft voice – and something in the tone drew the Atri-Ceda round. 'If I may, I will stand with you.'

She saw Aranict's eyes widen, and then flit away – as if she could no longer bear to see what was there in Faint's own face. The Atri-Ceda stared north. 'He's not yet touched on his power. But it's only a matter of time.'

'He may not have to,' Faint said, following Aranict's gaze. 'I don't know much about battles, but I can't see us winning this one.'

'We're not here to win,' Aranict replied. 'We're just here to take a long time to die.'

Precious Thimble moved past Faint then, mumbling chaining words under her breath. And there, three paces to the right, stood Amby Bole, his face a stone mask, his hands clenched into scarred fists.

And the ghost of Sweetest Sufferance spoke. *'Faint, I hear an echo of . . . of something.'*

'It's nothing,' Faint muttered in reply. *Nothing but the sound of all that we are about to lose. What is that sound like? When you hear it, you will know.*

Brys Beddict rode hard along the back of the reserve line. He wanted his soldiers to hear the hoofs of his horse behind them, wanted them to know he was there. So that they would understand that wherever they hesitated, he would ride to them; when they needed the strength of a commander's will, he would find them. Riding parallel to the ranks, he scanned the formations. Companies held tight in their rectangles, with broad avenues between them. Their discipline remained strong, resolute. There would be nothing subtle in the assault to come, and they had not yet wavered.

Horns sounded from the front ranks, to mark the last fifty paces from the enemy's forward earthworks. That forlorn cry sang through Brys and he almost faltered. *Is she alive? Do we give our lives to a cause already lost? Is my last gesture to be an empty one? Oh, beloved brother – I could do with some encouraging words right now.*

Better yet, make me laugh. What more fitting way to meet that moment when you fall to your knees than with sweet, unchained laughter? The kind that lifts you into the air, high above the grim violence of the land and all its sordid cruelty?

He was riding inward along the line, now, the ranks on his left, and in moments he would come into the clearing opposite the Perish-held centre, and before him, across the gap, he would see the Evertine Legion closing with the Kolansii lines. *Queen Abrastal, such a noble ally you have become. If my brother could but know of this – if your husband could witness this . . . some futures hold such promise as to convince you they can be nothing more than dreams, delusions built on wishful thoughts.*

You walk the steps of your life, and always that dream beckons, that dream waits. You don't know if it can ever be made real. You don't know that, even should you somehow stumble upon it, you won't find it less than it was, less than it could have been – if only you could have kept that distance, kept it just outside arm's reach. For ever shining. For ever unsullied by the all-too-real flaws of your own making.

Aranict. How could you have given me such a thing? How could you have let me take it close, feel it here in my arms, so warm, so solid?

When those dreams in that unreachable future suddenly rise up around you, how can you not be blinded to their truths? All at once, it is here. All at once, you are living in its very midst. Why then must you seek to pull away?

He rode on, waiting for the roar of clashing weapons, waiting for the awakening of the power of the Forkrul Assail – *and I must answer it, in the only way I know how. And when I am done, I know, there will be nothing left of me.* For so long, he had not understood what he was meant to do, but now, with energies crackling the air, it had all come clear.

Aranict, my love, you now hold the best in me. I pray that, for you, it is enough.

He bolted into the gap, sawed on the reins of his mount, and swung round to face the massive earthen fort where waited the Perish Grey Helms. But he could see nothing of what was happening behind the banked walls of earth.

In the centre of the maze of trenches and berms there was a broad marshalling area of packed earth cut with narrow slits to gather the blood of the wounded who would be brought here during the battle. Cutters waited standing close to stretchers, their faces smeared with ash to keep sweat from dripping into open wounds. Their sawing and cutting tools were laid out on skins beside leather buckets of steaming water. In all the trenches that Krughava could see into, her blessed soldiers stood with their eyes fixed on her as she made her way towards the centre, where waited Shield Anvil Tanakalian and, a dozen paces behind him, a young woman whom Krughava had never seen before.

There was something strange about her eyes, but the Mortal Sword could not yet determine what gave them such a disquieting regard. She was barely into womanhood, dressed in ragged deerskins, her hair long and ropy with filth, and the smile curving her lips looked faintly ironic.

Krughava ascended a ridged ramp and stepped out on to the hard ground. She set her helm down, and drew off her gauntlets.

Tanakalian spoke, 'It is our hope, Krughava, that you have come seeking to return to the fold. That you will fight with us on this day. That you will lead us in battle.'

She drew herself up, settling one hand on the pommel of her sword. 'Yes, I would lead the Grey Helms in battle, Shield Anvil Tanakalian. But not against the Letherii or Bolkando. Rather, I would our soldiers quit these trenches.' She lifted her gaze, studied the avenues leading back up the slope, and scowled. 'Do you not see what they have done? The Assail have made the Grey Helms a forlorn hope.'

Tanakalian sighed, tilting his head as he regarded her. 'There is another way of seeing our position here, Krughava. Simply put, Brother Diligence does not trust us – and you would prove to him that the Perish are as treacherous as he suspected.'

'Treachery? Now, that is a curious thing, Shield Anvil. I am not surprised the Assail does not trust you, given your precedents.'

The Shield Anvil's face flushed. 'The betrayal was yours, not mine – but have we not already been through all of this? The Grey Helms heard your arguments. They heard mine. They voted.'

Krughava looked round. Hard expressions, unyielding, on all sides. 'On this day, brothers and sisters, our allies will seek to break the tyranny of the Forkrul Assail. But that is not the only reason for this war – indeed, it is the least of them. Hear me, all of you! Long ago, a foreign god was brought down to this earth. He was torn to pieces, but they would not let him die – no, instead they chained him, as one would bind a wild beast. *As one might chain a wolf.* And so bound, so caged, that god has known nothing but unending pain and anguish. The gods feed upon him! The wretched among us mortals sip his blood in prayer! And these Forkrul Assail, they hold his heart in their cold, cruel hands!

'My brothers and sisters! On this day we shall seek to shatter those chains. We shall seek to free the Fallen God! But more than that, we shall endeavour to return him to his realm!' She pointed upslope. 'And yet, where do you stand? Why, you stand at the side of torturers, and

723

all the words of justice they so eagerly whisper in your ears – they are nothing but lies!'

The young woman came forward then, and Krughava saw now what gave her gaze such strangeness. *Wolf eyes. One silver, one amber. Blessed Throne – she is our Destriant! The Wolves of Winter look out from those eyes!* Where had she come from?

The Destriant spoke in the Letherii trader tongue, 'Mortal Sword, we are stirred by your words. But then, what do we know of mercy? We who have never felt its gentle touch? We who are hunted and ever hunted down? Shall I tell you of the memories rushing through me now? Will you hear my words?'

Krughava felt the blood draining from her, the heat of her passion stealing away. Beneath her heavy armour, she was suddenly cold. *This woman is my foe. Tanakalian is as nothing compared with her.* 'Destriant, I will hear your words.'

The young woman looked round. 'In your mind, see a herd – so many! Great, strong beasts – and they see us, they see us running beside them, or standing off in the distance. They see our shaggy heads sink low. Yet to all their nervous attention we are indifferent. Our eyes study the beasts. We seek scents on the wind. And when at last we drive that herd into flight, whom do we single out? Which of these great, terrible animals do we choose?'

Tanakalian answered with unfeigned excitement. 'Destriant Setoc, the wolves ever choose the *weakest* among the herd. The old one, the *wounded* one.'

Krughava stared at Setoc. 'The Wolves would feed on this day, Destriant? Upon the heart of the Crippled God?'

Setoc gestured, a loose wave of one hand. 'Tell your allies – ignore us in this battle. We'll not leave this nest. And when this day is done, we shall see who remains standing. It does not matter which of you has won – for you will be bleeding, your head will be hanging. You will be on one knee.'

'And then shall the Grey Helms strike!' cried out Tanakalian. 'Can you not see the truth of this, Krughava? Are you so blind as to still hold to your foolish conceit?'

Krughava was silent. After a long moment, wherein the only sounds came from the advancing armies on the plain, she approached the Shield Anvil, halting only when she stood directly before him. 'Tankalian,' she said in a low rasp, 'we are not wolves. Do you understand? When we act, we are privileged, or cursed, to know the consequences – the Wolves of Winter are not. They have no sense, no sense at all, of the future. There can be no worship of the Wild, Shield Anvil, without the *knowledge of right and wrong.*'

Tanakalian shook his head, avid pleasure gleaming in his eyes. 'You have lost this, Krughava. You cannot win – it is not just me any more, is it? Not even just the Perish. Now, you face a Destriant, and through her, our very gods.'

'That child is mad, Tanakalian.'

'I do not fear her, Krughava.'

That struck her as an odd thing to say. Deeply shaken, she lifted her gaze, studied Setoc. 'Destriant! Shall this be the only game the Wolves play?'

'This game they know well.'

Krughava pushed past Tanakalian, pushed him out to the side – no longer important, no longer relevant. 'Yes, they do, don't they? The glory of the hunt, yes? I will speak to the wolf gods now, and they would do well to hear me!'

Shouts from the Perish Grey Helms, offended, indignant, shocked, but Setoc simply shrugged.

Krughava drew a deep breath – the ground was trembling beneath her now, and in moments the forces beyond this fort would collide. 'You wolves think yourselves masters of the hunt – but have you not seen? We humans are better at it. We're so good at it that we have been hunting down and killing you for half a million years. But we're not content with just the weak among you, or the wounded. We kill every damned one of you. It may be the only game you know, but hear my words. *You're not good enough at it!*' She advanced on Setoc now, and saw the Destriant flinch back. *I have found my moment. I see the comprehension in her eyes – the Wolves of Winter have heard me. They finally understand.* 'Let me show you another way! Let me be your Mortal Sword once again!'

But it was not the wolf gods who understood. It was only Setoc, and in the moment before the wolf gods poured through her, she spun round in her mind. *NO! Heed her words! Can you not see the truth – you cannot hunt here!* But then they were upon her, tearing her apart in their frenzy to reach through, to close jaws on the hated human.

No! I loved you! I wept for you!

She screamed, and it was the last sound Setoc ever made.

Krughava's eyes widened upon seeing the woman's face transform into something unhuman. The flesh of her arms burst as the bones seemed to twist their way free, black tendons writhing like serpents. Her body stretched, the shoulders hunching. The eyes flared. Shrieking, she launched herself at the Mortal Sword.

Fangs – welters of boiling blood and thick saliva – a sudden burgeoning of mass, black-furred, looming huge before her – and then a figure

725

slipped past Krughava – Tanakalian, *forgotten Tanakalian*, his knife flashing, the blade plunging deep into Setoc's chest.

A deafening howl thundered, staggering Krughava back.

Blood sprayed from Setoc's eyes – she leapt away from the knife, suddenly flailing, groping blind. Another howl sounded, battering the air. Dark blood spilling down from her mouth and nose, the woman fell on to her back on the earthen steps, and then curled up like a child.

Krughava stumbled forward. 'Tanakalian! *What have you done?*'

He had been thrown to the ground by that terrible death cry, but now he clambered back to his feet, the knife still in his hand. The face he turned to Krughava horrified her. 'This was supposed to be my day! Not yours! Not hers! *I am the hero! I am!*'

'Tanak—'

'This is *my* day! *Mine!*' He rushed her.

She threw up an arm, but the gore-smeared blade slipped beneath it, punched hard, stabbing through her neck from one side to the other.

Krughava fell back, struggling to stay on her feet, and then pitching round to land hard on one knee. The side of her face where the hilt had struck throbbed – she could feel that. One hand reached up, collided with the leather-bound grip. The knife was still stuck through her throat, and her lungs were filling with blood. She opened her mouth, but could draw no breath.

Tanakalian was shrieking. '*They were coming through! I couldn't allow that! The Assail! The Assail! He would have taken them! He would have killed them!*'

She fought back to her feet, dragged free her sword.

Seeing her, he backed away. '*I saved our gods!*'

You fool – you killed one of them! Did you not hear it die? The world was growing black on all sides. Her chest was heavy, as if someone had poured molten lead down into her lungs. *Blessed Wolves! I did not intend this! Foul murder! This day – so sordid, so . . . human.* Rearing upright, blood pouring down her chin, Krughava advanced.

Tanakalian stared at her, frozen in place. 'We needed her out of the way! Don't you see? Don't you—'

Her first swing smashed into his right side, shattering ribs, slicing through the lung before jamming halfway through his sternum. The blow lifted him from the ground, flung him three paces to the right.

Astonishingly, he landed on his feet, scattering the cutters – blood and unidentifiable pieces of meat were spilling from the enormous cut in his chest.

Krughava closed again. *Enough for one more. Enough—* Her second swing took off the top half of his head, the blade slicing across just beneath his eyes. The broken bowl spun over the slick back of her blade, then off to one side, loosing the brain it held and with it both eyes, swinging on their stalks. What remained of Tanakalian then pitched forward, landing on his chin.

She sank down on to her knees. All breath was gone. The world roared in her skull.

Someone was at her side, fumbling with the knife still thrust through her neck. She feebly pushed the hands away, and then fell forward. Her face settled against the hard clay – and there, a gouged furrow, no wider than a knuckle, running out from under her eyes. She watched it fill with blood.

I wanted . . . I wanted a better . . . a better death . . . But then, don't we all?

Two thunderous howls erupted in quick succession from the Perish position, their ferocity plunging Brys Beddict's horse into a blind panic. He was almost thrown from the lunging, terrified animal, but then he managed to set his heels in the stirrups, drawing tight the reins.

The horse bucked, and then, unexpectedly, it ran straight towards the fort's high bank.

He looked to the top edge of the high banked wall – but he could see no Perish soldiers watching him, no one preparing for his arrival – he saw no one at all.

Brys eased the reins – there was no fighting this bolting beast, not yet. He rose in the saddle as the animal tackled the slope. The ascent was steep, uneven, and the straining effort burned out the horse's fear as it lunged upward.

Reaching the top of the berm, Brys checked his mount's advance, pulling on the reins hard enough to make the animal rear once more. His heels took his own weight as he shifted to take the movement, his eyes already studying the array of faces, turned now towards him.

Where was Krughava? Where were all the officers?

He saw the nearest Grey Helms – almost directly below in the first trench – reaching for their pikes. Swearing, Brys wheeled his horse round while it still stood high on its hind legs, sent it stumbling back down the slope. Stones and clouds of dirt followed the frantic descent. *Gods, they could have ended this for me right then!*

Wasn't anyone watching? No, they had all been facing the other way. I caught them completely by surprise – what was happening in that camp?

He suspected that he would never know. He was riding across level ground again, his horse's hoofs kicking through the dusty plough tracks – and ahead and to his right, his Letherii soldiers had reached the first of the earthworks. Behind the companies, crews swarmed to position the heavy onagers, driving wedges beneath the front runners to lift the arc of fire.

The enemy had begun releasing their own salvos of heavy bolts from raised fortlets flanking the trenches. Those deadly quarrels tore deep gashes into the advancing ranks.

His soldiers had begun dying. *Because I asked them to. Dying, in the name of a failed wish. I have brought them to this.*

But . . . why? Why do they follow? They are no more fools than I am. They know – my title means nothing. It is an illusion. No, worse, a delusion. Nobility is not something you can wear, like a damned cloak of jewels. You can't buy it. You can't even be born into it. The nobility we talk about is nothing but a mockery of all that it used to mean.

By no measure am I noble.

Why do you follow?

Gods, why do I presume to lead? Into this?

Brys Beddict drew his sword, but the taste of ashes filled his mouth. So many conceits, gathering here, crowding this moment and all the moments to come. *Now then, shake yourself awake, Brys. The time has come . . . to find us a name.*

He twisted his horse round, headed for the nearest avenue between companies, and rode to meet the enemy.

High Cutter Syndecan was still kneeling beside the body of Krughava, staring down into her pale, lifeless visage. In the clearing behind him all the officers and veterans had gathered, and the arguments were raging fierce on all sides. Horror, shock and confusion – the Perish was moments from tearing itself apart.

Syndecan was the eldest among them all. A veteran of many campaigns, a soldier in the long, hopeless battle that was staunching wounds, breathing life into dying lungs. And, once more, he could only sit, silent, looking down at yet another of his failures.

She came among us. A brave, brave woman. We all knew: her pride was ever her enemy. But see here, she came to us – imagine how doing that must have stung that pride. And yet, even over this powerful flaw within her, she finally triumphed.

What could be more heroic than that?

When at last he straightened – though in truth it was no more than thirty heartbeats since Krughava's fall – all the voices fell away. He was the veteran. He was the one they would now turn to, desperate for guidance. *Oh, all you fools. What to do? What to do now?*

He cleared his throat. 'I do not know what has happened here. I do not know if the Shield Anvil slew a young woman, or a god. Nor can I judge his reasons for doing so – this, this is beyond all of us.'

A young soldier called out, 'Brother Syndecan! Do we fight this day?'

He'd been thinking about that, from the moment of Krughava's fall, and he recalled looking across to the hacked corpse of Tanakalian, and thinking, *you are only what we deserved*. 'Brothers, sisters, on this day, yes, we must fight!'

Silence answered him.

He had expected as much. They would not follow blindly – not any more. *Not after this.*

'Brothers, sisters! There has been murder in our fold – we were witness to it! And in witnessing, we are made part of this crime. We must be cleansed. Today, we must fight to regain our honour!'

'*But who is the damned enemy?*'

And here, the old veteran found himself at an impasse. *Wolves help me, I don't know. And I'm not the one to decide. Veteran, am I? Yes, but the only wise veterans are the ones who have left war and killing behind them. No, I'm just the biggest fool among you all. Oh, fine then! Time to fall back on useless superstition. Isn't that what old soldiers turn to when all else fails?* 'Brothers, sisters! We must seek a sign! We must look to the world – here and on this day! We must—'

And then his eyes widened.

Faces turned. Eyes stared –

– as the Prince of Lether lunged into view atop the high berm at the fort's facing wall. Surging up and on to the narrow, ragged edge – and how the horse found purchase there was a mystery. That beast then reared, hoofs scything the air, with the prince glaring down at them all. And at that moment, from either side of the valley's length, came the sound of battle's clash.

Gods take me! Think I just pissed my breeches.

Abrastal sat astride her charger – the beast felt thin beneath her, but was still quivering in anticipation. *Bastard loves this – the stench of blood, the screams – wants at them. Gods, war is a fever!* She glanced back at Spax and his mass of warriors. 'Hold them, Warchief! Wait for it!'

The Gilk Barghast glared up at her. 'But how long? Your damned soldiers are dying on that front – at least let us charge and take out one of the fortlets. Those onagers are carving you bloody!'

She knew that – she could see the terrible casualties those perfectly emplaced weapons were delivering as her legion struggled to overrun the first line of defences. 'I said wait, Spax! I will need you and the Teblor to move fast when that Assail finds out—'

'But what if it's all gone wrong at the Spire? Firehair! We can collapse this flank – just let us loose, damn you!'

But something had caught her eye – she wheeled her mount round, stared towards the centre. 'Jheckan's fat cock! The Perish are pouring out of their trenches! Spax!'

'I see them! Do you see Krughava?'

Abrastal shook her head. 'They're too far away – listen, form a line to hold our inside flank, Warchief. If I was commanding that position and saw it uncontested, I'd do precisely what they're doing right now – out and into our unprotected sides.'

'They'll see us' – Spax was now at her side, a heavy axe in his hand, a spear in the other, his face half hidden by his ornate shell helm – 'and wheel round to bite the Letherii flank – Brys has no reserves to guard against them.'

'If they do that,' Abrastal said in a snarl, 'you know what to do, Spax.'

'Climb up their hairy asses, yes. But—'

'Just ready your warriors,' she cut in, and then jabbed her spurs into her mount's sides. 'I'm going for a closer look!'

'Not too close!'

She pushed her horse into a canter, the beast's armour cladding a weaponsmith's clamour around her. When four bodyguards rode to join her she waved them back. She hated the fools. Worse than hens. But the one messenger who drew close she gestured forward.

Beyond the Perish, the Letherii army had locked jaws with the first line of defenders, but they too were being savaged by the Kolansii onagers. She saw that the prince had deployed his own artillery, and the rate of fire from these heavy weapons was superior to the enemy's. At least three positions were concentrating fire on the nearest fortlet, and the raised redoubt was studded with heavy quarrels. Foot archers and skirmishers had advanced under the cover of that counterfire and were now assaulting the position.

The prince knew his business. But would it matter? Already the losses were appalling – and she knew her own Evertine soldiers were suffering the same behind her.

And now, these Perish . . . a part of her wanted to sink her teeth into the throat of the Grey Helms. For all that betrayal and treachery thrived in the court games of the Bolkando kingdom, out here it was a far deadlier indulgence. *Maybe this is teaching me a lesson. About backstabbing, lying and cheating to get your way.*

No, try as I might, I can't swing it across. The palace is my world and I'll run it the way I like.

Hoofs thundering, she was fast closing on the Perish – the soldiers were smoothly forming up now that they'd cleared the fort, and she saw them wheeling to face her. 'You want us first, do you? Spax will be so pleased!'

But that wasn't tactical – no, clearly they should have swung to face the Letherii. And as she drew yet closer, the front ranks before

730

her made no effort to draw weapons. *Can it be? Has Krughava won them over? Where is she? Where is Tanakalian? Errant's nudge, who's commanding this army?*

Abrastal waved up the messenger. 'Stay close, until we're within earshot, and then halt yourself. I will ride on. Listen well to this parley, soldier – the lives of thousands may well count on it, should I fail to win clear.'

The young woman, selected for her riding ability, was pale beneath the rim of her helm, but she nodded.

'Your eyes are better than mine – do you see a commander anywhere?'

'Highness, there is one – with the grey face. He has been gesturing – sending out orders. There,' and she pointed.

'I see him. What's with the face paint?'

'He's a cutter, Highness. A field medic.'

Whatever. 'No matter. Looks as if he's the one wanting to talk – I don't like this. What has happened to Krughava?'

They slowed to a canter, and at the appropriate distance the messenger halted, whilst the queen trotted forward. She studied the cutter. An old man, at least in so far as these Grey Helms went. His face was well worn with tracks of sorrow and loss, and she saw nothing in that face to suggest that anything had changed in his outlook. Her unease deepened.

The cutter raised a hand in greeting. 'Highness, the Grey Helms welcome you. I am Syndecan, elected commander following the tragic deaths of the Mortal Sword and the Shield Anvil.'

Abrastal felt her jaws clench. The words had struck like a blow to her chest. *Leave it, woman. Now is not the time.* 'You are arrayed. State your intentions, Syndecan – as you can see, we've got us a fight here and I really cannot waste any more time while you decide which way the fucking wind's blowing.'

The man recoiled as if slapped, and then he drew a deep breath and slowly straightened. 'The Perish Grey Helms humbly place themselves under the command of you and Prince Brys.' He made a faint gesture to the troops behind him. 'We face you because we could not determine the whereabouts of the prince. Highness, the Pure Forkrul Assail was injured in a clash with our Destriant. It is safe to assume, however, that he will recover. And when that happens . . . we anticipate an awakening of dire sorcery.'

'Can you defend against it?'

The old man shook his head. 'I fear not, Highness. We have lost our place as the weapon of the wolf gods. You see us as we are – simple soldiers seeking to regain our honour as men and women. That and nothing more.'

'As soon as that Pure is made aware of the attack on the Spire, he will disengage as many soldiers as he feels he can spare.'

'We understand this, Highness.'

'Are your soldiers rested, Syndecan? Can you fast-trot down this valley, and find an undefended ascent?' She made her voice louder, addressing the soldiers waiting behind the cutter. 'Grey Helms! Can you stand in the path of the Kolansii who will soon drive east to the Spire?'

In answer the soldiers shipped their shields on to their backs, began tightening straps.

Abrastal grunted. *Who needs words?*

Syndecan spoke. 'Do you require that we delay the enemy, or stop them in their tracks?'

'There are not enough of you to stop them, Commander, and you know it. If I can, I will spare you my Barghast, and the Teblor – but they may be arriving late to the fight.'

'We shall hold until they arrive, Highness.'

Abrastal hesitated, and then called, 'What I've seen of you thus far, Perish, has been sticks up the ass and plenty of proper marching and not much else. Well, now's your chance to show the world what you can do in a real fight.'

They seemed to weather this, either in humility or in shame. She had expected a wave of anger, but saw not a single spark. Her gaze fell once more to the cutter. 'Syndecan, you'll need to work hard at inspiring this lot – they're broken.'

'Yes, Highness, we are. But on this day, I believe that this is no weakness. We shall answer the world.'

She studied him for a moment longer, and then collected her reins. 'I trust you'll forgive my Barghast if they face you while you pass.'

The man simply nodded.

'Fare you well, then. If justice truly exists, perhaps your Mortal Sword will stand with you, if only in spirit. Seek to match her measure, all of you, and perhaps you will indeed find your honour once more.'

Dragging her mount round, she set off.

The messenger fell in alongside her. Abrastal glanced over. 'You've the lighter burden here. Ride ahead and inform Warchief Spax that the Perish march to take position in the expected path of the Kolansii relief force. They will pass south of our position at a fast-trot – but he is to face his warriors on them the entire time. Repeat my words back to me.'

The messenger did so, without error.

'Ride then. Go!'

Abrastal watched the younger woman swiftly pulling away. *Was I ever that young? It's the curse of nobility that we must be made to grow up all too fast. But then, look at you – tits barely budding and you're in the middle of a damned war.*

And I can't even remember your name.

But should we both survive this, I'm sending you to learn embroidery, and a year or two of flirting with artists and musicians and other ne'er-do-wells.

Growling under her breath, the queen of Bolkando shook her head. Rose in her saddle to glare at the forward lines of her beloved legion.

They'd yet to even take the first entrenchments – and that slope was a mass of dead and dying soldiers, getting deeper with every moment that passed. *Errant's tug – they've got us by the balls here. We need to push harder – no let-up on this pressure. Time for the Saphii, then – assuming they've gotten all yellow-eyed on that brave-spit they guzzle before battle. They should be well primed.*

But were they all doing little more than going through the motions? *Fourteenth Daughter – can you hear me? . . . Thought not. I could use your eyes right now, just to see where things stand over there. You should be in the damned bay by now. You should be in a good position to witness . . . everything.*

Once more she shook her head – too many things in her damned skull!

Her horse was tiring and she slowed her pace a fraction – she might need one more charge out of this beast. *The queen takes the sword and shows her face beneath the mask. But the world does not tremble as it should, for the mask only comes off in the face of death. Husband, dear me, your wife's strayed too far this time.*

She drew her sword as she closed – the Saphii commander was standing to the right of the royal entourage, his eyes upon her as were the eyes of virtually everyone else. She pointed her sword directly at him, saw him suddenly straighten as if in delight, raising his spear in one hand, and then he was moving, his tall dark figure speeding across the ground, back to his troops.

And she saw them now, too, leaping and dancing in a frenzy of excitement. *Oh, Kolansii, you have no idea what is about to hit you.*

Captain Feveren, Ninth Cohort of the Evertine Legion, slid back down the slope on a greasy mass of bodies, swearing all the way down to the base, where he was thrown up against the shins of the soldiers struggling to do what he'd just tried. He'd lost sight of his own troops – those that remained alive – but such details barely mattered now. The only cohesion left was the one that defined the living from the dead.

This was slaughter. Twice they had momentarily overrun the first trench, only to be thrown back by indiscriminate fire from ranks of onagers, the huge quarrels tearing through multiple bodies, blood and

733

gore exploding in torrents, men and women flung about like rag dolls. Shields shattered with impacts, breaking the shoulders behind them, driving soldiers down to their knees. The bank of the first berm was a ceaseless mudslide of all that could spill out from a human body, streaming over pale limbs, over staring, sightless faces, ruptured armour and tangled embraces.

Cursing, he struggled to find his feet again. He could feel another push coming from the ranks pressing against him, and wanted to be in a position to ride that tide upward. They were going to take that damned trench, no matter—

But the Evertine infantry were being jostled, the solid lines broken apart – and Feveren swore upon seeing tall Saphii pushing through, their eyes bright yellow with that infernal drug they took before battle, the froth thick on their lips.

'Clear paths!' the captain bellowed. 'Clear paths!'

But the command was not needed – nothing would stop the Saphii spear-wielders, not this close to the enemy.

Lighter-armoured, lithe and fleet of foot, the warriors seemed to clamber like spiders up the slope of the berm. In one hand they held their spears, and in the other a pick of some sort – its business end a splay of talon-like hooks that they swung down into dead and dying flesh alike, pulling themselves yet higher.

In moments the first line of Saphii had reached the top, and over and out of sight.

The screams from the first trench intensified.

'Follow!' bellowed Feveren. 'Follow!'

And up they went.

Somehow, they'd lifted him to his feet. But his mind remained lost in a deafening roar. Brother Diligence raised his head, struggled to find his balance. Officers surrounded him, healers crowded close, and, from a great distance, the sounds of battle took hold of the air above the valley, shaking it without pause.

He sought to make sense of the cacophony in his head. He heard screams, horrified screams, rising in waves of panic and dread, but even that seemed far away. *Far away, yes. That voice – so far away.* Abruptly he shoved his helpers from his side, and then staggered as at last he could make out the words, the sources of those desperate screams.

Sister Reverence!

Her answer came in a savage torrent. *'Brother Diligence! Your battle is feint! We are attacked! K'Chain Che'Malle! T'lan Imass! We cannot hold – gods, the slaughter!'*

He silenced her hard as a slap. *You must hold, Sister! We are coming!*

Looking around, he saw the panic in the eyes of the Watered – they had felt her, had heard her frantic cries. 'Attend!' he bellowed. 'Maintain the defences of the two lowest tiers – the rest are to withdraw to the high road – they must march east to the Spire with all haste! Weapons and armour and one skin of water and nothing more! You have one bell to get twenty-five thousand soldiers on the road!'

'Blessed Pure, the Perish have betrayed us!'

He waved a dismissive hand. 'Leave them. I shall awaken Akhrast Korvalain – I shall obliterate the enemies before us! Wait! I want the forces on our left to counter-attack – lock on to the enemy flank – I want those Bolkando and Barghast driven from the field! Now, clear me a path down to the second tier!'

The world seemed to be trembling beneath his feet. As he made his way down, choosing the right flank, he quickly scanned the battle before him. The damned Letherii fought as if blind to defeat – and they would be defeated, of that there was no doubt. Even without his voice, they could not hope to overrun his defences.

But I want them on their knees, empty-handed, heads bowed. And my soldiers shall rise from the trenches and walk among them, their weapons swinging. Not one Letherii shall leave this place – not one!

And when I have driven them down, I shall turn to the other flank – it is stronger, I can see that, the White Faces remain in reserve – but none there can hope to stop me. They will be held in place by the counter-attack. I will have them all!

Almost directly below, he saw a tight mass of Letherii, a standard waving above them, and there, to his amazement, two K'Chain Che'Malle. Ve'Gath soldiers, one being ridden by a scale-armoured figure, the other revealing an empty saddle. They were flanking a lone Letherii on a horse, a man struggling to form the tip of a wedge pushing its way up the first berm.

The K'Chain Che'Malle we shall have to cut down the hard way – and Sister Reverence faces an army of these creatures! We were complacent. We were fools to think them without cunning – are they not humans, after all?

I see you, Commander. I will take you first.

The first to kneel. The first to submit to execution.

He continued his rapid descent of the earthworks, feeling his warren awakening within him.

Below, Letherii sorcery crackled in a grey wave, swept up and over an onager redoubt. Bodies erupted in crimson mists. Furious, Diligence reached out, found a handful of squad mages. With a single word he crushed their skulls.

Reaching a ramp, he made his way across, and took position atop the second tier. Across a distance less than a bowshot, the Letherii commander had attained the top of the berm, his Ve'Gath clearing a path with vicious, sweeping strokes of their halberds that sent bodies spinning through the air.

'*I see you!*' roared Diligence.

Brys Beddict felt his horse crumpling under him, and as he flung his feet clear of the stirrups and twisted to evade the falling beast he saw an enormous quarrel driven deep into its chest. Landing in a crouch, he readied his blood-smeared sword.

The trench below was a mass of Kolansii infantry, pikes thrust upward and awaiting their descent. On either side of the prince, the Ve'Gath were fending off flanking counter-attacks, and their ferocity forced the breach yet wider.

The moment he straightened, three shouted words struck him like a fist, snapping his head back, and all at once he was under siege.

The Forkrul Assail had found him. *At last. You saw. You saw and wanted me first. Oh, friend, you are most welcome to me.*

He rose under the barrage, lifted his head, and met the eyes of the Pure.

'I see you! Kneel! YIELD TO MY WILL!'

'You see me? Tell me, Assail, whom do you see?'

'I will command you – I will take all that is within you—'

Brys Beddict, King's Champion and prince of Lether, spread open his arms, and smiled. 'Then have me.'

And from his soul, from a deep, unlit world of silts and crushed bones, there came a stirring, a sudden billowing of dark clouds, and from this maelstrom . . . *names.* A torrent, a conflagration. 'Saeden Thar, Lord Protector of Semii, Haravathan of the River People, Y'thyn Dra the Mountain of Eyes, Woman of Sky above the Erestitidan, Blessed Haylar Twin-Horns of the Elananas, Horastal Neh Eru SunBearer and Giver of Crops in the Valley of the Sanathal, Itkovas Lord of Terror among the K'ollass K'Chain Che'Malle of Ethilas Nest . . .' And the names rose unending, flowing through Brys Beddict's mind, one after another. 'Tra Thelor of the Twin Rivers, Sower of Spring among the Grallan. Adast Face of the Moon among the Korsone . . .'

All the forgotten gods, and as each name whispered out, sweeping into the torrid current of the Forkrul Assail's warren – his terrible power of the voice, of words and all their magic – Brys felt part of himself tearing away, snatched loose, drowned in the swirling flow.

There was no stopping this. The Pure had found him in the manner that Brys had desired – as he rode to the forefront of his army, as he fought between two K'Chain Che'Malle, as he delivered unopposable slaughter. *Find me*, he had prayed. *Find me – I am waiting for you. Find me!*

Once begun, once the warren was a torrent between the Assail and the prince, there was no stopping it. Power fed power, and its fuel was justice. *Let them be known. All the forgotten gods. All their forgotten people. All the ages past, all the mysteries lost. This unending stream of rise and fall, dream and despair, love and surrender.*

They deserve utterance, one more time. One last time.

Take them, take me. You with your power in words, me with my power in names. Without me, your words are nothing.

Come, let us devour each other.

He could see the Pure now with a sudden clarity, a tall, ancient male, one arm outthrust, one finger pointing across at Brys, but the Assail was motionless, frozen in place – no – Brys's eyes narrowed. He was *crumbling*. His face was a stretched mask, thin over the bizarre skeletal structure underneath. His eyes wept red, his mouth was open, pulling taut as the jaw angled down – as if the names were pouring down the Pure's throat, as if he was drowning in their deluge.

Brys's own soul was shredding apart. The world – this valley, this battle – all fell away. He could feel the pressure of the sea now, could feel his legs planted in shin-deep mud, and the current rushed past him, scouring the flesh from the bones of his soul, and still he had more to give.

Clouds of silt billowed and seethed around him – he was losing his vision – something was blinding his soul, something new, unexpected.

No matter. I am almost done with him – no, the names do not cease, they can never cease, and once my voice is gone there will be another. Some day. To guard what would otherwise be for ever lost. For you, Forkrul Assail, I have held back on one final name – the one to gather up your own life and carry it into the darkness.

This is the name of your god, Forkrul Assail. You thought it a name forgotten.

But I remember. I remember them all.

Blinded, deafened by some unknown roar, feeling the last of his soul ripping free, Brys Beddict smiled and spoke then the last name. The name of the slain god of the Forkrul Assail.

He heard the Pure's shriek as the power of the name reached out, clutched him tight. For this one god, alone among them all, did not come bereft of its people. This god flowed into the soul of its own child.

It does not do, to abandon one's own gods, for when they return, so unexpected, they are most vengeful.

The current pulled him from the silts, drove him forward into a darkness so complete, so absolute, that he knew it to be the Abyss itself.

I have saved my people, my dear soldiers – let them fight on. Let them take breaths, in owning and in release, in all the measures of living. I have done as a prince should do – Tehol, be proud of me. Aranict, do not curse me.

The sorrow of the ages closed around him. This was one river from which there could be no escape. *Do not grieve. We all must come to this place.*

My friends, it is time to leave—

Impossibly, he felt hands close from behind, hard as iron over his shoulders. And a harsh voice hissed in his ear. 'Not so fast.'

Faint stood close to Aranict. The Atri-Ceda was standing, head bowed, her arms out-thrust – but her hands and forearms had vanished inside a billowing, grey-brown cloud, and water was streaming down from her elbows. The air around her was rank, thick with the decay of tidal flats.

Faint could see the veins standing out on Aranict's taut neck, could see the muscles of her shoulders straining. And the Atri-Ceda was slowly being pulled forward – whatever was inside that swirling cloud was seeking to drag her into its maw.

Off to one side, Precious Thimble was on her knees, shrieking without surcease.

They had seen Brys Beddict, there atop the first earthen embankment – they had seen the standing stones rise from the ground around him, pushing upward through dirt and rocks, almost black with slime and filth. They had seen the prince's armour and clothing disintegrating, and then on the man's pallid skin dark swarms – tattoos, runes – emerging only to be torn free, spinning wild around him, and then rushing across, hammering into the Forkrul Assail.

And then, as if within a whirlwind, Brys Beddict vanished inside swirling gloom that was so thick as to be impenetrable. It spread out, devouring the huge menhirs.

Aranict now began howling – she was being pulled forward – and Faint suddenly understood. *She has him. She has hold of the prince! Gods below—*

Faint staggered towards the Atri-Ceda – but something resisted with devastating pressure, bitter cold, and she was flung back, gasping, spitting out blood. On her hands and knees, she lifted her head and looked across.

Most of Aranict's arms had disappeared inside the cloud. And now Faint could make out words in the Atri-Ceda's cries.

'Mael! Damn you! Help me!'

Faint crawled over to Precious Thimble. 'Stop that screaming, witch! Look at me! No, here, look at me!'

But the eyes that fixed on Faint belonged to a mad woman. 'I can't help her! Can't you see that? She's gone too far – too deep – how is she even alive? It's impossible!' Precious Thimble pulled away, scrabbling like a crab. 'He's lost! He's for ever lost!'

Faint stared at the witch, as the words slowly sank deep. *But that's not fair. Not a love like that – no! You can't take it away – don't you dare kill it!* 'Precious! What can I do? To help? Tell me!'

'Nothing!'

Go to Hood then.

She spun round, drawing a dagger. *Mael's an Elder God – but Aranict must understand this. He cannot answer this prayer, not the way it is now. I won't stand here to see this love die. I won't.* The blade cut a glistening slash along her left arm, and then, fumbling to take the knife in her left hand, she carved deep diagonally across her right forearm. Forcing herself forward, she reached for Aranict.

Mael – take my blood in offering. Just fucking take it!

The pressure sought to rebuff her, but she pushed harder – and then she was through, floundering, unable to breathe, the cold crushing her – she saw her blood billowing out as if under water, saw it spin on currents – so much of it – she almost lost sight of Aranict.

Desperate, feeling her bones cracking, Faint pushed closer, reached out and took the Atri-Ceda into an embrace.

Mael . . . don't you dare . . . don't you dare tell me this is not enough.

Precious Thimble had stared, disbelieving, as Faint struggled to reach Aranict. Her blood was a thick billowing cloud streaming out from her, curling round to whirl into the dark cloud. There seemed to be no end to it.

Someone had taken hold of the witch – strong arms closing round her, lifting her from the ground. Twisting now, she looked up.

Amby Bole's face was almost unrecognizable. 'This is bad magic,' he said.

'Save Faint! Save her!'

But the man shook his head. 'No one can live in there.'

'Save her, Amby! For my love – save her!'

His frown deepened, his eyelids suddenly fluttering, and he met her eyes. 'What?'

'You want me? I'm yours, damn you – just save Faint!'

Bole threw her down, visage darkening. 'All the fun ended with you! I don't want you, witch! I don't ever want to see you again!'

Precious stared up at him, and then she snarled. 'I will chase you, Amby! I'll hunt you down, no matter where you go! Year after year, I will follow you, I swear it! There's nowhere you can run to – you understand me? Nowhere!'

'I hate you!'

'The only place you could hope to escape me – is *there*!' and she pointed at that billowing cloud of blood now obscuring Faint and Aranict.

Amby made an animal cry, spun and ran heavy-footed – straight into the crimson cloud.

Precious Thimble fell back. *Gods below but that man is stupid!*

'Hold on, my love,' whispered a voice close to Faint's ear. '*Some laws even an Elder God cannot easily defy. But he's trying.*'

Faint felt the life leaving her. She was lying against the legs of Aranict – she could feel them cold as bars of ice. Were her eyes open? All she could see was the redness of her own blood. 'Sweetest, is that you?'

'*Always knew you had a romantic streak. What a thing to do!*'

'I'm dying.'

'*Looks like it. Regretting your moment of madness?*'

Faint shook her head – or tried to. 'Only if it fails.'

'*Well, how often do we regret successes?*'

'Is it enough, Sweetie? It's all I have.'

'*You're in water, fool, of course it looks like a lot – and if you stay in here any longer you'll bleed out for sure. Now, wish I could help you – wish I could help both of you, but I'm just a ghost. Well, not even that. Could be I'm just a voice in your head, Faint, born out of some bizarre misguided guilt.*'

'Oh, thanks for that.'

A foot slammed into the side of her head, half stunning her, and she struggled feebly as hands groped across her body, briefly closing on one of her tits before moving on – and then back again for a second squeeze.

Abruptly someone was lifting her from the muddy silts, throwing her over one bony shoulder. She felt one hand clutch and then leave her thigh, felt the fingers brush her knee as the arm reached out.

A deep grunt seemed to thrum through Faint, and she felt the stranger's feet slip suddenly, as if pulled by some inexorable pressure – and then the heels planted firm, and – impossibly – she felt him heave back against the current. One step, and then another. Another . . .

Amby Bole reappeared from the crimson cloud, Faint hanging limp over one shoulder. His other arm was stretched back behind him, and Precious saw him strain, saw him leaning hard, and then out from the cloud emerged Aranict, held by the back of her collar, and after her – the naked form of Brys Beddict.

The cloud erupted, burst apart in a welter of icy water.

The four figures fell to the ground, Faint rolling out almost to the witch's knees. Precious Thimble stared down, saw the blood still pumping from the woman's slashed arms. She closed trembling hands on both wrists, healing spells tumbling out on her breath.

Soldiers were rushing up. Shouts filled the air.

Precious Thimble's hands tightened on the wounds, but now there were only scars beneath her palms, and she could feel Faint's pulse. *But . . . gods, it's there – I can feel it. It's . . . faint.* A sudden giggle escaped her – but that was just relief. She'd always hated puns. Proper women did. She scowled down at the scars. *Hold on, where did I get* that *power?* Looking up, she saw Amby Bole lying motionless on the muddy ground. Beyond him soldiers crowded round Aranict, who knelt with her prince, cradling his head on her lap.

And then Precious Thimble caught a glimpse of motion from one of Brys's hands, out from under the cloak someone had thrown over him.

I can't believe it.

Faint stirred, groaned, eyes opening, stared unseeing for a moment, and then focused on the witch. She slowly frowned. 'I'm not dead?'

'No. I've just healed you. The Atri-Ceda made it out, too. So did the prince. Your blood bought passage – though how that watery piss you call blood ever passed muster in the eyes of an Elder God, I'll never know.'

'What – but how? Who saved us? Who dragged us free?'

Sudden coughing from where Amby Bole lay sprawled.

Precious Thimble shook her head. 'The only one who could, Faint, some idiot from Blackdog Swamp.'

The dozen menhirs erupting from the earthworks around Prince Brys Beddict had ruptured the embankment for sixty paces, driving fighting soldiers from their feet – bodies tumbling into the trenches even as enormous mounds of earth and stones poured down, burying scores alive.

The Ve'Gath beneath Grub elected to escape the chaos by leaping forward, across the entire trench, and landed close to where the Forkrul Assail stood. The K'Chain Che'Malle had shattered its halberd some time earlier, and now wielded a double-bladed axe in one hand and a falchion in the other.

The Forkrul Assail stood with his face stretched as if in agony, tilted back, the eyes shut and the mouth stretched wide open. When the Ve'Gath advanced, he gave no sign of awareness. Two swift thumping strides and the falchion swung down, taking the motionless Pure between his right shoulder and neck. The blade tore down through the chest, ripped free in a spray of bone shards.

The other Ve'Gath had followed its kin and now came in from the left. An instant after the first Ve'Gath's attack, its heavy single-bladed axe slammed into the side of the Assail's head in an explosion of skull fragments and gore.

The Forkrul Assail collapsed in red ruin.

Even as Grub struggled to wheel the beast round, two heavy quarrels hissed across – between him and the Ve'Gath's head – and punched into the side of the other Ve'Gath. The impact staggered the giant reptile, and then it fell over, hind legs scything the air.

'Back! Back across!'

The K'Chain Che'Malle burst into motion, sprinting down the length of the berm – fifteen, twenty paces, and then wheeling to plunge down amidst crowds of Kolansii in the first trench. Weapons hammered down, slashed and chopped a carnage-strewn path through to the other side.

Pike blades glanced across the armour encasing Grub's legs and girdling his hips – and then they were clawing up the other side, winning free atop what remained of the first bank.

Grub looked round for the prince – for any officer – but the chaos reigned on all sides.

Had Brys fallen? There was no way of knowing.

But Grub now saw Letherii soldiers lifting their heads, saw them tracking his thumping trek across the front of the warring forces – watching the Ve'Gath clear attackers from its path with devastating sweeps of its bladed weapons.

They're looking to me.

But I know nothing.

Fool! Nothing but a life of war! Look well – decide what must be done! Twisting in the saddle, he scanned the climbing slope to his left, squinted at the succession of fortified tiers – and saw soldiers streaming from the highest positions.

But between them and the Letherii . . . *four trenches. No, this is impossible. We've lost a third of the army against this first trench alone!*

Grub faced the Letherii ranks once more. 'Withdraw!' he shouted. 'By the prince's command, withdraw!'

And he saw, all along the front, the Letherii soldiers disengaging, shields up as they backed away, others dragging wounded comrades with them.

Another quarrel hissed past – too close. Cursing, Grub kicked at the sides of the Ve'Gath. 'Down from the ridge – along the front – put those weapons away and find us some shields! Better yet, pick up some of the wounded – as many as you can carry!'

The beast skidded down the slope, righted itself and, staying low beneath the cover of the first berm, began picking its way through heaps of bodies.

Grub stared down at the terrible carnage. *I remember on the wall and that man and all the ones who fell around him – he fought and fought, until they overcame him, brought him down, and then there was a cross and he was nailed to it and the crows spun and screamed and fell from the sky.*

I remember the old man on his horse, reaching down to collect me up – and the way he wheeled outside the gate, to stare back – as if he could see all the way we'd come – the bloody road where I was born, where I came alive.

I remember that world. I remember no other.

All of the brave soldiers, I am yours. I was always yours.

The Kolansii counter-attack from troops stationed in the next two trenches met the advance of Saphii and Evertine legionnaires in an avalanche of iron fury. Rolling down with the slope, along the wide descent tracks or up and over the berms, they slammed into the Bolkando forces like a storm of studded fists. For all the wild fury of the Saphii, they were not sufficiently armoured against heavy infantry, and the Evertine soldiers were unable to close a solid shieldwall with the Saphii in their midst.

The first lines were overwhelmed, driven underfoot, and the entire Bolkando front reeled back, yielding once more the second berm and then the first trench, and, finally, the first bank of earthworks. With the enemy gaining momentum, the legion was pushed back still further.

Almost none of the Saphii remained by this time, and as the Kolansii rolled out on to level ground they rushed across, only to collide with the legionnaires. They met a solid shieldwall. The impact sent bodies and weapons into the air and the crush made both sides recoil, before closing once more in savage fighting.

Queen Abrastal, still mounted, her sword and forearm painted with blood, forced her charger away from the inside edge of the Evertine line – the animal's muzzle was gushing blood from a frenzied bite against a visored face and its hind flanks were slashed through the cladding, spattering blood with every muscle surge. But she could feel the pounding of its heart and she knew that her horse had never felt more alive than at this moment – it was impossible for her not to grin at the terrible joy in the beast she rode. Impossible to not find herself sharing it.

Still, they'd arrived upon the crux – and looking to the west, she saw the Letherii forces withdrawing from the assault, though their onager salvos continued unabated.

The Pure had done as she had expected – seeking to break her hold here, forcing the Letherii away from any hope of marching to the Spire by blocking the valley – but only if they could succeed in turning the Evertine Legion.

She rode hard round to the back of her legion.

Still held in reserve, the Barghast ranks were readying weapons, and Abrastal caught sight of Warchief Spax, standing atop a small hill of bundled supplies and straining to see over the Evertine ranks to the front of the battle. She saw him turn to her upon hearing her horse's drumming hoofbeats.

She reined in before him.

'I've never swum in a sea of blood before, Firehair. How was it?'

The queen glanced down to see herself lathered in gore. She shook her sword clear. 'How fast were those Perish moving?' she asked.

'A good clip – almost as quickly as a band of White Faces on the raid. If they have anything left after tackling the valley side, they should be almost in position – but Highness, you've seen how many are headed their way.' He shook his head.

'Can they even slow them down?'

The Warchief shrugged. 'Depends on the lay of the land, I suppose. If it's a broad front they need to hold . . . no, they'll barely slow 'em.'

Abrastal cursed under her breath as she swung her mount round. Thought furiously for a moment, and then nodded. 'Very well. Warchief, take your warriors and the Teblor and move with all haste to support the Perish – whatever you can manage, understood?'

'You send us to our deaths, Highness.'

'Aye.' She bared her teeth at him. 'I show you my coin. You show me your love.'

'I wasn't complaining, just saying.'

'We will screen you here.'

'Highness, you can't hold against this counter-attack – we can see that.'

'We will screen you for as long as is needed,' Abrastal said firmly. 'Now get going, Warchief.'

'If we do not meet again, Firehair, I should tell you' – and Spax leapt down from the mound of supplies – 'I went and knocked up your daughter.'

'Gods below!'

'You'll have years of doting on that little runt – you'll know it for mine 'cause it's got my eyes.'

'Just get going for Errant's sake!'

Laughing, Spax raised his axe and waved it in a circle over his head.

As one, the White Faces lunged into motion – eastward.

Impressed in spite of herself, Abrastal watched in silence for a moment.

Spax was following her gaze. 'Aye, we live for this, Firehair. We'll give a good account of ourselves, I promise you.' He looked up at her. 'Sing songs about us, and remember to tell your court poets, that's Gilk with one k.'

She frowned down at him. 'How else would it be, you fool?'

'Fare you well, my queen,' Spax said, bowing even as he turned away.

When he'd trotted a dozen paces Abrastal called out, 'Spax!'

The Warchief glanced back.

'Boy or girl, I'll make sure it's named after you – but that's the only favour you'll get!'

Smiling, the Barghast waved his weapon, and then was on his way again.

She watched the Teblor falling in alongside the mass of White Faces, and then she swung round to study her legion.

Sure enough, they were being driven back – these Kolansii heavies were anything but soft. Abrastal adjusted her grip on the sword in her hand, collected the reins once more. *Let us make them remember us.*

She was about to kick her horse forward when a rider thundered up on her left. 'Highness!'

Abrastal stared. A damned Letherii! 'That was a long ride – what news?'

The messenger – a Bluerose Lancer – saluted. 'Felicitations from the prince, Highness—'

'Felicitations? Gods take me – sorry, go on.'

'Highness, the Pure Forkrul Assail is dead. Only mixed-blood Assail remain in command. The prince hereby informs you that he has disengaged his forces from the Kolansii positions. And that he has established dug-in defences along the onager line on the valley floor and will commit a third of his remaining forces there—'

'Excuse me, a third?'

The Letherii nodded. 'Prince begs to inform you, Highness, that he is on his way to your position.'

Abrastal looked round, and then cursed. 'Take a moment to rest your horse, sir, and then ride with all haste back to Prince Brys. Inform him he'd better hurry.'

But the messenger wasn't interested in resting, and he wheeled his weary horse round and set out at the gallop.

Damn but those lancers know how to ride. And damn me, young man – if we both survive this, I'm going to give you a ride you'll never forget.

Abrastal sighed, and then shook herself. With a low growl, she kicked her horse forward. 'My standard to the front! Get on with you – follow your damned queen!'

Someone had found clothing and armour for the prince. With Aranict close by his side, he stood on the high ground and watched his troops swarming to entrench all along the line of onagers. Lines of soldiers were moving the wounded back on stretchers, while still others retrieved serviceable weapons from the field. And overseeing it all, a young man riding a K'Chain Che'Malle.

Brys was still struggling to regain himself – he did not know how Aranict had managed to save him, or how she even survived her descent into that lifeless warren. While still only half conscious he had heard fragments of conversation, and it seemed that the three foreigners, Faint, Precious Thimble and Amby Bole, had all had a hand in his resurrection. And then he'd caught the name *Mael*.

Old man, we owe you so much. Why are we Beddicts so important to you? But . . . it wasn't me you did this for, was it? It was for Tehol. Your chosen mortal, the one you would have wanted as your own son.

Rest assured, I'm not complaining.

Someone brought him a helm and he took it with a grateful nod. Tugged it on and fastened the clasp.

An officer crowded close. 'Sir, we have found you a horse – it would do the troops good to see you again as soon as possible.'

Brys shook his head. 'Our Malazan guest has things well in hand, Lieutenant.'

'He has issued orders in the prince's name, sir!'

'A clever thing to do, under the circumstances. He may be young, but he does command a presence on the back of that lizard. From this moment forward, he is to be considered my second – make this clear to all the other officers.'

'Yes sir.'

Brys glanced over to see that a horse had been brought forward.

Aranict spoke, 'Still, beloved, it would be good for them to see you.'

'I am tempted to place Grub in command of our relieving force,' he replied. When she stepped closer he held up a hand. 'I am *not* recovered – I feel as likely to fall off that horse as stay on it. Oh, I'll mount up, and as long as the beast isn't moving under me, why, I should cut a strikingly inspiring figure.' He shot a look up at the imperial standard and winced. 'So long as no one looks too carefully.' He reached out and took hold of her hand. 'Aranict . . . I am glad you fought for me.'

'It was Mael,' she said. 'And Faint's blood. And then, if not for Amby Bole, we still would have failed.'

'Will you think less of me if I choose to remain here, commanding these defences?'

'Brys, if I had to, I'd have tied you down to keep you here. Close to me. We're not saving you just to see you fall to some errant arrow – no, you stay back, issue orders and leave the rest to everyone else.'

He smiled. 'You have begun to show a stubborn side, Atri-Ceda.'

'Idiot.' She lit a stick of rustleaf. 'The only thing just begun is you noticing it – but that's what makes the first flush of love so dangerous, and once it fades and you start seeing clearly again, why, it's too late.'

Still smiling, he took the reins and set a foot in the stirrup, pulling himself up to slump in the saddle with a low groan.

From all sides voices rose upon seeing him. Grimacing, Brys straightened, and then raised one gauntleted hand. The roar redoubled in its intensity.

He saw Grub riding up the slope towards him. The boy didn't look much like a boy any longer. He was splashed with drying blood, and from somewhere he'd found a Bluerose lance, and its iron point had swum in blood not long past.

'Prince Brys – I didn't know you— I mean—'

'There is little time to waste,' Brys cut in. 'I am placing you in command of the relief force. They're almost assembled – in fact' – he squinted eastward – 'they can shake themselves out on the march – the Bolkando are losing ground. Lead them, Commander, and be quick about it.'

Grub saluted. 'Sir, when we close, I may ride ahead.'

'Would any of us expect otherwise?' Brys asked. 'Just don't get yourself killed.'

Nodding, the Malazan youth kicked at the flanks of the Ve'Gath, and the huge beast wheeled round and set off.

Faint studied the defenders opposite, watching as they regrouped, drawing reinforcements down from the higher earthworks. 'They're going to break cover,' she muttered. 'They're going to charge us.'

Precious Thimble glanced over. 'What? Why would they do that?'

'Because most of us are headed east, down the valley – they can't let us chase after their own relieving force. They need to wipe out both the Letherii and the Bolkando.'

The witch's gaze was darting back and forth along the hasty defences thrown up by the Letherii. 'We're badly outnumbered.'

'Haven't you been paying attention? Assaulting costs dear – we're about to turn the tables on them, and they're not going to like it.'

'It's only the mixed-bloods who're keeping them fighting at all,' Precious said under her breath.

'What? What did you say?'

'It's the mixed-bloods, feeding off this cursed warren – using it to bend the Kolansii to their will. I doubt they'd fight this hard without it.'

'Now you say all this!' Faint looked about, saw the prince sitting on a horse twenty paces away, his back to them as he observed the departing

747

companies. Stepping forward, Faint stumbled slightly, recovered. But her head was spinning. 'What's wrong with me?'

'Blood loss,' snapped Precious Thimble.

Hissing in frustration, Faint made her way – slowly – towards Brys Beddict. *Find the damned mixed-bloods. Aim a few onagers at them. Tear them to pieces. And this battle is done.* 'Prince Brys!'

The man turned his head.

Faint hobbled forward. 'A word with you, Highness . . .'

Ascending a valley side at the run and in full armour left the Perish staggering once they'd reached the top. Heart hammering in the cage of his chest, Syndecan pulled clear of the others and then halted, studying the lay of the land.

Shit. It's all shit.

Forty paces away was a raised road, running parallel with the valley, its steep side facing them banked with water-worn stones. In between was a strip of furrowed field, left fallow for two years or more. Off to the right, a hundred paces along, rose a cluster of buildings – farmstead facing on to the field, public stables and inn facing the road.

Syndecan continued on, bleakly eyeing the sharp slope of the roadside. Reaching it, he sheathed his sword and scrambled his way to the top.

Beyond the road the unplanted fields stretched on for at least a third of a league, broken up by walled hedgerows forming a chaotic patchwork. 'Now that's better,' he grunted. No army would be happy crossing that – the walls alone would slow them up, since they were as high as a man was tall. The Perish could break up into half-cohorts and contest one after another, and by the time the Kolansii won through the battle at the Spire would be long over.

Still leaves the road and this side, though. Narrow enough, but where do I weight my defence? Road or field? And what about this infernal stony bank? Can't defend it worth a damn. That said, trying to breach along it would be a nightmare – until they won through. So I throw a cohort five steps back of the line, waiting for them. We bottle them up, don't let them spill out to the sides. It'll work. It'll have to.

Hands on his hips, he turned round, looked down on his Grey Helms. Winded, most of them bent over, or on one knee, gulping air like beached carp. He pointed at the buildings. 'Wounded go there. Cutters on your way – set up fast as you can. Rest of you, drink down the last of your water if you haven't already. Chew on some food while you're at it. We're going to hold on the road and this side of it – mostly. I want two cohorts on the other side in case they send anyone that way. If they do, make them pay, brothers and sisters. Now, march to twenty paces from the buildings and form up there.'

Not a single groan as the Perish picked themselves up again and set off along the rippled, weed-knotted field.

Swinging round, Syndecan looked up the road.

Was that a glitter of pike points?

He glared back at his Grey Helms. 'Step lively! Enemy sighted on the road!' *Wolves preserve us this day.*

High Watered Festian gestured, watched as the columns plunged down off the road on the inland side, breaking up as they entered the hedge-row fields. He saw crews rushing ahead with picks to ensure that the passage gates through the walls were serviceable.

Seven hundred paces up the road he could see the cursed Perish – but they had fully discounted the enclosed fields.

Festian intended to lock fiercely with the Grey Helms, pushing forward with the weight of fifteen thousand Kolansii heavy infantry, and then send eight thousand through the enclosures, to take the road behind them. They would first crush the defenders on the road itself, and then drive the rest south across the field, to the very edge of the valley – where the only retreat was a deadly tumble down the steep valley side.

He intended to make quick work of this.

In the distance to the east, he could make out the top third of the Spire. Everything below that, on the ridged ascent of the isthmus, was obscured in clouds of dust or smoke. The sight chilled him.

And now Brother Diligence is dead. Slain by some foul trap of sorcery. It all falls to you, Sister Reverence. But we shall prevail. Justice is a sword without equal. I pray to you, Sister, hold on. We are coming.

Gillimada slowed her pace to match that of the Warchief, and he glared up at the huge woman as he struggled for breath.

'I sent a scout up to the road – there are soldiers on it.'

Spax nodded but could manage little more. He couldn't remember the last time he'd led a raid, and while his warriors were thumping along in his wake with all the infernal ease of youth, his own legs were cramping, there was a stitch in his side, and sweat was stinging the vicious bite Abrastal's daughter had delivered to his penis the night before. That she'd been trying to tear it off with her own teeth was only because of her frustration and anger at getting pregnant – nothing to do with him, really – and it was just his bad luck that his champion was the nearest thing at hand on which to vent all her anger and whatnot.

'We could attack,' suggested the Teblor in her stentorian voice. 'A surprise!'

'Can – can we overtake 'em?'

'Teblor can – but not you. They are using the road. There is a road up there. My scout saw it and there were soldiers on it. Running.'

'Did your scout – did your scout see – the Perish?'

'No. Kolansii soldiers! On the road. Running!'

Oh, my cursed gods of the Barghast, am I wallowing in the muck with you? Feels like it! With some brainless backwoods harridan for company too! 'Felled any trees lately, woman?'

'What? No trees anywhere! I'd hit my head if there were trees. I'm glad there are no trees!' And she bellowed a laugh, only to then shake her head. 'Your language – it is so clumsy!' She drew a sudden deep breath and out from her came a smooth flow of sounds Spax had not imagined possible from this Teblor.

'What was that?' he demanded when she'd finished.

'I make up poem songs in my own language. I am famous for it, hah hah!'

'Care to translate what you just said?'

'No. Useless. You have one word for one thought. We have many thoughts for one word! You all speak too slow and we have to slow down too and we get bored talking to you humans!'

Gasping, Spax shook his head. 'Right now – no more words from me – at all!'

'I should carry you?'

Oh, and watch me try and live that down – in front of all my warriors? They'd die laughing, never mind enemy pikes and swords! 'Don't even touch me!' he growled.

'Hah hah hah!'

The Kolansii wasted little time, pouring down from the road to form up opposite the Perish on the field, and then, once the shields were locked and swords drawn, they advanced, matching step by step the troops remaining on the road.

Syndecan stood one row back from the front line. Much as he wanted to be with his fellow cutters amongst the buildings, he was now commanding and his place was here, with his brothers and sisters.

They were still winded, their legs sagging under them – he knew the signs of muscle exhaustion and there was no time to fully recover. *This is going to be unpleasant.*

The Kolansii closed to within six paces and then charged.

Gillimada dropped back again. 'There is fighting!'

'For Hood's sake, Teblor – we may be slow but we're not deaf!'

'Should we join them from here?'

'Not unless you want to fight on the damned slope! No, we'll move

750

past the whole mess and come up behind the Perish, and then move forward.'

'But I want to kill the mixed-blood!'

'Maybe you'll get a chance at that—'

'No! I want to kill him right away! It's important!'

'Fine! You can lead a counter-attack once we're up there, all right?'

Gillimada smiled broadly, her teeth even and white as snow. 'And we will cut down every tree we see!'

He glared at her back as she loped ahead. His heart felt ready to burst and he wondered if it might, the moment he stepped up to fight – a sudden clenching in his chest, or whatever happened when the thing seized up. He was certain that it'd hurt. Probably a lot.

Glancing upslope to his left, he saw rising dust, and there – the flash of spears or perhaps pikes, or even swords. Ahead, the Teblor raised a shout – and Spax squinted to see bodies sliding down the slope, limbs flailing, weapons skirling away.

'Go past! Go past!'

His warriors were pressing up behind him. Spax snarled. 'Go round me then, damn you all! I'll catch up!' They poured past on either side in a clatter of armour and drawn weapons.

My beloved fools, all of you.

Forty more heaving paces, another ten, five, and then, looking up, he saw his Barghast scrambling in the wake of the Teblor, up the valley side, many of them using their hands where they could. And above them the Perish falling back, spinning away from blows, tumbling and skidding down into the midst of the climbing warriors.

Gods curse us all!

'Climb! Get up there!'

He saw the Teblor reach the summit, saw them plunge forward and out of sight, weapons swinging. And then, behind them, the first of the Gilk, armour grey with dust, their white faces running with stained sweat.

Spax reached the base, clambered upward. His legs were half numb under him. Blisters roared with pain on his ankles, his heels. He coughed out dust, was almost knocked over by a descending corpse – a Perish, most of his face cut away – and struggled yet higher.

Is there no end to this damned hillside?

And then a hand reached down, took hold of his wrist, and Spax was dragged on to level ground.

They were in the midst of farm buildings, and the Kolansii were on all sides, sweeping down from the road, driving the buckling clumps of Perish back towards the valley edge.

His first sight of this told him that the Grey Helms had been flanked, and though they fought on, with a ferocity worthy of their gods, they

751

were dying by the score. His Gilk had slammed into this press, but even as they did so more Kolansii surged forward, fully encircling the defenders – with the valley side the only possible retreat.

Dark fury raged in Spax as he staggered forward, readying his weapons. *We failed, Firehair. May all the swamp gods rot in Hood's own bog! We should have set out earlier – we should have marched with the Perish!*

The Teblor had formed a solid square and were pushing through the enemy, but even they were not enough.

On the road, Spax could see massive elements of the Kolansii army simply driving forward, eastward, ignoring the vicious last stand on their right.

We didn't even slow them down.

'Withdraw! Barghast! Perish! Teblor! Withdraw – down the hillside! Back down the hillside!'

Seeing warrior and soldier stumbling back, seeing them twist and pour down from the summit, the Warchief's heart felt cold, buried in ashes. *Gesler, 'ware your flank. We couldn't hold them. We just couldn't.*

The press of retreating warriors, bloodied and desperate, gathered him up and they all slid ragged paths back down the slope. He was pulled along unresisting. *All this way – for this? We could have done more.* But he knew that any stand would have been doomed – there were just too many Kolansii, and they fought with demonic valour.

He had lost both his weapons on the descent, and his soul howled at the appropriateness of that. Tilting his head back, he stared up at the sun.

It was barely noon.

In the depths of night rain was pouring down in Darujhistan. Karsa Orlong had walked into the city, and now he stood, water streaming from him, waiting. Opposite him was the temple, and the vow that he had made so long ago now, in the savage intensity of youth, was a heat in his flesh, so fierce that he thought he could see steam rising from his limbs.

Almost time.

He'd seen no one else in the street since dusk, and during the day, while he had stood in place, the people of this city had swept past, unwilling to fix eyes upon him for very long. A troop of city guards had lingered for a time, nervous, half circling his position where he had stood, his huge stone sword resting point down, his hands wrapped about its leather-bound grip. Then they had simply moved on.

He would have been irritated at having to kill them, and no doubt there would have been alarms, and yet more guards, and more killing.

752

But, rather than being heaped with the dead, the cobbled width of the street before him remained unobstructed.

Eyes half closed, he experienced again the echo of the life he had watched seething back and forth in the day now gone. He wondered at all those lives, the way few would meet the gazes of their fellows, as if crowds demanded wilful anonymity, when the truth was they were all in it together – all these people, facing much the same struggles, the same fears. And yet, it seemed, each one was determined to survive them alone, or with but a few kin and friends offering paltry allegiance. Perhaps they each believed themselves unique, like a knot-stone in the centre of the world's mill wheel, but the truth was there were very few who could truly make claim to such a pivotal existence.

After all, there was only one Karsa Orlong. Standing here across from a modest temple with stained walls and faded friezes, standing here with the fate of the world in his hands.

He had known a time in chains. He had lived in that wretched house, his hands closed into fists against the slavery in which so many insisted he reside – meek, uncomplaining, accepting of his fate. He thought back to the citizens he'd seen here. So many had been dragging chains. So many had walked bowed and twisted by their weight. So many had with their own hands hammered tight the shackles, believing that this was how it was supposed to be. Sweating at another person's behest, the muscles and will given away and now owned by someone claiming to be their better in all things. Year after year, a lifetime of enslavement.

This was the conversation of the civilized, and it repulsed Karsa Orlong to the very core of his being.

Who was the slavemaster? Nothing but a host of cruel ideas. Nothing but a deceitful argument. A sleight of hand deception between things of value, where one wins and the other always loses. He had heard bartering, had witnessed bargains made, and it all had the illusion of fairness, and it all played out as if it was a ritual deemed necessary, made iron like a natural law.

But where was the joy in that ceaseless struggle? Where was the proper indolence of the predator, and just how many fangs needed pulling to make this precious civilization?

Of course, not everyone suffered the same emasculation, and this was where all the lies finally gathered. The hungriest maws, fangs dripping, hid in the cool upper rooms of the estates, in the fountained gardens of the rich – and these ones, oh, they indulged all the indolence they desired. While the crowds of their lessers looked on, wide-eyed and ever eager for details.

A broken and suffering god in chains had haunted him. It had flung weapons in his path. It had whispered all manner of enticements. It had, in all its desperate pain, rushed down a thousand tracks, only to find not a moment of blessed relief.

Karsa now understood that god. The times that he had been chained, he had felt that terrible panic, that animal frenzy to escape. No mortal, human or Toblakai, should ever feel such feelings. Nor, he knew now, should a god.

'He cannot know compassion, from whom compassion has been taken. He cannot know love, with love denied him. But he will know pain, when pain is all that is given him.'

Compassion. Love. It was not civilization that birthed these gentle gifts – though its followers might claim otherwise. Nor was civilization the sweetest garden for such things to blossom in – though those trapped within it might imagine it so. No, as far as he could see, civilization was a madman's mechanism that, for all its good intentions, ended up ensnaring the gentle gifts, stifling them, leaving them to wander mazes only to die alone and in the dark.

A mechanism, a cagework, and in its chaos the slaves bred like flies – until the world itself groaned under the assault of their appetites.

'You have made many vows, Karsa Orlong.'

A civilization was the means by which too many people could live together despite their mutual hatred. And those moments where love and community burgeoned forth, the cynics descended like vultures eager to feed, and the skies soured, and the moment died away.

'Upon my heart, Karsa Orlong. Do you hear me? Upon my heart!'

Blinking, Karsa looked down to see a crippled man drawn up against his feet. The rain streamed around him, gushed and swirled, and the face that had twisted up to look at him seemed to be shedding from blinded eyes the tears of the world.

'Is it time then?' Karsa demanded.

'Will you kill it all?'

The Toblakai showed his teeth. 'If I can.'

'It will simply grow up again, like a weed from the ashes. For all that we are made to kneel, Karsa Orlong, we yearn to fly.'

'Yes, rare and noble and precious as pigeons. I've seen the statues of old heroes in the square, old man. I've seen their crowns of bird-shit.'

'I – I was an artist once. These hands – so deformed now, so bent and frozen – can you understand? All this talent, but no way to release it, no way to give it shape. But perhaps we are all like that, and only the lucky few are able to find talent's path unbarred.'

'I doubt it,' Karsa replied.

Thunder rumbled from beyond the lake.

The crippled man coughed. 'I am drowning. I have enjoyed our conversation on the merits of the civilized, Karsa Orlong, but now

I must surrender. I must die. Sick. Fevered. The needs burn too hot. I have given you the words you shall use. Upon my heart. Upon my heart.'

Karsa stared at the wretched shape at his feet. He set his sword to lean against the wall behind him, and then crouched down.

The crippled man's face lifted, the sightless eyes white as polished coins. 'What are you doing?'

Karsa reached down, gathered the skeletal figure into his arms, and then settled back. 'I stepped over corpses on the way here,' the Toblakai said. 'People no one cared about, dying alone. In my barbaric village this would never happen, but here in this city, this civilized jewel, it happens all the time.'

The ravaged face was turned upward, the last of the raindrops dripping away as he huddled beneath the cover Karsa provided. The mouth worked, but no sounds came forth.

'What is your name?' Karsa asked.

'Munug.'

'Munug. This night – before I must rise and walk into the temple – I am a village. And you are here, in my arms. You will not die uncared for.'

'You – you would do this for me? A stranger?'

'In my village no one is a stranger – and this is what civilization has turned its back on. One day, Munug, I will make a world of villages, and the age of cities will be over. And slavery will be dead, and there shall be no chains – tell your god. Tonight, I am his knight.'

Munug's shivering was fading. The old man smiled. 'He knows.'

It wasn't too much, to take a frail figure into one's arms for those last moments of life. Better than a cot, or even a bed in a room filled with loved ones. Better, too, than an empty street in the cold rain. To die in someone's arms – could there be anything more forgiving?

Every savage barbarian in the world knew the truth of this.

Behind their massive shields the Ve'Gath soldiers of the K'Chain Che'Malle advanced into a hailstorm of arrows and heavy quarrels. Impacts staggered some of them, quarrels shattering against the shields. Others reeled, heads, necks and chests sprouting shafts, and as they fell their kin moved up to take their places, and the reptilian assault drew ever closer to the trenches and redoubts.

In the centre of the advance, the T'lan Imass weathered a similar deluge of missile fire, but they held no shields, and where the oversized quarrels struck the bodies shattered, bones exploding into shards and splinters. Those that could then picked themselves back up and continued on. But many were too broken to rise again, lying amid the wreckage of their own bones.

The withering fusillade lashed into the attacking forces again and again. Scores of Ve'Gath went down, legs kicking, tails whipping or striking the ground. Deep gaps opened in the T'lan Imass lines. Yet there were no screams, no terrible cries of agony or horror.

Sister Reverence stood high above the battle, winds both hot and bitter cold whipping about her, and watched as the enemy forces pushed ever closer to her soldiers waiting in their trenches and raised redoubts. The sorcery of Akhrast Korvalain streaming from her, she held fast her Kolansii heavy infantry, leaving no room for fear, and she could feel them bristling as she fed them her hunger. *Do not yield. Slay them all! Do not yield!* They would hold – they had to – and then High Watered Festian would arrive, to strike at the K'Chain flank, driving deep a mortal wound against these hated enemies of old.

She swore under her breath upon seeing masses of K'ell Hunters break out along the high rock-studded sides, rushing the fortified onager positions – and she watched as the crews frantically swung the heavy weapons round. They managed a single salvo, the scores of quarrels tearing into the ranks of Hunters, before the rest reached the base of the hill and swarmed upward, their terrible swords lifting high.

As the helpless crews were slaughtered, their machines smashed into splinters, Sister Reverence dismissed the scene from her mind. She had seen ten or more K'ell Hunters go down, and if each fortlet could match or better that toll, then she was satisfied. She would rely on attrition – there was no other choice.

Now that the battle was under way, her panic had subsided, though the murder of Brother Diligence still sent trembling waves of shock through her. She remained uncertain as to the manner of his death, and that still disturbed her; if she gave her dread free rein, she knew her fear would return. Humans were duplicitous and brazen – they should have known better than to underestimate their treacherous, deceitful natures. His power had been turned back upon him. Somehow. He had drowned in a deluge of words, and she could not comprehend how that was even possible.

But in this battle below she could see but *two* humans. *Riding Ve'Gath, by the Abyss. Do they command? No, that cannot be. The K'Chain Che'Malle would never yield to human rule. They are ever commanded by their Matron and none other. It has always been so and so it remains.*

A formidable Matron, however, to have spawned so many Ve'Gath. She stays hidden. She evades my questing. That alone speaks of impressive power.

But when this is done, when her army is destroyed, I will find her. I will eviscerate her. This day is the last gasp of the K'Chain Che'Malle.

There are no other Matrons left – I am certain of it. They must have discovered the alliance I made with the Nah'ruk, and so they have come here, seeking vengeance.

Am I a child with a hand to be slapped?

Of the four ancient races, who was always the most feared, if not the Forkrul Assail?

She knew there were other Pures, on distant continents. And, once Akhrast Korvalain's power was made unassailable in this place, she would quest to find them. She would invite them to share in this power, and the cleansing could begin in earnest. *We shall unleash such justice as to—*

A frigid blast of air swept up around her and Sister Reverence turned from the battle below. Facing into that icy wind, she made her way across the platform to the side looking out over the sea.

What she saw stunned her.

Kolanse Bay was filling with ice. Mountains, glowing emerald and sapphire, were rising up from the depths, and as she stared she saw the churning water bleach white, saw every wave freeze solid. The Perish ships, which had been broken and smashed and swallowed by the sea, had now reappeared, the wreckage sealed in ice – and there were more ships, ones long buried in the silts of the sea bottom, heaving to the surface. Directly below, the sheltered Kolansii galleys and triremes, now locked in ice, began to shatter, hulls collapsing. The sound of that destruction, rising up to where she stood, was a chorus of detonations, as of trees battered down by winds.

The entire bay was now solid ice, the surface a crazed landscape of jagged translucent crags, welling fissures, and flat sweeps of dirty snow. Mists poured from it in roiling clouds.

And, with the voice of grinding mountains, it had begun lifting higher, tilting, the nearest end reaching upwards. The mole and break-waters of the harbour directly below were suddenly obliterated, torn and crushed to rubble – and as the ice shifted, reaching the base of the Spire, Sister Reverence felt the stone tremble beneath her feet.

This cannot be!

Omtose Phellack – what Jaghut dares this? No! They are gone! Extinct – there is not one Jaghut left with this kind of power – we would have found the threat, we would have destroyed it!

Sister Reverence staggered back from the precipice as she felt the Spire sway under her. Hearts pounding, hips aching, she stumbled across the platform. Reaching her previous position, she glared down at the battle.

In time to see the Ve'Gath soldiers pouring up the embankment.

Rise! Kolansii – my blessed children – rise to meet them!

Fists clenched, she flung her humans into the K'Chain Che'Malle.

757

Buffeted to one side by a collapsing Ve'Gath, Gesler struggled for balance as his mount stumbled. He could see that the front line had plunged into the trench – and from higher up the tiers, hundreds of Kolansii were rushing down to support their besieged comrades.

He saw Stormy, dragging his axe upward, a cloven helm jammed on the blade. The man's face was red as his beard, a berserk rage upon him. His Ve'Gath stood atop the berm, its own weapons hammering down at the Kolansii swarming up to assail it.

Fool's going to get himself killed. He'll do it, too, just to spite me!

He commanded his Ve'Gath forward. Amidst the swirling flavours in his mind, he spoke to his K'Chain Che'Malle. 'Take this trench! Push! All of you – push!'

Off to his right he saw the T'lan Imass chopping their way through the defenders, overrunning the redoubts. Once they were able to close in hand-to-hand fighting, their battle turned into slaughter. Gesler saw Onos T'oolan – enemy weapons rebounding from him – wade forward, flint sword swinging. He seemed to be walking through a mist of blood.

Bastards are showing us up. Of course, we're all flesh and blood, and they're not. Nothing's more irritating than an unfair advantage on the field. At least they're on our side – gods, why am I even complaining?

'Push!'

The Ve'Gath advance stalled in the trench. The sheer mass of armoured bodies had blocked the huge reptilian warriors – their weapons tore through the Kolansii, but more of the enemy kept arriving. Ascending the berm, Gesler could see that the next tier of earthworks had been abandoned, all the forces pouring down to slam into the K'Chain Che'Malle. Yet beyond those entrenchments, the remaining infantry stayed in their positions. He could see high redoubts on enfilading angles, onagers loaded and waiting.

This is going to take all day.

Worse yet. We might even lose.

The T'lan Imass had taken the trench at the centre and were now seeking to broaden the breach. A salvo of heavy bolts slashed through their ranks.

'K'ell Hunters – Sag'Churok – we need you at the centre – we need those onagers destroyed! The T'lan Imass can break this wide open. Flow in behind them – Ve'Gath rear ranks, form up on the centre and advance into the breach!'

An arrow skidded off his left shoulder. Swearing, he kicked his Ve'Gath forward, down into the trench to join Stormy.

The slaughter was appalling, close and packed with heaving bodies, slashing and stabbing weapons. His Ve'Gath landed on corpses – already the trench was at but half its normal depth – and the smeared limbs and torsos slipped beneath his mount's weight until its claws dug in for purchase.

A half dozen shield-locked Kolansii held the top of the ramp directly opposite, short-handled spiked axes at the ready – they were attacking the Ve'Gath low, chopping at legs and thrusting at underbellies. *This is how the Malazans did it. Why couldn't these Kolansii be stupid?*

Howling, he drove his Ve'Gath forward.

'*We kill and we kill still more, and yet they do not break. Destriant, these soldiers are under a geas. The pure-blood Forkrul Assail commands their souls.*'

Kalyth slowly nodded. She could see that well enough – no army could withstand this kind of ceaseless slaughter. She knew that thousands of Kolansii had fallen. The battle for the first trenches had consumed almost half the morning, and now, as the sun blazed directly overhead – in the very midst of the Jade Strangers – the K'Chain Che'Malle and T'lan Imass had advanced no further than crushing the last defenders of the third entrenchment.

Only halfway through the defences.

Beside her the Matron Gunth Mach spoke in a mélange of flavours. '*My Ve'Gath are beginning to tire, Destriant. A thousand have fallen and will not rise again. And now Gu'Rull informs me that more Kolansii are on the way – upon the inland high road to the west.*'

Kalyth hugged herself. What to do, what to say? 'Then the Letherii and Bolkando have failed.'

'*No. They pursue, but they are much reduced and exhausted – they will not arrive in time to assist us. Destriant, it is difficult to reach the Shield Anvil and the Mortal Sword. They are in battle frenzy – again and again they call upon a name I do not know, but each time it is voiced, something trembles in the air. A flavour pungent and bestial.*

'*Destriant, we must withdraw an element of our forces to meet this threat from the west. You must reach through to our human commanders – you must break their fury and speak with a voice of reason. Ride the minds of the Ve'Gath – they will guide you to them.*'

Kalyth drew a deep breath, and then closed her eyes.

The tattoos on Gesler's forearms were burning, as if splashed with acid, but he barely noticed as he leaned over the shoulders of his reeling Ve'Gath. He had never been so tired, so . . . demoralized. The enemy would not break. The enemy fought with a rage to match his and Stormy's, and though they died and died, still more came.

An axe spike had plunged deep into his mount's gut and the animal was dying beneath him, yet somehow it remained on its feet, somehow it continued advancing, weapons bashing foes aside.

They had drawn closer to the centre – to where the T'lan Imass still pushed forward, their tireless arms rising and descending. Never before had Gesler been so close to the ancient undead warriors in the midst of battle, witness to this devastating . . . implacability.

And the Emperor had almost twenty thousand of them at his command. He could have conquered the world. He could have delivered such slaughter as to break every kingdom, every empire in his path.

But he barely used them at all.

Kellanved – is it possible? Did even you quail at the carnage these creatures promised? Did you see for yourself how victory could destroy you, destroy the entire Malazan Empire?

Gods below, I think you did.

You took command of the T'lan Imass – to keep them off the field of battle, to keep them out of human wars.

And now I see why.

He still held his heavy sword, but had no strength left to even so much as lift it.

The battle lust was fading – something was assaulting it, tearing it down, away from his eyes, and all at once the redness of his vision fragmented, vanished.

And he heard Kalyth's voice. *'Gesler. There is another Kolansii army on the high inland road. They are fast-marching – we must guard our flank.'*

'Guard our flank? With what?' He angled his mount round, lurched as it staggered. 'Ah, shit, my Ve'Gath's finished.' He pulled his boots from the scale stirrups, slid down from the beast's slathered back. Landing, his knees buckled and he fell to one side. Fighting to regain his breath, he stared up at the strange – and strangely crowded – sky. 'All right. Listen, Kalyth. Draw the K'ell back and send them over there, all of them. Tell Sag'Churok – I'm sending him the T'lan Imass.' He forced himself to his feet. 'Did you hear all that?' He flinched as his Ve'Gath fell over, legs flailing, half its guts hanging out in thick ropes. He saw the life empty from its eyes.

'Yes. Gu'Rull says you must hurry. There is little time.'

'That damned rhizan's finally come back, has it?'

'Gu'Rull says there is a storm coming, Gesler. He says you called it.'

'Like Hood I have!' He looked around, but Stormy was nowhere to be seen. *A storm? What's she going on about? Whatever it is, it's probably that red-bearded bastard's fault.*

Cursing, the Mortal Sword set off to find Onos T'oolan. His forearms, he saw with faint alarm, were sweating beads of blood.

Onos T'oolan cut diagonally in a downward chop, through the torso of the Kolansii opposite him, dragging his blade free as he stepped over the crumpling body. An axe head slammed into his ribs on his left side, bounced off, and he turned and slashed through his attacker's neck, watched the head roll off the shoulders. Two more strides and he was atop the fourth berm, his warriors coming up alongside him.

Looking down into the trench, he stared at a mass of upturned faces – all twisted with inhuman hatred – and weapons lifted as he prepared to descend into the press.

'First Sword!'

Onos T'oolan paused, stepped back and turned round.

The Malazan named Gesler was stumbling towards him.

'Gesler,' said Onos T'oolan, 'there are but two more tiers left – and the number of enemy in those positions is sorely diminished. We shall prevail. Draw your Ve'Gath into our wake—'

'First Sword – we are about to be flanked to the west. I have sent what remains of my K'ell Hunters there, but they are not enough.'

Onos T'oolan lowered his sword. 'I understand.'

'We will push on here without you,' Gesler said. 'You've split the defences in two, and when all is said and done, the Ve'Gath can out-climb and out-run humans – we will fight to the foot of the stairs. We will assault the Spire.'

'Akhrast Korvalain is wounded now, Mortal Sword. Tellann is awake – Olar Ethil is near. It seems that this shall be a day of ancient powers. Malazan, beware the voice of the Pure who awaits you atop the Spire.'

The man revealed red-stained teeth. 'Once I get up there, she won't have time to get a single damned word out.'

'I wish you success, Mortal Sword. Tell the K'Chain Che'Malle, we are honoured to have fought at their side this day.'

Onos T'oolan reached out to his followers, and as one they fell to dust.

Sister Reverence could hear the grinding ascent of the ice against the Spire off to her left, while before her she saw the K'Chain Che'Malle carve their way ever closer to the base of the stairs. The T'lan Imass had vanished, but she knew where they were going – *and High Watered Festian will have to face them. He will have to find a way to encircle them, to win past and strike the K'Chain Che'Malle.*

Then she looked skyward, where enormous dark clouds were building almost directly overhead, forming huge, towering columns bruised blue and green. She saw flashes of lightning flaring from their depths – and the blinding light was slow to fade. Two remained, burning luridly, and instead of diminishing, it seemed that those actinic glares were growing stronger, deepening in hue.

All at once, she realized what she was seeing.

There is a god among us. A god has been summoned!

The eyes blazed with demonic fire, and the clouds, ever massing, found form, a shape so vast, so overwhelming, that Sister Reverence cried out.

The argent gleam of tusks, the clouds curling into swirls of dark fur. Towering, seething, building into a thing of muscle and terrible rage, the eyes baleful as twin desert suns. Dominating the entire sky above the Spire, Fener, the Boar of Summer, manifested.

This is no sending. He is here. The god Fener is here!

With dawn paling the grey sky overhead and water running in streams along the gutters, Karsa Orlong looked down at the peaceful face of the old man cradled in his lap. He slipped a hand under that head and lifted it slightly, and then moved away, settling it once more on the hard cobbles of the street.

It was time.

He rose, taking hold of his sword. Fixing his eyes on the temple opposite, he walked towards the barred door.

The city was awakening. Early risers out on the street paused upon seeing him crossing their path. And those who could see his face backed away.

He reached for the heavy brass latch, grasped hold of it, and tore it away from the wooden door. Then he kicked, shattering the door's planks like kindling, the sound of the impact like thunder, its echoes tumbling down the passageway within. Voices shouted.

Karsa entered the temple of Fener.

Down a once-opulent corridor, past the flanking braziers – two priests appearing with the intent of blocking his passage, but when they saw him they shrank from his path.

Into the altar chamber. Thick smoke sweetly redolent with incense, a heat rising from the very stones underfoot, and to either side the paint of the murals was crackling, bubbling, and then it began to blacken, curling away from the walls, devouring the images.

Priests were wailing in terror and grief, but the Toblakai ignored them all. His eyes were on the altar, a block of rough-hewn stone on which rested a jewel-studded boar tusk.

Closing on the altar, Karsa raised his stone sword.

'Upon his heart.'

When the blade descended, it smashed through the tusk and then continued on, cracking the altar stone with the sound of thunder, shattering the block in half.

Onos T'oolan could hear weeping, but this was the sound of something unseen, something long hidden in the souls of the T'lan Imass. He had never expected it to awaken, had never expected to feel it again. In his mind he saw a child, clothed in mortal flesh, lifting a face to the heavens, and that face was his own – so long ago now. There had been dreams, but even as they faded the child boy wept with shuddering convulsions.

Things die. Dreams fall to dust. Innocence bleeds out to soak the ground. Love settles in cold ashes. We had so much. But we surrendered it all. It was . . . unforgivable.

He rose again, on a broad, level stretch of land where a village had once stood. It had been made mostly of wood and that wood had been taken away to build engines of war. Now only the foundation stones remained. The raised road that ran into it sloped until it was level with the cobbled street at the village's edge.

His kin rose around him and they moved out to present a broad front facing on to that road, there to await the army they could now see to the west. The sound of thousands of marching boots on cobbles was a solid roar underfoot.

We shall fight here. Because the fighting and the killing goes on for ever. And the child will shed his tears until the end of time. I remember so many loves, so many things lost. I remember being broken. Again and again. There need be no end to it – there is no law to say that one cannot break one more time.

When he raised his weapon, his kin followed suit. Seven thousand four hundred and fifty-nine T'lan Imass. *Another battle, the same war. The war we never lost, yet never knew how to win.*

The concussion that clove through the heaving clouds behind them staggered the T'lan Imass, a thunder so loud it shivered through their bones. Wheeling round, Onos T'oolan stared up to see a stone sword – an *Imass* sword – descending as if held in the hand of the Jade Strangers, impossibly huge, slicing down through a vague bestial shape – that then *staggered*.

Twin embers of crimson – *eyes* – suddenly blossomed as if filling with blood.

A roar sounded, filling the air with such fury and pain that it pounded the entire army of T'lan Imass back a step, and then another.

The death cry of a god.

And the heavens erupted.

Onos T'oolan watched the waves of blood descending, falling earthward. He watched the crimson sheets rolling across the land, watched them roll ever closer – and then with yet another roar, the rain slammed down upon the T'lan Imass, driving them to their knees.

Head bowed beneath the deluge, Onos T'oolan gasped. One breath. Another. And his eyes, fixed now upon the hands on his knees, slowly widened.

As the withered skin softened, thickened. As muscles expanded.

Another terrible gasp of breath, deep into aching lungs.

From his kin, sudden cries. Of shock. Of wonder.

We are remade. By the blood of a slain god, we are reborn.

Then he lifted his gaze, to look upon the Kolansii ranks, fast closing on their position.

This . . . this was ill-timed.

The blood of a slain god rained from the sky. In torrents, cascading down from the ruptured, now shapeless clouds. The air filled with the terrible roar of those thick drops, falling heavy as molten lead. The armies fighting near the highest level of the isthmus were staggered by the downpour. The vast shelf of ice, ever rising towards the pinnacle of the Spire, now streamed crimson in growing torrents.

Bowed beneath the onslaught, Sister Reverence staggered towards the altar stone. Through the carmine haze she could see the Crippled God's heart – no longer a withered, knotted thing of stone – now pulsing, now surging with life.

But the sorcerous chains still held it bound to the altar.

This – this changes nothing. My soldiers shall hold. I still have their souls in my hands. I have the chains of their fallen comrades, their slain souls – all feeding my power. At the foot of the stairs, they shall make a human wall. And I will take this unexpected power and make of it a gift. I will feed this blood into the soul of Akhrast Korvalain.

She drew up against the altar stone, slowly straightened, and held her face to the sky, to feel that hot blood streaming down. And then, laughing, she opened her mouth.

Make me young again. Banish this bent body. Make all that is outside as beautiful as that which was ever inside. Make me whole and make me perfect. The blood of a god! See me drink deep!

It was as if the heavens had been struck a mortal wound. Kalyth cried out, in shock, in dread horror, as the deluge descended upon the land – to all sides, devouring every vista, as if swallowing up the entire world. The blood – on her face, on her hands – felt like fire, but did not burn. She saw the heavy drops pounding into the lifeless earth, saw the soil blacken, watched as streams of thick mud slumped down the hillsides.

She could barely draw breath. 'Gunth Mach! What – what will come of this?'

'*Destriant, I cannot give answer. Immortal rituals unravel. Ancient power melts . . . dissolves. But what do these things mean? What is resolved? No one can say. A god has died, Destriant, and that death tastes bitter and it fills me with sorrow.'*

Kalyth saw how the K'Chain Che'Malle, momentarily stunned, now resumed their assault upon the highest defences of the Kolansii. She saw the defenders rise to meet the Ve'Gath.

A god dies. And the fighting simply goes on, and we add to the rain with blood of our own. I am seeing the history of the world – here, before me. I am seeing it all, age upon age. All so . . . useless.

There was low laughter behind her, cutting through the dull roar, and Kalyth turned.

Sinn had stripped naked, and now she was painted in blood. 'The Pure has made a shining fist,' she said. 'To block the ascent. The lizards cannot break it – their oils are fouled with exhaustion.' Her eyes lifted to Kalyth. 'Tell them to disengage. Order them to retreat.'

She walked past.

The Imass reeled back. The Kolansii heavy infantry pushed forward, over Imass corpses. With shields and armour they weathered blows from stone weapons. With iron sword, axe and spear, they tore apart unprotected flesh, and on all sides the rain of blood – cooled now, lifeless – hammered down.

Driven past the remains of the village, the Imass forces contracted, unable to hold the enemy back. Pincers swept out to either side, seeking to encircle the increasingly crowded, disorganized warriors. Onos Toolan sought to hold the centre in the front line – he alone remembered what it was to defend his own body – now so vulnerable, so frail. His kin had . . . forgotten. They attacked unmindful of protecting themselves, and so they died.

Reborn, only to live but moments. The anguish of this threatened to tear the First Sword apart. But he was only one man, as mortal as his brothers and sisters now, and it was only a matter of time before—

He saw the Kolansii line opposite him flinch back suddenly, saw them hesitate, and Onos Toolan did not understand.

Low, deep laughter sounded from somewhere on his right, and even as he turned, a voice spoke.

'Imass, we greet you.'

Now, pushing through to stand in the foremost line – *Jaghut.*

Armoured, helmed, bristling with weapons, all of it dripping blood.

The Jaghut beside Onos Toolan then said in a loud voice, 'Suvalas! Are you as beautiful as I remembered?'

A female shouted in answer, 'You only remember what I told you, Haut! And it was all lies!'

Amid Jaghut laughter, the one named Haut tilted his head to regard

765

Onos Toolan. 'To draw breath was unexpected. We thought to fight with you – two lifeless but eternally stubborn peoples. A day of slaughter, hah!'

The Jaghut beyond Haut then said, 'And slaughter it shall be! Alas, the wrong way round! And there are but fourteen of us. Aimanan – you are good with numbers! Does fourteen dead Jaghut constitute a slaughter?'

'With five thousand Imass, I would think so, Gedoran!'

'Then our disappointment is averted and I am once more at ease!'

The Jaghut drew weapons. Beside Onos Toolan, Haut said, 'Join us, First Sword. If we must die, must it be on the back step? I think not.' His eyes flashed from the shadows of his helm. 'First Sword – do you see? Forkrul Assail, K'Chain Che'Malle, Imass and now Jaghut! What a fell party this is!'

Gedoran grunted and said, 'All we now need are a few Thel Akai, Haut, and we can swap old lies all night long!'

And then, with bull roars, the Jaghut charged the Kolansii.

Onos Toolan leapt forward to join them, and behind him, the Imass followed.

Gillimada, who had been chosen to lead because she was the most beautiful, looked back on the way they'd come. She could barely make out the Barghast. 'They are slow!'

'If only you were taller, Gilli,' bellowed her brother, Gand, 'you could look the other way and see the fighting!'

Scowling, Gillimada faced forward again. 'I was about to – impatient runt, Gand! Everyone, enough resting – we shall run some more. Do you all see?'

'Of course we do,' shouted one of her brother's mouthy friends, 'we're all taller than you, Gilli!'

'But who's the most beautiful? Exactly!'

'Gilli – there are Jaghut with those Imass!'

Gillimada squinted, but the truth of it was, she *was* the shortest one here. 'Are they killing each other?'

'No!'

'Good! All the old stories are lies!'

'Surely just that one, Gilli—'

'No! If one is a lie then all of them are! I have spoken! Is everyone rested? Good! Let us join the fight, just like in the old story about the war against Death itself!'

'But it's a lie, Gilli – you just said so!'

'Well, maybe I was the one doing the lying, did you think of that? Now, no more wasting of breath, let us run and fight!'

'Gilli – I think it's raining blood over there!'

'I don't care – you all have to do what I say, because I'm still the most beautiful, aren't I?'

With the remaining K'ell Hunters – cut and slashed, many with the snapped stubs of arrow shafts protruding from their bodies – Sag'Churok advanced at a cantering pace. Before them, he could see the Imass – granted the bitter gift of mortality – locked in fierce battle against overwhelming numbers of Kolansii heavy infantry. Among them, near the front, there were armoured Jaghut.

To see these two ancient foes now standing side by side sent strange flavours surging through the K'ell Hunter, scouring away his exhaustion. He felt the scents flowing out now to embrace his kin, felt a reawakening of their strength.

What is this, that so stirs my heart?

It is . . . glory.

We rush to our deaths. We rush to fight beside ancient foes. We rush like the past itself, into the face of the present. And what is at stake? Why, nothing but the future itself.

Beloved kin, if this day must rain blood, let us add to it. If this day must know death, let us take its throat in our jaws. We are alive, and there is no greater power in all the world!

Brothers! Raise your swords!

Reaching level ground, the K'Chain Che'Malle K'ell Hunters stretched out their bodies, swords lifting high, and charged.

Two hundred and seventy-eight Teblor smashed into the flank of the Kolansii forces near the line of engagement. Suddenly singing ancient songs – mostly about unexpected trysts and unwelcome births – they thundered into the press, weapons swinging. Kolansii bodies spun through the air. Entire ranks were driven to the ground, trampled underfoot.

Wild terrible laughter rose from the Jaghut upon seeing their arrival. Each of the fourteen led knots of Imass, and the Jaghut themselves were islands amidst slaughter – none could stand before them.

Yet they were but fourteen, and the Imass fighting close to them continued to fall, no matter how savagely they fought.

The K'ell Hunters struck the inside envelopment, driving the enemy back in a maelstrom of savagery. They swarmed out across the pasture and over the paddocks to swing round and plunge into the Kolansii flank, almost opposite the Teblor.

And in answer to all of this, High Watered Festian ordered his reserves into the battle. Four legions, almost eight thousand heavy infantry, heaved forward to close on the enemy.

Bitterspring, crippled by a sword thrust through her left thigh, lay among the heaps of fallen kin. There had been a charge – it had swept over her, but now she saw how it had stalled, and was once more yielding ground, step by step.

There were no memories to match this moment – this time, so short, so sweet, when she had tasted breath once again, when she had felt the softness of her skin, had known the feel of tears in her own eyes – how that blurred her vision, a thing she had forgotten. If this was how living had been, if this was the reality of mortality . . . she could not imagine that anyone, no matter how despairing, would ever willingly surrender it. *And yet . . . and yet . . .*

The blood still raining down – thinner now, cooler on her skin – offered no further gifts. She could feel her own blood, much warmer, pooling under her thigh, and around her hip, and the life so fresh, so new, was slowly draining away.

Was this better than an inexorable advance into the enemy forces? Better than killing hundreds and then thousands when they could do little to defend themselves against her and her immortal kind? Was this not, in fact, a redressing of the balance?

She would not grieve. No matter how short-lived this gift.

I have known it again. And so few are that fortunate. So few.

The Ship of Death lay trapped on its side, embraced in ice. Captain Shurq Elalle picked herself up, brushing the snow from her clothes. Beside her, Skorgen Kaban the Pretty was still on his knees, gathering up a handful of icy snow and then sucking on it.

'Bad for your teeth, Pretty,' Shurq Elalle said.

When the man grinned up at her she sighed.

'Apologies. Forgot you had so few left.'

Princess Felash came round from the other side of the ship's prow, trailed by her handmaid. 'I have found him,' she announced through a gust of smoke. 'He is indeed walking this chilly road, and it is safe to surmise, from careful gauging of the direction of his tracks, that he intends to walk all the way to that spire. Into that most unnatural rain.'

Shurq Elalle squinted across what had been – only a short time ago – a bay. The awakening of Omtose Phellack had been like a fist to the side of the head, and only the captain had remained conscious through the unleashing of power that followed. She alone had witnessed the freezing of the seas, even as she struggled to ensure that none of her crew or guests slid over the side as the ship ran aground and started tilting hard to port.

And, alone among them all, she had seen Hood setting out, on foot.

A short time later, a storm had broken over the spire, releasing a torrential downpour of rain that seemed to glisten red as blood as it fell over the headland.

Shurq Elalle regarded Felash. 'Princess . . . any sense of the fate of your mother?'

'Too much confusion, alas, in the ether. It seems,' she added, pausing to draw on her pipe and turning to face inland, 'that we too shall have to trek across this wretched ice field – and hope that it does not begin breaking up too soon, now that Omtose Phellack sleeps once more.'

Skorgen scowled. 'Excuse me . . . sleeps? Cap'n, she saying it's going to melt?'

'Pretty,' said Shurq Elalle, 'it is already. Very well then, shall we make haste?'

But the princess lifted a plump hand. 'At first, I considered following in Hood's footsteps, but that appears to entail a steep and no doubt treacherous ascent. Therefore, might I suggest an alternative? That we strike due west from here?'

'I don't know,' said Shurq Elalle. 'Shall we spend half a day discussing this?'

Felash frowned. 'And what, precisely, did I say to invite such sarcasm? Hmm, Captain?'

'My apologies, Highness. This has been a rather fraught journey.'

'It is hardly done, my dear, and we can scarcely afford the luxury of complaining now, can we?'

Shurq Elalle turned to Skorgen. 'Get everything ready. There truly is no time to waste.'

The first mate turned away and then glanced back at Shurq. 'If that's the case, then why in Mael's name is she—'

'That will be enough, Pretty.'

'Aye, Cap'n. Sorry, Cap'n. On my way, aye.'

Queen Abrastal, I will deliver your daughter into your keeping. With every blessing I can muster. Take her, I beg you. Before I close my hands round that soft delicious neck and squeeze until her brains spurt from every hole in her head. And then her handmaid will have to chop me into tiny pieces, and Skorgen will do something stupid and get his head sliced in half and won't that be a scar worth bragging about?

She could just make out Hood's trail towards the spire, and caught herself looking at it longingly. *Don't be a fool, woman. Some destinies are better just hearing about, over ales in a tavern.*

Go well on your way, Hood. And the next face you see, well, why not just bite it off?

*   *   *

769

He had passed through the Gates of Death, and this rain – in its brief moments of magic – could do nothing for ghosts. No kiss of rebirth, *and no blinding veil to spare from me what I now see.*

Toc sat on his lifeless horse, and from a hillside long vanished – worn down to nothing but a gentle mound by centuries of ploughing – he watched, in horror, the murder of his most cherished dreams.

It was not supposed to happen this way. We could smell the blood, yes – we knew it was coming.

But Onos Toolan – none of this was your war. None of this battle belonged to you.

He could see his old friend – there at the centre of less than a thousand Imass. The fourteen Jaghut had been separated from kin, and now fought in isolation, and archers had come forward and those Jaghut warriors were studded with arrows, yet still they fought on.

The K'ell Hunters had been driven back, pushed away from the Imass, and Toc could see the Toblakai – barely fifty of them left – forced back to the very edge of the slope. There were Barghast on that far side now, but they were few and had arrived staggering, half dead with exhaustion.

Toc found that he was holding his scimitar in his hand. *But my power is gone. I gave the last of it away. What holds me here, if not some curse that I be made to witness my failure? Onos Toolan, friend. Brother. I will not await you at the Gates – my shame is too great.* He drew up his reins. *I will not see you die. I am sorry. I am a coward – but I will not see you die.* It was time to leave. He swung his mount round.

And stopped.

On the high ridge before him was an army, mounted on lifeless war-horses.

Bridgeburners.

Seeing Whiskeyjack at the centre, Toc kicked his mount into a canter, and the beast tackled the hillside, hoofs carving the broken ground.

'Will you just watch this?' he cried as his horse scrabbled up on to the ridge. He drove his charger towards Whiskeyjack, reined in at the last moment.

The old soldier's empty eyes were seemingly fixed on the scene below, as if he had not heard Toc's words.

'I beg you!' pleaded Toc, frantic – the anguish and frustration moments from tearing him apart. 'I know – I am not a Bridgeburner – *I know that*! But as a fellow Malazan, please! Whiskeyjack – *don't let him die!*'

The lifeless face swung round. The empty eyes regarded him.

Toc could feel himself collapsing inside. He opened his mouth, to speak one more time, to plead with all he had left—

Whiskeyjack spoke, in a tone of faint surprise. 'Toc Younger. Did you truly imagine that we would say *no?*'

And he raised one gauntleted hand, the two soldiers of his own squad drawing up around him – Mallet on his left, Trotts on his right.

When he threw that hand forward, the massed army of Bridgeburners surged on to the hillside, lunged like an avalanche – sweeping past Toc, driving his own horse round, shoving it forward.

And one last time, the Bridgeburners advanced to do battle.

The thunderous concussion of the god's death had driven Torrent's horse down to the ground, throwing the young warrior from the saddle. As he lay stunned, he heard the thumping of the animal's hoofs as it scrambled back upright and then fled northward, away from the maelstrom.

And then the rain slammed down, and out over the rising ice beyond the headland he could hear shattering detonations as the ice fields buckled. Whirling storms of snow and sleet lifted from the cliffside, spun crimson twisters – and the ground beneath him shifted, slumped seaward.

All madness! The world is not like this. Torrent struggled to his feet, looked across to where the children huddled together in terror. He staggered towards them. 'Listen to me! Run inland – do you hear me? Inland and away from here!'

Frozen blood slashed down from the sky. Behind him, the wind brought close the sound of laughter from Olar Ethil. Glancing back, he saw that she was facing the Spire.

Absi suddenly wailed.

Storii cried, 'Don't leave us, Torrent! You promised!'

'I will catch you up!'

'Torrent!'

'Just run!'

Taking up Absi in her thin arms, Stavi plucked at her sister's filthy tunic. And then they were on their way, vanishing in moments as the red sleet intensified, flinging curtains down that rolled deeper inland, one after another.

Turning to the east, Torrent stared in astonishment. The entire edge of the headland now sloped steeply towards the bay – but ice was rising beyond that edge, now level with the top of the cliff. Off to his right, the Spire was engulfed in the downpour.

Hearing the witch's laughter again, he looked across to where Olar Ethil stood.

But the ancient hag was no more – a young woman stood in the deluge. *'Reborn!'* she shrieked. *'My kin – all reborn! I shall lead them – we shall rise again!'* She spun to face Torrent, blood like paint on her bold features, and then her head darted like a bird's. 'Where are they? Where are the children! My gifts to him – and I will give him more! More children! We shall rule together – the Bonecaster and the First Sword – *where are they?*'

Torrent stared at her, and then, slipping treacherously on the icy ground, he collected up his bow and quiver. 'They slid,' he said. 'They panicked – went down the slope. Down on to the ice – I couldn't reach them—'

'*You fool!*'

When she ran towards the ice field, Torrent followed.

The frozen blood lacerated his face as the wind howled up from the bay. One forearm held up to shield his eyes, he stumbled after Olar Ethil.

You will give him more? *Is that what all this was about? You love him? You took his life and made him a thing of skin and bones – you stole his children away – maybe even killed his wife, their mother. You did all this – thinking you could win his heart?*

But he had seen her – enough of her, anyway. Reborn, made young, she was not displeasing to the eye, solid, full-breasted and wide-hipped, her hair – before the blood soaked it – so blonde it was almost white, her eyes the colour of a winter sky. *No longer undead. So too, then, Onos Toolan? Now reborn? She took everything away from him, and would now replace it with herself – with the world she would make.*

Toc Anaster, did you know this? Did you understand her reasons for all that she has done?

Does it matter?

He reached the ice – she was still ahead, fleet as a hare as she danced her way down the broken, jagged slope. He thought he could hear her, crying out for the children.

Fissures were opening up as the field's own weight began to crush the ice, and the descent was growing ever steeper – off to his right he could see one part of it still climbing as if would reach to the very summit of the Spire itself. Was there a speck there, halfway up that ramp of ice? Someone ascending? He could not be sure.

His feet went out from under him and he slid, rebounding from spars of rock-hard ice. In a blur he was past Olar Ethil, hearing her shout of surprise. His head struck something, spinning him round, and then his feet jammed against a hard edge that suddenly gave way. He was thrown forward, the upper half of his body pitching hard, as what felt like jaws closed on the lower half – snapping shut on his hips and legs.

He heard and felt both thigh bones snap.

Torrent screamed. Trapped in a fissure, the edges now rising above his hips as he sank deeper. He could feel blood streaming down, could feel it freezing.

He had lost grip on his bow and the hide quiver – they lay just beyond his reach.

Olar Ethil was suddenly there, standing almost above him. 'I heard bones break – is it true? Is it true, pup?' She reached down and took a handful of hair, twisting his torn face around. 'Is it? Are you useless to me now?'

'No, listen – I thought I heard them – the children. Absi – I thought I heard him crying.'

'Where? Point – you can still do that. *Where?*'

'Pull me out, witch, and I'll show you.'

'Can you walk?'

'Of course I can, woman – I'm simply jammed in this crack. Pull me out – we can find them! But quickly – this entire field is shattering!'

She cackled. 'Omtose Phellack in all its glory – yet who dares face it? A Bonecaster, that is who! I will destroy it. Even now, I am destroying it – that fool thinks he will take that wretched heart? I will defy him! He deserves no less – he is *Jaghut!*'

'Pull me free, witch.'

She reached down.

Her strength was immense, and he could feel frozen blood splitting, could feel massive sections of skin and flesh torn away as she lifted and dragged him out from the fissure.

'Liar! You lied!'

Torrent lay on his back. The red sleet was diminishing now – he could see the Jade Strangers and the sun itself. From below his hips he could feel nothing. *Frozen. Bloodless. I haven't got long.*

'Where are they?'

He forced himself on to one elbow, pointed off to the right and slightly downslope. 'There, behind that rise – stand atop it, witch, and you may see them.'

'That is all I need from you – now you can die, pup. Did I not say you would?'

'You did, Olar Ethil.'

Laughing, she set off for the rise of hard-packed snow and ice. Twenty-five, maybe thirty paces away.

Torrent twisted round, dragged himself closer to his bow. 'I promised,' he whispered. Half-numb fingers closed about the bow's shaft. He scrabbled one-handed for the quiver, drew out a stone-tipped arrow. Rolling on to his back, he lay gasping for a moment. It was getting hard – hard to do anything.

Ice squealed and then cracked and he slid half a pace – back towards that fissure, but now it was wider – now it could take all of him.

Torrent forced the nock's slitted mouth round the gut-string.

She was almost there, tackling the ragged side of the rise.

He used his elbows and shoulders to push himself up against a heap of rubbled ice. Brought the bow round and drew the arrow back. *This is impossible. I'm lying all wrong. She's too far away!* Wretched panic gripped him. He struggled to calm his breath, deafened by the pounding of his own heart.

Olar Ethil scrambled on to the rise, straightened and stared downslope.

He saw her fists clench, half-heard her howl of fury.

Squinting, his muscles starting to tremble, he stared at her shoulders – waiting, waiting – and when he saw them pivot, he released.

I will make him pay for the lies! Olar Ethil, eldest among all the Bonecasters and now reborn, spun round towards Torrent—

The arrow caught her in the left eye.

The stone tip tore through the eyeball, punched through the back of the socket, where the bone was thin as skin, and the spinning chipped-stone point drilled a gory tunnel through her brain, before shattering against the inside of the back of her skull.

He saw her head snap back, saw the shaft protruding from her face, and by the way her body fell – collapsing like a sack of bones – he knew that she was dead – killed instantly. Gasping, he sagged back. *Did you see that, Toc? Did you see that shot?*

Ah, gods. It's done, brother.

It's done. I am Torrent, last warrior of the Awl.

When he slid towards the fissure, he was helpless to resist.

Torrent. Last warrior of the . . .

Stormy bellowed in agony as Gesler dragged him away. The red-haired Falari had been stabbed through his right thigh. But the blood was slow, gushing only when the muscles moved, telling Gesler that the fool wouldn't bleed out before he got him away.

The Ve'Gath were all drawing back – and back . . .

Because she's coming. Because she's finally joining this fight.

Gods help us all.

Pulling Stormy on to the blood-soaked embankment of the third trench, he looked back upslope.

She was walking alone towards the massed Kolansii. Little more than a child, stick-thin, looking undernourished. Pathetic.

When Gesler saw her raise her hands, he flinched.

With a terrible roar a wall of fire engulfed the highest trench. Scalding winds erupted in savage gusts, rolling back down the slope – Gesler saw the corpses nearest the girl crisp black, limbs suddenly pulling, curling inward in the heat's bitter womb.

And then Sinn began walking, and, as she did so, she marched the wall of fire ahead of her.

Kalyth stumbled to her knees beside Gesler. 'You must call her back! She can't just burn them all alive!'

Gesler sagged back. 'It's too late, Kalyth. There's no stopping her now.'

Kalyth screamed – a raw, breaking sound, her hands up at her face – but even she could not tear her eyes from the scene.

The fire devoured the army crouched against the base of the Spire. Bodies simply exploded, blood boiling. Thousands of soldiers burst into flames, their flesh melting. Everything within the fire blackened, began crumbling away. And still the firestorm raged.

Gunth Mach was crouched down over Stormy, oil streaming from her clawed hands and sealing the wound on his leg, but he was already pushing those hands away. 'Gesler – we got to reach those stairs—'

'I know,' he said. *Through fire. Well, of course it has to be us.*

'She won't stop,' Stormy said, pushing himself to his feet, swaying like a drunk. 'She'll take it for herself – all that power.'

'I know, Stormy! *I know, damn you!*' Gesler forced himself to his feet. He squinted inland. 'Gods below – what is that?'

'A ghost army,' Kalyth said. 'The Matron says they simply came down from the sky.'

'Send the Ve'Gath that way – all of them, Kalyth! Do you understand – you need to get them as far away from this as possible. If Sinn reaches the heart, that fire's likely to consume the whole fucking land for leagues around!'

She pulled at him. 'Then you can do nothing. Don't you see – you can't—'

Gesler took her face in his hands and kissed her hard on the lips. 'Teach these lizards, Kalyth, only the best in us humans. *Only the best.*' He turned to Stormy. 'All right, let's go. Forget any weapons – they'll get too hot in our hands. We can tear off this armour on the way.'

'Stop ordering me around!'

Side by side, the two old marines set out.

They climbed across greasy bodies, over ground that steamed, and through air hot as the breath of a smithy's forge.

'Can't believe you, Ges,' gasped Stormy. 'You called on Fener!'

'I wasn't the only one, Stormy! I heard you—'

'Not me – must've been someone else. You called him and someone fucking killed him! Gesler, you went and killed our god!'

'Go to Hood,' Gesler growled. 'Who crossed his finger bones when he swore off that cult? Wasn't that you? I think it was.'

'You told me you did the same!'

'Right, so let's just forget it – we both killed Fener, all right?'

Five more strides and there could be no more words – every breath scalded, and the leathers they now wore as their only clothing had begun to blacken. *Now it's going to get bad.*

But this is Telas. I can feel it – we've been through this before. He looked for Sinn, but could not see her anywhere. *Walked out of the flames at Y'Ghatan. Walked into them here. It's her world in there, it always was. But we knew that, didn't we?*

I swear I can hear her laughing.

The two men pushed forward.

Kalyth cried out when Gesler and Stormy vanished into the flames. She did not understand. She had looked on in disbelief as they had stepped over bodies reduced to black ash – she had seen their tunics catch fire.

'Matron – what gift is this? What power do they possess?'

'*Destriant, this surpasses me. But it is now clear to me – as it is to all of us – that you chose most wisely. If we could, we would follow these two humans into the firestorm itself. If we could, we would follow them to the edge of the very Abyss. You ask what manner of men are these – Destriant, I was about to ask this very same question of you.*'

She shook her head, shrugged helplessly. 'I don't know. Malazans.'

The flames drove him back. And this was a source of fury and anguish. He tried again and again, but his beloved master was beyond his reach. Howling, he raced back and forth along the third berm, the foul stench of his own burnt hair acrid in his nostrils.

And then he saw the pup – the one of tangled hair and piercing voice, the pup that never grew up – running towards the cold, towards the frozen sea.

Had the pup found a way round this burning air?

The Wickan cattledog with the scarred face tore off in pursuit.

There would be a way round – he would find his master again. To fight at his side. There was, for Bent, no other reason to exist.

The base around the Spire had been reduced to scorched bedrock – not a scrap of armour remained, nothing but molten streaks of iron tracking the slopes of the blackened stone.

Yet Gesler and Stormy walked through the conflagration. Their leathers had melted on to their bodies, hard and brittle as eggshells, and as the two marines pushed closer to the stairs the clothing's remnants cracked, made crazed patterns like a snake's shedding skin.

Gesler could see the stairs – but she wasn't there. His gaze tracked upward. *Shit.* She was already a quarter of the way up. He punched at Stormy's shoulder and pointed.

They reached the base, set foot on the baked, crumbling stone.

Stormy edged into Gesler's path and began gesturing – the hand language of the marines. *'Leave her to me – I'll slow her up, hold her back, whatever. You go past. You go fast as you can – get to the top.'*

'Listen – this was almost too much, even for us. She'll cook you down to bones—'

'Never mind that. I'll hold her back – just don't fuck up up there, Ges! Throw the hag off the edge. Get that damned heart!'

Gesler's legs ached with every step – he was too tired for this. A whole day of fighting. The strain of command. The seemingly endless slaughter. By the time he reached the top – assuming they even got past Sinn – he'd have nothing left. Weaponless, face to face with a damned Forkrul Assail.

Sinn had not looked back down, not once. She had no idea she was being pursued. Her steps were measured, relentless but slow, almost casual.

They had all climbed above the flames, which had at last begun dying below them.

The girl would hold it back now – saving it for the Forkrul Assail. Telas to wage war against the Assail's warren. *Old old shit, all of this. Can't they all just go away? Back into their forgotten graves. It's not right, us having to fight in wars we didn't even start – wars that have been going on for so long they don't mean a thing any more.*

You took a foreign god's wounded heart. I see the blood on your lips. It's not right. It just isn't.

Adjunct. I know you ain't dead. Well, no, I don't. But I refuse to believe you failed. I don't think there's a thing in this world that can stop you. We'll do our part. You'll know that much – you'll know it.

Make this right. Make it all right.

Stormy was one step up from Gesler. He saw his friend reaching out, saw his hand close about Sinn's ankle.

And then, visibly snarling, Stormy tore her from the stairs, swung her out into the air behind him, and let go.

Gesler saw her plummet – saw her mouth open wide in shock, and then that visage darkened.

Now you got her mad, Stormy.

But he was reaching now for Gesler, grasping his arm and lifting him past. 'Go, Gesler! Climb your sorry arse off!'

A push that almost sent Gesler sprawling against the steps, but he recovered, and pulled himself upward, leaving Stormy in his wake.

Don't look down – don't look at him, Gesler. You know why – don't— Instead he paused, twisted round, met his friend's eyes.

Their gazes locked.

And then Stormy nodded, and flashed a half-mad smile.

Gesler made a rude gesture, and then, before his heart could shatter, he turned back to the stone steps and resumed his ascent.

Hood pulled himself over a splintered ridge of ice and looked up once more. Not far now. The ice road was groaning, cracks spreading like lightning. He had felt the assault of Olar Ethil – her hatred of Omtose Phellack unleashing power that raked through him sharp as talons – and then it had vanished, and he knew that she was dead. But the damage had been done. There was the very real chance that he would not make it, that this spar of ice would shatter beneath him, sending him down to his death.

Death. Now, that was an interesting notion. One that, perhaps, he should have been more familiar with than any other being, but the truth was, he knew nothing about it at all. The Jaghut went to war against death. So many met that notion with disbelief, or confusion. They could not understand. Who is the enemy? *The enemy is surrender.* Where is the battlefield? *In the heart of despair.* How is victory won? *It lies within reach. All you need do is choose to recognize it. Failing that, you can always cheat. Which is what I did.*

How did I defeat death?

By taking its throne.

And now the blood of a dying god had gifted him with mortal flesh – with a return to mortality. Unexpected. Possibly unwelcome. Potentially . . . *fatal. But then, who has a choice in these matters?*

Ah, yes, I did.

A rumble of laughter from deep in his chest followed the thought. He resumed his climb.

Ahead was a broad fissure cutting diagonally across his path. He would have to jump it. Dangerous and undignified. His moment of humour fell away.

He could sense the nearby unleashing of Telas – could see how the air around the Spire was grey with smoke, and the stench of burnt flesh swept over him on an errant gust of wind from inland. *This is not by the hand of an Imass. This is something . . . new. Foul with madness.*

This could defeat us all.

He reached the fissure, threw himself over its span. His chest struck the edge, the impact almost winding him, and he clawed handholds in the rotted ice beyond. And then waited for a moment, recovering, before dragging himself from the crevasse. As he cleared it a solid shape flashed past on his left, landed with a crunch, claws digging into the crusted snow – *a dog.*

A dog?

He stared at it as it scrabbled yet higher, running like a fiend from the Abyss.

From behind him, on the other side of the fissure, Hood heard furious barking, and looking back he saw another dog – or, rather, some shrunken, hair-snarled mockery of a dog, rushing up to the edge only to pull back.

Don't even try—

And then, with a launching leap, the horrid creature was sailing through the air.

Not far enough—

Hood cursed as jaws clamped on his left foot, the teeth punching through the rotted leathers of his boot. Hissing in pain he swung his leg round, kicked to shake off the snarling creature. He caught a blurred glimpse of its horrid face – like a rat that had been slammed headfirst into a wall – as it shot past him, on the trail of the bigger animal.

He glared after it for a moment, and then the Jaghut picked himself up, and resumed climbing.

With a limp.

She had been hurt by the fall, Stormy saw, watching as she laboriously made her way back up the stairs. Her left arm was clearly broken, the shoulder dislocated, skin scraped off where she had struck the unyielding bedrock. Had they been a dozen steps higher, she would be dead now.

The marine swore under his breath, twisted round to glare up at Gesler. He'd reached some kind of rest platform, maybe twenty-five steps below the summit. *What's he doing? Taking a damned breather? There's no time for that, you idiot! Go!*

'I will kill you!'

At the shriek Stormy looked back down. Ten steps between him and Sinn. Her face was lifted towards him, made demonic by hatred and rage.

A billowing gust of scorching heat rushed up to buffet him. He backed up the steps. Two, three, five.

She climbed closer.

The air ignited around Sinn, red and orange flames, white-hot where her body had been. Yet from that raging, incandescent core, he could still see her eyes – fixed on him.

Gods below, she is not even human! Was she ever human? What manner of creature is this?

The fire roared words. '*I will kill you! No one touches me! I will burn you – I will burn all who touch me! I will burn you all! You will know what it is to hurt!*

'*You said you wanted the fire inside me – you said you would kiss it – but you lied! You hurt me! You hurt me!*

'*You wanted the fire in me? You shall have it!*'

779

The flames exploded out from her, stormed up the steps and engulfed Stormy.

He howled. This was not Telas – this *burned*. This *reached* for him, took hold of him, bursting and cracking open his skin, tearing into his flesh, burrowing to clutch at his very bones. His screams vanished though his mouth remained open, his head thrown back in the stunning agony of the fire – his lungs were burned, useless. His eyes erupted and boiled away.

He felt her drawing closer – knew she was directly below him now. He could feel the stone steps against his back, could feel his body melting, pouring down as if molten.

Her hand closed on one ankle, crushed it to dust.

But he had been waiting for that touch. He had been holding on – to what he knew not – and with a silent sob that seemed to tear his soul in half Stormy threw himself forward. Closed what remained of his arms about her.

Her shriek filled his skull – and then they were falling.

Not like the first time – he'd drawn her almost half the way to the top – and he could feel her body inside that fire, or thought he could.

They plummeted.

Ges – take this – all I could—

He was dead before they struck, but enough of Stormy's corpse remained to hammer Sinn against the bedrock, though it was not needed. The impact split her skull, sent burning meat, blood and flesh spraying out to sizzle on the superheated rock. Her spine broke in four places. Her ribs buckled and folded under her back, splintered ends driving up through her lungs and heart.

The raging fires then closed on her, consuming every last shred, before dying in flickering puddles on the bedrock.

Gesler could not keep the tears from his eyes as he climbed the last few steps – he would not look down, would not surrender to that, knowing it would break him. The fury of heat that had lifted up around him moments earlier was now gone. *He's done it. Somehow. He's killed her.*

But he didn't make it. I feel it – a hole carved out of my soul. Beloved brother, you are gone.

I should have ordered you to stay behind.

Not that you ever listened to orders – that was always your problem, Stormy. That was – oh, gods take me!

He pulled himself on to the summit, rolled on to his back, stared up at the chaotic sky – smoke, the Jade Strangers, a day dying to darkness – and then, gasping, numbed, Gesler pushed himself on to his feet. Straightening, he looked across the flat expanse.

A female Forkrul Assail stood facing him. Young, almost incandescent with power. Behind her was a mass of bone chains heaped over something that pulsed with carmine light. The heart of the Crippled God.

'Where is your sword?' the Forkrul Assail demanded. 'Or do you think you can best me with just your hands?'

My hands. 'I broke a man's nose once,' Gesler said, advancing on her.

She sneered. 'It is too late, human. Your god's death assured that – it *was* your god, wasn't it? By your own prayers you summoned it – to its execution. By your own prayers you lost your war, human. How does that feel? Should you not kneel before me?'

Her words had slowed him, then halted him still three paces from her. He could feel the last remnants of his strength draining away. *There is no magic in her voice, none we would call so, anyway. No, the only power in her voice resides in the truth she speaks.*

I killed Fener.

'When this day began,' continued the Forkrul Assail, 'I was an old woman, frail and bent. You could have pushed me over with a nudge then – look at you, after all. A soldier. A veteran of many battles, many wars. I know this not by the scars you bear, but by the endless losses in your eyes.'

Losses. Yes. So many losses.

The woman gestured behind her. 'There can be an end to the pain, soldier, if you so desire. I can grant you that . . . sip.'

'I – I need a way out,' said Gesler.

She nodded. 'I understand, soldier. Shall I give it to you? That way out?'

'Yes.'

She cocked her head, her forehead seeming to flinch inward momentarily, as if about to vertically fold in half. 'I sense no duplicity in you – that is good. I am indeed become your salvation.'

'Yes,' he replied. 'Lead me from here, Pure.'

She raised one bony, long-fingered hand, reaching for his brow.

His fist was a blur. It smashed into her face. Bones snapped.

The Fokrul Assail reeled back, breath spraying from a crushed nose – and that fold dividing her face was deeply creased. Shaking her head, she straightened.

Gesler knew he was fast – but she was faster. She blocked his second punch and countered. The blow broke his left shoulder, threw him six paces back. He landed hard, skidded and then rolled on to his broken shoulder – the agony that ripped through him took with it all of his strength, his will. Stunned, helpless, he heard her advance.

A strange skittering sound, and then the sound of two bodies colliding.

He heard her stumble. Heard bestial snarling.

Gesler forced himself on to his side. Looked across.

Bent had struck the Forkrul Assail from one side, with enough force to drive her to one knee. The cattledog's jaws had closed on the side of her face, its canines tearing through flesh and bone. One eye was already gone, a cheekbone pulled away – spat out and lying on the blood-stained stone.

He saw her reach round, even as she staggered upright, and one hand closed on Bent's throat. She dragged the beast from the ruin of her face.

The cattledog, held out at the end of that long, muscled arm, struggled desperately in her choking grip.

No.

Somehow Gesler found his feet. And then he was rushing her.

Her lone eye locked with his glare and she smiled.

He saw her flexing her free arm – drawing it back to await him. He could block that blow – he could try to take her down – but Bent was dying. She was crushing his throat. *No.* In a flash, he saw a battlefield filled with corpses, saw Truth dragging a limp dog free of the bodies. He heard the lad's shout of surprise – and then that look in his eyes. So hopeful. So . . . young.

No!

Ignoring her fist, even as it shot out for his head, Gesler sent his own blow – not into her face, but into the shoulder of the arm holding the dog.

The hardest punch he ever threw.

Crushing impacts, and then—

The soldier's punch spun Reverence round, the stunning power behind it shattering her shoulder, even as her own blow connected with his forehead, splitting it, snapping his head back and breaking the vertebrae of his neck.

He was dead before he struck the ground.

But her right arm was useless, and she sagged to one knee as the dog pulled itself free of her numbed hand.

No matter. I will kill it next. A moment – to push past this pain – to clear my thoughts.

Bent kicked free, stumbled away. Air filled his lungs. Life flooded back into him. In his mind, a red mist, yearning need, and nothing else. Head lifting, the beast turned back to his master's enemy.

But his master was lying so still, so emptied of all life.

The Wickan cattledog was not bred for its voice. It rarely barked, and never howled.

Yet the cry that now came from Bent could have awakened the wolf gods themselves.

And the white-skinned woman straightened then and laughed, slowly turning to face the beast.

Bent gathered his legs beneath him. The scarred nightmare of his muzzle peeled back, revealing misshapen, jagged fangs.

And then someone stepped past him.

Hood advanced on the Forkrul Assail even as she was turning towards the dog. When she saw him, she cried out, took a step back.

He closed.

Her left fist snapped out but he caught it one-handed, crushed both wrist bones.

She screamed.

The Jaghut then reversed his grip on that wrist and added his other hand. With a savage lunge he whirled her off her feet, slammed her body down on the stone.

Yelping, the dog backed away.

But Hood was not yet done with her. He swung her up again, spun and once more hammered her on to the stone. '*I have had*,' the Jaghut roared, and into the air she went again, and down once more, '*enough*' – with a sob the crushed, broken body was yanked from the ground again – '*of*—

'*your*—

'*justice!*'

As the stranger dropped the limp arm he still held, Bent crawled over to his master's side. He lay down, settling his heavy head across the man's chest.

The stranger looked at him, but said nothing.

Bent showed his teeth to make his claim clear. He is mine.

The heavy thud of wings made Hood turn round – to see a Shi'gal Assassin descend to the Great Altar. Half crouched yet still towering over the Jaghut, it regarded him with cold eyes.

Hood glanced over at the heart of the Crippled God.

The Pure's ancestral chains were gone – destroyed with her own death. The heart was finally free, lying pulsing feebly in a pool of blood.

The smaller dog arrived, rushing over to worry at the torn face of the Forkrul Assail.

Grunting, Hood gestured towards the heart, and then turned away, to stare out over the lands to the west. Beyond the fields heaped with corpses, beyond the armies now gathered, virtually motionless with exhaustion. And now figures were climbing the stairs.

He heard the winged assassin lifting into the air and he knew that the creature now clutched that pathetic heart. The Shi'gal's shadow slipped over the Jaghut, and then he could see it, rising yet higher, winging towards the setting sun. Then his gaze fell once more, looking down on the devastation below.

I once sat upon the Throne of Death. I once greeted all who must in the end surrender, with skeletal hands, with a face of skin and bone hidden in darkness. How many battlefields have I walked? Must I walk one more?

But this time, they are the ones who have left.

Guardians of the Gate, will you tell all these, who come to you now, that it all meant nothing? Or have you something to give them? Something more than I ever could?

Others had arrived. He heard the wailing of a woman in grief.

And was reminded that there was, in truth, no sadder sound in all the worlds.

Bitterspring, Lera Epar of the Imass, lay propped up against cold bodies. Her wound had been bandaged, the flow of blood staunched. Around her the survivors were moving about, many simply wandering, while others stood motionless, heads lowered, scanning the ground for familiar faces.

She saw her kin. She saw Thel Akai. She saw K'Chain Che'Malle and Jaghut.

And she watched Onos Toolan leaving them all, stumbling northward, on to the stretch of flat land edging the walled port city that had once been the capital of the Forkrul Assail empire.

None of the Imass called after him. None asked where he was going. He was the First Sword, but so too was he a man.

She tilted her head back, studied the procession up the scalded stone stairs of the Spire. Prince Brys Beddict, Aranict, Queen Abrastal, Spax of the Gilk Barghast, the priest-woman of the K'Chain Che'Malle. The eleven remaining Jaghut were also making their way in that direction.

It is done, then. It must be done.

There is peace now. It must be peace – what other name for this terrible silence?

More rain began to fall, as the day's light slowly died, but this rain was pure and clear. She closed her eyes and let it rinse clean her face.

Onos Toolan walked past the city, out on to a barren headland of gorse and heather. The day's light was fast fading, but he was indifferent to that, and the ground underfoot, which had been soaked in blood, was now slick with simple rain.

The sun spread gold across the western horizon.

And then, in the distance, he saw three figures, and Onos Toolan's eyes narrowed. Like him, they seemed to be wandering. Like him, lost in the world. He drew closer.

The sword in his right hand, thick with gore but now showing its gleaming stone as the rain washed down its length, then fell to the ground, and he was running. His heart seemed to swell in his chest, seemed to grow too large for the bone cage holding it.

When they saw him, he heard childish cries, and now they were rushing towards him, the girl not carrying the boy winging ahead. All three were crying as they ran to meet him.

He fell to his knees to take them into his arms.

Words were tumbling from the twins. A saviour – an Awl warrior they had lost in the storm. A witch who had stolen them – their escape – and he had promised them he would find them, but he never did, and—

Lifting his gaze, still facing into the north, Onos Toolan then saw something else.

A vague shape that appeared to be sitting on the ground, curled over.

He rose, the girls reaching up to take his arms, the boy clinging to one shin. And then he moved forward, taking them all with him. When the boy complained, Storii picked him up in her arms. But Onos Toolan walked on, his steps coming faster and faster.

It was not possible. It was—

And then once more he was running.

She must have heard his approach, for she looked up and then over, and sat watching him rushing towards her.

He almost fell against her, his arms wrapping tight round her, lifting her with his embrace.

Hetan gasped. 'Husband! I have missed you. I – I don't know where I am. I don't know what has happened . . .'

'Nothing has happened,' he whispered, as the children screamed behind them.

'Onos – my toes . . .'

'What?'

'I have someone else's toes, husband, I swear it—'

The children collided with them.

In the distance ahead, on a faint rise of land, Onos Toolan saw a figure seated on a horse. The darkness was taking the vision – dissolving it before his eyes.

And then he saw it raise one hand.

Straightening, Onos Toolan did the same. *I see you, my brother. I see you.*

When at last the light left the rise of land, the vision faded from his eyes.

CHAPTER TWENTY-FOUR

I have heard voices thick with sorrow
I have seen faces crumble with grief
I have beheld broken men rise to stand
And witnessed women walk from small graves
Yet now you would speak of weakness
Of failings worth nothing but scorn
You would show all the sides of your fear
Brazen as trophies in the empty shell of conquest
But what have you won when the night draws close
To make stern your resolve among these shadows
When at last we are done with the world
When we neither stand nor fall nor wake from stillness
And the silent unknowing waits for us?
I have heard my voice thick with sorrow
I have felt my face crumble with grief
I have broken and turned away from graves
And I have grasped tight this hand of weakness
And walked in the company of familiar failings
Scorn lies in the dust and in the distance behind
Every trophy fades from sight
The night lies ahead drawing me into its close
For when I am done with this world
In the unknowing I will listen for the silence
To await what is to come
And should you seek more
Find me in this place
Before the rising dawn

Journey's Resolution
Fisher kel Tath

BANASCHAR REMEMBERED HOW SHE HAD STOOD, THE SWORD IN ITS scabbard lying on the map table before her. A single oil lamp had bled weak light and weaker shadows in the confines of the tent. The air was close and damp and it settled on things like newborn skin. A short time earlier, she had spoken to Lostara Yil with her back to that weapon, and Banaschar did not know if Tavore had used those words before and the question of that gnawed at him in strange, mysterious ways.

If they had been words oft repeated by the Adjunct, then what tragic truths did that reveal about her? But if she'd not said them before – not ever – then why had he heard them as if they were echoes, rebounding from some place far away and long ago?

Lostara had been to see Hanavat, to share in the gift of the son that had been born. The captain's eyes had been red from weeping and Banaschar understood the losses these women were now facing – the futures about to be torn away from them. He should not have been there. He should not have heard the Adjunct speak.

'It is not enough to wish for a better world for the children. It is not enough to shield them with ease and comfort. Lostara Yil, if we do not sacrifice our own ease, our own comfort, to make the future's world a better one, then we curse our own children. We leave them a misery they do not deserve; we leave them a host of lessons un-earned.

'I am no mother, but I need only look at Hanavat to find the strength I need.'

The words were seared into his memory. In the voice of a childless woman, they left him more shaken, more distraught than he perhaps would otherwise have been.

Was this what they were fighting for? Only one among a host of reasons, surely – and in truth he could not quite see how this path they'd chosen could serve such aspirations. He did not doubt the nobility of the Adjunct's motivations, nor even the raw compassion so driving her to seek what was, in most eyes, virtually impossible. But there was something else here, something still hidden.

How many great compassions arose from a dark source? A private place of secret failings?

After she had sent Lostara away, Tavore had turned once more to the sword, and after a time Banaschar had stirred from his seat on the war-gear chest, risen and walked to her side.

'I have stopped running, Adjunct.'

She was silent, her eyes fixed on the weapon in its battered, scratched scabbard.

'I – I wish to thank you for that. Proof,' he added with a sour smile, 'of your gifts of achieving the impossible.'

'Priest,' she said, 'the Chal'Managa – the Snake – that was a manifestation of D'rek, was it not?'

He found himself unable to meet her eyes, but managed a simple shrug. 'I think so. For a time. Her children were lost. In her eyes, anyway. And that made her just as lost, I suppose. Together, they needed to find their way.'

'Those details do not interest me,' she said, tone hardening. 'Banaschar, tell me. What does she want? Why is she so determined to be here? Will she seek to oppose me?'

'Why would you think I have answers to those questions, Adjunct?'

'Because she never left you either. She needed at least one of her worshippers to live on, and for some unknown reason she chose you.'

He wanted to sit down again. Anywhere. Maybe even on the floor. 'Adjunct, it is said that a worm finding itself in a puddle of ale will get drunk and then drown. I've often thought about that, and I admit, I've come to suspect that any puddle will do, and getting drunk has nothing to do with it. The damned things drown anyway. And yet, oddly enough, without any puddles the worms don't show up at all.'

'We have left the new lake behind us, Priest. No one drowned, not even you.'

'They're just children now.'

'I know.'

Banaschar sighed, nodded down at the sword. 'She will protect it, Adjunct.'

He heard her breath catch, and then, 'But . . . that might well kill her.'

He nodded, not trusting himself to speak.

'Are you certain of this, Demidrek?'

'Demi— Gods below, Adjunct – are you a student of theology as well? Tayschrenn was—'

'As the last surviving priest of the Worm of Autumn, the honorific belongs to you, Banaschar.'

'Fine, but where are the gold-stitched robes and the gaudy rings?'

An aide entered behind them, coughed and then said, 'Adjunct, three horses are saddled and waiting outside.'

'Thank you.'

Suddenly Banaschar was chilled, his hands cold and stiff as if he'd left them in buckets of ice-water. 'Adjunct – we do not know if the heart will be freed. If you—'

'They will succeed, Demidrek. Your own god clearly believes that—'

'*Wrong.*'

She was startled to silence.

'It's simpler than that, Adjunct,' Banaschar went on, the words tasting of ashes. 'D'rek doesn't care if the Crippled God is whole or not – if he's little more than a gibbering fool, or a gutted body with a huge hole in his chest, it doesn't matter. Whatever you have of him, *she wants it gone.*'

'Then . . .' Her eyes narrowed.

'Correct. Listen to her last Demidrek, because he knows when his god has lost all faith.'

'They won't fail,' Tavore whispered, eyes once more on the sword.

'And if the Perish betray them? What then?'

But she was shaking her head. 'You don't understand.'

'All our putative allies, Adjunct – are they strong enough? Wilful enough? Stubborn enough? When the bodies start falling, when the blood starts flowing – listen to me, Tavore – we have to weigh what we do – all that we do here – on the likelihood of their failing.'

'I will not.'

'Do you think I have no respect for Prince Brys Beddict – or Queen Abrastal? But Adjunct, they are striking where Akhrast Korvalain is at its strongest! Where the most powerful of the Forkrul Assail will be found – has it not once occurred to you that your allies won't be enough?'

But she was shaking her head, and Banaschar felt a flash of fury – *will you be nothing more than a child, hands over your ears because you don't like hearing what I have to say?*

'You do not yet understand, Demidrek. Nor, it seems, does your god.'

'So tell me then. Explain it to me! How in Hood's name can you be so sure?'

'The K'Chain—'

'Adjunct – this is the last gasp of those damned lizards. It doesn't matter who *seems* to be commanding them either – the Matron commands. The Matron *must* command. If she sees too many of her children dying, she will withdraw. She has to! For the very survival of her kind!'

'They are led by Gesler and Stormy, Banaschar.'

'Gods below! Just how much faith have you placed in the efforts of two demoted marines?'

She met his eyes unflinching. 'All that I need to. Now, you have indulged your moment of doubt, I trust. It is time to leave.'

He studied her for a moment longer, and then felt the tension draining from him. Managed a lopsided smile. 'I am Demidrek to the Worm of Autumn, Adjunct. Perhaps she hears you through me. Perhaps, in the end, we can teach D'rek a lesson in faith.'

'Better,' she snapped, picking up the sword.

They stepped outside.

The three horses were waiting, two saddles as yet unfilled. Slouched in the third one . . . Banaschar looked up, nodded in greeting. 'Captain.'

'Priest,' Fiddler replied.

He and the Adjunct swiftly mounted up – the scrawny animals shifting beneath them – and then the three of them swung away. Rode out from the Malazan encampment on the grassy plain.

Riding northwest.

There had been few words on that journey. They rode through the night, alternating between canter and trot. The western horizon was lit on occasion with lurid lightning, the flashes stained red, but overhead the Jade Strangers commanded the night sky, bright enough to expunge the stars, and the rolling grasslands around them bore a hue of healthy green the day's light would reveal as false. There had been no rain in this place for years, and the hoofs of their horses kicked up broken blades of grass like scythes.

When they came in sight of a lone rise that dominated all the others, the Adjunct angled her horse towards it. The lesser hills they crossed as they drew closer all bore signs of ancient camps – boulders left in ragged rings to mark where the sides of tipis had been anchored down. A thousand paces to the northwest the land dropped down into a broad, shallow valley, and its far slope was marked by long curving stretches of rocks and boulders, forming lines, blinds and runs for herd beasts now long gone, as vanished as the hunters who had preyed upon them.

Banaschar could feel the desolation of this place, like an itch under his skin, a crawling unease of mortality. *It all passes. All our ways of doing things, seeing things, all these lost ways of living. And yet . . . could I step back into that age, could I stand unseen among these people, I would be no different – no different inside . . . gods, could I explain this, even to myself, I might someday make a claim to wisdom.*

Our worlds are so small. They only feel endless because our minds can gather thousands of them all at once. But if we stop moving, if we hold to one place, if we draw breath and look around . . . each one is the same. Barring a few details. Lost ages are neither more nor less profound than the one we live in right now. We think it's all some kind of forward momentum, endless leaving behind and reaching towards. But the truth is, wherever we find ourselves – with all its shiny gifts – we do little more than walk in circles.

The thought makes me want to weep.

They drew rein at the base of the hill. The sides were uneven, with projections of rust-stained bedrock pushing up through the thin skin of earth, the stone cracked and fissured by untold centuries of frost and heat. Closer to the summit was a crowded chaos of yellow-white dolomite boulders, their softer surfaces pecked and carved with other-worldly scenes and geometric patterns. Spikewood and some kind of prairie rose bushes, skeletal now and threatening with thorns, filled the spaces between the boulders.

The Adjunct dismounted, drawing off her leather gloves. 'Captain.'

'Aye,' he replied. 'It will do.'

When Fiddler slipped down from his horse, Banaschar followed suit.

The Adjunct in the lead, they ascended the hillside. Now closer to the rotted outcrops, Banaschar saw bleached fragments of human bone trapped in cracks and crevasses, or heaped on ledges and in niches. On the narrow, winding tracks between the up-thrust bedrock, his boots crunched on beads made from polished nuts, and the ground was littered with the withered remnants of woven baskets.

Reaching the summit, they saw that the dolomite boulders formed a rough ring, perhaps ten paces across, with the centre area more or less level. When the Adjunct walked between two boulders and stepped into the clearing, her lead boot skidded and she lurched back. Righting herself, she looked down, and then crouched to pick something up.

Banaschar reached her side.

She was holding a spear point made from chipped flint, almost dagger length, and the priest now saw that the entire stretch of level ground was carpeted in thousands of similar spear points.

'Left here, all unbroken,' muttered Banaschar, as Fiddler joined them. 'Why, I wonder?'

The captain grunted. 'Never could figure out holy sites. Still, those tools are beautifully made. Even an Imass would be impressed.'

'Here is my guess,' Banaschar said. 'They discovered a technology that was too successful. Ended up killing every animal they saw, until none were left. Why? Because we are all equally stupid, just as short-sighted, twenty thousand years ago or tomorrow, makes no difference. And the seduction of slaughter is like a fever. When they finally realized what they'd done, when they all began starving, they blamed their tools. And yet,' he glanced across at Fiddler, 'even to this day, we think efficiency's a good thing.'

Fiddler sighed. 'I sometimes think we only invented war when we ran out of animals to kill.'

Dropping the spear point – it broke in half when it struck the layer of its kin – the Adjunct stepped forward. Stone snapped with every stride. When she was at the very centre, she turned to face them.

'This is not a matter of sacredness,' she said. 'There is nothing worth worshipping in this place, except perhaps a past that can never again exist, and the name for that is *nostalgia*. I am not a believer in innocence, either.'

791

'Then why here?' Banaschar asked.

But it was Fiddler who answered, 'Because it is defendable, Priest.'

'Demidrek?' Tavore asked, one hand now on the grip of her sword.

He looked round, stepped over to one of the dolomite boulders. Swirling patterns, grooves flowing like hair. Demonic, vaguely human figures, faces composed of staring eyes and open mouths filled with sharp teeth. He sighed, looked back at the Adjunct, and then nodded. 'She can . . . I don't know . . . wrap herself round the base of this hill, like a dragon-worm of legend, I suppose.'

'To what end, Demidrek?'

'Containment.'

'For how long?'

Until she dies. He shrugged.

He saw her studying him for a moment longer, and then the Adjunct Tavore drew out her Otataral sword.

The rust-coloured blade seemed to blaze in Banaschar's eyes, and he staggered back a step.

Nearby, Fiddler swore under his breath. 'Adjunct – it's . . . awake.'

'And,' whispered Banaschar, *'it shall summon.'*

Tavore kicked a space clear on the ground with one boot, and then set the sword's tip against the earth. She pushed down using all of her weight.

The blade slid, as if through sand, down to half its length.

Stepping back, the Adjunct seemed to reel.

Banaschar and Fiddler reached her at the same time, taking her weight – *gods, there is so little left of her! Bones and skin!* She slumped unconscious in their arms.

'Here,' grunted Fiddler, 'let's drag her back – find somewhere clear.'

'No,' said Banaschar. 'I will carry her down to the horses.'

'Right. I'll go ahead, get her some water.'

Banaschar had picked Tavore up. 'Fiddler . . .'

'Aye,' he growled. 'Like a starved child under that armour. When she comes round, Priest, we're making her eat.'

The soldier might as well have said, 'We're laying siege to the moon,' and been absolutely convinced that he would do just that, and then take the damned thing down in ruin and flames. *It's how a soldier thinks. At least, this one, this damned marine.* Saying nothing, he followed Fiddler down the narrow, twisting track.

She had been laid down on a threadbare saddle blanket. Banaschar had unstrapped and removed her helm, and rested her head on the worn saddle they'd pulled from the Adjunct's horse. Off to one side, Fiddler was splintering wood and building a small fire.

Taking a waterskin, the priest soaked a bundle of bandages from the sapper's kit bag and began tenderly wiping the sweat and grime from Tavore's brow and those so-plain features. With her eyes closed, he saw the child she had once been – serious, determined, impatient to grow up. But the face was gaunter than it should have been, too old, too worn down. He brushed tendrils of damp, lank hair from her forehead. Then glanced over at Fiddler. 'Is it just exhaustion, do you— Gods below, Fiddler!'

The man was breaking up his Deck of Dragons, using his knife to split each card. He paused, looked across at the priest. 'She's getting a cooked meal.'

Banaschar watched as the sapper fed the splinters into the fire. The paints filled the flames with strange colours. 'You don't expect to survive, do you?'

'Even if I do, I'm done with this. All of it.'

'You couldn't retire from soldiering even if you wanted to.'

'Really? Just watch me.'

'What will you do? Buy a farm, start growing vegetables?'

'Gods no. Too much work – never could figure out soldiers saying they'd do that once they buried their swords. Earth grows what it wants to grow – spending the rest of your life fighting it is just another damned war.'

'Right, then. Get drunk, tell old stories in some foul tavern—'

'Like you was doing back in Malaz City?'

Banaschar's smile was wry. 'I was about to advise against it, Captain. Maybe it sounds good from here – being able to live every moment without purpose, emptied of all pressure. But take it from me, you'd do just as well topping yourself – it's quicker and probably a lot less miserable.'

Fiddler poured some water into a pot and then set it on the flames. He began dropping shreds of dried meat into it. 'Nah, nothing so . . . wasteful. Thought I'd take up fishing.'

'Never figured you for a man of the seas.'

'You mean, like, in a boat with lines and nets? Out on the waves and o'er the deeps? No, not that kind of fishing, Priest. Sounds like work to me, and dangerous besides. No, I'll stay ashore. I'm thinking hobby, not livelihood.'

Glancing down at Tavore's lined face, Banaschar sighed. 'We should all live a life of hobbies. Doing only what gives us pleasure, only what rewards us in secret, private ways.'

'Wise words, Priest. You're just filled with surprises tonight, aren't you?'

When Banaschar shot the man a look, he saw his faint grin and the tension eased out from him. He grunted. 'I went into the priesthood looking for wisdom and only then did I realize I'd gone in precisely the wrong direction.'

'Piety not all it's made out to be, then?'

'Is soldiering, Fiddler?'

The man slowly settled back, stirring with his knife blade. 'Had a friend once, tried warning an eager little boy away from the soldier's life.'

'And did your friend succeed?'

'Doesn't matter if he did or didn't. That's not the point.'

'So, what is the point, then?'

'You can't steer anyone away from the path they're going to take. You can show 'em that there's plenty of other paths – you can do that much – but past that? They'll go where they go.'

'Your friend should have scared that boy rigid. That might've worked.'

Fiddler shook his head. 'Can't feel someone else's terror, either, Banaschar. We only know terror for what it is when it looks us dead in the eye.'

There was a sigh from Tavore and the priest looked down. 'You fainted, Adjunct.'

'The – the sword . . .'

'It's done.'

She struggled to sit up. 'Then we must leave.'

'We will, Adjunct,' Fiddler said. 'But first, we eat.'

Tavore pushed Banaschar's hands away and struggled upright. 'You damned fool – do you know who that sword is summoning?'

'Aye. Just burned that card, as it happens.'

Banaschar almost felt the Adjunct's shock, like a jolt of sparks snapping through the air between them.

The priest snorted. 'You've gone and made her speechless, sapper.'

'Good. Can't eat and talk at the same time. Come over here, Adjunct, else me and the priest will have to hold you and force this stew down your throat. Won't do anyone any good if you go and collapse at the wrong moment, will it?'

'You – you should not have done that, Fiddler.'

'Relax,' the man replied, tapping his satchel. 'Saved one House – the only one that means anything to us now.'

'Ours is a house still divided, Captain.'

'The King in Chains? Never mind him – the fool's too busy under-mining the throne he happens to be sitting on. And the Knight is with us.'

'Are you certain?'

'I am. Be at ease on that count.'

'When that god manifests, Fiddler, it will be upon a battlefield –

thousands of souls will feed its shaping. We are speaking of a god of *war* – when it comes, it could well fill half the sky.'

Fiddler glanced across at Banaschar, and then he shrugged. 'Beware the vow of a Toblakai.' And then, with a half-smile, he filled a tin bowl with stew and handed it up to the Adjunct. 'Eat, dear Consort. The rest are with us. Reaver, Fool, the Seven . . . Leper . . .' and his gaze fell for a moment with that title, before he looked back up, grinned over at Banaschar. 'Cripple.'

Cripple. Oh. Well, yes. Been staring me in the face all this time, I suppose. Been thinking it was terror, that old mirror reflection. And surprise, it was.

While they ate, Banaschar's memories wandered back, to the moment in her tent, and her words with Lostara, and all that followed.

Children, gather close. Your mother's days are fraught now. She needs you. She needs us all.

Glancing up, he saw Tavore studying him. 'Banaschar, was it you who removed my helm? Wiped down my face and combed through my hair?'

His gaze dropped. 'Yes, Adjunct.'

She made an odd sound, and then said, 'I am sorry . . . I must have looked a mess.'

Oh, Tavore.

Fiddler rose suddenly and said in a gruff voice, 'I'll saddle your horse, Adjunct.'

Hedge watched as the three riders rode back into the camp. 'Bavedict, distribute the munitions.'

The alchemist turned and in a startled voice asked, 'All of them?'

'All of them. And get 'em kitted out – water, a little food, armour and weapons and nothing else.'

'I'll go talk to the sergeants.'

Nodding, Hedge set off.

He found Fiddler on foot, just outside the Adjunct's tent. The man was alone, standing looking down at the ground.

'We're coming with you,' Hedge said.

Fiddler looked up, scowled. 'No, you're not.'

'The Bridgeburners are coming with you – nothing you can do about it.'

'It's all over with, Hedge. Just leave it alone.' And he turned away.

But Hedge reached out, pulled the man round. 'I already asked the Adjunct – I did it last night, once I figured out what was going on. You need me there, Fiddler. You just don't know it yet – you don't know the half of it, but you'll just have to trust me on this. *You need me there.*'

Fiddler stepped close, his face dark. 'Why? Why the fuck do I?'

Passing soldiers paused, turned to stare.

'You just do! If you don't – I swear this, Fid, I *swear* it – you'll spend the rest of your days poisoned with regret. Listen to me! It's not only us, can't you see that? You need the Bridgeburners!'

Fiddler pushed him back with both hands, staggering Hedge. 'They're *not* Bridgeburners! It's not just a fucking name! You can't just pick up any old useless fools and call them Bridgeburners!'

'Why not?' Hedge retorted. 'It's what we were, wasn't it? At the beginning? Young and wide-eyed stupid and wanting to be better than we were!' He waved an arm to take in the camp. 'No different from these Bonehunters – don't you see that?'

'Don't follow me!'

'You're not listening! I went through – I came back! I have no choice, damn you!'

There were tears glistening in Fiddler's eyes. 'Just don't.'

Hedge shook his head. 'I told you. No choice, none at all.'

When Fiddler pushed past him, Hedge let him go. He looked round, scowled. 'It's almost noon – go eat something, you slack-jawed bastards.' Then he headed back for his company's camp.

Fiddler cut between two staff tents, and made it halfway down before he stopped and slowly sank to one knee, his hands over his face. As tears broke loose, shudders drove through him, wave upon wave.

We're going to die – can't he see that? I can't lose him again – I just can't.

He could still feel Hedge's shoulders where he'd pushed him, and see the hurt look on the man's face – *no, don't.* His hands stung, his hands burned. He balled them into fists, head hanging, forcing himself to draw deep breaths, forcing all the rawness away, and with it the terrible anguish that threatened to break him, crush him down.

He needed to go to his soldiers now. The sergeants would have them ready. Waiting. Marines and heavies, the last of both. *One more thing to do, and then we'll be done. All of it, finished.*

Gods, Hedge, we should have died in the tunnels. So much easier, so much quicker. No time to grieve, no time for the scars to get so thick it's almost impossible to feel anything at all.

And then you showed up and tore them all open again.

Whiskeyjack, Kalam, Trotts – they're gone. Why didn't you stay there with them? Why couldn't you just have waited for me?

Still the tears streamed down his face, soaking his beard. He could barely see the matted dead grasses beneath him.

End this. One more thing to do – they'll try and stop us. They have to. We need to be ready for them. We need – I need . . . to be a captain, the one in charge. The one to tell my soldiers where to die.

Wiping at his face, he slowly straightened.

'Gods,' he muttered. 'First the Adjunct, and now this.' He sighed. 'Let's just call it a bad day and be done with it. Ready, Fid? Ready for them? You'd better be.'

He set out.

There was glory in pissing, Corabb decided as he watched the stream curve out and make that familiar but unique sound as it hit the ground.

'Doesn't look like you need both hands for that,' Smiles observed from where she sat nearby.

'Today, I shall even look upon you with sympathy,' he replied, finishing up and then spitting on his hands to clean them.

'Sympathy? What am I, a lame dog?'

Sitting leaning against his pack, Bottle laughed, earning a dark look from Smiles.

'We are going somewhere to fight,' Corabb said, turning to face her and the others sitting on the ground beyond. 'Today, you are all my family.'

'Explains the sympathy,' Koryk muttered.

'And I will stand at your side, Koryk of the Seti,' Corabb said.

Smiles snorted. 'To what, keep him from running?'

'No. Because, this time, he will stand with us. He will be a soldier again.'

There was a long moment of silence from the gathered squad, and then Koryk rose and walked a short distance away.

'There's demons crouched in his brain,' Cuttle said under his breath. 'All that whispering must be driving him mad.'

'Here comes the sergeant,' Corabb said. 'It's time.' He went to his kit bag, checked the straps once again, picking up the crossbow and admiring it for a moment before tying it on to the satchel. He re-counted the quarrels and was satisfied to find that they still numbered twelve.

'Load up,' Tarr said when he arrived. 'We're headed northwest.'

'That's damn near back the way we came!' said Smiles. 'How far? If I even come within sight of that desert, I'll slit my own throat.'

'It's a big lake now, Smiles,' Bottle pointed out.

Tarr said, 'Should be there by noon tomorrow, or so the captain says. Take food for two days, and as much water as you can carry.'

Corabb scratched at the beard covering his jaw. 'Sergeant – the regulars are getting ready to break camp, too.'

'They're going east, Corporal.'

'When do we rendezvous?'

But the sergeant's only reply was a sharp glance, and then he went to his own gear.

Smiles edged up close to Corabb. 'Should've used that thing for more than just pissing, Corporal, and now it's too late.'

Oh. I get it. We're not coming back. 'Then we march to glory.'

'Hood's breath,' Smiles sighed.

But he caught a look on her face – quickly hidden. *She is afraid. She is so young.* 'And you, Smiles, shall stand on my other side.'

Did she almost sag towards him then? He could not be sure, and she kept her face down, turned away as she worked on her satchel.

'You have let your hair grow long,' he said. 'It makes you almost pretty.'

Cuttle edged close. 'You really don't know when to keep your mouth shut, do you, Corabb?'

'Form up,' Tarr said. 'We're in the lead to start.'

Cuttle met his sergeant's eyes and gave a faint nod. Tarr turned and looked ahead to where Fiddler waited. The captain looked ill, but he held Tarr's gaze without expression, and then Fiddler swung round and set off.

Their march would take them through the entire camp of regulars, down the central, widest avenue between the uneven rows of tents, awnings and blinds. The sapper looked up at the sky, then back down again – those blazing slashes seemed closer than ever, unnerving him.

Cuttle waved the others in their squad forward, then glanced back to see Balm leading his own soldiers, and beyond them Sergeant Urb. And then the rest of them. Hellian, Badan Gruk, Sinter, Gaunt-Eye, and the heavies falling in wherever they felt like it.

He stepped in behind Shortnose – the man had a way of wandering off, as if forgetting which squad he'd joined, but now he was here, trudging along under a massive bundle of rolled chain armour, weapons and shield. The heavy had tied a Nah'ruk finger bone to his beard and it made a thumping sound on his chest as he walked. His maimed shield hand was bound up in leather straps.

As they walked, the regulars to either side began converging ahead, as if to line their route, as if to watch in that Hood-damned silence of theirs as the marines and heavies passed. His unease deepened. *Not a word from them, not a thing. As if we're strangers.* As the troop approached the broad avenue, the only sound came from their marching – the hard impact of their boots and the clatter of equipment – and through his growing anger Cuttle had an uncanny sensation of walking through an army of ghosts as the regulars drew up on either side. He didn't see a single youthful face among all the onlookers. *And not a nod, not even a tilt of a head.*

But we look just as old and ruined, don't we? What are they seeing? What are they thinking?

Tavore, I don't envy you these soldiers. I can't read them at all. Do they understand? Have they worked it out yet?

They're heading east – to block the army the Assail are sending after us – to buy us the time we need. But if they can't do it – if they can't slow the bastards down – it's all lost. This whole damned thing falls apart.

You're headed for a fight. And we won't be there for you – any of you. No fist of heavies. No knots of marines in the line. So if that's a look of betrayal in your faces, if you think all this is about abandoning all of you, then Hood take me—

The thought ended abruptly, and Cuttle's growing anger simply disintegrated.

The regulars began saluting, fists to their chests. Standing at attention, in suddenly perfect rows to either side.

The few muttered conversations among the marines and heavies fell off, and suddenly the silence became oppressive in an entirely different way. Cuttle felt more than heard the company's footfalls slipping into cadence, and in the squad directly in front of him he now saw the soldiers edging into paired rows behind Captain Fiddler, with Corabb and Tarr in the lead, Smiles and Koryk behind them, followed by Bottle and Shortnose.

'You just had to be uneven,' growled Balm in a low voice as he came up on his right.

'Then drop back.'

'And shake this out all over again? Can't even remember the last time I found myself on a parade – no, we just hold this, sapper, and hope to Hood no one trips over their own Hood-damned feet.'

'Wasn't expecting this.'

'I hate it. I feel sick. Where we going again?'

'Stop panicking, Sergeant.'

'And who in the White Jackal's name are you, soldier?'

Cuttle sighed. 'Just march, Sergeant. Once we get through this, we can relax again. Promise.'

'We getting medals or something?'

No. This is something else. This is what the Adjunct said wouldn't happen. Look at these regulars.

They're witnessing us.

'Did you see this?' Kisswhere asked.

Sinter kept staring straight ahead, but she frowned. 'What do you mean?'

'Your visions – did you see any of this? And what about what's coming – what about tomorrow, or the next day?'

'It's not like that.'

Her sister sighed. 'Funny. *I* can see what's coming, right through to the very end.'

'No you can't. That's just fear talking.'

'And it's got a lot to say.'

'Just leave it, Kisswhere.'

'No. I won't. Tell me about a vision of the future, with us in it. Here's mine. You've got a baby on your hip, with a boy running ahead. It's the morning walk down to the imperial school – the one they were building before we left. And I got a girl who looks just like me, but wild, a demon in disguise. We're exhausted, in the way of all mothers, and I'm getting fat. We brag about the runts, complain about our husbands, bitch at how tired we are. It's hot, the flies are out and the air smells of rotted vegetables. Husbands. When are they going to finish fixing the roof, that's what we want to know, when instead of doing something useful the lazy bastards spend all day lying in the shade picking their noses. And then if that's not—'

'Stop it, Kisswhere.'

To Sinter's astonishment, her sister fell silent.

Was that the first time? Must've been. Sorido the miller's boy. I'd woken up that morning with tits. We went behind the old custom house annexe, on that burnt stubble where they'd toasted an infestation of spiders only a few days before, and I lifted up my shirt and showed them off.

What was that boy's name? Rilt? Rallit? His eyes got huge. I'd stolen a flask from the house. Peach brandy. You could set your breath on fire with that stuff. I figured he needed loosening up. Hood knows I did. So we drank and he played with them.

I had to fight him to get his cock out.

And that was the first time. Wish there'd been a thousand more, but it didn't work out that way. He was killed a year later in his father's shop – some rushed order on ship fittings, rumours of another crackdown on Kartoolii pirates because the Malazan overlords were losing revenues or something.

They weren't pirates. That's just a name for people being obvious about theft.

There could have been other boys. Dozens of them. But who wants to lie down on the ground on an island crawling with deadly spiders?

Rallit or Ralt or whatever your name was, I'm glad we fucked before you died. I'm glad you had at least that.

It's not fair, how the years just vanish.

I love you, Hellian. How hard could it be to just say those words? But even thinking them made Urb's jaw tighten as if bound in wire. Sudden

800

sweat under his armour, a thudding heart, a thickening sensation of nausea in his throat. She had never looked better. No, she was beautiful. Why wasn't *he* the drunk? Then he could blather out all he wanted to say in that shameless way drunks had. But why would she want him then? Unless she was just as drunk. But she wasn't anything like that now. Her eyes were clear and they never rested, as if she was finally seeing things, and all that slackness was gone from her face and she could probably have any man she wanted now so why bother looking at him?

He kept his gaze ahead, trying not to notice all these regular soldiers with their salutes. Better to pretend they weren't even there, weren't paying them any attention, and they could walk out of this army, off to do whatever it was that needed doing, and no one needed to notice anything.

Attention made him nervous, when the only attention he really wanted was from her. But if she gave it to him, he'd probably fall to pieces.

I'd like to make love. Just once. Before I die. I'd like to hold her in my arms and feel as if the world's just slid and shifted into its proper shape, making everything perfect. And I could see all of that, right there in her eyes.

And looking up . . . I'd see all these soldiers saluting me.

No, that's not right. Don't look up, Urb. Listen to yourself! Idiot!

Widdershins found that he was walking beside Throatslitter. He'd not expected an actual military march, and already his bare feet inside his worn boots were raw. He'd always hated having to throw his heels down with every step, feeling the shocks shooting up his spine, and having to lift his knees higher than usual was wearing him out.

He could see the end ahead, the edge of the damned camp. Once out of sight of these wretched regulars going all formal on them, they could relax again. He'd happily forgotten all this shit, those first months of training before he'd managed to slip across into the marines – where discipline didn't mean striding in cadence and throwing the shoulders back and all that rubbish. Where it meant doing your job and not wasting time on anything else.

He remembered the first officers he'd encountered, bitching about companies like the Bridgeburners. *Sloppy, slouching slackers – couldn't get 'em to stand in a straight line if their lives depended on it, and as likely to slit their officers' throats as take an order.* Well, not quite. If it was a good order, a smart order, they'd step up smart. If it was a stupid order, an order that would see soldiers die for no good reason, well, the choice was not doing it and getting hammered for insubordination, or quietly arranging a tragic battlefield casualty.

Maybe the Bridgeburners had been the worst of the lot, but they'd also been the best, too. No, Widdershins liked being a marine, a Bonehunter in the tradition of their unruly predecessors. At least it had put an end to this kind of marching.

His heels were already bloody in his boots.

Deadsmell didn't want to say goodbye, not to anyone. Not even Throatslitter limping one row ahead of him, whom with a choice comment or two he could make yelp that laugh – like squeezing a duck. Always entertaining, seeing people flinch on hearing it. And Deadsmell could do it over and over again.

It'd been a while since he'd last heard it, but now was not the time – not with all these regulars on either side. *All these men and women saying goodbye to us.* The Bonehunters were in their last days. This tortured army could finally see the end of things – and it seemed to have come up on them fast, unexpected, appallingly close.

But no. We marched across half a world. We chased a Whirlwind. We walked out of a burning city. We stood against our own in Malaz City. We took down the Letherii Empire, held off the Nah'ruk. We crossed a desert that couldn't be crossed.

Now I know how the Bridgeburners must have felt, as the last of them was torn down, crushed underfoot. All that history, vanishing, soaking red into the earth.

Back home – in the Empire – we're already lost. Just one more army struck off the ledgers. And this is how things pass, how things simply go away. We've gone and marched ourselves off the edge of the world.

I don't want to say goodbye. And I want to hear Throatslitter's manic laugh. I want to hear it again and again, and for ever more.

Hedge had drawn up his Bridgeburners just outside the northwest edge of the encampment. Waiting for the marines and heavies to appear, he scanned his collection of soldiers. They were loaded down, almost groaning beneath the weight of their gear. *Way too many kittens.*

Sergeant Rumjugs caught his eye and he nodded. She moved up to position herself at his side as he turned to face the Bonehunter camp. 'Ever seen the like, sir? Who do you think gave the command for that? Maybe the Adjunct herself?'

Hedge shook his head. 'No commands, Sergeant – this came from somewhere else. From the regulars themselves, rank and file and all that. I admit it, I didn't think they had this in them.'

'Sir, we heard rumours, about the marines and heavies . . . that maybe they won't want us with them.'

'Doesn't matter, Sergeant. When it comes right down to it, we don't even take orders from the Adjunct.'

'But didn't she—'

'I lied,' Hedge said. 'I ain't talked to nobody. This is my decision.' He glanced over at her. 'Got a problem with that, Sergeant?'

But she was grinning.

Hedge studied her. 'You find that funny, do you? Why?'

She shrugged. 'Sir, we heard rumours – other ones – about us not being real Bridgeburners. But you just proved 'em wrong, didn't you? We don't belong to nobody – only to each other, and to you, sir. You lied – hah!'

Behind them Sweetlard said, 'Last night I took a man t'bed for free, sir, and y'know why? When he asked me how old I was and I said twenty-six, he believed me. Lies are sweet, ain't they?'

'Here they come,' said Hedge.

Fiddler had appeared, leading his troops out from the camp. Even from this distance, Hedge could see the faces of the marines and heavies – sickly, grim. They'd not been expecting any sort of send-off. *And they don't know what to do with it. Did Fiddler throw a salute back? No, he wouldn't have.*

Fid, I see you. You're as bad off as the rest of 'em. Like you're headed for the executioner.

Us soldiers only got one kind of coin worth anything, and it's called respect. And we hoard it, we hide it away, and there ain't nobody who'd call us generous. Easy spenders we're not. But there's something feels even worse than having to give up a coin – it's when somebody steps up and tosses one back at us.

We get antsy. We look away. And part of us feels like breaking inside, and we get down on ourselves, and outsiders don't understand that. They think we should smile and wave or stand proud. But we don't want to do anything of the sort, even when we're made to. It's because of all the friends we left behind, on all those battle-fields, because we know that they're the ones deserving of all that respect.

We could sit on a king's hoard of those coins and still stay blind to all of 'em. Because some riches stick in the throat, and choke us going down.

When he saw Fiddler look up and see him, Hedge strode over.

'Don't do this, Fid.'

'Do what? I told you—'

'Not that. You halt your company now. You form 'em up facing those regulars. You're captain now and they're looking to you. It's the coin, Fiddler. You got to give it back.'

The captain stared at Hedge for a long moment. 'Didn't think it'd be this hard.'

'So you thought to just run away?'

Fiddler shook his head. 'No. I didn't know what to do. Wasn't sure what they wanted.'

Cocking his head, Hedge said, 'You're not convinced they're worth it, are you?'

The captain was silent.

Hedge shook his head. 'We ain't made for this, you and me, Fid. We're sappers. When I get in trouble on all this stuff I just think what would Whiskeyjack do? Listen, you need those regulars to stand up, you need them to buy you the time needed. You need them to buy it with their own blood, their own lives. It don't matter if you think they've not earned a damned thing. *You got to give the coin back*.'

When Fiddler still hesitated, Hedge swung round and gestured to his Bridgeburners, then turned back. 'We're forming up, Fid, faces to the camp – you just gonna stand there, with all your marines and heavies mobbing up and not knowing where to fucking look?'

'No,' Fiddler replied in a thick voice. 'Hedge – I think . . . I just faltered a step. That's all.'

'Better now than a few days from now, hey?'

As Hedge moved to join his squads, Fiddler called out. 'Wait.'

He turned back. 'What now?'

'Something else everyone needs to see, I think.' And Fiddler stepped forward and held out his hand.

Hedge eyed it. 'You think that's enough?'

'Start there, idiot.'

Smiling, Hedge grasped that forearm.

And Fiddler pulled him into a hard embrace.

Badalle stood atop a wagon, Saddic at her side, watching the scene at the edge of camp.

'What's happening, Badalle?' Saddic asked.

'Wounds take time to heal,' she replied, watching the two men embracing, feeling a vast tension seem to drain away on all sides.

'Are they lovers?'

'Brothers,' she said.

'The one with the red beard – you called him Father, Badalle. Why?'

'It's what being a soldier is all about. That is what I have seen since we found them. You do not choose your family, and sometimes there's trouble in that family, but you don't choose.'

'But they did. They chose to be soldiers.'

'And then they come face to face with death, Saddic. That is the blood tie, and it makes a knot not even dying can cut.' *And that is why the others are saluting.* 'Soon,' she said, 'very soon, we are going to see this family awaken to anger.'

'But Mother is sending those ones away. Will we ever see them again?'

'It's easy, Saddic,' she said. 'Just close your eyes.'

Walking slowly, Pores made his way to the edge of the camp so that he could look out on the marines and heavies, who were now forming up to face the regulars. He looked round for the Adjunct but could not see her. Nor was Fist Blistig anywhere in sight – *the man who tried to murder me.*

There is nothing more dangerous than a man without a sense of humour.

As Fiddler and Hedge drew apart and headed for their respective companies, Faradan Sort came up alongside Pores, and then, on his other side, Fist Kindly.

Pores sighed. 'Fists. Was all this by your command?'

'I was barking orders when they just stood up and left me standing there,' said Faradan Sort. 'They're as bad as marines, these regulars.'

'We will see if that's true soon enough,' Kindly said. 'Master-Sergeant Lieutenant Pores, are you recovered?'

'Some additional healing proved possible once we were away from the desert. As you see, sir, I am up and about.'

'It is your innate laziness that still needs addressing.'

'Yes sir.'

'Are you agreeing with me, Master-Sergeant Lieutenant Pores?'

'I always agree with you, sir.'

'Oh, enough, you two,' Faradan Sort said. 'We're about to be saluted.'

All the regulars had drawn to this side of the camp and stood in an uneven mass. There was an ease to all of this that Pores found . . . peculiar, as if the entire structure of the military, in all its rigidity and inane affectation, had ceased to be relevant. The regulars no longer held their own salute and now stood watching, for all the world like a crowd drawn down to the docks to see a fleet's departure from the bay, while Captain Fiddler moved out to stand in front of his marines, facing them all. He lifted his hand in a salute, held it for a moment as his soldiers did the same, and then let the hand fall.

And that was it. No answering gesture from the regulars. Pores grunted. 'It's the old coin thing, isn't it?'

'Indeed,' replied Kindly in a rough voice. He cleared his throat and said, 'That tradition was born on the Seti Plain, from the endless internecine warfare among the horse clans. Honest scraps ended in an exchange of trophy coins.' He was silent for a few breaths, and then he sighed. 'Seti combs are works of art. Antler and horn, polished to a lustre—'

'I feel another bout of laziness coming on, sir. Isn't it time you ordered me to do something?'

Blinking, Kindly faced Pores. Then shocked him with a hand on his shoulder. 'Not today.' And he walked back into camp.

Faradan Sort remained at his side for a moment longer. 'If he had a son to choose, Pores . . .'

'I've already been disowned once, Fist, and regardless of what you might think, I'm not a glutton for punishment.'

She studied him. 'He was saying goodbye.'

'I know what it was,' Pores snapped, wincing as he turned too quickly away. When she reached to take his arm, he waved her off. Both gestures made his chest hurt, but that was the kind of pain he welcomed these days. Keeping the other kind at bay.

Forgot to thank him. Deadsmell. And now it's too late. And now Kindly goes all soft on me. Where's the fun in that?

'Go back to your wagon,' Faradan Sort said. 'I'll detail three squads for the harness.'

No heavies now. 'Better make it four, Fist.'

'It is my understanding,' she replied, 'that we do not have far to go today.'

Despite himself, he glanced over at her. 'Really? Has she announced our destination, then?'

'She has.'

'And?'

She looked across at him. 'We're looking for a suitable field of battle.'

Pores thought about that for a few moments. 'So they know we're here.'

'Yes, Lieutenant. And they are marching to meet us.'

He looked to the departing column of marines and heavies. *Then . . . where are they going? This is what I get for lying half dead for days, and then spoon-feeding old Shorthand, waiting for a word from him. Just one word. Something more than just staring into space – that's not a proper way for a man to end his days.*

And now I don't know what the Hood's going on. Me, of all people.

The camp was breaking up behind him. Everything coming down for the march, with barely a single word spoken. He'd never known an army as quiet as this one. 'Fist.'

'Yes?'

'Will they fight?'

She stepped close, her eyes cold as ice. 'You don't ask that kind of question, Pores. Not another word. Am I understood?'

'Aye, Fist. I just don't want to be the only one unsheathing my sword, that's all.'

'You're in no condition for that.'

'That detail hardly matters, Fist.'

Making a face, she turned away. 'I suppose not.'

Pores watched her head back into the camp.

Besides, I might need that sword. If Blistig gets close. It's not like he'll be of any use in the scrap – the very opposite, in fact. But I'll choose the perfect moment. It's all down to timing. All of life is down to timing, and that was always my talent, wasn't it?

I'm mostly a nice guy. Made a career of avoiding blood and fighting and all the unpleasant stuff. The challenge was pulling that off while being in an army. But . . . not as hard as it sounds.

No matter. It's not as if I'm afraid of war. It's the chaos I don't like. Kindly's combs . . . now, you see, those I do understand. That man I understand. Through and through. And being his one unruly comb, why, how perfect was that?

Mostly a nice guy, like I said. But Blistig tried killing me, for a few empty casks.

I don't feel like being nice any more.

'Adjunct wishes to see you, Fist,' said Lostara Yil.

Blistig glanced up, saw the look in her eyes and decided to ignore it. Grunting, he straightened from where he had been sitting amidst discarded equipment.

He followed the woman through the camp, paying little attention to the preparations going on around them. These regulars were good at going through all the motions – they'd done enough of it, after all, and had probably walked more leagues since forming up than most people did in a lifetime. But that didn't add any notches on the scabbard, did it? For all their professionalism – suddenly rediscovered since the Blood for Water miracle, and not just rediscovered, but reinvented with a discipline so zealous it bordered on the obsessive – these regulars looked fragile to Blistig.

They would melt away before the enemy at the first hint of pressure. He'd seen them lining the route taken by the marines and heavies; he'd seen their pathetic salutes. Good for gestures now, these soldiers, but their faces were empty. They had the look of the dead. Every man, every woman.

When Lostara reached the entrance to the Adjunct's tent, she halted, gesturing him inside.

He moved past her, stepped within.

Only the front chamber remained standing – the back end of the tent was already unstaked and hanging in a thick creased wall behind Tavore, who stood facing him. There was no one else present, not even that smirking priest, and Lostara Yil had not followed him in.

'What is it, Adjunct? I have troops to oversee if you want us up and on the way before noon.'

'Fist Blistig, I am placing you in command of the centre. You will have Fist Kindly on your right and Fist Faradan Sort on your left. War-leader Gall will hold the Khundryl in reserve, along with the skirmishers and archers.'

He stared at her, dumbfounded. 'You are describing the presentation for battle,' he said. 'But there won't be any battle. It will be a rout. We will face Forkrul Assail – and you've gone and given up your sword. Their sorcery will overwhelm us.'

Her eyes held on his, unwavering. 'You will hold the centre, Fist. That is your only task in the upcoming engagement. You will be attacked by normal soldiers – Kolansii – a conventional army. Expect them to be highly disciplined and well trained. If there are heavy infantry among the enemy then you can be certain that they will strike for your position. You will not yield a single step, is that understood?'

Blistig drew off his helmet, contemplated throwing it at the woman standing opposite him. Instead, he clawed a hand through his thinning hair. *I could kill her. Right now, here in this tent. But she bought their souls again, didn't she? I'd never get away alive. Better to wait, find a more perfect moment. But then, who am I trying to fool?* 'Put me there, Adjunct, and I'll take a knife to the back before the Kolansii even crest the horizon.'

There was a look in her eyes that made him wonder if she'd seen right through to his thoughts, if she knew how close she was to being murdered, and simply did not care enough to feel fear. 'Fist, I was advised when in Aren to leave you in command of the city garrison. Indeed, there was talk of promoting you to the city's Fist, and had that occurred it is possible that you would then be touted to become High Fist, overseeing all of South Seven Cities. I understand that what I have just described would have suited you perfectly. At least until the next uprising.'

Blistig's voice was a rasp, 'What is the point of this, Adjunct?'

'However, your proponents – the officers and functionaries in Aren – couldn't see a span beyond their city's walls. They could not imagine that Jhistal Mallick Rel would not rot away the rest of his days in a gaol cell, or lose his head to a pike above the main gate. In other words, they had no comprehension of the extent of the man's influence, how it had already corrupted the Claw, or that his agents were even then positioned within reach of Laseen's throne.

'Furthermore,' she continued, still studying him, 'that his hatred for you and your . . . betrayal at Aren, following Coltaine's fall, pretty much assured your eventual assassination. You may indeed be unaware that between the Fall and my arrival in the city three attempts were made on your life. All of them successfully intercepted, at the cost of four valuable agents.

'Your transfer to under my command was in fact the only means of keeping you alive, Fist Blistig. The fourth time your life was saved was at Malaz City; had we failed in extricating ourselves you would have been arrested and executed. Now, you may choose to believe that I undertook such efforts because I value you as a commander, and be sure that to this day I remain impressed and admiring of your quick wit and decisiveness when refusing to yield Aren to the rebels. But that was not my primary reason for saving your life. Mallick Rel, High Fist Korbolo Dom and their interests would seek to revise the events at Aren – the outlawing and castigation of the Wickans was but the beginning.

'Fist Blistig, there are few who know the truth of those events. I saved your life to keep that truth alive.'

He was silent following this speech. A part of him wanted to disbelieve every word, wanted to call her a damned liar, and a self-serving one at that. But . . . how could any of this be self-serving? She was placing him in command of the centre – probably facing heavy infantry – among Malazan soldiers who despised him. She'd saved his life only to throw it away now, and how did that make sense, any sense at all? 'Adjunct, are you expecting me to thank you?'

'The only expectation of any importance, Fist, concerns commanding the centre to the best of your abilities.'

'They won't follow me.'

'They will.'

'Why should they?'

'Because they will have no one else.'

No one . . . 'Where will you be, Adjunct?'

'I will be facing the Forkrul Assail and their sorcery. I will be fighting the power of their will. I will be preventing it from reaching my soldiers.'

'But you gave up your damned sword, woman!'

'There are residual effects to bearing such a weapon, Fist. In any case, none of that is your concern.'

'Except when you fail. When you fall.'

'Even then, Fist.'

His eyes narrowed on her. 'That only works if you take them down with you. Is that the plan, Adjunct? One final sacrifice to defend an army that doesn't even like you? That doesn't want to be here? That doesn't even know what it's supposed to be fighting for? And then you expect me and the other Fists to hold them together? With you dead and gone?'

She cocked her head. 'You are contradicting yourself.'

He waved a dismissive hand, the gesture chopping the air.

Tavore seemed to flinch slightly at that, but the tone of her next words belied the impression. 'Maintain your line with the flanks, Fist.'

'We're going to get cut to pieces.'

Turning away, she reached for her leather gloves. 'If so, Fist, just make sure you take a long time dying.'

He left without bothering to salute, walked with his helm dangling from one hand.

Three foiled attempts on my life? A corrupted Claw?

Then who did the foiling?

Banaschar stood twenty paces away from her tent, motionless while figures moved in measured haste around him, wanting to be a heavy stone in the stream, a place to set a foot and find an instant or two of rest. But his was a lifeless island, until Lostara Yil found him, taking his arm in hers and pulling him round – Henar Vygulf grinning off to one side.

'What is this?' Banaschar demanded, only vaguely resisting as she led him away – he'd just seen Blistig exit Tavore's tent, his stride echoing that of a lifeless T'lan Imass, and he'd been considering going to the Adjunct again, to see what he could glean of what had taken place between her and the Fist. Instead, he was being pulled away.

And there, ahead, stood a small group of officers. Skanarow. Ruthan Gudd, Raband and Faradan Sort.

Banaschar sought to disengage his arm. 'You keep forgetting, I'm not actually in this army.'

'Our last palaver,' said Lostara. 'Make it mocking, make it solemn, however you like it, Priest. But it will happen, and you will be in attendance.'

'Why?'

They'd reached the others, and Banaschar saw the expectation in their faces and wanted to hide under a shield.

Ruthan Gudd, fingers combing his beard, was the first to speak. 'Priest. We've all been given our orders. Will you be at the Adjunct's side through all of this?'

All of what? The dying? 'I don't know. I doubt it.'

'Why?' asked Faradan Sort, the word sharp, accusing.

He shrugged. 'I expect she will be fighting. Eventually.'

Lostara Yil cleared her throat in the silence that followed, and then said, 'She has ordered me, Henar and Ruthan Gudd to attend to her at all times.'

'That makes sense,' Banaschar said.

'It's the Forkrul Assail, isn't it?'

To Lostara's question Banaschar simply shrugged again.

'She has surrendered her sword, somewhere,' said Faradan Sort. 'How does she expect to defend herself against the sorcery of the Assail?'

'I don't know.'

Raband voiced a raw curse and looked ready to leave, but Skanarow shook her head at him and he subsided, scowling.

Lostara caught Banaschar's eye – he could see fear in hers. 'Priest, I do not think I will again Shadow Dance. Not the way I did before. If she is expecting such a thing from me – perhaps against the Forkrul Assail—'

'Captain, I don't know what she is expecting,' said Banaschar quietly. 'You and Ruthan Gudd, you have both shown exceptional abilities. Is that why she wants you close? I imagine that it is, and at the moment of greatest need, will she look to you two? Why wouldn't she?'

'I can't do it again!'

Banaschar glanced over at Ruthan Gudd. 'And what of you, Captain? Besieged by the same uncertainties, are you? Or will the gift of the Stormriders reawaken to protect you?'

'The Adjunct clearly believes that it will,' he replied.

'Have you told her otherwise, Captain?'

'It's complicated.'

'Is it not why you're here?' Banaschar asked. 'Was this not the reason for their gift?'

The others were studying Ruthan Gudd now, and the man looked decidedly unhappy. 'It depends. Nobody's ever as forthcoming on these things as one might like. Did they know what was hidden in Kolanse? Probably. Are they interested in . . . liberation?'

'Hardly,' growled Faradan Sort, one hand now on the sword belted at her side.

Ruthan Gudd's eyes flicked down to that weapon and his smile was wry when he lifted his gaze to Faradan's. 'I suspected you had a sound reason for forswearing the Wall.'

'I fought three links from Greymane.'

Ruthan Gudd nodded but said nothing more.

Breath hissed from Lostara Yil. 'This isn't fair. Ruthan – do you fear using what the Stormriders gave you?'

'The Stormriders are not a people given to compromise,' Banaschar said, when it was clear that Ruthan Gudd had no intention of replying. 'The captain senses the ambivalence in what is to come. And the risk of failure. He anticipates that the power of the Stormriders will, if unleashed, conclude that said risk is too great – with too much to lose should the Adjunct's plan fail.'

Lostara said, 'Ruthan – do you not *control* that power?'

Finally, the man scowled and said, 'Ask that of yourself and the Shadow Dance, Lostara Yil.'

'But that is the will of a god!'

'And whom do the Stormriders serve? Does anyone even know? You, Faradan? Are they mindless, senseless creatures? You have stood the Wall. Tell her – tell her what you have seen with your own eyes.'

'They have purpose,' she said slowly. 'They are driven. More than that, I cannot say.'

'This is getting us nowhere,' said Raband. 'The fact is this: you and me, Skanarow, we're in command of our companies. Is there anything more that you and I need know? Then I suggest we head back to our troops and leave the rest of their discussion to our superiors.'

Banaschar watched him dragging Skanarow away by one arm – she threw a look back at Ruthan Gudd but he either did not notice or chose not to, and so did not see the crushing grief take her face.

Sighing, Faradan Sort drew her gauntlets from her belt. 'Fare you well, captains.'

The priest looked up at the morning sky, squinted at the Jade Strangers. *Never been closer. We only have a day or two. Not more, surely.*

'Cotillion swore to me that he would never again take possession,' said Lostara Yil.

Banaschar shot her a searching look. 'Too tempting, I imagine?'

'What's given and what's taken away, Priest.'

He nodded, understanding her meaning.

'I was expecting to survive all of this,' said Ruthan Gudd. 'Now I am not so sure.'

'So you know how the rest of us feel,' snapped Lostara Yil.

But the man simply turned to Banaschar. 'If you will not be with her, Priest, then where will you be? What is your reason for being here?'

'There is a question that has been haunting me,' he replied over the sound of the first horns announcing column formation. 'How does a mortal win over a god? Has it ever happened before, even? Has the old order been overturned? Or is this just . . . special circumstance? A moment unique in all of history?'

'You have won the Worm of Autumn to her cause, Priest?'

At Lostara's question, Banaschar frowned. He studied her for a moment, and then glanced at Ruthan Gudd. 'You look shocked,' he said to him. 'Is it that I somehow possessed that power? Or is it the very idea that what we do in this mortal world – with our lives, with our will – could make a god kneel before us?' Then he shook his head. 'But you both misunderstood me. I was not speaking of myself at all. I cannot win over a god, even when I am the last priest in that god's House. Don't you understand? It's her. *She did it*. Not me.'

'She spoke to your god?'

Banaschar grunted. 'No, Lostara. She rarely speaks at all – you of all people should know that by now. No. Instead, she simply refused to waver from her path, and by that alone she has humbled the gods. Do you understand me? *Humbled* them.'

Ruthan Gudd shook his head. 'The gods are too arrogant to ever be humbled.'

'A year ago, lying drunk on my cot, I would have agreed with you, Captain. So tell me now, will you fight for her?'

His eyes were thinned as he studied Banaschar, and then he said, 'With all my heart.'

The gasp that came from Lostara was almost a sob.

The Bonehunters formed up into column. Alone by express order, the Adjunct mounted her horse and remained motionless on it until the last of the wagons they were taking trundled past, and then she took up her reins and swung the animal to face west.

She could see the worn path taken by the marines and the heavies, angling slightly northward but still on a westerly track. They were already out of sight, vanishing into the deceptive folds of the plain. Her hand brushed the empty scabbard at her side, and then away again. She adjusted the strap of her helm, and looked down to examine her worn, oft-mended Malazan uniform. The burgundy was faded, the grey worn to white in places. The leather of her gloves was cracked, sweat- and salt-stained. The armour bands protecting her thighs had rubbed through the underpadding here and there.

She had clasped her cloak to the fittings situated on the harness over her breastbone, and the black wool hung heavy, drawing her shoulders back. Adjusting its weight until it was even, she straightened and ran a hand across the fittings she could reach, tightening them where needed. Reached up and pushed stray wisps of thin hair from her cheeks.

Guiding her horse round, she nudged the animal into a slow trot.

As she passed her soldiers on her left, the Adjunct held her gaze straight ahead.

Faces turned to watch her.

No one called out. Not a word of encouragement, not a single jest, not a question rising up above the thump of boots and the rustle of gear to which she might respond with a word or two.

She held herself straight, moving slowly, making her way towards the head of the column. And of all the journeys she had undertaken, since the very beginning, this one – from the back of the column to its head – was the longest one she had ever travelled. And, as ever, she travelled it alone.

Riding bone-white Jhag horses, the three Forkrul Assail reined in a third of a league ahead of their armies. In their minds, they could hear distant clamour, and they knew that the assault against the Great

Spire had begun. But Akhrast Korvalain was trembling with blows from foreign magics, both ancient and new, and so details evaded their questing. The unease drifting between them was, alas, palpable.

'It does not matter,' Brother Aloft announced. 'We have before us a singular task, and in this we shall prevail. If it follows that we must retrace our steps to win once more the Altar of Judgement, then we shall do so.'

Sister Freedom spoke. 'Brothers, I sense three threats before us, but one will not reach us in time to affect the forthcoming battle, so we can for the moment discount it. It is, however, the smaller of the two elements before us that troubles me. Clearly, they have a specific intention, and the main force marching towards us is positioning itself with the aim of blocking our advance. From this, I conclude that the purpose of the smaller force is of vital importance.'

Brother Aloft slowly nodded. 'What do you propose, Sister?'

'We each possess an army, Brothers. If my senses are accurate – and I assure you that they are – any one of us alone is more than a match for the main force ahead of us. However, bearing in mind that our enemy is perhaps formidable in ways we have not yet been made aware of – they did manage to cross the Glass Desert, after all – I advise that we commit two armies to their destruction. The third, perhaps yours, Brother Grave, sets off at a faster pace to hunt down the smaller force – and prevent them from doing whatever it is they plan to do.'

'And this small force,' Brother Grave said in his thin voice, 'they flee northwest, yes?'

'I doubt it is flight as such, Brother,' Freedom said, frowning. 'I continue to sense a measure of confidence in you, Brother Grave, perhaps somewhat overinflated under the circumstances.'

The older Pure snorted. 'We shall face humans. Thus far, in all my thousands of years of life, I have yet to be impressed by these creatures.'

'Nevertheless, I implore you to engage with surety tempered by caution, Brother.'

'I shall be suitably exact in the execution of my mission, Sister Freedom. I shall hunt down this handful of humans and destroy them.'

'Your words reassure me,' she replied. 'Brother Aloft, I welcome your advice in the matter to follow, as much as I do Brother Grave's. That third element – so disturbingly efficacious against our northern forces – is, as I said, too far away to affect the engagements we anticipate. However, there is the slight risk – as it is known that certain companies among them are mounted – that they would in fact intercept Brother Grave should he lead his forces north from here in his effort to reach his target as quickly as possible. You see, my instincts are that Brother

Grave's foe – despite its paltry size – is in fact the most dangerous element now arrayed before us.'

'Understood, Sister Freedom. Then, might I suggest the following? That Brother Grave divide his army on the basis of speed of travel. That he personally lead his light and medium infantry not northwestward, but southwest skirting the force you and I shall engage, and then striking due north behind said enemy; while in turn his heavy infantry take the shorter northwest route – being heavy infantry, they can well successfully withstand incursions by cavalry should the unexpected happen. If led by the purest of the Watered, the heavy infantry element can coordinate their arrival at the target to coincide with Brother Grave's own companies, as rudimentary communication should be possible.'

Sister Freedom turned to Brother Grave. 'Does this suit you, Brother?'

'Light and medium elements constitute a little over two thousand soldiers – my force was ever weighted on the heavier elements, organized as it originally was for sieges and set battles. Sister Freedom, how accurate is your gauging of the complement of this smaller enemy force?'

'No more than a hundred, I believe, Brother Grave.'

'Well then.' The man smiled, face folding with the expression. 'Two thousand against a hundred. Will you both forgive me for a small meas-ure of confidence regarding those odds?'

Brother Aloft said, 'Since we are certain that there is nothing like a pass or any other similar feature into which to force attackers, then I cannot but share your confidence, Brother Grave. At best, the enemy will be defending a hill – perhaps one of the ancient Elan barrow camps – and so can be attacked from all sides. And of course, even should the light and medium forces fail, the heavy infantry companies will re-join you and thereby contribute to subsequent assaults. Given all this, I believe we have successfully addressed the matter of the smaller enemy force.' Aloft faced Freedom. 'Only a hundred, you say? Perhaps they are deserters.'

'It is possible,' she conceded. 'Yet my instincts say otherwise.'

'With vehemence?'

She glanced at him. 'Yes, Brother Aloft, with vehemence.'

'Then, if I may,' said Aloft, 'we should perhaps discuss another concern. The third force, which has so thoroughly negated our efforts at defeating or even containing it, is now marching with the clear intention of joining this battle – though as you say, Sister, they will be too late. My thoughts are these: it is too great a reach to imagine that there has been no coordination here. To begin, the strongest fortress in Estobanse is taken, thus threatening our north and, more important, our primary source of food, being the valley province. We respond by sending armies against them, only to have them crushed. Now, from what we are able to glean from Sister Reverence and Brother Diligence, at the Spire, two distinct elements have engaged us from the south. And we of course now march to block an incursion from the west. For all we know, a foreign fleet is even now entering Kolanse Bay.' He surveyed the expressions before him and slowly nodded. 'This was well planned, do you not agree? Its principal aim, to draw apart our active armies, has already succeeded. In each instance, we are forced to react rather than initiate.'

'A proficient high command, then,' said Sister Freedom, nodding.

But Aloft shook his head. 'In truth, this has the feel of a grand strategy, and just as your instincts speak with vehemence to you about the matter of the smaller force, Sister Freedom, so now my instincts have been shouting that this invasion – this strategy and each and every tactical engagement – is in fact the product of a single individual's will.' He nodded to Brother Grave. 'I accept your assessment of humans, in general. But is it not also true that, on rare occasions, there rises from the multitude of mediocrity that is humanity a single person of extraordinary vision conjoined with the will to achieve that vision, who presents a most formidable presence. One to shape the course of history.'

Brother Grave grunted. 'Charismatic tyrants, you mean. Indeed, they do appear from time to time, burning bright and deadly and expunged just as quickly. Such individuals, among humans, are inevitably self-corrupting, and for all that they may shape history, that shaping is more often than not simply born out of that tyrant's indulgence in destruction. Brother Aloft, you may well be right that we face such a person behind all of this. But does it matter in the end? And is it not that unbridled ambition that assures the fool's demise? I would venture, with considerable amusement, that we now represent that fatal overreaching on that tyrant's part.' He faced Sister Freedom. 'Have you not confirmed that the northern threat is too far away? This grand execution of coordinated invasions has failed, in fact.'

'It may be as you say,' acknowledged Brother Aloft. 'But what if our eyes deceive us? What if what we are seeing is in fact precisely what our opponent wants us to see?'

'Now you are too generous by far,' Sister Freedom admonished him. 'This is a breakdown in timing, perhaps precipitated by our detecting this western threat almost the instant it stepped out from the Glass Desert, and already being in perfect position to strike them with little delay.'

'I accept the wisdom of your words, Sister.'

'I will not castigate you, Brother, for listening to your instincts.

Although, as we all know, if left unrestrained instincts have a way of encouraging panic – as they lie beyond the control of the intellect to begin with, theirs is the shorter path to fear.'

The three Forkrul Assail were silent then, each preoccupied with their own thoughts.

And then Sister Freedom said, 'I shall seek to enslave the soldiers we face. They could prove useful.'

'But not the hundred I hunt,' said Brother Grave.

'No,' she agreed. 'Kill them all, Brother.'

Ben Adaephon Delat reined in hard, his horse's hoofs skidding through the parched grasses.

Cursing, Kalam wheeled his mount round, the beast pitching beneath him in its exhaustion. He glared back his friend. 'What is it now, Quick?'

But the wizard held up a hand, shaking his head.

Settling back to ease his aching spine, Kalam looked round, seeing nothing but empty, rolling land. The taint of green from the jade slashes overhead made the world look sickly, but already he was growing used to that.

'Never mind the Adjunct,' Quick Ben said.

Kalam shot him a startled look. 'What? Her brother—'

'I know – you think this was easy? I felt them pulling apart. I've been thinking about that all morning. I know why Ganoes wants us to find her – I know why he sent us ahead. But it's no good, Kalam. I'm sorry. It's no good.'

The assassin stared at his friend for a moment longer, and then he sagged, spat to clear the taste of ashes from his mouth. 'She's on her own, then.'

'Aye. Her choice.'

'No – don't even try that, Quick. This is *your* choice!'

'She's forced my hand, damn you!'

'How? What has she done? What's all this about pulling apart? What in Hood's name does that even mean?'

Quick Ben's horse must have picked up some of its rider's agitation, for it now shied beneath him and he fought to regain control for a moment. As the animal backed in a half-circle, the wizard swore under his breath. 'Listen. It's not with her any more. She's made herself the sacrifice – how do you think I can even know this? *Kalam, she's given up her sword.*'

Kalam stared. 'What?'

'But I can feel it – that weapon. It's the blank place in my vision. That's where we have to go.'

'So she dies, does she? Just like that?'

Quick Ben rubbed at his face. 'No. We've been doing too much of this – all of us. From the very start.'

'Back to the fucking riddles.'

'Underestimating her! From damned near the first day I ended up with the Bonehunters, I've listened to us all second-guessing her, every damned step she took. I did my share, Hood knows. But it wasn't just me, was it? Her officers. The marines. The fucking camp cook – what did you tell me a while back? About that moment in Mock's Hold, when she asked you to save her? You did it, you said, because she just asked you – no bargaining, no reasons or explanations. She just went and asked you, Kalam. Was it hard saying yes? Tell me the truth. Was it?'

Slowly, Kalam shook his head. 'But I sometimes wondered . . . did I just feel sorry for her?'

Quick Ben reacted as if he'd been slapped. In a soft voice he asked, 'Do you still think that, Kalam?'

The assassin was silent, thinking about it. Then he sighed. 'We know where Ganoes wants us. We even know why – he's her brother, for Hood's sake.'

'We know where she wants us, too, Kalam.'

'Do we?'

Quick Ben slowly nodded.

'So which of the fucking Parans do we obey here?'

'Which one would you rather face – here or other side of the Gates – to tell 'em you failed, that you made the wrong choice? No, I don't mean brazening it out, either. Just standing there, saying what needs saying?'

Fuck. 'I feel like I'm back in Mock's Hold,' he said in a growl. 'I feel as if I never left.'

'And she meets your eyes.'

Abruptly a sob took the assassin, vicious as a body blow and just as unexpected.

His friend waited, saying nothing – and Kalam knew that he wouldn't, because they'd been through it all together. Because true friends knew when to keep silent, to give all the patience needed. Kalam struggled to lock down on his emotions – he wasn't even sure what had taken him, in that moment. *Maybe this unrelenting pressure. This endless howl no one else even hears.*

I stood looking down on the city. I stood knowing I was about to walk a path of blood.

The betrayal didn't even matter, not to me; the Claw was always full of shits. Did it matter to her either? No. She'd already dismissed it. Just one more knife in her chest, and she was already carrying plenty of those, starting with the one she stuck there with her own hands.

Kalam shook himself. 'Same direction?'

'For now,' Quick Ben replied. 'Until we get closer. Then – south-west.'

'To the sword.'

'To the sword.'

'Anyone babysitting it, Quick?'

'I hope not.'

Kalam gathered his reins, drew a deep breath and slowly eased it back out. 'Quick – how did she manage to cross that desert anyway?'

The wizard shook his head, half smiled. 'Guess we . . . under-estimated her.'

After a moment, they set out once again.

Wings crooking, Silchas Ruin slid earthward. After a moment, Tulas Shorn followed. To the south they could see something like a cloud, or a swarm. The air hissing past their wings felt brittle, fraught with distant pain rolling like waves across the sky.

Silchas Ruin landed hard on the ground, sembled almost immediately, and staggered forward, hands held over his ears.

Taking his Edur form, Tulas Shorn studied his friend, but drew no closer. Overhead, one of the jade slashes began edging across the face of the sun. A sudden deepening of shadow enveloped them, the gloom eerie and turgid.

Groaning, Silchas finally straightened, stiff as an old man. He looked across. 'It's the Hust sword,' he said. 'Its howling was driving me mad.'

'I hear nothing,' Tulas said.

'In my skull – I swear I could feel bones crack.'

'Unsheathe it, friend.'

Silchas Ruin looked over with wide eyes, his expression filling with dread.

'Grasp it when you veer.'

'And what will that achieve?'

'I don't know. But I cannot imagine that this gift was meant to torture you. Your only other choice, Silchas, is to discard it.' He gestured southward. 'We are almost upon them – I am, frankly, astonished that she still lives. But if we delay here much longer . . .'

'Tulas, I am afraid.'

'Of dying? A little late for that.'

Silchas smiled, but it was more of a grimace. 'Easy for you to say.'

'I dwelt a long time in the House of Death, tormented by the truth that I failed to achieve what I most wanted in my life. That sense, of terrible incompleteness, overwhelmed me many times. But now I stand with you, my brother, and I will fall in your stead if I can in this battle to come. Oblivion does not frighten me – I see only its blessed release.'

Silchas Ruin studied him. Then he sighed and reached for the sword. Hand closing on its plain grip, he slid the weapon free.

The Hust sword bucked in his hand, voicing a deafening shriek.

Tulas Shorn was driven back a step, and he stared in shock as enormous ghostly chains appeared, writhing from the sword's patterned blade. Those chains seemed to be anchored deep into the ground, and suddenly the land beneath them was shaking, pitching them about as if the world was rolling its shoulders. From below, a rising thunder—

A blast of dirt and stone lifted skyward off to Tulas Shorn's left, and he bellowed in shock upon seeing a dragon clawing its way free of the steaming earth. And then, off to the right, another erupted in a shower of debris, and then a third – each one chained as it rose from the ground, wings hammering the dust-filled air.

Their roars – of release – ripped across the plain.

Silchas Ruin stood, both hands now on the sword, as the ethereal chains snapped taut, scissoring wildly above him like the strands of a wind-whipped thread.

Eloth. Ampelas. Kalse.

Tulas Shorn staggered forward. 'Veer! Silchas Ruin – veer! We have our Storm! He has given us our Storm!'

Screaming, Silchas Ruin blurred, pungent clouds roiling out from him. Sword and chains vanished – yet the three dragons held close in the air above them.

Veering, Tulas Shorn launched himself into the sky.

Eloth's voice filled his skull. *'Brothers! It is as Cotillion promised! We are freed once more!'*

'Only to die!' cried another voice – Ampelas – yet there was nothing of frustration in its tone.

'Should we prevail – Silchas Ruin, will you vow to break our chains?'

And Silchas replied, *'Eloth, I so swear.'*

'Then we have a cause worth fighting for! He bargained true. He is a god with honour!'

The five Ancient Dragons wheeled then, climbing ever higher as they winged southward. The shadow cast down by one talon slash in the heavens above them marked their path, true as an arrow into the heart of the battle.

'My leg!' Telorast shrieked. 'Curdle! I am crippled! Help me!'

The other skeletal lizard halted so quickly it fell over, rolled once, twice, and then leapt back to its feet. 'Aaii! See the shadow? It hunts us! It chases us! Webs across the sky! Telorast – you are doomed!'

'I see Eleint! They are coming for us! This was a trap! A lie! A deceit! Betrayal! Bad luck! Help me, Curdle!'

Curdle leapt up and down as if eating flies on the wing. 'They only pretended! Those two usurpers – they are venal and vicious, selfish! Not-Apsalar was their servant, was she not? She was! This has been planned from the very start – Telorast, I will weep for you. My sister, my lover, my occasional acquaintance – I promise, I will weep for you.'

'You lying bitch! Carry me! Save me! I would save you in your place if I was you and you were me and I wanted to run because that's the smart thing to do – except when I'm me and you're you! Then it's not smart at all!' She clawed furiously at the ground, one leg kicking, trying to reach Curdle, her small hands clutching the air, her serrated jaws clacking in a manic frenzy. 'Come closer, I beg you!' *Snap snap snap.* 'I only want to say goodbye, I swear it!' *Snap snap snap snap.*

'The shadow!' Curdle shrieked. 'I've waited too long! Help!' She began running, leaping over tufts of dead grass, dodging boulders and small stones. Her rush startled a grasshopper into the air and she bit it in half in passing. 'Did you see that? Telor—'

Both creatures veered. Chains cracked like lightning, lifting them skyward.

'*Storm! Five Ancients – now seven!*'

'*Eloth greets you, betrayers! Telorast Anthras! Kerudas Karosias!*'

'*Eloth! Ampelas! Kalse! They still hate us! Telorast, look what you've done!*'

Korabas, the Otataral Dragon, was being driven earthward as dragon after dragon crashed down on her from above, their talons raking through her hide, flensing her wings. She had killed hundreds, but now, at last, she was failing. The land beneath her loomed, every detail a bitter language of death. She could no longer give voice to her fury, her crushing frustration, and was too exhausted to strike out at the Eleint harrying her on all sides.

Blood streamed down her flanks, rained like acid on the lifeless earth below.

The summons dragged her forward, but she was blind to its purpose. Perhaps nothing more than a lure. Yet the imperative was absolute and she would strive to answer it. With her last breath, she would seek that fated place. *A trap, or a promise? An answer to my prayers, or the making of my barrow? No matter. I fail. I would even welcome chains, but they will not grant me that mercy. I feel Mother awakening. I feel T'iam, so close now – the Storms gathered, the power building. She is coming – she will see me killed!*

She pitched as yet another Eleint slammed down on her. With

one last surge, she swung her neck round, lacerated jaws stretching wide—

And saw seven dragons, descending from high above the swarm surrounding her. Another Storm. *This ends it, then.*

The creature clinging to her back tore itself away, flinching from her jaws – she caught a hind limb, ripped the flesh from the bone.

The seven Ancients plunged into the maelstrom – and suddenly Eleint were screaming in shock and pain, bodies twisting as they plummeted, blooms of blood like clouds—

They fight to save me! But why? Do not draw near, friends! I am poison!

But – more – do not die for me!

I, whose touch is death, beg you – do not die for me!

Yet on they fought, but now their foes were recovering, and scores lifted higher to close on them.

And should T'iam manifest – she will take even you.

East, the place of the summons, called to her. Torn fragments of meat falling from her jaws, Korabas fixed her gaze upon that beckoning horizon. Her allies had drawn away her assailants, won her a reprieve with fatal sacrifice. She did not understand, but she would honour them in the only possible manner available to her.

If this be a destiny offered me, I shall meet it. I shall face it, and, if I can, I shall speak to the world.

And if this be the place of my death, so be it.

I was free, even if only for a moment.

I was free.

He had pushed them hard, marching them through half the night and without pause through most of this day, and the marines and heavies were staggering as they came within sight of the hill. The muscles of his legs leaden, Fiddler angled towards it. Vast bands of shadow were still tracking the landscape, cast down by the Jade Strangers spanning the entire sky, leaving the captain with a sense that the world was unravelling before his very eyes.

He had worked hard not to think about the army they had left behind, and the fate that awaited them. Before the captain now was all that mattered. That forlorn hilltop with its fractured flanks, the lone sword of Otataral thrust deep into the ground at its very centre.

He feared that it would not be enough – they had all feared as much, those among them who understood what she was attempting here. The chains that bound the Crippled God had been forged by gods. *A single sword to shatter them all? Tavore, you must have believed it was possible. Or that some other force would awaken here, to lend us a blessed hand in this.*

Without this – this breaking of chains – all that we do here is for naught.

Tavore, I am trusting you. With the lives of my soldiers – with the meaning to their deaths. I know, it's unfair, asking this of you. You're mortal, that and nothing more. But I know – I feel it – I am setting my weight upon your shoulders. We all are, whether we care to admit it or not.

And it's that unfairness that's tearing me apart.

He glanced off to his left. Hedge walked there at the head of his own troop – Letherii and Khundryl cast-offs, a mix of half-bloods from a dozen subdued tribes of the Lether Empire. They'd had trouble keeping up, so loaded down were the soldiers – Hood knew why they'd felt the need to carry so much. *All those kittens, I expect. Hope they're worth it.*

Hedge had been keeping his distance, and Fiddler knew why – he could feel his own face transforming whenever his friend drew near, becoming a mask, bleak and broken, and the anguish and dread clawed at him with a strength he could not match. *So much of this is unfair. So much.* But now Hedge shifted his track, came closer.

He pointed at the hill. 'That's it? Damned ugly, Fid.'

'We can defend it.'

'We're too thin, even for a knoll as puny as that one. Listen, I'm breaking up my company. I ain't making too many big promises here, but my Bridgeburners got a secret—'

'Kittens, aye.'

Hedge scowled at him. 'You had spies! I knew it!'

'Gods below, Hedge, never met anyone as hopeless with secrets as you.'

'Go ahead and think that. You're in for a surprise, I promise you.'

'Can they match the Moranth munitions, that's the only thing I need to know.'

But Hedge shook his head. 'Not them. Never mind.' And then he shrugged, as if dismissing something. 'You was probably too busy last time, but we made a mess of those Short-Tails.'

'And you didn't use most of them up? That's not like you, Hedge.'

'Bavedict concocted more – the man's a genius. Deranged and obsessive, the best kind of genius. Anyway, we're packing them all.'

'I'd noticed.'

'Sure, it's wore us out, all that stuff. Tell me, Fid, we going to get time to rest up first?'

'Little late asking me that now.'

'So what? I'm still asking you.'

'To be honest, I don't know. Depends.'

'On what?'

'Whether the Spire's fallen to us. Whether they got the heart un-damaged. Whether they managed to break its own set of chains, or whatever geas is protecting it – could be twenty Kenyll'rah demons for all we know, and imagine the scrap that'd be.'

'Twenty Kenyll'rah demons? What is this, some bad fairy tale? Why not a demon king? Or a giant three-headed ogre with scorpion tails at the end of every finger, and a big one on his cock for added measure? Breathing fire outa his arse, too.'

'Fine, so my imagination's failed. Sorry about that – I ain't no spinner of decent tales, Hedge.'

'I'll say. What else should I know? We got to kiss that fucking heart awake once we get it? Put a hat on it? Dance in fucking circles round it? Gods, not more blood sacrifice – that stuff creeps me out.'

'You're babbling, Hedge. It's what you always do before a fight – why?'

'To distract you, of course. You keep chewing on yourself there'll be nothing left but wet gristle and a few pubic hairs I really don't want to see. Oh, and the teeth that did all the chewing.'

'You know,' Fiddler said with a sidelong glance, 'if you wasn't here, Hedge, I'd have to invent you.'

'What's that?'

'Just saying thanks, that's all.'

'Fine. Now can I babble some more? 'Cause I'm terrified, y'see.'

'This will work, Hedge. Get your kitten throwers spread out through my squads, and we'll make a mess of whoever tries to take us down.'

'Exactly. Good idea. Shoulda thought of it myself.'

The man moved off again, and Fiddler's gaze tracked him until he reached his original position at the head of the Bridgeburners. *Bless ya, Hedge.* He swung round to face his troops. 'That's the place, soldiers. That hill. Let's quick-time it now – only a bell or two before dusk and I want us digging and piling stones in a solid perimeter.'

'Aye, Captain,' barked out a heavy. 'Could do with some fucking exercise.'

Another soldier answered. 'Knew I should never have carried you, woman!'

'If you'd been carrying me, Reliko, I'd be pregnant by now – any chance y'get, right, you rat-eating piece of elephant dung.'

'Maybe if I closed my eyes. But then, can a man even breed with a warthog?'

'If anybody'd know the answer to that—'

'Save your breaths, damn you,' growled Fiddler.

*   *   *

824

They trudged over the lesser rises, tackled the hillside. Bottle moved up past Corabb and made the climb alongside Sergeant Tarr. 'Listen, Sergeant . . .'

'Now what, Bottle? Pull out your shovel – we got work to do.'

Soldiers were throwing down their kits on all sides, muttering and complaining about sore backs and aching shoulders.

'It's this ground,' Bottle said, drawing close. 'I need to talk to the captain.'

Tarr scowled at him, and then nodded. 'Go on, but don't take too long. I don't want you dying 'cause you dug your hole too shallow.'

Bottle stared at the man, and then looked round. 'They that close?'

'How should I know? Care to risk your life that they aren't?'

Swearing under his breath, Bottle set out to where he'd last seen Fiddler – up near the crest of the hill. Hedge had gone up there as well.

Taking a narrow, twisted route between outcrops of bedrock, he heard boots behind him and turned. 'Deadsmell. You following me for a reason or is it my cute backside?'

'Your cute backside, but I need to talk to Fid, too. Two joys in one, what can I say?'

'This hill—'

'Barrow.'

'Right, fine. Barrow. There's something—'

'Sunk deep all the way round it, aye. Widdershins damn near shit himself the moment he hit the slope.'

Bottle shrugged. 'Us other squaddies call him Widdershits, on account of his loose bowels. What about it?'

'Really? Widdershits? That's great. Wait till Throatslitter hears that one. But listen, how come you're keeping secrets from us like that? Names like that? We wouldn't do it to you, you know.'

'Stifflips and Crack? Scuttle and Corncob? Turd and Brittle?'

'Oh, you heard them, huh?'

They reached the crest, stepped out on to level ground. Ahead, standing near a long sword thrust into the ground, Fiddler and Hedge. Both men turned as the soldiers approached, hearing the stones snapping underfoot.

'Forgot how to dig holes, you two?'

'No, Captain. It's just that we got us company.'

'Explain that, Bottle. And be succinct for a change.'

'There's a god here with us.'

Hedge seemed to choke on something and turned away, coughing, hacking and then spitting.

'You idiot,' said Fiddler. 'That's the whole fucking point.'

'Not him, Captain,' said Deadsmell.

'What do you mean, not him? Of course he's here – as much of him as there is, I mean. The Adjunct said this was the place.'

Deadsmell met Bottle's eyes, and after a moment Bottle turned away, his mouth suddenly dry. 'Captain,' he said, 'the Crippled God ain't here. We'd know it if he was.'

Fiddler gestured at the sword. 'That's the Adjunct's, Bottle. Otataral, remember? Why should you think you'd be able to sense anything?'

Deadsmell was rubbing at the back of his neck as if he wanted to wear off two or three layers of skin, checking to see if he still had a backbone. Then he drew a fortifying breath and said, 'He's foreign – we'd know it anyway, Captain.'

Fiddler seemed to sag.

Hedge clapped him on the back. 'Relax, Fid, it's just the usual fuck-up. So we go through the motions anyway – you're still a damned sapper, you know. Who said you were supposed to be on the thinking side of things? We don't know that all this isn't how it's supposed to be right now, anyway. In fact, we don't know a damned thing about anything. The way it always is. What's the problem?' He faced Bottle then. 'So which turd-chewing god's got the nerve to horn in our business?'

But Deadsmell was the first to respond. 'Smells like old death.'

'Hood? Wrong. Impossible.'

'Didn't say that, did I?' Deadsmell retorted, scowling. 'Just smells old and dead, right? Like brown leaves in a cold wind. Like a barrow's stone-lined pit. Like the first breath of winter. Like—'

'Worm of Autumn,' growled Bottle.

'I was working up to that, damn you!'

'What does D'rek want with us?' Hedge demanded.

'Doesn't matter,' said Fiddler, turning back to stare at the sword. 'We've had that priest crouching on our shoulders ever since Malaz City. When we were here he said something about his god, I seem to recall. Wrapping round the base of the hill. Him and the Adjunct seemed to think we'd need help. Anyway, it's not like we can do anything about it. Fine, what you said, Hedge. We go through the motions. Deadsmell, is this place a barrow?'

'Aye, but no longer sanctified. The tomb's been looted. Broken.'

'Broken, huh?'

'Trust the Adjunct,' said Hedge.

Fiddler rounded on him. 'Was that you saying that?'

Hedge shrugged. 'Thought it worth a try.' Then he frowned. 'What's that smell?'

'Probably Widdershits,' Bottle said.

'Gods, downwind, damn him – always downwind!'

*　　*　　*

826

Masan Gilani threw herself down near Sinter and Kisswhere. 'Balm just tried putting his hand down my breeches. Said he forgot where he was. Said he wasn't even looking. Said he thought he was reaching into his kit bag.'

Kisswhere snorted. 'And with that sharpness of wit, Dal Honese men won an empire.'

'I should've stayed with the cavalry.'

'There was no cavalry.'

'The Khundryl, then.'

Sinter slowly straightened, studied the darkening sky. 'See any clouds?' she asked, slowly turning as she scanned the heavens.

'Clouds? What's up, sister?'

'Not sure. I keep expecting . . .'

'Clouds?'

Sinter made a face. 'You were the one asking me what I was seeing, remember? Now I'm telling you, I got something.'

'Clouds.'

'Oh, never mind.' She settled back down lengthways in the slit trench she'd hacked out of the stony barrowside. 'But if anyone sees . . .'

'Clouds, aye,' said Masan Gilani, rubbing at her eyes.

Rejoining his squad, Bottle glanced over at Shortnose. 'Joined us again, have you?'

'I brought a shield,' the heavy said.

'Oh, that's nice.'

'You need to tie it to my hand.'

'What, now?'

'Tie it so it doesn't come loose. Use . . . knots and things.'

'With rawhide.'

'And knots and things.'

Bottle moved over to the man, crouched down.

'You do that,' Smiles observed, 'and next he'll be asking you to give him a shake, too.'

'Make sure it's after the little shudder,' Cuttle advised. 'Else you get wet.'

'I once shuddered so hard,' said Shortnose, 'I shit myself.'

Everyone looked over, but it seemed that no one could think of a rejoinder to that.

Koryk had drawn his sword from its scabbard and now began running a stone down the length of the blade's edge. 'Someone make us a fire,' he said. 'We're facing east here – if they come in from the morning sun . . . I want charcoal under my eyes.'

'Sound enough,' replied Cuttle, grunting to his feet. 'Glad you're back thinking like a soldier, Koryk.'

The Seti half-blood said nothing, lifting the weapon to squint at its edge.

'Once that's all done,' Tarr said, 'eat, drink and sleep. Corporal, set the watch.'

'Aye, Sergeant. Listen all of you! I can taste it in the air!'

'That'd be Widdershins.'

'No! It is glory, my friends. Glory!'

Koryk said, 'If that's the smell of glory, Corabb, I knew an anaemic cat that was queen of the world.'

Corabb frowned at him. 'I don't get it. Was it named Glory?'

Corporal Rim settled down beside Honey. 'I can hold a shield,' he said. 'I'll cover you one side.'

'Not if it's going to get you killed.'

'A soldier who's lost his weapon arm isn't much good to anyone. Just let me do this, will you?'

Honey's brow creased. 'Listen, you've been moping ever since the lizards. It's obvious why, but still, show us a smile, will you? If you die here you won't be the only one, will you?'

'So what's the problem if my guarding you gets me killed?'

'Because I don't want it on me, right?'

Rim scratched at his beard. 'Fine then, I'll shield-bash the fuckers.'

'That's better. Now, I got a watch here – go to sleep, sir.'

Fiddler walked the crest of the hill, doing a full circuit, studying where his troops had dug in and fortified defensive positions using boulders and stones. Hedge was right, he saw. They were too thin, and the footing was precarious at best. *Should've brought spears – like those Bridgeburners did.*

Admit it, Fid, having Hedge here may hurt like a stuck knife, but you're glad of it anyway.

He studied the sky – the setting of the sun had passed almost unnoticed, so bright were the Jade Strangers overhead. Sighing, the captain moved to find a place to sit, his back against a carved stela. He closed his eyes. He knew he should try to sleep, but knew as well that such a thing was impossible.

He'd never wanted any of this. Handling a single squad had been burden enough. *And now everyone here's looking to me. If only they knew, the fools. I'm as lost as they are.*

In the ghoulish light he drew out the House of Chains. The lacquered wooden cards slipped about in his hands as if coated in grease. He squinted down at them, slowly worked his way through each one, studying it in turn. Seven cards. Six felt cool to his touch. Only one glistened with sweat.

Leper.
Aw, Hedge. I'm so sorry for that.

The Shi'gal Assassin had left a place of flame far behind him now. Flame and the blood of a slain god raining down from a tortured sky. He had witnessed the deaths of thousands. Humans, K'Chain Che'Malle, Imass. He had seen the fall of Forkrul Assail and Jaghut warriors. Toblakai and Barghast. All for the scarred thing he now clutched in his hands.

It dripped blood and there seemed to be no end to that flow, trickling down his fingers, painting his claws, spattering his thighs as the rhythmic beat of his wings carried him westward, as if chasing the sun's eager plunge beyond the horizon. The heart was once more alive, heavier than any stone of similar size – the weight of a skystone, such as fell from the sky. But that seemed an appropriate detail, since it belonged to the Fallen God.

Gu'Rull's mind tracked back to the last scene he had witnessed atop the Spire, moments after he had torn loose the heart from those dying chains. The body of the Mortal Sword lying so motionless on the blood-splashed platform. The dog guarding what had already left the world.

It is only the dumb beast that understands futile gestures – the cold necessity for them, in the face of all the hard truths. We who hold to the higher aspirations of the intellect, we surrender too quickly. And yet, in looking upon that dog – a creature knowing only loyalty and courage – we find flavours to wound our own souls.

I now wonder, is it envy we feel?

He had underestimated the Matron's choices. Destriant Kalyth, Shield Anvil Stormy and Mortal Sword Gesler – were these not worthy humans? *They have shown us a path, for all the children of Gunth Mach. Two are fallen. Two gave their lives, but one remains.*

I am not likely to see her again. But in my mind, in this moment and all the moments that remain to me, I will honour her, as I honour Gesler and Stormy. They lived as brothers, they fell as brothers. I shall call them kin, and of the tasks awaiting me, I shall in turn strive to see this through.

Destriant, in your sorrow and grief – which I even now taste – I will seek to give meaning to their deaths.

His wings shifted slightly at a sudden twist in the currents, and all at once the air seemed to thicken around the Shi'gal Assassin, filling with a strange susurration – heavy whispers, a sudden darkness that swarmed and swirled, blotting out the entire sky.

And Gu'Rull realized that he would not be making this journey alone.

Sinter sat up, and then stood. She studied the sky – and there, to the east. A black cloud, vast and seething, growing. Growing. *Gods below.* 'Everyone!' she shouted. 'Get under your shields! Take cover! Everyone!'

'Beloved children! Listen to your mother! Hear her words – the words of Crone! We took inside us his flesh! All that we could find! We kept it alive on the blood of sorcery! All for this moment! Rejoice, my sweet children, for the Fallen God is reborn!'

And Crone gave voice to her joy, and on all sides her children, in their tens of thousands, cried out in answer.

The winged K'Chain Che'Malle, clutching its precious prize, was buffeted by the cacophony, and Crone cackled in delight.

Ahead, she could sense the fragments of bone scattered on the knoll – the bones of dozens of people once interred in crypts within the barrow. Would they be enough? There was no choice. The moment had come, and they would take what was available to them. They would make a man. A poor man. A weak man. But a man nonetheless – they would make a home for the god's flesh from these bones, and then fill it with their own blood, and it would have to be enough.

The Great Ravens whirled over the knoll, and then plunged downward.

Fiddler threw himself behind the carved stela. The thunder of wings was deafening, crashing down, and the air grew hot and brittle. He felt the stone shuddering against his back.

Something like fists struck the ground, concussive blows coming one after another. He clutched at his head, tried to block his ears, but it was no use. The world had vanished inside a storm of black wings. He was suffocating, and before his eyes small objects were flashing past, converging somewhere close to the sword. Splinters, bleached fragments – bones, pulled into the air, prised loose from tangles of grass and roots. One cut a vicious gouge across the back of his hand and he flinched it under cover.

Who had voiced the warning?

Whoever it had been, it had probably saved their lives.

Except for me – I stayed too close to the sword. I should have gone down lower, with my soldiers. But I held back. I didn't want to see their faces, didn't want to feel this terrible love that takes a commander before battle – love for his soldiers, every one of them, that builds and ever builds, trying to shatter his heart.

My courage failed – and now—

*   *   *

Gu'Rull circled high overhead. He watched as the Great Ravens launched themselves at the knoll, saw the blooms of raw power erupt one after another. The black-winged creatures were sacrificing themselves, one by one, to return their god to living flesh – to make for his soul a mortal house.

One of the birds swung up alongside him and he tracked her with his lower eyes.

'K'Chain Che'Malle! I am Crone, mother of all these blessed children! You bring a gift!' And she laughed.

Reaching for her mind, Gu'Rull recoiled at the first touch – so alien, so cold in its power.

Crone cackled. 'Careful! We are anathema in this realm! Heed me well now – your task is not done. Beyond this gift you carry, you will be needed on the morrow. But I tell you this – in your moment of dire need, look again to the skies. Do you understand?

'I promised a most noble lord. I have sent my sweetest daughter far away, but she will return. You will see – she returns!'

The huge raven banked up closer still. 'Look below! They are almost all gone. We have waited for this all our lives – do you see what we have made? Do you?'

He did. A figure, sprawled close to the Otataral sword, bound by chains to the earth. But its chest was a gaping hole.

Gu'Rull crooked his wings, plummeted.

Crone followed, cackling madly.

The last of the other ravens plunged into the man's body in a flash of lurid power.

Wings thundering to slow his descent, the Shi'gal landed straddling the man and looked down, appalled at this mockery the Great Ravens had made. Bent bones, twisted muscles, a sickly pallor, the face deformed as if by disease.

The hole in its chest was a pool of black blood, revealing the reflection of Gu'Rull's own elongated face, his glittering eyes.

He took the heart in his hands, slowly crouched, and settled it like a stone in that ragged-edged pit. The blood swallowed it.

Flesh knitted, bones growing like roots.

The K'Chain Che'Malle spread his wings once more, and then lifted skyward.

Crone watched from above. *Reborn! Reborn! Look down, all ye souls in the sky – look down upon the one taken from you! He is almost within reach – your lost wandering is soon to end, for his spark of life shall return, his eyes shall open!*

Witness, for I am that spark.

He was brought down. He was torn apart. Scattered across the world. He made us to keep him alive – we fed on his corpse, by his will.

Ye souls in the sky – your god did not lose faith. He did not.

As the K'Chain Che'Malle lifted away, Crone swept down, power burgeoning within her. All she had. Eyes fixed on the body below, she loosed one last cry – of triumph – before striking home.

One final detonation, of such power as to fling Fiddler away, send him rolling to the very edge of the slope. Gasping, drawing in the suddenly cold night air as the echoes died away, he forced himself on to his hands and knees. Astonished that he still lived.

Silence now swallowed the knoll – but no, as he looked up, he saw marines and heavies stumbling into view, slowly rising to their feet in bludgeoned wonder. The ringing in his ears began to fade, and through the fugue he could now hear their voices.

Pushing himself to his feet, he saw that the half-buried standing stone he had been hiding behind had been pushed almost on to its side by the blast – and all the others ringing the summit were similarly tilted back. On the ground, not a single spear point remained, leaving only scorched earth.

Seeing a figure lying close to the sword, Fiddler staggered forward.

A broken, deformed man. *The Crippled God.*

Heavy chains pinned him to the ground.

We'll never break those. Not with that sword. We've done nothing but make him more vulnerable than he has ever been. Now, he can truly be killed.

Perhaps that's a mercy.

Then he saw that the man's eyes were on him.

Fiddler drew closer. 'I'm sorry,' he said.

But the twisted face softened, and in a frail voice the Crippled God replied, 'No need. Come near – I am still so . . . weak. I would tell you something.'

Fiddler walked until he was beside the figure, and then he squatted down. 'We have water. Food.'

But the god shook his head. 'In the time when I was nothing but pain, when all that came from me was spite, and the hunger to hurt this world, I saw you Malazans as no better than all the rest. Children of your cruel gods. Their tools, their weapons.' He paused, drew a rattling breath. 'I should have sensed that you were different – was it not your emperor's champion who defied Hood at the last Chaining? Did he not cry out that what they sought was unjust? Did he not pay terribly for his temerity?'

Fiddler shook his head. 'I know nothing about any of that, Lord.'

'When he came to me – your emperor – when he offered me a way

832

out . . . I was mistrustful. And yet . . . and yet, what do I see now? Here, standing before me? A Malazan.'

Fiddler said nothing. He could hear conversations from all the slope sides of the barrow, voices raised in wonder, and plenty of cursing.

'You are not like the others. Why is this? I wish to understand, Malazan. Why is this?'

'I don't know.'

'And now you will fight to protect me.'

'We can't break these chains – she was wrong about that.'

'No matter, Malazan. If I am to lie here, bound for the rest of days, still – you will fight to defend me.'

Fiddler nodded.

'I wish I could understand.'

'So do I,' Fiddler said with a grimace. 'But, maybe, in the scrap to come, you'll get a . . . I don't know . . . a better sense of us.'

'You are going to die for me, a foreign god.'

'Gods can live for ever and make real their every desire. We can't. They got powers, to heal, to destroy, even to resurrect themselves. We don't. Lord, to us, all gods are foreign gods.'

The bound man sighed. 'When you fight, then, I will listen. For this secret of yours. I will listen.'

Suddenly so weary that his legs trembled beneath him, Fiddler shrugged and turned from the chained man. 'Not long now, Lord,' he said, and walked away.

Hedge was waiting, seated on one of the tilted standing stones. 'Hood take us all,' he said, eyeing Fiddler as he approached. 'They did it – her allies – they did what she needed them to do.'

'Aye. And how many people died for that damned heart?'

Cocking his head, Hedge drew off his battered leather cap. 'Little late to be regretting all that now, Fid.'

'It was Kellanved – all of this. Him and Dancer. They used Tavore Paran from the very start. They used all of us, Hedge.'

'That's what gods do, aye. So you don't like it? Fine, but listen to me. Sometimes, what they want – what they need us to do – sometimes it's all right. I mean, it's the right thing to do. Sometimes, it makes us better people.'

'You really believe that?'

'And when we're better people, we make better gods.'

Fiddler looked away. 'It's hopeless, then. We can stuff a god with every virtue we got, it still won't make us any better, will it? Because we're not good with virtues, Hedge.'

'Most of the time, aye, we're not. But maybe then, at our worst, we might look up, we might see that god we made out of the best in us.

Not vicious, not vengeful, not arrogant or spiteful. Not selfish, not greedy. Just clear-eyed, with no time for all our rubbish. The kind of god to give us a slap in the face for being such shits.'

Fiddler sank back down on to the ground. He leaned forward and closed his eyes, hands covering his face. 'Ever the optimist, you.'

'When you been dead, everything after that's looking up.'

Fiddler snorted.

'Listen, Fid. They did it. Now it's our turn. Ours and Tavore's. Who'd have thought we'd even get this far?'

'Two names come to mind.'

'Since when didn't their empire demand the best in us, Fid? Since when?'

'Wrong. It was as corrupt and self-serving as any other. Conquered half the fucking world.'

'Not quite. World's bigger than that.'

Fiddler sighed, freed one hand to wave it in Hedge's direction. 'Go get some rest, will you?'

The man rose. 'Don't want anyone interrupting all that feeling sorry for yourself, huh?'

'For myself?' Fiddler looked up, shook his head, and his gaze slipped past Hedge, down to where his soldiers were only now settling once again, desperate for sleep.

'We're not finished yet,' Hedge said. 'You plan on talking to 'em all? Before it all starts up?'

'No.'

'Why not?'

'Because this is their time, from now to the end. They can do the talking, Hedge. Right now, for me, I'll do the listening. Just like that god back there.'

'What do you expect to be hearing?'

'No idea.'

'It's a good knoll,' Hedge said. 'Defendable.' And then he departed.

Closing his eyes again, Fiddler listened to the crunch of his boots, until they were gone. *Chains. House of Chains. Us mortals know all about them. It's where we live.*

Calm could see the rise where she had left him, could see a darker shape low across its summit. The chains of her ancestors still bound him. Distant deaths tracked cold fingers across her skin – Reverence was no more. Diligence was gone. They had lost the heart of the Fallen God.

When a building is so battered and worn that no further repairs are possible, it needs tearing down. As simple as that, now. Their enemies might well stand filled with triumph at this very moment, there on the heights of the Great Spire, with a fresh clean wind coming in from the sea. They might believe that they had won, and that no longer would the Forkrul Assail make hard the fist of implacable justice – to strike at their venal selves, to crush their presumptuous arrogance. They might now imagine that they were free to take the future, to devour this world beast by beast, tree by tree, emptying the oceans and skies of all life.

And if the victory on this day just past tasted of blood, so be it – it was a familiar taste to them, and they were still not weaned from it and perhaps would never be.

But nature had its own weapons of righteousness. Weapons that struck even when none held them. No god, no guiding force or will beyond that of blind destruction was even necessary. All it needed was freedom.

The time for Lifestealer had come.

Face the sea, you fools. Face the rising of the sun, imagining your new day.

You do not see what comes from the darkness in the west. The slayer is awakened. Obliteration awaits you all.

Innocence and ignorance. He had struggled with those two words for so long, and each time he had looked upon the face of Icarium Mappo had known his own war, there in his mind. They were places of being, that and nothing more, and long had sages chewed on their distinctiveness. But they understood little of the battle the Trell had fought. He protected innocence by making ignorance a weapon and shield. In the belief that innocence had value, was a virtue, was a state of purity.

So long as he remains . . . ignorant.

Knowledge is the enemy. Knowledge was ever the enemy.

Staggering through the gloom, shadow roads crossing the plain around him though there was no sun left to cast them, he looked up to see a figure in the distance, coming from the southeast.

Something cold whispered through him.

He's close. I feel him . . . so close! He forced himself to move faster – that stranger, the way it walked, the way it seemed a thing of bleached bone beneath this uncanny light – he knew. He understood.

With a soft groan, he broke into a run.

She saw him, after turning, after feeling his footfalls lumbering closer. Skin the colour of stained wood, a dark visage bestial by nature and ravaged by deprivation. The creature was emaciated, hunched beneath a heavy satchel, his clothes half rotted off. An apparition, yet one of weakness and pathos.

Calm faced him, waited.

When she saw him spot the body of Lifestealer – when he cried out a small animal sound, pitching as he changed direction, as he stumbled towards Icarium – Calm stepped into his path. 'It is too late, Trell. He is mine now.'

Haunted eyes fixed on her as the Trell stopped, only a few paces away. She could see the pain that had come from running, the way his chest heaved, the way he bent over, legs shaky beneath him. Then he sank down, pulled the satchel from his shoulder. His hands fumbled and a scatter of small objects spilled out from the sack – the shards of a broken pot. The Trell stared down at them, as if in horror. '*We'll fix that,*' he mumbled, visibly jerking as he pulled his gaze away from the fragments. Looking up, he glared at Calm. 'I won't let you, Assail.'

'Don't be a fool.'

He pulled a heavy mace from the satchel, struggled to his feet.

'I will kill you if you continue to stand in my way,' she said. 'I understand, Trell. You are his latest protector – but you lost him. All the ones before you – and there were many – they *all* lost him, eventually, and then they died.

'But none of you ever understood. The Nameless Ones weren't interested in Icarium. Each time, the one they chose – that one was the real danger. A warleader who threatened their hidden alliances. A rebel of terrible potential. Each time, for nothing more than squalid, immediate necessities – political expediency – they snatched away the maker of trouble, gave to him or her a task impossible to achieve, and a lifetime chained to it.

'You are the last of them, Trell. Made . . . harmless.'

He was shaking his head. 'Icarium—'

'Icarium Lifestealer is what he is and what he has always been. Uncontrollable, destined to awaken again and again, there in the midst of the devastation he has wrought. He cannot be stopped, cannot be saved.' She stepped forward. 'So, let me free him, Trell.'

'No.' The mace lifted in his hands. 'I will die first.'

She sighed. 'Trell, you died long ago.'

Roaring, he charged.

Calm evaded the clumsy swing, moved in close, one hand shooting out. The blow against his right shoulder punched the bone from its socket, ripped the muscles clean away. The Trell was thrown round by the impact. She drove her elbow into his face, shattering it. Angled a kick against his right shin, broke both bones.

The mace thudded on to the ground.

Even as he fell, he tried to grasp her with his left hand. She caught it by the wrist, clenched and twisted, crushed the bones. A savage pull snapped him closer. Calm plunged her other hand into his chest, up and under the ribs, the fingers stabbing through to sink deep. She pushed him back, her hand reappearing in a welter of blood, fingers clutching half a lung.

Another push sent him on to his back.

Calm dropped down over him, hands closing on his throat.

Mappo stared up at her. *Lies. I was nothing. Throwing away my life. They gave me a purpose – it's all anyone needs. A purpose.* She had stolen his breath and his chest raged with fire. His body was broken, and now the end was upon him.

Icarium! She's done something to you. She's hurt you.

Darkness closed around him. *I tried. But . . . too weak. Too flawed.*

They all hurt you.

I was nothing. A Trell youth among a dying people. Nothing.

My friend. I am sorry.

She crushed his windpipe. She crushed every bone in his neck. Her fingers pushed through wrinkled, slack skin – skin that felt like worn deerhide – and the blood welled out.

His dead eyes stared up at her from a blackened face, a face now frozen in a peculiar expression of sorrow. But she would give that no thought. Just one more warrior cursed to fail. The world was filled with them. They littered battlefields. They marched into the fray beating time with swords on shields. But not for much longer.

He is mine. I will awaken him now – I will free him to kill this world.

A sound to her left, and then a voice. 'That's not nice.'

She twisted, to fling herself away, but something massive slammed into the side of her head, hard enough to lift her from the ground, spin her in the air.

Calm landed on her right shoulder, rolled and came to her feet. Her face – her entire head – felt lopsided, unbalanced.

The backswing caught her left hip. Shards of jagged bone erupted from her pelvis. She folded around the blow, pitched headfirst downward, and once more landed hard. Fought to her knees, stared up with her one working eye to see a Toblakai standing before her.

But you freed me!

No. You're not him. That was long ago. Another place – another time.

'I don't like fighting,' he said.

His next swing tore her head from her shoulders.

'Brother Grave?'

'A moment.' The Forkrul Assail stared at the distant knot of hills.

This is where the cloud of birds descended. I see . . . shapes, there, upon the flanks of the Elan barrow. He spoke to the High Watered at his side. 'Do you see, Haggraf? We will now encircle – but maintain our distance. I want us rested before we strike.'

'Perhaps we should await the heavy infantry, Pure. They have prepared for us on that barrow.'

'We will not wait,' Grave replied. 'That hill is not large enough to hold a force of any appreciable threat. Before dawn, we shall form up and advance.'

'They will surrender.'

'Even if they do, I will execute them all.'

'Pure, will you make them kneel before our blades?'

Brother Grave nodded. 'And once we are done here, we shall return to Brother Aloft and Sister Freedom – perhaps the enemy they have now found will prove more of a challenge. If not, we will form up and march our three armies north, to eliminate that threat. And then . . . we shall retake the Great Spire.'

Haggraf strode off to relay the orders to the company commanders.

Brother Grave stared at the distant barrow. *At last, we will end this.*

Vastly Blank stepped down from the boulder, and then sat to adjust the leather bindings protecting his shins.

Fiddler frowned down at the heavy, and then across at Badan Gruk.

The sergeant shrugged. 'Just our luck, Captain, that it's him got the best eyes here.'

'Soldier,' said Fiddler.

Vastly Blank looked up, smiled.

'Captain wants to know what you saw from up there,' Badan Gruk said.

'We're surrounded.' He began pulling at a torn toenail.

Fiddler made a fist, raised it for a moment, and then let his hand fall to his side again. 'How many?'

Vastly Blank looked back up, smiled. 'Maybe three thousand.' He brought up most of the nail, which he'd prised off, and squinted at it, wiping the blood away.

'And?'

'Banded leather, Captain. Some splint. Not much chain. Round shields and spears, javelins, curved swords. Some archers.' He wiped more blood from the nail, but it was still mottled brown.

'They're getting ready to attack?'

'Not yet,' Vastly Blank replied. 'I smell their sweat.'

'You what?'

'Long march.'

'Best nose, too,' Badan Gruk offered.

Vastly Blank popped the nail into his mouth, made sucking sounds.

Sighing, Fiddler moved away.

The sky to the east was lightening, almost colourless, with streaks of silver and pewter close to the horizon. The sound of the Kolansii soldiers was a soft clatter coming at them from all sides. The enemy taking position, readying shields and weapons. Ranks of archers were forming up, facing the hill.

Sergeant Urb heard Commander Hedge talking to his own dozen or so archers, but couldn't quite make out what he was saying. Shifting his heavy shield, he edged closer to where Hellian sat. He couldn't keep his eyes from her. *She is so beautiful now. So pure and clean and the awful truth is, I liked her better when she looked like a bird that's flown into a wall. At least then I had a chance with her. A drunk woman will take anyone, after all, so long as they clean up after them and take care of them, and got the coin for more to drink.*

'Take cover – they're drawing!'

He worked his way back under his shield.

He heard Fiddler. 'Hedge!'

'After the first salvo!'

Distant *thrums*. Hollow whistling, and suddenly arrows thudded the ground and snapped and skidded on rock. One pained howl and a chorus of curses.

Urb looked across at her to see if she was all right. Two arrows were stuck in her shield and there was a lovely startled look on her face.

'I love you!' Urb shouted.

She stared at him. 'What?'

At that moment a thick rushing sound filled the air. He saw her flinch back down, but these weren't arrows. He angled himself up, saw a band of enemy archers on the ground, writhing, and, pelting back towards the barrow, one of Hedge's Bridgeburners, his shoulders covered in turf, his uniform grey and brown with dirt.

Dug a hole, did he? Hit the archers with some gods-awful grenado.

Hedge shouted, 'Archers down!'

'Gods below!' someone bellowed. 'What was that blue stuff? They're rotting to bones!'

Looking over, Urb saw the accuracy of that assessment. Whatever had splashed all over the archers had dissolved their flesh. Even the bones and quivers filled with arrows were nothing but paste.

Now an officer was stepping out from the ring of Kolansii infantry – tall, white-skinned.

Corporal Clasp crawled up beside him. 'That's one of those Fuckeral's, isn't it?'

'You!' shouted Hellian, pointing a finger at Urb. 'What did you say?'

The Forkrul Assail then roared – impossibly loud, the sound hammering against the hillside. Urb was driven into the ground by the concussion. He clawed at his ears. A second roar—

And then it seemed to dim, as if muffled.

A quavering voice lifted from a nearby trench. 'Worm says fuck you, Assail!'

'Is that you I'm smelling again, Wid?'

Urb uncurled, straightened up, though still on his knees.

He could see the Forkrul Assail. Watched him roaring for a third time – but the sound barely reached through.

A rock sailed out, landed well short of the Pure, bounced and rolled. The enemy commander seemed to flinch from it nevertheless, and then he whirled.

'Here they come!'

Hellian's voice was much closer and much louder. 'What did you say?'

He twisted round. Corporal Clasp was lying between them, staring back and forth.

'What in Hood's name is with you two?'

'I love you!' Urb shouted.

When he saw her delighted grin, Urb clambered over a grunting Clasp. Hellian pitched up to meet him, her mouth hard against his own.

Pinned by Urb's weight, Clasp squirmed and kicked. 'You idiots! The enemy's advancing! Get off me!'

Cuttle watched the lines closing in. At twenty or so paces javelins flashed out, colliding against uplifted shields, and then, at a signal from the company commanders, the Kolansii surged forward into a charge against the slope.

The sapper half rose from his position. The crossbow *thocked*, thick cord humming, the vibration a soft brush against his cheek. He saw his quarrel take a squad leader in the throat. The rest of the marines had also loosed quarrels into the rushing enemy. Bodies went tumbling among the crags and outcrops.

The sapper set his weapon down behind him, swung his shield round, slipping his arm through the straps, and drew his short sword. These four motions were done before the squad leader hit the ground. 'Hold and at 'em!' he shouted, rising as the first Kolansii arrived.

*   *   *

An arrow had pinned Saltlick's left foot to the ground, but he didn't want to move anyway. The soldier arriving directly in front of him stumbled at the last moment. Saltlick pressed his shield down on the man and drove the pommel of his sword through the top of his helm and then the bones of his skull. When he pulled his weapon free, the helm was stuck to the pommel.

A spear thrust at him. He batted it aside with the helm, put his shoulder behind his shield-bash, and flattened the soldier's face. As the man reeled back, Saltlick stabbed him low in the gut. Dragged the weapon free and began hacking at another Kolansii – they seemed to be everywhere.

He never even saw the spear that impaled his neck and tore out his throat.

Koryk swore, swinging his left arm to shake off the remnants of his broken shield. He drew a Seti long knife from his harness, kicked away the man whose skull had broken his shield, and looked up in time to meet the next attacker.

Blades flashed out, the heavier one batting aside the jabbing spear, the thinner one thrusting through leather armour to sink a hand's width into the Kolansii's chest, and then back out again. As the soldier staggered back, sagging, Koryk brought his long sword down between head and neck, the blow of such power that he cut through a clavicle and down through three ribs where they met the breastbone.

Koryk twisted to avoid another spear point, then heard a laugh and saw Smiles spin away again, leaving behind her a toppling corpse.

Another surging mass of Kolansii rushed up towards them.

The blued Letherii blade seemed to shout as it clove through the side of a helm, crushing the cheek-guard and then the bones it was meant to protect. Blood spat out from the soldier's gaping mouth, the eyes bulging, and then Corabb kicked the man away, watched as he pitched backward to collide with the next soldier.

The echo of that shout raced back and forth in his skull. He bellowed in answer to it, lifted the weapon crossways over his shield and awaited the next fool.

I am a marine! A heroic soldier on a day of glory! Come to me and die!

Swearing, Throatslitter cut off an arm to his right, then another to his left. Blood sprayed him from both sides, making him curse some more. He shifted to avoid a spear thrust, kicked under a jaw hard enough to snap the head back, and then slashed across that exposed neck.

Beside him, Deadsmell staggered to repeated blows on his shield from a Kolansii wielding a heavy spiked axe. Throatslitter's sideways thrust drove his long knife over the attacker's shoulder, into the gap behind the corner of jaw and the flared helm, angling slightly upwards to slice through the spinal cord just below the base of the skull.

Righting himself, Deadsmell lunged with his shield, blocking an attacker trying to take Throatslitter from the flank. The enemy soldier grunted at the impact, knees buckling. Having broken his own weapon, Deadsmell now held the spiked axe, and he hammered it down, splitting the Kolansii's round shield, and then thrusting the spike into the man's shoulder.

Ducking low, Throatslitter cut through the Achilles tendon of the Kolansii's right leg, and as the screaming man fell he stabbed down through the eye socket, silencing the cries.

'Stay down!' shouted Widdershins behind him.

A quarrel hissed over Throatslitter, caught the next foe in the chest.

From Deadsmell's other side, Balm shouted, 'Where'd you get that stupid axe, soldier! Find a sword! You end up hanging out there and you're finished!'

'I'm looking, damn you! I'm looking!'

Kisswhere fell on to her back. She heard the blocked thrust above her, and then Sinter's snarl as her sister backslashed across the Kolansii's face. Kicking herself clear of his collapsing body, her hand closed on a javelin. She grasped it, pushed herself back on to her feet, and leapt into the press yet again.

Sinter was taking blows on her shield, righting herself from that sideways lunge against Kisswhere's assailant. Badan Gruk then flung himself at her attacker, pushing his short sword deep into the man's side.

An axe came down on the back of the sergeant's helm, splitting it, driving Badan Gruk face first into the ground. The half-moon blade sobbed free, its edge dragging free hair, scalp and fragments of bone.

Howling, Sinter cut off the hand holding it, and then the flailing arm, and then opened wide the man's belly with a single savage slash. Intestines tumbled out over Badan Gruk's corpse.

And still she howled.

A spear transfixed Lap Twirl, drove him against a tilted standing stone. The Falari cutter shrieked as the iron point bit through to grind against the rock. He chopped down with his short sword, slicing off the fingers of the nearer hand along the spear's shaft. The pressure from the weapon released all at once. He slid forward on the slick wood until he was close to the Kolansii, and slashed halfway through the woman's neck, severing the jugular.

As the woman fell, the cutter dropped sword and shield, grasped hold of the butt end of the spear. Feeling the point dig at an angle into the ground at the base of the stone behind him, he flung out his feet and fell straight down. The shaft snapped just past his back. Leaving it there, he gained his knees, wiping his hands on dead grasses, and took up shield and sword again.

Spitting out a mouthful of blood from a cut tongue, he gasped, 'Now that wasn't so bad.'

More Kolansii clambered into view between the outcrops. Lap Twirl went forward to meet them, stepping over Burnt Rope's body. He had enough left in him to take a few more down. Maybe.

Skulldeath sailed sideways through the air, gliding over the hunched back of a Kolansii engaged in a fierce battle with Reliko. Lashing down, his blade bit deep beneath the flared rim of the man's helm, cutting through his vertebrae. Spinning round, Skulldeath landed in a crouch, and then screamed as he lunged forward. He saw a face – staring – directly ahead, and the Kolansii ducked down behind his round shield, slashing out with his scimitar, but Skulldeath leapt high, one hand landing atop the enemy's helm, and used that to pivot round above him. Cutting downward, he sliced through the Kolansii's hamstrings.

Striking the ground, the desert prince rolled—

He heard Sinter shouting – heard Kisswhere's cursing—

Gaining his feet, Skulldeath found himself surrounded. He twisted, slashed, ducked, kicked and closed. Bodies fell away. Blood sprayed.

Then a blow hammered his lower back, lifted him from his feet. He tried curling away from the blow, but something was jammed in his body, a hard edge crunching and grinding against his spine. He was driven to the ground face first, and then they were beating on him – heavy edges chopping into his muscles and bones.

One struck the back of his head and there was darkness, and then oblivion.

Hedge stood over the corpse of Bavedict – the damned fool had been killed outright by that first shower of arrows, taking one through an eye. From his vantage point Hedge could see the ring of defenders contracting as the enemy pushed higher up the slope. He watched Fiddler moving down to block an imminent breach where most of a squad had gone down.

'You – archers – keep an eye on there. If they get through it's a straight path to the Crippled God.'

'Yes sir!'

'Now, the rest of you – we got to relieve the pressure. Take those coppery ones and throw for the fifth and sixth ranks – use 'em all up. If we don't make 'em reel right now we're done for.'

'What's the copper kittens do, sir?'

Hedge shook his head. 'I forget, and the alchemist's dead. Just go – spread out, get moving!'

As they left, the sapper took up his crossbow – he only had half a dozen quarrels left. The occasional arrow still sailed down here and there, but either the sappers he'd dug in below the slope were all dead or they'd used up their munitions – it'd be just his luck if some errant arrow took him or Fiddler out now.

Loading his weapon, he moved down past his four remaining archers, who were sending arrows into the breach. He could see Fiddler, there with those Dal Honese sisters and a lone heavy infantryman shorter than any of them. The Kolansii who'd been advancing to flank them were all down, feathered with arrows. 'Good work,' barked out Hedge to his archers. 'Now find somewhere else you're needed.'

A stone turned underfoot and Fiddler's left ankle gave way in a stab of pain. Cursing, he stumbled. Looked up to see a Kolansii closing – the eyes manic and wild beneath the helm, a heavy axe lifting high.

The quarrel punched the man back a step, and he looked down in astonishment at the heavy bolt buried in his chest.

One hand closed on Fiddler's collar, dragged him clear. An all-metal crossbow landed in his lap, followed by a quiver. 'Load up, Fid,' said Hedge, drawing his short sword. 'Keep 'em off my left flank, will you?'

'You getting mad, Hedge?'

'Aye.'

'Gods help them.'

His attacker had pushed his spear right through Bottle's right thigh, pinning him down, but Bottle had replied with a sword through the stomach, and as the Kolansii sagged back voicing terrible screams the marine decided he'd come away the winner of the argument.

Is that what this is? An argument? But look at them – they're slaves. They're not asking for this.

Tarr dropped down beside him, blood streaming from a gash in his face. 'You want that spear out, Bottle? It ain't bleeding much for the moment, but if I take it out . . .'

'I know,' Bottle said. 'But it's pushed right through – I want it gone, Sergeant. I'll stuff rags in.'

'A bleeder—'

'It ain't one, Sergeant. It's just a big fucking hole.'

Tarr pushed Bottle on to his side, and then quickly drew out the spear. 'Bleeding,' he said after a moment, 'but not spurting. When I see Deadsmell I'll send him your way.'

Nodding, feeling faint, Bottle pushed himself upright, fumbling at the pouch at his side, where he found a roll of bandages. He was working a wad into one end of the hole when there was a flash of heat from downslope and then blood-chilling screams.

Brother Grave stared, in shock, furious at his own helplessness, as copper-hued grenados sailed down from the defenders to strike the Kolansii ranks at the foot of the barrow and on the level ground beyond it. The emerald fires that erupted when they shattered seemed almost demonic as they spread with terrible ferocity through the ranks.

The attack was a shambles – he saw his soldiers reeling, flinching back.

This is going to take longer than I anticipated.

He looked to the northeast, seeking that telltale sign of dust on the horizon. *Where are they?*

'Haggraf. Sound the recall. We shall wait until the fires burn down. Then strike again, and again, until they are all dead!'

The stench of burnt flesh carried with it a strange flavour, something between sulphur and limes.

The Crippled God listened to the clamour of battle on all sides. He heard the cries of pain and anger, but these were sounds he had expected. Amidst the clash of iron and the splinter of wooden shields, amidst the whistle of arrows – some of them striking close – and the splinter of shafts against insensate stone, he heard soldiers shouting to each other, heard their desperate breaths as they struggled to stay alive and to kill those who rose up against them in seemingly endless waves.

And overhead the sky was almost blinding with all the souls abandoned by his descent to this world. He thought to hear them as well, but they were too far away, lost in the heavens. Did they still struggle to hold on to their faith, with their god vanished for so long? Or had they surrendered to the cruel malice that came to so many of the spiritually vacant? Did they now wander without purpose, in the horror of a meaningless existence?

Fires erupted around him – not so close that he could feel their heat – and now shrieks rushed out to fill the air.

Sounds of dying, from all sides. He had heard these sounds before. There was nothing new, nothing to give him comprehension. That mortal lives could so willingly extinguish themselves, in the name of causes and noble desires – was this not the most profound, most baffling sacrifice of all? The one sacrifice every god has long since forgotten;

the one sacrifice that they, in their callous indifference, could not even comprehend.

Their flesh is all they know – all these men and women here. Flesh as now clothes me. Feel our limits, our terrible limits. So frail, so temporary. A flitting light, a moment's breath.

I hear you surrendering it. This one gift that is the only gift ever given you – you yield it back into the firmament. And the world passes on, barely taking notice.

Will no one notice?

I will heed your deaths. I will remember.

The Crippled God listened, past the horns of retreat, past the cries for healers, past the clashing signals announcing the next wave to advance upon these beleaguered few. The Crippled God listened, and he waited.

Seven of the Dead Fires, the T'lan Imass stood on a bare rise to the east of the Malazan regulars. Nom Kala and Kalt Urmanal were now among them, as bound as true kin, and in Nom Kala's mind it was well. She did not feel like a stranger. She did not feel alone.

Urugal the Woven spoke. 'She prepares for the enemy's approach. We have listened to her silence and we know that there are no lies within her soul. Yet she is mortal.'

'Many who see her,' said Beroke, 'believe her weak – not in her will, but in her flesh and bones. She has yielded her sword. I sought to give her mine, but she refused me.'

'We understand the power of a formidable will,' observed Kahlb the Silent Hunter.

'Nevertheless,' said Beroke.

Urugal said, 'I have elected that we remain with her. To stand here rather than join the fate of the marines. Should the Crippled God indeed rise once more, we shall not even witness that moment.' He faced the others. 'You did not agree with me on this – my command that we remain with her.'

'It is what we may lose, Urugal,' said Thenik the Shattered. 'To see him reborn.'

'Must our faith show its face to us, Thenik?'

'I have longed for proof,' the Shattered replied. 'That all that we have done has purpose. Is this not what the Fallen One offered us? Yet we do not lend our swords to the defence of our god.'

'In the manner I have chosen,' countered Urugal, 'we will do just that.'

Nom Kala spoke, hesitantly. 'Kin, I have listened to the soldiers – these Malazans. At the campfires, in the times of rest.' They had turned to regard her now. 'They speak to each other rarely, yet when they do, it is of her words from long ago. When she spoke of being unwitnessed. They do not, I feel, quite understand her – nor do I – and yet, when I hear them, when I see what stirs in their eyes . . . the word awakens something in them. Perhaps it is no more than defiance. But then, is not defiance mortality's most powerful proclamation?'

There was silence for a time, barring the faint moan of the morning wind.

Finally, Beroke said, 'Unwitnessed. Then let us make this our cause, too.'

'One none of us understands?' demanded Thenik.

'Yes. One none of us understands.'

'Very well. Nom Kala, your words awaken in me . . . defiance.' Thenik turned to Urugal. 'We have been ghosts among them. We have given them so little, because we had so little to give. This day, let us give to her all that we have left.'

'The Fallen One,' said Beroke, 'has placed his trust in her. His faith. Urugal, I honour you. My kin, I honour you all.' The T'lan Imass paused, and then said, 'One must be sacrificed. The interference of Akhrast Korvalain remains and will do so until the last of the Forkrul Assail falls. But the sundering of the Vow, by one of us here, will grant us what we seek. I volunteer to be that sacrifice.'

'Soft-Voice,' said Urugal, 'you are most formidable in battle. One of lesser use should be the one to sunder the Vow. It shall be me.'

'You are both incorrect,' said Thenik. 'I am well-named the Shattered. There must be no sentimentality to this decision. Nor obstinate courage – after all, does any of us here *not* possess that? Beroke. Urugal. Kahlb and Halad. Nom Kala of the wise words. Kalt Urmanal of Trell blood. I shall open the way for you all, in the name of defiance. The discussion ends.'

The T'lan Imass were silent.

And in silence they fell to dust.

The enemy had been sighted. The enemy was closing. Lostara Yil stood with the Adjunct in Tavore's tent, watching as the woman prepared for battle. The Adjunct had selected a standard issue long sword from the depleted stores. Its last wielder had scorched uneven patterns down the length of the leather-backed wooden scabbard. An eye bereft of talent but possessed of boundless discipline and patience. Not an artist. A soldier.

The captain had enquired of Tavore about her selection of this particular weapon – was it the scabbard's elaborate pattern that caught her interest? The well-honed blade edges? The solid-looking cross-hilt and firm grip? – and had earned nothing more than a blank look in reply. And Lostara understood, when Tavore had a moment later glanced back at the scabbard, that the Adjunct had not even noticed any of these details.

Her coat of chain waited on the wooden chest that had held it, with the leather-cuffed gauntlets folded over the glistening iron links. The plain shirt Tavore was now wearing was worn through in places, revealing pale, almost bloodless skin and the ripples of bone so close beneath it. Her iron helm with its grilled cheek-guards sat waiting on the map table.

Tavore finished binding her boot laces, and then walked to stand before a small wooden box beside the helm, one that bore a silver-inlaid family crest of House Paran. The fingertips of her right hand settled upon the lid, and then the Adjunct closed her eyes for a moment.

Lostara suddenly felt an intruder on this, Tavore's private readying for what was to come, and almost turned to leave before recalling that the Adjunct had ordered her to attend her preparations, to help with the chain coat and its fastenings.

The lid creaked as Tavore opened it, startling Lostara.

Reaching inside, she drew out a necklace – a simple leather string and an eagle's talon of brass or gold. Then she turned to the captain. 'Would you tie this for me, please?'

But Lostara simply stared at the talon.

'Captain.'

She looked up, met Tavore's eyes.

The Adjunct sighed. 'I am a child of the Emperor – what more is there for you to understand, Lostara Yil?'

'Nothing, Adjunct.' She moved forward, took the necklace in her hands. As she stepped close, drawing it up round Tavore's neck, Lostara caught a faint scent of perfume from the woman's thin, straight hair and her knees came close to buckling, a rush of ineffable sorrow taking hold of her.

'Captain?'

'A moment – sorry, sir.' She struggled to tie the knot, but it was harder than it should have been, as her vision wasn't clear. 'Done.'

'Thank you,' Tavore replied. 'Now, the chain.'

'Of course.'

Banaschar stood holding the reins of the Adjunct's horse. A Khundryl breed, tough and stubborn, but it was gaunt, aged by suffering, its coat matted and dull. Even the Burned Tears had, in the last days on the desert, failed in their diligence. This beast had no running left in it – the damned thing might well collapse beneath Tavore as she rode out to address her army.

Address her army. Is this truly the Adjunct? When did she last speak to all of her soldiers? Now I remember. On the ships. Confusing words, the awakening of an idea few could even grasp.

Will she manage better this time?

He realized that he was nervous for her – no, he was sick with anxiety. *So I stand here holding the reins of her horse, outside her tent. I am . . . gods, the word is pathetic. But what does it matter? I am also priest to a god about to die on him.*

I once vowed that I would meet this day cold sober. What a miserable vow to make.

The tent flap was drawn back and Captain Lostara Yil stepped outside, looked round until she saw Banaschar, and then gestured.

He led the beast forward by the reins.

The Adjunct stepped into view. Met his eyes and nodded. 'Demidrek. You have stood here for some time, I should think – I was expecting one of my aides to attend to this, and they're used to standing around and waiting. My apologies.'

He blinked. 'Adjunct, you misunderstand. I drove the poor man away.' He handed her the reins. 'I am and always will be honoured, Tavore Paran.'

'If I could,' she said, 'I would order you away from here.'

'But I am not one of your soldiers to be bullied around,' he said, smiling. 'So I will do as I damned well please, Adjunct.'

She studied him, and then said, 'I wonder.'

'Adjunct?'

'Is this not the true purpose of a priest? To take faith from the one hand and place it into the next? To stand between a god and one such as myself?'

His breath caught. 'A few remain,' he managed. 'Most go through the motions, but see themselves as privileged . . . from both sides. Closer to their god than to their unordained flock.'

'But that is not you, is it?'

'Adjunct, I am kneeling beside you.'

There was the flicker of something in her eyes, something raw swiftly suppressed, and then she was setting a boot in the stirrup and drawing herself into the saddle.

Banaschar stepped back. Looking away, he saw rank upon rank of soldiers turned, facing them, and now they slowly shifted as Tavore trotted her mount forward. She reached the southwest corner of the formation before wheeling inward to pass along the back line. She rode straight in her saddle, a figure in tattered chain, upon a starved, dying horse.

The image seemed to sear itself in Banaschar's mind.

Reaching the far end, she swung round the corner – making her way up to face the front of the three, much-reduced, legions. She would speak to her soldiers now. And, much as he yearned to hear her words, he knew that they were not for him.

Chest aching, the priest turned away.

As she rode towards the head of her forces, Tavore could see the dust cloud from the approaching army, and it was vast. Wheeling her horse, she walked the animal on a course parallel to the presented ranks, slowing the beast's steps enough to move her gaze from one face to the next in the front line.

When the Adjunct finally spoke, her voice carried firm on the wind. 'Does anyone know you? You, who stood in the shadows of the heavies and the marines. Who are you? What is your tale? So many have seen you – marching past. Seen you, standing silent and unknown. Even now, your faces are almost lost beneath the rims of your helms.' She was silent for a long moment, her eyes tracking each and every visage.

And then she halted, gaze fixing upon one man. A Falari. 'Corporal Grid Ffan, Third Squad, Eleventh Company. Bonehunter. You carried Sample – the soldier on your left – on your back. The last day in the desert. And, before the Blood for Water, the only thing that kept you – and her – alive was your love for her.'

The man seemed to sway before her words. She nudged her horse forward. 'Where stands Wreck-Eye?'

'Here!' cried out a voice from a dozen ranks back.

'When Lostara Yil lost consciousness protecting my life on the day of the Nah'ruk, you led your squad to recover us. Myself. Henar Vygulf. Captain Yil. You lost a brother, and to this day you can find no tears for him. But be at ease. There are those in your squad who have wept in your stead. At night, when you sleep.'

She walked her horse forward a few more steps, found another face. 'Sergeant Ordinary Grey. When Sergeant Gaunt-Eye's squad of marines broke and tried to murder him, you and Could Howl held them all off – you cut them down to save Gaunt-Eye. Because once, long ago on the Holy Desert of Raraku, he showed kindness to you.'

She reached the end of the ranks, turned her mount round and began retracing her route. 'Who are you? I know who you are. What have you done? You have stayed with me since the very beginning. Soldiers, hear me! This day is already lost to history, and all that happens here shall remain for ever unknown. On this day, you are unwitnessed.

'Except for the soldier to either side of you. *They* shall witness. And I tell you this, those soldiers to either side of you, *they* are all that matters. The historians' scrolls have no time for soldiers like you – I know, for I have read hundreds of them. They yield a handful of words to speak of defeat or victory. Perhaps, if so warranted, they will make mention of great valour, extraordinary courage, but the weight of those words is no more and no less than those used to speak of slaughter and murder. Because, as we all know, one soldier can be hero and villain both.

'We have no place in their histories. So few do. They are not us – they were never us, and we shall never be them.

'You are the Unwitnessed, but I have seen what you see. I have felt what you feel. And I am as much a stranger to history as any of you.'

The Adjunct reined in again, at the very centre, and swung her horse round to face the silent troops. 'On the day of the Na'ruk, they stood for you. Today, here, you shall stand for them. And I shall stand with you, my beloved soldiers.' She held up a gauntleted hand. 'Say nothing. We are walls of silence, you and me. We are perfect reflections of the one we face, and we have faced each other for so long now.

'And the meaning of that silence is none of the enemy's business.'

Behind her she could feel the tramp of thousands of boots reverberating up from the ground, but she would not turn, would not face the enemy. Her eyes belonged only to her soldiers, and, she could see, theirs belonged in turn to her and her alone.

'Bonehunters. Yield only in death on this day.'

When she rode to take her position on the south flank, Fist Blistig watched her, his eyes following her as did the gazes of every soldier round him.

Gods below. What kind of rousing speech was that? Salvage it, Fist – before it's too late. He swung round. 'For'ard ranks! Dr—'

But he got no further. Weapons snapped out of sheaths and scabbards, shields lifting on to shoulders.

And in the faces around him he saw the coldest iron he had ever seen.

Sister Freedom surveyed the enemy position. They had done the best they could given the limits of the land, arrayed along a modest ridge, and before them the ground stretched more or less level, although just to the north rose a series of low hills. Her scouts had informed her that the land beyond those hills was cut by ravines – if not for that obstacle to ordered retreat, no doubt the enemy commander would have positioned his or her troops on those heights. But movement would have been too restricted, and in a battle that could prove deadly.

She saw no heavily armoured infantry among the foreign soldiers facing them, and no cavalry. The ranks of archers anchoring each flank looked pitifully small.

'This is barely an army,' ventured Brother Aloft, who rode at her side. 'I might well believe that they crossed the Glass Desert – see how

851

disordered and worn they are, how few in number. They must have left a road of corpses behind them.'

'Of that I have no doubt,' Freedom replied, eyes narrowing upon seeing a lone rider – a slight, frail-looking figure – out in front of the facing line of soldiers. 'Yet,' she added, 'crossing that desert should have been impossible.'

'The foes who destroyed our kin at the Great Spire were known to Brother Diligence. Bolkando. Letherii. I do not recognize those standards.'

'Nor I, Brother Aloft. From what land have they come, I wonder?' She looked round, baffled. 'To this place. To die.'

'Brother Grave draws close to the smaller force.'

She nodded. Though faint, his sending had reached through to her. Akhrast Korvalain was in a tumult – disturbed and thinning with weakness. *There is something still to come. I feel its assault.* She looked up at the sky but saw only those slashes of jade. Icy worlds flung across the heavens. They had last appeared on the day the foreign god was brought down.

And that is the truth of this – all of this. They seek to return him to the heavens.

But the fate of the Fallen God belongs to the gods, not to humans. We could have wrested that privilege away from those gods – with our ancient power, our Elder Warren – but that has been taken from us. For the moment.

'Whose game was this?' she wondered, eyes still on that frail commander – who was clearly addressing his or her troops. *Her. That is a woman.*

'Sister?'

She shook her head. 'Audacity rarely goes unpunished.' She reined in. 'The way to the south is open. Brother, I want you there – I no longer trust that we shall have the power to make these foreigners yield.'

'But . . . why?'

'We shall strike them, yes, but not seeking to enslave. Voice no words in your cries, Brother. Instead, flense the flesh from their bones. I trust nothing more subtle.'

'As you wish.'

'Lead your forces round to the south, to encircle – the ranks we see are no doubt screening reserves, and I would know their strength. I in turn will leave the centre to High Watered Melest and take the north, where I will lead the dead king's elite infantry into the crook between the enemy's flank and the hills.'

'There is great risk in that, Sister Freedom.'

'No one hides behind those hills, Brother. Furthermore, with me in the lead, we can drive that flank inward. Shatter the hinge on your side while I break the one on mine, and we shall make quick work of this.'

Aloft faced the north. 'Do you sense anything from High Watered Kessgan? Have they encountered the other army? Brother Grave cannot find them at all.'

'Nor can I. If they are in battle, then we must trust that they can delay or even drive back the enemy.'

The woman commanding the foreigners was now riding to take position on the south flank. Whatever she had said to her soldiers had elicited no cheers, no defiant roars.

'She has lost them!' cried Brother Aloft.

'So it seems. Brother – see where she goes? She understands the weakness of that side. Ride straight for her when you advance. Kill her.'

'She might well be alone by then – I believe this army is moments from routing.'

'Such is the failing of their kind,' Freedom replied. 'Humans have the qualities of vermin – you will find them everywhere, but they share a belief in the virtue of running away when threatened. We shall have to hunt them down, Brother, and rid us of them once and for all.'

'I will ride to my vanguard now, Sister. When next we meet, it shall be standing upon the corpses of these wretched upstarts.'

'The ground will welcome their bones,' she replied, nodding.

Warleader Gall surveyed his paltry force of horse-warriors, and then, helm tucked under one arm, he walked over to Hanavat. The foundling Rutt was beside her, the unnamed baby cradled in his arms. His thin face was white with fear.

'Wife,' said Gall in greeting.

'Husband.'

'I will die today.'

'I know,' she replied.

'Will you flee this battle? For our child?'

'No,' she said.

'Please. I beg you.'

'Husband, we have nowhere to go. We shall find you in the Ancestral Hills, beneath a warm sun, and the desert flowers will fill our eyes with the colours of spring.'

At the ancient parting words of the Khundryl, Gall slowly closed his eyes. 'I have fallen,' he said, looking up once more to meet her level gaze. 'You have seen my weakness.'

'I have only seen what can be found in all of us, beloved. Does not a Warleader of the Khundryl walk the same ground as the rest of us? Your gift was courage and cunning on the field of battle. That gift remains. Take it with you this day, in the name of Coltaine, and in the spirit of the Wickans, who were the greatest horse-warriors this world has ever seen. Did we not proclaim that? With your own words, did you not cry their name to the heavens – until even the Ancestral Hills stirred in the awakening of our ghosts?'

'I did, my love.'

'We burned tears upon our faces to mark their passing from the world. But I see Khundryl warriors behind you, husband. I see the best of what remains. Lead them. I give to you the courage of my own heart, to join with yours. Today, I am proud.'

Trembling, he stepped forward and took her in his arms.

Fist Faradan Sort watched the massive army form up on the plain beyond. By numbers alone the centre dominated. Medium infantry along with skirmishers and crescents of archers: she judged seven or eight thousand. The wings belonged to heavy infantry, and she could see a pure-blooded Forkrul Assail commanding each one. Her eyes narrowed on the Pure opposite her – a female, mounted on a bone-white horse, from which she was now dismounting.

'They have power in their voice!' Faradan Sort shouted. 'By command alone they will seek to make you yield. To drop your weapons. Defy them, Malazans!' *Easy enough to say. Probably impossible to achieve. This could turn into horror very quickly.* She drew her sword. Ancient scars from the sorcery of the Stormriders marred the blade, forming a crazed mottling of pattern welding and watermarking.

In her mind, a faint echo rose up – the crash of massive waves, shuddering the treacherous, icy stone underfoot. The bitter cold bite of the shackles round her bandaged ankles. Explosions of foam – and then, rising through the blue-white foment, a shape, a figure armoured in ice— she shook herself, mouth suddenly dry.

It's a warm day. Nothing to slip on. No numbness to steal all feeling from my hands. No raw patches where my skin has torn away at the touch of metal.

I have faced worse. Remember that – it's what has kept you going battle after battle.

The Forkrul Assail was walking ahead of her troops now, up towards a low rise.

Faradan Sort suddenly looked down, studied the yellow, brittle grasses, the countless rodent holes. 'Soldiers – anyone see any scorpions hereabouts?'

A chorus of grunts answered her, all in the negative.

'Good. That will do, then. Shields high – seems she's got something to say to us!' *Gods, this is where it gets unfair.*

*   *   *

854

Smiling, Sister Freedom studied the enemy forces. *Ah, we were wrong. They are not moments from routing.* There was rage and stolid determination in the faces across from her, but none of that would help – not now. Shields and armour would resist the power she was about to unveil, would protect them – for a time. Perhaps a handful of heartbeats. But then her voice would tear through, claw away skin and muscle, spray blood into the air. Bones would snap, skulls would shatter.

They were all about to die, and nothing they did would prevent that.

As here, so too the rest of the world.

Glancing to her left, she saw the centre advancing – now less than thirty paces distant from the motionless line of defenders. Archers were loosing arrow upon arrow, with the enemy's own archers countering here and there. Soldiers were falling, though for most shields fended off the deadly rain. *Twelve paces, and then the charge. Its weight will drive them back, break up that facing line, and into the gaps we will pour, splitting the formation apart. And then will come the slaughter.*

Returning her attention to the flank opposite her, she raised her arms, began drawing breath.

The flint sword that erupted from the ground beneath the Forkrul Assail ripped into the inside of her left thigh, lifting her into the air as the tip cracked and pierced her hip bone. As its wielder rose in a shower of earth, stones and roots, others burst from the ground surrounding the Forkrul Assail.

Weapons hammered into her.

Howling, writhing still on that sword, she lashed out. The back of one hand struck the forehead of Urugal the Woven, collapsing it inward, pitching the T'lan Imass from its feet.

Kalt Urmanal's bone mace caught the Forkrul Assail under her left arm, spun her entirely around, boots skyward, and off from the skewering sword.

She landed with a roar, surging back to her feet.

Beroke's obsidian-tipped spear slid through her, exploding out from her lower belly. Twisting round, the Assail grasped hold of the spear shaft and lifted it into the air, taking Beroke with it. Releasing the wood, she reached up to trap Beroke's skull between her hands as he slid closer to her.

With a bellow she crushed the warrior's skull.

In her mind, Sister Freedom shouted commands to her officers. '*Charge the enemy – break through and encircle them! Kill every damned one of them! Leave these bone-bags to me!*' The T'lan Imass with the

855

crumpled forehead came towards her again. Snarling, she flung herself at him.

Blistig could feel the desperate rage growing in him, and as the enemy ranks suddenly seemed to build like a rising wave and rush howling towards him, he screamed his own fury.

The collision lifted soldiers from their feet, shoved them into the air. Blood misted, weapons hammered down, and the front ranks of the Malazans recoiled, and then stiffened. The clamour was deafening – weapons and shrieks – and the world was crazed before the Fist's eyes, frantic with motion, the flash of faces, teeth bared, sudden gushes of blood from mouths and gaping throats. Bodies pushing up against his shins. Staggering, flaying with his sword, buffeted by repeated blows against his shield, Blistig fought with the ferocity of a rabid dog.

He was going to die. They wanted to kill him – every damned one of them wanted to kill him, drag him down, trample his corpse. His life wasn't supposed to end like this. He would fight, and fight. This was not going to be the end – he wouldn't let it. *I will not let it!*

Chaos spun wild around him and the soldiers pressing against his sides.

They were pushed back another step.

Lostara Yil moved up alongside the Adjunct, drawing her swords. *Another dance. All I can do. The dance of the world – this fucking, miserable, murderous world.* She saw Ruthan Gudd take Tavore's other flank, and behind her she could hear Henar Vygulf – the fool was singing some damned Bluerose sea shanty.

Ahead, advancing now, leaning forward and striding on stiff legs like a madman, came the Forkrul Assail. His eyes were feral and they were fixed on the Adjunct.

When he roared, the sound hammered them back.

Blood sprayed into the air and Lostara staggered, blinded. *Whose blood? What—* And now it was pouring down her cheeks and she saw Henar thump down, turning to her a shredded face. *Oh, gods, it's my blood – we're all—*

Impossibly, the Adjunct straightened against that devastating onrush of wordless sound, drew her sword round, and sought to close.

The Forkrul Assail was still almost forty paces away.

We can't do this. Even Tavore – we can't—

Ruthan Gudd reached the Adjunct's side in his armour of ice – but that too was riven with cracks, breaking away in a hail of shards. He seemed to be reaching for her, as if to drag her back – away from this – but no retreat was far enough.

The Assail roared again.

Lostara Yil's own scream was lost even to her own ears.

She felt her body skidding across the broken, tortured ground.

Against this – we are done with. Not even the Adjunct. Not even Ruthan Gudd. He slays us. Cotillion—

But not even a god could hear her prayers now.

Fifty paces behind, driven to his knees by the power of Akhrast Korvalain, Banaschar wiped blood from his eyes. He had tried to get closer – tried to move up and join with the Adjunct and her companions – but he had failed.

Failure. I know that word – spent many a night sitting at its table—

A figure stepped past him.

Badalle hummed softly to herself, and that gentle sound pushed away all that the Quisitor flung at her. Ahead, she could see how the power was hurting Mother – even with all her magic-deadening blood, her extraordinary will, Mother was being torn apart.

She gave words to her wordless song. Simple words, three to find the fourth, when the fourth was all that mattered. 'Opals gems diamonds shards. Opals gems diamonds shards.' *You have forgotten so much. Until only hunger and pain remains. I know those two things. I know them well. We have shared them, you and I.*

'Opals gems diamonds shards. Opals gems diamonds shards.'

I sent you away once. I told you to take your hurt and your hunger away from us. Because we deserved neither.

Someone hurt you long ago. Someone hurt Rutt long ago. Someone hurt Saddic, and Held, and all the others. Someone must have hurt me, too.

'Opals gems diamonds shards. Opals gems diamonds shards.'

I sent you away. Now, I summon you. See the bringer of pain. See the deliverer of hunger. The Quisitor. I know him. I remember him. He came among my people. He told them they had to die. To answer ancient crimes.

Perhaps he was right.

But that did not mean he had *the right.*

'Opals gems diamonds shards. Opals gems diamonds shards.'

Do you know his kind? I think you do. Do you awaken now to ancient hurts? I think you do. I summon you. They like their justice. Now, my friend, deliver it.

'Opals gems diamonds shards. Opals gems diamonds *Shards*!'

And above the Forkrul Assail, the sky darkened.

*   *   *

857

Banaschar stared as the swarm of locusts descended – where they had come from, how they had been summoned, he knew not. Their sound was a seething whisper, and then a swarming, howling cacophony. He saw the Forkrul Assail cease his attack, saw the man look up.

And then the swarm plunged down in an enveloping cloud, a storm of wings that suddenly blossomed crimson.

Brother Aloft screamed, and as he screamed the locusts crawled into his mouth, poured inside, mandibles slashing. Blood soaked the creatures, helped them slide down his throat. Choking, blinded and deafened, he fell to his knees. They chewed inside – his windpipe, and now his stomach. They blocked his nostrils, fought to enter his ears. Their bites cut through his eyelids and burst the eyes behind them. They swarmed into the sockets.

The god of the Forkrul Assail was coming home.

The locusts formed a seething pillar, which fell as the body it shrouded toppled to one side. Flashes of red gristle, of pink bone, and then the creatures were lifting away on their wings, rushing into the Kolansii infantry – but those soldiers, well armoured, their shields up before their faces, pushed through and the locusts spun, the whirr of their wings reaching a higher pitch, as if giving voice to their frustration.

Abruptly the swarm lifted, swirled into the air overhead.

Badalle could feel their need – it was without end – and she knew that if they remained in this place she would lose control of them – they would devour everyone.

Go now. You cannot stay.

The roar reached a pitch that shivered the air – a scream of impotence – and then the whirling cloud spun away.

Just beyond the bones of the Forkrul Assail, the Kolansii infantry advanced, and before them stood four figures sheathed in blood.

Mother, when this is done – when you and all your children have fallen – I shall with my last breath summon them again. To deliver our revenge.

Warleader Gall sat on his horse, eyes on the heavy infantry pushing past the embattled female Forkrul Assail. Their ranks were disordered, broken by the steep pitch of the hillside on their right, crowding to avoid the hill where fought their commander and the T'lan Imass. Large stones that had long ago rolled down from the summit further slowed their advance.

He could see the flank of Malazans turning to ready for the inward attack – but he could also see that the intention of the enemy was to win through to the rear of the defenders.

Beside him, Shelemasa said, 'Warleader – the south flank—'

'We must choose one or the other,' Gall cut in. 'Do you see the ones before us? They cannot hold their lines – but see how, once they are past the Malazans, they will be able to spread out, once more on level ground. They will then form up.'

'Warleader, the Adjunct—'

'We cannot help her,' he said. 'If there were three thousand of us, yes, we could challenge that flank. But these ones here – at the threshold of open ground – we will meet them there.' He drew his tulwar, rode out ahead of his pitifully small army, and then wheeled.

'In the name of Coltaine and the Fall!'

He needed say nothing more. Weapons flashed, the horses tossing their heads as they caught the sudden fever of their riders.

Gall sawed on his reins, pitching his mount round. The beast reared, hoofs scything in the air.

And the Warleader laughed.

Faradan Sort had pushed her way to the edge of the flank – once the Kolansii broke through, she would need to be there, to hold her soldiers, to maintain their resolve – *but they do not need me. See their faces! The enemy seeks our underbelly and will be met with iron. And I will be there – this battle shall be mine, to the end.*

And then she heard the sound of horse's hoofs. Looked up, twisted round – and saw the Khundryl Burned Tears at full charge. Even as the first of the Kolansii spilled out from the narrow passage, the horse-warriors – with Gall in the lead – crashed into them.

The impact shook the ground, rippled through bodies all the way to the Malazan ranks.

'Hold fast!' Faradan Sort shouted. 'Now push! Into the enemy! *Push!*'

The Kolansii advance had been checked – but not for long, she knew. *It has to be enough. Now let's make them pay for that bad footing.*

The north-facing side of the Malazan phalanx surged forward, Faradan Sort in their midst, and the Kolansii heavy infantry turned to meet them. But they were staggering, stones rolling underfoot, boulders trapping their legs.

And the Khundryl were in a frenzy, driving ever deeper into their ranks.

Gods! See them fight!

Sergeant Ordinary Grey grasped hold of the corporal's jerkin, pulled him close. 'Grid Ffan – where's your squad?'

The Falari's eyes were wild, his face bright red. 'All around us, you Kartoolii spider bait!'

859

'Where's your sergeant?'

'Dead! Where's your fucking squad?'

'With your sergeant,' snapped Ordinary Grey. 'Except for my Semk here . . .'

They were being jostled, ever losing ground. Grid Ffan's eyes shifted past the sergeant and then widened. 'Someone sewed up his fucking mouth!'

'He likes it that way. Now listen – the south flank—'

'We ain't got a south flank!'

'She's over there – her and that Shadow Dancer and that captain with piss-ice in his beard. The Assail's finished, but the heavy infantry's about to fold us up. She named you, Ffan! Just like she named me and Could Howl. You understanding me?'

Grid Ffan shifted round. 'Hare Ravage! Sample! Find the others – we're pulling out of this press!'

The squad's huge mailed fist turned to the corporal. 'I barely got a swing in! Been waiting for fucking ever, Corporal!'

'We'll get you your Hood-damned fight, you Kanese squid-eater – we're taking on a whole army of heavies!'

'How many of us?' Sample demanded, her blue-tinted skin ashen with dust.

Ffan turned back to Ordinary Grey, who answered, 'Maybe ten.'

The Napan's grin flashed white, and in a sharp, piercing voice, she cried out, 'Shades, Brutan, Asp, Shipwreck and Gill Slime! With us! Move, damn you all!'

Pores sagged beside Kindly, who risked a moment to glower down at the man. 'Get out of here! You're a damned liability!'

'Just need – to – catch my breath!'

Beyond Pores, in the seething press, Kindly saw a dozen or so soldiers moving through the ranks away from the front line. 'What in Hood's name are they doing?' But he saw no panic in the faces of the soldiers closest to them – words were shouted back and forth, and the ranks shifted to make room for them to pass.

Pores straightened once more, followed Kindly's glare. 'Ordinary Grey . . . Ffan and Sample. And there's that scary Semk – it's the ones she called on, sir.'

'Is it now?'

Another hard shove from the front staggered them back again.

'Head back to the camp, Pores – do something useful. Protect the children.'

'I don't think – oh, right. Sir—'

'I'm moving up again – get out of here.'

'Sir—'

'That's it – you're up on report, soldier! Now go before I kill you myself!'

Lesser Watered Trissin moved past the bones of Brother Aloft – she struggled to not look down, yet could not help herself. Locusts still crawled here and there, out from under the bones or the slack skins of intestines, still crowded the gaping jaws.

She could feel Sister Freedom's fury and pain as the wounded Pure lashed out – the T'lan Imass would not win that battle – but they were taking all the Forkrul Assail's concentration. In truth, it was High Watered Melest who was commanding the assault, from the centre.

She saw, ahead of them, a line of four soldiers, and her eyes widened – *this is all they have for us? They are mad!*

Off to the right, spilling out from the enemy phalanx, came a dozen or so medium infantry.

A laugh burst from her. 'This is what they offer in opposition?' She gestured, her mind snapping out the command to spread out, widen the facing line.

They would sweep past these fools, and then wheel round to close on the flank from behind.

The battle was as good as done.

'Adjunct,' said Ruthan Gudd, 'we need to fall back – into the phalanx. We can't stay out here – we can't hold that advance—'

But Tavore Paran seemed to be beyond words. Blood flowed down her face, as if all that she had contained, all that she had held inside, was now pushing free.

Gods below. 'Take her left, Lostara – with Henar on yours. I've got the right. Adjunct! Fuck this waiting, let's charge.'

Her head snapped round, the eyes raw and wild.

And then the four of them were moving forward.

Trissin shouted in shock – they were attacking!

And now she saw – one of the soldiers was sheathed in ice, even unto the long sword in his hand. And another was coming forward with the fluid grace of water, two swords seeming to flow from her hands. Apart from the ice-bound figure, the others were covered in blood – these were the ones who had stood against Brother Aloft. *That woman – she commands this army.*

What is she doing?

What are they all doing?

Grid Ffan swore in a stream of languages and then yelled, 'Run, you fools! Catch up to 'em!' And as they pelted forward, ten regulars racing to join up with their Adjunct and her officers, the corporal found breath to bark out orders.

'Hare Ravage – go far end and arrive hard! Sample – follow him up! Shades Elar and Brutan Harb – back up the Shadow Dancer and the Bluerose. Shipwreck and Could Howl, stay with me for the Adjunct! You too, Grey.'

Sergeant Ordinary Grey cursed. 'I outrank you, Ffan!'

'So what?'

'Right,' the man gasped. 'You all, what Ffan said! Carry on, Corporal!'

'Asp Slither – got any magic? How 'bout you, Gill?'

''S coming back,' hissed Gill Slime.

And Asp Slither cackled like a strangled swan. 'Just watch me!' she crowed.

'No!' Ffan shouted – they were only a dozen or so paces away now. 'Hold back, both of you! Find their fucking commander and hit the fucker with all you fucking got, you fucking got it?'

The Kartoolii mage cackled a second time and loomed close. 'No, sir. What do you mean?'

A strange burbling sound spat out from Could Howl.

Ffan shot the Semk a look. 'That's some laugh you got there.'

They arrived like a whirlwind, into the front line of the Kolansii. Swords were a blur in the hands of the dancer, and, where they touched, blood sang forth and bodies tumbled back. The ice-clad soldier waded in, blows bouncing from him unnoticed, and cut deep into the ranks, his sword seemingly everywhere. The tall soldier on the dancer's left was bellowing as he beat down the Kolansii in front of him, shield-slamming another and knocking the two men off their feet, where they fouled those coming up behind them. And the commander fought with breathtaking precision, every motion either evading a thrust or dealing death, on her face an expression that struck ice through Trissin's heart.

And then the other soldiers arrived, four coming up around the commander, three of them howling like demons, the fourth with his mouth horribly sewn tight. They struck in a manic frenzy, driving the Kolansii back.

She saw a huge soldier collide with the heavies who had swung round the ice-bound man, somehow knocking three of them to the ground. His short sword lashed down, seemingly little more than touching each Kolansii on the side of the neck – and from three throats blood sprayed out.

'Surround them!' screamed Trissin from three ranks behind the fighting. 'Cut them—'

A ball of flames engulfed the Kolansii commander, raging wild, and from the cloudless sky above lightning crashed down, the impact thundering, flinging soldiers to the ground, the strike creating a vast hole in the ranks. Burnt flesh and parts of bodies rained down.

Three demons clawed up from the ground beneath the burning woman, their bodies covered in protruding mouths filled with dagger-length fangs, the talons on the ends of their fingers long as sabres, their heads swarming with coal-red eyes. Roaring, they lunged into the raging flames, tearing the commander to pieces.

Seeing all this, Grid Ffan shot a wild look back at his mages – saw them convulsed with laughter. *Fucking illusionists!* 'Tone it down, you fools! You want t'give it all away?'

Gill Slime and Asp Slither looked up, suddenly straight-faced.

'Got anything else?' Ffan demanded.

Both shook their heads.

'Then get up here and fight!'

The Kolansii had recovered, were now pushing to close once again. And more were swinging round on the far side, forcing Sample and Hare Ravage to back up.

Swearing, Ffan worked up close to the Adjunct.

'Sir! We need to fall back into the phalanx! Adjunct!'

When she did not reply – or even seem to hear him – he cursed and said to the sergeant beside him, 'Grey, listen. We come up and around her, either side – we make us a wall so she can't get past us. Shipwreck, go there – and you, Semk, right here – we're going to force her back and into the ranks, understood?'

'It's the battle lust, sir!' shouted Shipwreck, staggering drunkenly as was his way in moments of high excitement, when his damaged inner ear started acting up.

'I know what the fuck it is, idiot. Now, let's do this!'

Lostara Yil was being pulled away from the Adjunct's flank – Henar Vygulf was hard pressed, now defending himself from attackers on two sides. The sudden arrival of the regulars had eased the threat, but only momentarily – there were simply too many of the bastards.

Sobbing, bearing countless wounds, Lostara Yil drew closer to her love.

Don't die. Please. Don't die.

A sword blade clipped Henar's head. He staggered, stunned.

Lostara screamed, now fighting blind to the threats pressing in around her, her gaze fixed on Henar.

The two regulars collapsed in to fend off the blows rushing down towards Henar. A woman and a man, the former Nathii, the latter

Seven Cities – she had never seen them before, but they fought the attackers to a standstill above her love, who'd dragged off his cracked helm, blood gushing down from a scalp wound, and was trying to regain his feet.

Lostara hacked down a Kolansii on her left, leapt over his crumpling form. The grace was gone now. Only brutal savagery remained. She opened another man's throat.

The Nathii woman shrieked, a sword driven through her chest. Dropping her weapon she took hold of the arm gripping that sword, and pulled her attacker down as she fell. Her companion's short sword licked out, cut through half his neck; the man was shouting, trying to drag Henar back to his feet, until an axe crushed the back of the regular's head, through helm and bone, and flung him forward, limbs flopping. But Henar was on his feet once more – and Lostara reached his side. Just beyond, a row of faces: Malazan regulars, shouting from their line on the flank, screaming and beckoning. *Close! Hurry! Come to us!*

Lostara spun round, blades whipping out. 'Henar! To the ranks! Go!'

She saw the other regulars spilling back, all of them arrayed protectively round the Adjunct as they forced her towards the ranks. Ruthan Gudd and one huge regular were fighting to prevent the group from getting cut off, enveloped, but even they were being pushed back.

Take me, Cotillion! Please, I beg you! Take me!

But from her patron god . . . nothing. She twisted to her left, marched ahead to hold the enemy.

A dozen Kolansii rushed her.

The Khundryl had pushed as deep as they could into the press of heavy infantry. They had gone farther than Warleader Gall had thought possible. But now the horses were all dead, and so too the last of his warriors. But the advance had been blocked – bodies alone were enough to prevent the enemy from swinging round the Malazan wing – so now they were simply pushing inward, forcing the regulars into an ever-contracting formation.

A sword had ripped open everything below his ribcage. He was lying on his back, on the corpses of strangers and kin, his intestines spilled out and tangled round his legs.

Something was pulsing in the air – he could not be certain if it came from outside or from somewhere deep inside him. *No. Outside.* Voices, rising in rhythm, but he could not quite make out the word. Again and again, the sound rising and falling, coming from somewhere off to his right.

He found the pounding of his heart falling into that pulse, and warmth flowed through him, though he knew not the reason for it.

Darkness was drawing close.

That sound. That sound . . . voices. They are voices. Rising from the Malazans. What are they saying? What do they shout, again and again?

Abruptly, thick blood crackled in one ear, opened a way through, and he could at last hear the endlessly repeated cry.

'*Khundryl! Khundryl! Khundryl!*'

A word for his fading heart, a song for his ending life. *Coltaine, I shall stand before you. We shall ride with your Wickans. I see crows over the Ancestral Hills—*

Sister Freedom strode forward as the huge Imass toppled. She kicked him on to his back, plunged her battered hands down, closed her fingers through torn, papery skin and ripped sinews, and took hold of his spine. She paused a moment, glaring at the one with the flint-studded harpoon who was rising yet again a few paces away.

The Forkrul Assail was a mass of wounds and broken bones, but she was far from dead. Bellowing, she lifted the T'lan Imass from the ground and broke his spine like a branch, twisting it amidst snapping, grinding sounds. Flinging the corpse away, she advanced on the last undead warrior.

'This ends now!'

The female warrior backed away.

They were both down from the rise, down among heaps of bodies – cold flesh and thick, cooling blood underfoot, limbs that flopped away with each step.

Fury filled Freedom. At the murder of Brother Aloft. At the pathetic audacity and stubbornness of these T'lan Imass. At this army of foreigners who refused to break, who did nothing but die where they stood, killing her soldiers and killing yet more of them.

She would destroy them – soon, once this last Imass was crushed and torn apart.

She stepped over a dead horse-warrior, one boot cracking into the side of the man's head.

The blow rang loud, and Gall opened his eyes. Blinked up at the sky. *I should be dead. Why am I not yet dead?*

Behind him he heard someone speak. 'Surrender to me, T'lan Imass. Your kin are all gone. There is no point in continuing this fight. Stand and I will destroy you. But I will give you leave to depart. Be done with this – it is not your battle.'

Gall reached down, took hold of a handful of his intestines, just under his ribcage and tore it free. He groped, slicing open the palm of his hand on a discarded sword – a Kolansii blade, straight and tipped for thrusting. *A child's toy. Not like my tulwar. But it will have to do.* He climbed to his feet, almost folded as a weight slipped behind his ribs and sternum – with his free hand he reached in, to hold everything up.

Turning, he found himself staring at the back of the Forkrul Assail. Beyond her stood a T'lan Imass, the one he knew to be named Nom Kala. Her left thigh had been shattered, bent and splintered, yet still she stood, her spear held at the ready.

Gall stepped forward, and drove the sword through the Forkrul Assail, through her spine. She arched in shock, the breath rushing from her.

The Khundryl fell back, his lungs slipping past his spread fingers to flop in his lap.

He was dead before his head hit the ground.

Nom Kala stepped forward. The Forkrul Assail's eyes were wide, staring into her own. The T'lan Imass had been watching those eyes for what seemed an eternity, since the moment they had risen up from the ground beneath her. She had studied the malice and ferocity in that unhuman glare. She had witnessed the flares of pleasure and triumph each time the Assail had shattered another of her kin. She had seen their delight when breaking Kalt Urmanal's spine.

But now there was a sword thrust through the Forkrul Assail, iron gleaming blue-red, and those eyes held nothing but astonishment.

Nom Kala took one more step closer. Then drove her harpoon into the bitch's eye.

Hard enough to drive through, punching out the back of the Assail's skull.

The Malazan army was crumbling. Driven back, pushed ever tighter inward, they left bodies heaped in ribboned mounds with every step they yielded. Joined by a stumbling Pores, Banaschar led the non-combatants – the children of the Snake and the Khundryl – as far back as they dared, but it was clear that the Kolansii sought only to annihilate the Bonehunters. All the heavy infantry now working round from the south were ignoring the huddled mass of unarmed onlookers.

Blistig was still fighting, a hard, defiant knot at the front of the centre phalanx. Banaschar could see Kindly, there on the right, doing the same. And Faradan Sort on his left. These three Fists, chosen by the Adjunct, simply refused to fall.

The ex-priest could no longer see Tavore, but something told him that she still stood – somewhere in the ranks on the south-facing line.

That attack, with the squad of regulars coming up to join it, had been . . . extraordinary.

And that magic was . . . ridiculous. But see that commander – lying dead. That's real enough. Not much Assail blood in that one, to have succumbed to nothing but invented nightmares. Nice play, regulars.

But it was all hopeless. All that he'd seen here, all that he'd witnessed.

He felt a presence to his right and turned to see Hanavat, and a step behind her and to one side, Rutt carrying the child. 'Your husband – I am sorry,' said Banaschar.

She shook her head. 'He stopped them. They all did. And now – see? The Forkrul Assail herself has fallen.'

'It was well fought, was it not?'

She nodded.

'Tell me, have you named the child?'

Hanavat met his eyes. 'I believed . . . what is the point? Until this moment. Until you spoke.' Then her eyes fell from his. 'Yet for the life of me, I cannot think of one.'

'Gall?'

'Gall bears but one face in my life, and so it shall ever be. Priest, I am lost.'

He could say nothing to that.

We are all lost.

Banaschar faced the terrible battle once more, Hanavat upon one side with the boy and the baby, Pores upon the other. They looked on, silent.

To where the Bonehunters were dying. Every one of them.

The air swirling brittle with outrage, High Fist Ganoes Paran rode to the top of the ridge, Fist Rythe Bude at his side. Behind them the Host was drawing up at the trot – he did not need to look behind him, or listen to Bude's desperate breaths, to know that they were exhausted.

That legion of heavy infantry had savaged them. Without Kalam and Quick Ben's deadly antics, the High Watered who had commanded the Kolansii had proved a stubborn foe, refusing to yield to the inevitable – they had been forced to kill every last one of them before finally cutting down the commander.

And now his army was bleeding, dragging itself up the slope like a wounded dog.

They reached the rise and reined in.

Before them, the Bonehunters formed a crumbling core under sustained attack from three sides, and in moments the fourth side would be engulfed as well. Ganoes could barely comprehend the magnitude of the slaughter he was seeing – corpses made low hills around the combatants, as orderly as the berms of an earthworks fortification.

Shock and horror tightened like a fist round his heart.

His sister's army had been reduced to less than half a thousand, and they were falling fast.

'High Fist—'

Rythe Bude's mouth snapped shut when he spun to her and she saw his face. Paran swung his mount round as the first line of soldiers reached the summit. 'To the edge! To this damned edge! Close up, damn you! Those are fellow Malazans dying down there! Look on them! All of you, *look on them!*'

His horse staggered beneath him, but he righted it with a savage sawing of the reins, then reached up and dropped the full visor over his face. Drew out his sword and rose in his stirrups as still more soldiers crowded the ridge.

'Draw breath, you bastards! And *CHARGE!*'

As he and Fist Rythe Bude drove their mounts down the slope, Ganoes Paran angled close to her. 'Into that flank – leave the south alone!'

'Yes sir!'

'Look for any mixed-bloods.'

The look she shot him was venomous. 'Oh really, sir?'

Behind them the ground shook as the Host thundered down the slope.

'High Fist! If we take down their commanders! Mercy?'

He glared ahead, drawing his mount away from the woman, angling towards the unoccupied flats between the fighters and the non-combatants. 'Today, Fist, I don't know the word!'

But he knew he would change his mind. Cursed with softness. *I got it all. Left nothing for Tavore, my sister of ice-cold iron. We should have shared it out. Like coins. Gods, so many things we should have done. Is it now too late? Does she live?*

Sister, do you live?

High Watered Melest, still shaken by the deaths of the Pures, turned at the cries of shock and dismay from the Kolansii on the right flank, and his eyes widened upon seeing another foreign army pouring down from the hills. Even as he watched, they slammed into the heavy infantry – and these attackers were as heavily armoured, and with the weight of the downhill charge behind them they shattered the wing with the force of an avalanche.

Howling in rage, he pushed back through the ranks – he needed one of the Pures' horses, to attain a higher vantage point. They still held the centre and fully commanded the south side of the field. Victory was still possible.

And he would win it.

In his mind, drawing as much strength as he could from Akhrast Korvalain, he exhorted his soldiers into a battle frenzy.

'Kill them! All these who have so defied us on this day – destroy them!'

His horse lagging beneath him, beginning to weave, Paran cursed and slowed the beast. He fumbled in the saddlebag on his left, drew out a lacquered card. Glared at the lone rider painted on it. 'Mathok! I know you can hear me! I'm about to open the gate for you. But listen! Come at the charge, do you understand? You wanted a damned Hood-balled blood-pissing fight, and now I'm giving it to you!'

Paran kicked his horse forward again, pushing the poor beast into a gallop. He fixed his eyes on the place where he would tear open the gate, and then rose in his stirrups. 'There,' he said to the card, and then threw it.

The card sailed out, level as a quarrel from a crossbow, so fast it blurred as it cut through the air.

Beneath Paran, his horse stumbled. Then collapsed.

He threw himself clear, struck hard, rolled and was still.

Ruthan Gudd fought to defy the envelopment, but even with this unknown brute of a soldier fighting at his side he could not prevent the hundreds of Kolansii from swinging round, well beyond the reach of their swords.

Behind him he felt a sudden surge rip through the regulars, pushing everyone forward a step. Twisting round, Ruthan strained to see the cause – but dust filled the air, and all he could see was the reeling mass of Malazans, now breaking apart, spilling out, as if in a berserk fever they now sought to charge – but before these soldiers there were no Kolansii.

They are broken. They are finally—

Thunder spun him round, and he stared, disbelieving, as thousands of warriors rode out from an enormous gate – but no, this ragged tear in the fabric of the world did not deserve so lofty a title. It was huge, opened to a howling wind – and it was barely thirty paces from the first ranks of the enemy.

The riders bore lances, their mounts heavily armoured across chest and neck. They struck the disordered mass of heavy infantry – there had been no time to wheel, no time to draw shields round – and the concussion of that impact shuddered through the Kolansii. The wing split, broke apart – and suddenly all cohesion was lost, and the horse-warriors were delivering slaughter on all sides.

The regular infantryman beside him stumbled then, leaned hard against Ruthan Gudd's hip. Startled, he stared down, saw the man pressing his forehead against his ice-sheathed side.

Eyes closed, the gasping Kanese breathed, 'Gods below, that feels good.'

Lostara Yil saw Adjunct Tavore stumbling away from the ranks. The pressure was gone – the enemy had other foes to deal with, and those foes were driving them back, away from the Bonehunters. She stared after Tavore.

The Adjunct was barely recognizable. Covered in blood and gore, her helm torn off, her hair stained red, she staggered into the clear. Ten jerking, almost manic steps, her sword still in her hand but held out to one side, as if the arm had forgotten how to relax.

Lostara pulled free of the ranks, moved after her – but a hand grasped her, dragged her back, and Henar's voice was close by her ear. 'No, love. Leave her. Just . . . leave her.'

Her steps ran out, lost all momentum, and then she was standing, alone, her back to her army. The sounds of battle seemed to be falling away, as if thick, heavy curtains were being drawn across every side of the world, shutting away every scene, every swirl of motion and dust.

She was alone.

The sword, still held out so awkwardly, and her head slowly tilting back, to lift her face to the sky.

Eyes were upon her now, but she saw them not.

Tavore's mouth opened, and the cry of anguish that tore from it held nothing human.

It rang across the field of battle. It pushed past the witnessing Bonehunters, reached out and caressed countless corpses. It fought with the dust, rising up to vanish in the lurid green hue of the sky's fading light.

When her voice gave out, all could see that cry continuing in the stretched contortion of her face. Silent now, she gave nothing to the sky, and in that nothing, there was everything.

Half stunned by the fall from the horse, Paran staggered towards her. That sound had not come from his sister. Too terrible, too ravaged, too brutal, and yet it dragged him towards her, as if he was caught in a rushing current.

Off to his left, a few hundred Bonehunters still alive, motionless, unable even to sag or settle to the ground. They looked upon his sister and he could make no sense of their meaning, of what they still wanted from her.

Is this not enough? This one weakness, breaking loose so raw, so horrifyingly, from her?

Is it never enough?

I don't – I don't understand what you want from her! What more are you waiting for?

Through the bars of his helm's iron grille, she was directly ahead, a prisoner still.

Someone was rushing towards her. Another enemy. She could not even open her eyes, could not turn to meet him. One more death seemed too much, but she knew what waited within her. This need. This need . . . *to finish.*

Do not attack me. Please. Someone stop him. Please.

I will kill him.

She heard him arrive and she dropped down into a crouch, spinning round, eyes opening – a heavy helm, an armoured body lunging for her.

Her blade was a blur.

He caught her wrist, was rocked back by the force of the swing.

Pulled her close as she struggled.

Fumbled at his helm's strap.

'Tavore! Stop! It's me – it's Ganoes!'

The helm came away, left his hand to thump on the ground – she stared up at him, disbelieving, and then, in her face, everything shattered.

'I lost her! Oh, Ganoes, *I lost her!*'

As she collapsed into his arms, frail as a child, Ganoes held her tight. One hand against the back of her sweat-matted head, her bloodied face now pressed into his shoulder as she broke down, he found himself sinking to his knees, taking her within him.

And when he looked up, over at those Bonehunters, he saw that whatever they had been waiting for they had now found.

Like him, like her, they were settling down, to their knees. They were . . . surrendering.

To whatever was left inside them.

Muffled against his shoulder, through her sobs, she was saying his name. Over and over again.

On a distant part of the field, as High Watered Melest swung his Jhag horse round, seeking to flee, Mathok's lance took him in the side of the head.

And the final battle of the Bonehunter Regular Infantry was done.

*   *   *

871

'Corporal! Get over to those fat women!'

'Dead, Sergeant!'

'Then the other one, damn you!'

'Both corporals are dead – I told you!'

Cursing, Hellian sidestepped a lunging attacker, drove her knee into the man's jaw. The head snapped upward and the body beneath it sagged. She stabbed him in the neck and then turned to glare at her squad's last soldier. 'Well what good are you, damn it? What's your name?'

'You stupid brain-dead cow – I'm *Maybe*! I been with you from the start!'

'And you're still here – just my luck. I'll hold this track – go find someone to spell those two whales. Most of those Bridgeburners are dead.'

Swearing, Maybe moved off.

Hellian took a moment to dry the sweat and blood from her palm, and then picked up her sword again. Where was Urb? If that fool was dead she'd kill him. *No, that's not right. No matter.*

Below, she saw more helmed heads lurching into view on the narrow, winding incline.

Come on, then. One of you's gotta have a flask. Something, for Hood's sake. See what happens when I'm sober?

Corabb heard Maybe shouting behind him and turned – saw weapons flashing, Kolansii soldiers pouring up on to the summit. Marines were going down all round Maybe – Mulvan Dreader, Ruffle, Honey – 'Breach!' he screamed. 'Breach!'

And then he was running.

Maybe stumbled, stabbed through one calf, buckling to blows against his shield. Corabb saw Ruffle push herself on to her hands and knees – but then an axe descended, bursting her skull. She flopped back down, limp as a rag doll.

Now he could see the breach. The two Bridgeburner sergeants had both gone down at the top of the trail they had been defending.

Corabb leapt over the chained god.

Kolansii faces turned towards him – and then he was among them, his sword singing. The shield was torn from his left arm by an axe blade. A point bit deep into his side. Howling, he slashed open a shoulder, cutting through chain, the links scattering, and then drove another man to his knees on the backswing.

A heavy grunt from someone on his right – Shortnose had arrived, shield-bashing two foes, sending both to the ground. He'd collected up a Kolansii axe and now used it to dispatch the stunned soldiers.

More of the enemy rushed them.

The Crippled God was able to turn his head, was witness to the savage, desperate defence from these two Malazans. He watched the enemy driven back in one instant, then pushing closer in the next. The sweat of one of his protectors had splashed his face when the man had sailed over him, and those droplets now ran down in trickles, leaving tracks that felt cool as tears.

It seemed that there would be no reinforcements to this modest engagement – the enemy was upon them on all sides. They had finally come within sight of his chained body – and now the Forkrul Assail understood the purpose behind all this. The Crippled God could feel the Assail's hunger.

I am almost all here, within this bag of skin. And I remain in chains.

He can wound me. He can feed on my power for all time – and none could challenge him. He will unleash my poison upon the world.

The Malazan with the cut-off nose-tip staggered, pierced through by a sword, and then another. Only to then straighten, his axe lashing out. Bodies reeled, toppled in welters of gore. He stumbled forward, and the Crippled God saw his face in profile – and saw the man's smile as he fell face first on to the ground.

Leaving but one defender, harried now by three Kolansii, with a fourth and fifth soldier appearing from behind them.

His lone stalwart marine cut one down with his singing blade. And then another – crippled by a thigh chopped down to the bone.

The axe that caught the marine was swung from the shield side – but the Malazan held no shield, could not block the swing. It cut clean through his left shoulder, severing the arm. Blood spraying, the man stepped back, his torso held pitched to one side, unbalanced. A second swing slashed through half his neck.

Somehow, the marine found the strength to drive the point of his sword into his killer's throat, the tip bursting out below the back of the skull. The thrust toppled him forward, into the dying man's arms. They fell as one.

Even as the remaining two Kolansii moved towards the Crippled God, weapons lifting, quarrels flashed in the air, knocked both men down.

The god heard the scuff and thump of boots, and then someone landed and slid up against him, and he turned his head to the kneeling saviour, looked up into Captain Fiddler's eyes.

'They reach you, Lord?'

The Crippled God shook his head. 'Captain, your soldiers . . .'

As if the word alone wounded him, Fiddler looked away, and then scrambled back on to his feet, cranking back the claw on the crossbow, his eyes fixing on the breach. Those eyes then went wide. 'Hedge!' he screamed.

Hedge fell against the hacked bodies of Sweetlard and Rumjugs. The trail just below where the two women had fought was jammed with corpses – but beyond them he could see more Kolansii soldiers, dragging the way clear. They'd be through in moments.

Too many. Fuck.

How long had they been fighting? He had no idea. How many waves of attacks? It seemed like hundreds, but that wasn't possible – they still had daylight above them. Dying daylight, aye, but still . . .

Eyes on the mass of enemy below, an enemy heaving ever closer, he drew round the satchel he had collected from the mound of gear close to the feet of the Crippled God. Drew out the cusser. *Always keep one. Always.*

Sapper's vow. If you're going down, take the bastards with ya.

He lifted it high.

Behind him he heard Fiddler shriek his name.

Aw, shit. Sorry, Fid.

Hedge plunged down the trail, rushing the mob of Kolansii.

And then heard someone behind him, and whirled. 'Fiddler, damn you! No! Go back!'

Instead, his friend tackled him. Both went down, the cusser flying from Hedge's hand.

Neither man ducked for cover, instead turning to watch the munition take its leisurely, curving path down to the press of soldiers – and all those bobbing iron helms.

It struck one of those helms clean as a coconut falling from a tree.

Burst open to spill insensate carmine powder.

The two sappers stared at each other, faces barely a hand's width apart, and in unison they cried, 'Dud!'

And then a Malazan slammed down beside them in a clatter of armour – a man if anything shorter than Reliko, yet pale and thin, his ears protruding from the sides of his narrow head. He faced them and offered up a yellow, snaggle-toothed smile. 'Got your backs, sirs. Get on wi'yee now!'

Fiddler stared at the man. 'Who in Hood's name are you?'

The soldier gave him a hurt look. 'I'm Nefarias Bredd, sir! Who else would I be? Now, get back up there – I'll cover yee, aye?'

Fiddler turned and dragged Hedge back on to his feet, pulling him up the trail. As they scrabbled to the edge, hands reached down and dragged them up. The faces of the marines now surrounding them – Tarr, Bottle, Smiles and Koryk – were the palest he had ever seen. Deadsmell arrived and fell to his knees beside the prone bodies of Rumjugs and Sweetlard, looked up and muttered something to Tarr.

Nodding, Sergeant Tarr pushed Hedge and Fiddler from the edge. 'We got this breach taken care of, sirs.'

Fiddler grasped Hedge's arm, yanked him as he dragged him away. 'Fid—'

'Shut the fuck up!' He rounded on Hedge. 'You thought to just do it all over again?'

'It looked like we was finished!'

'We ain't never finished, damn you! We drove 'em back again – you hearing me? They're pulling back – we drove them back *again*!'

Hedge's legs suddenly felt watery beneath him. He abruptly sat down. Gloom was settling round them. He listened to gasping breaths, cursing, ragged coughs. Looking about, he saw that the others within sight were also down on the ground, too tired for anything more. Heads fell back, eyes closed. His sigh was a rasp. 'Gods, how many soldiers you got left, Fid?'

The man was now lying beside him, back propped against a tilted stone. 'Maybe twenty. You?'

A shudder took Hedge and he looked away. 'The sergeants were the last of 'em.'

'They ain't dead.'

'What?'

'Cut up, aye. But just unconscious. Deadsmell figures it was heat prostration.'

'Heat— Gods below, I told 'em to drink all they had!'

'They're big women, Hedge.'

'My last Bridgeburners.'

'Aye, Hedge, your last Bridgeburners.'

Hedge opened his eyes and looked over at his friend – but Fid's own eyes remained shut, face towards the darkening sky. 'Really? What you said?'

'Really.'

Hedge settled back. 'Think we can stop 'em again?'

'Of course we can. Listen, you ain't hiding another cusser, are you?'

'No. Hood take me, I been carrying that one for bloody ever. And all that time, it was a dud!'

Faces floated behind Fiddler's eyes. Stilled in death, when so many memories of each one gave them so much life – but that life was trapped now, inside Fiddler's own mind. And there they would remain, when in opening his eyes – which he was not yet ready to do – he would see only that stillness, the emptiness.

He knew which world he wanted to live in. But, people didn't have that choice, did they? Not unless they killed the spark inside themselves first. With drink, with the oblivion of sweet smoke, but those were false dreams and made mockery of the ones truly lost – the ones whose lives had passed.

Around him, the desperate gulps of breath were fading, the groans falling off as wounds were bound. Few soldiers had the strength to move, and he knew that they were now settled as he was, here against this stone. Too tired to move.

From the slope on all sides, the low cries and moans of wounded Kolansii lifted up, soft and forlorn, abandoned. The Malazans had killed hundreds, had wounded even more, and still the attackers would not relent, as if this hill had become the lone island in a world of rising seas.

But it's not that.

It's just the place we chose. To do what's right.

But then, maybe that alone gives reason to take us down, to destroy us.

Hedge was silent beside him, but not asleep – if he had been, his snores would have driven them all from this place, the Crippled God included, chains be damned. And from the army still surrounding them, down on the lower ground, nothing more than a sullen mutter of sound – soldiers resting, checking weapons and armour. Readying for the next assault.

The last assault.

Twenty-odd soldiers cannot stop an army.

Even these soldiers.

Someone coughed nearby, from some huddle of stones, and then spoke. 'So, who are we fighting for again?'

Fiddler could not place the voice.

Nor the one that replied, 'Everyone.'

A long pause, and then, 'No wonder we're losing.'

Six, a dozen heartbeats, before someone snorted. A rumbling laugh followed, and then someone else burst out in a howl of mirth – and all at once, from the dark places among the rocks of this barrow, laughter burgeoned, rolled round, bounced and echoed.

Fiddler felt his mouth cracking wide in a grin, and then he barked a laugh, and then another. And then he simply could not stop, pain clenching his side. Beside him, Hedge was suddenly hysterical, twisting over and curling up as the laughter poured out of him.

Tears now in Fiddler's eyes – wiping them frantically – but the laughter went on.

And on.

* * *

Smiles looked over at the others in her squad, saw them doubling over, saw faces flushed and tears streaming down. Bottle. Koryk. Even Tarr. And Smiles . . . smiled.

When her squad-mates saw that, they convulsed as if gut-stabbed.

Lying jammed in a crack between two stones a third of the way down the slope, half buried beneath Kolansii corpses, and feeling the blood draining away from the deep, mortal wounds in his chest, Cuttle heard that laughter.

And in his mind he went back, and back. Childhood. The battles they fought, the towering redoubts they defended, the sunny days of dust and sticks for swords and running this way and that, where time was nothing but a world without horizons – and the days never closed, and every stone felt perfect in the palm of the hand, and when a bruise arrived, or a cut opened red, why he need only run to his ma or da, and they would take his shock and indignation and make it all seem less important – and then that disturbance would be gone, drifting into the time of before, and ahead there was only the sun and the brightness of never growing up.

To the stones and sweat and blood here in his last resting place, Cuttle smiled, and then he whispered to them in his mind, *You should have seen our last stands. They were something.*

They were something.

Darkness, and then brightness – brightness like a summer day without end. He went there, without a single look back.

Lying beneath the weight of the chains, the Crippled God, who had been listening, now heard. Long-forgotten, half-disbelieved emotions rose up through him, ferocious and bright. He drew a sharp breath, feeling his throat tighten. *I will remember this. I will set out scrolls and burn upon them the names of these Fallen. I will make of this work a holy tome, and no other shall be needed.*

Hear them! They are humanity unfurled, laid out for all to see – if one would dare look!

There shall be a Book and it shall be written by my hand. Wheel and seek the faces of a thousand gods! None can do what I can do! Not one can give voice to this holy creation!

But this is not bravado. For this, my Book of the Fallen, the only god worthy of its telling is the crippled one. The broken one. And has it not always been thus?

I never hid my hurts.

I never disguised my dreams.

And I never lost my way.

And only the fallen can rise again.

He listened to the laughter, and suddenly the weight of those chains was as nothing. *Nothing.*

'They have resurr—' Brother Grave stopped. He turned, faced the dark hill.

Beside him, High Watered Haggraf's eyes slowly widened – and on all sides the Kolansii soldiers were looking up at the barrow, the weapons in their hands sagging. More than a few took a backward step.

As laughter rolled down to them all.

When Brother Grave pushed harshly through the soldiers, marching towards the corpse-strewn foot of the hill, Haggraf followed.

The Pure halted five paces beyond the milling, disordered ranks, stared upward. He flung Haggraf a look drawn taut with incredulity. 'Who are these foreigners?'

The High Watered could only shake his head, a single motion.

Brother Grave's face darkened. 'There are but a handful left – there will be no retreat this time, do you understand me? No retreat! I want them all cut down!'

'Yes sir.'

The Forkrul Assail glared at the soldiers. 'Form up, all of you! Prepare to advance!'

Suddenly, from the hill, deathly silence.

Brother Grave smiled. 'Hear that? They know that it is over!'

A faint whistling in the air, and then Haggraf grunted in pain, staggering to one side – an arrow driven through his left shoulder.

Brother Grave spun to him, glared.

Teeth clenching, Haggraf tore the iron point from his shoulder, almost collapsing from the burst of agony as blood streamed down. Staring down at the glistening sliver of wood in his hand, he saw that it was Kolansii.

Snarling, Brother Grave wheeled and forced his way back through the press of soldiers. He would join this assault – he would ride his Jhag horse to the very top, cutting down every fool who dared stand in his way.

In his mind, seeping in from the soldiers surrounding him, he could hear whispers of dread and fear, and beneath that palpable bitterness there was something else – something that forced its way through his utter command of their bodies, their wills.

These were hardened veterans, one and all. By their hands they had delivered slaughter, upon foes armed and unarmed, at the command of the Forkrul Assail. They had been slaves for years now. And yet, like a black current beneath the stone of his will, Brother Grave sensed emotions that had nothing to do with a desire to destroy the enemy now opposing them.

They were in . . . *awe.*

The very notion infuriated him.

'Silence! They are mortal! They have not the wits to accept the inevitable! You will fight them, you will take them down, every last one of them!' Seeing them wither before his command, a surge of satisfaction rushed through him and he moved on.

'And I will claim the Crippled God,' he hissed under his breath, finally pushing clear of the troops, marching towards his hobbled horse. 'I will wound him and Akhrast Korvalain shall be reborn, and then none will be able to oppose me. None!'

Motion off to his left caught his attention. He halted, squinted into the green-tinted gloom.

Someone was walking towards him across the plain.

What now?

At forty paces he saw the figure raise its arms.

The sorcery that erupted from him was a blinding, coruscating wave, argent as the heart of lightning. It tore across the ground between them, struck one edge of the Kolansii ranks, and scythed through them.

Bellowing in answer, Brother Grave threw up his hands a moment before the magic struck.

He was flung backwards through the air, only to slam into something unyielding – something that gave an animal grunt.

Strength fled Brother Grave. He looked down, stared at two long blades jutting from his chest. Each knife had pierced through one of his hearts.

Then a low voice rumbled close to one ear. 'Compliments of Kalam Mekhar.'

The assassin let the body sag, slide off his long knives. Then he turned and slashed through the rope hobbling the horse. Moved up alongside the beast's head. 'I hate horses, you know. But this time you'd better run – even *you* won't like what's coming.' He stepped back, slapped the animal's rump.

The bone-white Jhag horse bolted, trying a kick that Kalam barely managed to dodge. He glared after it, and then turned to face the Kolansii soldiers –

– in time to see another wave of Quick Ben's brutal sorcery hammer into the press of troops, tearing down hundreds. The rest scattered.

And the High Mage was shouting, running now. 'Through the gap, Kalam! Hurry! Get to that barrow! Run, damn you!'

Growling, the assassin lumbered forward. *I hate horses, aye, but I hate running even more. Shoulda ridden the damned thing – then this would be easy. Better still, we should never have let the other one go. Quick's going on soft on me.*

A Kolansii officer with Assail blood in him stepped into his path, clutching his wounded shoulder.

Kalam cut the man's head off with a scissoring motion of his long knives, knocked the headless body to one side, and continued on. He knew that tone from Quick Ben. *Run like a damned gazelle, Kalam!*

Instead, he ran like a bear.

With luck, that would be fast enough.

Hedge knew that sound, recognized that flash of blinding magefire. He rose, dragging Fiddler to his feet. 'Quick Ben! Fiddler – they're here!'

On all sides, the last few marines were rising, weapons hanging, their faces filling with disbelief.

Hedge pointed. 'There! I'd know that scrawny excuse for a man anywhere! And there – that's Kalam!'

'They broke the Kolansii,' Fiddler said. 'Why are they running?'

As Hedge spun round – as if to shout to the marines – his hand suddenly clenched on Fiddler's arm, and the captain turned.

He looked skyward.

'*Gods below!*'

She was the finder of paths. There were ways through the worlds that only she had walked. But now, as she forced her will through the warren's veil, she could feel the pressure behind her – a need that seemed without answer.

Instinct had taken her this far, and the world beyond was unknown to her.

Has my course been true? Or nothing but a lie I whispered to myself, over and over, as if the universe would bend to my will?

I promised so much to my lord.

I led him home, I led him to the throne of his ancestors.

I promised answers. To all of the hidden purposes behind all that his father had done. I promised him a meaning to all this.

And I promised him peace.

She emerged into a dying day, trod lifeless grasses beneath her moccasin-clad feet. And the sky above was crazed with emerald comets, the light stunning her eyes with its virulence. They seemed close enough to touch, and in the falling rain of that light she heard voices.

But a moment later those actinic arcs were not alone in the heavens. Vast shadows tore ragged trails through the green glow, coming from her right with the fury of clashing storm clouds. Blood and gore spattered the ground around her like hail.

She spun in that direction, and the breath escaped Apsal'ara in a rush.

A blight was taking the land, faster than any wildfire – and above it was a dragon, appallingly huge, assailed on all sides by lesser kin.

Korabas!

She saw the front of that blight rushing towards her.

She turned and ran. Reached desperately for warrens, but nothing awakened – it was all being destroyed. Every path, every gate. Life's myriad fires were being snuffed out, crushed like dying embers.

What have I done?

They are following – they trusted in me! My lord and his followers are coming – there is no stopping that, but they will arrive in a realm which they cannot leave.

Where flies Korabas, there shall be T'iam!

What have I done?

Suddenly, in the distance ahead, sure as a dreaded dawn, the rift she had made tore open wide, and five dragons sailed out, their vast shadows rushing towards her. Four were black as onyx, the fifth the crimson hue of blood.

Desra. Skintick. Korlat. Silanah. Nimander.

And awaiting them, in the skies above this world, between earth and the fiery heavens, the air swarmed with their kin. And Korabas.

At war.

She saw her lord and his followers drawn into that maelstrom – all lost, stolen away by what was coming.

Where flies Korabas, there shall be T'iam.

And the goddess of the Eleint had begun to manifest.

Panicked, weeping, Apsal'ara began running again, and there, in the distance, beckoned a hill crowded with crags and boulders, and upon that hill there were figures.

As Fiddler turned to face the west, he found himself staring at the most massive dragon he had ever seen. Harried by scores of lesser dragons, seemingly torn to shreds, it was labouring straight for them.

He spun – the Adjunct's sword was now bleeding coppery, rust-stained light, visibly trembling where it was driven into the earth. *Oh no. We're all dead.*

The land beneath the Otataral Dragon was withering, crumbling to dust and cracked, bare clay. The devastation spread out like flood-waters over the plains.

The sword wasn't enough. We all knew that. When we stood here – her, me, the priest . . .

The priest!

He whirled round.

At that moment Quick Ben reached the crest. 'No one leaves the barrow! Stay inside the ring!'

The ring? 'Gods below. D'rek!'

The wizard heard him and flashed a half-panicked grin. 'Well said, Fid! But not *gods* below. Just one.'

Kalam stumbled into view behind Quick Ben, lathered in sweat and so winded he fell to his knees, face stretched in pain as he struggled to catch his breath.

Hedge threw the assassin a waterskin. 'You're out of shape, soldier.'

Fiddler saw his marines drawing up – their eyes were on the approaching dragon, and the hundreds of other, smaller dragons swooping down upon it in deadly waves. When some of them saw the blight, spreading out and now rushing closer, they flinched back. Fiddler well understood that gesture. 'Quick Ben! Can she protect us?'

The wizard scowled across at him. 'You don't know? She's here, isn't she? Why else would she be here?' He then advanced on Fiddler. 'Didn't you plan this?'

'Plan? What fucking plan?' he retorted, unwilling to budge. 'Banaschar said something . . . his god was coming – to offer protection—'

'Exactly – wait, what kind of protection?'

'I don't know!'

The blight struck the lower ground, caught the scattered Kolansii soldiers. They disintegrated in billows of dust.

The Malazans threw themselves to the ground, covering their heads.

Fiddler simply stared, as the Otataral Dragon voiced a terrible cry that seemed to hold in it a world's pain and anguish, age upon age – and its tattered wings, snapping like torn sails, thundered wildly in the air as the creature halted directly above the barrow. Quick Ben pulled him down to the ground.

Nearby the earth shook as the corpse of a dragon slammed into it. A curtain of blood slapped the hillside.

The wizard dragged himself close. 'Stay low – she's fighting it. *Gods, it's killing her!*'

Twisting round on the ground, Fiddler looked over at the Crippled God. His eyes widened.

Forged by the gods, the chains shattered like ice, links exploding, flinging shards in a vicious hail. Soldiers cried out, flinched away. The Crippled God remained lying on the ground, motionless. He had carried that weight for so long, he felt unable to move.

Yet his chest filled with air, the unyielding constriction now gone. The sudden release from pain left him hollow inside. Trembling took his body, and he turned his head.

The mortals were screaming, though he could not hear them. They looked upon him with desperate need, but he no longer understood what they desired of him. And then, blinking, he stared up, not at the hovering, dying dragon, but beyond it.

My worshippers. My children. I hear them. I hear their calls.

The Crippled God slowly sat up, staring down at his mangled hands, the uneven fingers, the nubs where nails should have been. He studied his scarred, seamed skin, the slack muscles beneath it. *Is this mine? Is this how I am?*

Rising to his feet, his attention was caught by the hundreds of dragons now massing to the south. They had drawn back from the Otataral Dragon, and now had begun writhing, swarming against each other, forming spiralling pillars of scale, wings and dragon flesh, twisting above a more solid mass. The shape towered into the sky, impossibly huge, and from the flattened, elongated ends of those pillars, high above them all, eyes suddenly flared awake.

A word whispered into the Crippled God's mind – faint, yet still voiced in a howl of terror.

T'iam.

Manifesting. Awakening to slay the Otataral Dragon.

The Crippled God saw a man fighting his way closer to where he stood, as if against a whirlwind. Iron in his beard, a familiar face he vaguely recalled, and with that recollection vague emotions rising into his thoughts. *There have been sacrifices this day. Made for me, by these strangers. Yet . . . asking for nothing. Not for themselves. Still, what do they now want from me?*

I am free.

I can hear my children.

And yet they are trapped in the heavens. If I call them down, all will be destroyed here.

There were others, once – they fell as I did, and so much was damaged, so much was lost. I see them still, trapped in jade, shaped to make a message to these mortal creatures – but that message was never understood, and the voices stayed for ever trapped within.

If I call my children down, this world will end in fire.

Craning, he stared beseechingly into the heavens, and reached up, as if he might fly into them.

The uneven fingers strained on the ends of his misshapen hands, pathetic as broken wings.

The bearded man reached him, and now at last the Crippled God could hear his words, could understand them.

'You must chain her! Lord! She will accept your chains! You must – T'iam is manifesting! She will destroy everything!'

The Crippled God felt his face twisting. 'Chain her? I, who have known an eternity in chains? You cannot ask this of me!'

'Chain her or she dies!'

'Then death shall be her release!'

'Lord – if she dies, then we all die! I beg you, chain her!'

He studied this mortal. 'She accepts this?'

'Yes! And quickly – D'rek is dying beneath us.'

'But my power is alien – I have no means of binding it to this world, mortal.'

'Find a way! You have to!'

He was freed. He could walk from this place. He could leave these mortals – not even the deadly power of the Otataral Dragon could harm him. *Otataral, after all, is nothing more than the scab this world makes to answer the infection. And what is that infection? Why, it is me.*

The Crippled God looked down upon this mortal. *He kneels, as all broken mortals kneel. Against the cruelty of this and every world, a mortal can do nothing but kneel.*

Even before a foreign god.

And what of the love I possess? Perhaps there is nothing – but no, there is no such thing as foreign love.

He closed his eyes, released his mind to this world.

And found them waiting for him.

Two Elder Gods, each taking a hand – their touches heartbreakingly gentle. The crushing pressure in this place had levelled every feature, darkness and silts swirling in unceasing dance. Currents raged on all sides, but none could reach through – the gods held them at bay.

No, only one of these Elders possessed that power, and he was named Mael of the Seas.

They led him across this plain, this ocean bed lost to the sun's light.

To where knelt another mortal – but only his soul remained, though for the moment it once more occupied the body it had abandoned long ago: rotted with decay, swirl-tattoos seeming to flow in the currents from the naked form. He knelt with his hands thrust down, buried deep in the silts, as if seeking a lost coin, a precious treasure, a memento.

When he looked up at them, the Crippled God saw that he was blind.

'Who is this?' the mortal asked. 'Who is this, nailed so cruelly to this tree? Please, I beg you – I cannot see. Please, tell me. Is it him? He tried to save me. It cannot have come to this. It cannot!'

And the Elder God who was not Mael of the Seas then spoke. 'Heboric, you but dream, and this dream of yours is not a conversation. Only a monologue. In this dream, Heboric Ghosthands, you are trapped.'

884

But the mortal named Heboric shook his head. 'You don't understand. All I have touched I have destroyed. Friends. Gods. Even the child – I lost her too, to the Whirlwind. I lost them all.'

'Heboric Ghosthands,' said Mael, 'will you fill this ocean with your tears? If you believe this notion to be new, know this: these waters were so filled . . . long ago.'

The other Elder God said, 'Heboric, you must awaken from this dream. You must free your hands – they have waited for this moment since the island. They have touched and taken the Jade and now within you reside a million lost souls – souls belonging to this foreign god. And, too, your hands have touched Otataral, the summoner of Korabas.'

But Heboric sank back down, groping in the silts once more. 'I killed my god.'

'Heboric,' said Mael of the Seas, 'even gods of war will tire of war. It seems that only mortals will not. No matter. He has absolved you of all blame. His blood has brought life to dead lands. He deems it a worthy sacrifice.'

'But that sacrifice will fail, Heboric,' said the other Elder God, 'if you do not awaken from your dream.'

'Who is upon the tree?'

'Heboric, there is no one upon the tree.'

The sightless eyes lifted once again. 'No one?'

'Let us see your hands, old friend. I have awakened all the warrens, and all now lead to one place. A cavern far beneath a barrow, made by the jaws of D'rek. Shall we walk there now, Heboric?'

'A barrow?'

'A barrow.'

'No one dreams within a barrow.'

Both Elder Gods were silent to that, and when the Crippled God looked at each of them in turn he saw that they were weeping – he could see the tears on their weathered faces, as if they stood, not at the bottom of an ocean, but upon a desert.

Or upon the broken skin of a barrow.

When Heboric dragged his hands from the silts, one glowed emerald through the billowing clouds, the other the hue of Otataral. The face he now turned to the Elder Gods was filled with sudden fear. 'Will I be alone there? In that cavern?'

'No,' replied Mael of the Seas. 'Never again.'

'Who was upon the tree?'

'We go to her now, Heboric Ghosthands.'

They began walking, and the Crippled God could feel the sorceries of this realm drawing towards them, gathering, conjoining to make this road.

Then, ahead on the path, he saw the glimmer of a lantern – a figure, now guiding them forward, but from a great distance.

The journey seemed to take an eternity. Things sank down from time to time, coming from the darkness above, stirring clouds of silt into the currents. He saw ships of wood, ships of iron. He saw the carcasses of serpentine monsters. He saw a rain of human corpses, shark-gnawed and dragged down boots first to land upon the bottom as if to walk – perhaps even to join this procession – but then their legs folded beneath them, and the silts made for them a soft place to rest.

He thought he saw mounted warriors, glimmering green and blue, tracking them from a distance.

The lantern light was suddenly closer, and the Crippled God saw their guide standing before a cave chewed into the face of a massive cliffside.

When they reached the mouth of that cave, the two Elder Gods paused and both bowed to their guide, but that ghastly figure gave no sign of acknowledgement, only turned away, as if to take its light on to some other path. As if to lead others to their own fates.

They strode down a winding tunnel, and emerged in a vast cavern.

The Elder God who was not Mael of the Seas faced the Crippled God. 'Long have you wandered the blood I gave to this realm. I am K'rul, the Maker of Warrens. Now it is time for you to leave, to return to your home.'

The Crippled God considered this, and then said, 'I am flesh and bone. Made in the guise of a human. Where my children call down to me, I cannot go. Would you have me summon them down?'

'No. That would mean our deaths – all of us.'

'Yes. It would.'

'There will be a way,' K'rul said. 'It begins with Heboric, but it ends at the hands of another.'

'This flesh you wear,' Mael of the Seas added, 'is unsuited to your return. But it was the best that they could do.'

'Fallen One,' said K'rul, 'will you trust us?'

The Crippled God looked at Heboric, and then he released his grip on the hands of the Elder Gods. Reached for Heboric's.

But the mortal stepped back, and said, 'Not yet, and not both of them. Both of them will kill you. I will reach for you, Lord, when the moment arrives. This I promise.'

The Crippled God bowed, and stepped back.

And with his Otataral hand, Heboric, once named Light-Touch, reached through the waters above him. Copper light burst forth, filled the entire cavern.

*   *   *

The vast fingers that erupted from the barrow encompassed the entire mound – but they did not tear the ground. Ghostly, translucent, they arced high overhead, and closed about the Otataral Dragon.

Korabas loosed a deafening scream – but if it was a cry of pain, torment or release Fiddler could not tell.

Beyond the Otataral Dragon, which was even now being drawn closer down above them, the manifestation of T'iam – growing ever more corporeal, forming a multi-headed leviathan – began to tear itself apart once more. Distant shrieks, as dragons pulled away, lunged free.

Most fled as if their tails were on fire. Fiddler stared, now unmindful of the vast, descending form of the Otataral Dragon, as they raced away, while others, too badly damaged, spun earthward, striking the ground with thunderous concussions. *It's fucking raining dragons.*

Quick Ben stared upward, praying under his breath, and then his eyes narrowed – he could see through Korabas. *He has her – whoever you are, you have her now.*

Gods, this is going to work.

I promised, Burn. I promised you, didn't I?

All right, so maybe I can't take all the credit.

Maybe.

For modesty's sake, if I ever talk about it, I mean. But here, in my head . . . I did it!

Kalam saw the infernal pride burgeoning in the wizard's face and knew precisely what the scrawny bastard was thinking. The assassin wanted to hit the man. At least ten times.

Crouched, even as the ghostly body of the Otataral Dragon slipped down around them all, Kalam turned to look at the Crippled God. Who stood motionless, eyes shut, hands still raised into the sky.

Maybe a dragon can fly you up there, friend. They're not all fleeing, are they?

A woman he'd never seen before slumped down beside him, offered him an inviting smile. 'I like the look of you,' she said.

Gods, not another one. 'Who in Hood's name are you?'

Her smile flashed wider. 'I am the woman who stole the moon. Oh, I see that you don't believe me, do you?'

'It's not that,' he replied. 'Fine, you stole it – but then you broke the fucking thing!'

Fury lit her face most becomingly. 'I am Apsal'ara, the Mistress of Thieves!'

He grinned at her. 'Never liked thieves.' *Frustrate them. Works every time.*

*   *   *

887

Hearing the exchange, Quick Ben snorted.

Kalam, you never learn, do you? Or maybe you just can't help your-self.

The roof of the cavern suddenly glowed white-hot, and Heboric spun to the Crippled God. 'Now! Open your eyes – you can't be down here when she arrives. No one can!'

The Crippled God turned. He sensed the two Elder Gods were gone.

Farewell, Mael of the Seas and K'rul Maker of Warrens.

'Open your eyes!'

And so he did, and in that moment he felt Heboric take his hand.

Koryk had dragged himself behind a tilted standing stone, his eyes fixed upon the Crippled God not five paces away. There was a need inside him, unbearable, savage. It wanted to devour him. It wanted to annihilate the world, the one he lived in, the one that had nothing but the thinnest skin between what hid inside and what lay outside.

There was no answer. None but the obvious one – the one he dared not look at. If he did, he would have to face his own story – not as some nostalgic bravado, but as the succession of hurts that he was not unique in carrying. And he would see all the scars – the ones he bore, the others he had made on those close to him.

He stared at the Crippled God, as if it could somehow save his soul.

And the Fallen One opened his eyes – and stared directly into Koryk's.

Jade fire lit a whirling pillar round the god, spinning ever faster, the glow brightening, the air howling.

Their gazes were locked together through the emerald flames.

And Koryk saw something – there, awakening, a look . . . *a promise.*

He felt his soul reaching forth – closer . . . closer – reaching to touch.

The Crippled God smiled at him, with such love, such knowing.

The shadow rising behind him was out of place – it could not belong inside those raging fires. Yet Koryk saw it lifting, taking form. He saw two arms rising from that shape, saw the raw, dull gleam of dagger blades.

Shadow.

Koryk's scream of warning ripped raw his throat – he flung himself forward—

Even as Cotillion's knives plunged down.

To sink into the Crippled God's back.

Shock took that otherworldly face – as if the smile had never been – and the head rocked back, the body arching in agony.

Someone slammed into Koryk, dragged him to the ground. He fought, howling.

The green fire ignited, shot spiralling into the sky – so fast it was gone in moments.

Koryk stared after it, one hand stretching upward.

Beside him, too close to bear, he heard Fiddler say, 'It was the only way, Koryk. It's for the best. Nothing you can—'

Suddenly sobbing, Koryk pushed the man away, and then curled up, like a child who lived in a world of broken promises.

Hedge pulled Fiddler away from the sobbing soldier. Fiddler shot him a helpless look.

'He'll shake out of it,' Hedge said. 'Once it all settles and he works it out, he'll be fine, Fid.'

Quick Ben and Kalam joined the two sappers, and Fiddler fixed his eyes on the wizard. 'Was it real, Quick? What I saw – did I . . .'

The wizard gestured and they followed him to one edge of the summit. He pointed down to a lone figure standing some distance away, little more than a silhouette, its back to them. 'Care to ask him, Fid?'

Ask him? After all we've done . . . how to see this? Ask him? What if he answers me? 'No,' he said.

'Listen, you were right – it had to be this way.'

Yes! It had to – we didn't do all this for nothing!

Fiddler stepped back, eyed the three men standing before him. 'Look at us,' he whispered. 'I never thought . . .'

'Send them down, Fid,' said Hedge. 'Your soldiers – get 'em to carry the wounded down off this fucking barrow.'

'What?'

Quick Ben and Kalam were now eyeing Hedge suspiciously.

The man scowled at the attention. 'Fid, send them down, will you? This is just for us – don't you see? What's coming – it's just for us.'

When Fiddler turned, he saw his soldiers. And, feeling grief grip his heart, he forced himself to look from one face to the next. In his mind, he spoke their names. *Tarr. Koryk. Bottle. Smiles. Balm. Throatslitter. Deadsmell. Widdershins. Hellian. Urb. Limp. Crump. Sinter. Kisswhere. Maybe. Flashwit. Mayfly. Clasp. Nep Furrow. Reliko. Vastly Blank. Masan Gilani.* 'Where's Nefarias Bredd?' he demanded.

Sergeant Tarr tilted his head. 'Captain?'

'Where is he, damn you?'

'There is no Nefarias Bredd, sir. We made him up – on the march to Y'Ghatan. Got us a bad loaf of bread. Someone called it nefarious. We thought it was funny – like something Braven Tooth would've made up.' He shrugged.

'But I—' Fiddler turned to Hedge, saw the man's blank look. 'Oh, never mind,' he sighed, facing his soldiers again. 'All of you, go down – take Sweetlard and Rumjugs with you. I'll . . . I'll be down shortly.'

He watched them walk away. He knew their thoughts – the emptiness now overtaking them. Which would in the days and nights ahead slowly fill with grief, until they were all drowning. Fiddler looked back up at the sky. The Jade Strangers looked farther away. He knew that was impossible. Too soon for that. Still . . .

A faint wind swept across the summit, cool and dry.

'Now,' said Hedge.

Fiddler thought he heard horses, drawing up, and then three figures were climbing into view. Ghostly, barely visible to his eyes – he could see through them all.

Whiskeyjack. Trotts. Mallet.

'Aw, shit,' said Kalam, kicking at a discarded helm. It spun, rolled down the hillside.

Whiskeyjack regarded him. 'Got something to say, Assassin?'

And the man suddenly grinned. 'It stinks, sir, from here to the throne.'

The ghost nodded, and then squinted westward for a moment before turning to Hedge. 'Well done, soldier. It was a long way back. You ready for us now?'

Fiddler felt something crumble inside him.

Hedge drew off his tattered leather cap, scratched at the few hairs left on his mottled scalp. 'That depends, sir.'

'On what?' Whiskeyjack demanded, eyes fixing hard on the sapper.

Hedge glanced over at Fiddler. 'On him, sir.'

And Fiddler knew what he had to say. 'I let you go long ago, Hedge.'

'Aye. But that was then and this isn't. You want me to stay? A few more years, maybe? Till it's your time, I mean?'

If he spoke at all, Fiddler knew that he would lose control. So he simply nodded.

Hedge faced Whiskeyjack. 'Not yet, sir. Besides, I was talking with my sergeants just the other day. About buying us a bar, back in Malaz City. Maybe even Smiley's.'

Fiddler shot the man a glare. 'But no one can find it, Hedge. Kellanved went and hid it.'

'Kitty-corner to the Deadhouse, that's where it is. Everyone knows, Fid.'

'But they can't find it, Hedge!'

The man shrugged. 'I will.'

'Fiddler,' Whiskeyjack said. 'Pay attention now. Our time is almost done here – sun's soon to rise, and when it does, we will have left this world for the last time.' He gestured and Mallet stepped forward, carrying a satchel. He crouched down and removed the straps, and then drew out a fiddle. Its body was carved in swirling Barghast patterns. Seeing that, Fiddler looked up at Trotts. The warrior grinned, showing his filed teeth.

'I did that, Fid. And that mistake there, up near the neck, that was Hedge's fault. He tugged my braid. Blame him. I do.'

Mallet carefully set the instrument down, placing the bow beside it. The healer glanced up, almost shyly. 'We all had a hand in its making, Fid. Us Bridgeburners.'

'Take it,' ordered Whiskeyjack. 'Fiddler, you were the best of us all. You still are.'

Fiddler looked over at Quick Ben and Kalam, saw their nods, and then at Hedge, who hesitated, as if to object, and then simply shrugged. Fiddler met Whiskeyjack's ethereal eyes. 'Thank you, sir.'

The ghost then surprised him by stepping forward, reaching down and touching the fiddle. Straightening, he walked past them, to stand facing the lowland to the west.

Fiddler stared after him, frowning.

Sighing, Hedge spoke low at his side. 'She's out there, sembled now – they're keeping their distance. They're not sure what's happened here. By the time she comes, it'll be too late.'

'Who? By the time who comes?'

'The woman he loves, Fid. Korlat. A Tiste Andii.'

Tiste Andii. Oh . . . no.

Hedge's grunt was strained with emotion. 'Aye, the sergeant's luck ain't never been good. He's got a long wait.'

But wait he will.

Then he caught a blur of motion from a nearby jumble of boulders. A woman, watching them.

Fiddler hugged himself, looked over once more at Mallet and Trotts. 'Take care of him,' he whispered.

They nodded.

And then Whiskeyjack was marching past. 'Time to leave, you two.'

Mallet reached down and touched the fiddle before turning away. Trotts stepped past him, squatted and did the same.

Then they were down over the edge of the hill.

Moments later, Fiddler heard horses – but in the gloom he could not see his friends riding away.

* * *

A voice spoke beside Cotillion. 'Well done.'

The patron god of assassins looked down at the knives still in his hands. 'I don't like failure. Never did, Shadowthrone.'

'Then,' and the ethereal form at his side giggled, 'we're not quite finished, are we?'

'Ah. You knew, then.'

'Of course. And this may well shock you, but I approve.'

Cotillion turned to him in surprise. 'I knew you had a heart in there somewhere.'

'Don't be an idiot. I just appreciate . . . symmetry.'

Together they turned back to face the barrow once again, but now the ghosts were gone.

Shadowthrone thumped his cane on the ground. 'Among all the gods,' he said, 'who do you think now hates us the most?'

'The ones still alive, I should imagine.'

'We're not done with them either.'

Cotillion nodded towards the barrow. 'They were something, weren't they?'

'With them we won an empire.'

'I sometimes wonder if we should ever have given it up.'

'Bloody idealist. We needed to walk away. Sooner or later, no matter how much you put into what you've made, you have to turn and walk away.'

'Shall we, then?'

And the two gods set out, fading shadows as the dawn began to awaken.

Toc Younger had waited astride his horse, halfway between the motionless ranks of the Guardians and Whiskeyjack and his two soldiers. He had watched the distant figures gathering on the barrow's gnarled summit. And now the three ghostly riders were returning the way they had come.

When they reached him, Whiskeyjack waved Mallet and Trotts on and then reined in.

He drew his mount round, to face the barrow one last time.

Toc spoke. 'That was some squad you had yourself there, sir.'

'My life was blessed with fortune. It's time,' he said, drawing his horse round. He glanced across at Toc. 'Ready, Bridgeburner?'

They set out side by side.

And then Toc shot Whiskeyjack a startled look. 'But I'm not a—'

'You say something, soldier?'

Mute, Toc shook his head.

Gods below, I made it.

*   *   *

In the luminescent sky high above the plain, Gu'Rull sailed on the currents, wings almost motionless. The Shi'gal Assassin studied the world far below. Scores of dragon carcasses were strewn round the barrow, and there, leading off into the west as far as Gu'Rull's eyes could see, a road of devastation almost a league wide, upon which were littered the bodies of Eleint. Hundreds upon hundreds.

The Shi'gal struggled to comprehend the Otataral Dragon's ordeal. The flavours that rose within him threatened to overwhelm him.

I still taste the echoes of her pain.

What is it in a life that can prove so defiant, so resilient in the face of such wilful rage? Korabas, do you crouch now in your cave – gift of a god wounded near unto death – closing about your wounds, your sorrow, as if in the folding of wings you could make the world beyond vanish? And with it all the hate and venom, and all that so assailed you in your so-few moments of freedom?

Are you alone once more, Korabas?

If to draw close to you would not kill me – if I could have helped you in those blood-filled skies, upon that death-strewn road – I would join you now. To bring to an end your loneliness.

But all I can do is circle these skies. Above the ones who summoned you, who fought to free a god, and to save your own life.

Those ones, too, I do not understand.

These humans have much to teach the K'Chain Che'Malle.

I, Gu'Rull, Shi'gal Assassin of Gunth'an Wandering, am humbled by all that I have witnessed. And this feeling, so strange, so new, now comes to me in the sweetest flavours imaginable.

I did not know.

Settling the last stone down on the elongated pile, Icarium brushed dust from his hands and slowly straightened.

Ublala – with Ralata sitting nearby – watched the warrior walk to the edge of the hill, watched as Icarium dislodged a small rock and sent it rolling down the slope. And then he looked back at the barrow, and then at Ublala. The morning was bright but there were clouds building to the east and the wind carried the promise of rain.

'It is as you said, friend?'

Ublala nodded.

Icarium wiped at the tears still streaming down his face from when he'd wept over the grave. But the look on his face wasn't filled with grief any more. Just empty now. Lost. 'Ublala, is this all there is of me?' He gestured vaguely. 'Is this all there is to *any* of us?'

The Toblakai shrugged. 'I am Ublala Pung and that is all I ever am, or was. I don't know if there's more. I never do.'

Icarium studied the grave again. 'He died defending me.'

'Yes.'

'But I don't know who he was!'

Ublala shrugged again. There was no shame in weeping for the death of a stranger. Ublala had done it many times. He reached down, picked up a potsherd, examined the sky-blue glaze. 'Pretty,' he said under his breath, tucking it behind his belt.

Icarium collected up his weapons, and then faced north. 'I feel close this time, Ublala.'

Ublala thought to ask close to what, but already he was confused, and so he put the question away. He didn't think he'd ever go back to find it. It was where all the other troubling things went, never to be gone back to, ever.

'I am glad you found a woman to love, friend,' Icarium said.

The giant warrior smiled over at Ralata and received a stony stare in return, reminding him how she'd said she liked it better when it was just the two of them. But she was a woman and once he sexed her again, everything would be all right. That's how it worked.

When Icarium set out, Ublala collected up the useful sack he'd found, shouldered it, and went to join the warrior.

Ralata caught up a short time later, just before Icarium happened to glance at the pottery fragment Ublala had taken out to admire again, and then halted to face one last time the low hill they'd left behind. Icarium frowned and was silent.

Ublala was ready to turn away when Icarium said, 'Friend, I have remembered something.'

EPILOGUE I

Perched upon the stones of a bridge
The soldiers had the eyes of ravens
Their weapons hung black as talons
Their eyes gloried in the smoke of murder

To the shock of iron-heeled sticks
I drew closer in the cripple's bitter patience
And before them I finally tottered
Grasping to capture my elusive breath

With the cockerel and swift of their knowing
They watched and waited for me
'I have come,' said I, 'from this road's birth,
I have come,' said I, 'seeking the best in us.'

The sergeant among them had red in his beard
Glistening wet as he showed his teeth
'There are few roads on this earth,' said he,
'that will lead you to the best in us, old one.'

'But you have seen all the tracks of men,' said I
'And where the mothers and children have fled
Before your advance. Is there naught among them
That you might set an old man upon?'

The surgeon among this rook had bones
Under her vellum skin like a maker of limbs
'Old one,' said she, 'I have dwelt
In the heat of chests, among heart and lungs,

And slid like a serpent between muscles,
Swum the currents of slowing blood,
And all these roads lead into the darkness
Where the broken will at last rest.

Dare say I,' she went on, 'there is no
Place waiting inside where you might find
In slithering exploration of mysteries
All that you so boldly call the best in us.'

And then the man with shovel and pick,
Who could raise fort and berm in a day
Timbered of thought and measured in all things
Set the gauge of his eyes upon the sun

And said, 'Look not in temples proud,
Or in the palaces of the rich highborn,
We have razed each in turn in our time
To melt gold from icon and shrine

And of all the treasures weeping in fire
There was naught but the smile of greed
And the thick power of possession.
Know then this: all roads before you

From the beginning of the ages past
And those now upon us, yield no clue
To the secret equations you seek,
For each was built of bone and blood

And the backs of the slave did bow
To the laboured sentence of a life
In chains of dire need and little worth.
All that we build one day echoes hollow.'

'Where then, good soldiers, will I
Ever find all that is best in us?
If not in flesh or in temple bound
Or wretched road of cobbled stone?'

'Could we answer you,' said the sergeant,
'This blood would cease its fatal flow,
And my surgeon could seal wounds with a touch,
All labours will ease before temple and road,

Could we answer you,' said the sergeant,
'Crows might starve in our company
And our talons we would cast in bogs
For the gods to fight over as they will.

But we have not found in all our years
The best in us, until this very day.'
'How so?' asked I, so lost now on the road,
And said he, 'Upon this bridge we sat

Since the dawn's bleak arrival,
Our perch of despond so weary and worn,
And you we watched, at first a speck
Upon the strife-painted horizon

So tortured in your tread as to soak our faces
In the wonder of your will, yet on you came
Upon two sticks so bowed in weight
Seeking, say you, the best in us

And now we have seen in your gift
The best in us, and were treasures at hand
We would set them humbly before you,
A man without feet who walked a road.'

Now, soldiers with kind words are rare
Enough, and I welcomed their regard
As I moved among them, 'cross the bridge
And onward to the long road beyond

I travel seeking the best in us
And one day it shall rise before me
To bless this journey of mine, and this road
I began upon long ago shall now end
Where waits for all the best in us.

Where Ravens Perch
Avas Didion Flicker

THIS HAD, IN THE END, BEEN A WAR OF LIBERATION. KOLANSII CITIZENS
had emerged from the city, and after five days of hard labour the
vast trenches, revetments and redoubts had been transformed
into long barrows. Three such barrows now stood to mark the Battle of

Blessed Gift, where the Letherii, Bolkando, Gilk and Teblor had fought the army of Brother Diligence; and at the foot of the fissured ruin of the Spire, three large barrows of raw earth rose to commemorate the fallen Imass, Jaghut, K'Chain Che'Malle and Kolansii, with one smaller mound holding the remains of two Malazans. And it was at this last place that figures now gathered.

Remaining at a respectful distance, close to the now-abandoned work camps of the diggers, Lord Nimander stood with Korlat and his uncle, Silchas Ruin. Along with Skintick and Desra, and Apsal'ara, they had accompanied the troops commanded by Captain Fiddler on this long, tedious journey to the coast.

It was not hard to mourn the death of brave men and women. Nor even reptilian soldiers bred for war. There was no shame in the tears that ran from Nimander's face when he came to learn of the slaughter of the Imass in the moment of their rebirth. The survivors had departed some days ago now, into the north – seeking their leader, he had been told, whose fate after the battle remained unknown.

And the brother of his father, standing now at his side, had grieved over the destruction of an old friend, Tulas Shorn, in the draconic War of Awakening. The sword strapped to Silchas Ruin's hip still held bound to its blade the souls of three surviving Eleint from Kurald Emurlahn. The details of this binding were still unclear to Nimander, and his uncle seemed to be a man of few words.

More rain threatened from the east, and Nimander watched the dark grey wall of clouds drawing ever closer. He glanced over at Korlat. Something had awakened her own grief, and it had struck deep in the Sister of Cold Nights. And as the distant figures now closed about the small barrow, he saw her take a half-step forward and then halt.

'Korlat,' said Nimander.

She caught herself, turned to him wretched eyes. 'Lord?'

'It is not our place to intrude upon them at this time.'

'I understand.'

'But I believe it is nevertheless fitting that we convey our respect and honour in some fashion. I wonder, could I ask you, Sister of Cold Nights, to represent us by attending their ceremonies on our behalf?'

Something was released from her face, suddenly softening it, awakening once more her extraordinary beauty. She bowed to him. 'Lord, I shall go at once.'

Nimander watched her make her way towards the ceremony.

Beside him, Silchas Ruin said, 'She was ever favoured by your father, Lord.'

'Silchas, she gave her heart to a human, a Malazan, who died in the conquest of Black Coral.'

The white-skinned man was silent for a moment, and then said, 'He must have been . . . formidable.'

'I imagine so.'

'My experience with these Malazans has thus far been brief – I recognize the uniforms from my . . . attempt on Letheras. To say that they have earned my respect is something of an understatement. I would not willingly cross them again.'

Nimander looked at his uncle, wondering.

Tentative, weakened by a sudden feeling of temerity, Korlat's steps slowed when she was still forty or more paces away from the gathering of dignitaries. Off to her left, assembled in formation, stood the ranks of Malazans – the army known by the name of Bonehunters. Beyond them, arrayed on a higher vantage point, were the far more numerous ranks of the second Malazan army, the Host.

To her right, where the K'Chain Che'Malle had encamped, the Ve'Gath and K'ell Hunters had formed up in a facing line, the Matron foremost among them. A human woman was walking out from that formation, on a route that would intersect Korlat's own.

Perhaps she would find strength in that company. Failing that, she doubted she would manage to get much closer. Her heart felt laid bare – she had believed her days of deepest grief were past. But seeing those Malazan marines – seeing Hedge, Quick Ben and Kalam – had cut her open all over again. When they had seen her – when at last Nimander had judged it time to approach that fated barrow – they had but nodded in greeting, and she could admit now that the distance they had maintained since had hurt her in some way.

Perhaps they thought that she had been intent on stealing their sergeant away from them. Perhaps, even, they blamed her for his death. She did not know, and now she had been commanded to join them once more, at this place where two Malazan marines were interred.

She had selected a polished jet stone from her modest collection – knowing how the humans would smile at that, these small leather bags the Tiste Andii always carried, with a stone to mark each gift of the owner's heart. She possessed but a few. One for Anomander Rake, one for her fallen brother, Orfantal; one for Spinnock Durav – who cared nothing for her low birth – and one for Whiskeyjack. Soon, she had begun to suspect, she would set out to find two more. For Queen Yan Tovis. For Lord Nimander.

These stones were not to be surrendered.

To give one up was to set down a love, to walk away from it for evermore.

But it had been foolish, finding a stone for a man whose love she had known for so brief a time. He had never felt the way she had – he could

899

not have – she had gone too far, had given up too much. They'd not possessed the time to forge something eternal.

Then he had died, and it was as if he had been the one doing the walking away, leaving his own stone behind – the dull, lifeless thing that was her heart.

'The dead forget us.' So said Gallan. 'The dead forget us, and this is why we fear death.'

She had thought . . . there on that distant barrow now called the Awakening . . . a whisper of something, a presence arriving old and achingly familiar. As if he had looked upon her – as if she had felt his eyes – *no, you foolish woman. It was his soldiers gathered on that hill. If he was there at all, it was for them.*

Her thoughts were interrupted by the arrival of the woman from the K'Chain Che'Malle ranks. Korlat had come to a halt with her memories, and now she looked on this stranger, offering a rueful half-smile. 'My courage fails,' she said.

The human woman, plain, past her youth, studied her for a moment. 'What is that,' she asked, 'in your hand?'

Korlat thought to hide it away again, but then sighed and showed the black stone. 'I thought . . . a gift. For the barrow. I have seen such practices before . . .'

'Did you know them?'

After a moment, Korlat turned to retrace her steps. 'No. I am sorry. I did not.'

But the woman took her arm. 'Walk with me, then, and I will tell you about Mortal Sword Gesler and Shield Anvil Stormy.'

'I was presumptuous—'

'I doubt it,' the woman replied. 'But you can hold on to your tale, if you like. I am Kalyth.'

Korlat gave her own name.

'They won free the heart of the Crippled God,' said Kalyth as they drew closer. 'But that is not how I remember them. They were stubborn. They snapped at each other like . . . like dogs. They mocked their own titles, told each other lies. They told me lies, too. Wild stories of their adventures. Ships on seas of fire. Dragons and headless Tiste Andii – whatever they are . . .'

Korlat turned at that, thought to speak, then decided to remain silent.

'In the time I knew them,' Kalyth went on, not noticing her companion's reaction, 'they pretty much argued without surcease. Even in the middle of terrible battle they bickered back and forth. And all the while, these two Malazans, they did all that needed to be done. Each and every time.' She nodded towards the Spire.

'Up there,' she said, 'they climbed through walls of fire, and at that

900

moment I realized that all those wild tales they told me – they were probably all true.

'Stormy died on the stairs, keeping a wild witch away from the heart. Those flames he could not in the end defeat. Gesler – we are told – died saving the life of a dog.' She pointed. 'That one, Korlat, the one guarding the barrow's entrance. See how they await me now? It is because I am the only one the dog will let pass into the chamber. I dragged Gesler's body in there myself.'

When the woman at her side stopped talking then, Korlat looked down and saw how her face had crumpled – with her own words, as if their meaning only now struck true. She very nearly collapsed – would have done so if not for Korlat's arm, now flexing to take the woman's weight.

Kalyth righted herself. 'I – I am sorry. I did not mean – oh, look at me . . .'

'I have you,' Korlat said.

They went on.

This side of the small round barrow, the group of humans parted before them, as many eyes on Korlat as on Kalyth. She saw Hedge there, along with Quick Ben and Kalam, and the grey-bearded man she now knew to be Fiddler, Whiskeyjack's closest friend. Their expressions were flat, and she weathered their regards with as much dignity as she could muster. Near them stood a mother and daughter, the latter, though little more than a child, pulling hard on a stick of rustleaf – and on this one's other side stood an older woman doing the same with her own, beside a handsome young man. She saw a White Face Barghast chieftain grinning openly at herself – his desires made plain in the amused glint in his eyes.

Just beyond Whiskeyjack's old squad stood a man and a woman – possibly siblings – in the company of an older man weighed down in the robes of a High Priest, the gold silk patterned in the sinewy forms of serpents. Behind this group stood a man picking at his teeth and beside him, seated on a stool, was an artist, sketching frantically on bleached lambskin with a wedge of charcoal. At his feet was a bloated toad.

Arrayed in a semicircle around this group was an honour guard of some sort, facing outward, but as Korlat and Kalyth approached they smartly turned round, gauntleted hands lifting to their chests in salute. And she saw that they were the soldiers who had fought at the Awakening.

Kalyth leaned close against Korlat and disengaged her arm. 'I believe there are burial gifts,' she said, nodding to a soldier's chest waiting beside the barrow entrance. 'I will take it inside.' She looked up at Korlat. 'I will take your gift, Korlat, if you like.'

She held up her hand, opened it to look at the gleaming stone in her hand.

There was a commotion from Whiskeyjack's squad and Korlat faced them, ready to retreat – to flee this place.

'Captain!' snapped the plain woman behind the marines.

Korlat saw that the squad had reached for their weapons, swords now half drawn. At that woman's bark they had halted their motions, and Korlat stared, frightened and dismayed by what she saw in their faces.

The plain woman stepped round to place herself between Korlat and the squad. Standing directly in front of Fiddler, she said, 'What in Hood's name do you think you're doing?'

'Forgive us, Adjunct,' Fiddler replied, eyes still on Korlat.

'Explain yourselves! High Mage! Kalam – one of you, speak!'

'Your pardon, Adjunct,' Fiddler ground out. 'I would ask the Tiste Andii a question.'

'By your threat,' snapped the Adjunct, turning to Korlat, 'should she refuse the courtesy, I will defend her decision.'

Korlat shook her head, drawing a deep, fortifying breath. 'No, thank you, Adjunct. This soldier was Whiskeyjack's closest friend. If he would ask me something, I shall answer as best I am able.'

The Adjunct stepped back.

Fiddler's gaze fell to the stone in her hand. 'You mean to give that up? Did you know Gesler and Stormy?'

Korlat shook her head.

'Then . . . why?'

Her thoughts fumbled, words failing her, and her eyes fell from Fiddler's.

'Is it his?'

She looked back up, startled. Behind Fiddler the marines of the squad stared – but now she saw that what she had taken for rage in their expressions was in fact something else, something far more complicated.

'Korlat, is it *his*?'

She faced the barrow entrance. 'They were marines,' she said in a weak voice. 'I thought . . . a measure of respect.'

'If you give that up, you will destroy him.'

She met Fiddler's eyes, and at last saw the raw anguish in them. 'I thought . . . he left me.'

'No, he hasn't.'

Hedge spoke. 'He only found love once, Korlat, and we're looking at the woman he chose. If you give up that stone, we'll cut you to pieces and leave your bones scattered across half this world.'

Korlat stepped close to Fiddler. 'How do you know this?'

His eyes flickered, were suddenly wet. 'On the hill. His ghost – he saw you on the plain. He – he couldn't take his eyes off you. I see now – you thought . . . through Hood's Gate, the old loves forgotten, drifting away. Maybe you even began questioning if it ever existed at all, or meant what you thought it meant. Listen, they've told me the whole story. Korlat, he's waiting for you. And if he has to, he'll wait for ever.'

Her hand closed about the stone, and all at once the tension fell away, and she looked past Fiddler to the soldiers of the squad. 'You would have killed me for forsaking him,' she said. 'I am reminded of the man he was – to have won such loyalty among his friends.'

Hedge said, 'You've got centuries – well, who knows how long? Don't think he expects you to be celibate or anything – we ain't expectin' that neither. But that stone – we know what it means to your kind. You just shocked us, that's all.'

Korlat slowly turned to the barrow. 'Then I should leave here, for I have nothing for these fallen soldiers.'

The Adjunct surprised her by stepping forward and taking her arm. She led her to the chest. 'Open it,' she invited.

Wondering, Korlat crouched down, lifted back the lid. The chest was empty. Baffled, she straightened, met the Adjunct's eyes.

And saw a wry smile. 'They were marines. Everything of value they've already left behind. In fact, Korlat of the Tiste Andii, if Gesler and Stormy could, they'd be the first ones to loot their own grave goods.'

'And then bitch about how cheap we were,' Fiddler said behind them.

'We are here to see the barrow sealed,' said the Adjunct. 'And, if we can, get that Wickan demon to yield, before it starves to death.'

A thousand paces away from this scene, a gathering of Jaghut warriors stood facing a barrow raised to embrace the fallen Imass.

They were silent, as befitted the moment – a moment filled with respect and that bone-deep loss for comrades fallen in a battle shared, a time lived to the hilt – but for all that, it was a silence riotous with irony.

After a time, a small creature looking like a burst pillow of rotted straw came up to lie down at the feet of one of the Jaghut. From the filthy tangle out came a lolling tongue.

One of the warriors spoke, 'Varandas, our commander never tires of pets.'

'Clearly,' replied another, 'he has missed us.'

'Or does the once-Lord of Death return with alarming appetites?'

'You raise disquiet in me,' said Sanad.

'You promised to never speak of that – oh, you mean my query on appetites. Humblest apologies, Sanad.'

'She lies, Gathras, this I swear!'

'The only one lying here is the dog, surely!'

The warriors all stared down at the creature.

And then roared with laughter. That went on, and on.

Until Hood whirled round. *'Will you all shut up!'*

In the sudden silence that followed, someone snorted.

When Hood reached for the sword at his hip, his warriors all found somewhere else to look. Until the ratty dog rose and lifted a leg.

Weathering their raucous laughter and the steady stream tapping his ankle, Hood slowly closed his eyes. *This is why Jaghut chose to live alone.*

Brys Beddict turned at the sound of distant laughter. Squinted at the Jaghut warriors standing at the Imass barrow. 'Errant's nudge, but that's hardly fitting, is it?'

Aranict frowned. 'Theirs is an odd humour, my love. I do not think disrespect is the intention. Indifference would have managed that succinctly enough. Instead, they walked out there, and requested solitude.'

'Ah,' murmured Brys, taking her hand, 'it is, I believe, time.'

He led her towards the Adjunct, where Queen Abrastal, Felash and Spax now joined Tavore. Just beyond them, Aranict saw, was Ganoes – not one to join in these moments, yet never far from his sister.

Brys spoke as soon as they drew near. 'There was some tension at the barrow, Adjunct. I trust all is well?'

'A misunderstanding, Prince.'

'The cattledog—'

'No – once the barrow was sealed, the beast joined Destriant Kalyth, and at her side I believe it will stay until its life is done.'

'There is word,' said Abrastal, 'of a tribe on the plateau north of Estobanse, remote kin of Kalyth's Elan. Bhederin herders.'

'They will journey alone?' Brys asked in concern.

'With only a few hundred K'ell Hunters as escort, yes,' replied the Bolkando queen.

'Prince Brys,' said Felash, 'your brother the king's fleet is only days away.' Her languid gaze flicked to Aranict.

'I've not yet told him,' Aranict replied, lighting a stick. 'Beloved,' she now said, 'your brother is with that fleet.'

'Tehol hates the sea – are you certain of that?'

But Felash was coughing, her eyes wide on the prince. 'Excuse me, King Tehol *hates* the sea? But – rather, I mean, forgive me. Bugg – his— Oh, never mind. My pardon, Prince Brys.'

Abrastal was regarding her daughter sidelong. 'You're as plump as you ever were,' she said. 'Smoke more, girl!'

'Yes, mother. At once.'

'And where is your handmaid?'

'Down with Captain Elalle, Mother, shipshaping a boat or whatever they call it.'

Brys spoke to Tavore. 'Adjunct . . . there were times when I . . . well, I doubted you. This seemed so vast – what you sought—'

'Forgive me for interrupting, Highness,' Tavore replied. 'The deeds that have won us this victory belong to every soul on this journey, and it has been a rather long journey. A sword's tip is nothing without the length of solid steel backing it.' She hesitated. 'There have been many doubts to weather, but this is a weakness we all share.'

'You said you would be unwitnessed. Yet, that proved untrue, did it not?'

She shrugged. 'For each moment recorded in the annals of history, how many more are lost? Highness, we shall be forgotten. All of this, it will fade into the darkness, as all things will. I do not regret that.'

'In Letheras,' said Brys, 'there will be a statue of bronze raised in your likeness. I know, few will know what it means, what it signifies. But I will, Adjunct.'

'A statue?' Tavore cocked her head, as if considering the notion. 'Will I be beautiful?' she asked, and before Brys could answer she formally bowed before him and then Queen Abrastal. 'I thank you both, for making my cause your own. For your losses, I grieve. Goodbye, Highnesses.'

They let her depart.

And only Aranict heard Brys say, 'Of course you will.'

'A Hood-damned dog,' muttered Deadsmell as the marines and heavies walked from the barrow.

'That's Gesler for you,' replied Throatslitter. 'Brainless to the end.'

'He wouldn't have liked things without Stormy, anyway,' observed Balm.

Bottle considered this brief exchange, and then nodded to himself. *There's a point when there's nothing left to say. When every word does nothing more than stir the ashes.* He glanced over at Smiles, and then Koryk, and finally Tarr. *We finally took some losses, our squad. Cuttle – never thought he'd die, not like that. In some whore's bed, maybe. Corabb – gods below, how that man could fight.*

Limp says he saw him, there at the end – he'd blown his knee again, was looking over at the Crippled God – and there was Corabb, his face all lit with the glory of his last stand over the chained body of a god.

Really, what could be more perfect than that?

Well done, Corabb Bhilan Thenu'alas.

'Heard she's retiring us,' ventured Sinter. 'Priest's paying us out – a damned fortune for each and every one of us.'

'Where'en ne faareden? Eh? War bit ana dem?'

'To the families if they got any, Nep. That's how it's done. Stand or fall, you still get paid.'

'G'han nered pah vreem!'

Sinter made a startled sound, and beside her Kisswhere leaned forward to shoot Nep Furrow a shocked look.

'Really, Nep?' Kisswhere asked.

'Nepel!'

'Gods below,' Sinter whispered. 'I never . . .'

Reaching the road, they came within sight of the Bonehunter regulars. Glancing back, Bottle saw the Adjunct on her way up, with Banaschar at her side. Behind these two walked Lostara Yil, Henar Vygulf, the three Fists, Skanarow and Ruthan Gudd.

'She wants a last word with them,' Tarr said, evidently noticing Bottle's backward look. 'But we're not going to be there for that. Between her and them – you others all hear that? We walk through.'

'We walk through,' Hellian echoed. 'Crump, go back and help Limp – he's lagging. Let's just get this over with.'

They strode into the loose ranks of the regulars.

'Wish we had it as easy as you did!' someone shouted.

Koryk yelled back, 'You never would've hacked it, Ffan!'

'Hey, Hellian, found me this big spider here – wanna see it?'

'Call it whatever you want, soldier, it's still small.'

Bottle shook his head. *Aw, fuck. They're soldiers – what did you expect?*

It was dark by the time Korlat returned to the small Tiste Andii camp. They were seated round a fire, like hunters out from the wood, or harvesters at day's end. A fresh rain had cleansed the air, but its passage had been brief and now overhead tracked the Jade Strangers – as she had learned to call them – casting down a green light.

Nimander looked up, made room for her on the Kolansii workbench they had found in one of the work camps. 'We were wondering if you would ever return,' he said.

She drew her cloak about her shoulders. 'I watched the Bonehunters depart,' she said.

'Have ships arrived, then?'

Korlat shook her head. 'They're moving to a camp at this end of the Estobanse Valley. The Adjunct spoke to her regulars. She thanked them. That and nothing more. She was the last to leave – she bade the others go ahead, even her brother, and she walked alone. There was something . . . something . . .' She shook her head. 'It broke my heart.'

906

A voice spoke from the darkness behind her. 'She does that, does Tavore.'

They turned to see Fiddler stepping into the firelight, carrying something wrapped in skins. Behind, arrayed but drawing no closer, Korlat saw the rest of Whiskeyjack's old squad. They seemed to be muttering to each other in low tones, and then Quick Ben pointed up past the road, and in a sharp voice said, 'There, that hilltop. Not too far, but far enough. Well?' He looked at his companions, and both men grunted their assent.

Returning her attention to Fiddler, she saw that he had been watching, and now he nodded, faced Korlat. 'It's not far – in this air it'll carry just fine.'

'I'm sorry,' said Korlat, 'what are you doing?'

'See the hill they indicated, other side of the road? Go there, Korlat.'

'Excuse me?'

Nimander made to rise, but a look from Fiddler stilled him. 'Just her,' he said. 'I'll take that stump there – mind, sir?'

Silchas Ruin, seated on that stump, rose, shaking his head and then gesturing an invitation.

Fiddler went over and settled down on it. He began unwrapping the object on his lap, and then looked up and met Korlat's eyes. 'Why are you still here?'

'What are you going to do?' she demanded.

He sighed. 'Said it was the last time for him. Said it like it was an order. Well, he should know by now, we're lousy with taking orders.' He slipped away the final layer of skin, revealing a fiddle and bow. 'Go on now, Korlat. Oh, and tell him, this one's called "My Love Waits". I won't take credit for it – one of Fisher's.' Then he looked round at the gathered Tiste Andii. 'There's another one that I can slide into it easily enough, a bit sadder but not too sad. It's from Anomandaris. You'll forgive me, please, if I get the title wrong – it's been a long time. "Gallan's Hope"? Does that sound right to you all? . . . Seems it does.'

Korlat backed away, felt a hand touch her shoulder. It was Hedge. 'Hilltop, Korlat. Fid's gonna call him back. One more time. But listen, if it's too much, walk the other way, or stay off the hill. He'll see you anyway – we're doing that bit no matter what. For him.'

He would have babbled on, but she moved past him.

Eyes on the hill on the other side of the road.

Behind her, the strings drew a song into the night air.

When she reached the road and saw her beloved standing on the hill before her, Korlat broke into a run.

EPILOGUE II

FOR ONCE THE SEAS WERE CALM ON THE BEACH BELOW, AND WITH THE tide out many of the Imass had ventured on to the flats to collect shellfish. Off to one side the twins played with Absi, and the sound of the boy's laughter reached up to the shelf of stone where sat Udinaas.

He heard footsteps coming down the trail nearby and turned to see Onos and Hetan. They were carrying reed baskets to join in the harvest. Udinaas saw Onos pause, look out towards the children.

'Relax, Onos,' Udinaas said. 'I'll keep an eye on them.'

The warrior smiled. Hetan took his hand to lead him down.

Reclined on a high shelf of limestone above Udinaas, Ryadd said, 'Stop worrying, Father. It'll wear you out.'

From one of the caves higher up the climb behind them, there drifted out the sound of a crying baby. *Poor Seren. That's one cranky baby she has there.*

'We're safe,' Ryadd said. 'And if some damned mob of vicious humans shows up, well, they'll have Kilava, Onrack, Onos Toolan and me to deal with.'

'I know,' Udinaas replied. He rubbed and massaged his hands. The aches were coming back. Maybe it was time to try that foul medicine Lera Epar kept offering him. *Ah, it's just years of cold water. Sinks in. That's all.*

Glancing over, he grunted to his feet.

'Father?'

'It's all right,' he said. 'The twins have buried Absi up to his neck. Those girls need a good whipping.'

'You've never whipped a child in your life.'

'How would you know? Well. Maybe I haven't, but the threat still works.'

Ryadd sat up, looked down on Udinaas with his young, sun-darkened face. Squinting, Udinaas said, 'In the bright sun, I see your mother in your smile.'

'She smiled?'

'Once, I think, but I won't take credit for it.'

Udinaas set off down to the beach.

Absi had clambered free and tackled one of the girls and was now tickling her into a helpless state. Trouble passed, but he continued anyway.

Out in the sea beyond the small bay, whales broached the surface, sending geysers into the air, announcing the coming of summer.

The rider paused on the road, glancing down at the untended turnips growing wild in the ditch, and after a moment he kicked his horse onward. The sun was warm on his face as he rode west along Itko Kan's coastal track.

In his wake, in the lengthening shadows, two figures took form. Moments later huge hounds appeared. One bent to sniff at the turnips, and then turned away.

The figure with the cane sighed. 'Satisfied?'

The other one nodded.

'And you imagine only the best now, don't you?'

'I see no reason why not.'

Shadowthrone snorted. 'You wouldn't.'

Cotillion glanced over at him. 'Why not, then?'

'Old friend, what is this? Do you still hold to a belief in hope?'

'Do I believe in hope? I do.'

'And faith?'

'And faith. Yes. I believe in faith.'

Neither spoke for a time, and then Shadowthrone looked over at the Hounds, and cocked his head. 'Hungry, are we?' Bestial heads lifted, eyes fixing on him.

'Don't even think it, Ammeanas!'

'Why not? Remind that fop on the throne who's really running this game!'

'Not yet.'

'Where is your impatience? Your desire for vengeance? What sort of Patron of Assassins are you?'

Cotillion nodded down the road. 'Leave them alone. Not here, not now.'

Shadowthrone sighed a second time. 'Misery guts.'

The shadows dissolved, and a moment later were gone, leaving nothing but an empty road.

*   *   *

The sun set, dusk closing in. He'd yet to pass any traffic on this day and that was a little troubling, but he rode on. Having never been this way before, he almost missed the side track leading down to the settlement on the shelf of land above a crescent beach, but he caught the smell of woodsmoke in time to slow up his mount.

The beast carefully picked its way down the narrow path.

Reaching the bottom, now in darkness, he reined in.

Before him was a small fishing village, though it looked mostly abandoned. He saw a cottage nearby, stone-walled and thatch-roofed, with a stone chimney from which smoke drifted in a thin grey stream. An area of land had been cleared above and behind it where vegetables had been planted, and working still in the growing gloom was a lone figure.

Crokus dismounted, hobbled the horse outside an abandoned shack to his left, and made his way forward.

It should not have taken long, yet by the time he reached the verge of the garden the moon overhead was bright, its effervescent light glistening along her limbs, the sheen of her black hair like silk as she bent to gather up her tools.

He stepped between rows of bushy plants.

And she turned. Watched him walk up to her.

Crokus took her face in his hands, studied her dark eyes. 'I never liked that story,' he said.

'Which one?' she asked.

'The lover . . . lost on the moon, tending her garden alone.'

'It's not quite like that, the story I mean.'

He shrugged. 'It's what I remember from it. That, and the look in your eyes when you told it to me. I was reminded of that look a moment ago.'

'And now?'

'I think,' he said, 'the sadness just went away, Apsalar.'

'I think,' she replied, 'you are right.'

The boy watched the old man come down to the pier as he did almost every day whenever the boy happened to be lingering along the water-front at around this time, when the morning was stretching towards noon and all the fish were asleep. Day after day, he'd seen the old man carrying that silly bucket with the rope tied to the handle for the fish he never caught – and the fishing rod in his other hand would most likely snap in half at a crab's tug.

Bored, as he was every day, the boy ambled down to stand on the edge of the pier, to look out on the few ships that bothered sheltering in the harbour of Malaz City. So he could dream of the worlds beyond, where things exciting and magical happened and heroes won the day and villains bled out in the dirt.

He knew he was nobody yet. Not old enough for anything. Trapped here where nothing ever happened and never would. But one day he would face the whole world and, why, they'd all know his face, they would. He glanced over to where the old man was sitting down, legs over the edge, working bait on to the hook.

'You won't never catch nothing,' the boy said, idly pulling at a rusty mooring ring. 'You sleep in too late, every day.'

The old man squinted at the hook, adjusted the foul-smelling bait. 'Late nights,' he said.

'Where? Where you go? I know all the taverns and bars in the whole harbour district.'

'Do you now?'

'All of them – where d'you drink, then?'

'Who said anything about drinking, lad? No, what I do is *play*.'

The boy drew slightly closer. 'Play what?'

'Fiddle.'

'You play at a bar?'

'I do, aye.'

'Which one?'

'Smiley's.' The old man ran out the hook on its weighted line and leaned over to watch it plummet into the depths.

The boy studied him suspiciously. 'I ain't no fool,' he said.

The old man glanced over, nodded. 'I can see that.'

'Smiley's doesn't exist. It's just a story. A haunting. People hearing things – voices in the air, tankards clunking. Laughing.'

'That's all they hear in the night air, lad?'

The boy licked his suddenly dry lips. 'No. They hear . . . fiddling. Music. Sad, awful sad.'

'Hey now, not all of it's sad. Though maybe that's what leaks out. But,' and he grinned at the boy, 'I wouldn't know that, would I?'

'You're like all the rest,' the boy said, facing out to sea once again.

'Who are all the rest, then?'

'Making up stories and stuff. Lying – it's all anybody ever does here, 'cause they got nothing else to do. They're all wasting their lives. Just like you. You won't catch any fish ever.' And he waited, to gauge the effect of his words.

'Who said I was after fish?' the old man asked, offering up an exaggeratedly sly expression.

'What, crabs? Wrong pier. It's too deep here. It just goes down and down and for ever down!'

'Aye, and what's down there, at the very bottom? You ever hear *that* story?'

The boy was incredulous and more than a little offended. 'Do I look two years old? That demon, the old emperor's demon! But you can't fish for it!'

'Why not?'

'Well – well, your rod would break! Look at it!'

'Looks can be deceiving, lad. Remember that.'

The boy snorted. He was always getting advice. 'I won't be like you, old man. I'm going to be a soldier when I grow up. I'm going to leave this place. For ever. A soldier, fighting wars and getting rich and fighting and saving people and all that!'

The old man seemed about to say one thing, stopped, and instead said, 'Well, the world always needs more soldiers.'

The boy counted this as a victory, the first of what he knew would be a lifetime of victories. When he was grown up. And famous. 'That demon bites and it'll eat you up. And even if you catch it and drag it up, how will you kill it? Nobody can kill it!'

'Never said anything about killing it,' the old man replied. 'Just been a while since we last talked.'

'Ha! Hah! Hahaha!'

High above the harbour, the winds were brisk coming in from the sea. They struck and spun the old battered weathervane on its pole, as if the demon knew not where to turn.

A sudden gust took it then, wrenched it hard around, and with a solid squeal the weathervane jammed. The wind buffeted it, but decades of decay and rust seemed proof to its will, and the weathervane but quivered.

Like a thing in chains.

This ends the Tenth and Final Tale of the
Malazan Book of the Fallen

And now the page before us blurs.
An age is done. The book must close.
We are abandoned to history.
Raise high one more time the tattered standard
of the Fallen. See through the drifting smoke
to the dark stains upon the fabric.
This is the blood of our lives, this is the
payment of our deeds, all soon to be
forgotten.
We were never what people could be.
We were only what we were.

Remember us

APPENDIX

DRAMATIS PERSONAE
Characters appearing in both *Dust of Dreams* and
The Crippled God

THE MALAZANS

Adjunct Tavore Paran
High Mage Quick Ben
Fist Keneb
Fist Blistig
Captain Lostara Yil
Banaschar
Fist Kindly
Captain Skanarow
Fist Faradan Sort
Captain Ruthan Gudd
Lieutenant Pores
Captain Raband
Sinn
Grub

THE SQUADS

Captain Fiddler
Sergeant Tarr
Koryk
Smiles
Bottle

Corabb Bhilan Thenu'alas
Cuttle
Sergeant Gesler
Corporal Stormy
Shortnose
Flashwit
Mayfly
Sergeant Cord
Corporal Shard
Limp
Ebron
Crump
Sergeant Hellian
Corporal Touchy
Corporal Brethless
Maybe
Sergeant Balm
Corporal Deadsmell
Throatslitter
Widdershins
Sergeant Urb
Corporal Clasp
Masan Gilani
Saltlick
Burnt Rope
Lap Twirl
Sad
Sergeant Sinter
Corporal Pravalak Rim
Honey
Lookback
Sergeant Badan Gruk
Corporal Ruffle
Nep Furrow
Reliko
Vastly Blank
Corporal Kisswhere
Skulldeath
Drawfirst
Sergeant Gaunt-Eye
Corporal Rib
Himble Thrup
Dead Hedge

Alchemist Bavedict
Sergeant Sweetlard
Sergeant Rumjugs

THE HOST

Ganoes Paran, High Fist and Master of the Deck
High Mage Noto Boil
Fist Rythe Bude
Imperial Artist Ormulogun
Warleader Mathok
Bodyguard T'morol
Gumble
Skintick
Desra
Nemanda
Kalam Mekhar

THE KHUNDRYL

Warleader Gall
Hanavat (Gall's wife)
Shelemasa
Jastara

THE PERISH GREY HELMS

Mortal Sword Krughava
Shield Anvil Tanakalian
Destriant Run'Thurvian
Commander Erekala

THE LETHERII

King Tehol
Queen Janath
Brys Beddict
Atri-Ceda Aranict
Henar Vygulf
Shurq Elalle
Skorgen Kaban
Ublala Pung

THE BOLKANDO

Queen Abrastal
Spultatha
Felash, Fourteenth Daughter
Handmaid
Gilk Warchief-Spax

THE BARGHAST

Hetan
Stavi
Storii
Absi
Skincut Ralata
Awl Torrent
Setoc of the Wolves

THE SNAKE

Rutt
Held
Badalle
Saddic
Yan Tovis (Twilight)
Yedan Derryg (the Watch)
Witch Pully
Witch Skwish
Brevity
Pithy
Sharl
Corporal Nithe
Sergeant Cellows
Withal

THE IMASS

Onrack T'emlava
Kilava Onass
Ulshun Pral

THE T'LAN IMASS

Warleader Onos T'oolan
Bitterspring (Lera Epar)
Kalt Urmanal
Rystalle Ev
Ulag Togtil
Nom Kala
Urugal the Woven
Thenik the Shattered
Beroke Soft Voice
Kahlb the Silent Hunter
Halad the Giant

THE K'CHAIN CHE'MALLE

J'an Sentinel Bre'nigan
K'ell Hunter Sag'Churok
Matron Gunth Mach
Shi'gal Assassin Gu'Rull
Destriant Kalyth (Elan)

THE TISTE ANDII

Nimander Golit
Spinnock Durav
Korlat
Dathenar Fandoris
Prazek Goul
Skintick
Desra
Nemanda
Sandalath Drukorlat
Silchas Ruin

THE JAGHUT: AMONG THE FOURTEEN

Bolirium
Gedoran
Daryft
Gathras

Sanad
Varandas
Haut
Suvalas
Aimanan Hood

THE FORKRUL ASSAIL: THE LAWFUL INQUISITORS

Reverence
Serenity
Equity
Placid
Diligence
Abide
Aloft
Calm
Belie
Freedom
Grave

THE WATERED: THE TIERS OF LESSER ASSAIL

Amiss
Exigent
Hestand
Festian
Kessgan
Trissin
Melest
Haggraf

THE TISTE LIOSAN

Kadagar Fant
Aparal Forge
Iparth Erule
Gaelar Throe
Eldat Pressen

OTHERS

Rud Elalle (Ryadd Eleis)
Telorast

Curdle
The Errant (Errastas)
Knuckles (Sechul Lath)
Kilmandaros
Mael
Olar Ethil
Udinaas
Bent
Roach

Shadowthrone (Ammeanas)
Cotillion
Draconus
K'rul
Kaminsod (the Crippled God)
Karsa Orlong
Silanah
Apsal'ara
Tulas Shorn
D'rek, the Worm of Autumn
Gillimada (Teblor leader)
Faint
Precious Thimble
Amby Bole
Gruntle
Mappo
Icarium
Korabas, the Otataral Dragon
Absi
Spultatha
Spindle
Munug

ABOUT THE AUTHOR

A graduate of the Iowa Writers' Workshop, archaeologist and anthropologist **Steven Erikson** recently moved back to the UK from Canada and now lives in Cornwall. His début fantasy novel, *Gardens of the Moon*, marked the opening chapter in the epic 'Malazan Book of the Fallen' sequence, which has been hailed as one of the most significant works of fantasy of this millennium.

To find out more, visit www.stevenerikson.com and www.malazanempire.com